THOMAS MANN

JOSEPH AND HIS BROTHERS

THE STORIES OF JACOB
YOUNG JOSEPH
JOSEPH IN EGYPT
JOSEPH THE PROVIDER

TRANSLATED FROM THE GERMAN BY
JOHN E. WOODS

EVERYMAN'S LIBRARY
Alfred A. Knopf   New York   London   Toronto

287

THIS IS A BORZOI BOOK

PUBLISHED BY ALFRED A. KNOPF

First included in Everyman's Library, 2005
Copyright © 2005 by Alfred A. Knopf
Bibliography and Chronology Copyright © 2005 by Everyman's Library

Joseph and His Brothers, in a different translation, was first published in
Great Britain as four separate titles by Secker & Warburg (I. *The Tales of
Jacob* II. *Young Joseph* III. *Joseph in Egypt* (2 vols) IV. *Joseph the Provider*).
The collected edition was first published by Secker & Warburg in 1956.

Originally published in German as *Joseph und Seine Brüder*
in four volumes, as follows:
Die Geschichten Jaakobs © 1933 by S. Fischer Verlag, Berlin
Der Junge Joseph © 1934 by S. Fischer Verlag, Berlin
Joseph in Ägypten © 1936 by Berman-Fischer Ges. M.b.H, Vienna
Joseph, Der Ernährer © 1943 by Bermann-Fischer, A.B., Stockholm

US website: www.randomhouse.com/everymans

ISBN: 1-4000-4001-9 (US)
1-85715-287-5 (UK)

A CIP catalogue reference for this book is available from the
British Library

Library of Congress Cataloging-in-Publication Data
Mann, Thomas, 1875–1955.
[Joseph und seine Brüder. English]
Joseph and his brothers / Thomas Mann ; translated
by John E. Woods.
p. cm.
ISBN 1-4000-4001-9
1. Joseph (Son of Jacob)—Fiction. 2. Bible. O.T. Genesis—History of
Biblical events—Fiction. I. Woods, John E. (John Edwin) II. Title
PT2625.A44J7813 2004
2004043226

Book design by Barbara de Wilde and Carol Devine Carson

Typeset in the United States of America

Printed and bound in Germany by GGP Media GmbH, Pössneck

EVERYMAN'S LIBRARY

EVERYMAN,
I WILL GO WITH THEE,
AND BE THY GUIDE,
IN THY MOST NEED
TO GO BY THY SIDE

CONTENTS

CONTENTS

YOUNG JOSEPH

CONTENTS

CONTENTS

INTRODUCTION

Between 1926 and 1942, Thomas Mann labored off and on for a total
of ten years at what he called his "pyramid," *Joseph and His Brothers*,
the great literary monument that he hoped would tower over all the
other works for which he is now remembered. It is half a century now
since Mann's death, and although *The Magic Mountain, Doctor Faustus*,
"Death in Venice," and *Buddenbrooks* still find their readers, a mere
five decades have apparently sufficed to raze the pyramid of *Joseph*,
leaving few traces of what Mann intended as his magnum opus.

Why? For starters, there is the book's publishing history—
Germany's history. The first volume, *The Stories of Jacob*, appeared in
October 1933. The Nazis had spent their first nine months tightening
the terror, Thomas Mann and his family were already in exile, and
there were few who dared express open approval of the book. Despite
mounting difficulties, S. Fischer Verlag managed to publish a small
edition of volume 2, *Young Joseph*, in April of the following year. By
1936, however, S. Fischer had already been forced to move to Vienna,
where *Joseph in Egypt* was published. The Nazis allowed the work to
be sold inside the Reich, but permitted no reviews and engaged in
bureaucratic chicaneries to make sure it did not sell. *Joseph the Provider*
appeared, then, in neutral Stockholm, in 1943. After the war, modest
editions were offered once or twice a decade, the first in 1948, but the
work never recovered from its shaky early years.

The sheer bulk of the thing surely worked against it as well: four
formidable volumes, a veritable encyclopedia of ancient Near Eastern myth, history, theology, and cultural anthropology—and all just
to retell a (once) familiar Bible story? And who in postwar Germany
would read it? Many Christians found it heterodox to the point of
heresy; any Jewish readership had been largely exterminated in the
death camps. Communists in the East had no use for a "religious"
Thomas Mann. Intellectuals in the West were not particularly keen
on "biblical" novels, either. Besides, in 1947 Mann's *Doctor Faustus* had
become the focus of interest for Mann's readers. It spoke directly to
the evil that had befallen Germany and the world. *Joseph* seemed
more remote than ever.

On this side of the Atlantic, the book's reception, if seldom enthusiastic, was somewhat warmer—Mann was living, after all, among us
as the representative of the "good Germany," and volume 4, *Joseph the*

Provider, was written under the California sun. A single-volume edition incorporating all four novels was first published in 1948 and remained in print into the 1990s. But over the years, the larger American reading public, accustomed to historical biblical novels in the *Ben-Hur* and *Silver Chalice* mode, has quite understandably viewed *Joseph* as forbiddingly Germanic. And more intrepid readers, who find an intellectual home in *The Magic Mountain* or *Doctor Faustus*, have been just as reluctant as their European counterparts to embrace a work that seems so far removed from the concerns of our time. Beyond the issue of subject matter, there is another difficulty. However unfairly, Americans have tended to think of Mann as a writer of turgid and dense, if not almost unreadable prose. And here are almost fifteen hundred pages that, in Helen Lowe-Porter's translation, can often read rather like the King James Bible run amok—replete with "he saith" and "thou knowest."

Joseph and His Brothers deserves a far better fate. It is, by my lights, an epic comedy of extraordinary grandeur. If Thomas Mann regarded it as his magnum opus, that was in part because he wrote *Joseph* as a master craftsman at the height of his powers. He knew it to be, he said, a work of "quality." Here is a vast canvas of mythic sweep, dark beauty, and historical complexity, and Mann applies each stroke with incomparable skill—with a sovereignty revealed most especially in the work's humanity and, yes, its humor.

And yet the question remains how best should a reader approach a work so monumental and complex—plunge in at page 1 and devil take the hindmost? That is, after all, the way Mann wrote it to be read. With considerable trepidation, I would like to suggest a different strategy for first-time readers of this great novel. I propose you start with "The Story of Dinah," part 3 of *The Stories of Jacob*. Based on a Bible story (Genesis 33:17–35:5) never taught in the Sunday schools of my youth, this tale of passion and revenge becomes, in Mann's hand, a marvelous epitome of the virtues of the novel as a whole. My hope, and my guess, is that you will be irrevocably caught up in this great literary adventure and eager to climb the "pyramid." But beware: don't begin at the beginning even yet. For those just getting their climbing legs in shape, "Prelude: Descent into Hell" may well turn out to be literally that. This opening chapter's larger historical and theological perspectives introduce many of the themes that Mann will weave into his four novels, but without a story to hang them on, you may well feel he has pushed you over the edge and down a well that is indeed bottomless. So, "Dinah" first, then back to part 1, "At the Well"—and at some point, halfway up volume 1 or so, you will want to look back, and give the Prelude its due, for it has monumental rewards. If I read it right, Mann has woven his own Gnostic myth here in order to show not only myth's mystery, grandeur, and ineffability, but also its ultimate fragility, even untrustworthiness—not unlike the story of Joseph he is about to tell. One more hint: take time to reacquaint (or acquaint) yourself with Genesis, reading it a chapter or two at a time in step with the story as Mann tells it. This will enhance one of the special pleasures of *Joseph and His Brothers:* watching as Thomas Mann deftly reshapes one people's account of its beginnings and its faith in its God, turning that ancient text into richly detailed stories about splendidly vivid characters, each a manifestation of Mann's faith in our common humanity.

And now a word about something no translator should explicitly talk to readers about—translation. The craft should speak for itself, but perhaps a footnote is in order here. This is only the second translation of *Joseph* into English, and for those familiar with the previous one, it will come as something of a surprise. There is precious little "biblical" language here, but instead, or so I hope, a rich polyphony of voices, ancient and modern—for that is what Mann himself said he was trying to achieve. He almost never quotes Luther's translation of the Bible verbatim; instead he tinkers with it, teasing out its images and heightening its effects for his own purposes. In translating *Joseph,* Helen Lowe-Porter often chose to limit herself, and Mann, to a diction modeled on the King James Bible—perhaps the only choice she thought possible at a time when that version was still the language in which English-speaking people imagined a biblical narrative had to be told. But it is not Mann's language. The voice of *Joseph* is an exuberant hodgepodge, happily at home with both anachronisms and archaisms, now elegantly sublime, now comically coarse. And always, there is the prose of Thomas Mann, flowing in grand periods of thought, each resembling nothing so much as a movement in a Mozart sonata, with themes and counterthemes unfolding in vivid conversation. I hope I have been able to provide some echo of that music in this translation.

Joseph and His Brothers is a novel of innumerable, complex delights, and yet there are also passages here—and who more than the translator should know this—that seem to defy many readers' sensibilities of what a novel should be. At times Mann's novel simply stops and ponders. Mann—or at least this is my suspicion—wanted to make sure he had readers worthy of him. As a result, some passages resemble nothing so much as a pyramid hulking in the desert—do take time to contemplate the riddles. And then, within a page or two, you are sure to be swept up again in Mann's grand narrative, in our common human enterprise told as the story of Jacob, Esau, Laban, Leah, Rachel, Eliezer, Re'uben, Judah, Tamar, Benjamin, Montkaw, Peteprê, Mut-em-enet, Mai-Sakhme, Ikhnatôn—and Joseph. Thomas Mann calls this epic comedy "God's invention"—by which, of course, he also immodestly imputes a certain divinity to its human coinventor.

John E. Woods
2 September 2003

SELECT BIBLIOGRAPHY

WORKS BY THOMAS MANN

There are two good German editions of Mann: the East German Aufbau Verlag edition in twelve volumes (Berlin, 1956), long out of print; and the more complete Stockholmer Ausgabe, published by S. Fischer Verlag, in twenty volumes (Frankfurt am Main, 1965). For dates of first publication, see the chronology.

During Thomas Mann's lifetime most English editions of Mann were translated by Mrs. Helen Lowe-Porter, whom the author made the exclusive copyrighted translator of almost all his works. Over the past thirty years, and especially within the last decade, new editions of Mann's earlier works have appeared, most notably the four principal novels, *Buddenbrooks, The Magic Mountain, Doctor Faustus*, and now *Joseph and His Brothers*, translated by John E. Woods. The works listed below, with dates of first publication in English, are still in print:

Royal Highness, 1916
Buddenbrooks, 1924
Death in Venice, 1928
Tonio Kröger, 1929
The Magic Mountain, 1930
Mario and the Magician, 1930
Joseph and His Brothers, 1934–1944
Lotte in Weimar / The Beloved Returns, 1940
The Transposed Heads, 1941
Doctor Faustus, 1947
The Holy Sinner, 1951
The Black Swan, 1954
The Confessions of Felix Krull, Confidence Man, 1955

Thomas Mann Diaries, 1918–1939, edited by Hermann Kesten, translated by Richard and Clara Winston (André Deutsch, 1983). Fragmentary but still eloquent testament of Mann's inner life.

Thomas Mann: Pro and Contra Wagner, translated by Allan Blunden, introduction by Erich Heller (Faber & Faber, 1985). Documents the lifelong obsession of an imperfect Wagnerite.

GENERAL BIBLIOGRAPHY

BLACKBOURN, DAVID, and EVANS, RICHARD J., eds. *The German Bourgeoisie*, Routledge, 1991. Historical essays on Mann's milieu.

BRUFORD, W. H., *The German Tradition of Self-Cultivation. "Bildung" from Humboldt to Thomas Mann*, Cambridge University Press, 1975. Chapters on *The Magic Mountain* and "The Conversion of an Unpolitical Man" by a great scholar.

CARNEGY, PATRICK, *Faust as Musician: A Study of Thomas Mann's Novel "Doctor Faustus,"* New Directions, 1973. Subtle investigation of Mann and music by a leading opera critic and producer.

DE MENDELSSOHN, PETER, *Der Zauberer. Das Leben des deutschen Schriftstellers Thomas Mann*, Frankfurt, 1975. The standard German biography.

GRAY, R. D., *The German Tradition in Literature 1871–1945*, Cambridge University Press, 1965. A highly critical account of Mann's contemporaries and their ideas.

HAMILTON, NIGEL, *The Brothers Mann*, Yale University Press, New Haven, Conn., 1978. A biographical study of Thomas Mann and his elder brother Heinrich, an eminent novelist in his own right.

HAYMAN, RONALD, *Thomas Mann: A Biography*, Scribner, 1995. Reliable life and times by the author of biographies of Kafka, Brecht, Nietzsche and Proust.

HEILBUT, ANTHONY, *Thomas Mann: Eros and Literature*, Knopf, 1995. Revisionist biography, emphasizing links between Mann's homosexualitiy and his works.

HELLER, ERICH, *The Ironic German. A Study of Thomas Mann*, Little, Brown, 1958. This remains far and away the best book on Mann. Heller's best-known book, *The Disinherited Mind*, Barnes and Noble, 1971, gives the intellectual background to Mann. His German collection, *Die Wiederkehr der Unschuld und andere Essays*, Suhrkamp, Frankfurt am Main, 1977, contains three essays on Mann. One of this is "Thomas Mann in Venice," published in *The Poet's Self and the Poem*, Athlone Press, 1976. Heller, who died in 1991, also wrote an introduction to the earlier Everyman volume of *Thomas Mann: Stories and Episodes*, Dent, 1960.

HOLLINGDALE, R. J., *Thomas Mann. A Critical Study*, Bucknell University Press, 1971. The author, a Nietzsche scholar and translator, is especially worth reading on Mann's debts to the philosopher.

JOHNSON, DANIEL, introduction to Thomas Mann's *Death in Venice and Other Stories*, Everyman's Library, 1991. Background to Mann's most celebrated story.

SELECT BIBLIOGRAPHY

LAWRENCE, D. H., "German Books: Thomas Mann" (1913), in: *A Selection from Phoenix,* Peregrine, 1971. Among the first English reviews of *Death in Venice.* Lawrence rampant: "Thomas Mann is old—and we are young."

MANN, GOLO, *Reminiscences and Reflections: Growing Up in Germany,* Norton, 1990. Chilling, unsparing account of Thomas Mann as a father by his historian son.

PASCAL, ROY, *From Naturalism to Expressionism. German Literature and Society 1880–1918,* Oxford University Press, 1973. Fine on background to the young Mann.

PRATER, DONALD, *Thomas Mann: A Life,* Oxford University Press, 1995. The best of the recent crop of biographies, placing Mann in his literary, social and political context.

REED, T. J., *Thomas Mann: The Uses of Tradition,* Oxford University Press, 1974. Careful scholarship by the author of a critical edition of *Death in Venice.*

REICH-RANICKI, MARCEL, *Thomas Mann and His Family,* Fontana Press, 1989. Provocative essays on Thomas, Heinrich, Klaus, Katja, Erika and Golo Mann by Germany's most influential literary critic, based in part on personal acquaintance.

SONTHEIMER, KURT. *Thomas Mann und die Deutschen,* Fischer, Frankfurt am Main, 1965. A lively German apologia for Mann the political contortionist.

STERN, J. P. *Hitler. The Führer and the People,* University of California Press, 1975; *A Study of Nietzsche,* Cambridge University Press, 1979. Opposite poles of Mann's cosmos.

TAYLOR, RONALD, *Literature and Society in Germany, 1918–1945,* Barnes and Noble, 1980. Reliable work on the period of Mann's triumph and exile.

WYSLING, HANS (ed.), *Letters of Heinrich and Thomas Mann, 1900–1949,* University of California Press, 1998. Riveting chronicle of fraternal rivalry.

CHRONOLOGY

DATE	AUTHOR'S LIFE	LITERARY AND MUSICAL CONTEXT
1871		
1872		Nietzsche: *The Birth of Tragedy.*
1875	Paul Thomas Mann born on 6 June as the second son of Johann Heinrich Mann, a leading businessman and senator of the north German Hanse city of Lübeck.	
1876		First complete performance of Wagner's *Der Ring des Nibelungen.* Tolstoy: *Anna Karenina.*
1883		Death of Wagner.
1889		Hauptmann: *Before Sunrise.* Beginnings of naturalism in German literature.
1890		Wilde: *The Picture of Dorian Gray.*
1892	On the death of Senator Mann, the family grain firm goes into liquidation. Thomas Mann and his brother Heinrich are left with sufficient means to live independently and try to establish themselves as writers.	Ibsen: *The Master Builder.*
1893	Leaves school and moves south to Munich, where his mother has settled.	
1894	His first story, "Fallen," is published in a naturalist literary journal, *Society* (*Die Gesellschaft*).	Heinrich Mann's first novel, *In a Family.*
1895		Fontane: *Effi Briest.*
1896		Chekhov: *The Seagull.*
1896–8	Prolonged stay in Italy—Rome and Palestrina—with his brother Heinrich. Further short fiction appears in the leading literary journal of the day, *The New Review* (*Die Neue Rundschau*), published by the house of Samuel Fischer.	

Germany unified: the Wilhelmine/Bismarckian Reich. The boom "foundation years" (*Gründerjahre*) begin, confirming Germany as a leading industrial power.

Birth of Hitler.

Fall of Bismarck. Wilhelm II's personal rule begins.

Wilhelm II announces German pursuit of "world politics."

DATE	AUTHOR'S LIFE	LITERARY AND MUSICAL CONTEXT
1897	At Fischer's invitation, begins work on his first novel.	
1898	Publishes his first volume of collected short fiction, *Little Herr Friedemann*.	
1900	May: completes the novel *Buddenbrooks*. Samuel Fischer, sceptical about the chances of such a massive work by a barely known author, suggests that Mann abridge it. The young author persuades him to publish it as it stands.	Freud: *Interpretation of Dreams*. Death of Nietzsche. Conrad: *Lord Jim*.
1901	*Buddenbrooks* appears, in two volumes, and is well received.	Chekhov: *Three Sisters*.
1902	Fischer brings out a single-volume cheap edition of the novel. It becomes a best seller, establishing Thomas Mann's fortunes and a broad popular reputation.	Gide: *The Immoralist*. James: *The Wings of the Dove*.
1903	The volume *Tristan* appears, with six works including *Tonio Kröger*.	
1905	Marriage to Katia Pringsheim, daughter of a wealthy Jewish academic family. Mann completes his only drama, *Fiorenza*, set in Renaissance Florence. Melodramatic and stylistically overelaborate, it never succeeds on the stage.	Heinrich Mann: *Professor Unrat*. Wharton: *The House of Mirth*.
1905–10	Works on a number of projects that are destined never to be completed: a novel on Munich society, *Maya;* a historical novel on Frederick the Great of Prussia; a major aesthetic essay "Intellect and Art" ("Geist und Kunst"). Frustrated by his inability to make progress with them.	
1906		Galsworthy: *The Man of Property* (*Forsyte Saga*).
1907–8		Rilke: *New Poems*.

CHRONOLOGY

DATE	AUTHOR'S LIFE	LITERARY AND MUSICAL CONTEXT
1909	Publishes the novel *Royal Highness*, on the surface a romance about an imaginary prince but meant as an allegory of the artist's life. As the second novel from the author of the highly regarded *Buddenbrooks*, it is judged to be lightweight.	Gide: *Straight Is the Gate*. Heinrich Mann: *The Little Town*.
1910	Starts a further artist allegory, the story of the confidence trickster *Felix Krull*. Progress is difficult. Mann feels increasingly worried about how to repeat the success of *Buddenbrooks* with a comparable masterpiece.	Forster: *Howards End*. Rilke: *The Notebooks of Malte Laurids Brigge*.
1911	May/June: a stay at the Lido, Venice. Begins to write *Death in Venice*.	
1912	June: *Death in Venice* completed and published. Begins work on *The Magic Mountain*, planned as a similar-length novella and comic pendant piece ("satyr play") to *Death in Venice*.	Hofmannsthal: *Everyman*. Hauptmann: *Atlantis*.
1914	November: First polemical essay in defense of Germany against her critics.	Joyce: *Dubliners*.
1915	Polemics continue, in particular against his brother Heinrich. In no mood for fiction, devotes himself to a long, brooding work of cultural-political-autobiographical reflections.	Kafka: *The Metamorphosis*. Ford: *The Good Soldier*. Woolf: *The Voyage Out*. Lawrence: *The Rainbow*.
1917		Joyce: *A Portrait of the Artist as a Young Man*.
1918	*Reflexions of an Unpolitical Man* appears just before the war ends.	Heinrich Mann: *Man of Straw*. Spengler: *The Decline of the West*, part 1 (part 2, 1927).
1918–22	At first, bitter withdrawal and a search for any remaining congenial forms of conservatism. Disturbed by increasing right-wing violence, resolves to make the best of the new sociopolitical situation.	

CHRONOLOGY

Death of Edward VII.

Morocco crisis.

Sinking of the *Titanic*. German Social Democratic Party polls more votes in general election than any other party.

August: Outbreak of World War I.

Russian Revolution; Russia and Germany make separate peace.
Salzburg Festival inaugurated.
End of World War I; Wilhelm II abdicates; declaration of a German republic.

DATE	AUTHOR'S LIFE	LITERARY AND MUSICAL CONTEXT
1919		
1920		
1921–2		
1922	Public statement in speech "On the German Republic." From then on moves steadily toward social democracy.	Joyce: *Ulysses.* Eliot: *The Waste Land.* Brecht: *Drums in the Night.*
1923		Rilke: *The Duino Elegies; The Sonnets to Orpheus.*
1924	Publishes *The Magic Mountain.* The intended novella has grown into a massive novel, taking issue allegorically with the social and political problems of the day.	Forster: *A Passage to India.* Ford: *Parade's End* (to 1928).
1925		Woolf: *Mrs. Dalloway.* Kafka: *The Trial.*
1926–33	Active as a member of the Literary Section of the Prussian Academy of Arts, where the cultural and ideological issues of the Weimar Republic are fought out by leading writers of left and right.	
1927		Hesse: *Steppenwolf.* Final part of Proust's *Remembrance of Things Past.*
1928		Brecht/Weill: *The Threepenny Opera.*
1929	Publishes "Mario and the Magician," an allegorical tale of Italian fascism. Receives the Nobel prize for literature—but expressly for his first novel, *Buddenbrooks.* (The prize committee's most influential member disapproves of the liberalism implicit in *The Magic Mountain.*)	Döblin: *Berlin Alexanderplatz.* Remarque: *All Quiet on the Western Front.*
1930		Freud: *Civilization and Its Discontents.* Musil: *The Man Without Qualities.*
1931–2		Broch: *The Sleepwalkers.*

CHRONOLOGY

HISTORICAL EVENTS

Versailles treaty signed; Weimar Republic constituted; a "Soviet Republic" established in Munich and swiftly repressed.
The Kapp putsch.
Political assassinations—of Erzberger, Rathenau—by right-wing extremists: the Republic threatened by violence.
Mussolini's march on Rome; Italian Fascists come to power.

High point of German inflation; Hitler's Munich putsch fails.

Hindenburg elected as second Chancellor of the Republic, in succession to Friedrich Ebert.

Trotsky expelled from Russian Communist Party.

Wall Street crash; world economic crisis.

Growing electoral support for Nazis.

DATE	AUTHOR'S LIFE	LITERARY AND MUSICAL CONTEXT
1933	February: Mann travels abroad with a lecture on Richard Wagner. Reports of the lecture become the pretext for a hate campaign against him by Nazis and fellow-travelers. (Since the early thirties, he has been prominent as a defender of the Weimar Republic and an opponent of rising Nazism.) Mann's family warn him to stay abroad. It is the beginning of exile. Autumn: after short stays in various places in France and Switzerland, settles in Küsnacht near Zürich. Publication, still in Germany, of *The Stories of Jacob*, the first volume of the four-part novel *Joseph and His Brothers*.	Lorca: *Blood Wedding.* Malraux: *Man's Fate.*
1934	May–June: first visit to the United States. Publishes the second volume of the tetralogy, *Young Joseph*.	
1936	*Joseph in Egypt* appears. The Nazis deprive Mann of his German nationality. He takes Czech citizenship.	Klaus Mann: *Mephisto.*
1938	Emigrates to the United States and holds a visiting professorship at Princeton.	Freud: *Moses and Monotheism.* Sartre: *Nausea.*
1939	Publishes *The Beloved Returns,* a novel about the older Goethe.	Joyce: *Finnegans Wake.* Steinbeck: *The Grapes of Wrath.* Isherwood: *Goodbye to Berlin.*
1940	Moves to Pacific Palisades, California.	Greene: *The Power and the Glory.*
1941	Becomes Germanic consultant to the Library of Congress.	Brecht: *Mother Courage and Her Children.*
1942		Camus: *The Stranger.*
1942–3		
1942–5	Anti-Nazi broadcasts to Germany for the BBC.	
1943	*Joseph the Provider* completes the Joseph tetralogy. Begins writing *Doctor Faustus*.	Hesse: *The Glass Bead Game.* Brecht: *Galileo.*

CHRONOLOGY

January: Nazis come to power by constitutional means, but swiftly establish one-party state with violent suppression of opponents. Beginning of the Third Reich.

Outbreak of Spanish Civil War.

Austrian *Anschluss*.

Germany occupies parts of Czechoslovakia; attacks Poland, ignores Anglo-French ultimatum. September: World War II begins.

German *Blitzkrieg* conquers France.

Germany invades Soviet Union.

Tide of war turns against Germany in Russia and North Africa.

DATE	AUTHOR'S LIFE	LITERARY AND MUSICAL CONTEXT
1944	Takes U.S. citizenship.	
1945		Broch: *The Death of Virgil.*
		Orwell: *Animal Farm.*
		Sartre: *The Age of Reason; No Exit.*
1946		
1947	*Doctor Faustus* published.	Camus: *The Plague.*
		Gruppe 47 founded by young German writers.
1949	Publishes *The Genesis of Doctor Faustus,* which describes the roots of the work in the events of the time.	Orwell: *Nineteen Eighty-four.*
1950	Death of brother Heinrich.	
1951	Publishes *The Holy Sinner,* a parodistic retelling of the medieval legend of Pope Gregory.	Beckett: *Molloy; Malone Dies.*
1952	Disturbed by McCarthyism and drawn to Europe for cultural reasons, but unwilling to return to Germany. Settles in Switzerland for his remaining years.	Beckett: *Waiting for Godot.*
1954	Publishes *Confessions of Felix Krull, Confidence Man,* a completed first part of the novel begun in 1911 and abandoned in the twenties.	
1955	12 August: Thomas Mann dies in Zürich.	Nabokov: *Lolita.*

CHRONOLOGY

SIXTEEN YEARS

(For the 1948 American edition of *Joseph and His Brothers* in a single volume)

This piece of work is not unlike a pyramid—differing from its brothers, those monsters on the edge of the Libyan desert, only in that it did not demand the sacrifice of hecatombs of lashed and gasping slaves but was built by the patience of *one* man over long years—and to see the entire enterprise, previously divided in four parts, presented now as the unity it is between the two covers of a single volume, evokes in me, apart from justifiable amazement at a scarcely imaginable achievement of the bookbinder's craft, many memories and a pensive, autobiographical state of mind.

Long years—and upon closer reflection, their tally, including interruptions, some of which were rather extended, comes to a good sixteen: a period of time whose history has been as "rich with stories" as the willfully independent product that grew out of them, though rich in ways that one might expect to prove quite detrimental to epic equanimity. Is it too much to expect that posterity (assuming we can expect posterity to emerge yet in something like decent intellectual shape) may on occasion pause to wonder how during those years, from 1926 to 1942, when heart and brain were besieged daily by the wildest demands, such a narrative as this—a great, calm current of seventy thousand lines, bearing tidings of primal events shared by all humankind, stories of love and hate, blessing and curse, fraternal strife and paternal suffering, arrogance and repentance, of lives cast down to be raised up again—how such a comedic song of humanity (if one may be permitted to call a spade a spade) could be nurtured and completed under those turbulent circumstances? As for me, my feelings are not those of wonder, but of gratitude. I am grateful to this work, which was my staff and my stay along a path that often led through many a dark valley—it was my refuge, my comfort, my homeland, a symbol of stability, the guarantee of my own steadfastness amidst a storm of change.

The Magic Mountain was completed in Munich in 1924 and published that same year. Between its conclusion and the day when I found the courage to put to paper the words "Deep is the well of the past," the first sentence of "Descent into Hell," my overture to *Joseph and His Brothers*, the only thing I produced was a short story, "Despair and Early Sorrow," improvised for the magazine *Neue Rundschau* on the occasion of my fiftieth birthday and arising from one of those states of active relaxation that have come over me with a certain regularity whenever I have been released at last from a task of many years. In much the same way *The Beloved Returns* was followed by the metaphysical jest of *The Transposed Heads* and the completed Joseph stories by a defense of human civilization directed against Nazism and entitled *Tables of the Law*. Slowly—from that first day when I commenced the fantastical essay that forms my story's introduction and is itself reminiscent of an intrepid expedition equipping itself for its mission—slowly and with considerable worry as to how much time and space it was all taking, the parts of my mythological novel grew until it saw the light of day as *The Stories of Jacob*—simply because there was manuscript enough for a rather substantial volume, but not because my opus had been planned as a multivolume work, as a series of novels or as a "tetralogy." Ah, it had all been quite different in the planning—different, just as always. Just as *Buddenbrooks* was intended to be a mercantile tale, some two hundred fifty pages long, and then got out of hand; just as *The Magic Mountain* was really supposed to be a story only the size of "Death in Venice" and to serve as its grotesque sequel, and then hypertrophied all on its own—in much the same way, then, I had first imagined a triptych of novellas with a religious hue, the first of which was to have been of a mythic, biblical character, and in it I had decided to offer a lively retelling of the story of Joseph. *Habent sua fata libelli* [books have their own fates]—not just after their publication, but especially during their creation. When he sets his hand to them, the author knows little about them. They have a will of their own and know better. The novellas from the days of the Reformation and Counter Reformation vanished, and for more than a decade and a half I was to remain under the spell of my mythic, biblical story, which, as long as the plan remained at all tenable, was conceived as an ongoing, unified narrative, as a single volume, though now swelling to unfortunate size—so that one can well say that only here and now, after years of a "mutilated" existence, has the story appeared in its true form.

It has been my custom to accompany fictional works with essayistic offshoots, which often may be inspired or demanded by external events, but in essence have no purpose other than to strengthen me in my fictional task. And so the treatises "On the German Republic" and "Goethe and Tolstoy"—to name only two—belong to *Magic Mountain*, just as the essays on "Germany and the Germans" or on

Dostoyevsky and Nietzsche belong to *Doctor Faustus*. It would be te-dious to list all the critical escapades and glosses that belong to *Joseph* and are colored by it, for they fill volumes and make up the majority of what has appeared in English in the collections *Order of the Day* and *Essays of Three Decades*. As if a sixty-page preface to *The Stories of Jacob* had not been sufficient to get me into the mood and equip me for a journey into the land of myth, in 1926, the year I began my novel, I followed up with an infatuated analysis of Kleist's *Amphytrion;* and one need only read the mythicizing sentences that introduce my Lessing lecture to see that it also belongs to the "theme," or, shall we say, just a little gentle pressure establishes a connection with it. I even inter-rupted my narration at that time with another independent narra-tive, with *Mario and the Magician*, a story with a strong political cast, for its core concern is the psychologies of fascism and "freedom" and how the latter, being devoid of will, is left at such a great disadvantage over against its opponent's robust will.

One must keep in mind that at the time I began *Joseph* postwar political tension in Germany had already grown very acute and that during the decade of the twenties I had, thanks to my political writings, subjected my artistic work to pressures, to the psychological disruptions and encumbrances, of nationalist hatred—pressures un-altered by official honors that were awarded me by the German Re-public, but that in turn placed me under obligation for all sorts of academic speeches on festive occasions. Along with these came un-official statements, articles, and lectures that eschewed all politics. *The Stories of Jacob* was already finished and part of *Young Joseph* written when, in early 1930, I embarked on a journey to the Near East, to Egypt and Palestine, though it could hardly have still been seen as a research trip, and instead served merely as on-the-spot verification of relevant studies in which I had immersed myself from a distance. All the same, I did see the Nile's landscapes with my own eyes, from the Delta all the way up (or down) to Nubia, plus sites in the Holy Land, and my impressions were put to good use in the third volume, *Joseph in Egypt*, part of which was written in Germany. To it belongs the essay "Sufferings and Greatness of Richard Wagner." Fifty years had passed since that great musician of the theater had closed his eyes in Venice, and cities in various countries had invited me to lecture on his art. I wrote much more than I could deliver orally and first read an abridged version of my critical adulation before a quite sympathetic audience at the University of Munich on February 10, 1933, only to depart the next day with little baggage for a trip to Amsterdam, Brussels, and Paris, from which I was never to return to Germany.

Hitler was already chancellor when I left Munich, but it was not until we stopped for a holiday in the mountains of Switzerland that disaster struck: the Reichstag fire, the Nazi Party's calamitous electoral victory, the establishment of a dictatorship, the "National Revolution." A brutal campaign unleashed against me in the press and on the radio because of my portrait of Wagner cut off all possibility of my returning home. I have told the story of this chaotic epoch in my life elsewhere. For my work on *Joseph* it meant an interruption of several months. A brave daughter, who risked a return to our now confiscated house in Munich, found the manuscript left behind there and brought it to the south of France. Slowly, despite disjointed, provisional circumstances, I was able to resume work on the enterprise that was the sole guarantee of continuity in my life.

Despite frequent and sometimes long interruptions, my labor on *Joseph in Egypt* came to an end at Kusnacht on the Lake of Zurich, to which we had moved in the fall of 1933, and the book was published in 1936 in Vienna, the temporary refuge of the Berlin publishing house with which I was under contract. It was the period of my expulsion from the German state and the revocation of my honorary doctorate (since restored), to which I responded in a letter, now translated into many languages, to the dean of the Faculty of Philosophy at the University of Bonn. It was, moreover, the period when émigrés in Zurich founded a periodical for free German civilization, *Mass und Wert* (Measure and Value), of which I was a signatory editor and which published large portions of *The Beloved Returns,* the Goethe novel I had meanwhile begun—once again intending only a brief intermezzo. At the time I was a member of the Comité Permanent des Lettres et des Arts established by the League of Nations and had taken part in meetings of this body in Geneva and Frankfurt am Main before the incursion of the Third Reich. For a discussion in Nice, which I did not attend in person, I contributed a memorandum of a political nature, which caused a certain sensation when it was read and was later included under the title "Achtung, Europa!" (Europe, Beware!) in a collection of essays bearing the same name. I attended further sessions of the committee held in Venice and Budapest, and it was at an open meeting in the Hungarian capital that I was able to rouse myself to make an extemporaneous speech condemning the murderers of freedom and advocating militant democracy, a statement that—given the very academic nature of the conference and, especially, the way everyone was tiptoeing around the fascist delegates—verged on tactlessness, but that was greeted with several minutes of applause by the Hungarian audience and that earned me the enthusiastic embrace of the Czech poet Karel Čapek, who died of a broken heart when democracy betrayed his country.

By 1934 I had made contact with America. The travel diary "Voyage with Don Quixote" was the literary product of my first transatlantic trip. From then on I crossed the ocean almost every year, and the preponderance of my life began to shift to its farther shore. For America I wrote "The Coming Victory of Democracy," a lecture I delivered on a tour of fourteen cities of the United States during the winter of 1938. For America, too, I wrote an introduction to an abridged New York edition of my essay on Schopenhauer, the thinker who made such a deep impression on me in my youth. It can be found today in the collection *Essays of Three Decades*.

My two essays on Freud, the second given as a lecture in Vienna to commemorate the great researcher's eightieth birthday, likewise come from those years of moving back and forth between Europe and the New World, as does my second Wagner lecture on the *Ring of the Nibelung*, which I was asked to deliver at the University of Zurich for a production of the entire colossal work—all of them interpolations into the work on my Goethe novel, which in turn was an interpolation into my chief epic enterprise, the stories of Joseph. It is no insignificant psychological burden to work with a system of boxes within boxes—inevitable, it would seem, if one wishes to economize one's productivity. A great work is set aside for the sake of a smaller one, whose demands could not be anticipated and which itself then devours years. One is forced to set it aside as well in response to the many demands of the day; one gives oneself over to secondary tasks, some of which require not weeks, but months, and, wouldn't you know, one is then required to insert still other smaller improvisations, without ever losing sight of one's larger and still larger concerns. But the result is that bit by bit one comes to bear on one's shoulders and in one's mind the *entire* burden, the weight of every task and concurrent task. Patience is all—an equanimity that, should a man not possess it by nature, must be wrested from a nervous constitution given to despair. Endurance, stamina, perseverance is all, and every hope bears the name "time." "Give me time" is one's prayer to the eternal gods "and it will all be done."

It was in 1938, amid the most dreadful political circumstances, in the days of "Munich," when democracy capitulated to fascism, sacrificing the Czech state and all political morality for "peace in our time," that we settled in Princeton, New Jersey. Out of profound despondency, which was not without outrage, I wrote "This Peace," a bitter indictment of how the policies of Western nations were being debased by a fear of Russian socialism. Despite the difficulty of acclimatizing myself to new surroundings, I continued work on *The Beloved Returns*. But the duties associated with a guest professorship at the university were light: I put together a series of public addresses and lectures for advanced students on Goethe's *Faust* and *Werther*, on Freud, on the history of the European novel, even on *The Magic Mountain*. We were still able to spend the summer of 1939 in Europe, in England, Switzerland, and Holland; and on the beach at Noordwijk I wrote an introduction to Tolstoy's *Anna Karenina* for Random House in New York—it, too, has been incorporated in both German and English collections of my literary essays.

Caught by surprise in Sweden by the war—if one could speak of surprise—we embarked on our stressful, indeed perilous journey home, first by air to London and then on board the overcrowded *Washington*. I had with me a great many papers, lecture manuscripts, and books that became an object of tedious inspection at the camouflaged London airport well outside the city. An object of particular interest and misgiving in the inspectors' eyes was a sketch of the seating arrangements for a luncheon that Goethe gives for the sweetheart of his youth at his home on the Frauenplan in Weimar. It was suspected to be of strategic value, and I had to offer a brief lecture on my novel to convince these people that the sketch was completely harmless.

At the time *The Beloved Returns* was nearing completion. That same year, while still at Princeton, I brought the book to its close with a ghostly conversation between Lotte and Goethe in a carriage, and now, after an interruption of some five years, I was free to begin the final volume of *Joseph and His Brothers*. I was highly motivated to complete this narrative—which, surviving everything, had come with me from Germany—and my desire to do so was only strengthened by certain mythic memories, playful parallels not inappropriate to the subject matter. I stood where Wagner had once stood when, after the grand interpolation of *Tristan* and *Meistersinger*, he again took up work on his dramatic epic, the vast fairy tale of *The Ring of the Nibelung*. True, my method of dealing with myth was in essence closer to the humor of Goethe's "Classic Walpurgis Night" than to Wagnerian pathos; but the unanticipated evolution that the story of Joseph had taken had, I am certain, always been secretly influenced by memories of Wagner's grand edifice of motifs, was a successor to its intentions. Playing with themes invented long before, I needed to reshape and elaborate them all for a crowning convergence and conclude my three previous fairy-tale operas with a *Götterdämmerung* of high delight. I was looking forward to it—and yet I hesitated to begin.

It was not that the clay had dried out after so many tumultuous years. Despite all those diversions, I had clung tooth and nail to the old task, and it was still alive in me. The reason for my timidity was simply that I feared an anticlimax, a lesser fourth volume in comparison to the third. For almost without question *Joseph in Egypt* seemed to me the poetic high point of the work, if only because of my humane attempt to salvage a woman's honor by making a human figure of Potiphar's wife, by telling the painful story of her passion for the Canaanite steward of her pro forma husband. In my stock of characters I had no female who could match the Rachel of volumes 1 and 2, and the Mut-em-enet of 3—and it took a long time before I realized I did have one after all. It was Tamar, the daughter-in-law and seductress of Judah, whom I turned into a disciple of Jacob, into an Astarte-like figure with added characteristics taken from the Book of Ruth, and, in the same semicomedic style that informs the whole, developed her into the prototype of historical ambition. In her, who then gave her name to an entire segment of the book, a self-contained novella, I found courage and a synthesis of the charms of all that remained to be told. Even today I do not think it an exaggeration to repeat what is said in the text: "If someone were to call her the most astonishing person in this entire story, we would not venture to contradict him."

While still at Princeton and before resuming my main task, however, I wrote a "long short story," the Indian legend of *The Transposed Heads*. Then finally in Brentwood, California, where we spent the spring and part of the summer of 1940, I found the voice that I had not used for so long and began to sing my biblical saga again—and the first chapter of *Joseph the Provider* was written.

The story of the genesis of this volume, whose mood is the most translucent and cheerful of all, is no less tumultuous, indeed is even more so, than that of the other three and is filled with still more interruptions, to all of which I yielded unwillingly and yet with my whole heart. The story came into being under the awful tension of a war on whose outcome the fate of the world, of Western civilization, indeed of everything in which I believed, appeared to hang—of a war with such dark prospects at the start and into which, after the fall of

France, the country whose citizen I was about to become now entered, much like Achilles leaving his tent after the death of Patroclus—of a war whose cause I constantly felt called to serve with my words. The impromptu essays that belong to the period spent writing the fourth volume of *Joseph* deal with the war and the world it promised to create, texts like "This War," "The Problem of Freedom," and so forth, and I used them as the basis for the lectures that were part of my duties as a Fellow of the Library of Congress in Washington. Even before our move to California after my guest professorship at Princeton had come to an end, I had begun to compose radio speeches broadcast monthly to Germany by the British Broadcasting Corporation—there would be fifty-five in all by war's end. It was always twenty-eight days of *Joseph*, four weeks of freedom and mythical play—and then a day or two when I was no longer a novelist but, with all my soul, a herald in battle, when I could give free rein to my hatred of those who had corrupted Germany and Europe and then, in a state of excitement that comes not from art but only from life and the passion of the moment, record that hatred on a spinning disk. Then—back to the work of peace and my "temple theater," the unreal made real in the humorous detail of staging and discussion.

My work proceeded beneath the blue of the California sky—so like that of Egypt—and to it my narrative surely owes much of its serenity and cheerfulness; and even while some alarmists were fleeing the West Coast for fear of a Japanese attack, we did the opposite, and at the last possible moment when construction was still feasible, we took heart and built our house in the hills above Santa Monica. *Joseph the Provider* is the part of the work that was written in America, from first word to last, and there can be no doubt that it shares here and there in the spirit of this nation—and not only as the "success story" to which its nature predestined it, or even in the occasional Anglo-Saxon coloring that I gladly incorporated into its German voice. The spirit of this narrative—if anyone wishes to hear my mythic opinion—is an unrestrained spirit that borders on abstraction and whose medium is language per se, and in that sense it is language itself posited as an absolute, with little regard for idioms and local linguistic gods. I have no problem with someone deciding, for instance, that the German in "Prelude in Higher Echelons" in *Joseph the Provider* is "not really German at all." I am satisfied that it is language, satisfied that what the entire opus offers, above all else, is a work of language in whose polyphony sounds of the ancient Near East are blended with something very modern, with the accents of a fictive scientific method, satisfied with how it delights in changing linguistic masks the way its hero changes the masks of his gods—the last of which has something strikingly American about it. It is, after all, the mask of an American Hermes, of a masterly messenger of cleverness, whose New Deal is unmistakably reflected in Joseph's magical administration of Egypt's economy.

The year 1942 was well advanced when I came to the end. Eighteen years before, I had appended, not without a certain solemnity, the words *"Finis operis"* to the last lines of *The Magic Mountain*. Style— it is a cordial but stubborn power, and determinative to the last! This time it led me to disguise my "finis" with a very old-fashioned narrative trick, so that I could make the title of the whole, *Joseph and His Brothers*, the long-delayed phrase of the last sentence.

Here, then, is the entire work between two book covers in Helen Lowe-Porter's admirable translation—an achievement of loyalty and dedication that this woman could not have managed without *faith* in the worthiness of her task. Dare I share that faith? How will posterity view this work? Will it become a curiosity for archivists that quickly gathers dust, an easy prey to transcience? Or will its humor continue to delight those who come after us, its emotion still touch the emotions of later generations? Will it indeed be counted among the great books? I do not know, and no one can tell me. As the son of a merchant, however, I have an abiding faith in quality. What has helped so many products of the human hand to last through the ages and defy the centuries? What has induced humankind, even in the maddest of times, to protect them? Why, this quality. My song of Joseph is good, faithful work, done with the sort of sympathy to which humankind has always responded with fine feeling. Some measure of endurance, I think, is innate to it.

JOSEPH AND HIS BROTHERS

DESCENT INTO HELL

1

Deep is the well of the past. Should we not call it bottomless?

Indeed we should, if—in fact, perhaps only if—the past subjected to our remarks and inquiries is solely that of humanity, of this enigmatic life-form that comprises our own naturally lusty and preternaturally wretched existence and whose mystery is quite understandably the alpha and omega of all our remarks and inquiries, lending urgency and fire to all our speech, insistence to all our questions. And yet what happens is: the deeper we delve and the farther we press and grope into the underworld of the past, the more totally unfathomable become those first foundations of humankind, of its history and civilization, for again and again they retreat farther into the bottomless depths, no matter to what extravagant lengths we may unreel our temporal plumb line. The salient words here are "again" and "farther," because what is inscrutable has a way of teasing our zeal for placing it under scrutiny; it offers us only illusory stations and goals, behind which, once we reach them, we discover new stretches of the past opening up—much like a stroller at the shore whose wanderings find no end, because behind each backdrop of loamy dunes that he strives to reach lie new expanses to lure him onward to another cape.

Thus some origins are of a conditional sort, marking both in practice and in fact the primal beginning of the particular tradition kept by a given community, people, or family of faith, but in such a way that memory, even when advised that the well's deeps can in no way be considered earnestly plumbed, may find national reassurance in some primal event and come to historical and personal rest there.

For example, for his part the young Joseph, son of Jacob and his beloved Rachel, who had departed into the West far too soon, Joseph in his day—when Kurigalzu the Kassite reigned in Babel, lord of the Four Regions, king of Sumeria and Akkadia, highly agreeable to Bel–Marudug's heart, a ruler both stern and extravagant, his beard's curly locks set in such artful rows that they resembled a division of shield-bearers in finest dress rank; when in Thebes, in the lower lands that Joseph was accustomed to call Mizraim or even Kemi, "the black land," there beamed, radiant upon the horizon of his palace, His Holiness the Good God, called Amun-is-content, the third of that name, the sun's very son, dazzling and delighting all those born of dust; when Assyria was waxing strong thanks to the power of its gods and when royal caravans, following the great highway by the sea, then ascending from Gaza to the passes of cedar-clad mountains, conveyed tokens of courtesy, contributions of lapis lazuli and stamped gold, back and forth between Pharaoh's throne and the court in the Land of the Rivers; when Amorites served Astarte in their cities, in Beth-shan, Aijalon, Taanakh, and Urusalim, when at Sichem and Beth-lachem seven days of wailing resounded for the mutilated True Son and at Gebal, the city of books, El was worshipped, though needing neither temple nor cult—Joseph, then, residing in the district of Canaan in the land the Egyptians called Upper Retenu, living in his father's family camp near Hebron, in the shade of terebinths and evergreen holly oaks, a young lad famed for his pleasing ways, pleasing because of the inheritance passed on to him by his mother, who had been handsome and beautiful as the moon when it is full and as Ishtar's mild star floating gently in the pure aether, but pleasing as well by way of his father, bearing his spiritual gifts, indeed in some sense surpassing him with their aid— so, for the last time now, Joseph (and we take satisfaction in naming his name a fifth and sixth time, for there is a mystery about that name and in possessing it we feel as if we have been given a sorcerer's power over the person of this boy, who, though now sunk deep in time's depths, was once so full of life and speech)—Joseph, for his part, was accustomed to seeing the beginning of all things or, better, of all things of personal importance in a southern Babylonian city called Uru, which in his dialect he called Ur-Kashdim, meaning Ur of the Chaldees.

It was from there that long ago (Joseph himself was not clear just how far in the past it lay) a man made restless by his ponderings had set out together with his wife—whom presumably out of tenderness he liked to call his "sister"—and other members of his family and in imitation of the moon, the divinity of Ur, began to wander, thinking this the most proper thing to do given his disgruntled, doubt-filled, indeed tormented state of mind. His departure, which had a vague but undeniable sense of opposition and rebellion about it, was connected with certain structures that impressed him as impertinent and that, although they had not been erected by Nimrod, the current ruler of the locality and a mighty man on earth, had been restored and made exceedingly taller by him, less in honor of the divine heavenly lights to which they were dedicated—or that at least was the private opinion of the man of Ur—than as a deterrent to the inhabitants' scattering over the land and as a heaven-aspiring monument to King Nimrod's amassed power, from which the man of Ur had now escaped by scattering with his household all the same, to wander who knew how long. The tradition handed down to Joseph was not definite as to whether what had specifically annoyed this malcontent had been the great moon citadel of Ur, the towered temple of the god Sin—whose name had also been given to the entire land of Shinar and was likewise echoed in place-names closer to home, as in, for instance, a Mount Sinai—or whether it had been the lofty house of the sun, the Marduk temple Esagila in Babel itself, an exact description of which, including the pinnacle that Nimrod had also raised to rival heaven, had been passed down in the stories told to Joseph. There had evidently been several other things that offended this man as he pondered them: beginning with Nimrod's mightiness in general on down to various customs and usages that to others appeared part of a sacred, inalienable tradition, but that had filled his soul with increasing doubt—and since it is not easy to sit still with doubt in one's soul, he had set himself in motion.

He arrived in Haran, the moon city of the north, the City of the Way, in the land of Naharina, where he remained for several years and gathered souls, bringing them into a close relationship with his own family. This was, however, a relationship that brought with it uneasiness, and almost nothing else—an uneasiness of the soul expressed in a restlessness of the body that had little to do with the fickleness of everyday wanderlust and light-footed adventures, but was instead the obsession of one driven man, in whose blood there stirred the dark beginnings of fateful developments, the irresistible force and scope of which may well have stood in some mysteriously precise proportion to the torment that left him no peace. Which was also why Haran, a city still within Nimrod's sphere of influence, proved in fact to be merely a "city of the way," a station from which the moon man again set out after a while, together with Sarai, his sister-wife, and all his kin and his and their goods, to continue his hegira as their leader and mahdi, uncertain of his goal.

And so he had come to the western land, to the Amurru who resided in Canaan, where the rulers in those days were men from Heth, had moved by stages across the land, and forged ahead far into the south, beneath another sun, into the Land of Mud, where the water runs backwards, not like the water of Naharina, and boats float downstream to the north, where an ancient, stiff-necked people prayed to their dead and where there had been nothing for a man of Ur to search out or accomplish in his distress. He had returned to the western land or, better, to the middle country that lay between the mud and Nimrod's domains, with desert not far to the south, came to a mountainous region where there was little tilling of the soil, but abundant pastures for his flocks, where he and the inhabitants dealt fairly with one another, and he settled superficially after his fashion.

Tradition has it that his God—the God on whose essential image his mind was hard at work, the highest among all the others; whom alone he was determined to serve out of pride and love; the God of the eons, for whom he had sought a name and, finding none to his satisfaction, had assigned him a plural, tentatively calling him Elohim, the Godhead—that this God, then, had made him both far-reaching and tightly circumscribed promises to the effect that not only would he, the man of Ur, become a nation numberless as sand and stars and a blessing to all nations, but also to the effect that the land in which he now dwelt as a stranger and to which Elohim had led him out of Chaldea would be given to him and his seed as an eternal possession in all its parts—whereby the God of gods must have expressly listed all those peoples and current inhabitants of the land whose "gates" this Ur man's seed was to possess or, better, all those whom God clearly intended be subjugated and reduced to servitude in the interest of the man of Ur and his seed. All this is to be accepted only with caution—or at least must be correctly interpreted. We are dealing with late and tendentious interpolations, whose purpose is to find in God's intention from earliest times a sanction for political arrangements established much later by force of arms. In reality this moon-wanderer's personality was not the sort that either receives or generates political promises. There is no proof that from the very start, upon leaving his homeland, he had viewed the land of the Amurru as the future setting for his actions; indeed, his trial wandering into the land of tombs and the crop-nosed lion-maid would appear to prove the contrary. And even if—after putting Nimrod's all-powerful state behind him, but also quickly turning back out of the celebrated empire of the double-crowned king of oases—he intentionally returned to the western land, to a country, that is, whose fractured national existence condemned it to hopeless political impotence and dependency, this is a testimony to anything but a personal taste for imperial greatness or a gift for political vision. What had set him in motion was spiritual uneasiness, a need for God; and if prophecies were made to him—and of that there can be no legitimate doubt—these referred to the wider effects of his novel and personal experience of God, for whom he had sought to gain sympathy and adherents from the very beginning. He suffered, and in comparing the measure of his own interior discomfort with that of the great majority, he concluded that his suffering bore the future within it. Your torment, your restlessness, so he learned from his newly discerned God, is not to be in vain—for it will impregnate many souls, will bring forth proselytes countless as the sand upon the seashore and provide the impulse for amplitudes of life contained like a seed within it—in a word, you will be a blessing. A blessing? It is unlikely that this word correctly renders the sense of the one that came to him in his vision or corresponds to his own temperament and sense of self. The word "blessing" implies values that should be kept separate from the characterization of the nature and significance of men of his kind—of men, that is, who know an inner unrest, an urge to wander, and whose novel experience of God is destined to shape the future. The life of these men, with whom a new history begins, seldom or never means a pure and unquestioned "blessing," nor is that what is whispered to them by their own sense of self. "And you shall be a *destiny*"—that is the purer and more correct translation of the word of promise, whatever language it might have been spoken in; and whether this destiny may be a blessing or not is a question whose secondary importance is revealed by the fact that always and without exception there can be different answers to it—although of course a "yes" was always the answer of the community, growing by both physical and spiritual means, that recognized the true Baal and Adad of the grand cycle in the God who had led the man of Ur out of Chaldea. And it was to that cohesive community that Joseph traced his own spiritual and physical existence.

2

At times he considered the moon-wanderer even to be his own great-grandfather, but that must be most sternly dismissed from the realm of possibility. From instruction of all sorts he himself knew perfectly well that it was all more far-reaching. Not, to be sure, so far-reaching that that mighty man of earth—whose boundary stones decorated with signs of the zodiac the man of Ur had left behind him—had in fact been Nimrod, the first king on earth, who had sired Bel of Shinar. Rather the tablets told that it was Hammuragash the Lawgiver who had restored those citadels of sun and moon, and if young Joseph equated him with the far earlier Nimrod, this was merely a charming play of fancy that nicely suited his mind but is barred to us, for it would ill become our own. The same holds true for his occasionally confusing the man of Ur with his own father's grandfather, who had borne a similar or the same name. In terms of chronology, a system of which was certainly not unknown in his own cultural sphere and era, there lay between the boy Joseph and the wanderings of his spiritual, physical ancestor a good twenty generations, some six hundred Babylonian rounds of the year, a time span stretching back as far as the Gothic Middle Ages are from us—that far, and yet again not really.

For although we have adopted intact the mathematical sidereal time of that place and period—that is, from days far preceding the travels of the man of Ur—and shall likewise bequeath it to our most distant posterity, earthly time's meaning, gravity, and fullness have not always and everywhere been one and the same; despite all the objectivity of Chaldean measurement, the size of time is uneven. Six hundred years in those days and under that sky did not signify what they do to our history in the West; those expanses of time were more silent, more mute, more alike; time was less active, the efficacy of its constant work to effect change in things and the world was both

milder and more restricted—though, naturally, over those twenty
generations it had brought about significant changes and revolutions, even *natural* revolutions, changes in the earth's crust in
Joseph's immediate environs—as we know, and as he himself knew.
For where in his day were those licentious towns Gomorrah and
Sodom, the home of Lot of Haran, whom the man of Ur had received into his close kinship? A leaden, briny sea now lay where
their lewdness had once flourished, the result of an upheaval that
had flooded the region in fiery pitch and brimstone so dreadful and
all-destroying that Lot's daughters, who had escaped in the nick of
time with him—the same women he had tried to offer up to the lusts
of the Sodomites in lieu of certain staid visitors—had been crazed
enough to believe that there were no other humans left on earth and
out of feminine concern for the continuance of the human race had
lain with their own father.

Time in its course had, after all, left behind just such visible
transformations. There had been periods of blessing and periods of
curse, of plenty and scarcity, with campaigns of war, changing rulers,
and new gods. Yet, on the whole, the mind of the age was more conservative than ours. The shape of Joseph's life, his modes of thought,
his customs were far less different from his ancestors' than ours are
from the crusaders'. Memories based on oral tradition passed from
generation to generation were more direct, unimpeded, intimate;
time was more uniform, the eye could pierce through its vista more
easily. In short, there is no reason to be annoyed with Joseph for
dreamily collapsing time and, at least occasionally, when his mind
was less exact, at night perhaps or by moonlight, for considering the
man of Ur to be his father's grandfather—nor given such imprecision, did matters rest there. For in all probability, we should add,
the man of Ur was not the real and original man of Ur. Probably—
probable even to young Joseph, when, by day, he was more precise—
the former had never seen the moon citadel of Uru, but rather it had
been *his* father who had gone up from there, toward the north, to
Haran in the land of Naharina; and it was from Haran, then, that our
imprecisely called man of Ur had, at the bidding of the Lord of the
gods, departed for the land of the Amorites, together with Lot, who
was later to reside in Sodom and whom communal tradition dreamily declared to be a nephew of the man of Ur, inasmuch as Lot was a
"son of Haran," his brother. To be sure, Lot of Sodom was a son of

Haran, since he came from that city, just as had the man of Ur. But to turn Haran, the City of the Way, into a brother of the man of Ur, making a nephew out of Lot the proselyte, was purest dreaming— a fancy not tenable by day, yet it goes a long way to explain how it was so easy for the young Joseph to make his own little mistakes.

He made them in the same good faith, for instance, as the star-worshipers and astrologers of Shinar, when for their prognostications they followed a principle of astral representation, substituting one heavenly body for another—for example, exchanging the sun, once it had set, with Ninurta, the planet of war and state, or the planet Mardug with the constellation of Scorpio, blithely calling the latter Mardug and naming Ninurta the sun. In his desire to put a beginning to the events of which he was part, Joseph did much the same as a practical makeshift, for he was met with the same difficulty that confronts every such endeavor—the fact that everyone has a father and nothing is first, comes of itself, or is its own cause, but rather everything has been engendered and points backward, deeper into the first foundations, the depths and abysses of the well of the past. Joseph knew, of course, that the Ur-man's father, that genuine man of Uru, also had to have had a father with whom his own personal history would then have had to begin, and so forth, back to Jabel, Adah's son, the primal ancestor of those who live in tents and breed cattle. And so for Joseph the departure from Shinar also meant only a conditional and particular primal beginning, for he had been well instructed, in song and saga, how behind it things went on and on toward universality, by way of many stories, as far back as Adapa or Adama, the first man, who according to Babylonian lore—lies told in verse that Joseph even knew partly by heart—had been the son of Ea, the god of wisdom and the watery depths, and was said to have served the gods as baker and cup-bearer, but about whom Joseph knew more hallowed and accurate things; as far back as the garden in the East, where had stood two trees, one of life and the other an unchaste tree of death—back to the beginning, to the origin of the world, of heaven and the earthly universe formed out of a formless void by the Word that was moving above the primal waters and was God. But was not this, too, only a conditional, particular beginning of things? There had been beings even then to watch the creator in wonder and amazement: the sons of god, astral angels— about whom Joseph knew some remarkable and even comic stories—and foul demons. They must have come from a past world eon, which in perishing of old age had provided the raw material for the formless void—and had that even been the very first eon of all?

At this point the young Joseph grew dizzy, just as we do when leaning over the edge of the well; and despite those little imprecisions that ill become us but that his handsome and beautiful head allowed itself, we feel him close to us, our contemporary in relation to that underworldly gorge of the past, into which he too, now so distant, has already peered. He was a human being like us, so it appears to us, and despite being so early in time was, mathematically speaking, as far as we from the beginning foundations of humanity (not to mention, yet again, the beginning of all things), since those in fact lie in the abysmal darkness of the well's gorge. And so in our scrutiny either we shall have to hold to conditional pseudo-beginnings that we confuse with real beginnings in much the same way that Joseph confused the wanderer from Ur on the one hand with the man's father and on the other with his own great-grandfather, or we shall be lured backward, ever backward, from one coastal backdrop to another and into immeasurable depths.

3

We mentioned the example of those lovely Babylonian verses that Joseph knew by heart and that were taken from a larger written tradition full of spurious wisdom. He had learned them from travelers passing through Hebron, whom in his amiable fashion he had engaged in conversation, and from his tutor, old Eliezer, a freed slave of his father's—not to be confused (as Joseph sometimes did—a confusion in which the old man himself probably indulged on occasion) with the Eliezer who was the oldest servant of the wanderer from Ur and who had once wooed Bethuel's daughter by the well for Isaak. In point of fact, we know these verses and legends; we possess the texts on tablets found in Nineveh, in the palace of Assurbanipal, King of All That Is, son of Assarhaddon, son of Sennacherib, several of which provide, in delicate cuneiform inscribed on grayish yellow clay, our earliest recorded source for the Great Flood in which the Lord destroyed the first human race because of its depravity—and which also played such a significant role in Joseph's own personal tradition. To be frank, however, the word "source," at least in its most literal sense, is somewhat out of place here; for those little cracked tablets are copies that date from a mere six hundred years before the common era and that Assurbanipal (a sovereign fond of all thought fixed in writing, an avid collector of clever works of wisdom, and himself an "arch-clever" man, to use the Babylonian term) had ordered learned slaves to transcribe from an original a good thousand years older—meaning it had originated in the days of the Lawgiver and the moon-wanderer and so was about as easy or as difficult for Assurbanipal's scribes to read and understand as a manuscript from the days of Charlemagne would be for us today. A hieratic document, executed in a very obsolete and rudimentary script, it must have been difficult to decipher even then, and it remains a matter of doubt whether in preparation of the copy original meanings were fully preserved.

Except that this original was itself not actually an original, not *the* original if viewed correctly. It was itself already a copy of a document from God knows what ancient time, upon which, therefore, one might, without precisely knowing where one is, come to rest, declaring it the true original—if it were not for the fact that in its own day a scribal hand had doctored it with glosses and addenda intended as an aid for a better understanding of yet another text from still more ancient times, though probably achieving just the opposite by his "modern" transmogrification of its wisdom. And so we might continue on and on, were it not for the hope that our listeners already grasp what we have in mind at the mention of coastal backdrops and the gorge of the well.

The people of Egypt had a term for this, a word Joseph knew and occasionally used. For although no Hamites were tolerated in Jacob's camp—because of the sin of their ancestor, who had been turned black all over for shaming his father, and also because Jacob disapproved of the morals of Mizraim on religious grounds—Joseph, being a curious young lad, nevertheless often associated with Egyptians in the cities of Kiriath-Arba and Sichem and picked up a thing or two in a language he would one day speak with such brilliant perfection. Speaking of things of indefinite and very great age or, better, from time out of mind, Egyptians said "From the days of Set," referring, of course, to one of their gods, the conniving brother

of their Mardug or Tammuz, whom they called Osiris, the martyr—
a sobriquet given him because Set, having first lured him into a burial chest, had tossed him into the river and then like some wild beast
torn him to pieces besides, murdering him for good and all, so that
Usiri, his victim, now reigned in the underworld as lord of the dead
and king of eternity. "From the days of Set"—the people of Mizraim
had all sorts of uses for the idiom, since the origin of everything they
knew was inexplicably lost in that same darkness.

At the edge of the Libyan desert, near Memphis, there brooded a
colossus hewn from rock, a fifty-three-meter-tall hybrid of lion and
maiden, with female breasts and a man's beard—its headcloth displaying the royal serpent rising to strike, its giant paws stretched out
before its feline body, its nose cropped and gnawed away by time. It
had always brooded there, had always had that nose cropped by
time, and it was impossible to remember an age when that nose had
not been cropped or that the sphinx itself had not been there. Thutmose the Fourth, Golden Sparrow-Hawk and Strong Bull, King of
Upper and Lower Egypt, Beloved of the Goddess of Truth, from the
same eighteenth dynasty from which the aforementioned Amun-is-
content would come, had ordered—following instructions received
in a dream before ascending the throne—that the desert sands that
had long since drifted in to cover most of the oversized sculpture be
dug away. But one and a half thousand years before him, King
Khufu of the fourth dynasty, who had built the Great Pyramid as his
burial monument and offered sacrifices to the sphinx, had found it
half in ruins, and no one knew of a time when it had not existed or
had even existed with its nose intact.

Had Set himself hewn the stone to create this monster, which
later generations would regard as an image of the sun god and call
"Hor in the Mountain of Light"? That is quite possible, for like
Osiris the Martyr, Set presumably had not always been a god, but a
man at one time, and indeed a king over Egypt. As for the contention one hears not infrequently that a certain Menes or Hor-Meni
founded the first Egyptian dynasty approximately six thousand
years before our common era and that anything prior is a "pre-
dynastic period"; that he, Meni, first united the lands, both upper
and lower, the papyrus and the lily, the red and the white crowns,
and ruled as the first king of the Egyptians, whose history begins

with his reign—as for that notion, presumably every word of it is false, and to the more acute and penetrating eye the primal king Meni becomes a mere backdrop in time. Egyptian priests told Herodotus that the written history of their land went back 11,340 years before his day, which for us would mean about fourteen thousand years, a number aptly suited for virtually ripping the garb of ancient primacy from King Meni's figure. The history of Egypt falls into periods of division and impotence and those of power and brilliance, into epochs without a sovereign and many petty rulers and those in which all its energies are called together in majesty; and it becomes increasingly clear that these forms of existence alternated far too often for King Meni to have been the first representative of unity. The fragmentation that he healed had been preceded by an older unity, and it by an older fragmentation; we cannot say how many times one must speak here of "older," "again," and "farther," but only that unity first flourished under a dynasty of gods, whose sons most likely were the aforesaid Set and Osiris, and that the story of Usiri, of his martyrdom, murder, and dismemberment, alludes in legendary fashion to struggles for the throne that followed and were finally settled with criminal cunning. It was that past, shaped by deep, mythic, theological processes leading to its spectral and supernatural spiritualization, that became the present and an object of devout veneration in the form of certain animals—a few falcons and jackals cherished at Butto and Nekhab, the ancient capitals of the two lands—and within those creatures the souls of these prehistoric beings were said to have been mysteriously preserved.

4

"From the days of Set"—the phrase pleased young Joseph and we share his delight in it, for like the people of Egypt we, too, find it highly suitable and applicable to absolutely everything; indeed it lies close at hand wherever we look, in every sphere of human activity, and upon closer inspection the origin of all things is lost in the days of Set.

At the point in time when our story begins—a point chosen rather arbitrarily, but we must start somewhere and leave the rest behind, otherwise we, too, would have had to begin "in the days of

Set"—Joseph was already tending flocks beside his brothers, though called to this labor within gentle limits: whenever it pleased him, he would join them in shepherding his father's herds of sheep, goats, and cattle in the pastures of Hebron. What did these animals look like? In what way were they different from those we keep and tend? They weren't the least different. They were the same tamed and penned creatures, bred at the same stage of development, just as we know them now; and in young Joseph's day, the entire history of cattle's domestication from varieties of buffalo lay so far in the past that "long ago" would have been an outright ridiculous term for such expanses of time. It has been proved that cattle were being bred in that early stage of the culture that made its tools of stone, before the Iron or Bronze Ages, and that for an Amurru lad like Joseph, educated in Babylonian and Egyptian ways, lay almost equally far in the past as for us today—the difference is imperceptible.

If we were to inquire about the breed of these wild sheep from which the animals in Jacob's and our present-day flocks were "once" bred, we would be told that it is extinct. It ceased to exist "long ago." Its domestication must have occurred in the days of Set; and be it the horse, the ass, the goat, or even the pig—bred from the wild boar that mutilated Tammuz, the shepherd—domestication goes back to that same misty past. Our historical records date back approximately seven thousand years—during this period, at least, not a single wild animal has been domesticated to serve us. All that lies beyond memory.

In that same past lies the cultivation of wild and simple grasses to yield the grains that give us bread. To its regret, botanical science declares itself unable to trace our cereal grains, which also nourished Joseph—barley, oats, rye, corn, and wheat—to their wild-growing original state, and no nation can claim to have been the first to develop and cultivate them. We are told that in Stone Age Europe there were five different varieties of wheat and three of barley. And as for the taming of the wild grape for wine—an incomparable feat in terms of human achievement, whatever else one may think of it—the tradition echoing up from the abyss ascribes this to Noah, the righteous man who survived the Flood, the same man whom the Babylonians called Utnapishtim, as well as Atrahasis, "the arch-clever man"—and it was he who told his late-born grandson Gilgamesh, the hero of those tablet sagas, about the beginning of things. This righteous man had also been, as Joseph likewise knew, the first to plant vineyards—which Joseph did not regard as all that righteous. For could he not have planted something of real use? Fig trees or olive trees? No, he was the first to make wine, got drunk on it, and in his drunkenness was mocked and gelded. But if Joseph thought it had not been all that long ago that those monstrous events had occurred and the noble grape developed—a dozen generations or so before his own "great-grandfather"—that was a reverie of error and a pious foreshortening of an inconceivably distant primal past. Though it leaves us blanching in amazement, we can only point out that even that primal distance must in turn have come much later, at a very long interval after the origins of the human race, for it to have brought forth a degree of cleverness capable of so civilizing an act as the ennobling of the wild grape.

Where do the first foundations of human civilization lie? How old is it? We ask this in relation to the distant Joseph, whose stage of development—apart from little dreamy imprecisions that bring a friendly smile to our lips—already no longer differed in its essentials from our own. The question, however, needs only to be posed, and that taunting vista of backdrop dunes opens up before us. When speaking of "antiquity" we usually mean life in the Greco-Roman world—a period, by comparison, of bright and shiny modernity. Moving back to the so-called "aboriginal" peoples of Greece, the Pelasgi, we discover that before they took possession of its islands, these were inhabited by the *true* aborigines, a race of people who were forerunners to the Phoenicians in mastering the sea, reducing the latter's distinction as the "first buccaneers" to a mere backdrop. As if that were not enough, science is increasingly inclined to the hypothesis and conviction that these "barbarians" were colonists from beyond the Pillars of Hercules, from Atlantis, the submerged continent that long ago joined Europe to America. But whether that had been the region first settled by humankind is so very uncertain that it approaches improbability, and what becomes more probable instead is that the early history of civilization, including that of Noah, that arch-clever man, must be linked to far more ancient continents that had fallen and perished much earlier still.

Those are foothills that we shall not venture to wander, that can be only dimly suggested by that Egyptian turn of phrase, and the peoples of the Orient displayed equal wisdom and piety in ascribing

to the gods their first instruction in civilized life. The red-hued people of Mizraim saw their benefactor in the martyr Osiris, who had
first taught them to till the soil and had given them laws, his deeds
having been interrupted only by the insidious attack of Set, whose
behavior toward him was that of a ravening boar. And the Chinese
see the founder of their realm in an imperial demigod named Fu Hsi,
who introduced cattle among them and taught them the precious art
of writing. This same divine being evidently did not consider them
mature enough at the time—2,852 years before our era—to be instructed in astronomy, for according to their annals this was first
shared with them some thirteen hundred years later by the foreign
emperor, Tai Ko Fokee; whereas it is certain that the astrologer
priests of Shinar were skilled in reading the signs of the zodiac several hundred years before, and we are told that a man who accompanied Alexander the Macedonian to Babylon sent to Aristotle baked
clay tablets with Chaldean astronomical inscriptions whose data
would be 4,160 years old today. That is easily possible; for it is
probable that celestial observations and calendric calculations had
already been made on the continent of Atlantis, whose destruction
the scholar Solon dated to nine thousand years before his own
lifetime—meaning that humankind had advanced to the study of
these high arts a good 11,500 years before our era.

Clearly, then, writing is to be regarded as no more recent, and
quite possibly much older still. We speak of it because Joseph had a
particular and lively fondness for it and, unlike all his siblings, had
early on—at first with Eliezer's assistance—perfected himself in not
only the Babylonian but also Phoenician and Hittite scripts. He had
a true partiality, a weakness for the god—or idol—who in the east
was called Nabu, the writer of history, but was known as Taut in
Tyre and Sidon, being viewed in both regions as the inventor of symbols and the chronicler of primal beginnings, but who in Egypt was
Thoth of Khmunu, scribe of the gods and patron of science, whose
position in the land below was esteemed more highly than all
others—a truthful, temperate, and cautious god, who at times took
the charming shape of a white-haired monkey, but at times also had
the head of an ibis, and, moreover, much to Joseph's liking, maintained very subtle and solemn relations with the moon. The young
man did not even dare admit this fondness to his father Jacob, who
was unbending in his prohibition of dalliance with any such riffraff

idols and was probably more stern in this regard than certain highest powers to which his sternness was dedicated, for Joseph's story teaches us that such powers did not seriously hold against him—or at least not for long—these little excursions into what were actually proscribed areas.

By way of suggesting the murky origins of the art of writing, it might be better to employ a variation of that Egyptian phrase and say that it comes "from the days of Thoth." The scroll can be found depicted on the most ancient Egyptian monuments, and we know that a papyrus belonging to Horus-Send, a king of the second dynasty there, some six thousand years ago, was already considered so old that it was said Send had inherited it from Set. During the reigns of Sneferu and the aforementioned Khufu, solar sons of the fourth dynasty, when the pyramids of Giza were built, knowledge of writing was so common among the lower classes that today we can study simple inscriptions scratched by workers into the gigantic building blocks. It should come as no surprise, however, that such knowledge was widespread even in those remote periods, not when one recalls that priestly testimony concerning the age of Egypt's written history.

And if the days of fixed symbolic language are beyond our counting—where, then, would one search for the beginnings of the spoken word? The oldest language, the primal tongue, is said to be the Indo-Germanic, Indo-European, Sanskrit. But it is as good as certain that the "primal" is as premature in this case as in many another, and that there was yet again an older mother tongue that contained within it the roots of Aryan as well as Semitic and Hamitic dialects. It was probably spoken on Atlantis, whose silhouette forms the last backdrop of foothills still vaguely discernible in the distant haze of the past, and yet even it can hardly be the primal homeland of man the speaker of words.

5

Certain discoveries have induced experts in the history of the earth to estimate the human species to be five hundred thousand years old. That is cutting it fine—first, in light of what science teaches to be

true today, that man qua animal is the oldest mammal and already
during the later ages of prehistoric life, prior to any cerebral development, lived his life on earth clad in various zoological fashions, including amphibian and reptilian; and second, in light of what vast
expanses of time beyond our ken must have been required for a kind
of semi-erect, somnambulant, web-fingered marsupial twitching
with protoreason, such as humans surely must have been before the
appearance of that arch-clever man Noah–Utnapishtim, to become
the inventor of the bow and arrow, the master of fire, the smith of
meteoric iron, the breeder of domestic animals, the cultivator of
grain and wine—to become, in a word, the precocious, skillful, and
in every definitive sense modern creature that stepped out to meet us
as a human being in the first dawn of history. A sage in the temple at
Sais explained to Solon that the Greek legend of Phaethon stemmed
from a deviation in the course of heavenly bodies moving in space
around the earth, a deviation that human beings had experienced as a
devastating conflagration on earth. And it surely becomes ever more
certain that in its dreams—shapeless, yet constantly reshaped in fab-
ulous forms—human memory reaches back to incredibly ancient ca-
tastrophes, traditions of which, fed by later and smaller events of a
similar sort, found a home among various peoples, giving rise to that
same series of backdrops that lure and excite the wanderer through
time.

The verses from those tablets that were recited for Joseph and
that he learned by heart told, among other things, the story of the
Great Flood. He would have known this tale even had it not come to
him clad in Babylonian language and form; for it was alive everywhere in his western land, and especially among his own people,
though in a somewhat different form and with other details from
what people in the land between the rivers believed to be true. During his youth, in fact, it was on the verge of being fixed by his tribe
into a particular version, a variant on the eastern form. And Joseph
knew very well what had happened back then, when all flesh, animals not excepted, had corrupted its way in indescribable deeds, and
even the earth itself had committed whoredom and brought forth
deceitful tares where wheat had been sown—and all of this despite
Noah's warnings, so that the Lord and Creator, who had to watch as
even His angels became involved in this abomination, could finally

no longer justify or tolerate it and much to His pain, after a final grace period of one hundred twenty years, had to dispense His watery justice. And how in His marvelous kindness—in which His angels shared not a whit—He had left open a back door through which life might escape, in the form of an ark covered with pitch, into which Noah and the animal world climbed. Joseph knew that as well, and knew the day on which the creatures had entered the ark: the tenth day in the month of Marcheshvan, and on the seventeenth the flood burst, at the time of the spring thaw, when Sirius rises by day and water begins to surge in the wells. On that very day—Joseph had learned the date from old Eliezer. But how often had that day returned since then? He did not think of that, nor did old Eliezer think of it—and here lies the beginning of the illusion of piercing through the vista of time, of the foreshortenings and confusions that govern tradition.

Heaven knows when the Euphrates, always prone to irregularity and violence—or perhaps the Persian Gulf, bursting over the flatlands amid whirlwinds and earthquakes—had invaded to drown everything and, though not the source of the tradition of the Flood, had provided that story nourishment for a final time, enlivening it with the awful look of reality and establishing itself as *the* Flood for all following generations. Perhaps the most recent horror-filled incident of this sort had occurred not all that long before, and the closer it lay, the more intriguing the question whether—and if so, how—the generation for whom this was a personal experience was able to confuse its present affliction with the subject matter of a tradition, with *the* Flood. It happened, and that it happened should not be cause for any amazement or intellectual disparagement. The experience consisted not so much in something out of the past being repeated, as in its becoming the present. But the attainment of such a present reality was based in the fact that the circumstances leading to it were present at all times. The ways of the flesh were corrupted at all times, or could be despite the greatest piety—for do people even know if they are doing good or evil in God's eyes or if what appears good to them may not be an abomination before heaven? In its stupidity humankind knows neither God nor the decrees of the underworld; at any time forbearance may prove to be exhausted and judgment enacted. Nor, more than likely, had the warning voice been missing, the voice of a knowing and arch-clever man who could interpret the signs and, taking wise measures beforehand, is the only one of tens of thousands to escape—but not before first entrusting the tablets of knowledge to the earth as the seed of future wisdom, so that once the waters have dispersed, everything can begin anew from this written seed. At any time—that is the word of mystery, a mystery that knows no time. But the form of timelessness is the now and the here.

The Flood took place on the Euphrates, but it took place in China as well. Around the year 1300 before our era, there was a dreadful mutiny of the Huang Ho—which, by the way, led to measures controlling its course—a repetition of the Great Flood that had occurred some one thousand fifty years before, under the fifth emperor, whose Noah was named Yao; but, in terms of time, it was a long way from being the true, the first Flood, for the memory of that original event is common to all peoples. Just as the Babylonian tale of the Flood that Joseph knew was only a postscript to ancient and ever more ancient originals, so, too, the flood experience itself can be traced back to ever more remote primal scenes, and presumably one is being especially thorough if one designates the sinking of the land of Atlantis beneath the ocean's waves as the final, the true original— ghastly news of which, spreading to all the regions of the earth whose inhabitants had once come from there, became fixed forever in human memory as a variable tradition. That is, however, only an illusory station and preliminary goal. One set of Chaldean calculations shows that a period of 39,180 years lay between the Flood and the first historical dynasty in the land of the two rivers. Therefore the sinking of Atlantis—a mere nine thousand years before Solon and thus a very recent catastrophe within the perspective of earth's larger history—cannot possibly have been *the* Flood. It, too, was but a repetition, a moment when something from the deep past became the present, a terrible refresher of memory; and the real origin of the story must be moved back to at least that incalculable moment in time when the continental island called Lemuria, itself only a remnant of the old continent of Gondwanaland, vanished into the billows of the Indian Ocean.

Our concern is not time that can be enumerated, but rather its abrogation in the mystery of the transposition of tradition and prophecy, lending the word "sometime"—or, better, the word "once"—its double meaning of past and future and thus its import as potential present. Here the idea of reincarnation has its roots. The kings of Babel and of the two lands of Egypt, both curly-bearded Kurigalzu and Horus, whose name was Amun-is-content, in his palace at Thebes plus all their predecessors and successors, *were* the sun god manifested in the flesh—which is to say, myth became *mysterium* in them, without the tiniest space left for differentiating between being and meaning. It would be three thousand years before a time came when people could dispute whether the Eucharist's host "is" or merely "signifies" the body of the sacrificial victim; but even those terribly futile discussions have been unable to change the fact that the essence of the mystery is and remains the timeless present. That is the meaning of the solemn rite, of the feast. Every Christmas the child who is to save the world, who is destined to suffer and die and rise again, is born on earth in a manger once more. And when at midsummer, at the Feast of the Weeping Women, the Feast of the Burning Lamp, the Feast of Tammuz—in Sichem or at Bethlachem—Joseph experienced in the enlarged present the murder of the "lost and lamented son," of the young god, of Osiris–Adonai, followed by his resurrection amid the many sobbing flutes and joyful cries, what reigned over all that was the abrogation of time in mystery, the same nullification that interests us here, because it removes every logical stumbling block from a mode of thought that simply recognized the Flood in each new calamity of rising waters.

6

Alongside the story of the Flood stands the one about the Great Tower, shared, like the first, among many people. Situated in the localized present of there and then, it likewise offered as much occasion for forming backdrops and dreamy transpositions. It is as certain as it is excusable that Joseph, for example, plainly believed the tower of the sun citadel in Babel, called Esagila or House of the Raising of the Head, to be the Great Tower. Even the wanderer from Ur had doubtless believed as much; and not only in Joseph's immediate circle, but indeed in the land of Shinar as well, people believed it without question. This ancient and monstrous seven-storied tower of Esagila—built, as everyone agreed, by Bel, the Creator, though with the assistance of the black-haired people he first had to make;

renovated and enlarged by Hammuragash the Lawgiver; and enameled in a brightly colored splendor that Joseph could picture in his
mind—was for every Chaldean the embodiment of a tradition of
great antiquity now made visible and experienced in the present: a
Tower built by human hands and reaching to the heavens. That in
Joseph's particular world the Tower saga was joined with other notions not actually intrinsic to it—with the idea of "scattering," for
instance—can only be explained by the personal behavior of the
moon man, by his annoyance and emigration, since for the people of
Shinar such a concept had nothing whatever to do with the *migdal*s
or citadel towers of their cities. On the contrary, Hammuragash the
Lawgiver had expressly ordered it be written down that he had made
their spires so high in order "to gather" a fickle people dispersing in
all directions back under his sway, under the rule of "heaven's
envoy." But, given his views of divinity, the moon man had taken offense at this and scattered, in defiance of Nimrod's royal policy of
gathering; and thus in Joseph's homeland something out of the past,
but still present in the form of Esagila, took on an aura of the future
and prophecy. Judgment hovered over that heaven-high, defiant
monument to Nimrod's royal presumption; not one stone would be
left upon another and its builders would be confounded and scattered by the Lord of the gods. That is what old Eliezer taught Jacob's
son, thus preserving the double meaning of "once" and achieving
out of a mixture of saga and prediction a timeless presence in the
present—the Tower of the Chaldeans.

For Joseph, then, this structure was bound up with the story of
the Great Tower. But it is clear, of course, that on the immeasurable
journey back to the original tower, Esagila is only a backdrop of
dunes—one of many. The people of Mizraim also viewed the Tower
as part of the present, in the form of King Khufu's astounding desert
tomb. And in nations of whose existence neither Joseph nor old
Eliezer had even the vaguest notion, in the middle of America, in
fact, people had their "Tower" as well—or their image of the
Tower—the great pyramid of Cholula, whose ruins reveal dimensions that certainly would have had to rouse anger and jealousy in
King Khufu. The people of Cholula always denied that they themselves built this gigantic edifice. They declared it to be literally the
work of giants, for, they maintained, it was wanderers from the East,
a superior people drunk with longing for the sun, who had set their

fervor and energy to work in raising it up out of clay and bitumen in order to draw near to their beloved star. Several things speak for the supposition that these advanced strangers were colonists from Atlantis; and it would seem that wherever these sun-worshipers and inveterate astronomers went, their most urgent task was to raise up, before the marveling eyes of the natives, mighty observatories built after the model of their high towers at home—in particular, of one in the middle of their land, the soaring mountain to the gods of which Plato speaks. So perhaps the prototype of the Great Tower should also be sought in Atlantis. At least we cannot follow its history any farther back and have reached the end of our study of this strange object.

7

But where did Paradise lie? The "Garden in the East"? The place of serenity and happiness, man's home, where he had tasted of the evil tree and been driven out—or, better, driven himself from it and scattered over the earth? Young Joseph knew this as well as he knew about the Flood, and from the same sources. He had to smile a little whenever he heard inhabitants of the Syrian desert claim that the great oasis of Damascus was Paradise—for one could not dream of a more heavenly place than that, green with orchards and sweetly watered gardens nestled between majestic mountains and seas of meadows, teeming with all sorts of people, rich in luxurious commerce. Nor, out of courtesy, did he actually shrug, though he did so in his mind, whenever men from Mizraim declared the site of the garden had obviously been Egypt, for it was the center, the navel of the world. The curly-bearded men of Shinar implied the same thing, that Babel was the sacred middle point of the world, when they called their royal city "Gate of God" and "Bond Between Heaven and Earth"—as a boy Joseph could fluently imitate their sophisticated dialect, repeating it after them: "*Bab-ilu markas šamê u irsitim.*" But Joseph had better information from closer to home, taken directly, in fact, from the life of his good and solemnly pondering father, who, while still a young man—on his journey from his family home at Well of Seven to Naharaim to see his uncle in Haran—had unexpectedly and unwittingly stumbled upon the real Gate of Heaven, the true navel of the world: at the hilltop city of Luz, with its sacred circle of stones, which he had then named Beth-el, House of God, because there, while fleeing from Esau, he had been granted the grandest and most dreadful revelation of his life. Ever afterward, that hilltop—where Jacob had stood his stony pillow on end as a monument and anointed it with oil—was for Joseph and those around him the middle of the world, the place of the umbilical cord between heaven and earth. Paradise, however, had not lain there, either, but in regions of the beginning and of home, somewhere there—so Joseph's childish conviction, one that enjoyed wide support, by the way—in the land from where the man of the moon city had once set out, in lower Shinar, there where the river divided and the moist soil between its arms abounded in trees that bear sweet fruit even today.

It has long remained the view favored by theological science that it was here, somewhere in southern Babylonia, that one should search for Eden, that Adam's body was formed from Babylonian clay. And yet once again we are dealing with the familiar backdrop effect—the same system of overlapping, of localizations referring us back farther still—that we have had numerous opportunities to study. Except that in this case, we are dealing with a truly extraordinary and, in the most literal sense, alluring version of it, for it lures us above and moves us beyond anything earthly. Except that here the gorge of the well of human history is revealed in all its depths, in depths beyond all measure—indeed a bottomlessness to which one ultimately can no longer apply the concepts either of depth or darkness, but, on the contrary, only images of height and light—those bright heights, that is, out of which could come a *Fall*, the story of which is inextricably linked with our souls' memory of the Garden of Happiness.

The traditional topography of Paradise is precise in one respect. There was, it is said, a river that went out of Eden to water the garden, and from there divided into the world's four rivers: the Pishon, the Gihon, the Euphrates, and the Hiddekel. The Pishon, so one interpretation adds, is also called the Ganges; it encompasses all of India and bears gold with it. The Gihon is said to be the Nile, the greatest river of the world, which encompasses the whole land of the Moors. The Hiddekel, then—its current swift as an arrow—is the Tigris, which flows toward the east of Assyria. There is no dispute as to this last. Disputed, however, and by credible parties, is the equation of the Pishon and Gihon with the Ganges and Nile. Instead, they say, what is meant is the Araxes, which empties into the Caspian Sea, and the Halys, which flows into the Black Sea; for Paradise is indeed to be thought of as situated within a Babylonian perspective, yet not in Babylonia itself, but in the Armenian alpine country north of the Mesopotamian plain, where those rivers have sources close together.

Reason greets such information with a certain amount of applause. For if, as the most venerable report has it, the "Phrat," or Euphrates, arose within Paradise, it is untenable to think of the latter as located at that river's mouth. But having awarded the palm to the land of Armenia on the basis of that insight, we would at best have made one step leading to the next truth—only to come, then, to a halt one backdrop, one confusion farther on.

God gave the world, as old Eliezer himself instructed Joseph, four sides: morning, evening, noon, and midnight, watched over from the throne of dominion by four holy beasts and four guardian angels, who keep an unswerving eye upon this fundamental order. Did not the pyramids in Lower Egypt likewise have their four sides, each covered with sparkling cement, turned precisely toward the earth's four quarters? That same arrangement held for the rivers of Paradise. Their courses were to be thought of as serpents, the tips of whose tails touched but whose mouths lay far apart, each directed toward one of the four points of heaven. This is an obvious adaptation. Transferred to anterior Asia, it repeats the geography of another place now lost from sight, but with which we are very familiar: Atlantis, of course, where, according to Plato's descriptive report, the same four rivers flowed in the same fashion—pointing at right angles to the four quarters of the earth—from the towering mountain of the gods at the center of the island. By tracing back in this way, we lend every such learned dispute as to the geography of those "headwaters" or the site of the garden the mollifying stamp of idle speculation, for it becomes clear that the idea of Paradise—located now here, now there—ultimately owes its graphic description to various peoples' memories of a land now vanished, where a wise and advanced race of humans once spent blissful centuries under an order as gentle as it was holy. One cannot fail to recognize that at work here is a mixing of the tradition of an actual paradise with the saga of humankind's Golden Age. The memory of such a place refers, quite justifiably it would seem, to a Hesperian land, where— if all reports do not deceive us—a great people once lived a wise and pious life under favorable conditions never again achieved. But this could not possibly have been the Garden of Eden, man's home and the place of his Fall; it forms only a backdrop, another illusory goal on our temporal and spatial journey to Paradise—for the study of earth's earliest history looks for primal man, for the Adamite, in eras and places that perished before Atlantis itself was ever settled.

A journey of alluring and taunting delusion! For even given the excusable, though misguided, possibility of equating Paradise with the land of golden apples where the four rivers flowed, how could such a blunder—even granting the self-deception was made in good faith—have succeeded when confronted with the wraithlike world that forms the next, most distant promontory, where the tormented larva of the human species (a figure in which the handsome and beautiful Joseph would have refused, with the most justifiable outrage, to recognize himself) endured his lustful, fearful nightmare of a life, in desperate battle with armored mountains of flesh, with flying lizards and ravening salamanders? That was not the Garden of Eden; that was hell. Or rather, it was the first, accursed state after the Fall. It was not here, not at the beginning of time and space, that the fruit of the Tree of Lust and Death was plucked and tasted. That came before. The well of time, it turns out, has been plumbed before we ever reach the goal, the end and the beginning, we seek. The history of man is older than the material world that his will has worked, older than the life that rests upon his will.

8

A long tradition of thought—based on humankind's truest self-perception and arising early on, to become incorporated as an heirloom into the long succession of religions, prophecies, and epistemologies of the East, into Avesta, Islam, Manichaeism, Gnosticism, and Hellenistic cults—deals with the figure of the first or perfect human being, *adam qadmon* in Hebrew, who is to be thought of as a youthful creature of pure light, created before the beginning of the world as the prototype and epitome of humanity, with which, then, variable but ultimately concordant doctrines and reports become associated. This primal man, so it is said, had from the very beginning been God's chosen warrior in the battle against the evil invading the newly created world, but had come to harm, had been chained by demons, imprisoned in matter, estranged from his origins, but had been freed again from his earthly, bodily existence by a second emissary of the Godhead, who in some mysterious way was himself yet again, his own higher self, had then been led back into the world of light, but in the process had had to leave behind portions of his own light, which was then used for forming the material world and humankind on earth. What marvelous stories—in which, to be sure, the already discernible religious element of redemption is still overridden by cosmogonic intentions; for we hear how this primal human Son of God contained within his body of light the seven metals, each corresponding to one of the seven planets, from which the world was formed. This is also expressed by the fact that this being—who in emanating from the first paternal cause was both light and man—descended through the seven planetary spheres and from the ruling power of each sphere received some portion of its nature. But, then, as he gazed downward, he noticed his reflection in matter, became enamored of it, descended to it, and thus found himself ensnared in the bonds of lower nature. This explains, then, man's double nature, whereby the hallmarks of a divine origin and essential freedom are forever entangled beyond unravelment in the heavy fetters of the lower world.

It is in this narcissistic image so full of tragic charm that the tradition begins to achieve some refinement of meaning. This refinement occurs at that moment when the descent of the divine child out of his world of light and into nature ceases to be a matter of pure obedience to a higher injunction—and thus innocent—and gains instead the stamp of an independent and voluntary act of longing—that is, of guilt. At the same time we begin to understand the puzzling meaning of that "second emissary," who, being identical with the man of light in a higher sense, has come to free him from his ever-growing entanglement in darkness and to lead him home again. For here the doctrine proceeds to divide the world into the three personal elements of matter, soul, and spirit, out of whose inter-action with one another and the Godhead there unfolds the romance that has as its true hero the adventurous soul of man—so creative in its adventures—and that, as a complete myth uniting knowledge of the beginning with a prophecy of last things, provides clear informa-tion as to the true location of Paradise and the story of the Fall.

It is stated that the soul—that is, the primal human state—was, like matter, one of the principles ordained from the beginning, pos-sessing life, but not knowledge. Indeed, it had so little knowledge that, dwelling in proximity to God in a lofty world of peace and hap-piness, it let itself be agitated and confused by its inclination—in the literal sense of moving in a direction—toward formless matter, be-came eager to mix with matter, and to generate out of it those forms by which it could achieve physical desires. But even after the soul had let itself be seduced to descend from its home, the desire and pain of its passion did not abate, but instead became so strong that it was pure torment—due to the fact that matter, being indolent and stubborn, wanted nothing more than to remain in its primal form-less state, did not wish to know anything whatever about taking on form merely to please the soul, and offered every conceivable resis-tance to being formed into any shape. And here God intervened, for surely He found that, given this state of affairs, He had no choice but to assist the soul, which, though errant, was His concomitant. To support it in its amorous struggle with obstinate matter, He created the world; that is to say: as a means of assisting the primal human state, He generated within it solid, long-lived forms, thus enabling the soul to gratify its physical desires on these forms and generate human beings. Immediately thereafter, however, and pursuant to a loftily considered plan, He did something else. He sent into the world and to man—and these are the very words of the source upon which we are drawing—the *spirit* taken from the substance of His own divinity and intended to awaken the soul from its sleep within the shell of man, so that it might show the soul that, by the will of the Father, this world was not its abode and that its sensual enter-prise in passion had been a sin—and that the creation of the world should be regarded as that sin's consequence. In truth, the spirit is forever admonishing the human soul imprisoned in matter, is steadfastly trying to make clear to it that the formation of the world is the result of its having foolishly mingled with matter and that, if it were to separate itself from matter, the world of forms would immediately be bereft of existence. It is therefore the duty of the spirit to awaken the soul to this insight; it is its hope and the goal of its pursuit to impart knowledge of this entire state of affairs to the passionate soul, so that the latter will finally recognize its home in the world above, drive out every thought of this lower world, and strive to return to the sphere of peace and happiness in order to regain its home there. The moment that occurs, this lower world will render itself null and void; matter will regain its indolent stubborn will, will be freed from its union with form, be left to enjoy the same formlessness it knew at the beginning of eternity, and so be happy once again in its own fashion.

That, then, is the doctrine and romance of the soul. There can be no doubt we have arrived at the final step "backward," have gained man's loftiest past, defined Paradise, and traced the story of the Fall, of knowledge and of death, back to its pure and truthful form. The soul of the primal man is the oldest of things or, more precisely, an oldest of things—for it was always there, before time and form, just as God was always there, and matter, too. As for the spirit, in which we recognize that "second emissary" appointed to bring the soul home, it is in some indefinite sense closely akin to the former, but is not that same self yet again, for it is younger, an emanation of God to instruct and liberate the soul, rendering the world of forms null and void in the process. And if in certain phrases of this doctrine the claim or allegorical hint is made for a higher unity of soul and spirit, there is nonetheless a good reason behind it—that good reason is not exhausted, however, in an awareness that the primal man's soul was originally a warrior for God against evil and that this assigned role is related to the one that later devolved upon the spirit as the emissary sent to liberate the soul. In fact, the doctrine fails to provide an explanation for its reasoning because it has not yet arrived at a full development of the role that the *spirit* plays in the romance of the soul and thus clearly requires supplementation in this regard.

In this world of forms and of death, conceived in the nuptial recognition of soul and matter, the spirit's mission is unequivocally and clearly outlined. Its divine charge is to awaken in the soul—still entangled in form and death—the memory of its higher origin, to convince it that its having become involved with matter was a blunder that gave rise to the world, and finally to strengthen its sense of homesickness until it one day frees itself totally from pain and carnal desire and floats homeward—and with that, the end of the world would be instantly achieved, matter given its old freedom back, and death removed from the world. But just as it can happen that an ambassador, who is sent from one kingdom to another hostile realm and remains there for a long time, can become corrupted in terms of his own country's welfare, and in settling in and adapting can—without ever noticing it himself—take on the color of thought, slide into the self-interested standpoint of the enemy nation, so that he becomes unfit for representing the interests of his homeland and has to be called back, the same thing or something very like it happens to the spirit in the course of its mission. The longer its assignment takes and the longer the spirit remains at its diplomatic post here below, the more obvious the inner flaw, analogous to that ambassador's corruption, in its activity becomes, until the rupture can hardly remain hidden from the higher sphere and must lead, one can only surmise, to its recall—if, that is, the question of a practical replacement were more easily solved than it apparently is.

There can be no doubt that as time goes by the spirit finds itself increasingly troubled by its role as the world's destroyer and gravedigger. Colored by the duration of its stay, the spirit's viewpoint changes to such an extent that, though it perceives itself as having been sent to remove death from the world, it learns to regard itself as just the opposite, as the deadly principle, as that which brings death upon the world. That is indeed a question of viewpoint and perception—one can judge the matter now one way, now another. Except that one should know the appropriate mode of thought to which one is inherently duty-bound, otherwise precisely the phenomenon we straightforwardly called corruption will take root, and one will estrange oneself from one's natural tasks. A certain weakness in the spirit's character becomes evident here, inasmuch as it has difficulty bearing up under its reputation as the deadly principle intent on destroying all forms—a reputation, moreover, that it largely brought upon itself, given its own nature and its own judgmental impulses, including those directed against itself—

and makes it a point of honor to be rid of that reputation. Not that it deliberately sets out to betray its own mission; but against its best intentions and under the coercion of both that impulse and an inner agitation that might be termed an illicit infatuation with the soul and its passionate ways, words get twisted around in its mouth until they come out sounding like flattery of the soul and its enterprise and, with a kind of tendentious wit directed against the spirit's pure goals, speak out in favor of life and forms. Whether, to be sure, such traitorous or near-traitorous behavior is of any use to the spirit; whether, in any case, it cannot avoid, even by these means, serving the purpose for which it is sent (that is, to render the material world null and void by freeing the soul from it); and whether it does not know all this perfectly well itself and only acts in this way out of an ultimate certainty that it can allow itself to do so—such questions must remain open. In any case, in this witty and self-abnegating union of its own will with that of the soul, one can spot the explanation behind the allegorical turn the doctrine takes in saying that the "second emissary" is another self of that man of light sent to do battle with evil. Indeed, it is possible that hidden within this maneuver is a prophetic allusion to secret counsels of God that the doctrine considers too holy and impenetrable to be spoken straight out.

9

But when all this is regarded calmly, to speak of a "Fall" into sin by the soul or the primal man of light is possible only as starkly moralistic overstatement. At most the soul sinned against itself—by foolishly sacrificing its original peaceful and happy state—but not against God, not by disobeying any prohibition that He might have set down against its passionate behavior. Such a prohibition was never issued—at least not according to the doctrine we have adopted. If nevertheless pious tradition reports such a thing—that is, a divine prohibition against the first human beings' eating of the Tree of the Knowledge of "Good and Evil"—one must first bear in mind that we are dealing here with a secondary and already earthly event and with human beings, who with God's own creative assistance had arisen out of the soul's knowledge of matter; and if God really did put them to this test, there can be no doubt whatever that He knew what the result would be beforehand, and the only obscure issue is why, by setting forth a prohibition that was certain not to be observed, He chose not to avoid arousing the schadenfreude of the angelic entourage, given its already very unfavorable opinion of humankind. Second of all, since the phrase "good and evil" is without any doubt an acknowledged gloss and addition to the pure text and that, in fact, the issue was one of knowledge per se, resulting not in the moral ability to distinguish between good and evil, but rather in death itself, there is nothing to stand in the way of our declaring the information about the "prohibition" itself to be a well-intended but inappropriate addendum of the same sort.

Everything speaks in favor of this view, but principally the fact that God was not angered by the soul's acting upon its yearnings, did not cast it out or inflict any punishment that might have gone beyond the measure of suffering that it voluntarily drew upon itself, while, to be sure, also finding compensation in desire. Instead, it is clear that upon beholding the soul's passion, He was touched, if not by sympathy, then by pity; for immediately and unbidden He came to its aid, personally intervened in its loving struggle to know matter by allowing death's world of forms to issue from it, so that the soul could then satisfy its desire in them—conduct on God's part in which it is indeed very difficult, if not impossible, to distinguish between sympathy and pity.

To speak in this connection, then, of sin in the sense of an offense against God and His explicit will is relevant only in part, especially when one includes God's peculiar zeal in His relations with the race that arose from the mixing of the soul and matter, with human beings who unquestionably and for good reason were an object of the angels' jealousy from the start. It made a deep impression on Joseph when old Eliezer told him of these relationships, speaking of them along the lines of what we can read even today in Hebrew commentaries on the stories of the beginning. If God had not remained silent, they say, wisely keeping to Himself the fact that out of humankind would arise not only just but also evil things, permission for the creation of human beings would not even have been granted by the Realm of Sternness. Such a term gives us important insight into the relationships involved. Above all, it instructs us that "sternness" is a concern not only of God, but indeed of His entourage as well—on whom He appears to be dependent in some (though of course in no way decisive) degree, since out of worry that there might be some difficulty from that side He decided to neglect to tell them the plain truth about what was in store, announcing some things, but keeping mum about others. But does this not indicate all the more that He was interested in the creation of the world rather than that He was opposed to it? So that if God might not exactly have enjoined and encouraged the soul in its enterprise—it certainly did not act against His intention, but rather only against that of the angels, whose less than friendly attitude toward humankind is, to be sure, an a priori certainty. To them God's creation of a living world of good and evil and His concern for it seem some sort of majestic whim that nettles them, for they assume—probably more rightly than wrongly—that behind it lay a weariness with their psalm-singing purity. Constantly hovering about their lips are amazed and reproachful questions like: "What is man, O Lord, that You are mindful of him?" And God's replies are indulgent, soothing, evasive, sometimes even annoyed— and definitely humiliating to them. There is certainly no easy explanation for the downfall of Sammael, one of the great princes among the angels, for he possessed twelve pairs of wings whereas the holy beasts and the seraphim each had only six, but—as was evident from Eliezer's lessons, to which Joseph listened with great attentiveness— its immediate cause must be traced to these conflicts. It had been Sammael in particular who had fanned the fires of the angels' sensitivity toward human beings or, better, toward God's concern for them; and on that day when God demanded that His hosts bow down before Adam because of his reason and because he knew how to give names to all things, though all the others obeyed the order, some smiling covert smiles and some with knitted brows, Sammael did not. For with savage candor he declared it absurd that those created from the effulgence of glory should sink down before something made of dust and earth—and it was on that occasion that he was overthrown, which, according to Eliezer's description, had from a distance looked like the falling of a star. But the shock of it must have remained with the other angels forever; and if ever since they have exercised the greatest caution when it comes to humankind, it nevertheless remains manifestly clear that sin's rampant spread over the earth, as for instance before the Flood and at Sodom and Gomorrah, is a regular cause for triumph among the holy entourage and of embarrassment for the Creator, who is then forced to wreak dreadful havoc—less out of His own sense of the matter than under the pressure of heaven. But if this presentation of things is correct, what then is the task of the "second emissary," of the spirit, and has it truly been sent to render the material world null and void by separating the soul from it and leading it home?

A possible supposition is that this is not God's intention and that in fact the spirit was not, as its reputation would have it, sent after the soul to play gravedigger for the world of forms created by the soul with God's gracious assistance. It is perhaps another mystery, and one perhaps based in the doctrine's contention that the second emissary was once again the first man of light sent to do battle with evil. We have long known that mystery uses time's tenses freely and may very well speak in the past when it means the future. It is possible that in saying that soul and spirit were once one, the actual intention is to say that they will be one at some point. Yes, this appears all the more plausible since the spirit represents in and of itself the principle of the future, the "It will be," the "It shall be," whereas the piety of the soul, which is bound up in forms, refers to the past and to the sacred "It was." It remains debatable just where life and death are to be found here, since both parts (the soul woven into nature and the spirit external to the world, one the principle of the past and the other of the future) claim, each in its own way, to be the water of life and each accuses the other of being on death's side—and neither unfairly, since nature without spirit, just as spirit without nature, can scarcely be called life. But the mystery—and God's quiet hope—lies perhaps in their union, that is in the spirit's genuinely entering into the world of the soul, in the mutual penetration of both principles, and in the hallowing of the one through the other, thus actualizing in the present a humanity that would be blessed with blessings of heaven above and blessings of the deep that lies below.

This, then, would be worthy of consideration as the secret possibility and final meaning of the doctrine—though strong doubt remains whether the proper path to such a goal is the spirit's self-abnegating and fawning behavior, stemming from its aforesaid all-too-lively sensitivity to the reproach of having sprung from death. And let the spirit lend its wit to the mute passions of the soul, let it celebrate the grave, call the past the sole source of life, and confess and expose itself as the evil zealot, as the murderous life-enslaving will—it remains, no matter how it presents itself, what it is: the mes-

senger of warning, the principle of opposition, umbrage, and wandering, which stirs up within the breast of one individual, among all
the great host of the lustily complacent, an uneasiness at our preter-
natural wretchedness, drives him out of the gates of the past and the
given and into the extravagant adventure of uncertainty, and makes
him like the stone that, once it has broken away and begins to roll, is
destined to set in motion an ever-growing, rolling, incalculable cas-
cade of events.

10

In this way, then, the beginnings and promontories of the past are
formed, where a particular memory may come to historical rest, as
Joseph's did at Ur, the city, and with his ancestor's departure from it.
It was a tradition of spiritual restlessness that was in his blood, that
defined his personal life, his world, and his father's actions, and that
he recognized whenever he recited a verse from the tablets:

> "Why have you instilled this uneasiness
> within my son Gilgamesh,
> Given him a heart that knows no rest?"

This knowing no rest, this questioning, listening and searching, this
wooing of God and bitter, doubt-filled striving after the true and the
just, the whence and the whither, after his own name, his own nature, the real intention of the Most High—all of it, bequeathed by
the wanderer from Ur through the generations—was expressed in
the face of the aged Jacob, in his lofty brow, in the anxious peering
gaze of his brown eyes; and how intimately Joseph loved these attributes of his father's nature, the nobility and excellence of which
his own nature was well aware—for precisely as an awareness of
higher cares and worries they lent his father's person all the dignity,
reserve, and solemnity that perfected it. Restlessness and dignity,
that is a seal of the spirit, and with a child's fearless fondness Joseph
recognized the traditional imprint upon the brow of his father and
master, although his own stamp was not the same, but—determined
more strongly by his charming mother—was more cheerful and less
anxious, and his congenial nature was more open to conversation
and sociability. But how could he have feared an anxious father lost

in pondering, when he knew how very much his father loved him? Being loved and preferred was a habit crucial to his nature, lending it color and tone; it also determined his relation to the Most High, whom, to the extent one was allowed to ascribe Him any form, Joseph imagined to be exactly like Jacob, experienced Him, so to speak, as his father repeated in a higher form, and, in his ingenuousness, was convinced that he was loved by Him in just the same way. We would like to anticipate from afar his relationship to the Adon of heaven by saying it had a "bridelike" quality—just as Joseph knew of Babylonian women, consecrated to Ishtar or Mylitta, who were pledged to unwedded lives of pious devotion in temple cells and were called "pure" or "holy," but also *enitu*, the "brides of God." There was something of the *enitu* in his own sense of life, something, too, of the strict bonds of betrothal, and, connected with that, there was moreover a certain element of fanciful playfulness that will give us considerable trouble once we are down there below with him— and indeed may be the form in which the inheritance of spirit expressed itself in his case.

On the other hand, despite his attachment, Joseph did not understand or approve the form this same inheritance had taken in his father's case: the worry, fretting, and restlessness expressed both in an overwhelming dislike of the solid, settled existence that most certainly would have suited his dignity and in an always provisional, shifting, impromptu, seminomadic attitude toward life. Without doubt, Jacob, too, was loved, looked after, preferred by Him— indeed, if that was also true of Joseph, then surely it was for his father's sake. God Shaddai had made Jacob rich in cattle and all sorts of goods in Mesopotamia, and amid his band of sons, his assemblage of wives, his shepherds and servants, he might have been a prince among the princes of the land, and indeed he was one, except not in terms of external trappings, but of his spirit and mind, as a *nabi*— a "prophet," as one who knows and has experienced God, as an arch-clever man, as one of those spiritual leaders and elders, upon whom had been bestowed the inheritance of the Chaldean and each of whom people took to be the Ur-man's physical descendant. In negotiations and business contracts they spoke with him only in the finest circumlocutions, calling him "my lord" and speaking of themselves in the most disparaging terms. Why did he and his family not live as propertied citizens in one of the cities, in Hebron itself, in

Urusalim or Sichem, and dwell in a solid house of stone and wood, beneath which he could have buried his dead? Why did he live in tents, like some Ishmaelite and Bedouin of the desert—in open country, so far outside the city that he could not even see the citadel of Kiriath-Arba, out beside wells and burial caves, oaks and terebinths, always ready to strike camp as if he dared not stay in one spot and so take root with others, as if awaiting from hour to hour the instructions that would drive him onward: to take down his tents and stalls, pack the poles, the felt, and the hides on pack camels, and move on? Joseph knew why, of course. It had to be that way because one served a God whose nature was not rest and comfortable repose, a God of future plans, within whose will grand and indefinite and far-reaching things were in the making, who, along with His brooding plans and His will for the world, was Himself actually only in the making and thus a God of unsettling uneasiness, a problem God, who wanted to be sought out and for whom one had to make oneself ready to move at all times.

In short: It was the spirit—the spirit that brings dignity, but yet again disgrace—that forbade Jacob from living a city-based settled life; and if little Joseph, who did not lack for a sense of worldly magnificence, or indeed of pomp, sometimes regretted this, we shall accept it as we do several traits of his character that are compensated for by others. As for ourselves, in setting out to tell of all these things and so, under no external duress, plunge into an adventure whose end is not in sight—"plunge" in its precise sense of downward direction—we wish candidly to express our natural and unbounded appreciation for the old man's restless opposition to remaining in one spot, to a permanent dwelling. Do we ourselves know the feeling? Have we not also been ordained to restlessness and given a heart that knows no repose? And this storyteller's star— is it not the moon, the Lord of the Way, the wanderer, who, in his stations, frees himself from each to move on? Whoever tells a story wanders through many stations in his adventures, but only pitches a tent at each, waiting for further directions, and soon feels his own heart pounding, in part out of desire, but in part also out of fear and the apprehension in his bones, yet always as a sign that the road now opens onto new adventures that he must experience precisely, in all their incalculable detail, for that is the will of the restless spirit.

We have been under way for some time now and have already

left far behind the station where we briefly lingered, have forgotten it, and, after the wont of travelers, have already established a connection with the world to which we have set our gaze and that gazes back at us, so that when it takes us in we shall not be totally stilted, bungling strangers. Is it already taking much too long, this journey? No wonder, for it is a descent into hell! Down it goes, hurling us, ashen-faced, into the dark depths, deep into that well of the past whose gorge has never been plumbed.

Why do we turn pale now? Why is our heart pounding, not just since we set out, but since receiving our first instructions to break camp, and not just out of desire, but very much with apprehension in our bones as well? Is not the past the storyteller's element, the air he breathes, a tense to which he takes like a fish to water? Yes, true enough. But why does our curious and cowardly heart refuse to be calmed by these words of reason? Surely because the element of the past, by which we are customarily carried farther, ever farther, is a different past from the one into which we now begin our trembling descent: life's past, the world that was, the dead world to which—deeper, ever deeper—our life will one day belong and to which its beginnings are already consigned to considerable depths. Granted, to die means to lose time and be hurled out of it, but in return to gain eternity and a timeless present, and thus, for the first time, real life. For the essence of life is presentness, and only by means of myth does it represent its mystery in past and future tenses. That, as it were, is life's popular method for revealing itself, whereas the mystery belongs to the initiated. Let the people be taught that the soul wanders, but those with knowledge are aware that this doctrine is but the garment of the mystery by which the soul enjoys a timeless present, with all of life belonging to it once death has released it from its solitary cell. When as adventurous storytellers we plunge into the past, we taste death and the knowledge of it—that is, the source of both our desire and our ashen-faced apprehension. But desire has more life—nor do we deny that it is bound up in the flesh. But the object of desire is the first and last of all our remarks and inquiries, of all our zeal: humanity—for which we shall search in the underworld and in death, just as Ishtar had searched there for Tammuz, and Isis for Osiris, in order to know it there where the past is.

For it *is,* always *is,* though the common phrase may be: It *was.* That is how myth speaks, for it is merely the garment of the mystery.

But mystery's festal garment is the feast itself, the ever-recurring feast that spans all of time's tenses, making both past and future present in the mind of the people. Is it any wonder that on those feast days human beings were all in a ferment and custom accepted degenerate, lewd behavior, for it is then that death and life know one another? Feast of Storytelling, you are the festal garment of life's mystery, establishing timelessness in the mind of the people and evoking the myth to be played out in the very present. Feast of Death, descent into hell—you are truly a feast, the reveling of the flesh's soul, which not for nothing clings to the past, to the grave and the "It was" of piety. But may the spirit be with you as well, and enter into you, so that you may be blessed with blessings of heaven above and blessings of the deep that lies below.

So down then, and no wavering! Is there no stopping in the plunge to the bottomlessness of the well? Of course there is. Not much deeper than three thousand years down—and what is that compared to fathomless depths? The people there do not have horned armor or an eye in the middle of their foreheads, do not do battle with flying lizards, but are human beings just like us—allowing for a few easily pardoned dreamy imprecisions in their thoughts. Someone who is not a great traveler says much the same to himself before a journey, but when the time comes is plagued by fever and a pounding heart. After all, he says, am I going to the end of the world, leaving every convention behind? Not at all, but only someplace where others have been before, a day or two from home. And it is the same for us in terms of the land that awaits us. Is it some Shangri-la, some never-never land, so alien that one can only clasp one's head in utter bewilderment? No, it is, rather, a land as we have often seen it, a Mediterranean land, not exactly like home, a bit dusty and stony, but certainly not crazed, and passing above it are the same stars we know. There it lies—with mountain and valley, cities, roads, and hills clad in vineyards, with its murky river gushing swiftly through green thickets—spreading out over the past like the spring-fed meadows of the fairy tale. If you squeezed your eyes tight during the descent, open them now! We have arrived. Look—a night of sharp-edged moonlit shadows above a peaceful hilly landscape! Feel the gentle freshness of the spring night blazoned with summer's stars!

THE STORIES OF JACOB

Part One

AT THE WELL

Ishtar

It was beyond the hills to the north of Hebron, a little to the east of the road from Urusalim, in the month of Adar, on a spring evening flooded by moonlight bright enough to render writing legible and to reveal—in precise tracery yet shimmering like gossamer—the smallest detail of the leaves and clustered blossoms of a solitary tree, an aged and mighty terebinth, which despite a rather short trunk flung its sturdy branches wide. This beautiful tree was sacred. Beneath its shade counsel might be obtained in various ways, both from the mouths of men—because those who were moved to share their experience of the divine would gather listeners beneath its branches— and by higher means. For those who had slept with their heads leaning against its trunk had, in fact, repeatedly received instruction and prophecy, and during the many years of burnt sacrifices offered at this spot—as attested by the blackened surface of a stone slaughtering table where a slightly sooty flame guttered—the behavior of the smoke, a telling flight of a bird, or even some sign in the heavens had often reinforced the particular fascination that such pious acts at the foot of the tree enjoyed.

There were other trees in the vicinity as well, though none so venerable as the one standing off to itself. Some were of the same species, but there were large-leaved fig trees, too, and stone pines, whose trunks sent aerial roots down into the well-trodden soil and whose evergreen boughs—halfway between needle and foliage, but pallid now in the moonlight—formed thorny fans. Behind the trees, to the south in the direction of the hill concealing the town and partway up its slope, were dwellings and stables, from where the night's silence was occasionally broken by the muffled lowing of an ox, the snorting of a camel, or the initial agonized strains of an ass's complaint. To the north, however, the view lay open. A good-sized enclosure, its moss-covered walls set in two courses of roughly hewn stones, gave the precinct of the oracle tree the appearance of a terrace with low parapets; the plain beyond—bathed now in the luster of a moon at three-quarters and high in the heavens—extended as far as low rolling hills closed by the horizon. The landscape was sprinkled with olive trees and tamarisk copses and crossed by dusty paths, but in the distance it became treeless pasture where here and there the blaze of a shepherd's fire could be seen. Cyclamens, their purples and pinks bleached by the moon, blossomed along the walled parapet; white crocus and red anemone dotted the moss and grasses at the foot of the trees. The air here bore the scent of flowers and aromatic herbs, of moist vapors from the trees, of wood smoke and dung.

The skies were glorious. A broad ribbon of light encircled the moon, whose glow was so intense in its gentleness that it was almost painful to gaze directly into it; and stars had been sown and scattered by the handfuls, so to speak, across the wide firmament—here more sparsely, there more lavishly in thronging, glittering ranks. In the southwest Sirius–Ninurta stood out, a living blue-white fire, a radiant gemstone that seemed to be set in array with Procyon, standing higher to the south in the Lesser Dog. Such splendor might have been matched by King Marduk, who had taken the field shortly after the sun withdrew and would shine all night long—but the moon dimmed his brilliance. Not far from the zenith and a little to the southeast was Nergal, the foe with seven names, the Elamite, who decrees pestilence and death and whom we call Mars. But Saturn, the constant and just, had preceded him above the horizon and now sparkled to the south in the meridian. Orion, with his dominant red light, presented his familiar, showy self—he, too, a hunter, girded and well-armed, sinking toward the west. And there as well, but more to the south, the Dove hovered. Regulus in the constellation of the Lion saluted from directly overhead, to where the yoked oxen of the Wagon had likewise climbed, while reddish yellow Arcturus in the Herdsman stood lower in the northeast and both the yellow light of the Goat and the constellation of the Charioteer had already slipped down toward the realms of evening and midnight. But far lovelier than these, fierier than any portent or the whole host of *kok-abim,* was Ishtar, the sister, wife, and mother—Queen Astarte, low in the west in pursuit of the sun. Her blaze was silver, casting fleeting rays, flaring spikes, and one tall flame seemed to stand atop her like the point of a spear.

Fame and Reality

There were eyes here, skilled at differentiating and making sense of all this, dark eyes lifted upward and mirroring such manifold luster. They moved along the causeway of the zodiac—that sturdy embankment where order was established in the surging heavens and the arbiters of time stood watch—along the sacred array of signs that in quick succession had now begun to grow visible after the brief twilight of these latitudes. First came the Bull, for since those eyes were shining on an early spring night, the sun stood in the sign of the Ram and both had descended together into the depths. Those knowing eyes smiled to the Twins as they turned now from the zenith toward evening; glancing eastward, they found the ear of wheat in the Virgin's hand. But irresistibly drawn by the pure and soft dazzle of the moon, they turned back to its domain of light and shimmering silver shield.

They were the eyes of a young man sitting on the edge of a stonework well not far from the sacred tree. An arch vaulted above the open watery depths of the well, and leading up to it were circles of cracked steps, where the young man was resting his bare feet, wet now with the same spilled water dripping from the stones along that side. Nearby, where the wall was dry, lay both his coat, its wide rust-red pattern set against a yellow background, and cowhide sandals, which, with their tapering sides that allowed heel and toes to be thrust deep into them, were almost shoes. The youth had let fall his shirt of bleached but coarse rustic linen and had wrapped its wide sleeves around his hips. In proportion to his childlike head, his upper body seemed rather heavy and full—with shoulders so square and high-set that there was something Egyptian about them—and in the moonlight his tanned skin took on an oily sheen. For beside him stood an opaque iridescent glass pot filled with scented olive oil, and, after having washed himself with very cold water from the cistern, raising its roped pail several times and drenching himself with the dipper—to bring desired relief from the day's intense sun and at the same time to observe a holy precept—the lad had rubbed his limbs supple with the oil, but he had not removed either the myrtle wreath plaited loosely in his hair or the amulet hanging by a bronzed cord from around his neck to the middle of his chest—a small packet, into which potent threads of protective roots had been sewn.

He appeared now to be engaged in devotions, for with his face lifted to the moon shining full upon it, he held both arms against his ribs, but with forearms erect and open palms turned up and out; and as he sat there rocking gently back and forth, his voice added a kind of low chant to the words or sounds formed by his lips. He wore a blue ring of glazed stoneware on his left hand, and the nails on his fingers and toes showed traces of brick-red henna, presumably applied on the occasion of the town's most recent festival—a dandy's attempt to please the ladies on the rooftops—although he could easily have done without such cosmetic precautions and depended solely on the handsome face God had given him, which despite a still childlike oval was really very charming, thanks in particular to the gentle look of his black, slightly slanting eyes. Beautiful people think they need to enhance nature and "spruce themselves up," presumably as a way of conforming to the pleasing role they play in life or of providing a service for gifts received—which, when taken as a kind of piety, is certainly excusable, whereas there is something sad and foolish about ugly people decking themselves out. But beauty, too, is never perfect and for that very reason incites to vanity; for beauty works hard to achieve what it finds lacking in its own self-imposed ideal—yet another error, for beauty's secret actually consists in the attraction that comes from imperfection.

Around the head of this young man whom we see before us now in reality, hearsay and poetry have woven a veritable halo of fabled beauty, giving us some cause for wonder in the presence of flesh and blood—even with the moon's precarious magic of soft dazzling light lending its aid. As days have multiplied upon days, what all has not been proclaimed and asserted, in song and saga, in apocrypha and pseudepigrapha, in praise of his appearance—praise which, now that we behold him, might well cause us to smile. That his countenance could have shamed the splendor of sun and moon is the least of what became fixed in memory. It has been said that he literally had to cover his brow and cheeks with a veil so that people's hearts might not be ignited by earthly passion for this man sent from God, and that whoever had seen him without his veil would—"now lost in deep and blissful contemplation"—no longer recognize the lad. Oriental tradition does not hesitate to declare that one-half of all potential beauty was bestowed upon this young man, and the other half doled out to the rest of humankind. A Persian bard of great authority outdoes even that conception with the eccentric notion that if all the world's beauty were melted into a single coin weighing twenty-four drachms, then twenty drachms, so our poet enthuses, would have fallen to him, the incomparable paragon.

Fame so extravagant and overweening that it no longer assumes it will be verified is somehow both confusing and alluring to anyone beholding the reality. It can prove dangerous to a sober observation of fact. There are many examples of the power of suggestion inherent in an exaggerated evaluation that gains such general acceptance that individuals allow themselves to be dazzled by it, even to the point of frenzy. Some twenty years before the time now engaging our attention, a man very closely related to this lad had, as we shall hear later, offered sheep for sale in the region of Haran in the land of Mesopotamia, sheep that he had bred himself, but that enjoyed such a reputation that people paid him absolutely absurd prices for them, although anyone had to have seen that these were not heavenly sheep, but quite normal and naturally bred specimens, however excellent. Such is the power of our human need to submit to others! Although determined not to let our minds be darkened by fame that, given our situation, allows us to compare it with reality, we ought not err in the opposite direction either and yield to an exaggerated desire to find fault. Posthumous enthusiasm of the kind that we sense can threaten healthy judgment does not, of course, come out of nothing and nowhere; it has roots sunk firmly in reality and was demonstrably offered, at least in part, to that person while still alive. In order to comprehend this, we must above all accommodate ourselves to the viewpoint of a certain darkling Arabic taste, the aesthetic perspective operative at the time, according to which the young man was indeed so handsome, so beautiful that on many an occasion he was taken at first glance to be, more or less, a god.

We wish therefore to be careful with our words and, yielding to neither a feckless indulgence of rumor nor a hypercritical spirit, shall offer the statement that the face of the moon's young devotee beside the well was a pleasant one, even in its defects. The nostrils, for example, of his rather short and very straight nose were too thick; but since that gave them a flared effect, they added to his countenance a certain liveliness, passion, and fleeting pride that corresponded nicely to the cordiality of the eyes. We shall not censure the expression of haughty sensuality caused by the pout of the lips. That can be misleading, and besides, when it comes to the shape of the lips, we must maintain the viewpoint of the land and its peoples. Whereas we would consider ourselves justified in finding the area between the mouth and nose as too fully arched—or we would, had it not been part and parcel of an especially appealing contour at the corners of the mouth, so that a simple meeting of the lips, without any tightening of muscles, produced a serene smile. Above the strong and handsome line of the brows, the lower part of the forehead was smooth, but farther up it bulged slightly beneath the thick, black hair, which was adorned, of course, with that myrtle wreath and tied back in a pale leather band that gathered the hair at the nape of the neck, but left the ears free—ears that would have been perfectly in order had the lobes not turned out a bit fleshy and too long, evidently the result of unnecessarily large silver rings inserted in early childhood.

So was the lad praying now? He was seated too comfortably for that. He should have been standing. The murmurs and sotto voce singsong with raised hands seemed more a diversion lost in self-forgetfulness, rather like a soft dialogue with the heavenly body that he was addressing. He rocked and mumbled: "Abu—Hammu—Aoth—Abaoth—Abirâm—Haam-mi-ra-am . . ."

The ideas muddled together in his improvisation were elaborated and associated in every conceivable way, for although he included within it the Babylonian pet names for the moon, calling it *Abu,* father, and *Hammu,* uncle, he was also playing both with the name of Abram, his true and presumed ancestor and, in a chain of permutations on that name, yet another honored by tradition: the legendary name of the Lawgiver Hammurabi, which means "My divine uncle is exalted." Although these syllables proceeded by way of the star worship practiced in ancient eastern homelands to a commemoration of family, they were also intended to move beyond the concept of fatherhood, culminating in stammered attempts at something new and yet to be, something that shared the spirit of what was so passionately cherished, debated, fostered by those closest to him . . .

"Yao—Aoth—Abaoth—" the chant intoned. "Yahu, Yahu! Ya-a-we-ilu, Ya-a-um-ilu—" But as it continued with raised hands, swaying body, rocking head, and loving smiles lifted to the light-spending moon, something remarkable, almost frightening became noticeable about the solitary figure. He seemed to be carried away by his devotions, by this lyrical diversion or whatever it was; the increasing self-forgetfulness into which he was lulling himself now took on an eerie aspect. He had not put much voice into his chant, nor would he have had much to give. His still high-pitched, half-childish voice was brittle and immature, its organic resonance still youthful and inadequate. But now every tone left it, it died away in a throttled cramp; his "Yahu! Yahu!" was just a whispered gasp from lungs that were totally devoid of air and that he failed to fill again. At the same time his body wrenched, the chest collapsed, the muscles of his abdomen began a strange rotating motion, neck and shoulders rose in contortion, hands trembled, biceps stood out like strands of rope, and in a flash the black of his eyes had rolled back—leaving the ghastly glint of white voids in the moonlight.

One must add that no one would easily have misinterpreted the irregularity of the lad's behavior. His seizure, or whatever one chose to call it, seemed incongruous, a disquieting surprise, an improbable contradiction to the cordial, reasonable, well-mannered impression that the agreeable young man—at worst something of a dandy—convincingly made at first glance. If this was serious, then the question became who was to take responsibility for the state of his soul, which in this case could conceivably be regarded as bewitched, or at least as imperiled. Even as a game or a whim, this was dangerous business—and it appeared likely that it was at least something of the sort, to judge from the moonstruck lad's behavior in circumstances now to be described.

The Father

From the direction of the hill and its dwellings his name was called: "Joseph! Joseph!" twice, three times, the distance dwindling with each cry. He heard the third call, or at least only first acknowledged it, and quickly extricating himself from his state, he muttered, "Here I am." His eyes rolled back into place, and as he dropped his arms and lowered his head, he smiled an embarrassed smile down at himself. It was his father's mild voice, slightly plaintive and charged with emotion as always. It now sounded close at hand. Although he had already spied his son beside the well, he repeated his question, "Joseph, where are you?"

Jacob—or Yaaqov ben Yitzchak, as he wrote when signing his name—was standing now between the well and the oracle tree, but close enough to the latter for the shadows of its leaves to dapple his long robes; and the fantastically clear moonlight, which can exaggerate any image, provided so sharp an outline that he appeared majestically, almost superhumanly tall. The figure's impressiveness was enhanced, whether intentionally or not, by his pose, for he was leaning on a long staff, grasping its hilt so high that his arm—adorned with a copper bracelet, but already that of an elderly man—was raised above his head and the wide sleeve fell back against the heavy folds of his coat, a wool and cotton outer garment with narrow, pale blue stripes. This brother of Esau, this preferred twin, was sixty-seven years old at the time. His sparse beard had no curl, but was long and wide—for just below the temples wisps of it stood out from his cheeks and it had been left to grow without any shaping until it now reached his chest at full width. Thin lips were visible under the beard glistening silver in the moonlight. The nose was sharply ridged and deep creases ran from both nostrils to the beard below. Beneath a brow half veiled by a hooded shawl of dark and gaudy Canaanite cloth that fell in folds to his chest and was then flung over one shoulder, were small bright brown eyes—already weary with age above the soft pouches of sagging lower lids and keen solely because of a keen mind—and they gazed anxiously now at the lad beside the well. The pose of the arm pushed the coat back, opening it enough to reveal an undergarment of dyed goat's wool, sewn with a hem that fell to the tips of his cloth shoes and arranged in long, fringed pleats, making it look as if it were several garments, one beneath the other. The old man's garb was heavy and diverse, the work of a very arbitrary, eclectic taste: elements of an Eastern cultural heritage were joined with those belonging more to the Ishmaelite or Bedouin traditions of the desert.

Joseph was prudent enough not to answer the last call, for its

question had obviously been asked even as his father saw him. He
contented himself with the response of a smile—lips separated, his
teeth sparkling white, the way teeth always gleam in a dark face,
though not set closely together, but with small gaps—and accompanied it with the usual gestures of greeting. He raised his hands yet
again, just as he had to the moon, rocked his head and gave a click of
his tongue to express delight and admiration. Now he put his hand
to his brow, palm up, and let it glide earthward in one smooth and elegant motion. Then, half closing his eyes and laying his head back,
he put both hands to his heart and without separating them extended
them several times toward the old man, each time circling back to
the region of the heart, offering it in service to his father as it were.
He also pointed with both forefingers to his eyes and touched his
knees, the top of his head, his feet, each time returning hands and
arms to the pose of devoted greeting—a lovely performance, carried
out with both the casualness and formality prescribed by good manners and yet also with personal art and charm, expressing an amiable,
courteous nature, but certainly not devoid of feeling either. Along
with the intimacy of the accompanying smile, it was a pantomime of
filial submission to his sire and master, the head of the clan, but it
was also enlivened with the genuine joy afforded by such an opportunity for paying homage. Joseph knew well that his father had not
always played a dignified and heroic role in life. Jacob's love of loftiness in word and demeanor had at times been undone by a gentle
timidity of the soul; he had known moments of humiliation, of
flight, of naked fear—situations in life that, though they proved to
be the very ones transparent to grace, were also ones in which the lad
he loved did not like to imagine him. And although Joseph's smile
was not entirely free of coquetry and a sense of triumph, it came primarily from the joy of beholding his father—a sight intensified by
moonlight and enhanced by the old man's regal pose on his long
staff. Such childlike satisfaction showed a sensitivity for pure effect,
absent any consideration of profounder factors.

　　Jacob stayed where he was. Perhaps he noticed his son's delight
and wanted to prolong it. His voice—we described it as "charged
with emotion" because it always carried a tremolo of inner
anxiety—called out again from a short way off. Its statement was
half a question.

　　"My child is sitting beside the depths of the well?"

A strange, uncertain declaration, like some faux pas in a dream. It sounded as if the speaker found it improper or at least surprising that anyone so young would sit beside depths; as if the words "child" and "depth" were at odds. But the question's true intent, what it wanted to express, was a nursemaid's worry that Joseph, whom his father saw as a much smaller child than he had become by now, might carelessly fall into the well.

The lad's smile broadened, so that even more of his gapped teeth became visible, and he offered a nod in lieu of a reply. But his expression quickly changed, for Jacob's second statement was much sterner. "Cover your nakedness," he commanded.

Raising his arms to form a circle, Joseph gazed down at himself in half-playful dismay, then hastily undid the knotted sleeves of his shirt and pulled the linen up over his shoulders. And it looked as if the old man had indeed been keeping his distance because his son was naked, for he stepped closer now. He used his long staff in earnest as a cane, lifting and setting it down firmly, for he limped. He had been lame, halt in one thigh, for twelve years now, ever since an encounter—in which he had prevailed—while on a journey undertaken amid dire circumstances and at a time of great fear and distress.

The Man Jebshe

It had indeed been only a short time since the two had last seen one another. As usual, Joseph had sat in his father's tent, fragrant with the scent of musk and myrrh, and eaten his evening meal with whoever of his brothers and half brothers happened to be at home; for in order to guard other flocks some of them were living in the country farther to the north, near a stronghold and shrine in the valley overlooked by Mounts Ebal and Gerizim, and called Sichem, or Shechem, "the nape of the neck," and probably Mabartha as well, which meant "the pass." Jacob maintained religious connections with the people of Shechem; for although the divinity worshiped there was a variant of the Syrian shepherd, the handsome Lord Adoni or Tammuz—a strapping youth who was mutilated by the boar and whom people in the Lower Lands called Osiris, the Martyr—as far back as the days of Abraham and Malkizedek, king and priest of Sichem, this divine personage had assumed particular conceptual contours that earned him the title of El-Elyon, Baal-Berith, the name of God Most High, the Lord of Hosts, maker and owner of heaven and earth. This was to Jacob's mind a correct and pleasing viewpoint, and he was inclined to regard Shechem's mutilated son as the true and highest God, the God of Abraham, and to see the Shechemites as brothers covenanted in faith, particularly since according to a firm tradition passed from generation to generation that ancient wanderer had engaged the Lord Mayor of Sodom in a learned conversation in which he, Abraham, had equated the God whom he knew and called El-Elyon with Malkizedek's Baal and Adon. And years before, upon his return from Mesopotamia, Jacob, Abraham's grandson in the faith, had himself erected an altar to this God near where he set up camp outside the city of Sichem. He had also built a well there and purchased pasturing rights with good silver shekels.

There had later been serious altercations between Sichem and Jacob's people, with dreadful results for the city. But peace had been established and their relationship reinstated, so that a portion of Jacob's flocks now grazed on Shechem's commons and for the sake of those flocks some of his sons and shepherds had to remain far from the light of his countenance.

Besides Joseph, two of Leah's sons had shared in the meal, raw-boned Issakhar and Zebulun, who had no use for the shepherd's life, nor did he wish to be a tiller of the soil, but wanted only to be a sailor. For ever since he had seen the sea at Askalon, he knew of no finer calling and carried on at length about nautical adventures and horrible mongrel creatures that lived across the water and that only sailors could visit—humans with the heads of bulls or lions, or two heads, or two faces, one of which was human, the other that of a sheepdog, so that they took turns speaking and barking, or people with feet like sponges and other such monstrosities. Also present were Bilhah's son, the nimble Naphtali, and Zilpah's two boys: outspoken Gad and Asher, who as usual had kept an eye out for the best morsels and made sure to agree with everyone. As for Joseph's full brother, the child Benjamin, he still lived with the women and was too small to join in a feast for guests, for that is what this evening's meal had been.

A man named Jebshe, who called Taanakh his home, had told over dinner of the flocks of doves and the fishponds at the temple there, and of how he had been on the road for several days, bearing a stone tablet inscribed on all sides by Ashirat-Yashur, the lord of the city—the title of king was an exaggeration—and intended for his "brother," the Prince of Gaza, whose name was Riphath-Baal, with words to the effect that Riphath-Baal might enjoy a happy life and that all the more important gods might join together in concern for his welfare, and for that of his house and his children as well, but that he, Ashirat-Yashur, could not send the timber or money more or less justly demanded of him by his "brother," in part because he did not have it, and in part because he himself had urgent need of it, but was sending in its stead via this man Jebshe an uncommonly powerful clay image of the goddess Asherah, his personal guardian and protector of the city of Taanakh, that it might bring him blessing and help comfort him for the loss of the timber and the money. This same Jebshe, with his pointed beard and bright-colored woolens wrapped round him from throat to ankle, had stopped at Jacob's tent to hear his opinions, to break bread with him and spend the night before continuing his descent toward the sea; and Jacob had hospitably taken the messenger in, suggesting only that the image of Astarte—a female clad in trousers, crown, and veil, and clutching her tiny breasts with both hands—not be brought near him but left somewhat aside instead. Otherwise Jacob greeted him without prejudice, recalling an old tale handed down about Abraham, who had angrily chased off an aged idolater, sending him into the desert, but upon being rebuked by the Lord for his intolerance, had fetched the deluded old man back again.

Attended by two slaves in freshly laundered linen smocks, the old man Madai and the youth Mahalaleël, and seated on cushions placed around the banquet carpet—for Jacob held fast to this custom of his forefathers and would not hear of sitting on chairs, as had become common among elegant people in cities, who followed the fashions of the great empires to the East and South—they had dined on olives and a roasted kid, served with the good bread made of *kemach,* and then on a compote of plums and raisins in copper goblets accompanied by Syrian wine in bowls of colored glass. Meanwhile the host and his guest carried on a serious conversation, to which Joseph at least had paid closest attention and which touched upon matters private and public, with topics ranging from the divine to the earthly, but to political rumor as well. They talked about the

man Jebshe's own family and his official relation with Ashirat-
Yashur, the lord of the city; about his journey, for which Jebshe had
taken the road leading across the plain of Yezreel and into the highlands, then, mounting donkeys, had followed the route along the
ridge of the watershed, although he was thinking of continuing his
journey to the land of the Philistines by camel, on beasts to be purchased the morning he arrived in Hebron; about the price of cattle
and grain at home; about the cult of the Blossoming Rod attached to
Asherah of Taanakh, her "finger" as it was called, her oracle, by
which she had granted permission for one of her images to be sent
on a journey as "Asherah of the Way," so that it might delight the
heart of Riphath-Baal of Gaza; about her festival, which had been
celebrated recently with universal and unbridled dancing as well as a
feasting on fish beyond all excess and during which men and women
had exchanged clothes in token of Asherah's male-femaleness, her
twofold sexual nature as taught by the priests. At this Jacob stroked
his beard and interjected questions of circumspect subtlety: what
about the defenses of the city of Taanakh now that Asherah's image
was on a journey; how was one to understand the relationship between the traveling image and the patron goddess of his homeland,
and might not the latter have suffered a considerable loss of her
powers now that part of her presence had wandered off? To which
Jebshe replied that if that were the case, Asherah's finger would
hardly have indicated she should be sent on her way, and that the
priests taught how the divinity's full power was present with equally
perfect efficacy in each of her images. Moreover Jacob had gently
pointed out that if Ashirta was both male and female, that is, both
Baal and Baalat at once, mother of the gods and king of heaven, one
would have to revere her as the equal not only of Ishtar, renowned in
Shinar, but also of Eset, renowned in the unclean land of Egypt, as
well as the equal of Shamash, Shalim, Addu, Adon, Lachama, or
Damu—in short, of the lord of all worlds and the highest god, so
that the upshot was that in the end one was dealing with El-Elyon,
the God of Abraham, the Creator and Father, whom one could not
send on journeys because He ruled over all, and who was to be
served not with a feast of fish but only by walking before Him in purity and by falling upon one's face to worship Him. But such a viewpoint was met with little understanding by the man Jebshe. Instead,
he explained that just as the sun always followed a given direction

and appeared along that one path, lending its light to the planets so that each could in its particular way influence the fate of humankind, so, too, the divine was split apart and had transformed itself into divinities, among whom the Lord–Mistress Ashirat was in fact, as everyone knew, the one divinity who actualized that divine energy by making plants fertile and by resurrecting nature from the bonds of the underworld, by transforming herself from a dry stick into a blossoming branch each year, so that on such an occasion a little immoderate eating and dancing was surely in order, as were other liberties and amusements associated with the Festival of the Blossoming Rod—just as purity was ascribed solely to the sun and to primal undivided divinity, but not to its planetary manifestations, and so reason had to make a sharp distinction between what was pure and what was holy, and he himself had noticed that the holy and the pure had nothing, or at least did not necessarily have anything, to do with one another. To which Jacob responded with the greatest circumspection: When it came to convictions inculcated by parents and scribes, he did not wish to offend anyone—and least of all a guest in his humble abode, the bosom friend and messenger of a mighty king. But the sun was also merely the work of El-Elyon's hands—divine, but not God, a distinction reason had to make. In worshiping one or another of the Lord's works, one contradicted reason and risked rousing His wrath and jealousy; and with his very own lips his guest Jebshe had characterized the gods of the country as lesser deities, for which there was a nastier name, but one which he, the speaker, would forbear from speaking out of charity and courtesy. If the God who had established the sun, the signs along its path, and the planets, including the earth, was the highest God, then He was also the only God, and it would be best not even to speak of other gods in such a case, otherwise one would be forced to label them with the name Jacob had refrained from using, precisely because reason demanded that the term and concept of "the highest God" be equated with the only God. The issue of whether these two ideas, the highest and the only, were the same or different notions gave rise to one of those longer discussions that the host could never get enough of and that, had it been up to him, would have lasted half or even all the night. Jebshe, however, had brought the conversation around to events out in the world and its empires, to commerce and intrigues, about which he, as a friend and relative of a Canaanite city prince, knew more than the average man: how pestilence was raging on Cyprus, which he called Alashia, and had carried away a great many people, but not all of them, as the ruler of that island had written to the Pharaoh of the Lower Lands by way of excuse for the almost total cessation of his tribute of copper; how the king of the Empire of the Chetites or Hittites was named Suppiluliuma and commanded such a vast military force that he was threatening to crush King Tushratta of Mitanni and make off with his gods, even though the latter was related by marriage to the Great House of Thebes; how the Kassite of Babel had begun to tremble before the power of the priest-prince of Assyria, who was striving to loosen his ties to the Empire of the Lawgiver and to found a state of his own along the river Tigris; how Pharaoh had enriched the priests of his god Amun with the wealth of Syria's tribute, erecting for that god a new temple of a thousand columns and portals with those same moneys, the flow of which, however, would soon be a mere trickle, for not only had the cities of that country been plundered by Bedouin thieves, but Chetite power was also expanding from the north and vying with devotees of Amun for dominance in Canaan, while at the same time a good number of Amorite princes were seeking to come to an accommodation with these foreigners against Amun. Jebshe gave a wink at this point, presumably to indicate, just among friends, that Ashirat-Yashur was also moving down that same clever political path; but once God was no longer the subject of discourse his host's interest had diminished greatly. As the conversation languished, people left their cushions—Jebshe to make certain that in the meantime no harm had come to Astarte of the Way and then to lie down to sleep; Jacob, supporting himself on his staff, to make his rounds of the camp and tend to the women and the cattle in their stalls. As for his sons, Joseph had parted from the other five outside the tent, although it had looked at first as if he intended to remain with them. But outspoken Gad had abruptly said, "Run along, you little dandy, you harlot, we don't need you!"

To which, after pausing to order his thoughts, Joseph replied, "Gad, you are like a beam of wood that has not yet been planed, and like a butting billy goat in the herd. Were I to report your words to Father, he would punish you. Were I to report them to our brother

Ruben, however, he would, as a just man, reprimand you. But let it be as you have said. If you five go to the right then I shall go to the left, or the other way round. For indeed I do love you all, yet you have an abhorrence of me, and today most especially, because Father served me up pieces of the kid and cast friendly glances at me. And for that reason I find your suggestion good, for by that means any offense may be avoided and you will not fall unwittingly into sin. Farewell."

Glancing disdainfully over his shoulder, Gad had listened to it all, for he was curious as to what sort of clever things the boy would think to say this time. Then he had made a crude gesture and walked off with the others. Joseph, however, went his way alone.

He had taken a pleasant little evening stroll—or took what pleasure he could in it, given the downcast state into which Gad's coarse behavior had now put him, mitigated only in part by the satisfaction he took in his own well-formed reply. Ambling up the hill by following the easier slope on its eastern side, Joseph had soon arrived at the crest and its view to the south, so that to his left lay the valley and moon-whitened town, with its thick walls and four-cornered towers and gates, its palace extending out into a pillared courtyard, and its temple set on a rocky promontory surrounded by a broad terrace. He liked to gaze down at the town, where so many people lived. And at his family's burial place, the two caves that Abraham had once bought with some difficulty from a Hittite and where the bones of his ancestors, of his ancient Babylonian mother from Ur and of later heads of the clan, were laid to rest—he was just able make it out from here: the cornices of the stone portal to the rocky double grave were barely visible at the far left of its encircling wall. And in his breast he had felt a mixture of the piety that has its source in death and the sympathy that the sight of a populous town inspires. Then he had walked back, sought out the well, refreshed himself, washing and rubbing himself with oil, and afterward had paid his somewhat dissolute court to the moon, at which his ever-attentive, ever-anxious father had discovered him.

The Tattletale

And now the old man was standing next to him, and after shifting his staff to his left hand, laid his right hand on Joseph's head. His aged, but penetrating eyes gazed into the lovely black eyes of the lad, who had at first raised them—meanwhile displaying yet again a good many gapped and gleaming teeth—but now lowered them again, in part out of simple respect, but in part, too, because of an uneasy sense of guilt bound up with his father's demand that he cover himself. In fact it was not just because of the pleasant breeze, or not for that reason alone, that he had delayed putting his clothes back on, and he guessed that his father had seen through the urges and notions that had led him to direct his salutations skyward half-naked. He had in fact found it both sweet and auspicious to offer his youthful nakedness up to the moon, with which he felt certain ties due to his horoscope and for all sorts of other speculative and intuitive reasons, for he was convinced that the moon would be pleased and had intentionally tried to bribe it and gain its favor—or even that of the power on high in general. The sensation of its cool light joining the evening air to brush his shoulders had, or so it seemed to him, confirmed the success of his childish attempt, which ought not be called shameless, because it was itself tantamount to a sacrifice of shame. One must keep in mind that the rite of circumcision as adapted by Joseph's clan and family from an external custom practiced by the Egyptians had long since acquired a special mystical meaning. Commanded and instituted by God himself, it was the marriage of man with the deity, performed on the part of the flesh which appeared to constitute the crux of his being, and indeed every vow was physically confirmed by a hand placed upon it. Many a man bore the name of God bound to his reproductive organ or inscribed it there before taking a wife. The bond of faith with God was sexual, and since it had been established with a demanding Creator, with a Lord insistent upon exclusive possession, it had the civilizing effect of weakening the male of the human species in the direction of the feminine. The bloody sacrifice of circumcision is related more than just physically to the concept of castration. This sanctification of the flesh carries with it both the idea of chastity and its loss, and therefore has a feminine meaning as well. Moreover, Joseph was, as he knew and heard everyone say, handsome and beautiful—a state that in any case includes a certain feminine consciousness; and inasmuch as "beautiful" was an adjective commonly applied above all to the full, unclouded, uneclipsed moon—a moon word, if you like, more at home really in heavenly realms and, if one is to be precise, conferred upon human beings only in a wider sense—the concepts of "beautiful" and "naked" were thus almost interchangeable in his mind; and it seemed to him both wise and pious to respond to the beauty of that heavenly body with the nakedness of his own, so that the pleasure and admiration might be mutual.

We would prefer not to judge to what extent that certain dissolute quality in his behavior may have been connected with these shadowy sentiments. They originated in any case from the primal meaning attached to a cultic nakedness that was still regularly practiced before his eyes; and so when he was confronted by his father and his reprimand, they stirred in him a vague sense of guilt. For he loved and feared the old man's spirituality, and he had a clear suspicion that a world of thought to which he himself still felt some connection, if only a playful one, was for the most part considered sinful by his father, who had put such things behind him as pre-Abrahamic, applying to them a term he had ever at the ready, his most dreadful word of scorn, the word "idolatrous." Joseph was prepared to hear just such a reproach that expressly called things by their name. But given the worries that, as always, he felt for this son, Jacob chose other words. He began:

"Truly it would be better had my child said his prayers and were now sheltered and sleeping. I do not like to see him alone in the deepening night, and beneath stars that shine upon both the good and the evil. Why did he not remain with Leah's sons and why did he not go with the sons of Bilhah?"

He knew very well why Joseph had once again not done so, and Joseph also knew that only worry over this familiar state of affairs had compelled his father to ask the question. Pursing his lips, he replied, "My brothers and I discussed the matter and resolved it peaceably."

Jacob continued, "The lion of the desert that lives in the reed banks where the river flows into the salt sea has been known to come across and attack the sheepfolds when hungry and to snatch his prey when thirsting for blood. It is but five days now since the shepherd Aldmodad lay upon his belly before me and confessed that a ravenous beast of prey had fallen upon two young ewes during the night and dragged one off to devour it. Aldmodad swore true to me without any oath, for he showed me the bloodied ewe that had been preyed upon, so that it stood to reason that the other had been stolen by the lion and that the loss was upon my own head."

"A small loss," Joseph said to flatter him, "and as nothing when compared with the riches with which the Lord chose to favor my lord in Mesopotamia."

Jacob lowered his head and let it fall to one side a bit, as a sign that he did not boast of this blessing—although without some clever assistance on his part it would not have come to pass. He replied, "From one to whom much is given, much can be taken away. And if the Lord has made silver of me, He can make me into clay, poor as the potsherds upon the rubbish heap; for He is mighty in His ways, and we do not comprehend the paths of His justice. Silver has a pallid light," he continued, but avoided looking at the moon, although Joseph immediately cast it a sidelong glance. "Silver is grief, and the bitterest fear of the fearful is the folly of those who are sick for it."

Looking up imploringly, the lad made a caressing gesture to mollify him.

Jacob did not let him finish, but said, "It was out in those pastures there, a hundred or two hundred paces from here, that the lion crept near and pounced upon the old dam's ewes. But my child is sitting beside the well at night, careless, naked, with no weapon and no thought to his father. Are you steeled for danger and armed for battle? Are you like Shimeon and Levi, your brothers—God protect them—who attack their enemies with a shout, sword in hand, and who burned the cities of the Amorites? Or are you like Esau, your uncle in the wastelands of Seïr to the south—a hunter and a man of the plains, red of skin and hairy like a billy goat? No, you are gentle, and a child who dwells in tents, for you are flesh of my flesh. And when Esau came to the ford with four hundred men and my soul did not know how it would all turn out before the eyes of the Lord, I put my handmaids in front with their children, your brothers, then Leah with her sons, but as for you, behold, I put you at the very rear, beside Rachel, your mother . . ."

His eyes were full of tears already. He needed only to mention the name of the wife he had loved more than anything, and they would well up, though it had been eight years now since God had incomprehensibly taken her from him, and his voice, charged as always with emotion, faltered, and broke with a sob.

The young man stretched out his arms to him and then put clasped hands to his lips.

"How needlessly the heart of my dear papa and lord is troubled," he said in gentle reproach, "and how overwrought is his concern. When our guest wished us good health and left to look after his precious image"—he gave a sneer to please Jacob, adding—"which to my eyes looked rather wretched and helpless and of no more account than some piece of crude pottery at the market—"

"You saw it?" Jacob interrupted. This in itself displeased him and darkened his mood.

"I begged our guest to show it to me before the meal," Joseph said with pouted lips and a shrug. "The work is mediocre, with impotence written all over it . . . When you had finished talking, you and our guest, I left with my brothers, but one of the sons of Leah's handmaid, Gad I think, who is by nature blunt and curt, suggested that I set my feet along paths that theirs did not tread, and it pained my soul somewhat, for he did not call me by my name, but rather by a false and foul one to which I do not gladly answer . . ."

Suddenly and quite unintentionally he found himself playing tattletale, though he knew this to be a propensity that only detracted from his own sense of satisfaction—that he genuinely wanted to control and only moments before had successfully though temporarily overcome. First, there was his unrestrained need to communicate, which became a vicious circle given his bad relations with his brothers; for inasmuch as this set him apart and pushed him closer to his father, it created a state halfway between them that only spurred him on as a tattler. This in turn made his estrangement that much worse, over and over again, so that one could not say whether the damage had first begun with one or the other of them, but that in any case the older brothers could hardly look at Rachel's son without grimacing. The origins can without doubt be traced to Jacob's partiality to the child—and noting that fact is not intended as any real offense to this tender-hearted man. For by its very nature tender feeling tends to know no bounds and to form a delicate cult of itself; it cannot be concealed, cannot keep its tongue, but seeks out ways to confess and announce itself, to "rub itself under the nose," as we say, of the entire world, so that everyone may be caught up in it. Such is the excessive indulgence of people of tender feeling; and Jacob found himself encouraged all the more by his tribe's tradition, the prevailing view of God's own self-indulgence and majestic moodiness in matters of feeling and in the objects of His partiality. El-Elyon's choice and preference of some individuals, absent, or at least beyond any merit on their part was absolute and splendid; by any human measure, it was hard to comprehend and unjust, a sublime emotional reality that was not to be quibbled with, but to be honored with trembling and rapture in the dust. And Jacob, himself aware—though in all humility and fear—that he was the object of such favor, imitated God by insisting exuberantly on his own predilection and giving it free rein.

Joseph had inherited from his father an emotional man's tender lack of self-control. We shall have more to say about his inability to tame the fullness of his feelings and the lack of tact that would become so extremely dangerous to him. As a nine-year-old child it was he who had told his father about how the tempestuous but kindly Ruben had burst into a rage at Jacob—who had made Bilhah his favorite by taking to the bed of Leah's handmaid, rather than to that of Leah, Ruben's rejected, red-eyed mother, cowering in her tent—and had torn his father's bed from its new location, cursing and maltreating it. A rash act, committed by a son whose pride had been hurt, committed on Leah's behalf—and he was soon sorry for it. The bed could easily and quietly have been put back in place, and Jacob would have needed to be none the wiser. But Joseph had witnessed it all, and could think of nothing better than to carry the tale to his father; so that from that hour on, Jacob—who himself was not the firstborn son by nature, but only in name and in the legal sense—had toyed with the plan of cursing Ruben and divesting him of his firstborn's status, but not in order to let the next eldest, Leah's second son, Shimeon, take his place, but instead, in an exercise of the most arbitrary freedom of emotion, Joseph, Rachel's first.

The brothers were wrong to claim that by being a chatterbox the boy was intentionally trying to influence such paternal decisions.

Rather, he simply could not hold his tongue. Which made it all the harder to forgive him and only fueled the brothers' suspicions when, at the very next opportunity, he was again unable to keep silent, despite his awareness of such intentions and the charges laid against him. Few people know just how Jacob came to find out that Ruben had "sported" with Bilhah.

What happened then, well before their settling in Hebron, at a stopover between there and Beth-el, was far worse than the story about the bed. Ruben, twenty-one at the time and with overflowing urges and energy, had been unable to resist his father's wife, the same Bilhah against whom he had felt such bitter spite because of the neglected Leah. He had spied upon her in her bath, at first purely by accident, then for the pleasure of shaming her without her knowledge, then with slowly overpowering lust. The sturdy youth had been seized with a sudden and brutal desire for Bilhah's ripe, but artfully maintained charms, for her still-firm breasts, her dainty belly, and his obsession was not to be quelled by any handmaid, any slave obedient to his every command. He crept in upon his father's concubine and current favorite wife, taking her by surprise if not by force, though indeed his strapping youthful vitality surely seduced this handmaid, who trembled before Jacob.

Joseph had been loitering nearby and, with no real intention to spy, had observed enough of this scene of passion, fear, and misconduct that, in his naive eagerness, he was able to report to his father as an oddity of some note: that Ruben had been "sporting" and "laughing" with Bilhah. These words literally said less than he knew had occurred, but in common usage they implied everything. Jacob blanched and gasped. Only minutes after the boy had told his tale, Bilhah lay before the clan's leader whimpering her confession and clawing her fingernails at those same breasts that had bewitched Ruben, but that for her master would now remain forever sullied and untouchable. Then the malefactor himself lay there, with only a sack cinched about him in token of his humiliation and submission; and raising his hands in true contrition above dust-strewn, disheveled locks, he let the sublime thunderstorm of his father's rage pass over him. Jacob called him Ham, the profaner of his father, called him the dragon of chaos, Behemoth, and a shameless hippopotamus—this last because of an Egyptian fable, according to which it was the hippopotamus's wicked practice to slay its father and then ravish its mother. By pretending that Bilhah was Ruben's real mother, simply because he himself slept with her, Jacob imbued his tirade with the ancient, dark notion that in cohabiting with his mother Ruben had intended to make himself lord of all—and now proclaimed to him the opposite. For with arms outstretched above the groaning man, he wrested from him the rights of the firstborn—though, to be sure, temporarily retaining them for himself, without bestowing that dignity on anyone else, so that the matter had remained unsettled ever since and, for now at least, a father's intense and majestic partiality for Joseph took the place of any legal fact.

The remarkable thing was that Ruben bore the lad no ill feelings, and of all the brothers was the most indulgent of him. He quite correctly did not ascribe the boy's actions to pure malice but sincerely saw it as Joseph's right to be concerned for the honor of such a loving father and to inform him of events whose shamefulness he, Ruben, would be the last to deny. Conscious of his own fallibility, Re'uben was kind and just. Moreover, like all of Leah's sons he was, despite his physical strength, rather ugly—he had his mother's feeble eyes, too, and, though it did not help, was forever rubbing ointment on the lids, which tended to fester. He was more susceptible than the others to Joseph's universally admired charms and, in his own oafishness, was touched by them and sympathetic to the idea that the forever shifting legacy, the chosen status as head of the clan, the divine blessing bestowed on its great patriarchs, was being passed on to the boy rather than to him or any other of the twelve. So that, hard as it had been for him, his father's wishes and plans in regard to the firstborn had always seemed understandable.

Joseph had known perfectly well, then, what he was doing in threatening Zilpah's son—who though outspoken was certainly not the worst—with Ruben's justice. For the latter had often spoken, if disparagingly, on Joseph's behalf to his brothers, had defended him by force several times from abuse and reprimanded them when, enraged by one of his acts of disloyalty, they had made vengeful plans to attack him. For the ninny had learned nothing from his earlier serious episodes with Ruben, nor had Ruben's magnanimity improved his behavior; and as he grew older he became a more dangerous observer and talebearer than he had been as a child. Dangerous to himself as well, especially since the role he had become accustomed to playing daily exacerbated his ostracism and exclusion, diminished

his happiness, called down upon him a hatred he was unable by nature to cope with, and created every reason for him to fear his brothers, which only meant that he was tempted yet again to secure his
position against them by flattering his father—all despite repeatedly
resolving not to dip his tongue in poison, to improve his relationship
with the ten of them, of whom none was a scoundrel and who, together with himself and his little brother, were as many as the houses
of the zodiac, a number with which he felt a deep and holy bond.

But in vain. Whenever Shimeon and Levi, who were hot-
tempered men, picked a quarrel and brawled with shepherds from
foreign parts or even with the residents of nearby towns, bringing
shame on the clan; whenever, much to Jacob's displeasure, Jehuda, a
proud but long-suffering fellow who was tormented by Ishtar and
found nothing funny in what others found so humorous, had got involved in a clandestine affair with some country lass; whenever one
of the brothers transgressed against the One and Most High God by
surreptitiously burning incense before an image, thus endangering
the fertility of the flocks and calling down upon them the pox, the
mange, or the staggers; or whenever at a sale of culled cattle, whether
locally or at Shechem, the sons quietly tried to secure and divide
profits over and above what was rightfully Jacob's—their father
would hear of it from his favorite. He even heard falsehoods from
him that stood counter to reason but that, gazing into Joseph's
lovely eyes, he was inclined to believe. The boy claimed that several
of the brothers had repeatedly cut pieces from the flesh of living
rams and ewes in order to eat it, that all four born of the concubines
had done so, but that Asher had been the worst offender, for he was
known in fact to be a glutton. Asher's appetite was the only thing
that spoke for such an accusation, which in and of itself seemed
highly unbelievable and could never have been proved true against
any of the four, either. It was, objectively speaking, simple slander.
Perhaps from Joseph's point of view, however, the incident did not
quite deserve that name. Presumably he had dreamed the tale; or
more correctly, at a period when he had every right to expect a
thrashing, he had let himself dream it, hoping to get his father to
shield him with it against his brothers' intentions, and now neither
could nor would rightly distinguish between truth and a mere vision. It goes without saying, of course, that in this case the brothers'

outrage took especially lavish forms. They were almost too fero-
cious in declaring themselves innocent, as if this were not totally the
case and there might have been something true behind Joseph's fantasies after all. We are bitterest about accusations that are indeed
false, yet not entirely so.

The Name

Jacob came close to flying into a rage upon hearing about the coarse
name that Gad had called Joseph and that the old man was instantly
ready to take as a punishable offense against his holiest feelings. But
with just a cheerful face and a deft turn of phrase, Joseph could re-
lent, mollify, and move on so swiftly and charmingly that Jacob's
wrath abated before it truly flared up, and he could only smile
dreamily as he continued to gaze into those black and slightly slanting eyes, narrowing with sweet guile now as Joseph spoke.

"It was nothing," he heard his son say in that austere yet lan-
guorous voice he loved because it held much of the timbre of
Rachel's voice. "I offered him a brotherly reproach for his coarse-
ness, and since he wisely accepted my admonition, it is to his credit
that we parted so amicably. I walked up the hill to view the city and
Ephron's double dwelling; I cleansed myself here with water and
with prayer, and as for that lion, that ravener of the underworld
and offspring of the black moon with which it pleased my dear papa
to unsettle me, he has kept to the thickets of the Jardên"—he pronounced the river's name with different vowels from those we use,
called it the "Jardên," with a rather open "e" and an "r" formed at
the palate but without being rolled—"and has found his supper in
the clefts of the cliff, and the eyes of the child have not seen him,
either near or far."

He called himself "the child," a name that had remained with
him from his earliest days, because he knew it would especially
touch his father.

"Had he come with his tail whipping and voice rumbling with
hunger like the voices of the seraphim raised in hymns of praise," he
went on, "the child would have been only slightly terrified of his
fury, or perhaps not at all. For, thief that he is, he surely would once

again have set upon some little lamb—assuming Aldmodad had not already driven him off with rattlings and flames—and would wisely have avoided the human child. Does my dear papa not know that animals fear and avoid man because God has given him the spirit of understanding and instilled in him the order and kind to which each of them belongs? And does he not recall how Sammael shrieked when the man of clay first learned to put names to creation, as if he were its master and maker, and how all the fiery hosts were amazed and cast down their eyes, for they know quite well how to cry 'Holy, holy!' in chorus arrayed, but lack any understanding of the ranking of higher and lower orders? And the animals, too, are ashamed and tuck their tails, for we know them and have command over their names and can deprive each of its roaring demeanor simply by presenting it with its name. And if he had approached with gruff, panting, abhorrent muzzle and long slinking stride, I certainly would not have let his terror rob me of my good sense or cause me to blanch before his riddle. 'Is not your name Bloodthirst?' I would have asked, just to make sport of him. 'Or are you perhaps called Death-pounce?' But then I would have sat up tall and cried, 'Lion! Behold, you are a lion after your order and kind, and your secret lies bare before me, so that I can speak it and dismiss you with a smile on my lips.' And he would have blinked at that name and slunk away at that word, powerless to answer me. For he has no learning whatever and knows nothing of the tools of writing . . ."

He was playing on words, something he always enjoyed, but, as with his boasting just now, he did it at the moment to amuse his father. His own name contained the sounds of the word "sepher," meaning book, writing material—which was a source of constant satisfaction, by the way, for unlike his brothers, none of whom could write, he loved composing with the stylus and was so skilled at it that he could have served as a junior scribe at some place where documents were collected, at Kiriath-Sepher or Gebal, that is, if Jacob could conceivably ever have given approval for such a profession.

"And if my dear papa," he continued, "would deign to ease himself into a comfortable seat beside his son at the well, here on the rim of its depths for instance, while his bookish child slips down to sit at his feet, what a truly delightful order and ranking that would be. For then he could entertain his lord and tell him a fable that he has learned, a tale of names that he knows how to tell most engagingly. For in the days of the generations of the Flood, the angel Semhazai saw upon earth a maid whose name was Ishchara and whose beauty made a fool of him, so that he said, 'Hearken unto me!' But she answered and said, 'I would not think of hearkening unto you unless you first teach me the true and undisguised name of God, which at its mere mention causes you to mount up on high.' And, fool that he was, since all his lust was for her to hearken unto him, the messenger Semhazai indeed taught her the name. But no sooner did Ishchara find herself in its possession, and what does my dear papa suppose the chaste maid then did to snap her fingers in the face of the persistent angel? . . . This is the moment of highest suspense in my tale, but, sad to say, it would seem my dear papa is not listening, that his ears are sealed by his thoughts and that he is lost in his deep pondering?"

And in fact Jacob was not listening, but "pondering." It was a mighty and eloquent pondering, the essence of pondering, its very definition so to speak, an emotional self-absorption of the highest degree—he never did less than that. When Jacob pondered, then it had to be a pondering visible at a good hundred paces, a pondering so grand and strong that not only was it obvious to anyone that Jacob was lost in thought, but also people realized for the first time in their lives what it truly means to ponder and were left awestruck by such a state and sight: the old man leaning with both hands grasping his long staff, his head bent over one arm, an ardently dreamy bitterness playing upon the lips within his silver beard, the brown aged eyes burrowing and probing deep into memory and thought, their self-absorbed and blunted gaze directed from so far below that it appeared caught in his overhanging brows. . . . Emotional people are expressive people, for emotions, in their need to be taken seriously, find expression by casting off silence and inhibition; expression arises from a tender but great soul, where languor and boldness, sensuality and nobility, naturalness and mannerism, all blend to form the most sublime theatricality, which other people may regard with slightly amused awe. Jacob was very impressive—much to Joseph's delight, for he loved and was proud of such stirring flights of emotion, but much to the alarm and shock of those who had dealings with him, and in particular his other sons, who, whenever there was a disagreement with their father, feared nothing so much as just such expressiveness. That had been the case with Ruben, when he had had to present himself before the old man because of that nasty episode with Bilhah. For even if fear and awe before such over-wrought expression were deeper and darker in those days than in ours, even back then, if threatened by such expressive reactions, the ordinary fellow was filled with a lowbrow desire to keep them at bay—which might best be put in words as "For heaven's sake, this could get serious!"

Jacob's power of expression, however, as well as the emotional charge in his voice, the elevation of his speech, the solemnity of his person in general, were all connected with the same predisposition and tendency that explained why he could so often be found lost in such strong and picturesque pondering. This was his gift for con-necting ideas, which governed his inner life to such a degree that it more or less shaped it, so that he thought almost exclusively in such associations. At every step, reminiscences and correspondences struck hard at his soul, diverted and abducted it into elaboration, mixing within the present moment both what was past and what was promised, creating the distortion and refraction of vision so typical of brooding. It was almost an illness, although he was not the only one to suffer from it, for it was so very prevalent, though in varying degrees, that one might say that in Jacob's world intellectual worth and "significance"—using that word in its most literal sense—were defined by the wealth of ideas formed by mythical association and by their power to permeate every moment. Recall how strange, high-flown, and significant it had sounded when the old man spoke those broken words to express his worry that his son might fall into the cistern. But that was because he could not think of the depths of a well without ideas of a netherworld and the realm of death merging with that thought, deepening and sanctifying it—an idea, which, though it played no role in his own religious opinions, was certainly lodged in the depths of his soul and imagination as the ancient myth-ical heritage of many peoples: the idea of a land below, where the dismembered Osiris reigned, the home of Namtar, god of plagues, the kingdom of terrors from where all evil spirits and scourges came. It was the world into which the stars and planets submerged them-selves upon setting, so that they might rise again from it at their proper hour, whereas no mortal who walked the path to this house ever found the way back. It was the place of filth and excrement, but also of gold and riches; the womb in which the seed corn was bedded and from which it sprouted as nourishing grain, the land of the black moon, of winter and scorched summer, into which Tammuz, the shepherd in the spring of life, had sunk—and sank again each year when the boar slew him, so that all conception was dried up and the tear-drenched world lay barren, until Ishtar, his spouse and mother, undertook her descent into hell to look for him, burst open the dusty bars of his prison, and with great laughter led her beloved and beautiful Tammuz out of hell, out of the pit, as lord of the new age and of fields freshly decked in blossoms.

How could Jacob's voice not have quivered with emotion, how could his question not have acquired a strangely resonant significance? For he had seen that well—if not in his mind, then in his emotions—as an entrance to the netherworld, and all this and more resounded within him at the word "depths." A stupid, uneducated man with a soul of no significance might doltishly utter such a word free of any association, thinking only of the immediate and actual reference. But it lent dignity and intellectual solemnity to Jacob's person, rendered it expressive to a fearful degree. There are no words for how the fallible Ruben must have been cut to the quick when his father flung the notorious name of Ham at him that day. For Jacob was not a man to avail himself of such a curse merely as a feeble allusion. His mind had the power to merge the present most dreadfully into the past, to reestablish the full force of that prior event and to effect a personal oneness between himself and Noah—a father spied upon, mocked, and dishonored by his son's own hand. Ruben, too, had known beforehand that this would be so and that he would truly, actually be lying as Ham before Noah, and for that very reason he had shuddered in such horror as he entered.

What had caused the old man to fall into his current and manifest state of pondering were memories that his son's chatter about "names" had awakened in his mind—lofty and panicky memories with the weight of a dream but from days long past, when in great fear for his life he had been awaiting yet another encounter with his desert-dwelling brother, whom he had tricked and who was doubtlessly thirsting for revenge. For he had so fervently longed for spiritual power that for the sake of a name he had wrestled with the extraordinary man who had attacked him. It was a heavy, terrible, and highly sensual dream of desperate sweetness, not something airy and transient that leaves no traces, but a dream so hot with body heat, so dense with reality that it had left behind a twofold lifelong legacy, like creatures of the sea stranded by the ebbing tide: first, the lameness in Jacob's hip, in the hollow of his thigh, put out of joint by that extraordinary man, leaving him halt; and second, the name—not the name of that peculiar stranger, which had been denied him with might and main, until dawn, until that painfully dangerous moment when it would have been too late, no matter how insistently, violently the hot, panting Jacob had demanded it of him; no, not that name, but his own other and second name, the surname the stranger had bequeathed to him in battle in order to prevent a delay that would have proved most painful and to depart before sunrise, the title of honor that people had used ever since, whenever they wanted to flatter him and see him smile: Yizrael, "God goes to war" . . . He saw the ford of the Jabbok before him again, where he had remained among the bushes on the near side after having first led across his wives, eleven sons, and the flocks he had selected as a gift of atonement for Esau; saw the unsettled, cloudy night, in which, restless as the sky itself, he had wandered about after two attempts at sleep, still trembling, despite the passable outcome of his encounter with Rachel's outfoxed father, and tormented now by his grave concern at the approach of yet another man he had duped and defrauded. How he had admonished the Elohim in his prayers, more or less declaring it Their duty to stand beside him. And he also saw that man—with whom he had unexpectedly found himself, God knew why, wrestling for his life—by the garish light of that night's moon as it had suddenly emerged from behind the clouds—saw him again so close, almost breast to breast, with his wide-set ox eyes that never blinked, with that face, and those shoulders, shining like polished stone. And entering his heart again was something like the ghastly lust he had felt while his groaning whispers demanded that name. . . . How strong he had been—with the desperate strength of dreams, with the stamina of unexpected reserves of energy in his soul. He had held out the whole night, until dawn, until he saw that it had now grown too late for the distraught man, until he heard him beg, "Let me go!" Neither had prevailed over the other, but had that not meant victory for Jacob, who was no extraordinary man, but a man from here and now, born of man's seed? It seemed to him as if the wide-eyed stranger had had his doubts. That painful blow when he had grabbed his hip had felt like an examination. Maybe it had been meant to determine if there was a ball and socket there, a mobile joint, not one fixed and ill fashioned for sitting, like those of his own kind. . . . And then the man had been clever enough to turn things around so that although he did not yield up his own name, he bestowed one upon Jacob instead. He could hear, as clearly as he had that morning, the high and brazen voice that had spoken to him: "Henceforth you shall be called Yizrael"—whereupon he had released the owner of that extraordinary voice from his arms, in the hope that the stranger might just barely still make it in time. . . .

Monkey-Faced Egypt

The way in which the solemn old man ended his pondering and returned from his profound absence was no less impressive than his descent into it. With a heavy sigh, with grave dignity, he rose out of it, standing erect and shaking it off, his head lifted to gaze grandly and vacantly about, like a man awakening, obviously collecting his thoughts, and finding himself in the present again. He appeared not to have heard Joseph's proposal that he take a seat. Nor, as the lad was forced to realize to his embarrassment, was this the moment for engaging little stories. The old man had something else, something more serious to speak with him about. Worries about the lion had not been his sole concern; Joseph had given him cause for others as well, and he was going to hear about it. What he heard was:

"There is a land far below, the land of Hagar the handmaid, the land of Ham and also called the Black Land, monkey-faced Egypt. For the souls of its people are black, though their faces be red, and they emerge from the womb already old, so that their suckling babes resemble little aged men and begin to babble of death within an hour. They carry, or so I have heard, their god's manhood, three ells in length, through the streets, with drums and harps, and lie with rouged and painted corpses in their graves. Without exception they are arrogant, wanton, and unhappy. They clothe themselves according to the curse placed upon Ham, who was made to go naked with private parts exposed, for linen thin as gossamer covers their nakedness without hiding it, and they think very highly of themselves for it, saying they are clad in woven air. For they are not ashamed of their flesh and have no word for sin, neither do they understand it. They stuff the bellies of their dead with spices and in place of the heart they lay—and justly so—the image of a dung beetle. They are rich and filthy like the people of Sodom and Amorrah. Whenever they like, they place their beds beside those of a neighbor and exchange wives. If a woman goes to the market and sees a lad after whom she lusts, she lies with him. They are like animals and bow before animals in the innermost places of their ancient temples, and I was told that there, in the view of everyone, a maiden, who was chaste until that day, allowed herself to be covered by a billy goat named Bindidi. Does my son approve such customs?"

Since Joseph was well aware to what offense these words referred, he hung both head and lower lip, like a little boy being scolded. But in that look of half-pouting contrition he also concealed a smile, for he knew that Jacob's description of the customs of Mizraim contained grand generalizations, personal biases, and exaggerations. After a bit of remorseful silence, he felt called upon to reply and lifted his eyes to search those of his father for the first gleam of a smile of reconciliation and attempted to lure it out with cautious overtures, by turns risking and retracting tokens of his own amusement. It was his way of playing at negotiation.

At last he said, "If that is what it is like down there, my dear lord, then this imperfect child here would indeed be certain not to commend it in his heart. It does seem to me, however, that the fineness of Egyptian linen, which is like the air itself, is a testament to the skill that those aged dung beetles display at their handicrafts, and might, when seen from another viewpoint, if only conditionally, speak in their favor. And if they find no shame in their flesh, someone willing to be overindulgent might perhaps excuse them by noting that they are usually quite slender of frame and lean of flesh, whereas plump flesh has more cause for shame than gaunt, because . . ."

But it was now time for Jacob to turn serious. A lively battle between tenderness and impatient rebuke could be heard in his voice as he replied, "You speak like a child! You are deft at putting words together and your speech is beguiling, like that of a shrewd camel dealer at barter, but the sense of it is thoroughly childish. I do not want to believe that you intend to mock me in my distress, for that sets me trembling for fear you may displease the Lord and arouse His anger against you and Abraham's seed. My eyes beheld you sitting naked beneath the moon, as if the Most High had not planted knowledge of sin in our hearts, and as if the spring nights were not chilly after the heat of the day upon these heights, so that you could catch a bad catarrh overnight and be rendered senseless by fever before the cock crows. Which is why I want you to put your coat on over your shirt at once, as is the pious practice of the children of Shem. For it is woolen, and a wind comes from Gilead. And I want you to cease to give me cause to worry, for my eyes beheld even more, and I fear they saw you blowing kisses to the stars. . . ."

"By no means!" Joseph cried in great dismay. He had jumped up from the edge of the well in order to slip into his knee-length brown and yellow robe, which his father had picked up and handed to him; but his standing up and moving so swiftly also looked as if they were meant to rebuff the old man's suspicions, which it was necessary to refute at any cost—and by any means. We should indeed take special note here, for all this was very characteristic. Jacob's mode of thought, with its several layers and interlocked associations, was confirmed in the way he united three charges in one: carelessness in regard to health, a lack of modesty, and religious backsliding. This last was the deepest and most awful layer of his bundle of worries, and Joseph—both arms halfway into the sleeves of his coat, his fingers searching frantically for the slit for his head—used his struggle with his garment to demonstrate how important it was to him to deny behavior that he at once set about justifying in his most artful fashion.

"Never ever have I done that! Most definitely not!" he maintained, while his handsome, beautiful head found its way through the slit; and in an attempt to make his protest all the more convincing by a choice turn of phrase, he added, "My dear papa's opinion is, I assure him, darkened by clouds of gloomiest error."

In his agitation, he tugged the coat into place around his shoulders and pulled it down with both hands, reached for the rumpled myrtle wreath on his head to cast it aside, and without looking began to fasten the coat with the cords placed just below the opening at the neck. "As for blowing kisses, why nothing even vaguely of the sort . . . Why would I do such an evil thing? May my dear lord be gracious enough to tally my errors, behold, he will find these do not enter into the account. I was looking up, true, that is correct. I beheld the radiance of the light, watched the splendid rays in motion, and my eyes, wounded by the fiery darts of the sun, cooled themselves in the gentle glow of night's fabric. For as the song that passes from mouth to mouth says:

> Great Sin, in your radiance, appointer of time,
> In all of your changes, he wed you with night
> And crowned with high splendor your festive completion."

Standing one step above the old man, he chanted the song, his hands raised, his body bending low for each half line of verse, first to one side then to the other.

"Shapattu," he said. "That is the day of festive completion, the day of beauty. It is very close, it will be here tomorrow, or the day after. But even on the Sabbath I would not think of blowing the smallest, the most furtive kiss to the arbiter of time, for it is not said that it shines on its own, but rather that He made it to shine and set a crown upon it—"

"Who?" Jacob asked softly. "Who made it shine?"

"Marduk–Baal!" Joseph cried all too hastily, but followed this at once with a long, drawn-out "Aeh-h-h-h," shaking his head to undo it, and now continued, ". . . as He is called in the old tales. It is, however—as my dear papa has no need to learn from his poor child—the Lord of the gods, who is stronger than all the Anunnaki and Baals of other nations, the God of Abraham, who defeated the dragon and created the threefold world. When He turns away in wrath, He does not bend His neck again, and when He is angry no other god can oppose His fury. He is generous of heart, His understanding is all-embracing, evildoers and sinners are a stench in His nostrils. But He showed favor to the man who went up out of Ur and made a covenant with him, that He would be his God, his and his seed's after him. And His blessing has come upon Jacob, my Lord, who properly bears the title of Yizrael, the beautiful name known to all, and he is a great expounder, full of insight, and far be it from him to instruct his children so falsely that they would even think of blowing kisses to the stars, for kisses should be reserved for the Lord alone, always presupposing, which one cannot, that they might be fitting for Him, which is so little the case that one might say, still by way of comparison, that it were more proper to blow kisses to mere stars. But even if one could say that, I will not say it, and if I placed my fingers at my mouth for a kiss of that sort, then let me never do so again even to eat, but let me starve. And I shall likewise never eat again, but shall prefer starvation, if my dear papa does not at once take a comfortable seat, here beside his son on the rim of this deep well. My lord has been standing on his feet far too long as it is, for in his hip he has a holy weakness, acquired, as everyone knows, in a most highly peculiar way . . ."

He ventured to step down to the old man and carefully placed an arm around his shoulders, convinced he had enchanted and placated him with his chatter; and Jacob, who had been standing there pondering his God and playing with the little stone signet cylinder dangling at his chest, sighed and, yielding to the pressure, set one foot on the circular step and then sat down on the rim of the well, resting his staff against his arm, ordering his robes, and turning his face now to the moon, with its clear light brightening his gentle aging majesty, its gleam mirrored in his wisely worried chestnut-brown eyes. Joseph sat at his feet, completing the scene he had imagined and suggested earlier. He felt Jacob lower a hand onto his head, and as the old man began, probably quite unconsciously, to move it in a stroking motion through his hair, Joseph commenced to speak again in a softer voice.

"You see, how fine and agreeable this is. I would like to sit like this through all three watches of the night, for that has been my desire for so long now. My lord gazes up into that countenance on high, and I do equally well in gazing up into his own, for I regard it, too, as a divine face, shining now in reflected light. Tell me, did not the face of my hairy uncle Esau look to you much like the face of the moon, when, as you report, he met you at the ford and, against all hope, was gentle and brotherly? But that, too, was but mildness reflected upon a hairy, heated face, the reflection of your countenance, dear lord, which is like that of the moon, and of Abel the shepherd, whose offering was pleasing to the Lord, but not like Cain's or Esau's, whose faces are like a field burst by the sun, and like a clod cracked by drought. Yes, you are Abel, the moon, and the shepherd, and all your family, we too are shepherds and herdsmen, and not people of the sun who till the soil, not like farmers, who walk sweating behind the wooden plow and the plow's oxen and pray to the

Baalim of the land. We, however, look up to the Lord of the Way, the wanderer who rises gleaming in white robes. But do tell me," he continued without pause, almost without taking a breath, "did not Abiram, our father, go up from Ur in Chaldea out of vexation, and did he not leave the moon citadel of his city in anger, because to the displeasure of Sin's people, the Lawgiver greatly exalted his god Marudug, the fire of the sun there, elevating him above all the gods of Shinar? And tell me, do not people there also call him Shem when they want to exalt him highly—the same name given Noah's son, whose children are black, but lovely, as was Rachel, and dwell in Elam, Assur, Arpachsad, Lud, and Edom? But wait now and listen, for your child has thought of something else. Was not Abram's wife named Sahar, that is, the moon? Do but look, and I shall reckon it up for you. Seven times fifty days, those are the days of the round, and four besides. Each month, however, has three days when people do not see the moon. Let my lord, if I may ask, take three times twelve from those three hundred fifty-four days, which leaves three hundred eighteen nights of the visible moon. But three hundred eighteen is the number of servants born in Abraham's house, with whom he defeated the kings of the East, pursuing them beyond Damascus and freeing Lot, his brother, from the hand of Kudur-Laomor, the Elamite. So then behold, Abiram, our father, loved the moon as well, and was so devout that in battle he counted his servants exactly according to the days of its shining. And presuming I might have blown it kisses, not one, but three hundred and eighteen—though in truth I blew not a one—tell me then, would that have been so great an evil?"

The Test

"You are clever," Jacob said, and his hand, which had lain still during the task of reckoning, began to stroke Joseph's head again even more vigorously than before. "You are clever, Yashub, my son. On the outside your head is handsome and beautiful, just as Mami's was"—this had been the young Joseph's nickname for his mother, a name of Babylonian origin, the earthly, familiar name for Ishtar—"and inside very quick and godly. When my years counted no more than yours do now, mine was just as merry, but it has grown rather weary with all these stories, not just new ones, but those that have been kept for us from the old days and are worthy of thought; weary, too, with troubles and Abraham's legacy, which gives me cause to ponder, for the Lord has not been clear. And even though one may behold His countenance as the face of gentleness, it is also like the fire of the sun and like a blazing flame; and it destroyed Sodom with its heat, and in order to cleanse himself a man passes through the fire of the Lord. He is the devouring flame that burns outside the tent at nightfall and consumes the fat of the firstborn at the feast of the equinox, while we sit inside faint of heart and eat of the lamb whose blood stains the doorposts, because the Destroyer is passing by . . ."

He broke off, and his hand slid from Joseph's hair, who looked up only to behold the old man with his face in both hands, and saw that he was quivering.

"What is it, my lord!" he cried in dismay, swiftly wheeling around and extending his hands up to those of the old man, without daring to touch them. He had to wait and ask yet again. Jacob changed his position only with some hesitation. When he revealed his face it was lined with dreadful pain, and his sorrowful eyes peered beyond the boy into space.

"I thought of God, and it was terrible," he said, and he seemed to have difficulty moving his lips. "It was as if my hand were the hand of Abraham lying upon Yitzchak's head. And as if His voice had called to me and commanded . . ."

"Commanded?" Joseph requested, tossing his head with a quick birdlike motion.

"Commanded and instructed—but you know what it was, for you know the stories," Jacob replied with faltering voice, as he sat there bent forward, his brow resting on the hand that held his staff. "I heard that command, for is He less than Molech, the bull-king of the Baalites, to whom in their need they bring the firstborn of men and deliver babes into his arms at a secret feast? And may he not demand from his own what Molech demands from those who believe in him? And he demanded it, and hearing his voice I said: 'Here I am!' And my heart stood still, my breathing stopped. And early in the morning I saddled an ass and took you with me. For you were Isaak, my late-born and my firstborn, and the Lord had prepared laughter for us when He announced you, and you were my one and all, and all the future lay upon your head. And now it was His right to demand this, though it ran counter to the future. And so I split wood for the burnt offering and loaded it on the ass and set the child upon it as well and departed with servants from Beersheba, traveling for three days in the direction of Edom and the land of Muzri, and toward Horeb, His mountain. And when I saw the mountain of the Lord from afar and the top of the mountain, I left the ass behind with the young lads, who were to wait for us, and laid the wood for the burnt offering on you, and took fire and a knife, and we went off alone. And when you spoke to me, asking 'My father?' I was unable to say, 'Here I am,' and instead my throat suddenly let out a whimper. And when you asked in your voice, 'We have fire and wood; but where is the sheep for a burnt offering?' I could not answer, as I should have answered, that the Lord would be sure to provide a sheep, for I was so grieved and sick that I could have wept and vomited out my soul, and I whimpered yet again, so that your eyes cast me a sidelong glance. And when we came to the place, I built a table of sacrifice with stones and laid the wood on it and bound the child with ropes and laid him on top. And took the knife and covered both your eyes with my left hand. And when I drew out the knife and put the knife blade to your throat, I faltered before the Lord, and my arm fell from above my shoulder, and the knife fell, and I tumbled to the ground, falling on my face and biting the earth and the grass of the earth and striking it with my feet and fists, and I cried, 'Slay him, You slay him, O Lord and Destroyer, for he is my one, my all, and I am not Abraham, and my soul falters before You!' And while I struck and cried, thunder from above the place rolled across the heavens, and its rolling died far off in the distance. And I had the child, but I had the Lord no longer, for I could not do it, for Him, no, no, could not do it," he moaned, shaking his head against the hand holding the staff.

"At the last moment," Joseph asked, raising his brows, "your soul faltered within you? Yet in the next moment," he continued, since the old man simply turned his head away in silence, "in the very next moment, the voice would have sounded and called out to you, 'Do not lay your hand upon the boy and do him no harm!' and you would have seen the ram in the thicket."

"I did not know that," the old man said, "for it was as if I were Abraham, and the story had not yet happened."

"Aha, but did you not say that you cried out, 'I am not Abraham!'?" Joseph responded with a smile. "But if you were not, then you were Jacob, my dear papa, and the story was an old one and you knew how it came out. And so it was not the lad Yitzchak, either, whom you bound and were about to slay," he added, with another delicate toss of his head. "But that is the advantage of these later days, that we know the great rounds in which the world rolls ever on, and the stories in which it all comes to pass and that the fathers established. You could have trusted the voice and the ram."

"Your answer is facile, but false," the old man replied, forgetting his pain in the heat of argument. "First, you see, if I was Jacob and not Abraham, I could not know that it would turn out as it had that day, and I could not know if the Lord might not want to allow what He had once prevented to proceed to its ending. Second, do but consider: What would have been my strength before the Lord if it had come from my counting on the angel and the ram rather than from my great obedience and the faith that God can let the future pass through fire unscathed and burst the bars of death and is the Lord of resurrection? And third—was God testing me? No, he tested Abraham, who stood fast. I, however, tested myself with the test of Abraham, and my soul faltered within me, for my love was stronger than my faith, and I could not do it," he lamented again, bending his brow to the staff once more, for having now justified his reasoning, he again gave himself over to his emotions.

"Most certainly I have spoken nonsense," Joseph said humbly. "My stupidity is without doubt greater than that of most sheep, and in comparison with this brainless lad a camel surely has the insight of Noah, the cleverest of men. My reply to your embarrassing rebuke will be no more enlightened, but it does seem to this stupid child that if you were testing yourself, you were neither Abraham nor Jacob, but—how fearful to say it—you were the Lord, who was testing Jacob with the test of Abraham, and you had the wisdom of the Lord and knew which test He intended to inflict upon Jacob, that is, the one that He had no intention of letting Abraham endure to the end. For He said to him, 'I am Molech, bull-king of the Baalites. Bring me your firstborn!' But when Abraham set about to do so, the Lord said, 'How dare you! Am I Molech, bull-king of the Baalites? No, rather I am Abraham's God, whose countenance is not like a field burst by the sun, but like the countenance of the moon, and what I commanded I did not command so that you would do it, but that you might learn that you should not do it, because it is nothing but an abomination in My sight, and here, by the by, is a ram.' My dear papa was diverting himself by testing whether he might be able to do what the Lord forbade to Abraham, and is now fretting because he has discovered that he could never, ever do it."

"Like an angel," Jacob said, sitting up straight, so touched that he shook his head. "You speak like an angel near to the throne, Jehosiph, my child of God! I wish that Mami could hear you; she would clap her hands, and those same eyes that you have would shimmer with laughter. Only half the truth is in your words, and the other half remains with what I said, for I proved weak in my trust. But you clothed your part of the truth with grace, anointing it with the oil of wit, so that it is a delight for the understanding and a balm for my heart. How is it that my child can speak words so full of wit that they fall merrily over the rocks of truth and splash in my heart to make it leap for joy?"

Oil, Wine, and Figs

"That comes from the fact," Joseph replied, "that wit is by nature a messenger who goes back and forth, like the intermediary between sun and moon and between the power that Shamash and the power that Sin hold over the body and mind of man. That is what Eliezer, your wise servant, taught me when he showed me the science of the stars and their conjunctions and their power over the hours, depending upon their aspects one with the other. And when he showed me the horoscope of my birth in Haran in Mesopotamia at midday in the month of Tammuz, Shamash was standing at the zenith and in the sign of the Twins, and the sign of the Virgin was rising in the east." Looking up, he pointed a finger to these constellations, of which the one was just leaving its apex and declining toward the west, while the other was about to begin its ascent in the east. Then he went on: "That is a sign of Nabu, my dear papa should know, a sign of Thoth, the scribe, who is a nimble, resourceful god, the one who advises good counsel among all things and promotes intercourse. And the sun likewise stood in one of the signs of Nabu, who was the lord of that hour and was in conjunction with the moon, which is favorable to him according to the priests and interpreters, for through it his cunning is given mildness and his heart receives tenderness. Nonetheless, Nabu, the go-between, was in opposition to Nergal, that fox and mischief-maker, through whom his dominion takes on a hardness and is sealed with the cylinder of fate. As for Ishtar, whose contribution is moderation and charm, love and grace, she was at her zenith at that hour, in an exchange of friendly aspects with Sin and Nabu. She also was standing in the Bull, and experience teaches that this lends tranquillity and persevering courage and gives delightful shape to the understanding. But she also stood, or so Eliezer says, in a trine aspect to Nergal in the sign of the Goat Fish, which Eliezer found a cause for rejoicing, because then her sweetness, so he says, is not bland, but is like strained honey spiced by the fields. The moon stood in the sign of the Crab, its own sign, and all interpreters stood, if not in their own, then in signs with which they were allied. But if Nabu in his shrewdness joins the moon in a powerful position, this brings great journeys out into the world. And if, as at that hour, the sun is in trine aspect to Ninurta, the warrior and hunter, that is an indication of a share in the events of the empires of this earth and in the administration of authority. It would not make for a bad horoscope according to these rules, that is, if the folly of this disappointing child does not ruin it all."

"Hmm," the old man said, letting his hand pass gingerly over Joseph's hair and looking off to one side. "That is a matter for the Lord," he said, "who guides the stars. But what He announces through them cannot be the same every time. If you were the son of a great and powerful man in this world, one might then perhaps read that you should have a share in affairs of state and governance. But since you are but a shepherd and the son of a shepherd, it stands to reason that it must be interpreted in some other fashion, on a smaller scale. But what was that about wit as a messenger going back and forth?"

"I was just coming to that," Joseph replied, "and shall now guide my words in that direction. For my father's blessing was a birth with the sun at the zenith and its aspect toward Marduk in the Scales and toward Ninurta in the eleventh house, in addition to the aspect these two paternal interpreters, king and armed warrior, shared with one another. That is a strong blessing! But my lord should also realize how powerful my mother's was as well, and the moon's blessing, given the strong positions of Sin and Ishtar. And that is surely the source of wit, produced, for example, when Nabu is in opposition to Nergal, when the reigning Scribe opposes the hard light of that retrograde scoundrel in the Goat Fish; and it is produced so that he can act as ambassador and mediator between the father's legacy and the mother's legacy, balancing the forces of the sun and moon and happily reconciling the blessing of day with the blessing of night . . ."

The smile with which he broke off was slightly awry but Jacob, sitting above and behind him, did not see it.

His father said, "Old Eliezer has had much experience, has gathered many words of wisdom and has, so to speak, read the stones from before the Flood. He has also taught you all sorts of true and worthy things about the beginnings, about origins and relations, all sorts of practical knowledge that can be put to use in the world. But about many things it cannot be said with certainty that truth and usefulness are to be accounted to them, and my heart wavers, doubting if it was good for him to show you the arts of the astrologers and magicians of Shinar. For though I consider my son's head worthy of all knowledge, I never knew that our fathers read the stars or that God taught Adam to do so, and I have my worries and doubts if it is not perhaps very like the worship of heaven's lights and an abomination before the Lord, a thing dubious and demonic, halfway between piety and idolatry." He shook his head in distress, caught up in his most private concerns—that is, in his worries about what was right and his brooding uneasiness about God's lack of clarity.

"Much is doubtful," Joseph answered, if what he said can be called an answer. "There is, for example, the night, which hides the day, or is it the other way round, so that day conceals night? It would be an important matter to determine, and I have often considered it when out in the fields and in the tent, so that if I should ever gain certainty I might draw conclusions as to the virtue of the sun's blessing and the virtue of the moon's blessing, as well as to the beauty of the legacies from father and mother. For my dear mother, whose cheek smelled as sweet as the petal of a rose, descended into the night when she gave birth to my brother, who still dwells in the tents with the women, and in dying wished to call him Ben-Oni, for it is known that On in the land of Egypt is the home of the sun's dearest son, Osiris, who is king of the lower realms. But you named the little boy Ben-Yamin, so that it might be known that he is a son of your true and dearest wife, and that, too, is a beautiful name. And yet I do not always obey you, but sometimes call my brother Benoni, a name he likes to hear, because he knows that for a moment as she lay dying Mami had wanted it so. She is now in the realm of night and loves us from the night, the boy and me, and her blessing is the moon's blessing and a blessing from the depths. Does not my lord know of the two trees in the garden of the world? From one comes the oil with which the kings of the earth are anointed that they may live. From the other comes the fig, green and pink and full of sweet garnet-hued seeds, and whoever eats of it will surely die. From its broad leaves Adam and Heva made aprons to cover their nakedness, for knowledge had become their portion beneath the full moon of the summer solstice, when it passes through its highest splendor, so that it may then wane and die. Oil and wine are sacred to the sun, and happy the man whose brow drips with oil and whose drunken eyes glisten from red wine. For his words will ring bright and bring laughter and comfort to the nations, and he will provide for them the ram in the thicket instead of the firstborn as a sacrifice to the Lord, so that they may be healed of their torment and fear. But the sweet fruit of the fig is holy to the moon, and happy is he whose dear mother nourishes him out of the night with its flesh. For he will grow as if beside a spring and his soul will have its roots at the source of the waters, and his word will be substantial and lusty like an earthly body, and the spirit of prophecy will be with him . . ."

How was he speaking? He was whispering. It was as it had been earlier that evening, before his father found him, and it was eerie. He wrenched his shoulders, his hands lay trembling on his knees, he smiled, but at the same time his eyeballs incongruously rolled back to show the white. Jacob did not see this, but he had been listening. He bent down to him, holding his hands above and beside the lad's head, discreetly protecting it at a distance. Then he laid his left hand on the boy's hair again after all, and at once there was a relaxation in Joseph's state.

While Jacob's other hand groped for his son's right hand where it lay on his knee, he said with cautious intimacy, "Yashub, my child, listen to what I want to ask, for my heart is anxious for our cattle and the welfare of our herds. The early rains came even before the onset of winter, and were pleasing, for there were no cloudbursts that flood the fields and fill only the wells of those who live unsettled lives, for it came as a soft drizzle, beneficial to the land. But the winter was dry, and the sea would not lend its mildness to the air, but rather the winds came from the plains and deserts, and the sky was clear, delighting the eye, but bringing care to the heart. And woe to us if the late rains are also delayed and do not come, for that would be the ruin of the farmers' harvest, of seed sown by the tillers of the soil, and the grass would wither before its time, so that the cattle would find nothing to eat, and the udders of the ewes would hang limp. Let my child tell me what he thinks of wind and weather and of their prospects, and what his state of mind is in regard to whether the late rains will still arrive in time."

And then he bent down even lower to his son, turning his face aside to hold one ear above Joseph's head.

"You are listening just above me," Joseph said, without being able to see it, "and your child is still listening as well, to what is both within and without, and he brings tidings and news to your listening ear. For in my ear is the sound of branches dripping and of drizzle falling upon the plains, though the moon is exceedingly bright and the wind comes from Gilead. For this rustling sound is not of the present time, but near in time, and my nose is certain it can smell how, before the moon of Nisan has waned by a quarter, the earth will be pregnant by the manly water of heaven and will give off the steamy mists of lust, for I can smell them, and the pastures will be full of sheep and the meadows will stand thick with grain, causing rejoicing and singing. I have heard and learned that in the beginning the earth was watered by the river Tavi, which flowed from Babel and flooded the earth once every forty years. But then the Lord ordained that it should be watered from the heavens, for four reasons, one of which was that all eyes would then look upward. So that we would gaze in thanksgiving to heaven's throne on high, where the devices of weather, the chambers of whirlwinds and tempests, are found, just as I beheld them in my dream as I lay sleeping beneath the oracle tree yesterday. For a *cherubu* calling himself Jophiel was kind enough to take me by the hand and lead me there, so that I might look about and gain some insight. And I saw caves filled with steam and their doors were made of fire, and saw the laborers at their business. And heard how they said one to the other: 'Orders have gone out in regard to the feast and the clouds of the heavens. Behold, a drought reigns over the lands to the west and the plains and pastures of the highlands are parched. Preparations are to be made that it rain right soon upon the land of the Amorites, Ammonites, and Pherrizites, of the Midianites, Hivites, and Jebusites, but especially over the region of the city of Hebron, higher up where the waters divide, where even my son Jacob, whose title is Yizrael, pastures his countless flocks.' I dreamt it with such vividness that there is no mocking it, and seeing as it was beneath the tree as well, my lord can be confident and certain in the matter of quenching waters."

"Praise be to the Elohim," the old man said. "We shall in any case select animals to slaughter for a burnt offering and present Them with a meal, and burn the entrails with incense and honey, so that it may turn out as you say. For I fear that otherwise those who dwell in cities and upon the land may spoil everything by doing things in their fashion and by announcing a debauchery in honor of Baalat and a feast of coupling, with cymbals and shouts in the cause of fertility. It is a fine thing that my boy is blessed with dreams; that is because he is my firstborn by my true and dearest wife. I too received revelations when I was younger—and what I saw as I journeyed from Beersheba against my will and, all unawares, came upon that place with its entrance gate, is surely a match for what you were shown. I love you because you have spoken comfort to me in regard to the rains, but do not tell just anyone that you dream beneath the tree, do not tell it either to the children of Leah or to the children of the handmaids, for they might take offense at your talent."

"I swear it, and lay my hand beneath your thigh," Joseph replied. "Your word is a seal upon my lips. I know well enough that I am a chatterbox, but when reason demands it, I can most certainly master my tongue; and that will prove all the easier since my little visions are hardly worth mentioning compared with what was granted my lord at the city of Luz, when the messengers ascended and descended between earth and the gates and the Elohim revealed Themselves to him . . ."

Duet

"Ah, my dear papa and lord," he said, turning with a happy smile to throw one arm around his father, enchanting him more than a little.

"How splendid it is that God loves us and delights in us and lets the smoke of our sacrifices ascend to His nostrils! For though Abel did not have time to sire children, but was slain in the field by Cain for the sake of their sister Noema, yet we are of the lineage of Abel the tent-dweller, and of the lineage of Isaak, the younger son, who was given the blessing. And that is why we have both reason and dreams, which two are a great delight. For it is precious to possess wisdom and words, so that one understands to speak and to reply and to name all things. And it is equally precious to be a fool before the Lord, so that one may stumble all unawares upon the place that binds heaven and earth, and be given to know in a sleep the purposes of His counsel and to interpret dreams and visions, as far as they indicate what will happen from moon to moon. And so it was with Noah, the arch-clever man, to whom the Lord announced the Flood, so that he might save his life. And so it was with Enoch as well, son of Jared, for he walked in paths of purity and washed himself in living water. That was the boy Hanok, and do you know of him? I know it well, all that transpired with him, and that God's love for Abel and Yitzchak was lukewarm compared with His love for him. For Hanok was so very clever and pious and learned in the secret tablets that he set himself apart from mankind and the Lord took him so that he was seen no more. And made of him an angel in His sight, who became Metatron, the great scribe and prince of this world . . ."

He fell silent and turned pale. Toward the end he had fought for breath as he spoke and in breaking off, he hid his face on his father's breast, who gladly tended it there, speaking out over it and up into the silvered air above.

"I do indeed know Hanok, who was of the first lineage of men, the son of Jared, who was the son of Mahalaleël, who was born to Kenan, who was born to Enos and Enos to Seth, who was Adam's son. That is Enoch's descent and lineage back to the beginnings. But the son of his son's son was Noah, the second first man, and he sired Shem, whose children are black, but lovely, and from whom in the fourth generation came Eber, so that he is the father of all the children of Eber and of the Ebrews and is our father . . ."

It was familiar; there was nothing new in his summary. Any child in the tribe and clan could rattle off the lesson of generations by heart, and the old man was merely using the occasion to repeat and witness to it in conversation. Joseph understood that their talk was to turn "fine" now, become "fine discourse" that no longer served the purpose of useful exchange and agreement on practical or intellectual issues, but merely listed and recited things already known to them both—in the service of memory, sanction, and edification—a spoken antiphon like those that shepherds exchanged by the fire in the fields at night and that began: "Do you know of this? I know it well." And so he sat up straight and joined in:

"And behold, from Eber came Peleg and he sired Serug, whose son was Nahor, the father of Terah, rejoice and be glad! He sired Abraham at Ur in Chaldea and departed from there with Abraham, his son, and with his son's wife, whose name was Sahar, like the moon, and who was barren, and with Lot, his son's nephew. And he took them and led them out of Ur and died at Haran. And there God commanded Abraham that, together with the souls he had won for the Lord, he should journey on, across the plain and across the river Phrat, following the road that joins Shinar and the land of Amurru."

"I know it well," Jacob said, taking up the story again himself. "It was the land that the Lord would show to him. For Abraham was God's friend, who with his spirit had discovered among the other gods the Lord who was in truth the Most High. And he came to Damascus and there sired Eliezer with a handmaid. Then he wandered across the land with his people, who were God's people, and he sanctified anew, and in his own spirit, the places where the people of the land worshiped and made holy their altars and circles of stone and instructed the people under the trees and taught them about the coming of the time of blessing, so that others were added to him from those regions and the Egyptian handmaid Hagar came to him, the mother of Ismael. And he came to Shechem."

"I know that as well as you," Joseph sang, "for the father went up out of the valley and came to that place whose fame is great and that Jacob also found, and there built for Yahu the Most High a table of sacrifice between Beth-el and Ai, city of refuge. And from there he traveled southward, to the land of Negeb, and that is here where the mountains descend toward Edom. And he went all the way down them and came into the filthy land of Egypt, the land of Amenemhet, the king, and there he became silvered and gilded, for he was very rich in cattle and treasures. And returned toward Negeb, where he separated from Lot."

"And do you know why?" Jacob asked, but only in pretense. "Because Lot was also very rich in sheep, oxen, and tents, and the land could not support them both. But behold how kind the father was, for when there was strife among the herdsmen about the pastures, it was not as it is among the thieves of the desert, who come and seize by the throat people whose pastures and wells they desire, but rather he said to Lot, his nephew, 'Let there be no strife between your people and my people. The land is wide, and we shall separate so that one goes here and the other there, without hatred.' And Lot journeyed toward the sunrise and availed himself of all the meadow-land of the Jordan."

"In truth that is how it was," Joseph chimed in again. "And Abraham dwelt near Hebron, the Fourfold City, and he made holy the tree that gives us both shade and dreams, and it became a refuge to the wanderer and a shelter to those who had no shelter. He gave water to those who thirsted and set those who had strayed upon the right path and repelled thieves. And took neither payment nor thanks, but taught them to pray to his God El-Elyon, the Lord of his House, the merciful Father."

"You have told it rightly," Jacob confirmed in a chant. "And it came to pass that as Abraham was making a sacrifice at sunset, the Lord made a covenant with him. For he took a heifer, a she-goat, and a ram, all three years old, and a turtledove and a young pigeon. And he divided those with four feet and spread the halves apart and put a bird at each side, leaving open the path of the covenant between the halves and kept watch for eagles that tried to pounce upon the pieces. And a sleep came over him that was like no other, and he was seized with terror and darkness. For the Lord spoke to him in that sleep and let him see the distant places of the world and the nation that would go out from the seed of his spirit and grow large out of the truth and vigilance of his spirit, and great things, of which the princes of empires and the kings of Babel, Assur, Elam, Hetti and Egypt knew nothing. And in the night passed like a flame of fire along the path of the covenant between the pieces of the sacrifice."

"Your knowledge is unrivaled," Joseph's voice commenced again, "but I also know something more. For that is Abraham's inheritance, which fell upon the heads of Isaak and of Jacob, my lord: the promise and the covenant. But it was not for all the children of Eber, nor was it given to the Ammonites, Moabites, and Edomites, but to this tribe alone, whom the Lord chose by seeking out the firstborn, not according to the flesh and the womb, but according to the spirit. And those He chose were the gentle and the clever."

"Yes, yes! You tell it as it was," Jacob said. "For what happened with Abraham and Lot, their separation, that occurred yet again, and the nations were divided. Moab and Ammon, whom Lot had sired by his own flesh, did not remain together upon his pastures, for Ammon was fond of the desert and the life of the desert. Nor did Esau remain on Isaak's pastures, but went forth with his wives, sons, and daughters and the souls of his household and his goods and cattle to another land and became Edom on the mountains of Seïr. And what did not become Edom, was Yizrael, and it is a special people, unlike those who roam the land of Sinai and the ragged thieves of the land of Arabaia, but also unlike the people of Canaan, unlike the tillers of the soil and those who dwell in the fortresses of their cities, and instead are lords and herdsmen and free men, who drive their herds in between and tend their wells and remember the Lord."

"And the Lord remembers us, and that we are special," Joseph cried, throwing back his head and spreading his arms in his father's embrace. "Full of rejoicing is the heart of this child in his father's embrace, and he is enraptured by what he knows well and drunk on edifying exchange. Do you know the sweetest dream, which I have dreamt many thousand times? It is the dream of preeminence and of being the child. For much will be granted the child of God, what he begins shall turn out well for him, he will find grace in the eyes of all, and kings will praise him. Behold, my desire is to sing to the Lord of Hosts with a nimble tongue, nimble as the stylus of the scribe. For in their hatred they sent for me and laid snares for my steps, they dug a pit before my feet, and thrust my life into the pit, where darkness became my dwelling place. But I called upon His name out of the darkness of the pit, and He healed me and He rescued me out of the underworld. He made me great among strangers, and a people I did not know serves me, touching their brows to the ground. The sons of strangers flatter me, for without me they would perish . . ."

His chest was heaving. Jacob gazed at him wide-eyed.

"Joseph, what is it you see?" he asked uneasily. "My child's words are imposing, but do not accord with reason. For what does it mean that a strange land will serve him lying upon its face?"

"These were merely pretty words," Joseph replied, "that I spoke to say something grand for my lord. And it is the moon, too, which beguiles me somewhat."

"Watch over your heart and mind and be wise!" Jacob said fervently. "Then it will come to pass as you have said, that you will find approval in the eyes of all. And I intend to give you something that will make your heart rejoice and that will become you. For God has poured His grace upon your lips, and I pray that He will keep you holy forever, my lamb."

As they spoke the moon, its shimmering light so pure that it transfigured its own materiality, had continued its high journey; the position of the stars had changed according to the law of hours. Night wove peace, mystery, and the future out into far expanses. The old man sat a while yet with Rachel's boy at the rim of the well. He called him Damu, "Little Child," and Dumuzi, "True Son," just as the people of Shinar called their Tammuz. He also called him Nezer, a word from the Canaanite language meaning "sprout" and "blossoming twig," and flattered him. But as they sought out their tents, he urgently advised him not to brag before his brothers and not to announce to Leah's sons and the sons of the handmaids that he had spent so long a time with his father, exchanging intimate words with him. And Joseph promised him, too. But the very next day he not only told them that, but he also babbled on without a second thought about his dream of the weather. And they were all the more annoyed when his dream was fulfilled, for the late rains were abundant and pleasing.

Part Two

JACOB AND ESAU

Moon Grammar

During the "fine discourse" we had the opportunity to listen in on—
that evening antiphon at the well between Jacob and his imperfect
favorite—the old man made passing mention of Eliezer, who had
been borne to his ancestor by a slave woman during his sojourn with
his family in Damashki. Nothing can be clearer than that he cannot
have meant the aged scholar Eliezer who lived in his own camp—
likewise the freed son of a slave and presumably a half brother of
Jacob—and who, though he had two sons of his own, Damasek and
Elinos, used to sit beneath the oracle tree with Joseph in order to
further the lad's knowledge of many useful and some more than useful things. Surely one can say it is as clear as day that Jacob meant the
Eliezer whose own firstborn son had perforce been regarded for
years as the heir of Abraham, the wanderer from Ur or Haran, that is
until first Ismael and then—much to the laughter of both Sarai, for
whom life was no longer after the manner of women, and Abraham,
who himself was so old one might call him a centenarian—Yitzchak
or Isaak, the true son, beheld the light of this world. But the sun's
clarity is one thing and the moon's another, for the latter had indeed
ruled most marvelously over that more than useful discourse.
Things look different by moonlight than by the bright of day, and its
clarity may indeed have seemed the true clarity to those minds in
that time and place. So let us admit, though keeping it to ourselves,
that in mentioning Eliezer, Jacob had in fact meant the steward of his
own household, his chief servant—or him *too,* that is, both at once,
and not just both, but Eliezers *in general,* for since the days of the
eldest of them, in the camps of the heads of the clan there had often
been a freed slave named Eliezer, and he had often had sons named
Damasek and Elinos.

This attitude, this opinion of Jacob's was also—and the old man
could be sure of this—the same as Joseph's, who did not make an
even remotely clear distinction between Eliezer the original servant

and his own aged teacher, and had still less cause to do so since Eliezer did not make it himself, so that when he spoke of "himself" it was, at least in large part, Eliezer, Abraham's servant, that he had in mind. More than once, for example, he had told Joseph the story of how he, Eliezer, had been sent to the clan's relatives in Mesopotamia to woo Rebekah, the daughter of Bethuel and Laban's sister, on Yitzchak's behalf, had told it in exact detail, down to the little moons and crescents that had jingled from the necks of his ten dromedaries, down to the precise value in shekels of the nose rings, bracelets, festal raiment, and spices that had made up the dowry and purchase price for the virgin Rebekah; had told it as his own story, a memory from his own life, and could not get enough of describing Rebekah's charming gentleness and how she had stood that evening at the well of the city where Nahor dwelt, had taken her pitcher from her head and, bending down, held it in her hand to offer water to him, a thirsty man whom she had called "my lord"—something he had regarded as very much in her favor; had told of her modest manners and how upon first seeing Isaak in the field, where he had gone to lament the recent death of his mother, she had sprung from her camel and veiled herself. Joseph listened to it all with a delight that could not be diminished in the least by the grammatical form in which Eliezer presented it; he was far from being offended by the fact that the old man's "I" did not turn out to be solidly encompassed but, as it were, stood open to the rear, overflowed into earlier times, into areas beyond his own individuality, and incorporated experiences that, when given shape as memory and narration, should have actually—viewed by the light of day—been cast in the third person, rather than the first. But what does "actually" mean in this context, and is the human ego something closed sturdily in on itself, sealed tightly within its own temporal and fleshy limits? Do not many of the elements out of which it is built belong to the world before and outside of it? And is the notion that someone is no one other than himself not simply a convention that for the sake of good order and comfortableness diligently ignores all those bridges that bind individual self-awareness to the general consciousness? Ultimately, the idea of individuality stands in the same chain of concepts that includes unity and entirety, totality, universality; and the differentiation between human spirit in general and the individual spirit has not always had anything like the power over the mind that it has in today's world, which we have left behind in order to tell of a different mind, whose mode of expression provided a faithful image of its understanding, as when for notions of "personality" and "individuality" it knew only more or less objective terms like "religion" and "confession."

Who Jacob Was

Within this context it is quite appropriate then to bring our story around to the origin of Abraham's wealth. For, you see, when he went down into Lower Egypt (it must have been during the twelfth dynasty), he was in no way so weighed down with goods as he was when he separated from Lot. The extraordinary increase in wealth that he experienced there came about as follows:

From the start he was filled with the deepest mistrust of the morals of that nation, which he considered, whether rightly or not, a reed-clogged swamp, like one of the mouths of the Nile. He was afraid—in particular because of Sarai, his wife, who accompanied him and was very beautiful. He was terrified by the lewd eagerness of the people there, who would presumably lust after Sarai on sight and kill him in order to take possession of her; and tradition has preserved for us how, with that in mind—that is, out of concern for his own welfare—he immediately spoke with her upon entering that country and, as a way of diverting the jealousy of its shameless populace from himself, commanded her not to call herself his wife, but rather his sister—which she might do without its being an outright lie, since it was a popular custom, especially among Egyptians, to call one's beloved wife one's sister. Second, however, Sarai was a sister of Lot, whom Abraham regarded as his nephew, but called his brother; so if need be he could also consider Sarai his niece and apply to her the common name of sister in its larger sense, which he then did, both to mislead others and to protect himself. What he expected, happened—in fact far more happened than he had anticipated. Sarai's dark beauty catches the attention of those of both high and low rank in the land, the news finding its way to the very throne of its ruler, and the ember-eyed Asian is taken from her "brother's"

side—not by force, not by robbery, but for a very high price—
meaning she is bought from him, for she has been found worthy as
an enhancement to the choice inventory of Pharaoh's house of
women. And there she is brought, and her brother—who, so it is believed, should not be offended by such an arrangement, but rather, as
everyone said, should consider himself lucky—is not only allowed
to remain close by, but as a member of the court is also continuously
showered with favors, gifts, reparations, which he intrepidly accepts, so that he is soon rich with sheep, cattle, jack and jenny asses,
male and female slaves, and camels. Meanwhile, however, an unpar-
alleled scandal, which is carefully hidden from the populace, has occurred at court. Amenemhet—or Senwosret; it cannot be stated with
absolute certainty, which of the victors over Nubia it was who was
then lavishing the blessings of his rule over both lands—His
Majesty, then, a god in the full flower of his years, sets about to taste
this novelty, and is struck down by impotence, not once, but repeatedly; moreover word slowly leaks out that his entire court, the highest dignitaries and administrators of the empire, have simultaneously
succumbed to this same ignominious and—if one likewise considers
the higher cosmic implications of a man's procreative powers—
thoroughly terrifying malady. Something is wrong here, there's been
a blunder, a magic spell has been cast, some higher power is revealing
its opposition—that is patently clear. The brother of the Hebrew
woman is summoned before the throne, is asked, is interrogated, and
he confesses the truth. No praise can be high enough for the reason-
ableness and dignity of His Holiness's conduct. "Why," he asks,
"have you done this to me? Why did you subject me to this unpleasantness by your ambiguous words?" And without so much as a
thought that Abraham ought to forfeit even one of the gifts that have
been so generously heaped upon him, Pharaoh hands him his wife
back and bids them, in the name of the gods, to go their way, even
providing the party safe conduct to the borders of his realm. The father, however, now in possession not only of an unsullied Sarai, but
also of a wealth of goods greater than before, has the pleasure of
knowing he has pulled off a successful shepherd's trick. For it is far
better to presume that from the start he had counted on God's preventing Sarai's defilement in one way or another, had raked in the
gifts only on the basis of that supposition, being certain, even as he

initiated it, that this was the best way to outfox Egyptian lust, since only when viewed from this aspect is his behavior—the denial of his married state and the sacrifice of Sarai for his own welfare—set in its proper, and indeed very witty, light.

This, then, the story, whose truth is particularly underscored and corroborated by tradition, since it reports it a second time, with the difference that it takes place not in Egypt, but at the court of King Abimelek at Gerar, the capital of the land of the Philistines, to which the Chaldean had come with Sarai after leaving Hebron, and where, from Abraham's first request to his wife down to the happy ending, everything plays out just as before. Repetition of a report as a way to emphasize its truthfulness is unusual, but not extraordinary. Far more remarkable is the fact that according to this tradition (whose fixed written form, to be sure, is from a later period, but which, of course, always existed *as* tradition and so must be traced back to the statements and reports of the patriarchs themselves), the same experience, when told a third time, is ascribed to Isaak, meaning that he, too, bequeathed it to memory as his experience—or as likewise his experience. For at some time after the birth of his twin sons and because of a scarcity of food, Isaak also came to the land of the Philistines, to the court at Gerar, with his beautiful and very clever wife; and once there, for the same reasons that Abraham had done so with Sarai, he passed Rebekah off as his "sister"—not entirely falsely, since she was the daughter of his cousin Bethuel. But in his case the story continues with King Abimelek's gazing through a window—meaning, he was secretly spying and eavesdropping—and seeing Isaak "sporting" with Rebekah, which left him horrified and disappointed as only a lover can be when he realizes that the object of his desires, whom he has assumed to be available, is already firmly in other hands. His words betray him. For when Yitzchak admits the truth under interrogation, the Philistine cries out in reproach, "What peril have you called down upon us, stranger! How easily it could have happened that one of my people might have made bold with this woman, and then what guilt would have come upon us!" The phrase "one of my people" is transparent. In the end, however, the spouses found themselves placed under the special and personal protection of this pious, if lascivious, king, so that Isaak's wealth increased in the land of the Philistines, just as had once happened to

Abraham either there or in the land of Egypt, and his possessions in herds and servants grew so great that it became too much even for the Philistines, who gently forced him out of the country.

Assuming that Abraham's adventure also took place in Gerar, it is hard to believe that the Abimelek with whom Yitzchak dealt was the same king who found himself prevented from defiling Sarai's marital purity. The characters are well differentiated; for while Sarai's princely lover adds her to his harem without any ado, Isaak's Abimelek is far more modest and shy; and the notion that they were one and the same could be maintained, at best, only if the king's caution in Rebekah's case could be traced, first, to his having grown much older since Sarai's days and, second, to his already having been forewarned by his experience with her. But at issue here is not Abimelek's character, but Isaak's, as well as the question of his relation to this story about women—though strictly speaking, it, too, is unsettling only as it pertains indirectly to the question of who *Jacob* was: the Jacob, that is, whom we have heard chatting in the moonlight with his young son Joseph, Yashub, or Jehosiph.

Let us consider the possibilities. Either Yitzchak experienced in Gerar the same thing, with minor modifications, that his father had experienced there or in Egypt—in which case what we have before us is a phenomenon we might call imitation or devolution, a view of life, that is, that sees the task of individual existence as pouring the present into given forms, into a mythic model founded by one's forefathers, and making it flesh again. Or, however, Rebekah's husband did not "himself" experience the story, not in the narrower fleshly confines of his own ego, but nevertheless regarded it as part of his own life story and passed it on to those who came later because he differentiated less sharply between "I" and "not-I" than we are accustomed to doing (with what dubious right has already been indicated), or at least were accustomed to doing before stepping into this tale; since for him the life of the individual was separated more superficially from that of the race, birth and death meant a less profound alteration of existence—as in the previously examined case of the later Eliezer, who told Joseph the adventures of the primal Eliezer in the first person. In a word, it is the phenomenon of a more open identity, which stands alongside that of imitation or devolution and, locking arms with it, defines one's sense of self.

We labor under no delusion as to how difficult it is to talk about people who do not rightly know who they are; but neither do we doubt the necessity of taking such a vacillating state of consciousness into account; and if in reliving Abraham's Egyptian adventure Isaak took himself to be the same Isaak that the ancient wanderer had wanted to sacrifice, that is for us no conclusive proof that he was not deceiving himself—that is unless that sacrifice-temptation was itself part of the model and so occurred repeatedly. The Chaldean emigrant was Isaak's father, who wanted to slay him, but just as it is impossible for the latter to be the father of Joseph's father, whom we observed by the well, it is equally possible that the Isaak who imitated Abraham's shepherd's trick or incorporated it into his own life was at least in part confusing himself with the Isaak who came within an inch of being slain, although in reality he was a much later Isaak, standing removed by many generations from the primal Abiram. There is convincing certainty, which though it perhaps requires some clarification, needs no proof, that the story of Joseph's ancestors, as offered by tradition, represents a pious abridgment of the actual state of affairs, which is to say: a succession of generations that must have filled centuries and that lie between the Jacob we saw and the primal Abraham. Just as the primal Abraham's natural son and steward Eliezer had often appeared in the flesh since the days when he had wooed Rebekah for his young master—indeed had probably often courted a Rebekah beyond the waters of the Euphrates, but now again enjoyed the light of day as Joseph's teacher—so, too, many an Abraham, Isaak, and Jacob had witnessed the birth of day out of night since then without any of them being excessively precise about time and the flesh, neither differentiating with daylight clarity between the present he experienced and a present experienced in the past, nor very clearly demarcating his own "individuality" from the individuality of earlier Abrahams, Isaaks, and Jacobs.

These names were inherited from one generation to the next—if "inherited" is the correct or adequate word in regard to the community in which they repeatedly occurred. For it was a community whose growth was not that of a family tree, but rather of a cluster of trees, depending in large part as well on the ancient practice of winning souls, of propagating the faith. One needs to understand the tribal paternity of an Abraham, the primal immigrant, principally in spiritual terms, and whether he was truly related to Joseph in the flesh, whether he was his forefather—in the same direct line that they assumed—is definitely uncertain. As it was for them themselves; except that this twilight of theirs, this dusk of a generalized consciousness, allowed them to let it remain uncertain in some dreamy or piously dazed sense, to take words for reality and reality merely partially for a word, and to call Abraham the Chaldean their great- and great-great-grandfather in the same spirit that he himself had called Lot of Haran his "brother" and Sarai his "sister," which likewise had been both true and not true. Yet not even in a dream could the people of El-Elyon attribute their interconnection to a unity and purity of blood. Something Babylonian-Sumerian—and so not exclusively Semitic—had passed through Arabian desert stock; further elements from Gerar, from the land of the Muzri, from Egypt itself, had been blended in, as in the person of the slave Hagar, who was found worthy of sharing the bed with the great head of the tribe himself and whose son, then, married an Egyptian; and it was so universally known that one hardly needed to waste words on how sorely vexed Rebekah must have been by Esau's Hittite wives—daughters from a tribe that likewise did not call Shem its primal father, but that at some point came from somewhere in Asia Minor, pressing into Syria from the Ural-Altaic region. Many a branch was cast off early on. It is certain that the primal Abraham sired more children after the death of Sarai, and in particular—not being particular himself—with Keturah, a Canaanite woman, though he had not wanted his son Isaak to wed a Canaanite. Of Keturah's sons, one was named Midian, whose descendants lived out their lives south of the Seïr mountains of Edom—Esau's region— bordering on the Arabian desert, much like Ismael's children this side of Egypt; for Yitzchak, the true son, had been the sole heir, while the children of concubines had been bought off with gifts and pushed off to the east, where they lost any feeling for El-Elyon—if they ever had clung to Him—and served their own gods. But it was divine matters, the inherited task of thinking about God, that formed the spiritual bond that, whatever its motley makeup in terms of blood, held this clan together, who among all the Hebrews—be it the sons of Moab, Ammon, or Edom—ascribed that name to themselves in a special and narrow sense, especially insofar as they had now begun, at the very period into which we have entered, to restrict it and link it with another name, that of Israel.

For the name and title that Jacob had once wrested for himself

was no invention of his extraordinary opponent. Warriors of God—
that was the name that a bellicose and plundering desert tribe with
extremely primitive customs had always called itself. Driving their
herds of small animals before them, moving from pasture to pasture
in the plains among the settlements of the fertile land, small groups
of them had exchanged the purely nomadic life for a more or less settled state and, having been won over by spiritual wooing and accommodation, had become an essential part of Abraham's clan of faith.
Their god back at home in the desert was a snorting warlord and
rouser of storms named Yahu, an intractable kobold, cunning,
tyrannical, unpredictable, with traits more demonic than divine, before whom his brown-skinned tribe—who were proud of him, by
the by—lived in fear and trembling, employing magic and bloody
rites in an effort to control the harum-scarum nature of their demon
and guide him into useful paths. With no apparent provocation of
any sort, Yahu could happen upon a man by night, a man whom
he had every good reason to treat well—and throttle him; and yet he
could be moved to desist from his vile intentions if the wife of the
man being attacked hastily circumcised her son with a stone knife,
touched the fiend's genitals with the foreskin, and murmured a mystical formula, which—though anything close to an intelligible translation into our language has thus far presented insurmountable
difficulties—immediately mollified the Destroyer and scared him
off. So much by way of characterizing Yahu. And yet a great theological career awaited this dark divinity, so totally unknown in the
civilized world, precisely because fragments of that group who believed in him found themselves within the world of Abraham's conception of his God. For just as these families of herdsmen, drawn
into spiritual speculations set into motion by that first immigrant,
had with their own flesh and blood strengthened the basis of the
Chaldean's tradition of belief, so, too, some of their god's desert
quality had seeped in to nourish the divine nature struggling to realize itself through the human spirit—just as Osiris of the East, Tammuz, and Adonai, the mutilated son and shepherd of Malkizedek
and his Shechemites, had also delivered intellectual substance and
color. Did we not just hear his name, which was once a battle cry,
chanted lyrically by handsome and beautiful lips? This name—both
in the form brought by a brown-skinned tribe from out of the desert
and in abbreviations, derivations, and combinations derived from

conditions of popular Canaanite culture—was one of the sounds by which people sought to approach the inexpressible. For ages now, one town in the region had been called Be-ti-Yah, House of Yah, which is the same as Beth-el, House of God; there is also documentation that well before the days of the Lawgiver, the Ammuru who migrated into Shinar bore names in which the divine name of "Ya'we" played a role—in fact, primal Abraham had once named a tree growing near the holy Well of Seven *Yahweh el olam*— "Yahweh is the god of all the ages." But the name that Yahu's Bedouin warriors applied to themselves was to become the decisive hallmark of a purer and higher Hebraism, the designation for Abraham's spiritual seed—precisely because in the depth of night beside the Jabbok, Jacob had allowed its claim to apply to him.

Eliphaz

There may have been good reason for people like Shimeon and Levi, Leah's strapping sons, to smile furtively at their father's having acquired precisely this bold and rapacious name, wrenching it from the heavens, so to speak. For Jacob was not a warlike man. He had never been a man to do what the primal Abram had done when, in the name of overdue tributes, mercenaries from the East—the troops of Elam, Shinar, Larsa, and regions beyond the Tigris—had overrun the land of Jordan, plundered its cities, and dragged Lot away from Sodom as their prisoner. In a plucky, determined, and loyal response, Abram had scraped together a few hundred of his household servants and neighbors, fellow believers in El-Berith, the Most High, and set out with them from Hebron at a forced march, caught up with the retreating Elamites and *goyim,* and caused such confusion in their rearguard that he was able to free many prisoners and return home in triumph with both Lot and a great deal of the plundered goods. No, that would not have been for Jacob; he would have failed in a situation like that, as he had once silently admitted to himself when Joseph brought up the old often-told story. He "could not have done it," no more than, as he had also confessed, he could have done with his son what the Lord demanded. He would have left Lot's liberation to Shimeon and Levi; but if they had carried out a bloodbath among the worshipers of the moon, all the while emitting those horrifying cries they kept in reserve for just such occasions, he would have covered his face with his shawl and said, "May my soul not join in your counsels." For his was a weak and fearful soul; it abhorred violence, it trembled at the thought of enduring it, and was full of memories of the defeats his manly courage had met—memories, however, that did not impair his soul's dignity, its solemnity, because in just such situations of physical humiliation it had always been struck by a ray of light, by a consistent spiritual flood, a powerfully comforting revelation and reconfirmation of the grace that had been granted it and now gave it every right to lift its head once again, for such grace had been created and wrested out of his soul's own unhumiliated depths.

How had things gone with Eliphaz, Esau's splendid son? Eliphaz had been borne to Esau by one of his Hittite-Canaanite wives, worshipers of Baal, whom he had brought home to Beersheba early on and about whom Rebekah, Bethuel's daughter, used to say, "It wearies me to live among the daughters of Heth." Even Jacob was no longer certain which of them Eliphaz called his mother; it had probably been Adah, Elon's daughter. In any case, Yitzchak's thirteen-year-old grandson was strong for his age and an uncommonly likable young man—a simple spirit, but brave, openhearted, high-minded, upright in body and soul, and devoted to his wronged father with a proud love. Life had proved hard for him in more ways than one—because of both the complicated situation of his family and issues of religion. For no fewer than three creeds battled for his soul: the El-Elyon of his grandparents, the Baalim of his mother's clan, and a thundering, arrow-shooting divinity named Kuzach, honored by the mountain tribes to the south, the Seïrim or people of Edom, with whom Esau had had ties from early on and to whom he then later converted completely. The awful pain, the helpless rage that that hairy man had endured as a result of the decisive events in the dark tent of his almost blind grandfather—events that had been initiated by Rebekah and would drive Jacob from his home and herds and into foreign lands—had cut the boy Eliphaz to the very quick; and his hatred of his falsely blessed young uncle so completely consumed him that it had become life-threatening, was obviously more than his tender years could handle. At home, under the eye of the watchful Rebekah, there was nothing he could do about the thief who had stolen the blessing. But when it turned out that

Jacob had fled, Eliphaz ran to Esau and in hurried words demanded that he pursue the traitor and slay him.

But Esau, damned to the desert, was far too broken a man, far too weakened by bitter tears shed over a fate in the netherworld to be in the mood for the deed demanded of him. He wept because tears were his due, because they fit his role. His way of looking at things and at himself was conditioned and ordered by inborn rules of thought that firmly bound him, as they did the whole world—for their pattern had been stamped by the signs of the circling cosmos. Blessed by his father, Jacob had finally become the man of the full and "beautiful" moon, but Esau was now a man of the dark moon, and thus a man of the sun, a man of the underworld—and in the underworld one wept, though one might possibly become very rich in treasures there. When he later joined up with the people of the southern mountains and their god, he did so because it was fitting for him, since the south lay within the conceptual aura of the underworld, just as did the desert into which Ismael, Isaak's fraternal rival, had been driven. But long before, while still in Beersheba, Esau had entered into relations with the people of Seïr—well before receiving the curse—proving that both blessing and curse simply confirmed what was already so: that his character, that is, his role on earth, had been determined far in advance and that he had long been perfectly aware of both his character and its role. He had become a hunter, a roving guest of open country, the opposite of Jacob, who lived in tents and was a shepherd of the moon—had become a hunter by his very nature, on the basis of his strongly masculine physical traits. But it would be a mistake, an injustice to the mythical pattern that had shaped his mind, if one were to assume that it was his profession as a hunter that first suffused him with these feelings and this self-understanding of his role as a sunburned son of the underworld. Just the reverse—or at least reversed to that extent—he had chosen his calling because it fit him, as a man formed by myth and obedient to the pattern. If one viewed his relation to Jacob on a more cultivated level—which Esau, despite his rough hairiness, was always ready to do—then it was the return or the present manifestation, or timeless presence, of the relationship between Cain and Abel; and in that case Esau was in fact Cain, was so already in his capacity as the elder brother, to which the more recent laws of the world lent their support and honor, although he probably felt and knew that as a legacy from ancient matriarchal days, humanity's deep affection still belonged to the younger, the youngest son. Yes, if a certain story about a pottage of lentils is to be taken as having actually occurred and not having been added later to the facts as a way to justify the blessing subterfuge—which is why Jacob could most definitely have still believed in its truth—such an affection might very well explain Esau's apparent folly in surrendering his birthright to his brother so cheaply: he did it in hope of at least gaining for himself sympathies traditionally accorded the younger son.

In short, hairy, reddish Esau wept and showed absolutely no inclination for any attempt at pursuit and revenge. He simply had no desire to slay his Abel-brother and thereby carry to extremes a parallel that in any case his parents had used for playing out the whole relationship from the beginning. But then when Eliphaz offered, or rather fervently demanded that he himself be allowed to catch up with the son of blessing and slay him, Esau could recall no reason why not, and amidst his tears he waved his permission. Because for him a nephew's killing of his uncle would be a salutary breaking of the troublesome pattern and a new historical foundation that might serve as a parallel for later young Eliphazes—but at least would ultimately relieve him of the role of Cain.

And so Eliphaz scraped together a few people, five or six who sided with his father and usually accompanied him on his excursions into Edom, armed them from the camp's supply of long cane spears with very long, menacing points just above brightly dyed tufts of hair, commandeered some camels from Yitzchak's stalls well before dawn, and before the break of day the avenging troop was fast on the heels of Jacob—who, thanks to Rebekah's assistance, was likewise riding a camel and amply furnished with two slaves, a supply of food, and lovely items for barter.

His whole life long Jacob never forgot the terror that seized him when the intent of the approaching riders became clear. Upon spotting them, he had at first flattered himself that Yitzchak had become aware of his departure a bit too soon and had sent someone to call him back. But when he recognized Esau's son, he realized the gravity of the situation and lost all heart. A life-and-death race now began—on long-striding dromedaries grunting fervently and stretching their necks out horizontally, with tassels and moons bobbing and flying. But Eliphaz and his group had not packed as heavily as Jacob, who watched as the lead on which his life hung dwindled from one moment to the next. And when the first spears came flying past, he signaled surrender, dismounted along with his men, and—face in the dust, empty hands raised—awaited his pursuer.

What now happened was the most wretched and disgraceful event in Jacob's life and would have been enough to undermine forever the dignity and self-esteem of some other man. If he wished to live, and he did, at any price—but not, let it be remembered, out of ordinary cowardice, but because he was consecrated, because the promise that came from Abraham lay upon him—then he would have to plead with this lad burning with rage, soften the heart of his nephew, who was so much younger, so much lower in rank, but was now brandishing a sword above him, would have to beg in self-abasement, with tears, with flattery, with whimpering appeals to his magnanimity, with a thousand apologies, in a word, with convincing proof that it was not worth his effort to thrust a sword into such a bundle of misery. Which is what Jacob did. Like a madman he kissed the boy's feet, tossed whole handfuls of dust in the air, letting it fall on his head, and all the while his tongue never ceased casting its spell and imploring, for it was driven by fear to an ultimate glibness aimed at and indeed capable of preventing the lad—so instinctively astounded by such a flow of words, by such felicity of speech that he stood there thunderstruck—from his rash deed.

Had he wanted the deception? Had he initiated it, was it his invention? Let his bowels be ripped from him if that was even remotely true. His mother—Eliphaz's grandmother—had desired and planned it all alone, out of an excessive and undeserved fondness for him, and he, Jacob, had resisted and opposed the plan with might and main, had remonstrated with her that the danger was too great and dreadful, that Isaak would discover it all and curse not only him, but also the all-too-resourceful Rebekah. Nor should it be forgotten that he had reminded her with desperate urgency of what it would mean for him, even should the plan succeed, to stand before the majestic face of his firstborn brother. Yes, dressed in Esau's best raiment, kidskin wrapped around his wrists and neck, he had entered his father's, Eliphaz's beloved grandfather's, chambers with the dish of savory kid and the wine—yet not gladly, not happily, not blithely, not at all, but with trembling and trepidation. In his fear and anguish, sweat had run down his thighs, his voice had died in his constricted throat when Isaak asked him who he was, ran his hand over him, smelled him—but Rebekah had not even forgotten to salve him with Esau's wildflower fragrance. A deceiver? Not he. But rather a victim of female cunning, Adam seduced by Eve, friend of the serpent! Ah, Eliphaz, the good lad should beware his whole life long— God grant it should be several hundred years and more—of women's counsel and prudently avoid the snares of their guile. He, Jacob, had stumbled in that snare, and it was all over with him now. Blessed? Him? First, what sort of father's blessing was that, one so erroneous, obtained so underhandedly, so totally against the wish and desire of the man blessed? Was it of any worth? Had it any weight, any efficacy? (He knew very well that a blessing was a blessing, and that it had its full worth and weight, but he asked the question just to confuse Eliphaz.) And second, had he, Jacob, looked like a man who wanted to play the beneficiary of such a blunder by strutting around the house as the bearer of the blessing and pushing aside Esau, his lord? Ah, not in the least, quite on the contrary! He was voluntarily leaving the field to his brother. The penitent Rebekah had herself driven him off; he was now on his way, never to return, to places unknown, into exile, straight into the underworld, and tears would be his portion for ever and ever. Did Eliphaz— a cock pigeon on radiant wings, a young mountain bull in his splendor, an exquisite buck antelope—wish to strike him with the blade of his sword? Even though the Lord had instructed Noah that he would demand blood in payment for shed human blood, and even though it was no longer as in the days of Cain and Abel, but the land was now ruled by laws that it might be highly dangerous for a noble young man like Eliphaz to violate? For that young man was the sole concern of his already sufficiently punished uncle, a man destroyed and of no worth, and inasmuch as he was now about to go to a land where he would be a stranger and a servant, why then Eliphaz would be exceedingly fortunate and his mother blessed among the children of Heth, if he were to hold back his hand from bloodshed and turn his soul away from wrongdoing.

The fear-inspired words streamed from the babbling, pleading Jacob, leaving Eliphaz astonished, his head spinning in their eddy.

He had expected to meet up with a laughing thief and had found a
wretch whose humiliation appeared to restore Esau's dignity completely. Eliphaz was a kind lad, just as his father was, really. One ardent emotion quickly took the place of another in his soul,
generosity superseded anger, and he cried out that he would spare
his uncle—at which Jacob wept tears of joy and covered the hem of
Eliphaz's robe, his hands and feet with kisses. Eliphaz's lofty benevolence was tinged with embarrassment and slight disgust. He found
himself annoyed at his own vacillation and gruffly demanded that
the runaway's baggage be handed over to him, everything that Rebekah had secretly packed for his uncle belonged to Esau, the injured party. Jacob was about to try eloquent words to turn this
decision around as well, but Eliphaz shouted at him with contempt
and had him plundered so thoroughly that he truly had nothing left
but his skin. The gold and silver vessels, the jars of finest oil and
wine, the necklaces and bracelets of malachite and carnelian, the incense, the honeyed sweets, and all the woven and knitted cloth his
mother had ordered packed for him—it all had to be handed over to
Eliphaz; even the two slaves who had fled the camp with him, one of
whom was bleeding from a spear wound to the shoulder, were made
to join up with his pursuers and return home, along with their animals. And then, with only a couple of earthenware jars of water at
his saddle, Jacob was allowed to go his way alone, taking the dark
road to the east—but who knows in what frame of mind.

His Head Is Raised Up

He had saved his own life, his precious life of promise, for God and
for the future—of what value were gold and carnelian in comparison? Everything depended on life, and ultimately young Eliphaz
had been far more brilliantly swindled than the man who had sired
him, but at what a price! Surely one greater than some baggage—his
very honor as a man. And no one could have been more disgraced
than Jacob, who with his face disfigured by smeared tears and dust
had had to grovel and whimper before a fuzzy-cheeked boy. And
then? And immediately following such humiliation?

Immediately thereafter, or only a few hours later that evening,
he arrived by starlight at the town of Luz—a place he did not know,

for this entire region was unfamiliar to him—which was set on a hill-side in rolling country mostly terraced and planted in vineyards. The few square houses of the town were crowded halfway up the hillside crisscrossed by paths, and when some voice within him told the impoverished traveler to spend the night here, he started up the hill behind his obstinate camel—of which he was a bit ashamed, for it was being obstinate, still quite bewildered by that sorry and stormy incident. He watered the beast at the well that lay outside the town's encircling clay wall and washed the traces of shame from his face, which improved his mood considerably. All the same, feeling like a beggar, he avoided asking the people of Luz to admit him inside their walls and instead took the only possession he now had by the reins and, still on foot, led it up above the town, to the very top of the hill's flattened summit—and at the sight of it he regretted not having arrived here earlier, in the nick of time. For a sacred stone circle, a *gilgal,* marked the place as a refuge and sanctuary, and young Eliphaz, that highwayman, would have been unable to touch him here.

In the middle of the *gilgal* a peculiar coal-black, cone-shaped stone had been erected, one that had evidently fallen from heaven and in which slumbered the power of the stars. Since its form was reminiscent of his procreative member, Jacob piously raised his eyes and hands heavenward and felt even more strengthened. Here, this is where he wanted to spend this night, until day hid it again. For his pillow he chose one of the stones in the circle. "Come, old stone," he said, "comfort me, raise up this troubled head by night!" He covered it with his headscarf, stretched out with his head raised in the direction of that phallic scion of the heavens, blinked briefly up into the stars, and fell asleep.

And then it happened, something high and marvelous—at some point in the middle of the night, after a few hours of deepest sleep, his head was truly raised up, exalted above every disgrace, to a sublime vision that united all the royal and divine thoughts lying hidden in his soul, which, though humiliated, secretly smiled at its humiliation and for comfort and strength enlarged upon these things within the space of its own dream. . . . He dreamt fixed to that very spot. Even in his dream he lay asleep, his head propped up. But his eyelids were transparent to an extravagant brightness; he saw through them, saw Babel, saw the umbilical cord between heaven and earth, the

stairway to the highest palace, a ramp of numberless fiery and broad
steps, each with its astral guard, leading up to the highest temple, the
throne of dominion. The steps were neither of stone nor wood, nor
of any other earthly substance; they appeared to be of molten brass,
to have been fashioned from the fire of the stars; their planetary brilliance melted and faded across the measureless expanses of earth, but
increased as it rose on high and spread to an overpowering dazzling
light that would have been unbearable to eyes wide open and could
be beheld only through the protection of his eyelids. Winged creatures, part man part beast, cherubim, crowned cows with the faces of
maidens, stood with folded wings at both sides, immobile, staring
straight ahead; and the spaces between front and hind legs set apart
at angles were filled with bronze tablets inscribed with glowing sacred words. Bull-gods—with strings of pearl across their brows and,
dangling at their ears, locks as long as the fringe-trimmed beards that
covered their cheeks and ending in rolls of curls—crouched there,
gazing at the sleeping man from serene long-lashed eyes. Alternating
with them were lionlike creatures that sat upon their tails, their
barrel chests covered with flaming tufts. From their wide, square-
shaped mouths appeared to come loud hisses that made the whiskers
beneath their fierce blunted noses bristle. The broad ramp between
these beasts, however, roiled with servants and messengers, ascending and descending, taking the stairs in the measured strides of a
slow dance whose movements declared the joyous law of the stars.
Their lower bodies were veiled in garments inscribed with sharp-
pointed characters, and their breasts seemed too soft for those of
young lads, too flat for female breasts. With arms upraised, some
bore bowls upon their heads, others carried tablets in the crooks of
their arms and pointed fingers at them; many, however, played flutes
and harps, strummed lutes or tapped drums, and behind them came
singers who filled the vastness with the whir of high, metallic voices
and kept time by clapping their hands. And so the whole expanse of
this stairway of the worlds throbbed and rang with surging harmonious chords sinking and rising up to the fiercest flames of light, to
the narrow arch of fire and the gate of the palace with its pillars and
lofty pinnacles. The pillars were made of golden bricks that stood
out in relief as scaly beasts whose front paws were those of leopards,
but whose hind feet were those of eagles; and the beams of the fiery
gate were supported at each side by oxen-hoofed men, whose

crowns bore four horns and whose eyes were precious stones and whose curly beards were coiled against their cheeks in tight rolls. But before them stood the seat of royal power and the golden foot-stool before it, and behind them was a man who bore a bow and quiver and held the fan above the caplike crown of the Almighty, whose raiment was of moonlight and fringed with little flames. And God's arms were sinewy with great power, and in one hand He held the Sign of Life and in the other a drinking vessel. His beard was blue and bound in ribbons of brass, and beneath His high-arching brows was a terrifying countenance of fierce goodness. Before Him was yet another man with a wide band encircling his head, like a vizier or the servant nearest the throne, who gazed into the Almighty's face and pointed with an open palm to Jacob sleeping upon the earth. And the Lord nodded and set down one sinewy foot, and the highest servant swiftly bent low to pull away the footstool so that the Lord might stand up. And God stood up from His throne and held the Sign of Life out to Jacob and drew air deep into His chest, raising it up. And His voice was splendid, sonorously blend-ing with the psaltery and the star-born music of those who ascended and descended to form one mild and mighty harmony. But what He said was: "I am! I am the Lord of Abiram and of Yitzchak and I am your Lord. My eye falls upon you, Jacob, with farseeing favor, for I will make your seed as the dust of the earth and you shall be blessed by Me above all men and possess the gates of your enemies. And I will keep and watch over you wherever you go, and will bring you home a rich man to the land upon which you sleep, and will never leave you. I am and I will!" And the harmonious thunder of the King's voice died away, and Jacob awoke.

What a dream and vision it had been, what a raising up of his head! Jacob wept for joy, meanwhile laughing at Eliphaz, and there beneath the stars he walked around the circle of stones and inspected the one that had propped up his head for such a spectacle. What sort of place is this, he thought, that I have come upon by chance? Chilled by the fresh night air and moved by profound excitement, he shivered and said, "It is right that I shudder, right indeed! The peo-ple of Luz have only a vague notion what sort of place this is, for though they have made of it an asylum and set up a *gilgal*, they know as little as I did that it is quite simply a place of the Presence, the gateway to splendor binding heaven and earth." He then slept a few hours, a sturdy and proud sleep full of private laughter, but at dawn he arose and went down to Luz and stepped under the arch. For in the fold of his girdle he kept a ring with a seal of deep blue lapis lazuli that Eliphaz's men had not found. He sold it now for less than its value, for some dry grain and a few jars of oil—for he needed oil to carry out a plan he considered his duty. Before proceeding on to the east and the river Naharina, he once more climbed up to the place of his dream, set the stone on which he had slept on end, as a monument, poured oil generously over it, saying as he did so: "Beth-el, Beth-el, shall be the name of this place and not Luz, for it is a house of the Presence, and God the King revealed Himself here to one who had been brought low and strengthened his heart beyond measure. For surely it was exaggerated and beyond measure when He called out above the harps that my seed would be countless as the dust and my name would triumph high in honor. But if He will be with me, as He promised, and watch over my footsteps in a strange land; if He will give me bread and raiment for my body and allow me to return safely to Yitzchak's house, then shall He, and no other, be my God, and I will give Him one-tenth of all that He gives me. And if all these things with which He has strengthened my heart beyond measure prove true, then will I take this stone and build a sanctuary in which food shall be offered without ceasing and pungent incense constantly burned for His nostrils. This is a vow and a promise in return for the other, and may God the King now do whatever may seem to Him to be in His interest."

Esau

That was how it had gone with the splendid Eliphaz, who really was but a poor lad when compared with Jacob, whom in his pride he had humiliated; but thanks to supplemental spiritual resources of which Eliphaz had not the vaguest, Jacob had triumphed with ease over whatever disgrace a boy might be capable of inflicting on him, for revelation always came to him in the states of his deepest misery. Had things gone any differently with the father than with the son? By which we mean his meeting with Esau himself, to which we have heard Jacob refer in conversation. In that case his head had been raised up and his heart greatly strengthened ahead of time, at Peni-el, during that fearful night when he had wrestled for the name that gave Shimeon and Levi something to smile about. And in possession of that name, victorious in advance, he had gone out to meet his brother—armed in his deepest soul against any humiliation that might prove unavoidable and armed as well as against the indignity of his own fear of a meeting that would so tellingly reveal how dissimilar in character the twins were.

Although Jacob had sent his messengers on ahead to Esau, since some clarification of the situation seemed absolutely necessary, he did not know in what frame of mind Esau was approaching him. All he knew from his spies was that he was at the head of a troop of four hundred men—which could be taken as an honor, in response to the flattering message Jacob had sent in great humility, or, possibly, as a great danger. He had made his own preparations. He had hidden his dearest treasures, his wife Rachel and her five-year-old son, with the beasts of burden at the rear, had placed Dinah, his daughter by Leah, in a chest as if she were dead, almost smothering her, and put the other children behind their respective mothers, with the concubines in the lead. He had divided up his gifts of livestock, and had herdsmen drive them on ahead: two hundred he-goats, two hundred she-goats, the same number of ewes and rams, thirty nursing camel mares, forty cows with ten young bulls, twenty she-asses and their foals. He had had them driven in separate herds at intervals, so that as Esau met each herd he could learn in response to his question that these were gifts for him, the lord Esau, from Jacob, his servant. And that was what happened. And even if Esau may still have been very indecisive, ambivalent, and even uncertain himself about his attitude as he left the mountains of Seïr to meet the wanderer returning home, when he finally caught sight of Jacob for the first time after twenty-five years, he was already in the most cheerful of moods.

True, Jacob had himself gone to the trouble of making arrangements to produce this cheerfulness, but he found it highly disagreeable, and no sooner did he realize that, for the moment at least, he had nothing to fear than he began to have difficulty hiding his disgust at Esau's brainless and guileless good nature. He never forgot the scene of Esau's approach. Rebekah's twin sons were fifty-five years old at the time—the "fragrant grass" and the "thorny weed" as they had been known even as boys in the region between Hebron and Beersheba. But the "fragrant grass," smooth-skinned Jacob, had never been much for youthful high jinks, had kept to the tent, proving himself thoughtful and timid even as a boy. But he had lived through a great deal now, and Jacob was a man in his best years, to whom stories and events had lent dignity, a man whose concerns were spiritual and who came laden with the goods that had accrued to him—whereas Esau, although grown gray like his brother, appeared still to be the same natural lad from long ago, still a mindless and unimportant fellow, who vacillated between howls and animal foolishness. Even his face was not changed in the least: just as aging in the physiognomy of the majority of our youthful companions consists of their growing a beard and probably adding a few wrinkles to their boyish faces—but it is a boy's face with beard and wrinkles, and otherwise nothing new has been added.

Jacob's first impression was a sound he knew from early youth: Esau playing upon his flutes, a high and hollow trilling on a bundle of reed pipes of various lengths bound in a row by crossbands—a favorite instrument of the mountain people of Seïr, perhaps even of their invention, which Esau had taken up as a boy and from which, given his thick lips, he knew how to draw quite ingenious music. But Jacob had always despised these silly and riotously idyllic tones, this inexcusable tra-la-la native to the underworld of the south, and disdain rose upon within him as his ears now picked up the sound again. Besides which, Esau was dancing. Pipes at his lips, a bow upon his back, and a tattered goatskin around his loins, but without another stitch of clothing—which he really didn't need, for he was so hairy that his own pelt literally hung from his shoulders in grayish red tufts—he danced and leapt at the head of caravan and troops, approaching his brother on foot across open country with piping, waving, laughing, and weeping, so that at the sight of those pointy ears and that flat nose pressed against a bare upper lip, what Jacob thought—in scorn, embarrassment, pity, and impatience—was something like "Oh good God in heaven!"

He, too, by the way, had dismounted, as quickly as his swollen hip allowed, in order to hasten toward the goatish musical oaf, but as he gathered up his robes and limped eagerly ahead, he was also practicing all the declarations of submission and self-abasement that he had resolved to make and that now, following his victory the night before, he could perform without any real impairment of his self-esteem. Some seven times, despite his pain, he fell to his knees, the palms of his hands above his head, and that was also how he landed at Esau's feet, against which he pressed his brow, while his hands groped upward to touch his brother's knees—where tufts of hair dangled—and his mouth constantly repeated words intended to portray their relationship as being completely in Esau's favor, despite blessing or curse, and so disarm and reconcile him: "My Lord! Your servant!" Esau, however, displayed not just reconciliation, but also a tenderness beyond all expectation, very likely including his own—for upon receiving news of his brother's return home, his first reaction had been one of general and vague agitation, which even shortly before their meeting could very easily have turned to rage rather than to gentler emotions. He forcibly raised Jacob from the dust, pressed him to his shaggy breast with noisy sobs, and planted smacking kisses on his cheeks and lips—caresses that were soon all too much for their recipient. And yet Jacob wept too—partly because the tension of uncertainty and fear had melted away, partly as well out of nervous weakness, but mostly he wept over life and time and the human condition. "Dear brother, dear brother," Esau babbled between kisses. "All forgotten! Let all the roguery be forgotten"—an embarrassingly explicit statement of generosity more likely to stop Jacob's tears at once than to set them flowing more fervently—and then he began to ask questions, but put aside the one closest to his heart: that is, about the meaning of the herds that had been driven on ahead—and raising his eyebrows, first inquired about the women and children sitting on the camels behind Jacob. And so next came dismountings and introductions: first the concubines with their four boys bowed low before the hairy tufted man, then Leah with her six, and finally sweet-eyed Rachel with Joseph, who was brought up from the rear; and at the mention of each name Esau gave a thick-lipped swipe across his rank of pipes, praised the sturdy limbs of the children and the breasts of the women, and expressing loud amazement at Leah's feeble eyes, offered an Edomite herbal salve for the chronic inflammation of her eyelids, for which she thanked him with an angry heart and kissed the tips of his toes.

The brothers had difficulty with even the outward forms of communication. As they spoke, both searched for the words of their childhood and had trouble finding them, for Esau spoke in the rough dialect of the people of Seïr, which, through influences from the Midianite and elements taken from the deserts of Sinai, differed

from the language spoken in the region of their youth, and in the
land of Naharaim Jacob had grown accustomed to speaking Akkadian. They both had to make do with lots of gestures, but when it
came to the matter of those fat herds up ahead, Esau was very good
at putting his curiosity into words; and the coyness he showed about
accepting such a lavish gift, when Jacob indicated he hoped it would
bring him favor in the eyes of his lord, was evidence of good manners. This coyness took the form of lighthearted indifference about
possessions and riches and all such encumbrances. "Ah, dear
brother, I couldn't!" he cried. "It's yours to have, yours to keep. I
give it right back to you. I don't need it to make me forget the pain of
that old nasty scampish trick. It's forgotten, the pain is gone. I've
reconciled myself to my fate and am content. Do you think we
southerners down below are the sort who mope about our whole life
long? Ho-ho-ho and pshaw! You're badly mistaken there. True, we
don't strut about and roll our eyes with blessings on our head, but
we live life, too, and right lustily in our own way, believe me. We too
find it sweet to sleep with a woman, and we too have our share of
love in our hearts for a bevy of children. Do you suppose that the
curse for which I have you to thank, dearest rascal, turned me into a
scabby, starving beggar in Edom? Anything but! I am a lord there
and great among the sons of Seïr. I have more wine than water, and
honey to spare, and oil and fruits, barley and wheat, more than I can
eat. My underlings bring me of their crops and send me bread and
meat every day, and fowls already prepared for my meal, and I have
game as well, what I kill and what they hunt for me in the desert
with their dogs, and milk and cheese until I spend half the night
belching. Gifts? Herds and flocks as atonement and whitewash for
that old shabby prank you and that woman pulled on me? I don't
give a fig or a whistle about that—tra-la-la-la"—and he gave a flourish on his flute. "What need is there for gifts between you and me?
The heart is what matters, and my heart has forgiven and forgotten
that vile trick from years gone by, and how you mimicked my shag-
giness with a goat hide around your wrists to fool the old man, you
rapscallion you, so that I can only laugh at it in my old age now,
though I wept bloody tears at the time and sent Eliphaz after you,
turning you so pale with fear that even a woman would mock you."

And he embraced his brother yet again and smacked more kisses on his face, a torment that Jacob endured with no responding pressure or tenderness. For he was thoroughly disgusted by Esau's words, found them excruciatingly asinine and slovenly and could think of nothing but how to get away with all due speed from his uncouth kinsman, but not without having finally settled accounts and applying the tribute he had rendered as payment for the birthright yet again—and all Esau really wanted was to be persuaded. And so more courtesies, expressions of humility, and offers were pressed upon him. But when Esau finally agreed to please his blessed brother and receive this gift from his hand, the poor devil's heart really was finally won over, and he proved far more sincere and earnest about their reconciliation than Jacob could ever bring himself to be.

"Ah, dearest brother," he cried, "and now not one word more of the old shabby misdeed! Did we not slip from the same womb, one after the other, as good as at the same time? For, as you know, you were holding my heel, and I, as the stronger, pulled you into the light. We had, to be sure, buffeted each other a little in her belly, and have buffeted each other outside as well, but from now on we'll not think of it. Let us live henceforth together as brothers and as twins before the Lord, and dip hands in the same bowl and never depart from one another again our whole life long. So come, let us journey now toward Seïr and there we shall dwell side by side."

Thanks but no thanks, Jacob thought. Am I supposed to become a flute-playing goat in Edom as well, and hole up there forever, you dolt? That is neither God's intention, nor my soul's. Everything you say is excruciatingly asinine to my ears, for what happened between us cannot be forgotten. You mention it yourself with every twitch of your tongue. Yet your feeble mind deludes you into thinking that you can forget and forgive?

Aloud he said, "The words of my lord are a delight and each seems to have hearkened to the most secret wishes of his servant's heart. But my lord can see that I have half-grown children with me and small ones, too, like this five-year-old, named Jehosiph, who is weakened by the journey; moreover, one dead child, sad to say, here in this chest, and it would be irreverent to hasten over hedge and ditch with her, plus suckling lambs and calves. All of which would die if I were to go too fast. And so let my lord go on before me, and

I will slowly follow after according to the pace of my cattle and children, until I arrive in Seïr somewhat later, and we can dwell side by side in heartfelt affection."

That was a refusal in supple words, and Esau, with a bit of a glower, immediately took it as such more or less. He made yet another attempt by suggesting he would leave a few men with his brother by way of escort and protection. But Jacob replied that would be quite unnecessary, if only he found grace in the eyes of his lord—and with that it was clear as day that his promises were empty phrases. So Esau shrugged his shaggy shoulders, turned his back on his fine and false brother, and departed with herds and retinue for his mountains. Jacob, however, first straggled a while behind him, but then at the first opportunity he turned off and went his own way.

Part Three

THE STORY OF DINAH

The Little Girl

Since he then went on to Sichem, this is now the place to present the stories describing the serious troubles of his sojourn there—that is, to report them as they really happened, correcting those little embellishments on the truth that were later believed obligatory during those "fine discourses" when someone asked, "Do you know of this? I know it well," and that were then incorporated into the tribe's and the world's tradition. We have undertaken to enlarge upon these grave and ultimately bloody events—inscribed in the lines of the aged Jacob's weary face along with other experiences that formed the worthy burden of memory in his dignified later years—because it is part and parcel of our examination of the stamp of his soul and because, given his behavior in the course of them, nothing is better suited for explaining why Shimeon and Levi nudged each other whenever their father made use of his honorary name, his divine title.

The hapless heroine of the adventures at Shechem was Dinah, Jacob's only daughter, borne to him by Leah at the beginning of her second period of fertility—at the beginning, then, and not at the end, not after Issakhar and Zebulun, as the sequence is recorded in the version set into writing much later. That chronology cannot be correct, because if it were correct Dinah would not have reached physical maturity at the time of her misfortune, but would have been a mere child. In reality she was four years older than Joseph, and so nine when Jacob's household arrived at Sichem and thirteen at the time of the catastrophe—two significant years older than the arithmetic of the traditional timetable would have it, for it was during those two years that she blossomed and became a woman, as attractive as could be expected of any child of Leah—indeed, for a short time, more attractive than one would ever have expected from that robust but ill-favored stock. She was a true child of the Mesopotamian plains, which enjoy an early spring with an extravagant bounty of flowers, followed by a lifeless summer, for already in May the merciless sun has burned all the magical splendor to a crisp. These, then, were Dinah's physical attributes; and events did their part to exhaust her before her time and make a wilted young woman of her. As for her place in the sequence of Jacob's descendants, it is of no real consequence what position the scribes have given her. Simple haste or indifference guided their pens to set the girl's name at the end of the list of Leah's children rather than at the appropriate spot—so as not to break the sequence of sons with something so irrelevant, indeed disruptive, as a girl's name. Who is going to be so punctilious about a girl? There was no significant difference between the birth of a girl and a closed womb, and Dinah's appearance, when rightly ordered, formed the transition, so to speak, between Leah's brief period of barrenness and her body's renewed fecundity, which first began in earnest with the delivery of Issakhar. Even today every schoolchild knows that Jacob had twelve sons and can rattle off their names, whereas large segments of the populace scarcely even suspect the existence of unfortunate little Dinah and seem surprised at the mention of her name. Jacob, however, loved her as well as he loved any of the children of his wrong wife, hid her from Esau in a coffin—and when the time came, he was sick at heart for her.

Beset

And so Israel, the man blessed by the Lord—together with his goods and chattel, his flocks, of which the sheep alone numbered five and a half thousand, with his wives and children, slaves, male and female, drivers, herdsmen, goats, asses, pack- and riding-camels—or Jacob, the father, coming now from the Jabbok and his meeting with Esau, crossed the Jardên and, having left behind the extreme heat of that river valley, having escaped the wild boars and leopards of its thickets of poplar and willow, was happy to find himself in a moderately mountainous country of fertile valleys that abounded with blossoms, rushing springs, and wild barley and in one of which he came upon the city of Shechem, an easygoing town that lay beneath the shadow of the cliffs of Mount Gerizim and was already hundreds of years old, its thick wall of unmortared stones encircling both a

Lower City in the southeast and, to the northwest, an Upper City, so named because it was set upon an artificial mound some five double ells high, but also in a wider, respectful sense because it consisted almost totally of the palace of Hemor, prince of the city, and the rectangular massive temple of Baal-Berith—and it was those two towering structures that caught the eyes of Jacob's people as they entered the valley and approached the city's eastern gate. Shechem had about five hundred inhabitants, not including the Egyptian garrison of some twenty men, whose commander, a very young officer from the region of the Delta, had been assigned here for the sole purpose of collecting an annual tax that was exacted directly from Hemor the city prince, but indirectly from the great merchants of the Lower City and took the form of several ring-shaped bars of gold that then had to be sent on to the city of Amun—and their failure to appear would have meant great personal unpleasantness for young Weser-ke-Bastet, that being the name of the commander.

One can imagine the ambivalent feelings of the people of Shechem upon being informed both by watchmen on the walls and citizens returning from outside the city of the slow, swaying approach of this nomadic tribe. They could not know whether the roving band was up to good or ill; and in the latter case, only a modicum of experience on its part, a little practice at raiding and pillaging, would suffice to put Shechem—despite its mighty walls—in a precarious situation. The spirit of the locals was less martial and more commercial, comfortable, and peaceable; and Hemor, the city prince, was a peevish old man with painfully swollen joints, whose son, the young Sichem, was a coddled young nobleman with his own harem, a layabout with a sweet tooth, an elegant drone. So that under such conditions, the inhabitants would have been all the happier to trust in the soldierly merits of its occupying garrison had there been even the least possible basis for that trust. But this troop, which rallied round a falcon banner trimmed in peacock feathers and called itself the Shining Solar-Disk Division, inspired not the least hope if worse should ever come to worst—beginning with its commander, the aforementioned Weser-ke-Bastet, who had nothing whatever of the warrior about him. A close friend of Sichem, the princeling, he was a man with two passions, cats and flowers—and made a fool of himself over both. He came from the city of Per-Bastet in Lower Egypt, or Pi-Beset, as the name was reshaped to suit tongues in these parts, which is also why the Shechemites simply nicknamed their commander "Beset." The local god of his city was the cat-headed goddess Bastet, and thus his devotion to cats knew no bounds. With every step he took he was surrounded by these animals, not just living cats of all colors and ages, but also by dead ones, for propped against the walls of his quarters were several cat mummies, to which, weeping loudly, he would offer sacrifices of mice and milk. This weakness was matched by his love of flowers, which might have been called a handsome trait as a complement to or in compensation for more manly preferences, but was unnerving in their absence. He walked about with a broad necklace of fresh flowers, and even the humblest article of daily life had to be wreathed in flowers—all in all, the effect was downright absurd. He never wore anything but civilian garb: a white batiste tunic, under which his loincloth was visible, with his arms and waist wrapped in ribbons, and no one had ever seen him in a coat of mail, or with any other weapon than a light cane. It was only due to a modicum of skill as a scribe that Beset had ever become an officer.

As for his men—for whom, by the way, he showed almost no concern—they were forever bragging, in phrases worthy of inscriptions, about the martial deeds of a previous king of their land, Thutmose the Third, who had led his Egyptian army in seventeen campaigns and conquered the region as far as the river Euphrates; but their own prowess lay chiefly in polishing off roast goose and beer. On all other occasions—a serious fire, a raid by Bedouins on the open villages attached to the city—they had proved out-and-out cowards, in particular the Egyptians among them, for there were also a few yellow-skinned Libyans and even a couple of Moors from Nubia. When, just for show and decked out in leather bucklers, spears, scythes, and triangular leather shields at their tunics, they would come running bent low at a double-time pace that looked more like a retreat, forcing their way through Shechem's crooked narrow streets—through a throng of people on asses and camels, water and melon vendors, peddlers bartering under the arches of the market—the locals would wink at one another derisively behind their backs. The rest of the time, Pharaoh's warriors amused themselves with games like "How many fingers?" and "Who hit you?" interspersed with songs about the hard lot of the soldier, especially the lad forced to eke out an existence in the wretched land of

Amurru, instead of enjoying life on the banks of the Spender of Life, where countless barques plied beneath the colorful columns of the city of No, the city of cities, the incomparable city, No-Amun, the city of the god. Sad to say, there could be no doubt that for them the fate and protection of Shechem weighed less than a kernel of grain.

The Rebuke

The city's residents would have been even more fidgety in their unease, however, had they been able to listen in on the conversations of the approaching chieftain's older sons—for these dusty young men with an enterprising look in their eyes had plans that touched all too closely on Shechem and that they weighed in low voices before bringing them to their father, who, to be sure, forbade them any such thing in no uncertain terms. Ruben—or Re'uben, as the eldest was actually called—was seventeen at the time, Shimeon and Levi sixteen and fifteen; Bilhah's Dan, a young and wily trickster, was likewise fifteen; and slender, swift Naphtali was the same age as the strong but melancholy Judah, that is, fourteen. Those were the sons of Jacob who were in on the secret plot. Gad and Asher, though they too were sturdy lads and, for their eleven and ten years, of mature and quick intellect, had been left out, not to mention the three youngest boys.

And what was it all about? Well, about the same thing bothering people in Shechem. Those who were putting their heads together outside the walls—lads tanned almost black by the sun of Naharina, with well-greased hair and shaggy belted tunics—had grown up more or less wild as sons of the plains, shepherd boys fond of their bows and knives, used to encounters with wild oxen and lions, to wholesale brawls with strange herdsmen over a bit of pasture. Little of Jacob's gentleness and God-mindedness had been passed on to them; their thoughts were directed to practical, tangible things; and boasting of a spiritual nobility that was not theirs in any personal sense, they were full of a youthful defiance and tribal pride forever on the lookout for any affront, any call to battle. As wanderers without a home, under way for some time now, they considered themselves nomads, who in their boldness and freedom were the superiors of the settled inhabitants of this fertile land into which they had come—and their thoughts were of pillage. Dan had been the first to suggest it out of the corner of his mouth: take Shechem by surprise and plunder it. Ruben, who, though an honorable fellow, had always been the prey of his own sudden urges, was quick to join in; Shimeon and Levi, the biggest ruffians and always ready for adventure, shouted and danced in delight; the others were all the more eager out of their pride at being included.

What they were considering was certainly not unheard-of. Though perhaps not a daily occurrence, cities of the region were attacked and even temporarily occupied by rapacious invaders from the desert to the south or east, by the Habiru or Ibrim, on a fairly regular basis. But tradition, whose source is not the urbanites, but the Habiru and Ibrim in the narrower sense of the word, that is the *bene Israel,* has no qualms of conscience whatever—being convinced that it has been given permission to purify reality on an epic scale—about not mentioning the fact that from the start the intention in Jacob's camp had been to settle matters with Shechem by means of war and that only resistance by the head of the tribe delayed those plans a few years—that is, until the sad incident with Dinah.

This resistance was, however, majestic and indomitable. Jacob was in an especially lofty state of mind at the time—the result of experiences that had shaped him and of the significance of his soul, itself shaped by his fondness for an all-embracing association of ideas. And to his pondering mind, the past twenty-five years of his life, when viewed in the light of cosmic analogy, seemed like an allegory of the great circle—the rise and fall of ascent into heaven, descent into hell, and rising yet again—like a supremely happy fulfillment of a pattern of growth found in myth. Fleeing Beersheba, he had arrived at Beth-el, where he had had his vision of the great stairway—that was an ascent into heaven. From there he had descended into the underworld of the plains, where, sweating and freezing, he had served seven years twice over, and afterward had become very rich by outfoxing a devil named Laban, who was as sly as he was stupid. As a cultured man, Jacob could not help seeing his Mesopotamian father-in-law as a black moon demon, an evil dragon, who had cheated him and whom he had in turn carefully cheated and robbed; and then, with a heart full of great and godly laughter as he burst the bars of the underworld, he had risen up out of it, taking his stolen goods with him—and in particular his liberated Ishtar, the sweet-eyed Rachel—and arrived in Sichem. Its valley needn't have been so rich in blossoms as it presented itself on his arrival for his senses to have perceived it as a new spring, a station in this new cycle of life; in calling to mind that Abraham had stood on this very spot, he felt his heart soften greatly toward this place, and that, too, played a role in his reverence for it. And if his offspring were re-minded of Abraham's exploits of war, of his bold raid on the armies of the east and of how he had set those star-worshipers' teeth on edge, Jacob himself thought of the primal father's friendship with Melchizedek, the high priest of Sichem, of the blessing Abram had received from him, of the acceptance and recognition he had rendered unto Abram's god. And so the reception that his older boys found for their crude plan—even in the almost poetical version they cautiously allowed him a peek at—had been bad beyond telling.

"Depart from me," he cried, "and do so at once! Sons of Leah and Bilhah, you should be ashamed of yourselves. Are we thieves of the desert who come over the land like locusts and like a plague from God to eat the harvest of those who till the soil? Are we riffraff, with no names, sons of nobody, whose choice is to beg or steal? Was Abraham not a prince among princes and a brother to the mighty? Or did you intend to sit down beside the lords of the cities, your swords still dripping, to live amid warfare and terror—how will you pasture our lambs upon meadows that defy you and our goats upon mountains that echo with hate? Begone, you dolts! How dare you! See if things are in order outside, if our three-week-old lambs will accept fodder so that their mothers may keep their milk. Go and col-lect the hair of the camels so that we may have stuff to clothe the ser-vants and shepherd boys, for it is now the season for shedding. Go, I say, and inspect the ropes of the tents and the eyelets of the tent roofs to see that nothing has rotted, so that no mishap may occur, sending the house falling upon Israel. I, however, so that you may know, shall gird my robes and enter beneath the city gate and speak in peace and wisdom with the citizens there and with Hemor, their shepherd, so that we may come to an understanding with them and purchase land from them in a valid and written agreement and trade with them both to our benefit and with no harm to them."

The Agreement

And that is what happened. Jacob had pitched his camp not far from
the city, near a group of old mulberry trees and terebinths that
seemed sacred to him and that stood out from the rolling, open
country of meadows and fields from where one could view the bare
bluffs of Mount Ebal, while nearby rose Mount Gerizim with its
boulder-strewn heights, but richly blessed lower slopes. From here
he sent three men, three shepherds, to Shechem, with pretty presents
for Hemor: a sack of doves, pressed loaves of dried fruits, a lamp in
the shape of a duck, and a pair of lovely ewers painted with fish and
birds. And he told them to say that Jacob, the great traveler, wanted
to meet with the leaders of the city beneath its gate, there to negotiate his sojourn and rights to pasture here. The people of Shechem
were relieved and delighted. The hour of the meeting was set, and
when it came round, from the city's east gate emerged gout-ridden
Hemor, with all the trappings of his position, and Sichem, his fidgety
young son, as well as Weser-ke-Bastet, who also appeared in a flower
necklace and with several cats; and from the other side Yaaqov ben
Yitzchak came forward with great dignity, accompanied by Eliezer,
his eldest servant, and surrounded by his older sons, whom he had
enjoined to absolute courtesy for the duration. And so they met at
the gate and conferred both under and before it, for the gate was a
massive structure, with hall-like extensions both inside and out, the
inner one serving as a market and court of law; and a great crowd
formed behind these great men; for people wished to watch them
discuss a business arrangement that began with all the ceremonial of
fine manners, but was actually addressed only very hesitantly, so
that the meeting lasted six hours, during which the peddlers in the
crowded marketplace did a good business themselves. After first
bowing low, the parties took their places, facing each other on camp
stools, mats, and cloths; refreshments were served: spiced wine and
curds with honey; there was a long discussion of nothing but the
health of the chief participants and their loved ones, then of traveling
conditions on both sides of the "drain," then of even more remote
subjects. They approached the matter about which they had come
together, however, only reluctantly and with shrugs, skirting and
backing off the issue several times, as if each side wished to suggest

to the other that it would be better not to speak of it—precisely because the topic to be addressed, the matter at hand, was a subject
about which it was necessary to maintain the appearance of disdain
for the sake of a higher humanity. For, ultimately, it is the luxury of
exaggerated objectivity, a pretense of priorities honoring refined formality, including a generous casualness about wasting time for formality's sake, that defines what is worthy of humankind: those
things that are more than merely natural and therefore civilized.

Jacob's personality made a splendid impression on the city's
populace. If not at first glance, then shortly after the initial exchanges, they knew whom they had before them. This was a lord
and a prince of God, of refined intellectual gifts that likewise ennobled his social personage. At work here was the same nobility that
in the eyes of the people had always been the hallmark of the successor or reincarnation of Abraham—a nobility that, by being quite independent of birth and based solely on spirit and form, had assured
spiritual leadership to this race of men. The touching gentleness and
depth in Jacob's eyes, his perfect bearing, his exquisite gestures, the
tremolo in his voice, the cultured and flowery speech in which his
thoughts moved, rhyming in theme and countertheme, filled with
mythical allusions—these so won over gout-ridden Hemor in particular that in scarcely no time he stood up and walked across to kiss
the sheik, to the accompanying applause of the crowd in the gate's
inner hall. As for the stranger's requests, which as was well-known
in advance were aimed at his settling legally here, that, to be sure,
presented the head of the city with some difficulty, for if some distant higher-up were to be notified that he, Hemor, was handing land
over to the Habiru, that might bring vexation to his old age. But reassured in this regard by silent glances exchanged with the commander of the occupying garrison, who for his part was equally
warmed by Jacob's manner, Hemor opened the negotiations with
the lovely suggestion, accompanied, needless to say, by the segue of
a low bow, that Jacob should simply accept both land and pasture
rights as a gift, then followed up by naming his exorbitant price, demanding one hundred shekels of silver for cropland encompassing
some nine acres, and, since he was prepared for some serious bargaining, closed with the question of what was such a paltry sum between the two of them. But Jacob did not haggle. His soul was
moved and exalted by thoughts of emulation, recurrence, the past

made present. He was Abraham coming from the east to buy a field with its double grave site from Ephron. Had the founder haggled with the leader of Hebron and with the children of Heth? The centuries did not exist. What had been was now again. The rich Abraham and Jacob, the rich man from the east, they both struck a bargain with dignity and no further ado. Chaldean slaves dragged the scale and the weighing stones over; Eliezer, the steward, approached with a clay pot full of rings of silver; Hemor's scribes rushed forward, squatted down, and began to prepare the commercial documents and articles of peace in best legal fashion. Payment for the field and pasture rights was weighed out, the contract made valid and sacred, and cursed be he who contested it. Jacob's people were now Sichemites, citizens with full rights. They might enter and leave the city gate as they pleased. They might come and go and do business in the land. Shechem's sons might take their daughters to be their wives, and Shechem's daughters their sons to be their husbands—all by force of law, and he who opposed it would forfeit his honor for the rest of his life. The trees upon the purchased field were Jacob's as well—he who doubted it was an enemy of the law. In witness thereto Weser-ke-Bastet pressed the scarab on his ring into the clay, Hemor applied his stone, Jacob the seal cylinder hanging from his neck. It was done. Kisses and compliments were exchanged. And thus it was that Jacob settled outside the city of Shechem in the land of Canaan.

Jacob Dwells at Shechem

"Do you know of this?"—"I know it well." Israel's shepherds knew nothing of the sort when they later made it the subject of "fine discourses" by the fire. In good conscience and for the sake of the purity of the story, they rearranged some things and were silent about others. They said nothing of what wry faces Jacob's sons, particularly Levi and Shimeon, pulled that day at the signing of articles of peace; they pretended as if the contract had been drawn up only after the incident with Dinah and Sichem, the princeling, had already begun—and in fact it also began rather differently from how they "knew" it. They told it as if there had been an additional point in the document of agreement, a certain condition demanded of Sichem in regard to Jacob's daughter—whereas that stipulation had been a totally separate matter, a demand made at a quite different point in time from the one they pretended to "know well." As we shall now explain. The treaty came first. Without it neither the settlement there by Jacob's people nor subsequent events could ever have come about. They had been living in tents outside Shechem, at the entrance to its valley, for almost four years before the trouble started; they planted wheat in their field and barley in its rich soil; they won oil from their trees, they grazed their herds out in the country, dealt in sheep and goats; they dug a well where they settled, fourteen ells deep and very wide, lining it with stones, Jacob's Well. . . . A well that deep and wide? What did the children of Israel even need with a well? After all, the city with which they were allied had one at its gates and the valley was likewise full of them. Yes, true, they didn't need it right away, they did not dig it immediately after settling in, but rather a little later on, when it turned out that, when it came to water, being independent and having a plentiful supply of it in their own ground, a source that would not run dry even in the worst drought, was one of life's necessities for them, the Ibrim. The treaty of concord had been concluded, and anyone who quibbled with it would pay with his bowels. But it had been concluded by the chiefs, though to the approval and applause of the citizenry, and in the eyes of the people of Shechem Jacob's people would remain strangers in the land, immigrants—who, moreover, were not all that tractable and harmless, but rather arrogant and preachy, the sort who thought they had some spiritual precedence over the rest of the world, who knew how to see to their own advantage when trading in cattle and wool, to the point that one's self-esteem actually suffered when one dealt with them. In short, the amity did not go very deep, it suffered certain setbacks, as for instance when, by way of keeping the Ebrews somewhat in check, they were soon denied access to the available sources of water—which, by the way, had not been mentioned in the treaty. And that was the reason for Jacob's large well, itself a monument to the fact that even before more serious trouble broke out, relations between the tribe of Israel and the people of Shechem stood as they usually stood between encampments of Habiru tribes and older legitimate residents of the land—and not as they should have stood after the meeting beneath the city gate.

Jacob both knew and did not know this, which is to say: he

looked the other way, turning his gentle interest to family and spiritual matters. Sweet-eyed Rachel, won at great cost, abducted at great
peril, and rescued and brought to the land of his fathers, was still
alive at the time, his true and dearest wife, the delight of his eye, the
banquet upon which his heart feasted, the balm to his senses. Joseph,
her branch and offspring, the real son, was growing up; the toddler
was becoming a boy—and what a charming time it was!—a boy so
beautiful, witty, beguiling, and enchanting that Jacob's soul overflowed at the sight of him; and even then the older sons began to exchange glances at the folly the old man displayed in his dealings with
his glib scamp of a son. Jacob was away from the business of the
tribe several times, by the way—he went on journeys. He established relations with comrades in the faith in both the city and countryside, visited places sacred to Abraham's God in the valleys and
upon the mountains, and engaged in many discussions about the nature of the One and Most High. And above all it is certain that, after
a long separation lasting almost a generation, he turned toward the
south, there to embrace his father, to show himself in his fullness,
and to reconfirm a blessing that had so obviously benefited him. For
Yitzchak still lived, an ancient man who had long ago become totally
blind, whereas Rebekah had descended into the realm of death years
before. That, however, was also the reason why Isaak had transferred the altar of his burnt offerings from the tree *Yahweh el olam*
at Beersheba to the oracle terebinth near Hebron, that is, to the immediate vicinity of the double cave where he had laid to rest his
cousin's daughter, his sister-wife, and where in due time he himself,
Yitzchak, the averted sacrifice, would, after a long and eventful life,
be interred and wept over by Jacob and Esau, his sons—but that
would happen later, when a broken Jacob would depart from Beth-
el after Rachel's death, bringing with him the little murderer, her
newborn son, Ben-Oni, Ben-Yamin. . . .

The Grape Harvest

Four times the wheat and barley grew green and turned yellow on
the fields of Shechem, four times the anemones in the valley
bloomed, and Jacob's people had sheared their sheep eight times, for
Jacob's spotted spring lambs grew fleece in the wink of an eye and he

took abundant wool from them twice a year, both in the month of Sivan and again in Tishri come autumn. And for the inhabitants of Shechem it was the time of grape harvest, of the festival of wine in the city and on Mount Gerizim's terraced slopes, held at the first full moon after the fall equinox, for the year was beginning anew. The world of both city and valley was all shouting and processions and harvest offerings, for they had picked the grapes, singing as they went, and had stomped them with bare feet in the stone winepress, turning their legs purple up to their hips and sending the sweet blood through the trough and into the vat, where they knelt and laughed, filling jars and wineskins to let it ferment there. And now that the wine was working, they announced the Feast of Seven Days, sacrificing a tenth of their firstling cattle and sheep, of their grain, must, and oil; they ate and drank, brought lesser gods into the house of Adonai, the great Baal, to wait upon him, and carried the god himself upon their shoulders in his ship, leading him in procession with drums and cymbals across the countryside, so that he might renew his blessing of the mountain and the fields. But in the midst of the festival, on the third day, they announced music and dancing outside the city, beneath the castle and in the presence of all who wished to come, including women and children. Out of the city came Hemor, carried on his chair, and fidgety Sichem—likewise carried—along with a panoply of women and eunuchs, with petty officials, merchants, and ordinary people, and from his tented camp came Jacob with his wives, sons, and servants. They all came together, sitting down at the spot where the music rang out, but leaving areas open for the dancing—there beneath olive trees in a wide part of the valley, where the Mount of Blessing with its rocky heights and sweet slopes made a grand curve, while in the cleft of the Mount of Curses goats scrambled in search of dried grasses. The late afternoon was blue and warm, its light gently enhancing every object, every person, turning golden the bodies of the dancing girls, who with embroidered ribbons around hips and hair, eyes artfully lengthened by paints, and glittering metallic dust in their lashes, danced before the musicians, rolling their bellies and turning their heads away from the little tambours they beat with their hands. Squatting musicians strummed lutes and lyres, filled the air with the shrill whistle of their short flutes. Others behind them simply clapped to the rhythm, still others sang, holding quivering hands

against their throats to produce a tight, supple sound. Men joined
the dance as well. They were bearded and naked, with animal tails
wrapped around them, and they leapt like goats as they tried to catch
the girls, who escaped by arching their bodies. Balls were tossed,
too, and the girls could deftly juggle several spheres in the air at
once, even with arms crossed or with one sitting astride the hips of
another. Great was the satisfaction of city-dweller and tent-dweller
alike, and though Jacob was no lover of hubbub and jangle, for it
numbed one's awareness of God, he put a good face on it for the sake
of the others and now and then even politely clapped in time to the
music.

And so it was that Sichem, the princeling, beheld Dinah, the
thirteen-year-old daughter of the Ibrim, and came to desire her until
he could not ever cease to desire her. She was sitting with Leah, her
mother, on a mat close to the musicians, directly across from
Sichem's chair, and he could not keep his dazed eyes off her. She
was not beautiful—she was a child of Leah—but at the time there
was charm in her youthfulness, a viscous sweetness, like dripping
threads of date honey; and as he watched Sichem was soon like a fly
on honey-coated paper—he tugged at his sticky little legs to see if he
might be able to get away if he wanted, though he didn't really want
to, because the paper was so sweet, and was also frightened to death
by the realization that, try as he might, he could not escape. And he
hopped and squirmed on his little camp chair and blushed a hundred
times over. She had a dark little face, with black bangs dangling at
her brow from under the scarf covering her head; long dusky-sweet
eyes that were almost sticky black and kept going cross-eyed under
the smitten fellow's stares; a wide nose, a gold ring dangling from between the flared nostrils; an equally wide mouth, its red high-
vaulted lips pulled in an agonizingly broad smile; and almost no
chin. Her unbelted tunic of blue and red wool covered only one
shoulder, while the other—bare—shoulder was utterly charming in
its daintiness, the epitome of charm. And things got no better, but
only worse, whenever she lifted that shoulder's arm to set it behind
her head and Sichem could see the damp curls of her little armpit and
her delicately firm breasts jutting out beneath her shirt and tunic.
And there was more trouble—she had dark little feet with copper
ankle bracelets and soft golden rings on every toe except the big

ones. But worst of all were her small, golden-brown hands—the nails painted and likewise decked out in rings—and the childish yet clever way she would play with them in her lap; and when Sichem thought of what it would be like to lie beside her on their wedding bed, with those hands caressing him, his senses reeled and he fought for breath.

But it was of a wedding bed that he thought at once—and then of nothing else. Custom did not allow him to speak to Dinah himself or flirt with her with anything other than glances. But even on the way home and then continuing once back in the palace, he dinned his father's ears with how he could not live, how his body would surely wither, without that Habiru lass, and asked old Hemor to go out and buy her as a wife for his bed, or he would wither in an instant. What else could gout-ridden Hemor do but have two men carry him out to Jacob's house made of felt, bow down before him, call him brother, and after much circumlocution finally come round to speaking of his son's heart's desire, while also offering a rich dowry should Dinah's father consent to the match? Jacob was both surprised and dismayed. The offer embarrassed him, awakened conflicting emotions. In worldly matters he was a respectable man, interested in establishing kinship relations between his house and one of the princely houses of the land if that might be of use to him and his tribe. But the transaction also called up memories of bygone days, of his wooing of Rachel with Laban, and how that devil had stalled him off, lied to him, and exploited his desires. And now he had slipped into Laban's role himself; it was his child who was the object of some lad's desires, and he did not want his behavior to resemble Laban's in any way. On the other hand he had very lively doubts about the higher propriety of this match. He had never worried much about Dinah, that little monkey, since his heart belonged to the enchanting Joseph, nor had he ever received any instructions from on high concerning her. But nonetheless she was his only daughter. For a prince to request her increased her value in his eyes, and he was mindful that before God he should not waste even this less appreciated possession. Had not Abraham made Eliezer place his hand under his thigh and swear that he would not seek a wife for his true son, Yitzchak, from among the daughters of Canaan where he lived, but rather fetch a wife from among his kin in the homeland to the east? Had not Yitzchak handed that same prohibition on to him, the chosen son, saying, "Do not take a wife from among the daughters of Canaan"? Dinah was only a girl and a child of the wrong wife besides, and whom she wed was probably not of the same importance as for the bearer of the blessing. Nonetheless, it was imperative that one keep one's self-respect before God.

The Condition

Jacob called his sons together in council, all the way down to Zebulun, ten in all, and they sat before Hemor, their hands raised, rocking their heads. The eldest of them, who set the tone, were not the sort to reach out and grab, as if they could imagine nothing better than this. Without consulting among themselves they were unanimous that one ought not hurry a decision about what to make of this matter. Dinah? Their sister? Leah's daughter, lovable, priceless Dinah, only recently become a woman? For Sichem, Hemor's son? That was obviously worth the most careful consideration. They asked for time to think. They did so out of common commercial hardheadedness, but Shimeon and Levi had ulterior motives and half-formed hopes of their own besides. For they had certainly not given up on their old plans, and what the cutting off of water had not yet accomplished might, so they thought, grow in the soil of Sichem's wishes and courtship.

Three days, then, to think things over. And, slightly offended, Hemor had himself carried home. But when three days had passed, Sichem himself, riding a white ass, arrived in camp to advance his own cause, both because his father, who had lost interest, demanded it of him and because, in his impatience, it seemed the amiable and natural thing to do. He advanced it not as a business matter, but without hiding his heart in the least, frankly admitted that he was being consumed by a veritable fire for the maid Dinah. "Make your demands," he said, "brash and shameless demands—gifts, a dowry. I am Sichem, son of the palace, maintained in splendor in my father's house, and by Baal, I will give them." And they named him the condition they had agreed upon among themselves in the meantime, that had to be fulfilled prior to any further discussion.

One should pay close attention to the sequence of events here, which is different from the order the shepherds later passed on in their "fine discourse." According to them Sichem immediately and with no cause did the evil deed that demanded a cunning act of violence in return; in reality, however, he did not resolve to create an irrevocable state of affairs until Jacob's people had proved themselves in the wrong by what he saw as delay tactics, if not outright deception. They told him, then, that first of all he would have to be circumcised—that was mandatory—just as they themselves were, for they firmly believed that it would be an abomination and an offense to their eyes to give their daughter and sister to an uncircumcised man. It was the brothers who had suggested this stipulation to their father, and Jacob, pleased by this postponement, could on principle find no objection to it, though he was surprised by his sons' display of piety.

Sichem laughed out loud and then apologized by placing his hands over his mouth. "Nothing more than that?" he cried. That was all they demanded! But, good gentlemen, seeing as he was prepared to sacrifice an eye, his right hand for Dinah, how much more willing then was he to offer such an insignificant bit of flesh as his foreskin? By Suteh, no, that would present no difficulty whatever! His friend Beset was also circumcised, and he had never thought the least bit about it. Not a single one of Sichem's little sisters in his house of sport and delight would take the least offense at its absence. It was as good as done—in the temple of the most high, by the hand of a priest versed in matters of the body! As soon as his flesh was healed, he would return. And he ran out, waving to his slaves to bring him his white ass.

When he reappeared seven days later—as early as possible and beaming with confidence although hardly healed and still impeded by the sacrifice he had made—he found that the head of the family had ridden off somewhere on a journey. Jacob was avoiding the encounter. He had left his sons in charge. He found that despite himself he had slipped totally into the role of Laban, that devil, and preferred to play it in absentia. But when poor Sichem cheerfully announced that the condition was now fulfilled—though hardly the trifle he had imagined, indeed rather bothersome—that it was done and he was awaiting his sweetest reward, what did Jacob's sons reply? Done, yes, they said. Quite possibly done, they were prepared to believe it. Yet not done in the right spirit, but without any higher meaning and understanding, superficially, meaninglessly. Done? Perhaps. But done solely for the purpose of marriage with the woman Dinah, and not in the sense of marriage to "Him." What was more, most probably not even done with a stone knife, as was obligatory, but with a metal one, which in itself rendered the deed questionable, if not null and void. Besides, Sichem, prince of the palace, already had a chief wife and sister, his first and true spouse, Rehuma the Hivite, and Dinah, Jacob's daughter, would therefore serve only as one of his concubines—which was unacceptable.

Sichem fidgeted. How could they know, he cried, in what spirit and understanding he had performed that unpleasant act, and how dared they bring up the stone knife after the fact, when it had been their duty to point that out at the time. Concubine? But the king of Mitanni himself had given his daughter, Gulichipa by name, to be Pharaoh's wife and had sent her down to him with great pomp, not as queen of the Two Lands, for Tiy, the goddess, was queen of both lands, but as a concubine, and if King Shuttarna himself—

Yes, the brothers said; that, however, had been Shuttarna and Gulichipa. But this concerned Dinah, the daughter of Jacob, the prince of God, Abraham's seed, and that she could not be a concubine in the palace of Shechem—why his own reason would tell him as much if he thought about it.

And Sichem was to take that as their final word?

They shrugged, they spread their hands wide. Would he like a gift of some sort, two or three castrated rams perhaps?

With that his patience was at an end. He had already suffered a great deal of vexation and annoyance because of his desires. That priest in the temple had turned out not to be so well-versed in matters of the body as he had claimed and had been unable to prevent Hemor's son from having to put up with inflammation, fever, and dreadful pain. And this was the result? He hurled a curse, the intent of which was to reduce Jacob's sons to weightless light and air—which they in turn endeavored to ward off with a few deft, rapid gestures—and he bolted. Four days later Dinah had vanished.

The Abduction

"Do you know of this?" Pay attention to the sequence! Sichem was simply a pretty, shambling lad who had not been raised to deny himself the wishes of his senses. But that is no reason that certain tendentious shepherds' tales, casting him in the most unfavorable light, must forever be taken literally. And if this tale traced such deep lines in Jacob's worried face, it was precisely because—though he himself may also have been the first to abridge it and to tell and even believe its sugar-coated form as he told it—he secretly knew who had first planned robbery and violence, who had intended to move events in that direction from the very start, and that Hemor's son had in no way simply carried Dinah off, but had first courted her honestly and only upon being repulsed had considered himself justified in making his happiness the basis for further negotiations. In a word, Dinah was gone, stolen, abducted. By broad daylight, out in the open field, indeed within view of her family, men from the palace had crept up on her while she was playing with some lambs, gagged her with a cloth, tossed her on a camel, and were well on their way back to the city before Israel's men even could saddle their mounts to follow in pursuit. She was gone, locked up inside Sichem's house of sport and delight, and, moreover, surrounded by all sorts of unimagined urban comforts; and Sichem hastily brought her to the marriage bed of his desires—to which she had no real objections. She was an insignificant thing, submissive, lacking both good judgment and any power of resistance. If what happened to her happened clearly and vigorously, she accepted it as quite natural, as a given. Besides, Sichem did her no harm—on the contrary; besides, the rest of his sisters, including Rehuma, his first and true wife, were friendly to her.

But her brothers! Especially Shimeon and Levi! Their rage was boundless, it seemed, and a confused and despondent Jacob was subjected to the worst of it. Dishonored, raped, villainously deflowered—their sister, their black turtledove, their purest, their one and only, Abraham's seed. They ripped the jewelry from their chests, rent their clothes, put on sackcloth, disheveled their hair and beards, howled, and carved long gashes on their faces and bodies—what a horrible sight they were. They threw themselves on their bellies, beat their fists on the ground, and swore neither to eat nor to empty their bowels until Dinah had been snatched away from that debauched Sodomite and the city of her violation made a wasteland. Revenge, revenge, attack, carnage, blood, and torture—they knew nothing else. Jacob was shaken, deeply perplexed, painfully embarrassed—feeling, by the way, as if he had behaved like Laban, and knowing full well that the brothers now saw themselves nearing the goal of their original wishes—but found it difficult to keep them temporarily in check without opening himself to the charge of a lack of fatherly feelings, a lack of honor. He took part in the demonstrations of their aggrieved anger to a certain degree, likewise donning a soiled robe and mussing his hair a bit, but he also reminded them that forcefully removing Dinah from the palace did not promise to be of much use, since that would not resolve, but in fact first give rise to, the question of what to do with the violated, dishonored girl once she was home. Now that she had fallen into Sichem's hands, her return would, upon careful consideration, not be desirable, and to dampen one's sorrow and wait things out was far wiser—a course of action whose advisability he also claimed to have seen hinted in the liver of a sheep slaughtered for that purpose. Doubtless, given how things stood on the basis of the pact between the city and the tribe, Sichem would send word soon enough, make some new suggestions, present some opportunity for putting a moderately good, though surely not fine, face on such an ugly affair.

And behold, to Jacob's own amazement, his sons suddenly yielded and consented to wait for a message from the palace. Their silence immediately unnerved him, almost more than their fury—what lay behind it? He anxiously observed them, but did not share in their counsels, and he learned of their new decisions hardly any sooner than did Sichem's messengers, who, just as he had expected, presented themselves a few days later, bearing a letter written in Babylonian on several clay shards, very polite in form and likewise very obliging and accommodating in its sentiments. It read:

> To Jacob, son of Yitzchak, the Prince of God, my father and lord, whom I love and upon whose love I lay such great weight. Sichem son of Hemor, your son-in-law who loves you, the heir to the palace, exalted by his people, speaks: I am well. May you also be well. May your wives, your sons,

your household servants, your cattle, sheep, and goats, and all else that is yours enjoy the highest degree of well-being. Behold, Hemor, my father, once established and sealed a covenant of friendship with you, my other father, and sincere friendship has existed between us and you for four rounds of the year, during which my constant thought was: May the gods, at the bidding of my god Baal-Berith and your god El-Elyon, which are almost one and the same god, differing only in trifles, so order it that just as we are befriended now, so may we be for all eternity, and as for the sincerity of our friendship may it remain thus for numberless years of jubilee.

But when my eyes beheld your daughter Dinah, child of Leah, daughter of Laban of Chaldea, I wished most ardently that our friendship, beyond its endless duration, might also increase a million times over. For your daughter is like a young palm tree by the water and like a pomegranate blossom in the garden, and my heart trembles with desire for her, so that I understood that without her my breath would be of no use to me. Therefore, as you know, Hemor, Prince of the City and exalted by his people, came out to you to speak with his brother and to take counsel with my brothers, your sons, and departed with hopes. And when I myself came out to woo Dinah, your child, and plead for breath for my nostrils, you and your sons said: "Dear sir, you must be circumcised in your flesh before Dinah can be yours, for we find anything else an abomination before our god." Behold, I did not insult my father's heart nor that of my brothers, but in friendship I said: "I will comply." For I rejoiced beyond measure and delegated Jarah, the scribe of god's book, to do unto me as you had said, and endured pain both at his hands and thereafter, so that my eyes overflowed, all for the sake of Dinah. But when I returned, behold, it counted as nothing. And so Dinah, your child, came to me, because the condition had been fulfilled that I might prove my love for her upon my bed and to my greatest pleasure, nor was her pleasure small, as I learned from her lips. But that there may be no discord between your god and mine, let my father swiftly name the price and marriage stipulations for Dinah, who is sweetness to my heart, so that there may be a great feast held in the palace at Shechem and we may celebrate the marriage with laughter and song. For Hemor, my father, wishes to have three hundred scarabs inscribed with my name and the name of Dinah, my spouse, in memory of this day and in token of the eternal friendship between Shechem and Israel. Ordered at the palace on the twenty-fifth day of the month of the harvest. Peace and Health to its receiver!

The Repetition

So the letter. Jacob and his sons waved the palace's couriers out and studied it. And when Jacob looked to his sons, they told him what action they had already agreed upon if such a case arose. Although amazed, he could find nothing in their suggestion with which to disagree on principle; for he realized that the fulfillment of the new condition they were proposing would mean, first of all, a significant spiritual achievement, and, second, it also incorporated both atonement and satisfaction for the crime committed. When they then sat down together again with the letter's bearers, he let Dinah's aggrieved brothers speak, and it was Dan as their spokesman who announced and laid out the decision to the messengers. They were already rich by the grace of God, he said, and placed no great importance on the size of the payment for their sister Dinah, whom Sichem had quite rightly compared to a palm tree and a fragrant pomegranate blossom. As for that, Hemor and Sichem could themselves decide what was commensurate with their honor. But Dinah had not "come" to Sichem, as he had chosen to put it, but rather she had been stolen, thereby creating a new situation which they, the brothers, were not prepared to accept out of hand. Therefore, in order for them to accept it, the same precondition by which Sichem had so meritoriously allowed himself to be circumcised should now be extended to all the males of Shechem—be they old men, adults, or boys—the act itself to be performed within three days, counting today, and with stone knives. If that were done, they would indeed celebrate the marriage at Shechem with a great feast and with laughter and tumult.

The condition sounded extreme, but at the same time it was easy to carry out, and the messengers immediately expressed their conviction that Hemor, their lord, would not hesitate to order whatever was necessary. But no sooner were they gone than Jacob suddenly felt dire misgivings rise within him as to the meaning and purpose of this seemingly pious provision, so that his very bowels trembled in terror and, had it been at all possible, he would have called the men from the city back. He did not believe either that the brothers had abandoned their old and original desires or that they had renounced their revenge for Dinah's abduction and defilement; and when he combined that fact with their sudden acquiescence just now and the demand that had now been spoken, and when he likewise recalled the look on their faces—still gashed in mourning—when their spokesman mentioned the tumultuous wedding feast they planned in Shechem once the condition was fulfilled, he was amazed at his own obtuseness and that he had not spotted their dark designs even as they spoke.

What had dazzled him was his delight in imitation and repetition. He had thought of Abraham and of how one day at the Lord's command and as part of the covenant with him, he had circumcised his entire household in its flesh—Ismael, his slaves, both those born to him and those bought from various strangers, every male child in his household, and he was certain that his own sons had also based their demand on that story—yes, surely that was it, that is where they got the idea, but what sort of ending were they planning? He repeated to himself how it was said that the Lord had visited Abraham on the third day, to look after him because of his pain. God had stood outside the tent where Eliezer did not see Him. But Abraham saw Him and warmly invited Him in. But when the Lord saw him unbinding and binding up his wound again, He said: "It is not seemly for Me to stay here." That is how gently God had behaved in the presence of Abraham's sacred shameful discomfort—but come the third day, what gentleness did they intend to display toward those indisposed urbanites in their pain? Jacob shuddered at such a repetition, and shuddered again at the sight of their faces when news came from the palace that the condition was accepted without hesitation, and that the general sacrifice would be made precisely on the day designated, three days from yesterday. More than once he wanted to raise his hands and implore them; but he feared the superior force of their brotherly pride, their well-founded right to revenge, and realized that behavior he once would have forbidden with overwhelming solemnity now, under these circumstances, had strong underpinnings. To put the question circumspectly: Did he secretly feel he owed them some little gratitude for not initiating him into their plans, for maintaining his purity, so that if he so wanted, he might know nothing or have only his suspicions and let happen what in fact was to happen? Had not God the King, called out above the harps at Beth-el that he, Jacob, would possess gates, the gates of his enemies, and—disregarding his personal love of peace—did not that perhaps mean that conquest, deeds of war, and the exhilaration of plunder might nevertheless belong to what the stars had decreed for his life? He no longer slept—out of dread, worry, and the most secret secret pride in the cunning manliness of his offspring. Nor did he sleep on the night of horror, the third after the set day had passed, as he lay in his tent wrapped in his coat and his apprehensive ear took in the muted sounds of armed conflict in the distance.

The Butchery

We have come to the end of our factual presentation of the interlude at Shechem, which later was the source of so much song and white-washed saga—whitewashed for Israel's benefit as regards the sequence of those events that led to its awful outcome, if not in terms of the outcome itself, which cannot be whitewashed—and indeed "fine discourse" insisted on bragging about and flaunting its unique horror. Thanks to their scandalous cunning, Jacob's people, although only about fifty in all and far outnumbered by the city's residents, had easy work with Shechem, both in taking its walls, which were almost stripped of guards and which they vaulted silently with ropes and scaling-ladders, and in the subsequent tumultuous dance, which suddenly erupted inside the city when secrecy was cast aside and for which the totally surprised inhabitants proved indisposed and less than agile. Every male child in Shechem, young or old, lay in a fever, "unbinding and binding up his wound," including the majority of the occupation forces. Whereas the Ibrim, sound of body and morally inflamed by the unifying cries of "Dinah!" that accompanied their bloody handiwork, raged like lions, for they seemed to be everywhere and from the start instilled in the souls of the inhabitants such a sense of inevitable calamity bursting in upon them that the invaders met with almost no resistance. Particularly Shimeon and Levi, the ringleaders of the operation, raised shouts—studied bull-like bellows convulsing the core of their bodies—that instilled in their victims the sort of holy terror that at best sees flight, not battle, as the only escape from death. People cried, "Alas, these are not men! Suteh has come amongst us! Glorious Baal lives in all their arms and legs!" And in midretreat they were bludgeoned to death. The Hebrews set to work literally with fire and sword. Smoke rose up from the city, the palace, the temple; houses and narrow streets were awash in blood. Only young people in good physical condition were taken prisoner, the rest were strangled—and if the stranglers went beyond mere slaying in their cruelty, it should be noted on their behalf that they were no less caught up in poetic images than their unfortunate victims, for they viewed such acts as a battle with the dragon, the victory of Marduk over Tiâmat, the worm of chaos, which also led them to indulge in the mythical practice of mutilation, with a great many limbs and members lopped off for "display." And so, barely two hours later, when the punishment had ended, Sichem the princeling lay shamefully battered in his bathroom, headfirst in the drain of the latrine; and in a street somewhere, draped in a necklace of tattered blossoms, the corpse of Weser-ke-Bastet lay in its own blood, but no longer intact, which from the viewpoint of his ancestral faith was an especially grievous blow. As for the old man Hemor, he had simply died of fright. Dinah, the irrelevant, innocent cause of so much misery, was now in the hands of her family.

The pillaging went on for a long while. The brothers' old wishful dream was fulfilled—they could gladden their hearts with plunder. Glittering booty, urban riches of very considerable note, fell into the victors' hands, so that their return home at the end of the last watch of the night looked like a straggling caravan of triumph—their prisoners bound in ropes and driven before them and their beasts packed high with golden sacrificial bowls and ewers, sacks of rings, bracelets, belts, buckles, and necklaces, delicate household items of silver, electrum, enamel, alabaster, carnelian, and ivory, not to mention the foodstuffs and supplies, the flax, oil, fine flour, and wine that was part of the take. Jacob did not leave his tent at their arrival. He had spent much of his restless night under the sacred trees near their camp making sacrifices of atonement to his God who bore no image, spilling the blood of a nursing lamb down over the stone and burning its fat with fragrant simples and spices. And when his sons, in their hot and puffed-up pride, now entered his tent with Dinah, whom they had retrieved amid such horrors, he lay face-down with his head covered and for some time could not be brought to look at the hapless girl, let alone at his barbaric sons. "Begone!" he said, waving them away. "Fools! . . . Cursed fools!" They stood there defiant, pouting their lips. "Should we allow our sister to be treated like a harlot?" one of them asked. "Behold, we have washed our hearts. Here is Leah's child. She is avenged seventy-seven times over." And since Jacob was silent and did not uncover himself, he went on: "Let our lord look at the goods outside. Much is yet to come, for we left several men behind to gather up the townspeople's flocks out in the fields and bring them back to Israel's tents." Jacob leapt up and raised balled fists above them, so that they shrank back. "Cursed be your anger," he cried with all his strength, "that it is so fierce, and your wrath that it is so stubborn! Wretches, what have you done to make me stink among the inhabitants of the land like a carcass in a swarm of flies? And what if they gather together in revenge against us, what then? We are few in number. They will slay us and destroy us, me and my house and all the blessing of Abraham that you were to bear further over the course of time, but what has been founded will now be crushed. How feeble your sight! Off you go and strangle the afflicted and make us strong and rich for the moment, but are too weak in the head to think of the future, of the covenant and the promise!"

They all just pouted their lips. All they knew to do was to repeat themselves: "Were we supposed to let our sister be dealt with like a harlot?"

"Yes!" he cried, beside himself, horrifying them. "Better that than to endanger life and the promise. Are you with child?" he snapped at Dinah, cowering in her nothingness on the floor. "How can I know that?" she wailed. "The child shall not live," he declared, and she wailed again. More calmly he announced, "Israel shall now break camp, with everything that is his, and he shall set forth with those goods and herds that you took with the sword for Dinah. For he shall not sojourn at the place of this abomination. I have had a vision this night, and the Lord spoke to me in my dream, saying, 'Arise and go up to Beth-el!' Now begone! Begin the packing."

The vision and command had truly been given to him, for after he had made his sacrifice by night and while his sons were still plundering the city, he had fallen into a light sleep on his bed. It was a reasonable vision and came from the heart, for Luz, that place of asylum he knew so well, held a great attraction for him under such circumstances, and in journeying there it was as if he were fleeing to be at the feet of God the King. Those refugees who had escaped Shechem and its bloody marriage feast were indeed on their way to surrounding towns to announce what had happened to their own. It was also during this period, then, that certain letters, prepared by various chiefs and shepherds of the cities of Canaan and Emor reached the city of Amun and unfortunately had to be placed before Hor in his palace, before his Holy Majesty Amenhotep the Third, although at the time the god was in a low and nervous state, suffering from one of the tooth abscesses that so frequently afflicted him, and was, moreover, so busy with the building of his own temple tomb over in the west that he simply could not find time to cast an eye upon such annoying news from that wretched land of Amurru concerning the "loss of the king's cities" and "the taking of Pharaoh's land by the Habiru, who are plundering all the lands of the king"—for that is what the chiefs and shepherds had written in their letters. And so these documents, which moreover were marked by a faulty Babylonian that had sounded rather ridiculous to the ears of the court, were made part of the archives without having produced any decision in Pharaoh's mind as to measures to be taken against these robbers—and Jacob's people could count themselves lucky for other reasons. The cities that lay about them, seized with holy terror at the extraordinary savagery of their behavior, took no action against them, so that Jacob, the father—after first instituting a general cleansing, collecting the countless idols that had found their way into his camp over the last four years and burying them with his own hands beneath the sacred trees—could set out with goods and chattel, leaving behind Shechem, the city of abomination, the vultures circling above it, and without disruption wend his way, a still richer man, along the well-maintained road toward Beth-el.

Dinah and Leah, her mother, rode the same clever and strong camel. They dangled in decorated baskets on both sides of its hump, shaded by a cloth roof that was looped across a cane rod and that Dinah almost always kept draped down over her, so that she sat in darkness. She was with child. The baby she brought into the world when her time came was left exposed, for so the men had decided. She herself grieved and withered away before her time. At fifteen her unhappy little face was that of an old woman.

Part Four

THE FLIGHT

Primal Bleating

What weighty stories! Jacob, the father in all his dignity, was as weighed down with them as with goods and chattels—both with new stories from the recent past as well as those that were old, indeed ancient—weighed down with stories and with history.

History is what has happened and what continues to happen on and on through time. But it is also layered in strata that lie beneath the ground we walk upon, and the deeper the roots of our being reach down into those unfathomable layers of history—which lie beyond and below the fleshly confines of our ego and yet determine and nourish it, so that in less precise moments we may speak of them in the first person and as if they belonged to our flesh—the more weighed down with meaning is our life and all the more dignity attaches to the soul of our flesh.

When Jacob returned to Hebron, also called the Fourfold City, when he came to the oracle tree, planted and sanctified by Abraham—by Abiram or by someone else unknown—and returned home to his father's tent after yet another far too weighty event that will be dealt with in due time, he found Isaak wasting away; and he died, a very old man, a blind patriarch who had inherited the name of Yitzchak, Abraham's son. And in the solemn hour of death he spoke to Jacob and all who were present in high and dreadful tones, in prophetic confusion, of "himself" as the averted sacrifice and of the blood of the ram that should be regarded as the blood of the true son shed in atonement for all. Yes, shortly before the end, he attempted to bleat like a ram, and with the most remarkable success, while at the same time his bloodless face took on an astounding resemblance to the physiognomy of that animal—or rather, it was as if one suddenly became aware of a resemblance that had always been there—so much so that they were all horrified and could not fall on their faces fast enough to avoid seeing the son become the ram, even as he began to speak again, calling the ram his father and God. "A god shall be slain," he babbled in ancient poetic words, and with head thrown back, eyes wide open and vacant, fingers splayed, he went on babbling about how they should prepare a banquet of the slaughtered ram's flesh and blood, about how he and Abraham had once done just that, the father and the son for whom the divinely paternal animal had intervened. "Behold, it was slaughtered," they heard the old man proclaim in his rambling death rattle, though no one dared gaze upon him, "the father and the animal instead of the man and the son, and we ate of it. But truly I say unto you the man and the son will be slaughtered instead of the animal and in place of God, and you will eat of it." Then he gave another realistic bleat and expired.

They remained lying on their faces for a long time after he fell silent, uncertain whether he was really dead and would bleat and proclaim no more. They all felt as if their bowels had rolled over within them, with the bottom upended and now at the top, making them want to vomit, for in the dying man's words and demeanor they had sensed something primal and obscene, ghastly and ancient, sacred and yet prior to all sacredness, something that lay beneath all the layers of civilization in the most forgotten, shunned, and suprapersonal depths of their souls and that the dying Yitzchak had roiled up, creating utter nausea. From remote and buried times had come a specter, an obscenity of an animal that was God, a ram in fact, that was the tribe's god and ancestor, out of which the tribe came and whose divine tribal blood they had shed and consumed in order to refresh the tribe's kinship with the divine animal, in those long-ago obscene times—before He had come, the God from far away, Elohim, the God from outside and beyond, the God of the desert and of the moon at its zenith, who had chosen them, who had cut the tie to their primal nature, who had wed them with the ring of circumcision and had founded a new beginning of God in time. That was why they been sickened by the dying Yitzchak's ramlike face and his bleating; and even Jacob felt sick to his stomach. Yet with feet unshod and head shaved and strewn with dust, he also felt his soul mightily raised up, for he would now have to attend to funeral rites, to lamentations and sacrificial dishes eaten for the dead—along with his brother Esau, the flute-playing goat, who had come from his goatish mountains to assist in burying their father in the double cave and to lift up his childish voice through his tear-stained beard, joining in the unrestrained wail of other men and women singing their *hoiadôn!* Together they sewed Yitzchak up in a goatskin with his knees drawn high and gave him over to devouring time, who eats his children so that they may not set themselves over him, but must also regurgitate them so that they may live again as the same children in the old and same stories. (For as he fingers them the giant does not notice that their clever mother has given him something like a stone, wrapped in skins, and not a child.) Their "alas for our lord!" was a lament that had been repeated many times over a dead Yitzchak, the averted sacrifice, and yet Isaak had lived in his stories and rightly told them in the first person, for they were his stories—in part because his self, in moving back and beyond, merged with the primal image of what once had been and in part because what once had been had become present again in his flesh and could repeat itself in accordance with its founding form. That is how Jacob and all the others had heard and understood it when the dying man once again mentioned the averted sacrifice—had heard it with a double ear, as it were, and yet understood its message as one, just as in reality we perceive a single speech with two ears, see one object with two eyes, but grasp both speech and object in a single meaning. Moreover, Yitzchak was a very old man who spoke about a little boy who had almost been slaughtered, and whether he himself had once been that boy, or whether it had been someone else long before, carried no real weight in their thoughts and understanding, because in any case the sacrificial child could have been no more strange to him in his old age or distanced from him to any greater degree than was the child he once was.

The Red One

And so Jacob's soul, though weighty and pondering, was raised up during the days when he and his brother buried their father, for all the stories rose up again before him and were present in spirit, just as they had once again been present in flesh molded according to their ancient archetype. And it seemed to him as if he were walking on transparent earth made up of countless, unfathomable layers of crystal descending into the depths and brightly lit by lamps hung in between. But here above them he walked in the stories of his own flesh, was present as Jacob, and he looked at Esau, cursed by means of trickery, who was also walking now in his archetypal mold—and his name was Edom the Red One.

And with that his personality is without doubt perfectly characterized—"without doubt" in a qualified sense, "perfectly" under the proviso that the precision of this "characterization" is that of moonlight, of which teasing illusion is very much a part; nor are we entitled to wander beneath such ambiguous precision bearing that same look of slightly pensive simplicity found on faces of persons in our story. We have told how even during his early years at Beersheba Esau, the red and hairy man, had established and cultivated relations with the land of Edom, with the people of the wooded and goatish mountains of Seïr, and how later with kith and kin, with his Canaanite wives Adah, Aholibamah, and Basemath, along with his sons and daughters, he had joined them, converting entirely to their god Kuzach. This people of the goats, then, already existed, had existed who knows how long, when Joseph's uncle Esau went over to them, and it is only with the magically ambiguous precision of moonlight that tradition—that is, the "fine discourse" spun out over generations and solidified as a chronicle only much later—calls him "father of the Edomites," the tribal primogenitor, the original goat of this goatish folk. But that was not Esau, not this Esau, not him personally—even if discourse and presumably, in a certain sense, even he himself considers him to be so. The Edomite people were much older than Joseph's uncle—whom we again call by that name, because it is much more reliable to establish identity by descendant rather than ascendant relatives—older than he beyond measure, for the primacy of a certain Bela, son of Beor, mentioned in the tables as the first king of Edom is assuredly no more certain than the primacy of the kingship of Menes in Egypt, a notorious backdrop chronology. The primogenitor of Edom was therefore not, in a precise sense, Esau; and when in a chanting verse it is expressly said of him that "he *is* Edom," but not, for instance, "he *was* Edom," the statement's present tense is not a matter of mere chance, but rather it explains the timeless and supra-individual consolidation of a given type. In terms of history, and thus of an individual, the primal goat of this goatish people had been an incomparably older Esau, in whose footprints our present primal goat wanders—well-worn footprints in which, one must add, many others later trod, footprints that, in conclusion, were probably not even those of the man of whom "fine discourse" might rightly have declared: "He *was* Edom."

And here, to be sure, what we have to say flows into a mystery in which our own information gets lost—the mystery, that is, of an endless past in which every origin proves to be just an illusory stopping place, never the final goal of the journey, and its mystery is based on the fact that by its very nature the past is not a straight line, but a sphere. The line knows no mystery. Mystery lies in the sphere. But a sphere consists of complements and correspondences, a doubled half that closes to a unity; it consists of an upper and a lower, a heavenly and an earthly hemisphere in complement with one another as a whole, so that what is above is also below and whatever may happen in the earthly portion is repeated in the heavenly, the latter rediscovering itself in the former. This corresponding interchange of two halves that together build the whole of a closed sphere is analogous to another kind of objective change: rotation. The sphere rolls; that is the nature of the sphere. In an instant top is bottom and bottom top, if one may even speak in the generalities of bottom and top in such a case. It is not just that the heavenly and the earthly recognize themselves in each other, but thanks to spherical rotation the heavenly also turns into the earthly, the earthly into the heavenly, clearly revealing, indeed yielding the truth that gods can become human and that, on the other hand, human beings can become gods again.

This is as true as it is true that Osiris, the dismembered martyr, was once human, was a king over the land of Egypt, but then became a god—though, to be sure, with an immutable tendency to become human again, which is clearly demonstrated in the very nature of the Egyptian kings, each of whom was god as man. But as to the question of what Usiri was at first, at the very beginning, god or man, there is no answer; for there is no beginning to a rolling sphere. It is no different with his brother Set, who, as we have already pointed out, was the murderer who dismembered him. This fiend, it is said, had the head of an ass, was warlike by nature and also a hunter, who at Karnak near the city of Amun instructed the kings of Egypt in the use of the bow. Others called him Typhon, and on occasion he was given the attributes of the *khamsin,* a hot desert wind, of the searing sun, fire itself, so that he became Baal-Hammon, the god of incandescent heat, known among the Phoenicians and Hebrews as Moloch or Melech, the bull-king of the Baalites, who devours children and the firstborn with his fire and to whom Abram was tempted to offer Yitzchak. Might it be said that Typhon–Set, the red hunter, was first and last at home in the heavens and none other than Nergal, the foe with seven names, Mars, the red planet, the fire planet? With equal justification someone might claim that he had been a man first and last—Set, the brother of King Osiris, whom he drove from his throne and murdered, and only afterward became a god and a star, though to be sure, by the law of the rotating sphere, always ready and on the verge of also becoming human again. He is first of all both and neither: ever changing by turn, god-star and human being in one. Which is why the present tense is the only verb form applicable to him, for it contains within it the rotation of the sphere, and quite correctly it is always said of him: "He is the Red One."

But if it is the case that Set, the archer, exchanges heavenly and earthly places with Nergal–Mars, the fiery planet, then it is obvious that the same relationship of rotating correspondences exists between Osiris, the murdered king, and Marduk, the royal planet, which only recently was likewise greeted by those black eyes at the rim of the well and whose god is also called Jupiter–Zeus. The story is told of him that he took a sickle, castrated his father, Kronos—the very same divine giant who devoured his children and did not do so in Zeus's case only because of a mother's cunning—and drove him from the throne in order to set himself up as king in his stead. That should offer a hint to anyone who does not wish to stop halfway in determining the truth. For it obviously means that Set or Typhon had not been the first regicide, that Osiris himself already owed his sovereignty to a murderous deed, and that what happened to him as king was what he himself had done as Typhon. This, you see, is part of the sphere's mystery, that by its rotation a person's unity and identity can go hand in hand with his change of role. One is Typhon as long as one remains the claimant to the throne plotting murder; after the deed, however, one is king in the manifest majesty of success, and the role and model of Typhon devolve on someone else.

There are many who claim to know it was the red Typhon and not Zeus who castrated Kronos and drove him from his throne. But that is a pointless argument, for it is all one and the same for the spinning sphere: Zeus is Typhon before he conquered. But included in the spinning is the interchangeability of father and son, so that it is not always the son who slays the father, but rather at any moment the son may be put in the role of the victim, who is then slain by the father instead. Typhon–Zeus, then, by Kronos. The primal Abram surely knew that when he set about to sacrifice his only son to Moloch the Red. It was apparently his gloomy view that he had to act on the basis of that story and fulfill its pattern. God, however, averted him from his deed.

There was a period when Esau, Joseph's uncle, was in constant contact with Ismael, his own uncle and Isaak's disowned half brother, visiting him conspicuously often in his desert underworld to the south and hatching plots—concerning the horrors of which we shall hear later. The attraction was, of course, no accident, and if our subject is "the Red One," then we must also speak of Ismael. His mother was named Hagar, which means "the wanderer," in and of itself an invitation for her being sent into the desert in fulfillment of her name—the immediate cause of which, however, was Ismael, whose netherworldly tendencies had long been all too clear for it to be even conceivable that he might remain permanently bathed in the higher light of a life pleasing to God. It is written of him that he was a "mocker," which however does not mean that he was too free with his tongue—that alone would not have made him ineligible for the upper spheres just yet, but rather in this case "mocking" denotes "sporting"; and what happened was that Abram looked "through the window" and saw Ismael sporting in netherworldly fashion with his younger half brother, an act certainly not without danger for Yitzchak, the true son, for Ismael was as beautiful as a desert sunset. Which is why the future father of many took even greater fright and saw the situation as ripe for drastic measures. Constant quarrels had marked the relationship between Sarah and Hagar, who at one time had flaunted her motherhood in front of Isaak's still-barren wife and on one occasion had had to flee before the latter's jealousy. And Sarah daily urged him to drive off the Egyptian and the fruit of her womb, if for no other reason than because the question of who was the true heir remained unsettled, a matter of dispute between the

elder son of the concubine and the younger son of the true wife, for
it was still very much a question whether Ismael ought not share the
inheritance with Yitzchak, or indeed take precedence over him—
a ghastly thought for the doting, jealous mother Sara and an uncomfortable one for Abiram as well. Which was why what he had
seen Ismael doing had set the scales of his decision out of balance;
and after giving arrogant Hagar her son—along with some water
and flatbread—he told her to have a look around in the world of no
return. How could it have been otherwise? Was Yitzchak, the
averted sacrifice, supposed to fall victim to the fiery Typhon in the
end after all?

That question needs to be properly understood. It sounds offensive to Ismael, but rightly so. For the offense lies in Ismael himself,
and it is indisputable that he was treading in perilous footsteps and
was "no fool," so to speak. The smallest alteration in one syllable of
his name suffices to reveal him in all his arrogance, and that he
proved to be such a good archer in the desert left an impression on
scholars, who compared him with a wild ass, the beast of murderous
Typhon–Set, Osiris's evil brother. Yes, he is the evil fiend, he is the
Red One. But although Abraham drove him off, protecting the son
of blessing from Ismael's ardently improper entrapments, when
Isaak sired sons in his wife's womb, the Red One returned to live in
his stories alongside Jacob, the pleasant son. For Rebekah gave birth
to twins: the "fragrant grass" and the "thorny weed," Esau, the hairy
red son, whom scholars and seers have reviled far more fiercely than
his everyday earthly persona deserves. For they call him the serpent
and Satan, even a swine, a wild swine, attempting to force an allusion
to the boar that mutilated the shepherd lord in the ravines of
Lebanon. Yes, in their erudite rage they even call him a "strange
god" so that the crude kindliness of his everyday persona will deceive no one as to what he is in the rotation of the sphere.

It rotates, and father and son, though unequal, are often the red
one and the blessed one; and the son castrates the father, or the father
slays the son. But then again they are often—though no one knows
what they first were—brothers as well, like Set and Usiri, like Cain
and Abel, like Shem and Ham; and it can happen that, as we have
seen, three of them build both pairs in the flesh, the father-son pair
on one side, the fraternal pair on the other. For Ismael, the wild ass,
stands between Abraham and Isaak. To the former he is the son with

the sickle, to the latter the red brother. But did Ismael want to castrate Abram? Of course he did. For he was about to seduce Isaak into netherworldly love, and if Isaak had not sired children in a woman's womb, there would have been no Jacob and his twelve sons. And then what would have become of the promise of those numberless descendants or of Abraham's name itself, which means "father of many"? But now they walked the earth again in the present time of real flesh, as Jacob and Esau; and if even the doltish Esau knew more or less what he was all about, how much more so, then, did such a cultured and ingenious man like Jacob?

Isaak's Blindness

The blurred and scattered gaze of Jacob's wise, brown, and already somewhat weary eyes rested on the hunter, his twin, who was helping him bury their father, and all the stories rose up in him again to become a brooding present: their childhood and how the decision that had hung so long in the balance had been made, sending blessing and curse and everything that followed after. He pondered dry-eyed, but at times his chest would tremble at life's adversities, and he would gulp for air. Busy as he was, however, Esau blubbered and wailed, though he owed little thanks to the old man being sewn into the goatskin, not when the only thing left for him after the blessing was to be cursed to live in the desert—much to his father's great sorrow, or so at least Esau was convinced, a conviction that had become a necessity of life for him, which was why he forever wanted to hear it, if only from his own lips. And so busy as they were, he wiped the snot from his nose and wailed, saying it ten times over: "The woman loved you, Yekev, but father loved me and was glad to eat of my game, that's how it was. 'Rough Hide, my firstborn' he would say, 'what you killed for me tastes good and you roasted it in a fire you fanned yourself. Yes, I do like it, Red Hide, and my thanks for your agile hard work. You shall be my firstborn all my life long and I will remember it.' Those were his very words, spoken a good hundred, a good thousand times over. But the woman loved you and said to you: 'Little Yekev, my chosen one!' And, the gods know, a man finds a softer bed in a mother's love than in a father's, that much I have learned."

Jacob was silent. And so Esau launched into more sobbing accounts of what his soul needed to hear. "And oh, oh, how dismayed the old man was when I arrived after you, bringing him what I had cooked so that he might be strengthened for the blessing, and he realized that it was not Esau who had been there first. He was dismayed beyond all measure, crying out over and over, 'Who was that hunter then, who was he? The blessing will remain with him, for I had strengthened myself mightily to bless him. Esau, my Esau, what shall we do now?'"

Jacob was silent.

"Enough silence, my smooth brother!" Esau cried. "Enough of your self-serving silence, which you even pass off as silent gentle forbearance, raising bile and rage within me. Was it not the case that the old man loved me and was dismayed beyond measure?"

"So you have said," Jacob replied, and Esau had to be content. But his having said it made it no more true than what had really happened, made it no less complicated, but left it only half-true and ambiguous. And it was not furtive malice that lay behind Jacob's silence and monosyllabic answers, but his own resignation before the complicated knot of the facts, which no amount of wailed exclamations and heartfelt sentimentality could undo—the apologetic and self-deceptive sentimentality of the survivor who in looking back tries to make the best of his relationship with the deceased. It might well have been true that Isaak had been dismayed that day when Esau arrived after he had already been there. For the old man may have feared that some stranger had been with him there in the dark, an impostor who was no relation whatever and had gained the blessing by trickery, which would indeed have to be regarded as a great misfortune. But whether he would have been dismayed, genuinely dismayed, had he been certain that it was Jacob who had preceded Esau and received his blessing, that was a different question, which was not easily answered to the satisfaction of Esau's needy heart and which had to be regarded more or less from the very same viewpoint as that other question: whether their parents' love had been actually divided as simply as Esau wanted and needed to believe—with "Little Yekev" here and "Little Red Hide" there. Jacob had his reasons to doubt it, even if it was not his place to insist on them with his weeping brother.

Cuddling her younger son to her, his mother had often told how difficult it had been to carry the brothers in those last months before their birth, and how she had dragged herself about, short of breath, badly misshapen, carrying too much weight on her feet, and constantly pummeled by the two of them, who had not lived in peace in her belly, but had battled for precedence. Isaak's God, she said, had meant for him, Jacob, to be the firstborn, but Esau had been so fierce in claiming that right for himself that Jacob had held back out of friendship and courtesy—and also probably out of the calm conviction that the minor difference in age between twins was itself of no great significance, did not yet determine any real decision, and that the question of who was the true firstborn in a spiritual sense, of whose sacrificial smoke would ascend straight up to the Lord, would only be decided over time outside the womb. Rebekah's tale sounded probable. Certainly Jacob might well have behaved in that fashion, and he thought he could even recall doing so. But in telling it, what his mother betrayed was that Esau's tiny, defiant head start in life had never been regarded as decisive and that the question of who would claim the blessing had remained in abeyance for a long time, until they were young men, until that fateful day, so that Esau might well have cause to complain of a decision made against him, but certainly not of any injustice in its having been rendered prematurely. Indeed for a long time in their father's eyes Esau's having been actually born first had weighed heavily enough to his advantage, counterbalancing all aversion arising from his character— whereby "character" is to be understood in a physical as well as a spiritual and moral sense—until the day it no longer carried such weight. He had had red hair from the first, all over his body, like a litter of bezoar goats, and came equipped with a full set of teeth— a truly eerie phenomenon, which Isaak, however, forced himself to greet and interpret as somehow splendid. He wanted very much to take the side of this firstling, and he himself originated and for many years carefully tended the assumption to which Esau clung: that is, that he was his son, whereas Jacob was his mother's little boy. He spoke to his smooth toothless son there, gave his soul a nudge, so to speak—for this little person, his second son, had a gentle radiance about him and smiled such a clever, peaceful smile, whereas the first one rolled about squalling insufferably and knitting his eyebrows in a ghastly arabesque. There was evidently not much to hope for in the pitiful smooth child, while the hairy one impressed him as having the makings of a hero who would surely do well in the eyes of the Lord. From that day on, he constantly and automatically said things of the sort, casting them in the usual adages and clichés, though soon enough it was often in a voice trembling with personal annoyance; for Esau's disgusting premature teeth dreadfully abused Rebekah's breasts, so that soon both teats were quite raw and inflamed and even little Jacob had to be fed with diluted goat's milk. And to that Yitzchak said, "He will be a hero, and he is my son and my firstborn. But the smooth boy is yours, daughter of Bethuel, heart within my breast." It was in this connection, then, that he named her "heart within my breast" and called the gentle child hers, and the rough child his own. Which did he prefer then? Esau. So it was said later in the shepherds' song, and that is also what people in the country roundabout said: Yitzchak loves Esau, Rebekah loves Jacob. That was the compromise Isaak established by his words and went on maintaining in words, a small myth inside a much larger and more powerful one, but in such contradiction to that larger and more powerful one—that it ended in Yitzchak's going blind.

How is that to be understood? In the sense that the fusion of body and soul is far more intense, the soul much more physical, the body's molding by elements of the soul far more extensive than has been believed on occasion. Isaak was blind, or as good as blind when he died, there is no contesting that. During the twins' childhood, however, his sight was not nearly so diminished by age, and if by the time the boys were young men, he had advanced farther on the road to blindness, it was because he had catered to his eyes for decades, had been overprotective, shielding or simply not using them, and offered as his excuse that they tended to inflame easily, a condition quite common in his world—indeed Leah and several of her sons also suffered from it all their lives—but in fact it was simple aversion on his part. Is it possible for someone to go blind or come as close to it as Yitzchak actually did in old age, because he does not want to see, because seeing is a torture to him, because he feels better in a darkness in which certain things can happen *that have to happen?* We do not claim that such causes can produce such effects, but shall content ourselves with stating that such causes were present.

Esau matured early like a young animal. While still a boy, one might say, he married again and again: daughters of Canaan, Chetites

and Hivites, as we have heard, first Judith and Adah, then Aholibamah and Basemath as well. He settled them in tents in his father's
camp, and was fruitful with them, and with total insensitivity allowed them and their brood to pursue their traditional and idolatrous worship of nature before his parents' very eyes. Lacking any
sense whatever for Abram's lofty inheritance, he also established a
friendship with the Seïrim to the south, basing it on both hunting
and religion and openly worshiping the tempestuous Kuzach. All of
which, as the song later put it and as can still be found in the traditional text, was a "grief of mind" to Isaak and Rebekah—to them
both, that is, but inevitably far more to Yitzchak than to his sister-
wife, although it was she who put words to her vexation while Isaak
kept silent. He was silent, and when he spoke it was in words to this
effect: "Mine is the red one. He is the firstborn, and I love him." But
Isaak—bearer of the blessing, keeper of the idea of God that Abram
had struggled to win, the man whom his spiritual family saw as the
son and reincarnation of the Chaldean—suffered greatly from what
he was forced to see, or to close his eyes to in order not to see, suffered, too, from his own weakness, which prevented him from putting an end to this mischief by suggesting Esau take to the desert, as
had been done with Ismael, his savagely beautiful uncle. The "small"
myth prevented it, Esau's actual priority of birth prevented it, for
that still weighed heavily in his favor, since the old question of which
twin was to be called upon and chosen still hung in abeyance. And
so Isaak complained of his eyes, that the lids burned and watered,
that his vision was blurred, like the waning moon, that any light was
painful—and he sought out darkness. Are we claiming that Isaak
became "blind" in order not to see the idolatry practiced by his
daughters-in-law? Ah, that was the least of what it pained him to see,
of what made the loss of sight desirable—for only in blindness could
those things happen that had to happen.

For the older the boys grew the more clearly defined—if one
looked—were the lines of the "great" myth, within which the
"smaller" became forced and untenable to an ever increasing degree,
in spite of all those fatherly principles favoring the elder of the two.
Over time it became that much clearer *who these two were,* in whose
footsteps they walked, and in which story they were grounded: the
red man and the smooth man, the hunter and the homebody. But as

for Isaak (who along with Ismael, the wild ass, had formed the fraternal pair himself, who had been not Cain but Abel, not Ham but Shem, not Set but Osiris, not Ismael but Yitzchak, the true son), if his eyes had been wide open to see, how could he ever have been able to maintain a compromise that gave preference to Esau? And so his sight grew dim, like the waning moon, and he lay in the darkness so that both he and Esau, his eldest, might be cheated.

The Grand Joke

In truth, no one was cheated, not even Esau. For if it is our ticklish task to tell of people who did not always know precisely who they were, and if Esau did not always know it all that exactly either, but at times took himself for the primal goat of the people of Seïr, speaking of it in the first person, this occasional lack of clarity really only affected what was individual and time-bound and was itself the direct result of the fact that each of them had an excellent understanding of who he was in his essence—that is, outside of time, mythologically, typologically—including Esau, of whom it has been said, and not without good reason, that in his way he was as pious a man as Jacob. Certainly he wept and raged after he had been "cheated" and laid snares in his blessed brother's path more deadly than those Ismael had laid in Isaak's—indeed it is true that he spoke with Ismael of his murderous plans against both Isaak and Jacob. But he did it all because it was part of his character's role, and because in his piety he was perfectly aware that everything that happens is a fulfillment, that what had happened had happened because it had to happen according to an established archetype. Which meant: this had not been the first time; it had happened as part of a ceremony and according to the pattern, had gained its reality in the present, like a festival, and had reoccurred just as festivals reoccur. For Esau, Joseph's uncle, was not the tribal father of Edom.

Which is why when the time came—the brothers were almost thirty by then—and from the darkness of his tent Yitzchak sent his slave attendant, a young lad missing an ear (which on account of several frivolous blunders had been cut off, much to his betterment), when this poor fellow, then, stood with arms crossed at his dark chest and said to Esau, who was toiling along with servants in the plowed fields, "My lord asks for my lord," Esau stood there as if rooted in place, and his red face turned pale beneath the sweat that covered it. He murmured the phrase of obedience, "Here I am." In his soul, however, he thought, "Now it begins!" And that soul was full of pride, dread, and solemn misgivings.

So he left his labor in the sunny fields, and entering the dim tent where his father was lying with two moist cloths over his eyes, he bowed and said, "My lord has called me."

Isaak replied rather peevishly, "That is the voice of my son Esau. Is it you, Esau? Yes, I called you, for the hour has come. Step closer, my eldest, that I may be sure it is you."

And Esau, dressed in a goatskin apron, bent down beside the bed and fixed his gaze on those cloths as if trying to bore through them into his father's eyes, while Isaak fingered his shoulders and arms and chest and said, "Yes, these are your hairy tufts, and this is Esau's red fleece. I can see with my hands, which for better or worse have learned to perform very nicely the tasks of my failing eyes. Listen then to me, my son, and open your ears wide to receive hospitably the words of your blind father, for the hour has come. Behold, I now lie covered so deep with years and days that I shall soon vanish beneath them. And since my eyes have failed over time, it can be presumed that I myself shall soon fail altogether and vanish into darkness, so that my life becomes night and is seen no more. Therefore, that I may not die before I give my blessing and share of my power and pass on the inheritance, let it be now as it has so often been. Go, my son, and take the weaponry of your bow, which you handle stoutly and cruelly before the Lord, and roam plain and field to slay me some game. Prepare it for me and make me a dish of meat, the way I love it, cooked with fine spices in sour milk and over a flaming fire and bring it here to me so that I may eat and drink and strengthen the soul of my body and that I may bless you with seeing hands. This is my instruction. Go."

"It is done." Esau murmured the well-worn phrase, but remained on his knees, bowing his head so low that those blind cloths were now staring into vacant space.

"Are you still there?" Isaak inquired. "For a moment I thought you had gone, which would not have surprised me, for the father is accustomed to having everyone swiftly follow his instructions out of love and fear."

"It is done," Esau repeated and left to go. But as he had pulled aside the goatskin at the entrance to the tent, he let it fall back and returned, kneeling once again at the bed and saying in a broken voice, "My father!"

"What now, something else?" Isaak asked, eyebrows arching above the cloths. "All is well," he then said. "Go, my son, for the hour has come, a great hour for you and for us all. Go, hunt, and cook, that I may bless you."

And Esau left with head held high, and stepping before the tent in the pride of the moment, he announced in a loud voice, for all within earshot to hear, the honor just bestowed. For stories do not happen all of a sudden, but point by point; they have their stages of development, and it would be wrong to call them sad throughout because the conclusion is sad. Stories with a sad ending have their moments, their episodes of pride, and it is right to view them not from the way they end, but each in its own light; for an episode's present is no less powerful than the present of the ending. Which was why Esau was proud of his hour, and letting his voice ring out, he cried:

"Hear this, people of the camp, hear, children of Abram whose incense rises to Yah, hear as well, you women whose incense rises to Baal, wives of Esau and your brood, the fruit of my loins. Esau's hour is come. The lord will bless his son yet today. Isaak sends me out into plain and field that with my bow I may provide a meal to strengthen him for my sake. Fall to your knees."

And while those closest fell upon their faces when they heard it, Esau saw one handmaid running off so fast it set her breasts bouncing.

This was the handmaid who, as she gasped for breath, then told Rebekah of what Esau had been boasting. And now the same handmaid, completely out of breath from running back and forth, came out to Jacob, who along with his companion, a pointy-eared dog named Tam, was tending sheep while lost in thoughts about God as he leaned on his long staff with a crook at the top. And with her brow pressed to the grass, she panted, "My mistress . . ." Jacob stared at her for a good while and then replied very softly after a long pause, "Here I am." During that pause, however, he had thought in his soul, "Now it begins!" And his soul was full of pride, dread, and solemnity.

Having told Tam to watch over his staff, he now entered the tent where Rebekah was waiting impatiently for him.

Rebekah, Sarai's successor, was a stately, strong-boned matron who wore golden earrings and whose well-defined features still preserved much of the beauty that had once proved so dangerous for Abimelek of Gerar. Beneath the high-arched, leaden sheen of evenly drawn brows separated by two vigorous creases, the gaze in her black eyes was quick-witted and firm. Her nose was robust, almost manly, with strong nostrils and a bold arch, her voice deep and resonant, and her upper lip shaded by delicate dark hairs. The silvery black curls of her hair, parted in the middle and falling in a mass over her brow, were covered by a brown scarf draped down her back, and her amber brown shoulders—their proud curves as little affected by the years as her nobly shaped arms—were bare, hidden neither by the scarf nor by an ankle-length patterned woolen dress, which she wore unbelted. Her small hands traced with many veins had just now quickly intervened to admonish and correct the fingers of the two women squatting there—one at each side of a loom with beams pegged to the ground outside—busily inserting and thrusting wooden shuttles through the taut warp of long flaxen threads. But she had stopped the women at their work, had sent them away, and was awaiting her son beneath the felt roof of a tent that befitted her status as mistress. With a decisive air she stepped across the mats to greet him as he respectfully entered.

"Yekev, my child," she said in a soft, deep voice, drawing his upraised hands to her breast. "It is indeed so. The lord wishes to bless you."

"He wishes to bless me?" Jacob asked, turning pale. "Me, and not Esau?"

"You in him," she said impatiently. "No subtleties now! Do not speak, do not quibble, but do as you are bidden, so that no mistake is made and no misfortune occurs."

"What is the command of my dear mother, from whom I draw life as I did during my days in her womb?" Jacob asked.

"Listen well," she said. "He told him to slay game and to prepare a meal of it to his taste, so that he may be strengthened for the blessing. You can do it more quickly and better. Go out to your flock at once, take two kid goats, slaughter them, and bring them to me. I shall use the best meat of them to make your father a meal of which nothing will be left uneaten. Now go!"

Jacob began to tremble and he did not stop trembling until it was all over. At certain moments he had the greatest difficulty keeping his chattering teeth under control. He said, "Merciful mother of men, your every word is like the word of a goddess to me, but what you say is dreadfully dangerous. Esau is hairy all over, and your child is smooth in all but a few places. If the lord were to take hold of me and feel my smoothness, how would I stand before him? Exactly as if I had wanted to deceive him—and instead of a blessing, his curse would be upon my head in an instant."

"Are you quibbling again already?" she snapped at him. "Let the curse be upon my head. I shall tend to things. Begone and bring the kids. A mistake is being made . . ."

And he ran. He hurried to a slope not far from camp where the goats were grazing, grabbed two kids, born that spring, as they gamboled about their dam, and he slew them with a cut to the throat, calling to their keeper that they were for the mistress. He let their blood spill out before God, then grabbed them by the hind legs, threw them over his shoulder, and started homeward, his heart pounding. They hung all the way down to the hem of his shirt—those still young heads, those little ringed horns, cleft noses, and glassy eyes, sacrificed early in life for a great cause. Rebekah stood waiting, beckoning.

"Quick," she said, "everything is ready."

Inside her tent were a stone hearth—the fire already burning under a bronze pot—and all the utensils of a kitchen and household. And his mother took the kids from him and began hastily to skin them and cut them up—a grand and energetic woman busy with her fork at the hearth, stirring, strewing seasoning, preparing the meal. And there was silence between the two while she worked. And as the meal cooked, Jacob watched her take folded clothes, a shirt and tunic, from her chest. These were Esau's festal garments, which were in her keeping, as Jacob now realized; and he turned pale again. Then he saw how she took the kid hides, still moist and sticky with blood on the inside, and cut them into pieces and strips—and he trembled at the sight. But Rebekah told him to take off his long shirt with its half-sleeves, his everyday garb at this season of the year, and now pulled his brother's short undergarment down over his trembling arms, and over that the finely woven blue and red woolen shirt that left one shoulder free and both arms bare. Then she said, "Now come here!" And while her lips moved in soft words and those vigorous creases stood out between her brows, she took cord and bound the pieces of hide—still offensively sticky all on their own— to wherever his skin lay bare and smooth: around his neck and arms, around his calves and on the backs of his hands.

She murmured, "I swaddle the child, I swaddle the lad, exchanged is the child, and changed is the lad, by the skin, by the hide."

And she muttered yet again, "I swaddle the child, I swaddle the lord, that the lord may touch, that the father may eat, brothers of the deep will now have to serve you."

Then with her own hands she washed his feet, just as she had surely done when he was small, then took oil fragrant of meadow and meadow flowers, Esau's scented oil, and anointed both his head and the feet she had just washed, while between clenched teeth she said, "Anointed the child, anointed the stone, that the blind man may eat, at your feet, at your feet must kneel the brothers of the deep."

Then she said, "It is done." And while a confused Jacob clumsily stood up in his bestial garb, standing there with arms and legs spread wide, his teeth chattering, she ladled the seasoned meat into its bowl, provided white bread as well, with clear golden oil in which to dip it, and a jug of wine, and putting it all in his hands and under his arm, she said, "Now go your way."

And balancing this load and terrified that the nasty sticky hides might shift under the cord, Jacob went his bowlegged, encumbered way—heart pounding, face contorted, eyes fixed to the ground. Many of the household servants who saw him crossing the camp like that rocked their heads with hands upraised and clicked their tongues, some even kissed their fingertips and said, "Behold, the lord!"

And so he came to his father's tent, put his mouth to the curtain, and said, "It is I, my father. May your servant lift his feet to approach you?"

From deep within the tent came Isaak's peevish voice, asking, "But who are you? Are you not perhaps a thief on the prowl and the son of a thief, who has come to my tent claming 'It is I'? For anyone can claim 'It is I,' but the question is who says it."

Clenching his teeth to keep them from chattering, Jacob replied, "It is your son who says I and who has hunted and prepared a meal for you."

"That is another matter," Yitzchak replied from inside. "Then come in."

So Jacob entered the twilight of the tent, along the back of which ran a raised and draped clay bench, on which lay Yitzchak wrapped in his robe, his eyes still covered by moistened cloths, and his head raised slightly by a headrest with a bronze half-ring. He asked again, "So who are you then?"

And in a breaking voice Jacob replied, "I am Esau, your older, your hairy son, and I have done as you bade me. Sit up, my father, and strengthen your soul; here is your meal."

But Isaak did not sit up yet. He asked, "What? You have encountered game so quickly and it ran before your strung bow this soon?"

"The Lord, your God, brought me good fortune in the hunt," Jacob replied—supporting only a few of the syllables with his voice, the others were whispers. But he said "your God" because of Esau; for Isaak's God was not Esau's god.

"But why does it seem to me," Isaak asked again, "that your voice is uncertain, Esau, my eldest, and that it sounds to me like Jacob's voice?"

And in his fear Jacob knew of no answer to that, and only trembled.

But Isaac said gently, "The voices of brothers are surely much alike, and the words from their mouths have the same or similar sound. Come here, that I may feel and see with my hands, which are seeing hands, whether you are Esau, my eldest, or not."

Jacob obeyed. He set down all the things his mother had given him, stepped closer, and offered himself to be felt. And from up close he could see that just as Rebekah had bound the unpleasant hides to him, his father had used cord to bind the moistened cloths to his head, so that they would not fall off if he sat up.

Spreading tapered fingers wide, Isaak's hands groped the air a little before he encountered Jacob, who presented himself. And those skinny, pale hands found him and felt where there was no garment—felt his neck, along his arms and the back of his hands, on down his thighs—and everywhere they touched the pelt of the kids.

"Yes," he said, "yes indeed, that surely has to convince me, for it is your fleece, the red tufts of Esau, I can see it with my hands. The voice resembles Jacob's voice, but the hairiness is Esau's, and that decides the matter. And so you are Esau?"

Jacob responded, "So you have seen and said."

"Then give me something to eat," Isaak said, sitting up. His robe hung down over his knees. And Jacob picked up the bowl, and crouching at his father's feet, he held it up to him. But Isaak first bent forward, placing a hand at each side, directly over Jacob's pelt-covered hands, and smelled the dish.

"Ah, good," he said. "Well prepared, my son. It has been cooked in sour cream, just as I ordered, and there's cardamom in it, and thyme, too, and a pinch of caraway." And he named several more ingredients that his nose could distinguish. Then he nodded, reached for the bowl, and ate.

He ate it all—which took a long time.

"Do you have bread, too, Esau, my son?" he asked, still chewing.

"But of course," Jacob replied. "Flatbread made of wheat, and oil."

And he brought him the bread, dipped it in oil, and held it to his father's mouth. Chewing it, Isaak took another bite of meat, then stroked his beard and nodded approval, while Jacob looked up into his face, observing it as he ate. That face was so frail and transparent, with delicately sunken cheeks from which only a sparse gray beard sprouted, and with a large and fragilely shaped nose, its thin nostrils spread wide, the arched bridge like a well-honed knife—it looked so spiritual, so holy, despite the cloths covering the eyes, that frugal meals and chewing seemed not to fit it really. It was slightly embarrassing to watch the eater as he ate, and one could imagine that he must be embarrassed that someone was watching him. It may well be that the cloths over his eyes spared him such uneasiness—at any rate, he kept chewing, his brittle jaw beneath its sparse beard moving at a relaxed pace, and since the bowl contained only the very best pieces, he left nothing in it.

"Give me something to drink," he then said. And Jacob hastened to hand him the jug of wine, even setting it to his father's lips, thirsty from the meal, and his father's hands rested on the pelts on the backs of Jacob's hands. And having come so close to him, Isaak spread his fine nostrils wide to sniff at the balm in his hair and the wildflower fragrance of his garments, but then fell back and said, "Indeed it is most deceptive—the scent that my son's fine garments always have! Like the meadows and the fields in the spring of the year, when the Lord has blessed them with flowers to delight our senses." And with the tapered tips of two fingers he lifted the edge of one of the cloths a little and said, "Are you truly Esau, my older son?"

To which Jacob gave a desperate laugh and asked in return, "Who else?"

"Then all is well," Isaak said and took such a deep breath that his fragile Adam's apple raised and lowered under his beard. Then he ordered Jacob to pour water over his hands. And when he had done it and dried the hands as well, his father said, "So let it be done!"

And greatly refreshed by food and drink, his face flush now, he placed his hands on the crouching, quivering man before him to bless him with all his might; and since his soul had been so strengthened by the meal, his words were full of all the power and riches of the earth. He gave him earth's fatness and womanly plenitude and dew and the male water of the heavens, gave him the fullness of the field, tree, and vine and the rampant fertility of flocks and a twofold shearing each year. He laid the covenant upon him, gave him the promise to bear, so that what had been founded might be passed on to the generations. His words were high-sounding and like a great current. He passed on to him dominance in the battle of the world's two halves, the light and the dark, victory over the dragon of the desert, and ordained him to be a beautiful moon and to be the bringer of the equinox, of renewal and great laughter. He, too, used the formula Rebekah had muttered, so ancient that it had become a mystery that did not exactly fit or accord with reason in this case, since only two brothers were involved, but Isaak spoke it solemnly over him all the same: The children of his mother would serve the bearer of the blessing, and all his brothers would fall down before his anointed feet. Then he called out the name of God three times, saying, "So may it be, so let it come to pass!" and released Jacob from his grip.

He stumbled away, to his mother. But a little later Esau returned home with a young wild goat that he had shot—and now the tale turns quite merry and quite horrid.

Jacob was an eyewitness to nothing of what then happened, nor did he wish to be; he kept himself hidden that day. But he knew it all exactly from what others told him and he could remember it as if he had been present.

The returning Esau was still in his state of glory. He knew not one thing of what had gone on in the meantime, for the story had not yet taken him that far. In happy arrogance and swollen pride he came strutting, the wild goat on his back, the bow in his hairy fist, and as he marched along he kicked his legs very high at each step and with a radiant glower turned his head from side to side to see if people were also watching him in his impressive superiority, and even at a distance began once more to boast and crow—and what a grand calamity and joke it was for all who heard. For they had gathered now, both those who had seen goat-pelted Jacob enter and then leave his lord's tent, and those who had not seen it themselves. But Esau's wives and children did not come out with them, though he called out to them again to come witness his grandeur and pomp.

People gathered and laughed at the way he was tossing his legs and crowded around him to see and hear him go about this. For he now began to shout incessantly like a peddler as he skinned his goat with much to-do, gutted and cut it up for all to see; he struck flint, set brushwood afire, hung a kettle over it, and ordered the laughing servants to bring him all the other items he needed to prepare his dish of honor.

"Ha-ha and ho-ho, you awestruck gawkers!" he blustered. "Bring me the big fork. Bring me sour milk from the nursing ewe, for his favorite feast is boiled in sheep's milk. Bring me salt from the salt mine, you sluggards, bring coriander, garlic, mint, and mustard seed to charm his palate, for I will pamper him until power bursts from his very pores. Bring me bread to serve with it, made of *solet* flour, and oil from the pressed fruit, and strain the wine, you idlers, so that no yeast is in the jug, or may the white jackass kick you! Run now and bring it here. For it is the feast of the feeding and blessing of Isaak, the feast of the son and the hero Esau, whom his lord sent out to hunt game for his meal, and whom he wishes to bless there in the tent before the hour is out!"

And so he went at it with hand and mouth, with ha-ha and ho-ho, with bombastic gestures and windy booming boasts of his father's love for him and of Red Hide's great day, till those in camp were bent over with laughter, writhing and weeping and hugging themselves. And when he departed with his fricassee, carrying it like the tabernacle before him, kicking his legs so ridiculously again, and bragging all the way to his father's tent, they screeched for joy, clapping their hands and stamping their feet, and then fell silent.

For from outside the curtain Esau said, "It is I, my father, and I bring you something so that you will bless me. Do you wish me to enter?"

And from within came Isaak's voice, saying, "Who is it who says I and wishes to enter the blind man's tent?"

"Esau, your Rough Hide," came his answer, "who has hunted and cooked for your strengthening, just as you commanded."

"You fool and robber," the voice resounded. "What are these lies you present me? Esau, my first son, was here long before you, he fed me and gave me drink, and went his way with the blessing."

Esau was so startled that he almost dropped the whole lot, and flinched with such a jerk that the creamy sauce spilled from the pot, soiling his clothes. People yowled with laughter. They shook their heads, for it was all much too absurd, they wiped tears from their eyes with their fists, then shook them, sprinkling the ground. Esau, however, lunged into the tent, unbidden, and then there was silence while all the others stood outside, hands clapped to their mouths, nudging each other with elbows. But not for long, for from inside there came a howl such as they had never heard before, and Esau burst out with upraised arms, his face not red but violet. "Damn, damn, damn!" he shouted with all his might, a quick burst of words that we might use at some minor annoyance nowadays, but at the time and coming from shaggy Esau's mouth, it was a new and inventive cry, filled with its original meaning, for he was truly was damned, not blessed, and solemnly deceived, a butt of jokes like no one else. "Damned," he screamed, "cheated, deceived, and overthrown!" And then he sat down on the ground and wailed with his tongue hanging out and tears thick as hazelnuts rolling down his cheeks, while people stood in a circle around him, clutching themselves in sheer pain at the grand joke, at how Esau, the red man, had been duped out of his father's blessing.

Jacob Must Journey

Then came flight, Jacob's escape from home and the camp, decreed and put into action by Rebekah, his determined and high-minded mother, who in sending her darling away was willing never to see him again perhaps, if only he had the blessing and could bear it on through the course of time. She was too clever and farseeing not to have known what would follow the solemn deception; but just as she knowingly had laid its burden upon her son, she also knowingly took it upon herself and sacrificed her heart.

She said not a word, and even in her conversation with Isaak to prepare what had to be done, not a word was spoken about the substance of the matter, essential realities were avoided. Nothing escaped her. It was certain, written in the stars so to speak, that within his own chaotic soul Esau was planning revenge, employing whatever imaginative powers he possessed to undo what had been done. She soon learned how he was pursuing his Cain-like goals. She learned that he had established mutinous contact with Ismael, the dark beauty, the spurned man of the desert. Nothing was more understandable. They were both of the same disadvantaged breed—Yitzchak's brother, Jacob's brother. They walked in the same set of footprints, excluded and disagreeable men—they had to find one another. The danger was worse, more far-reaching than Rebekah had anticipated, for Esau's bloody plans extended to Isaak as well. She heard how he had suggested to Ismael that he murder the blind man, and then he, Esau, would deal with his smooth brother. He was afraid of Cain's deed, afraid that it would make him even more himself, more clearly himself. So if his uncle acted first, that would embolden him. But Ismael raised objections—giving his sister-in-law time to act—for this was not to his liking. He hinted that tender memories of feelings that he once had for his gentle brother and that had served as the pretext for his exile, made it difficult for him to raise his hand against Isaak. That was for Esau himself to do, and then he, Ismael, would plant an arrow so neatly into the nape of Jacob's neck that it would come out at his Adam's apple, instantly sending the coddled brother sprawling dead in the grass.

The plan that savage Ismael suggested was typical of him. His idea was new, whereas Esau had only conventional fratricide in mind. He could not grasp what his uncle meant at all, thought he was babbling nonsense. Murder your father—that wasn't even a possibility to his way of thinking; it had never happened, didn't exist, was without rhyme or reason, was by its nature an absurd proposal. At most you could castrate your father with a sickle, the way Noah had been castrated, but to kill him—that was idle gibberish. Ismael smiled at his nephew's slack-jawed obtuseness. He knew quite well his plan was not idle, that it had roots, that perhaps it had been the source of all things and that Esau had stopped too soon on his journey into the past and, in saying that it had never happened before, was taking comfort in much later beginnings. He told him as much, and had more to say as well. Ismael said things that at first made the hairs of Esau's fleece stand on end and sent him running. He suggested that after slaying the father, one should eat abundantly of the flesh in order to incorporate his wisdom and power, the blessing of Abram within, and for that reason Esau should not first cook Isaak's body, but would have to devour him raw, blood and bones and all—which sent Esau running.

He returned again, it's true, but negotiations dragged on between nephew and uncle as to their assigned roles as murderers, giving mother Rebekah time to take precautionary measures. She told Isaak nothing of what she knew about designs that close, if unnamed, kinsmen harbored against him. The conversation between husband and wife was solely about Jacob—though not about the danger that, as Isaak himself surely knew, threatened him. There was never any talk about the deception of the blessing or Esau's rage—not a word in that regard, but only about how Jacob had to go on a journey, to Mesopotamia in fact, to visit his Aramaic relatives, for were he to stay, there was every reason to fear that he—he too!—might make a ruinous marriage. The parents found agreement at that level. If Jacob were to wed one of the daughters from the region, Rebekah said, a Hittite who like Esau's wives would arrive with her abominable idols in tow, what then, she asked Isaak in all earnest, would still be the point of her life? Isaak nodded and then admitted that yes, she was right, Jacob would have to go away for a while on that account. For a while, that's how she had put it to Jacob, too, and she meant it seriously, hoped she might be allowed to mean it seriously. She knew Esau, his chaotic, flighty nature, knew that he would forget. He was out for blood now, but he could be distracted.

She knew that on his excursions to the desert he had become infatuated with Ismael's daughter Mahalath and planned to make her his wife. Perhaps among his other fleeting thoughts that amiable matter would now assume a more important role than plans for revenge. Once it became clear that Esau had completely lost view of them and had calmed down again, Jacob would receive a message from her and return to her breast. But first, and for her sake, her brother Laban—Bethuel's son, seventeen days from here, in the land of Aram Naharaim—was to receive him with open arms. And so the flight was arranged, and Jacob was secretly readied for his journey to Aram. Rebekah did not weep. But she clasped him to her for a long time in the early morning darkness, stroking his cheeks and dangling amulets around him and his camels, pressed him to her again, and pondered in her heart that, if her God or some other god willed it, she might never see him again. It was destined to be so. But Rebekah had no regrets, either that day or later.

Jacob Must Weep

We know what happened to the traveler on that first day, have seen both his humiliation and his lifting up. But his being raised up had occurred within him as a great vision for his soul, whereas his humiliation had been real and physical, much like the journey itself, which he continued under its sign and as its victim—alone and a beggar. The way was long, and he was not Eliezer whom "the earth had leapt up to greet." He thought a great deal about that old man, Abram's chief steward and messenger, who, as everyone said, bore a considerable resemblance to the primal father and had made this same journey on a great mission, to fetch Rebekah for Isaak. How different his journey had been, how stately and befitting his rank, with ten camels and richly provided with all necessary and superfluous items, just as Jacob himself had been before that damnable meeting with Eliphaz. Why had God the King decreed this? Why had He punished him with such hardship and misery? For it seemed certain to him that it was a punishment, in repayment and satisfaction for Esau; and during his rigorous and wretched journey he thought a great deal about the nature of the Lord, who had doubtlessly willed and ordered what had happened, but was now harassing him for it, making him pay for Esau's bitter tears, if only for decorum's sake, so to speak, and in generously inexact proportion. For was his burden, however onerous, equal in value to the advantage he had gained over his permanently thwarted brother? At that question, Jacob smiled under his beard, which had grown considerably now during his travels and together with his damp and dirty headscarf framed a dark brown and lean face, shiny with sweat.

It was the height of summer, in the month of Ab, hopeless in its heat and drought. Dust lay thick as a man's finger on trees and bushes. Whenever other travelers passed him by, Jacob would cover his face and sag in his seat atop the high back of his intermittently and poorly fed camel, its large, shrewd, and sad eyes growing increasingly tired and plagued by flies. Or to lighten its burden, he would also lead the animal by the bridle as it strode along one of the parallel paths that made up these roads, while he walked in the one adjacent, his feet dusted by the stony powder. At night he would sleep in the open—in a field, at the foot of a tree, in an olive grove, beside a village wall, whatever offered itself—and could make good use of the body heat of his animal, against which he snuggled. For the nights were often cold desert nights, and being a coddled child of tents, he immediately caught cold as he slept and was soon coughing like a consumptive by the blazing heat of day. This greatly hampered his ability to earn his daily bread, for in order to eat he had to speak, tell stories, entertain people with descriptions of the dreadful adventure that had reduced a son of such good family to poverty. He told his tale in the towns, in the markets, or outside the wall at wells where he was allowed to water his camel and wash himself. Boys, men, and women with pitchers gathered around him and listened to words that, even when interrupted by coughing fits, were polished and vivid. He gave his name, praised his line of descent, described in detail the grand life he had led at home, lingered over the rich and spicy meals he had been served, and then provided a picture of the love and painstaking generosity with which he, as the firstborn of the family, had been provisioned for his journey to Haran in the land of Aram, toward the dawning east and darkening north, beyond the river Prath, where certain of his kinfolk dwelt, whose place of honor among the residents of that land should be no cause for wonder, since they owned a myriad of sheep and goats. And so he had been sent to them from home, and the purpose of his mission had combined partly commercial, partly religious and diplomatic elements of great import. The gifts and items for barter in his baggage, the ornaments on his animals, the weapons of his princely escort, the delicacies packed for him and his retinue—his precise account of it all set mouths and eyes gaping among an audience that was hungry for sensation and, although well aware that a man could indeed brag, unanimously refrained from differentiating between good bragging and the truth. That was how he had departed, but sad to say, certain regions of the land were teeming with robbers. These were very young robbers, but incredibly audacious. Moving through a ravine, his caravan found itself cut off both at the front and the rear, lacking any possibility of escape to either side and badly outnumbered. There ensued a battle, one of the most exciting that human memory would ever preserve, which Jacob then described in every particular, down to the last thrust, blow, and stab. The ravine was filled with the carcasses of men and beasts. He himself had brought low seven times seven young robbers, and each of his men had also slain a lesser number. But alas, the enemy's superior force was not to be tamed; one after another his men fell around him, and after a struggle of several hours, he was at last left all alone, pleading for the breath of life.

And why, one woman asked, had they not slain him as well?

That had been their intent. The chief of the robbers, the youngest and most insolent of all, was brandishing his sword above him, ready for the fatal blow, when he, Jacob, had cried to his God in his great need, had invoked the name of the God of his fathers—with the result that the bloodthirsty lad's sword burst into splinters in midair above him, was blasted into seven times seventy pieces. This had so confused the horrid child's mind, left him so stricken with fear, that together with his band he had beaten a retreat, though to be sure taking with him all that Jacob had possessed, so that he was left naked. Naked, but steadfast, he had continued on his way, certain that purest balsam awaited him at his goal—milk and honey and garments of purple and precious linen. But, alas, until then he had nowhere to lay his head, nothing with which to silence the shrill cry in his stomach, for his belly had seen far too little fodder for far too long.

He beat his breast, and his audience—standing at market booths or a well, hot yet moved by his tale—beat theirs, too, saying what a shame such things still occurred and roads were not safer. Here, they said, they posted guards on the highways, one every two hours. Then they gave the afflicted man something to eat: flatbread, dumplings, cucumbers, garlic, and dates, sometimes even a pair of pigeons or a duck, and hay was strewn for his camel to eat, even grain, so that it might marshal its energies to continue the journey.

And thus he would leave one spot and move on, toward the flow of the Jordan, into the vast hollow of Syria, to the gorge of the Orontes and the feet of the White Mountains. But it was a slow journey, for his means of earning bread took time. In cities he would visit temples, speak with the priests about divine matters, and his cultured and intelligent discourse would win them over and they would allow him to strengthen himself with provisions from the divinity's storehouses. He saw many beautiful and holy things along the way, saw the lordly mountain of the farthest north sparkling as if with fiery gemstones, and worshiped; he saw regions whose precious moisture came from the snow of the mountains, where the trunks of high, swaying date palms resembled scaly dragon tails, where forests were dark with cedar and sycamore and trees that offered clusters of sweet breadlike fruit. He saw cities and their throngs, saw Dimashki set amid its orchards and enchanted gardens. He saw a sundial there. And from there he also gazed with fear and loathing into the desert. It was red as was only proper. It extended toward morning in a murky reddish haze—a sea of uncleanness, the playground of evil spirits, the underworld. Yes, this, too, was now his lot. God was sending him into the desert because he had made Esau wail loudly and bitterly—according to God's will. The full circuit, which on Beth-el's heights had led to a comforting ascent into heaven, was now turning at its westernmost point, where it opened onto the world of hell below, and who knew what awful dragons awaited him there. As he swayed across this wasteland atop the hump of his camel, he wept a little. Ahead of him ran a jackal—with a long dirty yellow body, pointed ears, a tail extended behind—the animal of some doleful god, a disreputable specter. It ran ahead of him, but at times it let the rider get close enough for him to smell its acrid odor, turned its dog's head toward Jacob and looked at him out of small ugly eyes, then giving a short laugh, burst into a trot again. Jacob's knowledge and thoughts were far too rich in associations for him not to recognize the opener of the eternal ways, the guide into the realm of the dead. He would have been quite amazed had it not preceded him, and once again shed a few tears as he followed it into the empty desolation of the region where Syria merges into Naharina—amid gravel and cursed stones, between boulders, over stretches of loamy sand and parched plains with sparse thickets of scrub tamarisk. He was fairly sure of the path, the same route once followed in the opposite direction by his primal father, by Terah's son coming from the place where Jacob hoped to arrive, directed westward, just as he had been told to go east. The thought of Abraham comforted him somewhat in his solitude, which was broken here and there, by the by, with traces of human concern for the comings and goings of travelers. There was occasionally a clay tower to climb, primarily for a look around, but also as an escape if some wild beast threatened the wanderer. There was even a cistern here and there. Best of all, road signs had been set up, inscribed posts and upright stones that could guide one's journey even at night, by just a little light of the beautiful moon—stones that doubtless had once aided Abram on his path. Jacob praised God for civilization's good deeds and let himself be led by Nimrod's signposts pointing toward the river Prath, to the exact point he had in mind, the right and true point, where the Broadest One left its mountain ravines, breaking through from the midnight of the north to flow quietly upon the plain. Oh, it was a great hour when Jacob finally stood in the muck and reeds and could let his poor beast lap up the yellow flood. A pontoon bridge led across, and a city lay on the far side, but not yet the dwelling of the moon god, not yet the City of the Way, Nahor's city. It was still far to the east, beyond the plain across which, with the aid of signposts, he must yet pass, on into Ab's blazing skies. Seventeen days? Ah, the necessity of forever repeating his gory tale of robbers had already made it many more than that—Jacob did not know how many, he had stopped counting and knew only that the earth had certainly not leapt up to greet him, but on the contrary had done its best to deprive him of the goal of his weary wandering. But he never forgot—speaking of it even on his deathbed—how, when he still believed it far off, at a moment when he had the least hope of achieving it, his goal had suddenly, unexpectedly been reached or as good as reached—how it had leapt toward him, so to speak, and with it, the finest and dearest thing it had to offer, something that one day, after a sojourn beyond all surmising, Jacob was to take away with him.

Jacob Joins Laban

One day toward evening, in fact, as the sun set behind him in a pale haze and the towering shadows of rider and beast cast long silhouettes across the plain—on a late afternoon that refused to cool off, with not a breeze stirring under heaven's bronze vault, so that the air, as if on the verge of igniting, flickered above the sparse grasses and the rider's tongue lay parched in his throat, deprived of water now for a good day—Jacob gazed ahead with dulled senses toward two hills that formed a gateway onto wide, rolling country and in the level expanses far beyond he saw a moving dot, which even in his lethargy his eye immediately recognized as a herd of sheep, with dogs and shepherds, all gathered around a well. His good fortune startled him and he heaved a sigh of gratitude to Yah the Most High, but he had only one thought: water. His scorched throat called out the word and he clucked a command to his camel, and—already sensing this godsend, stretching out its neck, and flaring its nostrils—the beast lengthened its stride in a burst of joyous energy.

He was soon so close that he could make out the gaudy marks of ownership on the sheep's backs, the faces of the shepherds under their sun hats, the hair on their chests, the bracelets on their arms. The dogs growled and began barking, while at the same time making sure the sheep did not scatter. Showing no concern, the men hushed them, for they had nothing to fear from a solitary rider and could see that he had been courteously hailing them in peace while still a good way off. As best as Jacob could recall, there had been four or five of them—with perhaps two hundred sheep, a fat-tail breed as his expert eye told him—and they had been squatting or standing idly beside the well, which was still covered by its round stone. They all carried slings, and one of them had a lute with him. Jacob spoke to them right off, calling them "brothers," and with his hand at his brow he took his chances and called out that their god was great, although he was not certain which god they served. In response to which, as to everything else he said, they just looked at each other and shook their heads or, better, rocked them from one shoulder to the other, while clicking their tongues in apology—which was hardly surprising, since they did not understand him. But look there, one of them, with a silver coin at his breast, gave his name as

Jerubbaal, and he had been born in the land of Amurru, so he said. His speech was not exactly the same as Jacob's, but the kinship was close enough for them to understand one another, and Jerubbaal the shepherd could act as interpreter by translating what the traveler said into their own *ummu-ummu* language. They passed on their thanks for the power he had ascribed to their god, invited him to have a seat, and introduced themselves. Their names were Bullutu, Shamash-Lamassi, Ea's Dog, or something of the sort. But there was no need for them to ask him his name and origin, for he hastened to announce both, adding at once an initial bitter reference to the adventure that had plunged him into poverty, and above all a request for water for his tongue. He was given some from a clay bottle, and lukewarm as it was, he blissfully swallowed it. His camel, however, would have to wait to be watered, as was also apparently the case with the sheep, since the stone still lay atop the mouth of the well and for some reason no one had thought of rolling it aside.

And from where did his brothers come, Jacob asked.

"Haran, Haran," they replied. "Bel-Charran, Lord of the Way. Great, great. The greatest."

"One of the greatest in any case," Jacob said deliberately. "But I'm on my way to Haran! Is it far?"

It was not far at all. The city lay just beyond the slope of that hill there. An hour away, even with sheep.

"Wondrous are God's ways!" he cried. "Then I have arrived! After a journey of more than seventeen days. I can scarcely believe it." And he asked them, seeing as they were from Haran, whether they knew Laban, son of Bethuel, son of Nahor?

Indeed they did. He did not live in the city, but only a half hour from here. They were waiting for his sheep.

And was he well?

Quite well. Why?

"Because I've heard of him," Jacob said. "Do you pluck your sheep, or shear them with shears?"

They all responded disdainfully that of course they sheared. Did they perhaps pluck them where he came from?

"Not at all," he replied. Even in and round about Beersheba people had shears by now.

They then turned back to Laban and said they were waiting for Rachel, his daughter.

"I was going to ask you about that," he cried. "About the waiting, I mean. I've been perplexed for some time. You're sitting here around a covered well as if guarding the stone atop it, instead of rolling it away from the mouth, so that your flocks can drink. What is the point? It is a bit early to drive them home, I'll grant, but now that you're here, since you've arrived at the well, you could at least roll the stone away and let your lords' sheep drink, instead of lounging about, even if you are still waiting for the maid you spoke about, Laban's child—what was her name?"

He spoke to these servants reproachfully, like a man who was their better, even though he called them "brothers." For the water had put courage into his body and soul, and he felt himself their superior.

They exchanged *ummu-ummu*s and then let Jerubbaal speak for them: It was only proper that they should wait, it was a matter of courtesy. They could not roll the stone away and water their flocks and drive them home before Rachel arrived with her father's sheep, which she tended. For all the flocks had to be gathered together before they were driven home, and if Rachel came to the well first, ahead of them, she likewise waited until they arrived and rolled it away.

"I can well believe it," Jacob laughed. "She does it because she can't roll the cover off herself, for that requires the arms of men." But they replied that it did not matter why she waited, but that she did wait, and therefore they waited as well.

"Fine," he said, "it occurs to me you're right and that to do otherwise would surely seem improper to you. I'm only sorry my camel must go thirsty so long. What did you say the maid's name was, Rachel?" he repeated. . . . "Jerubbaal, you must tell them what that means in our language. Has this 'mother sheep' we're waiting for cast her first lamb yet?"

Oh no, they said. She was as pure as a lily of the field in spring, as untouched as the petal of a garden rose in the dewy morn, and as yet had never known any man's arms. She was twelve years old.

It was clear to see that they admired her, and Jacob automatically began to do so as well. He sighed and smiled—the curious pleasure of meeting his uncle's daughter made his heart leap lightly within him. With Jerubbaal's help, he chatted a while yet with the men about the local price for sheep and what five minas of wool might bring and how many silas of grain their lord allowed them a month—until one of them said, "There she comes." Jacob was just starting to pass the time by telling his gory tale of the young robbers, but broke off at this announcement and turned in the direction to which the shepherd's arm pointed. And for the first time he saw her, the destiny of his heart, the bride of his soul, the mother sheep of his lamb—for the sake of whose eyes he would serve fourteen years.

Rachel was walking amid a flock of sheep crowding around her, while a dog with its tongue lolling ran along the edge of the woolly throng. Raising her shepherd's staff—her weapon, which she held in the middle and whose metal crook was made from a sickle or hoe—she greeted the men looking her way, laying her head to one side and smiling, the first time, and from a good distance, that Jacob ever saw her very white, gapped teeth. As she drew near she moved past the sheep that had been trotting ahead of her, stepped out from among them, pushing them aside with the tip of her staff. "Here I am," she said, first squinting slightly the way nearsighted people do, but now, raising her eyebrows, she added in happy surprise, "Look there, a stranger!" Surely she must have noticed the incongruous camel and the added figure of Jacob some time before—that is, if her nearsightedness was not all too severe—but in that first moment there was no hint that she had.

The shepherds at the well said nothing and held themselves aloof from this meeting of children of rank. Even Jerubbaal evidently assumed they would manage matters on their own and chewed a few kernels as he stared into the air. While Rachel's dog continued to bark, Jacob greeted her with raised hands. She responded with a few quick words, and there beneath the high, wide, pale sky they stood, face to face, both looking very earnest—caught in the slanting, vivid light of late afternoon and enfolded in the gentle odor rising from the sheep all around them.

Laban's daughter was slight of build, as was evident despite her loose formless yellow robe or smock, which was trimmed with a red border decorated with black moons and running from neckline to the hem, which fell just above her little bare feet. Casually cut, indeed unbelted, the garment fell comfortably in a pleasant, artless flow, but was shaped enough at the shoulders to reveal how touchingly narrow and delicate they were. The sleeves were likewise fitted more closely and covered only half of the upper arm. The girl's black hair was more unkempt than curly. She wore it cut short, shorter at least than Jacob had ever seen women at home wear it, and only two longer strands had been left to fall from beside the ears and along both cheeks, ending in curls at the shoulders. She played with one of them as she stood there looking at him. What a delightful face! Who could describe its magic? Who can explain the interplay of the sweet, happy features out of which life, by drawing here and there upon heredity and adding unique touches, creates the grace of a human countenance—the charm that sits on the razor's edge, that, one might say, always hangs by a thread, so that if the smallest trait, one small muscle, were placed differently, though a great deal would still remain, all the bewitchment that delights others' hearts would be gone? Rachel was handsome and beautiful, in both sly and gentle ways, from within her soul. You could see—and Jacob saw it as she looked at him—that behind this loveliness, indeed at its source, were both will and intellect molded into feminine courage and wisdom. She looked at him now with such total expressiveness, such an alert eagerness for life. With one hand at a braid, the other clasping the staff that loomed over her, she measured the young man, gaunt from his long journey and dressed in a dusty, faded, ragged tunic; and as she gazed at his brown beard, at his dark sweaty face—which was not the face of a servant—the rather too thick nostrils of her little nose seemed to widen in a slight droll flair and her upper lip, extending just a bit beyond the lower and joining it at the corner of the mouth, formed, without any tightening of muscles, the dearest hint of a serene smile. But prettiest and most beautiful of all was the look in her black and slightly slanting eyes, sweetened and strangely transfigured by her nearsightedness, a look into which nature, let it be said without exaggeration, had poured all the charm it can lend to any human gaze—a deep, flowing, melting, cordial night that spoke both in earnest and in play—such as Jacob had never seen before, or had ever thought to see.

"Marduka, hush!" she called, bending down to scold the noisy dog. And she asked a question Jacob could easily guess without understanding the words. "And from where does my lord come?"

He pointed over his shoulder, toward the lowering sun, and said, "Amurru."

She turned around to Jerubbaal and signaled to him with her chin and a smile. "From so far," she said with gestures and lips. And then apparently inquired more closely as to his home, describing the western land as vast and naming two or three of its cities.

"Beersheba," Jacob replied.

Startled, she repeated the word. And her mouth, which he had already begun to love, named the name of Isaak.

His face twitched, his gentle eyes overflowed. He did not know Laban's people and had not been impatient to have dealings with them. He was a fugitive, abducted into the underworld, not here of his own free will, and there was little reason for him to feel happiness stirring within him. But worn down by the strain of his wanderings, his nerves gave way. He had arrived at his goal, and the girl whose eyes were filled with sweet darkness and who named the name of his faraway father was his mother's brother's child.

"Rachel," he said with a sob, and with trembling hands he extended his arms toward her, "may I kiss you?"

"And just why should you be allowed to do that?" she said, stepping back and laughing in astonishment. She was no more ready to admit what she surmised than she had been willing to admit noticing the stranger right off.

But with one arm outstretched to her, he kept pointing at his own breast. "Jacob! Jacob!" he said. "I! Yitzchak's son, Rebekah's son, Laban, you, I, mother's child, brother's child . . ."

She let out a soft cry. And while she still held him from her with one hand at his chest, they rehearsed the relationship for one another, both with tears in their eyes, laughing, nodding, calling out names, showing each other the line of descent by various signs—placing forefingers together, crossing them, or laying the left across the tip of the right.

"Laban—Rebekah!" she cried. "Bethuel, son of Nahor and Milcah, grandfather, yours, mine!"

"Terah! he cried. "Abram—Isaak! Nahor—Bethuel! Abraham, first father, yours, mine!"

"Laban—Adina!" she cried. "Leah and Rachel! Sisters, cousins, yours!"

They nodded over and over again and laughed amid their tears, united by the blood bond flowing from both his parents and her father. She presented him her cheeks, and he kissed them solemnly. Three dogs leapt up at them, barking with the excitement animals feel when people lay hands upon one another, whether for good or evil. The shepherds broke into rhythmic applause and rejoiced in resonant falsetto: "Loo, loo, loo!" And so he kissed her, first on one cheek and then the other. But as he did he forbade his senses to respond to anything more than the girl's tender cheeks; he kissed her reverently and solemnly. But what a fine thing that he was allowed to kiss her right off, for he was already smitten by the cordial night of her eyes. Many a man must look for a long time, must wish and serve, before the almost incomprehensible is made possible and he is permitted to do what simply fell into Jacob's lap because he was a cousin from far off.

When he let go of her, she laughed and rubbed the palms of her hands over where his beard from the journey had tickled her, and cried, "So be quick now, Jerubbaal! Bullutu! Roll the stone from the well, so that the sheep may drink, and make sure they do, both yours and mine, and water my cousin Jacob's camel and be swift and smart at it, my good men, for meanwhile I shall run without delay to Laban, my father, and tell him that Jacob has come, his sister's son. He is out in the fields not far from here and will come running in haste and joy to embrace him. Hurry, then, and follow after me, I shall run hotfoot . . ."

Jacob caught the sense of all this from her gestures and tone, and even some of the words. For the sake of her eyes, he had already begun to learn the language of the land. And as she was running off, he held the shepherds back in a voice loud enough for her to hear, and said, "Wait, brothers, leave the stone. That is Jacob's task! You have guarded it well as good watchmen, but I wish to roll it away from the hole for my cousin Rachel all by myself! For the journey has not consumed all the manly strength in my arms, and it is only just that I lend their strength to Laban's daughter and roll the stone, so that the blackness may be taken from this moon, and the circle of water may shine fair for us."

They let him pass, and calling on all his strength, he rolled the lid off, though it was not the work of just one man, and moved the heavy stone aside, even if his arms were not the strongest. The animals crowded around, all the voices of goats, sheep, and lambs rising in a many-toned chorus of bleats, and Jacob's beast of burden likewise grunted as it got to its feet. The men dipped and poured the living water into the troughs. With Jacob's help they watched over the watering, driving off those who had drunk their fill and letting the thirsty in, and when all the animals had had enough, they put the stone back over the hole, covering it with earth and grass, so that no one would recognize the spot and make use of the well without having asked, and drove all the sheep home together, both Laban's and their masters'—and atop his camel Jacob towered above the throng.

The Clod of Earth

It was not long before a man wearing a cap with a neck flap came running up, but then stopped short. It was Laban, Bethuel's son. He always ran on such occasions—it was a now a couple of decades, a generation that had simply flown past, since he had come running just like this, the day he found Eliezer, the matchmaker, with his ten camels and retinue waiting beside the well and had said to him, "Come in, O blessed of the Lord!" Though now a graybeard, he ran again, for Rachel had announced to him that Jacob was here from Beersheba—not a servant, but Abram's grandson, his sister's son. But he stopped short in order to let the man come to him, for he had seen no trace of a golden band on Rachel's brow, or bracelets at her hands like Rebekah had had, and he likewise noted that the stranger came not as a lord with a well-stocked caravan, but obviously all alone and riding a gaunt, worn-out beast. That was why he did not want to compromise himself by taking the last steps to greet his ostensible nephew, why he was full of mistrust and stood there with arms crossed, waiting for Jacob to approach him.

As ashamed and uneasy as he was, with a bad conscience about both his poverty and indigent dependence, Jacob understood all of it well enough. Ah, he had come not as a rich envoy, making a grand entrance, bewitching everyone with gifts of hefty value pulled from his saddlebags, and asking to remain a day, or perhaps ten. He found himself an empty-handed fugitive with no roof over his head and no possibility of returning home—a beggar in search of shelter, with every cause for faltering humility. And yet he at once saw through the sullen man standing before him and understood that it would not be wise to appear all too wretched to him. And so he was in no particular hurry as he got down off his camel and stepped before Laban exuding all the dignity of his lineage, greeting him properly, and saying, "My father and brother. Rebekah, your sister, has sent me that she might pay you her respects in bidding me to spend some time beneath your roof, and I greet you in her name and in the name of Yitzchak, her lord and mine, and in the name of those fathers we likewise share in common, and call upon Abram's God to safeguard your health and that of your wife and children."

"The same to you," said Laban, who had grasped the main essentials. "And so you are truly Rebekah's son?"

"Truly," he replied. "I am Yitzchak's firstborn, as you yourself have said. Might I suggest that you not be misled by my having arrived alone, or by my garment which has been rotted by the sun. You shall hear an explanation for all this from my lips in due time, and will see that though I have nothing except that which is most important, that I do indeed have—and if you were to say to me, 'O blessed of the Lord!' you would be hitting the nail on the head."

After first having the shepherd Jerubbaal repeat this for him in *ummu-ummu*, Laban sullenly said, "Then accept my embrace." He placed his arms on Jacob's shoulders, bent forward to one side—first to the right, then the left—and kissed the air. Jacob's immediate impressions of this uncle were very equivocal. Laban had two nasty creases between his eyes, one of which squinted and kept blinking, though he appeared to see more with this almost totally closed eye than with the other wide-open one. Beneath his grizzled beard and on that same side of his face, there was a pronounced underworldly set to the mouth, a slack droop at one corner that resembled a sour smile and likewise gave Jacob pause for thought. But for the rest, Laban was a strong man, with locks of fully gray hair curling out from under the neck flap. He was dressed in a knee-length tunic, with a whip and knife stuck in at the belt, and its narrow sleeves revealed his sinewy and heavily veined forearms. These, too, were covered with black and gray hair, as were his muscular thighs, and ended in broad, warm, and equally hairy hands, the hands of a man who held on to what he had, of a man confined by his gloomy earthbound thoughts—of a true clod of earth, so Jacob thought. Yet his uncle's face might indeed have been handsome, with its heavy, low-set, and still very black eyebrows, its fleshy nose joined in a straight line to the brow, and full lips under his beard. Rachel obviously had his eyes—as Jacob observed with that mixed sense of recognition, tenderness, and jealousy by which one is instructed about the inherited origins and natural history of those whose life and appearance are dear to us: a happy lesson, insofar as it allows us to probe the intimacy of such appearances, to get behind them, as it were, and yet again somehow offensive, so that our reaction to the bearers of the prototype is a peculiar combination of awe and antipathy.

Laban said, "Welcome, then, and follow me, stranger, you who call yourself—and, as I am ready to believe, rightly so—my nephew. As we once had room for Eliezer and straw and fodder for his ten camels, so we shall have room for you and your camel—your only one, evidently. Your mother sent no presents with you, then, no gold, garments, spices, and such?"

"She sent them in great abundance, of that you can be certain," Jacob replied. "And you shall hear why I do not have these things once I've washed my feet and had something to eat."

He spoke his demands quite deliberately as a way of asserting himself over against this clod of earth, who in turn was amazed at such self-confidence amid such poverty. They said nothing more then until they had arrived at Laban's farm, where the shepherds of the other flocks took their leave and continued on toward town, while Jacob helped the owner coop up his own sheep inside a pen of clay walls topped with wattle as a protection against beasts of prey. From the roof of the house three women watched them work; one of them was Rachel, the second Laban's wife, and the third Leah, the older daughter, who was cross-eyed. The house, indeed the entire settlement—for the dwelling was surrounded by several reed huts and beehive-shaped storehouses—made quite an impression on Jacob, who lived in tents, but who in the course of his trip had indeed seen far more beautiful dwellings in cities and was not about to let any sort of admiration be noticed. In fact he found fault with the house right off, remarking offhandedly that the wooden ladder leading to the roof from outside really ought to be replaced by a brick stairway, and the whole thing needed whitewashing and those ground-floor windows should be latticed.

"There's a stairway leading up from the courtyard," Laban said. "My house does well enough for me."

"Don't say that!" Jacob said. "If a man is easily content, then God is content for him as well and draws His hand of blessing from him. How many sheep does my uncle have?"

"Eighty," his host replied.

"And goats?"

"About thirty."

"But no cattle at all?"

Laban indignantly pointed his beard in the direction of a closed pen of clay and wattle, which was evidently a cow stall, but he offered no count.

"There will have to be more," Jacob said. "More of every kind of animal." And Laban cast him a sullen glance, but beneath their gloom his eyes were curious and probing. Then they turned toward the house.

The Evening Meal

Towered over by several tall poplars—the bark of one had been split from top to bottom by lightning—the house was a rude structure of fairly modest dimensions and made of clay bricks already crumbling a little, but its airy upper floor lent it a certain architectural charm; for the roof, covered with a layer of earth and furnished with a few reed sheds, rested directly on masonry only at the center and the corners, while the rest was set on wooden posts. It would be better to speak of several roofs, for the house was open in the middle and formed a quadrangle of four wings surrounding a small courtyard. A few steps of well-trodden clay led to the palm-wood door.

Two or three artisan slaves—a potter and a baker slapping barley dough against the interior wall of his little oven—were at work among the sheds in the courtyard, across which uncle and nephew now strode. A maid in a loincloth was carrying water, fetched from the nearest artificial waterway, called the Bel Canal, which was the source of irrigation for Laban's beloved field of barley and sesame some distance away, but which in turn drew its water from the Ellil Canal. The Bel Canal belonged to a merchant in town, who had had it dug, and for the use of its water Laban had to pay him onerous quantities of oil, grain, and wool. Beyond the field the open plain rolled on as far as the horizon, above which rose the tiered tower of the moon temple of Haran.

The women had descended from the roof and were awaiting their lord and his guest in the front hallway, onto which the house door opened and into whose plastered clay floor had been set a great mortar for pounding grain. Adina, Laban's wife, was an unprepossessing matron with a necklace of gaudy gemstones, a headscarf draped over her tight-fitting cap and covering her hair, and a face whose joyless expression was reminiscent of her spouse's, except that the set of her mouth was not so much sour as bitter. She had no sons, and that may well help explain Laban's gloominess as well. Later Jacob learned that early in their marriage the couple had indeed had a little son, but that when building the house they had sacrificed him by burying him alive in its foundation inside a clay pot, along with lamps and keys, so as to call down from on high blessing and prosperity for both house and farm. Not only had the offering not brought any special blessing, but ever since Adina had also proved incapable of giving birth to boys.

As for Leah, she appeared no less well-formed than Rachel, was in fact taller and more stately, but exemplified how a flawless body can be so strangely devalued by an ugly countenance. She certainly had extraordinarily rich ash blond hair, covered on top by a small cap and falling in a heavy gathered knot at the back of her neck. But her green-gray eyes crossed woefully as they gazed down her long and reddened nose, and the scabby lids of her eyes were red, too, as were her hands, which she tried to hide, just as she tried to hide the skewed look of her eyes by constantly lowering her lids in a kind of coy dignity. There we have it, Jacob thought, gazing at the sisters, the feeble moon and the beautiful moon. But it was to Leah and not to Rachel that he spoke as they crossed the little paved courtyard, in the middle of which stood a sacrificial altar; but like the shepherds in the field before, she just kept clicking her tongue in apology, obviously putting him off by letting the interpreter intervene, a man whose Canaanite name she repeated several times, a household servant named Abdcheba—the same man, as it turned out, who had been baking cakes in the courtyard outside. For once they had climbed the brick stairs, which led on up to the roof, and entered the open upstairs room where they were to have their meal, he brought Jacob water for his feet and hands and explained that he had been born in a village under the protection of Urusalim, but was sold into slavery by parents in direst need, and had since passed through many hands at the going rate of twenty shekels, which evidently defined his own middling sense of self-worth. He was short, gray-haired, and sunken-chested, but quick with his tongue and could immediately translate each phrase Jacob uttered into the local language, and just as promptly and fluently clarify the answer.

The room where they seated themselves was long and narrow, a quite pleasant, airy spot—between posts bearing the roof you saw to one side the darkening plains and to the other the peaceful quadrangle of the interior courtyard with its colorful awnings, pebbled floor, and wooden gallery. Evening was falling. The maid in the loincloth who had been carrying water now brought fire from the hearth and lit three clay lamps set atop tripods. Together with Abdcheba she then brought in the food: a pot of thick porridge seasoned with sesame oil—"Pappasu, pappasu," Rachel repeated with childish glee, clapping her hands and letting her little tongue wander droll and wanton between her lips. There were also warm barley cakes, radishes, cucumbers, and hearts of palm, with goat's milk and canal water to drink, supplied from a large clay amphora hanging from one of the roof beams. Set against the room's outer wall were two clay chests filled with various copper bowls, assorted vessels, a hand mill, and goblets. In varied positions and at irregular intervals, the family was seated for the meal around a table raised only slightly above the floor and covered in cow's leather. Laban and his wife squatted side by side on a couch, the daughters sat with their legs tucked under them on cane stools fitted with pillows, and Jacob had been given an armless chair of brightly painted clay and a footstool of the same material to prop his feet on. For the pappasu they shared two cow-horn spoons, each diner at once refilling it from the pot after use and passing it on to the next person. Jacob, who was sitting beside Rachel, filled her spoon so full each time that it made her laugh. Leah saw this, and her eyes crossed now in great and utter distress.

While they ate, almost nothing of importance was said, only such things as concerned the meal. For instance, Adina said to Laban, "Eat, my husband. It all belongs to you." Or she remarked to Jacob, "Help yourself, foreigner, and delight your weary soul."

Or one of the parents might say to one of the daughters, "I see that you are taking the lion's share and leaving nothing for the others. If you do not bridle your greediness, the witch Labartu will turn your innards upside-down and cause you to vomit."

Abdcheba did not fail to provide a precise translation of even these bagatelles for Jacob, and the latter was already taking part in the conversation, saying to Laban in the local language. "Eat, father and brother, all is yours." Or to Rachel, "Help yourself, sister, delight your soul."

Both Abdcheba and the maid in the loincloth took their meal, though with interruptions, at the same time they served their masters—now and then suddenly squatting down on the floor to quickly devour a radish, alternating this the next time with a drink from a bowl of goat's milk. The maid, who was named Iltani, frequently used the fingertips of both hands to brush crumbs from her long breasts.

When they had eaten, Laban ordered strong drink be brought for him and his guest. Abdcheba dragged over a skin full of fermented emmer beer, and as he filled two goblets from it—and placed straws in them as well, for a great deal of grain still floated on top—the women withdrew from the men, but not until Laban had perfunctorily laid his hands on the head of each of them. They likewise took their leave of Jacob for the night, and he once again gazed into the cordial night of Rachel's eyes—for she was looking into his—and at the white, gapped teeth of her mouth as she said with a smile, "Much pappasu, in spoon, heaped high!"

"Abraham—first father—yours, mine," he replied as if by way of explanation, and once again placed one forefinger across the tip of the other; and they nodded as they had out in the field—while her mother smiled a bitter smile, Leah gazed cross-eyed down her nose, and her father's face retained its blinking, slack gloom. The uncle and his nephew were now alone in the airy upstairs room, with only Abdcheba sitting close by on the floor, still short of breath from serving the meal, and fixing his gaze on the lips first of one and then the other.

Jacob and Laban Strike a Deal

"Speak now, my guest," the lord of the house said after he had taken a drink, "and reveal to me the circumstances of your life."

Thus in considerable detail Jacob reported to him all those matters, truthfully and precisely, just as they had happened. At most he glossed over particulars in his encounter with Eliphaz somewhat, although here, too, in light of his obvious naked and unburdened state, he gave truth its due. From time to time, after having offered a considerable, but still absorbable, quantity of material, he would break off and wave his hand down at Abdcheba, who would translate; and Laban, who drank a good deal of beer in the course of the narrative, gloomily listened to it all, blinking and sometimes nodding. Jacob stuck to the facts. He did not say that what had happened between him, Esau, and his parents was good or bad, but announced it frankly as a god-fearing man. For in the end he could depend on one great and decisive fact, which, however it may have come to pass, retained its full import in any case and even robbed his momentary naked and unburdened state of any higher significance—and that fact was: He and no other was the bearer of the blessing.

Laban listened, blinking gravely. He had sucked so hard at his straw and partaken of so much strong drink that his face was like a waning moon when it rises late for its journey, an ominous dark red; and his body was bloated as well, so that after loosening his belt and letting his coat fall from his shoulders, he now sat there in his shirt, his muscular arms folded across his half-bared, fleshy chest matted with black and gray curls. Bending forward ponderously and rounding his back, he squatted on his couch and, as a skilled practical businessman, countered with questions concerning this asset of which the man opposite him boasted and to which he, Laban, was careful to avoid giving any undue recognition. He deliberately raised doubts. This asset did not seem free of debt to him. Granted, Jacob had sufficiently stressed the point: In the end Esau was the man of the curse, and the blessing rested upon his brother. But even that blessing, given the manner in which it had been gained, came bound up with some curse, the consequences of which, whatever shape they took, were certain. Everyone knew the ways of the gods—and one was no different from the other, whether you were dealing with the local divinities, with whom Laban of course had to maintain good relations, or with the unnamed or, better, vaguely named God of Isaak's people, of whom he knew and whom he likewise conditionally recognized. The gods expressed their wishes and let them come to pass; but the guilt was all man's. The asset on which Jacob was relying was a possession encumbered with guilt, and the question was on whom that guilt would devolve. Jacob assured him that

he himself was free and pure. He had done hardly anything, but simply let happen what was meant to happen, and even that only with
the greatest inner reluctance. At most it was energetic Rebekah who
was encumbered by guilt, for she had initiated it all. "Let the curse
be upon my head," she had said, only just in case, of course—in case,
that is, his father had become aware of the deception. But that statement was an expression of her relationship to the enterprise in general, of the responsibility she had taken upon herself, and like a good
mother she had held him, the child, to be free of all guilt.

"Yes, like a good mother," Laban said. The beer was making him
breathe heavily through his mouth, and his upper body was tipped
forward and to one side. He sat up, swayed, and sagged to the other.
"Like a mother, a mother and a parent. Like a god." For parents and
gods blessed their darlings in the same ambiguous way. Their blessing was power and came from power, for love—in particular—was
sheer power, and gods and parents blessed their darlings out of love
with a powerful life, powerful in both its happiness and its curse.
That was the substance of it; that was the blessing. "Let the curse be
upon my head": those were merely fine words and a mother's chatter, spoken out of ignorance that love is power, that blessing is
power, that life is power and nothing else. Rebekah was only a
woman, but he, Jacob, was the blessed one—the fundamental guilt
of deception lay upon what was in his possession. "It will devolve
on you," Laban said with a heavy tongue, pointing a heavy arm,
a heavy hand, at his nephew. "You deceived, and you shall be
deceived—Abdcheba, put your mouth to work and translate that for
him, you wretch. I bought you for twenty shekels, and if you nod
off instead of translating, I will bury you in the ground up to your
lower lip for a week, you ninny."

"Stop. Shame on you," Jacob said, and spat. "Does my father
and brother curse me? What do you suppose this is all about—am I
your flesh and blood or not?"

"That you are," Laban replied, "you are right in that regard. You
have accurately told me about Rebekah and Isaak and Esau, the red
one, and you are Jacob, my sister's son, that has been proved. Accept
my embrace. But the facts of the case must be examined on the basis
of your statements, and consequences drawn both for you and me
according to the laws of commerce. I am convinced of the truth of
your report, but have no reason to admire your candor, for to

explain your situation you had little choice but to be candid. It is not correct, then, to say as you did before that Rebekah sent you so that she might pay me her respects. It was rather because you could not remain at home, for Esau threatened your life as a result of your and your mother's deed, the success of which I will not deny, but which for the present has made a naked beggar of you. You did not come to me of your own free will, but because you had nowhere to lay your head. You are at my mercy, and I must draw the consequences. You are not a guest in my house, but my servant."

"My uncle speaks justly, but without adding the salt of love to his justice," Jacob said.

"Fancy phrases," Laban replied. "These are the natural rigors of commercial life that I am accustomed to taking into account. The bankers in Haran, two brothers, Ishullanu's sons, likewise demand of me what they wish, because I have urgent need of their water, and knowing I need it, they make whatever demand suits them, and if I cannot meet it, they will sell me and my goods and pocket the takings. I'll not play the fool in this world. You are at my mercy, and I shall fleece you. I am not rich and blessed enough to puff myself up with love of charity and keep an open house for every fugitive. The only strong arm I have to drudge for me is that feeble toad there, plus Iltani, the maid, who is dumb as a chicken and cackles like a hen, for the potter is a journeyman and I have contracted his labor for only ten days, and when the time of harvest comes or of shearing, I do not know where I shall find strong arms, for I cannot pay. It long ago became improper to send my younger daughter, Rachel, to tend sheep and suffer the heat of day and the chill of night. That is for you to do, in return for a roof and provender, but nothing else, for you have nowhere to go and are not a man to set the conditions—those are the facts of the case."

"I shall gladly tend sheep for your child Rachel," Jacob said, "and serve for her sake, that her life may be easier. I am a born shepherd and understand the breeding of sheep and indeed wish to do it well. It was not my intent to play the sluggard, to be a useless mouth for you to feed. But now that I hear I shall exert the full manly strength of my arm for Rachel, your child, I am that much more willing to serve."

"Is that so?" Laban asked, the corner of his mouth drooping, and he stared at him, blinking hard. "Fine," he said. "You must do so for good or ill, such are the constraints of commercial life. But if you do it gladly, then it is to your advantage, yet with no inconvenience to me. We shall set it in writing tomorrow."

"You see?" Jacob said. "There is such a thing: advantages that serve both sides and ease natural rigors. You wouldn't have thought it. You did not wish to add salt's zest to justice, so I shall provide my own, naked and unburdened though I be at the moment."

"Fancy phrases," Laban concluded. "We shall draw up a contract and seal it in orderly fashion, so no one can contest it by illegal conduct. Go now, I am sleepy and bloated with beer. Douse the lamps, toad," he said to Abdcheba, stretched out on his couch, covered himself with his coat, and fell asleep with his mouth hanging open. Jacob could make his bed wherever he wished. He climbed to the roof, spread a blanket under the awning of a small reed tent erected there, and thought of Rachel's eyes, until sleep kissed him.

Part Five

IN LABAN'S SERVICE

How Long Jacob Remained with Laban

This marked the beginning of Jacob's sojourn in Laban's realm and in the land of Aram Naharaim, which he aptly and privately named Land of Kurungia: first, because from the start and in general it was for him a land of the underworld, to which he had hastily had to emigrate, but second because it turned out that with the passing years this land embraced by rivers held fast to its man, evidently never gave him up again and truly and literally proved to be a Land of No Return. Does "no" mean "never"? And what does "never" mean? It means no return for as long as the self retains its state and form, at least in rough contour, and is still the same self. A return that occurs twenty-five years later no longer affects the same self that, when it departed, expected to return in a half a year, or in three years at most and, with the episode now behind it, to be able to pick up the thread of life again where it had been broken off—for that self there is no return, ever. Twenty-five years are not an episode, they are life itself; they are, when they begin in a man's young years, the core and foundation of life, and though Jacob would live for a long time after his return and experience things most difficult and glorious—for, by our close calculation, he was one hundred and six years old when he solemnly departed this life in yet another underworldly land—one can say that it was while he was with Laban in the land of Aram that he did indeed dream the dream of his life. There he loved, he married, there four women bore him all his children, except for the youngest, twelve in number, there he became weighed down with goods and grew in dignity, and never returned as a young man, but as an aging man of fifty-five years, a nomadic sheik from the East, leading very great flocks, arrived in the western land, more or less a foreign country, and moved on toward Shechem.

That Jacob remained with Laban for twenty-five years is verifiably true, the certain result of any fair-minded investigation. In this regard both song and tradition betray the sort of imprecise thinking that we can excuse in them more easily than we would in ourselves. They would have it that Jacob spent a total of twenty years with Laban: fourteen plus six. In apportioning the time in this fashion they maintain that several years before bursting the dusty bars and fleeing, he had demanded his release from Laban, but having been denied it, had pledged himself to stay on under new stipulations. The point in time when he demanded this is said to have occurred "when Rachel had borne Joseph." But when was that? If only fourteen years had passed until then, all twelve children, including Dinah and Joseph, and excluding only Benjamin, would have to have been born to him within those fourteen or, more correctly, those last seven years—and with four women hard at work that would not have been impossible per se, but given the sequence of births arranged by God it did not happen that way. In that sequence, sweet-toothed Asher, Joseph's senior by five years, was born *after* the two times seven years had passed, that is in the eighth year of marriage, and as can be shown in detail it is not possible for Rachel to have borne Joseph earlier than two years after the appearance of sea-loving Zebulun, that is in the thirteenth year of marriage or in the twentieth year at Haran. How could it be otherwise? Joseph was a child of Jacob's old age, who therefore must have been fifty years old when his favorite appeared, which means that he must already have spent twenty years with Laban by then. But since of those twenty only two times seven, which makes fourteen, were actually years of service, that leaves between them and Jacob's giving notice and signing on to a new contract, yet another six years without a contract, a period that represents an unspoken continuance of Jacob's relationship with Laban, but that, given his ultimate riches, must be counted together with the final five years spent again under contract. For though those five years may help provide the best and most important explanation of how the man became so rich beyond measure, they would most definitely not have sufficed to create a fortune celebrated with the most opulent particulars in song and saga. Granted, considerable exaggeration has crept into the account—we immediately recognize as untenable the assertion that Jacob owned two hundred thousand sheep. But they did number many thousands, not to mention his holdings in other animals, precious metals, and slaves, and Laban's statement, once he had caught up with his fleeing son-in-law, that he should give back to him what he had "stolen" by day and "stolen" by night would not have been even vaguely justifiable, would have been totally meaningless, if Jacob had enriched himself solely on the basis of the new contract—that is, if previously, during that intervening period, he had not been engaged in business more or less for himself and thereby established the basis for his later wealth.

Twenty-five years—and for Jacob they passed like a dream, the way life passes as we live it, in yearning and achievement, in expectation, disappointment, and fulfillment, made up of days that are not counted, but each of which gives what it gives, of days completed one by one, in waiting and striving, in patience and impatience, and melting into larger units, into months, years, groups of years, each of which in the end is like a single day. It is debatable which makes time pass better and more swiftly: uniformity or articulating variety—the upshot, in any event, is that we pass our time. Alive, we strive onward, strive to put time behind us, strive in reality toward death, all the while thinking we are striving for life's goals and turning points. And though a man's time be articulated and divided into epochs, it is nevertheless and likewise monotonously uniform as *his* time, slipping by under the immutable preconditions of his ego, so that as he passes his time, passes his life, both beneficial energies—uniformity and articulation—are simultaneously at work.

Ultimately, apportioning time is a quite arbitrary act, not very different from drawing lines in water. You can draw them one way or another, and even as you draw them it all gathers again into a broad unity. We have already variously divided Jacob's five times five years at Haran into twenty plus five and into fourteen plus six plus five; he himself, however, may well have divided them into the first seven until his marriage, the thirteen during which the children arrived, plus the five supplemental years, much as the five leap days of the sun's year exceed twelve times thirty. In that way or perhaps in some other is how he would have reckoned it. In any case, there were twenty-five in all, uniform not only because they were all exclusively Jacob's years, but also because the external circumstances of one almost monotonously resembled that of another, and variations in viewpoint as they were being lived could not diminish their uniformity as they slipped away.

Jacob and Laban Cement Their Deal

A segment, an era if you will, was established almost immediately in Jacob's life only a month later, when the contract that had been concluded with Laban the day after his arrival was annulled and replaced by one whose totally different conditions bound him all the more firmly. The morning after Jacob's arrival Laban did indeed take steps to have the relationship between his house and his nephew legalized in writing and in accord with the earthbound practical decisions he had made over his beer. Early that morning, they departed on asses for the city of Haran: Laban, Jacob, and the slave Abdcheba, who was to serve as a witness before the judicial notary. This official had set up his chair in a courtyard crowded with people come to document the concluding or contesting of all sorts of contracts dealing with purchases and sales, leases, rental agreements, barter arrangements, marriages, and divorces, and, together with two other junior scribes or assistants who squatted at his side, he had his hands full satisfying the many demands of his urban and rural clientele, so that Laban's people had to wait a good while before it was their turn to do business—insignificant business, by the way, and quickly executed. In order to have a second witness, Laban had first had to disburse a little corn and oil in payment to a man who loitered about in the hope of just such exigencies. He and Abdcheba, then, were the guarantors of the contract, and both set their seal to it by pressing a thumbnail into the convex back of the clay tablet. Laban owned a cylinder seal, and Jacob, who had been relieved of his, used the hem of his coat as his seal. This legalized the simple text that had been scratched into clay by a junior scribe at the perfunctory dictation of the judicial notary: Laban, the breeder of sheep, took such and such a man from the land of Amurru, the homeless son of such and such a man, to be his indentured servant until further notice, the latter to place all the strength of his body and mind in the service of Laban's house and farm in return for no other payment than what his body required. No abrogation, no legal recourse, no lawsuits. Any party who might act illegally and attempt to rise up against and dispute this contract in the future would have his suit declared null and void, and for that there was a fine of five minas of silver. The end. Laban had to cover the costs of the written contract, and he did so with a couple of copper coins that he tossed onto the scales with a grumble and a curse. Secretly, however, he found this small expenditure well worth the bargain rate at which Jacob had obligated himself, for Laban laid far greater store by Yitzchak's blessing than had been apparent in his conversation with his nephew; and it would be underestimating his business acumen to assume that he did not realize from the very start what a good catch he had made in adding Jacob to his household. He was a gloomy man, without favor before the gods and without trust in his own good luck—which also explained why he had had so little success in his enterprises until now. Not for a moment did he fail to recognize what splendid use he could make of a co-worker who bore a blessing.

Which was why after signing the contract he was in a relatively good mood, purchasing a few items in the narrow streets—cloth, provisions, and small utensils—and demanding his companion express amazement at the city and its noisy bustle: at the thickness of its walls and bastions; at the charm of the encompassing, generously watered gardens, where grapevines entwined the date palms; at the sacred splendor of the walled temple E-hulhul, with its courtyards and silver-hammered gates guarded by bronze bulls; at the loftiness of the tiered tower set upon a huge raised mound and encircled by ramps, a tiled monster of seven hues, azure blue at the top, so that the crowning shrine—where the god could alight to find the wedding bed set up for him there—appeared to shimmer and melt into the blue of the upper air. But Jacob had only a few "hmms" and "my mys" for these sights. Cities were not to his taste, and he loved neither the clamor and confusion nor the pomp of extravagant buildings that put on airs of the eternal but that in his opinion were doomed—no matter how skillfully drained the brick mountain might be, how cleverly secured with pitch and reed mats—and would perish within a space of time that at least in God's eyes was very short. He was homesick for the pastures of Beersheba; but the pretensions of the city weighing heavily on his shepherd's sensibilities made even Laban's farm now seem almost like home—where, moreover, he had left behind a pair of black eyes that had gazed back at him with the most exceptional eagerness and with which, so it seemed to him, some highly important matters had yet to be arranged. It was of those eyes that he thought while casting distracted glances at ramshackle pomposities, of them and of the God who had promised to watch over his footsteps in foreign lands and bring him home a rich man, the God of Abram, for whom he felt jealous at the sight of Bel-Haran's house and court, that fortress of idolatry watched over by wild oxen and serpentlike griffins, in whose innermost chamber, a cell made of gilded cedar beams and sparking with gems, the bearded statue of the idol stood on its silver pedestal, content to be censed and flattered in formal royal rituals— while Jacob's God, whom he believed greater than all others, greater to the point of being the one and only, had no house upon earth whatever, but could be honored simply under trees and on hilltops. He doubtlessly wanted it no other way, and Jacob was proud that his God disdained and prohibited such earthly, urban ostentation, because none of it would have satisfied Him. But a suspicion was mixed with Jacob's pride, and together those feelings gave rise to his jealousy: the suspicion that God would indeed have liked very much to live in a house of enamel, gilded cedar, and carbuncles, but that it would have had to be seven times more beautiful than the house of this moon idol, and that God forbade it precisely because He could not yet have it, because His people were not yet countless and strong enough to build it for Him. "Just you wait," Jacob thought, "and meanwhile boast of the splendor of your great lord Bel. At Beth-el God promised to make me a rich man, and He has it in His power to make those who believe in Him heavy with riches, and once we are, we shall build Him a house, made of naught but gold, sapphire, jasper, and crystal inside and out, and all the houses of your divinities, your male and female idols, will pale before it. The past is dreadful and the present is powerful, for it springs up before our eyes. But without doubt what is greatest and most holy is the future, and it comforts the hard-pressed heart of him to whom it is promised."

Jacob's Prospects

As late as it was when uncle and nephew returned home, Laban still insisted that the contract tablet be placed in the cellar of his house that very night, for that was where such documents were stored. Jacob, like Laban carrying a lighted lamp, accompanied him. The chamber lay under the planks of the ground-floor room on the left side of the house, opposite the gallery where they had eaten the evening before, and functioned as archive, chapel, and crypt all in one—for Bethuel's bones had been laid to rest here in a clay chest that stood in the middle of the room, surrounded by bowls with offerings of food and incense pans set on tripods; and somewhere here as well, deeper in the ground or in a side wall perhaps, must likewise have been the clay pot with the remains of Laban's sacrificed little boy. There was a niche at the back of the cellar with a cube-shaped altar of bricks in front and low narrow benches to both sides, on one of which, to the right, lay all sorts of written tablets: receipts, bills, and contracts brought here for safekeeping. On the other bench, however, stood a row of little idols, some ten or twelve of them, curious-looking things, some with tall caps and bearded childlike faces, some bald and beardless and dressed either in scaly skirts with their upper bodies bare and their little hands peacefully crossed just beneath the chin or in pleated robes—though the modeled clay was not of the best craftsmanship—beneath the hems of which plump little toes were visible. These were Laban's household spirits and little soothsayers, his teraphim, to which he was fiercely attached and to which the sullen man would descend for consultation on all important matters. They protected his house, as he explained to Jacob, were fairly dependable at predicting the weather, advised him whether he should buy or sell, were capable of giving hints as to what direction a stray sheep had wandered, and so forth.

Jacob was not at all comfortable with the bones, the receipts, the idols, and he was happy to return back up the ladder leading down into this underworld through the hole of a little trapdoor and to find sleep in the world above. Laban had made devotions at Bethuel's chest, placing fresh water beside it for the refreshment of the deceased, which he called a "water offering," and had bowed in worship before the teraphim—it wouldn't have been all that surprising had he prayed to his commercial documents. Jacob, who approved of neither any sort of worship of the dead nor adoration of idols, was saddened by the lack of clarity and certainty in religious matters that apparently reigned in this house, for one ought to have been able to expect a decidedly more enlightened attitude toward God from Laban, the great-nephew of Abraham, the brother of Rebekah. In reality, Laban did have some knowledge of his western relatives' traditional faith, but it was so mixed up with local usages that it could be said to be the other way around, with these forming the core of his convictions, to which some Abrahamic notions had been added. Although he sat at the source, the very starting-point of their spiritual history, or indeed precisely because he had remained at that spot, he considered himself entirely a subject of Babel and its official faith and spoke to Jacob of Yah–Elohim simply as the "God of your father," all the while foolishly lumping him together with Shinar's chief god, Mardug. Jacob was disappointed by this, for he had assumed the house would be more progressive, more civilized, as evidently his parents at home had likewise believed. It troubled him in particular for Rachel's sake, inside whose handsome and beautiful head things surely did not look much better than inside the heads of the rest of her family; and from the very first day he took every opportunity to influence her as to what was true and right. For from the first day on, actually from the moment he first saw her at the well, he regarded her as his bride, and it is not too much to say that with the first little cry that had slipped from her when he revealed himself as her cousin, Rachel had seen him as her suitor and bridegroom.

Marriage between relatives, among members of the same tribe, was the general practice in those days, and for good reason. It was considered the only honorable, reasonable, and reliable thing to do—and we know what damage poor Esau had done to his own position with his eccentric marriages. It had not been on a personal whim that Abraham had insisted that Yitzchak, the true son, take a wife only from his own race and father's house, that is from the house of Nahor in Haran, where a man knew what he was getting. Now that Jacob had come into this house that sheltered daughters, he was walking in Isaak's or, more precisely, in the matchmaker Eliezer's footsteps, and the idea of courtship was for him, as for Isaak and Rebekah, bound up with his visit as a simple matter of course, as indeed it would have instantly been for Laban, too, had this man steeled by business been able to bring himself right off to see a son-in-law in this fugitive and beggar. For Laban, as for any other father, the idea of handing his daughters over to a totally unrelated and unknown race—or as he would have said, of selling them to foreigners—would have seemed both highly offensive and dangerous. It was far safer and more respectable to have them remain as married women within the bosom of the clan; and since a cousin did exist, and on the father's side, that same Jacob was more or less foreordained as their natural spouse—that is, not just for one of them, but for both. That was the tacit and general understanding in Laban's house when Jacob arrived. It was also, ultimately, that of the lord of the house as well, and in particular it was Rachel's, who had been the first to meet the new arrival and understood her role on earth well enough to know that she was handsome and beautiful, whereas Leah was feeble-eyed, but who had certainly not been thinking only of herself when she had cast that eager, probing look that had stirred Jacob so deeply there beside the well. From the moment of her cousin's arrival, life demanded of her that she enter into feminine competition with her sister and playmate, but not as regarded the crucial question of whom he would choose—though it might perhaps first be her task to exert the greater attraction on behalf of them both. No, the competition was in fact to come later, and it involved the question of which of them would be a better, more competent, fertile, and beloved wife to their spouse and cousin— a question in which she was in no way at an advantage and the answer to which certainly did not lie in determining who might prove more or less attractive at the moment.

That is how the matter was regarded in Laban's house, and only Jacob himself—and this, then, was the source of many a misunderstanding—did not see it that way. For first of all, he was well aware that besides one's true wife a man could have concubines and slaves with whom he could sleep and who could bear him semilegitimate children, but he did not know, and did not learn until much later, that in these regions, particularly in Haran and environs, marriage to two equally legitimate wives not only occurred frequently, but that among people of means it was also simply common practice. Secondly, his heart and mind were too filled with Rachel's loveliness for him even to have wanted to give a thought to the older, more stately, and ugly sister. He did not even think of her when he spoke to her out of politeness—something which she indeed did notice and in her dignified distress would smile a bitter smile and lower her lids to cover her crossed eyes. Laban noticed it as well, and felt jealous for his older daughter, even though he had reduced this suitor cousin to the legal status of a hired slave—and that delighted him, if only for the sake of his neglected Leah.

Jacob Makes a Discovery

Jacob, then, spoke as often as possible with Rachel, but that happened rarely enough, since they both had a great deal of work to do each day, and Jacob's situation in particular was that of a man who is filled with a great emotion that he would like to make his sole business, but who likewise finds himself kept seriously busy—so busy that he is forced to forget and sabotage the very love for which he labors. That is hard for a man of tender feeling like Jacob, for he wants to bask in his emotion and live entirely for it, but he may not and must do his duty for the sake of honoring that emotion, for what honor would remain if he did otherwise? Indeed it was one and the same—his feeling for Rachel and the work he did on Laban's farm, for how could he advance the former if he did not stand the test of the latter? Laban had to be thoroughly convinced of the genuine value of that on which his nephew rested his case, and it was Jacob's fondest wish that the firmest of ties be established between them. In a word, Isaac's blessing dare not be thwarted—for that is a man's job: to make certain that the blessing he has inherited is not thwarted and that the emotion of his heart is duly honored.

In those days, at the beginning of his sojourn, Jacob—accompanied by Marduka the dog, supplied with a few provisions in his shepherd's pouch, and armed with the sling at his belt and his long staff—would depart every morning with Laban's flocks to spend the day in nearby pastureland, about an hour distant from his uncle's farm. This had the advantage that Jacob did not have to spend the night there, but could drive the sheep home at sundown and let his own light shine, in both word and deed, around the farmstead, which he much preferred, since at first his shepherd's job offered little opportunity for him to awaken in his uncle the impression that with his arrival not only a fugitive but also a blessing had come to the farm. To be sure, not a lamb was missing each evening when he would count the herd with his staff as they were let into the pen while Laban looked on; and not only did he swiftly wean the summer's lambs to fodder, providing Laban with a good deal more milk and curds, but with much love and skill he also cured of the pox one of the two he-goats, a very valuable breeder. But Laban accepted these and other such modest feats of a useful shepherd without so much as a thank-you, just as he gave no notice to the pretty wooden latticework with which Jacob covered the ground-floor windows not long after he began his service. The frugal Laban likewise refused to pay for lime to whitewash the exterior brick walls, and so Jacob was unable to tie his arrival to such an obvious and handsome improvement to the property. He was truly at his wit's end in finding ways to prove the blessing; but the inner tension of his urgent wishes and searching may well have prepared him for a revelation and made him the man for the momentous event that he would recall with pleasure his whole life long.

He found water near Laban's grain field, living water, a subterranean spring, found it, as he well knew, with the help of the Lord, his God, although certain phenomena involved truly must have been an abomination to Him and had every appearance of a concession by His pure nature to the local spirit and its common usages. An equally gallant and candid Jacob had just finished a private conversation with Rachel outside the door of the house. He had told her that her charms were those of Hathor or Isis of Egypt, her beauty that of a young cow. She glowed with womanly radiance, he said poetically, for to him she was like a mother who nourishes the good seed with her moist heat, and to have her as his wife and to produce sons with her was his most fervent wish. She had accepted this with great sweetness, chastity, and sincerity. Her cousin and spouse had come, her probing eyes had tested him, and she loved him with youth's eagerness for life. And now, as he took her head between his hands and asked if it would also delight her to bear him children, she had nodded as tears welled up in her gracious black eyes, and he had kissed those tears from her eyes—his lips were still wet with them. He was walking toward the field in the dusk of twilight, for moonlight and daylight still stood at odds, when suddenly something seemed to catch hold of his foot and a peculiar burning spasm, as if he had been struck by lightning, ran from his shoulder to the tips of his toes. With eyes gaping wide, he saw a very strange figure standing directly before him. It had the body of a fish—slippery and silvery in the blend of moon- and sunlight—and the head of a fish as well. But beneath its fish head, as if it were only some kind of cap, was also a human head with a curly beard; and the creature had short human feet, too, growing from its fishy tail, and a pair of little arms. It was stooped over and appeared to be ladling and pouring something from the ground—it ladled and poured, over and over again. Then taking a few mincing steps to one side on its short feet, it slipped into the earth, or at least was no longer to be seen.

Jacob understood instantly that this had been Ea–Oannes, god of the watery depths, lord of the middle earth and of the ocean above the deepest deeps, the god whom the local people saw as the source of almost all useful knowledge and whom they considered very great, as great as Ellil, Sin, Shamash, and Nabu. For his part, Jacob knew he was not all that great in comparison with the Most High, whom Abram had come to know, if for no other reason than because he had a shape, and a rather ridiculous one at that. He knew that if Ea had revealed himself here and shown him something, it could only have been at the behest of Yah, the God of Isaak, the one and only God who was now with him. What this lesser divinity had shown him by its behavior, however, was also immediately clear to him—not just in and of itself, but also in all its consequences and associations. Pulling himself together, he ran back to the farm to fetch digging tools and roused Abdcheba, the twenty-shekel man, to come help him; and he dug half the night, with only an hour's sleep, continuing then to dig until dawn, when much to his distress he had to drive the sheep to pasture and leave his work lie for the rest of the day—and all day as he watched over Laban's grazing sheep, he found it impossible to stand, to lie down, to sit.

It was still some time before the winter rains would begin and people could start to prepare the soil again. Everything lay parched, nor was Laban concerned about his field, but busied himself at the farmstead. He did not come out to where Jacob was digging and so noticed and suspected nothing of Jacob's activities, which were taken up again that same evening and continued under the transit of moonlight until the rising of Ishtar. He set to work at various points around a small circle and by the sweat of his face had to probe deep into clay and stone. But as the sky was awakening in the east, before the topmost rim of the sun had risen into view, behold—water gushed forth, the well spurted up with great force, leapt three spans high inside the hole, and began to fill the shapeless, hastily dug pit and drench the soil roundabout. And its water tasted of the treasures of the underworld.

Jacob began to pray, but as he prayed he was already running to find Laban. When he saw him from a distance, however, he slowed his gait, greeted him when he had drawn near, and said with bated breath, "I have found water."

"What do you mean?" Laban replied with that slack droop of his mouth.

"A well from below," came Jacob's answer, "which I have dug between the farm and the field. It spouts a good ell high."

"You are mad."

"No. The Lord, my God, let me find it, according to my father's blessing. Let my uncle come and see."

Laban ran just as he had run when Eliezer, the rich envoy, had been announced. He arrived at the gushing pit long before Jacob, who followed at an easy pace. He stood there and gawked.

"This is the water of life," he said in shock.

"So you have said," Jacob confirmed.

"How did you do it?"

"I believed and I dug."

"This water," Laban said without lifting his eyes from the pit, "can be directed in an open ditch to irrigate my field."

"It will do that very nicely," Jacob responded.

"I can cancel the contract with Ishullanu's sons in Haran," Laban continued, "for I no longer need their water."

"Something of the sort," Jacob said, "went through my mind as well. And if you like you can wall in a pond, too, and plant a garden with date palms and all kinds of fruit trees, such as figs, pomegranates, and mulberries. And if it strikes your fancy and you are of a mind, you might even plant pistachio trees or pears or almonds, or perhaps a few strawberry trees. And the dates will yield not only their flesh, juice, and seeds, but also heart of palm for salad, leaves for weaving, ribs for all sorts of household purposes, bast for ropes and fabric, and wood for building."

Laban was silent. He did not embrace the bearer of the blessing, or fall to his knees before him. He said not a word, but stood there, then turned around and walked away. Jacob, too, hurried off to find Rachel, who was sitting in the stall, drawing milk from an udder. He told her everything and spoke of how they would now presumably be able to have children together. They joined hands and did a little dance and sang, "Hallelu-Yah!"

Jacob Sues for Rachel

When Jacob had been with Laban for a month, he came before him again and told him that since the worst of Esau's perilous rage had surely cooled by now he, Jacob, needed to talk to his master.

"Before you speak," Laban replied, "listen to me, for I was about to come to you with a proposal of my own. You have been with me now for one round of the moon, and we have been to the roof to sacrifice at its new light, its half light, its full beauty, and on the day of its disappearance. During this time I have hired for the interim, besides yourself, three more slaves, whom I pay as is only just. For water has been found, not without your assistance, and we have begun to wall in the spring and build an irrigation ditch of brick. We have also pegged out the size of the pond we wish to dig, and should there be plans for planting a garden there will be much work to do, for which I need strong arms such as yours and those whom I have also taken in, feeding and clothing them and rewarding each with eight silas of grain a day. You have served me thus far without pay, out of love as a kinsman in accordance with our contract. But behold, we wish to make a new one, for in the eyes of the gods and men it is no longer just that outside servants are paid, but not my nephew. Therefore tell me what you demand. For I shall give you what I give the others and a little more if you will seal an agreement to remain with me as many years as the week has days and as one reckons until a field must lie fallow and the soil rest without sowing or reaping. So shall you serve me seven years for the reward that you may demand."

Such were Laban's words and train of thought, judicious words clothing judicious thoughts. But even earthbound man's thoughts— and not just his words—merely clothe and gloss over his endeavors and interests, and in thinking them he sets them into judicious form, so that usually he lies before he speaks, and his words have an honest ring because they are not the lie, but rather his thoughts are. Laban was profoundly dismayed when it appeared that Jacob might depart, for ever since the spring had welled up he knew that Jacob was truly a bearer of blessing and a man whose hand was blessed, and his chief concern was to bind Jacob to him, so that his own business might continue to make use of the blessing Jacob took with him wherever he went. The discovery of water was a powerful blessing, fraught with consequences, of which the first, but not the greatest, was that it had relieved Laban of those burdensome payments to Ishullanu's sons. For under the sly pretext that the man could never have tilled his field without the water from their canal, they had in fact declared that he should make payments of oil, corn, and wool in perpetuity, whether he now used their water or not. But the judge upon his chair had feared the gods and decided in Laban's favor, which he then was inclined to see as yet another intervention by Jacob's god. But a great many things had been set in motion, were already under way; projects had been embarked upon that apparently required Jacob's blessed presence for their completion and further success. The economic balance of power between the two had shifted in the nephew's favor—Laban believed he needed him, and Jacob, well aware of that fact, could, merely by threatening to leave, exert the kind of pressure for which earthbound Laban was immediately ready to make allowances. That was why—even before Jacob could move to put such pressure into play—Laban had hastened within his soul preemptively to declare the stipulations under which Rebekah's son worked for him to be unworthy and interrupted his nephew with his own judicious suggestions about improving on them. In point of fact Jacob could not imagine returning home already, for no one knew better than he that conditions were definitely not yet ripe for that. And so he was quite pleased that his uncle was mistaken about the actual balance of power; he was sincerely grateful to him for his accommodating suggestions, though fully aware that they arose not out of Laban's sense of fairness or any personal love for him, but solely out of self-interest. His gratitude, then, was actually for the self-interest that bound the man to him, the bearer of the blessing, for it is man's nature that the cordiality in which such self-interest clothes itself is automatically reflected back upon him as love. Jacob, moreover, did love Laban for the sake of what he had to give and what he was about to demand of him, for it was far greater that silas and shekels. He said:

"My father and brother, if you wish for me to remain and not return to Esau, who is now reconciled, but to serve you, then give me Rachel, your child, to be my wife—that will be my reward. For as to her beauty she is like a young cow, and she for her part looks with favor upon me as well, and we have discussed and agreed that we would like to have children together after our likeness. Therefore, give her to me and I am yours."

Laban was certainly not surprised. The notion of courtship was, as we already noted, closely bound up from the start with the arrival of this cousin and nephew, and only Jacob's plight had pushed it farther back in Laban's mind. It was understandable that, with the balance of power now shifted in his favor, Jacob should speak of it; and Laban, that clod of earth, was very happy he had, for he immediately realized that in so doing Jacob had restored the lion's share of the advantage to him. For by admitting that he was fond of Rachel, Jacob had put himself as much in Laban's hands as Laban was in his, thereby weakening any pressure he might exert in threatening to depart. What annoyed the father, however, was that Jacob spoke of Rachel, of her alone, and passed over Leah completely.

"I am to give you Rachel?" he replied.

"Yes, Rachel. She herself would like that."

"Not Leah, my older child?"

"No, I am not quite so fond of her."

"She is the older and the first to be courted."

"To be sure, she is somewhat older. She is also stately and proud, despite minor shortcomings in her appearance or perhaps because of them, and would be very competent in bearing me the children I so desire. But the fact is that my heart hangs on Rachel, your younger child, for to me she is like Hathor and Isis, she literally glows in feminine radiance in my eyes, much like Ishtar, and her own sweet eyes follow me wherever I go. Behold, it was but an hour ago that my lips were wet with tears she wept for me. So give her to me, and I will toil for you."

"It is obviously better that I give her to you than to some stranger," Laban said. "But should I then give Leah, my older child, to a stranger, or should she perhaps wither away without a husband? Take Leah first, take them both."

"That is very kind of you," Jacob said, "but as incredible as it may sound, Leah simply does not enkindle my manly desires, but just the opposite, and your servant cares only for Rachel."

Laban squinted at him a while with his bad eye, then said gruffly, "As you like. And so you will seal an agreement to stay with me seven years, serving me for this reward."

"Seven times seven," Jacob cried, "until God's jubilee! When is the wedding to be?"

"After seven years," Laban replied.

Imagine Jacob's horror!

"What," he said, "I am to serve for Rachel seven years before she is given to me?"

"How else?" Laban responded, feigning utter amazement. "I'll not play the fool in this world and give her to you right off, so that you can pick up and leave with her whenever you like, and I am left the worse for it. Or where is the purchase price and portion, together with suitable gifts you would present me that I might bind them to the bride's sash or that remain with me by writ of law should you withdraw from the betrothal? Do you have it with you, the mina of silver and whatever else it may be, or if not, where is it? You are as poor as a field mouse, poorer even than that. And thus it will be documented and sealed before the judicial notary that I will sell you the girl for the seven years you shall serve me, and payment shall be made only at the end of that time. And the tablet shall be stored below in the house shrine and entrusted to the protection of the teraphim."

"How hard an uncle," Jacob said, "God has bestowed upon me."

"Fancy phrases!" Laban responded. "I am as hard as the facts in the case allow me to be, and if they so demand it, then I am weak. But if you want to have the girl for your wife—either depart without her, or first serve!"

"I will serve," Jacob said.

The Long Wait

And so that first, brief, and preliminary epoch of Jacob's long sojourn with Laban had been delineated—the prelude lasting only a month, at the end of which the new contract involving a longer, indeed a very much longer, period was drawn up. It was a marriage contract, but then again a contract of servitude, a mixture of both, of a sort that, if not an everyday occurrence, had surely appeared in some similar form now and then before the *mashkim*, or judicial notary, and that he had at any rate recognized as legitimate and, this being the will of both parties, legal. In order to make the case perfectly clear, the document itself—prepared in duplicate—was recorded directly in the form of a dialogue, with Laban and Jacob each stating his position, thereby making the basis of their amicable agreement patently obvious. This man had said to such and such a man: Give me your daughter to wife, whereupon such and such a man had asked: What will you give me for her? But the former man had nothing to offer. To which the latter man said: Since you lack a portion as well as any asset whatever to pay toward it that I might hang on the sash of the bride in token of the betrothal, you shall serve me for as many years as the week has days. That shall be the purchase price you pay to me, and the bride shall be yours to lie with at the end of that period, together with a mina of silver and a handmaid, which I will give to the woman as her dowry, and in such fashion that two-thirds of a mina of silver shall be reckoned in the value of the slave, but one-third mina be paid in ready money or in fruits of the field. To which the former said: So shall it be. Let it be so in the name of the king. They have each taken a written tablet. And may nothing good come to him who acts illegally and attempts to rise up against this contract.

The agreement was solid and sure, the judicial notary declared it fair, and from a purely economic point of view even Jacob had no cause for complaint. If he had owed his uncle a mina of silver, at sixty shekels the mina, seven years of toil would not have sufficed to cover the debt; for the average wage of an indentured slave came to six shekels a year, and thus the wages of seven years would not have equaled Jacob's liability. To be sure, he was profoundly aware how deceptive the economic aspect was in this case and that had there been a scale of justice, a scale set up by God, the pan in which his seven years lay would have sent the other with its mina of silver shooting upward. All in all, however, they would be years he would spend close to Rachel, years that cast the hue of love's joy over any sacrifice; what was more, from the very first day of his fulfilling the contract, Rachel would be legally promised and bound to him, so that any man who dared approach her would be as guilty as if he were seducing a married woman. Ah, these children of a brother and a sister would have to wait for one another for seven long years. Before they could have sons together they would have entered a stage of life very different from their present one—and that was bitter, a requirement that revealed either cruelty on Laban's part or his lack of imagination, marking him, in short, once again and most crassly as a man without heart or compassion. A second annoyance was the exceptional avarice, the desire always to be one up on the other fellow, evidenced by the contract's stipulation regarding the dowry— a father's nuptial gift due at the end of seven years, which proved a rotten bargain for poor Jacob, particularly since it placed the value of a handmaid, of who knew what quality, at twice the sum anyone would pay for a middling slave either here or in western lands. But there was no altering that or any other objectionable provision. A time for striking a better bargain would come soon enough, Jacob felt—he sensed in his soul the promise of good business and a secret power that most certainly exceeded that found in the breast of this underworldly devil of a father-in-law: Laban, the man of Aram, whose eyes had reappeared as the sweet eyes of Rachel, his child. And as for those seven years, he simply had to deal with them, put them behind him. It would have been easier to sleep through them; but Jacob did not even allow for such a wish, not only because it was an impossibility, but also because he found it better in any case to be alert and active.

Which he was, and the teller of the tale should be the same and not suppose he could sleep through the period, leap right over it with some brief statement that "seven years passed." That is presumably the casual style of the storyteller, but if such a magic charm must be spoken, then it should pass his lips only with somber thought and a hesitant reverence for life, so that it likewise makes the listener grow thoughtful and somber in his amazement at how those unforeseeable seven years—or if foreseeable, then only with the intellect, not with the soul—have passed as if they were but seven days. For that is how tradition puts it, that for Jacob those seven years, which at first he had feared to the point of despondency, seemed like days; and that tradition—being based, but of course, ultimately on his own statements—is, as they say, authentic and, by the way, totally plausible. At work here is not some "seven-sleeper" enchantment or any sort of magic other than that of time itself, whose larger units pass just as do its smaller ones—neither quickly nor slowly, but simply pass. A day has twenty-four hours, and although an hour is a considerable mass or expanse of time, embracing a great deal of life and thousands of heartbeats, a goodly number of them pass nevertheless from one morning to the next, in sleeping and in waking, you never know quite how, as little as you know how seven such days of life pass—a whole week, a unit of which only four suffice for the moon to move through all its phases. Jacob did not say those seven years had passed for him "as quickly" as seven days, he had no desire to belittle the weight of a day of life by such a comparison. The day itself does not pass "quickly," but it passes, one among many, with its times of day, with morning, noon, after-noon, and evening, and so, too, in that same unqualifiable way, as one among many, does a year, with its seasons, from spring to resur-recting spring. That is why Jacob told those who came after that the seven years seemed to him like days.

It is pointless to note that the year consists of more than just its seasons, of more than the circuit of spring, green pastures, and sheepshearing, of harvest and summer swelter, of first rain and new planting, of snow and frost at night until the tamarisk blossoms pink again; that is only the framework, one year—that is, a massive fili-gree of life, saturated with events, a sea to be drunk down. The day, too, is such a filigree of thinking, feeling, doing, and happening, just as is the hour—on a smaller scale, if you like; but any difference in size between units of time is hardly absolute, for their scale simulta-neously defines us, our emotions, our attitude and adaptation to life, so that under certain circumstances seven days or even hours can be more difficult to drink down, may present us with a more daring en-terprise in time, than seven years. But what does daring even mean! Whether a man is cheerful or irresolute as he climbs into the flood, nothing lives that must not give itself over to it—nor is anything more than that necessary. It bears us along in a rushing torrent with-out our even noticing, and when we look back, the point where we first climbed in is now "long ago"—seven years, for example, which passed the way days pass. Yes, it cannot even be stated or discerned how man actually gives himself over to time, whether happily or hesitantly; the necessity of doing so overwhelms such differences and undoes them. No one claims that Jacob should have undertaken or entered upon these seven years with joy, for only after they had passed would he in fact be able to have children with Rachel. But that was a worrisome thought that would be weakened and elimi-nated for the most part by the countervailing life-forces determining his relationship with time—and time's with him. For Jacob is said to have lived one hundred and six years, and though his mind did not know that, his flesh and the soul of his flesh knew it, and so the seven years ahead of him were, though certainly not so brief as in God's eye, definitely not so long as they would be for someone who would live to be only fifty or sixty, and so his soul could envision those years of waiting more calmly. Finally, however, by way of spreading a general calm over things, it should be pointed out that this was not a period of pure waiting that he had to endure, it was too long for that. Pure waiting is agonizing torture, and no one could bear just to sit there or pace the floor while waiting out seven years, or even seven days, the way any of us can surely manage to do for an hour or so. That cannot happen on a larger or grand scale because then the waiting becomes so prolonged and attenuated, and at the same time so strongly alloyed with the process of living, that for long periods of time the waiting itself falls victim to forgetfulness, that is, it recedes into the depths of the soul and is no longer a conscious act. That may explain why a half hour of pure, unadulterated waiting is a more ghastly and cruel trial of patience than a wait wrapped in seven years of life. Something imminently awaited, precisely because it is so near, is a far fiercer and more direct test of our patience than something far off, making of it an impatience that strains nerves and muscles, turning us into invalids literally uncertain of what to do with our arms and legs, whereas with long-term waiting we retain our calm, since it does not merely allow, but indeed forces us to think other thoughts, do other deeds, for we must live. All of which gives rise to the strange statement that with whatever degree of yearning we may wait, it is not harder, but easier to do, the farther ahead in time what we await may lie.

The truth of these comforting reflections—a truth whose ultimate meaning is that nature and the soul always know to come to their own aid—now found especially clear proof and confirmation in Jacob's case. He served Laban chiefly as a shepherd—and a shepherd, as we all know, has a great deal of time on his hands. For hours at least, sometimes half a day, his task is leisurely contemplation, and if there is anything he is waiting for, it is not wrapped in a great deal of active life. This, however, demonstrates the gentle nature of long-term waiting, for it was certainly not the case that Jacob did not know if he should sit or stand or lie down, or that he ran aimlessly about the plains, his head clasped between his hands. Instead, his mood was calm, if also a little sad at the same time, and waiting was not the treble, but rather the ground bass of his life. Even when far from her, of course he also thought of Rachel and the children they would have together. Lying beside Marduka the dog in the shade of a rock or a shrub, propped on his elbows, hand to his cheek or maybe both hands linked behind his neck, one leg across the raised knee of the other, or standing leaning on his staff amid the wide plain while sheep grazed around him—he would think not only of her, but also of God and all those stories, both nearest to him and farthest away: of his flight and wanderings, of Eliphaz and his own proud dream at Beth-el, of the Feast of the Cursing of Esau, of Yitzchak the blind man, of Abraham, the Tower, the Flood, Adapa or Adama in his Paradise garden . . . which reminded him of the garden that that devil Laban had planted with his help, a creation blessed with success and the source of considerable progress for the man's business and prosperity.

It might be useful to know that in the first year of his contract Jacob was not yet, or only rarely, a tender of sheep, and instead usually left that to Abdcheba, the twenty-shekel man, or even to one of Laban's daughters, whereas he, at his uncle's wish and behest, took part in the work resulting from his own blessed discovery: the construction of the irrigation ditch and of the pond, for which they used a natural sinkhole, leveling it with spades, then bricking up its walls, and caulking it with a pebbly cement. Finally the garden was done—and Laban had attached great importance to having his nephew's blessed hands put to work on these new facilities as well, for he was convinced of the efficacy of that blessing, however craftily obtained, and he prided himself on the cleverness with which he had engaged it in the service of his own economic interests for a long time to come. Was it not manifestly clear that Rebekah's son brought good luck, almost against his own will, and that his mere presence brought enterprises to life, rousing and directing them along unexpected channels, when it had seemed certain that they would drag along on permanent hold? What was all this activity and promising bustle on Laban's farm and in his fields all of a sudden—all this digging, hammering, plowing, and planting? Laban had borrowed money in order to enlarge his operation and manage the necessary purchases—Ishullanu's sons in Haran had advanced him the funds, even though they had lost their lawsuit. They were cool-headed men who never let personal emotions interfere with business and for whom a defeat in court was certainly no reason not to conclude a new deal with the man who had bested them, for that same economic asset by which he had won his suit against them now made him a good investment in their eyes and they lent him money without a second thought. That is how things work in economic life, which came as no surprise to Laban. He needed the bank's money just to pay and feed his three new farmhands, the indentured slaves who had been leased to him by a man in the city and whom Jacob supervised, both directing their labors and lending a hand himself to assist in the backbreaking work. Needless to say his position in the household was, by unspoken agreement, not for a moment comparable with that of these branded hirelings with their shorn heads and their owner's name indelibly inscribed on their right hands. The terms of that seven-year contract lying in a clay chest among the teraphim below were a long way from making him their equal. He was a nephew of the house, a future bridegroom, and also master of the well and therefore both waterworks engineer and head gardener—Laban had immediately ceded him those duties and knew full well what he was doing.

He also thought he knew why he had commissioned Jacob to purchase most of the tools, building materials, seeds, and saplings that these renovations required and in which the borrowed funds were invested. He trusted his nephew's lucky hand, and rightly so, for Jacob could always make the better deal for finer goods than when he himself—being a gloomy man lacking a blessing—did the bargaining, even though Jacob was also making a little profit and starting to put aside the foundation, however meager for now, of his later prosperity. For in his dealings with business partners in the city or on farms in the country roundabout, he never saw his task in the fixed and rigid sense of simply being Laban's employee or go-between, but rather he viewed himself more as the middleman, an independent merchant, and indeed was such a good, skilled, sociable, charming conversationalist that whether by a hard-cash purchase or the more usual barter he always managed to add some smaller or larger dividend to his own account, so that he in fact already owned a small private flock of sheep and goats before he actually began to tend Laban's herds. God the King had called out above the harps

that Jacob would return home to Yitzchak a rich man, and that was
both a promise and a command—the latter insofar as promises can,
of course, not be fulfilled unless a man does his part as well. Was he
supposed to make a liar of God the King and wantonly disgrace Him
by simply letting things ride and showing excessive scrupulousness
toward an uncle who gloomily applauded all the rigors of commercial life without ever having understood how to make them work to
his own advantage? Jacob was not even tempted to make such a mistake. Let it never be said that he cheated or duped Laban and secretly
took advantage of him. Laban generally knew what Jacob was doing,
and even when details of his behavior became clear as day, he literally winked an eye at them and let his slack mouth droop. For the
man saw that he almost always came out better for it than if he had
clumsily managed things on his own. He also had good reason to be
afraid of Jacob and look the other way. For Jacob was easily offended, wanted to be treated gently and indulged in his blessing. He
spoke of it quite openly, warning Laban once and for all about it.

"If, my lord, you wish to chide and admonish me," he said, "for
every trifle that falls my way when I am dealing in your service and
to look askance when on occasion it is not you alone who profits
from your servant's cleverness, then you shall vex both my heart
within my breast and the blessing within my soul, until your own affairs will no longer flourish in my hands. The Lord, my God, spoke
in a dream to Belanu, the very man from whom I bought the seed
corn that you needed to enlarge your field, saying to him, 'The man
with whom you are dealing is Jacob, who is blessed, whose head and
footsteps I watch over. And so you, too, shall mind your step and
charge him five shekels for the five cors of grain that he wishes to
buy from you, with two hundred and fifty selas to the cor and not
the two hundred forty or even thirty that you might possibly measure out for Laban, or else I will threaten you. Jacob will give you
nine selas of oil instead of one shekel and five minas of wool instead
of a second, plus a good ram valued at one and a half shekels and a
lamb from his herd for the rest. He will pay you all that for your five
cors of seed corn instead of five shekels, and will spend you many
friendly glances and merry words besides, so that your dealings with
your customer will be pleasant. But should you offer a worse price,
beware! I will then come upon your cattle and strike them with

every sort of pestilence and will visit your wife with barrenness and what children you have with blindness and idiocy, and you shall learn of Me and My ways.' And Belanu feared the Lord, my God, and did as he was told, so that I acquired the barley at a better price than it could have been acquired by any man—and by my uncle in particular. For let him search his heart and ask himself whether he would have come off with nine selas of oil for one shekel or five minas of sheep's wool for a second, when at the market twelve selas of oil or more and six minas of wool are to be had for that price, not to mention any additional rate of exchange. And would you not have had to give a good three lambs for the remaining one and a half shekels, or a pig plus a lamb? Which is why I have taken two lambs from your flock and have marked them with my mark and they are now mine. But what is that between you and me? Am I not your child's intended, and is not what is mine also yours through her? If you wish to benefit from my blessing and for me to serve you with goodwill and cunning, some reward must beckon me, some incentive must spur me on, otherwise my soul will be limp and lame, and my blessing will not be at your service."

"Keep the lambs," Laban said; and that was how it went between them on several occasions, until Laban decided to hold his tongue and let Jacob do as he pleased. For he certainly did not want Jacob's soul to be limp and lame, and so he had to pamper him. But he was glad when the ditch was finished, the pond filled, the garden planted, and the field enlarged, and he could send Jacob away from the farm, out onto the plain with the sheep, first nearby, but then farther away, so that for weeks and months on end he never entered under Laban's roof, but remained out on the vast expanses, erecting near a cistern his own light roof to ward off sun and rain, as well as sheepfolds of clay and reeds, and a simple tower as protection and lookout. With crooked staff and sling, he lived on scant rations, took care of both Marduka the dog and the grazing herds spread out in various smaller flocks, and gave himself over to time, talking to Marduka, who looked as if he understood him—and who really did understand him, at least in part. He watered his animals, penned them up at night, suffered heat and chill, and did not sleep all that well; for at night wolves would howl for lambs, or if a lion happened to slink in close, he had to rattle and shout with the noise of a dozen men to chase the robber from the sheepfold.

Laban's Increasing Wealth

When he drove his flocks home, a journey of a good day or two, to render an accounting to his lord of both the old flock and the new births, letting the sheep pass beneath his staff before him, he would see Rachel, who had also waited out the days, and they would walk off hand in hand to where no one saw them, and speak ardently about their fate, about how they had had to wait so long for one another and still could not have children together, with her letting him first console her, and then the other way around. It was usually Rachel, however, who needed to be consoled, for the time seemed longer to her and dealt her soul a harder blow, for she would not live one hundred and six years, but only forty-one, so that seven years were more than twice as much of her life as they were of his. And so tears welled up from the depths of her soul whenever the bridal couple came together secretly, and with her sweet black eyes overflowing, she would lament:

"Ah, Jacob, my cousin from afar who has been promised to me, how your little Rachel's heart aches with impatience. Behold, moons change and time passes, and that is both good and sad, for I shall soon be fourteen, but I shall have to be nineteen before the drums and harps are sounded for us and we may enter the bedchamber and I shall be before you as the spotless virgin before the god in his highest temple, and you will say, 'Like the fruit of the garden will I make this woman fruitful.' It is still such a long time away, for it was my father's will in selling me to you that I shall no longer be who I am when that day comes, and who knows if a demon may not touch me before then, making me fall ill, striking me to the very root of my tongue, and leaving me beyond all human help? But if I do recover from his touch, might it not perhaps be with the loss of my hair, or with blemished skin, left yellow and pockmarked, so that my friend will no longer know me? I am so dreadfully afraid of it and cannot sleep and toss the blanket from me and wander through the house and courtyard while my parents sleep, and grieve over the time that is passing and yet not passing, for I can feel so clearly that I would be fruitful for you, and before I am nineteen we could have six sons, or even eight, for in all likelihood I will bear you twins at some point, and I weep because it must be delayed so long."

Then Jacob took her head between his hands and kissed her just below both eyes—Laban's eyes, grown beautiful in her—kissed her tears away, leaving his lips wet. And he said, "Ah my good, clever little girl, my impatient mother sheep, take heart. Just look, I shall take these tears with me out into the field, and in my loneliness they shall be the pledge and guarantee that you are mine and entrusted to me and wait with the same patience and impatience as I. For I love you, and the night of your eyes is dearer to me than all else, and the warmth of your head when you rest it against mine touches me to the quick. In its silky darkness your hair is like the pelt of goats upon the slopes of Mount Gilead, your teeth are like the whitest light, and your cheeks are a living reminder of the softness of a peach. Your mouth is like young figs still reddening on the tree, and when I close it in a kiss the breath from your nostrils bears the fragrance of apples. You are indeed handsome and beautiful, but you will be all the more so when you are nineteen, believe me, and your breasts will be like clusters of dates and like grapes clustered on the vine. For you are of the purest blood, my darling, and no sickness shall beset you and no demon shall touch you. The Lord, my God, who led me to you and set you aside for me shall prevent it. But as for me, my love and tenderness for you is unshakable and is a flame that the rains of all those many years shall not extinguish. I think of you when I lie in the shade of a rock or a shrub or stand leaning on my staff, when I roam in search of a lost sheep, when I nurse the sick or carry the weary lamb, when I defy the lion or draw water for the herd. In all of it I think of you and slay time itself. For it passes ceaselessly in all that I do and undertake, and God does not permit me to remain still for even a moment, whether I rest or rouse myself. You and I, we are not waiting for what is empty and uncertain, but rather we know our hour, and our hour knows us, and it is coming toward us. In a certain sense some margin of time between that hour and us is perhaps not a bad thing, for when it has come we shall depart from here for the land to which our first father wandered, and it is a good thing if until then I do well in business and become somewhat weighed down with goods, so that the promise of my God may be fulfilled, that He would lead me home to Yitzchak a rich man. For to me your eyes are like the eyes of Ishtar, goddess of embraces, who said to Gilgamesh: 'Your goats shall be doubled, your sheep shall bear twins.' Yes, although we may not yet embrace one another and be fruitful, the flocks are fertile in the meantime and bring forth young for the sake of our love, so that I may do business for Laban and myself and grow rich before the Lord before we depart."

That is how he consoled her and delicately found the right words to express the surrogate fertility, as it were, of the sheep; for it really was as if the local goddess of embraces, restrained on a human level by Laban's gloomy hardness, had found a way to burst free and recoup her losses in other living things—that is, in the sheep and goats that Jacob tended for Laban, which flourished as no others, so that Yitzchak's blessing proved its value in them as never before, making Laban increasingly glad that he had made his nephew his servant, for he was very useful. When, after a journey of a day or two on his ox, Laban would arrive to check on his herds, he was astonished by such burgeoning, but he said not a word, for good or ill—certainly not for ill, since simplest prudence told him to look the other way when dealing with this sheep breeder, this man of blessing, even if the latter looked to his own advantage as well and privately put some of the gains from his dealings aside for himself, just as he had openly declared he would on principle. It would have been unwise to challenge that principle—if followed in moderation; for such a man wanted to be treated gently and one dared not vex the blessing in his body.

Jacob was truly in his element as a breeder of sheep, as a master of the sheepfold, far more than he had previously been on the farm as the supervisor of water and gardens. He was a shepherd by birth, by the stamp of his character, a moon man, not a man of the sun and the field. Life out in the pasture, despite its drudgery and even its dangers, matched the wishes of his nature—it was dignified and contemplative, it gave him the leisure to think of God and of Rachel. As for the animals, he loved them with heart and mind; yes, he was truly fond of them in his gentle and strong way. He loved their warmth, their life of gamboling and scattering only to huddle together again, the idyllic and many-toned chorus of their bleating under the wide skies—loved the meek reserve of those faces, the ears flared out to each side, the wide-set sparkling eyes, and the way the wool between them came halfway down the flat nose. He loved the massive, sacred head of the ram, the prettier, more fragile shape of the ewe, the naive childlike face of the lamb—loved the tufted, curly, precious commodity they patiently carried about, the fleece that never ceased to grow, that together with Laban and his servants he would first wash and then shear from their backs each spring and fall. And his compassion for them made him a master at tending and cleverly managing their rut and fertility, which with a breeder's knowledge and painstaking respect he could direct along certain lines, applying his perfect understanding of both the breed and individuals, of wool quality and body build—not that we would wish to claim the wonderful results he achieved were to be attributed solely to such skills. For it was not merely that Jacob improved the breed and produced splendid sheep valuable for both their meat and wool, but the sheer growth in numbers, the constant fecundity of his herd exceeded all common standards, became extraordinary in his hands. There was not a single barren ewe in his pens, they all gave birth, to twins to triplets, were still fertile at the age of eight; their rut lasted three months, their gestation only four, their lambs matured both to sire and bear after one year. And other shepherds claimed that in the herds of Jacob, the man from western lands, even the castrated males sired by a full moon. That was both a joke and a superstition, but it proves how manifestly exceptional Jacob's success in these matters was, going well beyond an expert's knowledge of them. But to account for the phenomenon—a source of much envy—did one truly have to ascribe it to the power of the local goddess of embraces? In our opinion, one should instead credit its source to the master of the sheepfold himself. He was an expectant lover; he dared not be fruitful with Rachel just yet; and just as so often in this world the very blocking and damming-up of wishes and energies has found an outlet in great creative deeds, so here, too, in a similar indirect transference, those energies found a substitute in the flourishing of natural life placed under the compassionate care of the man who suffered from their blockage.

The same tradition that functions as the original text for learned commentary and is itself a late literary version of the antiphonal songs of shepherds and their "fine discourse" is rhapsodic in its report of Jacob's successful dealings in sheep; it so glorifies them that it becomes guilty of exaggeration, from which, however—in our desire to present a clear and final version of the story—we cannot then detract all that much without distorting the truth yet again. The exaggeration actually lies for the most part not in glosses and particulars supplied by later sources, but rather in the original events themselves or, more precisely, in the persons involved. For we know how in every age people tend to excess when evaluating and counting such worldly goods as they agree it is fashionable to admire and covet. And that was likewise the case with Jacob's success at breeding sheep. Over time, rumor of their unique excellence spread among people much like Laban and himself, both in the area of Haran and beyond, though we shall have to leave uninvestigated the extent to which the power of the man's blessing may have helped dazzle some people. In any case, an obsession for owning just one of Jacob's sheep was universal. It became a matter of honor. People would pilgrimage from great distances to barter with him, and when they finally arrived and realized that rumor had overstated things, that these were quite normal and naturally bred specimens, however excellent, they nevertheless felt compelled by fashion to see them as miracle sheep and knowingly let themselves be deceived, accepting on his mere say-so that a sheep was a yearling or just full-grown, even when it was already losing its front teeth, which meant it was at least six years old. They paid him whatever he demanded. For one sheep he is said to have received an ass, even a camel, and indeed a slave, either male or female—all exaggerations, if one were to generalize and claim such deals were the rule. But concessions of that sort did occur, and there is even something to the report of slaves being offered in exchange for sheep. For as time passed Jacob needed help running his operation, and assistant shepherds were leased from his trading partners, the price being included in the goods he delivered: wool, curds, pelts, sinews, or live animals. As the years passed, he even made several of these assistants independent, commissioning them to pasture, care for, and tend his sheep in return for a set payment: sixty-six or seventy lambs each year per one hundred sheep, a sela of curds for the same number, or a mina and a half of wool per head—profits that belonged to Laban, of course, but some of which, since they had passed through Jacob's hands, remained there, if only because he knew how to use them to make far greater profits.

Was that the sum of the blessings that Laban, the clod of earth, received by way of Jacob's management? No—presuming, to be sure, that the happiest and most unexpected increase that the man could record had its fundamental basis in his nephew's presence, a solid assumption that is certainly warranted, whether one chooses to attach a rational or a more mysterious interpretation to the event. If this were an invented tale and we regarded it as our task—merely for the sake of momentary entertainment and with the tacit agreement of our audience—to lend the appearance of reality to spurious fables, what we have to report here would surely be taken as humbug, as immoderate bravado, and we would not be spared the reproach of having been carried away by the plot and of trumping it with a tall tale just to stun the reader's credulity, which surely has its limits. All the better then, that this is not our role, that instead we rely upon facts as reported by tradition, which are no less unshakable in that they are not known to everyone or that some of them will be news to some people. We are in a position to state our case in a voice that, though calm, is also insistent and confident that any such objection, which one might otherwise rightly fear, can be dismissed out of hand.

In a word, during the first seven years that Jacob served him, Laban, Bethuel's son, became a father yet again, and indeed the father of sons. The prospering man was recompensed for the miscarried and patently heinous sacrifice long past—for the little boy in the jar—and was repaid not once, but thrice. For three times in a row, in the third, fourth, and fifth years of Jacob's sojourn, Adina, Laban's wife, unprepossessing as she was, became pregnant, groaning proudly as she incubated and tended what she had conceived, wearing around her neck a metaphor for her condition, a hollow stone inside of which a smaller one rattled. With wails and prayers she gave birth in Laban's house and in his presence, kneeling on two stacks of two bricks each to make room for the child at the portal of her body—embraced from behind by one midwife, while another crouched beside her, guarding the portal. The births were successful, and despite Adina's advanced years her own life was not endangered by any complication. Sacrifices of food in the form of beer, emmer bread, and even sheep were offered repeatedly to red Nergal to induce him to keep his fourteen illness-bearing servants from any interference in the matter. And as a result in none of the three instances did the laboring woman's bowels upend, nor did the witch Labartu decide to obstruct her body's portal. These were three sturdy lads that she brought into the world, and their vehement demands turned Laban's once very dull house into a veritable cradle of life. The first was named Beor, the second Alub, and the third Muras. Not only did Adina suffer no harm from three pregnancies and deliveries in rapid succession, but as a result she even appeared younger and less unprepossessing than before and busily set to work adorning herself with the headscarves, sashes, and necklaces that Laban acquired for her when bartering in the city of Haran.

Laban's melancholy heart was greatly pleased. The man beamed—as best as he could. The slack droop at the corner of his mouth lost its sour expression and took on the look of a satisfied and smug smile. Considering how his farm was flourishing, how splendidly business was going, and how successfully fruitful his loins had proved—the shadow of that curse stemming from a failed spiritual gamble at last having been graciously removed from his household—his being so puffed up with himself is quite understandable. He had no doubt that, as with all his good fortune, the appearance of sons likewise had a direct connection with Jacob's proximity as part of his household, with Yitzchak's blessing, and he would have been very wrong to have doubted it. And though perhaps it was the prevailing good cheer of both spouses—and in particular of Laban, arising from the fine business their nephew was doing out in the fields—that revived their conjugal activities and caused the gates of fertility to open again, in one way or another it could all be traced back to Jacob's influence. That did not, however, prevent Laban from taking personal pride in it. It had been he who had been clever enough to apply both artifice and wisdom in binding to his household this bearer of blessing—this fugitive and beggar, who obviously promoted prosperity wherever he went, and indeed whether he wished to or not. From the modest tokens of joy and astonishment that Jacob thought it appropriate to display at the births of Beor, Alub, and Muras, Laban concluded that his nephew may not even have been especially anxious for his uncle to become a happy father.

"Now you tell me, my good nephew and son-in-law," Laban surely said on one such occasion when he arrived on the back of his ox to visit his herds in the field, or when Jacob happened to be at the farm to settle accounts, "you tell me whether I am worthy of praise, and whether the gods smile upon Laban or not. For in my gray old age they have awakened my powers to sire sons, and my wife Adina has exuberantly borne me boys, though only recently she was scarcely that impressive."

"And you may indeed rejoice in it," Jacob replied. "But such things are not all that unusual in the eyes of our God. Abram was a hundred years old when he sired Yitzchak, and, as everyone knows, life for Sarai was no longer after the manner of women when the Lord caused them to smile their smiles."

"What a dull way you have," Laban said, "to belittle great things and to diminish a man's joy."

"It is not fitting for us," Jacob responded coolly, "to make a fuss over strokes of good fortune to which we may ascribe some merit of our own."

Part Six

THE SISTERS

The Evil One

The seven years were coming to an end and the time approaching when Jacob was supposed to know Rachel, and he could hardly believe it, was so outrageously happy that his heart started pounding whenever he thought of that hour. For Rachel was now nineteen and had waited for him in the purity of blood that protected her against the evil touch and any illness that might have spoiled her for her bridegroom. Instead, all those things that Jacob had tenderly predicted had been fulfilled in her blossoming loveliness, and of all the daughters of the land she was the most charming to gaze upon—with the daintiness of her perfect and pleasing figure, her soft braids, the flare of her thick nostrils, the sweetly nearsighted look of her slanted eyes suffused with cordial night, and especially that smiling way her upper lip met the lower, lending that graciously promising contour to the corners of her mouth. Yes, she was the loveliest of all; if, however, we were to say, as Jacob always told himself, that she was above all lovely in comparison to her older sister, that would not mean that the latter was the ugliest of all, but only that Leah was the nearest point of a comparison that went against her solely in respect to loveliness, although one certainly could imagine a man who was less dependent on this point of view than Jacob, a man who would have shown preference to the older sister—despite the inflamed feebleness of those crossed blue eyes, over which she proudly and bitterly lowered her lids—because her hair was full and blond and her body stately and suited for motherhood. Nor can one emphasize enough that, to little Rachel's credit, she never lorded it over her older sister, boasting, for instance, of her own winning face merely because she was the child and likeness of the beautiful moon and Leah that of the waning. Rachel was not so unschooled that she would not have known rightly to honor that heavenly body even in its feebler phase; indeed, in a certain sense she disapproved of the way Jacob totally rejected her sister and showed his unbridled, one-sided fondness for her, though she could not banish from her heart a certain female satisfaction in that regard.

The nuptial feast was set for the full moon of the summer solstice, and Rachel, too, admitted that she was waiting expectantly for the great day. But the truth is that she also looked sad in the weeks preceding it, spilling silent tears on Jacob's cheeks and shoulder, with no other reply to his fervent questions than a weary smile and a shake of the head so quick that the tears flew from her eyes. What did she have upon her heart? Jacob did not understand it, although at the time he was often sad as well. Was she sad because the time of her virginity, of her blossoming, was drawing to an end and she would soon be a tree that bore fruit? Such a sadness in life would in no way have been incompatible with happiness, and Jacob had himself often felt much the same in those days. For marital union, life's highest point, is also the point of death and the feast of the solstice, for the moon celebrates its height and fullness only to turn its face again toward the sun, into which it must now sink. Jacob was to know the woman he loved, and begin to die. For all of life was not to be present exclusively in Jacob alone from now on, and he would no longer stand alone, the sole lord of his world; but instead, he was to dissolve into his sons, and his person be given over to death. Yet he would love those who bore his changed and dispersed life, because they were his sons, whom he had knowingly poured into Rachel's womb.

In those days he had a dream he would long remember for its strangely peaceful and consoling sadness. He dreamt it on a warm Tammuz night spent in the field near the sheepfold, and the same narrow-planked boat of a moon already floating in the sky would in its rounded beauty later shine upon his night of bliss. It seemed to him as if he were still fleeing from home, or was fleeing yet once more; as if he must ride out into the red desert anew; and before him trotted that pointy-eared, dog-headed beast with its tail extended, and it turned to look at him and laugh. It was a matter of both still and once more—the situation that had once never quite developed had returned to find its fulfillment.

Where Jacob rode there was only scattered gravel, scrub bushes were all that grew. The evil one loped ahead, winding its way between boulders and bushes, disappearing behind them, only to reemerge and look around. At one point it vanished, and Jacob blinked. No sooner had he blinked than the animal was sitting in front of him on a stone, and it still had the head of an animal, that nasty dog's head with its pointy ears erect and that almost beaklike protruding muzzle, the line of its mouth extending to the ears; but the body had a human shape down to its barely dusty toes—a boy's slight, delicate body that was a pleasure to behold. Sitting on the boulder, it struck an easy pose, bending forward slightly, with a little crease in the belly just above the navel and one forearm resting on the thigh of its drawn-back leg, while the other leg was stretched forward, with only the heel touching the ground. This outstretched leg, with its trim knee and the slight curve of its long, finely sinewed calf, was the most pleasant sight of all. But along the god's slender shoulders, across the upper part of its chest and neck, was the beginning of hair that became a pelt the color of yellowish clay covering the dog's head, with its broad cleft of a mouth and small malicious eyes—and it all fit together the way a foolish head has to fit a stately body, sadly debasing it, so that all the rest, that leg, that chest, *might* have been lovely, but certainly not with that head. And having ridden up close now, Jacob could smell in its full pungency the acrid jackal odor exuded, sad to say, by this dog-boy. And the strange sadness was complete when the broad mouth of the muzzle opened and the throaty labored voice began to speak: "*Ap-uat, Ap-uat.*"

"Don't trouble yourself, son of Osiris," Jacob said. "I know that you are Anup, the guide and opener of the ways. I would have been amazed not to have met you here."

"It was a mistake," the god said.

"How do you mean?" Jacob asked.

"They conceived me by mistake," that laboring mouth said, "the Lord of the West and Nephthys, my mother."

"I'm sorry to hear it," Jacob responded. "But how did it happen?"

"She was not supposed to have been my mother," the boy replied, his mouth gradually becoming more supple. "She was the wrong one. Night was at fault—she is a cow, it makes no difference to her. She bears the sun's disk between her horns, to show that the sun enters her each time in order to beget the young day, but giving birth to so many radiant sons has never interfered with her dullness and indifference."

"I am trying to understand," Jacob said, "how that might be dangerous."

"Very dangerous," the other rejoined with a nod. "In her blindness, in her bovine warmth and goodness she embraces everything that happens within her, and out of the fullness of her dull passivity simply lets happen what happens, if only because it is dark."

"Too bad," Jacob said. "But who would have been the right one to conceive you if not Nephthys?"

"You don't know?" the dog-boy asked.

"I cannot exactly tell the difference," Jacob replied, "between what I know on my own and what I am learning from you."

"If you did not know it," came the response, "I could not tell it to you. In the beginning, not the very beginning, but more or less the beginning, there were Geb and Nut. He was the god of earth and she the goddess of heaven. They had four children: Osiris, Set, Isis, and Nephthys. Isis, however, was the sister-wife of Osiris, and Nephthys the wife of red Setekh."

"That much is clear," Jacob said. "And did these four not keep a sharp enough eye on that arrangement?"

"Two of them didn't," Anup replied. "Unfortunately not. What can you expect? We are distracted creatures, born to live without care, inattentive and dreamy. Worry and precaution are dirty, earthly attributes, but on the other hand, just think of all the things that carelessness has caused in life."

"Only too true," Jacob agreed. "One must be careful. If I may be frank, in my opinion it is all because you are mere idols. God always knows what He wants and does. He makes promises and keeps them, He establishes a covenant and is faithful for all eternity."

"Which god?" Anup asked.

But Jacob replied, "Don't pretend with me. When earth and heaven join, that results at best in heroes and great kings, but not in a god, neither four nor one. Geb and Nut, as you've admitted, were not at the very beginning. Where did they come from?"

"From Tefnut, the great mother," came the quick, pat answer from the stone.

"Fine, you say that because I already know it," Jacob went on in his dream. "But was Tefnut the beginning? Where did Tefnut come from?"

"She was called into being by what is unbegotten and hidden, whose name is Nun," Anup replied.

"I did not ask as to the name," Jacob rejoined. "But now you are starting to speak reasonably, dog-boy. It was not my intention to dispute with you. After all, you're an idol. So now tell me about the error your parents made."

"Night was at fault," the foul-smelling beast repeated, "and he who bears the lash and the shepherd's crook was carelessly distracted. The majestic god was in pursuit of Isis, his sister-wife, and in the blindness of night inadvertently stumbled upon Nephthys, the sister of the Red One. So the great god embraced her, assuming she was his wife, and both embraced in the perfect indifference of a night of love."

"Can something like that occur!" Jacob cried. "What happened?"

"It can occur very easily," the other voice answered. "Even in her indifference, night knows the truth, and the awakened prejudices of day are nothing to her. For one female body is like another, good for loving, good for conceiving. Only the face marks the difference between one and the other, making us think that in conceiving we want the one and not the other. For the face belongs to day, which is full of awakened illusions, but it is nothing to night, which knows the truth."

"What crude and unfeeling words," Jacob said in anguish. "You have good reason to say such stupid things with a head and face like yours—why, a man must first hold a hand in front of it just to notice and concede that your outstretched leg is handsome and beautiful."

Anup looked down, placed his feet side by side, and thrust his hands between his knees. "You can leave me out of this!" he then said. "I'll get rid of this head of mine yet. So then, do you want to know what happened then?"

"What?" Jacob asked.

"In that night," he continued, "the Lord Osiris was for Nephthys like Set, her red husband, and for him she was just like Isis, his mistress. For he was made to beget and she to conceive, and night was indifferent to all the rest. And they delighted each other in begetting and conceiving, for in believing that they loved, they could not help conceiving. And that goddess became pregnant with me, whereas Isis, the true wife, should have been."

"Sad," Jacob said.

"When morning came they sped apart," the boy-beast said, "and things might have turned out all right if the majestic god had not left his lotus wreath with Nephthys. The red Set found it and bellowed. And ever after he sought to slay Osiris."

"You report it as I know it," Jacob recalled. "Then came the part with the casket, did it not?—into which the Red One lured his brother, using it to slay him, so that Osiris, the dead lord, floated down the river in the sealed coffin and out into the sea."

"And Set became king of the Two Lands and sat upon Geb's throne," Anup added. "But that is not what I wish to dwell upon, nor what lends this dream of yours its stamp. For the Red One did not long remain king of the lands, because Isis bore the child Horus, who slew him. But behold, she wandered the world searching for her lost, her murdered husband, wailing without surcease, 'Come to your house, come to your house, my beloved! O beautiful child, come to your house!' and beside her was Nephthys, the wife of his murderer, whom the slain god had mistakenly embraced, beside her at every step, and they ardently shared their pain and lamented together: 'O you whose heart no longer beats, I wish to see you, O beautiful lord, I wish to see you!'"

"An amiable and sad thing to do," Jacob said.

"Indeed," the dog-boy on the stone replied, "that is the very stamp of it. For who else was beside her, lost and wailing and helping in the search, both then and later, after Set found the hidden corpse and dismembered it into the fourteen pieces for which Isis had to search in order that her lord's limbs might be whole again? It was I, Anup, the son of the wrong wife, the fruit of the murdered man's loins, who was with her as she wandered and searched—always at Isis's side. And she laid her arm around my neck as we went, so that I could better support her, and we lamented together: 'Where are you, left arm of my beautiful god, and where are you, shoulder blade and right arm, where are you, his noble head and his sacred genitals that appear forever lost, so that it is our wish to replace them with images of sycamore wood?'"

"You speak obscenely, as befits the god of death of the Two Lands," Jacob said.

But Anup replied, "In your situation one should have a sense of such matters, for you are a bridegroom and you shall both beget and die. For sex is death and in death is sex, that is the secret of the crypt and sex rips open death's winding-sheets and stands up against death, just as happened with the lord Osiris, above whom Isis hovered as a female vulture, making seed flow from the corpse and impregnating herself by him even as she lamented."

A man should best awaken at this point, Jacob thought. And in thinking it, he saw the god swing down from his stone and vanish—and the lurch of his standing up and vanishing were all one motion—and awakened to the starry night, the sheepfold at his side. The dream of Anubis, the jackal, was soon erased from his mind, the details finding their way back, so to speak, into reality's simple journey, which was all that Jacob could still recall. The only part of the dream that remained in his soul for a while was a forgiving sadness—at how Nephthys had joined Isis to search and lament for him whom she had embraced by mistake and at how she who was bereft had allowed him who had been born by mistake to protect and support her.

Jacob's Wedding

During this period Jacob frequently discussed with Laban the imminent event of the nuptial feast, asking his master's intentions in all particulars, and learned that he planned to do things on a grand scale and was making arrangements for a wedding done in style and with no regard to the cost.

"It will cut deep into my purse," Laban said, "for the farm has many more mouths to feed now, but I shall stuff them all full. With no regrets, either, for as you see my business is not doing all that badly; indeed it's doing moderately well thanks to various circumstances, among which one might certainly also mention the blessing of Isaak that you bear with you. Which is why I have been able to add some strong arms and have bought two handmaids to help the slovenly Iltani: Zilpah and Bilhah, both attractive wenches. I want to give them to my daughters on the day of the wedding—Zilpah to Leah, my eldest, and Bilhah to my second daughter. And since you are the suitor, the handmaid will be yours as well, and I shall give her to you as a dowry, and the price will be reckoned at two-thirds of a mina of silver, as in our contract."

"Accept my embrace in return," Jacob said with a shrug.

"That is the least of it," Laban continued. "For the feast I wish to hold will be at my own expense, and I want to invite people from near and far for the Sabbath and bring in musicians who will both play and dance, and I want to split the backs of two bullocks and four sheep and cheer my guests with strong drink until they see double. I shall have to dig deep into my purse for it, but I will endure it without a grimace, for it is my daughter's wedding. I intend, moreover, to present the bride with something to wear that will delight her greatly. I bought it some time ago from a traveler, but have always kept it in the chest, for it is precious: a veil to veil the bride's face, so that she may sanctify and consecrate herself for Ishtar, but you shall lift the veil. It is said to have belonged long ago to the daughter of a king, to have been the virginal garment of a prince's child, and is artfully embroidered all over with every sort of symbol of Ishtar and Tammuz. And being unblemished, she shall wrap her head in it, and be as one of the unblemished *enitu*, like a bride of heaven, whom the priests bring to the god each year at the feast of Ishtar in Babel, leading her up the stairway and through the seven gates of the tower while everyone watches and removing a piece of her jewelry and attire at each gate, the cloth at her loins last of all, until they lead the holy naked girl into the highest bedchamber of the tower Etemenanki. There the god receives her upon his bed by the darkest darkness of night, and the mystery is very great."

"Hm," Jacob said, for Laban's eyes were wide, his fingers splayed at both sides of his head, and in his nephew's opinion that sublime look did not at all befit a clod of earth.

"It is indeed a fine and lovely thing," Laban went on, "when the bridegroom calls a house and farm his own or is held in high regard in the house of his parents and arrives in splendor to receive his bride and lead her off in pomp, by land or water, to his own property and inheritance. But you, as you know, are nothing but a fugitive without a roof, at odds with your family, and reside here with me as a son-in-law, yet I shall be content with that, too. There will be no bridal processions by land or water, for you two will remain here with me after the feasting and revelry; but when I have stepped between you and have touched both your brows, we then follow local custom in such a case and lead you alone about the courtyard with singing and to the bedchamber. There you sit upon the bed, a flower in your hand, and await the bride. For we then lead her, my unblemished daughter, round about the courtyard as well, with torches and singing, and at the chamber door we extinguish the torches, and I lead the consecrated bride to you and leave you both, so that you may present her the flower in the dark."

"Is that the custom and lawful usage?" Jacob asked.

"Far and wide, just as you say," Laban replied.

"Then that will be fine with me," Jacob responded. "I assume, by the way, that at least one torch will continue to burn or the wick of some little lamp, so that I can see my bride when I hand her the flower, and afterward."

"Silence!" Laban cried. "I would like to know how you can possibly speak so unchastely, and what's more to the father, for whom it is bitter and painful enough to lead his child to a man that he may uncover her and sleep with her. At least put a rein on your salacious tongue in my presence and keep your excessive lewdness to yourself. Do you not have hands to see, and must you also devour the unblemished girl with your eyes in order to sharpen your lust on her shame and trembling virginity? Think of the mystery of the tower's highest chamber."

"I'm sorry," Jacob said, "do forgive me. I did not mean it as unchastely as it sounds from your lips. I would merely have liked to behold my bride with my eyes. But if the custom far and wide is as you've described, I shall be content for now."

And so that day of perfect beauty, the nuptial feast, approached, and on the farm and in the house of Laban, the successful breeder of sheep, all the slaughtering, cooking, roasting, and brewing raised a great din and fumes that had every eye watering from the acrid smoke of the fires that burned under kettles and ovens—for Laban saved money on charcoal by burning almost nothing but thorns and dung. Masters and menials, including Jacob, set their hands to work preparing comestibles for the many guests of the prolonged banquet, for the wedding was to last seven days and during that time the household, if it was not to be shamed and mocked, had to prove its inexhaustible supply of pastries, twisted breads, and fish cakes, creamed soups, compotes, and milk puddings, beer, fruit juices, and strong schnapps—not to mention the roast mutton and haunches of beef. As they bustled about, they sang songs for Uduntamku, the plump god of the belly who presided over all feasting. They all sang and worked: Laban and Adina, Jacob and Leah; the slovenly Iltani and Bilhah and Zilpah, the daughters' handmaids; Abdcheba, the twenty-shekel man; and the newly acquired slaves. Laban's late-born sons ran yelping through the hubbub in their shirttails, but then slipped on blood spilled during slaughtering and soiled themselves, so that their father had to twist their ears until they howled like jackals; and only Rachel took no part, but sat quietly off by herself in the house—for she dared not see the bridegroom now, nor he his bride—and examined the precious veil her father had given her to wear at the feast. It was splendid to look upon, a masterwork of the weaver's and embroiderer's arts—what an undeserved stroke of good fortune that something like this had found its way into Laban's house and chest. The man who had been forced to sell it so cheaply to him must have been hard-pressed by circumstance.

It was long and ample, both a dress and a robe over that, cut with wide sleeves, if one chose to use them, and a section that could be pulled up to cover the head or simply wound around the head and shoulders, or left to hang down the back. Weighing this virginal garb in one's hands left one strangely uncertain, for it was both heavy and light, its weight varying here and there. The pale blue fabric itself was extremely light, as finely spun as if made only of a breeze, a vapor, of nothing, so that it could be balled up into the hand until not a trace was visible; and yet heavy from the embroidered images scattered everywhere across it and filling it with shimmering bright colors, each highly ingenious symbol and image executed in a tightly worked embossment of gold, bronze, silver and in every imaginable hue of thread: white, purple, pink, olive, plus black and white and medleys of color like those fused together in glass. Ishtar–Mami's figure was displayed in frequent variation—a small nude, squeezing milk from her breasts with her hands, sun and moon at each side. Repeated everywhere in a multitude of colors was the five-pointed star that means "god"; and the silvery sheen of the dove, the bird of the mother-goddess of love, dotted the fabric. Gilgamesh, the hero, two-thirds god and one-third man, was there, throttling a lion in one arm. Clearly visible was the pair of scorpion men who guard the gate at world's end, through which the sun enters the underworld. There were several different animals, former paramours of Ishtar, but transformed by her into a wolf, or a bat that had once been Ishal-lanu, the gardener. One brightly colored bird, however, was recognizable as Tammuz, the shepherd, her first partner in lust, for whom she had decreed weeping year in, year out; nor was heaven's fire-breathing bull missing, the one that Anu had sent out to battle Gilgamesh at the bidding of Ishtar, wailing in her rutting. As Rachel let the garment glide through her hands, she saw a man and a woman sitting on each side of a tree, stretching out their hands for its fruit, while behind the woman's back a serpent rose up. And another holy tree was embroidered there: next to it stood two bearded angels facing one another and touching it to impregnate it with the scaly cones of male flowers; but above this tree of life, surrounded by sun, moon, and stars, hovered a symbol of the female. And mottoes had been sewn on as well, in broad and sharp-pointed characters, some horizontal, others slanted or erect, crossing at various angles. And Rachel deciphered: "I have removed my garment, shall I put it on again?"

She played a great deal with this colorful gossamer, this masterly robe, this veil; she threw it around her, turning and spinning, inventively draping herself in the transparent fabric and its wealth of symbols. This was her amusement as she waited in seclusion while the others made ready for the feast. Occasionally she was visited by Leah, her sister. And she, too, would then try on the veil's beauty, and afterward they would sit together, the garment in their laps, and weep as they caressed one another. Why did they weep? That was for them to know. But this much we will say: each did so for her own special reason.

When, as on the day he joined his red twin to bury their father, Jacob's eyes would glisten with remembering and all those stories written in his face and lending weight and dignity to his life would rise up within him and become a pondering present—on such occasions, the day, the story, most present of all to him was one that had dealt him such a terrible, mind-boggling defeat and emotional humiliation that his soul took a long time to overcome it and was really only healed to believe in itself again by a feeling that was itself a resurrection of what had been mutilated and violated that day. More than all the other stories alive in him, then, was the story of his wedding day.

They had all—everyone in Laban's household—washed their

heads and limbs in the blessed water of the pond, had duly anointed their bodies and curled their hair, laid on their festal garments, and burned much sweet-scented oil so that arriving guests might be received with its fragrant haze. They had come on foot, on asses, and in carts pulled by oxen and mules—men by themselves, men with women, even with children, if they could not be left at home—neighboring farmers and cattle breeders, likewise anointed and curled and festively clad, men like Laban, with the same plodding manners and heads for business. Hands to their brows, they had extended greetings, inquired as to health, and then taken their seats in the house and in the courtyard, around kettles and decorated tables, so that water might be poured over their hands and they could begin the prolonged banquet with smacking lips and invocations of Shamash and praise for Laban, their host and the father of the bride. The banquet was laid out among the sheds and storehouses of the outside courtyard and in the paved interior court with its stone of sacrifice, in the surrounding wooden gallery and up on the roof of the house. Gathered around the sacrificial altar were musicians hired from Haran, who played harps, drums, and cymbals, but could dance as well. The day was windy, the evening was even more so. Clouds glided past the moon, covering it for a while, which not a few guests took as a bad omen, though without actually mentioning it; for these were simple people, for whom there was no difference between a moon whose face was darkened by clouds and an actual eclipse. The sultry wind sighed as it passed through the house, whistled whenever it got caught in the storehouse vents, set the poplars creaking and soughing, rummaged among the wedding feast's aromas—the fragrant balms of the diners, the steam rising from the food—blended them all in drifting gusts, and tried to snatch the flames from the tripods where spikenard and budulhu gum were burning. Whenever he recalled these events, Jacob always thought he could feel his nose tickled by that same pungency of smoke and spices, of festal sweat and roasting meat, all tangled up on the wind.

He sat with Laban's household among other banqueters in the upstairs room where he had first broken bread with his foreign kin seven years before, sat with the master of the farm, his fertile wife, and their daughters around a cloth-covered table piled with desserts and delicacies—sweet bread, dates, garlic, and pickles—and returned

the toasts of guests who raised their goblets of strong drink to him
and their hosts. Rachel, the bride he would soon receive as his own,
sat beside him, and now and then he would kiss the hem of the veil
concealing her in its folds heavy with images. Not once did she lift it
to eat or drink—the consecrated bride had evidently been fed before
the banquet. She sat quiet and mute, merely bending her covered
head meekly toward him whenever he kissed her veil; and Jacob,
too, sat silent and numbed by the feast, a flower in one hand, a twig
of blossoming white myrtle from Laban's irrigated garden. He had
drunk beer and date wine, his senses were dazed, and his soul could
not free itself for thought or look up to observe all this in gratitude,
but lay heavy inside his well-anointed body—and his body was his
soul. He would have liked to think, to have gained a true grasp of
how God had prepared all this, of how He had once led a fugitive
to his beloved, this human child whom he had needed only to behold for his heart to choose her for all eternity, to love her in the
present—and in the future beyond her, in the children she would
offer in return for his tenderness. He strove to rejoice in his victory
over time, over the long and bitter wait evidently required of him in
atonement for Esau's abasement and bitter tears, strove to lay his triumph at the feet of God, to praise his Lord—for the victory was
God's, who, just as He had defeated the worm of chaos, had used
him and his hardly indolent patience to conquer time, the seven-
headed monster, so that what had been a fervently awaited wish was
now the present, with Rachel sitting beside him in a veil that he
would lift in but a little while. He strove to let his soul take part in
his good fortune. But good fortune is much like the waiting for it—
the longer it lasts, the less it becomes pure waiting and is diluted with
having to live, with practical ambition. And when good fortune so
actively awaited finally arrives, it is not made of divine stuff, as it
once appeared in the future, but has become the physical present,
bearing the same heaviness of the body as all life. For life in the body
is never bliss, but dubious and unpleasant in part, and when good
fortune becomes physical life, the soul that waited so long must join
in, is itself nothing more than the body, which with its oil-clogged
pores is now in charge of that once distant and blissful good fortune.

Jacob sat there, tensing his thighs, thinking of his sexuality,
which was now in charge of his good fortune, but in a very little

while was to be permitted and required to prove its strength in a bedchamber's sacred darkness. His good fortune was the gaiety of a wedding ceremony, a feast of Ishtar, wrapped in a haze of spicy incense, celebrated with gluttony and drunkenness, whereas it had once been God's concern, had rested in His hand. Just as Jacob had once felt sorry that his waiting was forgotten in living and doing, he now felt sorry for God, the great Lord of life and the yearned-for future, who, now that the hour was realized, had to yield His lordship over it to the idols and divinities of the flesh, under whose sign the hour stood. Which was why Jacob kissed the nude likeness of Ishtar when he lifted the hem of Rachel's veil as she sat beside him as procreation's purest sacrifice.

Across from him sat Laban, leaning toward him with heavy arms resting on the table and a heavy gaze fixed on him.

"Rejoice, my son and sister's son, for your hour has come, the day of your reward, and payment shall be made you as legally required by contract for the seven years you toiled for my house and farm, to the reasonable satisfaction of him whose business it is. And the payment is not in goods or gold, but is a gentle maiden, my daughter, your heart's desire, who will lie obedient in your arms as your heart yearns for her to do. I am curious as to how your heart is beating, for the hour is a great one for you, truly an hour like the greatest in your life, I would think, as great as the hour when you won your father's blessing there in his tent, as you have told me, you sly fellow and son of a sly woman."

Jacob was not listening.

Laban, however, teased him roughly before his guests and said, "Tell me, son-in-law, hey now, hear now, how are you feeling? Do you shudder perhaps at the good fortune of embracing your bride, and are you not afraid as on the day when the blessing was at stake and you entered your father's tent on wobbly knees? Didn't you say that in your distress and fear sweat ran down your thighs, and your voice almost failed you when it came to gaining the blessing in the place of Esau, who was cursed? Lucky dog, let's hope your joy doesn't play a trick on you when it comes time, that your manly powers don't fail you! Your bride might take it amiss."

Laughter thundered through the upper room, and with a smile Jacob once again kissed the image of Ishtar, to whom God had given this hour.

Laban, however, got ponderously to his feet, and, swaying a little, he said, "Well then, all right, let's risk it. Midnight is here, step forward, I shall join you together."

And they all crowded around to see the bride and bridegroom kneel on the plastered floor before the bride's father and to hear Jacob speak the words according to custom. For Laban asked him if this woman was to be his wedded wife and he her husband, and if he wished to give her the flower, to which he said yes. And he asked if he was well born, if he wished to make this woman rich and her womb fruitful. And Jacob responded that he was the son of a great man and would fill the woman's lap with silver and gold and make her fruitful as the fruit of the garden. Whereupon Laban touched both their brows, stepped between them, and laid his hands upon them. Then he told them to rise and embrace, that they were wed. He gave the consecrated wife back to her mother, but grasped his son-in-law by the hand and, at the head of the guests who pressed in behind and took up a song, he led him down the brick stairway to the paved courtyard where the musicians now stepped out in front. After them came servants with torches and after them children in shirttails with incense pots strung on chains. Led by Laban, Jacob walked amid the clouds of fragrance billowing from them, and in his right hand he held the blossoming twig of white myrtle. He did not join in singing the traditional songs that rang out as they went, and not until Laban nudged him and told him to open his mouth, did he hum a little. Laban, however, sang in his booming bass and knew all the songs by heart, sweet and love-struck ditties about couples in love, about a lad and a lass on the verge of marriage and how both can hardly wait. The words told of the very procession they were now in, coming from the wide plain, sending the smoke of lavender and myrrh into the sky. There was the bridegroom, his head bearing the crown his mother had ornamented with her aged hands for his wedding day. This didn't match Jacob's case—his mother was far away, he was only a fugitive—nor did it fit his special situation when they sang of how he led his beloved to his mother's house, to the chamber of her who had given birth to him. But if only for that reason, it appeared, Laban sang lustily along, both to honor the norm in light of reality's deficiencies and to let Jacob feel the difference. And then it was the bridegroom of the song who spoke, and the bride who gave her ardent response, and they exchanged enraptured words of praise and yearning. Finally, however, they implored everyone else, pleading their cause one for the other, not to awaken them too early once they had fallen asleep in blissful desire, but to let the bridegroom rest and his bride slumber her fill, until they awakened on their own. That was the song's entreaty, sworn by the deer and hinds of the field, and everyone sang it with heartfelt emotion as they went—even the children carrying incense pots sang eagerly along without really understanding it. And so the procession moved about Laban's farm in the windy, dark-mooned night, passed by the house first once, then returned a second time to press through its palm-wood doors, the musicians out in front, and now arrived at the bedchamber on the ground floor, which also had a door—and Laban took Jacob by the hand and led him inside. He let it be illumined by torches so that Jacob could look about the room and see where the bed and table stood. Then wishing blessings upon his manly powers, Laban turned to the celebrants crowded in the doorway. They withdrew, taking up their song again, and Jacob was left alone.

Decades later in old age—and even as he solemnly asserted on his deathbed—there was nothing he recalled more clearly than standing alone in the darkness of that drafty, windy bridal chamber; for fierce gusts burst in through window slits just under the roof and out again through those on the courtyard side, got tangled in the curtains and tapestries with which, as Jacob had noticed by torchlight, the walls had been hung, and set them fluttering and flapping. It was the room beneath which lay the archive and crypt with its teraphim and receipts; through the thin carpet spread here for the wedding, Jacob's foot could feel the little ring of the trapdoor leading down to it. He had also seen the bed and stepped that way with an outstretched hand. It was the best bed in the house, one of three, the one Laban and Adina had sat on during that first evening meal seven years before—a couch with metal-sheathed legs and a rounded headrest of polished bronze. Blankets had been tossed over the wooden frame and, as Jacob could feel, linen over them, and cushions were propped against the headrest—but the bed was narrow. The table next to it had been laid with a light meal and beer. There were two low stools in the room, likewise draped in fabric, and lamp stands at the head of the bed. But there was no oil in the lamps.

Jacob established that fact as he groped in the drafty darkness,

while the procession filled the house and courtyard with songs and
noisy stomping on its way to fetch the bride. Then he sat down on
the bed, the flower in his hand, and listened. They were leaving the
house again to circle it, harps and cymbals in the lead, this time with
Rachel, his lovely beloved to whom he had given his heart entirely
and who walked in her veil. Laban was leading her by the hand—just
as Jacob had been led before—and perhaps Adina as well, and the
amorous wedding songs sounded again in chorus, now near, now far.
As they finally approached, they sang:

> My friend is mine, he is utterly my own.
> I am a locked garden and closed, am well-laden with fruits
>   and most fragrant spices abound.
> Come, beloved, into your garden!
> Pluck with daring its most tempting fruits, oh sip the
>   refreshing sweetness of their juices.

Those were the singers' footsteps outside the door. When the door
opened a little, song and strumming burst into the room for a moment, then the veiled bride was inside the room, let in by Laban,
who at once shut the door again; and they were alone in the dark.

"Is that you, Rachel?" Jacob asked after a little while, having
waited for those outside to withdraw somewhat. He asked the question the way you ask "Are you back from your journey?" even
though the person is standing before you and there can be no question but that he is back, so that the question is pure nonsense, just a
way to let your voice be heard, to which the traveler has no reply except a laugh. Yet Jacob heard her nodding her head in assent, heard it
in the soft rustle and patter of the light yet heavy veiled garment.

"My darling, my little dove, apple of my eye, heart within my
breast," he said fervently. "It is so dark and drafty . . . If you weren't
able to see, I'm sitting here on the bed straight ahead in the room and
a little to the right. Do come to me, but don't bump into the table,
leaving a dark bruise on your tender skin, and you'd knock over the
beer as well. I'm not thirsty for beer, not for it, but only for you, my
pomegranate—how wonderful that they have led you to me and I no
longer have to sit here alone in the wind. Are you coming now? I
would come to you, but I probably am not supposed to, for it is custom and lawful usage that I give you the flower while sitting, and

although no one will see us, we want to observe what has been prescribed, so that we are truly wed, as has been our unwavering desire
through so many years of waiting."

It overwhelmed him. His voice broke. This reminder of time endured in patience and impatience for the sake of this moment
touched him deeply and powerfully, and so touching was the
thought of how she had waited with him and likewise now saw herself at the goal of her wishes that it roused his heart. For that is love
when it is complete: tenderness and desire, to be touched by emotion and filled with lust at the same time, and even as tears of emotion welled up in Jacob's eyes he also felt the tensing of his manhood.

"There you are," he said, "you have found me in the dark, just as
I found you after a journey of more than seventeen days, and you
approached amidst your sheep and said, 'Look there, a stranger!'
And we chose one another from among all others, and I have served
for you for seven years, and the time now lies at our feet. Here, my
doe, my dove, here is the flower. You cannot see to find it, but I will
lead your hand to this little twig that you may take it, and I give it to
you—and now we are one. But I will keep your hand in mine, for I
love it so, and love the little bones of your wrist, so familiar to me
that I delight to recognize them again here in the dark, and to me
your hand is like you, is like your whole body—which is like a sheaf
of wheat garlanded in roses. Darling, my sister, sit down here at my
side, I shall move over to make room for two, and even for three if
need be. But how good of God to let us be but two, apart from all
others, to let me be with you and you with me. For I love only you,
love you for your face that I cannot see, but have seen a thousand
times and kissed out of love, for its loveliness is what garlands your
body with roses, and when I think that you are the same Rachel with
whom I have been so often, and yet never like this, the Rachel for
whom I have waited, and who has waited for me and waits for me
and my tenderness even now, I am caught up in a rapture stronger
than I, so that it overwhelms me. A gloom enfolds us thicker than
the veil with which they have adorned you, my pure one, and our
eyes have been bound with darkness, so that they cannot see beyond
themselves and are blind. But only they are blind, thank God, and
none of life's other senses. For we can hear one another when we
speak, and the darkness no longer divides us. Tell me, my soul, are
you also enraptured by the greatness of this hour?"

"I am yours, my dear lord, in bliss," she said softly.

"Leah, your older sister, could have said that," he replied. "Not the sense of it, but the way of speaking it, as is understandable. The voices of sisters are surely much alike, and the words from their mouths have a similar sound. For the same father begot them with the same mother, and they are somewhat parted by time and go their different ways, but they are one in the womb of their origin. Behold, I am a little afraid of my blind words, for it was easy for me to say that the darkness has no power over our speech, and yet I sense how this gloom thrusts itself into my words and drenches them so that they frighten me a little. Let us praise the difference, and the fact that you are Rachel and I am Jacob and, for instance, not Esau, my red brother. Both our forefathers and I have pondered many times beside the sheepfold just who God is, and our children and children's children will ponder after us. But may my words be bright in this hour so that the darkness retreats before them, and I say: God is the divider! And therefore I shall now lift your veil, my beloved, so that I may see you with seeing hands, and I shall lay it carefully on a chair that stands here, for it is precious with images, and we shall want to bequeath it down through the generations, and among all those countless numbers let those who are specially loved wear it. Behold, here is your hair, black, but lovely, I know it so well, I know its fragrance, which is like no other. I put it to my lips and what can darkness do now? It cannot thrust itself between my lips and your hair. Here are your eyes, laughing night in the night, and their delicate sockets, and I recognize that soft spot beneath them, where so many times I have kissed away the tears of impatience, leaving my own lips wet. Here are your cheeks, soft as down and like the most precious wool of goats from distant lands. Here are your shoulders, that seem almost more stately to my hands than they may appear to the eyes by day, your arms here and here—"

He fell silent. For as his seeing hands left her face and found her body and the skin of her body, Ishtar stirred them both to the core. The heavenly bull panted and his breath was the breathing of them both intermingled. And Laban's child was a splendid partner to Jacob all that windswept night, grand in her lust and lusty to conceive, and she received him often, over and over, until they lost count—but the shepherds told each other that it was nine times.

Later he fell asleep on the floor, nestled against her hand, for the bed was narrow and he wanted to leave her room for comfortable slumber. And so he slept hunched beside the bed, his cheek against her hand dangling at the edge. Morning dawned. Hushed and murky red, it stood at the window openings and slowly filled the bridal chamber with its light. It was Jacob who was awakened first, by daylight thrusting itself under his eyelids and by the silence, for the feasting had continued in the house and courtyard with much noise and laughter until deep into the night, and only toward morning, when the newlyweds were already asleep, had it grown quiet. He was uncomfortable as well, though joyfully so—and thus awakened more easily. He stirred, felt her hand, remembered how it all was, and turned his mouth to kiss her hand. Then he raised his head to tend his darling and watch over her slumber. With eyes unable to focus easily, heavy and sticky from sleep and still prone to roll back for more, he looked at her. It was Leah.

He lowered his eyes, shaking his head with a smile. My my, he thought—even as he felt a shudder pass through his heart and gut—look there, just look! Morning's teasing prank, an absurd bit of dazzlement. Curtains of darkness at my eyes—and now that they are free, they pull silly tricks. Are sisters secretly much alike perhaps, and even though the resemblance is not evident in their features, might one perceive it when they sleep? And so let's have a better look.

But he did not look yet, out of fear, and what he told himself was nothing but the babblings of dread. He had seen that she was blond and her nose a bit red. He rubbed his eyes with his knuckles and forced himself to look. It was Leah who lay there asleep.

Thoughts tumbled through his head. How did Leah get here, and where was Rachel, whom they had brought to him and whom he had known in the night? He staggered back from the bed, to the middle of the room, and stood there in his shirt, fists to his cheeks. "Leah!" he cried, and the word was strangled in his throat. She sat up. She blinked, smiled, and lowered her lids over her eyes just as he had often seen her do. One shoulder and breast were bare—they were white and beautiful.

"Jacob, my husband," she said, "let it be according to my father's will. For this was what he wished, and what he arranged, and may the gods grant me that you will still offer both him and them your thanks."

"Leah," he stammered, pointing to his throat, his brow, and his heart, "since when has it been you?"

"It has always been me," she replied, "and I was yours this night, ever since I entered here in my veil. Since I first saw you from the roof, I have always been ready for you, with a tenderness as good as Rachel's, and I proved that to you, I should think, all night long. For tell me yourself whether I served you or not, as well as any woman could, and was bold in my lust. I am certain in my heart of hearts that I have conceived by you, and it will be a son, strong and good, and his name shall be Re'uben."

And Jacob stopped to think and recalled how all night he had taken her for Rachel. And he walked over to one wall and laid his arm against it, and his brow to his arm, and wept bitterly.

He stood there a good while, his emotions torn and tossed, and each time he again thought of what he had believed and known, realized how all his happiness was a deception, how the hour of fulfillment for which he had served and conquered time was now desecrated, he felt as if his stomach and brain would upend, and he despaired to his very soul. Leah, however, knew nothing more to say and likewise wept now and then, just as she had with her sister before. For she saw how little it had been she who had received him time after time, and only the thought that at least in one of those times she had most likely received a strong son named Ruben strengthened her heart amid her tears.

Leaving her now, he stormed out of the room. He almost stumbled over the sleepers lying there and everywhere in the house and courtyard, strewn about on blankets and mats or even the bare ground amid the disarray of yesterday's feast, sleeping off their drunkenness. "Laban!" he shouted, climbing over the bodies that gave out peevish grunts, stretched, and returned to snoring. "Laban!" he repeated his cry more softly, for anguish and bitterness and a fierce need to call the man to account could not entirely stifle his consideration for these early morning sleepers after their high revelries. "Laban, where are you?" And he came to the chamber where Laban, master of the house, lay beside his wife Adina. He knocked and called, "Laban, come out here!"

"Hey there!" Laban replied from within. "Who hails me at dawn after I've been drinking?"

"It is I. You must come out here!" Jacob answered.

"Ah, yes," Laban said. "It's my son-in-law. To be sure, he says 'I' like a little child, as if someone could deduce it by that alone. But I know his voice and I will go out to hear what he has to tell me by the light of dawn, though I was enjoying my best sleep." And with hair still disheveled, he stepped outside, blinking.

"I was sleeping," he repeated. "A splendid and refreshing sleep. Why are you not sleeping as well, or doing what your new status requires?"

"It is Leah," Jacob said, his mouth trembling.

"But of course," Laban countered. "Have you come at daybreak, snatching me from wholesome slumber after strong drink, to tell me what I know as well as you?"

"You dragon, you tiger, you devil of a man!" Jacob cried, beside himself. "I do not tell you so that you may learn of it, but to show you that I know it as well, and in my anguish to call you to account."

"First off, mind your voice, and lower it considerably," Laban said. "I must require that of you, if you yourself choose not to let obvious circumstance require it of you. For if it is not enough that I am your uncle and father-in-law and your employer besides, before whom it is no way fitting for you to explode in such a frenzy, then you can plainly see that the house and courtyard are also filled with sleeping wedding guests, who in a few hours shall wish to join me in a hunt, so that they may amuse themselves in the wilderness and in the reeds of the swamp, where we hope to catch birds in nets, partridge or bustard, or capture a tusked boar and bring it down, that we may pour a libation of strong drink over it. And for that my guests are fortifying themselves with slumber, which is sacred to me, and our revelries will continue come evening. You, however, upon emerging from the bridal chamber after the fifth day, shall likewise join us in our joyous hunt."

"I will hear nothing about a joyous hunt," Jacob riposted. "It is the last thing on my poor mind, which you have baffled and desecrated till it cries from earth to high heaven. For in a cruel and shameless deception you have deceived me beyond all measure, and secretly brought Leah, your older daughter, to me instead of Rachel, for whom I served. What shall I now do with myself, and with you?"

"Give heed," Laban replied. "There are words you would do

better not to let pass your lips and had best be chary of speaking aloud, for in the land of Amurru, as I well know, there is a hairy man who weeps and plucks at his shaggy pelt and seeks to slay you, and he could surely speak of deception. It is unpleasant when one man must blush for another who does not blush for himself, and that is how things stand at the moment between you and me, given your poorly chosen words. I deceived you? In what regard? Did I bring to you a bride who was no longer spotless or unworthy to ascend the seven stairways into the arms of the god? Or did I lead to you one whose body was not well-formed and fit, or who started wailing at the pain you did her, or was not willing and obliging in your lust? Have I deceived you in any such fashion?"

"No," Jacob said, "not in that fashion. At conceiving, Leah is surely grand. But behind my back you doused the lights in order to cheat me, so that I could not see and all last night took Leah to be Rachel, and gave of my soul, gave my best to the wrong wife, which I now repent beyond telling. That is what you have done to me, you wolf-man."

"And you call that deception and brazenly compare me to beasts of the wilderness and to evil spirits, because I followed custom and as a just man did not presume to defy sacred tradition? I know not how it is done in Amurruland or in the land of Gog the king, but in our land it is not customary to hand over the youngest before the eldest—that would be a slap in the face of ancient custom, and I am a man of law, a man of decorum. And so I did what I did and acted wisely against your lack of reason, as a father who knows what he owes his children. For you basely offended me in my love for my eldest, for you said to me, 'Leah does not enkindle my manly desires.' Did you not deserve to be reprimanded and taught a lesson for that? And now you have seen whether she enkindles you or not!"

"I saw nothing whatever!" Jacob cried. "It was Rachel that I embraced."

"Yes, that is how it turned out come morning," Laban replied mockingly. "But that is the point—Rachel, my little one, has nothing to complain of. For the reality was Leah's, yet the intent was Rachel's. And yet I have also taught you an intent for Leah, and whichever you embrace in the future, hers will be both the reality and the intent."

"So you wish to give me Rachel as well?" Jacob asked.

"But of course," Laban said. "If you wish her and are willing to pay me the lawful price, you shall have her."

And Jacob cried, "But I served you seven years for Rachel!"

"You served me," Laban replied with dignity and firmness, "for one child. If, however, you wish the second, which I would also welcome, you must pay yet again."

Jacob was silent. But then he said, "I shall arrange for the purchase price and see to it that I can offer the portion. I shall borrow a mina of silver from people with whom I do business, and will also defray the cost of this or that present to hang on the bride's sash, for during that long time my worldly goods all unexpectedly met with an increase, and I am no longer quite so poor a mouse as when I first sued for her."

"Once more you speak with no delicate feeling," Laban replied with a dignified shake of the head, "and put scurrilous words to things you should lock deep within your bosom, rejoicing that others do not speak of them or call you to account. Instead you chatter loudly of them, serving them up to the world of late, until one man must blush for the other who prefers not to. I will hear of no unexpected increase and other such vexations. I don't want your silver as a portion or gifts for the bride, no matter to whom they belong, but rather you shall also serve me for the second child, as long as you did for the first."

"Wolf-man!" Jacob cried, barely able to restrain himself. "So you will only give me Rachel after another seven years?"

"Who says so?" Laban replied superciliously. "Who suggested anything of the sort to you? It is you alone who speaks absurdities and rashly compares me to a werewolf, for I am a father and do not wish for my child to pine for a man until he is old. Go now to where you belong and put in your week with honor. Then my second child shall quietly be brought to you as well, and you shall serve me another seven years as her husband."

Jacob was silent and lowered his head.

"You are silent," Laban said, "but cannot bring yourself to fall at my feet. I am truly curious whether I may still succeed at softening your heart to feel gratitude. For evidently my standing here in shirt-tails by the light of dawn, after being roused from much-needed sleep to settle affairs with you, does not suffice to awaken such a feeling in you. I have not yet mentioned that along with my second child you will also receive the other handmaid I bought. For I am giving Zilpah to Leah as a dowry, and Bilhah to Rachel, and wish in the second case as well to count her as two-thirds of the mina of silver I am giving you. And so overnight you have four wives, a house of women like the king of Babel and Elam's king, and only just now you were sitting in the pasture scrawny and alone."

Jacob was still silent.

"Hard man," he said finally with a sigh. "You do not know what you have done to me—do not know and, as I surely must believe, do not consider or even imagine it in your ironclad mind. I have squandered my soul and my best with the wrong wife this night—which crushes my heart for the sake of the true one, for whom it was intended. And I am supposed to tend to Leah for the rest of the week; and when my flesh is weary and sated, for I am only human, and my soul all too sluggish from high emotion, I am to have the true wife, Rachel, my jewel. And you think that makes it good again. But it can never be made good, not after what you have done to me and Rachel, your child—and last but not least to Leah, who sits upon her bed and weeps because she was not the one in my mind."

"Does that mean," Laban asked, "that after the honeymoon with Leah you will no longer be man enough to make the second fruitful?"

"Not at all, God forbid," Jacob answered.

"Whims, pure whims," Laban concluded, "and finicky twaddle. Are you satisfied with our new contract, and shall it be so established between you and me?"

"Yes, man, it shall be so," Jacob said and went back to Leah.

God's Jealousy

These, then, are the stories of Jacob, inscribed in his aged face and passing before his blurred gaze beneath knitted brows when he would fall into his solemn pondering, whether alone or in the presence of other people, who would inevitably be struck with holy awe at such an expression, so that they would nudge one another and say, "Hush, Jacob is pondering his stories." We have already unfolded and at last corrected some of them, even those that still lie far ahead,

including Jacob's return journey to the western lands and what happened after his arrival there; but seventeen years rich with stories
and changes of fortune remained to be filled, at the start of which
were Jacob's double wedding to Leah and Rachel and the birth of
Ruben.

Re'uben, however, was not Rachel's but Leah's, for she gave
Jacob his firstborn—who would later trifle away his birthright, for
he was like gushing water. It was not Rachel who conceived and
bore him, not the bride of Jacob's affection who gave this child to
him, nor, by God's will, was she the one who presented him with
Shimeon, or Levi or Dan or Jehuda or any of the ten, on down to
Zebulun, even though after the week of feasting was over, after Jacob
had departed from Leah on the fifth day and refreshed himself by
joining the bird-hunting party, she was likewise brought to him—
but we shall say nothing more of that. The story has already been
told of how Jacob received Rachel; for he first received her in Leah,
just as Laban, that devil, had arranged it; and it was indeed a double
wedding that Jacob celebrated, sleeping with two sisters, the one in
reality, but the other in intent—but what does reality mean in such a
case? From that point of view, then, Re'uben was indeed Rachel's
son, conceived with her. Yet although she had been so ready and
eager, she came away empty-handed, and Leah grew stout, contentedly folding her hands across her plump belly, tilting her head
meekly to one side, and lowering her eyelids to hide her crossed
eyes.

Kneeling on the bricks, she showed the greatest talent for giving
birth—a matter of a few hours, pure pleasure. Re'uben came gushing
forth like water. When Jacob, who was hastily informed, arrived
from the field—for it was sesame harvest—the newborn had already
been bathed, rubbed with salt, and swaddled. He laid his hand upon
him, and in the presence of the entire household he said, "My son."
Laban paid him his compliments, encouraging Jacob to be as vigorous as himself and to make his mark three years in a row, at which
the joyful new mother called across from her bed that she would be
fruitful for twelve years, and without a pause. Rachel heard her.

There was simply no keeping her away from the cradle, which
hung by ropes from the ceiling like a swing and which Leah could
direct from her bed with one hand. On the other side sat Rachel, observing the child. When it cried she would pick it up and give it to

her sister, laying it at her breast, richly veined and swollen with milk, and could not get enough of watching Leah feed the child, until it nursed its fill, turning red and puffy, and as she watched she would press her hands to her own tender breasts.

"Poor little thing," Leah might then say to her. "Don't fret, your turn will come. And your prospects are incomparably better than mine, for you are the one who is the apple of our lord's eye, and for every night he spends with me, there are four or six when he comes to you—how can it fail to happen?"

But though prospects favored Rachel, it was Leah in whom, according to God's will, they were fulfilled, for no sooner had she recovered from the first than she was fruitful again. Even as she carried Ruben upon her back, she bore Shimeon in her belly, was hardly sick at all when he began to grow, saw no reason to sigh at how he disfigured her body, and was vigorous and cheerful to the last, working in Laban's orchard when her time came, and with an odd look on her face she commanded the bricks be set up. And Shimeon appeared with ease, and sneezed. Everyone admired him, Rachel most of all—and how it hurt her to admire him. Things were different with him from the way they had been with the first, for without any deception, Jacob had consciously sired him with Leah, and he was hers entirely and beyond all doubt.

And Rachel, what was wrong with the little one? How earnestly and merrily she had once gazed up at her cousin, with such lovely courage and eagerness for life; with what confidence she had hoped and known that she would present him with children after their likeness, even twins on occasion! But here she stood empty-handed, and Leah was cradling her second now—how could that happen?

The letter of tradition is the only point of reference offered us when it comes to explaining these melancholy events of life. In brief it reads: because Leah was hated by Jacob, God opened her womb and made Rachel barren. That's why. It is one attempt at explanation like any other. It has the ring of supposition, not that of authority, for there is no direct and determinative utterance by El Shaddai as to the meaning of His decree, be it directed against Jacob or some other party—and without doubt He never offered one. All the same, it would be proper to cast this interpretation aside and offer another only if we knew a better, which is not the case. Indeed, we shall take the kernel of the one offered to be true.

That kernel is that God's action was not directed against Rachel, or at least not at first, nor was it done for Leah's sake, but rather was meant as instructive chastisement for Jacob himself, who was in fact rebuked inasmuch as the selectivity and gentle despotism of his emotions, the arrogance with which he nursed and proclaimed them, did not have the approval of the Elohim—even though such a tendency to single out by displaying unbridled preference, this pride of feeling that evaded all criticism and desired the whole world's reverent acceptance, could appeal to a higher model and indeed represented its earthly imitation. Even though? Jacob's emotional despotism was punished precisely because it was an imitation. Anyone attempting to address this matter must take care how he expresses himself; but after scrupulous examination of the text at hand there can be no doubt that the supreme motive for the action under discussion was God's *jealousy* of a privilege, which, in humbling Jacob's emotional despotism, He intended to designate as His privilege. This interpretation may well be censured and will surely not escape the objection that a motive as petty and passionate as jealousy is inappropriate for explaining divine decrees. People with such sensitivities, however, are free to understand a motivation they find offensive as the intellectually undigested vestige of an earlier and more savage state in the development of God's nature, an original state of affairs on which some light was shed on a previous occasion and according to which the countenance of Yahu—lord of war and thunderstorm for a host of brown sons of the desert who called themselves his warriors—boasted not just of holiness, but of worse and more monstrous traits.

The covenant of God with the intellectually active Abram, the wanderer, was a covenant whose ultimate purpose was the sanctification of both parties and in which human and divine need are so intertwined that one can scarcely say on which side, divine or human, the first impulse for cooperation originated—but a covenant in any case, and its establishment declares the double process by which both God and man are made holy and most intimately "bound" to one other. Why else, one may ask, should there even be a covenant? God's instruction to man, "Be holy, as I am holy," already presupposes the sanctification of God in humankind, its real meaning being "Let Me become holy in you, and you are to be holy as well!" In other words, the purification by which a shadowy, malicious god becomes a holy God includes, retroactively, humankind, in whom this is accomplished according to God's urgent wish. But this intimate linkage of man and God's affairs and the fact that God achieves His true dignity only with the aid of the human spirit, which in turn, however, enjoys no dignity without perceiving God's reality and its relationship to that reality—this amalgamation, then, this sublime marriage, this referential reciprocity sealed in the flesh and guaranteed by the ring of circumcision, allows us to comprehend why indeed jealousy, as a vestige of a passion antecedent to holiness, survived longest in God, whether as His jealousy of idols or, for instance, of His privilege of emotional despotism, which ultimately are one and the same.

For what is the unbridled feeling of one human being for another—such as Jacob allowed himself to feel for Rachel and later transferred in an even stronger form, if that is possible, to her firstborn—if not idolatry? What happened to Jacob through Laban may rightly, if only partially, be understood as a necessary balancing of the scales of justice in regard to Esau's fate, as compensation extracted from the man for whose sake the balance was disrupted to begin with. But when, on the other hand, one thinks of Rachel's dark destiny, and learns, moreover, what young Joseph had to endure—and how only by great astuteness and a charmer's finest skills at dealing with both God and man he managed to turn things around to the good—then one cannot doubt that it was a matter of jealousy in its purest meaning and finest luster, not jealousy in some general sense based on a privilege, but rather highly personal and directed in vengeance toward the objects of an idolatrous emotion. In a word, a matter of passion. Call it a vestige of the desert, but the truth remains that it is in passion, first and foremost, that the tempestuous term "living God" is actually and demonstrably fulfilled. And in retrospect, one will say that Joseph, however much his own flaws hurt him, had a better sense of this living God and was far more adept at taking Him into consideration than the father who begot him.

Rachel's Confusion

Little Rachel understood not a whit of all that. Weeping, she clung to Jacob's neck and said, "Give me children. Otherwise I shall die." He replied, "Dearest dove, what's all this? Your impatience only makes your husband a little impatient, and I would never have thought my heart could come to have such feelings toward you. It is truly unreasonable of you to cling to me with entreaties and tears. Am I in the place of God who has withheld from you the fruit of the womb?"

He blamed God, implying that it was not any deficiency on his part, was patently no fault of his, since he was fruitful with Leah. His proposing that the younger sister should turn to God, however, was tantamount to saying that she was to blame—itself a demonstration of his impatience, as was the quiver in his voice. Of course he was irritated, for it was silly of Rachel to plead with him for something that he himself so ardently desired, for it only turned his disappointed hopes into a reproach of her. And yet allowances surely had to be made for the poor thing in her distress, for hers was a sad plight if she remained barren. She was cordiality itself, but it would have been asking too much of feminine nature for her not to have envied her sister; and envy is a fusion of emotions in which, unfortunately, not only admiration but also other feelings are at work, so that the response from the other party cannot be the best, either. It had to undermine their sisterly relationship and had already begun to do so. In the eyes of the world the maternal Leah had such an advantage over her infertile co-wife, who still walked about very much the young maiden, that it would have been as good as hypocritical of her not to reveal in her behavior at least some awareness of her superior worth. In common parlance, simplistic though it may be, the wife blessed with children was the "beloved" and the lean one simply "despised"—a hideous turn of phrase to Rachel's ears, hideous because it was totally inapplicable to her situation. It was therefore only human that she was not satisfied with silent knowledge of the truth but needed to speak it aloud. And that, unfortunately, is what she did. Pale and with eyes flashing, she mentioned Jacob's undisguised preference for her and his more frequent visits at night—that, in turn, being a sore point with Leah, and once it was brought up, there was only one possible wincing retort: Yes, and what good had that done her? And that put an end to friendship.

Anxious and uneasy, Jacob stood in the middle.

Laban watched it all gloomily as well. It was fine by him that the child Jacob had chosen to disdain now stood in such honor; but then again he also felt sorry for Rachel—besides which, he began to fear for his purse. The Lawgiver had set it in writing that if a woman went childless, the father-in-law had to pay back her purchase price, for such a marriage was nothing but a failure. Laban could hope that Jacob knew nothing of this, but he might learn of it any day, and someday, when there was no longer any hope for Rachel, it might just happen that Laban or his sons would have to compensate Jacob in cash for his seven years of service. That stuck in Laban's craw.

And so when Leah became pregnant in her third year of marriage as well—the boy Levi was announcing himself—but nothing was stirring on Rachel's side, Laban was the first to suggest that some remedy was called for here and declared that measures must be taken, introducing Bilhah's name into the discussion and demanding that Jacob sleep with her, so that she might give birth on Rachel's knees. It would be a mistake to believe that Rachel herself had been the one to bring up or principally espouse what was, after all, an obvious idea. Her own feelings in this regard were too mixed for her to do anything more than tolerate it. But it is true that she was on very close and cordial terms with Bilhah, her handmaid—an attractive young thing, to whose charms Leah would one day have to abandon the field. And so Rachel's longing for the prestige of motherhood outweighed any other natural feelings of constraint she might have had in personally doing what her stern father had once done: leading a nocturnal surrogate to her cousin and spouse.

Actually, it was the other way around: Rachel took Jacob by the hand and led him to Bilhah, after first giving a sisterly kiss to her little handmaid—doused in too much perfume and so giddy with happiness that she did not know up from down—and saying, "If it must be so, dear heart, then you are the right one. Be mother to thousands!" This hyperbole was only a congratulatory phrase expressing the wish that Bilhah might prove receptive in her mistress's stead—and that is what the child promptly did. She announced her success to the mother of her future child, so that Rachel could then tell the news to the father and her parents. During the following months her body's plumpness from its cargo was only slightly behind Leah's. And Rachel, who was full of tenderness for Bilhah during this time and would often stroke her handmaid's body and lay an ear to its swollen contours, could see in everyone's eyes the respect that her successful sacrifice had brought her.

Poor Rachel! Was she truly happy? An accepted custom for such predicaments helped her minimize the decree from on high. But to the confusion of her eager, yearning heart, what gave her new worth was growing in the body of another. It was a half-worth, a half-happiness, a half-self-deception, with custom as its makeshift support, but with no solid foundation in Rachel's flesh and blood; and the children would be half-genuine as well, these sons that Bilhah would bring to her and the man she fruitlessly loved. The pleasure had been Rachel's, but the pain would be someone else's. That was convenient, but hollow and despicable, a silent abomination—not to her mind, which was obedient to law and custom, but to her honest and brave little heart. There was bewilderment in her smile.

Moreover, Rachel performed with joy and piety all that she was permitted and required to do. As ceremony demanded, she let Bilhah give birth across her knees. She wrapped her arms around Bilhah from behind and shared the long hours of labor, the groans and screams, acting as midwife and birthing mother in one. Bilhah had a difficult time of it, her labor lasted a full twenty-four hours, and at the end Rachel was almost as exhausted as the physical mother, but that suited her soul just fine.

And so the offspring of Jacob who was named Dan came into the world only a few weeks after Leah's Levi, in the third year of marriage. And in the fourth year, after Leah had been delivered of the son they called Jehuda—or "praise God"—Bilhah and Rachel joined forces to present their spouse with a second son, who would be a good wrestler from the looks of him, and so they named him Naphtali. And now Rachel had, in the name of God, two sons. After which there were no births for the time being.

The Dudaim

Jacob spent the first years of married life almost entirely on Laban's farm and let assistant shepherds and those who leased his flocks work the pastures, visiting them only occasionally to check things over with a sharp eye and receive payment in goods and animals—which then belonged to Laban, but not entirely, and not always even the bulk of them. For a great deal of the assets in the fields and even at the farm, where Jacob had erected several new storehouses to hold his own goods, now belonged to Laban's son-in-law, and one might speak of a virtual meshing of two flourishing businesses, whose interests were entangled in a set of complicated calculations, which Jacob evidently supervised and controlled, but which had long since lost any real transparency for Laban's gloomy eyes—not that he would have been willing to admit to it, in part out of a concern that it might show his intellectual weak points, but also in part out of his old fear that criticism and meddling might vex the blessing in his administrator's body. Things were, after all, going too well for him; he really had to look the other way, and indeed he hardly dared speak a word about business—it continued to be overwhelmingly obvious that Jacob was God's child. In just four years he had called into being six sons, six "spenders of water"—twice what Laban had managed living in proximity to the blessing. His secret esteem for Jacob was almost boundless, its only constraint being Rachel's closed womb. One had to let the man do as he pleased, and the lucky part was that he evidently had given scarcely any thought to departing and setting off on his own.

In reality Jacob's soul had never wandered far from thoughts of returning home, of resurrection out of his pit, this underworld that was Laban's realm—not after twelve years, any less than after twenty or twenty-five. But with an organic awareness of how much time he had—for he would live to be one hundred and six—he took his time, and had ceased to connect notions of travel with a given point in time when Esau's rage might presumably have died down. And his life had also necessarily become somehow rooted in the soil of Naharina, for he had experienced many things here, and the stories that happen to us in a given place are like roots that we send deep into the ground. Primarily, however, Jacob decided that he had not yet gained sufficient benefit from his descent into Laban's world, was not yet heavy enough with riches there. The underworld hides two things: filth and gold. He had come to know the filth—in the form of cruel waiting and of the even more cruel deception with which Laban, that devil, had cleft his soul on his wedding night. But he had also begun to load himself up with riches—but not enough, not in abundance. Whatever he could carry would be packed up, and there was still gold to be bled from Laban, that devil; they were not square yet, he needed to be cheated more thoroughly, not for the sake of Jacob's revenge, but simply for its own sake, because in the end it was only fitting for that deceiving devil to be deceived down to his toes—except that Jacob did not yet see the decisive method by which to make what was inevitable come to pass.

That kept him there, and his dealings kept him busy. He was back in the fields and on the plain a great deal again now, among shepherds and flocks, immersed in breeding and trading to Laban's and his own advantage; and that may have been one reason among others why the blessed tide of children came to a standstill, even though his wives frequently visited him at the sheepfolds along with both their own sons and Laban's growing boys and lived with him there in tents and huts. The fact was that Rachel, having acquired her makeshift sons, could not contain her jealousy toward Bilhah, who had helped her in her need, and no longer permitted intercourse between her lord and her handmaid, though both willingly complied with her ban. Her womb remained closed into the fifth, into the sixth year—and forever, or so it unhappily seemed. And Leah's body likewise remained fallow, much to her disgust—but it was simply resting, one year, two years.

And so she said to Jacob, "I do not know the source of this disgrace, that I am barren and useless. If you had only me this would not happen, and I would not have remained without a blessing for two long years. But there is my sister, who is everything to our lord, and she takes my husband from me, so that it is all I can do to keep from cursing her, though I do love her. Perhaps this strife has done harm to my blood so that I no longer bear fruit, and your God no longer wishes to think on me. But what was good for Rachel can only be fair for me as well. Take Zilpah, my handmaid, and lie with her, so that she may give birth upon my knees and I shall have sons through her. And as I am of no worth to you, I will nonetheless have children, by any means, for they are like balm to the wounds you inflict on me with your coldness."

Jacob barely contradicted her reproach. His statement that she, too, was of worth patently bore the stamp of feeblest politeness—and deserves censure. Could he not bring himself to show a little kindness to his wife, even though, to be sure, his soul had been sorely deceived through her? Did he have to regard every gentle word he might speak to her as somehow plundering his store of precious, coddled feelings? The day would come when he would bitterly repent the arrogance of his heart; but that day lay far off—indeed the day of greatest triumph would first have to dawn upon his feelings.

Leah presumably made this suggestion about Zilpah for form's sake, as a cover for her real desire that Jacob visit her more often. But being full of feeling, he felt nothing of that, and his arrogance led his feelings straight to simple and ready consent to revive the blessed tide of children with the help of Zilpah. He was granted immunity in the matter by Rachel, who could not refuse it to him, especially after the proud-breasted Zilpah—who bore a certain resemblance to her mistress and thus also never truly won Jacob's favor—fell to her knees and apologized to her, Jacob's favorite. And so Leah's hand-maid received her lord with humility and slavish diligence, conceived, and gave birth on the knees of her mistress, who helped her in her groans. In the seventh year of Jacob's marriage, the fourteenth of his sojourn with Laban, she bore Gad and wished him joy; and in the eighth and fifteenth came sweet-toothed Asher. Jacob now had eight sons.

It was during this time, after Asher's birth, that the episode of the *dudaim* occurred. The luck of finding them fell to Re'uben—eight years old at the time, a dark, muscular boy with inflamed eyelids. He was already helping with the summer harvest, for which Laban and Jacob, leaving the shearing behind, had come home and which likewise kept the rest of the household, including a few temporary hired hands, hard at work. Laban was a breeder of sheep, and until Jacob's arrival his tilling had been limited to cultivating a field of sesame; but once water was discovered he also sowed barley, millet, emmer, and especially wheat. His wheat field, enclosed by a clay wall and threaded with ditches and dams, was his most important piece of land, almost four acres that followed the slope of a low line of hills whose soil was rich and robust, and if left to rest from time to time, a holy and wise procedure that Laban never failed to observe, it bore more than thirtyfold.

This was a year of blessing. The honest labor of tilling, of the plow and the sowing hand, of hoe, harrow, and life-spending water pail had been divinely rewarded. Before ears of grain had begun to form, Laban's animals were granted lush green pastures—no gazelle, no raven came near to steal the fruit, no locust covered the land, no flood washed it away. In the month of Iyyar, the fields stood rich for harvest, especially since Jacob, though well aware that he was no tiller of the soil, had retained the vigor of his blessing in this sphere as well and had advised and implemented a denser planting than usual, so that despite somewhat fewer kernels per ear, the total yield would not be diminished but increased—so greatly that even after a portion of the harvest was measured out for his son-in-law, Laban would still come out ahead, at least as Jacob knew how to explain it in his calculations.

They were all out working in the field, even Zilpah, who stopped now and then to offer her breast to Gad and Asher; only the daughters of the house, Leah and Rachel, had remained at home to prepare the evening meal. With reed sun hats on their heads, tufted aprons at their loins, and bodies shiny with sweat, the people in the field sang hymns as they sickled the grain with wide sweeps of their arms. Others, however, cut straw or bound sheaves, loaded them on carts drawn by donkeys and oxen, so that once the blessing had arrived at the threshing floor it could be threshed by cattle, winnowed, sieved, and stored. And in this festival of labor even the boy Ruben had done his duty alongside Laban's children. But as the afternoon turned golden and his arms wearied, he ambled away to the edge of the field. There, beside the clay wall, he found the mandrake.

It took a sharp, indeed a schooled eye to spot it. The coarse weed with its oval leaves grew low to the ground, inconspicuous to an untrained eye. By its berries, however—*dudaim*, dark and the size of hazelnuts—Ruben recognized what grew underground. He laughed and gave thanks. He reached for his knife, drew a circle, and dug all around it, until the root was clinging only by thin threads. Then he spoke two words as a protective charm and with a quick jerk pulled the tuber from its earthbound realm. He had expected it to scream, but that did not happen. All the same, it was a fine and well-made magic little man, the size of a child's hand. He held it now by its top-knot: fleshy white, with two legs, a beard, and a skin of hairy filaments—a kobold inspiring wonder and laughter. The boy knew its properties. They were countless and useful—but especially beneficial to women, as Ruben was aware. Which is why he at once thought of giving his find to Leah, his mother, and he now bounded home with it.

Leah was very delighted. She praised her eldest, coaxing him, rewarding him with a fistful of dates, and warning him not to boast of his find to his father, or even his grandfather. "Silence is not a lie," she said. No need for everyone to know what was in the house; they would all sense its benefits, and that sufficed. "I shall wait," she decided, "and entice from it what it has to offer. Thank you, Ruben, my first, son of a first wife, thank you for thinking of her! There are others who do not think of her. But it's from them that you have your good luck. Now run along."

With that she dismissed him, intending to keep her treasure to herself. But Rachel, her sister, had been spying and seen it all. And who else would one day spy like that, and tattle till it almost cost him his life? Along with all her charms, this too was part of her nature, and she passed it on to her flesh and blood.

She said to Leah, "What did our son bring you?"

"My son," Leah said, "brought me nothing to speak of, a little something. Did you happen to be close by? Foolish boy, he brought me a beetle and a bright pebble."

"He gave you a little man out of the earth, with leaves and fruit," Rachel said.

"To be sure, that too," Leah replied. "Here it is. You can see how plump and jolly it is. My son found it for me."

"Ah yes, right you are, just look at how plump and jolly," Rachel cried, "and at all the *dudaim* it bears, such a wealth of seeds!" She had now put both hands to her handsome face, resting a cheek against them. All that was left to do was to stretch out her hands and beg for it. "What are you going to do with it?" she asked.

"I'll dress it in a little shirt, of course," Leah replied, "after I've washed and anointed it, and make a little box and faithfully wait for it to benefit the house. It will frighten off the riffraff of the air, so that none of them enter into a person or some animal in its stall. It will predict the weather and seek out those things that are hidden at present or still lie in the future. If I slip it in the pocket of our men, no knife can prick them, and it will bring them profit in their business and make it so that judges will speak in their favor even if they are in the wrong."

"What are you saying?" Rachel said. "I know such uses well enough. But what else will you do with it?"

"I will shear it of its leaves and *dudaim*," Leah answered, "and make a broth of them, one whiff of which brings on sleep, and anyone who smells too long of it is robbed of his speech. It is a potent infusion, my child, and whoever sips too much of it, be it man or woman, will surely die. But a little is good against snakebite, and if someone must have his flesh cut open, then it seems to him as if someone else's flesh is being cut."

"That is all quite beside the point," Rachel exclaimed, "and you make no mention of what you have most particularly in mind. Ah, Leah, my sister," she cried, and began coaxing and begging with her hands like a little child. "Little vein of my eye, most stately of daughters, give me a portion of your son's *dudaim* so that I may be fruitful, for my disappointment that I am not undermines my life, and bitter is my shame that I am of so little worth. Behold, my doe, my golden-haired sister among the black-tressed, you know the merits of this brew, and what it does to men, but it is like heavenly waters upon a woman's drought, so that she may happily conceive and deliver with ease. You have six sons in all, and I have two, which are not mine. Of what use to you are the *dudaim*? Give them to me, my wild she-ass, and if not all, then just a few, that I may bless you and fall at your feet, for my desire for them is a fever!"

Leah, however, clutched the mandrake to her breast and gazed at her sister with menacing crossed eyes. "I call that brazen," she said. "Here the little dear comes to spy on me, and she wants my *dudaim*. Is it not enough for you that you take my husband from me each day, each hour, and now you want my son's *dudaim* as well. Have you no shame!"

"Must you speak so hatefully," Rachel retorted, "and can you not do otherwise even if you were to try? Do not set me in a rage by distorting everything, for I would show you tenderness, if only for the sake of our childhood. I have taken Jacob, our husband, from you? You took him from me on that consecrated night, secretly going in to him in my place, and into you he blindly poured Ruben, whom I should have conceived. He would be my son now if things had been done rightly, and would have brought me the herb and its root, and if you were to come to me for some of it, I would give it to you."

"My, my, you don't say!" Leah said. "Would you actually have conceived my son? Why have you not conceived since then, and in your need would now use magic? You would give me nothing, that much I know. When Jacob is sweet with you and wants to take you to him, have you ever said, 'Dearest, do give a thought to my sister as well'? No, you merely melt away and give him your breasts to play with, your sole concern your wanton coquetry. And here you come begging, 'I would give it to you'!"

"Oh, how hateful!" Rachel replied. "How disgustingly hateful the things that your own character forces you to speak—they hurt me so, and yet it hurts me for your sake as well. It is indeed a curse to have to distort everything simply by opening one's mouth. That I did not send Jacob to you when he wanted to sleep with me had nothing to do with my begrudging you his company, may his God and our father's gods be my witness. But I am disconsolate, for I am still unfruitful for him after nine years, and each night that he chooses me I ardently await the blessing and dare not forgo it. But you, who might easily forgo it once or twice, what can you be thinking? You want to bewitch him for yourself with your *dudaim* and give me none of them, so that he forgets me and you have everything and I nothing. For I had his love, and you bore his fruit, and in that there was still a kind of justice. But you wish to have them both, love and fruit, and I am to eat dust. That's the thought you give to your sister!"

And Rachel sat down on the ground and wept loudly.

"I shall now take my son's little underground man and go inside," Leah said coldly.

And forgetting her tears, Rachel leapt up and cried in a low, fervent voice, "In God's name, do not do it, but stay and listen! He wishes to be with me tonight, he told me so this morning as he left me. 'Sweetest,' he said, 'my thanks for this. The wheat will have to be cut today, but after the scorching labor of a day in the field I would come to you, my dearest, and bathe in your gentle moonlight.' Ah, how he can speak, our husband! His words are pictures and full of majesty. Do we not both love him? But for tonight I shall leave him to you, in return for the *dudaim*. My very words: I leave him to you, if you will give me some of them. And I shall hide myself away, whereas you will say, 'Rachel is not of a mind, she has had enough billing and cooing. She says you are to sleep with me.'"

Leah blushed and then blanched. "Is this true?" she stammered. "You wish to sell him to me for my son's *dudaim*? So that I may say to him, 'Tonight you are mine'?"

Rachel replied, "You have put it perfectly."

And Leah gave her the mandrake, leaves and root, the whole thing, hastily thrusting it into her hand, and with a heaving breast she whispered, "Take it, go, and make yourself scarce!"

But as evening came on and people were returning from the field, she walked out to meet Jacob and said, "You are to sleep with me tonight, for our son found a turtle, and Rachel begged me to give it to her for just such a price."

Jacob replied, "My my, so I'm worth the price of a turtle and of the little dappled box that can be made from its shell? I don't recall being all that firmly resolved to spend the night with Rachel. And so she has purchased a certainty for an uncertainty, which I find praiseworthy. And if you both are agreed as regards me, then it shall be so. For a man should not set himself against woman's counsel, or kick against the decision and resolve of women."

Part Seven

RACHEL

The Oil Oracle

It was Dinah, the little monkey, who was then conceived—a hapless child. But through her Leah's body was reopened, returned to robust action after a pause of four years. In the tenth year of marriage she bore Issakhar, the raw-boned ass, and in the eleventh Zebulun, who did not want to be a shepherd. Poor Rachel! She had the *dudaim,* but Leah gave birth. That is how God willed it, and continued to will it for a while, until His will changed, or rather advanced to a new level, until another fragment of His fateful plan was revealed and Jacob, the man of blessing, was granted happiness—and on receiving it his time-bound human mind could never have dreamt how rich with life, how laden with suffering it would prove. Laban, that clod of earth, had surely been right when he ponderously expounded over his beer that blessing was power and that life was power and nothing more. For it is vapid superstition to believe that the life of the blessed is trivial happiness and shallow prosperity. Whereas blessing in fact is the very foundation of their nature, shimmering golden, as it were, through a wealth of torment and tribulation.

In the twelfth year of marriage or the nineteenth of Jacob's time with Laban, no child was born. In the thirteenth and twentieth, however, Rachel found she was expecting.

What a turnabout, what a beginning! Imagine her anxious, incredulous elation and Jacob's high emotion as he fell to his knees. She was thirty-one years old at the time; no one had believed God still held this laughter in store for her. In Jacob's eyes she was Sarai, who according to the threefold man's annunciation would bear a son, against all odds; and there at her feet, Jacob called her by the first mother's name, gazing in devotion through tears up into her face, which though pale and contorted seemed to him lovelier than ever. To this fruit of her body—conceived at last, but so long denied, withheld by an unfathomable interdiction that confounded confidence—to this child, even as she carried it, he gave the ancient, archaic name of a young god, who though hardly recognized officially now was still beloved by the people: Dumuzi, true and genuine son. Leah heard it. She had borne him six genuine sons and a thoroughly genuine daughter as well.

Even apart from that, she knew what to think. She gathered her four eldest, ages ten to thirteen at the time, sturdy and able young fellows, nearly adults and sure to be manly, though ill-featured men and all with a tendency to inflammation of the eyelids. She said to them, clearly and frankly, "Sons of Jacob and of Leah, it is over with us. If she bears him a son—and, may the gods protect my heart, I do wish her success—then our lord will no longer cast us a glance, not you, not the little ones, not the children of the handmaids, and certainly not me either, were I his first wife ten times over. For I am the first, and his God and my father's gods have made me a mother seven times. But she is his favorite, which makes her the first and only true wife, so he thinks in his pride, and her son, who has not yet beheld the light, he calls him Dumuzi, as you have heard. Dumuzi! It is like a knife in my chest, like a slap to my face, like a welt on the face of each of you, and yet we must bear it. That is how things stand, lads. We must remain calm, you and I, taking our hearts in both hands, so that they do not resort to violence against this injustice. We must love and honor our lord, even if in the future we become but dross in his eyes and he gazes through us as if we were air. And I will also love her and force my heart not to curse her, for it looks gently on a little sister, fondly recalling childish play, but it is also violently inclined to curse this favorite who would give birth to this Dumuzi, and my feelings for her are so divided, I am so sickened and repulsed, that I do not even recognize myself."

Ruben, Shimeon, Levi, and Jehuda awkwardly caressed her. They mulled this over, chewing on lower lips, blinking reddened eyes. That was when it started. That was when Ruben first planned in his heart the swift act of vengeance that he would perform one day for Leah, and it was the beginning of the end of his birthright. That was when the seed of hatred—of a life that was itself still a seed— was buried in the brothers' hearts and once sown would sprout as unspeakable heartbreak for Jacob, the man of blessing. Did it have to be that way? Might not peace and good cheer have reigned in the tribe of Jacob and everything have followed a smooth and steady course in equitable concord? Unfortunately no—not if what happened was meant to happen, not if the fact that it happened is likewise proof that it ought and had to happen. How manifold the happenings of this world, and since we cannot wish them to remain peacefully unhappened, we ought not curse the passions that cause them—for without guilt and passion nothing would ever move ahead.

A great to-do was made of Rachel's condition; that itself was annoyance and abomination enough for Leah, for whose robust pregnancies no cock had ever crowed. But in hers Rachel had become holy, so to speak—an attitude whose source was Jacob, of course, but that no member of the household, from Laban on down to the last slave in the courtyard or groom who cleaned stalls, could avoid. People walked about on tiptoe, spoke to her only in saccharine, sympathizing tones, tilting their heads and gesturing as if petting the air around her figure. All that was lacking was for palm fronds and carpets to be spread where she walked, so that her foot might not dash against a stone; and with a pallid smile she let them pay her court, less out of egotism than for the sake of Jacob's fruit, with which she had finally been blessed, and in honor of Dumuzi, the true son. But who can tell the difference between humility and conceit in those who are blessed?

Draped with amulets, she dared not lift a finger in the house, courtyard, garden, or field. Jacob forbade it. He wept if she did not eat or could not hold down what she ate, because for weeks on end she was wretchedly ill, and there was great fear of some riffraff demon's taunting influence. Her mother Adina constantly rubbed her with ointments concocted from old recipes, and the mixtures had a twofold purpose: both magically to protect and ward off evil and to provide healing and soothing by natural means. She ground together nightshade, dog's tongue, garden cress, and the root of the plant of Namtar, lord of sixty illnesses, stirred into the powder pure oils over which appropriate charms had been spoken, and rubbed it in the region of the expectant mother's navel, stroking upward and murmuring in slurred, jumbled, half-meaningless words, "Let evil Utukku, evil Alu step aside; evil spirit of death, Labartu, Labashu, heart's woe, belly's gripe, head's ache, tooth's pain, Asakku, grievous Namtaru, depart from this house, by heaven and by earth are you conjured!"

In her fifth month, Laban insisted Rachel be taken to Haran, to a seer and priest of Sin's temple, E-hulhul, so that he might foretell both her and her child's future through augury. In the presence of others, Jacob held to his principles and declined to participate, but ultimately he was no less feverish than his kin to know the results and always the first to demand nothing be left undone. Besides which, the old seer and temple-dweller in question was one Rimanni-Bel, which means, "Bel, have mercy on me," a son and grandson of seers, an especially popular and skillful clairvoyant and reader of oil, whose readings, it was generally agreed, were masterly and whose services were constantly in great demand. Jacob quite naturally refused to step before him as a supplicant and to sacrifice to the moon, but was far too curious as to what might be said—no matter from what corner—about Rachel's condition and prospects not to have indulgently allowed her parents to do as they pleased.

Thus it was Laban and Adina who walked beside the ass on which their pregnant daughter sat, one on each side, holding the bridle and leading the beast carefully to keep it from stumbling and giving its pallid rider a jolt. Behind them they had in tow the sheep they would sacrifice. Jacob, who had waved as they left, stayed at home in order not to see the pompous abomination of E-hulhul and be offended by its adjoining house of female prostitutes and boy lovers, who to honor their idol surrendered themselves to strangers for considerable sums. Without sullying himself, he awaited the verdict of this son of seers, who over a bowl spoke his thought-provoking prophecy, which they then brought home—and he listened silently to their story of what had happened to them in the temple precincts and then face-to-face with Rimanni-Bel, the reader of oil, or Rimut, as he was nicknamed. "Call me Rimut, short and sweet," the mild man had said. "For indeed my name is Rimanni-Bel, so that Sin may have mercy upon me, but I myself am full of mercy toward those who in their need and doubts are wise enough to make their sacrifice, and so simply address me as 'Mercy,' for the short form matches my face." And then he had asked what essential of life they had brought, inspected for any blemish the animal to be sacrificed, and directed them to booths in the main court where they could purchase such and such spices for the burnt offering.

An agreeable man, this Rimanni-Bel or Rimut, in his white linen garments and his cone-shaped cap, likewise of linen—an aged man now, but with a trim body free of any unsightly fat, a white beard, a reddened bulbous nose, and droll little eyes that made you merry just looking at them. "I am well-made," he had stated, "and with no flaw of limb or entrails, like the sacrificial animal when it is pleasing, and like the sheep to which no objection can be made. I am of straight stature and even proportion, and my leg is bent neither inward nor outward, nor am I missing so much as a single tooth, nor could my eyes be called crossed or my scrotum misshapen. Except my nose is a little red, as you can see, but only out of mirth and for no other reason, for I am as sober as clear water. I could step before the god naked, as was once the custom, so we have heard and read. Now we stand before him in white linen, and I am also glad of that, for it is likewise pure and sober and matches my soul. I harbor no envy against my brothers, the conjuring priests, who do their work in undergarments and cloaks of red, wrapping themselves in the luster of terror in order to confound demons and lurking riffraff. These others, too, are useful and necessary and worthy of their hire, and yet Rimanni-Bel, for I am he, would not wish to be any of them, nor to be a priest of baths and salves, nor one possessed, nor a priest of lamentation and wailing, nor indeed one whose manhood Ishtar has transformed into femaleness, as holy as that state may be. None of these awaken in me so much as a trace of jealousy, so content am I in my own skin, and I would choose to practice no other art of divination, but am solely given to the reading of oil, for it is by far the most sensible, the clearest and best. Just between ourselves, there is something very arbitrary about both augury with livers and the oracle of the arrow, and even the interpretation of dreams and spasms of the limbs do not lack for sources of error, so that I often make my little private jokes about them. As for you, father, mother, and pregnant child, you have chosen the right path and knocked on the right door. For my forebear is Emmeduranki, who was king of Sippar before the Flood, the wise keeper of the art—imparted to him by the great gods—of gazing into oil upon water and reading what will be from the behavior of the oil. I take my origin from him, in a direct line passed from father to son, an unbroken tradition—for each father had the son whom he loved swear with tablet and stylus before Shamash and Adad and had him learn the work entitled 'When the Son of the Seers'—on down to Rimut the Merry, the Unblemished, for I am he. And from the sheep I receive the hindquarters, the pelt, and one pot of broth—just so that you may know in advance; moreover the sinews and half the entrails as shown on these tablets and displays. The loins, the right shoulder, and a lovely piece of roast belongs to the god, and together we shall lift hands to share what remains at the temple meal. Is that satisfactory?"

The words of Rimut, son of seers. And they had sacrificed on the roof sprinkled with holy water, strewing the table of the lord with salt and placing upon it four jugs of wine, twelve loaves of bread, as well as a paste of curds and honey. Then they had strewn spices for burning on the incense candelabra and slaughtered the sheep: the suppliant held it, the priest dealt the blow, and requisite offering was made. How charmingly Rimut, the old man of unblemished limbs, had performed the final dance before the altar, cutting his judicious capers. Laban and the women could not praise it enough to Jacob, who listened and said not a word, silently eager to hear the verdict, but hiding his impatience.

Yes, the verdict, the judgment spoken by the oil—it was a murky and ambiguous matter; in possessing it, one was not much wiser than before, for it was both consolation and threat in one—but surely that was how the future had to sound if it could speak, and at least they had heard some sound from it, if only a buzzing, words spoken through lips shut tight. Rimanni-Bel had taken his cedar rod and bowl, had prayed and sung and poured oil on the water and water on the oil and cocking his head had observed the formations of the oil in the water. Two rings had emerged from the oil, one large, the other small—by every indication Rachel, the sheep breeder's daughter, would give birth to a boy. One ring had emerged from the oil toward the east and then stood still—the mother, having given birth, would return to health. A shake of the bowl, a bubble formed in the oil—her guardian god would stand by her in her need, for it would be great. Someone would escape from need, for the oil had sunk and risen, and when water was poured, it had divided and come together again, and thus someone would, though after terrible suffering, be well again. But since the oil, after water was poured, sank and then rose again and clung to the rim of the bowl, that meant that whoever was sick would rise again, but whoever was healthy would surely die. "Not the boy!" Jacob could not help crying out. No, for the child it was just the opposite—judging from the oil's signals, which in this instance were not easily comprehended by human understanding. The child would go down into the pit, and yet live; it would be like grain, which bears no fruit unless it dies. This reading, so Rimut had assured them, was indisputable—given how, when he had poured water into the oil, it had first separated, but then had rejoined with a strange sheen along the edge pointing toward the sun, for this meant the raising up of the head out of death. It was not very intelligible, the seer had said, he himself did not understand it, he would not pretend to be wiser than he was; but the signal was reliable. In regard to the woman, however, and judging from both test and countertest, she would not see the boy's star at its zenith, not unless she avoided the number two. For in general that number was unlucky, but especially for the sheep breeder's daughter, and according to the oil she should not undertake a journey under the sign of two, for otherwise she would be like an army that does not advance to the head of its field.

This was the verdict and muttered judgment, to which Jacob listened, nodding his head, but at the same time shrugging his shoulders. What was he to make of it? It was important that he hear it, because it concerned Rachel and her child, but for the rest he would have to let it be and leave the future to make of these mutterings whatever it intended to make. Destiny and the future maintained a more or less free hand in such things in any case. A great deal could happen or not happen, and it all still might be passably reconciled with the verdict, so that one might declare this to have been its meaning. For many an hour Jacob pondered the idea of oracles in general and also spoke about it to Laban, who would hear nothing of it. Was an oracle by its nature the revelation of some unalterable future, or was it an instruction to take care, a warning that a man should do his part to keep a predicted misfortune from occurring? But that would presume that providence and fate were not fixed, but rather that it was up to man to influence them. If that were so, however, then the future did not reside outside of man, but inside him, and in that case how could it even be read? Besides which, it had often happened that the taking of preventive measures more or less brought on the prophesied disaster, indeed, it evidently never could have happened without such measures, making both the warning and fate itself the sport of demons. The oil had spoken, Rachel would give birth, though with difficulty, to a son. But if one were to neglect her in labor, speak no charms, withhold the necessary anointings—how would destiny then go about being true to its happy verdict, yet remaining itself? For, in a most sinful fashion, evil would occur contrary to fate. But was not sin also the attempt to make good things happen contrary to fate?

Laban disapproved of such quibbling. This was not well thought out, merely skewed and oversubtle faultfinding. The future was simply the future, which meant it had not yet happened and so was not fixed, but it would happen someday, one way or the other, and was therefore fixed in only a certain sense, that is, according to its property as future—and that was all there was to say about it. Statements concerning it were illuminating and instructive for the heart, and seers and priests were engaged and paid to make them, after years of schooling under the sponsorship of the King of the Four Regions at Babel–Sippar on both sides of the river—the darling of Shamash, the favorite of Mardug, king of Sumeria and Akkadia, he who dwelt in a palace whose foundations were fathoms deep and in a throne room of unutterable splendor. So enough quibbling!

Jacob had already fallen silent. He held Nimrod of Babel in profound derision, a sentiment inherited from the primal wanderer. And so it did not make the oracle appear any more sacred for Laban to invoke in its favor this omnipotent ruler and how he himself never lifted a finger without first consulting seers and priests. Laban had paid for the oracle with a sheep and diverse nourishment for the moon idol, and if only for that reason alone he had to cling to its verdict. Jacob, who had paid nothing, necessarily treated it more casually; but, then again, he delighted in having heard something without having paid, and as for the future, one question at least, or so he thought, was already fixed: whether Rachel's fruit was to be a boy or a girl. That was already determined in Rachel's womb, except that one could not yet see it. There was such a thing as a fixed future, then, and that Rimanni-Bel's oil had indicated a boy was at least heartening. As for the rest, Jacob was grateful for practical instructions the seer had given; for as a true priest of the temple he also had knowledge of healing; and although without question there was a contradiction between these two capacities—for what good was medicine against the future?—he had not been chary in providing tried-and-true counsel for the delivery, with ritual incantations and medicinal prescriptions supplementing each other for full efficacy.

Little Rachel did not have it easy. Long before her hour had come—which almost became her last hour—the regimen was begun. She had to drink foul-tasting brews, quantities of oil, for example, containing pulverized pregnancy stones; and her body had to bear up under all sorts of compresses—packets of salve made from pitch, swine fat, fish, and herbs—or even the body parts of unclean animals, which like the salves were bound to her limbs with cord. Moreover, a kid of atonement always lay at her head as she slept, a substitute sacrifice to feed the greedy demons in her stead. Near her, day and night, stood a clay doll of swamp-born Labartu, a pig's heart in her mouth, so that the abominable demons would leave the pregnant woman's body where they had taken up residence and be lured into her image, which was smashed every third day with a sword and buried in a wall niche—and one made sure never to glance around behind. The sword was thrust into a basin of glowing coals, which likewise—though the season was very warm, with the month of Tammuz approaching—had to stand next to Rachel's bed day and night. Her bed was encircled by a low wall of flour paste; the three mounds of grain in her chamber were also there at Rimanni-Bel's suggestion. At the first labor pains, people hurried to smear the sides of her bed with pig's blood and the house door with gypsum and asphalt.

The Birth

It was summer, a few days into the month of the mutilated god, the Lord of the Sheepfolds. Since the grand moment when he had first learned that his true and dearest wife was to give birth, Jacob had not left her side, had personally helped tend her, refreshing the salve compresses and once even breaking the image of Labartu and burying it—measures and usages which, it was true, had not come from the God of his fathers, but could, after all, have come from Him by way of the idol and its seer, and were, in any case, the only ones available to observe. Pale, emaciated, and sturdy only in the middle of her body, where the fruit, in order to flourish, was sucking at all her energies and juices with oblivious ruthlessness, Rachel had often smiled and led his hand to where he could feel the child's faint kicks; and through the veil of flesh he had greeted Dumuzi, his true son, and told him to pluck up his courage for daylight soon, but to slip deftly from his refuge and spare his sheltering mother undue suffering. And when with a weak smile contorting her poor face and with shortness of breath she announced that the time was near, he became greatly agitated, called her parents and the handmaids, demanding the bricks be set up, bustling about pointlessly—and his heart was full of pleading.

Rachel's willingness and good courage cannot be praised enough. With joyous and brave determination to prove fit in deed and suffering, she entered upon the work of nature. Her zeal was not for the sake of appearances and because she no longer wanted to be seen by others as the childless and "hated" wife; it was, rather, from a deeper, more physical sense of honor—for it is not just human society that knows what honor is, but the flesh knows it, too, and even better than society, as Rachel herself had discovered when in her disgrace she painlessly became a mother through Bilhah. As her labor now began, her smile was not the confused smile of that day, when it had been painted by her flesh's grieved conscience. Transfigured both by happiness and nearsightedness, her handsome and beautiful eyes rested on those of Jacob, for whom she would give birth in honor, for this was the hour to which she had looked forward with her wide-eyed eagerness for life from the very first, from the day when the stranger, her cousin from a strange land, had stood across from her in the field.

Poor Rachel! How joyous her bravery, what a good will filled her to be strong in the work of nature—and nature repaid her with little goodwill, made it very hard for the brave woman. Was Rachel, who had been so honestly impatient for motherhood and so convinced of her talent for it, in truth, that is in the flesh, not made for it at all—far less so than Leah, the unloved wife—so that the sword of death hung over her as her first labor began, and indeed fell upon her and slew her the second time? Can nature be so at odds with itself, mocking the very wishes and happy faith it places in the human heart? Evidently. Rachel's joy was not accepted and her faith was proved false—such was this eager, willing woman's fate. She had waited with Jacob in faith for seven years, and then for thirteen years had met disappointment beyond all comprehension. But now, when nature had finally granted what she longed for, it did so at a ghastly price beyond all that Leah, Bilhah, and Zilpah combined had had to pay for the honor of motherhood. Her terrible labor lasted thirty-six hours, from midnight to noon and on through yet another night to the following afternoon, and had it lasted a mere hour or even half hour more, her breath would have left her. From the start Jacob was anxious about Rachel's own disappointment, for she had imagined she would complete this quickly, merrily, vigorously, but was quickly brought to a standstill. The first signals were obviously deceptive; the early contractions were followed by pauses of many hours, a barren time of emptiness and silence, during which, although Rachel did not suffer, she felt embarrassed and bored. She said to Leah several times, "How very different it was for you, sister!"—which Leah had to admit, casting Jacob, her lord, a sidelong glance. But then urgent pain grabbed at the mother-to-be, each clutch more cruel and protracted than before, yet when it ceased all the hard labor seemed to have been in vain. She exchanged the bricks for the bed, the bed for the bricks again. The hours of the night watches and of daylight came and went; she was aggrieved, shamed by her incompetence. Rachel did not scream when pain grabbed her and would not let go; clenching her teeth with mute integrity, she put her best energies to work, for she knew her lord's soft heart and did not want to frighten Jacob, who with his soul in tatters would kiss her hands and feet during those pauses of exhaustion. What good did integrity do? It was not accepted. And when things grew worse yet, she did scream—monstrous, savage cries so out of character, so unlike little Rachel. For by this point, as morning dawned a second time, she was not in her right mind, no longer herself, and they could easily tell by her hideous bellowing that it was not Rachel who was screaming, because the voice was utterly strange, the voice of demons that the pig's heart stuck in the mouth of the clay doll had been unable to lure out of her.

These spasms of pain accomplished nothing, but merely held her in her holy anguish and in the relentless torments of hell, until the screaming mask of her face turned blue and her fingers were talons clutching the air. Jacob wandered through house and courtyard, but kept bumping into things because he was holding his thumbs in his ears and the other eight fingers over his eyes. He pleaded with

God—not for a son, he was no longer concerned about that, but that Rachel might die, might lie peaceful in her bed, freed from her hellish distress. When their draughts and salves and massages had proved fruitless, Laban and Adina resorted in their bewilderment to reciting invocations, and while their daughter wailed in her labors, their rhythmic words reminded Sin, the moon god, that just as he had once helped a cow give birth he might now help loosen the knots entangling this woman and assist this maiden in the throes of childbirth. Leah stood bolt upright and silent in one corner of the room, arms straight at her sides, but hands raised at the wrist, while her blue crossed eyes watched the life-and-death struggle of Jacob's beloved.

Then from Rachel came a final shriek of utter demonic rage, a cry one cannot release a second time short of death and cannot hear twice without loss of reason—and Laban's wife had something to do besides recite the tale of Sin's cow, for Jacob's son, his eleventh and first, had come forth, emerging from life's dark bloody womb— Dumuzi–Apsu, the true son of the abyss. It was Bilhah, mother of Dan and Naphtali, who came running pale and laughing into the courtyard where Jacob had fled in vain, and with tongue aflutter she reported to her lord that a child was born to us, a son given to us, and that Rachel lived. His whole body trembling, he dragged himself into the mother's room, fell before her, and wept. Bathed in sweat and as if transfigured by death, she sang a panting song of exhaustion. The portal of her body was ripped and torn, her tongue bitten through, and her weary heart's life close to fading forever. But this was the reward for her eager joy.

She did not have the strength to turn her head toward him or even to smile, but she stroked the top of his head as he knelt beside her, and then let her eyes drift to one side, to the suspended cradle, signaling to him that he should behold his living child and lay his hand upon his son. Bathed now, the infant had stopped blubbering. It slept, wrapped in its swaddling clothes. It had long lashes, tiny hands with perfectly formed nails, and smooth black hair on the little head that had torn at its mother as it emerged. It was not beautiful at the time; how could one even hope to speak of beauty in such a small child. And yet Jacob saw something that he had not seen in Leah's children, had not perceived in the children of the handmaids, saw at first glance something that filled his heart with devout rapture—almost to overflowing the longer he looked. The newborn had something ineffable about him, something like the luster of clarity, loveliness, proportion, sympathy—of those things that are pleasing to God—so that although he could not comprehend it, Jacob thought he recognized it in its singularity. He put his hand on the boy and said, "My son." But as he touched the child, it opened its eyes, blue at the time, and their light reflected the rays of the sun of his birth, which stood at its zenith in the heavens. And with those tiny, perfectly formed hands it took hold of Jacob's finger, holding it in the tenderest of embraces while it went back to sleep. Even Rachel, its mother, had fallen into a deep sleep. Jacob, however, caught in that clasp gentle as breath, stood there for a good hour, bent low, gazing into his little son's lustrous clarity—until the infant began to whimper for food, and he lifted it up and across.

They named him Joseph, or Yashub, which means increase and addition, just as when we call our sons Augustus. His full name, incorporating God, was Joseph-el or Josiphyah, but they were inclined to see even its first syllable as hinting at the Most High and called his name Jehoseph.

The Speckled Flocks

Now that Rachel had given birth to Joseph, Jacob's emotions were very tender and running high; he spoke only in a solemn, emotionally charged voice—and the self-satisfaction of his mood was reprehensible. Since the child had appeared at the midday hour with the zodiacal sign of the Virgin rising in the east and standing, as he well knew, in corresponding aspect to the star of Ishtar, the planetary revelation of heavenly femininity, he stubbornly insisted that Rachel, the child's mother, should be regarded as a heavenly virgin, a mother goddess, a Hathor and Isis with the babe at her breast—and the child itself as anointed, a wonder-working boy, whose appearance was bound up with the beginning of an age of blessing and laughter and who himself would be fed by the strength of Yahu. We have no choice but to charge him with immoderation and extravagance. A mother and child make for a holy image, to be sure, but the simplest consideration toward certain sensitivities should have prevented Jacob from turning an image into an "image" in the word's most pejorative sense, from turning Rachel into a celestial divine maid. He knew, of course, that she was not a virgin in the ordinary and earthly sense of the word. How in the world could that ever happen! His use of the word "virgin" was merely mythical, astrological jargon. But he insisted on the metaphor with an all too literal enthusiasm, his obstinacy even bringing tears to his eyes. And since he was a breeder of sheep and, moreover, the darling of his heart was named Rachel, the "mother sheep," his calling her infant "the lamb" might have been acceptable as a quite pleasant, even charming flight of fancy. But his tone of voice when he did so, his talk about the lamb that came forth from the virgin, had nothing to do with fancy, but appeared to ascribe to that little urchin in his suspended cradle the holiness of the unblemished sacrificial firstborn of the flock. In his raptures he would declare that the lamb would be beset by the beasts of the wild, yet would conquer them all, spreading joy among angels and men throughout the earth. He also called his son a shoot and a twig broken from the tenderest root, which, in his hyperpoetical sensibility, joined together notions of the world's springtime and that same age of blessing now begun, in which the heavenly boy would cast down the violent and mighty with the rod of his mouth.

What overwrought emotions! Especially since on a purely personal level the "new age of blessing" had a very practical meaning. It meant the blessing of riches—Jacob was certain that he should regard the birth of the true wife's son as guaranty that, given the profits that had already come his way in Laban's service, the curve of his business affairs would now take a decided, indeed a very steep climb upward, was certain that after this turning point the filthy underworld would grant him without restriction all the treasures of gold it had to offer—all of which, to be sure, was closely connected with a higher, even more intensely felt idea: his return, laden with bounty, to the upper world, to the land of his fathers. Jehosiph's appearance was indeed a turning point in the course the stars of his own life had taken and should have coincided, strictly speaking, with his ascent out of Laban's realm. But that could not be, not straightaway, not as things stood. Rachel was unable to travel—was still pale and weak, recovering only with difficulty from the terrible delivery—and for now that also held true for the child, an infant whom one could not possibly presume to take on the exhausting Eliezer journey of more than seventeen days. It is amazing—indeed it is almost laughable—

how these matters have on occasion been viewed and reported so cavalierly. One hears, for example, that Jacob spent fourteen years with Laban, seven plus seven; at the end of which came Joseph's birth, followed by the journey home. Whereas it is explicitly stated that at the meeting with Esau beside the Jabbok, Rachel and Joseph also drew near and bowed down before the man of Edom. But how is an infant supposed to draw near and bow down? Joseph was five years old at the time, and those were the five years that Jacob spent there after the first twenty—five years under a new contract. He could not travel, but he could act as if he intended to depart at once in order to exert pressure on Laban, that clod of earth, who could be outmaneuvered only with pressure and ironclad exploitation of the rigors of commercial life.

Which is why Jacob addressed Laban, saying, "Might it please my father and uncle to incline his ear to what I have to say."

"Before you speak," Laban swiftly interrupted, "you would do better to listen to me, for I have something urgent to say. Things cannot go on as they now are. There is no longer a lawful order between men, and over time that has become an abomination to me. You have served for your wives seven plus seven years according to our contract still lying among the teraphim. For some years, however, I believe it is six now, both the agreement and its document have been outdated, and what is left is not law but custom and routine, so that no one knows what he can cling to. Our life has become like a house built without a plumb line, and, quite frankly, like the den of beasts. I am well aware, for the gods made me with eyes to see, that you have been amply rewarded, since you serve me without any conditions or contracted wage and yet have assembled all manner of goods and assets on your side, which I do not wish to enumerate, for they are yours. And when the children of Laban—Beor, Alub, and Muras, my sons—pulled faces because of it, I reprimanded them. For every effort deserves its reward—but one must impose a certain order. Which is why we shall go and conclude a new contract for, tentatively, seven years, and you see me ready to negotiate any condition you may be inclined to propose to me."

"That cannot be," Jacob replied, shaking his head, "and my uncle has unfortunately wasted precious words he might have spared himself had he listened at once to me. For it is not about a new contract that I come to speak with Laban, but rather about my departure and resignation. I have served you twenty years and must leave to you any testimony as to how well I did so, being unable to provide it myself—it not being fitting for me to use the only words appropriate. But they would certainly be most suitable for you to speak."

"Who denies it?" Laban said. "You've served me quite tolerably, that is not at issue."

"And I have grown old and gray in your service for no need," Jacob continued, "since the reason why I departed from Yitzchak's house and left my home was Esau's anger, which has long since evaporated, and so childish is that hunter's nature that he no longer even remembers those old stories. For many a year now I might have returned to my country at any moment, but I did not. And why not? Yet again, the only fitting words are those I dare not use, for they are words of praise. But now Rachel, the heavenly maid in whom you yourself have become beautiful, has born to me Dumuzi, Joseph, my and her son. And I will gather him, together with my other children, those of Leah and the handmaids, and what has accrued to me in your service, and we will mount up and embark upon a journey, so that I may come to my own country and my home and finally look after my own house, after having kept watch over yours alone for so long."

"That I would regret, in the truest sense of the word," Laban retorted, "and whatever I can do, I will do to keep this from taking place. And so let my son and nephew mince no words, but say directly what he demands in regard to new conditions, and I swear by Anu and Ellil that I will give due and most generous thought to even the most extreme propositions he might make—as long as they are more or less reasonable."

"I have no idea what you would hold to be reasonable," Jacob said, "considering what you owned before I came to you and how it has expanded under my hand, so that even your wife Adina was included in the growth and with unexpected vigor presented three sons to you in your gray old age. You would be perfectly capable of regarding all that as unreasonable, which is why I prefer to say nothing further and depart."

"Speak, and you will remain," Laban replied.

Then Jacob named his demand, said what he wanted if he were to stay another year or two. Laban was prepared for many things, but not for this. For a moment he was simply dumbfounded, and his mind hastily struggled first to get a good grasp on the demand and second immediately to limit its impact with sorely necessary countermeasures.

It was the famous story of the speckled sheep, told and retold a thousand times beside wells and campfires, celebrated and exchanged in a thousand "fine discourses" in honor of Jacob and his masterstroke of ingenious shepherd cunning—the tale that whenever even Jacob pondered it all in his old age he could not recall without those delicate lips beneath his beard curling into a smile. In a word, Jacob demanded the two-colored sheep and goats, the ones speckled black and white, not—let it be understood!—those already alive, but whatever among Laban's flocks would be born spotted in the future, they were to be his reward and added to the private property he had acquired in his uncle's service over so many years. It was a matter of dividing between master and servant those animals yet to be bred, though certainly not half and half; for the vast majority of the sheep were white, and only a small number speckled, so that Jacob pretended they were some sort of dregs. And yet even as they bargained they both knew that compared to the white sheep, the speckled sheep were lustful and fruitful, and though crushed by the shameless ingenuity of his nephew's demand, Laban said as much in his dismay and admiration.

"The things you think of!" he said. "A man might be struck blind and dumb by such particulars. So then, the speckled ones, who are so especially lustful. That is brazen! Not that I am saying no to it, don't misunderstand me. I gave you license to name your demands, and I will stand by my word. If it is a condition that you are hard set upon and would otherwise depart and tear my daughters and your wives, Leah and Rachel, from my heart so that I will never see them again in my old age, then let it be as you have said. And yet, I must admit it grieves me to the marrow."

And Laban sat down as if struck with palsy.

"Listen," Jacob said. "I can see that what I demand has struck a hard blow, and does not entirely please you. But seeing that you are my mother's own brother and that it was you who begot my Rachel for me, the virgin of the stars, my true and dearest wife, I will put conditions to my condition to make it less frightful. Let us go through your flocks and cull out all the speckled and striped animals, plus all the black ones, and set them apart from the white, so that the one group knows nothing of the other. And all that are born two-colored after that, they shall be my reward. Are you satisfied?"

Laban looked at him and blinked. "Three days' journey!" he suddenly cried. "There shall be the space of a three days' journey between the white and the speckled and black, and their breeding and tending shall be separated, so that one group knows nothing of the other, that is how I want it. And it shall be documented in Haran before the judicial notary and deposited underground with the teraphim, that is my immutable counterdemand."

"A hard one for me," Jacob said. "Yes, truly, truly hard and oppressive. And yet from the start I have been accustomed to how my uncle regards business matters so sternly and austerely, with no consideration of familial relationships. And so I accept your condition."

"You do well to do so," Laban replied, "for I would never have budged from it. Tell me, by the by, let me hear which herds you intend to pasture and which you will personally lead with your staff, the spotted or the white?"

"It is only just and natural," Jacob said, "that each tend the property from which he will benefit. I shall tend the speckled herd."

"No, you shall not!" Laban cried. "Definitely not! You made your demand, made it forcefully. It's my turn now, and I shall instead present what seems to me the easiest and fairest way to preserve honor in business. Once again in this contract you are hiring yourself out to me. But as you are my servant, good business sense would say that you and your staff should lead those animals that are to profit me—the white, not the speckled that will bear young for you. Let them be pastured by Beor, Alub, and Muras, my sons, whom Adina exuberantly bore me in her old age."

"Hm," Jacob said, "that might work, too. I'll not be quarrelsome and oppose it—you know my gentle nature."

They came to an agreement, and Laban had no idea what role he was playing—that from cowlick to toe he was the duped devil. How clumsy his calculations! He wanted to keep the use of Yitzchak's blessing, that above all else, and calculated that it would be stronger than the natural vigor of the speckled flocks. And under Jacob's hands, that much he knew, the white herds—which, now that they were separated from the spotted and black, could not be expected to bear any speckled lambs—would prosper and increase at a faster rate than the two-colored herds left under the solid, but less than brilliant care of his sons. The clod of earth! He cleverly took the blessing into account, but, once again, not thoroughly enough to form a true picture of Jacob's wit and invention, let alone to dream of the plan that stood behind not just his son-in-law's demand, but his concessions, too: a well-thought-out idea—and well-tested beforehand—that was at the bottom of it all.

For let no one think it was only after concluding the deal that Jacob first came up with his profound ruse for breeding speckled animals—even with white mixed only with white—in order, then, to exploit it to the full. No special purpose had lain behind the idea at first, it was an intellectual game, tested purely for its science, and was simply being put to clever commercial use in the bargain with Laban. The idea went back to the days before Jacob's marriage, when he was a lover in waiting and his sound breeder's judgment was at its fervent, clever best—an idea born from a continual state of impressionable inspiration and ardent intuition. One cannot value too highly the emotions and premonitions with which he enticed nature to reveal one of her oddest secrets and then confirmed it by experiment. He discovered the phenomenon of maternal misperception. He tested females in heat to see if the sight of something speckled would affect lambs conceived while gazing at it, so that these were born speckled and two-colored. His curiosity, it must be emphasized, was of a purely ideal sort, and in the course of his experiments he noted with sheer intellectual pleasure the countless cases that met with confirmatory success. Some instinct moved him to keep this magic empathy a secret from the rest of the world, and from Laban especially; but even when, in due time, the thought of turning this hidden knowledge into a source of definitively ample riches came to him, this was really secondary, solidifying only as the day approached for concluding a new contract with his father-in-law.

For the shepherds in their "fine discourses," to be sure, the practical application was everything, the point of this prank of cunning chicanery. How Jacob made a farce of Laban's conditions and systematically snatched up his flocks; how he had taken rods of poplar and hazel, peeled white streaks in them, and laid them in the watering troughs for the animals to see as they drank and, as was their wont, simultaneously copulated; how they conceived looking at the rods and then gave birth to speckled lambs and kids, though they themselves were all white; and how Jacob did this especially with the year's early flocks, leaving the later lambs, which were less valuable, to Laban—they told it all to one another, singing to the accompaniment of lutes, holding their sides as they laughed at this priceless swindle. For lacking Jacob's piety and knowledge of myth, they did not know the earnestness with which he had gone about it all: first, as his human duty to assist God the King in fulfilling the promise of prosperity, and second, because Laban, the devil who had deceived him in the dark with the stately but dog-headed Leah, had to be deceived himself—for one had to fulfill what was written: that one left the underworld only when laden with the treasures strewn there so abundantly alongside the filth.

And so it was: there were three grazing herds—the whites, tended by Jacob; the black and spotted, under the staff of Laban's sons; and Jacob's private flocks, acquired in trade over the years and tended by his assistant shepherds and servants, to which were added whatever was born speckled from among both the spotted and the enchanted white ones. And by such means the man became so heavy with riches that throughout the region people spoke with awe of him and of how many sheep, handmaids and servants, camels and asses he could call his own by now. In the end his wealth far exceeded that of Laban, the clod of earth, as well as that of all the business leaders who had once been invited to his wedding.

The Theft

Ah, how well Jacob remembered, how deeply and clearly! That was evident to everyone who saw him stand there, solemnly pondering, and they muffled their own life signs in awe of a life so heavy, so rich with stories. For things had now become quite ticklish for the wealthy Jacob—God Himself, El the Most High, had recognized that as a result of so much blessing the situation had become unstable and so had given him instructions in a vision. News had reached the man of blessing—all too plausible news concerning the feelings harbored against him in his growing strength by Laban's heirs, his brothers-in-law, by Beor, Alub, and even Muras: sullen remarks by all three, ominous remarks, passed on by his assistant shepherds and servants, who had heard of them during encounters with his cousins' people at the farm, remarks whose solid ring of truth made them no less disquieting. "This man Jacob, a distant cousin," so they had remarked, "came here before our time, a beggar with no home, with nothing to wear but his skin, and out of kindness and in deference to the gods our father gave shelter and work to him, the layabout. And now look at the turn things have taken under our very noses! He has stuffed himself on our flesh and blood and usurped our father's goods and has grown fat and rich, till it stinks to the high gods, for it is thievery in their eyes and fraud in the eyes of Laban's heirs. It is high time something be done to restore justice one way or another and in the name of this land's gods: of Anu, Ellil, and Marudug, not to mention that of Bel-Charran, whom we worship according to our fathers' custom—whereas our sisters, the stranger's wives, have also unfortunately sided to some extent with his god, the lord of his clan, who teaches him magic, so that the early lambs are born speckled and our father's property becomes his own by the terms of that filthy contract. But when things turn serious, we shall see who proves the stronger in this land and upon these plains: the gods of the land who have been at home here since days of old, or his god, who has no house except at Beth-el, which is no more than a stone atop a hill. For there is the possibility that something might happen to him in these parts, for the sake of justice, and that a lion might rend him to pieces out in the field—which would be no lie, for in our rage we are lions. Laban, our father, is far too loyal, to be sure, and fears the contract that rests among the lesser gods of our house. But one might say to him that it was a lion, and he would be satisfied. For this robber from the west has strapping sons, two of whom, Shimeon and Levi, can bellow to make a man tremble. But our gods have likewise put iron in our arms to strike with, even if we are the children of a graybeard, and we could strike of a sudden and without notice, at night, while he sleeps, and say it was a lion—father would have no trouble believing it."

Such were the remarks Laban's sons made among themselves, remarks not meant for Jacob, but brought to him by assistant shepherds and servants, who were rewarded. And he shook his head in objective disapproval, contemplating how these lads would never have known life or had breath in their nostrils without the blessing of Isaak, to which Laban owed all his affluence, and that they should be ashamed of such intrigues against him, their true sire. But he also felt apprehension and from that moment on attempted to read from Laban's behavior how things stood with the master himself, what his attitude might be, whether he would be ready to believe, on the say-so of his brothers-in-law, that some wild beast had torn Jacob to pieces. Jacob studied the man's face when he came out on his ox to check on the breeding; and deciding he must do so again, he rode to the farm himself to discuss the shearing and took another reading of that stolid face. And behold, it did not look on him as it had yesterday or the day before, the man no longer returned Jacob's searching gaze, his features sagged dark and heavy, and his eyes were not raised to him even once, but were averted and cast down beneath bulging brows whenever he had to make some necessary response to his son-in-law. And so after this second reading it was clear, Jacob was certain: the man would not merely believe in the ravening beast, but would also offer it dark gratitude in his heart.

Jacob now knew enough, and the moment he fell asleep he heard God's voice in a dream, saying, "See that you depart from here!" And it urged him: "Pack up all that you have, better today than tomorrow, and take your wives and children and everything that has become yours through Me over these many years, and make your heavy, swaying way homeward, in the direction of the mountains of Gilead, and I will be with you."

A command on a grand scale, but the planning and execution were left to man, and Jacob began quietly and cautiously to make arrangements for his flight from the underworld. First of all, he called his wives, Leah and Rachel, the daughters of the house, to join him in the field where he was tending his herd, so that he might come to an understanding with them both and make sure he could depend on their devotion. As for the concubines, Bilhah and Zilpah, their opinions did not count, they would be informed as needed.

"So it is," he said to his wives as the three of them squatted outside the tent, "so it is. Your late-born brothers seek to slay me for my goods, which are yours as well, and your children's inheritance. But when I study your father's countenance to see if he will protect me against their evil counsels, I find he does not look on me as he did yesterday or the day before, will not look at me at all; for he lets one side of his face sag as if palsied, and the other will know nothing of me. And why is that? I have served him with all my power. Three times seven plus four years he has deceived me whenever he could, and changed my wages as he pleased, appealing to the rigors of commercial life. But the God of Beth-el, my father's God, did not allow him to do me harm, and turned things in my favor instead. And when it was said: the speckled shall be your reward, behold, the rams covered the ewes, and the whole herd bore speckled young, so that your father's property was taken from him and given to me. For this I am now to die, and it will be said: a lion has eaten him. The Lord of Beth-el, however, for whom I anointed the stone, desires that I shall live and grow very old, which is why He instructed me in a dream to take what is mine and secretly depart across the water to the land of my fathers. I have spoken. Now you must speak."

And it turned out that the women were of the same opinion as God—how could it have been otherwise? Poor Laban! He would have come off second best even had they seen themselves confronted with something like a choice, which was scarcely the case. They were Jacob's. The purchase price had been paid for them over fourteen years. Had matters taken a normal course, their buyer and lord would long ago have led them from their father's house to the bosom of his own clan. They had become mothers of eight of his children before this perfectly natural turn of events by which Jacob asserted rights long since acquired. Were they to let him depart with his sons and Dinah, his daughter by Leah, and cling instead to the father who had sold them? Should he flee by himself with the riches his God had taken from their father to give to them and their children? Or should they betray to their father and brothers Jacob's plans to flee and so thwart them? All impossibilities—each more impossible than the next. Above all, they loved him, had loved him as rivals from the day he first appeared, and never had there been a finer moment for competitive devotion than this.

Cuddling against him on both sides, the two said in unison, "I am yours! What she may think, I do not know and shall not ask. But I am yours, wherever you are, wherever you may go. If you steal away, I shall also steal away with all the rest that Abraham's God has bestowed on you, and may Nabu, the guide, the god of thieves, be with us!"

"I thank you," Jacob replied, "with equal thanks to you both. Laban will be coming out to shear his herd with me three days from today. After which he will make a journey of three days to shear his speckled sheep with Beor, Alub, and Muras. While he is under way, I shall gather what is mine, which lies midway between here and there, the herds that God has given me, and on the sixth day from today, when Laban is far off, we shall steal away with all our heavy riches toward the river Prath and toward Gilead. Go, I love you both more or less equally. But you, Rachel, my very eye, take care that it be as soft a journey as possible for the virgin's lamb, Jehosiph, my true and genuine son, and think of warm coverings for him in anticipation of cold nights, for the shoot is as tender as the root from which it was broken amid such agony and pain. Go and let all my words stir you to action!"

Thus, and in still greater detail, they arranged the flight that even in old age Jacob would recall with sly excitement. But until the day he died, he was also touched whenever he thought and spoke about what Rachel, his little one, had done back then in her sweet innocence and cunning. She did it all on her own, without anyone's knowledge, and to free Jacob's conscience from sharing in her deed so that he could swear his oath to Laban with the purest of hearts, she admitted it only later even to him. What did she do? Since they were stealing away and the world stood in the sign of Nabu, she stole as well. In the quiet of the night, once Laban had left the farm to go shearing, she descended through the trapdoor into the chamber of graves and receipts, took Laban's little house gods, the teraphim, picked up one after the other by its bearded or female head, stuck them under her arm and into her sash pocket, and clasping a couple more in one hand, slipped off unseen to the women's quarters, where she buried the clay idols under utensils to be taken along on their thievish journey. For her little head was all a muddle, and that was precisely what so touched Jacob's heart when he learned all this—touched it and filled it with anxiety. Half of her, or so she had confessed, had indeed, out of love for him, been won over to his God, the One and Most High, and had renounced the customary deities of her land. The other half, however, was in its heart of hearts still idolatrous and thought at least: better safe than sorry. Just in case, then, she had taken Laban's advisors and prophets from him, so that they could not provide him information about the path the fugitives had taken and would instead offer protection against pursuit, for it was generally agreed that this was one of their powers and virtues. She knew how Laban depended on these little manikins and miniature Ishtars, in what high regard he held them, and yet she stole them from him for Jacob's sake. No wonder that a damp-eyed Jacob kissed her when she later confessed the deed to him, and only quite incidentally very gently reproved her for being so muddleheaded and for having allowed him to falsely swear his personal oath to Laban, once he had caught up with them—for in saying that the gods were not to be found under his roof, Jacob had blindly put all their lives at risk that day.

The Pursuit

In this case the teraphim did not, in fact, demonstrate their protective virtue in any way—perhaps because they did not wish to turn it against their true owner. Yitzchak's son had fled, westward of course, with his wives, his handmaids, his twelve progeny, and all that was his—Laban learned that much on the third day, shortly after his arrival for the shearing of his speckled and black flocks, learned it from hired shepherds who had hoped their faithful report would earn them a better reward than what they now received, for just the opposite happened: they came close to being thrashed instead. The furious man hastened home, where he discovered the theft of his idols, and from there, having gathered his sons and a number of armed men, he at once took up pursuit.

Yes, it was exactly like twenty-five years before, on Jacob's first journey, with Eliphaz hot on his heels. Once again he saw himself being fiercely pursued, and even more frightening was the fact that the forces at his rear could advance much more easily than he with his slow caravan—the flocks, pack animals, and oxcarts inching their dusty way forward. But mixed with the fear that overcame him as his scouts and spies at the rear reported Laban's approach was the intellectual pleasure he took in the correspondences and symmetry. It took Laban seven days, so it is written, to catch up with his son-in-law, who already had the worst part of his journey, the desert, behind him, and had now arrived on the wooded slopes of the mountains of Gilead, from where he needed only to descend to the valley of the Jordan, where it flows into Lot's Sea or the Sea of Salt—but now his head start was used up, and he had no choice but to deal with this meeting and confrontation.

Its scene is laid in this enduring landscape of river, sea, and hazy mountains, all of them bearing witness as silent, oath-bound guarantors to the stories that made Jacob's pondering so heavy, so full of dignity, so awe-inspiring, and of which we give this complicated account—that is to say, in all its complexities—just as they can be proved to have happened here in abiding harmony with mountain and valley. It was here, it is all correct, everything fits, we ourselves went down—how eerie—into the depths and to the sunset shore of Lot's Sea, sampling its foul taste and seeing with our own eyes that it all corresponds correctly. Yes, those bluish heights to the east, beyond this brine, are Moab and Ammon, the lands of Lot's children—outcasts that his daughters had procured by sleeping with him. There in the distance, far to the south of the sea, lies the dusk of Edom, of Seïr, the goat land, from where a bewildered Esau set out to greet his brother, meeting him at the Jabbok. Does that work—the placement of the mountains of Gilead, where Laban caught up with his son-in-law, in relation to the river Jabbok, to which Jacob then proceeded? Perfectly. People presumably applied the name Gilead to lands east of the Jordan as far north as the river Jarmuk, which joins its rushing waters with the Jordan not far from the Sea of Chinnereth or Gennesareth. But the mountains of Gilead are more particularly those heights stretching east to west on both banks of the Jabbok, and from them one descends to its thickets and the ford that Jacob chose for his family to cross; but he stayed behind that night and experienced the lonely adventure that left him with a limp for all time. How enlightening that in making his entrance into the hot region of Ghor, he did not first turn his weary caravan of people and animals toward his true homeland, but instead proceeded westward, into the valley of Sichem at the foot of Mounts Gerizim and Ebal, where he hoped to find rest. Yes, it is all demonstrably consistent and bears witness over time that there is no falsity in the songs of the shepherds and in their "fine discourses."

It will always remain unclear just what sort of mood Laban, that clod of earth, was in as he snorted and panted in pursuit; for his behavior upon arrival at his goal offered Jacob quite a few pleasant surprises and, what is more, corresponded nicely, or so he thought later, with Esau's unexpected conduct at their meeting. Yes, Laban's mood as he set out was evidently as bewildered as the red man's had been. He panted at the head of his armed force, following the runaway, but then declared Jacob's actions merely foolish, and in his discussion with his nephew admitted that a god, his sister's God, had visited him in a dream, threatening him if he dared speak with Jacob in any but friendly terms. That may be so, since for Laban it was enough simply to know of the existence of the God of Abram and Nahor for him to ascribe to Him a reality equal to that of Ishtar or Adad, even if he did not count himself a devotee. But it remains debatable whether he, as an outsider, actually saw and heard Yeho, the Only God, in a dream; teachers and commentators have expressed their puzzlement about it, and it is more probable that certain sentiments and fears overcame him on the way, considerations formed in the stillness of his soul, but given the name of a vision for emphasis— and Jacob himself saw little difference and let the turn of phrase be. Twenty-five years had taught Laban that he was dealing with a man of blessing, and if nothing is more understandable than that Laban snorted with rage because Jacob, by stealing himself away, had also robbed him of the efficacy of the blessing for which he had made such great sacrifices, it is equally understandable that Laban's original plan of a violent encounter very quickly evaporated before such disconcerting scruples. Nor could there be any real objection to Jacob's having taken his wives, Laban's daughters, with him. They had been bought, they were Jacob's, body and soul, and Laban himself had once disdained the beggar who had had nowhere to lead them in a wedding procession out of the house of their parents. And look how the gods had now decreed things otherwise and allowed the man to plunder him! When setting off in his rage, Laban was hardly thinking of taking back his riches by force of arms, but rather he was driven by the murky notion of softening this terrifying blow, the loss of all that had passed from his hand into Jacob's, by at least taking his leave of the lucky thief and making his peace with him— he would be better off that way. And only one matter made him snort with true outrage and demand restitution: the theft of his teraphim. Among the vague and confused motives for his pursuit, this alone was firm and palpable—he wanted his household gods back. And those who can still feel some sympathy—despite all his hardhearted clumsiness—for this Chaldean businessman and his contracts may even today feel the sad insult of his having never recovered them.

The formalities of this meeting between fugitive and pursuer were strangely peaceable and silent, considering the collision one might have expected from Laban's conduct upon departure. Night fell over Gilead, and Jacob had just set up camp on a damp highland meadow, driving pegs for the camels and herding the smaller animals into a fold so that they might stay warm together, when Laban arrived in shadowy silence, and just as silently had his tent pitched nearby and vanished into it—without hide or hair of him to be seen the rest of the night.

But come morning, he stepped out and trudged across to the draped entrance of Jacob's tent, where the latter awaited him in some perplexity. Each touched his own brow and chest, and they sat down.

"It is an occasion for thanksgiving," Jacob said to initiate their ticklish conversation, "that I may behold my father and uncle once again. May his journey's hardships have proved incapable of in any way diminishing his body's well-being."

"I am vigorous for my years," Laban replied. "Doubtless you had that in mind when you brought this journey upon me."

"How is that?" Jacob asked.

"How is that? Son of man, examine your heart and ask what you have done to me by stealing away unawares from me and our contract and roughly carrying off my daughters like captives taken by the sword. In my view you should have stayed with me forever according to our contract, which cost me my blood, but to which I held religiously, as is the custom of my land. But if you could not bear it and wished to depart so helter-skelter with your legacy and property, why did you not open your mouth and speak to me like a son? Even so late we might have made good on what your circumstances have prevented at the moment and would have accompanied you with cymbals and harps, whether by land or water according to good custom. But what have you done? Must you then always be stealing, by day and night—and have you no heart in your body and no feeling in your bowels that you begrudge me in my old age the farewell kisses of my children? I say unto you, you have behaved foolishly, that is the word that comes to me for your actions. And had I wished it and had a voice not come to me yesterday in a dream—quite possibly the voice of your God—and dissuaded me from quarreling with you, you may well believe that my sons and servants would have had enough iron in their arms to make you pay for your foolishness, now that we have caught up with you in your thievish flight."

"Oh yes," Jacob responded, "the truth must remain true. My master's sons are wild boars and young lions and would long since have liked to deal with me after the manner of boars and lions, if not by day, then by night, as I lay sleeping—and you would have gladly believed it was a ravening beast and would have wept great tears for me. You ask why I departed in silence and made no long speeches? Should I not fear you, then—fear that you would not have allowed it and would have snatched my wives, your daughters, from me or at the least have imposed new conditions to allow me to depart and taken my goods and chattels from me? For my uncle is hard, and his god is the implacable law of commerce."

"And why have you stolen my gods from me?" Laban suddenly shouted, veins of anger swelling up an inch thick on his brow.

Jacob was speechless and said as much. In reality, he felt easier in his soul now that Laban had put himself in the wrong with such an absurd claim—that was in Jacob's favor.

"Gods?" he repeated in astonishment. "The teraphim? I'm supposed to have pilfered your images from their chamber? That is the most preposterous and inane thing I have ever heard! Put your reason to work, man, and consider what you're accusing me of. What value or purpose would your idols, those bits of clay, have for me that I would become an evildoer for them? To the best of my knowledge they were turned on a potter's wheel and dried in the sun like any other utensil and aren't even good for stopping a slave brat's runny nose when it has the sniffles. I speak for myself; it may be different for you. But since they appear to have got away from you, it would not be polite to assess their virtue all too highly in your presence."

Laban replied, "That is simply clever deception on your part, to pretend as if you care not a whit about them, so that I may believe you have not stolen them. No man can hold their virtue in such low regard that he would not gladly steal them, that's impossible. And since they are not where they were, it is you who stole them."

"Now listen to me," Jacob said. "It is very good that you are here and did not think it a crime to follow after me for so many days for their sake, for the matter must be settled down to the last detail— I, the accused, demand it. My camp lies open to you. Go through it however you wish, and search! Do not shy from upending every-thing, just as you please—I give you the freest of hands. And with whomever you find your gods, be it me or one of my household, let him be put to death here before the eyes of all, and I do not care whether you choose iron or fire or burial to do the deed. Begin with me and be meticulous! I insist on the most thorough investigation."

He was in fine spirits, for he could shift everything to the teraphim, making them the only subject of discussion on all sides, and at the end of the search he would stand there grand in his af-front. He did not suspect just how slippery the earth beneath his feet was—and how deadly his misjudgment. Rachel, in her blameless in-nocence, was to blame; but with greatest deftness and determination she took responsibility for her own folly and the folly she now caused.

Laban, you see, replied, "Indeed, let it be so," stood up eagerly, and began searching the camp to find his earthenware gods. We know the precise sequence in which he went about it—with fierce thoroughness at first, but then, after hours of futile effort, weariness and dejection slowly set in. For as the sun rose he grew very hot, and although he wore no outer garment for the search, but only a shirt open at the chest and with rolled-up sleeves, sweat soon began to ap-pear from under his cap, and his face was so red that one might have feared the stout old man would have an apoplectic fit—all because of his teraphim! Had Rachel no heart, letting him torment himself that way, never letting him out of her mocking eye? But one must recall the power of suggestion and influence Jacob's imposing personage and spiritual ideas exerted on all around him, especially on those who loved him. By the power of his spirit and obstinacy, Rachel her-self played a holy role, that of astral virgin and mother of the heav-enly boy who bestowed blessing; and thus she was all the more inclined to view the rest of the world and her own father through Jacob's eyes and to approve as legitimate the role assigned to Laban. For her, as for her beloved, Laban was a deceiving devil and demon of the black moon, who in the end had been deceived on a still grander scale than he himself had deceived. And so Rachel batted not an eyelash, for the event happening here was devout, meaning-ful, and legitimate, one in which Laban—more or less consciously and willingly—played his own holy role. She felt as little pity for him as Yitzchak's household had felt for Esau, the butt of the grand joke.

Laban had arrived by night and had come to Jacob in the early morning—no doubt to demand what she had. Her father had arisen from the discussion and begun his search—this she learned from a little servant girl whom she had sent to spy and who, wanting to run faster, put the hem of her skirt between her teeth, leaving her body naked at the front as she ran. "Laban is searching!" she cried in a whisper. Rachel hurriedly grabbed up the teraphim, already wrapped in a cloth, and carried them outside her gray-black tent, where both and she and Leah had pegged their riding camels, exquisitely bred beasts of grotesque beauty, with sagacious serpentlike heads on long-arched necks and feet as wide as pillows that kept them from sinking into the sand. Beneath them servants had spread an abundance of straw, on which they now lay, superciliously chewing their cud. Rachel shoved her stolen goods under the straw, completely burying them in it, and then sat down where she had been rummaging—right on top, beside the camels, who gazed back at her over their shoulders, still chewing. And that is how she waited for Laban.

As we know, he had begun his search in Jacob's tent and had turned his son-in-law's traveling household topsy-turvy, airing the mat, lifting the mattress from the cot, and shaking out shirts, coats, and woolen blankets; in emptying a chest he spilled Jacob's board game of Evil Eye, which he loved to play with Rachel, dropping and breaking five of the stone pieces. Departing with a furious shrug he went to Leah's tent, then moved on to Zilpah's and Bilhah's, sparing no feminine secrets as he rifled their things, quivering so that he even stuck himself with tweezers and smudged his beard with a green cosmetic they used to extend the corners of their eyes—utterly clumsy in his fervor and in dim awareness that it was his role to look ridiculous.

Then he came to where Rachel was sitting and said, "May you be well, my child. You did not think you would see me."

"May you be perfectly well," Rachel responded. "My lord is looking for something?"

"I am searching all your shelters and sheepfolds for stolen goods," Laban said.

"Yes, yes, how awful," she nodded, and the two camels stared at her over their shoulders with haughty, sardonic smiles. "Why is not Jacob, our husband, helping you in your search?"

"He would find nothing," Laban riposted. "I must search all by myself and drudge here on a mountain in Gilead while the sun rises ever higher."

"Yes, yes, how awful," she repeated. "My little tent is that one. Look around inside if you think you must. But do be careful with my pots and spoons. Your beard is already a bit green."

Laban bent down and went inside. He soon came out again to Rachel and the animals, sighed, and said nothing.

"Are there no stolen goods there?" she asked.

"Not that my eye can see," he replied.

"Then they must be somewhere else," Rachel said. "I'm sure my lord has been wondering why I do not stand to greet him in reverence and courtesy. It is only because I am feeling qualmish, so that I am hindered in moving about freely."

"How then qualmish?" Laban wanted to know. "Are you hot and cold by turns?"

"Not really. I'm indisposed," she responded.

"But in what way exactly?" he asked again. "Have you a toothache or a boil?"

"Ah, my dear lord, it is but the way of women, I'm suffering from my period," she answered, and the over-the-shoulder smiles of the camels were truly sardonic and haughty.

"That is all?" Laban said. "Well, that doesn't count. I much prefer your having your period to your being pregnant. For you have little talent for childbirth. May you be well! I must search for my stolen goods."

With that he departed and ransacked himself half to death on into the afternoon, the sun rays already striking at an angle. Then—dirty, exhausted, and undone—he returned with his head hanging to Jacob.

"Well then, where were your idols?" Jacob asked.

"Nowhere, it seems," Laban replied, lifting his arms and letting them fall again.

"It seems?" Jacob said in indignation; for his mill was now turning full tilt, he stood there grandly and could swagger just as he pleased. "You say 'it seems' to me, and so refuse to recognize as proof of my innocence that you have found nothing, though you searched for ten hours, turning the camp upside down, rummaging in your rage, and hoping to slay me or one of my family? You have fingered all my household stuff—with my permission, to be sure, I gave you free rein, but that you did it was most discourteous all the same. And what did you find of your own? Set it down here and accuse me before your people and mine, that the voice of the public may judge between the two of us. How you overheated and soiled yourself—just to slay me! And what have I done to you? I was a young man when I came to you, but am now dignified by age, though I would hope the One and Only may grant me a long life yet—having spent all those years in your service as a head servant to you such as the world has never seen, which I say out of rage to you now, having kept it to myself out of modesty. I found water for you, setting you free from Inshullanu's sons and allowing you to throw off the banker's yoke, and you blossomed like a rose in the valley of Sharon and bore fruit like a date palm in the plains of Jericho. Your goats have given double their young and your sheep borne twins. If ever I ate a ram from your herd, then strike me, for I have plucked grass with gazelles and drank from the trough with your cattle. Thus did I live for you and serve fourteen years for your daughters and six for naught and nothing and five for the dregs of your herds. I languished beneath the heat of the day and shivered at night in the chill of the plains, and slept not at all in my watchfulness. But if by misfortune some ill touch visited the sheepfolds, or a lion murdered among them, you did not allow me to swear, proving my innocence, but made me pay for the loss and acted as if I stole from you day and night. And you changed my wages purely at your whim and substituted Leah when I thought I was embracing my true wife—that will sit in my bones my whole life long. Had the God of my fathers, Yahu the Almighty, not been on my side and turned some few things my way, I would have gone from you, God forbid, as naked as I came. But He indeed did not wish that and would not let His blessing be mocked. Never has He spoken to a stranger before, yet He has spoken to you for my sake and instructed you to speak to me in nothing but friendly terms. Yes, I certainly call it friendly of you to come here bellowing that I have stolen your gods from you. But when you do not find them, despite an excessive search, it only 'seems' so!"

Laban said nothing and sighed.

"You are so false and so clever," he declared wearily, "that there is no prevailing against you, and let no one pick a quarrel with you, for you will put him in the wrong, one way or another. When I look about me it is all like a dream. Everything I see is mine—daughters, children, herds and wagons and animals and slaves are all mine, but they have come into your hands, I know not how, and your departing from me with them seems but a dream. Behold, my thoughts are of reconciliation, I wish to come to an understanding and make a covenant with you, so that we may part in peace and I do not consume myself because of you all the rest of my days."

"That is worth hearing," Jacob replied, "and such words sound different from 'it seems' and similar insults. What you say accords with my own thoughts, for behold, you have sired the virgin, my son's mother—in her you have become beautiful. And the fruit of Laban ought not be alien to me, that would be abhorrent. Merely to make the farewell less difficult for you did I depart in secret and steal away with what was mine, but I would be very glad if we were to part amicably and I can think of you henceforth with peace of mind. I wish to erect a stone—shall I? I shall do so with pleasure. And four of your servants and four of mine shall make a heap of stones for the meal of promise that we shall eat before God and so be reconciled before Him. Are you satisfied?"

"I think so, yes," Laban said. "For I see no other way."

So Jacob went and set a handsome long stone on end, so that God might be present; but eight men had to collect the heap of stones for the covenant, gathering all sorts of mountain rubble and pebbles, and the two of them sat down and ate from it a dish of mutton, the fatty tail in the middle of the bowl. But Jacob let Laban eat almost the entire fatty tail and merely tasted it himself. So they ate together, alone under the sky, and with glances and hands were reconciled across the mound separating them. Laban made his daughters the subject of the oath, for he did not rightly know what else to choose. Jacob had to swear by the God of his fathers, by the Fear of Isaak, that he would not mistreat his wives and take no others besides them—the stone heap and the meal would be his witness. But Laban was not all that concerned about his daughters; they were a pretext for his desire to come to a passable conclusion with the man of blessing, so that he might be able to sleep.

He spent that night yet on the mountain with his family. The next morning he embraced the women, also spoke a last word over them, and turned homeward. Jacob, however, sighed a sigh of relief, followed by another of worry. For as the proverb says, out of the claws of the lion and into the mouth of the bear. And now came the red man.

Benoni

Two women in Jacob's caravan were pregnant when, in the wake of the grievous events at Shechem, he departed for Beth-el and later in the direction of Kiriath-Arba and Isaak's home—two, at least, who stand out in the light of history, for it is impossible to say whether at that moment there were also pregnancies among the women in his company of nameless household slaves. Dinah, that hapless child, was pregnant, made fruitful by Sichem, the unlucky prince, and a cruel decree loomed over her unhappy fruitfulness, so that she rode veiled from view. And Rachel was pregnant.

What joy! Ah, temper your jubilation, remember, and be still. Rachel died. It was God's will. During their wanderings that sweet thief—the girl who had stepped out from among Laban's sheep to meet Jacob at the well with childish, brave eyes—saw the time of her delivery arrive and did not survive it, for only with great difficulty had she been able to survive it the first time, and her breath failed her and she died. The tragedy of Rachel, the true and dearest wife, is the tragedy of a bravery that found no acceptance.

One almost lacks the courage to share in the feelings of Jacob's soul at this point, when the bride of his heart flickered and died, a sacrifice to his twelfth son, or even to try to imagine the blow to his reason, how deeply the gentle immodesty of his emotions was trodden in the dust. "Lord," he cried as he saw her die, "what are You doing?" Much good his cries did him. But the dangerous part, giving rise to our fears in advance, was that Jacob did not allow his precious feelings, his despotic selectivity, to be torn from him in Rachel's annihilation, did not bury them with her in the quickly dug grave beside the road, but rather, as if to prove to the Almighty that He would gain nothing by His cruelty, cast those feelings in all their voluptuous obstinacy upon Rachel's firstborn, the nine-year-old, dazzlingly beautiful Joseph, so that in loving him twice over in a perfect excess of emotion, he exposed to fate a new and alarming weak spot. It is worth pondering if this man of feeling is not truly and consciously disdaining freedom and peace, is not knowingly challenging destiny, having no other wish than to live in dread and beneath the sword. Evidently such an audacious will is a fixture of emotional transport, since, as everyone should know, it presumes a great readiness to suffer—and nothing is more reckless than love. The contradiction of nature at work here is simply that those soft souls who choose such a life are not created to endure what they provoke, whereas those who can endure it would never think of laying their hearts bare—that way nothing can happen to them.

Rachel had lived thirty-two years when she bore Joseph amid such holy agony, and thirty-seven when Jacob broke the dusty bars and carried her away. At age forty-one she was expecting again and had to depart from Shechem on a journey. That is, it is we who are counting, it was not the custom of her world to do so; she would have had to ponder a long while to say even approximately how old she was—a question of little importance to anyone at the time. At the morning side of the world the chronological vigilance of the Occident was almost unknown. With far greater composure, time and life were left to themselves and to darkness, without subjecting them to the discipline of measuring and counting; and the question as to a person's age was so uncommon that anyone putting it might well be prepared for the shrugging nonchalance of an answer varying as much as whole decades and for hearing something like "Forty maybe, or seventy?" Jacob, too, was no longer quite certain about his own age and had no problem with that. To be sure, certain years, those spent in Laban's land, had been counted, but not the others; and besides, he did not know, nor was he concerned, how old he had been upon arriving there. As for Rachel, the abiding present of their loving fellowship had not allowed him to perceive the natural changes that time, watched and counted or not, could not have been prevented from working on her handsome and beautiful person, transforming the lovely half-child of long ago to a mature woman. For him, as is usually the case, Rachel was always his bride by the well, who had waited those seven years with him, whose tears of impatience he had kissed from her eyelids. He looked at her with far-sighted eyes, at a blurred version of what his eyes had first sipped tenderly, and that essential nature could truly not have been touched by time—he saw the cordial night of her eyes, drawn happily together in their nearsightedness, the slightly too thick nostrils of her little nose, the contour of the corners of her mouth, her touching smile, that special way the lips came together, which had been passed on to the idolized boy. Above all he saw the carriage and character of this child of Laban—so shrewd, gentle, brave—and the eagerness with which she looked out on life, lifting Jacob's heart within his breast at first glance there beside the well and reemerging so sweetly once more the day that she confided her condition to him in the camp outside Shechem.

"Yet one more!" or "Lord, increase him!"—that had been the meaning of the name she had given her firstborn son as she lay exhausted almost to death. And now that Joseph was to be increased, she had no fear, but was happily prepared, for the sake of increase and her womanly honor, to endure everything she had endured back then. Her own cheerfulness was probably assisted by an organic amnesia peculiar to women, many of whom may loudly swear in the throes of childbirth never to know their husbands again so as to be spared such suffering—and yet are pregnant within a year; for the impression left by pain on the female sex has its special way of fading. Jacob, by contrast, had certainly never forgotten the hell of that day and was terrified at the thought of Rachel's body being ripped open so cruelly yet again after lying fallow for nine years. Granted, he rejoiced in the honor, and the idea that the number of his sons would now equal the signs in the temple of the zodiac amused his mind. But then again, he also felt he should regard it as a disruption that a still younger son would dare succeed the declared favorite, his youngest. For favoritism always best suits the youngest child, and something like jealousy on behalf of Joseph, his charming son, was mixed up in Jacob's paternal expectations—in short, almost as if some understandable dark foreboding were hovering around him from the very first, Jacob was not especially happy to hear Rachel's announcement.

It was still the season of winter rains, in the month of Kislev, when she told him. What was to happen to that little monkey Dinah still lay in the future. As he had once before, he wrapped his blessed wife in tender indulgence and reverent care, sadly clasped his head in his hands whenever she had to vomit, and called upon God as he watched her dwindle and grow pale, while only the vault of her belly grew—for the crude, natural selfishness of this human fruit was revealing itself in all its unconscious cruelty. The thing inside its cave wanted to grow strong no matter what; thinking ruthlessly only of itself, it sucked up juices and energies at the expense of her who bore it, ate her alive without a thought to good or evil; and had it known how to express its view of this state of affairs, or had so much as had one, it would have been to the effect that its mother was only a means to its own vigor, nothing more than protection and nourishing shelter to make it robust, destined to be cast aside as a useless pod and shell, once it, the sole important thing, had first slipped out into the world. It was unable either to think or say that, but its innermost opinion was quite unmistakable, and Rachel responded with an indulgent smile. It is not always true that motherhood equals sacrifice to such a degree; it does not have to be so. In Rachel, however, nature exemplified this attitude, having done so once very clearly in Joseph's case, yet not so obviously—not so frighteningly for Jacob—as it did this time.

His bitter feelings toward his older sons, toward Shimeon and Levi in particular, toward those headstrong Dioscuri and their atrocity at Shechem, was centered in fact on his worries about Rachel. It would never have entered his mind to embark upon a journey with this fragile pregnant woman, whose fruit alone was strong. And those crazy lads had served him up this mischief for the sake of honor and revenge. Mindless idiots! Now of all times they had to rise up in anger, slaying men and wantonly maiming cattle. Like Dinah for whom they destroyed, they were Leah's children. What did they care about the fragility of their father's true and dearest wife and his concern for her? Not one of their savage thoughts would have taken her into consideration. But it had come to this, and now they had to depart. It had been eight months and more since Rachel had told him; they had counted eight moons, Rachel moons, waxing and waning, just as the child waxed within her and she herself waned. The round of the year had begun again, bursting into flower anew, and it was now the sixth month, Elul, the reign of blazing summer—not a good time for a journey, but Jacob had no choice. Rachel had to ride an animal—but to spare her the swaying of a camel ride in her condition, he gave her an ass, a very wise beast. She sat on its hindquarters, where there is the least jostling, and had to be led by two slaves, who had been threatened with a beating if the ass should stumble or its foot so much as dash against a stone. And so they set out with their flocks. The goal was Hebron, and the majority of the tribe was to make for it directly. For himself, his wives, and a small retinue, Jacob had set his eye on Beth-el as the nearest refuge, an intermediate goal whose holiness would protect him against pursuit and attack, but where he also wished to rest in memory of the night when his head had been raised up and he had dreamt of the stairway.

That was Jacob's mistake. He had two passions: God and Rachel. And the one was at cross-purposes with the other, and by devoting himself to spiritual matters, he called disaster down upon the object of his earthly passion. He could have made straight for Kiriath-Arba, which could be reached in four or five days of steady travel; and if in fact Rachel had died there, at least she would not have died so helplessly, so wretchedly by the roadside. But he spent several days with her at the town of Luz, on the hill at Beth-el, where he had once fallen asleep in misery and dreamt in exaltation; for he was again in distress and danger now and intent on being greatly consoled, on having his head raised up from on high. The *gilgal* was undisturbed, its blackish star-born stone still in its midst. Jacob showed it to his family and also pointed to the spot where he had slept and been granted his extravagant vision. The stone that had raised up his head and that he had anointed was no longer there, which annoyed him. He set up another, sprinkling it with oil, and spent these several days in fact busying himself with all sorts of religious ceremonies, with burnt offerings and libations, taking great care in their preparation; for he insisted that this spot, which he had recognized as a place of the Presence—quite apart from the significance that had always been attached to it locally—be fitted out in a dignified and practical fashion for worship, that not just an earthen hearth be built where smoke could rise up to nourish Yah, but that the jutting rock on the hilltop also be hewn into an altar for God, with steps leading up to its platform, in the middle of which a sacrificial basin and drains would have to be bored and polished. All this required a great deal of work, and Jacob, acting as supervisor, took his time at it. His own people watched and listened as he gave his instructions; but there were also many curious souls from the town of Luz who climbed the hill and lay down or squatted on their heels in the open space before the altar to observe this wandering proclaimer of God and freelance priest, and they exchanged low-voiced and thoughtful opinions about his arrangements. They saw nothing especially new, and yet it was clear to them that this worthy stranger was determined to attach some exceptionally potent and even aberrant meaning to routine matters. For example, he told them that the horns at the sacrificial altar's four corners were not horns of the moon, and certainly not the bull horns of Mardug–Baal, but rather ram horns. They found this astounding and discussed it at length. Since he called upon his lord as Adonai, they believed for a while that it was the beautiful, mutilated, and re-arisen one who was meant, but were then persuaded that someone else must be intended. They did not hear the name El mentioned. That the god's name was Yizrael turned out to be a mistake; rather, the man Jacob himself was called that, both personally and together with all those for whom he was the leader of the faith. This was the basis of a briefly circulated view that he himself was or pretended to be the god of the ram horns, but that was soon corrected. One could make no image of this god, for though he had a body, it had no form—he was fire and clouds. That appealed to some, but repulsed others. In any case one could tell by looking at Jacob that he gave substantial thought to his god's nature, although at the same time a certain worry, a kind of painful anxiety, was written on his wise and solemn face. How marvelous he looked standing up there as he stabbed the kid with his own hand, letting the blood flow and smearing it on those four horns, which were not the moon's horns. Wine and oil were also poured in profusion for this unfamiliar deity, who was also offered bread—the man making such sacrifices must be rich, which said a great deal for both him and his god. The best pieces of the kid were burned to rise as smoke, the sweet odor of *samim* and *besamim*; the rest was prepared as a meal—and partly to be allowed to share in it and partly because they had truly been won over by the wanderer's grand personage, several of the townspeople declared themselves willing to sacrifice to Yizrael's god from now on, if only secondarily, while retaining their traditional worship. Upon closer approach during these proceedings, almost everyone was taken by the incredible beauty of the youngest of Jacob's sons, who was named Joseph. Whenever he appeared, they would kiss their fingertips, clap their hands above their heads, bless their eyes, and almost die with laughter, for with a winning lack of modesty he called himself his parents' favorite, basing such a preference on his own physical and intellectual charms. With the pedagogical irresponsibility characteristic of our relationship to other people's children, they delighted in his mischievous conceit.

Jacob spent the evening hours of these days withdrawn in contemplation, preparing himself for whatever revelatory dreams might be granted him by night. They occurred, too, though not with the overwhelming vividness of those he had dreamt here as a young man. Grand, general, uplifting, and vague was the voice that spoke to him of fertility and the future, of the covenant of the flesh with Abram and most insistently about the name that the sleeper had wrested for himself in panicky strength at the Jabbok and that was now confirmed in power by words more or less forbidding his old and original name, erasing it, elevating the new to exclusive use, and filling his listening heart with a turbulent sense of renewal, as if some caesura had occurred, as if the old were in retreat and the world and time beginning anew in their youth. This was visible in his manner during the course of the day, and everyone avoided him. Laboring with his profound thoughts, he seemed to have forgotten the urgency of Rachel's condition, and no one dared remind him, least of all the expectant mother herself, who in loving meekness subordinated her own physical need for moving on as quickly as possible to his spiritual ponderings. Finally he ordered them to break camp.

From the Mount of Olives near Jebus—also called Uru-shalim, a city where a Hittite named Putichepa played shepherd and tax collector under the aegis of Egypt's Amun—from there one might have seen, indeed probably did see, the caravan pass like a tiny band of figures following an arc that began at Beth-el, crossed a broad hilly landscape parched by summer sun, left Jebus behind on its left, and continued southward toward the house of Lachama or Beth-lachem. Jacob would very much have liked to stop at Jebus and speak with the priests of Shalem—the sun god at home here in the western parts of the land and after whom the city took its second name—for he also found conversations about strange and false gods both spiritually exciting and compatible with his own inner shaping of the image of the One True God. But it was more than likely that stories of

Shechem and what his sons had done to its occupation troops and Beset, their captain, had long since come to the ears of Putichepa, the city's shepherd and the deputy of Amun—which meant the traveler had best be cautious. On the other hand, in Beth-lachem, the "house of bread," he wanted to discuss with those who burned incense to Lachama the nature of this manifestation of the re-arisen and nourishing god, with whose cult Abraham had once maintained relationships of friendly interest, seeing in it a faith of limited kinship. He was delighted to see the city greeting him from its hill. It was late afternoon. Hidden behind a stormy, bluish wall of clouds and now sinking to the west, the sun sent out wide bundled rays of light across the mountain landscape, encircling the settlement higher up in a ring of shimmering white. Dust and stones were radiant in this obscured and sublimely broken revelation of light, filling Jacob's heart with still prouder and more pious feelings for the divine. On the right, behind a wall of loose stones lay vineyards tinged with violet. Small orchards filled gaps between the boulders to the left of the road. Distant mountains were about to take on a kind of transparent twilight hue and lose all substance. The trunk of a very old and mostly hollow mulberry tree was propped against a pile of stones and leaned out across the road. They were riding past it when Rachel fainted and slipped from her beast.

The pains had begun softly hours before, but in order not to upset Jacob and interrupt their journey, she had said nothing about them. Now, suddenly, the weakened woman, sapped of strength by her robust fruit, was overcome with an agony whose thrust and impact were so savage and rending that she lost consciousness. Without even a command, Jacob's tall and splendidly saddled dromedary went to its knees to let its rider dismount. He called for an old slave, a woman from Guta beyond the Tigris, who was skilled in female matters and had acted as midwife to many a delivery in Laban's household. In the hard labor of childbirth, Rachel was laid under the mulberry tree and cushions were dragged over. If it was not the spices that they made her inhale, then it was renewed pain that called her out of her unconscious state. She promised not to let that happen again.

"I wish to be alert and diligent from now on," she gasped, "so that I may assist in this and not delay your journey for long, my dear lord. To think that it should come upon me now, so close to our goal. But behold, the hour is not ours to choose."

"It doesn't matter, my dove," Jacob replied gently. And instinctively he began muttering a formula, appealing to Ea of Naharina in time of need: "You have made us, so let disease, swamp fever, ague, misfortune be turned away."

The woman from Guta recited the same prayer as she added one of her own time-tested amulets to those already hanging at her mistress's neck. But since poor Rachel was now in the throes of pain again, the midwife began chattering to her in broken Babylonian. "Take comfort, my fertile one," she said, "endure, no matter how savage the attack. You shall have this son as well as the other, for in my wisdom I see that, and your eye shall not fade before you behold him; for the child is very robust."

Robust it was, this sole important thing. In the certain knowledge that its time had come, it strove to find its way to the light and to throw off the maternal shell. It gave birth to itself, as it were, impatiently storming the narrow womb with almost no help from her who had so gladly conceived it and nourished it with her own life, yet did not know how to bring it forth despite a fervent willingness to do so. The old woman hummed and advised and arranged Rachel's limbs so that she might assist in the process, but to little avail; she gave her instructions on how to breathe, how to hold her chin and knees. The assaults of pain obliterated every attempt to assist her labor; tortured by random spasms of anguish, she tossed and writhed in a cold sweat, her teeth clenched, her lips blue. "Oh! Oh!" she screamed and called now on the gods of Babel, now on the God of the child's father. As night fell and the silvered barque of the moon came floating up over the mountains, she awoke from a faint and said, "Rachel will die."

Cries went up from all those crouching around her—Leah, the handmaids who were mothers of Jacob's sons, and other women who had been allowed near—and they stretched imploring arms toward her. Then their monotone murmuring of charms began again, stronger now and almost unbroken, like the humming of a swarm of bees in accompaniment to the event. The first to speak after a long pause was Jacob, in whose arm the despairing woman's head lay, and in a hollow voice he said, "What a thing to say!"

She shook her head and tried to smile. An armistice had set in, during which life's assailant appeared to take counsel with itself inside its cave. When the midwife expressed her semi-approval of this pause, adding that it could last a while, Jacob attempted to suggest that the interlude be used to construct a soft stretcher for Rachel and that they continue along the short path across the fields to the inn in Beth-lachem. But Rachel did not want this.

"It began here," she said with struggling lips, "it should be completed here. And who knows if there would be room for us in the inn? The midwife is wrong. I shall very soon be back at vigorous labor, Jacob my husband, so that I may bring you our second."

Poor woman—there was not even the remotest sense of vigor left in her, and she was not deceiving even herself in speaking of it. She had already said what she thought and knew in her deepest heart, and in the course of the night, between two periods of brutal martyrdom, she let her knowledge and secret thoughts show through again when—though barely able to move lips now swollen by a weakened heart—she began to speak of the name to be given her second son. She asked Jacob his opinion, and he replied, "Behold, he is the son of the only true wife and should be called Ben-Jamin."

"No," she said, "don't be angry with me, but I know better. Ben-Oni should be the name of this new life. That is what you should all call the lord I bring to you, and he should be mindful of Mami, who formed him beautifully in your and her image."

Jacob's skill at combining disparate spiritual ideas allowed him to understand this almost without having to think about it. Mami or "the wise Ma-ma" was one of the popular names for Ishtar, mother of gods and fashioner of men, of whom it was said that she formed both male and female to be beautiful after her own image. And in her weakness and mother wit Rachel had let the person of this divine fashioner blur and merge with her own maternal self, which was all the easier since Joseph often called her "Mami." For the initiated, however, for those whose thoughts could follow the arc of it, the name Ben-Oni meant "son of death." She most certainly no longer recalled that she had betrayed herself once already, and was trying now, before it happened, gently to nudge Jacob to brush up against what she knew was coming, so that it would not descend as a sudden blow that left him bereft of reason.

"Benjamin, Benjamin," he said weeping, "but never Benoni!" And it was here, for the first time, as if confessing he now understood, that he directed his question beyond her and up into the night of all those silvery worlds: "Lord, what are you doing?"

In such cases, no answer follows. Yet it is the glory of the human soul that in this silence it does not stray from God, but is able to grasp the majesty of what is incomprehensible and to grow from it. Off to one side the Chaldean women and slaves hummed the litany of magic charms by which they hoped to compel terrible and foolish powers to follow human wishes. But never before this hour had Jacob so clearly understood why that was wrong, and why Abram had set out from Ur. His view into monstrous vastness filled him with terror, but the looking itself was not without power; and on this dreadful night his laboring to understand the divine, which always left its careworn traces in his face, achieved an advancement that bore a certain kinship to Rachel's own agony. And it was very much in accord with her love that her husband Jacob should gain some spiritual advantage from her dying.

The child came into the world toward the end of the night's last watch, as the sky turned pale in the predawn light. To prevent strangulation the old woman had to rip it forcibly from the poor womb. Rachel, who could no longer scream, fell unconscious. Blood gushed in the child's wake, so that the pulse on her hand no longer came in beats but only in a thin trickle that died away. But she saw the child's life and smiled. She lived another hour. When they brought Joseph to her, she did not recognize him.

She opened her eyes one last time as the east began to blush and the red of dawn fell across her countenance. She looked up into Jacob's face bent low above her, squinted slightly, and began to babble: "Look there, a stranger! . . . And just why should you be allowed to kiss me? Is it because you are a cousin from far off, and because we are both children of the same first father? Well then, kiss me, and the shepherds beside the well stone rejoice, singing 'Loo, loo, loo!'"

Trembling, he kissed her for the last time. But she went on speaking.

"Look, you have rolled the stone away for me with your manly strength, Jacob my love. Roll it away from the pit once again and lay Laban's child in her bed, for I am leaving you. Look how every burden has been lifted from me, the burden of children, the burden of life, and night is coming on. Jacob, my husband, forgive me for being unfruitful and presenting you with only two sons, but two at least, Jehosiph the blessed and this little son of death, this babe—ah it is so hard to go now and leave them. And it is hard to leave you, too, Jacob my darling, for we were the true husband and wife for each other. You will have to ponder and discover who God is without Rachel now. Discover it and farewell. And forgive me, too," she whispered in her final breath, "for stealing the teraphim." And death crossed over her countenance and put out its flame.

The humming of the conjuring women stopped at a signal from Jacob's hand. They all fell to press their faces to the ground. But he sat there, her head still resting on his arms, and his never-ceasing tears fell silently on her breast. After a while they asked him if they should build a litter and carry the dead woman to Beth-lachem or Hebron for burial.

"No," he said, "it began here, let it be completed here, and where He has done this let her lie. Dig a grave and hollow out its pit there by the wall. Take fine linen from the baggage, wrap her in it, and choose a stone to place upon her grave and in her memory. Then Israel will journey onward, without Rachel and with the child."

While the men dug, the women loosed their hair and bared their breasts, mixed dust and water to soil themselves in token of this sorrow, and to the music of the flute they raised their lament, "Alas for our sister!" clapping one hand to the forehead and beating their breasts with the other. Jacob, however, held Rachel's head in his arm until they took her from him.

When the earth had closed over his beloved, there by the roadside, at the place where God had taken her from him, Yizrael took up his journey again and at one point made his camp near Migdal Eder, a tower from earliest times. There Ruben sinned with Bilhah, the concubine, and was cursed.

YOUNG JOSEPH

Part One

THOTH

Beauty

And so it is said that Joseph was seventeen years old and was tending the flock together with his brothers; and that the lad lived with the sons of Bilhah and Zilpah, who were wives of his father. That is correct, and as to something else added by "fine discourse," that he brought to his father any evil report of his brothers—of that we have seen evidence. It would not be difficult to take a point of view that makes him look like an insufferable scamp. That was his brothers' standpoint. We do not share it—or better, having assumed it for a moment, we immediately put it behind us. For Joseph was more. But these statements, being so precise, require, each in its turn, elucidation and clarification, so that a state of affairs compressed and shrunk by its having happened so long ago may now unfold fully.

Joseph was seventeen years old and in the eyes of all who beheld him the most beautiful among the children of men. To be frank, we do not like to speak of beauty. Does not the concept, the word, exude boredom? Is beauty not a sublimely pallid notion, a pedant's fantasy? It's said that it is based in laws; but laws speak to reason, not to emotion, which has no use for reason's strictures. That is why perfect beauty, which needs no apology, is so dreary. For emotion actually wants to find something it can forgive, otherwise it turns away with a yawn. Enthusiastic admiration for what is merely perfect demands a devotion to preconceived, prototypical norms—a pedant's devotion. It is difficult to ascribe profundity to such preconceived enthusiasm. The law's bonds are external and didactic; magic alone creates an inner bond. Beauty is magic worked upon the emotions—always half-illusionary, extremely precarious, and fragile in its very efficacy. Place a loathsome head atop a beautiful body, and the body itself will no longer be beautiful in terms of any emotional effect—or, at best, only in the dark, which is mere deception. Deceit, trickery, fraud—how great a role they play in the realm of beauty! And why? Because at the same time it is suddenly the realm of love and desire; because sexuality becomes involved and defines the concept of beauty. The world of anecdotes is full of tales of how lads dressed as women have turned men's heads, of how girls in trousers have ignited the passions of their own sex. But discovery sufficed to dampen any such feelings, for with it beauty had become impractical. Perhaps human beauty in its effect upon the emotions is nothing more than the magic of sex, the illustration of the idea of sexuality, so that one would do better to speak of a consummate man, of a supremely womanly woman, than of a beautiful one and to say that it understandably demands a great deal of a woman to speak of another woman's beauty, or a man of another man's. Cases in which beauty triumphs over the attribute of manifest impracticality and retains its unconditional effect upon the emotions are in the minority, but do demonstrably occur. The impulse of youth comes into play here, and with it a magic that emotion is very apt to confuse with beauty, so that youth, if some all too disconcerting flaw does not cripple its attraction, is usually simply perceived as beauty—even by youth itself, as its own smile unmistakably reveals. Charm is inherent in youth, a manifestation of beauty that by its very nature is suspended between masculinity and femininity. A lad of seventeen is not beautiful in the sense of consummate masculinity. Neither is he beautiful in the sense of a purely impractical femininity—that would attract only a few. But let us grant this much: Beauty as youthful charm always tends in both psychology and expression somewhat toward the feminine; that is part of its nature, which has its basis in its tender relationship with the world and of the world with it—it is painted in youth's smile. At seventeen, it is true, someone can be more beautiful than woman or man, beautiful both as woman and man, beautiful from both sides and in every way, handsome and beautiful enough to set any woman, any man gawking, tumbling head over heels in love.

And so it was with Rachel's son, and that is why it is said that he was the most beautiful among the children of men. That was exaggerated praise, for there have been and are a great many like him; and ever since humankind ceased to play the role of amphibian or reptile and has, for the most part, followed a path toward a more divine physicality, it has hardly been unusual for a lad of seventeen with such trim legs and small hips, such a well-formed torso, such golden brown skin to be greeted with approving looks—nothing unusual about being neither too tall nor too squat, but of just the right stature, about walking and standing in demigod-like fashion, about a form charmingly suspended between gentleness and power. It is also hardly extraordinary that no dog's head sits atop such a body, but rather something very appealing, with a smiling human mouth that approaches the divine—it happens every day. But in Joseph's world and immediate circle it was precisely his person and presence that exercised beauty's emotional effect, and people generally felt that the Eternal had poured out grace upon his lips—which would certainly have been too full if not for the movement that came with speaking and smiling. This grace was challenged, there was resistance to it here and there, but that resistance denied none of all this, nor can one claim that it actually excluded itself from the reigning emotion. There is much to be said at any rate for the notion that his brothers' hatred was essentially nothing other than that same universal infatuation, but with a negative prefix.

The Shepherd

So much, then, for Joseph's beauty and his seventeen years. That he tended the flock together with his brothers, that is, with the sons of Bilhah and Zilpah, also needs to be elucidated, with amplifications on the one hand, and qualifications on the other.

Jacob, the man of blessing, was a stranger in the land, a *ger*, as people called him, a tolerated guest of some repute—not because he had lived so long outside the country, but in his own right, by heritage and rank, as the son of his forefathers, who had likewise been *gerim*. His distinction was not that of a home-owning citizen from a highborn urban family; it had its source in wisdom and riches, together with the mark they left upon his personage and bearing, and not in his style of life, which was rather loose and, though always within the law, had about it, one might say, an orderly ambiguity. He lived in tents outside the walls of Hebron, just as he had once dwelt before Shechem's gates, and might one day pack up and once again seek out different wells and pastures. Was he then a Bedu and offspring of Cain, with the sign of the vagrant and robber upon his brow, an abomination and terror to cities and farmers alike? Not in the least. In dealing with the mortal enemy, the Amalekites, his God had proved no different from the local Baals—he, Jacob, had demonstrated that several times by arming his own household so that, together with city folk and cattle farmers, they might beat back that camel-breeding riffraff who came swarming up out of the southern desert, painted with tribal signs and bent on plunder. But all the same he was—intentionally, explicitly—not a farmer; that would have contradicted his religious sensibility, which was not in accord with that of the sun-reddened tillers of the soil. Besides, as a *ger* and tolerated, protected resident, he had no right to own land, except for that beneath his tents. He leased a little farmland, a parcel here, a parcel there, a wide level field or a steep rocky one, where fertile soil between the boulders yielded wheat and barley. He set his sons and servants to work it, so that Joseph was also a sower and a reaper on occasion, and not just a shepherd—but everyone knows that. And yet such casual farming scarcely defined Jacob's life, it was something done halfheartedly on the side, a ceremony to show some sort of permanence. What truly gave his life weight was the movable wealth teeming about him, his herds and what they yielded, which he then traded for lavish supplies of grain and must, figs, pomegranates, honey, even silver and gold—and these assets defined his relationship to both townspeople and country folk, a relationship established and regulated by numerous contracts that gave solidity to his loose form of citizenship.

Maintaining these herds required cordial business dealings with the locals, with urban merchants and the farmers who labored for or rented from them. If Jacob did not wish to live the vagabond life of a nomadic thief, breaking into the enclosures and destroying the fields of the propertied class, then Baal's people required agreements with binding and amicable terms as to pasturing rights in return for payments in kind: documents permitting his teeming herds to be driven through stubble and left to graze their way across fallow lands—which, however, were on the decrease in these mountains at the time. There had been a long season of peace and blessing, the highways were never still. Town-dwellers who had profited from the land now grew fat on the caravan trade, on fees paid for storing, reloading, and escorting wares that came from the land of Mardug by way of Damascus, down the highway east of the Jardên and through this region to the Great Sea, and on to the Land of Mud—or moved in the opposite direction. Town-dwellers kept accumulating land, which they then set their slaves and indentured servants to till, the harvests leaving them even fatter than commerce had and bringing free farmers under their control, just as Ishullanu's sons had done by lending money to Laban. Both settlements and land under cultivation increased; there were not that many pasturing places left. And so it came about that the land could no longer support Jacob, just as the meadows of Sodom had no longer been able to support both Abraham and Lot. He had to divide his flocks; large numbers of animals grazed peaceably elsewhere, some five days' journey to the north, there where Jacob had settled previously in the valley of Shechem with its abundance of wells; and it was usually Leah's sons, from Ruben to Zebulun, who cared for the animals there, while only the four sons of Bilhah and Zilpah, together with Rachel's two offspring, lived with their father—that is, just as happens with the signs in the zodiac, only six of which are visible at a time, while the other six are removed from view, a metaphor and model that Joseph never tired of mentioning. That is not to say that those living at a distance did not come when there was special work to be done at Hebron, at harvest for example—a detail of some importance. But usually they were four to five days' journey off—a matter of equal importance. That is the explanation for why it is said that the lad Joseph was with the sons of the handmaids.

The work Joseph did at his brothers' side in the fields and pastures, however, was not a daily routine—we ought not take it too seriously. He was not constantly tending the herd or plowing up soil for winter sowing after it had been softened by rain, but did so only now and again, on occasion, when it occurred to him, when he felt like it. Jacob, his father, did not begrudge him a great deal of free time for loftier pursuits, which will be described in a moment. But when he was with the others, what was the nature of his presence—was he helper or overseer? That remained, much to his brothers' indignation, undecided, for when told to do so—in rather gruff tones—he would, as the youngest, perform a little work for them; but when he was in their midst it was never really as an equal, not as someone who gladly joined in a fellowship of sons against the old man, but as his representative and emissary, who spied on them, so that they were hardly happy to see him—but, then again, they were annoyed whenever he stayed at home just as he pleased.

The Lesson

What did he do there? He sat with old Eliezer under God's tree, the great terebinth near the well, and pursued the sciences.

It was said of Eliezer that his countenance was much like Abraham's. Ultimately that was something people could not know, for none of them had ever seen the Chaldean, nor had any image or likeness of his face been passed down through the centuries; and Eliezer's alleged similarity to him could only be understood the other way around: When one tried to imagine the person of that ancient wanderer and friend of God, the features of Eliezer's face might have lent assistance, not only because they were as grand and imposing as his whole figure and bearing, but even more importantly because they also had something unique about them, a soothing universality, a divine vagueness, that made it easier to transfer his image to some venerable unknown out of the primal past. He was Jacob's age, or a little older, and dressed in much the same way as well—half Bedouin-like, half in the fashion of Shinar, with fringed tassels on his robe, but with a stylus always tucked in his sash. The portion of his brow left uncovered by his scarf was smooth and unwrinkled. His still dark eyebrows ran in narrow, low arcs from the shallow onset of the nose to the temples, while the almost lashless eyelids, both upper and lower, were so heavy and somehow swollen that they looked like lips from between which the black orbs of his eyes bulged. The small-nostriled, wide-bridged nose ended at a narrow mustache extending down over the corners of his mouth to join the whitish yellow beard below and revealing beneath it the reddish arc of his lower lip, an even line that extended from one corner of the mouth to the other. There was such regularity about the starting point of the beard on his prominent cheeks—whose yellowish skin was full of tiny fissures—that one might have had the impression it was attached at his ears and easily removable. Indeed, the whole face left one imagining it could be removed, and that only then would Eliezer's true face be discovered—certainly on many an occasion it had seemed that way to Joseph as a boy.

As to Eliezer's person and origins there were various erroneous reports in circulation, which will be refuted somewhat further on.

He was Jacob's steward and his oldest servant, skilled in reading and writing and Joseph's teacher—that should suffice for now.

"Tell me, son of the true wife," he might ask him as they sat in the shade of the oracle tree, "for what three reasons did God create man last, after all growing things and beasts?"

To which Joseph had to respond: "God created man last of all: first, so that no one could say he had shared in all the other works; second, so that man might be humbled and say, 'The blowfly came before me'; and third, so that he might at once sit down at the banquet table, as the guest for whom all has been prepared."

To which Eliezer replied in satisfaction, "So you have said." And Joseph laughed.

But that was the least of it. This was merely one example from among many of the training of the mind's acumen and memory to which Joseph was subjected, and of the ancient drolleries and anecdotes that Eliezer passed on while the boy was still of tender years and that, when repeated on Joseph's grace-filled lips, enchanted people already silly with wonder at the boy's beauty. That was how he had tried to amuse and divert his father beside the well, with the story and fable about names, about how Ishchara, the virgin, had extracted the Name from the lascivious messenger. For no sooner had she learned the true and undisguised Name than she cried it out and rose up on its power, her virginity intact, having snapped her fingers in the face of the Semhazai the Lustful. Once on high, she was received with great approval by the Lord God, who spoke to her: "Since you have fled from sin, We wish to assign you a place among the stars." And that is the origin of the constellation of the Virgin. But the messenger Semhazai had no longer been able to mount up, but rather had to remain behind in the dust, until the day that Jacob, son of Yitzchak, dreamt his dream of the heavenly stairway at Bethel. Only by means of those ladders and ramps had he been able to climb homeward again, deeply shamed that this was possible only within a human being's dream.

Could this have been called science? No, it was barely half true, a mere adornment for the mind, but suitable for preparing the temperament to receive sterner matters of holy precision. And so Joseph learned from Eliezer about the universe, the heavenly world perfectly constituted in its three parts—the higher heavens, the heavenly earth of the zodiac, and the heavenly ocean in the south; for it corresponded exactly to the earthly world, also divided into three parts—a heaven of air, the realm of earth, and the world ocean. This latter, he learned, surrounded the earth's disk like a ribbon, but was also beneath it, so that in the days of the Great Flood it had been able to burst up through all the cracks and unite these waters with those of the heavenly sea spewing down from on high. But the realm of earth was to be viewed as stamped firmly into place, while the heavenly earth above was a land of mountains with two peaks, those of the sun and the moon, its Horeb and Sinai.

Sun and moon plus five other wandering stars made seven, the number of the planets and bearers of command, moving in seven circles of varying size along the causeway of the zodiac, which was therefore much like a seven-storied circular tower, the rings of its terraces leading up to the highest heaven of the north and the throne of dominion—where God was, and his holy mountain flashed like fiery gemstones, just as the snows of Mount Hermon sparkled above the land to the north. And as he taught, Eliezer pointed to the glistening white mountain of power in the distance, visible from all points, including from the tree here—and Joseph did not differentiate between the heavenly and the earthly.

He learned of the wonder and mystery of numbers, the sixty, the twelve, the seven, the four, the three, of the divinity of measurement and how all things stood in accord and correspondence, setting man in amazement and adoration at such great harmony.

Twelve were the constellations of the zodiac, and they formed the stations of its great round. There were the twelve months of thirty days. But corresponding to this great circuit was a smaller one, which was also divided into twelve sections, and that made a space of time sixty times as large as the sun's disk, and that was the double hour. It was the day's month and proved divisible in the same ingenious fashion. For the visible path of the sun on the day of the equinox contained the diameter of the sun's disk exactly as many times as there were days in a year, that is three hundred and sixty, and indeed on such days the time between the rising of the sun, from the moment it first appeared above the rim of the horizon until its disk was perfect, comprised the sixtieth part of a double hour. And behold, that was the double minute; and just as summer and winter made the great circle, and day and night the smaller, so twelve double hours yielded twelve single ones for each day and each night, and sixty single minutes for each hour of the day and night.

Was that order, harmony, and well-being?

Now mark this as well, Dumuzi, true son! Let your mind be bright, keen, and clear!

Seven was the number of those wanderers and bearers of commands, and each had its own day. But seven was also most especially the number of the moon, which prepared the path for the gods, its brothers, for indeed each of its quarters numbered seven days. Sun and moon made two, as did all things in the world and life, as did yes and no. Which was why one could arrange the planets as two plus five—and how rightly so, in view of the five! For it stood in a most beautiful relationship with the twelve—since five times twelve made sixty, a demonstrably holy number—but also, and most beautiful of all, with the holy seven, for five plus seven made twelve. Was that all? No, for this same ordering and sorting yielded a planetary week of five days, and seventy-two such weeks made one year. Five, however, was the number that one had to multiply by seventy-two in order to produce the glorious three hundred and sixty—sum of both the days in the year and the number that resulted when the sun's path was divided by the longest line that could be drawn across its disk.

That was splendid.

But by following sublime authority concerning both terms, one could also order the planets as three plus four. For three was the number of the zodiac's regents: sun, moon, and Ishtar. Moreover it was the world number, determining the division of the universe above and below. On the other hand, four was the number of the world's regions, corresponding to the seasons of the day; it was also the number of segments into which the sun's course was divided, each ruled by a planet, and beyond that the number of the moon and Ishtar's star, for they each displayed four phases. What was the result, however, if you multiplied the three and the four? That produced the twelve!

Joseph laughed. Eliezer, however, raised his hands and said, "Adonai!"

How did it happen that if one divided the days of the moon by the number of its phases, that is four, the result yet again was a seven-day week? It was His finger at work.

Under the old man's watchful eye, young Joseph played with all this as if juggling balls, amusing himself profitably. He understood that man had been given reason by God in order that he might improve on something holy, if not quite consistent, so that man would have to balance out the three hundred sixty days of the sun's year with the addition of five days at its end. Those were evil and foul days, dragon days, curse days, stamped with the mark of winter's night; not until they had passed did spring appear and the season of blessing reign. This lent the five a noxious aspect. But thirteen was also a very evil number, and why? Because the moon's twelve months had only three hundred and fifty-four days, and from time to time a leap month had to be inserted, corresponding to the thirteenth sign of the zodiac, the raven. This superfluity made the thirteen an unlucky number, just as the raven was a malevolent bird. That explained why Benoni–Benjamin almost died as he moved through birth's narrow passageway—which is like the gorge between the two peaks of the world mountain—and was almost defeated in his struggle against the power of the underworld, for he was Jacob's thirteenth child. But Dinah was accepted as an offering in his place, and she withered.

It was good to understand necessity and thereby penetrate the nature of God's mind. For his miracle of numbers was not entirely flawless, and man had to temper it with his reason; but a curse and calamity lay over such corrections, turning even the twelve—so beautiful otherwise—into something ominous, for one had to use it to match the moon's year of three hundred fifty-four days to the lunar-solar year of three hundred sixty-six days. But if one adopted three hundred sixty-five as the number of days, that meant, as Joseph was made to calculate, that one-fourth of a day was missing, and this irregularity swelled over the course of the sun's circuits until one thousand four hundred and sixty of them created one entire year. That was the period of the Dog Star; and Joseph's perception of time and space now expanded to something superhuman, pressing past small circles into ever more monstrous ones that spun around them at vast distances, into cyclic years of terrifying size. The day itself was a small year with seasons, with summer brightness and winter night, and the days were enclosed within a great circle. Yet it, too, was only comparatively large, for one thousand four hundred sixty of them closed to form a Dog Star year. The world, however, was made up of an overpowering circuit, the turning cycle of the largest—or then again perhaps not the ultimately largest—year, each one of which had its summer and winter. The former occurred when all heavenly bodies met in the houses of the Water Bearer or the Fish, the latter when they met in the house of the Lion or the Crab. Each such winter began with a flood, and each summer with a conflagration, so that between these beginning and end points all the world's other periods and great circular orbits were completed. Each such cycle comprised four hundred thirty-two thousand years and was an exact repetition of all that had gone before, for by then all heavenly bodies had returned to position and thus had to bring about the same effects, large and small. Which is why the world's periods were called "renewals of life" and sometimes, as well, "repetitions of the past" or "eternal return." Its name, moreover, was *olâm,* the "eon"; God, however, was the Lord of the Eons, *El-Olâm,* He who lived through the eons, *Chai olâm,* and it was He who had put the *olâm* into the hearts of men, that is, had given them the ability to conceive of eons and thus, in some sense, likewise to rise up to be their master. . . .

These were lessons of majesty that entertained Joseph in grand style. For what all didn't Eliezer know! Secrets that made learning a great and flattering delight, precisely because they were secrets known to only a few tight-lipped and arch-clever men in temples and closed lodges, but not to the great masses. Eliezer knew and taught that the Babylonian double ell was the length of the pendulum that made sixty double oscillations in a double minute. Chatterbox though he might be, Joseph told no one else; for this revealed yet again the holy attribute of the sixty, which when multiplied by the beautiful six, gave the most sacred three hundred and sixty.

He learned measures of length and travel, deducing them from his own stride measured simultaneously with the course of the sun—which was not, as Eliezer assured him, a presumptuous act, since man himself was a little universe, perfectly corresponding to the great one—and thus the holy numbers of the cycles played their role in both the grand structure of measures and in time, which in turn became space.

This led to volume and so to weight; and Joseph learned the value and measurement of gold, silver, and copper according to Babylonian and Phoenician norms, in both royal and common usages. He practiced commercial accounting, transforming copper into silver values, exchanging an ox for quantities of oil, wine, and wheat equal to the beast's value in metal, and was so quick-witted at it that whenever Jacob listened in, he would cluck his tongue and exclaim, "Like an angel! Just like an angel of Araboth."

Added to all this, Joseph learned the essentials about sickness and simples, about the human body, which is constituted according to the cosmic triad of solid, fluid, and airlike substances. He learned to assign the body's parts to the houses of the zodiac and the planets, to hold in high regard the fat of the kidneys, since the organ it surrounded was the seat of vital energy and was also associated with the organs of procreation; to consider the liver the origin of emotion, and, with the aid of a clay model divided into heavily inscribed fields, to memorize a system that taught how the bowels mirrored future events and were a source of dependable omens. Then he learned the peoples of the earth.

These were seventy or, in all probability, seventy-two in number, since this was the number of five-day weeks in the year, and the manner in which some of them lived and worshiped was appalling. This was especially true of the barbarians of the far north, who lived in the land of Magog, far beyond Hermon's heights and even beyond the land of Khanigalbat, north of the Taurus. But the extreme West, which was called Tarshish, was horrible as well, a land to which the men of Sidon, casting aside all fear, had sailed, arriving after endless days on a straight course across the Great Green. In their obsession with faraway places and trade, these same people from Sidon and Gebal had traveled by the same means to Kittim, by which they meant Sicily, and had founded settlements there. They had done much to make the earth's disk known—not so that wise Eliezer might have matters to teach, but rather out of an eagerness to visit peoples who dwelt far beyond and to coax them into buying their purple cloth and elaborate embroidery. There were winds that guided them all on their own, as it were, to Cypress, or Alashia, and to Dodanim, as they called Rhodes. At no great peril, they had also made their way to Muzriland and Egypt, and their ships had returned home upon a current favorable to the spirit of commerce. But the people of Egypt had themselves overthrown Kush and opened to knowledge the lands of Negroes to the south, far up the Nile. They had summoned their courage and taken to ship themselves, and had found out the lands of incense at the far end of the Red Sea—Punt, the realm of the phoenix. Farthest south lay Ophir, the land of gold, so it was said. As for the land of sunrise, there was a king in Elam, whom they had not yet been able to ask whether he could see beyond his own lands in that same direction. Presumably not.

This is only a portion of what Eliezer impressed upon Joseph beneath the tree of God. The lad wrote it all down, just as the old man instructed, and tilting his head to one shoulder, read it himself until he had it down by heart. Reading and writing were, to be sure, the basis of and accessory to all else; for otherwise there would have been only hearsay scattered by the wind and quickly forgotten among men. Which was why Joseph had to sit up very straight under the tree, knees spread wide, writing utensils in his lap: the clay tablet on which he inscribed wedges with his stylus, or leaves of pasted reed fabric, or sometimes a smoothed piece of sheep- or goatskin, on which he set rows of crow's-foot marks with a reed—either sharpened to a point or chewed to a fibrous brush—that he first dipped into the red and black pots of his ink tray. He alternated writing in the common script of the land—good for noting everyday speech and dialect, for very neatly copying commercial letters and lists in the best Phoenician style—and in divine script, the official sacred script of Babel, appropriate for the law, for precepts and sagas, and for that there were the stylus and clay tablets. Of these Eliezer owned countless, lovely models to copy: treatises on the stars, hymns to the moon and sun, chronological tables, weather chronicles, tax registers, as well as fragments of the great fables in verse from olden times—which were lies, and yet cast in such audaciously solemn words that they became reality in one's mind. They dealt with the creation of the world and of humankind; with Mardug's battle against the dragon; with Ishtar's elevation from lowly servant to royal sovereign, and of her journey to hell; with the herb of procreation and the water of life; with the astounding exploits of Adapa, Etana, and that Gilgamesh whose body was divine flesh, but who nonetheless never succeeded in gaining eternal life. Hardly bending over, with only eyelids lowered, and tracing with his forefinger, Joseph read and modestly copied it all down. He read and wrote about Etana's friendship with the eagle that bore him up to Anu's heaven; and indeed they flew so high that the land below was like a cake, the sea like a breadbasket. But when both of these had vanished entirely, Etana had unfortunately been seized with fear, and plunged back into the depths along with the eagle—an ignominious end. Joseph hoped that, given the occasion, his behavior would be different from that of the hero Etana. But the story he liked even better was the one about the woodsman Engidu and how a wench from the city of Uruk converted him to civilized conduct, how she taught the brute beast to eat and drink with good manners, to anoint himself with oil and wear clothing, in short to become like a human being, like a man of the city. This attracted him, and he especially liked the way the girl docked the tail of this wolf of the steppes after first making him receptive to life's refinement with a love tryst lasting six days and seven nights. When he recited these lines, the language of Babel played on his lips in all its dark splendor, until Eliezer would kiss the hem of his pupil's robe and cry, "Hail, son of a lovely wife! You are making brilliant progress, and in but a short while will be the *mazkir* of a prince, the voice of memory for a great king. Remember me, when you come into your kingdom."

Afterward Joseph would stroll out to join his brothers in the field or pasture to offer them unstrenuous service as a young helper.

But, baring their teeth, they said, "Look there, how he comes strolling along, the dandy with fingers inky from reading stones from before the Flood. Will he be so kind as to milk the goats, or will he simply loll about, waiting to see if we cut pieces of flesh from the animals for our own stew pot? Ah, if we could give him the thrashing we'd like, he'd not do without one, as must sadly be the case for fear of Jacob!"

Body and Mind

If one were to trace how the relationship between Joseph and his brothers worsened over the years—from details to generality, from the day's annoyances and misunderstandings back to a fundamental basis—one would encounter envy and arrogance as the first and last causes; and anyone who loves justice will find it difficult to decide whether it was the former or latter failing—that is, whether, in personal terms, it was the individual or the group as it grew ever more menacing in its actions toward him—to which principal blame should be assigned for all this misfortune. Indeed, justice and the honest desire to cast off every possible seductive bias may perhaps lead a person to chastise arrogance as the primary iniquity and source of all evil; but then again, justice would demand that same person admit that, both now and at the time, the world has seldom seen so much cause for arrogance—and thus, to be sure, for envy as well.

Seldom are beauty and knowledge found together on earth. Rightly or wrongly, we are accustomed to imagine that erudition is ugly, and that charm lacks all intellect—indeed it is part of charm that it lacks intellect in all good conscience, since it not only has no need of letters, of intellect and wisdom, but in fact also runs the risk of being distorted or destroyed by them. But the exemplary bridging of the gulf set between mind and beauty, the unification of both such fine qualities in one individual seems to cancel a tension that we are accustomed to regard as based in what is naturally human, automatically leading us to thoughts of the divine. For the unbiased eye necessarily comes to rest with purest rapture on any such manifestation of this divine lack of tension, which is likewise so constituted as to arouse the bitterest emotions in those who have reason to believe they have been diminished or darkened by its light.

Such was the case here. The happy acceptance that certain phenomena arouse within the human heart and that is objectively called their beauty was so absolutely palpable in the case of Rachel's firstborn and people found him—whether we can share entirely in their enthusiasm or not—so handsomely beautiful that his charm became proverbial early on, well beyond his immediate vicinity. And that charm was such that it incorporated the mind and its related arts, grasped and assimilated them with cheerful eagerness, only to release them again under its own seal, the seal of charm, until no opposition and almost no difference remained between the two, between beauty and mind. We said that cancellation of this normal tension must have something divine about it. Let that be rightly understood. Not that this tension was then resolved *into* something divine—for Joseph was a human being, and a fallible one at that, and with far too healthy an understanding not to know it in his bones at all times; but it was resolved *in* something divine, that is, in the moon.

We were witnesses to a scene—one very characteristic of the physical and intellectual relationships that Joseph cultivated with that heavenly body—that took place, quite understandably, behind the back of his father, who, upon his arrival, felt it his most urgent task to censure the nakedness with which this boy who was everything to him had been ogling that naked beauty on high. But what bound the boy to the moon's nature was more than the mere thought of beauty's magic; what also bound him equally closely was the idea of wisdom and letters—for the moon was the heavenly image of Thoth, the white baboon and the inventor of the written sign, the speaker and scribe of the gods, the recorder of their words and patron of all who could write. It was the simultaneous magic of beauty and the written sign, and that unity had been what exhilarated him and gave his solitary worship its stamp—a somewhat out-of-the-way and confused cult, prone to degeneration (and sure to upset his father), but for that very reason easily leading to intoxication by its muddling the sensations of both mind and body in a most ravishing way.

Without doubt every person possesses and cultivates, more or less consciously, an idea, a favorite thought, that forms the source of his secret delight and is nourished and maintained by his sense of life. For Joseph this ravishing idea was the notion of body and mind, beauty and wisdom, abiding together, each mutually reinforcing consciousness of the other. Chaldean travelers and slaves had told him that in creating humankind Bel had had his own head cut off, letting his blood mix with the earth so that living creatures could be shaped from the bloody clods. Joseph did not believe this. But whenever he wanted to feel his own existence and privately take delight in himself, he would recall that bloody mixture of the earthly and the divine and feel strangely gladdened to know that he himself was of such a substance, smiling as he thought how consciousness of the body and of beauty could only be improved and fortified by consciousness of the mind—and the other way around.

What he believed was that the Spirit of God—what the people of Shinar called *Mummu*—had brooded over the waters of chaos and created the world through his Word. He thought: Just think of it! The world had come to be by the Word, the free and external Word, and, even today still, although a thing might be present, it was not actually present in truth till man bestowed existence to it with the word and gave it a name. And should a handsome and beautiful head then not likewise convince itself of the importance of the wisdom of words?

Such tendencies and the encouragement they received from Jacob—for several reasons to be discussed shortly—contributed much to Joseph's estrangement from the sons of Leah and the handmaids, and that isolation sowed many of the seeds of arrogance on the one side and of jealousy on the other. We are loath to lump the brothers together and brand tribal founders—whose names, even today, are still justly memorized in the sequence of their birth by every schoolchild—as strictly ordinary fellows. That would hardly apply to at least a couple of them—to Jehuda, for instance, a man of complicated and tormented character, or to the fundamentally decent Ruben. First off, however, beauty is a term not even vaguely applicable either to those closer to Joseph's age or those in their late twenties by the time he was seventeen, although they were all strapping fellows and Leah's offspring and especially Re'uben, but Shimeon, Levi, and Jehuda as well, gloried in their athletic build; but as for wisdom and the word, there was not a one of them who would not have prided himself on a total lack of regard or understanding of such things. Granted, it was said of Bilhah's Naphtali early on that he gave "goodly words," but that judgment is based on the modest demands of ordinary folk, and Naphtali's gift with words was, taken all in all, a rather trifling glibness with no basis in knowledge or affinity for higher things. One and all, they were (just as Joseph should have been to be properly integrated into their society) shepherds and occasionally, and secondarily, tillers of the soil—quite estimable in both those capacities and hostile to someone who, with his father's permission, imagined he could be that as well, but only incidentally, with one hand behind his back as it were, all the while playing the scribe and reader of tablets. Before they came up with the nickname that betrayed their bitterest hatred of him—"Dreamer of Dreams"—they mocked him as Noah-Utnapishtim, the archclever man, the Reader of Stones from before the Flood. By way of rebuttal on his part, he called them "dogs' heads" and "people who can't tell good from evil"—said it to their faces and was shielded only by their fear of Jacob, for otherwise they would have thrashed him black-and-blue. We would not have liked to see that; but his beautiful eyes should not mislead us into thinking his answer was any less censurable than their mockery. Just the opposite—for what good is wisdom if it cannot so much as keep a man from arrogance?

And how did Jacob, the father, react to all of this? He was not a learned man. To be sure, he spoke Babylonian as well as his southern Canaanite dialect—spoke it better, in fact, than his native tongue—but had no Egyptian, if only because, as we have noted, he detested and disapproved of all things Egyptian. From what he knew of that land it seemed to him the home of both immorality and drudgery under the lash. Service to the state, which evidently defined life there, offended his sense of independence and personal responsibility; and the cults of death and of beasts that flourished there were folly and abomination in his eyes, especially the cult of death, for any worship of what was under the earth—beginning already very early on, with the earthly, with seed corn rotting in the earth in order to become fertile—was for him the same as fornication. Keme or Mizraim were not his names for that muddy land down under, he called it Sheol, hell, the realm of death; and his spiritual and moral antipathy applied as well to the exaggerated regard in which, or so he had heard, they held the written word. His own skills in that arena went hardly any farther than putting his name to legal agreements he was required to sign, though he usually just stamped them with a seal. He left everything else of that sort to Eliezer, his eldest servant, and gladly so, for the skills of our servants are our own skills, and the weight of Jacob's dignity did not depend upon them. Its source was of a free, original, and personal nature; it was based on the power of his emotions and experiences that were the clever and momentous fulfillment of stories; it came from a natural spirituality radiating from him and apparent to everyone. It was the added special weight of a man of inspiration, of bold dreams, of direct contact with God, who could easily do without a knowledge of writing. It is hardly appropriate to make a comparison that would never once have occurred to Eliezer himself. But could it ever have possibly been Eliezer's office to dream the dream of the heavenly ramp or, with God's help, to make discoveries in the realm of nature, like the sympathetic magic that led to the birth of speckled sheep and goats? No, never!

Why, then, did Jacob encourage Joseph's literary education by his scribe and gaze with approval at erudition that carried with it dangers—for both the lad and his relationship with his brothers—that could not have escaped him? There were two reasons, both based in love—one a matter of ambition, the other of concern for how the lad was to be raised. Leah, the disdained wife, knew very well what she was saying when, at Joseph's birth, she had prophesied both to herself and the sons of her body that they would all become as nothing in Jacob's eyes and light as air. Since the day he was presented with the child of his true wife—with Dumuzi, the sprout, the son of the virgin—Jacob had had but one thing in mind: to place this latecomer before his previous sons, at their head, in the highest position, and slyly pass on to him, as Rachel's firstborn, primacy as the firstborn of them all. His rage at Re'uben's awful offense with Bilhah had been genuine enough—genuine and sincere, no doubt—but also feigned to some extent and purposefully exaggerated in expression. In revealing the episode to his father that day in his childishly malicious words, Joseph had not known it, or known it only in part, but Jacob's first thought was: Now I can curse the eldest and make room for the youngest! But precisely because he was aware of having thought it, and probably also because of his apprehension at embittering the others who came after Ruben, he had not dared use that opportunity to its fullest and expressly set Joseph in the evildoer's place. Rather he let things hang in the balance, and, by waiting, left the place of honor, left the election and position of his heir, open for his favorite, so to speak. For this was about the election of an heir, about the blessing of Abram, which Jacob himself bore, which he, and not Esau, had received from the blind man and wanted to pass on, but not in a manner so correct that it would be done wrongly. If it could be arranged somehow, then this loftiest good would belong to Joseph, who, both in flesh and in spirit, was manifestly better fit to receive it than Ruben, that man as unstable as he was ponderous. And Jacob considered any means justified if it made Joseph's higher fitness obvious to others as well, even to his brothers—knowledge of science, for example. Times were changing. Until now Abram's spiritual heirs had not needed erudition; in his own eyes, Jacob had never suffered from its lack. In the future, however, who knew if it might not prove, if not indispensable, useful and desirable for the man of blessing to be a man of learning as well. Great or small, it was an advantage, and Joseph could not have too many advantages over his brothers.

That was one reason for Jacob's approval. The other came from deeper paternal cares, was a matter of the lad's salvation, of his religious health. We were present on that evening by the well, when with gentle caution Jacob asked his favorite concerning a matter he hoped lay in the near future, about drenching rains, and in so doing had held a hand, protectively as it were, over the lad's head. He had not liked asking. Only a great impatience to learn about future weather—a matter of very great importance—had enabled him to make use of a character trait in his son that he regarded chiefly with worried aversion, though not entirely without wonder.

He knew of Joseph's proclivity for vaguely ecstatic states, which though not fully formed and even half pretended, were genuine prophetic seizures all the same, and he was very uncertain how a father profoundly aware of the holy and pernicious ambiguity of such tendencies ought to respond. The brothers—ah no, not a one of them had shown the least sign of being singled out in that way; God knows, they did not look like seers or men visited by spirits. One need lose no sleep on their account; raptures, whether viewed as pernicious or holy, were not for them. But in one sense it did in fact fit into Jacob's plans that Joseph stood out from them in this regard in a significant, if also dubious, fashion: this could be taken as a mark of distinction that, along with so many other virtues, made his election as heir all the more plausible.

Nevertheless, Jacob was not perfectly at ease with his observations. There were certain people in the land—the sort a father's heart would not want Joseph to be one of. These were holy fools possessed by God, who foamed at the mouth and made a living of their ability to prophesy in a slavering state—babblers of oracles, who roamed about or lived in caves visited by clients and who pocketed foodstuffs and money in exchange for prognosticating all sorts of lucky days and hidden signs. Jacob did not like them because of his God, but in fact no one liked them, though people were very careful not to offend them. They were filthy men of disorderly and crazed habits; children ran after them calling out, "Aulasaulalakaula"—the sort of sound they made when they prophesied. They wounded and maimed their own bodies, ate putrid food, walked about bearing a yoke on their shoulders or a pair of iron horns at their brow; a few went naked. That was just like them—both horns and nakedness. Both the nature of these men's behavior and what ultimately lay behind it were obvious enough: nothing but filthy Baal worship and holy whoredom, the magic fertility rites of country farmers and ecstatic sexual sacrifices at the feet of Melech, the bull-king. That was no secret; everyone was aware of such connections and relation-ships; except that people roundabout regarded them with a kind of amiable awe devoid of any of the sensitivity that was part of Jacob's religious tradition. He had nothing against oracles with arrows or lots cast to determine the lucky hour for this or that business and kept a close eye on the flight of birds or the rising smoke during a sacrifice. But whenever God-given reason broke down and lewd frenzy took its place, that was for him the beginning of what he called "folly," a very strong word in his mouth, strong enough to ex-press utter disapproval. It was "Canaan" who was involved in that murky story about his forefather in his tent and afterward, when naked with his manhood exposed, whoring after the Baals of the land. Nakedness, chanting circles of dancers, festal gluttony, wor-ship as fornication with temple women, the cult of Sheol, and "Aulasaukaulala" and vile oracular seizures—that was Canaan, it all belonged together, it was all the same thing, and it was folly in Jacob's eyes.

But how unnerving to think that Joseph, with his childish pro-clivity for rolling his eyes and dreamlike babbling, might be in con-tact with those unclean regions of the soul. Jacob was, of course, a dreamer as well—but to his honor! To be sure, he had seen God as a great king together with his angels in a dream and had heard the most heartening promise amidst the strains of harps. But it was plain as day that such a raising up of the head out of gloom and external humiliation differed greatly, both in terms of reason and spiritual decorum, from every such evil spasm. Was it not a cause of worry and pain to see how the honest and grace-filled gifts of fathers were diminished in unstable sons, to their refined perdition? Ah, it was heartwarming to behold a father in the form of a son, but also dis-maying and suspect when it became instability and diminishment. What a comfort, then, that Joseph was still so young; his instability would grow firm, more robust and steady, would mature with God-given reason to respectability. But as a father, Jacob's moral acuity did not fail to notice that the young man's proclivity for raptures of a less than model sort had been allied with nakedness, that is with abandonment, that is with Baal and Sheol, with an enchantment with death and netherworldly unreason—and it was for that very reason that he encouraged the scribe's influence on his beloved son. It was a very good thing that Joseph was learning, was gaining methodical practice in the word and literacy under skilled tutelage. He, Jacob, had not needed it; even his grandest dreams had been respectable and tempered. But the old man felt that Joseph's dreams could stand the precise discipline of what was letter-perfect and reasonable—it might prove a blessing for firming up his instability, and as an educated man he would bear no resemblance to horned men running about naked and foaming at the mouth.

Such were Jacob's considerations. It seemed to him that dark elements in the character of his favorite were in need of release and clarification on an intellectual level. Thus, as one can see, in his own anxious way, Jacob agreed with Joseph's own youthful speculations that consciousness of the body ought to be improved and corrected by consciousness of the mind.

Part Two

ABRAHAM

The Oldest Servant

Abram may actually have looked much like Eliezer—but then again perhaps quite different, perhaps he was a scrawny, poor man, twitching with restlessness and fretting himself sick. And the assertion that Eliezer, Joseph's teacher, looked like that moon-wanderer really had nothing to do with the person of the learned steward now visibly at hand. People spoke in the present, but they meant the past and transferred the latter to the former. Eliezer's countenance, it was said, "resembled" that of Abram, and such hearsay might have been vaguely justified in view of that commissioned wooer's birth and background. For allegedly he was Abraham's son. True, it was also claimed that Eliezer was the servant whom Nimrod of Babel had presented to Abram upon being obliged to let him depart; yet it was almost a certain improbability that this could have been the case. Abraham had never come into personal contact with the potentate under whose reign his emigration from Shinar had taken place; Nimrod had never bothered in the least with Abram. The conflict that had driven Jacob's spiritual ancestor from that country had been a very quiet, internal affair; and all tales of personal confrontations between him and the Lawgiver—of martyrdom, of a stay in prison, of his being subjected to a fiery ordeal in a limekiln—those stories (only a few of which are mentioned here, though Eliezer also liked to tell them to amuse Joseph) were based, if not on free conjecture, then at least on much older events from a far distant past, transported then to a nearer past only six hundred years previous. The king of Abram's day, who had renovated and raised the Tower higher still, had not been named Nimrod, which was merely a term of rank and lineage, but rather Amraphel or Hamurapi; and the real

Nimrod had been the father of that Bel of Babel of whom it was said he had built the city and the Tower, becoming a god-king after having first been a human one, much like Usiri of Egypt. The figure of the first Nimrod belonged therefore to a pre-Usirian age, which may help one discern the distance, or better the immeasurable distance, between his historical twilight and the time of Abram's Nimrod; and as for events that occurred under his rule—whether his astrologers predicted the birth of a boy who would imperil his rule, whereupon he decreed a general slaughter of boys, with a little Abram escaping this precautionary massacre, to be raised in a cave by an angel who let the babe suckle milk and honey from his fingertips, and so forth—about those events one can draw no scientific conclusions whatever. In any case, the situation with the figure of Nimrod the King is very similar to that of Edom the Red: it is a present transparent to increasingly ancient pasts, which lose themselves in a divinity that, in still deeper depths of time, emerged out of humanity. The time will come for us to note that it was much the same with Abraham. But for now it is best to stick to Eliezer.

He had not, therefore, been presented to Abram as a gift from "Nimrod"—that must be considered a fable. Instead, it is highly probable that he had been Abram's natural son, begotten with a slave and presumably born in Damashki during the period that Abraham's people sojourned in that flourishing city. Abram had later given him his freedom, and his rank within the family had been somewhat lower than that of Ismael, Hagar's son. Having remained childless for a long time, the Chaldean had originally had to regard the elder of Eliezer's two sons, Damasek and Elinos, as his heirs, until first Ismael and, after him, Yitzchak, the true son, were born. But even afterward, Eliezer had remained an important personage among Abraham's people, and to him had been given the honor of journeying to Naharina to woo a bride for Isaak, the averted sacrifice.

He enjoyed telling and retelling Joseph about his journey—yes, we shall let ourselves be seduced, perhaps all too readily, into simply using the word "he" here, although it was not Abram's Eliezer who spoke to Joseph, at least not according to our local standards. What seduces us is the natural ease with which he said "I" whenever he spoke about this bridal expedition and the way his student let this

grammatical form bathed in moonlight pass over him without contradiction. He smiled, to be sure, but he nodded, too, and it was uncertain whether the smile meant some kind of criticism, the nod
perhaps a certain polite indulgence. Upon closer look, we would like
to believe his smile more than his nod and are inclined to assume that
his attitude toward Eliezer's mode of speech was somewhat clearer
and keener than that of the old man himself, Jacob's venerable elder
half brother.

And so it is with clarity and reason that we call him Eliezer, for
that he was. Before he grew old and feeble, Yitzchak, the true son,
had been a man of robust senses, who certainly did not show exclusive attention to Bethuel's daughter. The very fact that, like his
mother Sahar, she too remained barren for a long time would have
had to induce him to look to an heir by other means from time to
time; and some years before Jacob and Esau appeared, a beautiful
slave had borne him a son, whom he later freed and who was named
Eliezer. Tradition demanded that this sort of son should one day be
given his freedom and be named Eliezer. Yes, Yitzchak, the averted
sacrifice, could be forgiven all the more readily as regards such a son,
for a man had to have an Eliezer—an Eliezer had always existed in
the tents of Abraham's spiritual clan, had always assumed the role of
steward and first servant, and, quite possibly, had been sent as an
envoy to court a bride for the son of the true wife. The head of the
family even made it a rule to provide a wife for the man as well, by
whom the latter then had two sons, Damasek and Elinos by name. In
short, he was an institution much like Nimrod of Babel. And so,
during lessons at the foot of the oracle tree and in its leafy shade,
rather odd feelings surely often crept over young Joseph as he sat
near the well with arms embracing knees and gazed attentively up
into the face of this lecturing old man—who "looked like Abraham"
and who knew how to say "I" in such an easy and grand manner.
The gaze from Joseph's handsome and beautiful eyes would fall
upon the man telling stories and break through to an unending perspective of Eliezer figures—and each of them said "I" through the
lips of the one seated before him. And since Joseph was sitting in the
dusk of the tree's vast shade while breezes shimmered hot in the sun
beyond Eliezer, this perspective of identities lost itself not in darkness, but in light. . . .

The sphere rolls, and one can never determine where a story has its first home: in heaven or on earth. Truth is served by stating that all stories take place both there and here, simultaneously and in correspondence. Only to our eyes does it look as if they might have first come down from on high and then ascended again. Stories descend, as when a god becomes man, are made earthly and bourgeois, so to speak. By way of example, let us again note one of Jacob's people's favorite stories for boasting: the so-called battle of the kings, in which Abram defeated the armies of the East in order to free his "brother" Lot. Later exegetes and learned commentators on the patriarchal stories are thoroughly convinced and state as fact that Abram pursued and defeated the kings, driving them on beyond Damascus, not with three hundred eighteen men, as Joseph understood, but rather all on his own with just his servant Eliezer, for the stars had done battle for them, giving them the victory and routing their enemies. Eliezer himself might even tell Joseph the story in this version—the lad was familiar with this variation. But one cannot fail to notice that in this form the story loses the earthly, albeit heroic character lent it by discoursing shepherds and takes on a different quality. Told this way, it sounds as if—and even Joseph had this same impression, more or less—two gods, master and servant, had battled superior numbers of giants or lesser elohim and defeated them. Without doubt, that means the event has been justifiably traced to its heavenly form, has been restored in the service of truth. But should one therefore totally deny its earthly reality? On the contrary, one might say that its superterrestrial truth and reality are proof of those same qualities on earth. For what is above descends to earth; but what is below would not know what must happen—would not even occur to itself, so to speak—without its heavenly model and counterpart. What had once been in the stars became flesh in Abram. In victoriously scattering those robbers from beyond the Euphrates, he stood upon the divine, found his support in it.

Did not, for example, the story of Eliezer's journey to woo a bride have a history of its own, upon which it stood and in which its hero and teller might find support in the experiencing and telling of it? The old man would transform this story, too, in a special way, and caretakers of tradition have passed it down to us in its transformed version as well. For they state that when Abram sent Eliezer off to Mesopotamia to woo a bride for Isaak, the journey from Beersheba to Haran, which normally takes twenty days and seventeen at the least, was accomplished in three—and that was because "the earth leapt up to greet him." This can be understood only metaphorically, for it is certain that the earth does not run toward or leap up at anyone; but it *appears* to do so to anyone who moves across it with great ease—on winged feet, as it were. The commentators likewise do not say that the journey was undertaken in usual fashion, as a caravan with animals and baggage; they make no mention of ten camels. Rather the light they cast upon the story awakens a definite sense that Abram's natural son and envoy covered the distance alone and as if on pinions—with a speed that even winged feet would not have sufficed to explain; one is instead automatically tempted to picture his cap having wings as well.... In short, by this light Eliezer's earthly journey in the flesh appears to be a story that had come down to him, one in which he stood on superterrestrial ground, so that later, in Joseph's presence, it was not just grammatical forms, but also the forms of the story itself that he got muddled up a bit, saying that the earth "leapt up to greet him."

Yes, as the student's gaze fell upon Eliezer, as he pondered the venerable man's appearance and presence, the vista of his personality was lost in light and not in darkness—just as happened at the same time with the identity of other people, one can easily surmise which others. We wish merely to remark, as we look ahead to Joseph's life story, that these kinds of impressions were the most abiding and effective ones he gained from instruction by old Eliezer. Children are not being inattentive when their teachers scold them for it; they are merely attending to things that are perhaps more essential than those their practical instructors have in mind. Although his gaze might seem to have been floating in oblivion, Joseph retained the attentiveness of the child, in a most particular fashion—whether entirely to his own welfare is another question.

How Abraham Discovered God

Our mentioning "other people" was a way of pointing, circumspectly and in advance, to Abraham, the messenger's master. What did Eliezer know about him? Many things—of great variety. He spoke of him with a double tongue, as it were, sometimes in one way, but then again quite differently. On occasion, the Chaldean was simply the man who had discovered God, making Him kiss His fingers and cry: "Until now no man has called Me Lord and the Most High, but so will I now be called!" The discovery had proceeded along a very arduous, indeed agonizing path; the primal father had fretted more than a little. And in fact his endeavors and strivings had been determined and driven by a notion peculiar to him alone: the idea that it was supremely important whom or what things a man served. That impressed Joseph, he understood it at once, and especially the part about importance. If one was to gain any sort of repute and significance before God and man, it was necessary that one attribute importance to things—or at least to one thing. The first father had attached unconditional importance to the question of whom man should serve, and his remarkable answer had been: "Only what is highest." Remarkable indeed! That answer spoke of a sense of self that one might have called almost arrogant and intemperate. The man might have said to himself: "What am I, of what value am I and, in me, is humankind? It is enough that I serve some El or other, some lesser or demi-god, it does not matter." It would have made things easier for him. But he said: "I, Abram, and, in me, humankind, may serve only what is highest." That's how it all began. (Which pleased Joseph greatly.)

It began with Abram's thinking that mother earth alone was worthy of service and worship, for she brings forth fruits and sustains life. But then he noticed that she needed rain from the sky. And so he looked about in the heavens, saw the sun in its splendor, in its power to bless and curse, and was at the point of deciding in its favor. But then the sun set, and he persuaded himself that surely it could not be the highest. And so he looked to the moon and the stars—at these, in fact, with special fondness and hope. This, quite possibly, had been the initial reason for his vexation and urge to wander: that his love for the moon, the divinity of Uru and Haran, had been scandalized by the exaggerated public favors shown toward the solar principle, toward Shamash–Bel–Mardug, by Nimrod of Babel at the expense of Sin, Shepherd of the Stars. Yes, it might have come from God's very own cunning, who in contemplating being glorified in Abiram and making a name for Himself through him, aroused this initial antagonism and unrest in him by means of his love for the moon, used it for His own divine purposes, and made it the secret starting point of Abram's career. But when the morning star rose, both Shepherd and sheep vanished, and Abram concluded: "No, even these are not worthy gods for me." His soul was weary from his efforts, and he concluded: "Might they, high as they are, not have above them yet a Lord who directs their courses, the rising and setting of each? It would be ill suited for me, as a man, to serve them and not that which perhaps rules over them." And so great was Abraham's sincere affliction and concern for the truth, that God the Lord was deeply moved and He said to Himself: "I will anoint you with the oil of gladness more than all your fellows!"

Thus Abraham had discovered God out of a desire for what is highest, had continued to shape that impulse in his thoughts and teaching, which proved to be of great benefit for all concerned: for God, for himself, and for those souls he won to his teachings—for God, by preparing the way for His actualization in the minds of men; but especially for himself and his proselytes, by reducing multiplicity and terrifying ambiguity to unity and something reassuringly familiar, to something definite from which all things came, both good and evil, both the suddenly terrible and the blessedly routine, and to which one had to cling no matter what. Abraham had gathered powers into one power and called it the Lord—excluding all others, once and for all, not just for a single feast day when one sang flattering hymns that heaped all power and honor upon the head of a god, of a Mardug, Anu, or Shamash, only to turn the next day to the next temple and sing to yet another: "You are the One and Most High, without you no judgment is rendered, no decision made, no god in heaven or earth can resist you, you are exalted above them all!" Surrendering to the truckling spirit of the moment, people often sang and said such things in Nimrod's realm. Abraham, however, discovered and declared that in truth this could and should be said to only one God—always to the same and surely quite familiar God, for everything came from Him and He revealed all things, each according to its source. The people among whom Abraham had grown up were terribly anxious not to leave out a single source when giving thanks and pleading for favor. If they did penance amid calamity, they would begin their prayers of distress by calling upon a whole list of gods, appealing painstakingly to each—some of whom were only a name—just to make sure they did not omit the one who had sent this scourge and was responsible for it, for they did not know which it might be. Abraham knew, and taught: It was always only He who was the Last and Most High, who alone could be the true God of all men and who would not fail to hear their cries of distress and hymns of praise.

Young as he was, Joseph understood quite well the boldness and strength of soul expressed in the first father's conclusions about God, before which many of those to whom he suggested them had pulled back in horror. Truly, whether Abram had been tall and beautiful in his old age like Eliezer or, perhaps, small, skinny, and bent, he had in any case had courage, the fullness of courage required to reduce divinity's manifold abundance to his God, to trace all sorrow and all grace directly back to Him, to rely solely upon Him and make himself exclusively dependent upon the Most High.

Even Lot had turned ashen pale as he said to him, "But if your God forsakes you, then you are utterly forsaken."

To which Abram had responded, "True enough, so you have said. And then there will be no forsakenness in heaven or on earth to compare in magnitude—it will be absolute. But keep in mind that if I appease Him and He is my shield, I can lack for nothing and will possess the gates of my enemies."

And Lot took heart and said to him, "Then will I be your brother."

Yes, Abram had knowingly shared his high optimism with his family. He was called Abirâm, which may have meant "my father is exalted," or, quite rightly and probably, "father of the Exalted." For in some measure Abraham was God's father. He had discovered Him and thought Him into being. Those mighty attributes that he ascribed to Him were surely God's original property, Abram was not their originator. But by recognizing them, teaching them, and realizing them in his own thought, was he not His father in a certain sense? God's powerful attributes were, to be sure, a given reality outside of Abraham, but at the same time they were also in him and from him; at certain moments the power of his own soul—deliberately shrinking and melting into one with them—was scarcely to be differentiated from them. Here lay the origin of the covenant that the Lord made with Abraham and that was merely the explicit confirmation of an inner reality; this was also, however, the origin of the peculiar quality of Abram's fear of God. For since God's greatness was indeed something terrible and real outside him and yet at the same time coincided in some sense with his own soul and was indeed its product, Abram's fear of God was not fear alone in the true sense of the word—it was not only trembling and quaking, but also attachment, intimacy, and friendship, all in one. And at times the first father did indeed have a way of dealing with God that, if one did not take into consideration the interlocking peculiarity of their relationship, must have aroused amazement in heaven and earth. For example, given God's terrible power and greatness, Abram's friendly rebuke of the Lord during the destruction of Sodom and Amorrah had verged on being offensive. But, to be sure, whom should it offend if not God? And He had taken it well enough. "Hear me, Lord," Abram had said on that occasion, "yes or no, one way or the other! If You want to have a world, You cannot demand justice; but if You care only for justice, then the world is done for. You grasp the cord by both ends, wanting both a world and justice in it. But if You are not more lenient, the world cannot stand." He had even accused the Lord of deception and reproached Him for having once sworn never to flood the world again, and yet here He came with a flood of fire. But God, who surely could not have dealt any differently with these cities after what had happened, or almost happened, to His messengers, had received it all, if not with good, at least not with ill will; to all of it He had wrapped Himself in benevolent silence.

This silence was the expression of a monstrous fact that belonged both to God's external presence and at the same time to the largeness of Abram's soul, which was perhaps its most proper source: the fact that the contradiction of a living world that was also supposed to be just resided within God's greatness itself. For He, the living God, was not good or merely good among other things, but was evil besides. His living presence embraced evil and was at the same time holy, was holiness in and of itself, holiness that demanded holiness.

The vastness of it! It was He who had dashed Tiamat in pieces, had cloven the dragon of chaos in two; the cries of jubilation with which the gods had greeted Mardug at creation and that Abram's countrymen repeated each New Year's Day belonged by rights to Him, the God of Abraham. Order and wholesome dependability originated in Him. That the early rains and late rains fell in their season was His handiwork. He had banned the hideous sea—once left behind by the Flood and now the abode of Leviathan—within limits

that even its fiercest blows could not exceed. He made the engendering sun to rise, climb to its zenith, and retreat each evening for its
journey through hell; made the moon to measure time by the
constant shifting of its phases. He arrayed the stars, uniting them
in sturdy constellations, and disposed the life of animals and men
by nourishing them according to the seasons. In places where no
one had ever been, snow melted to moisten the earth, whose disk
He had set upon the great waters, so that it never, or only very
seldom, shook or faltered. What a wealth of blessing, of benefit and
goodness!

Except that just as when a man slays an enemy, he is likely to
take on his foe's qualities in victory, it appeared that in cleaving the
monster of chaos in two, God had incorporated its nature. Perhaps
only then had He become complete and perfect, only then had He
grown into the full majesty of His living presence. The battle between light and darkness, between good and evil, horror and mercy,
was not, as Nimrod's people believed, the continuation of Mardug's
battle with Tiamat. Even darkness, evil, and unpredictable horror,
even earthquake, a crackling bolt of lightning, a swarm of locusts
darkening the sun, the seven evil winds, the Abubu of dust, the hornet, and the serpent were from God; and if He was called Lord of
Pestilence, then that was because He was both its sender and its
healer. He was not what is good, but what is all. And He was holy!
Holy not out of goodness, but out of being the living God, and more
than living, holy in His majesty and terribleness—uncanny, dangerous, deadly—so that one oversight, one mistake, one small slip in
one's conduct toward Him could have horrible consequences. He
was holy; but He also demanded holiness, and that He did so merely
by existing gave the Holy One a meaning beyond that of the danger
of holiness. The caution that He enjoined became piety itself and
God's living majesty became the measuring rod of life—the source
of guilt and of that fear of God that meant walking in purity before
God's great grandeur.

God was there, and Abraham walked before Him, his soul made
holy by God's nearness outside it. They were two, an I and a Thou,
each of whom said "I," and to the other "Thou." It is quite correct to
say that Abram discerned God's qualities with the help of his own
largeness of soul—without it he would not have discerned them or
known how to name them, they would have remained in darkness.

That, however, is also why God remained a powerful Thou who said "I" apart from Abraham and apart from the world. He was in the fire, but not the fire—which is why it would have been a very serious blunder to worship the fire. God created the world, in which there were things of powerful immensity, like the whirlwind or the Leviathan. One had to consider these things in order to have some picture, or if not a picture, some conception of His external greatness. He was of necessity much greater than all His works, and it was equally necessary that He be outside His works. He was called *makom,* space, because He was the space of the world, but the world was not His space. He was also in Abraham, who knew Him thanks to His power in him. But this very fact strengthened and fulfilled the first father's sense of saying "I," for in no way was this God-filled and courageous "I" inclined to vanish into God, to be one with Him and no longer be Abraham. Instead he very alertly and clearly held himself erect opposite Him—at a vast distance, to be sure, for Abraham was only a man, a clod of earth, but bound to Him by that knowledge and made holy by God's sublime there-ness and Thouness. It was on such foundations that God established an everlasting covenant with Abram, a contract that held such promise for both parties and of which the Lord was so jealous that He wished to be worshiped exclusively by His people, with never a sidelong glance toward other gods, of which the world was full. That was remarkable. Through Abraham and his covenant something had come into the world that had never been there before and of which the nations knew nothing: the damnable possibility that the covenant could be broken, that one could fall away from God.

The first father had many other things he could teach about God, but he did not know how to *tell* about God—not in the way others knew to tell stories about their gods. There were no stories about God. This was perhaps the most remarkable thing of all: the courage with which Abram posited God's existence as a given, without any attendant circumstances or stories, but simply by saying "God." God had not arisen, had not been born, of any female. Nor was there a female beside His throne, no Ishtar, no Baalat and mother of God. How could that be? Simple reason led one to realize that such a thing was inconceivable in view of God's entire nature. He had planted the Tree of Knowledge and of Death in Eden, and man had eaten from it. It was for man to give birth and die, but not for God, and He beheld no divine female at His side because He did not need to know one, and instead was Himself both Baal and Baalat in one. He likewise had no children. For neither the angels nor the *zebaoth* who served Him were His offspring, nor had those giants been—rather, they had been born of the daughters of men by a few angels seduced by the sight of female wantonness. He was alone, and that was a hallmark of His greatness. And to whatever extent God's solitary state without wife or child might serve to explain His great jealousy in regard to His covenant with man, it was in any case tied up with the lack of stories about Him, the fact that there was nothing to tell about Him.

And yet again, even this was to be understood only conditionally, for it was true only in terms of the past, but not as regarded the future—always presuming that the word "tell" can be applied to the future and that one can tell the story of the future, even if it must be in the form of the past. Nevertheless, God did indeed have a story, but it concerned the future, a future so glorious for God that His present, glorious as it was, could not match it; and *that* it did not match it lent God's grandeur and holy power a quality of expectation and of unfulfilled promise—a sorrowful quality, to put it bluntly, that was not to be ignored if one were fully to understand God's covenant with man and His jealousy of it.

There came a day, the last and final day, and only it brought the fulfillment of God. This day was both end and beginning, destruction and new birth. The world, this first or maybe not even first world, vanished amidst enveloping catastrophe, and chaos, the primal silence, returned. But then God would begin His work anew and more marvelous still—Lord of Destruction, Lord of Calling into Being. Out of formlessness and the void, *tohu* and *bohu*, mire and darkness, His Word called forth a new cosmos, and the jubilation of the watching angels sounded more overwhelmed than it had once before, for the newborn world surpassed the old in every respect, and in it God would triumph over all His enemies.

That was how it was: At the end of days God would be King, King of Kings, King over men and gods. But was He not that already now? To be sure, in the stillness and in Abram's perception. But not as a recognized and appreciated reality, and thus not in fully realized terms. The realization of God's absolute kingship was left to the last and first day, that day of destruction and of calling into being, when before all eyes His unconditional splendor would rise up out of bonds in which it still lay. No Nimrod would rebel against Him with shameless terraced towers, no human knee would bow but before Him, no human mouth give glory to any but Him. But that meant that God would finally and truly be—just as He had in truth always been—Lord and King over all gods. To the blaring of ten thousand trumpets tilted toward the heavens, amid a chorus of thundering flames, in a hailstorm of lightning bolts, He would stride past a prostrate and adoring world and, clothed in sovereignty and dread, ascend His throne, assuming possession—for all to behold and for all eternity—of a reality that was His truth.

Oh day of God's apotheosis, day of promise, expectation, and fulfillment! It would, let it be noted, also include the apotheosis of Abraham, whose name would henceforth be a word of blessing, a greeting to be shared among the races of men. That was the promise. That this thundering day was not yet the present, but only the ultimate future to be awaited until then—this was what lent a quality of suffering to God's countenance at present, a quality of not-yet and of expectation. God lay in bonds, God suffered. God was held prisoner. This softened His grandeur, making it an object of comforting devotion for all who suffered and waited, who were not great, but small in this world, and it put scorn in their hearts against anything that was like Nimrod and against all things shameless in their greatness. No, God had no stories like Osiris, the martyr of Egypt, who had been dismembered and buried, but rose again, or like Adon–Tammuz, over whom the flute mourned in the ravines, the lord of the sheepfold whose side was ripped open by Ninib the boar and who descended into captivity only to rise again. Therefore, let it be a remote, a forbidden idea that God ever had some tie to the stories of nature—withering in sorrow, freezing in suffering, only to be renewed by law and promise into laughter and a profusion of flowers—to grain rotting in the darkness of earth's prison, so that it might sprout and rise again; to dying and to sex; to the corrupted holiness of Melech–Baal and his worship at Tyre, where with eyes rolling in folly and with the shamelessness of death itself, men offered their semen to that hideous god. God forbid that He should ever have had anything to do with stories of that sort! All the same,

He lay in bonds and was a God awaiting the future—and this established a certain similarity between Him and these suffering divinities; and it was for this reason that Abram held long conversations at Shechem with Malkizedek, who was an attendant priest at the temple of the Baal of the Covenant and El-Elyon, concerning whether and, if so, to what extent there might be some similarity in the natures of his Adon and Abraham's own Lord.

God, however, had kissed His fingertips and—much to the secret vexation of the angels—cried out: "Unbelievable, how well this clod of earth understands Me! Have I not begun to make a name for Myself through him? Truly, I will anoint him!"

The Messenger's Master

Such a man, pure and simple—that was the portrait of Abraham that Eliezer's tongue painted for his pupil. But even as he spoke his tongue might suddenly fork, and he would speak differently about him, in other terms. It was still Abram, the man from Uru (or actually, Haran), about which that venerable serpent's tongue spoke—calling him Joseph's great-grandfather. But both the old man and the lad knew that by the light of day this had not been Abram—not the Abraham of whom the other tongue had just spoken, the restless subject of Amraphel of Shinar—just as they knew that no man's great-grandfather could have lived twenty generations before him. But they shared a wink over more than just this imprecision; for the Abraham of whom this tongue now spoke, alternating on occasion, moving back and forth in its forked fashion, was likewise not the one who had lived back then and had shaken the dust of Shinar from his feet, but rather a figure who came into view far behind him and for whom he grew transparent, so that as the lad's eyes fell on him they floated in a vista of personality just as they had in a vista named "Eliezer"—which, as nature demands, grew ever brighter, for transparency is light shining through.

What came to light, then, were all the stories that belonged to that half of the sphere in which master and servant had driven the foe beyond Damashki not with three hundred eighteen men but with the assistance of spirits from on high; the story of the earth's "leaping up to meet" Eliezer, the messenger; or of the prophecy of Abraham's birth, of babes slaughtered on his account, of his childhood in a cave, and of how the angel suckled him while his mother wandered about in search of him. It had the stamp of truth—somewhere and somehow it was true. Mothers have always wandered and searched; they have many names, but they roam the fields looking for the poor child who has been abducted to the underworld, murdered, dismembered. This time she was named Amathla, or probably Emtelai, names that Eliezer perhaps let be rendered in free form and dreamy combination; for they were less suitable for the mother than for the nursing angel, who—or so, for the sake of more colorful verisimilitude, the forked tongue said—had probably taken the form of a goat. Hearing the mother of the Chaldean called Emtelai put Joseph in a very dreamy state of mind as well and contributed to the look in his eye as he listened; for without doubt the name meant "mother of my exalted one," or in plain terms "mother of God."

Should the venerable Eliezer have been censured for speaking this way? No. Stories come down from above—just as a god becomes a man—become earthly and bourgeois, as it were, without ceasing to take place on high and be narratable in their higher form. And so the old man would sometimes claim that the sons of Keturah, the woman Abram took as a concubine in his old age—that is, Medan, Midian, and Jokshan, plus Zimran, Ishbak, and whoever—these sons had "flashed like lightning," and Abram had built them and their mother a city of iron, so high that the sun never shone into it and it was illumined only by gemstones. His listener would have had to be an awfully dull lad not to have realized that this referred to the dimly glimmering city of the underworld, whose queen, in this version, was named Keturah. An unassailable version! For Keturah was in fact simply a Canaanite woman, whom Abraham in his old age had honored with his bed; but she was also the mother of a long series of Arabian tribal fathers and lords of the desert, just as Hagar the Egyptian had been the mother of such a lord. When Eliezer said of her sons that they had flashed like lightning, that only meant that one had to view them with both eyes, and not with just one, to regard them under the sign of simultaneity and the unity of what is twofold—that is, both as Bedu chieftains roaming homeless and as sons and princes of the underworld, just as Ismael, the false son, had been.

There were also moments when the old man spoke in strange tones of Sara, the first father's wife. He called her "daughter of the castrated one" and "heaven's highest." He added that she had carried a spear, a perfect match for the fact that she had originally been called Sarai, that is "heroine," which God then later muted and diminished to Sara, a mere "mistress." The same had happened to her brother-husband; for Abram, which means "exalted father" and "father of the exalted," had been muted and diminished to Abraham, that is, father of a vast and teeming posterity of spiritual and physical offspring. Did he then cease to be Abram? Not at all. It was merely that the sphere was rolling; and that tongue, subtly forked into Abram and Abraham, spoke of him now in one way, now in another.

Nimrod, the father of his people, had wanted to devour him, but he had been snatched away from his gluttony, had been nourished in a cave by angelic goats, and when he grew up had played such a prank on that greedy king in his idolatrous splendor that one might well say Nimrod had felt the "tickle of the scythe." Before he had in any sense assumed his just place, he had had to suffer. He had been held captive—and what fun it was to hear how he had used even this stay to make proselytes and convert the guardians of that deep dungeon to the highest God. He was sentenced to be sacrificed in Typhon's blazing heat, thrown into a limekiln or, even better—Eliezer's details varied—sent to be burned at the stake, which also bore the stamp of truth, for Joseph knew very well that even in his own day a "feast of the stake" was celebrated in many cities. But do people celebrate feasts that commemorate nothing, unreal feasts with no roots? Were the pious masquerades acted out on New Year's or Creation Day representations of events that someone or some angel had woven from thin air and that had never happened? Man invents nothing. Ever since he had eaten from the tree, he was indeed arch-clever and in that regard little less than a god. But no matter how clever he was, how could he ever have come up with a thing that was not there? And so there was something to his having been burned at the stake.

According to Eliezer, Abraham had founded the city of Dimashki and had been its first king. A weakly flickering statement, for cities are not usually founded by a single man, and those beings one calls their primal kings do not usually have a human countenance. Even Hebron itself, or Kiriath-Arba, within whose domain they lived, had not been built by a man; instead—or so at least it was popularly asserted—it had been founded by the giant Arba or Arbaal. Eliezer, however, held strictly to his claim that Abram had also founded Hebron, which perhaps did not, nor was it meant to, contradict popular belief, for the primal father must have been of gigantic size, since it was Eliezer's testimony that his stride was a mile long.

Was it any wonder, then, that—at certain dreamily muddled moments—in Joseph's eyes the figure of his ancestor, this founder of cities, merged in that faraway vista with that of Bel of Babel, who had built that city and its Tower and who became a god after he had been a man and was buried in the tomb of Bel? Though with Abraham it seemed to be the other way around. But what does "other way around" mean in this case, and who can say what had come first and where the original home of his stories was, above or below? They are the present of the rotating sphere, the unity of what is twofold, the statue that bears the name "Simultaneous."

Part Three

JOSEPH AND BENJAMIN

The Grove of Adoni

A half hour's walk toward the city from Jacob's scattered settle-ment—from his tents, stalls, sheepfolds, and sheds—was a ravine filled with a dense growth of stunted but sturdy myrtle bushes, a grove that the people of Hebron considered sacred to Astarte–Ishtar, or rather to her son, brother, and husband, Tammuz–Adoni. An agreeably bitter, in the heat of summer sometimes peppery, fra-grance filled the air; and the venerated wilderness was not impene-trable, but rather a maze of twisting random openings suggestive of paths threaded through it in all directions, and if one aimed for the lowest point in the basin, one found an open area obviously cleared of undergrowth, and within it a shrine, a square stone obelisk rising taller than a man and inscribed with fertility symbols, a *massebah*—evidently itself a fertility symbol erected in the middle of the clear-ing, with offerings placed about its pedestal: earthenware pots filled with soil from which whitish green sprouts emerged or more elabo-rate objects of a similar sort, rectangular wooden frames stretched with canvas against which there stood out a crude, green human fig-ure wrapped in what looked like a shroud. The women who had placed it there had sketched a corpse on canvas, covered it with soil, sown it with wheat, moistened the seeds, then trimmed the sprouts even, leaving a figure set in green relief against the background.

Joseph often came to this place with Benjamin, his full brother, who at age eight now had begun to outgrow the watchful eye of women and enjoyed trying to match strides with his mother's first-born. He was a chubby-cheeked boy who no longer ran about naked, but wore a short-sleeved knee-length tunic of dark blue or rust red wool with embroidery along the hem. He had lovely gray eyes that held an expression of utter trust when he would look up at his older brother. His thick, almost metallic hair ran from midbrow to the nape of his neck and fit tightly to his skull like a sleek helmet with slits for the ears, which were as small and sturdy as his nose and his stubby-fingered hands, one of which he always gave to his brother when they walked together. An engaging boy, he had inherited Rachel's cordiality. But over his little person lay the shadow of a shy melancholy, for he had not grown up unaware of the hour and manner of his mother's death, of what he had done while still all unconscious; and the sense of tragically guiltless guilt he carried with him was nourished by Jacob's attitude toward him—which, though certainly not without tenderness, was imbued with a painful reticence, to the point where his father was more likely to avoid his gaze than seek it out. From time to time, however, Jacob would ardently press his youngest son to him, call him Benoni, and whisper words of Rachel in his ear.

And so as the boy began to step out from behind the women's skirts, he found he could not deal truly openly with his father. All the more affectionate, then, were his ties to his full brother, whom he admired in every way and who, though everyone he met greeted him with a smile and raised eyebrows, was in fact quite isolated and could certainly use this kind of devotion and, for his own part, likewise felt a strong natural sense of attachment to the boy, so that he accepted him as a friend and confidant—to such a degree, in fact, that Joseph would pay too little attention to the difference in their ages, leaving Benjamin more troubled and confused than proud and happy. Yes, the things that the clever and startlingly beautiful "Yossef" (which was how Benoni pronounced his brother's name) would say to him in confidence were more than a child's heart could hold; and eager as Benjamin was to take all this in, it only intensified the shadow of melancholy that lay over a little boy who had murdered his mother.

Hand in hand, they walked away from Jacob's hilltop olive garden, where the handmaids' sons were busy harvesting and pressing. They had banished Joseph from the place because he had gone to their father—who had been seated in the sheepfold while Eliezer stood before him rendering accounts—and accused them of having let the fruit on almost all the trees grow too ripe, so that it no longer yielded the best oil, especially since, in his opinion, his brothers were pressing the olives too hard in the mills, mashing rather than gently squeezing them. Upon being reprimanded, Naphtali, Gad, and

Asher had stretched out their arms and, skewing up their mouths, told this braggart—or, better, slanderer—to clear out.

But Joseph had called Benjamin to him and said, "Come, let us go to our spot."

On the way he said, "I did in fact say 'on almost all the trees'— fine, that was an exaggeration, the sort that just happens when you're speaking. Had I said 'on several' it would have been more precisely put, I admit. You see, I had climbed up into the old tree, the one with three trunks and masonry around the base, to pick fruit and toss it down into a cloth, while unfortunately our brothers were just throwing stones at the tree and banging the boughs with sticks, and I saw with my own eyes that the fruit on the old tree at least was already too ripe—I can't say as to the others. But they act as if I were lying in general and as if you get fine oil by rolling the stone clumsily like that and mashing God's gift to smithereens. Can a person look on and not protest?"

"No," Benjamin replied, "you know better than they do and had to tell Father so he could hear of it. But it's fine by me that you quarreled with them, little Yossef, for then you called your brother to take your right hand."

"And now, my noble Ben," Joseph said, "let's take a running jump over that wall in the field there—one, two, three . . ."

"All right," Benjamin responded. "But don't let go of me! It's more fun together, and a lot safer for a little fellow like me."

They ran, jumped, and walked on. It was Joseph's habit when Benjamin's hand became too hot and damp in his own to grab hold of the boy's wrist—which Benjamin would hold limp—and fan the whole hand to let it dry in the breeze. This airing procedure would always set the boy laughing so hard that he stumbled.

Upon arriving at the ravine of myrtle and the grove of the god, the brothers had to separate and walk single file—the narrow paths through the underbrush required it. They formed a maze that was always fun to wander; for it was fascinating to see how far a meandering corridor let you proceed before impenetrable barriers held you fast and to discover whether by veering uphill or down you could go any farther or would have to turn around despite the risk that you might lose the path that had brought you there and end up once again in a cul-de-sac. Fending off blows and scratches to their faces, they talked and laughed as they struggled along, and Joseph would also break off twigs from the bushes, which blossomed white in the spring, collecting them in his hand for later; for it was here that he always supplied himself with green myrtle for the wreaths he loved to wear in his hair. At first Benjamin had wanted to imitate him and had plucked twigs of his own, giving them to his brother so that he could weave a wreath for him as well. But he had noticed that Joseph did not like him to adorn himself with myrtle, wanting, without ever saying so, to keep this adornment for himself—behind which, or so it seemed to the boy, lay hidden some secret thought, like those others Joseph had, something Benjamin had also noticed, especially since in the company of his little brother Joseph did not always keep them to himself. Benoni guessed that Joseph's undeclared but obvious jealousy about the myrtle twigs might have something to do with the selection of an heir, with the nominal honor of the firstborn and the right to bear the blessing, which, as they all knew, their father had left hovering above his head—and yet that was evidently not the sole reason.

"Hush now, my boy," Joseph might say to him, giving his companion a kiss on his cool helmet of hair. "When we get home I shall make you a wreath of oak leaves or colorful thistles or a wreath of mountain ash with its red pearls—what do you say to that? Is that not prettier? Why bother with myrtle? It doesn't suit you. One must be careful how one adorns oneself, and make good choices."

Then Benjamin replied, "You're obviously right. I realize that, Josephyah, Yashub, my Jehosiph. You are clever beyond measure, and I could never say the things you say. But when you say them, then I realize it is so and defer to your thoughts, so that they become mine as well and I'm as clever as you make me. It is quite clear to me that choices must be made and that not every adornment suits everyone. I can tell that you wish to leave it at that and to leave me as clever as I have now become. But even if you were to go farther and speak out more explicitly to your brother, I would follow you. Believe your little brother; you can demand a great deal of him."

Joseph was silent.

"This much have I heard people say," Benjamin went on, "that the myrtle is a symbol of youth and beauty—that's what big people say, but if I say it, it makes you and me laugh, for what sort of phrases are those that they should be suitable to me, both in tone and meaning. I am truly young, indeed small, that is to say not even young, but only a whelp. You are young and beautiful, enough to set tongues wagging everywhere. Whereas I am more droll than beautiful—when I look at my legs, they are so short in relation to the rest of me, and I still have the potbelly of a suckling babe, and my cheeks are round, as if I were forever puffing them up with air, not to mention the hair on my head, which is like a cap of otter fur. And so if myrtle becomes youth and beauty, and if that is the nub of the matter, then indeed it suits only you, and it would be a mistake for me to wear it. I know very well that one can blunder and do oneself harm in such matters. You see, all by myself and without your even telling me, I understand some things, but of course not all, and I still need your help."

"My good little man," Joseph said, laying an arm around him, "your otter cap suits me fine, as do your belly and cheeks. You are my nearest and truest brother, flesh of my flesh, for we came from the same abyss, which is called *absu,* but which we call Mami, the sweet wife for whom Jacob served. Come, let us go down to the stone and rest."

"That we shall do," Benjamin replied. "Let's inspect the little garden the women have set in frames and pots, and you will explain the gravesite to me, for I love to hear about it. Most especially because Mami died on my account," he added as they descended, "and half the time I am called Little Son of Death—and at most the myrtle might suit me as well for that reason, for I have heard people say that it is also an adornment of death."

"Yes, there is lamentation in the world for youth and beauty," Joseph said, "and that is because Asherah makes her children weep and brings ruin upon those who love her. That is why the myrtle is also a shrub of death. But take note of the fragrance of this twig—do you smell its harshness? Bitter and acrid is the myrtle's adornment, for the whole sacrifice is dressed with it, and its green is set apart for those who have been set apart and chosen for those who are chosen. For the name of the whole sacrifice is consecrated youth. But myrtle in the hair, that is the herb touch-me-not."

"You no longer have your arm about me now," Benjamin remarked, "and have taken it from me, leaving this little fellow to walk all alone."

"Here is my arm again!" Joseph cried. "You are my true little brother, and when we are home I shall weave for you a wreath of many colors, from all the flowers of the field, so that everyone who sees you will laugh for joy—and shall that be a word given here and now between you and me?"

"That is sweet and dear of you," Benjamin said. "Grant me your robe for a moment, that I may touch my lips to the hem."

He thought: "Obviously what he has in mind is the firstborn and the election of an heir. Yet what strikes me as new and strange is how he has mixed it with talk of whole sacrifice and touch-me-not. It's possible that he's thinking of Isaak when he speaks of the whole sacrifice and of consecrated youth. At any rate he would have me understand myrtle as an adornment of sacrifice—which frightens me a little."

But aloud he said, "You are doubly beautiful when you speak as you have just now, and I in my folly can scarcely tell whether the scent of myrtle in my nose comes from the trees or your words. But we have arrived at the spot. Look, the gifts have increased since last time. There are two more seedling gods in their frames and two sprouting pots. Women have been here. They have planted little gardens before the grotto as well; I want to have a look at them. But the stone has not been touched or rolled away from the grave. I wonder where the Lord is—might he be inside in his beautiful form?"

For a little to the side of the slope and surrounded by shrubs, there was in fact a rocky cave—not very high, but long as a man and partially sealed by a stone—that served the women of Hebron in their festal rites.

"No, no," Joseph said in answer to the question, "his figure is not here and is not visible the whole year over. It is kept in the temple at Kiriath-Arba, and is brought forth only for the feast, on the day of solstice, when the sun begins to vanish and light is given over to the underworld, and then the women deal with him according to their rites."

"They lay the figure to rest here in the cave?" Benjamin inquired. Their first time here he had asked this same question, and Joseph had instructed him. Later, then, the boy often pretended to have forgotten, so that he might be taught anew and hear Joseph speak of Adonai, the Shepherd and Lord who had been murdered, for whom there was lamentation in the world. For he would listen between the words and attend to the tone and flow of Joseph's speech, as if in some vague way he were trying to find his brother's secret thoughts, which—it seemed to him—were dissolved in his words like salt in the sea.

"No, they bury him later," Joseph replied. "First they search for him." He was sitting at the base of the Ashtaroth shrine, a rough-hewn obelisk of blackish stone whose surface appeared covered with little mildewed blisters, and as he began to weave the gathered myrtle into a wreath, the delicate, agile tendons stood out on the backs of his hands.

Benjamin gazed at him from one side. A dark luster beneath Joseph's temple and on his chin revealed that he was already shaving his beard—with the help of a mixture of oil and potash and a stone knife. But what if he had let his beard grow? Presumably it would have changed him greatly. Quite possibly the beard would not have amounted to much yet; but still, what would then have become of his beauty, of the special beauty of his seventeen years? He might just as well have worn a dog's head atop his neck—it would have made no essential difference. Beauty, one must admit, is a fragile thing.

"They search for him," Joseph said, "for he is lost and he is sublime. Some of them have hidden his figure in the bushes, but they join in the search as well. They know where he is and they do not know, deliberately confusing themselves. They all lament as they wander about searching, they lament in chorus and each for herself, 'Where are you, my beautiful god, my husband, my son, my colorful shepherd-bird? I miss you! What has happened to you here in the grove, in the world, in the greenwood?'"

"But they do know," Benjamin objected, "that the Lord is mutilated and dead?"

"Not yet," Joseph responded. "That is the feast. They know it, because he was once discovered, and they do not know it, because the hour of rediscovery has not yet come. Each hour in the feast has its own knowledge, and each of the women is the searching goddess before she has made her discovery."

"But then they find the Lord?"

"Just as you say. He lies in the underbrush and is rent open on one side. They all crowd round, raising their arms and crying in shrill voices."

"Have you seen and heard it?"

"You know that I have heard and seen it twice now, but I made you promise not to tell Father. Have you kept silent?"

"I have indeed kept silent!" Benoni assured him. "Would I wound our father? I have wounded him enough with my life."

"And I will go out again when the time comes," Joseph said. "At present we are as far from the last time as from the next. When the oil is pressed, it is the solstice of return. And a wonderful feast it is. The lord lies prone among the shrubs, his deadly wounds gaping."

"What might he look like?"

"Just as I have described him for you. His is a beautiful figure, of olive wood, wax, and glass, for his eyeballs are of black glass, and have lashes."

"Is he young?"

"I told you, yes, he is young and beautiful. The grain of the yellow wood is like a network of fine veins over his body, his locks are black, and his loincloth is embroidered in many colors, worked in pearls and glass thread, with purple fringe at the hem."

"What does he have in his hair?"

"Nothing," Joseph replied curtly. "They have made his lips, nails, and birthmarks of wax, and the horrible wound from Ninib's tusk is lined with red wax. It bleeds."

"You said that the women's lamentation is great when they find him."

"It is very great. Thus far it was only the lament of loss, but now the great dirge of finding him begins, and is far more piercing. There is the mourning of flutes for Tammuz, the Lord, for here at this spot musicians sit and pipe with all their might on short flutes whose piteous wails cut to the quick. The women let down their hair and each gesture is excessive, as they mourn over the corpse: 'O my husband, my child!' For each of them is like the goddess, and each laments: 'No one loved you more than I!' "

"I must sob, Joseph, for the Lord's death is almost too grievous for one as small as I and it batters at me within. And why must this young, beautiful god be mutilated in the grove, in the world, in the greenwood, that such lamentation should be raised over him?"

"You do not understand," Joseph replied. "He is the martyr and the sacrifice. He rises from the abyss in order to go forth and be glorified. That was Abram's certainty when he raised the knife above his true son. But as he thrust downward, there was the ram in his place. That is why when we bring a ram or a lamb as a whole offering, we hang round its neck a seal with the image of a man, as a sign that it is his representative. But the mystery of representation is greater still, for it is determined by the position taken by the stars of man, god, and beast and is the mystery of substitution. As a man offers his son in the animal, so the son offers himself through the animal. Ninib is not cursed, for it is written: A god shall be slain. And the meaning of the animal is that of the son who recognizes his hour, just as in the feast, and also knows he will topple the house of death and come forth from the cave."

"If only the time were come," the little boy said, "and the feast of joy begun! Do they lay the Lord now in the grave and in that cave there?"

Joseph swayed back and forth from the hips as he worked. He began a nasal chant:

> "'In the days of Tammuz, play upon the flutes of lapis lazuli,
> and play as well upon the ring of carnelian! . . .'"

"Singing dirges, they bring him here to the stone," he went on, "and the musicians now play so loudly upon their flutes that it pierces the soul. I saw the women busy with the figure of the corpse in their laps. They washed it with water and anointed it with oil of nard, so that the Lord's face and grained body glistened and dripped with it. Then they wrapped him in swaths of linen and wool, shrouded him in purple cloths, and laid him upon a bier here beside the stone, never ceasing their lamentations and weeping to the sound of the pipes:

> 'Alas for Tammuz!
> Alas for the beloved son, my springtime, my light!
> Adon! Adonai!
> We sit ourselves down amidst tears,
> For you are dead, my God, my husband, my child!
> You are a tamarisk that has not drunk of the water in its bed,
> Whose tops have brought forth no shoots in the field!
> You are a sapling that has not been planted in its stream,
> A twig, whose roots have been ripped out,

An herb that has drunk no water from the garden!
Alas, my Damu, my child, my light!
No one loved you more than I!'"

"You know all the words to their lament."

"I know them," Joseph said.

"And they lie near to your heart, too, I think," Benoni added. "Once or twice as you sang, it seemed to me it came close to battering at you within as well, though the women of the city act only according to their understanding, and the son is not Adonai, the God of Jacob and Abraham."

"He is the son and the beloved," Joseph said, "and the sacrifice. But what are you saying? For it did not batter at me. I am no small, sniveling boy like you."

"No, rather, you are young and beautiful," Benjamin said meekly. "Now the wreath you have reserved for yourself is almost done. I see you have made it higher and wider at the front than at the back, like a crown upon the brow, as proof of your skill. I rejoice that you will put it on, more greatly than I shall rejoice at the wreath of mountain ash you will make for me. But the beautiful god now lies upon his bier for four days?"

"Just as you say and have remembered," Joseph replied. "Your understanding is waxing and will soon be round and full, so that one can discuss anything with you, without exception. He lies displayed here until the fourth day, and each day the townspeople and musicians come to the grove, beating their breasts at the sight and wailing:

'O Duzi, my Lord, how long you have lain here!
O Lord of the sheepfold, how long you have lain helpless here!
No bread will I eat, no water will I drink,
For dead is youth, and dead is Tammuz.'

And within the temple and in their homes their lament is the same. But on the fourth day they come and lay him in his ark."

"In a box?"

"One must call it 'the ark.' Another good word would be a 'chest'—a perfectly apt word, and yet inappropriate for this case. It has been called 'the ark' for ages. The Lord fits perfectly within it, for it is made to measure, the wood's grain a pattern of red and black, and it could not suit him better. As soon as he is laid in it, they clap the lid tight, seal it with pitch all around and, amidst their tears, inter the Lord in that cave there, roll the stone across it, and return home from the grave."

"Does the weeping now cease?"

"You have remembered poorly. The lament continues in the temple and in their homes, for two days and a half. But on the third day, as dusk falls, the Feast of Burning Lamps begins."

"I have been looking forward to it. So they light a few lamps?"

"Lamps without number, everywhere," Joseph said, "as many as they possess, around their houses and beneath the open sky, as well as along the paths to this place. And here, too, in these bushes encircling us, lamps are burning all around. They come to the grave and raise their lament yet again, and it is indeed the bitterest dirge of all, never before have the flutes blared so shrilly as they lament: 'O Duzi, how long you have lain here!' and the women's breasts will bear the scratches for a long time. At midnight, however, everything grows still."

Benjamin grasped for his brother's arm. "It suddenly becomes still?" he said. "And everything is silent?"

"They stand there motionless and hushed. The silence continues. But then from a distance a voice is heard, a single bright and joyful voice: 'Tammuz lives! The Lord is risen! He has toppled the house of the shadow of death! Great is the Lord!'"

"Oh, what tidings, Joseph! I knew that it would come at their hour of joy, and yet it still stirs me to the marrow, as if I had never heard it. Who is it that calls out?"

"It is a maiden of mild countenance, especially chosen and appointed each new year. Her parents glory in this and are held in honor. The proclaiming maiden draws nearer, a lute in her arm, she strums and sings:

'Tammuz lives, Adon is risen!
Great is He, great, the Lord is great!
His eye, which death had closed, He has opened it.
His mouth, which death had closed, He has opened it.
His feet, which lay in chains, wend their way again,

Herbs and flowers spring up where they have trod,
Great is the Lord, Adonai is great!'

But as the maiden comes forward singing, they all rush to the grave. They roll the stone away, and behold, the ark is empty."

"Where is the mutilated god?"

"He is no longer there. The grave could not hold him for but three days. He is risen."

"Oh! But how, Joseph, how—forgive this little chubby-cheeked boy, but what are you saying? Please don't deceive your mother's son! For you have told me now and again that the beautiful figure is kept in the temple from one year to the next. So then, what does 'risen' mean here?"

"Little dunce," Joseph replied, "it will be a while yet before your understanding is round and full, for though it is waxing, it is still very much like a barque rocking as it moves across the heavenly sea. Am I not describing the feast in each of its hours, and do you suppose the people deceive themselves as they celebrate it, hour by hour, knowing what the next will bring, but sanctifying each in its moment? Of course they all know that the figure is kept in the temple, but Tammuz is risen nonetheless. I almost think you mean that because the image is not the god, the god cannot be the image. Beware, he is that most indeed! For the image is the instrument of the present and of the feast. The Lord Tammuz, however, is the lord of the feast."

With that he set the finished wreath on his head.

Benjamin gazed at him with large eyes. "God of our fathers," he cried in admiration, "how well your brow is adorned with the crown of myrtle greens your skillful hands have made before my eyes. It suits only you, and when I think how it would look upon my otter cap, I can see what a blunder it would have been had you not reserved it for yourself. Tell me truly," he went on, "and tell me more: when the townspeople find the ark and grave empty, I suppose they then wend their silent way home, enrapt in joyful thoughts?"

"It is then that jubilation begins," Joseph corrected him, "and the feast of joy erupts. 'Empty, empty, empty!' they all cry. 'The grave is empty, Adon is risen!' They kiss the maiden and call out, 'The Lord is great!' Then they kiss each other in turn and cry, 'Tammuz is glorified!' Then they form a ring to dance and whirl in the lamplight around the monument of Ashtaroth here. And in the brightly illumined city is purest joy and revelry, feasting and drinking, and every breeze is filled with the cry of good tidings. Yes, even for the next day they greet one another with a twofold kiss and the salutation: 'He is risen indeed!' "

"Yes," Benjamin said, "that is how it is, and you have told me so. I had simply forgotten, thinking they returned home in silence. What a splendid feast in all its hours! And so the Lord's head is raised up for this year, but he knows the hour when Ninib will again attack him in the greenwood."

"Not 'again,' " Joseph instructed. "It is always the first and only time."

"Whatever you say, dear brother, it is so. The way I put it was immature, the words of a whelp. Always the first and only time, for he is Lord of the feast. But, when one considers it rightly, for there even to be a feast, it surely must have happened at one time, that first time, when Tammuz died and his beauty was mutilated, must it not?"

"When Ishtar vanishes from the heavens and descends to awaken her son, that is the occasion."

"Yes, yes, that is up above. But how is it here below? You call it the occasion. But tell me the story!"

"They say there was a king in Gebal," Joseph replied, "at the foot of the snowy mountains, and he had a daughter fair of face. But Nana, that is Ashtaroth, afflicted him with the folly of desire for the girl, so that he lusted after his own flesh and blood, and he knew his daughter." And as he said it, Joseph pointed back at the symbols etched in the obelisk where they sat.

"And she was pregnant with a child," he went on, "and when the king saw that he was the father of his own grandson, he was filled with confusion, rage, and remorse, and he rose up to slay her. But the gods, knowing full well that Asherah had caused this, transformed the pregnant girl into a tree."

"Into what kind of tree?"

"It was a tree or a shrub," Joseph said in annoyance, "or a shrub sturdy as a tree. I was not there, so I cannot tell you what sort of nose the king had or what earrings the nurse to his daughter wore. If you wish to hear, then hear and do not hurl immature questions like stones into my sheepfold."

"If you scold me, I shall cry," Benjamin protested, "and then you will have to comfort me. Therefore don't scold me first, but believe me when I say I wish only to listen!"

"Ten months later," Joseph said, continuing his tale, "the tree opened and burst after the appointed time, and behold the boy Adonai came forth from it. Asherah, who had caused all this, saw him and would yield him over to no one else. Which is why she kept him in the Lower Realm, ruled by Queen Ereshkigal. But she, too, would allow no one else to have him and said, 'I shall never give him back, for this is the land of no return.'"

"Why would these two rulers not yield him to anyone else?"

"To no one else, nor to each other. You need only ask and you will know all. If one thing can be inferred from another, then one merely mentions the first, and the other becomes evident. Adon was the son of a fair maiden, and Nana herself had had a hand in his conception, so words are not needed to explain how he was a source of envy. Which is why, when the queen of desire appeared in the Lower Realm to demand him back, Queen Ereshkigal was frightened in her deepest soul and grit her teeth. She said to the gatekeeper: 'Deal with her according to custom!' And so Queen Astarte was compelled to pass through the seven gates, leaving behind at each a piece of clothing in the hands of the gatekeeper—head scarf, robes, belt and buckles, and at the last her loincloth—so that she came naked before Queen Ereshkigal to ask for Tammuz. Whereupon the two rulers made talons of their fingers and flew at one another."

"They grappled and clawed at one another over him?"

"Yes, each twisted the other's hair round her hand, and they grappled—so great was their jealousy. But then Queen Ereshkigal ordered Queen Astarte locked up in her Lower Realm with sixty locks and assailed her with sixty sicknesses, so that Astarte waited in vain to return to earth and all sprouting lay in fetters and blossoming in chains. The pastures turned white by night, the fields bore salt. No herb came forth, no grain grew. The bull no longer covered the cow, nor the jackass its jenny, nor the husband his wife. The womb was sealed tight. Life, deserted by desire, froze in sadness."

"Ah, Josephyah, move on to other hours of this tale, and celebrate this one no longer. I wish to hear no more of how the jackass no longer covered the jenny and the earth was leprous with salt. I shall weep and then I would be only trouble to you."

"God's messenger wept as well when he saw it," Joseph said, "and amidst his tears showed it to the Lord of the gods. Who said: 'It is not good that blossoming should lie in chains. I shall intervene.' And he mediated between the two queens, Ashtaroth and Ereshkigal, decreeing that Adoni should spend one-third of the year in the Lower Realm, one-third on earth, and one-third wherever he chose. And then Ishtar led her beloved upward again."

"But where did he who had sprung from a tree spend the third part of the year?"

"That is difficult to say. In various places. There was much jealousy over him and many are the wiles of jealousy. Ashtaroth loved him, but more than one god led him away and would not yield him up to anyone."

"Gods made in the image of man, just as I am?" Benjamin asked.

"How you are made," Joseph replied, "is indeed clear and intelligible to all, but things are not so simple with gods and demigods. Many do not call Tammuz their master, but their mistress. They call him Nana then, the goddess, but at the same time the god who is with her, or even mean him instead of her, for is Ishtar herself a female as well? I have seen images of her and she had a beard. So, why should I not say I have seen images of 'him'? Jacob, our father, makes no images. Without doubt it is wisest not to make images. But we must speak and our clumsy choice of words is inadequate for the truth. Is Ishtar the morning star?"

"Yes, and the evening star."

"So she is both. I also read from a stone that said of her: 'Of evening a female and of morning a male.' How can one make an image of that—or choose words that accord with the truth? I have seen one god's image, depicting the water of Egypt that gives drink to the fields, and its breast was a woman's breast on one side, but that of a man on the other. Perhaps Tammuz was a virgin and is a lad by way of death."

"Is it within death's power to alter the nature of something?"

"The dead one is God. He is Tammuz, the shepherd, who is also called Adonis, but Osiris in the Lower Lands. There he has a squared-off beard, even if in life he may have been a woman."

"Mami's cheeks were, as you've told me, so very soft, and when you kissed them their scent was of rose petal. I don't want to have any such bearded image of her! If you demand it of me, I shall be naughty and not do it."

"Dear dunce, I don't demand it of you," Joseph said with a laugh. "I'm only telling you about the people in the Lower Lands and their thoughts concerning what is not easily understood by all."

"My chubby cheeks are tender and soft, too," Benjamin remarked, feeling his cheeks with the palms of both hands. "That's because I'm not even young yet, but merely a whelp. You, you are young. That is why you're keeping your face pure and free of a beard until you are a man."

"Yes, I keep myself clean and pure," Joseph replied. "You, however, *are* pure. You have cheeks like Mami's, so soft that it's as if you were an angel from the Most High, from God the Lord, who has betrothed Himself to our tribe and to whom we are betrothed in the flesh by the covenant of Abraham. For to us He is like a bridegroom by blood, full of jealousy toward Israel, His bride. But is Israel in fact a bride or a bridegroom? That is not easily understood by all, and one should make no image of it, for at best Israel is a bridegroom, circumcised as a bride, consecrated and set apart. When I try to make an image of Elohim in my mind, He is like the father who loves me more than my fellows. But I know that it is Mami that he loves in me, because I live, while she is dead—for she is alive to him now in a different nature. I and my mother are one. But Jacob means Rachel when he gazes at me, just as the people of the countryside mean Nana when they call Tammuz their mistress."

"I mean Mami, too—I do, too—when I am tender with you, Josephyah, dear Jehosiph!" Benjamin cried, wrapping his arms around Joseph. "You see, that is the substitute, that is representation. For the woman with soft cheeks had to go toward the west for the sake of my life, and so from the very start, the whelp is an orphan and an evildoer. But you are like her to me, you lead me by the hand into the grove, into the world, into the greenwood, you tell me about the god's feast in all its hours and make wreaths for me, just as she would have done—though, of course, you don't allow me each and every green, but reserve some for yourself. Ah, if only it had not come upon her so hard beside the road that she had to die! If only she had been like the tree that burst open with such ease and let the sprout emerge. What did you say, what sort of tree was it? My memory is as short as my legs and my fingers."

"Come now, let us go," Joseph said.

The Dream of Heaven

At the time his brothers did not yet call him Dreamer, but it came to that very soon. If for now they merely called him Utnapishtim and Reader of Stones, the mildness of these terms for expressing hostility can be explained by these young men's lack of invention and imagination. They would indeed have gladly called him nastier names, but they could come up with none, and so they were very happy once they could call him Dreamer of Dreams, which was nastier. But that day had not yet come; his gushing on about his dream of the weather, which had brought comfort to his father, had not been enough to make them notice this particular haughty characteristic, and, what is more, he had thus far held his tongue about his dreams, though he had been having them for some time now. He never said a word about the most powerful ones, either to them or to his father. The ones he did tell, to his detriment, were comparatively modest. But he poured it all out to Benjamin, who in their intimate times together would hear about the very immodest dreams as well, those that Joseph was otherwise prudent enough to keep to himself. No need to mention that the boy, being a curious fellow, listened with the most attentive delight and even prompted Joseph to tell them. But, having already to bear melancholy burdens demanded of him by all sorts of vague, myrtle-wreathed secrets, as he listened he could not help feeling anxious and apprehensive—which he wanted to ascribe to his own immaturity and thus tried to overcome. All the same, the legitimacy of such feelings was all too real, for no one can banish every worry when presented with the gross immodesty of a dream like the one that follows—which Benjamin, and he alone, heard more than once. And knowing that he alone shared in it obviously troubled the boy a good deal, however much he recognized the necessity, and great honor, of such exclusivity.

Joseph usually told this dream with eyes closed and in a low voice that could suddenly burst into fervor, with fists clenched to his chest and a heart evidently deeply moved, though he warned his listener not to be upset, but to accept it all calmly.

"You needn't be afraid, and there'll be no shouting or laughing or crying," he said, "otherwise I'll not speak."

"Oh, but I won't," Benjamin replied each time. "I may be a whelp, but I'm not a ninny. I know how to do it. As long as I'm relaxed, I can forget that it's a dream, and that way I can truly relish it. But the moment I feel afraid or turn hot and cold, I'll remember that it's only a dream you're telling me. That will cool my mind so that I will cause no disruption whatever."

"I dreamt," Joseph began, "that I was with the herds in the field and was alone with the sheep pasturing on the slopes and around the hill on which I lay. And I lay upon my belly, a straw in my mouth, my feet in the air, and my thoughts were as slipshod as my limbs. Then it happened that a shadow fell over me and my spot, as if from a cloud darkening the sun, and with it there came a powerful rushing in the air, and when I looked up, behold, it was an eagle hovering monstrously above me, as large as an ox and with the horns of an ox upon its brow—it was this that cast a shadow over me. And all about me was a raging of wind and power, for he was now just above me, grabbed me by the hips in his talons and, with pinions beating, swept me up from the earth and away from my father's herds."

"What a wonder!" Benjamin interjected. "Not that I would have been afraid, but did you not then shout, 'Help me, people below!'?"

"I did not, and for three reasons," Joseph responded. "First, there was no one in those wide pastures to hear me; second, my breath was taken away, so that I could not have shouted even had I wanted to; and third, I did not want to, for instead there was a great joy within me, and it seemed to me as if I had long expected this. Grasping me by the back of my hips, the eagle held me ahead of him by his talons, with his head above mine and my legs dangling in the wind of our ascent. At times he would lower his head to mine and gaze at me with one powerful eye. And then he spoke from his bronze beak. 'Am I holding you fast, my lad, but not all too tightly with my invincible talons? You should know that I am taking good care that they cause no harm to your flesh, for woe is me if I did so!' I asked: 'Who are you?' He answered: 'I am the angel Amphiel, to whom this shape has been given for my present task. For your biding place, my child, is not upon earth, but rather you shall be transported, that is the decree.'

" 'But why?' I then asked.

" 'Be silent,' the onrushing eagle said, 'and keep your tongue from asking questions, just as all are compelled to do in heaven. For this is the decree of omnipotent predilection, and there is no fancy reasoning or resisting against it—for if you speak and question, the decree casts it down with power, and let no one burn his tongue on that vast immensity!' So I fell silent before his words and said nothing. But my heart was full of terrible joy."

"I am glad you are sitting beside me in token that it was all a dream," Benjamin said. "But were you not rather sad to leave earth on the wings of an eagle, and did you not feel a little sorry for all of us whom you were leaving—for this little fellow here, for me, for example?"

"I was not leaving you," Joseph replied. "I was taken from you and could not change that, but it was as if I had expected it. And in a dream one is not aware of everything, but of only one thing, and that was the terrible joy in my heart. It was great, and what was happening to me was great as well, and so it may have been that those things about which you have asked might have seemed small to me."

"I am not angered by it," Benjamin said, "rather I am amazed at you."

"Many thanks, little Ben. You must also keep in mind that the ascent may well have erased my memory, for I was being carried ever upward in the talons of the eagle, who after two double hours said to me: 'Look down, my friend, to land and sea, to what they have become.' And the land had become the size of a mountain, and the sea like the water of a river. And after two double hours more, the eagle again said: 'Look down, my friend, at what has become of land and sea.' And the land was like a planting of trees and the sea like the ditch dug by a gardener. After two more double hours, however, when Amphiel the eagle showed it to me, behold and marvel, for the land had become a cake and the sea no more than a breadbasket. After this view, he bore me upward yet another two double hours and said: 'Look down, my friend, at how land and sea have vanished.' And they had vanished, but I was not afraid.

"On through *shehakim*, the sky of clouds, the eagle climbed with me, his pinions dripping with moisture. In the gray and white around us, however, were flashes of gold, for already some of heaven's children, members of the host with weapons of gold, stood about on the damp islands, laying a hand to their brows and peering out at us, while beasts bedded on cushions lifted their noses, and I saw them sniff at the wind of our ascent.

"Through *rakia,* the starry heavens, we rose, while a thousand-fold booming of harmony filled my ears, for all about us stars and planets were marvelously passing in the music of their numbers; and here and there angels with tablets of numbers in their hands stood on fiery footstools, pointing to the paths these raging wanderers were to follow, for they dared not turn around. And they called to one another: 'Praise the glory of the Lord in the place of His dominion!' But as we passed they fell silent and lowered their eyes.

"Terrified with joy, I asked the eagle: 'Where are you leading me, and how high is it still?' He replied: 'Boundlessly high and unto the topmost heights of the north of the world, my child. For it is the decree that I should bring you straightway and posthaste to the furthest heights and expanses of Araboth, there where the storehouses of life, of peace and of blessing are found, and to the uppermost vaults, in the heart of the Great Palace. There is the chariot and the Throne of Dominion, which you shall henceforth serve daily, and you shall stand before Him and have power over the keys, to open and close the halls of Araboth, and to do whatever else is intended for you.' I said: 'If I have been chosen and selected from among all mortals, then let it be so. It does not happen all unexpectedly.'

"Then I saw a fortress, dreadful and built of ice crystal, its battlements manned by warriors of the heights, whose wings covered their bodies to their feet, and whose legs were straight, but whose feet were round feet, so to speak, and sparkled like burnished bronze. And behold, two were standing side by side, with hands braced upon serpent swords and of bold countenance, and there were furrows of pride between their brows. The eagle said: 'Those are Aza and Azael, two of the seraphim.' And I heard Aza say to Azael: 'For more than sixty-five thousand miles I have smelled his coming. But tell me what is the odor of one born of woman and the value of one begotten by a drop of white seed, that he may enter the Highest Heaven and take up service among us?' And in horror, Azael sealed his lips with a finger. But Aza spoke and said: 'Not so, I shall fly with you before the face of the One and Only and will dare to speak, for I am an angel of lightning and am free to speak my word.' And they both took flight in our wake.

"And through whatever heavens the eagle carried me by my hips and through whatever ranks of hosts singing praises and squadrons of fiery servants, the hymn fell silent the moment we ascended past them; and a few of the children of these heights would join us at each level, so that soon there were swarms of winged creatures accompanying us, before and behind, and I heard the rustle of their wings like a mighty rushing of waters.

"Oh, Benjamin, believe me. I saw the seven halls of Zebul built of fire, and seven hosts of angels stood there, and seven fiery altars had been built. The Highest Prince ruling there is robed in the splendor of a priest and his name is Who Is Like God, and he made burnt offerings, sending up pillars of smoke from the altar of sacrifice.

"I cannot count the double hours nor put a name to the sum of miles before we reached the heights of Araboth and the Seventh Level and set foot on its soil, which was light and soft and spent grace through the soles of my feet, so that it rose up through me, even to my eyes, and I wept. And the Children of Light moved past us and behind us, so that they both led and followed us. And the one that took me and led me now by the hand was very strong and naked to the waist, wearing a golden skirt to his ankles, with armbands and a necklace and a round helmet set atop his hair, and the tips of his wings touched his heels. He had heavy eyelids and a fleshy nose, and his red mouth smiled when I gazed at him, but he did not turn his head toward me.

"And I lifted up my eyes in my dream—and in the vast expanse I saw the glistening of weapons and wings and endless hosts encamped about their standards, singing hymns of praise and war at full voice, and it all swam before my eyes like milk, gold, and roses. And I saw wheels turning, terrible in their height and rims, they gleamed like beryl, and one wheel turned within another, four together, without turning as they went. And their rims were full of eyes, round and about on all four wheels.

"In the middle, however, was a mountain, flashing with fiery stones, and atop it a palace made from the light of sapphire, where we entered with a great throng before and after. And its halls were full of messengers, guards, and stewards. But as we entered into the columned hall at the center, no end or background was visible, for they led me down its length, and cherubim were standing before each column at both sides, and between them as well, each with six wings covered over with eyes. And so we moved between them, I do not know for how long, toward the Throne of Dominion. And everywhere the air was overfilled with the cries of those beneath the columns and of those who stood in hosts about the throne: 'Holy, holy, holy, is the Lord Sabaoth, the whole earth is full of His glory!' The throng about the throne, however, was a throng of seraphim, and with two wings they covered their feet and with two their faces, but they peeked a little through the feathers. And he who had brought me said to me: 'Hide your countenance as well, for it is fitting!' And I put my hands to my face, but I also peeked a little through my fingers."

"Joseph," Benjamin cried, "for God's sake, did you behold the face of the One and Only?"

"I saw Him sitting upon His throne in the sapphire light," Joseph said, "in form like a man and made in the image of man, in His familiar majesty. For the beard and the hair at His temples glistened as they flowed to each side, and there were furrows there, deep and good. Lines of tenderness and weariness lay beneath His eyes, which were not all too large, but brown and bright, and they peered at me with concern as I approached."

"It seems to me," Benjamin said, "as if I see Jacob, our father, gazing at you."

"It was the Father of the world," Joseph replied, "and I fell upon my face. Then I heard a voice speaking, which said to me: 'Son of man, stand upon your feet. For from henceforth you shall stand before My throne as Metatron and God's child, and I will give you the power of the keys, to open and to close My Araboth, and you shall be set as commander over all the hosts, for the Lord takes delight in you.' And through the throng of angels there passed a rustling and rumbling like great armies. And behold those whom I had heard speaking together, Aza and Azael, stepped forward. And Aza the seraph said: 'Lord of all worlds, what sort is this that comes to these Upper Regions to take up service among us?' And Azael added, though he covered his face with two wings to diminish his words: 'Is he not begotten by a white drop of seed and by a race of those who drink iniquity like water?' And I saw displeasure pass over the face of the Lord, and His words flared up mightily, for He answered and said: 'What are you to interfere with Me? I show favor to whom I show favor, and mercy to whom I show mercy! Truly, sooner than any of you, I will make him prince and magistrate in the heights of heaven.'

"And again the rustling and rumbling passed through the hosts and was like a bowing and retreating. The cherubim beat their wings, and all the menials of heaven raised the resounding cry: 'Praise the glory of the Lord in the place of His dominion!'

"The King, however, now magnified His words and said: 'I lay my hand upon this man here and bless him with three hundred sixty-five thousand blessings and make him great and exalted. I shall make him a throne, like My own, and place upon it a covering of pure radiance, light, beauty, and glory. I shall place it at the entrance to the Seventh Level and set him upon it, for I will magnify still further. A cry shall go out before him, from heaven to heaven: Pay heed and take to your heart! I have named My servant Enoch to be a prince and a mighty ruler over all princes of My realm and over all the children of heaven, except at most the eight terrible powers that are named with the name of God as with the name of the King. And every angel who would petition Me shall first come before him and speak with him. But you shall heed and obey every word that he speaks to you in My name, for the princes of wisdom and understanding stand at his side. Such is the fame that shall precede him. Give Me the robe and the crown.'

"And the Lord cast over me a splendid robe, into which every sort of light was woven, and arrayed me in it. And took a heavy circlet with forty-nine gemstones of inexpressible luster, and with His own hands He set it upon my head to match the robe. And before the face of the entire heavenly tribe He named me by my title: Yahu, the Little One, Innermost Prince. For He was magnifying these things.

"And all the sons of heaven stepped back shuddering, quaking and bowing, and with them the princes among the angels, the powers, the mighty ones and the lions of God, who are greater than all the hosts and whose service is before the Throne of Dominion, and with them, the angels of fire, of hail, of lightning, of wind, of anger, and of rage, of storm, of snow and rain, of day, of night, of the moon and the planets, whose hands guide the destinies of the world—all of them trembled as well and, dazzled, hid their faces.

"The Lord, however, stood upon His throne and magnified to the uttermost and began to proclaim and say: 'Behold, there was a tender cedar sapling in the valley, which I transplanted upon a mountain, high and lofty, and made a tree of it, under whose boughs the birds can dwell. And by My incomprehensible will and out of predilection and election by grace, I took this boy, the youngest in days, months, and years from among all the hosts, and made him greater than all creatures. I commanded him to oversee every precious thing in the halls of Araboth and all the treasures of life that are kept in the highest heaven. It was his office, moreover, to bind wreaths around the heads of the holy beasts, to adorn the dazzling wheels with strength, to array the cherubim in splendor, to endow the fiery bolts with radiance and light, and to enfold the seraphim in pride. Each morning when I made ready to ascend My seat and survey My power from the height of heights, He set the throne of My dominion to rights. I cloaked him in a splendid robe and arrayed him in a coat full of pride and glory. I crowned his head with a heavy circlet and lent him something of the majesty, splendor, and radiance of My throne. And I regretted only that I could not make his throne larger than My own and his dominion greater than My own, for it is infinite! His name, however, was The Little God.'

"There followed upon this announcement a mighty crack of thunder, and all the angels fell upon their faces. But because the Lord had chosen me with such joy, my flesh had become a blazing flame, my veins burned brightly, my bones were like a fire of juniper, and the raising of my eyelashes like a lightning bolt. My eyes rolled like orbs of fire, the hair on my head was ablaze, my limbs had become fiery pinions, and I awoke."

"My whole body trembles at your dream, Joseph," Benjamin said, "for it is extravagant. And even you are trembling slightly, I should think, and are a bit pale—I can tell from the way the dark luster, where you pass the knife blade over your face, stands out clearly."

"Ridiculous," Joseph replied. "Am I supposed to tremble at my own dream?"

"And were you now glorified forever to the heights, never to return, and had you no thought at all of your family, of this little fellow here, for example?" Benjamin asked.

"Simple as you are, you can well imagine," Joseph responded, "that I was somewhat confused at such a despotic election by grace and had little time for thinking of what lay behind me. But after a time—of this I'm certain—I would have thought of you and have sent for you, so that you all might be raised up alongside me— Father, his wives, our brothers, and you. No doubt that would have been a trifle, given my full powers. But listen and take heed, Benjamin, in whom I have confided because of your maturity and understanding, that you do not prattle to our father or brothers about the dream I have told you, for they could interpret it to my disadvantage."

"Not for the world!" came Benjamin's response. "That would be dragon's work! You forget all too easily the difference between a whelp and a ninny, though it is a most important one. Not even in a dream would I consider prattling so much as a whit of what you let come to you in your dream. But you yourself, Joseph, should take greater heed still, and I beg you to do so for my sake, dear brother. For I have it easy, since gratitude prevents me from forgetting your trust in me. But nothing prevents you, for you dreamed on your own and are richer in the splendor and radiance of a dream that you have merely lent to me. Therefore think of this little fellow when you are tempted to tell how the Lord chose you with such great joy. For my part I find it only fitting, and am angry with Aza and Azael for interrupting. But Father might, as usual, be grieved and worried by it, and our brothers would spit and spew with displeasure and pay you back out of jealousy. For they are brutes before the Lord, as we both well know."

Part Four

THE DREAMER

The Coat of Many Colors

Not at harvest time as planned, but much sooner, on the night of the spring's full moon, the sons of Leah came hurtling head over heels back to Hebron from the pastures at Shechem. They arrived ostensibly to eat the Pesach lamb with their father and observe the moon with him, but in reality they came because they had received news affecting all the brothers, news so upsetting that they absolutely had to convince themselves on the spot of its truth and to learn if it might be altered. The matter was so important and frightening that the handmaids' sons could think of nothing more urgent than to delegate one of their own to embark on the four-day journey from Hebron to Shechem, for no other purpose than to bring news to their distant brothers. And of course they had entrusted fleet-footed Naphtali with the message. In terms of speed it was ultimately of no consequence, however, who made the journey. Naphtali had to ride an ass, too, and whether the pair of legs dangling at the ass's side were long or short made no difference, really—the journey took about four days in any case. But, in fact, it was Naphtali, Bilhah's son with whose person speed was associated, and by shared conviction his was the role of the messenger. And since his tongue was equally nimble, it is true that, at least in those final moments, the brothers would learn the facts somewhat more quickly than from any of the others.

What had happened? Jacob had given Joseph a gift.

That was nothing new. The "lamb," the "twig," the "heavenly boy," the "son of the virgin" (and whatever all those other willful, emotion-laden paternal designations for the Reader of Stones might be) had always been given special presents and tender mementos on the sly: tasty tidbits, pretty pieces of pottery, gemstones, purple cord for trimming, scarabs, and this and that—at which the brothers would scowl whenever they noticed them in his casual possession, feeling they had received the short end of things. They had had time enough to become accustomed to injustice, to a fundamental and almost pointedly purposeful injustice. But this was a gift of startling importance and, there was every reason to fear, of decisive significance—it meant a slap in the face for them all.

Here is the course of events. It was tent weather, the late rains had set in. Toward afternoon Jacob had withdrawn to his house of felt—a matted fabric woven from black goat's wool, spread over nine sturdy poles and fastened by strong ropes tied to deep-driven pegs—that provided him total and secure protection from the blessed damp. It was the largest in the rather scattered settlement, and, as a rich man who made a point of providing his wives shelter of their own, the master lived alone in his tent, though it was divided into two rooms by a curtain strung from the center posts, front to back. One room served as a private storeroom and pantry where camel saddles and bags, unused carpets—some rolled up, some folded—hand mills, and other gear lay strewn about. From the poles were hung skins filled with grain, butter, drinking water, and a palm wine fermented from soaked dates.

The other space served as the man of blessing's living room and, despite the casual semi-Bedouin style of life to which Jacob clung, revealed many comforts. He needed them. His rejection of the softer bonds of urban life did not prevent his requiring some pleasures whenever he withdrew from the world to his personal realm for contemplation and the work of thinking about God. With an opening the height of a man toward the front, the chamber had a warm floor of felt, over which were spread colorfully worked carpets, with some even hanging as tapestries along the walls. A bronze-footed cedar bedstead spread with blankets and cushions stood at the rear. Several clay lamps with shallow bowls, ornamental bases, and stubby spouts for the wick were always burning here, for it would have been a sign of poverty unbecoming a man of blessing to sleep in the dark, and even by day a servant tended to the oil so that no one might say—even in the literal sense of a phrase that had a deeper, blacker meaning—that Jacob's lamp had gone out. Painted limestone pitchers stood on the flat lid of a sycamore chest, whose sides were adorned with bits of blue-glazed pottery. Another carved and inscribed chest set on long legs had a vaulted lid. A glowing basin of coals in the corner had not been omitted, either, for Jacob tended to chill easily. There were low stools, too, but they were seldom used for sitting, but instead served as places to set things. On one stood a small incense tower, from whose tiny windowlike openings came clouds of curling smoke redolent of cinnamon, storax gum, and galbanum; another bore an object that witnessed to its owner's prosperity: a valuable piece of Phoenician artisanship, a shallow golden vessel that one grasped by a delicate stem in the form of a female musician.

Near the entrance Jacob was sitting with Joseph on cushions placed beside a low taboret, on whose engraved bronze surface the game board lay open. He had called his son to join him for this pastime, for which Rachel had once been his opponent. From outside came the patter of rain as it fell on olive trees, stones, and shrubs and, by God's grace, provided the moisture that the grain of the valley required in order to endure the early summer sun until harvest. The wind set up a light clatter in the wooden rings by which the ropes were attached to the tent roof.

Joseph let his father win at the game. He had intentionally landed in the "evil eye" square, putting him at a disadvantage, so that he fell behind until Jacob, much to his pleasant surprise—for he had been playing with a considerable lack of attention—finally beat him. He confessed to his own preoccupation, admitting that luck had played a greater role in the outcome than any keenness of mind.

"Had you not fallen into the trap so soon, child," he said, "I would certainly have had to lose, for my thoughts were wandering, and no doubt I made grave blunders, though you moved artfully and neglected nothing to make up for your misfortune. The way you play reminds me very much of Mami's, who often put me in a spot. It touches me to see again in you both the way she would bite her little finger while thinking and those certain tricks and sly moves she loved."

"Much good it does," Joseph replied and stretched, throwing back his head with one arm extended and the other bent around to his shoulder. "The outcome does not speak in my favor. Since my dear papa won while woolgathering, what would have happened to the child had your full attention been working against him? The game would have come to a speedy end."

Jacob smiled. "I am older in experience and have had the best training, for even as a boy I played against Yitzchak, your grandfather on my side, and later often even with Laban, your grandfather on the side of your lovely mother, in the land of Naharaim, beyond the great water, and he played with dogged deliberation."

More than once he, too, had intentionally let Yitzchak and Laban win, whenever he wanted to put them in a good mood, yet it never occurred to him that Joseph might have just done the same.

"It is true," he continued, "that I was not at my best today. A recurrent thought made me forget the placement of the stones, for I was thinking that the feast is near at hand and the night of sacrifice approaching when we slaughter the sheep after sundown and dip a sprig of hyssop in its blood so that when we paint the doorposts with it, the Destroyer may pass by. For it is the night of passing over and of life spared for the sake of the sacrifice, and the blood on the posts placates the Wanderer, for it is a sign that the firstborn has been offered in expiation and as a substitute for the men and beasts that he lusts to strangle. I fell to thinking of it several times—for a man does many things, and behold, he knows not what it is he does. But if he would know and consider it, it may well be that his bowels would roll over within him, with bottom upended and now at the top, making him sick to his stomach, just as has happened to me several times in life—and the first time was when I learned that Laban, at Shinar beyond the river Prath, had slaughtered his own firstborn son as an offering and buried him in a pot in the foundation of his house to protect it. But do you suppose it brought him blessing? No—ill luck, adversity, and standstill, and had I not come and spread a little life in his house and business, everything would have been deadlocked in misery and he would never again have been fruitful by his wife Adina. And yet Laban would not have placed his little son in the wall had that not brought blessing to his ancestors in times past."

"Just as you say," Joseph replied, having clasped his hands behind his neck, "and you've made it clear to me how it came about. Laban acted as outworn custom demanded and so made grave errors. For the Lord abhors what is outworn, and wants to move us beyond it as He Himself has done, for He casts it out and curses it. That is why if Laban had understood the Lord and the times, he would have slaughtered a goat kid instead of his little boy and have painted his threshold and doorposts with its blood, and it would have been acceptable and its smoke would have risen straight toward heaven."

"Just as you say yet again," Jacob responded, "and have preceded me in my thoughts and taken the words from my mouth. For the Destroyer lusts not only after our beasts, but after the blood of men as well, and it is not just in regard to our flocks that we assuage his thirst both with the blood of the animal on our doorposts and the sacrificial meal that we observe by eating all of it in haste at night, so that nothing is left of the roast come morning. For when one considers it, what sort of roast is this, and does the lamb we slaughter atone only for the flocks? What would we slaughter and eat if we were as foolish as Laban? And what was slaughtered and eaten in filthy times past? Do we in fact know what we do in celebration when we eat, and if we were to ponder it, would we not find the bottom upended and now at the top, so that we would vomit?"

"Let us celebrate and eat," Joseph said in a giddy high voice, rocking in his clasped hands. "Rites and roast are to our taste, and if they are an extrication, then let us happily extricate ourselves from that filth by understanding the Lord and the times. Look, there is a tree," he cried, pointing with an outstretched hand to the tent's interior, as if the tree of which he spoke were visible there, "splendid in trunk and crown, planted by our forefathers for the enjoyment of those who came after. The treetop sparkles, swaying in the wind, for its roots are stuck in the stone and dust of earth's realm, deep in its darkness. And does the merry treetop likewise know much about those murky roots? No, but rather it has moved beyond them with the Lord, rocking in the wind and paying them no heed. And so it is, to my mind, with custom and filth; and that we may enjoy the taste of our pious rites, we will let what lies far below remain nicely far below."

"A lovely, lovely parable," Jacob said, nodding his head and stroking his beard by placing his palms to both sides and letting them glide down over it, "a witty and pleasant invention! But that does not put an end to our need to ponder or to the concerns and restlessness that were Abram's portion and are ours as well for ever and ever, so that we may extricate ourselves from the things that the Lord wishes to move us beyond and is perhaps already beyond Himself—that is our concern. So tell me: Who is the Destroyer, and what is his passing over? Is not the moon full on the night of the feast, beautiful there in the pass at its northernmost point and zenith in its path, the very point where it turns in its fullness? But the northern point is Nergal's, the murderer; the night belongs to him. Sin rules over night for him, Sin is Nergal at this feast, and the Destroyer who passes over and whom we appease, he is the Red One."

"Evidently," Joseph said. "We scarcely think of it, but so he is nonetheless."

"That is the uneasiness," Jacob continued, "that distracted me from the game. For those are the stars that determine the feast, the moon and the Red One, which enter into an exchange on this night, the latter taking the place of the former. But should we then blow kisses to the stars and celebrate their stories? Ought we not be troubled about the Lord and the times, whether we still understand them and are not sinning against both by adhering out of lazy habit to some filthiness that they would have us move beyond? I am seriously considering whether it may not be my task to step beneath the oracle tree and call the people together for them to hear my concerns and listen to my doubts concerning the Feast of Pesach."

"My dear papa is all too punctilious in his soul," Joseph said, bending forward and placing his hand on the old man's, where it lay beside the game board displaying his son's defeat, "and one must plead with him not to be overhasty and led to disruption. If the child may regard himself as having been asked, then he counsels that the feast be spared, that it not be zealously assailed because of its past stories, which over time may perhaps be replaced by some other, which you might then tell during the eating of the roast—the sparing of Isaak, for instance, which would be very fitting. Or let us simply wait until such time as God may glorify Himself in some great act of deliverance and mercy, the story of which we will then make the basis of our feast, singing songs of jubilation. Has the foolish lad spoken comforting words?"

"Words of balsam," Jacob replied. "Very clever and consoling, which together are what I mean by balsam. For you spoke for both the custom and the future, much to your honor. And you argued for a waiting that is part of the journey at the same time, and my soul smiles upon you, Joseph-el, sprout from the tenderest stem. Let me kiss you."

And reaching across the board, he took Joseph's beautiful head between his hands and kissed him, profoundly happy to have him as his own.

"If I only knew," Joseph said, "where my cleverness, my poor sagacity, comes from at this hour in response to my lord's wisdom in conversation. You said your thoughts were distracted during the game, but to be frank, mine were no less so. They kept wandering off from the stones in one direction, and only the Elohim know how I managed to hold on for so long."

"And in what direction, my child, did your thoughts go?"

"Ah," the young lad responded, "you can easily guess. A word has been itching in my ear day and night, something my dear papa recently said to me beside the well. It has robbed me of my rest, until curiosity plagues me wherever I go, for it was a word of promise."

"What did I say, and what promise did I give you?"

"Oh, oh, you know it well! I can tell by looking at you that you know. You intended, you said—well? 'I intend,' you said, 'to give you something—that will make your heart rejoice—and that will become you.' That was it, word for word. It has remained with me only too precisely, and it continually itches in my ear. What might my dear papa have meant by his promise?"

Jacob blushed and Joseph saw it. It was a flush of soft pink that rose in the old man's delicate gaunt cheeks, and his eyes were clouded with tender confusion.

"How's that? It was nothing," he said defensively. "The child is worrying for no reason. It was merely said to no purpose, without any firm meaning or intent. Do I not give you this and that whenever my heart prompts me? Well then, it was meant only in the sense that I would give you some pretty thing on some fitting occasion . . ."

"That's not it, not it!" Joseph cried, leaping up and embracing his father. "This wise and good man here says nothing without purpose—that would indeed be new. As if I could not tell clearly and plainly as he said it that it was not an empty phrase, that he had his eye on one definite and lovely thing, not just anything—something special and splendid, and intended it for me. But you did not just think of it for me, but told me so and promised. Am I not to know what is mine and what awaits me? Do you believe I could find rest and leave you in peace so long as I do not know?"

"How you prod and press me," the old man said in his torment. "Do not shake me. And take your hands from my earlobes, so that it may not look as if you were knocking me about. Know—you want to know. I shall tell you and admit that I had one thing in mind, and not just this or that. Hear then, and take your seat upon the ground. Do you know of Rachel's *ketônet passîm*?"

"A garment of Mami's? A festal robe perhaps? Ah, I understand, you want to take her dress and make for me a . . ."

"Listen, Jehosiph! You understand nothing. So let me instruct you. When I had served seven years for Rachel and the day approached that I was to receive her in the Lord, Laban said to me: 'I shall give her a veil, so that the bride may veil herself, consecrating and sanctifying herself for Nana. Some time ago,' he said, 'I bought this head covering from a traveler and have kept it in a chest, for it is precious. It is said to have belonged long ago to the daughter of a king, to have been the virginal garment of a prince's child, which is quite believable, so artfully is it embroidered all over with all sorts of symbols of idols. And she shall wrap her head in it and be like one of the *enitu*, like a heavenly bride in the bedchamber of the tower Etemenanki.' These or similar words are what that devil said to me. And he did not lie in speaking them, for Rachel received the garment, and in it she was splendid beyond compare as we sat at the wedding feast and I kissed the image of Ishtar. But when I presented the flower to the bride, I lifted the veil that I might see her with seeing hands. It was Leah, whom that devil had cunningly let into the bedchamber, so that I was happy only in my intent, but not in truth—and what man's head would not grow muddled when he loses his way in there, which is why I shall pass over it. But I was prudent even in my presumed happiness, folding the holy garment and laying it on the chair that stood there. And I said these words to my bride: 'We shall want to bequeath it down through the generations, and among all those countless numbers let those who are specially loved wear it.'"

"Did Mami wear this cloth when her hour came as well?"

"It is not a cloth, it is a garment of splendor. It is a piece to be worn as one chooses, of ankle length, with sleeves that a person may deal with according to taste and beauty. Mami? She wore it and kept it. She faithfully packed and unpacked it when we departed and broke the dusty bars and duped Laban, that devil. It always accompanied us, and just as Laban carefully preserved it for a long time in his chest, so have we as well."

Joseph's eyes darted about the tent and among the chests. "Is it nearby?" he asked.

"Not all too distant."

"And my Lord wishes to give it to me?"

"I have intended it for the child."

"So you have said and promised!"

"But for later, not at present!" Jacob cried out in his uneasiness. "Be reasonable, child, and be content for now in the promise. Behold, things are in the balance, and the Lord has not yet decided in that regard within my heart. Your brother Ruben came to ruin, and I was forced to strip him of the title of firstborn. Is it now your turn, that I should robe you in it, giving you the *ketônet*? One could answer: No, for after Re'uben came Judah, and Levi and Shimeon appeared. One could answer: Yes, for since Leah's firstborn fell and was cursed, Rachel's firstborn now follows. It is debatable and as yet unclear; we must wait and look for the sign that clarifies it. But if I were to robe you with it, your brothers might interpret it wrongly, in the sense of a blessing and election, and in their fervor rise up against you and me."

"Against you?" Joseph asked in greatest amazement. "I almost think I no longer trust my own ears. Are you not their father and lord? If they grumble, can you not rise up and with incensed words say: 'I show favor to whom I show favor and mercy to whom I show mercy. Who are you to interfere with me? Sooner than any of you, I will array him in this robe and in his mother's *ketônet passîm*.' I do trust my ears, by the by; they are young and keen. That is, when my dear papa speaks, I prick them to their finest and sharpest. Did you once say to your bride: 'Among those countless numbers, let the firstborn wear the veil?' No, but what? But what? But what? Whom did you say should wear it?"

"Enough, you fiend! Begone and do not fawn upon me till your folly spreads to me."

"Dear papa, I want to see it!"

"See it? Seeing is not having. But seeing is wanting to have. Be reasonable!"

"Am I not to see what is mine and promised to me? Let us do

this: I shall crouch fettered here, and will not budge from the spot. But you will go and show me the festal robe and hold it out in front of you, the way the merchant under the arch in Hebron shows his wares to the buyer and lets the fabric drape down before greedy eyes. But the man is poor and cannot buy it. Then the merchant hides it away again."

"So let it be in the Lord's name," Jacob said. "Although to someone who might see us it might look as if you were knocking me about. Stay where you are sitting! Sit upon one leg, your hands at your back. You shall see what may one day be yours, under the right circumstances."

"What is already mine," Joseph called after him. "But that I simply do not yet have."

He rubbed his eyes with his knuckles, making ready to look. Jacob went to the vaulted chest, undid its bolts, and clapped the lid back. He took out several items for warmth that lay on top and somewhat deeper—coats and blankets, aprons, head scarves, shirts—and let them drop still folded to the floor. He found the veil where he knew it would be, picked it up and, turning around, spread it out and let it unfold.

The lad marveled. He sucked air between his open, smiling lips. The metallic embroidery glistened in the lamplight. As the old man held it between restless arms, flashes of silver and gold merged at times with the quieter colors—with the purple, the white, olive, pink, and black of symbols and images of stars, doves, trees, gods, angels, human beings, and animals set in the bluish haze of the fabric.

"Good heavenly lights!" Joseph exclaimed. "How beautiful it is! My dear merchant father, what are you showing your client here beneath your arch? That is Gilgamesh throttling a lion in one arm—I recognize him even at a distance. And there I can see someone battling a griffin and swinging a club. Wait, wait. Oh Sabaoth, what beasts! There are the paramours of the goddess—horse, bat, wolf, and colorful bird! Let me see—do let me see! I don't recognize it, can't make it out. The child's poor eyes are burning from looking across the distance separating us. Is that the pair of scorpion men with stinging tails? I'm not certain, but it appears to be so, even if my eyes, as might be expected, are tearing. Wait, merchant, I shall slide a little closer on one leg, but with hands at my back. Oh, Elohim, it grows more beautiful from closer up, and it all becomes clearer. What are those bearded spirits doing beside the tree? They're impregnating it . . . and what is written there? 'I have—removed—my garment, shall I—put it on again?' Wonderful! And always Nana, with her dove, sun, and moon. . . . I must get to my feet. I must stand up, merchant, for I can't see the top—that date tree, from where a goddess offers food and drink with outstretched arms. Might I touch it as well? It costs me nothing, I would hope, to hold it tenderly in my hand, testing how light or heavy it is, weighing the mixture to see if it's heavy or light. . . . Merchant, I am poor, I cannot buy. Merchant, give it to me. You have so many wares—let me have the veil. Lend it to me, be so good as to let me show it to people in honor of your booth beneath the arch. No? Definitely not? Or are you wavering perhaps? Are you wavering just the least bit and, despite all your severity, wishing again that I might wear it? No, I am mistaken, you waver only from having to hold it out and spread it wide. You've spent far too much effort on me. . . . Give it here. How does one wear it, how does one wrap it? Like this? And like this? And perhaps this, too? How do you like it? Am I a shepherd-bird in my robe of many colors? Mami's veiled garment—how does it suit her son?"

He looked like a god, of course. There had been every reason to expect the effect, and his secret wish to produce it did not strengthen Jacob's attempt to resist. No sooner had Joseph finessed the garment out of the old man's hands and into his own (using methods whose wiles and charms one had best calmly acknowledge), than—by just three or four tugs and tosses of such assurance that they proved his natural talent for dressing himself—it suited his person in an easy and becoming way, covering his head, wrapping around the shoulders, flowing down over his young figure in folds that sparkled with silver doves and glowing embroidery, and making him look taller than he was. Taller? If only that had been the whole of it! But the splendid veil so perfectly matched his face that it would have proved difficult to offer any critically sober argument to counter his popular fame. It made him so handsome and beautiful that it was almost eerie, indeed bordered on the divine. The worst part was that his resemblance to his mother—the forehead, the eyebrows, the contours of the mouth, the eyes—had never been so patently evident before as it was thanks to this attire—and was so evident to Jacob's eyes that they welled with tears, for he could believe only that he beheld Rachel there before him in Laban's hall on the day of fulfillment.

The mother goddess stood before him in this smiling lad, and asked, "I have put on my garment—shall I remove it again?"

"No, keep it, keep it!" his father said. And while the god leapt to escape, he lifted up his brow and hands, his lips moving in prayer.

The Fleet-Footed Runner

What a vast uproar there was. Benjamin was the first person to whom Joseph showed himself in his robe of colors. But Benjamin was not alone, he was with the concubines, where Joseph in all his finery found him. He entered the tent and said, "Greetings, I just chanced to stop by. Women, is my little brother here? Why look, there you are, Ben, my best greetings. I merely wanted to see how you all are. What are you doing, combing flax? And Turturra is helping as best he can? Does anyone know where old Eliezer might be?"

Turturra (which meant "little one"—Joseph sometimes called Benjamin by this Babylonian nickname) had already emitted drawn-out cries of wonder. Bilhah and Zilpah joined in. Joseph was wearing the robe very casually, gathered somewhat and tucked into the belt of his shirt.

"What's all this crowing?" he said. "All three of you are making eyes like cartwheels. Oh, I see: you mean my new outfit, Mami's ketônet veil. Well, yes, I'll be wearing it sometimes now. Yizrael gave it to me, bequeathed it to me, just a few minutes ago."

"Joseph-el, sweet lord, son of the true wife!" Zilpah cried. "Did Jacob bequeath you the colorful veil in which he first received Leah, my mistress? How justly and wisely done, for it suits you so well that it melts the heart and one can't imagine anyone else ever wearing it. One of those now distant, for instance, a son of Leah, from whose face Jacob lifted it that first time? Or my Gad or Asher, that I bore upon Leah's lap? The mere thought leaves one with only a mocking and wistful smile."

"Josephyah! Fairest of all!" Bilhah cried. "Nothing compares with how you look in it! One is tempted to prostrate oneself at the mere sight, especially if one is only a handmaid like me, though to be sure I was the favorite maid, like a sister, to Rachel, your mother, and by the power of Jacob bore for her Dan and Naphtali, your older brothers. They, too, will fall to their knees, or at least come very close to it, when they see this boy in their mother's festal robes. But do make great haste to show them, for they suspect nothing, thinking neither good nor evil, all unaware that their lord has chosen you. You should also travel across country and show yourself to Leah's six red-eyed sons, so that you may hear their cries of jubilation and let their hosannas fill your ear."

It seems almost implausible, but Joseph did not sense the thickly spread bitterness and cunning in the women's words. His sense of fulfillment, his childlike but nonetheless reprehensibly blissful self-confidence left him deaf and unreceptive to any warnings. He took pleasure in the sweetness of their words, convinced he deserved nothing but sweetness and incapable of making the least effort to probe any deeper. That was the reprehensible part! An indifference to, an ignorance of other people's inner lives reveals a fully skewed relationship to reality and gives birth to delusion. Since the days of Adam and Eve, when one first became two, no one has ever been able to live without wanting to put himself in his neighbor's place and to explore someone else's true situation by attempting to see it through his eyes. Imagination and the art of surmising the emotional life of others—that is, empathy—is not merely praiseworthy; to the extent that it bursts the ego's limitations, it is also an indispensable means of self-preservation. But Joseph knew nothing of such precepts. His blissful self-confidence was, despite all unambiguous signs to the contrary, a kind of self-pampering that told him everyone loved him more than they loved themselves and he therefore need not take them into consideration. To pardon such thoughtlessness for the sake of his beautiful eyes would be to reveal a great weakness.

It was somewhat different with Benjamin. Here, for once, insouciance was not amiss when the boy cried, "Jehosiph, heavenly brother! It's not like being awake, but like a dream, and our lord has cast a splendid garment over you, into which every sort of light is woven and arrayed you in a coat full of pride and glory. Ah, your little brother is enchanted! Don't yet go to Bilhah's sons, and leave Zilpah's sons unaware for a time. Stay here with your nearest brother so I can admire you the more and feast my eyes to the full."

And Joseph could, to be sure, take that at face value—it was meant no differently. Yet there was also a warning that Joseph might have gleaned from those candid words—for it would be a grave error for us not to hear in them both an astute anxiety about the beautiful lad's meeting his brothers and the wish to delay that meeting for a while at least. Moreover, Joseph possessed, if not enough insight, then at least enough instinct not to make an appearance before the handmaids' children right off, not to visit them in his garment straightaway. That day—with the exception of a few menials, who spotted him walking about and did not fail to respond with flattery, blown kisses, and benedictions—the only other person allowed to see him was old Eliezer, who fell into a protracted nodding that could have meant approval or merely a general contemplation of fate, but who then took on a most divinely inexpressive air and began losing himself in the so-called memories that the veiled garment called up in him. How, for example, "he," Eliezer, had once been the wooer who led Rebekah out of the netherworld of Haran, and how upon their arrival in the upper world, as they approached her future husband, she had taken a veil and covered herself. And why was that? So that Isaak might know her. For how could he have known her upon lifting her veil, if she had not veiled herself? "My child," he said—with a face so immobile it looked as if you could remove it and might find another beneath—"Yizrael has given you a great thing, for life and death are in this veil, but death is in life and life in death, and the initiate is he who knows this. The sister motherwife had to remove her veil and appear naked in death at the seventh door of hell; but in returning to the light, she veiled herself again, in token of life. Behold the seed grain: if it sinks to the earth, it dies, so that the harvest may grow. For very like the ear of grain is the sickle, which grows as young life in the black moon and which is death and castrates the father to establish a new dominion over the world, and from the sickle's harvest rolls the seed corn of death and life. And so within the veil there is life after nakedness in death, just as within it there is knowing and death, for, yet again, there is conception and life in knowing. The father has granted a great thing, light and life, for he has veiled you in the veil that your mother had to lay aside in death. Therefore take care of it, child, that no one rip it from you, lest death know you!"

"My thanks, Eliezer," Joseph replied. "Many thanks, wise steward, who defeated kings at Abram's side and for whom the earth leapt up. How impressively you jumble it all together in words of veils, sickles, and seed grain—and rightly so, for these things are bound up together and are one in God, whereas for us they are embroidered on the veil of diversity. But as for this lad, he will now take off his robe and cover himself with it upon his couch, so that he may slumber beneath it like the earth beneath the world's veil of stars."

Which he then did. And that is how they found him, sleeping under the veil—the handmaids' sons, that is, after having been informed by their mothers—when they entered the tent they shared with him. At first all four stood beside his bed—Dan, Naphtali, Gad, and Asher—and then one of them (it was sweet-toothed Asher, the youngest, barely turned twenty-two) held a lamp over him and illumined his sleeping face for the others, along with the coat of many colors covering him.

"There you have it, just look!" he said. "No different from what the women said, nor one word too many, when they informed us that this dandy appeared before them in his mother's *ketônet passîm*. He has spread it out and is sleeping the sleep of the just, with a sanctimonious look on his face. Can there be any doubt now? Father has given it to him—poor man, he wheedled it out of him with honeyed words. Fie on him! We are all equally enraged by this abomination, and Asher now takes our rage in his mouth and spits it out at this sleeping nuisance, so that he may at least have bad dreams."

He very much loved being of one mind and heart with others, Asher did, and to provide fervent confirmation of such unity with speeches matching the general opinion, so that in the glow of his words they felt bound up together and the steam of common satisfaction rose from their rage—it was all of a piece with Asher's love of good food, with his moist eyes and lips. And he went on to say, "So I cut pieces of living flesh out of rams and sheep, and ate them—did I? That's what he told our poor father, that pious, credulous man, and for that Jacob has bequeathed him the *ketônet* in payment for his lies. But the fact is, he has gulled the old man into believing some such thing about each of us, and the veil under which he lies is recompense for his falsehoods and the evil repute into which he has brought us all. Let us step closer and unite forces, brothers, embrace one another in our injury, and let me speak the curse that will bring some relief to us all—you puppy!"

He had wanted to say "you dog," but in the last moment, for

Jacob's sake, he took fright and hastily robbed the animal of some
years.

"True," said Dan (who at twenty-seven, the same age as Leah's
Shimeon, sported a goatee but no mustache and a tightly fitting, embroidered shirt, and whose piercing eyes were set close together at
the top of his hooked nose), "true, I may be called a serpent and an
adder, because I am held to be spiteful. But what is that compared to
what lies sleeping here? This is a monster! It acts as if it were a dear
sweet boy, but in reality it is a dragon. Damn his deceptive looks,
that make people gape and ogle, and enthrall our father! I wish I
knew the curse to force him to show his true ugly face!"

Strapping Gaddiel, one year older than Asher, had a face full of
rough honesty. His cone-shaped cap and short belted shirt, from
which armored scales dangled and to which he had sewn breastplates, lent him a martial air. His red and sinewy arms were thrust
out from the short sleeves and ended in stubby, equally sinewy
hands. He said, "I suggest, Asher, that you mind your lamp, so that
a boiling drop of oil may not accidentally land on him and he be
awakened by the pain. For if he wakes up, I shall whack him with all
straightforwardness, that is certain. One doesn't whack a sleeping
man—I don't know where that is written, but it's simply not done.
But if he wakes up, he shall have my hand in his mug at the same moment, enough to make his cheeks swell as if he had a dumpling in his
mouth, for a good nine days starting tomorrow—as surely as my
name is Gad. For the sight of him makes me furious and foul-
minded—as does the sight of that coat he's sleeping under and that
he impudently duped father out of. I am no coward, but I am unsure
what it is rumbling in the pit of my stomach, as a warning from my
bowels. Here we stand, brothers, and there lies the rascal, the fop,
the dandy, the coxcomb, the whippersnapper, the greenhorn, the
turner of every head, and he has the coat. Are we all to bow down
before him perhaps? I can't rid myself of those words 'bow down,'
as if some damnable pack were persistently whispering them in my
ear. That's why my hand itches to whack him—it would be just the
thing, and the loathing in my belly would be quelled."

Outspoken Gad expressed far deeper feelings than Asher (despite his need to consolidate emotions and bundle them into words)
had tried to touch, since the latter's sole concern was to find reasonable terms for what was simplest and most easily grasped so as to

garner affection and warming unity. Gad had tried harder. He wrestled to suggest a worrisome, tormenting something beneath their simple anger and envy, to put a name to dark memories, anxieties, threats, to a phantom of relationships that was haunted by concepts like "firstborn," "deception," "substitution," "world dominion," and "fraternal servitude" and that odiously engendered—though recognizable neither as past or future, as nightmare or prediction—the term "bow down": "They shall bow down before you."

The others felt strongly, and strangely, attracted to Gad's words. Especially Naphtali—a tall, slightly stooped man, who had been shifting from one foot to the other for some time now—felt them in the marrow of every bone, intensifying to its limits his urge to jump up and run. His instinct to play messenger, his need to report and communicate had been violently aroused from the start—it tugged at his calves till they twitched. Naphtali was obsessed with the notion of space and its divisive nature. He regarded it as his most intimate enemy and himself as the authorized agent for overcoming it—that is, for removing the differences in men's knowledge that distance created. When something happened at the spot where he was, in his mind he immediately joined it to some faraway place where no one knew of it, which in his eyes was an intolerable, oblivious, vegetative state that he felt compelled to correct by the propulsion of his legs and the nimbleness of his tongue, in order that, if possible, he then might also bring back some still disgracefully unknown bit of news from there to here and thus equalize the sum of human knowledge. In this case, then, it was the locale of his distant brothers that his thoughts—his before any of the others'—had speedily connected with his present location. Thanks to the intolerable consequences of space, they as yet knew nothing, but they had to know, posthaste. In his soul, Naphtali was already running.

"Listen, brothers, hearken, children and friends," he prattled away in his soft, hasty voice. "Here we stand staring at what has happened, for we are at the very spot. Yet at the same moment our brothers sit red-eyed around the fire in the valley of Shechem discussing this and that, but not how Jacob has raised up Joseph's head, much to their disgrace, for they have no way of surmising it, and however loud the cry of that disgrace, theirs and ours, they cannot hear it. But is it fair that we should be content with our advantage, saying, 'They are distant, and thus foolish, for distance is foolish, and that is that'? No, rather they must be told, so that it is the same there as here and they no longer live as if it were not. Send me, send me! I shall travel across country and bring them tidings to lighten their darkness and to make them shout in a loud voice. But on my return I shall also report to you what they shouted."

They agreed with him. Their red-eyed brothers must learn of this. It concerned them almost more than it did these four. Naphtali knew the road; but they would tell their father urgent business had sent his fleet-footed son across country. In his impatience he barely slept and saddled his ass before dawn. When Joseph awoke beneath his cloak of worlds, Naphtali was well on his way, and knowledge was advancing toward the faraway brothers. Nine days later, on the very day of the full moon, there they were, along with the messenger: Ruben, Shimeon, Levi, Judah, Issakhar and Zebulun—all looking about them, scowling and searching. Shimeon and Levi, who were called "the twins" although they were a year apart, had, so Naphtali assured the others, bellowed like bulls at the news.

Ruben Is Appalled

Joseph had sufficient reason and understanding not to approach them in his coat right off, though he very much wanted to. What had enabled him to leave the veil aside for the moment and welcome them in his everyday shirt was a glimmer of doubt—as to whether they really did love him so much more than they loved themselves for them to feel anything but pure joy at the sight of how his head had been raised up.

"Greetings, dear sons of Leah, strong brothers!" he said. "Welcome to our father's house. Let me kiss at least a few of you."

And he walked around among them and kissed three or four on the shoulder, though they stood stiff as poles and did not touch him. Only Re'uben—a large, heavy man of twenty-nine at the time, supported on powerful legs wrapped in leather straps and wearing an apron of pelts, whose close-shaven, flushed, and muscular face was blunt in profile and wore a gruff, uneasy, but dignified expression under a low brow darkened by dangling locks of black hair—only he, without so much as a wince, lifted a heavy hand when he felt

Joseph's lips on his shoulder and let it pass over his brother's head with one light and, as it were, furtive stroke.

Jehuda, three years younger than Ruben but just as tall, though somewhat stooped and marked by traces of suffering about the nostrils and lips, wore a coat that allowed him to keep his hands hidden. He had on a close-fitting cap, from beneath which burst a mane of thick hair of the same reddish brown as his goatee and a narrow mustache slanting down beside his red, fleshy lips. Those lips betrayed sensuality, but the finely chiseled, arched nose that flattened as it descended to them expressed a wary intellect, and melancholy lay in heavy-lidded eyes bulging brightly like a stag's. At the time Judah, like several of his brothers and half brothers, had already taken a wife in marriage. Ruben, for instance, had wooed a maid from the countryside and with her had produced several children for Abraham's God—for example, two boys, Hanoch and Pallu, whom Jacob would occasionally dandle on his knee. As part of the booty of Shechem, Shimeon had carried off a merchant's daughter named Bunah and made her his own. Levi had married a maiden who believed in Yahu and was held to be a granddaughter of Eber; Naphtali had married a young wife whose origins Jacob rather ingeniously traced to Nahor, a brother of the ancient Chaldean; and Dan had simply chosen a Moabite woman. It had been impossible to arrange for every match to be religiously unobjectionable; and as for Judah, his father had to be happy that he had found in marriage some sort of mollifying stability in regards to matters of the flesh, for from youth onward his sexual life had been marked by confusion and torment. He stood on cheerless, strained terms with Ashtaroth, suffered beneath the lash with which she pursued him, submitting to it without loving her—which rent his soul and left him at odds with himself. His association with the consecrated temple whores of Ishtar brought him into proximity with the sphere of Baal and its folly and abominations, with the sphere of shameless Canaan; and no one, not even Jacob his father, could have fretted worse over this than Jehuda himself, who not only was a pious man, longing for godly and reasonable purity and deeply despising Sheol and all the follies and mysteries with which the nations defiled themselves, but who also believed he had reason to think well of himself, for after Ruben had stumbled and now that the so-called twins could likewise regard themselves as cursed after the mayhem at Shechem, there was good cause to think that Judah, the fourth son, stood in line to be the bearer of blessing and promise, though nothing of the sort was ever said among the brothers and any such claim was evidenced only in the form of shared ill will toward the son of Rachel.

It was through one of his shepherds, who was named Hirah and came from the village of Adullam, that Judah became acquainted with a man named Shuah, whose daughter pleased him, and he took her as his wife with Jacob's approval. He instructed the sons that she gave him—two, thus far—in the understanding of God. But they took after their mother, much as Ismael had taken after Hagar, and not their father. Or at least that is how Judah saw it as a way of explaining to himself why they were nasty, children of Canaan, brats of Baal, scoundrels of Sheol, fools of Molech—though perhaps his grief came not solely from Shuah's daughter. She had now promised him yet a third child, and he was afraid of how it would turn out.

And so there was sadness in Judah's eyes, but it did not make his mood any kindlier or lead him furtively to ruffle Joseph's hair as Ruben had. He had said, "So this is how you come out to us, scribe? Does one approach in a common ink-stained shirt to greet one's elders, though they have been gone so long and have just returned? Do you care so little to please us, seeing as usually your greatest concern is to bewitch people into smiles? It is said you have in your chest garments so precious they make people blink, robes worthy of a prince's child. Why do you offend us by being so niggardly with them in receiving us?"

Scarred, fire burning in their eyes, oiled chests covered in tattoos—Shimeon and Levi leaned on their massive cudgels and broke into a brief bellow of laughter. "Since when do seductresses stroll about without their veils?" one shouted. "And since when do temple whores not cover their eyes?" the other chimed in—oblivious to Judah's wince.

"Ah, you mean my robe with pictures?" Joseph asked. "Did our brother Naphtali tell you en route of the mercy that Jacob has shown to me? Be so kind as to forgive me," he said, and with his arms crossed made a charming humble bow. "It is hard to do right, whether in doing or leaving undone, and a man falls into sin whatever he does. Foolishly I thought, 'Should I give myself airs before my lords? No, but I will approach them without pomp, so that they may take no offense at my arrogance, but love me instead.' And look, I have done a stupid thing. I should have adorned myself to greet you—I understand. But believe me, when we gather to eat the roast come evening, when you, too, have washed and put on your festal garments, I shall sit at Jacob's right hand in the *ketônet,* and you will see our father's son in all his glory. Would you have me promise it?"

And the savage twins again broke into bellowing laughter. The others bored angrily into his eyes, trying to distinguish between the naiveté and impudence in his words, which proved very difficult.

"A golden promise!" exclaimed Zebulun, the youngest, who did his best to emulate a Phoenician, with a close-cropped round beard, a mop of short locks, a gaudily patterned tunic that covered only one shoulder and was cut under the other arm to reveal his shirt—for his heart was set on the sea, on harbors, and he would rather not have been a shepherd. "A tasty promise. A promise like a sacrificial cake of fine wheat and strained honey, I must say. Do you know I would enjoy cramming it down your throat till you choked on it?"

"Come, come, Zebulun, what a coarse joke!" Joseph replied, lowering his gaze and smiling awkwardly. "Did you get it from pitch-stained galley slaves at Ashkelon or Gaza?"

"He called my brother Zebulun a pitch-stained galley slave!" cried Issakhar, a long-limbed, heavy-boned man of twenty-one, whom they called the "raw-boned ass." "Ruben, you heard him, and you must stop his mouth for him, if not with your fist, as I would like, then with words of rebuke that he will remember!"

"What you say is not exact, Issakhar," Ruben replied in a high and gentle voice, the kind sometimes found in men of powerful build, and he turned his head away. "He did not call him that, but rather asked if he had the phrase from such men. That was impudent enough."

"It was my understanding that he wanted to choke me with a sacrificial cake," Joseph replied, "which would be both blasphemous and very unfriendly. But if he did not say and mean it, then I most certainly did not tease him, either, I swear."

"Then let us go one way and the other," Re'uben concluded, "so that our being together does not lead to further taunts and misunderstandings."

They separated, ten and one. But Ruben followed after the

solitary lad and called him by name. They stood off to themselves, Ruben towering over him on leather-strapped legs like columns and Joseph gazing with polite attention up into that muscular face, whose uneasy dignity was marked by an awareness of both strength and fallibility. Ruben's eyes with their inflamed lids were close to him now. His gaze seemed to lose itself as it studied Joseph's face, or actually stopped short of it and turned back upon itself, and all the while his powerful right hand kneaded gently at his brother's shoulder, a habit he had when speaking to him with whom he now spoke.

"The garment is in your keeping, my boy?" he asked with his lips, scarcely opening his mouth.

"Yes, Ruben, my lord, I am caring for it," Joseph replied. "Israel gave it to me, for he was in high spirits after beating me at the game."

"His stones defeated yours?" Ruben asked. "You play deftly and shrewdly, for your mind has been well trained by Eliezer in all sorts of mental work, and that is to your favor in the game as well. Does he defeat you often?"

"Now and then," Joseph said, baring his teeth.

"When you want him to?"

"It doesn't depend on me alone," the lad replied evasively.

"Yes, that's how it's done," Ruben thought to himself, his gaze turning farther inward than before. "Such is the deceit of men who are blessed, that is their sort of deception. They must keep their lamp under a bushel to prevent its light from doing them harm, while others must lie about their own brightness just to stay even." He gazed at his half brother. "Rachel's child," he thought. "How charming he is! People do well to smile at him. He's the perfect height and bats those handsome and beautiful eyes up at me with veiled mockery, if I read them rightly, standing here before him like a tower in the pasture, much too tall and burly, with this oafish body of mine and all my veins almost bursting with energy, so that like a bull I forgot myself with Bilhah, not even noticing if anyone was watching. So he went and told Israel, in his innocent, cunning way, and I ended up on the ash heap. For he is wise as the serpent and gentle as the dove, as a man should be. Cunning in his innocence and innocent in his cunning, so that his innocence is dangerous and his cunning holy—the unmistakable sign of blessing, and there is nothing you can do to counter it even if you wanted to, but you don't, for God is there.

With a single blow I could strike him down for good and all; the energy that ravished Bilhah would work well for that, too, and the thief of my rights as the firstborn would feel that energy as a man, just as Bilhah did as a woman. But what good would it do me? Abel would lie slain, and I would be the man I do not wish to be—Cain, whom I don't understand. How can a man act against his own conviction, as Cain did, and with eyes wide open slay what is pleasing because he himself cannot please? I will not act against my conviction, I will be just and fair, something more agreeable to my soul. I will not compromise it. I am Re'uben, my veins full of energy, Leah's firstborn, Jacob's eldest, the head of the twelve. I will not cut a doting face for him and humble myself before his charm—patting his hair just now was foolish enough a mistake. I will not lay a hand on him, one way or the other. I stand before him like a tower, oafish for all I care, but in dignity."

With the muscles of his face drawn taut, he asked, "You coaxed the garment from him, did you?"

"He promised it to me recently," Joseph replied, "and when I reminded him he took it from the chest and gave it to me, saying, 'Keep it, keep it.'"

"So, you reminded him and begged for it. He gave it to you against his will, having been tempted by yours. Do you know that it goes against God to misuse the power one has been given over another, so that he agrees to do wrong and does what he will repent?"

"What power do I have over Jacob?"

"You lie even in asking. You have the power of Rachel over him."

"Then I did not steal it."

"Nor earn it."

"The Lord says, 'I show favor to whom I show favor.'"

"Oh, you are brazen!" Ruben said, drawing his thick eyebrows into a scowl and slowly shaking the lad back and forth by the shoulder. "It is rightly said of me that I am like gushing water and sin is not far from me. But recklessness, obstinate recklessness such as yours, that indeed is far from me. You brag of God, and yet you mock the heart there in your hand. Do you know the anxiety and distress you have caused the old man by coaxing this garment from him?"

"But, great Ruben, what sort of distress?"

"I know it well, how you can *lie* even as you *ask*. Does it give you great joy that a man is capable of that? He is distressed for you, who are his favorite not by merit, but as it pleases his heart, which is both weak and proud. He was blessed instead of Esau, his twin, but has he not had cares enough, with Rachel's dying but a little way from Ephron, with Dinah, his child—and with me, with what I did to him, since I can tell you are perfectly capable of reminding me of it?"

"Not so, strong Ruben. I was not even thinking of how you sported that day with Bilhah, so that in his ill humor father took you for a hippopotamus."

"Silence! How can you mention it when I expressly took the words from your mouth and spoke of it first? You are forever inventing new kinds of lies, saying, 'I was not even thinking of it,' so that you can speak of it in detail. Is that what you learn from reading stones, what you practice when studying temple wisdom with Eliezer? Your lips move, who knows how, and have been carved by the Creator like this and this, and your teeth sparkle in between. But what comes out is pure impudence. My boy, my boy, take heed!" he said, kneading at Joseph until he swayed back and forth on heels and toes. "Have I not rescued you ten times from the hands of your brothers, and ten times from the wrath of those who trampled Shechem for the sake of our ravished sister, each time they were about to thrash you for tattling on them to Father and lying about 'pieces of flesh from living rams' and still more such things—and now you go and swindle yourself the garment, because we are in far-off pastures, and shamelessly provoke fury against you, if not from ten, then at least from nine? Tell me who you are, and what is this arrogance that you set yourself off and walk apart from all others? Are you not afraid that your conceit will gather above you the cloud from which lightning comes? Do you have so little notion how to thank those who would be gracious to you that you put them in distress, like someone climbing up into rotten branches and mocking those standing below, who worriedly call up to him for fear the branch will crack beneath him and he will fall and spill out his bowels?"

"Set me down, Ruben, and listen! Believe me, I do know how to thank you for having spoken for me against our brothers' malice. I am also grateful to you for holding on to me, and for upending me, both at once. But now set me upon the soles of my feet, that I may speak! Good. There can be no coming to terms amid such shaking. But now that I am standing I wish to do so, and am certain that as a just man you will agree with me. I neither swindled the garment, nor stole it. Ever since Jacob promised it to me at the well, I knew it was his wish and intent to present it to me. But when I saw that, being a gentle soul, he was somewhat at odds with his own will, I held him to it and was able to make it easy for him to hand it to me—hand it, I say, not give, for it was mine before he gave it."

"And why yours?"

"You ask? I shall answer. From whom did Jacob first lift the veil, bequeathing it in that very hour?"

"It was Leah!"

"Yes, in reality. But in truth it was Rachel. Leah was merely clad in it, but the mistress of the garment was Rachel, and she kept it until she died but a little way from Ephron. But now that she is dead, where is she?"

"Where dust is her nourishment."

"Yes, in reality. But the truth is otherwise. Do you not know that death has the power to change the nature of things, and that Rachel lives for Jacob in a different nature?"

Ruben was taken aback.

"I and my mother are one," Joseph said. "Do you not know that Mami's robe is also her son's and that they wear it by turns, each in place of the other? Name my name, and you name hers. Name what is hers, and you name what is mine. And so, to whom does the veil belong?"

He had spoken from a thoroughly modest pose, simply standing there with eyes lowered. But afterward, after he had said his piece, he suddenly looked up, returning his brother's gaze with large and open eyes—not forcing himself upon him, not in a piercing attack, but rather simply submitting himself quietly and candidly to view, accepting in his own inscrutable, unfathomable way and without any rebuttal the alarmed stare of those blinking, inflamed Leah eyes.

The tower swayed. Hulking Ruben shuddered. What sort of words were these that the lad had used, what was he driving at, where did it all come from? Ruben had asked him about his arrogance—he regretted it now, for he had his answer. He had angrily demanded to know just who this lad was—if only he hadn't! For now he had been informed, but so ambiguously that chills ran down his spine, long as it was. Had those words taken their shape in the boy's mouth merely by chance? Had he been trying to allude to the divine, to appeal to it, to justify his subterfuge, or . . . And it was this "or" that stirred in Ruben the same eerie queasiness in the pit of his stomach that had been the source of their brother Gaddiel's cursing complaint beside Joseph's bed, except that for Ruben it was even stronger—both profound shock and admiration, both gentle, tender terror and amazement.

One must try to understand Ruben. He was not unique in this world in misjudging the importance of the question that asks who someone is, in whose footsteps he walks, on what past he bases his present, in order thereby to establish his real identity. Joseph had established his identity—in such a monstrously presumptuous way that it made Ruben dizzy. But this sorcery of words, bringing what lies above to the world below, this free and easy and doubtlessly genuine malleability by which language plays its confounding magic, made the footsteps in which his young brother walked shimmer brightly before Ruben's eyes. At that moment, he did not exactly consider Joseph a veiled twofold divinity of both sexes—we do not wish to go that far. Yet his love for him was not far from faith.

"Child, child," he said in that tender voice within a massive body, "spare your soul, spare our father, be sparing of your lamp. Place it under a bushel so that it may not light the way to ruin!" Then, lowering his head, he took three steps backward and only then did he turn away from Joseph.

But at the evening meal Joseph wore his festal robe, so that his brothers sat there like logs and Jacob was afraid.

The Sheaves

After these events and many more days, the season had come for cutting wheat in the valley of Hebron, for harvest and the time of cheerful sweat and rejoicing until the day of first fruits and the offering of leavened wheat bread from new flour, seven weeks after the full moon of spring. For the late rains had been abundant, but

shortly thereafter the windows of heaven were shut, the waters sub-
sided, and the land dried up. The triumphant sun, Marduk–Baal,
drunk from victory over the dripping Leviathan, established his
fiery reign in the heavens, hurling his golden spears into the blue;
and by the time of the turning from the second to the third month,
his dominion was already so scorching that there would have been
reason to fear for the sown grain had not a wind come up, whose
welcome approach Zebulun, Leah's sixth son, could scent in the
distance.

And he said, "My nose is pleasantly brushed by this wind, for it
brings moisture from afar and carries the soothing dew. As I always
say—behold, what good comes from the sea. A man should live beside the Great Green and near to Sidon, and travel the waves instead
of tending lambs—which gives me less joy. Riding the waves aboard
well-turned planks, one can reach people who have tails and shining
horns on their brows. And beyond them, those who have great ears
that can cover their entire bodies and others whose bodies are overgrown with grass—a man from the harbor at Chazzati told me so."

Naphtali agreed with him. It would be good to exchange news
with people covered with grass. Presumably neither they nor those
with tails or floppy ears knew anything of what was happening in
the world. The others dissented, wishing to know nothing of the sea,
even if it did offer dewy winds. It was a region of the underworld,
full of the monsters of chaos, and Zebulun might just as well revere
the desert. Particularly Shimeon and Levi, rough but pious men, advocated this viewpoint, although they, too, ultimately had little use
for the shepherd's life, pursued it only for the sake of chance conquest, and would have preferred more savage handiwork.

The labors of the harvest, which began with the cutting of the
barley, offered a welcome change, and they sweated with good cheer,
as men do in these weeks of reward, so that despite themselves even
their relationship to Joseph, who also helped sickle and bind, began
to relax and soften somewhat—until once again the incredible loose-
ness of his tongue ruined it all, pushing matters to their worst. Of all
that, in a moment. As for Jacob, he was less affected by the merry
mood the calendar induced in those around him and by the high
spirits of the harvesting farmers, in whose midst his family tended to
its own affairs. Indeed his attitude, which was the same every year,

had a certain dampening effect on things—without his ever even appearing in the field. That happened only rarely, although, to be sure, it was to occur once this year yet, the result, in fact, of a special request by Joseph, who had his reasons for making it. But in general Jacob showed no concern for sowing and mowing, but went about his bit of farming without casting it a glance, so to speak, simply out of prudence, not out of some inner partiality to it, inasmuch as his relationship to this realm was determined by just the opposite—that is, by indifference, indeed an aversion of the moon-shepherd to the red-faced tiller's drudgery of turning soil. Harvest resulted in real embarrassment, since, for his part, he profited from the fertility cult that, from one spring to the next, the children of the land dedicated to the Baals of the sun and the lovely women in their temples, but that was so foreign to his own soul. Sharing in such profits brought with it a certain shame that closed his lips when those bringing in the harvest erupted in hymns of thanksgiving.

And so now, after the barley, he ordered the wheat harvested for household use, and since every pair of arms was needed—even hired laborers had been brought in by Eliezer for these weeks—Joseph interrupted his studies with the old man so that he, too, special though he was, might work in the field from rosy dawn until evening, sweeping at clustered ears of grain with his sickle, gathering them up in his right hand, binding the sheaves for straw, and helping brothers and servants load them onto carts or hang them on asses that bore them to the threshing floor. It should be acknowledged that he did not regard this as theft of his time, but worked willingly and gladly and in all modesty—granted, a modesty that stood in gross contrast to certain revelations that concerned his inner life and in which he was basking at the time. It would have been easy, after all, for him to have got Jacob to release him from his drudgery in the field, but he never gave it a thought, in part because he took healthy pleasure in the work, and in part—indeed primarily—because it brought him closer to his brothers; and he took pride and joy in working together with them, hearing them call his name, lending them a hand as best he could. All that is literally true. Their common labor, which on a practical level improved their relationship, raised up his heart and made him happy. None of that is refuted by certain contradictions, which despite their destructive irrationality, could not negate the fact that he loved his brothers and, however unreasonable, indeed totally deluded it may sound, he so trusted in their love that he believed he could demand things of it—just a few things, for unfortunately, he did not think he was demanding much.

Work in the field exhausted him, and often he would take an occasional nap. He also napped one midday when all of Jacob's sons, except for Benjamin, had gathered to rest and eat in the shade of a brown awning stretched between crooked poles. They had broken bread and were chatting as they sat crouched on their heels, all of them clad just in aprons, their bodies reddened by the power of Baal, who blazed down from among white summer clouds, searing the half-harvested fields, where the patches of stubble that sickles had left amidst the suntanned host of grain were dotted with sheaves leaning up against one another and hemmed by low walls of stone rubble, beyond which other farmers had taken up their work. Rising at some distance was a hill that served as the threshing floor for Jacob's people. Laden asses were moving toward it, and up top stood men with pitchforks, spreading the stalks before oxen that trod the grain, threshing it.

And so Joseph, likewise in his work apron and with sunburned skin, lay asleep in the shade too, crouching there, head cradled on his arm. In all guilelessness he had asked Issakhar, the "raw-boned ass," who sat closest to him, to lend him one of his knees as a prop for his head. But Issakhar had asked if he might like his head scratched, too, and maybe he should keep the flies off—and told him to bed down wherever he liked, just not on him. Joseph responded with a child's laugh, as if at a good joke, and went to sleep without anything to raise up his head. That he found elsewhere, it turned out, but no one could tell by looking at him, especially since no one paid him any attention. Only Ruben cast a glance his way now and then. The sleeper was turned toward him—and his was not a calm face. The brow, the eyelids twitched, and the slack mouth moved as if to speak.

Meanwhile the brothers discussed advantages and disadvantages of an implement recently come into wide use for threshing—the threshing board, which was pulled by oxen while sharp stones set in its underside tore at the ears of grain. There was no question the method was faster. But several of them claimed that the winnowing afterward was more work than simply driving animals over the grain often and thoroughly enough. They also spoke of a threshing cart many farmers used, which moved on rollers fitted with iron plates. At this point Joseph awakened and sat up.

"I have had a dream," he said, looking around at his brothers and smiling in amazement.

They turned their heads, turned them away again, and went on talking.

"I have had a dream," he repeated, passing a hand across his brow and gazing into space, but still with a smile of confusion and happiness. "A vivid and wonderful dream!"

"That's your affair," Dan replied, briefly directing his piercing gaze at him. "If you must nap, you'd do better to do so without dreaming, for a sleep of dreams does not refresh."

"Don't you want to hear about my dream?" Joseph asked.

No one responded. Instead, one of them—it was Jehuda—resumed their discussion of agriculture in a tone that more or less contained an answer befitting such a question.

"It is necessary," he said in a cold, loud voice, "to keep the little iron plates very sharp, otherwise they don't cut, but simply smash, and the grain doesn't slip from the ear as it should. But you tell me if we can depend on people, hired people at that, to keep them sufficiently sharp. But if the wheels are too sharp then they cut the grain as well, and then the flour turns out . . ."

Joseph listened a while to this discussion that blatantly ignored him. At last he interrupted them and said, "Beg pardon, brothers, but I really would like to tell you the dream that I dreamt during my nap. I feel compelled to. It was very short, but so vivid and wonderful that I don't want to keep it to myself, but heartily wish for it be to be as real before your eyes as before mine, so that you may laugh in amusement and slap your thighs."

"Now listen here," Judah said again with a shake of his head. "What ails you that you want to vex us with your affairs, which we don't give a fig about? For we could care less about your innermost thoughts and the pap of your sleep—the stuff that climbs from your belly to your head after you eat. It's unseemly and is of no concern to us, so be silent!"

"But it does concern you!" Joseph cried eagerly. "It concerns all of you, for you are all in it, and me, too, and my dream is so worth the pondering and amazement of us all that you will bow your heads and think of almost nothing else for three days."

"Should he not recite it in a few words, with no further ado, so that we can hear it in brief?" Asher asked. Sweet-toothed people are always curious, too. But they were all curious and actually liked very much to be told stories, whether real or invented—the sagas, dreams, and songs from ancient times.

"Fine," Joseph said happily, "if you like I shall tell you my vision, it is worth telling, if only for the sake of interpreting it. For the dreamer should never interpret, but rather someone else. If any of you dream, I'd be glad to interpret the meaning, it costs me nothing, for if I ask the Lord, He provides it. But it's different with one's own dreams."

"Do you call that 'no further ado'?" Gad asked.

"So listen . . ." Joseph began. But Ruben tried to stop him at the last moment. He had not let the master of the veil out of his eye the whole time, and he did not think this boded any good.

"Joseph," he said, "I don't know your dream, for I was not lost in sleep with you, for you alone were there. But it seems to me it would be better that each be left with his own dreams and that you keep to yourself what you dreamt, so that we can go to work."

"We were at work," Joseph said, picking up on his words, "for I saw us, the sons of Jacob, all together out in the field, and we were harvesting wheat."

"Magnificent!" Naphtali cried. "The things you dream, eminently dreamable—let no one deny it. Miraculous, one must say—so remote, so wild and gaudy is your dream!"

"But it was not our field," Joseph continued, "but someone else's, a curiously strange field. And yet no one remarked on it. We went silently about our work and bound sheaves, after first cutting the grain."

"Well, that is a dream to set before the Lord!" Zebulun said. "A vision beyond compare! Were we supposed to bind them first and then cut the grain, you fool? Do we really have to hear this to the end?"

Some of them had already stood up with a shrug and were about to leave.

"Yes, hear it to the end!" Joseph cried with upraised hands. "For now comes the marvelous part. Each of us bound one sheaf of wheat, and there were twelve of us, for Benjamin, our youngest brother, was with us in the field and bound his little sheaf along with you in the circle."

"Enough rubbish!" Gad demanded. "How can it be 'with you in the circle'? What you mean to say is 'with us in the circle.'"

"No, not at all, Gaddiel, but rather just the opposite. For you eleven had formed the circle and were binding sheaves, but I stood in the middle binding my own sheaf."

He fell silent and looked into their faces. Every man of them had arched his eyebrows and, shaking his head, laid it back until his Adam's apple protruded. There was scoffing amazement, warning, and worry in those shaking heads and raised eyebrows. They waited.

"Now hear what happened and how wonderful my dream was," Joseph said again. "Since we had bound our sheaves, each his own, we left them and walked away as if we had nothing more to do, but said not a word. We had walked together about twenty paces, or forty, and behold, Ruben looked around and silently raised his hand to point back at the place where we had been binding. It was you, Ruben. Everyone stood and looked, shading his eyes. And behold: my sheaf is standing in the middle, straight up, but yours, gathered round it in a circle, bend low to it, bend low, bend low, but mine stands upright."

A long silent pause.

"Is that all?" Gad asked curtly, his low voice breaking the silence.

"Yes, then I awoke," Joseph replied, crestfallen. He was rather disappointed with his dream, which as he dreamt it—especially when Ruben silently pointed back at the sheaves acting all on their own—had about it something quite exceptional that both troubled and cheered him; but now, put into words, it looked comparatively meager, indeed foolish, and to Joseph's mind could not have had any effect on his audience whatever—a feeling reinforced by Gad's "Is that all?" He was embarrassed.

"What a this and a that," Dan said after another silent pause, in a choked voice, or more precisely, with only the first syllables anything more than a strangled whisper.

Joseph raised his head. He found new courage. It looked as if the dream, just as he had told it, had not entirely missed its effect on his brothers after all. "Is that all?" had been disheartening enough, but Dan's "this and that" was comforting and full of hope, for it meant "You don't say!" and "Quite a mouthful!"—meant "Damnation!," that sort of thing. He looked into their faces. They had all turned pale, with deep vertical creases between each pair of eyebrows, a strangely impressive effect against their pallor, the same effect that comes from widely flared nostrils in a pale face or a lower lip clenched between the teeth—and these, too, were much in evidence. And they were all breathing hard besides, but since it was not in unison, the sound was a tenfold irregular muddle of snorts there beneath the awning, all the result of his storytelling—and taken with the general pallor it surely ought to have disconcerted Joseph.

Which to a certain degree it did, but in the sense that it all seemed to him like a continuation of his dream, whose peculiar twofold nature, encompassing both an eerie joy and a joyful eeriness, reinforced this impression. For the effect achieved on his brothers was not one of joy, true, but it was obviously much stronger than Joseph had momentarily dared hope, and his relief that his story had not been a failure, as he had first had to fear, acted as a counterbalance to his uneasiness.

Nor did anything change when, after another general pause full of snorting and lip-gnawing, Jehuda exclaimed in a throaty, hoarse voice, "I have never heard more disgusting nonsense in all my life!" For this, too, was without doubt an expression of high—if not exactly happy—emotion.

And again, silence, pallor, gnawing reigned.

"You brat! You toadstool! Blowhard! Stinking breakwind!" Shimeon and Levi suddenly roared. Unable to speak in tandem, one after the other, as they usually did, they outshouted one another, both at the same time, their faces crimson, the veins on their foreheads swollen—and it turned out the rumor was true, that when they were enraged, the hair on their chests bristled, as it had, for example, during the frenzied attack on Shechem. It was really true, one could suddenly and clearly see the hair along their collarbones stand on end. And meanwhile their oxlike voices bellowed in confusion:

"You sack of filth, upstart, dog's ass, and bald-faced liar! What do you claim you dreamt? What happened there behind your eyelids, you scoundrel, you thorn in the flesh, you stumbling block, that we are supposed to interpret and explicate it for you no less, you putrid sheaf? 'Bend low, bend low!' What? You dare dream it, you vile sneak, and force us honest men to listen? So our sheaves all waggle limply in a circle, while yours stands upright! Has anything more disgusting ever been heard in the world? Sheol, filth, and spit upon you! You want to rule as father and king, do you? Here over us? Because, charlatan and pilferer of birthrights that you are, you viciously stole the *ketônet* behind the backs of your older brothers. We'll teach you a lesson in standing and bending. We'll show you who's master, till you admit your name to us and own up to your insolent lies!"

These, then, the savage bellows of the Dioscuri. And with that all ten emerged from under the awning and still pale and red, still gnawing at their lips, walked out into the field. Ruben, however, said as he departed, "You heard it, boy." Joseph sat there a while yet in a brown study, confused and depressed, because his brothers had not wanted to believe his dream. For that is in fact how he had heard it— they didn't believe him, since the twins had shouted several times something about lying and sneaking. That depressed him, and he asked himself how he could prove to them that he had said not one word too many and had merely honestly told what he had actually dreamt in their midst. If only they would believe him, he thought, the foul mood they had displayed would abate. For had he not openly proved his brotherly faith in them by informing them what God had showed him in the dream, so that they might share in the wonder and joy that he felt and advise him as to its meaning? It was impossible that they could fault him for believing in the unshakable basis of their fellowship, for that was what had moved him to reveal to them God's thoughts. He was, to be sure, raised up over them in the dream; but the idea that his older brothers, to whom in a certain sense he had always looked up, might not be able to bear the thoughts of God—that would have been too great a disappointment for him even to imagine it. Since he realized that for today it was impossible to rejoin them in cheerful, untroubled work, he decided not to return to the field with them, but instead went home, seeking out Benjamin, his dear little brother, to report to him how he had told the older men a, so to speak, thoroughly modest dream—adding its particulars. But they had not wanted to believe him, and the twins had been furious, although when compared to his dream of the journey to heaven, about which he had said not a word, the vision of sheaves had been the humblest thing in the world.

Turturra was glad no mention had been made of that stupendous dream of heaven, and for his part took such sincere delight in the dream of the sheaves that Joseph felt fully compensated for his rather lackluster success with his older brothers. For, you see, the little boy was so pleased that his sheaf had been in the circle with the others and had also bent low, that he leapt about and laughed at how perfectly it all corresponded to his own way of thinking.

The Conference

Meanwhile out in the field, the ten stood huddled together in distress and rage, propping themselves on their tools and deliberating beneath a setting sun. At first, in accord with signals given by Shimeon and Levi in their diatribe, the prevailing view—or, better, unspoken agreement—had been that the detestable fellow had invented the dream, or related it only in his lying fashion. They would gladly have held to this presumption, since it provided them all a means of defense. But it had been Judah who—just to make certain, so to speak, that nothing was omitted from their deliberations—pointed out the possibility that the lad had really dreamt the dream and was not bragging. From then on they all had to reckon with that view, and not just tacitly, but explicitly as well, dividing it, however, into two contingencies: either the dream, if actually dreamt, came from God, which was unanimously regarded as the greatest conceivable objective catastrophe, or it had nothing to do with God, but rather its sole source had been the smart aleck's gross arrogance, so gorged by possession of the *ketônet* that it was now conjuring up intolerable visions. During this debate, Ruben suggested that if God were involved, they were powerless and should worship Him—not Joseph, but the Lord. But if the dream were born of arrogance, they could simply shrug it off, leaving the Dreamer to his own folly. At the same time, however, he returned to the probability that the boy had childishly invented the dream and was teasing them, and for that he deserved a thrashing.

Indeed, big Ruben's proposal was for thrashing as punishment for chronic lying. But since at the same time he also recommended shrugging it off, his could not have been a very serious suggestion, for one cannot shrug and at the same time thrash with any vigor. It should be evident, by the way, that Ruben was determined to believe the one possibility that, in his opinion, led to a thrashing. But if one listened more intently, it appeared as if he intended this linkage of ideas as a way to distract his brothers from other assumptions and wanted to entice them as well into holding fast to the lie hypothesis, out of worry that if they assumed God Himself had sent the dream they might very well not be inclined to regard humility and worship to be the best course, but rather something vaguely worse than a mere thrashing. And in fact he found them less than willing to separate the personal from the factual and thus allow their conduct toward Joseph to be determined by the distinction of whether he had dreamt out of pure arrogance or whether his dream cast light upon a real state of affairs, that is, upon God's will and plans. From what they said it was not apparent in which of these two instances Joseph would appear to them more despicable and serpentlike—though presumably this was more likely in the latter case. If the dream really came from God and was a token of election, then, to be sure, nothing could be said against God—just as there was nothing to be said against their father Jacob, given his venerable weakness. To their minds, it all came back to Joseph. If God had chosen him to their detriment and let their sheaves waggle ignominiously before his, then God, just like Jacob, had been duped by Joseph's plying the same dissimulation by which he undermined them with their father. God was great, holy, and beyond responsibility. But Joseph was a viper. One can see (and Ruben saw it, too) that their notion of Joseph's relationship to God perfectly matched the one the lad himself cultivated—they viewed it as the same relationship he had with their father. That was how it had to be, for only shared assumptions create real hatred.

Re'uben feared these trains of thought, which was why he did not try to defend Joseph by conceding that perhaps God had sent him the dream, but hoped to persuade them to believe these were fibs and to punish the rascal for them, albeit with a shrug. In reality he was no more of a mind to shrug things off than were the others. There was that queasiness in the pit of the stomach, the feeling that outspoken Gad had first put into sketchy words and that not just the handmaids' four sons but all of ten of them felt now—and Ruben's soul perhaps endured the greatest measure of this eerie feeling, which arose from a deeply inbred horror attached to legends and prophecies associated with bartered birthrights, world dominion, and fraternal servitude, a horror that normally lay quiet but had now been stirred and awakened anew. Unlike the others, however, for him it was not translated into an unnamable rage against the man who aroused this queasiness, but into both an equally unnamable compassion for the chosen one's babbling innocence and an awestruck reverence for destiny.

"The only thing missing was for him to have said 'bow down,'" Gaddiel exploded between clenched teeth.

"He said 'bend low,'" raw-boned Issakhar remarked. He basically loved his peace and quiet, was willing to accept and suffer some things for its sake, and had now mentioned a detail that might possibly have a mitigating effect.

"I know that," Gad replied. "But first, he may have said it merely out of cunning, and second, it's the same filth either way."

"Not quite," Dan rebutted. He was a quibbler—that was part of his image, and in pious devotion to his image he never failed to display it. "Bending low is not exactly the same as bowing down—it is, we must admit, something less."

"Why's that!" Shimeon and Levi shouted, determined to manifest their savage obtuseness, whether the occasion suited or not.

Dan and a few of the others, including Ruben, advanced the theory that "bending low" carried less import than "bowing down." They said that with "bending low" it was not certain if it was done out of inner conviction or if it was not an external and empty gesture instead. One also "bent low" only now and then; whereas one was constantly "bowing down" with one's heart, for that was a way of sincerely paying facts their due, so that, as Ruben explained, one could "bend low" out of prudence without truly "bowing down," but that one could also "bow down" and yet remain too proud actually to "bend low." Jehuda disagreed, saying that this distinction could not be maintained in practice, for they were dealing with a dream after all, and in a dream "bending low" was merely the pictorial expression for the behavior that Ruben wanted to reserve for the term "bow down." Sheaves in a dream were, of course, not too proud to "bend low," if those who bind them have been ordered to "bow down." At which point young Zebulun objected that they were now happily engaged in the very work that Joseph had so shamelessly proposed and that they had utterly scorned to do—that is, interpreting his dream. And this statement—amid cries by Shimeon and Levi that it was all hemming and hawing, that a man neither bent low nor bowed down to such insults, but put an end to them, just as they had done at Shechem—provoked such exasperation that the conference was broken off on the spot, its only upshot an unappeased bitterness.

Sun, Moon, and Stars

And Joseph? Quite unaware of how the ten were agonizing over his dream, he was worried only by the notion that they had not wanted to believe him, and so could think of nothing but of how to confirm their belief—in a twofold sense: in both the reality of his dream and its truth. How best to do that? He urgently asked himself that question and was later amazed to realize that he had no answer, but that the answer had to be given to him or, rather, had had to give itself to him. He simply dreamed, you see, another dream, actually the same dream, but in a form so much more grandiose that the confirmation it carried was far more impressive than if his vision of the sheaves had simply repeated itself. He dreamed it at night, under a starry sky, lying on the threshing floor, where during this season he often spent the night with several brothers and servants, guarding grain that had not yet been fully threshed and returned to storage pits in the fields. It is in no way an explanation for the source of dreams to note that viewing the scene of heaven's hosts before sleep may well have shaped and influenced his dreams. The proximity of his companions in sleep, some of whom were those he wished to convince, may also have secretly provided a strong stimulus to the mechanism of dreaming. Nor should it be left unmentioned that on that same evening he and old Eliezer had discussed the subject of Last Things beneath the oracle tree, touching on topics like the judgment of the world and the time of blessing, on God's final victory over all those forces to whom the nations had been burning incense for so long, on the triumph of the Savior over heathen kings, astral powers, and zodiacal gods, which He would break and cast down, locking them in the lower depths, to mount up, then, in glorious and sole dominion over the universe. . . . It was of this that Joseph dreamt, but in such a confused fashion that he drifted into a childish mistake, equating the eschatological divine hero with his own dreaming person and beheld himself, the boy Joseph, as lord and ruler over all the rolling worlds spinning through the zodiac—or better, he felt it, for it really was quite impossible to narrate the dream as a visible scene, and in telling it Joseph was forced to put it in the simplest, briefest words and simply describe his inner experience without developing it as a sequence of events. None of which helped make it any more acceptable to his hearers.

He already started worrying about the proper form for communicating his dream the moment he startled up from it during the night, full of joy that he now had in his hands such decisive proof for the credibility of his previous vision. Above all, his immediate worry was whether his brothers would even give him a chance to justify himself, that is, whether they would allow him to tell another dream—this seemed doubtful to him. Even the first time they had come very close to paying him no attention, or withdrawing it too soon. How much greater his fear, then, given that the experience of satisfying their curiosity had evidently not brought them unalloyed pleasure.

That was why it was necessary to take precautions to counter their refusal to listen, and that very night on the threshing floor Joseph conceived a plan by which to do it. The next morning he went as usual to his father, for Jacob liked to see him each morning, to look him in the eyes to assure himself that his son was well, and to bless him for the day.

"A right good morning, my dear papa and prince of God," Joseph said. "Behold, a new day born of the night—I think it will be quite warm. One day follows another much like a string of pearls, and the child is pleased with life. It delights him particularly during this time of harvest. It is beautiful in the fields, whether one toils or rests, and men become friends over common tasks."

"What you have said is pleasant to hear," Jacob replied. "And so you are getting on well together on the threshing floor and in the fields and have come to understand one another in the Lord, you and your brothers?"

"Excellently," Joseph responded. "Apart from minor disagreements such as the day brings with it and the world's fragmentation furnishes, it is all running like a top; for an honest word, even if somewhat coarse, will clear up any confusion, and then harmony reigns again. I wish my dear papa might witness it sometime. You are never there—something that, when we join company, we often regret."

"I do not love the tilling of the soil."

"But of course, but of course. And yet it is a shame that those assembled never see their lord and his eye does not know their work, particularly that of the hired hands, on whom one cannot depend. My brother Jehuda complained to me in confidence only recently that they usually don't keep the wheels on the threshing cart properly honed—they mash instead of cutting. So it goes when the master does not show his face."

"I must admit your reproach is just."

"Reproach? May God guard my tongue! It is a request that the sprout presumes to make, in the name of the eleven. Nor should you share in our labors, the drudgery of the soil, Baal's work—who would expect it of you?—but only in our fine rest, when we break bread, shaded from the sun at its zenith, chattering away, sons of one and of four. And if someone knows a joke or a dream, he tells it to the others. We have often nudged one another with elbows and nodded among ourselves at how delightful it would be to entertain our father at the head of our circle."

"I will come sometime."

"Hurrah! Come today, then, and honor your sons! Our work is already drawing to a close, there's no time to lose. Today then—agreed? I shall say nothing to my red-eyed brothers and divulge not a word to the handmaids' sons—let joy overtake them. The child, however, will know in his heart whom they all have to thank and who so prettily contrived it in his loyalty and ingenuity."

Such was Joseph's plan. And indeed, that same noon Jacob was sitting out in the field beneath the awning and among his sons, having first surveyed the grain pits and run his thumb across the wheels of the threshing cart, checking for sharpness. The brothers were dumbfounded. Over the last few days, the Dreamer had not joined them for their hour of rest. But now he was back, his head in his father's lap. It was clear he had to be there when their father visited, but the question was: What had suddenly brought the old man here? There they sat, very stiff and silent, all in proper dress out of consideration for Jacob's views. He was surprised to find no evidence whatever of the healthy intimacy that, according to Joseph, should have characterized the hour. It might have been respect that held them back. Even Joseph had nothing to say. He was afraid, although he lay in his father's lap and in arranging for his presence had created the support he needed to speak freely. Truth to tell, he was worried about his dream and its success. It could be told in one sentence and allowed for no embellishment. If Gad would ask him, for instance, if that was all, he would be trounced. Brevity had the advantage that it was all out at once before anyone was even aware, and no one could interrupt. But any effect on their hearts and minds might easily be shattered by a certain grand spareness of the report. His heart was pounding.

He came close to letting the moment for his coup pass, for as the rest hour proved boring, things threatened to come to a premature end. Even hints that this could happen might very possibly not have enabled him to overcome his justifiable hesitation, had not Jacob at last made an amiable inquiry: "How was that? Did I not hear that you tell one another droll tales and dreams here in the shade at this hour?"

Bewildered, they said not a word.

"Yes, droll tales and dreams!" Joseph cried excitedly. "To think how they usually just trip from our lips on occasion. Does anyone know some untold tale?" he asked cheekily of all present.

They stared at him and said not a word.

"I know something, however," he said, sitting up from his father's lap, an intent look on his face. "I know a dream that I dreamt last night on the threshing floor, and you shall hear it, my father and brothers, and be amazed. I dreamt," he began again, and faltered. He felt an ominous shifting and twitching in his limbs—a cramp that lifted neck and shoulders, a wrenching at his arms. He lowered his head and the smile on his lips seemed intended to mitigate and excuse the way his eyes suddenly showed only the white. "I dreamt," he repeated, short of breath, "and what I saw in my dream—was this. I saw: the sun, the moon, and eleven *kokabim* waiting upon me. They came forward and bent low before me."

No one stirred. Jacob, their father, kept his gaze firmly lowered. It was very still; but into the stillness came an ugly sound, furtive and yet audible to all—it was the brothers gnashing their teeth. Most of them gnashed with lips closed. But Shimeon and Levi even bared their teeth as they gnashed.

Jacob heard the gnashing. Whether Joseph also grasped its meaning is uncertain. Tilting his head to his shoulder, he smiled to himself, a modest, unruffled smile. It was out now, let them do with it as they pleased. Sun, moon, and stars, eleven of them, had waited upon him. Let them think about that.

Jacob looked nervously around. He found what he had expected: ten pairs of eyes directed at him, their gaze wild and piercing. He collected himself, made himself strong. As roughly as he could possibly manage, he said from behind the boy's back, "Jehoseph! What sort of dream is this that has come to you, and what might it mean that you've dreamt and told us such tasteless nonsense? Am I and your mother and brothers supposed to come and worship you? Your mother is dead—that's the first absurdity, but a long way from the last. Shame on you! By all human standards what you have served up to us is so preposterous you might just have well simply babbled 'Aulasaulalakaula'—it would have served the same purpose. I am disappointed in my soul that, despite your good seventeen years and all the enlightenment your mind has received through words of written reason bestowed upon you by my permission through Eliezer, my oldest servant, you have advanced no farther in your understanding of God, so that you allow yourself to dream disreputable things and play the buffoon before your father and brothers. You are hereby punished! I would punish you more harshly still and perhaps even tug painfully at your hair if your babbling were not far too childish for a mature man to let himself be troubled by it or for a man of sober years to be tempted to repay you with severity. Farewell, sons of Leah! And greetings to conclude the meal, sons of Zilpah and Bilhah!"

And with that he stood up behind Joseph and left. His chastisement, coerced by the glances of his sons, had cost him a great deal, and he could only hope that these boys were satisfied. If there was any real anger in it, it was directed toward the fact that Joseph had not confided his dream to him alone, but had been so foolish as to make witnesses of his brothers. Had he intentionally set out to embarrass his father, Jacob thought, Joseph could not have made a better start of it. He would tell him that face-to-face yet, for he had not been able to tell him that just now, and presumably even realized that the rascal had used his brothers as a shield against his father, and vice versa. For on the way home he had trouble squelching under his beard a tender and delighted smile at such chicanery. And though the concerns evident in his reprimand were genuine—concern for the child's spiritual well-being, for his penchant for dreams and crowing for effect—both his anger and worry were feeble emotions in comparison with the tender, semireligious pleasure he took in Joseph's overweening dreams. Quite irrationally he pleaded with God that the dream might have come from Him—which, if He had not been involved, as was quite probably the case, would be a totally absurd prayer; but Jacob was close to shedding tears of love when he imagined that these might be real presentiments of future greatness that had taken on visionary form and that the child, in total innocence and without taking into account their full impact, had simply blurted out. The poor father! Surely he should have been enraged at the idea that he and all the rest would come forward to worship the good-for-nothing. But it would have disconcerted him to have been told that—for did he not adore him?

As for the brothers, no sooner was Jacob gone than they also retreated to a man, pushing their way into the open. Twenty tempestuous strides into the field, they stopped for a brief, heated discussion. Big Ruben spelled it out, told them what was to be done now. Away from here—that was it. Away with them all, in self-imposed exile from their father's hearth. That, said Ruben, would be a dignified and powerful demonstration, the only possible answer on their part to this abomination. What he thought was: Away from Joseph, that no disaster may occur. But he did not say that, and instead tried to put these measures entirely in the light of a chastening protest.

That very evening they appeared before Jacob and announced that they were leaving. A place where such dreams were dreamt and where someone was allowed to tell about them while risking at most, at the very worst, getting his hair mussed perhaps—they had nothing to gain in such a place, they would not stay. The harvest, they said, was over, thanks to their strong efforts, and now they would move on to Shechem—not just the six, but the four as well, all ten. For the meadows of Shechem were fertile and good, and with unshakable, if unappreciated, loyalty they would tend their father's flocks there, but would not return again to the camp at Hebron, given the thoroughly slanderous dreams dreamed there. In paying their farewell respects, they said that they bent low and bowed down to him, their father—and did as they said. They had no worries, they added, that their departure would cause him pain or even regret, for everyone knew that Jacob, their lord, would give ten for one.

Jacob bowed his head. Had he perhaps begun to fear that the despotism of emotion into which he had fallen by way of imitation was being taken amiss in the place of its divine origin?

Part Five

THE JOURNEY TO HIS BROTHERS

An Extraordinary Demand

We have heard how Jacob bowed his head as his embittered sons cut their ties with their father's home—and from then on he raised it only seldom. The oncoming season, the time of baking heat, of the sun's fiercest searing of the land—for the day was approaching when the sun would begin to decrease, and though it was the point in the year when his true wife had once bestowed Joseph upon him, in the month of Tammuz, Jacob's spirit nevertheless usually flagged beneath the singed bleakness of this quarter of the circle—the season, then, may well have contributed to his downcast state, even serving to help him explain it to himself. But the real reason for his depression was actually the unanimous decision of his sons to depart, an event about which it would be saying too much to claim that it had caused Jacob great pain—no, it was not so. In his heart he truly was willing to give "ten for one." But it was a different matter to deal with the reality of it, with having to realize that the cancellation of fraternal fellowship was final and that he, Jacob, now stood there with two sons instead of twelve, like a tree stripped bare. First of all, it was detrimental to his majesty; but beyond that, it left him with the worry of being put in an embarrassing position with God, for he wondered how great was the responsibility with which he had burdened himself in the eyes of the planning Lord of promise. Had the future-filled Lord not wisely prevented things from proceeding according to Jacob's heart, kept him from being fruitful in Rachel alone? Had He not given him many sons, by way of Laban's wiles and despite his own heart, and were they not all, even those of an unloved wife, fruits of the blessing and bearers of a future beyond reckoning? Jacob certainly realized that his choosing of Joseph was a matter of extravagant obstinacy, a private indulgence of the heart. But might it also, in all its consequences, be culpable presumption? Only as yet unknown and devastating blows in some ruinous altercation with God could reveal that—but it appeared as if this were about to happen. For though Joseph's folly might have been the direct cause for both the strife and Jacob's pained anger toward him, Jacob did not delude himself—he knew that he and he alone had to answer for that folly before God and man. In bickering with Joseph he was bickering with himself. If misfortune had been the result, the boy had only been its mediator, and it was Jacob's loving heart that had been at fault. And what good would it have done to hide this from himself? God knew it, and you could hide nothing from God. To honor truth was Abram's heritage, and that meant you did not gloss over something God already knew.

These were questions of conscience that Jacob put to himself in the days after the wheat harvest and that influenced his resolve. His heart had done harm; now he had to bring himself to turn the coddled object of its weakness, the mediator of that harm, into a mediator of reconciliation as well, to make a rather extraordinary demand of him to that end, to treat him a little roughly as an act of penitence for both his own heart and the boy.

And so, seeing him at some distance, he called him to him in a rather firm voice, saying, "Joseph!"

"Here I am," the lad answered and was at his side at once. He was glad to be called, for since his brothers' departure his father had said little to him, and, fool though he was, their last meeting had left him with uneasy forebodings.

"Listen now," Jacob said, blinking his eyes in thought and stroking his beard with one hand, pretending absentmindedness for one reason or another. "Do I not recall that your brothers, those older than you, are all tending flocks together in the valley of Shechem?"

"Indeed," Joseph replied, "I seem to recall that myself, and if memory is not playing a trick on me, they all intended to go to Shechem to tend your herds grazing there because of its rich meadows and because this valley here will not support all that is yours."

"That is so," Jacob confirmed, "and it is for that reason that I have called you. For I have heard nothing from Leah's sons and there are no tidings from the children of the handmaids. I have no knowledge of the state of the meadows there, whether Yitzchak's blessing was upon the summer lambing or if liver rot and bloating have ravaged what is mine. I know nothing of the health of my children, your brothers, and have not heard whether they exercise pasturing rights in peace within a jurisdiction where, as I recall, grave events once occurred. It gives me pause for thought, and it is out of such thoughts that I have decided to send you to them, so that you may greet them for me."

"Here I am," Joseph cried again. He flashed his white teeth at his father and kicked up his heels, almost hopping about for sheer eagerness.

"By my estimation," Jacob continued, "you are about to enter the eighteenth year of your life, and it is time that you were treated a bit more roughly and that your manhood was put to the test. Which is the reason behind my decision to make this extraordinary demand of you, that you leave me for a short while and go to your brothers in order to ask them all the things I do not know, and return to me again, with God's help, in ten or nine days and report to me."

"Ah, here I am indeed," Joseph rejoiced. "My dear papa's ideas are gold and silver. I shall journey across country, I shall visit my brothers, and see if things are in order in the valley of Shechem— what fun! Had I been allowed to wish whatever my heart desires—it would have been this and none other!"

"You shall not see if things are in order with your brothers," Jacob said. "They are man enough to do that themselves, and have no need of the child for that. Nor is that my intention in sending you. Rather you shall bend low before them as is seemly custom and say, 'I have come several days' journey in order to greet you and inquire about your health, both of my own volition and at our father's direction, for our meeting was held in the spirit of that wish.'"

"Give me Parosh to ride! His legs are long and he is tough and strong-boned, much like my brother Issakhar."

"It speaks for your manliness," Jacob replied after a pause, "that you are looking forward to this mission and do not consider it an extraordinary demand that you will be taken from me for a number of days, during which the moon will change from sickle to semicircle without my seeing you. But tell your brothers: 'It is our father's wish.'"

"Do I get Parosh?"

"Although I am willing to treat you roughly as befits your years, I shall not give you the ass Parosh, for he is stubborn, and his wits are not as quick as his temper. Much better for you is Hulda, the white jenny, an amiably cautious beast, and of dapper appearance when you are traveling amongst others—you shall ride her. But so that you may realize just what I expect of you, and so that your brothers may see it as well, I charge you to ride alone the entire journey, from here to Shechem's pastures. For I shall not give you any servants, nor allow Eliezer to ride at your side. But you shall travel by yourself, all on your own, and say to your brothers, 'I have come alone on a white ass to visit you, as our father wished.' It may be that you will then not have to return to me by yourself, but that your brothers will travel with you, several or all of them. That, in any case, is what I have in the back of my mind in making this extraordinary demand."

"I shall surely manage that," Joseph promised, "and I pledge to bring them back to you, indeed I warrant it and dare to say: I shall not return unless I bring them to you!"

Joseph followed his asinine chatter with a little dance around his father, rejoicing in the name of Yah that he would be traveling all on his own and seeing the world. Then he ran to Benjamin and to old Eliezer to tell them everything. But Jacob nodded as he watched him go and saw quite well that if his demand was extraordinary, its challenge applied to himself and that he was treating no one more roughly than himself. And yet was it not the right thing to do, did not his heart's answerability for Joseph desire it? He would not see the child for several days, that seemed penance enough for his culpability—he had no idea, for it was beyond his imaginings, what "rough treatment" meant in higher realms. He took into account that Joseph's mission might fail, inasmuch as he considered it possible he might return without his brothers. The terrible opposite never entered his mind. For its own sake, fate excluded that notion. Since everything turns out differently from what we intend, destiny is greatly hampered by man's fearful apprehensions, which are almost conspiratorial. Destiny cripples our anxious imagination by allowing it to anticipate everything except its fate—fate that thus avoids being turned aside by vigilant thoughts and retains all its primordial power and crushing blows.

During the brief preparations that Joseph's excursion demanded, Jacob was sensibly reminded of fateful days from his own past, of the measures Rebekah took to prepare his departure from home after the switch in blessings she herself had initiated, and his soul was filled with a solemn sense of recurrence. One must say that it was a risky correlation he was making here, for his role did not compare with that of Rebekah, his heroically courageous mother, who knowingly sacrificed her own heart by arranging a deception that set things right and then, fully aware that she might never see her favorite again, sent him off to strange lands. That theme underwent a good many mutations. It was indeed true that Joseph had to leave home because of aggrieved fraternal anger, and yet he was not fleeing from their rage, but rather Jacob was sending him, so to speak, into Esau's arms. It was the scene beside the Jabbok that Jacob had in mind and whose recurrence he was trying to hasten—an external humbling, the forms of a makeshift reconciliation filled with reservations, the cobbling-over of an irreparable breach, the sham resolution of something never to be resolved. In his dignified weakness he was a long way from the determined Rebekah, who had acted regardless of consequences. His goal in sending Joseph on a mission was indeed the restoration of a previous situation—already abundantly proved untenable. For no one can doubt that once the ten had returned home, the old game—consisting of Jacob's weakness, Joseph's blind arrogance, and the brothers' fatal rancor—would have continued its hopeless course, leading inevitably to the same consequences.

Nonetheless, the golden son was readied for a journey rooted in fraternal strife—to that extent it was a recurrence and Jacob saw to other similarities as well, making sure that Joseph rode off in the early morning, before sunrise, just as he had done in his own day. He was scarcely even Jacob as they said their farewells, but rather was Rebekah, was the mother. He held his departing son for a long time, murmured blessings against his cheek, took a protective amulet from his own neck and hung it around the boy's, and hugged him yet again—behaving more or less as if Joseph were traveling for who knew how long or forever, seventeen days or more, toward the utterly strange world of Naharaim, when in fact the lad, provisioned with more than ample food, was setting out on a jaunt over safe roads to the hardly distant Shechem—much to his delight. Which shows how excessive a man's behavior can appear when one's awareness is one's yardstick, but how, when observed from the viewpoint of a fate still quite unknown to the man, the same conduct seems all too fitting. This can even offer consolation once the conscious mind clears and we learn what was truly meant. Therefore people should never say their farewells lightly, for then, no matter what, they will be able to say: At least I pressed him to my heart!

No need to record that the farewell taken that morning at the side of Hulda—packed to the full and adorned in colorful woolen flowers and glass beads—was but the last of several occasions when advice, recommendations, and warnings were offered. Jacob had taught the boy the way and its stations in every detail he knew and, just as a mother would, warned him of getting too hot or taking a chill, had given him the names of men and fellow members of the faith in various towns where the traveler could spend the night and warned him sternly that, when passing the city of Urusalim and beholding there the temple of Baal and its house of consecrated women, he should not even enter into the smallest conversation with any of those who wove for Asherah, and above all constantly impressed on him the need to treat his brothers with particular courtesy. It would do no harm, he had instructed, if Joseph would prostrate himself seven times before them and frequently address them as his lords—presumably they would then henceforth decide to dip hands with him in the bowl, never leaving his side for the rest of their lives.

Jacob–Rebekah repeated many of these things during his final farewell at the break of day, before allowing the lad to swing his leg over the ass and, with a click of the tongue, ride off toward the midnight of the north. He even strode a little way alongside Hulda, fresh with morning vigor, but could not keep pace for long and gave up, standing there with a heart heavier than seemed suitable. He caught the flash of teeth turned in a last smile and raised a hand to wave. Then a turn in the path removed his son's figure from view, and he would see no more the Joseph who had ridden off.

Joseph Rides to Shechem

The lad, now out of his father's eye, feeling comfortably at home and yet all by himself, trotted along the road to Beth-lachem astride the animal's croup, his slender brown legs stretched forward and his upper body tilted saucily back under the gentle light of the morning sun bathing the hills round about. His mood perfectly suited the circumstances as he saw them, and he accepted his father's excessive farewell with the cheerful forbearance of a coddled favorite, his heart burdened not in the least by the knowledge that he had responded to his father's worries about their first separation with a little trick of his own.

Jacob, you see, had expatiated at length on how the traveler should conduct himself, overlooking not a single precept or warning—except that he neglected one thing, for which a peculiar and not totally blameless lapse in memory was at fault. He had forgotten to advise the boy concerning one particular act of consideration and requisite tact and did not think of it until the day when the object that his admonishment would have concerned was suddenly, and horribly, presented to his view again: the veiled *ketônet*. He should have suggested Joseph leave it at home, but Joseph had slyly, silently taken advantage of Jacob's lapse and taken it with him. He so longed to show himself to the wider world in it that he had literally trembled for fear his father might decide at the last moment to deny it to him—yes, we consider it possible that in that case he would have lied to the old man and declared that the sacred embroidery lay in its chest, whereas in truth it was hidden among his baggage. Dangling from the back of his beast of burden, milk-white Hulda, a charming three-year-old, clever and obliging, though inclined to harmless bits of mischief, with that touching good humor that sometime peeks through the nature of such reserved creatures, with eloquent velvet ears and a droll woolly forelock growing down over her large and merrily mild eyes, where only too quickly flies began to gather— Hulda, then, had dangling from both sides of her back all sorts of travel necessities and provisions: a goatskin with soured skim milk for thirst, lidded baskets and clay pots with wheat and fruit cakes, parched grain, salted olives, cucumbers, roasted onions, and fresh cheeses. All this and more, both for the traveler's own refreshment and as gifts for his brothers, had been carefully inspected by his father, who had failed to peer into just one container, an utterly ordinary, age-old item of traveler's luggage: a round piece of leather that served as a tablecloth or, better, as the table itself, for dining, with metal rings sewn around its edge. Even the Bedouin of the desert, they in particular, used it—it came from them. A cord was drawn through the rings, and during a journey the dining table was hung from the animal as a bag. Joseph had done the same, but in his dining bag, much to his gloating delight, his *ketônet* was tucked.

Why did it belong to him, why had he inherited it, if he was not to let himself be seen in it on his journey? Close to home, people along the road and in the fields knew him and called his name in delight. But farther on, when after a few hours they no longer knew him, it was a good idea not to rely solely on the plentiful provisions he had with him as evidence that a man of refinement was passing by. Which was why, especially as the sun climbed higher, he soon pulled out his splendid attire and put it on to suit his mood, protecting his head, but with the myrtle wreath he usually wore no longer in his hair, but set atop the veil framing his face.

That day he did not reach the place for which he had also donned his robe and where, following both Jacob's fervent instructions and his own desires, he had planned to spend the night, offering sacrifices and praying; and yet it was only a short distance from Beth-lachem, where he found shelter with a friend of Jacob's, a carpenter and believer in God. The second morning, however, after saying good-bye to his friendly host, the man's wife, and their household, he was soon at the spot, and Hulda waited beneath the propped-up mulberry tree, while Joseph, clad in his bridal heirloom, offered prayers and libations at the stone erected beside the road—a memorial stone for God, that He might be reminded of what He had once done here.

Morning stillness lay upon the vineyards and rock-strewn fields, and as yet no traffic was passing to and from Urusalim. A breeze casually played in the tree's shining foliage. The landscape was silent, and the spot where Jacob had once laid Laban's child to rest accepted in silence his son's gifts and tokens of devotion. Joseph placed water beside the stone, added a loaf of raisin bread, kissed the ground beneath which an eager life had vanished, and stood up again, raising heavenward hands, eyes, and lips—all inherited from this vanished woman—and muttering litanies of veneration. There was no answer from the depths. What had vanished was silent, spellbound in indifference, incapable of caring. What it possessed of the present in this place was Joseph himself, who wore her bridal dress and turned her eyes heavenward. Might it not have warned him, that maternal part of his own flesh and blood alive in him? No, it lay within him, in the thrall of blind, coddled, boyish folly, and could not speak.

And so in a cheerful mood Joseph continued on his way, along roads and mountain paths. It was the smoothest journey in the world; neither misfortune nor unforeseen accident marred its success. It wasn't exactly as if the earth leapt up to greet him; but it extended obligingly before him and offered joyous greetings through people's eyes and mouths wherever he went. They had long since ceased to know him personally, but his type is extraordinarily popular in these climes, and his appearance—enhanced by the power of the veil—awakened favor and delight in all those who saw him, particularly among the women. Sitting in the garish sun beside village walls of honeycombed baked clay and dung, they suckled their children, and the pleasure they took in nursing their brood was reinforced by the sight of the handsome and beautiful young man riding by.

"Good health to you, apple of every eye!" they called to him. "Blessed be she who bore you, warmer of hearts!"

"Perfect health to you!" Joseph responded, showing them his teeth. "Your son shall rule over many!"

"A thousand thanks!" they called after him. "May Ashtaroth show you favor. You are like one of her gazelles." For they were all devotees of Asherah and thought of worshiping only her.

In other instances—because of his veil, but also because of his ample provisions—some simply considered him to be a god and showed an inclination to worship him. But that was the case only in the countryside, not in walled cities that bore names like Beth-shemesh or Kiriath-Ayin or even Kerem-Baalat and the like, beside whose ponds and gateways he would stop to chat and soon be surrounded by large numbers of people. For he amazed them with the kind of learning that city people love, spoke with them of the miracles God performed with numbers, of eons, of the secret of the pendulum, and of the peoples of the earth, and also, to flatter them, told them of the wench from Uruk who converted the woodsman to civilized conduct, all the while displaying so much engaging charm in speech and manners that they agreed he might very well be the *mazkir* of a city prince or the voice of memory for a great king.

He brilliantly displayed the knowledge of languages he had gained with Eliezer's help, and there beneath the gate he spoke Hittite with a man from Hetti, Mitannite with a man from the north, and a few words of Egyptian with a cattle trader from the Delta. It was not much that he knew, but a clever man can say more with ten words than a stupid one with a hundred, and he understood that those who were listening would be impressed with him as a marvelously facile polyglot even if his conversational partner was not. He served as interpreter for a woman at the well, who had dreamt a terrifying dream. In it her little three-year-old son had suddenly appeared larger than she herself, and had had a beard. That meant, he told her, his eyes rolling back briefly to show the whites, that her son would soon leave her, but that she would indeed see him again, but only after many years, as a grown man with a beard. Since the woman was very poor and might possibly be forced to sell her son into slavery, the interpretation had a certain probability, and people marveled at the union of beauty and wisdom embodied in this young traveler.

There were always several who invited him to their homes, asking him to be their guest for a few days. But following his father's traveling instructions as best he could, he neglected his duty no more than common courtesy demanded. Of the three nights separating his four days of travel, he spent only one other in a house, as the guest of a silversmith named Abisai, whom Jacob had once visited and who, though not unconditionally and exclusively a follower of Abraham's God, was strongly inclined in His favor and noted, by way of excuse for fashioning idols from the moon's metal, that a man had to make a living somehow. As a man of the world, Joseph conceded the point and slept under his roof. The third brief period of darkness he spent in the open, making his bed in a grove of fig trees, for he had rested during the day because of the excessive heat and was so late in arriving at his third way station that he did not want to ask admission into the city. Something similar happened on the last night as he was nearing his goal. For the sun's ferocity had forced him to rest during the afternoon hours of the fourth day too, and since he had slept the day away under trees and set forth again only toward evening, it was already the second watch of the night when he arrived at Shechem's narrow valley. But if his journey had thus far proceeded so favorably, it turned mad and bedeviled from the first hour he entered the valley and, by the light of a moon still floating like a trim barque, beheld the walled city with its fortress and temple set on the slopes of Mount Gerizim—from that moment on, nothing went quite right; indeed things went so awry and at such utter cross-purposes that Joseph was tempted to connect this turnabout in fortune's mood with the person of a man who met him that night outside Shechem and who forced himself upon him as a companion for this final period preceding the transformation of all things.

The Man in the Field

We read that Joseph was wandering in the field. But what does "wandering" mean here? Had his father demanded too much of him, and did young Joseph go about it so poorly that he made mistakes and lost his way? Not at all. To wander is not the same as to lose one's way, and when one is looking for something that is not there, one need not go astray in order not to find it. Joseph had spent several boyhood years in the valley of Shechem and was no stranger to the area, though it was with a kind of dreamy familiarity that he recognized it again, particularly by night and faint moonlight. He was not lost, he was searching. And since he found nothing, his search was pointless exploration of a maze. Leading his animal by the bridle through the silence of night, he wandered the rolling expanses of meadow and field, beneath darkly brooding starlit mountains, and he thought, "Where can my brothers be?" He came across sheepfolds, where the flocks inside slept as they stood. It was uncertain whether these were Jacob's sheep, and there was no one there—the silence was remarkable.

Then he heard a voice, heard a question asked by a man whose footsteps he had not noticed approaching from behind, but who had now caught up with him and was at his side. Had the man been coming toward him, Joseph would have asked him a question, but as things stood the man allowed no questions, but asked one instead: "Whom are you looking for?"

He did not ask "What are you looking for here?" but simply "Whom are you looking for?" And it may be that the emphatic way he posed the question helped shape Joseph's childish and thoughtless answer. The boy's mind was weary, and his joy at meeting someone in this cursed maze of night was so great that he immediately turned the man—simply because he was another person—into an object of ingenuously obliging and illogical trust. He said, "I am looking for my brothers. Tell me, good man, please, where they are grazing their flocks."

The "good man" took no offense at the simplicity of this

entreaty. He seemed capable of rising above that and refrained from pointing out to the questioner just how vague were the details provided. He replied, "Certainly not here, nor in the vicinity, either."

A confused Joseph gazed at him from the side. He could see him quite clearly. The man was actually not yet a man in the fullest sense of the word, but only a few years older than Joseph, yet taller for all that, very tall indeed. He was clad in a sleeveless linen tunic that had been tucked in bunches up under the belt, baring the knees to make walking easier, and flung over one shoulder was a short robe. His head, perched atop a rather massive neck, seemed small in proportion to the rest, with brown hair and curls that partially covered his forehead and fell at an angle to the eyebrows. The nose was large, straight, and firmly chiseled, the space between it and his little red mouth was quite insignificant, but the indentation beneath his lips so pronounced and yet so soft that the chin jutted out below it like a plump round fruit. He turned his head with somewhat affected curiosity to gaze down over his shoulder in languid courtesy at Joseph. The eyes, though not unattractive, were only halfway open and their sleepy, blurred expression was like that of someone who has neglected to blink. His arms were nicely contoured, but pale and rather weak. He wore sandals and had a walking stick that he had apparently cut to size himself.

"Certainly not here?" the boy repeated. "How can that be? When they left home they were so definite in saying they were all coming to Shechem. Do you know them then?"

"Slightly," his companion replied. "To the extent necessary. Oh no, I'm not on very familiar terms with them, not very familiar at all. Why are you looking for them?"

"Because my father has sent me to them, that I might greet them and see if things are in order with them."

"You don't say. So then you're a messenger. I'm one myself. I often take stick in hand and act as messenger. But I am also a guide."

"A guide?"

"Yes indeed. I guide travelers and open pathways for them, that is my business, and that is why I addressed you with a question when I saw you were gone astray in your search."

"You seem to know that my brothers are not here. But do you also know where they are?"

"I believe I do."

"Then tell me!"

"Are you so eager to see them?"

"Certainly, I long to reach my goal and my brothers to whom my father sent me."

"Well, then, I shall give it a name, your goal. The last time I was passing by here as a messenger, only a few days ago, I heard your brothers say, 'Come, let us go to Dothan with part of our sheep, just for a change.'"

"To Dothan?"

"And why not Dothan? The idea came to them and they did it. There are lush pastures in the valley of Dothan, and the people of the hillside town are glad to do business. They buy sinews, milk, and wool. Why does that surprise you?"

"I am not surprised, for there is no surprise in it. But it is an unlucky omen. I was certain that I would meet my brothers here."

"So it's rare, then," the stranger asked, "for things not to go just as you've planned? You appear to me to be a mother's boy."

"I have no mother," Joseph responded peevishly.

"Nor do I," the stranger said. "In that case, you would appear to be a father's boy."

"That may be as it may be," Joseph replied. "Tell me instead what I should do now?"

"Very simple. You go to Dothan."

"But it is night, and we are tired, Hulda and I. It is more than just a short way from here to Dothan, as I recall from before. It is a leisurely day's journey."

"Or a night's. Since you slept the day away under trees, you must make use of the night to arrive at your goal."

"How do you know that I slept under trees?"

"Begging your pardon, but I saw you. Striding past on my walking stick, I saw where you lay, and I left you there. Now I find you here."

"I don't know the way to Dothan, especially at night," Joseph protested. "My father did not describe it for me."

"Well then," the man responded, "be glad I found you. I am a guide and I will guide you if you like. I shall open the pathways to Dothan for you quite free of charge, for as a messenger I must go there in any case, and I shall show you the shortest way, if that is all right with you. We can take turns riding the ass. A handsome beast," he said, gazing at Hulda with partially opened eyes expressing such languid disapproval that they stood in contradiction to the man's words. "As handsome as you. Except her pasterns are too weak."

"Hulda," Joseph said, "is the best ass in Yizrael's stall, except for Parosh. No one has ever found her pasterns too weak."

The stranger made a face. "You would do better," he said, "not to contradict me. It is foolish for several reasons—for example, you must depend entirely on me to reach your brothers, and besides, I am older than you. Both these reasons are surely clear to you. When I say that your jenny here has frail pasterns, then they are frail, and there is no cause for you to defend them as if you had made this beast, since all you can do is walk before it and call it by name. And speaking of names, I would like to ask you here and now not to call good Jacob 'Yizrael' in my presence. It is unseemly and a vexation to me. Give him his natural name and leave aside the high-flown titles."

Pleasant the man was not. It seemed as if—and for no predictable reason—his languid, over-the-shoulder courtesy might at any moment turn into rankled bad temper. This propensity for a foul disposition was at odds with the eagerness to help that he had shown a lad gone astray in his search, invalidating it more or less, since it left the impression that it contradicted the man's own intentions. Or had this wanderer on foot simply been looking for a ride to Dothan? And in fact he was the first to take a seat on the ass as they started off, and Joseph walked alongside.

Offended that he had been forbidden to call his father Yizrael, Joseph remarked, "But it is his title of honor, which he wrested for himself at the Jabbok in a hard-won victory."

"I find your speaking of victory absurd," the other replied, "when such a thing is out of the question in every case and everywhere. A pretty victory, when a man is left halt in his hip for the rest of his life and, to be sure, comes away with a name, but not that of him with whom he wrestled. Anyway," he suddenly said with a peculiar motion of his eyes, not just opening them wide, but also rolling them about in cross-eyed circles, "go right ahead and call your father Yizrael—please do. There's a rightness to it, and my objection simply burst out like that. I am also aware," he added, letting his eyeballs roll yet again, "that I am sitting upon your beast. If you'd like I shall dismount so that you may sit on her."

A peculiar man. He seemed to repent his own unfriendliness, yet his repentance had none of the marks of gravity and sincerity—no more than had his readiness to help. Joseph, however, was friendly by nature and held to his principle that the best response to such peculiarity was increased cordiality. "Since you are my guide and are showing me the way to my brothers out of the goodness of your heart," he replied, "you have every right to my animal. Remain seated, I beg you, and we shall change places later. You have been walking most of the day, whereas I was able to ride."

"Many thanks," the young man said. "Your words are no more than proper, to be sure, but my best thanks to you all the same. I have been temporarily deprived of certain items that facilitate my progress," he added with a shrug. "Do you enjoy being sent on missions and playing the messenger?" he then asked.

"I was very glad when my father called me," Joseph replied. "But who has sent you?"

"Ah, as you know, there are many messengers who are sent by rulers to the east and south and move back and forth through this land," the young man responded. "You don't even know who it is that has actually sent you; the message passes through many mouths, and it is of little help to follow it back to its origins—you must take to your feet in any case. I am now on my way to Dothan with a letter," he said, "which I carry in the fold of my belt. But I can see it coming that I shall also have to play the watchman yet as well."

"The watchman?"

"Yes, no one can assure me that, for example, I shall not have to guard a well or some other place of significance. Messenger, guide, and watchman—I am employed as needed and according to the whim of him who commissions me. Whether one enjoys it and feels that one was made for the task is another question, which I shall leave unanswered—as well as whether one is of one mind with the original purposes out of which such missions arise. I shall, as I have said, leave these questions open, but just between us there is much incomprehensible zeal at work here. Do you love humankind?"

He asked it out of the blue, and yet the question did not surprise Joseph; for his guide's languid, peevish way of speaking was that of someone haughtily dissatisfied with humankind, of an individual annoyed by the necessity of having to pursue his business among men.

"We usually smile at one another," Joseph replied, "the rest of humanity and I."

"Yes, because as everyone knows you are handsome and beautiful," his companion said. "That is why they smile at you, and you smile back to encourage them in their folly. You would do better to put on a glum face and tell them, 'What's there to smile about? Sadly, my hair will fall out someday, as will these now white teeth. These eyes are but a jelly of blood and water that will ooze away, and this hollow charm of the flesh will shrivel and perish ignominiously.' The decent thing to do would be to disabuse them, reminding them of something they already know, but about which they delude themselves in that moment of fawning smiles. Creatures like you are but a fraud, who conceal beneath a fleeting, glittery surface the inner abomination of all flesh. Not that this skin, this husk, with its reeking pores and sweaty hair is all that appetizing—let it be rent but a little, and the salty brew gushes out in its red wickedness, and it only grows more abominable deeper within—sheer guts and stench. What is handsome and beautiful must be handsome and beautiful through and through, massive and of noble stuff, not crammed with glue and garbage."

"Then you will have to stick with images of iron and carved wood," Joseph said, "for example with the beautiful god that the women hide in the greenwood and search for with lamentation so that they may inter him in his cave. He is handsome through and through, of massive olive wood, not bloody and sweaty. But so that he may appear as if he is not massive, but bleeding from the tooth of the boar, they paint him with red wounds and deceive themselves, so that they may weep for this dear lost life. That is how it is—life is either deception or beauty. You do not find both united in reality."

"Pah!" the guide said, wrinkling his round fruit of a chin and looking down over his shoulder with half-closed eyes at the lad walking beside the ass. "No," he added after a pause, "say what you will, it is a disgusting race that drinks iniquity like water and has long since deserved another Flood, but without an ark to save it."

"You are probably right about the iniquity," Joseph responded. "But consider how everything in the world comes in twos, part and counterpart, so that one may distinguish between them, and if the one were not alongside the other, there would be neither. Without life there would be no death, without wealth no poverty, and if stupidity were to be lost, who would want to speak of wisdom? But it is also true of what is clean and unclean, surely that is clear. The unclean beast says to the clean one, 'You may thank me, for if I did not exist how would you know that you are clean, and who would call you that?' And the evil man says to the just, 'Fall at my feet, for without me where would be your advantage?' "

"Precisely," the stranger replied. "That is precisely the point. I disapprove of it from the ground up, this world of duality, and I cannot comprehend zeal on behalf of a race whose cleanliness can be described only in comparative and reflexive terms. And yet that race must always be kept in mind and there are always new and wondrous plans for it, so vast that one must prepare the way for this and that and I know not what, all on behalf of its scrap of future, just as I must guide you along your way now, you bag of wind, so that you may arrive at your goal—how truly boring!"

What a peevish fellow. Why is he showing me the way, then, if it's such a bother? Joseph thought. It is really stupid to play the obliging stranger and then pout about it. He definitely was just looking for a ride. He could climb down now, too—we were going to trade off. He certainly talks like a human being, he thought, smiling to himself at how people like to quarrel with their own kind, while exempting themselves, just as this fellow rendered judgments of his fellow man as if he were not one himself.

That is why he said, "Yes, you speak of the human race and sit in judgment over how it is made of poor stuff. But there was a time when man was not made of too poor a stuff even for the children of God, for they visited mankind's daughters, from which there came giants and mighty men."

With his usual affectation, the guide turned his head toward the shoulder opposite Joseph. "My, all the little tales you know!" he replied with a titter. "For your years you know a thing or two about such episodes, I must say. For my own part, let it be noted, I regard the story as mere gossip. But if it is true, then I shall tell you why the Children of Light did what they did and cast an eye on the children of Cain. They did it out of unrestrained disdain, yes indeed. Do you know the extent to which depravity flourished among Cain's daughters? They went about with private parts exposed—men and women mating like animals. Their whoredom made a mockery of every constraint, until one could not watch, so to speak, without being caught up in it—I don't know if you can understand that. They went beyond all bounds, threw their clothes upon the ground and strutted naked in the marketplace. If they had not known what shame is, then perhaps it might not have been so bad, and the Children of Light would not have been stirred to the quick by the sight. But they knew exactly what shame is, by God's decree they were very shamefaced, and the very essence of their lust was that they trampled shame underfoot—can such a thing be endured? Men copulated in the streets with their mothers and daughters and their brothers' wives. They all had but one thing on their minds: their abominable delight in profaned shame. How could that have not stirred the Children of God to the quick? They were seduced by contempt—can you not understand that? They cast aside their last remnant of respect for a race that had been set down in front of their noses—as if they themselves had not been sufficient for this world—and that they were supposed to esteem for the sake of the zeal shown from on high. They discovered that man existed solely for the sake of lewdness, and their contempt took on a wanton character. If you do not understand that, you are no more than a calf."

"I can understand it if need be," Joseph rejoined. "But how do you know all this?"

"Do you likewise ask your Eliezer how he knows what he teaches you? I know as much as he about such episodes, and probably a little bit more as well, for one gets around in this world as a messenger, guide, and watchman and experiences a great variety of things. I can assure you that the Flood came at last only because it turned out that the contempt the Children of Light felt for humankind had itself become wanton—that tipped the scale. It might never have happened otherwise, and I just want to add that, for their part, the Children of Light intentionally brought on the Flood. Unfortunately there was also the rescuing ark, and man slipped in through the back door again."

"Let us be glad of that," Joseph said. "Otherwise we would not be chatting away on our journey to Dothan and *taking turns* riding the ass, in accord with our agreement."

"Yes, right!" the other man responded and again rolled his eyes around in cross-eyed circles. "I forget everything when I'm chatting away. I must lead you on the right paths and watch over you that you may come to your brothers. Who, however, is more important, the watchman or the person watched? Not without bitterness I must answer: It is the one who is watched, the watchman is there for him, and not vice versa. And thus I shall now climb down so that you may ride and I shall walk alongside in the dust."

"I can bear watching that," Joseph said, taking his seat. "It is by pure accident, after all, that you too can ride now and then and don't have to walk the whole way in the dust."

They went on beneath stars and faint moonlight, northward from Shechem toward Dothan, through valleys narrow and wide, over steep mountains forested with cedar and acacia, past sleeping villages. Seated on the ass, Joseph slept an hour or so, too, while his guide walked in the dust. When he awoke again from one such sleep—it was already the dusk of dawn—he saw that a basket of pressed fruit and another with roasted onions were missing from the ass's baggage, and could not help noticing that the bunched fabric above his guide's belt had a corresponding bulge. The man was a thief! That was a disconcerting discovery, and it proved how little reason the fellow had had to exclude himself from his censure of the human race. Joseph said not a word, particularly since in their conversation he had defended wrongdoing for the sake of its opposite. And the man was a guide after all and thus consecrated to Nabu, lord of the westernmost point in the circuit that led to the underworldly half of world, was a servant of the god of thieves. One might easily assume that in stealing from his sleeping ward he had performed a pious symbolic act. Joseph therefore said nothing about his discovery, but respected the man's dishonesty as a possible act of piety. All the same, he did find it disconcerting that his guide had categorically stolen. It implied something about both the means and the goal of his guidance that gave Joseph an unpleasant feeling, an uneasiness about the heart.

But it was not long before something worse than theft occurred. The sun had risen from behind field and forest, and Dothan's green hill was already in view a little off to the right, the town upon its crest bathed in the sun's dawning rays. Joseph, who was riding the ass at the time, while the thief held the reins, was looking in that direction—there was a jolt and a pitch, and it had happened. Hulda caught one of her front feet in a hole, she buckled and could not get up again. She had broken a pastern bone.

"Broken," his guide said after a brief examination by both. "Just look at this mess. Didn't I say that her pasterns were too frail?"

"This misfortune should give you no cause for rejoicing in

having evidently been right, and there was no need to even mention it at the moment. You were leading her and were paying no attention, and that's why she had the bad luck to step into the hole."

"I wasn't paying attention, and you're accusing me? That's typically human, to have to find someone to blame when things go awry just as could be predicted."

"It is also typically human to claim to have predicted an accident and to look for some pointless triumph in it. Be glad I've accused you of no more than inattention. There are other things I might charge you with as well. You shouldn't have advised me to travel by night, then we wouldn't have tired Hulda and the clever beast would not have stumbled."

"Do you suppose your complaints will heal her pastern?"

"No," Joseph said, "that's not what I mean. But I am to the point of asking what am I to do now? I cannot leave my animal here with its baggage of provisions that I intended to give my brothers as gifts in Jacob's name. There is still a great deal, even though I ate some of it and other things disappeared in other ways. Is Hulda to lie here helpless while the beasts of the field devour my treasures? I am close to weeping in exasperation."

"And once again who but I has good advice," the stranger responded. "Did I not say that I occasionally also acted as a watchman if need arose? Well then, off with you! Here I shall sit, the watchman of an ass, and of these edibles as well, fending off birds and robbers. Whether I feel I was originally made for such duties is another question that need not be discussed here. Enough. I shall sit here guarding the ass until you have found your brothers and return with them or a few servants to fetch your treasures and take care of the beast, whether to heal it or slay it."

"Thank you," Joseph said. "That is how we'll do it. I can already see that you are a proper man, that you have your good sides—and we'll not speak of the rest. I shall make haste as best I can and return again with others."

"I shall depend on it. You cannot go astray—around the hill there and some five hundred paces up the valley behind, through brush and clover, you'll find your brothers there, not far from a well in which there is no water. Consider if there's anything you need from the ass here. Something to protect your head from the sun as it climbs higher?"

"You're right," Joseph cried, "the accident has robbed me of every thought. I'll not leave *this* here," he said, pulling the *ketônet* from its ringed leather pouch, "not even under your protection, whatever good sides you may have. I'll take this along for my walk through Dothan's valley, so that I shall arrive in splendor even if not upon white Hulda, as Jacob wanted. I'll wrap it round me here right before your eyes—like so—and so—and then just this bit here! How do you like it? Am I not a colorful shepherd-bird in my robe? Mami's veiled garment, how does it suit her son?"

Lamech and His Wound

Meanwhile, behind the hill in the floor of the valley, Leah's sons and the handmaids' sons were sitting together, all ten, staring into the embers of the fire that had cooked their morning porridge. They had emerged from their striped tents a little distance off in the underbrush to greet the day—not all at the same time, but all quite early, some even before dawn, for they were not much in the mood for sleep. Seldom had any of them slept well since they had left Hebron, and the desire for variety that had moved them to exchange the pastures of Shechem for Dothan's meadows had arisen solely out of the illusory hope that sleep might be more refreshing elsewhere.

Sullen and stiff-limbed, stumbling at times over creeping, tangled roots of broom, they had gone to the well farther ahead, where their flocks covered the field and there was fresh water, for the cistern close by was dry and empty at this time of year. They had drunk, washed, and prayed, looked to the lambs and then found their way back to where they usually took meals in the shade of a group of red-trunked pines with many wide-reaching branches. There was a clear view from here across the plain dotted only with shrubs and a few trees, to the hill crowned by the town of Dothan, to the distant throng of sheep and gentle mountain slopes farthest off. The sun had already climbed fairly high. There was an odor of warmed herbs, of fennel, thyme, and those other fragrances of the field that sheep love.

The sons of Jacob were squatting on their heels in a circle—in its center, the pot set over still faintly glowing brushwood. They had long since finished eating, and sat there, red-eyed, doing nothing.

Their bodies were sated, but in their souls there gnawed a hunger and an unslaked thirst to which they could not have given a name but that ruined their sleep and undid the nourishment their morning meal should have provided. Every one of them felt a thorn in his flesh, festering, tormenting, consuming him—and it could not be pulled out. They all felt lethargic, and most had headaches. If they tried to clench their fists, they found they couldn't. When those who had once created a bloodbath to revenge Dinah asked themselves if they were men enough for such a deed here and now, they found that, no, they were no longer such men. That rancorous worm, that festering thorn, that gnawing hunger within them unnerved and unmanned them. What ignominy this condition must have brought with it, particularly for Shimeon and Levi, the savage twins. The latter poked his shepherd's staff glumly in the last embers. Shimeon rocked his body back and forth, breaking the silence in a low singsong, and one by one some of the others joined in, humming, for it was an ancient song, a fragment of some scattered ballad or epic, scraps of which had been passed down from time out of mind.

> Lamech, the hero, took unto him two wives,
> Adah and Zillah were their names.
> "Adah and Zillah, hear my song,
> You wives of Lamech, hearken to what I say.
> I have slain a man because he wounded me,
> I have brought a young man low for striking me.
> Cain was avenged sevenfold,
> Truly Lamech seven-and-seventyfold!"

They no longer knew what preceded or followed it, and so fell silent. But they let their thoughts play with the sound as it broke off, and in their mind's eye they saw Lamech, the hero, return armed and hot with pride from his deed and announce to his wives bowing before him that he had washed his heart clean. They also saw the man he had slain lying in the bloody grass—a man of little guilt, but nonetheless a sin-offering for Lamech's savagely sensitive honor. The robust "man" had been turned in the next line into something gentler by the word "young," which might have inclined the listener to sympathy for charm left bleeding. But sympathy was at most something for women, for Adah and Zillah, and in fact may only have served to spice their adoration of Lamech's incorruptibly murderous manhood and inflexible vengefulness, the ancient and pitiless emotion that ruled both the song and its character.

"His name was Lamech," Leah's Levi said, poking brushwood charcoal to pieces. "Do you like him? I ask because I do, indeed find him an excellent fellow. That was still a man, a lion-heart, the genuine thing, the sort you don't find anymore. It's only found in song nowadays, you sing and cheer yourself and think of times past. He could step before his wives with a heart washed clean, and when in his vigor he sought them out, one after the other, they knew whom they were receiving, and trembled with desire. Do you step forward like that before Shuah's daughter, Judah, or you, Dan, before your Moabite? Tell me what has become of the human race since those days, that all it brings forth are subtle thinkers and pious prayers, but no men?"

In reply Ruben said, "I will tell you what has taken revenge out of man's hand so that we are no longer like Lamech the hero. It is two things: Babel's decree and God's jealousy, both of which say 'Vengeance is mine.' For revenge must be taken away from man, otherwise it goes on breeding wildly, rank as a swamp, and the world is filled with blood. What was Lamech's fate? You do not know, for the song no longer tells us. But the young man that he slew had a brother or a son, who then laid Lamech low, so that the earth might receive his blood as well, and again from Lamech's loins came one who slew Lamech's murderer out of revenge, and so on, till nothing was left of Lamech's seed or of the seed of him who was first slain, and the earth could close its maw, for it was sated. But it is not good so—it is revenge's swampy brood and it knows no law. That is why when Cain slew Abel, God marked him with a sign showing that he was His, and said, 'If anyone slays Cain, vengeance shall be taken sevenfold.' But Babel established the court of law so that man may submit to its judgment for his deeds of bloodguilt and that vengeance not run wild."

To which, in his outspokenness, Zilpah's son Gad responded, "Yes, so you say, Ruben, in that thin voice that comes from your powerful body, all unexpectedly no matter how often one hears it. If I had your limbs I would not speak as you do, defending time's circuits and changes, which unman heroes and remove their lion hearts from the world. Where is the pride in your body that you speak in that thin voice and leave revenge to God or the court of bloodguilt? Are you not ashamed before Lamech, who said: 'This matter is a matter for three, for it is between me, him who wounded me, and the earth'? Cain said to Abel, 'Will God comfort me if Naëma, our sweet sister, accepts your gifts and smiles at you, or shall a court decide to whom she should belong? I am the firstborn, so she is mine. You are her twin, so she is yours. Neither God nor Nimrod's court can settle it. Let us go out into the field that we may settle it.' And he settled it with him, and as sure as I sit here, Gaddiel by name, whom Zilpah bore on Leah's lap, I am for Cain."

"And for my part I would no longer wish to be a young lion as people call me," Jehuda said, "if I were not for Cain as well, and even more for Lamech. On my honor, he respected himself and did not hold his pride in low esteem. 'Sevenfold?' he asked. 'Pah! I am Lamech. Seven-and-seventyfold will I be avenged, and there he lies, the dandy, in token of my wound!'"

"What sort of wound might it have been," Issakhar, the raw-boned ass, inquired, "and in what way did that wretched youngster offend valiant, strapping Lamech that he did not leave revenge to God or Nimrod, but took it into his own hand many times over?"

"No one knows anymore," his half brother Naphtali, son of Bilhah, replied. "The young man's impudence is unknown, and what Lamech washed away with that blood has been lost to the world's memory. But I've heard it said that men in our own day swallow shame far more disgusting than what Lamech suffered. They swallow it, the cowardly wretches, and then depart, so it's said, for somewhere or other, and there they sit, gorged on a shame that rages within them, till they cannot eat or sleep, and if Lamech, whom they so admire, were to see them, he'd kick them in the backside, for that is all they're worth."

He said it with a maliciously nimble tongue, his face distorted. The twins groaned and tried to clench their fists, and yet could not.

Zebulun said, "There were Adah and Zillah, Lamech's wives. Adah is to blame, let me tell you. For she bore Jabal, the father of those who live in tents and keep cattle, Abram's ancestor, and Yitzchak's, and Jacob's, our gentle father. That's what ruined things and made a mess of them, so that we are no longer men, just as you say, brother Levi, but subtle thinkers and pious prayers, as if we'd been castrated with a sickle, God help us! Yes, if only we were hunters or even seafarers, that would be different. But with Jabal, Adah's son, the coziness of tents came into the world, the keeping of sheep and Abram's pondering on God—that has unnerved us, until we tremble for fear of offending a worthy father. Until big Ruben says, 'Vengeance is God's.' But can one rely on God and His justice if He takes sides in the argument and even uses disgusting dreams to instill impudence in that good-for-nothing lad? We can do nothing against dreams," he cried in agony, his voice breaking, "if they are from God and it is ordained that we are to bow down!"

"But we could do something about the Dreamer," Gad shouted, he, too, with torment in his breast. "So that," Asher added for him, "the dreams would have no master and no longer know how to come true."

"That would have meant," Re'uben retorted, "setting oneself against God, either way. For it is the same thing to rise up against the Dreamer or against God, if the dreams are from Him." He used the past tense, saying "would have meant" and not "would mean," as a sign that the matter was already settled.

It was Dan who spoke next. He said, "Listen, brothers, and heed my words, for Dan is called a serpent and an adder and, by reason of a certain craftiness of mind, is fit to be a judge. It is certainly true, and Ruben is right: If one were to retaliate, leaving the Dreamer's dreams helpless and without a master, one would, I grant, be exposing oneself to the wrath of those whose ways are arbitrary and call down upon oneself the vengeance of those whose will is unjust— there's no denying it. But one must take that risk, so Dan says, for one cannot imagine what could be worse, or at least as bad as the fulfillment of those dreams. But one has at least deprived arbitrary power of their fulfillment, and though it rage in its fury—the dreams will search for their dreamer in vain. Deeds shape events, that we know from the past. Did not Jacob suffer one thing or another for his deception, and because of Esau's bitter tears find little to laugh about in Laban's service? Well, he endured it, for he already had the chief advantage, the blessing, it was safely put away, and no God, no god whatever, could have done anything to undo it, try as He might. One must endure tears and revenge for the sake of a future good, for what has safely been put away will not return again . . ."

His words, however crafty at first, now got tangled up. But

Ruben replied, and it was strange to see this man strong as a tree turn so pale. "You have spoken, Dan, and may now be silent. For we have departed from there and separated ourselves from our father's hearth. What vexed us is safely far away, and we sit here in safety as well, in Dothan, five days distant from there. Those are deeds that shape events."

And with that, after the many speeches, they all bowed their heads, very low, almost between their knees, which jutted up from their crouching positions, and there they sat crumpled up around the ashes like ten bundles of misery.

Joseph Is Cast into the Well

But it happened that Asher, Zilpah's son, curious despite his distress, peeked out over his knees, letting his gaze roam out across the land. And there in the distant light he saw something flash like silver lightning, vanishing only to reappear, and when he looked more closely there were two and more bolts, shimmering now singly, now concurrently at different points, but very close together.

Asher nudged Gad, his full brother sitting beside him, and pointed a finger toward this will-o'-the-wisp, in hopes that he might help him understand. And as they inspected it, hands shading their eyes and one face seeking advice of the other, the rest were alerted by their uneasiness. Those with their backs to the plain turned around. They exchanged glances, each pair of eyes following the direction of another, until all heads were raised and they peered together toward a figure strolling toward them and glittering as it came.

"A man is coming, and he glitters," Judah said.

After a pause, during which they watched and waited for the figure to grow in size, Dan remarked, "More like a young man."

And in that same moment every tanned face turned as ashen as Ruben's had only minutes before, and their hearts beat at the same wild, accelerated rhythm, like drums in a kind of muffled concert, and the hollow rumbling filled the breathless silence around them.

Joseph came directly toward them across the plain, dressed in his coat of many colors, a wreath set atop its veiled hood.

They did not believe it. They sat there with thumbs pressed to cheeks, fingers crossed before mouths, elbows propped on knees, and stared bug-eyed out over their hands at the approaching dazzlement. They hoped and feared it was a dream. In terror and hope, several refused even to grasp its reality, until the approaching figure smiled at them from so near now that there could no longer be any doubt.

"Yes, yes, greetings!" he said in his own voice and stepped before them. "Go ahead and trust your eyes, my good men. I have come at Father's behest on Hulda, the she-ass, to see if things are in order with you and to—" He faltered in dismay. There they sat, not saying a word, not even stirring, but staring—an eerily bewitched group of men. But as they sat there, though with neither a sunrise nor sunset to paint them, their faces turned as red as the twisted trunks of trees at their back, red as the desert, dark red like that star in the sky, and their eyes seemed about to spurt blood. He stepped back. Then came the sound of a booming roar, the twins' bull-like bellow that sent terror through men's bowels, and with a long-drawn-out scream as if from *one* tormented throat—a desperately exultant "ahhh" of rage, of hate, and of release—they all leapt up in savagely precise simultaneity and hurled themselves at him.

They fell on him like a pack of starved wolves on their prey; there was no holding them back, no second thoughts tamed their blood-blinded lust, they looked as if they were about to tear him into at least fourteen pieces. In the depths of their souls they truly were intent on ripping, ripping off, ripping apart. "Off, off, off!" they gasped and shouted, and it was clear they meant the *ketônet*—the robe of symbols, the veiled garment—it had to come off him. But even in the midst of the melee it stayed on, for he had wound it about himself, fastening it at head and shoulders, and they were too many for just *one* deed, getting in each other's way, with brother shoving brother off their pummeled victim, who staggered and flew among them as they exchanged blows intended for him—though, to be sure, plenty of them landed on their mark. Blood streamed from Joseph's nose at once, and one eye closed shut in a blue welt.

In their midst, however, towering above everyone and shouting "Off, off!" along with the rest, Ruben made good use of the hurly-burly. He howled with the wolves. He did what people have always done when trying to gain makeshift control over a mob on the loose, joining in with apparent zeal in order to maintain influence over events and prevent worse. He gave every appearance of being jostled about, but in truth was himself doing the jostling, shoving back, as best he could, those who tried to strike Joseph and rip his coat off him and doing what he could to protect him. He paid particular attention to Levi, who had his shepherd's staff, and kept stumbling into him. Despite his maneuvers, however, the terrified lad was doing worse than a coddled son could ever have dreamed. He lurched about in bewilderment, head tucked between shoulders, elbows splayed, trapped beneath this hailstorm of ugly brutality—that came from out of the blue and was hideously, totally oblivious of where its blows landed—thundering down upon him and smashing to pieces his beliefs, his image of the world, his conviction, firm as natural law, that everyone must surely love him more than they loved themselves.

"Brothers!" he stammered, blood from his split lip and nose running down over his chin, "What are you—" A blow to his head that Ruben had been unable to prevent ripped the word from his mouth; he crumpled under an utterly reckless fist to the soft belly between his ribs—and vanished under the pack. It cannot be denied, indeed it should be emphasized, that the behavior of Jacob's sons, despite whatever justice stood on their side, was absolutely shameful, indeed it must be termed atavistic. They descended below their humanity and, since their hands unfortunately had more than enough to do, in their attempt to rip his mother's garment from Joseph's bloody, semiconscious body, they remembered their teeth. They were not mute as they went about it, and "Off, off!" was not their only cry. Just as laborers dull their senses with monotonous shouts as they haul and heave together, they too called up tags of words from the depths of their rancor, erupting over and over into groans that fed their rage and banished thought. "Bend low, bend low!" "See if things are in order!" "You thorn in the flesh!" "Lingering malady!" "This—is for your dreams!" And the wretched lad?

For him what was happening to the *ketônet* was the most horrible and incredible thing of all, more painful and hideous than all the bruising insult accompanying it. He desperately tried to preserve the garment, to keep its tatters and rags about him, screaming several times "My robe!," and was still begging "Don't rip it!" even as he stood there naked, like a fearful virgin. For the veil's removal was all too violent for it to have been limited to the veil alone. Shirt and loincloth went with it, their shreds lay scattered about in the moss, along with those of wreath and veil. And while he covered his face with his arms to little benefit, the pack's blows mercilessly pummeled his naked body—"Bend low, bend low!" "This—is for your dreams!"—but were deflected, their force slightly diminished, by big Ruben alone, who went on playing the man being jostled about while pushing the others away from Joseph and pretending they were preventing him from hammering away at their victim to his own heart's and wrath's content. "Thorn in the flesh!" and "Lingering malady!" were his cries too. But then he shouted something else that came to him on the spur of the moment, shouted it loudly and repeatedly, so that they all might hear it and be distracted from their mindless rage. "Tie him up! Tie him up!" "By his hands and feet!" It was a new slogan that he provided—new and invented in greatest haste to serve a good purpose. It was intended as a temporary goal for a deed of unpredictable scope, was meant to create a breathing spell in which Ruben might gain time in his anxious desire to avert the worst. In fact, as long as they were busy with tying Joseph up, they would not beat him; and once he lay bound, they could take satisfaction in something accomplished for the moment, a stage of events that would demand they step back and consider further action. That was Ruben's hasty calculation. And so he propagated his solution with a desperate zeal, as if it were the only expedient and reasonable action to be taken now, and as if anyone who didn't listen to it was a fool. "This—for your dreams!" he shouted. "Tie him—tie him up!" "You blockheads!" "You take revenge like ninnies!" "Instead of hitting me, tie him up!" "Is there no rope here?" he cried yet again at the top of his voice.

There was. Gaddiel, for example, wore a piece of rope around his body and he unwound it. Since their heads were empty, there was room for Ruben's slogan. They tied the naked man up, securing his arms and legs with the same piece of rope, trussed him up properly until he moaned—and Ruben diligently joined in their labors. When it was done he stepped back, breathing a sigh and wiping away the sweat, as if he had outdone them all from the start.

Temporarily removed from battle, the others stood there beside him, gasping as they took a savage pause. Before them lay Rachel's son, wretchedly battered. He lay on his own bound arms, the back of his head angled into the grass, his knees drawn up, his ribs heaving, his entire body, to which clung moss and dirt and the slobber of his brothers' fury, soundly battered and thrashed; and meandering down over it were trickles of the red juice that gushes out of beauty when its surface is damaged. His unscathed eye searched out his assailants in horror, blinking at times in reflex, as if defending itself against new acts of violence.

The malefactors stood about huffing and exaggerating their exhaustion to conceal the uncertainty taking hold as they began to come to their senses. They mimicked Ruben, wiping sweat with the backs of their hands, puffing their lips, and making faces to express the vast justice of the outrage that still lingered from their act of revenge, as if to say, "Whatever may happen, can anyone reproach us for this?" They said it in words as well, panted exclamations of self-justification, for one another and for any other judge who might have power to hear their case: "What a scoundrel!" "What a thorn!" "We showed him!" "We thrashed it out of him!" "Can you believe it!" "Comes strolling up!" "Comes strolling right up to us!" "In his coat of many colors!" "Right before our eyes!" "Wants to see if things are in order!" "Well *we* saw to that!" "And he won't forget it, either!"

But even amid their exclamations, there were stirrings—simultaneous in all of them—of a horror that all these blurted-out phrases were actually meant to deaden, and a closer look at this secret dread revealed that it was the thought of Jacob. God Almighty, what had they done to their father's lamb—not to mention the state Rachel's bridal heirloom was currently in? How would that man of forceful words react when he saw or learned of it, how would they stand before him, and how would they all fare then? Re'uben thought of Bilhah. Shimeon and Levi thought of Shechem and Jacob's wrath, how it had come over them as they had returned home from their heroic deed. Naphtali, he especially, took fleeting comfort in the thought that Jacob was five days off and suspected nothing whatever; yes, for the first time in his life Naphtali considered space, which divided and kept people in ignorance, to be a blessing. That power of space, however—as they all understood—could not be maintained. All too soon, when Joseph stepped before him again, Jacob would learn of everything, and the inevitable emotional storm with its bolts of curses and rolling thunder of words would be unbearable. Grown men though they were, they had a child's deep fear of that, fear of the curse as a gesture and fear of its meaning and consequences. They would all be cursed together, that was clear, because they had lifted a hand against the lamb, and the hypocrite would finally, explicitly be raised above them as the chosen heir.

The fulfillment of those shameful dreams—the work of their own hands! Precisely what event-shaping deeds were supposed to have prevented God from doing. They began to realize that big Ruben had made fools of them with his slogan. There they stood now, and there lay the thief of the blessing, nicely punished, true, and tied up, but could these be called deeds that shaped events for good and all? It would be a different matter if Joseph were *never* to appear before the old man again, if Jacob were to be told of an irrevocably accomplished deed. Granted, his distress would then be even more horrible—unimaginable in fact. But it would then pass over them—that could be arranged. Half a deed, and they would be blamed. But not necessarily if they went the whole way. They stood there considering this, the same thought running through all their heads—even Ruben's. He could not help recognizing facts. The cunning that had brought their deeds to a halt had come from his heart. Reason told him that so much had happened already that still more would have to happen now. It had to happen, and yet for God's sake it could not happen, not for any price—that was the confusion in his soul. Big Ruben's muscular face had never worn so stormy and baffled an expression.

He feared that at any moment he would hear spoken the inevitable words to which he had no answer. They were spoken, and he heard them. Someone said them, it makes no difference who. Ruben did not look to see who it might be. The imperative belonged to them all: "He must be gone."

"Gone," Ruben nodded in fierce confirmation. "So you say. But not where."

"Gone for good," the voice replied. "He must go down into the pit, so that he is no more. He ought not to have been for a long time, but now he cannot be at all, ever again."

"I perfectly agree!" Ruben responded with bitter scorn. "And then we will come before Jacob, his father, without him. 'Where is the boy?' he will ask at some point. 'He is no more,' we shall then answer. But if he asks, 'And why is he no more?,' we shall answer, 'We have slain him.'"

They said nothing.

"No," Dan said, "not like that. Listen to me, brothers, I am called a serpent and an adder and a certain craftiness cannot be denied me. We shall do it this way: We shall put him into the pit, let him down into a pit, into this dry well here, half filled with earth, but with no water in it. We'll put him safely away there, and then let him see what dreams he has. But we shall lie to Jacob and say with assurance, 'We have not seen him and do not know whether he is alive or not. If not, perhaps some ravenous beast has eaten him. Alas, how awful!' We shall have to add that 'Alas!' for the sake of the lie."

"Hush," Naphtali said. "There he lies close by and can hear us."

"What does that matter?" Dan replied. "He will tell no one. That he can hear us is one more reason why he cannot depart from here, but then we dared not let him depart before, so it's all one. We can go ahead and speak before him, for he is already as good as dead."

From Joseph came a plaintive cry, torn from a chest thrust upward by the tight ropes and with nipples like frail, red stars. He wept.

"You hear that, and feel no pity?" Ruben asked.

"Ruben, what is your point?" Judah rejoined. "Why speak of pity, even if one or the other of us may feel a tinge of it just as well as you? Does his weeping at this moment undo the fact that he has been a shameless toad all his life, offensive to heaven and beyond, and has denigrated us before Father with his vile dissembling? Does pity counter what is necessary, and is it a decisive reason why he should depart from here to accuse us all? And so what use is there in speaking of pity, even a tinge of it? Has he not already heard that we will lie to Jacob? Just for him to have heard is more than enough to cost him his life—and Dan spoke the truth, with or without pity. He is already as good as dead."

"You are right," Ruben then said. "We shall throw him into the pit."

Joseph gave another wretched wail.

"But he's still wailing," someone thought it necessary to remind them.

"Is he not to be allowed even to weep?" Ruben cried. "Let him go down into the pit wailing, what more would you want!"

And here words were said that we shall not provide verbatim, since they would horrify modern sensibilities and, in a more direct form, cast the brothers, or some of them, in disproportionately bad light. The fact is that Shimeon and Levi, as well as outspoken Gad, offered to polish off the bound lad on the spot. The twins wanted to use their staffs, swinging back with the full power of both arms in good Cain fashion, to put an end to him. Gad, however, asked to be permitted to swiftly cut his throat with a knife, just as Jacob had once done to the kid whose pelt he needed for that exchanged blessing. Such suggestions were made—there is no denying it; but we do not wish the reader to have an irrevocable falling-out with Jacob's sons and refuse ever to forgive them, which is why we do not supply the brothers' words verbatim. These things were said because they had to be said, because, to use contemporary terms, they were the logical consequence. And it was only appropriate, then, that those who managed to utter such words and offer their services were the brothers whose earthly role best suited such actions and who, so to speak, proved obedient to their myth: the savage twins and strapping Gad.

But Ruben did not permit it. It is a known fact that he resisted and did not want what had happened to Abel and the goat kid to happen to Joseph. "I oppose and protest this," he said, invoking his standing as Leah's firstborn, which allowed him, despite downfall and father's curse, to have his say. The boy was as good as dead— they had said so themselves. He would weep a little more, that was all, and it sufficed to cast him into the well. Let them have a look for themselves to see if that was still Joseph the Dreamer. He was already unrecognizable after what had happened—events in which he, Ruben, had taken part, and would have taken a greater part still had they not jostled him on all sides. But what had happened had simply happened, they had not done anything, no one could say that. It had happened through his brothers, but they had not done it, rather events had simply pulled them along. But now with clear heads and by deliberate decision, they wanted to do an abominable deed and lift their hands against the boy—which meant shedding their father's blood, which until now had merely flowed, though they had been involved. But just as with doing and happening, there was a difference in this world between flowing and shedding, and if they could not see the difference they had been shortchanged on reason. Had they been appointed as a court over life and death, he asked, to judge in their own case and then to carry out the bloody sentence themselves? No, no bloodshed, he would not stand for it. Given what had happened, what they needed to do was put the boy in the pit—and leave the rest to happenstance.

So said big Ruben, but no one has ever believed that he was deceiving himself, that he was a strict adherent of some fundamental difference between "do" and "happen" or supposed that letting the boy perish in the pit did not mean lifting a hand against him. When, a little later, Jehuda raised the issue of what was to be gained by slaying their brother and concealing his blood, he was not telling Ruben anything new. Humanity has long since looked into Ruben's heart and seen that he wanted nothing more than to gain time—he could not have said for what—just time to nurture a scant hope that he might rescue Joseph from their hands and, one way or another, bring him back to his father. It was both his fear of Jacob and a grim, embarrassed love for the hated brother that secretly drove him—and that allowed him to consider treason against the tribe of his brothers, for it could be called nothing less. Re'uben, the son like gushing water, had all sorts of amends to make to Jacob because of Bilhah. But if he were to bring Joseph back to him from here, would not that past affair be more than compensated for, the curse lifted from him, and his rights as a firstborn restored? We do not presume to know all that lay behind Ruben's thoughts and plans, nor do we wish to disparage the motives behind his actions. But do we disparage them by submitting the possibility that he privately hoped both to save and to triumph over Rachel's child?

Moreover, he met with scarcely any resistance from his brothers in demanding that they set doing aside and let happening take over. It probably would have suited them all fine if what they were doing—seeing as it was already happening—had led to its goal in *one* fell swoop; but having once paused to consider things, to end it now with a pure deed based on an explicit decision to shed blood—no one really had the heart for that, not even the twins, savage as they were, or Gaddiel, however strapping. They were quite happy that they had not been assigned tasks in regard to head or throat, and that Ruben's authority and catchphrases prevailed—first with the tying-up, and now with the well.

"To the pit!" was their cry, and they grabbed the rope by which

Joseph was bound, took hold here and there and dragged the poor lad cross-country to the spot beyond the meadow where they knew the cistern stood empty. A few of them had yoked themselves at the front to pull, several assisted alongside, and a couple trotted behind. Re'uben was not trotting, but walked with long strides at the rear of the transport, and if there was a stone in the path, a nasty stump, or thorny shrub, he would grab hold of their cargo and raise him up to prevent needless suffering.

So off they went to the pit with Joseph, with a heigh! and a ho!, for a kind of merriment took hold of the brothers on the trip, the mindless sport of shared labor, so that they laughed and joked and shouted nonsense to one another—about how they were dragging a well-bound sheaf, and would it ever bend low into the hole, into the well, into the deep. But this was merely because they all felt a sense of relief at not having to follow the model of Abel or the kid, and also so that they might not hear the pleas and plaintive wails that constantly came from Joseph's split lips.

"Brothers! Have pity! What are you doing! Stop! Oh, oh, what's happening to me!"

Which helped him not in the least. Away they trotted with him through weeds and shrubs, a good distance across open country to where a mossy slope descended to a cool hollow that had once been walled in, but was now only rubble, cracked tiles, shrub oaks, and stunted fig trees, with several steep and broken steps leading down to it—over which they dragged Joseph, who had now begun a desperate struggle to free himself from the ropes and their arms, for he had a horror of the well built there and of the hole of the well, but most especially of the mossy, damaged well stone now resting on tiles off to one side, but intended as a cover for the well. But no matter how Joseph resisted and wept, gazing in terror with his one good eye at the black circle, they heaved him up on its edge with a heigh! and a ho! and thrust his weight forward so that he had to fall, who knew how deep.

It was deep enough, though not an abyss, not a bottomless gorge. Such wells often reach depths of a hundred feet and more, but this one had long been out of use and was now silted with soil and gravel—perhaps the result of some old feud about the spot. But the five or six fathoms that Joseph had to descend into the shaft were quite enough, and certainly too many for a bound man ever to climb out of again. He had fallen with all the caution and fear for his life that he could summon, with feet and elbows finding some little purchase here and there, breaking his fall to a slide, so that he landed relatively unscathed in the rubble, much to the fright of all sorts of beetles, crickets, and other cellar denizens unprepared for such a visit. But even as he was thinking about his having landed, one way or another, the brothers up top were putting strength of arm to work to do the rest, shouting as they labored to cover his house with the stone. For it was heavy and rolling it over the pit was not work for one man, but rather they all took hold and shared in the task, since it was a piecemeal job in any case. For the old cover, green with moss and a good five feet in diameter, was split into two parts, and when they had rolled each half over the round hole, the two did not meet, but left a gap, narrow here, wider there, though which a little daylight fell into the well. Joseph looked up at it with his one good eye—at how he had somehow fallen into these circular depths, to lie here naked and exposed.

Joseph Cries from the Pit

Their work done, the brothers now sat down to rest on the steps leading to the recess of the well, and a few of them pulled bread and cheese from their belt pouches to enjoy some breakfast. Levi, a rough but pious man, suggested that they ought not eat in the presence of shed blood; but they responded that there was no blood, that was the advantage of the method, blood had neither flowed nor been shed—and so Levi ate as well.

They chewed, blinking and thinking. Their thoughts were directed now toward something quite secondary—but for the moment it seemed the most impressive matter of all. The hands and arms that had been busy burying a man still bore the memory of touching Joseph's bare skin, and the memory was remarkably tender, although their touch had been anything but; and as they sat there blinking they could feel the gentle message it shared with their hearts, but could not rightly understand it. Nor was anything said about it, for when they spoke it was only to assert that Joseph was now set aside, that both he and his dreams were now in safekeeping, and mutually to comfort one another in that regard.

"He is no more now," they said. "Pfff, so that's done, and we can sleep in peace now." The more dubious the matter appeared to them, the more emphatically they repeated the assertion that they could now sleep peacefully. They would sleep because the Dreamer was now eliminated and would say nothing to their father. But even this calming thought included thought of their father, who would be waiting in vain, forever in vain, for Joseph's return home—and the mere idea, despite all the security it provided, was certainly not an invitation to sleep. It was for all ten, without exception, even for the savage twins, a horrible thought, its most conspicuous component their childish fear of Jacob, fear of both the tenderness and the power of his soul, and the price paid for Joseph's being unable to speak had been an attack on that passionate soul, which they called to mind only with terror. In the end, what they had done to their brother they had done out of jealousy—and everyone knows what emotion is wrenched and distorted into jealousy. To be sure, when one looked at Shimeon's and Levi's well-oiled brutality any reference to that emotion might seem quite inept, which is why we need to speak obliquely, in half-words. Some instances are best served with only half-words.

They brooded, chewing and blinking, the gentle touch of Joseph's skin still on hands and arms. Thinking was difficult, and made more difficult by disruptive, muted wails and pleas that found their way up to them from the man lowered into his grave. For after his fall, he had collected his senses enough to remember the need to wail in protest, and he implored them from below:

"Brothers, where are you? Oh, don't go, don't leave me alone in this grave, it's so full of rot and horrors! Brothers, take pity on me and save me yet from the night of the pit where I'm perishing. I am your brother Joseph. Brothers, do not close your ears to my sighs and shouts, for you do me wrong. Ruben, where are you? Ruben, I call out your name, from here in the pit below. They have misunderstood me. You have misunderstood me, dear brothers, so do help me and save my life. I came to you for our father's sake, a journey of five days on Hulda, the white jenny ass, to bring you gifts, parched grain, and fruit cakes—ah, how it all went wrong. And that man is to blame for its having gone wrong, the man who guided me. Brothers in Jacob, hear and understand me, I did not come to you to see if things were in order, you don't need the child for that. I came to bend low before you as is seemly custom and to inquire about your health, that you might return home to Father. Brothers, those dreams . . . was it so rude of me to tell you my dreams? Believe me, I told you only relatively very modest ones, when I could have . . . Ah, that's not what I wanted to say. Oh, oh, my bones and sinews, right and left, and all my limbs! I thirst! The child is thirsty, for he has lost a great deal of blood because of a mistake. Are you still there? Have I been deserted already? Ruben, let me hear your voice. Tell them I won't say a word if they rescue me. Brothers, I know you think you have to leave me here in the pit because otherwise I would tell. By the God of Abraham, Yitzchak, and Jacob, by your mothers' heads and by Rachel's head, my own dear mother, I will not tell, never ever, if you will only yet save me from this pit, just this one time."

"Oh, he's certain to tell, if not today, then tomorrow," Judah muttered between his teeth, and there was no one who did not share his certainty, not even Ruben, however much his own unsettled hopes and plans might contradict theirs—but that meant he had to keep them all the more secret and strongly deny them. Which is why he put cupped hands to his mouth and cried, "If you don't keep quiet, we shall throw stones down on you, and that will really be the last of you. We don't want to hear anything more from you, for you are finished."

Hearing and recognizing Ruben's voice, Joseph took fright and fell silent, leaving them to go on blinking and fearing their father without disruption. As things had stood, had their intent been to hold to self-exile and live in ongoing discord with their father's hearth, they would not have had to deal with Jacob's waiting and slowly gathering despair, with the whole emotional misery in preparation at Hebron. But now the very opposite was the case. Their having sunk Joseph into the pit could serve but one purpose—to do away with the obstacle between them and their father's heart, for which they all felt a truly childlike concern; and the basis of their confusion was that they had found themselves compelled to do utmost harm to that gentle and powerful heart in order to win it for themselves. And indeed this was the viewpoint taken by all of them now. The chief concern that had taken hold of them was not to punish the smart aleck or seek revenge, or even primarily to destroy his dreams; they were, instead, unanimous in wanting to open the way

to their father's heart. The way lay clear now, and they would return—without Joseph, just as they had departed without him.
Where was he? He had been sent to find them. If someone is sent to
find those whose departure was a protest against his very life, and
they now return without him, there is something suspicious about
that. They would be asked—and not without a certain horrible justification—as to the whereabouts of the person without whom they
were returning. To be sure, they could reply with a shrug. Were they
their brother's keepers? But the question would not then be answered—no, it would go on, fixing large, piercing, mistrustful eyes
at them, and beneath its gaze, beneath the eyes of that question they
would witness both agonizing waiting, which they knew to be in
vain, and a gradual despair that, given the nature of things, could be
its sole result. They shuddered at such a penance. Should they stay
away, then, until hope had been burned out and waiting had yielded
to a realization that Joseph would never return? That would take a
long time, for waiting is stubborn, and meanwhile the question
might easily answer itself and become a curse upon them all. The essential thing, it was clear, was an immediate and brief announcement
that the boy would never return, but this also carried within it conclusive proof of their innocence, cleansing them of any suspicion.
The thought was at work in all of them, and in Dan, who called
a serpent and an adder, it matured to a proposal. For he combined
his own ideas from before, about telling the old man that a wild beast
had slain Joseph, with Gad's suggestion as to how he was reminded
of the goat kid Jacob had sacrificed for the exchange of blessings.

Dan said, "Listen to me, brothers, I am fit to be a judge and
know how we shall do it. We shall take an animal from the flock and
slay it by cutting its throat, so that blood flows. But into the animal's
blood we shall dip that nuisance, the coat of many colors, Rachel's
bridal garment that lies ripped to shreds at our camp. We shall bring
it before Jacob and say to him, 'We found this in the pasture, torn
and drenched in blood. Is this not your son's robe?' Then he may
draw his conclusions from the condition of the robe, and it will be
the same as when a shepherd shows his master the remains of a sheep
that a lion has slain—for he is then absolved and need not even swear
to his innocence."

"Hush," Judah muttered in painful discomfort. "Under the

stone are ears to hear what you say and to understand what we are planning."

"Where's the harm?" Dan replied. "Should I whisper and lisp for his sake? It's all about things beyond his life—our business, but no longer his. You forget that he's as good as dead and finished. If he understands that as well as what I am saying now in my natural voice, he'll keep it all nicely to himself. We have never been able to speak freely and unreservedly when he was among us, for we had to bear in mind that he would report it to Father and we would end up on the ash heap. That's the point, that we finally have him among us as a brother whom we can trust and who may hear everything. Why, I'd like to blow him a kiss there in the pit. So what do all of you think of my inspiration?"

They wanted to discuss it, but Joseph began to wail again and entreat them in weeping pleas from below not to do it.

"Brothers," he cried, "do not do that with the animal and the robe, do not do that to Father, for he will not survive it. Ah, I'm begging not for me, my body and soul have been broken, and I lie in my grave. But spare our father and do not bring him the bloody garment—it will be his death. Ah, if you only know how in his fears he warned me about lions whenever he found me alone at night, and now I'm supposed to have been eaten by one! If you had seen how he sent me on my journey with such anxious care, for which I made lame allowances. Woe is me, for it is surely not wise of me to speak to you of his love for the child—yet what am I to do, dear brothers? Advise me how best not to vex you. Why, indeed, is my life so intertwined with his that I cannot entreat you to spare his life without also begging for my own. Ah, dear brothers, hear my weeping and do not terrify him in his fears with that bloody robe, for his gentle soul will not bear it, and he will fall back in a faint."

"Well now," Ruben said, "I can't take this, it's unbearable." And he stood up. "If you like, let us go elsewhere, farther away. No one can talk amid his wailing, or even think amid his cries from the depths. Come, let's go to our tents." He said it angrily so that the pallor of his muscular face might look like the pallor of rage. But in fact its source was the realization of how right the boy was about his father. For he, too, could foresee Jacob's literally falling back in a faint at the sight of the garment. Apart from that, however, Ruben was particularly moved by the awareness that in his distress Joseph's thoughts were of his father, that his fearful petitions concerned the vulnerability of the old man's soul—that above all else, and himself only secondarily. Might he have thrust that to the fore in order to save himself, hiding himself behind it out of old habit? No, no, it was different this time. The cries from under the stone came from a Joseph different from the boy whose shoulders he had once shaken, trying to awaken him out of his vain folly. What shaking had not accomplished, the fall into the pit evidently had—Joseph was awakened, was pleading for his father's heart, no longer mocking it, but repentant and anxious for it; and this discovery offered Ruben an extraordinary reinforcement for his unsettled plans, at the same time making him doubly sensitive to their helpless and hopeless uncertainty.

Which was the reason for his pallor when he stood up and invited them all to leave the place where Joseph was now concealed. And they did so, too. Departing together, they went to gather up the veil's tatters at the spot where the thrashing had taken place, to bring them to their tents and there deliberate Dan's inspiration. And Joseph was left alone.

In the Grave

He was terrified to his very soul to be left alone in his hole, and he wailed for a long time as his brothers moved off, begging them not to desert him. He scarcely knew, however, what it was he cried out in his weeping, and that was because his true thoughts were not with his automatic and superficial pleas and wails, but rather somewhere below them; and below these true thoughts others truer still moved as their shadows, their ground bass, their deepest current, so that all together, arranged vertically, they resembled agitated music that his mind was occupied with directing—top, middle, and bottom—all at once. That was also the explanation for his having let slip that blunder amid his entreaties, saying that he had told his brothers only very modest dreams compared to others he had also dreamt. Anyone who could consider this a mitigating circumstance for even a moment, indeed blurt it out, would have to be someone whose thoughts were not entirely with his words, but in whom several things were happening—as was the case with Joseph.

A great deal had been happening in him since that startling and terrifying moment when his brothers had fallen upon him like wolves and he had gazed into their enraged and aggrieved faces out of the one eye that they had not immediately blinded with their fists. Those faces had been very close to his own as the furious men ripped the garment of symbols from his body with nails and teeth—terribly close; and the torment of hatred that he had been able to read in them had counted for the major part of the horror he had felt at their abuse. It goes without saying that he had been utterly terrified as he wept in pain at their blows; fear and pain, however, were thoroughly drenched with sympathy for the torment of hatred that he could read in those sweating, masklike faces as they came and went all too close before him—and sympathy with pain that we must admit we have caused is very much like repentance. Ruben had been quite correct in his perceptions. This time Joseph had been shaken so roughly that his eyes had been opened and he saw the damage he had done, and that he had done it. All the while he was being tossed back and forth under the fists of his furious brothers and losing his robe, all the while he was lying tied up on the ground and enduring the excruciating transport to the well, his thoughts never stood still despite all those numbing terrors; his mind had definitely not remained solely in the frightening present, but had also hastily skimmed back over a past in which all of these things—though hidden to his soul's trustfulness and yet somehow also brashly half-known to it—had been in preparation.

My God, his brothers! To what had he brought them? For he understood that he had brought them to this—many and grave mistakes had been committed in the assumption that people loved him more than they loved themselves, an assumption that he had believed and yet not quite actually believed, but according to which he had at any rate lived and that, as he plainly realized, had landed him in this pit. With his one good eye he had clearly read in his brothers' distorted, sweating faces that it had been an assumption beyond human capacities, that he had taxed their souls with it for a long time and caused them great suffering, until finally it had come to this end—so terrible both for him and doubtlessly for them as well.

His poor brothers! What they must have endured until desperation had driven them to lay violent hands on their father's lamb and cast it into this pit. Into what a situation had they now put themselves—not to mention his own, which, to be sure, was hopeless, as he himself admitted with a shudder. For he would never be able to make them believe that once returned to his father he would hold his tongue and not report all this—it was not believable, not even to himself—and so they had had to leave him in this pit to rot, they had no other choice. He understood that, which may make it seem all the more remarkable that his horror at his own fate still left room for sympathy with his murderers. And yet that is the proven state of affairs. Joseph knew precisely, and admitted it openly and honestly to himself as he sat there at the bottom of the well, that the shameless "assumption" by which he had lived had been a game in which he himself had never seriously believed, or ever could have believed, and that, to take just one example, he ought never to have told his brothers his dreams—how impossible, tactless, devoid of all legitimacy. Indeed it was—and he had been silently, privately aware of that, as he now admitted to himself, both always and in the very moment of telling them. And yet he had done it. Why? He had felt an irresistible itch to do it; he had had to do it because God had created him expressly to do it, because He had designed it all with and through him, so that, in a word, Joseph would go down into the pit—or put even more precisely, God had wanted it that way. But why? Joseph did not know. Evidently so that he would perish. But ultimately Joseph did not believe that. He was fundamentally convinced that God looked farther than just to this pit, that as usual He had far more extensive plans and was following some purpose of the distant future, and to serve it he, Joseph, had had to drive his brothers to the uttermost. They were being sacrificed to that future, and he felt sorry for them, despite how bad things were for him. Those unhappy men would send their father the garment, after first rolling it in the blood of the goat kid as if in Joseph's own, and Jacob would fall back in a faint. The thought made Joseph start up in an attempt to protect his father from the sight of it—the upshot of which was, of course, that he sank back in his bondage against the wall of the well, pain stabbing at him like the bites of beasts, and began to weep again.

He had the anguish of leisure to put fear, remorse, and sympathy to the test, and, though despairing for his life, to believe nevertheless in God's wise and healing future purposes. For, awful as it is to say, he was to remain in his prison for three days, three days and nights, naked and exposed and bound, lying in rot and dirt, among the insects and reptiles of the well's floor, without sustenance or solace, without comfort or any reasonable hope of ever seeing the light again. And he who would tell of it must take care to picture it rightly and with a shudder paint what that means, particularly for a father's boy who had never dreamt of such hard extremity: how the hours dwindled miserably away until his wretched scrap of daylight through the gap in the stone died and in its place a compassionate star sent a diamond spark down to him in his grave; how new light from above awakened there a second time, feebly endured, and perished again; how in the twilight he peered intently up at the round walls of his house to see if there might not be some thought of ascent and escape with the help of chinks in the wall and bushes rooted in the mortar, or at best some hope of it—even though the covering well stone and his ropes, each for itself and certainly taken together, nipped every hope in the bud; how he twisted in his ropes, trying to find some less painful position to sit or lie, which even when found after a fashion was soon as unbearable as its predecessor; how thirst and hunger tormented him and his empty belly burned, sending pains through his back; how, like a sheep, he soiled himself with his own filth, sat in it sneezing and shivering until his teeth chattered.

We are greatly concerned to impress upon everyone's imagination a lively and real sense of such all-embracing discomfort. And yet, precisely for the sake of life and reality, it is likewise our task to ameliorate things out of a concern that imagination not gain the upper hand and lose itself in empty emotion. Reality is sober and unimaginative—that is its character as reality. As the epitome of facts—undeniable facts with which we must come to terms—reality demands that we adjust and quickly hews its man to the needs of the moment. We are easily moved to call some situation unbearable—it is the protest of fiercely outraged humanity, well intended and even beneficial for the person suffering. Yet such protest may easily also seem a bit ridiculous to someone whose reality is "unbearable." Those who feel outraged sympathy find themselves in an emotionally impractical relationship with a reality that is not their own; they

put themselves in the situation of someone else who is already in it—
an error of imagination, for precisely because of his situation he is no
longer like them. And what does "unbearable" mean when it must
be borne and one has no choice but to bear it as long as one's senses
are intact?

Young Joseph had not been fully and clearly in his right senses
for a long time now, not since the moment when his brothers turned
into wolves before his eyes. The storm that had broken over him had
greatly dazed him, resulting in the diminishment that something
"unbearable" requires in order for it to be borne. The thrashing he
received had left him numbed, as had his incredible transport down
the well hole. The condition induced was one of painful despair, but
at least the horrible events themselves had come to a standstill, had
advanced to a certain fixed state, and his condition, however objectionable, at least had the advantage of security. Hidden in earth's
womb, he did not have to fear further acts of violence and had time
to pursue his thoughts—which at times almost entirely excluded
physical discomforts from his conscious mind. Security, moreover
(if that word is permissible in the face of probable, indeed almost
certain death—although death is always certain at some point, despite which we still somehow feel secure), that sense of security,
then, helped him sleep. Joseph's exhaustion was so great that it vanquished all the terrible discomfort of his circumstances and submerged him in sleep, so that for long periods of time he knew little
or nothing of himself. When he awoke, his amazement at the refreshment sleep was able to provide all on its own, without any assistance from food or drink—for sleep and nourishment can replace
each other for a while—was mixed with his horror at his ever present
and ongoing misery, which had never left him entirely even in his
sleep, but whose worst rigors had begun, if only in a manner of
speaking, to ease a bit. There are no rigors, no bonds that do not
loosen a little over time, providing small concessions in terms of
freedom of movement. We are thinking of the rope and of how by
the second and third day, its loops and knots no longer retained the
tautness of that first hour, but provided a little slack and reached a
kind of accommodation with the needs of Joseph's poor limbs. This,
too, is noted in order to bring sympathy and sober reality into balance. Even when we add that Joseph was, of course, growing ever
weaker, we do so only in part to keep sympathy alive and not let our

cares fade, for on the other hand, his increasing weakness and de-cline also meant practical alleviation of his sufferings, so that, in his own eyes, the longer the situation lasted the better things got, so to speak, since in the end he scarcely still noticed his misery.

His thoughts, however, continued to work actively despite the almost forgotten life of his body, and in such a way that the musical composition that they represented, those "shadows," that "ground bass" that lay beneath all the rest emerged ever more strongly thanks to his dreamy weakness, finally almost drowning out the treble voices entirely. That upper voice was the fear of death, which, as long as his brothers had been nearby, had poured out as urgent wails and entreaties. But once the ten had moved off, why had it fallen en-tirely silent to the world outside, and why did Joseph no longer re-lease haphazard cries of help and distress from the depths? The answer is: He completely forgot it given the urgency of those trains of thought that we have already hinted at and that concerned expla-nations for his sudden downfall, for the past and his own past mis-takes—perhaps willed by God, but no less grave and serious for all that.

The garment his brothers had ripped from his body—at times, horribly enough, even using their teeth—played a prominent role in all this. That he should not have paraded before them in it, not have forced them to see it as his possession, and, most especially, not have approached them in it here and now, was so overwhelmingly obvi-ous to him that he would have clapped a hand to his forehead if his ropes had not prevented it. But even as he did so in spirit, at the same time he admitted the pointlessness and peculiar hypocrisy of such a gesture, for it was clear that he had always known this and yet had done such things anyway. He gazed in amazement at the riddle of self-destructive arrogance offered by his own perplexing behavior. It was more than his reason could solve—indeed, it is beyond all rea-son, since far too many incalculable, irrational, and perhaps even holy factors are involved. When he had trembled for fear that Jacob might discover the *ketônet* in his table pouch, he had been trembling for fear he might be rescued. For he had deceived Jacob, taken ad-vantage of his lapse of memory by secretly packing the heirloom, not because his view of the effect the sight of the veil was sure to have on his brothers was any different from his father's. He had been of the same opinion and had packed it nonetheless. Could that riddle be solved? But since he had not forgotten to assist in his own down-fall—why had Jacob forgotten to prevent it? Here was another riddle. Surely it should have been as important to a loving and anxious father for the coat of many colors to be left at home as it was to an overeager Joseph to smuggle it with him. Why had love and anxiety failed to upset overeager plans and prevented something so important from coming to mind? If Joseph had succeeded in wheedling the splendid garment from the old man in his tent, it was only because they were playing the *same* game, and Jacob wanted the robe to be his son's as much as Joseph desired it for himself. The practical application followed soon enough. Together they had brought the lamb to the pit, and now Jacob would fall back in a faint.

That could very well happen to him, and, afterward, he might consider the great mistakes of the past they shared in common, as Joseph was doing now here below. Yet again he admitted to himself that his oaths, swearing that he would report nothing of this to his father if he should be given back to him, had been made only out of a superficial fear for them both and that if the old state of affairs before the pit were ever restored—something Joseph fervently desired, of course, with one part of his being—he would inevitably and without fail tell Jacob everything and his brothers would end up on the ash heap. Which is why another part of his being did not want such a restoration, which was out of the question in any case—as to that he was in agreement with this brothers, so much so that he would have liked to return the blown kiss that Dan had wanted to send down into the pit to him, because for the first time he was among them as if among brothers and was allowed to hear about everything, including the blood of the kid that was to represent his blood, for all this went beyond his own life and was kept safe with him as if in the grave.

A strong impression had been left on Joseph by Dan's declaration that they could speak in front of him however they pleased, since every word only enhanced the impossibility of his returning home, that it was in fact a good idea to say things in his presence that went beyond his life, because this was a way of firmly binding him to the underworld, like a dead spirit to be feared; and in his own mind those ideas played the role of a counterpart to and reversal of the assumption that had ruled his life until now—that he need not take other people into account because they all loved him more than they loved themselves. And now it turned out that they no longer needed to take him into account, and this experience shaped the flow of that shadowy ground bass that ran below the upper and middle voices of his thoughts and, the weaker he became, gained ever more sonorous dominance over them.

But they had already been set into motion along with others much earlier, at the first moment when the provocation he never suspected became reality, as the slaps and blows landed and he had reeled back and forth among his brothers while they ripped the robe of symbols from his body with nails and teeth—for voices had spoken from the start, and in the midst of that pelting hail of horror his ear had heard them in large part. It would be wrong to assume that Joseph might cease to play and dream under such deadly earnest circumstances—if playing and dreaming may still be called that given such conditions. He was the true son of Jacob, the man of dignified ponderings and mythic knowledge, who always knew what was happening to him, who in all his earthly dealings gazed up at the stars and knotted his life into the divine fabric. Granted, Joseph had a different, less emotional and more wittily calculating method for linking his life to the world above in order to lend it rightness and reality than was the case with his father; but he, too, was convinced that life and action that lacked proof of the authenticity of a higher reality, that did not base and support itself on what was sacred and known, that was incapable of finding its reflection in the heavens in order to recognize itself, was not life and action at all; just as he was totally serious in his belief that what is below would not even know to happen and never occur to itself without its starry model and counterpart, for the principal certainty of his life, too, was the unity of duality, the constant present of the revolving sphere, the interchangeability of above and below, with each becoming the other, with gods capable of becoming men and men of becoming gods. It was not for nothing that he was a pupil of Eliezer, the old man who knew how to say "I" in such a bold and easy way, till one's gaze was lost in pondering his appearance. The transparency of being, its character as repetition and return of the prototype—this fundamental creed was also in Joseph's flesh and blood; and every sense of spiritual dignity and significance seemed to him bound to that same self-awareness. That was in the order of things. What was no longer quite in the order of things, what playfully deviated from dignified significance, was Joseph's tendency to take advantage of this general scheme of thought and thereby dazzle people in the very process of consciously shaping himself.

He had paid close attention from the first moment on. Believe it or not, in the most turbulent confusion of the surprise attack, in the worst rush of fear and looming death he had opened his spiritual eyes to see what was "actually" happening. Not as if fear and distress were in any way diminished by this, but there was also a kind of joy, indeed of laughter, added to them, and a rational serenity had illuminated the terror in his soul.

"My robe!" he had screamed, and begged in fearful anxiety, "Don't rip it!" Yes, they had ripped and shredded it, the mother's garment, and the son's as well, so that both wore it by turns, becoming one by means of the veil, god and goddess. His furious brothers had unveiled him without mercy—as love unveils the bride in the bedchamber, so their rage had unveiled him and known him as he stood there naked, shudders of deadly shame passing through him. In his mind the ideas of "unveiling" and "death" dwelt close together—how could he not have held the tatters of the garment to him and begged, "Don't rip it!" And how in that same moment could the joy of reason not have filled him as it found the coupling of those ideas confirmed in what was happening, made present in them? No agony of flesh or soul could kill his mind's attentiveness to the accumulation of allusions through which what was happening revealed itself as a higher reality, as transparent and prototypical, as the present of the revolving sphere—in short, as star-born. And such attentiveness was very natural, for these allusions dealt with being and identity, with the vista onto his own self, which recently he had opened slightly to Ruben—much to his great bewilderment—and which grew ever brighter in the course of events. He had wailed in his misery when big Ruben had given his consent to have him thrown into the pit, but in that same moment his reason had laughed at the joke, for the word Ruben had used was replete with allusions. "*Bôr*" was the word his brothers spoke in their language, a monosyllable that expressed multiple meanings, for that one syllable contained both the concept of the well and the prison; and the latter, then, was so closely associated with the idea of the lower world, the realm of death, that prison and underworld were one and the same thought and each was merely another word for the other, particularly since a well by its very nature was tantamount to being an entrance to the lower world and the round stone that usually fit over it even suggested death itself, for the stone covered its circle like the shadow that is the dark moon. Shimmering through what was happening to light Joseph's attentive reason was the archetype of the dying star—with the dead moon that one did not see for three days until its gentle rebirth and, more especially, the dying of the gods of light, who fall prey to the underworld for a period of time. And when that horrible concept became reality and his brothers heaved him up on the open well, at the rim of the pit, and he had to descend into its shaft with whatever tense agility he could summon, his quick mind had clearly grasped the allusion to the one star that of evening is a female and of morning a male and that then sinks into the well of the abyss as the evening star.

It was the abyss into which the true son had descended—he who is one with his mother and wears the robe with her by turns. It was the underworldly sheepfold, Etura, the realm of the dead, where the son becomes Lord, shepherd, martyr, victim, the mutilated god. Mutilated? They had only ripped open his lip and lacerated his skin here and there, but they had torn the robe from him and ripped it with nails and teeth, those red murderers and conspirators, his brothers, and they would dip it in goat's blood, which was to represent his own, and bring it before their father. God demanded from the father the sacrifice of his son—demanded it of the gentle man who had admitted with a shudder that he "could not do it." That poor man would have to be able to do it, and it was just like God to pay so little regard to what humans imagine themselves capable of.

At this, Joseph wept amid the transparent misery over which his reason presided. He wept for poor Jacob who would have to be able to do it, and over his brothers' trust in death. He wept, weakened and dazed by the vapors of the well; but the more wretched his condition grew in the course of the seventy-two hours he spent here below, the more strongly the lower voices of his thoughts emerged and the more deceptively his present state was mirrored in heavenly prototypes, so that in the end he no long distinguished at all between above and below and in the dreamy vainglory of death saw only the unity of duality. This may rightly be understood as a measure taken by nature to tide him over something unbearable. For natural hope needs some reasonable justification for clinging to life to the very end, and Joseph found it in these confusions. To be sure, it went beyond life, this hope that he would not perish for good and all, but somehow be rescued from the pit—for on a practical level he regarded himself as dead. He found the proof that he was dead in the confidence his brothers shared, in the blood-soaked garment that Jacob would receive. The pit was deep, and there could be no thought of rescue and return to the life before his plunge into the depths—a thought as absurd as for the evening star to return from the abyss into which it has sunk or the shadow to be drawn away from the black moon, making it full again. But the concept of a star's death—the descent of the darkening son who then takes up residence in the underworld—included the idea of light's return, of new light and resurrection; and it was in this sense that Joseph's natural hope for life justified itself by faith. His hope was not pinned upon the return from the pit to what had been—and yet the pit was vanquished in that faith all the same. And Joseph no longer nurtured that faith for and by himself alone, but he nurtured it in the old man's stead, together with whom he had been brought down into the pit and who would fall back in a faint at home. Jacob's receiving the bloody garment surely meant something beyond the son's life. And if only his father, following ancient expectation, might simply have faith in something beyond death, so Joseph thought in his grave, the blood of the animal would, as once before, nonetheless be accepted as the blood of the son.

Part Six

THE STONE AT THE GRAVE

The Ishmaelites

And rocking to the gait of their beasts, men came from beyond Gilead, that is, from the East and beyond the river—four or five of them, along with a couple of extra camels laden only with wares, plus porters and boys to hold the reins, bringing the total to twice that number. They were traveling merchants, at home neither here nor in the lands they had come from, foreigners, with deeply tanned faces and hands and felt rings to hold their head scarves in place, who cloaked themselves in diagonally striped desert robes, their white eyes in constant observant motion. Riding at their head was a man of worthy years with a white beard; a thick-lipped boy in a white, rumpled cotton shirt, his head wrapped in a hood, led his animal by a long rein, while his heavily robed master sat high in the saddle, hands resting hidden from view, head tilted thoughtfully to one side. As anyone could see, he was the ruling head of the party. The others were his nephew, his brother-in-law, and his sons.

What sort of men were these? One can respond both more precisely and more generally. They were at home to the south of the land of Edom-Seïr, on the edge of the Arabian desert, this side of Egypt, in a region also called Mizraim—itself another name for Egypt—a land of passage and transit to the Land of Mud. It was also called, more properly, Musri, or in another dialect Mosar, as well as Midian, after the son of Abram and Keturah, a land settled by people who came from Ma'in farther to the south, somewhere near the land of frankincense, and traded between Arabia and the kingdom of animals and death. They had stockpiles not only in Musri, but also in western Canaanite lands and in the land of two rivers, passing through them as Midianites, who traded among peoples and served as guides for royal and official caravans passing from nation to nation.

These travelers, then, were Ma'onites from Ma'in or Minæans, better known as Midianites. But since Medan and Midian—children of the desert, Abraham's lesser sons born of Keturah—were more or less the same, with one easily taking the other's place, one could also call them Medanim instead of Midianites. It made no difference to them. Yes, they were even willing to accept the simple and general designation Ishmaelite, which encompassed all things having to do with the desert and the steppes and was based on the assumption that it was not Keturah, but Hagar the Egyptian, that other woman of the desert, who was their tribal mother. It was, in fact, not important to them what they were called or who they were. The main thing was that they were part of this world and could do business along its major highways. There was even solid reason to call the old man and his fellow travelers Ishmaelites, for as men of Musri they were half-Egyptian, as had been Ismael himself, that fiery and beautiful man, so that, taking some liberties, one could say that they had descended from him.

Coming from out of the East, this was not some royal or official caravan—far from it. These were private travelers, and theirs was a small-scale, self-supported enterprise. At markets set up as part of the sacrificial feasts held by people of the plains beyond the Jordan, they had sold Egyptian linen of varying quality and pretty trinkets of glass and used their tidy profit to buy all sorts of balsamic exudates, tragacanth, frankincense, gum, and labdanum. And if on this side of the river they could purchase local goods—a little honey and mustard, a camel-load of pistachios and almonds—at reasonable prices, that would be fine by them. As to their route, they were still undecided. They were debating whether to take the north-south road that followed the crest of the mountains and took them by way of Urusalim and Hebron to Gaza and the sea, or if it might not be better to keep to the north and east for now and pass through the plain of Megiddo to quickly gain the coast, and from there descend to the land of transit that was their home.

On this day, then—it was now past noon—with the old man in the lead and the others in a long single file behind him, they entered the valley to see if the people of Dothan might be holding a market fair and have goods to trade, and now let their beasts plod across a low spot where a mossy slope fell away to the left. And since their rolling eyes were so observant, they spotted some crumbling stairs and walls in the underbrush below. With his head tilted, the old man saw it first, pointed it out, ordered a halt, and sent the hooded boy down to investigate the spot. For travelers are explorers and curious by nature—they must nose around in everything.

The boy was not gone long, bounding down and back up again, and his thick lips reported that there was a covered well down there.

"It's covered and concealed," the old man said wisely, "so it's worth uncovering. The children of this land are evidently covetous and somewhat greedy, so that I think it possible this well has water that is uncommonly cool and tasty—we can drink some of it and also fill our containers. I see no one who would deter us, and why should they call us Ishmaelites if we cannot make quiet use of such opportunities for a little thievish activity to circumvent greed? Take a goatskin and a few bottles, and let us go down."

Which they did, for they always followed the old man's lead. They made their beasts lie down, untied their drinking vessels, and climbed down to the well's precincts—uncle, nephew, son-in-law, and sons, together with a couple of slaves. Looking about, they saw that there was neither pail nor ladle; but that did not matter—they would lower the goatskin and let it fill up with precious coveted water. The old man sat down on a stone that had broken away from the wall, set his robes to rights, and motioned with his dark hand for the stone to be rolled from the well. The stone was cracked, broken in two.

"This well," the old man said, "is covered and concealed, it's true, but is in a truly dilapidated state. The children of this land seem both covetous and careless. But I shall not yet doubt the quality of the water, it is too soon for that. That's right, one half is off. Now remove the other with your young arms and lay it here on the tiles beside its green sister. Well? Is clear water smiling up at you out of the circle, and is its mirroring surface clean?"

They stood on the low step that encircled the well and bent down over its depths.

"The well is dry," said the son-in-law, never turning to look at the old man but continuing to peer down into the well. And even as he said it, they all pricked up their ears. A whimper rose up out of the depths.

"Surely it cannot be," the old man said, "that something is whimpering in this well. I do not trust my own ears. Let us make not the least motion, but let silence reign, and listen whether the sound is confirmed by repetition."

There was another whimper.

"I am now compelled to trust my ears," the old man declared. He stood up, strode to the circular step, waving his arms to push those aside who stood in the way of his having a look into the pit for himself.

Out of courtesy the others waited for him to express an opinion, but his eyes were already dim with age, and he saw nothing.

"Do you see anything, Mibsam, my son-in-law?" he asked.

Now allowed to reply, Mibsam said, "I see something whitish at the bottom, it is moving and seems to be a creature with limbs."

Kedar and Kedma, the merchant's sons, confirmed this observation.

"Amazing!" the old man said. "I shall depend on your keen eyes and call out to see if it answers us. . . . Hey there!" he called down into the well, straining his old man's voice. "Who or what is that whimpering in the well? Is this your natural abode, or would you prefer to avoid it?"

They listened. A little while passed. Then they heard a feeble, distant voice: "Mother! Save your son!"

They all sprang into bustling action.

"To work, make no delay!" the old man shouted. "Bring a rope to let down and pull this creature up to daylight, for evidently this is not the habitation to which it was born. There is no mother here," he cried down again now, "but pious people are here above you, who indeed wish to rescue you, if that is your wish. Just look," he said, alternating his attention now to his own men, "what all can happen and what may befall one in one's travels. This is among the strangest things I've encountered between the rivers. Admit it—we were right to investigate this covered and concealed well. Do you still recall that it was I who suggested it? Fearful sorts might hesitate . . . or take flight, and I can clearly tell from your expressions, which are more than dumbfounded, that you yourselves are not free of such spasms of timidity. Nor will I deny that it is uncanny to be spoken to from the depths, and the thought lies only too close at hand that the genius of this neglected well or some other spirit of the abyss has spoken to us. And yet one must see the matter from its practical side and deal justly with it, inasmuch as it demands we take action, for to my ears those whimpers were sounds of someone in dire need of help. . . . Where is that rope? Do you think yourself capable, creature," he asked down into the pit, "of grasping a rope and tying it round you, so that we may pull you up to us?"

It was another good while until the faint sound of an answer came: "I lie here tied and bound."

The old man had to have it repeated for him, though he had held a hand to both ears.

"There you have it!" he then said. "Tied and bound! As much as that makes our intervention more difficult, it equally increases its necessity. We shall have to let one of us down, so he can put things in order and rescue this creature. Where's that rope? Here it is. Mibsam, my son-in-law, I select you to be dangled downward. I shall see to it that you are bound securely, until you are like a limb of my body that we extend into the deep and pull out again with our catch. As soon as you have a secure hold on the catch, you must cry 'Pull!' and with energies united we shall pull you, our limb, back to us with your catch."

Mibsam declared himself willing, for good or ill. He was a young man with a squat face, a rather long but pinched nose, and bulging eyes, the whites strongly contrasting with his dark complexion. He removed a head scarf from his curly hair, took off his outer cloak, and raised his arms to let himself be harnessed in the rope, which he knew to be of dependable quality—not hemp, but cordage of Egyptian papyrus, wonderfully softened and pounded, supple and unbreakable. The men carried several coils as wares to be traded.

The son-in-law was soon wrapped and harnessed, ready to be dangled. They all took part in harnessing him, even Epher, the old man's nephew, as well as his sons and slaves. Then Mibsam sat down on the rim of the well, let go, and dived into the dry depths, while those holding him braced themselves with one leg forward and let the rope pass through their hands in short jerks. It was not long before the rope slackened, for Mibsam was at the bottom. Pulling their legs back in, they walked over to peer after him. They heard muted words as he spoke to the creature and went to work on him, huffing and puffing. "Pull!" he cried as instructed. They did their best and, crying out as on a single note, hauled up their double burden, while the old man directed the operation with anxious gestures. The son-in-law came swaying up over the edge, the well's inhabitant in his arms.

And how amazed the merchants were when they beheld the bound boy! They raised eyes and hands to heaven, rocking their heads and clicking their tongues. Then they placed their hands on their knees to inspect their catch more closely, for they had lowered him to the circular step, propping him against the well. His head drooping low, there he now sat in his bonds, giving off a musty odor. He wore an amulet on a bronzed cord around his neck and a lucky gemstone on one finger—that was his costume in toto. His wounds had scabbed and healed over somewhat down below, and the swelling around his eye had gone down enough that he could open it, which he did now and then. But mostly he kept his eyes closed, though occasionally he raised his weary eyelids and gazed up at an angle, quite doleful and yet curious about his liberators. He even smiled at their astonishment.

"Merciful mother of the gods!" the old man said. "What have we fished up from the deep? Is he not like the spirit of this neglected well, half perishing in his misery because his water has dried up and left him stranded? Let us, however, deal justly with the practical side of the matter and do what is needed for this creature. For from an earthly standpoint he appears to me to be a boy of a refined sort, if not of the most refined, and to have fallen into misfortune, I know not how. Look at these eyelashes and the charming line of his limbs, though they are sullied and stink of these depths! Kedar and Kedma, it is rude to hold your noses, for now and then he opens his eyes and will see it. First off, remove his ropes, cut through them, that's right, and fetch milk to refresh him. Does your tongue obey you, my son, so that you may inform us who you are?"

Joseph might possibly have spoken, feeble as he was. But he did not want to, having no intention of revealing his family quarrel to these Ishmaelites, for it certainly was none of their business. So he merely looked at the old man as if close to perishing and smiled helplessly, putting his now free hand to his lips in a gesture of failing strength. He was given milk, drinking it from a jar that a slave held for him, for his arms were still stiff from having been bound. He drank so greedily that, no sooner had he finished, than like a suck-ling babe he softly regurgitated a good portion of the milk. When, in the wake of this, the old man asked him how long he had dwelt in the well, he held up three fingers to indicate that it had been three days, which the Minæens found more than a little significant and ingenious, given the three days that the new moon spent in the underworld. And since they also wanted to know how he had ended up in the well—in other words, who had thrown him down it—he confined his answer to the gesture of raising his brow heavenward, leaving it unclear if men had done this to him or if heavenly powers had been at work. But when they asked him a second time who he was, he whispered, "Your servant!"—and then fell to one side, leaving them no wiser than before.

"Our servant," the old man repeated. "To be sure, insofar as he is our foundling and without us would have no breath for his nostrils. I know not what you think, but as far as I can see, there is a mystery here, like many such that haunt the world and whose traces one is amazed to come across on one's travels. What remains for us to do is no less than to take this creature with us, for we cannot leave it here, nor pitch our tents here until it regains strength. I am aware," he added, "that this boy from the well touches my heart in some way, bathing it in a kind of pleasantness, I know not how. And it comes not from pity alone, nor even the mystery that he bears. Rather every person is possessed of an encompassing ring—this is not the stuff he is made of, and yet is of that stuff, bright or dark. Old, experienced eyes perceive it better than young, feeble eyes, which see but do not perceive. And now that I give this foundling my steadfast observation, I find his encompassing ring exceedingly light, and am well aware that this is a find one does not cast away again."

"I can read stones and write cuneiform," Joseph said, sitting up again somewhat. Then he fell back.

"Do you hear that?" the old man asked, after first having it repeated for him. "He can read and write and is well-bred. This is a valuable find, just as I've said, and not made to be left lying here. We shall take it with us, for thanks to the inspiration that told me to investigate this well, we are its finders. I would like to see the man who would call us robbers because we exercise finder's rights and make little inquiry as to who cast aside or carelessly lost what we have found. But if they should come forward, we have a right to reward and a respectable ransom, and there is some profit in the matter in any case. Come, throw this robe over him, for he came naked and sullied from the depths, as if from a mother's womb, and is born a second time as it were."

It was the robe that Mibsam, the son-in-law, had cast aside to which the old man pointed, and its owner grumbled that the boy from the well should have it and soil it so badly. But to no avail, for they followed the old man's wishes, and slaves bore the robed child up to where the animals stood waiting and placed him on one of the camels. Kedma, the son who wore a white head scarf with a black ring, a lad of calm, regular features and a dignified tilt to his head, so that he gazed down at things from under half-lowered eyelids, set Joseph in front of him as the old man bade. And the merchants rode off again now in the direction of Dothan, where there might be a market.

Ruben's Plans

During these same days, Jacob's sons were not in a good mood, indeed, in a very bad mood, certainly no better than before, when the thorn had sat in their flesh and, spiteful from unslaked outrage, they had stumbled through the broom. The thorn had been pulled, and yet the wound in which it had sat was not doing well—it continued to fester, as if its barb had been poisonous—and they would have been lying had they claimed they were sleeping better since having assuaged their hearts. But they said nothing of that.

They had of late become taciturn in general, exchanging words only when necessary, and then grudgingly, gritting their teeth. They avoided one another's eyes, and when one had to speak to another, he glanced here and there, but not into the other's face, so that afterward no one knew whether the matters addressed were binding for either, since agreements made only with the lips and not with the eyes as well can hardly be considered valid and settled. But whether settled for certain or no, such things seemed irrelevant, for they often were heard to say phrases like "All's well," or "So far, so good," or even "That's the least of it!"—gloomy allusions to the essential matter that stood in the background behind any topic addressed and, as long as it was not cleared up, made every word they said disgustingly cheap.

But that essential matter had to settle itself—an equally disgusting, obstinate, and wretchedly long process, a perishing and dying somewhere in the depths, of which no one could say when it would come to an end and which in one sense they were inclined to hasten, but in another they wished to delay, so that at least the possibility of a less ugly settlement might remain open for a little while longer, even when that was, to be sure, unimaginable. Once again, let readers be warned that they ought not consider Jacob's sons to be especially hardened louts and deny them every sympathy. Even the most partisan weakness for Joseph (a weakness of the centuries, from which this factual presentation strives to keep itself free) should avoid such a one-sided position—he himself thought otherwise. They had simply stumbled into this and would much rather have not been caught up in it—that we can all believe. Granted, more than once during these agonizing days they wished things had been brought to an end then and there, had been settled for good and all, and were angry with Ruben for having thwarted that. But this gloomy regret arose simply from the predicament in which they were stuck, an imprisoning quandary with no escape, one of those checkmates that life produces and for which chess is the purest visual model.

Big Ruben was certainly not alone in his wish to rescue Rachel's child from the pit; indeed there was not one of the brothers who was not seized, in a sudden fit of the jitters, with that same wish every few hours. But was that even possible? Unfortunately it was not—and the hasty decision died under the implacable objections of reason. What could they possibly do with the Dreamer, once they had pulled him out, only this far from perishing? It was a wall, and there was no exit; he would have to remain in the pit. They had not only cast him into it, but in every way bound him to the grave and resolutely prevented his rising again. He was logically dead, and now they had to wait and do nothing, so that he really would be dead—an unnerving task and one with vague limits besides. For it was not a matter of "three days" for these piteous men. They knew nothing about three days. They did, however, know of people who had spent seven, even twice seven days wandering about in the desert with no food or water, before they were found. It was good to know this, for it left room for hope. It was detrimental to know it, for the hope was absurd and self-contradictory. Seldom has there been such a predicament, and anyone who might think here only of Joseph's sufferings is playing favorites.

So, then, on this afternoon the tormented brothers were sitting under those red trees at the spot where the thrashing had taken place and where recently they had spoken of Lamech, hero of olden days, and felt shamed by him—which they would have done better not to feel. There were eight of them. Two were missing: fleet-footed Naphtali, who was wandering about somewhere in the area, acquainting himself perhaps with new tidings, knowledge that he might then spread, planting it from place to place; and Ruben, who had been gone since early morning. He was off to Dothan "on business," as he had declared between his teeth, to exchange, or so he said, the products of their labor for bread and a little spiced wine; and particularly in regard to the latter the brothers had seconded Ruben's business trip. Contrary to their usual habits, they had of late imbibed eagerly of the myrrhed wine produced in Dothan, a strong and numbing drink that blurred the mind.

Just between us, Ruben had left them behind to pursue very different activities, and had mentioned spiced wine merely to sugarcoat his departure. The night before, as he had tossed about sleeplessly, the decision had ripened in big Ruben's mind to go behind them all and rescue Joseph. Walking in the traces of light, while Jacob's lamb perished in the well, he had held out for three days. It was enough now, and God grant that he was not too late! He would steal away and all by himself rescue the buried lad; he would take him and lead him back to their father and say to him: "I am like gushing water, and sin is not far from me. But behold, I have gushed forth to do good and bring you back your lamb, which they wished to mutilate. Has my sin been blotted out, and am I your firstborn again?"

Ruben tossed about no longer, but lay there with open eyes, not stirring a muscle for the rest of the night, hatching the smallest details of rescue and flight. It was not simple: the boy was bound and weak, he could not grab hold of any rope that Ruben might toss him; a rope alone would not do it, it would need a hook attached, to catch in the knots of the boy's fetters, so that he could be hauled up like a prize fish; a mesh of ropes might be even better, a net for fishing and catching the prey; or a plank tied among the ropes like a swing, on which the all but helpless lad might be able to sit and so be drawn up to the well's rim. Ruben debated the smallest matters of equipment and other necessary preparations, including the clothes he planned to take from his own supply and have at the ready for the naked boy;

and in his mind's eye he picked the strong ass that he would drive to Dothan, laden for show with wool and cheeses, but on which he would then set the boy in front of him and under the shelter of night flee with him to Hebron, to their father, five days away. Big Ruben's heart was filled with violent joy at his decision, dampened only by his worry that Joseph might not survive the day until it had grown dark; and in taking leave of his brothers that morning, he had difficulty keeping to the crabbed and grumpy monosyllables that had now become their habit when speaking.

The Sale

And so the eight of them sat beneath the spreading branches of the pines, blinking glumly as they gazed out into that same distant plain from which the glittering had come, the dancing will-o'-the-wisp that had bewildered and lured them into this damned predicament. They saw their brother Naphtali, Bilhah's son, bounding in long strides on sinewy legs through the underbrush on their right and could tell even from afar that he bore knowledge to share with them. But they were not eager to learn it.

"Brothers, children, friends," he launched in, "hear my tidings. A train of Ishmaelites has come riding out of Gilead, noses directed this way, and must soon be here, passing within three stone's throws from where you now sit. They appear to be peaceable heathen, laden with wares, and trade might well be possible if we were to call out to them."

And having listened, they turned their heads wearily away again.

"So far, so good," one of them said. "Fine, Naphtali, thanks for the news."

"That's the least of it!" another added with a sigh. In troubled peevishness, they fell silent, having no desire to do business.

After a while, however, they grew uneasy, fidgeting back and forth and letting their eyes wander. And when Jehuda—for it was he—raised his voice and called out to them, they all flinched and turned to him, saying, "Speak, Judah, and we shall listen."

And Judah said, "Sons of Jacob, I have something to ask you and this is my question: What is to be gained by slaying our brother and concealing his blood? I shall answer for you all—we gain nothing whatever by it. For it is senseless, if not abominable, to throw him into the pit and try to persuade ourselves that his blood has been spared and that we might eat beside the well, when in fact we were far too timid to shed it. Do I denounce our timidity? No, rather I denounce our lying to ourselves about it, the way we find differences in this world between 'doing' and 'happening,' so that we may hide behind them and yet stand naked and exposed, for they are but wind. We wanted to emulate Lamech in the song and slay a young man as our plunder. But behold what comes of trying to do things as in ancient song and of taking their heroes as a model. We had to yield somewhat to the times, which are no longer those of old, and instead of slaying a young man, we are merely letting him die. Fie on us, for it is a filthy mongrel, begotten of song and the times. Thus I say to you: Since we did not know how to emulate Lamech and had to sacrifice something to the times, let us now be totally honest and act according to the times. Let us sell the boy!"

A stone fell from every heart, for Judah had spoken the thoughts of all and completely opened eyes that had still been squinting into the light as they silently considered Naphtali's news. Here at last was the way out of their predicament—simple and clear. Naphtali's Ishmaelites showed it to them: it was these merchants' way, leading God knew where, moving on to the measureless vastness of foreign lands lost in mist, from where there was as little chance of return as from the pit! As much as they had wanted to, they had been unable to pull the boy out—but now suddenly they could; for he would be handed over to these wanderers coming this way, and would depart from view with them, just as the falling star and its trail vanish into nothingness. Even Shimeon and Levi thought it a relatively good idea, seeing as their old-fashioned heroism had now truly gone awry.

So that all at once they burst into a muddle of low, eager agreement: "Yes, yes, yes, yes, as you say, Judah, excellent words! Sell him, sell him—to the Ishmaelites. What a practical way to help ourselves and be rid of him! Bring Joseph here, pull him up into the light, they're coming, and one may well believe there is still life in him, a man's sure to last twelve days, or fourteen, as experience has shown. Some of us must go at once to the well, while others . . ."

But behold, here were the Ishmaelites already. The man in the lead came into view some three stone's throws away—an old man, his hands in his robes, on a tall animal led by a boy, and behind him the others: riders, pack animals, and drivers. It was not a particularly majestic train, nor did they appear to be very rich traders—there were even two sitting on one camel. They were evidently just quietly passing through, eyes fixed on the slopes of Dothan's hill.

Too late to fetch Joseph, too late for now. But Jehuda was determined, as were the others as well, not to let this opportunity pass, but to grab it by the hair and attach the boy to this train of Ishmaelites, who might then lead him from view and save the brothers, for they simply could no longer endure things as they stood. The patriarch of these travelers—had Abraham not banished him to the desert along with Hagar, because he had sported in underworldly fashion with Isaak, the son of the true wife? Joseph was now to be shunted off into the desert with Ismael's sons—the deed was not without its roots, it existed, and was now recurring. The new and original ingredient, so to speak, was the idea of selling him. Yet for thousands of years this has been booked as all too high a sum in the brothers' debit column. Selling another human being! Selling their brother! Let us not overreact in sensitive revulsion, let us, rather, be fair to life and to the powerful element of ordinary custom that robbed the idea of almost all its ugly originality. A man in need might sell his sons—and one might, after all, concede that this need applied as well to the predicament in which the brothers were stuck. A father sold his daughters in marriage—and these nine would never have taken a living breath and would not have been sitting here if Jacob had not bought their mothers from Laban with fourteen years of labor.

It was, however, a bit awkward that their merchandise was not readily at hand, but rather stored, so to speak, in a pit in the field. But it could still be delivered at the right moment, and in any case one first of all had to make the acquaintance of these strangers and determine how ready they were to buy.

Which is why all nine put their hands to their mouths and called out across the field, "Hallo, men! Whence? Whither? Beg pardon, but here is shade from trees and people it will pay you to talk to."

The sound found its way across to the ears of the passersby. For they turned their eyes from the hill of Dothan and their heads toward those calling to them. The leader nodded, pointed, and steered toward the children of this land, who had risen to greet the travelers and now laid fingers beneath their eyes to signal that they would like

to see their guests, touched brows and chests to indicate that everything both here and there was handsomely at the ready to receive
them. Gesticulating slaves ran back and forth among the animals and
clucked for them to kneel and lie down. The Ishmaelites dismounted, paid the standard courtesies, and then sat down facing
their hosts—the brothers in their usual spot, the strangers across
from them. The old man sat in the middle, his family—son-in-law,
nephew, and sons—in a line to his right and left. The rest of the company kept farther back. Between them and their masters, in the space
directly behind the strangers, right between the old man and one of
his sons, was another man in a robe pulled up over his head and face,
so that only the brow was revealed by one folded opening in the
mask.

Why in the course of the first exchange of courtesies with their
visitors should the brothers have felt compelled to keep looking at
this shrouded person in the second row? Surely the question is superfluous. The figure's mute isolation automatically attracted their
gaze; no one would have behaved any differently from the brothers—and why on such a pleasant day would anyone wrap up his
head like that as if a dust Abubu were approaching? The brothers
were not at ease during this exchange, but distracted to some extent.
Not because of that special figure—it might have its reasons for
avoiding the light and could keep them to itself. But at issue was how
best to prepare the way for a sale, and it would have been very helpful if a few of them, two or three, could have stood up now to go
fetch the merchandise from its container and, while still out of sight,
to freshen it up a bit for the sale, as had been agreed in a few soft,
quick words before the Ishmaelites had turned their way. And why
did no one leave? Presumably because it had not been decided just
who was to go—though each could have decided that for himself
now. Perhaps, too, out of fear that it might seem impolite. An excuse
could have been found, however. Dan, Zebulun, and Issakhar, for
example—why were they stuck there, glued to the spot and peering
absentmindedly at the figure in the space behind the merchant and
his son?

In unassuming, proud turns of phrase that held boasting and
self-deprecation in balance, both sides recounted their mode of life.
They were very simple shepherd folk, Jehuda and his brothers declared, really only dregs in comparison to the lords sitting before

them, but also sons of a very rich man in the south, a veritable king of flocks, a prince of God, of whose countless possessions these grazing in this valley were but a small portion—though the eye could scarcely take them all in—inasmuch as the land down there could not support them all, of course. Whom, then, did they, insignificant as they were, have the undeserved privilege to entertain?

If one turned one's eye, the old man said, from such splendor to gaze upon him and his troupe, one could see nothing at all, first because one was already dazzled and, secondly, there was almost nothing there. They were sons of the mighty empire of Ma'on in the continent of Arabia, dwellers of the land Mosar or Midian—that is Midianites, though, in God's name, one might also call them Medanim or quite simply Ishmaelites—what did it matter what title one gave to a nothing. They equipped caravans that had roamed more than once to the end of the world, trading back and forth between empires the precious treasures on which many a king had cast an eye—the gold of Ophir, the balsam of Punt. They asked royal prices of royalty, but for strangers their goods came cheap. And now their camels were bearing milk-white flake tragacanth of finest fracture, such as this valley had surely never seen, and frankincense, irresistibly seductive to the nostrils of the gods, who once they had smelled it would desire no other fumes. So much for the insignificance of the guests.

The brothers kissed their fingertips and indicated a connection between their brows and the earth.

The land of Mosar, or in fact the land of Ma'on, Jehuda wanted to know—it was surely very distant in this world, a foreign land truly lost in mist?

"Very distant in terms of space and thus of time as well, to be sure," the old man confirmed.

"Seventeen days distant?" Judah asked.

"Seven times seventeen," the old man replied, but that described its remoteness only very roughly. Both in motion as well as at rest—for rest was likewise part of a journey—one must abandon impatience and give oneself over to time, for time alone can overcome space. Eventually, at some point, and before one has even thought it so, time has accomplished this.

One might well say, Judah suggested, that these regions and

goals lay beyond all view, in the measureless vastness of God knew where?

One could put it that way, the old man concurred, if one had as yet never measured the distance in question and was unaccustomed to ally oneself with time against space, never making use of the one in dealing with the other. If that distant land was one's home, one thought of it more matter-of-factly.

He and his brothers, Jehuda said, were shepherds and not merchants—but not merely that, he begged to note, for they also understood the patient alliance with time that conquered space. How often was the shepherd not compelled to change pastures and wells and to imitate the wanderings of the Lord of the Way, and in that regard was quite different from the farmers of the field, the settled sons of Baal. Their father, the king of flocks, as already noted, dwelt five days from here toward the south, and how often had they measured that distance themselves—though unworthy of comparison with a distance of seven times seventeen days—in both directions, so that they knew by heart every boundary marker, well, and tree to be found within it and no longer marveled at anything along the way. Wandering and overcoming space? They did not wish to compare themselves to traveling merchants from misty foreign lands, but as boys they had left the land of the rivers, far toward the dawn, where their father had once amassed the basis of his wealth, and come to this land, dwelling in the valley of Shechem, where their father had dug and built a well of his own, fourteen ells deep and very wide, because the children of that city had been jealous of all the watering places at their disposal.

"May they be rebuked unto the fourth generation!" the old man said. What good fortune, he added, that the children of the valley had not violated the well, filling it up again in their jealousy and leaving it dry.

Oh, but they, the brothers, had known how to spoil their games, the nine responded. Oho, they had spoiled quite a few things for them later on.

Were they then such fierce heroes, the old man asked, stalwart and ruthless in their resolve?

They were shepherds, came the answer, but valiant as well, accustomed to doing battle with lions and robbers if need be, and to holding their ground in quarrels over pastures and wells. As for the matter of space, Judah continued—after the old man had showed due respect for their manliness—and as regarded the traveler's courageous heart, their own forebear had had wanderlust in his blood, had departed from Ur in the land of Chaldea, and had come to these valleys, taking their measure in all directions, though little inclined to settle down, so that if one counted all his wanderings together, they might indeed come to seven times seventy days. But to woo a bride for his miraculously late-born son he had sent his oldest servant on a journey with ten camels, to the land of Naharaim, that is, to Shinar; and he had been such a nimble world traveler that, to exaggerate only slightly, the earth had leapt up to greet him. And at a well in the field he had found the bride and recognized her by how she refreshed him with the pitcher she held in her hand and then watered his ten camels. There had been so much traveling and conquest of space by his own race—not to mention by their father and lord, who as a young man had shown plucky resolve by departing from his home on a journey of seventeen days and more, likewise to Chaldean lands. There he had come upon a well . . .

"Beg pardon," the old man said, taking his hand from his robe to halt this flow of speech, "beg pardon, my friend and good shepherd, but allow your elder servant a remark concerning your words. When I listen and attend to what you tell of your race and its stories, it seems to me that wells have played in them a role equally as remarkable and prominent as has the experience of journeying and wandering."

"How is that?" Judah asked and stiffened his back. All his brothers did the same.

"Why in this way," the old man responded, "you speak, and the word 'well' falls upon my ear from moment to moment. You change pastures and wells. You know the wells of the land by heart. Your father built a well, very deep and wide. Your grandfather's steward wooed a bride beside a well. Your father, too, so it appears. My ear is veritably buzzing with the wells you have mentioned."

"My lord the merchant," Judah replied with a stiffened back, "wishes to say that what I have said is a monotonous droning, for which I am sorry. We brothers and shepherds are no spinners of fairy tales beside the well . . .—we are not the vendors of lies at the market, who have studied that art and ply it for wages. We speak and tell our stories without tricks and trappings, and without mincing words. I would also like to know how one should tell of a man's life, of a shepherd's life in particular, and of his journeys and yet never mention wells, without which nary a step can be taken and . . ."

"Very true," the old man interrupted. "The response of my friend, the son of the king of flocks, is most apt. What a prominent role wells do play in human life, and how many droll stories and re-markable events are likewise tied up with such places for me, your elder servant, whether they contain spring water or rain water or are even dry and filled up. Believe me, my ears, which have grown weary and dull with years, would not have been so alert to the word 'well' and to its place in your reports, if I had not recently, on this very journey in fact, encountered a curiosity in that regard, indeed one of the most amazing within my memory, concerning which I would hope you might kindly offer me advice and explanation."

At that the brothers recoiled yet again. Their backs were now so stiff they were concave, and they stared without blinking an eye.

"Is there not perhaps," the old man asked, "in this land where you graze your flocks, a human child missing, whom his family can-not find and who is thought stolen or abducted or is believed to have been lost to a lion or some other bloodthirsty beast, because he has not returned home for three days?"

"No," the brothers answered. Not that they knew.

"And who is this?" the old man said, reaching back and pulling the robe from Joseph's head. . . . There he sat, behind and between the men, wrapped in fallen folds of cloth, his eyes directed chastely to the ground. His expression was somewhat reminiscent of the one he had worn that day in the field when, under his father's protection, he had told his shameless dream of stars. His brothers at least were reminded of it.

Upon recognizing the figure, several of them had jumped to their feet; but then they shrugged and took their seats again.

"You meant him," Dan said, seeing that it was time for him to prove himself a serpent and an adder, "when you spoke of the well and of missing persons? You meant no one else? Well, in that case you've got something there. That is a slave, a son of a nobody, a me-nial of the lowest sort, a kennel boy, whom we had to punish for re-peated thievery, lying, blasphemy, belligerence, stubbornness, fornication, and moral corruption by the bushel. For young as he is, he is a storehouse of wickedness. So you found him, did you, and pulled him from the pit in which we were keeping this gallows bird for his betterment? Behold, you have anticipated us, for his sentence had run out at this very hour, and we were just about to grant him life and to see if his chastisement had struck home."

These, then, the words of Bilhah's crafty son. He spoke out of brazen desperation, for there sat Joseph, who could open his mouth whenever he liked. But it appeared as if the trust that the brothers had been able to place in him once he was in the pit still held; and Dan's effort did not miscarry, for Joseph in fact said nothing, but just sat there with meek, downcast eyes, behaving on the whole like a lamb being sheared without a bleat.

"Oh, oh! My, my!" the Midianite said, rocking his head, letting his eyes pass back and forth between the culprit and his harsh judges; but the rocking gradually became a shaking of the head, for something didn't fit here, and the old man would have liked to ask his foundling whether all this was true, but tact forbade it. Which is why he said, "What do I hear, what do I hear! We've taken mercy on such a scoundrel as this and helped him from his hole in the last moment. For I must say, you go a bit too far with your amends, pushing them to the extreme. When we found him he was already so weak that he spat up the milk we gave him, and his release dared not have been deferred much longer—that is, if you place any value in his worth, which, to be sure, may be next to nothing, given his wickedness, of which there can be no doubt, since the severity of the punishment proves an extraordinary degree of villainy."

At this Dan had to bite his lip, for he saw that he had said too much and, quite apart from whether Joseph was to be trusted, had spoken imprudently, as a sullen poke in the ribs by Judah had tried to inform him. Dan had been thinking only of a way to make the boy's cruel treatment plausible to the Ishmaelites. Judah, however, was thinking of the sale, and it was difficult to do justice to both points of view at the same time. For, contrary to all good business sense, the merchandise had to be disparaged in front of those on whom one hoped to unload it. This had never happened to Jacob's sons before, and they were embarrassed by their own folly. But it seemed as if when it came to Joseph there was no end of predicaments. No sooner was one resolved than you were stuck in yet another.

Judah took it upon himself to rescue their commercial honor from this impasse. He said, "Now, now, truth must be served, the degree of punishment may have exceeded his villainy somewhat and could lead one astray as regards his worth—but never mind. We sons of the king of flocks are somewhat impetuous and hotheaded masters, strict, perhaps even too strict in reproving wickedness and, as we admitted, a little too stalwart and ruthless in our resolve. The misdeeds of this kennel boy, if taken singly, were not all too serious; but by the bushel, the sum of them gave us pause and determined the severity of his punishment, from which you may conclude the value we place in him, and thus of our concern to preserve his worth. For the lad's intelligence and aptitude are remarkable, and once cleansed of wickedness—as you see him sitting here now, thanks to our severity—he is without doubt a useful property, a fact I really would like established in the interest of truth," Jehuda concluded. And Dan, though not a little abashed by his own miscarried craftiness, was glad that Leah's son had wisely known how to breach the impasse.

"Hmm, hmm," went the old man, shifting his gaze back and forth between Joseph and his brothers, while continuing to shake his head. "A scoundrel with aptitude, then. Hmm, you don't say. And what is the kennel boy's name?"

"He has none," Dan replied. "Why should he? He's had no name at all thus far, for as we said, he is the son of a nobody, a bastard, and a wild reed from the swamps, without tribe or family. We call him 'Hey There' and 'You' or simply whistle. Those are the names we use for him."

"Hmm, hmm, so our convict is a little son of the swamp and of dissolute growth, is he?" the old man said. "Strange, strange—how amazing the truth can be! It is counter to all reason and courtesy, and yet one is amazed. But when we pulled him from his prison, this son of the bulrushes announced that he could read what was written and write himself. Was that a lie on his part?"

"Not an all too impudent one," Judah replied. "We've noted that he is of remarkable intelligence and of more than common aptitude. He can probably keep a list and the accounts for jars of oil and bales of wool. If he said no more than that, he avoided the lie."

"May it be avoided on all occasions," the old man responded, "for truth is god and king, and Neb-má-rê is its name. One must bow down before it, even when it seems puzzling. Can my lords and masters of this kennel boy read and write as well?" he asked, narrowing his eyes.

"We consider it a task for slaves," Judah replied curtly.

"And it is that at times," the old man conceded. "But the gods also write the names of kings on trees, and great is Thoth. Quite possibly it was he himself who sharpened the reeds for this swamp lad and instructed him—may he of the ibis-head not count that jest against me. But this much is true: All ranks of men are ruled, except for the scribe in his house of books, he rules himself and need not toil. There are nations where this child of the bulrushes would be set over you and your sweat. Just think, I can well imagine—and my fantasy does not fail me entirely when I posit the case by way of jest—he might be the master and you his slaves. You see, I am a merchant," he went on, "and a shrewd one, as you may well believe; for I have grown old in appraising and estimating whether things are of high or low quality, so that one does not easily make a fool of me when it comes to wares, for I can tell between thumb and forefinger what they are worth, and these fingers here tell me if the weave is of coarse, fine, or medium grade. My head is tilted to one side out of an old habit of testing things, so that no one can sell me inferior goods as quality. Now behold, this lad is of fine fiber and grain, though unkempt due to severe punishment—I can tell that with my head set atilt and these rubbing fingers are a perfect test. I am not speaking of aptitude, of intelligence, or of the art of writing, but of fabric and weave—I am an expert in that. Which is why I made my bold jest and said that my reason would not come to a standstill were I to hear that Hey There was the master and you were his slaves. But, to be sure, it is the other way around, is it not?"

"Most certainly!" the brothers responded, stiffening their backs.

The old man was silent.

"Well," he then said, narrowing his eyes again, "since he is your slave, sell the boy to me." He was putting them to a little test. There was something mysterious here; and all on his own, for sly but vague reasons, he made his proposal, curious as to its effect.

"He is yours as a gift," Judah muttered automatically. And once the Midianite had proclaimed that his head and heart were receptive to such flourishes, Judah continued, "Granted, it is unfair that we have had such vexation from the boy and that now, cleansed of his wickedness, you should glean the fruit of our schooling. But since you are of a mind to have him, make us an offer."

"You name your price instead," the old man said. "I never proceed otherwise."

And now the bargaining and haggling over Joseph began, with each side so stubborn that it lasted five hours, until late in the day just before sundown. On behalf of his family, Judah demanded thirty pieces of silver; but the Minæen retorted that this must surely be a jest over which one might laugh for a while, but certainly that could be one's only response. A mere Hey There, a kennel boy born in the bulrushes, who as they themselves admitted had proved he suffered from serious character defects—and he was to pay for that in the moon's metal? This was requital for Dan's overeager explanation for the punishment in the well and his having discounted the merchandise's value far too much. The old man exploited it to lower the price. But he, too, had left himself badly exposed by failing to refrain from rubbing his fingers, by boasting of his ability to recognize quality and having committed himself to an appraisal of the ware's fiber and grain, which proved very useful to the sellers. Jehuda took him at his word, on his reputation as an expert, and ballyhooed the boy's superior quality as if he and his brothers had never entertained the least disregard for it, or cast the object of their dealings into the pit on that account. The heat of bargaining left them immune to shame; indeed, Judah had no scruples whatever in shouting, "How can a lad so fine that he might be the master of us all and we his slaves be tossed aside for less than thirty shekels?" He pretended to be totally infatuated with his merchandise, and when he named twenty-five silver coins as his lowest possible price, he walked over and kissed silent, blinking Joseph on the cheek, crying that he could not and would not surrender such a treasure of cleverness and charm for fifty!

But the old man would not rise to the bait of a kiss, and kept the upper hand, particularly since he could see that the brothers' fundamental desire was to be rid of the lad no matter what, which was easily determined by his feigning to break off the bargaining. He had offered fifteen shekels of silver, and those according to the lighter Babylonian weight; but when the brothers used his exposed position to raise this to twenty shekels Phoenician, he stopped there and could not be forced any higher. He had found the boy, he said, in ultimate danger of perishing and might now claim finder's rights and demand ransom; it was pure business courtesy on his part not to take that sum into account and deduct it from the price, but be willing instead to pay the full, heavy sum of twenty shekels Phoenician. If they could not appreciate that, he would withdraw from the deal entirely and wished never again to hear of this scoundrel born in the bulrushes.

And so they struck an agreement for twenty pieces of silver of standard weight, and there beneath the trees and in honor of their guests the brothers slaughtered a lamb from the herd, letting the blood flow out and roasting the flesh over coals fanned hot, so that they might lift their hands and eat together in celebration and confirmation of the sale—and even Joseph received a bit of the meat from his master, the old Minæen. But what was he forced to behold? He had to watch as his brothers quite casually—though furtively, so that the Ishmaelites would not even notice—dragged the remnants of the garment of symbols through the blood of the slaughtered lamb, drenching and soiling them with it. They did it brazenly before his eyes, trusting both in death and the certainty of his silence; and he ate of the lamb whose blood was to represent his own.

A meal for the guests and general refreshment were called for, since their business was far from complete. Only the rough outline had been decided, the price itself established; but now the petty details had to be worked out, the conversion of the agreed-upon sum into commodities. Here we must correct an ingrained notion that many a pious description has spread abroad, as if in selling Joseph his brothers were paid the price in coins that the Ishmaelites took from their purse to let them fall clinking into their fraternal hands. The old man had no intention whatever of paying in silver, not to mention "coins," and for good reason. Who would haul so much metal around with him on a journey, and what customer would not rather pay his debt in commodities, since each item offered as part of the total price gave him an opportunity to improve on the deal and serve his interests as a buyer by becoming a seller? Using a fragile scale that he carried at his belt, the Minæan weighed out one and a half shekels in silver coin for the shepherds—all the rest would have to be made up for by the goods his camels carried. And so the wares to be offered were unpacked and spread out on the grass: incense and beautifully fractured resins from beyond the river and all those amusing objects one could use—razors and knives of copper and flint, lamps, spoons for ointment, inlaid walking sticks, beads of blue glass, castor oil, and sandals—a booth, a whole bazaar, that the merchants laid out before the greedy eyes of their customers, who could select from it goods worth up to eighteen and a half silver coins in exchange for their one piece of merchandise. They haggled over every item, as if it alone were at issue, so that in fact evening had fallen before they had finished and Joseph was sold for a little silver and a great many knives, shavings of balsam, lamps, and walking sticks.

With that, the Ishmaelites packed up and prepared to take their leave. They had leisurely gone about this business, paying the hours little heed; but now time needed to give birth to space again, and they intended to journey some distance into the evening before setting up camp for the night. The brothers certainly did not hold them back. But they did offer advice as to the route they should choose and which roads to take.

"Don't travel inland," they said, "along the mountain crest that divides the waters, leading on to Hebron and so forth—we don't recommend it and warn our friends against it. The roads are rough, animals stumble, and riffraff lies in wait everywhere. Follow this plain and turn onto the road that leads down through the hills at the foot of Mount Orchard, to the borders of the country. You'll be safe that way and can continue south in the gentle sand of the sea, for seven times seventeen days or as far as you like. It is a pleasure to travel beside the sea, one never gets enough of it, it's the only sensible route."

The merchants promised they would and said farewell. Their camels rose up beneath them, and Joseph, the bartered slave, rode with Kedma, the old man's son. He kept his eyes lowered, just has he had done the whole time, even while eating lamb. And his brothers likewise stood there with downcast eyes while the caravan quickly vanished in the falling dusk. Then they all took a deep breath and puffed the air out again.

"Well, now he is no more!"

Ruben Comes to the Grave

But as dusk fell and murmuring evening arose with its great stars, Ruben, Leah's son, was driving his jackass, laden with everything needed, along byways leading from Dothan to Joseph's grave, so that he might carry out the decision he had made out of fear and love the night before.

His heart pounded in his chest, as broad and mighty as it was; for Ruben was strong, but also weak and excitable, and afraid that his brothers would catch him and prevent his work of rescue, which was also a work of purification and reinstatement. That was why his muscular face was pale in the darkness and the leather-strapped columns of his legs moved stealthily across the land. From his tightly pressed lips came no commands for his beast, but to keep it moving ahead, he would angrily poke the even-tempered animal's rump from time to time with the tip of his staff. For Ruben feared one thing above all: that it might be deathly still inside the well when he arrived and softly called out the name, that Joseph might not have held on to his soul this long, but have already perished, and that all his preparations would have been in vain, especially the rope ladder that he had had the rope maker in Dothan knot together while he looked on.

For that was the rescue apparatus that Ruben had finally decided upon. It was useful for various contingencies—if one had sufficient energy, one could climb up it from the bottom of the well, or, if that was not the case, sit between rungs and be drawn up above ground by Ruben's brawny arms, which had once embraced Bilhah and would surely be capable of pulling this lamb out of the depths for Jacob. There was a robe for the naked lad, and hung at the ass's flanks were provisions for five days—days of fleeing before his brothers, whom Ruben intended to betray, sending them all to the ash heap. And admitting as much, he bowed his head as he slunk to the grave by night. In doing good, was big Ruben behaving so badly? It was a good and necessary thing to rescue Joseph—his soul was filled with that certainty, and if something evil and self-serving had crept into his cause, then he simply had to make the best of it, that was the mix of life. Besides, Ruben wanted to turn evil to good, and was confident he could. If only he could stand before his father in good stead and be the firstborn once again, he would try to save his brothers as well and extricate them from their adversity—for his word would then carry weight, and he would use it to gain pardon for his brothers and spread the guilt to include everyone, including even his father, so that there would be a great shared insight, and mutual forgiveness and justice would reign forever.

That was how Ruben sought to quiet his pounding heart and console himself for the welter of motives that made life so murky. Arriving at the slope and the masonry walls, he looked about to see if anyone was watching, pulled out ropes and robe, and, brushing obstructing fig saplings aside, edged his way down to the broken steps that led to the well.

Stars shone down into the cracked tiled precincts, but not the moon. Watching his feet to keep from stumbling, Re'uben had already drawn breath into his tightened chest so that he could call out in a furtive, urgent voice, "Joseph! Are you alive?"—in joyful expectation of his brother's reply, in anxious fear that none might follow—when he suddenly was so startled it was as if he were flung back, and his fervent call became a hoarse cry of terror. He was not alone down here. Someone else was sitting there, a white shimmer in the starlight.

How could that be? Someone was sitting beside the well, and the cover had been removed. The two halves of the well stone lay on the tiles, one atop the other, and on them sat someone in a tunic, leaning on his staff, and gazing directly at Ruben with silent lips and sleepy eyes.

His legs still tangled from stumbling, big Ruben stood there, staring at this apparition. He was so dazed that the thought came to him for a moment that this was Joseph that he saw before him, that he had died and his ghost was sitting beside his grave. And yet the disturbing presence bore no resemblance to Rachel's son—even as a ghost he surely would not have been so inordinately tall nor, by human standards, would his neck have been so massive with that little head set atop it. But then why had the stone been rolled back from the well? Re'uben no longer understood anything.

"Who are you?" he stammered.

"One of many," the seated figure answered coolly, and the chin that was now lifted beneath delicate lips had a sculpted look. "I am nothing special, and you need not be afraid. But whom do you seek?"

"Whom do I seek?" Ruben repeated, losing his temper at this unexpected turn of events. "What I want to know first off is what *you* seek here?"

"You do, do you? I am the last to presume that there is anything to seek here. I have been put here as a watchman over this well, which is why I am sitting here watching. If you think that it gives me any special amusement and that I'm sitting in the dust for the sport of it, you are mistaken. One does one's duty and follows instructions and sets aside many a bitter question."

At these words, curiously enough, Ruben's anger over the stranger's presence abated. The fact that someone was sitting here was itself so annoying and unwelcome that he was glad to hear that the man did not enjoy doing it. It created a certain common bond between them. "But who put you here?" he asked, with more measured irritation. "Are you one of the people of the place?"

"Of the place, yes. It doesn't matter where such an order comes from. It usually passes through many mouths, and there is little benefit in tracing it to its original source—you must take up your position in any case."

"A position beside an empty well!" Ruben cried in a choked voice.

"Empty, to be sure," the watchman replied.

"And uncovered, too!" Ruben added and in his agitation pointed a trembling finger at the well's hole. "Who rolled the stone from the well? You perhaps?"

Smiling, the man looked down at himself, at his arm emerging nicely contoured but weak from his sleeveless linen tunic. No, that was certainly not the manly strength of an arm to roll the covering stone, either on or off.

"I've rolled the stone neither on or off," the stranger said, still smiling and shaking his head. "You know about the former, and you can see the latter. Others went to the trouble, and I would not have had to play watchman here if the stone on which I sit were still in place. But who can say what the true position for such a stone is? Sometimes it is over the hole; but must not the cover be rolled away if refreshment is to come from the well?"

"What are you talking about?" Ruben cried, racked with impatience. "I think you're just chattering away to steal precious time from me with your babble. How is a dry well supposed to provide refreshment—there's nothing but dust and rot inside."

"It all depends," the seated figure replied, calmly pouting his lips and tilting his little head, "on what has first been committed to the dust and lowered into its womb. If it was life, then life and renewal will come forth a hundredfold. A grain of corn, for example—"

"Listen, my man," Ruben interrupted with a quivering voice—the rope ladder shook in his hands, the robe Joseph would need still dangled over one arm—"it is intolerable for you to sit there and start talking about first principles that a child is taught at his mother's knee and that everyone knows by heart. I am asking you—"

"You are quite impatient," the stranger said, "and are, if you will allow me the comparison, like gushing water. But you should learn patience and expectation based upon first principles of concern to all creatures, for anyone who simply gushes forth out of expectation has nothing to seek either here or elsewhere. For fulfillment proceeds only slowly, and begins with first one attempt and then another, and its present is provisional both in heaven and on earth, not yet the true present, but merely a trial attempt and a promise. And so fulfillment rolls ponderously along, much like a stone, if it is heavy, rolled from a well. It would appear that people were here who went to the trouble of rolling the stone away. But they will have to roll it for a long time before it is truly rolled away from this hole, and I, too, am sitting here only provisionally and in a trial attempt."

"You should not sit here any longer at all!" Ruben shouted. "Do you finally understand? Begone, toddle on your way, for I wish to be alone with this well, which concerns me more than it does you, and if you do not get up this very moment, I shall help you to your feet. Do you not see, you weakling—who has to let other people do his rolling and can only sit there and gawk—that God has made me strong as a bear and that I have rope in hand besides, good for various things. Get up, vanish, or I shall gush straight for your throat!"

"Do not touch me!" the stranger said, extending a long, softly contoured arm toward the angry man. "Remember that I am of the place and that you will have to deal with all the others of the place if you lay a hand on me. Did I not tell you that I have been put here? I could indeed vanish, and with ease, but I am not about to do so at your bidding, neglecting duty, which demands that I sit here and watch by way of practice. Here you come with your robe and rope-work and do not even notice how ridiculous you appear bringing all that to an empty well—empty by your own characterization."

"Empty as a well," Ruben explained vehemently. "Empty of water!"

"Completely empty," the watchman said. "The pit will be empty when you and yours come."

Ruben could contain himself no longer and rushed over to the well, bending down into it and calling into its depths in an urgent, muted voice, "My boy! Pssst! Are you alive, do you have any strength left?"

But the figure on the stone shook his head, smiling and clucking his tongue in sympathy. He even imitated Ruben, calling out, "Boy! Psst!" and clucked his tongue again. "Walks right up and talks to an empty hole," he then said. "What a lack of good sense. There is no boy here, my man, far and wide. If one was here, then this place did not hold him. Won't you finally stop making a fool of yourself with your gear and talking into an empty hole!"

Ruben was still standing over the gorge, from which no sound came in response.

"How horrible!" he groaned. "He is dead or gone. What shall I do? Ruben, what will you do now?"

And all his pain, all his disappointment and fear suddenly erupted.

"Joseph," he cried in despair, "I wanted to save you and help you out of this pit with my own arms. Here is the ladder, here is the robe for your body. Where are you? Your door is open. You are lost. I am lost. Where shall I go now that you are gone—stolen or dead? . . . Young man, you of this place!" he called out in unrestrained distress, "don't sit there mute on that stone that thieves rolled away, but advise and help me! There was a boy here, Joseph, my brother, Rachel's child. His brothers and I, we lowered him into his well three days ago as punishment for his arrogance. But his father is expecting him—his expectation is beyond all measure, and if they tell him that a lion has ripped his lamb apart, he will fall back in a faint. Which is why I have come with coat and cord to pull the boy from the well and take him to his father, for he must have him back. I am the eldest. How shall I come before my father's face if the boy does not return, and where shall I go? Help me, tell me, who rolled the stone away, and what has happened to Joseph?"

"You see?" the stranger said. "When you entered the well's precincts you were annoyed at my presence and angry because I was sitting on the stone; but now you come to me for advice and consolation. You are quite right to do so, and perhaps it is for your sake that I have been put here beside this pit, so that I may bury one or two seed corns in your understanding, that it might silently preserve the germinating bud. The boy is here no more, as you can see. His house stands open, it could not hold him, none of you will see him anymore. But there should be one of you who will nurture the seed of expectation, and since you came to rescue your brother, then you shall be the one."

"What am I to expect, if Joseph is gone, stolen, and dead!"

"I don't know what you understand 'dead' and 'alive' to mean. You do not wish to hear about childish first principles, it's true, but allow me to remind you of the grain of wheat lying in the womb, and to ask what you think of 'dead' or 'alive' in regard to it. Those are mere words after all. For it is so, that if the seed falls into the earth and dies, it bears much fruit."

"Words, mere words," Ruben shouted, wringing his hands. "Those are mere words that you present to me. Is Joseph dead, or is he alive? That is what I must know!"

"Dead, evidently," the watchman retorted. "You have bedded him in the earth, so I hear, and then he was probably stolen besides—either that, or mutilated by wild beasts. You and your brothers have no other choice but to report it to your father and make it tangibly clear to him, so that he may grow used to it. But it will always remain a doubtful thing, not made for getting used to, but rather hiding within itself the seed of expectation. People do a great many things to approach the mystery, laboring to celebrate it. I saw a young man descend into the grave in festal garments and wreath, and they slaughtered an animal from the herd over him, letting the blood drip down upon him, until it drenched him entirely and he captured it with all his limbs and senses. And afterward, as he climbed out again, he was divine and had attained life—at least for a time. Then he had to descend into the grave again, for a man's life revolves several times, bringing the grave and birth with it once more. Man must become several times over, until he has fully become."

"Ah, the wreath and the festal garment," Ruben groaned, burying his face in his hands, "lie ripped to shreds, and the boy went naked to his grave."

"Yes, and that's why you've come here with that robe," the watchman responded, "wishing to clothe him anew. God can do that as well. He, too, can clothe those stripped bare, and better than you. Which is why I advise: Go home and take your robe with you. God can provide even more garments to him who has not been stripped bare, and in the end the stripping of your boy did not matter all that much. With your permission, I would like to bury a seed of thought in your understanding—that this story is itself play and festival, like the lad spattered with blood, merely a beginning, an attempt at fulfillment, and a present not to be taken all too seriously, but is instead a jest and an allusion, so that in response we may nudge one another with a wink and a laugh. It could be that this pit is but a grave that comes with life's smaller revolution, that your brother may still be very much in the becoming and has not yet become at all, just as this entire story is still becoming and has not already become. Receive it, please, into the womb of your understanding and let it die peacefully there and germinate. But if it bears fruit, then give your father some for refreshment as well."

"Father, father!" Ruben cried. "Don't remind me! How shall I come before my father without the child?"

"Look up!" the watchman said. For it had grown brighter around the well, and the barque of the moon—its dark half traced invisibly visible against the sky, hidden and yet manifest—had just now floated up above them. "Look at it, how it moves along, shimmering to light the way of its brothers. Allusions are constantly occurring in the heavens and on earth. He who is not dull-witted but knows how to read them will live in expectation. But the night proceeds apace, and he who must not sit and play the watchman would do well to get some sleep, wrapped in his robe, his knees comfortably drawn up, so that he may rise again in the morning. Go, my friend. You haven't anything whatever to seek here, and I am not about to vanish at your bidding."

Shaking his head, Ruben now turned away and hesitantly plodded up the stairs and slope, returning to his animal. He kept on shaking his dazed head almost the entire way back to his brothers' tents, half in despair, half in puzzled deep thought, hardly able to separate one from the other, but shaking his head.

The Oath

And so he arrived at their tents and roused the nine, snatching the drowsy first sleep from their eyes, and with trembling lips said to them, "The boy is gone. But where shall I go?"

"You?" they asked. "You speak as if he were only your brother, yet he was that to us all. Where shall we all go? That is the question. And just what do you mean by 'gone'?"

"'Gone' means stolen, vanished, mutilated, dead," Ruben shouted. "Which means, lost to his father. The pit is empty."

"Were you at the pit?" they asked. "For what purpose?"

"For the purpose of investigation," he rejoined angrily. "The firstborn is surely free to do that much! Could what we have done leave a person in peace, and not unsettle him? In any case, I wanted to check on the boy and am now telling you that he is gone and that we must ask ourselves where we shall go now."

"Calling yourself the firstborn," they replied, "is rather bold, and mention of the name Bilhah should suffice for you to recall the facts. We were in danger of letting the rights of the firstborn fall to the Dreamer; but now it is the twins' turn, and Dan might also lay claim to the title, for he appeared in the same year as Levi."

They had, however, noticed the jackass with its robe and ladder, which Ruben had not even tried to conceal, and had no difficulty putting two and two together. So then, big Ruben had wanted to undermine them by stealing Joseph—had thought of raising up his own head and sending them to the ash heap. Now wasn't that pretty. They came to an understanding with glances. But that being the case—and their silent understanding included this as well—they did not owe Ruben an account of what they had done in the meantime. Betrayal for betrayal: Ruben did not need to know anything about the Ishmaelites and how they were on the verge of removing Joseph beyond all view. The man might well be capable of setting off after them. And so they said nothing, shrugged at his news, and declared their indifference.

"Gone is gone," they said, "and it doesn't matter what 'gone' means. Stolen, vanished, mutilated, betrayed, sold—it's not worth a snap of the fingers, a sniff of the nose. Was it not our just demand, did we not yearn that he be no more? So then, that has been granted us, the pit is empty."

Amazed, however, by their cold reception of this latest monstrous news, Ruben searched their eyes and shook his head. "And Father?" he suddenly erupted, flinging his arms into the air.

"That has been arranged and settled," they said, "according to Dan's wise counsel. For he should not be left sitting in doubt, but it should be told him point-blank, with tangible proof, that his Dumuzi, his coddled pet, is no more. But we wish to be made clean in his eyes by that same token of proof. Look at what we have prepared, while you went your own way."

And they brought out the tatters of the veil, stiff with half-dried blood.

"Is it his blood?" Ruben cried in his high voice, his mighty body shuddering in horror. For a moment all he could think was that they had preceded him to the pit and had slain Joseph.

They exchanged smiles.

"What delusions and drivel!" they said. "It was done according to our agreement, and an animal from our herd gave its blood as a token that Joseph is gone. We shall now bring it to Father and leave it to him to interpret it in the way he must, for his only choice will be that a lion surprised Joseph in the field and mutilated him."

Ruben sat with his massive knees drawn up and rubbed his fists in his eye sockets.

"Wretches," he groaned, "what wretches we are. You easily chatter on about the future, but do not see it and cannot know it. For it lies before you, blurred and pale in the distance, and your minds lack the strength to bring it nearer and to experience, if only for the twinkling of an eye, what it will be when that hour has come. Otherwise you would be horrified and prefer to have been struck down by lightning beforehand or to have been cast into the water where it is deepest, a millstone around your neck, rather than bear the consequences of what you have done and spoon the broth you have cooked. But I have lain before him, for I had done evil and he cursed me, and I know the fervor of his soul in anger—and I can see, as exactly as if it were already real, his soul's dreadful response to this anguish. 'We shall bring it to Father and let him interpret it.' Chatterboxes! Yes, he will interpret it. But let any of you watch when he does, and endure it when his soul expresses itself. For God created it both tender and great and taught it to reveal itself in overwhelming power. But you see nothing and can imagine nothing clearly that has not already occurred. Which is why you go ahead and babble on about the future, without the slightest fear. But I am afraid," he cried and stood up before them strong as a bear, tall as a tower, his arms widespread. "And where shall I go when he interprets it?"

The nine sat there disconcerted, abashed, each staring down into his own lap.

"Fine then," Jehuda replied softly, "there's not a man here who would spit on you for being afraid, Re'uben, son of my mother, for it is also brave to admit one's fear, but you are mistaken if you think that there is boldness and merriment in our hearts and around our kidneys and that we know nothing of your fear of Jacob. But what does it avail us to curse what has happened or attempt to undo the inevitable? Joseph is removed from the world, and this bloody garment says so. Tokens are milder than words. That is why we are bringing Jacob this token and are thus spared words."

"You mention bringing it, but must we," Asher, Zilpah's son, asked, licking his lips out of habit, "must all of us bring the token to Jacob at once, and all be present when he interprets it? Let one of us precede the others with the garment and bring it to him; but we others will arrive in due time and appear before him once he has already interpreted it—that seems to me milder still. I suggest fleet-footed Naphtali be the bearer and messenger. Or perhaps we should let the bearer be decided by lot."

"By lot!" Naphtali quickly shouted. "I'm for lots, for I do not chatter about the future without imagining it, either, and boldly admit my fears!"

"Listen, men," Dan said, "for now I will speak a judgment and save you all. For since the plan came from me and took shape in my hand like wet clay and potter's earth—I wish to improve upon it. For we need not bring Jacob the garment, neither one nor all of us. But instead, let us give it to strangers, to those we hire, people of this place and region who are receptive to kind words and a little wool and curds. Then we shall impress upon them what they are to say to Jacob: 'Such and such, and we found this in a field near Dothan and stumbled on it by chance in the desert. Do look more closely at it, my lord, to see if it is not your son's garment.' In that fashion. And having said it, let them take to their heels. But we shall delay a few days before we follow after, until he has fully interpreted the sign and knows that he has lost one and gained ten. Are you satisfied?"

"This is good," they said, "or at least worth hearing. Therefore let us accept it, for in this case anything just worth hearing must surely be regarded as very good."

They all accepted it, including Ruben, although he had let out a bitter laugh when Dan spoke of the ten that Jacob would gain in place of one. But they went on sitting outside their tents beneath the stars, unable to bring their deliberations to an end, for they were all uncertain of their fellowship, each unable to trust the others. The nine gazed at Ruben, who had evidently wanted to steal the lad lowered into the pit and undermine them—and they were afraid of him. He gazed at the nine, however, who had remained so strangely unmoved at the news that the pit was empty, and did not know what to think.

"A fierce oath," said Levi, who was coarse but pious and liked to put his expert piety to work by arranging holy ceremonies, "a gruesome oath, that's what we must swear, that none of us will ever breathe a word to Jacob or anyone else about what happened here and what we did with the Dreamer, nor with a wink, blink, or twitch of the eye, will hint at, intimate, or insinuate anything of this story, to his dying day."

"He has said it, we must do it," Asher confirmed. "And this oath must join us ten together, binding us together as *one* body in *one* silence, as if we were not individuals here and there, but *one* man, who presses his lips tight, refuses to open them even in death, and dies biting them shut to keep his secret. One can suffocate what has happened and slay it with silence, which is rolled over it like a boulder. And for lack of air and light it runs out of breath and ceases to have happened. Believe me, a great deal of what has happened perishes this way. The silence need only be sufficiently inviolable, for without the breath of the word nothing can endure. We must be silent as *one* man, and with that our story is over and may Levi's fierce oath assist us in this—for it shall bind us together."

This suited them fine, for not one of them would gladly have been left alone in his silence, and each in his weakness preferred to share and be secure in a common and powerful inviolability. That is why Levi, Leah's son, devised hideous terms for their oath, and they drew so close together that their noses bumped and their breath mingled. They piled hands atop one another and with one voice invoked the Most High, El-Elyon, the God of Abraham, Yitzchak, and Jacob, but also called upon the several local Baals they knew—such as Anu of Uruk, Ellil of Nippur, Bel-Charran, and Sin, the moon—to witness their oath, swearing, almost mouth to mouth and in unison chant, that he who did not keep silent about "it" or with so much as a wink, blink, or twitch of the eye hinted at, intimated, or insinuated "it" should straightaway become a whore: Sin's daughter, mistress of women, was to take his bow, that is, his manhood, from him; he would become like a mule, or better still, a whore, who earned her wages in the streets, be driven from land to land, never knowing where to bed his whore's head, unable either to live or die, with life and death vomiting upon him in disgust for eon upon eon.

This was their oath. And when they had sworn it, they felt both easier and steadier of heart, for they had provided themselves extraordinary security. But as they separated from their bond and each left to sleep his own sleep, one of them said to another (it was Issakhar who said it to Zebulun), "I am envious, envious of Turturra, the little one, of Benjamin, our youngest at home, of his knowing nothing and having remained outside this story and this alliance. He has it good, I think, and I envy him. Don't you?"

"I do indeed," Zebulun replied.

Ruben, however, tried to recall the words of that vexing young man, the man of the place, who had sat atop the well stone. It was not easy to remember them, for they were really quite vague and full of twilight, more verbiage than speech, and he could not reconstruct them. And yet somewhere in Ruben's deepest understanding a seed had been left to germinate, though it knew nothing of itself, just as the seed of life knows nothing in its mother's womb—and yet the mother knows of it. It was the seed of expectation that Ruben nourished, secretly feeding it with his own life, both awake and asleep, until he was a gray-haired old man—for as many years as Jacob had served Laban, that devil.

Part Seven

THE MUTILATION

Jacob Mourns for Joseph

Are tokens milder than words? That's highly debatable. Judah had spoken from the standpoint of the bearer of terrible tidings, who might well prefer a token that spares him the use of words. But what about the receiver? Out of ignorance, he can toss words to the winds, trample them underfoot as lies and ghastly drivel, ban them to the hell of inconceivable nonsense, where, as he says with a mighty laugh, he is convinced they belong—that is, until it dawns on the poor wretch that they have a claim to light in the upper world. A word penetrates only slowly; especially if it is incomprehensible, its meaning is not to be grasped or realized; you are free for a while to prolong your ignorance, and your life, and to thrust the devastation that it wants to cause your brain and heart back at the messenger and declare him mad. "What are you saying?" you can ask. "Are you not well? Come, I will tend to you and give you a little something to drink. Then you may speak again, but in a fashion worth hearing." That is offensive to the messenger, but given your situation, of which he is the master, he indulges you, and gradually his reasonable and pitying gaze causes you to waver. You cannot hold up under his eyes, you realize that the exchange of roles you wanted to impose for your self-preservation cannot be achieved, and that instead it is you who must accept a sip from his hand. . . .

Words allow for this kind of temporizing struggle against truth. But nothing of the sort is possible if a token is employed. Its amassed cruelty does not allow for the fiction of delay. It is unmistakable and has no need of realization—it is already real. It is tangible and disdains the soothing attribute of incomprehensibility. It refuses to leave open a temporary escape hatch. It forces you to conceive in your mind what you would reject as madness were you to hear it stated in words, until you must either consider yourself mad or accept it as truth. What is circuitous and what is direct interact differently in word and token, and it may well remain undecided which is the more brutally direct. The token is mute—for the anything but mild reason that it is the thing itself and need not speak to be grasped. Its silence sends you falling back in a faint.

It is a certain fact that, just as could be predicted, Jacob fell in a faint at the sight of the garment. No one saw it happen, however, for the men of Dothan, a pair of indigent, callous fellows who, for a bit of wool and curds, had assumed the role of finders, had taken to their heels as soon as they rattled off their little text of lies, not even waiting to observe its effect. They had left Jacob, the man of God, standing at the same spot where they had met him outside his house of felt, the veil's blood-stiffened tatters in his hands, and beaten a hasty retreat, first taking two deliberately slow steps backward, then turning to run off as fast as they could. No one knew how long he had stood staring down at scraps of what, as he was gradually forced to realize, was all that was left of Joseph in this world. But in any case, he had fainted, for women passing by found him lying on his back—wives of his sons, Bunah the Shechemite, Shimeon's spouse, and the so-called granddaughter of Eber, Levi's bride. Terrified, they picked him up and carried him into his tent. What he held in his hands quickly informed them of the reason for his collapse.

But it was not a usual faint into which he had fallen, but a kind of rigidity that had seized every muscle and fiber, turning his entire body to stone, so that any attempt even to bend a joint would have shattered it. The phenomenon is rare, but occurs now and then as the reaction to the extraordinary demands fate can make; and the spasm is much like a barrier, an act of desperately defiant obstinacy against the unacceptable, easing then after a few hours at the latest—capitulating, as it were, to the implacable pain of truth that lies in wait and must at some point be granted admission.

People from the camp, both men and women, were called and came running from all sides—to watch in alarm as this pillar of salt softened into a man of sorrows, defenseless now against his misery. His voice was toneless, still a mere whisper, when, as if it were a confession, he finally responded to those who, though now long vanished, had brought him this token: "Yes, it is my son's coat!" Then he screamed in a terrible voice that rose to a shriek of despair: "A wild animal has devoured him, a ravenous beast has mutilated Joseph and torn him to pieces!" And as if the words "torn to pieces" had provided him the cue as to what he must do, he began tearing his own clothes.

It being the height of summer, his light clothing offered little resistance. But although he set all the energy of his anguish to the task,
it took a good while, given the eerily silent thoroughness with which
he carried it out. Horrified and gesturing in vain to prevent these excesses, those standing about him were forced to watch as, against all
reasonable expectation, he did not stop at his outer robe, but, evidently pursuing some savage plan, in fact tore to shreds everything
he had on, casting the tatters aside one after the other, and stripped
himself naked. As the act of a modest man, whose aversion to any
sort of naked flesh the whole world had come to respect, it all
seemed so highly unnatural and debasing that they could not watch,
and family and servants turned away wailing in protest and, covering their heads, pushed their way out of the tent.

The word "shame" is the correct, applicable term for what drove
them away only if it is understood in its ultimate and largely forgotten meaning: as a monosyllabic paraphrase for the horror that wells
up when the primal state breaks through the layers of civilization,
where it lives on only in superficial, muted traces of allegory. One
such civilized trace can be found in the rending of the outer garment
as a sign of deep mourning—it is the subdued, bourgeois form of the
original, precivilized custom of casting off every bit of clothing, of
disdaining every covering and adornment as symbols of a human
dignity now destroyed and, so to speak, cast to the dogs by external
tribulation. It is debasement to the state of the naked creature. That
is what Jacob did. In deepest pain, he returned to the foundations of
the custom, moving from symbol to crude reality and terrible fact;
he did what "one no longer does," did what, when rightly considered, is the source of all horror: upending what is at the bottom and
bringing it to the top. And if, in trying to express the profundity of
his misery it had occurred to him to bleat like a ram, his family and
servants could not have felt more nauseated.

They fled, then, in shame; they left him—and it can be debated
whether that was precisely what the pitiful old man wanted, whether
the engendering of horror was not in fact his deepest desire, whether
being left alone now to continue his crude demonstration was exactly what he had counted on. He was not alone, however, and his
performance needed no human witnesses to retain its true nature
and purpose—that is, the engendering of horror. The desperate father knew perfectly well to Whom, or better, against Whom all this

was directed, in Whom it was actually intended to create a sense of horror, and before Whose eyes this expression of a return to a state of nature was being performed in order to show Him what a throwback to primal desert ways His own behavior had been. Those around him gradually became aware of these intentions, particularly the man who looked after him, Eliezer, "Abraham's oldest servant"—that aged institution, who knew how to say "I" in such a special way and whom the earth had leapt up to greet.

His heart, too, had been pierced by the terrible news, confirmed by its bloody token, that Joseph, his beautiful and apt pupil, the son of the true wife, had come to grief and been killed on his journey, prey to a ravaging beast; but his strange personal constitution, his peculiar extended sense of self, allowed him to receive the blow with a certain equanimity; moreover, the need to care for Jacob, this man of sorrows, meant that he regarded his own distress as of little importance. It was Eliezer who saw to his master's meals, although Jacob refused to eat anything for days, and to make sure that at least for the night Jacob returned to his tent and bed, where he never left his side. For during the day, Jacob had found a place on a dust heap littered with shards and located in an out-of-the-way, totally unshaded corner of the settlement; and there he sat naked, clutching the veil's tatters in his hands, strewing hair, beard, and shoulders with ashes, and from time to time picking up a loose shard of pottery to scrape his body as if he were afflicted with boils and leprosy—a purely symbolic procedure, for there was not the least sign of boils, and the scraping was part of his performance intended for that other witness.

The sight of this wretched penitent's body was woefully touching enough even without the unclean state such actions were supposed to illustrate, and everyone except the aged steward avoided Jacob's place of abandonment with awe and reverence. Jacob's body was no longer that of the delicately robust young man who had wrestled beside the Jabbok with the ox-eyed stranger and not been defeated, or who had spent a windblown night with the wrong wife—nor was it the body of the man who later sired Joseph with his true wife. Seventy years of life—not precisely or attentively counted, to be sure, but effective for all that—had now passed, inflicting all the touchingly homely disfigurements of old age that made his nakedness so painful to behold. Youth gladly and candidly shows itself naked; beauty allows for a clear conscience. Old age wraps itself in dignified shame, and knows why. That exposed body—with its chest reddened by the heat, overgrown with white hair, and, as happens in later years, resembling more and more a woman's breast; with its weakened arms and thighs, its sagging, wrinkled belly—was not a sight for anyone but perhaps old Eliezer, who accepted it calmly and raised no objection, for he did not want to disturb his master's performance.

Still less was he the man to keep Jacob from other measures that did not go beyond the usual scope of deep mourning—in particular, his long stay on the dust heap and his repeated soiling of himself with ashes, which were then mixed with sweat and tears. These were to be sanctioned, and Eliezer made a point only of erecting a makeshift awning over the place of penance, so that at the height of the day Tammuz's sun would not assail his master all too cruelly. Despite which, Jacob's sorrowful countenance—with its open mouth, slack jaw and drooping beard, eyes constantly rolled up and back from uncomprehending depths of pain—was swollen and red from heat and affliction, just as he himself noted, the way those who are tenderly self-aware are wont to do when it comes to their own condition, convinced it might go unnoticed unless put into words.

"Weeping has left my face bright red and swollen," he said in a trembling voice. "Bent low with weeping, I take my seat, and tears run down my countenance."

Those were not his own words, as was readily apparent. According to ancient song, Noah himself spoke these or similar words when looking out upon the Flood, and Jacob made them his own. For it is good, consoling, and useful that phrases of lamentation from the early days of beleaguered humanity are preserved and lie at the ready, suitable for later and present occasions as if made for them, in order to ease the pain of life to whatever extent words can ease it, so that one may make use of them and join one's own suffering with ancient and ever-present pain. Indeed, Jacob could pay his misery no greater honor than to equate it with the Great Flood and apply to it words coined for that occasion.

In his despair he spoke a great many such preformed, or partially preformed words of lamentation. In particular, he would erupt again and again into a wailing cry—"A ravenous beast has devoured Joseph! Mutilated and torn to pieces is my son!"—that bore the marks of an older coinage, though no one should for that reason think that it lessened the immediacy of his pain in the least. Ah, there was no lack of that, despite all coined words.

"Lamb and mother sheep are slain!" Jacob recited in litany, rocking back and forth and weeping bitterly. "First the mother and now the lamb! The mother sheep left her lamb, though it was but a little way to the inn; now the lamb has strayed and is lost as well. No, no, no, no! Too much, too much! Alas, alas! Raise a lament over the beloved son. Over the sprout whose roots have been ripped up, over my hope that has been ripped up like a seedling—oh lament, lament! My Damu, my child! The underworld has now become his dwelling. No bread will I eat, no water will I drink. Mutilated and torn is Joseph . . ."

Wiping his master's face from time to time with a cloth dipped in water, Eliezer shared in the wailing—as long as it kept to these set formulas and coinages or phrases closely modeled on them—by at least murmuring or half singing repetitive words, the cries of "Lament! Lament!" or "Mutilated and torn!" The entire camp joined in the wailing for hours on end as well, by the way, and would have done so even if their sadness at the loss of a beloved son of the house had been less unfeigned. "*Hoi achî! Hoi adôn!* Alas for our brother! Alas for our lord!" The chorus drifted across to where Jacob and Eliezer were, and they also heard, though these were not to be taken literally, words refusing food and drink, for the seedling was uprooted and the green grass withered in the desert wind.

It is a good custom, there is something soothing about the ordering of exultation and sorrow by prescribed texts that provide a firm bed through which emotion may flow and prevent us from degenerating into wild, floundering excess. Jacob likewise experienced the blessing and usefulness of binding tradition; but Abraham's grandson was too original a spirit, and everyday emotion was too intensely bound up with his personal thought, for him to have found satisfaction in uniformity. He also spoke and grieved freely, without prescribed formulas, and Eliezer wiped his face then, too, inserting from time to time a word of reassurance or admonishing with a contrasting traditional phrase.

"What I feared," Jacob exclaimed in a voice diminished, raised, and half choked by suffering, "has come upon me, and what most disquieted me has come to pass. Do you understand it, Eliezer? Can you grasp it? No, no, no, no—no one can understand it when what one has feared has actually happened. Had it not disquieted me, but burst upon me without warning, I would believe it. I would say to my heart, 'You were thoughtless and did not prevent this evil by setting your eye on it and banishing it in time.' Behold, surprise is believable. But for forebodings to come to pass, brazenly to occur nonetheless—to my eyes that is an abomination and against the arrangement."

"Nothing is ever arranged in matters of affliction," Eliezer replied.

"No, not as regards the law. But as regards human feeling, which also has reason and outrage on its side! For why has man been given fear and foresight if not to ban evil and to prevent fate early on from even thinking its wicked thoughts? To fate's vexation, but to its shame as well, for it says to itself, 'Are these still my thoughts? These are human thoughts, and I no longer like them.' But what shall become of man if foresight is no longer in force and his fears are in vain—that is, justified? Or how shall a man live if he can no longer depend on events turning out differently from what he has thought?"

"God is free," Eliezer said.

Jacob closed his lips. He picked up a shard he had dropped and began to scrape again at his symbolic boils. For now, this was his only response to the name of God. He went on: "What cares and dread I had that a wild beast from the thickets might come upon the child one day and harm him. I disregarded that I had become a laughingstock because of my fears, paying people no mind when they said, 'Look at the poor old wet nurse!' And I was as ridiculous as a man who constantly repeats, 'I am sick, I am sick unto death,' but looks healthy and does not die, and no one takes him seriously, finally not even he himself. But then they find him dead and rue their mockery and say, 'Behold, he was not a fool.' Can the man still relish their humiliation? No, for he is dead. And would rather have been a fool in their eyes and his own, than justified in so unpalatable a fashion. Here I sit on the dust heap, my face bright red and swollen from weeping, ashen tears running down my countenance. Can I rejoice at my tears because this has come to pass? No, for it has come to pass. I am dead, for Joseph is dead, torn to pieces, mutilated . . .

"Here, Eliezer, take this and see—the tatters of his coat and veil of images! I lifted it from my true and dearest wife in the bridal chamber, and gave her the blossom of my soul. But then, because of Laban's trickery, it turned out to be the wrong wife, and my soul was unspeakably reviled and torn for a long time—until amid ghastly pain, the true wife gave me this boy, Dumuzi, my all. And now he too has been torn from me and the apple of my eye is slain. Can anyone grasp it? Is it acceptable, this outrageous demand? No, no, no, no, I no longer desire to live. I would choose for my soul to be hanged, and death rather than these bones."

"Do not sin, Israel!"

"Ah, Eliezer, teach me to fear God and worship His overwhelming power! He lets Himself be paid in names and blessings and Esau's bitter tears—paid mightily! He sets the price as He pleases, and is moved by a peculiar forbearance. He did not negotiate with me, or let me bargain as to what price would be too high. He takes what I can pay as He sees it, and claims to know better than I what my soul can bear. Can I argue with Him as equal to equal? I sit here on an ash heap, scraping my body—what more does He want? With my lips I say, 'What the Lord does is well done.' Let Him heed my lips! What I think in my heart is my own affair."

"But He reads the heart as well."

"That is not my fault. He, and not I, made things so that He sees the heart. He would have done better to leave man a refuge from His overwhelming power, so that he could grumble against what is unacceptable and think his own thoughts as to justice. This heart was His refuge and tent of comfort. When God came to visit, it was properly adorned and swept with brooms, and a seat of honor prepared for Him. Now there is nothing but ashes in it, mixed with tears and the rubbish of misery. Let Him avoid my heart, that He may not soil Himself, and heed only my lips."

"Surely you would not sin, Yaaqov ben Yitzchak."

"Words, words, old servant, do not thresh them, for they are nothing but straw! Take my part and not God's, for He is too great and laughs at your concern, whereas I am but a mound of sorrow. Do not appeal to me from what is outside, but speak to me from your soul, I can bear nothing else. Do you know and have you understood that Joseph is gone and will never return to me, never,

never? Only when you ponder that can you speak to me from your soul and not speak empty words. My own lips sent him on this journey, saying, 'Go to Shechem and bow down before your brothers, that they may come home and Israel not stand as a tree stripped bare.' I made this extraordinary demand of him and of myself and treated us both roughly, sending him on his journey alone, without servants; for I recognized his folly as my own and did not hide from myself what God knew. God, however, hid from me what He knew, for He told me to command the child, 'Go there!' and withheld His knowledge and brutal intent. That is the faithfulness of a powerful God, and that is how He repays truth with truth!"

"Guard your lips at least, son of the true wife!"

"My lips were made for me that I may spit out what is unpalatable. Speak not from the outside, Eliezer, but rather from inside. What is God thinking to lay this upon me so that my eyes roll and I lose my senses because it is nothing I can bear? Have I the strength of stones, or is my flesh of brass? If only in His wisdom He had made me of iron, but this is nothing for me. . . . My child, my Damu! The Lord has given him, the Lord has taken him away again—if only He had not first given him or not let me have come from the womb, or given nothing at all! What is a man to think, Eliezer, and where can he twist and turn in his distress? If I were not, then I would know nothing, and it would be nothing. But since I am, it is better that Joseph is gone than that he had never been, for at least I still have what remains to me, my grief for him. Ah, God has seen to it that one cannot be against Him and that one must say 'yes' in saying 'no.' Yes, He gave him to me in my old age, may His name be heartily praised for that! He fashioned him with His hands and gave him his charms. Like milk He milked him and skillfully crafted his frame, clothing it with skin and flesh and pouring out grace upon him, so that he could take hold of me by the earlobes, laughing and saying, 'My dear papa, give it to me!' And I gave it to him, for I am not made of iron or stone. And when I called him to go on the journey and made my demand, he cried, 'Here I am!' and kicked up his heels—and when I think of it, my groaning pours from me like water. For I might just as well have laid the wood for the burnt offering upon him and taken him by the hand, carrying fire and the knife myself. Oh, Eliezer, I have confessed to God, contritely, honestly admitting that I could not have done it. And do you think He graciously accepted my humble heart and showed mercy on my confession? No, but rather He snorted at it and said, 'Let what you cannot do be done, and though you do not wish to give it, I shall take it.' That is God!

"Here, look—the coat and its tatters, stiff with blood. It is the blood of his veins that the monster tore apart along with his flesh. Oh the horror, the horror! And God's sin! Oh savage, blind, senseless crime! . . . I demanded too much of him, Eliezer, too much of the child. He went astray in the fields and lost his way in the desert—where the monster fell upon him, pouncing upon him to devour him, with no thought of his fear. Perhaps he screamed for me, perhaps for his mother, who died when he was small. No one heard him, God saw to that. Do you think it was a lion that fell upon him or a brutish boar that attacked with bristles flared and buried its tusks in him . . ."

He shuddered, fell silent, and fell back into brooding. The word "boar" necessarily established certain connections of thought that lifted this one ghastly event ripping at his emotions to a higher level, to a model and prototype, to the ever-revolving, ever-abiding sphere, transported it, so to speak, to just below the stars. The boar, the raging swine of swine, was Seth, the deicide, it was the Red One, was Esau whom he, by way of exception, had known how to mollify when he had wept at Eliphaz's feet, but who in true prototypical fashion had dismembered his brother and may also have been dismembered himself, only to appear here below in ten different pieces. And at that moment a premonition, a kind of mythic suspicion rising from the depths where it had rested since he had first received the bloody remnants, tried to emerge into Jacob's conscious mind: a dark inkling as to who that damned boar had been who had mutilated Joseph. But he let it fall back down into the darkness before it ever reached the surface, even helped a little to suppress it himself. Strangely enough, he did not want to know anything about it and fought off its knowledge, which would have meant recognizing something from above in the world below, for the suspicion of guilt, had he allowed it, would have been directed against himself. His courage, his love of truth, had sufficed for him to recognize his own liability for Joseph, which was why he had demanded of himself that Joseph be sent on his journey. But a recognition of his shared guilt in the child's death, which would have ineluctably resulted from any suspicion of a brother, of brothers—for that his courage and love of truth were pardonably insufficient. The admission that he himself had been the swine of swine whose foolish doting, born of emotional pride, had slain Joseph—in his secret heart he called that demanding too much, and in his bitter pain he would hear nothing of it. And yet the unbearable bitterness of that pain was rooted in that same inadmissible suspicion now banned to the darkness, just as the urge to act out his misery before God could primarily be traced to it as well.

But God was Jacob's real concern, for He stood behind everything and it was to Him that his brooding, weeping, despairing eyes were directed. Lion or boar—God had willed, permitted, or, in a word, *done* the horrible deed, and Jacob found a certain satisfaction, familiar to all, in the fact that his despair allowed him to argue with God—it was in reality an elevated state that stood in contradiction to his external abasement in nakedness and ashes. To be sure, in order to argue he had first to be abased. Jacob scraped at his misery—but in return did not mince words or keep a watch on his lips.

"That is God!" he repeated with an exaggerated shudder. "The Lord did not ask me, Eliezer, and did not command I be put to the test, saying, 'Offer me your son whom you love.' Perhaps, contrary to my humble expectation, I would have been strong and would have led the child toward Moriah despite his question about where the sheep for the burnt offering was; perhaps I could have heard it without falling into a faint, and have been able to raise the knife above Isaak, trusting in a ram—it would at least have come to a test. But not like this, not like this, Eliezer. He did not even dignify me with a test. But rather He lured the child away from my heart on the basis of my honest insight that I was not without guilt in his strife with his brothers, and He led him astray so that the lion might surprise him and a wild boar thrust its tusks into his flesh and root its snout in his bowels. It is, you should know, a beast that devours everything. It devoured him. It even brought some of Joseph back to its nest, to its children, the little swine. Can one grasp that, accept that? No, it is unpalatable! I vomit it up as a bird vomits its castings. There it lies. Let God do with it what He will, for it is nothing for me."

"Compose yourself, Israel."

"No, I am beyond composure, my steward. God has torn it from me, so now let Him hear my words. He is my creator, I know that. He has milked me like milk and curdled me like cheese, I admit that. But what about Him, and where would He be without us, my fathers and me? Is His memory so short? Has He forgotten man's torments and labor for His sake, and how Abram discovered Him by the impulse of thought, so that God might kiss His fingers and cry, 'Finally I have been called Lord and Most High!' I ask you: Has He forgotten the covenant, so that He gnashes me between His teeth, acting as if I were His enemy? Where is my transgression and my iniquity? Let Him show them to me. Have I made smoke to rise for the Baals of the land round about and blown kisses to the stars? There was no wrong in me, and my prayer was pure. Why do I suffer violence instead of justice? Let Him crush me at once in His willfulness and cast me into the pit, for that is a small thing to Him, even if unjust, and I no longer wish to live if violence reigns. Does He mock the spirit of man, that He slays the godly and the wicked for sport? But then where would He be without the spirit of man? Eliezer, the covenant is broken! Do not ask me why, for I would have to give you a sorrowful answer. *God has not kept pace*—do you understand me? God and man have chosen one another and made a covenant, that they may rightly become what they are, each in the other, and grow holy, one in the other. But if man has become gentle and refined in God, his soul well-mannered, whereas God seems to him an abomination of the desert that he cannot accept, but must spew from his mouth, saying, 'This is nothing for me'—it is thereby proved, Eliezer, that God has not kept pace in His own sanctification, but has stayed behind and is still a fiend."

Eliezer was understandably horrified at such words and prayed on high for leniency for his master, who was now out of all bounds and whom he resolutely admonished.

"You prattle on," he said, "saying impossible words no one would want to hear and tugging at God's robes beyond all seemliness. *I* say this to you—I, who with God's help routed the kings of the East with Abram and for whom the earth leapt up on my journey for a bride. For you call God a desert fiend and set yourself up against Him as refined and gentle, but it is from your words that the desert howls, and in abusing Him and permitting yourself the most abominable license, you trifle away any sympathy with your pain. Do you determine what is right and wrong and sit in judgment over Him Who has made not only Behemoth, its tail extending like a cedar, and Leviathan, whose bared teeth are a horror and whose scales are like shields of brass, but also Orion, the Seven Sisters, the rosy dawn, hornets, snakes, and the Abubu of dust? Did He not give Yitzchak's blessing to you instead of to Esau, who was a little older, and confirm His promise in your splendid vision of the stairway at Beth-el? You were happy to accept that, and your gentle and refined human spirit found nothing to which it could object, for it was to your liking. Did He not make you rich and fat in Laban's house and open the dusty bars that you might come forth with chick and child, and was not Laban like a lamb before you on the mountain in Gilead? But now that you have suffered injury—grievous injury, as no one will deny—you rise up in defiance, kicking like a stubborn jackass, recklessly tossing all that aside and saying, 'God's manners have not kept pace.' Are you, being made of flesh, free of sin, and is it so certain that you have practiced justice your life long? Are you determined to understand what is too high for you and fathom the riddle of life, riding roughshod over it with human words and saying: 'It is nothing for me, and I am holier than God'? Truly, I should not have heard such words, son of the true wife."

"Yes, you, Eliezer," Jacob riposted with intemperate scorn, "you are the very truth to me, and may you remain so! You have gobbled down wisdom by the spoonful and sweat it out of every pore. It is truly edifying that you scold me and remind me how you drove off those kings with Abram—which is patently impossible. For reason tells me that you are my half brother by a handmaid, born in Dimashki, and never beheld Abram with your own eyes any more than I. Behold, how in my misery I make short work of your edification! I was pure, but God has drenched me in dung, over and over, and such people hold fast to reason, for they can make nothing of the guise of pretty piety and they let truth go naked. And I declare my doubts as to whether the earth leapt up to greet you. It is all over."

"Jacob, Jacob, what are you doing! You destroy the world in the conceit of your grief, you smash it to pieces, heaping them upon the head of your admonisher—for I will not say on Whose head you would in fact heap them. Are you the first man ever to know sorrow, and may you above all not know its affliction, else you puff up your

belly with blasphemy and rebel and butt against God with head lowered? Do you think mountains will be moved for your sake and
water made to run uphill? I believe you will burst with malice on the
spot, calling God godless and He Who Is Exalted unjust."

"Silence, Eliezer! I beg you, do not speak in such skewed words
about me, I am sore with pain and cannot endure it. Did God have to
give up His only son to be fodder for swine and for the offspring of
swine in their nest, or did I? Why do you console Him and take His
part, instead of mine? Do you even understand what I mean? You
understand nothing at all and would speak on God's behalf. Ah, defender of God, He will repay you and will credit you highly for cunningly protecting and glorifying His deeds, because He is God! But
I say to you: He will cast it in your teeth. For you are unjustly trying
to speak in His cause and deceive Him, as one deceives a man, all the
while secretly looking to your own person. Hypocrite, He will rebuke you for treating Him that way for His sake and for toadying to
espouse His cause, when what He has done to me in casting Joseph
before swine shrieks to high heaven. What you say, I could say as
well, and I am no more stupid than you—think on that before you
utter platitudes. But I speak differently—and in doing so am closer
to Him than you are. For one must defend God against His defend-
ers and protect Him before those who would excuse Him. Do you
think He is a man, albeit an overpowering one, and that you must
take His part against a worm such as I? If you call Him eternally
powerful, then you are merely blowing words if you do not know
that God is even above God, eternal beyond Himself, and will bring
punishment down upon you from that place where He is my salvation and my refuge, and where, if you regard yourself as between
Him and me, you are not!"

"We are altogether corrupt flesh and naked before sin," Eliezer
replied softly. "Each must deal with God as best he understands and
as far as understanding reaches, for no one reaches Him. One may
assume we have both spoken culpably of Him. But come now, dear
master, and return to your house, this is enough of uttermost
mourning. Your face is all swollen from the heat of this place of
potsherds, and you are too gentle and refined for this degree of
mourning."

"From weeping!" Jacob said. "My face is bright red and swollen
from weeping for my beloved son." But he went along anyway and

let himself be led to his tent. For he, too, had no more interest in
rubbish, stark nakedness, and scraping—they were of service only
so that he could dispute with God at length.

The Temptations of Jacob

After the first three days, he at least put on sackcloth and assumed a
life somewhat less desolated by suffering, so that when his sons finally arrived they no longer found him in his most extreme state.
But they took their time in coming, and those who mourned and
lamented with him, who supported and comforted him, were primarily his sons' wives—those in the camp, that is, since Judah's wife,
Shua's daughter, was not there—as well as Zilpah and Bilhah and
also Benjamin, the little boy, whom he would take in his arms while
they both sobbed together. He did not love his youngest even remotely as much as he had loved Joseph, and had never been able to
hide the gloom in his eyes when their gaze fell on the boy who had
cost him Rachel. But now he pressed him fervently to his breast,
called him Benoni for his mother's sake, and swore to him that he
would never, under any circumstance, send him on a journey, either
alone or even with an escort—no matter how old, even as a married
man, he was always to remain here under his father's eye, cherished
and protected, and not to take a step from the safest path, for nothing and no one could be relied upon in this world.

Benjamin accepted this reassurance, although it depressed him a
little. He thought of his excursions with Joseph to the grove of
Adonai; and the thought that his beloved, beautiful brother would
never again leap at his side or air his little hand when he sweated, that
he would never again tell him grand dreams of heaven or make him,
a mere whelp, proud by trusting in his understanding—it all unleashed bitter tears. Ultimately, however, he was not capable of realizing in his own mind what they meant by saying Joseph would
never return, that he was no longer alive, but dead—did not even believe it despite the horrible token of the veil, which his father always
kept with him. The natural inability to believe in death is the negation of a negation, and deserves to be called a positive affirmation. It
is helpless faith, for all faith is helpless and strong in its helplessness.
As for Benjamin, he dressed his invincible faith in the notion that

Joseph had been carried off somehow. "He will come back," he assured the old man as he caressed him. "Or he will send for us to come." For his part, Jacob was no child, but a man who was laden with the stories of his life and whose experience of death's unmerciful reality had been all too bitter for him to greet Benoni's consoling words with anything more than a melancholy smile. But he, too, was ultimately incapable of an affirmative to death's negation, and his efforts to fend it off and evade its necessity—to reconcile himself with the inhuman contradiction between the reality and its impossibility—were so excessive that in our own day we would be forced to speak of mental derangement. For his own household, to be sure, that would have meant going too far; but Eliezer had his hands full with the desperate plans and speculations that Jacob was rolling over in his mind.

It has been handed down to us that his reply to everyone was: "I shall go down to the pit, to my son, mourning." Both then and later, that was generally understood to mean that he wished to live no longer, but to die as well and join his son in death—especially in light of his other lament that it was all so sad and hard that a man could only bed his gray head in death out of grief. Quite possibly, his words were intended to be so understood. Eliezer, however, heard them in a different and more precise fashion. As mad as it sounds, Jacob was brooding over the possibility of descending into the pit, that is, into death, in order to *fetch Joseph back*.

The notion was all the more absurd since it was not the father, but the mother-wife who set about to free her true son from his underworld prison and restore him to the devastated earth. But in Jacob's poor head, ideas were equated in the boldest ways, and his inclination not to regard sex all too precisely, but to treat it with a certain freedom in his thoughts, was anything but recent. He had never known how to differentiate clearly between Joseph's and Rachel's eyes—they were truly one and same, and he had once kissed away the tears of impatience from beneath them. In death they merged completely into one pair of eyes, while the beloved figures themselves merged into a hermaphroditic image, the object of a yearning that was itself suprasexual, both male and female, like all highest things, like God himself. But since that yearning was part of Jacob and he part of it, so Jacob, too, partook of this same nature—a conclusion with which he had long felt emotionally compatible.

Since Rachel's death he had been both father and mother to Joseph, had assumed her role in their relationship as well, with maternal love in fact predominating; and his equating of Joseph with Rachel found its counterpart in his own identification of himself with the departed woman. Only a double love can truly respond to a double object of love, its feminine side calling forth the masculine, its masculine the feminine. Paternal emotions that see in their object both the son and the beloved—that is, which incorporate a tenderness more befitting the love of a mother for her son—are masculine insofar as they are directed toward the beloved in the son, and yet maternal, insofar as they are love for the son. This balancing of emotions assisted Jacob in the mad enterprise with which he filled Eliezer's ears and that concerned his leading Joseph back into life by following the mythic model.

"I will go down," he declared, "to my son. Look at me, Eliezer—has the shape of my breasts not already become somewhat more like that of a woman? At my age, nature balances things out. Women grow beards and men breasts. I shall find the way to the Land of No Return, I shall set out tomorrow. Why do you look at me so doubtfully? Might it not be possible? One must only keep moving westward, then cross the river Kubur, and one comes to the seven gates. I beg you, do not doubt me! No one loved him more than I. I will be like his mother. I will find him and descend with him to the bottommost place, where the river of life has its source. I will sprinkle him with its water and loosen the dusty bars for his return. Did I not do it once before? Am I not expert at outwitting others and fleeing? I will deal with the queen of that realm just as I dealt with Laban, and she shall likewise send me off with fair words. Why must I watch as you shake your head?"

"Ah, dear master, I try to agree with your endeavors as best I can, and I assume that at least at the start all will go according to your plan. But at the seventh gate at the latest, usages there will inevitably determine that you are not the mother . . ."

"To be sure," Jacob replied and, despite all his anguish, could not entirely suppress a smile of satisfaction, "that is unavoidable. It will be obvious that I did not suckle him, but rather sired him . . . Eliezer," he said, following a new line of thought, which had turned away from the maternal-female to the phallic, "I will sire him once again! Ought it not be possible to sire him anew, just as he was, the very same Joseph, and in that way, then, to lead him back from below? After all, I am still here, from whence he came; is he to be lost then? As long as I am, I cannot give him up for lost. I will awaken him anew and in siring him restore his image on earth."

"But Rachel is no longer here, who received you for that work, and both of you had to unite for this boy to have sprung into being. If she, however, were still alive and you two would beget a child, it would still not be the same hour and placement of the stars that awakened Joseph. You would not call him forth, or a Benjamin, but a third whom no eye has ever seen. For nothing happens twice, and everything here is forever only like itself."

"But then it dare not die and be lost, Eliezer! That is impossible. Whatever is only once, that is like nothing else either with or after it and that no great cycle can restore, cannot be destroyed and cast to the swine—I cannot accept that. What you say is true—Rachel was necessary for Joseph's begetting, as was the hour of it as well. I knew that, but knowingly provoked your reply. For he who sires is only a tool of creation, blind and unaware of what he is doing. When we begot Joseph, my true wife and I, we did not beget him, but rather a something, and that it became Joseph was God's work. Begetting is not creating, but is merely the blind lust of life plunging into life. But He creates. Oh, if only my life could plunge into death and know it, so that I might sire in it and awaken Joseph, just as he was, out of it! That is where my thoughts are tending, and that is what I mean when I say: I will go down. If only I could sire backwards into the past and into the hour that was Joseph's hour! Why do you shake your head? I know myself that I cannot do it; but you should not shake your head because I wish it, for God has so arranged that I am and Joseph is not, a flagrant contradiction that rends the heart. Do you know what that is, a heart that has been rent? No, you merely babble away when you say it, and at most you mean 'truly sad.' But my heart has literally been rent apart and mutilated, so that I am compelled to think against reason and to ponder the impossible."

"I shake my head, my lord, out of pity, because you defy what you call a contradiction—that is, that you are and your son no longer is. Together, that is the sum of your grief, which you manifested to such a high degree and demonstrated for three days on the heap of potsherds. But after all that, it would be better now if you would gradually begin to surrender to God's design, if you were to gather up the pieces of your heart and no longer speak words that are torn and rent, such as 'I will sire Joseph once again.' How can that ever be? In siring him, you did not know him. For man only begets what he does not know. If he would try to beget knowingly and mindfully, then it would be creation, and in that he would be presumptuous, daring to be God."

"Well, Eliezer, what then? Must not man therefore be presumptuous, and would he still be man if he did not always aspire to be like God? You forget," Jacob said in muted voice, edging closer to Eliezer's ear, "that I secretly know more about creating life than many a man, and that indeed, if need be, I know means and ways to blur the difference between begetting and creating, and can make a bit of creating flow into the begetting, just as Laban learned when I had white sheep and goats conceive while looking at peeled rods, so that they bore speckled young to my advantage. Find me a wife, Eliezer, whose eyes and limbs resemble Rachel's—there must be such women. I will conceive with her, my eyes firmly and knowingly fixed on the image of Joseph as I know it. And she will bear him again to me from among the dead."

"What you say," Eliezer replied in an equally low voice, "makes me shudder in revulsion, and I prefer not to have heard it. For it seems to me that it comes not only from the depths of your grief, but from deeper still. Besides, you are well on in years and for dignity's sake should no longer even been thinking of begetting, let alone with any tinge of creation added—it is unseemly in every regard."

"Make no mistake about me, Eliezer. I am an old man, but I am alive and not even close to being like the angels, definitely not—I know better. I would very much like to beget. But I grant," he added dejectedly after a brief pause, "that my vital powers are somewhat dampened at present by my grief for Joseph, so that perhaps out of grief I would not yet be able to beget, even though I wish to do so precisely because of my grief. There, you see the contradictions God arranges to rend and mutilate me."

"I see that your grief has been set as a watchman to guard against great sacrilege."

Jacob brooded.

"In that case," he said, his lips still at his servant's ear, "the watchman must be deceived and one must snap one's fingers in his face, which may be easy to do, since he is both obstacle and motive.

For it must be possible, Eliezer, to make a man without begetting him, if one is prevented from it by grief and suffering. Did God create man in a woman's womb? No, for there was none, and it is disgraceful even to think of it. But with His own hands He made him according to His wishes, out of clay, and blew the breath of life into his nostrils, so that he might rise and walk. But what if, Eliezer—listen, let me win you over—we were to make a figure of clay, to form a thing of earth, like a doll, three ells long and with all its limbs, just as God imagined and envisioned them, for He conceived man in His mind and made him after His image. God saw and made man, Adam, for He is the creator. But I see Joseph, one man, just as I know him, and long far more to awaken him than I did to beget him, not knowing him. And there it would lie before us, Eliezer, this doll, stretching out the length of a man, an artificial figure lying on its back, its countenance directed heavenward; but we would stand at its feet and gaze into its face of clay. Ah, eldest servant, my heart beats high and fast, for what would it be like if we did this?"

"If we did what, my lord? What are these new and strange things your sorrow conceives?"

"Do I even know yet, my steward, and can I tell you? Let yourself be won over, and help me to do what I still don't rightly know myself. If we were to walk around the image, one and seven times, I to the right and you to the left, and lay a slip of papyrus in its mouth, inscribed with God's name . . . But I would kneel down and embrace the clay in my arms and kiss it with all my might, from the depths of my heart. . . . There!" he cried. "Eliezer, look! The body turns red, red like fire, it glows, it scorches me, but I don't let go, I hold it tightly in my arms and kiss it again. The fire goes out, and water courses through the clay body, it swells and gushes with water, and behold, hair sprouts from its head, and nails sprout from its fingers and toes. Then I kiss it a third time and blow my breath into it, which is God's breath, and fire, water, and gentle air, these three, cause the fourth, the earth, to be awakened to life and to open its eyes in amazement upon me, the awakener, and it says, 'Abba, dear father' . . ."

"I find this all very, very uncanny," Eliezer said, trembling slightly, "for indeed it is as if you had earnestly won me over to something new and dubious and the *golem* were alive before my eyes. Truly you worry the life out of me, and what strange thanks you offer for my waiting with you in your sorrow and faithfully supporting your head, that you have now come to idols and sorcery and have me join in, whether I will or no, so that I see it all with my own eyes."

And Eliezer was glad when the brothers arrived; but they were not glad.

The Inurement

They came on the seventh day after Jacob had received the token—they, too, with sackcloth about their loins and hair full of ashes. They were in grim spirits, for not one of them understood how they could ever have thought and persuaded themselves that they would have it good, that their father's heart would belong to them, if only his coddled pet was no more. This delusion had by now long since fallen away, and they were amazed they could ever have entertained it. Even under way, they had admitted, both privately to themselves and in scraps of exchanged words, that as far as Jacob's love was concerned, getting rid of Joseph had been completely pointless.

They could well imagine, and fairly precisely, what was going on inside Jacob as regarded them—it was clear to them how troublesomely complicated their life would be. In some way or other, in the depths of his soul but quite possibly without drawing a final conclusion, he surely believed them to be the boy's murderers, even if he did not assume that they had slain their brother with their own hands, but instead had somehow got the animal to do it for them, acting according to their wishes and yet relieving them of the bloody deed, so that in his eyes they were still guiltless and unassailable—and therefore all the more despicable—murderers. In reality, as they well knew, it was just the opposite: They were guilty, but were not murderers. But they could not tell their father that, for in order to cleanse themselves of a dark suspicion of murder they would have had to confess their guilt—and the very oath that bound them already prevented that, though, to be sure, there were moments when they were close to finding their oath as stupid as all the rest.

In short, they would know no more good days, presumably not a one—they saw it clearly. A bad conscience is bad enough, but an aggrieved bad conscience is almost even worse, for it creates a sullen confusion of the soul, filled with both foolishness and anguish, and cuts a sorry figure. That is how they would stand there before Jacob their whole life long, all ten, never knowing a moment's peace. For he suspected them, and they would learn what that means: suspicion and distrust—how they make a man mistrust himself in others and others in himself, so that he begrudges them the peace he cannot find in himself, and must nag and skulk, poke, prod, and pry without rest, vexing himself by appearing to vex them—that is the meaning of suspicion and incurable distrust.

As they stepped before Jacob, they saw at first glance that this was how things stood and would stand from now on. They saw it in the look his eyes gave them as he lifted his head a little from the arm on which it lay—eyes inflamed by weeping, both keen and clouded, fearful and hateful, that tried to pierce through them, yet knowing they could not—a look that lasted a long time before a matching word followed: a question, unanswerable and yet answered all too well, pathetically empty, wretchedly absurd, its only purpose pointless torment.

"Where is Joseph?"

They stood there, hanging their heads in response to his impossible question, aggrieved sinners, sorry figures. They saw that he intended to make things as difficult for them as possible and to spare them nothing. They had been announced to him, so he certainly could have prepared himself and sat up to receive them; but he still lay stretched out before them, a week now after having received the token—lay there, his face buried in his arm, lifting it only after a considerable time, to give them this look and ask the brutal question that his sorrow allowed itself. He was using his sorrow, they saw that. He lay before them like that in order to ask it, so that, if need be, his question of distrust might also be taken as a question of sorrow—and they understood it very well. People have always had a sharp eye for one another, each painfully seeing through the other—in those depths of time no less keenly than today.

They wrenched their mouths to reply, but it was Jehuda who answered for all of them: "We know, dear lord, what suffering and great sorrow has been visited upon you."

"Me?" he asked. "And not you as well?"

A genuine question. A quibbling, insidious question. But, of course, them as well.

"Of course us as well," they replied. "But we do not wish to speak of ourselves."

"Why not?"

"Out of respect."

A wretched conversation. They shuddered to think it might go on like this forever.

"Joseph is no longer here," Jacob said.

"Sad to say," they replied.

"I sent him on this journey," he said again, "and he was elated. I told him to go to Shechem so that he might bend low before you and persuade your hearts to return home. Did he do that?"

"Sad to say and beyond all sadness," they replied, "he never got to do it. Before he could, the wild beast had slain him. For we were no longer pasturing our flocks in the valley of Shechem, but in the valley of Dothan. The boy lost his way and was slain. We have not seen him with our own eyes since that day in the field when he announced to both you and us what he had dreamt."

"The dreams that he dreamt," Jacob said, "were surely an offense to you, a heavy offense, so that you held a great grievance against him in your hearts, did you not?"

"Something of a grievance," they replied. "A grievance to be sure, but within measure. We saw that his dreams were a vexation to you, for you scolded him and threatened to tug at his hair. Which is why we were also aggrieved by him to some degree. But now, sad to say, the cruel beast has tugged at him far more than you threatened."

"It tore and mutilated him," Jacob said and wept. "How can you say 'tugged,' when it tore him apart and devoured him? For any of you to say 'tugged' instead of 'mutilated' is mockery and scorn, and bears the sound of approval."

"It can also happen," they replied, "that one says 'tugged' for 'mutilated' out of bitter sorrow, and a tender desire to spare feelings."

"That is true," he said. "You are right to reply in that fashion, and I must fall silent. But since Joseph could not persuade your hearts, why have you come?"

"To lament with you."

"Then let us lament," Jacob responded. And they sat down beside him to raise a lament that began "How long have you lain there?" And Judah supported his father's head on his knees and dried his tears.

But after a short while Jacob interrupted their lament and said, "I do not wish for you to hold my head and dry my tears, Judah. Let the twins do it."

Offended, Judah let the twins take over his father's head, and they supported it a while as they lamented, until Jacob exclaimed, "I don't know why, but I find it unpleasant for Shimeon and Levi to perform this service for me. Let Re'uben do it."

Very offended, the twins passed their father's head on to Ruben, who tended to it for a while. But then Jacob said, "It does not suit or comfort me for Ruben to do the holding and drying. Let Dan do it."

But things went no better with him; he had to pass the head on to Naphtali and he, with the offense not long in coming, on to Gad. And so it went via Asher and Issakhar down to Zebulun, and each time Jacob would say something like "For some vague reason it goes against my grain that this one or this one is holding my head—let another do it."

Until they had all been spurned and offended—then he said, "Let us cease to lament."

After that, they could only sit around him in silence with pouting lips; for they understood that he halfway held them for Joseph's murderers, which they were halfway—and not entirely only by accident. And so they were mightily offended that he halfway held them for full murderers—and turned hard and sullen.

So, they thought, this is how they would live from now on, as misunderstood sinners, victims of an unreasoned suspicion that would never listen to reason—that was what they had gained by getting rid of Joseph. Jacob's eyes—those bright, brown paternal eyes, reddened now and with soft swollen pouches below, those troubled eyes, usually immersed in pondering on God—were, as they well knew without even looking up, now focused upon them, brooding and searching with inconsolable mistrust, only to turn away with a squint if their own eyes met them.

As they ate, Jacob began to speak, saying, "If a man has hired an ox or an ass, and it is beset in some way, or a god assails the animal so that it dies, then the man must swear an oath and cleanse himself of guilt, before he can be held blameless."

Their hands turned cold, for they understood where this was leading.

"Swear?" they said, dejected and sulky. "He should swear an oath if no one saw how the animal died and there is no blood or wound, such as a lion or some other ravenous beast would leave. But if there is blood or a paw print—who would blame the man who hired the animal? It is the owner's concern."

"His affair then?"

"So it is written."

"But it is also written: If a shepherd is tending flocks belonging to another, and a lion murders within the sheepfold, the shepherd has to swear an oath in order to cleanse himself, and only then is the loss to be that of the owner. From which I draw what conclusion? Should not the hired shepherd also swear if it seems clear and certain that the lion did the murdering?"

"Yes and no," they replied, and their feet turned cold now, too. "More no than yes, if you please. For if it is a sheepfold that the lion attacks, then he drags his victim away and no one sees it, and an oath must be sworn. But if the shepherd can produce the slain animal and show this or that of the mutilated sheep, then he does not have to swear."

"You could all be called judges, you know the statutes so well. But if the sheep belonged to the judge and was of value to him, but of no value to the shepherd—is it not enough that it was not his and of no value to him for him to have to swear an oath?"

"Never before in this world was that sufficient reason to compel an oath."

"But what if the shepherd hated the sheep?" he said, and stared at them with wild and skittish eyes. . . . Wild, skittish, and gloomy, they countered his gaze, but they found some relief even in their discomfiture, for while he let his eyes pass from one to the other, each of them in his turn had to bear the look of suspicion only briefly.

"Can a man hate a sheep?" they asked, and their faces were cold and sweaty. "That does not happen in this world and no statute covers it, so that it cannot be a topic of discussion. But we are not hired shepherds, but rather sons of the king of flocks, and if one of our sheep is lost, our suffering is the same as his, and there can never ever be any question of a forced oath, before any judge whatever."

Cowardly, idle, wretched talk! Was it to go on like this forever? In that case, it would be better if the brothers moved on again, toward Shechem, Dothan, or somewhere else, for their remaining here without Joseph was of no more value to them than with him.

But did they move on? Not at all; they remained, and if one of them did go his own way, he returned soon enough. Their bad consciences needed Jacob's suspicions, and vice versa. They were bound to one another in God and in Joseph, and though it was surely a great agony to live together at first, they accepted it as their penance, both Jacob and his sons. For they knew what they had done, and if they were guilty, he knew his guilt as well.

Time passed, however, and with it came inurement. Time erased the probing suspicion from Jacob's eyes and left the ten brothers no longer exactly sure of what they had done, for they grew less precise in distinguishing between happening and doing. What had happened was that Joseph had got lost—the question of how slowly receded behind the fact itself, as father and sons became inured to it. That the boy was no longer present was a given, an awareness in which they all felt at home and at rest. The ten knew that he had not been murdered as Jacob believed. This gap in knowledge, however, no longer retained much meaning, because for them, too, Joseph was a mere shadow who had wandered off into the distance, beyond all view, never to return—in that idea they were united, both father and sons. The poor old man—God had robbed him of his precious feelings, so that his heart no longer knew the beauty of springtime and was ruled instead by parched summer and dreary winter, ultimately leaving him as "rigid" as he had been at the beginning of his seizure; but he did not cease to weep for his lamb, and when he wept his sons wept with him, for their hatred had been taken from them, and in time they were left with only vague recollections of how greatly the ninny had angered them. They could afford to weep for him too, for they knew him to be safe in a world of shadows, securely hidden in his absence from the circle of their life—which was also what Jacob knew.

He gave up his idea of "going down" as a mother to fetch Joseph; in the end he no longer alarmed anyone with mad plans of trying to sire him or to play God by creating him anew from clay. Life and love are beautiful, but death has its advantages, too, for it shelters and secures the beloved in absence and in what has been, and where once worry and fear ate away at happiness, there is now perfect calm. Where was Joseph? In the bosom of Abraham. With God, who had "taken him to Himself." Or whatever other words man finds for final absence, all those studied attempts to put a soft and safe—if also rather hollow and bleak—name to our most profound security.

Having done its work of restoration, death preserves. What had Jacob striven to do by restoring a dismembered Joseph? Death itself very quickly took care of it in a most loving way. It made his image whole again out of fourteen pieces or even more, restored it to smiling beauty, preserving him better and more sweetly than the people of the wicked land of Egypt preserved the body with wrappings and balms—inviolable and unchangeable, removed from harm's way, the dear, vain, clever, wheedling lad of seventeen, who had ridden off on white Hulda.

Removed from harm's way and unchangeable, no longer an object of worry and always seventeen years old—no matter how many circuits came round, no matter the sum of years added to the life of the living after his departure—that is how Joseph appeared to Jacob. And let no one say that death does not have its advantages, though they be rather hollow and bleak. Jacob grew very used to them. In silent embarrassment he recalled his reckless bickering and arguing with God in that first flowering of his sorrow and found it in no way an act of a God holding to His old ways, but rather regarded it as truly refined and holy of Him that He had not crushed him on the spot and instead in silent forbearance had let him sport with his misery.

Ah, pious old man! Could you ever have imagined what bewildering goodwill is hidden yet again behind the silence of your curiously majestic God, and, by His counsel, with what incomprehensible rapture your soul is to be mutilated? When you were young in the flesh, morning revealed to you that your most ardent happiness was deception and illusion. You will have to grow very old in order to learn that, by way of compensation, your bitterest suffering was also deception and illusion.

JOSEPH IN EGYPT

Part One

THE DESCENT

The Silence of the Dead

"Where are you leading me?" Joseph asked Kedma, one of the old man's sons, as they set up tents to sleep among the moonlit low hills at the foot of Mount Orchard.

Kedma looked him up and down.

"A fine one you are," he said, shaking his head to show he didn't mean "fine," but several other things, like "simple," "cocky," and "odd." "Where are we leading you? So we're leading you, is that it? We're not leading you at all! You happen to be with us because Father bought you from harsh masters, and you're traveling with us wherever we go. You can't very well call that 'leading' you."

"No? Well then, not," Joseph replied. "I only meant: Where is God leading me by having me travel with you?"

"What a fellow, always good for a laugh," the Ma'onite rejoined. "You have a way of putting yourself in the middle of things that leaves a man not knowing whether to be amazed or angry. Do you suppose, Hey There, that we journey simply so that you may arrive somewhere your god wants you to be?"

"I wouldn't think of it," Joseph responded. "I know quite well that you, my masters, journey on your own, for your own purposes, and to wherever you have a mind, and certainly would not detract from your dignity and authority with my question. But behold, the world has many middle points, one for every creature, and makes its own circle around each. You are standing but half an ell from me, but the circle of your world lies around you, and I am not its center, but rather you are. I, however, am in the middle of my own circle. Therefore there is truth to both, whether spoken from your middle or from mine. For our circles are not so far apart that they do not touch, but instead God has pushed them deeply into one another and interlocked them, so that you Ishmaelites indeed travel on your own authority and wherever you have a mind to go, except, however, by our being interlocked, you are the means and tool by which

I am to arrive at my goal. That is why I asked you where you are leading me."

"I see, I see," Kedma said, still looking him over from head to toe, his face turned away from the peg he was about to drive. "So that's the stuff you invent, your tongue waggling like a mongoose's. I shall tell the old man, my father, how you, the kennel boy, dare to speculate and stick your nose into wisdom that says you have a world circle all to yourself and that we have been ordained to be your guides. Watch out, I will tell him."

"Do that," Joseph replied. "It can do no harm. It will give your master, your father, pause for thought, so that when he decides to trade for me, he won't sell me too cheaply or to the first comer."

"Are we here to chatter," Kedma asked, "or to put up a tent?" And he ordered him to lend a hand.

But at one point, he said, "You ask more than I know in asking me where we are going. I would have nothing against giving you such information if I knew it myself. But it is a matter for the old man, my father, who keeps his own counsel, from which everything then follows, and we find out soon enough. But this much is clear, that we're holding the course your harsh masters, those shepherds, suggested, and shall not travel inland, along the water divide, but head toward the sea and the coastal plain, descending, day after day, until we come to the land of the Philistines, to the cities of seafaring traders and the fortresses of pirates. Perhaps you'll be sold there somewhere to row as a slave."

"I would not want that," Joseph said.

"Wanting has nothing to do with it. It's all according to the old man's counsel, whatever he may decide, and as to where the journey may end, he may not know that himself yet. But he wants us to think that he knows every detail well ahead of time, and so we all pretend we do—Epher, Mibsam, Kedar, and I . . . I'm telling you this because we happen to be putting up this tent together. I have no reason to tell you otherwise. I would hope the old man does not exchange you all too soon for purple dye and cedar oil, but that you remain with us a while yet for part of the way, so that one might hear more from you about people's world circles and how they interlock."

"Anytime you like," Joseph replied. "You are my masters and for twenty silver coins have purchased me, together with my wit and my tongue. They stand at your disposal. And as to each individual's world circle, I can add many other things about God's not entirely flawless miracle of numbers, which man has to improve upon, and, what's more, tell about the pendulum, the Dog Star year, and the renewals of life . . ."

"But not now," Kedma said. "The tent simply must be set up, for the old man, my father, is weary, and so am I. I fear I could no longer follow your tongue today. Are you still queasy from hunger, and do your limbs still hurt where you were bound with ropes?"

"Hardly at all now," Joseph replied. "I spent only three days in the pit, after all, and the oil with which you allowed me to rub my limbs did them much good. I am healthy and nothing detracts from the value and usefulness of your slave."

Indeed he had been given an opportunity to cleanse and oil his body, had received from his masters a loincloth and, for cool hours, the same sort of white, rumpled, hooded cloak that the thick-lipped camel boy wore—and afterward, the phrase "feeling born anew" suited him perhaps better than it has ever suited a human being from the creation of the world until today. For was he not truly born anew? A deep cleft, an abyss, divided his present from his past—it was his grave. And since he had died young, his vital energies were quickly and easily restored on the far side of that pit; but that did not prevent him from sharply differentiating between his present life and the previous one that had ended in the pit, so that he no longer regarded himself as the old, but as a new Joseph. If "dead and gone" means to be bound to an inviolable state that permits no backward wave, no greeting, not the slightest resumption of relationships with one's former life; if it means to have vanished, to be forever silent to that former life and never to be given permission, or any conceivable chance, ever to break the ban of silence by any signal whatever— then Joseph was dead, and the oil with which he had been allowed to cleanse himself of the dust of the pit had been no different from the oil laid in the grave of a dead man in order that he may anoint himself in the next life.

We give weight to this aspect because it seems imperative that we defend Joseph, both now and later, from a charge that those pondering his story have often leveled against him—that is, the question, itself a rebuke, of why, once he had escaped from the hole, he did not exert all his energies to find some way of establishing contact with his pitiable father Jacob and letting him know that he was alive. Surely some opportunity must have soon presented itself; indeed, over time, the means for sending his disappointed father word of the truth grew increasingly easy for his son, and it remains incomprehensible, to the point of offense, that he refrained from taking advantage of it.

This charge confuses what is outwardly feasible with what is inwardly possible, and ignores those three black days that had preceded Joseph's rising anew. They and their cruel pains had forced him to see the fatal error of his previous life and to renounce any return to it; they had taught him to affirm his brothers' trust in death; and his decision, his resolve, not to disappoint them was all the firmer since it was not voluntary, but as automatic and logically necessary as the silence of a dead man, who is silent before those whom he loves not out of a lack of love, but because he must be—so it was not out of cruelty that Joseph was silent before his father. In fact, silence proved very hard for him—and, one may well believe, even harder over time—as hard and heavy as the earth that covers the dead. He was sorely tempted by the sympathy he felt for the old man—who, he knew, loved him more than he loved himself and whom he in return loved with the most natural and grateful love, but whom he had brought down with him into the pit—a sympathy that would happily have persuaded him to take steps contrary to his reasoning. But our sympathy for the pain our own fate has caused someone has about it a special quality, something distinctly harder and colder than is found in our sympathy for the sufferings of strangers. Joseph had gone through something terrible, he had been taught a lesson so cruel that it eased the pity he felt for Jacob; indeed the awareness of their shared liability allowed him to see his father's misery as more or less part of the order of things. His bond with death prevented him from making a lie of the bloody token his father must have received. But that Jacob must, of necessity, have believed the animal's blood to be incontestably Joseph's blood also had a reverse effect on Joseph, practically removing in his eyes any difference between "This is my blood," and "This signifies my blood." Jacob believed him dead; and since his belief was incontestable—was Joseph then dead or not?

He was. And the most compelling proof of it was that he had to keep silence before his father. He was held within the realm of death—or rather would be held there, for he was soon to learn that he was still on his way there and to regard the Midianites who had bought him as his guides to that land.

Before the Master

"You must come before the master," a groom named Ba'almahar said to Joseph as he busied himself one evening baking flat cakes on hot stones—they had left Mount Kirmil behind and for several days now had been plodding in the sand beside the open sea. He had claimed that he was extraordinarily good at baking them, and although he had never tried it before—since no one had expected it of him—with God's help he actually proved to be excellent at it. By sundown their camp for the night had been set up at the foot of the reed-covered line of dunes that had monotonously accompanied their caravan on the landward side for days now. It had been very hot; milder air was settling now out of a sky turning pale. The beach stretched ahead in violet hues. The sea, dying slowly from sight, sent flat, broad waves to break with a silky murmur along the rim of wet sand, its reddish gold a reflection of scarlet remnants from the blazing splendor the sun had unfolded as it said its farewell. The pegged-down camels were resting. Not far from the beach a lumbering barge, evidently loaded with construction timber and manned only by two steersmen, was being towed southward by a sailing ship with many oars, a short mast, a long yard, a great deal of rigging, and the head of an animal set on a prow sweeping high above the water.

"Before the master," the groom repeated. "He bade you be summoned through my mouth. He is sitting on his mat in his tent and says that you should come before him. I was passing by, and he called me by my name, Ba'almahar, and said, 'Send me that newly purchased convict, that son of reedy swamps, our Hey There from the well. I wish to question him.'"

Aha, Joseph thought, so Kedma had told him about the world circles, and that was very good. "Yes," he said, "that's how he put it because he assumed he could not otherwise get you, Ba'almahar, to understand whom he meant. When speaking with you, my good fellow, he must use words you can grasp."

"To be sure," the slave responded, "and how else should he speak? If he wishes to see me, he says, 'Send Ba'almahar to me.' For that is my name. But it's harder with you, since you are called only with a whistle."

"So he is constantly asking to see you," Joseph said, "although the top of your head is somewhat scabby? But be on your way now. Thanks for the message."

"What are you thinking!" Ba'almahar cried. "You have to come along at once, so that I may bring you before him. For if you don't come, things will go bad with me."

"Before I go, I still have to brown this cake," Joseph replied. "I want to take it with me, so that the master can sample my extraordinarily fine baked goods. Hold still and wait!"

While the slave kept up his urgent cries, Joseph finished baking the flat cake, then stood up from his crouch and said, "I'm coming."

Ba'almahar accompanied him to the old man, who was sitting pensively on a mat at the low entrance to his portable tent. "To hear is to obey," Joseph said, greeting him. Gazing into the vanishing glow of the sunset, the old man nodded and then raised a hand from his lap and extended it at shoulder level, signaling Ba'almahar to withdraw.

"I hear," he began, "that you have said you are the navel of the world?"

Joseph shook his head and smiled.

"What can be meant by that," he replied, "and what may I have said in passing to enliven a conversation that could be so misconstrued when reported to my lord? Let me see. Yes, I know, I said that it has many middle points, this world does, as many as there are people who say 'I' upon the earth, one for each."

"That amounts to the same thing," the old man said. "It is true, then, that you have uttered such madness. I have never heard the like in all my wide travels and it is perfectly clear that you are a blasphemer and a wicked lad, exactly as your former masters told me. What do you suppose would happen if every dunce and dullard in the great muddle of mankind were to walk about regarding himself as the navel of the world, and what would we do with so many middle points? When you were stuck in the well—where, as I now see, you ended up only all too justly—was that well then the world's holy middle point?"

"God made it holy," Joseph replied, "in that He had one eye on it and did not let me perish within it, but sent you along the path so that you might rescue me."

"So that?" the merchant asked. "Or in order that?"

"So that and in order that," Joseph rejoined. "Both, and however you wish to take it."

"You are a chatterbox! Until now the question has been uncertain as to whether Babel with its tower is the middle of the world or perhaps the city of Abôt on the river Hapi, where the first man of the West lies buried. You have multiplied the question. To which god do you belong?"

"To God, the Lord."

"So, to Adôn, and you mourn for the setting of the sun. That I am willing to accept. It is a least a statement worth hearing and better than if a man says, 'I am a middle point,' as if he were mad. What have you there in your hand?"

"A flat cake that I baked for my lord. I am extraordinarily good at the art of baking cakes."

"Extraordinarily? Let me see."

And the old man took the flat cake from Joseph's hand, turned it back and forth and then took a bite from it with his back teeth, for he had none left up front. The cake was as good as it could be, but no better.

The old man, however, declared, "It is very good. I would not say 'extraordinary,' because you have said so. You should have left that to me, but it is good. Indeed excellent," he said as he went on chewing. "I set you the task of baking them, often."

"It shall be done."

"Is it true or not that you can write and keep a record of all sorts of wares?"

"Nothing easier," Joseph replied. "I can write in human and divine letters, with a stylus or a reed, just as you like."

"Who taught you this?"

"The steward of our house. A wise servant."

"How many times does seven go into seventy-seven? Two times, I presume?"

"Two times only in the writing of it. But in the true sense, I must take the seven first once, then twice, and then eight times so that I can arrive at seventy-seven, for seven, fourteen, and fifty-six, make the sum of it. One, two, and eight, however, are eleven, and so I have it: seven goes into seventy-seven eleven times."

"You can find a hidden number so quickly?"

"Quickly or not at all."

"But you surely knew that from practice. Let us presume, however, that I have a field that is three times as large as the field of my neighbor Dagantakala, who then buys a yoke of land to add to his field, and mine is now only twice as large. How many yokes are there in these two fields?"

"Together?" Joseph asked and set to work . . .

"No, each by itself."

"Do you have a neighbor named Dagantakala?"

"That is merely the name I gave to the owner of the second field in my problem."

"I see, and I understand. Dagantakala—judging by the name, he must be a man from the land of Peleset, home to the Philistines, to which, it seems, we are now descending according to your counsel and decree. He does not even exist, but he is named Dagantakala and is content to till his field, which of late has become three yokes large, being incapable of envying my lord and his field of six yokes, since he has, after all, increased his own from two to three, and what is more, because he does not exist, nor his little field either, taken altogether it comes to nine yokes—that's what's so funny. Except my lord does exist, as do his deep counsels."

Still uncertain, the old man blinked, for he had not really noticed that Joseph had solved the problem already.

"Well?" he asked . . . "Ah, yes, that's it! You've already said it and I hardly realized it, because you wove it into your speech and chattered all around the solution, so that I almost missed hearing it. That is correct: six, two, and three are the numbers. They were hidden and concealed—how did you pull them out so swiftly in the midst of your chatter?"

"One must merely keep an eye on what is unknown, then what enfolds it will fall away, and it becomes known."

"I have to laugh," the old man said, "at how you wove the solution into things and made no to-do about it. I truly have to laugh most heartily." And he laughed—with a toothless grin, his head shaking and inclined to one shoulder. Then he grew serious again and blinked, his eyes still moist.

"Now listen, Hey There," he said, "and answer me honestly for once and in keeping with the truth. Tell me, are you truly a slave and the son of a nobody, a kennel boy, a menial of the lowest sort, severely punished for crimes and moral corruption by the bushel, as those shepherds told me?"

Joseph veiled his eyes and pursed his lips as he often did, the lower lip protruding.

"My lord," he said, "you presented me with an unknown in order to test me, and did not provide the solution, for that would have been no test. But now that God is testing you with an unknown—do you wish to have the solution along with it, and should the questioner answer in place of him who is questioned? That is not how the world works. Did you not pull me from the pit, where I had soiled myself like a sheep with its own filth? What sort of kennel boy must I then be and how great my moral corruption! I shifted your twofold and threefold around in my brain and weighed the relationships, until I saw the solution. So then you, if it please you, should reckon back and forth between punishment, guilt, and wickedness, and from two givens you are sure to arrive at the third."

"My problem was in agreement with itself and bore its solution within. Numbers are pure and final. But who will guarantee me that life can be solved as well and that what is known does not deceive me about the unknown? There is much here that speaks against such an agreement of relationships."

"Then that must be taken into account as well. If life cannot be solved like numbers, it is at least presented to you so that you may see it with your eyes."

"Where did you get that gemstone on your finger?"

"Perhaps the kennel boy stole it," Joseph proposed.

"Perhaps. But you must surely know where you got it."

"I've had it forever and couldn't say there was ever a time I didn't."

"So you brought it with you from the reeds and the wild swamp of your conception? For you are a son of the swamp and a child of the reeds, are you not?"

"I am the child of the well out of which my lord pulled me, then raised me on milk."

"Have you known no mother except the well?"

"Yes," Joseph said, "I did indeed know a sweeter mother. Her cheek smelled of rose petal."

"You see. And did she not name you with a name?"

"I have lost it, my lord, for I have lost my life. I dare not know my name just as I dare not know my life, which they pushed into the pit."

"Tell me the offense that brought your life down into the pit."

"A punishable offense," Joseph replied, "and it is called trust. Culpable trust and blind expectation, that is its name. For it is blind and fatal to trust men beyond their power and to expect of them what they cannot and will not hear. In the face of such love and respect their gall overflows and they become like ravening beasts. Not to know that or not to wish to know it is most destructive. But I did not know it or, rather, I cast it to the winds, so that I did not keep my mouth shut and told them my dreams in order that they might marvel with me. But 'in order that' and 'so that' are sometimes two different things and do not always go together. The 'in order that' did not happen, and the 'so that' was called the pit."

"The expectation that made men ravening," the old man said, "is surely called arrogance and insolence, or so I am prone to think, and it does not surprise me in someone who says, 'I am the navel and middle point of the world.' But I have traveled much between the two rivers that flow in different directions, the one from south to north, the other just the opposite, and I know that many a mystery holds sway in an apparently so obvious world and that strange silent powers are at work behind the world's loud chatter. Yes, it has often seemed to me as if the world is so full of loud chatter precisely so that unspoken silence may hide all the better beneath it, that the babble may drown out the mystery that lies behind men and things. I have come across many things without having looked for them, and what I had not sought found its way to me. Yet I let things be, for I am not so curious that I must fathom it all. Rather, it suffices for me to know that mystery fills the garrulous world. Here I sit, a doubter, not because I have believed nothing, but because I consider everything possible. Such am I, an old man. I know of fables and events considered improbable that nevertheless occur. I know of a man of such noble and handsome rank that he clothed himself in the linen of kings and anointed himself with the oil of joy, who was driven into the wilderness and misery—"

Here the merchant broke off and began blinking, for the necessary and appropriate conclusion to his words, the continuation that was still outstanding but that he had not thought through, gave him pause. There are deep ruts of thought from which one does not stray once one is in them—ideas whose connections have been fixed since ancient times, fit together like the links of a chain, so that whoever says A cannot avoid saying B or at least thinking it; they are also like chain links because the earthly and the heavenly are so interlocked and enmeshed that one inexorably moves from one to the other, whether one speaks or falls silent. It is simply a fact that human beings think primarily in patterns and formulas, that is, not as they purposely choose, but in remembered commonplaces; and no sooner had the old man spoken of the man driven from his lofty rank into the wilderness and misery, than he found himself slipping into a divine pattern. And ineluctably attached to that pattern was its conclusion, telling how the abased man rose up again as the savior of humankind and the bringer of a new age, and the good man now halted in silent perplexity.

But it was no more than a mild perplexity—merely a decent, pious pause by a practical, but good-natured man contemplating the holy. If it did increase to a kind of uneasiness, a deeper puzzlement, indeed, to alarm—though, to be sure, only fleeting and hardly even acknowledged—the blame lay solely in the meeting taking place between the blinking eyes of the old man and those of the lad standing before him, even if it did not actually deserve to be called a true meeting, because Joseph's gaze did not "meet" the other man's, did not return it, despite its direct assault on him, but merely received it, simply offered itself, quietly and openly, for the other man to look into—an ambiguously provocative darkness. Others had also blinked in bewilderment, just as the Ishmaelite did now in his attempt to understand this quiet provocation—unsettled by the question of what sort of slightly out-of-the-ordinary or perhaps even risky deal he had made with those shepherds, and just what all his purchase entailed. But the investigation of this question was the purpose of the evening's entire conversation, and if the point of view from which the old man examined it had shifted for a moment into supernatural and fabled matters, that was because ultimately there is nothing that cannot be regarded from that side as well; a competent man, however, surely makes his distinctions among such spheres and aspects and turns again with no difficulty to the practical side of the world.

It took only a clearing of the throat for the old man to accomplish this adjustment.

"Hm," he said. "All in all, your master has traveled and experienced much between the rivers and knows what all can be found there. He does not need to be instructed about such things by you, child of the reeds and son of the well. I bought your body and whatever skills you may boast of, but not your heart, that I could force it to reveal your affairs. Not only is it unnecessary for me to delve into you, it is also inadvisable and might be to my harm. I found you and gave you breath again; yet it was not my intention to buy you, if only because I did not know if you were for sale. I had no commercial advantage in mind other than maybe a finder's fee or, possibly, a ransom. And yet it turned out that I did come to barter for your person—I suggested it as a test. By way of inquiry I said, 'Sell him to me,' and that test would decide it for me, and it was so decided, for the shepherds entertained my offer. I purchased you after difficult and detailed bartering, for they were stubborn. Twenty shekels of silver, by customary measure, is what I weighed out for you, and owed them nothing more. And what about that price, how do I stand now? It is a middling price, not terribly good, not all that bad. I could reduce it because of those errors that, so they said, had consigned you to the pit. Given your talents, I can sell you for more than I paid for you and enrich myself at a price I fix. What does it profit me to delve into your affairs, only to learn perhaps that your nature is such, the gods alone know why, that you could not be sold to me at all or cannot be sold again, and that I have lost what is mine, or that if I were to sell you again it would be unjust and trading in stolen goods? Go now, I wish to know nothing about your affairs, in detail—that is, so that I may remain unsullied and in the right. It suffices for me to assume that they are probably rather peculiar and counted among those things I am doubter enough to consider possible. Go, I have spoken with you longer than needed, and it is time for sleep. But be sure to bake such cakes for me often, they are truly good, if not extraordinary. I command you, moreover, to instruct Mibsam, my son-in-law, to supply you with writing tools—pages, reed, and ink—and that you prepare me a record, in human letters, of the wares we carry, each after its kind: balsam, salves, knives, spoons, walking sticks, and lamps, as well as footwear, lamp oil, and also glass trinkets—by piece and weight, the items in black, but weight and quantity in red, without errors or smudges, and to bring me that record within three days. Understood?"

"Commanded is as good as done," Joseph said.

"Then go."

"A sweet and peaceful slumber," Joseph said. "May it be interwoven now and again with light, amusing dreams."

The Minæan grinned. And he went on thinking about Joseph.

Conversation by Night

After three more days of traveling southward beside the sea, it was evening again and time to rest in tents, but where they rested was unchanged and looked exactly like three days before—it could have been the same spot. Joseph, cakes and scroll in hand, appeared before the old man, sitting on his mat at the entrance to his quarters.

"A nameless slave brings his master what he has ordered," he said.

The Midianite laid the stone-baked cakes to one side. He unrolled the scroll and examined the record, his head slightly tilted. His approval was evident.

"No smudges," he said, "that is good. But one can also see that the letters are drawn with pleasure and a sense for beauty, and are an ornament. Let us hope they accord with reality, so that they are not merely decorative, but practical as well. A man enjoys seeing his assets arranged so figuratively in rows, with various items neatly listed. Goods themselves are greasy and sticky, the merchant does not dirty his hands with them, but deals with them in written form. The things are there, but they are also here, odorless, pure, and all within view. Such a written record is like the *ka*, the spiritual body of things, which exists alongside the body. What a good thing, too, Hey There, that you know how to write and can also reckon with figures a bit, as I noticed. Nor, given your circumstances, do you lack a facility with words, for your master took pleasure in your good-night wish of three days ago. What were your words again?"

"I no longer recall them," Joseph replied. "I probably wished you a peaceful sleep."

"No, it was more pleasant than that. But in any case, there will be other occasions for such turns of phrase. But what I wanted to say is: When I have nothing more important to think about, I may at times, in third or fourth place, think of you as well. Your lot may be hard, since you most likely have seen better days and now serve a traveling merchant as his baker and scribe. Which is why, inasmuch as I shall be selling you and—free of any knowledge of your affairs—thereby enrich myself as much as possible, I intend to look out for you."

"That is very kind of you."

"I wish to bring you to a house that I know from having been allowed to offer it my services on several occasions, to our mutual advantage—a good house, a well-kept house, a house of honor and distinction. It is a blessing, I tell you, to belong to this house, if only as the lowest of its slaves, and if ever there was a house where a servant might show his finer talents, then this is it. If you are lucky and I can place you in this house, then your lot will have fallen out as graciously as it possibly could, given your blame and culpability."

"And to whom does this house belong?"

"Yes, to whom. To a man—it is a man—or rather a lord. A great lord over great men, decorated with tributes of gold, a holy, strong, and good man, whose grave awaits him in the West, a shepherd of men, the living image of a god. Fan-Bearer at the King's Right Hand is his name, but do you think he carries a fan? No, the man lets others do that for him, he himself is too holy for the task, he bears only the title. Do you think I know the man, this gift of the sun? No, I am but a worm before him, he does not even see me, and I have seen him only once from a distance, seated in a great chair in his garden, stretching out his hand to give commands, and I made myself small so he would take no offense at me and be distracted from his commands—how could I ever answer for that? But face to face and word to word I know the high steward of his house, who oversees the servants, warehouses, and craftsmen, and is in charge of it all. He loves me and offers cheering words when he sees me, and says, 'Well, old man, so we see you yet again, and you've come before our gates with your odds and ends to swindle us?' He says it only in jest, you should know, because he thinks a merchant is flattered to be called a sly swindler, and then we laugh together. I wish to show you to him and offer you to him, and if my friend, the steward, is in a good mood and can use a young slave for the house, you are taken care of."

"Which king is it," Joseph asked, "who has decorated the master of the house with tributes of gold?"

He wanted to know where he was being taken and where the house the old man planned for him was located; yet it was not that alone that gave rise to his question. He did not know it, but his thoughts and inquiries were governed by a mechanism that came from a distant time of beginnings and forefathers—speaking through him was Abraham, who had thought so presumptuously of man that he was of the opinion that he ought to serve solely and directly only what is highest, and whose ponderings and strivings therefore were directed exclusively to what is highest, to Him Who Is Most High, with utter disdain for all idols and minor divinities. The voice of his grandson here inquired in an easier, more worldly tone, and yet it was his ancestor's question. With sheer indifference Joseph heard about the house steward, on whom after all, according to the old man, his fate directly depended. He felt disdain for the old man because he knew only the overseer and not the man who bore that high title and owned the house. But he was not concerned about this man, either. Above him was one still higher, the highest, of whom the old man's account had spoken, and he was a king. Joseph's curiosity and zeal were aimed exclusively and directly at him, and it was of him that his tongue had made inquiry, unaware that it did not do so by random chance, but out of tradition and heritage.

"Which king?" the old man repeated. "Neb-maat-rê-Amunhotpe-Nimmuria," he said in a liturgical chant, as if it were a prayer.

Joseph was taken aback. He had been standing there with his arms crossed behind him; he quickly loosened them and clasped both cheeks between his palms.

"That is Pharaoh!" he cried. How could he have failed to understand? The name that the old man had prayed was known to the

ends of the earth and to the alien peoples whom Eliezer had taught
Joseph about, as far as Tarshish and Kittim, as far as Ophir and Elam,
where the East ended. How could it have meant nothing to a well-
instructed Joseph? If certain parts of the name the Minæen had spoken had been incomprehensible—the "Lord of Truth Is Rê," the
"Amun is content"—he would surely have been enlightened by the
Syrian title Nimmuria, which meant "He goes to his fate." There
were many kings and shepherds; every city had one, and so Joseph
had calmly inquired about the one in question here, because he had
expected to hear the name of some lord of a coastal citadel, some
Zurat, Ribaddi, Abdasharat, Aziru or other. He had not been prepared to apprehend the royal name in such a gloriously sublime
sense, cloaked in so godlike a splendor as the name demanded to be
apprehended. Inscribed in the vertical oval of a ring, protected by
falcon wings spread over it by the sun itself, that name stood at the
end of a list of glorious names, some lost now in the eternity of the
past, but all set in oval rings and each associated with the notion of
all-conquering campaigns, far-advanced boundary stones, and edifices whose splendor was the talk of the world; and for its part, this
name carried with it such a heritage of sacred rank and elevated luxurious living, such a demand that one fall to one's knees, that
Joseph's agitation was understandable. But was nothing else stirring
within him except the alarmed awe that would have moved anyone
in his place? Oh yes, there were other, antagonistic, feelings as well,
which were as old as his question about the highest and with the help
of which he at once automatically attempted to correct his initial reaction: mockery of those who are shamelessly mighty upon the
earth; secret rebellion in God's name against Nimrod's amassed
royal power—that is what caused him to remove his hands from his
cheeks and to repeat his cry much more calmly now, as a simple
statement, "That is Pharaoh."

"To be sure," the old man said. "That is the Great House that has
made great the house to which I would bring you and there offer
you to my friend, the high steward, that you may try your luck."

"So you want to lead me to Mizraim, all the way down to the
Land of Mud?" Joseph asked, and could feel his heart pounding.

The old man's head was inclined to his shoulder, and shaking.

"Such words," he said, "are once again just like you. I have been
told already by Kedma, my son, that in your childish arrogance you

imagine we are leading you here or there, whereas we would take the path that we shall take, even without you, and you will simply arrive wherever that path takes us. I am not traveling to Egypt in order to take you there, but rather because I have business there that should bring me riches. I wish to buy charming things that are produced there and are in demand elsewhere: glazed collars, camp stools with trim legs, headrests, game boards, and pleated linen skirts. These things I shall purchase in workshops and markets, as cheaply as the gods of that land allow, and shall take them back out again across the mountains of Kenan, Retenu, and Amor into the land of Mitanni on the river Phrat and to the land of King Hattusil, where they have an eye for such things and will pay me with blind abandon. You speak of the 'Land of Mud' as if it were a filthy land, like a bird's nest baked from dung or like an unswept stall. Whereas the land to which I have once again resolved to travel, and where I shall perhaps be able to leave you, is the finest land upon the circle of earth, with such exquisite manners that you will think yourself an ox before whom lutes are strummed. What eyes you will make, wretched man of Amu, when you behold the land to both sides of the divine river, which there is called the Two Lands, because it is twofold and doubly crowned, but Mempi, the house of Ptah, is the balance scale of the Two Lands. There great bastions stand in rows before the desert, incredible, and beside them lies the lion in his head scarf, Hor-em-akhet, created before all else, the mystery of the ages, on whose breast the king, the child of Thoth, fell asleep, and in his dream his head was raised up in highest promise. Your eyes will bug out of your head when you see the wonders and all the splendor and exquisiteness of the land that is called Keme because it is black with fertility and not red like the wretched desert. But whence comes its fertility? From the divine river, and from it alone. For it is its rain, and its manly fluid is not in heaven, but on earth, and it is the god Hapi, the strong bull, who spreads out gently over it and stands in blessing above it for a whole season, leaving behind the blackness of his strength, so that seed can be sown in it and fruit harvested a hundredfold. But you speak as if it were a latrine."

Joseph lowered his head. He had learned that he was on his way to the Realm of Death; for the custom of regarding Egypt as the land of the underworld and its inhabitants as the people of Sheol had been born with him, and he had never heard otherwise, particularly from

Jacob. He was to be sold into that sad lower world, his brothers had already sold him to its depths, the well had been a fitting entrance. He was very sad, and tears would have been justified. His joy at how fitting it was, however, held his sadness in check; for his view that he was dead and that the blood of the animal had truly been his own blood was now ingeniously confirmed in the old man's revelation. He had to smile—despite how close he was to tears for both himself and Jacob. Down there, of all places, was where he was to go, to the land his father most resolutely abhorred, to Hagar's homeland, to monkey-faced Egypt! He recalled the fiercely tendentious descriptions with which Jacob, without ever having seen this land, had attempted to make it equally intolerable to him, on the basis of its hostile and cruel doctrines—the worship of the past, the courting of death, the insensibility to sin. Joseph had always tended to view the fairness of this picture with a cheerful mistrust, with a sympathetic curiosity that is the usual consequence of a father's moralistic warnings. If that worthy man, so full of goodness and principle, only knew that his lamb was on his way to Egypt, to the land of Ham, the naked son, as he called it, since it bore the similar name "Keme" due to the black and fertile soil his own God had bestowed on it. That confusion was quite characteristic of the pious prejudices of Jacob's judgment, Joseph thought with a smile.

But his filial bonds were preserved in more than contradiction alone. To be sure, he found a certain furtive pleasure in being on the way to a land forbidden on principle, felt a kind of youthful triumph in flirting with the moral horrors of the underworld. Those same bonds, however, contained within them a silent resolve in his blood that would also have restored joy to his father's heart: the determination of a child of Abraham not to let his eyes well up in tears before the refined wonders the Ishmaelite had proclaimed, and most certainly not to admire all too greatly the splendid civilization awaiting him. The scorn of a very ancient spirituality drew his lips into a sneer at the exquisite mode of life that ostensibly lay ahead; and at the same time his scorn acted as a defense thrown up early on against the helpless intimidation that is the product of unbounded admiration.

"Is the house to which you wish to bring me," he asked, looking up now, "in Mempi, the house of Ptah?"

"Oh no," the old man responded, "we will have to go still farther up—which is to say down—upriver, I mean, out of the Land of the Serpent into the Land of the Vulture. Your question reveals how simpleminded you are, for I told you that the master of the house is Fan-Bearer at the King's Right Hand, and so he must be where His Majesty, the good god, is. So it is in Wase, the city of Amun, that the house stands."

Joseph learned many things that evening by the sea, and a wealth of information was thrust upon him. He would be taken to No itself, to No-Amun, the city of cities, the talk of the world, a topic for boasting in the conversations of even the remotest peoples, and of which it was said that it had a hundred gates and more than a hundred thousand inhabitants. Would Joseph's eyes not well up with tears after all upon beholding this metropolis? He was indeed aware that he would have to resolve very firmly beforehand not to fall into dumbfounded admiration. He pursed his lips in great indifference, but although he strove—for the sake of God's honor as well—to put a careless look on his face, he could not entirely ban embarrassment from it. For he was a little afraid of No, especially because of the name of Amun, that mighty name, laden with intimidation for anyone, imperious in its efficacy even where he was an alien god. The news that he would end up within the sphere of this god's cult and power filled him with anxiety. Amun was, as Joseph knew, lord of Egypt, the imperial god of the Two Lands, king of the gods—a status so unique was cause for bewilderment. Amun was the greatest, though only in the eyes of the children of Egypt, to be sure. But Joseph would be living among the children of Egypt. And so he thought it would be useful to speak about Amun, to try to get his tongue around him.

"Wase's lord in his shrine and on his barque," he said, "is surely one of the more lofty gods here in this world?"

"One of the more lofty?" the old man rejoined. "Your words are truly no better than your understanding. What all do you suppose Pharaoh has set before him to devour in the way of bread and cakes, beer, geese, and wine? He is a god without compare, I tell you, and my breath would give out were I to count the treasures he calls his own, both movable and immovable, and the number of scribes who administer it all is like to that of the stars."

"Wonderful," Joseph said. "A very important god, to judge by what you tell me. But I asked, to be precise, not about his importance, but about his loftiness."

"Bow down to him," the old man's voice advised, "for you shall be living in Egypt, and do not make so great a distinction between important and lofty, as if the one did not stand for the other and both were not the same. For all the ships of the sea and rivers, and the rivers and seas, are his. He is the sea and the land. He is also Tor-Neter, the Cedar Mountains, whose trunks grow for his barque, which is called *Amun's Brow Is Mighty*. In the form of Pharaoh he goes into the Great Wife and sires the god Hor within the palace. He is Baal in all his members—does that impress you? He is the sun, Amun-Rê is his name—does that satisfy your demands for loftiness, or not completely?"

"But I have heard," Joseph said, "that in the darkness of his innermost chamber he is a ram."

"I have heard, I have heard . . . your words are exactly like your understanding, and not one whit better. Amun is a ram, just as Bastet in the land of the Delta is a cat, and the Great Scribe of Shmun is both an ibis and a monkey. For they are sacred in their animals and their animals sacred in them. You will have to learn a great deal if you want to live in the land and endure there, even if only as one of the lowest of its young slaves. How would you behold a god, if not in an animal? The three are one: god, man, and animal. For if the divine is wed to the animal, then so, too, is man, when at the feast and according to ancient custom Pharaoh puts on an animal's tail. And so when, in turn, the animal is wed with the human, it is a god, and the divine is not to be viewed or understood except in such a marriage, so that you see Heket, the great midwife, sitting on a wall and with a head like that of a toad, and Anup, the opener of the ways, with the head of a dog. Behold, god and man find themselves in the animal, and the animal is the sacred point of their connection and union, each revered at its feast according to its nature, and among the most revered feast of feasts is when the ram breeds with the pure virgin in the city of Djedet."

"I have heard of that," Joseph said. "Does my lord approve of the custom?"

"Me?" the Ma'onite asked. "Leave an old man in peace. We are traveling merchants, middlemen, at home everywhere and nowhere, and our motto is: 'If my belly you feed, I'll honor your creed!' Take note of that in this world, for it will serve you as well."

"Never, in all Egypt or in the house of the Fan-Bearer," Joseph replied, "will I say one word against the honor due to the Feast of Covering. But just between us, allow me to mention that there is a trap and a snare looped about the word 'honor.' For people find it easy to consider what is old to be honorable, simply because it is old, and they let one stand for the other. But ancient honor is at times a snare, that is, when it has merely survived over time and gone to rot—for then it merely feigns honor, but is in truth filthiness and an abomination before God. Just between you and me, the sacrifice of a human virgin at Djedet seems more like filthiness to me."

"How would you decide between the two? And what would become of us if every dullard wished to place himself at the middle point of the world and set himself up as judge over what is holy in the world and what is merely old, what is still worthy of honor and what is now an abomination? Soon nothing would be holy! I do not believe that you will hold your tongue and conceal your impious thoughts. For the peculiar thing about ideas such as those you cherish is that they want to be spoken—that I know."

"In your presence, my lord, it is easy to learn to equate age and honor."

"Fiddle-faddle. Do not flatter me with sweet talk, for I am but a traveling merchant. Pay heed instead to my admonishments, so that you do not collide with the children of Egypt and talk yourself out of your good fortune. For it is certain that you cannot keep your thoughts to yourself; therefore you must take care that first your thoughts, and not just your words, are correct. Nothing is more obviously sacred than the unity of god, man, and animal in the sacrifice. Reckon it both forward and backward among these three in relation to the sacrifice, and you will find they offset one another. All three are in the sacrifice, and each takes the place of the other. That is why Amun stirs as the sacrificial ram in the darkness of his innermost chamber."

"I don't really know how I feel, my lord and purchaser, honored merchant. Darkness has fallen so hard while you have been instructing me, and scattered light, like the dust of gemstones, trickles down from the stars. I have to rub my eyes—forgive me for doing so—for I am dazed by it, and sitting before me on your mat, broadly squatting there as wise and plump as a toad, you look to me to be wearing the head of a tree frog."

"You see how you cannot conceal your thoughts, no matter how

offensive they may be? Why should you, why would you want to
see in me a toad?"

"My eyes do not ask if I want to. Here under the stars you look
exactly like a squatting toad to me. For you were Heket, the great
midwife, since it was the well that gave me birth and you lifted me
from out of my mother."

"Ah, you chatterbox! That was no great midwife who brought
you into the light. Heket, the frog, is called great because she helped
at the second birth and resurrection of the mutilated one, since the
lower world was assigned to him, but the upper to Hor, or so the
children of Egypt believe, and Osiris, the sacrifice and martyr, became the First of the West, king and judge of the dead."

"I like that. If one is to go to the West, then one should at least
become the *first* of those who dwell there. But teach me, my lord: Is
Osiris, the martyr, so great in the eyes of the children of Keme that
Heket became a great frog, acting as a midwife at his rebirth?"

"He is indeed very great."

"Great above the greatness of Amun?"

"Amun is great because of the empire; his glory terrifies alien
peoples, who cut down their cedars for him. But Usiri, the mutilated
one, is great in the love that people bear him—all the people, from
Djanet in the Delta as far as Yeb, the Elephant Island. There is no
one among them all, from the gasping slave dragging stones in the
quarry, of whom there are millions, on up to Pharaoh, of whom
there is but one alone and who worships himself in his temple—I tell
you, there is no one who does not know and love him or does not
wish, if it were only possible, to have his grave beside the grave of
the mutilated one at his shrine in Abôt. But since that is not possible,
they all cling to him with fervor, confident that in their hour they
will become like him and live eternally."

"To be like God?"

"To be like the god, to be the same as him—that is, united with
him, so that the dead person is Usiri and is called by his name."

"What you don't say! Go lightly with me, lord, in my instruction and help my poor reason just as you helped me out of the womb
of the well. For there is no common sense in what you would teach
me here in the night beside a slumbering sea about the opinions of
Mizraim's children. Am I to understand that they believe it is within

the power of death to change our nature, and that a dead man is a god with the beard of a god?"

"Yes, that is the firm belief of all the people of the Two Lands, and they love it with such fervent unanimity, from Zo'an to Elphantine, because they had to wrest it for themselves in a long struggle."

"Did they wrest their belief in a difficult victory, holding out for it until dawn?"

"They prevailed. For in the beginning and originally it was only Pharaoh, he alone, as Hor in his palace, who came to Osiris and became one with him, so that he was like the god and lived eternally. But all the gasping workers, the draggers of statues, the brick makers, the pot reamers, those behind a plow and those in the mines, would not rest, but struggled on until they prevailed and secured the doctrine that when their hour came they would all be like Usiri and after death they would be called Usir Khnemhotpe, Usir Rekh-me-rê, and live eternally."

"Once again I like what you have said. You chastised me for my opinion that every child of earth has around him his own special world circle, of which he is the center. But in one way or another it seems to me that the children of Egypt shared my opinion, since each wanted to be Osiris after his death, just as only Pharaoh was at the beginning, and they have prevailed."

"The words you speak are still foolish. For it is not the child of earth who is the middle point, Khnemhotpe or Rekh-me-rê, but rather this faith and confident belief that they share, one and all, up and down the river, from the Delta to the sixth cataract, the belief in Usiri and his resurrection. For this, too, you must know: This very great god did not die just once and rise again; he does so over and over in measured ebb and flow and before the eyes of the children of Keme—descends and reemerges in his might, to stand as a blessing over the land, Hapi, the strong bull, the divine river. If you count the days of winter, when the river is small and the land lies dry, that makes seventy-two, and seventy-two is the number of those who conspired with Seth, that spiteful jackass, to put the king in his coffin. But at his hour he arises from the lower world, he is the growing, the swelling, the flooding, the one who increases himself, the Lord of Bread, who sires all good things and lets all things live, and his name is Provider of the Land. They slaughter oxen and cattle for him, and from that you can see that the god and the sacrificed animal are one; for he is himself an ox and a bull before them upon the earth and in his house—Hapi, the black bull with the sign of the moon on his flank. But when he dies, he is preserved in balsam and wrapped and laid away and is called Usir-Hapi."

"Look there!" Joseph said. "Did Hapi, like Khnemhotpe and Rekh-me-rê, also prevail, so that in death he, too, becomes Usiri?"

"I believe you're mocking, aren't you?" the old man asked. "I see only a little of you in the glimmering night, but when I hear you, it sounds very like mockery. I tell you, do not mock in the land to which I wish to bring you because I am traveling there in any case, and do not vaunt your dullard's opinion over those of its children because you think you know better with your Adôn, but adapt to its pious customs, otherwise you will suffer a most grievous collision. I have taught you a few things and initiated you and exchanged a few words with you this evening for my own amusement, to pass the hours; for I am already well on in years, and sleep deserts me from time to time. I had no other reason for speaking with you. You may now say good-night to me, so that I may attempt to sleep. But be mindful of your turns of phrase."

"Commanded is the same as done," Joseph responded. "But how could I have mocked, when my lord has shown such kindness this evening, so that I may endure and not suffer a collision in the land of Egypt, and has taught this convict things of which I, a child of the rabble, would never have dreamt, so new are they to me and so unlike common sense. If I knew how to thank you I would do so. But since I do not, I shall do something else for you today yet, my benefactor, that I had not intended to do, and shall answer one of your questions that I previously evaded when you asked it. I wish to tell you my name."

"Do you?" the old man asked. "Do it or not, as you please. I did not delve into you for that reason, for I am old and cautious, and I prefer to know nothing of your affairs, because I would have to worry that I might be caught up in them and be guilty of an injustice through such knowledge."

"Not at all," Joseph replied. "You run no such danger. But you must at least be able to name the slave when you pass him on to that blessed house in Amun's city."

"So then, what is your name?"

"Osarsiph," Joseph replied.

The old man was silent. Although there was no more than a respectful distance between them, they could perceive one another only as shadows now.

"That is well done, Usarsiph," the old man said after a while. "You have told me your name. Take your leave now, for we wish to set out again at the rising of the sun."

"Farewell," Joseph saluted in the dark. "May the night cradle you in its gentle arms and your head fall asleep upon its breast, in that same sweet peace you once knew as a child upon your mother's heart."

The Temptation

And after Joseph had told the Ishmaelite his name in death and revealed to him how he wanted to be called in the land of Egypt, their party continued on, for a few days, for several, for many more, at an indescribably leisurely pace and with total indifference to time, for they knew that, with just a little effort on their part, time would one day take care of space and was most certain to do so if they did not worry about it, but rather left to it the secret task of allowing bits of progress, which were nothing in themselves, to amass into a great sum, while they lived out their lives and held tolerably to their direction.

Their route was dictated by a sea that, beneath a sky fading into the hallowed distance, stretched out forever to the right of their path, now pausing to rest in a silvery mantel of glistening blues, now surging against the well-populated coast in waves strong as bulls and flaring with foam. And into it set the sun, ever changing yet unchangeable, the eye of God, often a clear disk glowing in pure solitude and, as it went under, casting a glittering pathway across the endless water to the shore and to those worshipfully passing by, but often joining a great wide feast of lambent gold and pink so wonderfully vivid that the soul was strengthened with heavenly convictions, but saddened sometimes, too, by murky, smoldering vapors and hues that announced the god's melancholy, menacing mood. Its rising, in contrast, did not occur in open view, but behind hills and even higher mountains that bounded the travelers' view to their left; there too, in the interior of the land—a rolling countryside, where extensive fields were tilled, wells dug, and orchards adorned the terraces— there, too, some distance from the sea and fifty ells above its surface, they would often wend their way among villages that paid tribute to fortified cities united in a federation of principalities—and Gaza in the south, Khazati, the strongest citadel, headed the federation.

These were the mother cities—each, surrounded by white walls, shaded by palm trees, and set atop a hill—and they served both as refuges for rural people and as fortresses of the Sarnim; and just as they had done in the fields outside villages, so here, too, the Midianites would set up for business in the gates of these large cities, home to throngs of people and many temples, and offer the residents of Ekron, Yabne, and Ashdod their transjordanian wares. Joseph acted as scribe. There he sat, wielding his ink brush and entering each transaction completed with the haggling children of Dagon—fishermen, sailors, craftsmen, and the citadel's mercenary soldiers clad in copper armor—Usarsiph, the literate young slave, obliging his good master. The sold and bought slave found his heart beating higher from day to day—one can well imagine why. It was not his nature to immerse himself thoughtlessly in the impressions thronging in upon his senses and not abstract some conceptual notion of where he was and how this place stood in relation to others. Despite their many stops and protracted, sluggish pauses, he knew that he was returning from the same journey—in the opposite direction and via a route through different country several leagues farther toward evening— that he had taken on Hulda, the poor beast, to visit his brothers, that he was moving toward his home, indeed would be passing beyond it, and that they would soon arrive at the point where he would have completed the circuit, his father's hearth lying only a little off to one side, a distance no more than half as long as his journey to his brothers. Somewhere near Ashdod—home of Dagon, the fish-god who was worshiped here, a lively settlement two hours from the sea, which was reached by a harbor road filled with shouts and jammed with men, oxcarts, and teams of horses—would be the spot, for Joseph knew that the coastline turned more and more westward as it ran down toward Gaza, so that the distance to the mountainous interior to the east would increase with each day, not to mention that by afternoon they would have passed the high point at which they would be even with Hebron.

That was why, in anxiety and temptation, his heart pounded as they moved through the region and continued their unhurried advance toward the rocky citadel of Askuluna. He took in this landscape. They were now crossing Shephelah, the lowland running parallel to the coast; but the chain of mountains that glowered down at them from the east and toward which his pensive eyes, Rachel's eyes, now gazed, formed the second, higher, valley-threaded level of the land of the Philistines, rising ever more steeply above the sea and toward the dawn, to a rougher, harder world of pastures avoided by the palms of the low plain, to upland meadows spicy with herbs, populated by sheep, by Jacob's sheep.... And how was it all playing out? There sat Jacob in despair, crushed by his tears, suffering anguish sent by God, the bloody token of Joseph's death and mutilation in his poor hands—while at his feet, down here, Joseph, his stolen son in the company of strange men, was mutely passing Jacob's camp, was moving from one Philistine city after the other, yet never giving so much as a sign on his way down to Sheol, to the house where death was worshiped. And the thought of escape—how close at hand it lay! How the urge itched in his limbs, tugged at him, half stirred in the ferment of his mind and impetuously forged ahead to accomplished deeds in his imagination—especially in the evening, after he had said his good-night salute to the old man who had bought him, something he had to do every day now, for it had become one of his duties to wish the Ishmaelite pleasant slumbers in ever-new variations, since otherwise the old man would say he had already heard that one. Especially in the dark, then, as they camped outside a village or a Philistine city and his fellow travelers were lost in sleep, the idea would grab hold of their captive and try to snatch him away, into the fruitful hills of night and on across ridges and wooded ravines, eight marches away, surely it couldn't be more than that, and Joseph would scramble until he found the path—up into the mountains, into Jacob's arms, where he would dry his father's tears with the words "Here I am" and be his favorite again.

But did he carry it out and steal away? No, of course not, we know he didn't. He reconsidered, once or twice rejecting the temptation only at the last moment, renounced his plan, and stayed where he was. This was, by the way, easiest at the moment, for escape on his own brought with it great peril—he could die of hunger, fall prey to thieves and murderers, be eaten by wild beasts. But one would be belittling his renunciation to reduce it to the dictum that, given man's natural passivity about making decisions, doing nothing easily gains the upper hand over doing something. There were instances in Joseph's life when he refused to engage in a physical act that would have been considerably sweeter than a wild escape across the mountains. No, both at that moment and in the future crucial instance we have in mind, his refusal, despite such stormy temptation, came from the very special way Joseph had of considering things, which, if put into words, would have been something like "How could I do such a foolish thing and sin against God?" Or put another way, it was insight into the absurdly sinful error of thinking about escape, a clear, intelligent perception that it would have been an oafish blunder, an attempt to erase God's plans. For Joseph was imbued with the certainty that he had not been carried away for no purpose, but rather that He who had planned this, wrenching him from his old life and leading him to the new, intended to deal with him in one way or another in the future, and that to kick against this goad, to escape these troubles, would have been a sin and a great mistake—which were the same in Joseph's eyes. He had truly been born with the concept of sin as a mistake, a blunder in life, an oafish offense against God's wisdom, and experience had only strengthened him greatly in it. He had made enough mistakes—he had become aware of that in the pit. But if he had escaped that hole and been carried away according to some apparent plan, then all his prior mistakes might perhaps have been part of the plan, have had a purpose, that is, and, blind as they were, have been steered by God. Any more such mistakes, however, such as escaping, for instance, would be blatant and foolish evil; it would literally mean wanting to be wiser than God—which, according to Joseph's prudent insight, was simply the height of stupidity.

To be his father's favorite again? No, to still be the favorite—but in a new sense that he had long yearned for and dreamt of. It was a new, higher favor and election, in which he was meant to live now, after the pit, in the bitter-scented adornment of a rescue set apart for those who have been set apart and chosen for those who are chosen. The torn wreath, the adornment of the whole sacrifice, he wore it anew now—no longer in dreamy play, but in truth, and that meant: in his spirit. And should he now renounce it for the sake of some foolish fleshly instinct? So silly, so devoid of wisdom about God, Joseph was not—not so stupid as to trifle away at the last moment the benefits of his new status. Did he know the feast in all its hours, or did he not? The instrument of the present and of the feast—was he that, or was he not? With the wreath in his hair—should he now run from the feast to be a shepherd of sheep again with his brothers? The temptation was great only in the flesh—in the spirit, however, it was weak. Joseph withstood it. He traveled on with his owners, on past Jacob and away from his nearby presence—Usarsiph, born of the reeds, Joseph-em-heb, which in plain Egyptian simply means Joseph in the Feast.

A Reencounter

Seventeen days? No, it was a journey of seven times seventeen—not counted, but understood in the sense of a great weary duration; and over time one could not determine how much of it was the fault of the Midianites' sluggishness and how much was due to the distance measured. They journeyed through fruitful land bustling with people, garlanded with olive groves, with heavy stands of palm, walnut, and fig trees, with fields of grain irrigated from deep wells visited by camels and oxen. Here and there in the fields were small royal fortresses, called way stations, with walls and battle turrets, on whose parapets stood archers and from whose gates charioteers drove forth with snorting teams; and the Ishmaelites did not hesitate to do business even with these royal warriors. Everywhere were villages, farms, and *migdal* settlements inviting them to tarry, and they tarried by the week, it made no difference to them. And summer was already waning before they came to the spot where the low coastal border was steeply abutted by a high precipice, at the top of which lay Ashkelon.

Holy and strong was Ashkelon. The hewn stones of its surrounding walls, which fell in a semicircle to the sea and embraced the harbor, appeared to have been heaved into place by giants; its house of Dagon was a compact square with many courts, beloved for its grove and the pond in the grove, teeming with fish; and the dwelling place of Ashtaroth boasted that it was older than any other site ded-icated to the Baalat. A spicy kind of small onion grew wild here in the sand beneath the palm trees—the gift of Derketo, Ashkelon's di-vine mistress—and it could be sold to outsiders. The old man had them gathered in sacks, on which he wrote in Egyptian letters: "Finest Ashkelon Onions."

From there they traveled through gnarled forests of olives, in whose shade great herds were pastured, and arrived in Gaza, or Khazati—they had truly come a long way now. They were almost within the sphere of Egypt itself; for whenever Pharaoh had burst forth from below with his chariots and foot soldiers and advanced through the wretched lands of Zahi, Amor, and Retenu to arrive at the end of the world, so that he could then be depicted in giant deeply engraved reliefs across the walls of temples, suddenly grab-bing five barbarians by their hair with his left hand and, to their holy amazement, swinging a club in his right hand over their heads—on such occasions, Gaza was always the first stage of the enterprise. One also saw a great many Egyptians in Gaza's pungent streets. Joseph eyed them carefully. Broad-shouldered people, they kept their noses in the air and wore white. Excellent and inexpensive wine came from these coasts and from far inland in the direction of Beer-sheba. The old man traded for numerous jugs of it, enough for two camels to carry, and wrote on the jugs: "Eightfold Good Wine from Khazati."

But no matter how far they may have come in reaching the city of Gaza and its mighty walls, the worst part of their journey—com-pared with which the dawdling trip through the land of the Philistines had been child's play—still stood before them; for as the Ishmaelites knew, having traveled this stretch several times, beyond Gaza to the south the sandy road that hugged the coast and led to Egypt's great brook passed through an utterly inhospitable world, and before one came to nourishing fields among the branches of the Nile, there lay a profoundly doleful underworld, an accursed, dan-gerous, and horrid expanse, nine days wide: a dismal desert that al-lowed for no dallying, but that had to be covered and left behind as quickly as possible, making Gaza the last resting place before one ar-rived in Mizraim. Which was why the old man, Joseph's master, was in no hurry to move on, since, as he said, they would be moving on in great hurry for far too long. Instead he remained in Gaza for a goodly number of days, particularly since he needed to make serious preparations for the desert journey, taking on a supply of water and a special guide to open the ways, and actually should have stocked up as well on weapons to fight marauding bands and the thievish denizens of the sand, though our old man dispensed with these: first because in his wisdom he considered them useless, for, he said, either you escaped these villains entirely—in which case you had no need of weapons—or, unfortunately, they caught up with you—and then no matter how many you killed, there were always enough left to rob you naked. The merchant, he said, must depend on his luck, not on spears and toy bows, that was not for him. Second, the guide they had hired at the city gate, there where such men offered their services to travelers, had reassured him greatly about such marauders, pledging that under his escort there was no need for weapons whatever, because he was a perfect guide and would open the safest ways through that horrid world, rendering it absolutely absurd to secure him as a guide and drag along weapons besides. So then, when the hireling joined the little caravan as they set out early one morning and took his place at their head, how startled, indeed both frightened and pleased, Joseph was to recognize him, incredibly enough, as the peevishly helpful young man who, only recently, yet prior to so many other things, had led him from Shekem to Dothan.

It was he beyond a doubt, although the desert robe he wore altered his appearance. The little head and massive neck, the red mouth and the chin like a plump fruit, but especially the languid eyes and the strangely affected poses were all unmistakable; and the startled Joseph thought he had also caught a wink that the guide had directed his way by briefly closing one eye in his otherwise immobile face, both alluding to their old acquaintance and requesting discretion. That greatly comforted Joseph, for their acquaintance reached back farther into his previous life than he wished the eyes of the Ishmaelites to penetrate, and he could take the wink to mean the man understood this.

And yet he felt a great need to exchange a word with the man, and when, to the songs of the drivers and the sound of the lead camel's bells, the band of travelers had left green land behind them and dry wastes opened up before them, Joseph asked the old man, behind whom he was riding, if he might be allowed yet once more, just in case, to ask their guide if he was entirely sure of what he was doing.

"Are you afraid?" the merchant asked.

"It concerns us all," Joseph replied. "But I'm traveling for the first time into this accursed land, and so am close to tears."

"Then ask him."

And so Joseph directed his animal to the lead camel and said to their guide, "I am my master's mouthpiece. He wishes to know if you are sure of the route."

The young man gazed in the same old way over his shoulder with barely opened eyes. "You could have reassured him from experience," he replied.

"Hush!" Joseph whispered. "How is it that you're here?"

"And you?" came the answer.

"Well, yes . . . but not a word to the Ishmaelites that I was on my way to my brothers," Joseph whispered.

"Not to worry," the other man rejoined just as softly; and that was that for now.

But after they had proceeded farther into the desert, one day and then another—a murky sun was sinking behind chains of dead mountains, and armies of clouds, gray in the middle but with edges inflamed by evening, covered the sky above a waxen yellow, sandy plain with a few hills scattered in the distance ahead like little bushy cushions covered with dry grass—another opportunity presented itself for speaking with the man unobserved. For a few travelers had camped around one of those cushions of grass and lit a fire of brushwood to ward off the sudden cold; and since their guide was among them, though he did not usually keep company with either masters or servants, scorning small talk and consulting only with the old man each day about the path ahead, Joseph, having completed his duties for the day and wished his master pleasant slumbers, joined the group, sat down beside their guide, and waited until the monosyllabic exchanges had died out and they were all evidently beginning to be wrapped in dozing semisleep. Then he gave his neighbor a little nudge and said, "Listen, I'm sorry I was unable to keep my word that day and had to leave you in the lurch, waiting for me."

The man cast him only a languid glance over his shoulder and then returned to gazing at the glow of the fire.

"I see, so you were unable to?" he replied. "Well, let me tell you, I've never met such a faithless fellow in all the world before. Had it been up to him, he would have let me sit there watching over a jackass for seven jubilee years, and he never returned as promised. I'm amazed that I'm even speaking with you; I'm amazed at myself, in fact."

"But I'm apologizing as you can hear," Joseph muttered, "and truly have an excuse, which you do not know about. Things turned out differently from what I supposed and went as I had not expected. I could not return to you despite my best intentions."

"Yes, yes, yes, gibberish and empty excuses. I could have sat there for seven of God's jubilee years waiting for you . . ."

"But you didn't sit there for seven jubilee years waiting for me, but went your way when you realized that I was not going to appear. Don't exaggerate the hardship that I reluctantly caused you. Tell me instead what became of Hulda after my departure."

"Hulda? Who is Hulda?"

"'Who' is asking a bit too much," Joseph said. "I'm asking you about Hulda, the ass that bore us, my little white riding jenny from Father's stall."

"Little ass, little ass, white riding jenny!" the guide mimicked softly. "You have a way of speaking so tenderly of things you hold dear that one may conclude it comes from your love of yourself. Such people then behave so faithlessly that . . ."

"Not at all," Joseph countered. "I do not speak tenderly of Hulda for my own sake, but for hers, for she was such an amiably cautious animal, entrusted to me by my father, and when I think of how the curls of her forelock grew down over her eyes, it makes my heart melt. I have not ceased to worry about her since taking leave of you, and continued to ask about her fate even in moments and long hours that were not without some terror for me. You must know that since I came to Shekem my unlucky star has never left me, and sore tribulation has been my lot."

"Impossible," the man said, "and unbelievable. Tribulation? My reason comes to a halt, and I am firmly convinced that I did not hear rightly. You were going to your brothers, were you not? Other people and you, you're forever smiling at one another, because you are handsome and beautiful as a graven image, and you possess sweet life itself on top of it, do you not? Where is there an unlucky star in that and where should sore tribulation come from? I ask myself, but without any sort of answer."

"It is at any rate so," Joseph replied. "And, I'm telling you, despite everything I have never stopped worrying about poor Hulda's fate for a moment."

"Well," the guide said, "well, fine." And Joseph recognized that strange movement of his eyeballs that he had noticed before, the way the man rolled them in cross-eyed circles. "Fine then, Usarsiph, young slave, you will speak and I shall listen. One might well think it quite futile also to worry about an ass amidst these many other adversities, for what sort of role can she play and what was so incomparable about her? But I consider it possible your worries might be to your credit and that it might be recorded as praiseworthy for you to think of a dumb beast despite your own troubles."

"So what became of her?"

"Of the dumb beast? Hm, it is rather a distressing matter for the likes of us first to have to play watchman over an ass to no purpose and then to give an account of what happened besides. One would like to know how it has come to that exactly. But you can put your mind at ease. My last impression tended to the conclusion that her pastern was not so bad off as we initially feared. Apparently it was only sprained, but not broken—which means, apparently broken and actually only sprained, if you understand me. While waiting for you I had nothing but time to care for the ass's foot, and by the time I had finally lost all patience, your Hulda was well enough again that she could trot, though chiefly on three legs. I rode her myself to Dothan and stabled her at a house where I have been able to be of service on several occasions to our mutual advantage—the first one in the village, which belongs to a farmer, where she will have things as good as in the stall of your father, the so-called Israel."

"Really?" Joseph cried softly and joyfully. "Who would have thought! So she stood up and walked, and you saw to it that she was well taken care of?"

"Very well," the other man confirmed. "She can happily say that I stabled her at the farmer's house, and that her lot has proved to be a happy one."

"Which means," Joseph said, "that you sold her in Dothan. And the price?"

"You're asking as to the price?"

"Yes, now I am."

"I took it as pay for my service as a guide and watchman."

"Oh, I see. Well, I shall not ask how much it was. And the baggage Hulda was carrying, full of delicacies?"

"Is it really true that you are thinking of tidbits amidst these adversities, and do you find them of comparative importance?"

"Not so much, but they were with her."

"I also reimbursed myself with them."

"Well," Joseph said, "you had already begun to reimburse yourself behind my back in any case—I'm referring here to certain quantities of onions and pressed fruit. But let it be, perhaps it was well intentioned, and in any case I wish to dwell on whatever good sides you may show. That you got Hulda on her feet again and filled her belly in the country, for that I truly owe you my gratitude and also thank good fortune that I've unexpectedly met you again to learn of it."

"Yes, and now I must guide you along your way again, you bag of wind, so that you may arrive at your goal," the man countered. "As to whether it is truly fitting and proper for someone like me, one does privately ask oneself that question in passing, but to no avail, since no one else asks it."

"Are you being peevish again," Joseph rejoined, "just as that night on the way to Dothan, when you offered to help me find my brothers, but with such ill humor? Well, this time I need not reproach myself for annoying you, for you have hired yourself out to the Ishmaelites to lead them through this desert, and by chance I happen to be with them."

"It amounts to one and the same—you or the Ishmaelites."

"Do not tell the Ishmaelites that, for they think highly of their dignity and authority and do not like to hear that they are traveling more or less so that I may come to wherever God wants me."

The guide said nothing and lowered his chin into his scarf. Was he rolling his eyes again in that way of his? Quite possibly, but darkness made it difficult to tell.

"Who likes to hear," he said with a certain reluctance, "that he is a tool? Most especially, who likes to hear it from a jackanapes? Coming from you, it is indeed sheer impudence, Usarsiph, young slave. But on the other hand, it is just as I say—that is, it all amounts to the same thing and it might just as well be Ishmaelites who come along. And that once again it is you for whom I must open the ways—that makes no difference to me. I have also had to watch beside a well, not to mention that jenny ass."

"A well?"

"I had come to expect a role of that sort the whole time—that is, as regards the well. It was the emptiest hole I've ever come across, couldn't have been emptier, the more absurd for its emptiness—keep that in mind when judging the dignity and propriety of my role. In any case, perhaps it was the very emptiness of the pit that was of importance."

"Had the stone been rolled away?"

"Of course, I sat on it, and remained sitting there no matter how much that man would have liked for me to vanish."

"What man?"

"Why, the one who in his foolishness stole secretly to the pit. A man of towering stature, with legs like temple columns, but with a thin voice for such a shell."

"Ruben!" Joseph cried, almost forgetting to be cautious.

"Call him what you will, he was a foolish tower of a man. Came slinking up with his ropework and his robe to such a perfectly empty pit . . ."

"He wanted to rescue me!" Joseph exclaimed.

"For all I care," the guide said with a ladylike yawn, holding his hand primly to his mouth and adding a delicate sigh. "He played his role too," he added indistinctly, for he had thrust chin and mouth still more deeply into his scarf and evidently wanted to sleep. Joseph heard him mutter some more ill-humored tatters of words—"Not to be taken seriously . . . mere jests and insinuations . . . jackanapes . . . expectations . . ."

Nothing more useful was to be got out of him, and for the rest of their desert journey Joseph had no further conversation with the guide and watchman.

The Fortress of Zel

Day after day they moved patiently across the dismal land, following the bell of the lead camel from well station to well station, until nine days had passed and they could count themselves lucky. Their guide had not been wrong in recommending himself, he knew what he was doing. He never lost his way, never strayed from the road, even when it passed through a maze of mountains that weren't mountains at all, but merely a jumble of ghastly sandstone boulders, grotesque and up-thrust masses that glistened with the blackness of ore instead of stone, a gloomy sheen that made them look like a towering city of iron. He did not lose his way even when for days there could be no talk of a path or road in an upper-worldly sense, and instead theirs was a world damned beyond all reckoning, a seabed enclosing them in their fear and filled with corpse-pale sand to a far horizon pallid with heat. They crossed dunes, down whose backs the wind had evidently left repulsively dainty waves and folds, while above the plain below them the hot air played and flickered as if about to burst into dancing flames and the sand was lifted in whirling vortices so that the men covered their heads in order to pass through such ghastly terrors, preferring to ride blind rather than gaze upon so vicious a delight in death.

Bleached bones often lay along the way, the rib cage and thighbone of a camel or desiccated human limbs jutting up out of the waxy dust. They blinked as they passed and went on nourishing their hope. Twice, for half a day each time, from noon until evening, a pillar of fire preceded them, seeming to lead them. They knew the nature of this phenomenon, but did not allow their reactions to be determined only by its natural cause. These were, as they well knew, whirling eddies of dust turned fiery by the sun shining through. All the same they spoke to each other of this important honor—"a pillar of fire goes before us." If the sign were to collapse suddenly before their eyes it would be dreadful, for then in all probability this would be followed by an Abubu of dust. But the pillar did not collapse and, like a kobold, merely changed its shape, slowly fluttering away on the northeast wind, which remained faithful to them through all nine days. Good fortune held the south wind captive, preventing it from drying out goatskins and devouring life-giving water. By the ninth day they were out of danger, had escaped the wasteland's horrors, and could count themselves lucky, because this portion of the desert road, for a good stretch out into the desert, was already occupied and watched over by the eye of Egypt, which protectively guarded every step taken upon it with bastions, breastworks, and watchtowers beside the wells, manning them with small garrisons of Nubian archers with ostrich feathers in their hair and Libyan ax-bearers under the command of Egyptian captains, who called out in surly voices to the approaching caravan and officially questioned them as to their whence and whither.

The old man had a cheery and clever way of speaking with such troops, of establishing beyond all doubt the innocence of his intentions, and of winning their goodwill with little gifts from his wares—knives, lamps, Ashkelon onions. And so they moved ahead from garrison to garrison, with some bother, but smoothly enough, since exchanging jokes with guards was far better than passing through the city of iron and over the pale seabed. But the travelers were well aware that putting these stations behind them was only a preliminary step and that the sternest test of their innocence and harmlessness to the security of a civilized society still lay ahead—at the massive and unavoidable barrier that the old man called the Sovereign's Wall and that had been built ages before on the neck of land between the two Bitter Lakes to protect against Shosu savages and denizens of the dust who might try to drive their animals onto Pharaoh's fields.

From a rise where they halted at sunset, they looked out across to those menacing precautionary measures, structures of anxious but arrogant defense, which the amiable, loquacious old man, having conquered them several times now, both coming and going, therefore did not fear too greatly, and so, with a calmly outstretched hand, he could point out to his company the long line of a wall, jagged with pinnacles, broken here and there by towers and set behind canals that linked a chain of larger and smaller lakes. At about midpoint in the wall a bridge spanned the water, but here too, on both sides of the crossing the precautions were prodigious, for there, surrounded by their own encircling walls, stood massive, imposing, two-storied fortified citadels, whose walls and ramparts rose to the parapets in an intricate zigzag, making them all the more invincible, and bristled on all sides with battlement turrets, sally ports, and bastions, with barred windows set into smaller structures on top. This was the fortress of Zel, the precautionary bulwark erected out of fear and strength by a refined, happy, but vulnerable Egypt against desert, depredation, and destitution to the east—the old man spoke the name to his company without fear and then went on to talk about how easy it ought to be, would be, for his innocence to slip, as so often before, through this barrier, but spoke at such length that one had the impression he was plucking up his own courage.

"Do I not have a letter from a merchant friend in Gilead beyond the Jordan," he said, "for another merchant friend in Djanet, which is also called Zo'an and was built only seven years after Hebron? Indeed, I have it, and you will see it open gates and portals for us. It all depends on being able to present something written, so that the people of Egypt can write something else and send it on somewhere, where it will be copied yet again and entered into their ledgers. Granted, without written matter you will not get through; but if you can present a shard, a scroll, a document, they brighten up. For, to be sure, they claim that Amun or Usir is for them the highest of gods, the Eye Enthroned, but I know them better, for ultimately it is Thoth, the scribe. Believe me, if only Hor-waz, the young staff officer, comes to the wall, an old friend of mine from before, and I can speak with him, there will be no difficulty and we'll slip right through. And once we are inside the wall, no one will question our innocence again and we shall move freely upstream through every district, as far as we like. Let us set up our tents and spend the night here, for my friend Hor-waz will not be returning to the wall again today. But tomorrow, before we step forward and request passage through the fortress of Zel, we must wash ourselves with water and shake the desert dust from our clothes, dig it from our ears, and scrub it from under our fingernails, so that they may see us as human beings and not sand rabbits; and you youngsters must also pour sweet oil in your hair, add a little eye makeup, and make yourselves savory; for poverty is suspect in their eyes and a lack of culture an abomination."

Such were the old man's words, and they acted upon them, remaining there for the night and making themselves as beautiful the next morning as they could after so long and dreadful a journey. But during their preparations something unusual and surprising happened: at some point the guide whom the old man had hired in Gaza and who had led them so safely was no longer among them, though no one could say definitely when he had absented himself, whether during the night or while they were sprucing up for Zel. At any rate, when they happened to look around for him, he was no longer there, although the belled camel he had ridden still was—nor had he collected his wages from the old man.

This was no cause for lamentation, but only for head-shaking, since they no longer required a guide and the man had also been a cool, taciturn companion. They wondered about it for a while, and the old man's satisfaction at having saved some money was slightly diminished by the murkiness of the matter and the unease that comes with a piece of unfinished business. He assumed, by the way, that the man would show up again at some point to claim his pay. Joseph thought it possible that he had perhaps already secretly laid claim to more than just that, and suggested they check their wares; but the result of this inventory proved him wrong. He was the one who was most surprised, in particular by how out of character this was for his acquaintance and how hard it seemed to reconcile this indifference to matters of profit with his usual manifest greed. He took more than his due for friendly services rendered voluntarily, but, or so at least it appeared, let wages honestly earned carelessly slip through his fingers. But Joseph could not speak with the Ishmaelites about these discrepancies, and what is never put into words is soon forgotten. They all had other things to worry about besides their eccentric guide; and after they had cleaned their ears and put on eye makeup, they advanced toward the water and the Sovereign's Wall, arriving around noon at the bridge to the fortress of Zel.

Ah, it was even more terrifying from close-up than from a distance, doubly impregnable, with its zigzag ramparts, towers, and bastions, its high parapets occupied all round by warriors clad in battle tunics and carrying shields made of hides on their backs; there they stood, spears clenched in fists, chins resting on fists, and stared in contempt down at the approaching caravan. Officers fitted out in half-length wigs, white shirts, and skirts with leather groin guards could be seen walking back and forth behind them, a cane in one hand. They paid no attention to the approaching band, but the first line of sentries raised their arms and then, cradling their spears in their arms, cupped their hands to their mouths and called out, "Back! Turn back! Fortress of Zel! No passage! We will shoot!"

"Pay no heed," the old man said. "Just stay calm. It's not half so bad as it looks. Let us show gestures of peace, while advancing slowly, but undeterred. Do I not have the letter of my merchant friend? We shall get through."

Following his instructions and signaling that they came in peace, they moved ahead to the loopholed wall, directly in front of a gate, behind which was a great portal of iron that led to the bridge. Above the portal glistened a deep carved relief, painted in bright fiery colors—the giant figure of a bare-throated vulture with outspread wings, a joist ring in its talons; and jutting out from the bricks to its right and left were four-foot-high pedestals with stony cobras, their heads raised above their bellies and hoods spread—symbols of defense terrible to look upon.

"Turn back!" the sentries called down from the outer gate wall with its vulture relief. "Fortress of Zel! Return, you sand rabbits, to your misery! There is no passage here!"

"You are mistaken, warriors of Egypt," the old man replied, still seated on his camel, from the midst of his band. "It is precisely here that one finds passage and nowhere else. Where else could one find it on this neck of land? We are knowledgeable people, who do not knock at the wrong smithy door, but know exactly how one passes into the country beyond, for we have crossed this bridge many times, going both forward and back."

"Yes, back!" they shouted from up top. "Just keep going back, it's nothing but back to the desert with you, that is our order—let no riffraff into the country!"

"To whom do you tell this?" the old man replied. "To me, who not only knows it well enough, but also expressly approves of it? For I despise riffraff and sand rabbits as fervently as you and have only high praise for how you prevent them from ravaging the land. Do but examine us closely and study our faces. Do we look to you like marauding thieves and Sinai's rabble? Is our appearance such that it could awaken the presumption we come to reconnoiter the land for some evil purpose? Or where are our herds that we intend to drive onto Pharaoh's pastures? Not for a fleeting moment can there be any question of that. We are Minæens from Ma'on, traveling merchants, of particularly honorable intentions, and we carry with us charming wares from abroad, which we would spread before you, hoping to trade for them among Keme's children, that in return we may bring the gifts of the Yeôr, which here is called the Hapi, to the ends of the earth. For it is an age of commerce and of exchanged gifts, and we travelers are its servants and priests."

"Tidy priests you are! Dusty priests! All lies!" the soldiers shouted down to them.

But the old man did not lose his courage and only shook his head indulgently.

"As if I did not know all this," he said in an aside to his followers. "They always act like this on principle and create difficulties just so that people may decide to toddle off instead. But I have never turned back here, and will pass through again this time as well. . . . Listen, warriors of Pharaoh," he called up to them again, "you doughty men of reddish brown hue! I particularly enjoy speaking with you here, for you are merry men. But the man with whom I would really rather speak is your youthful staff officer, Hor-waz, who let me in the previous time. Be so good as to call him to the wall. I wish to show him the letter for Zo'an that I carry with me. A letter," he repeated. "Written matter! Thoth! Djehuti, the baboon!" He smiled as he called to them in the way we do when speaking to people we know not as individuals but as representatives of a given nationality familiar to the world at large, and half in teasing, half in flattery invoke some name of popular fancy, the recollection of which, by way of proverb or fable, provides everyone with an amusing link to their conception of that people as a whole. And then they laughed, too, if only perhaps at the standard prejudice of foreigners who believed every Egyptian to be totally obsessed with writing and written matter, but at the same time they were impressed by the old man's familiarity with the name of one of their leaders; for they consulted among themselves and called down to the Ishmaelites that staff officer Hor-waz was on an official trip, was at present in the city of Sent, and would not return for three days.

"How dreadful!" the old man said. "What an awkward mischance, O warriors of Egypt! Three black days, three days of the new moon, without Hor-waz, our friend! That means we must wait. We shall wait here, my good armed friends, for his return. When he has come back from Sent, call him at once to the wall, if it so pleases you, with news that the famed Minæans from Ma'on are here and carry written matter."

And they did indeed set up their tents in the sand outside the

fortress of Zel, and remained there three days, waiting for the lieutenant, while staying on good terms with the men of the wall, who
came out to them at various times to view their wares and trade with
them. Their number was also increased by the arrival of another
band of travelers who had come out of the south, probably Sinai
and, having followed the route along the Bitter Lakes, likewise
wanted to be admitted into Egypt—a very ragtag lot, by the way,
and short on refinement. They waited with the Ishmaelites, and
when the hour came and Hor-waz had returned, the soldiers opened
the wall gate and allowed all those desiring admission to gather in a
courtyard before the portal to the bridge, where they had to wait another few hours until the youthful, skinny-legged officer came
bounding down an open stairway and halted on one of its lower
steps. He was accompanied by two men, one carrying writing utensils, the other bearing a standard with a ram's head. Hor-waz signaled for the petitioners to approach.

His head was covered by a light brown wig cut straight across
the forehead and lying smooth as glass to the ears, where it suddenly
became a mass of little curls that fell to his shoulders. His overshirt
of scaly armor—at which hung a medal, a fly cast in bronze—did not
really match the delicate folds of the short-sleeved, dazzling white
linen tunic that showed underneath or the just as delicately pleated
skirt that fell at an angle to the hollows of his knees. They greeted
him with earnest sincerity, but as wretched as they might appear in
his eyes, he returned their greetings with even greater courtesy, indeed with fatuous politeness, hunching forward while tossing his
head back, smiling insipidly as if blowing kisses into the air with
pursed lips, and raising one very thin brown arm, adorned with a
wrist bracelet, from out of a pleated sleeve. To be sure it was all done
so swiftly and fluently that the strained grace and exaggerated eloquence of the pose lasted only a moment and vanished at once; but it
was immediately apparent—especially to Joseph—that it was done
not in their honor, but as a token of refined culture and for his own
self-esteem. Hor-waz had the short face of an aging child, with a pug
nose, eyes lengthened with cosmetics, and conspicuously deep
creases at both sides of his still pursed but smiling mouth.

"Who is this?" he asked rapidly in Egyptian. "Men of wretchedness in such great numbers who would enter the Two Lands?" He
did not mean the word "wretchedness" as an aspersion, really; he

simply meant everything foreign. But his "great numbers" referred
to both groups of travelers, since he saw no difference between the
Midianites, including Joseph, and the band from the Sinai, all of
whom had thrown themselves down before him.

"There are too many of you," he continued, scolding. "Every
day there are people from here or there, whether from the land of the
god or the mountains of Shu, who want to enter the land, or, if daily
is a bit exaggerated, then almost daily. Only the day before yesterday
I let through some from the land of Upi and from Mount User, since
they were bearing letters with them. I am a scribe of the Great Gate,
who provides reports on the concerns of the Two Lands, fine and
lovely reports for those who read them. Mine is a weighty responsibility. Where do you come from and what do you want? Are your
intentions good or less than good, perhaps even evil, so that we must
either drive you back or perhaps change your complexion to that of
corpses at once? Do you come from Kadesh and Tubichi or the city
of Her? Let your head man speak. If you come from the port of Sur,
I know that wretched place well, where water has to be brought in
by boat. We know all these foreign lands quite well, for we have conquered them and accept their tribute. . . . Above all, do you know
how you will live? I mean, have you brought food and are you able
to provide for yourselves one way or another, so that you do not
become a burden to the state or be driven to steal? If the former is
the case, where then is your proof and written guarantee that you
know how to live? Do you bear letters for a citizen of the Two
Lands? Then hand them over. Otherwise there is only an immediate
turnabout."

The old man drew near with prudent meekness. "You are as
unto Pharaoh here," he said, "and if I do not take fright before the
authority you exercise or stand in stammering confusion in view of
your power to render decisions, then it is merely because I do not
stand before you for the first time, but have experienced your kindness before, wise lieutenant." And he reminded him how, at such
and such a time, perhaps two or four years before, he, a Minæan
merchant, had last passed through here, that being the first time
commanding officer Hor-waz had cleared him to pass on the basis of
the purity of his intentions. The lieutenant appeared to have at least
some partial recollection, too—the little beard, the tilt of the old
man's head, the way he spoke Egyptian like a real human being; and

so he listened with goodwill to the answers the old man gave to the questions posed him—that not only had he come with no evil intentions, or even less than good ones, but indeed with only the very best; that he had come, by way of the land of Peleset and the desert, as a traveling merchant from beyond the Jordan; that he knew how to live and provide for himself and his family most excellently, as attested by precious wares to be found on the backs of his beasts of burden. But as for his connections with the Two Lands, here, then, was a letter—and he unrolled a piece of polished goatskin before the officer, on which his merchant friend in Gilead had written a few sentences in Canaanite script recommending him to a merchant friend in Djanet in the Delta.

Hor-waz's slender fingers—of both hands—reached to receive the written material with the gentlest of gestures. He could make very little of it; but he could certainly tell from a visa written in one corner in his own hand that this parchment had been presented to him before.

"You are bringing me the very same letter, old friend," he said. "That will not do, you cannot pass through forever with this. I wish to see this scribble-scrabble no more, it is outdated, you must provide me with something new."

In response, the old man suggested that his connections were not exclusively with the man in Djanet, but rather extended as far as Thebes itself, Wase, the city of Amun, to which he planned to travel, to a house of honor and distinction, with whose steward, by the name of Mont-kaw, son of Ahmose, he had been closely acquainted for countless years, having often been permitted to supply him with foreign goods. The house, however, belonged to a great lord over great men, to Peteprê, Fan-Bearer at the King's Right Hand. Mention of even so roundabout a connection to the royal court made a visible impression on the young officer.

"By the king's life!" he said. "That would mean that you are not just anyone, and should your Asiatic mouth not be lying, it would, to be sure, alter the matter. Have you nothing in writing about your acquaintance with this Mont-kaw, the son of Ahmose, who is steward over the house of this fan-bearer? Nothing at all? What a great shame, for that would have simplified your case not a little. All the same, you know to name these names, and your peaceable face provides your words a reasonable attestation of credibility."

He gestured for his writing utensils, and his aide hurried over to hand him the wooden tablet on whose smooth clay surface the lieutenant was accustomed to scribble notes with a sharpened reed. Hor-waz now dipped it into the inkwell of a palette that the soldier held out for him, shook off a few excess drops, brought his hand in a grand sweep to the surface, and recorded basic information about the old man as it was repeated to him. With the standard planted beside him, he held the tablet on one arm and wrote standing, bent delicately forward, pursing his lips, squinting elegantly, and devoting himself to the task with obvious smug pleasure. "You may pass!" he now declared, handing tablet and pen back. Saluting them once again in the same fatuously refined fashion, he bounded back up the steps by which he had come. The Sinai sheik with the disheveled beard, who had spent the entire time lying on his face, was not even interrogated. Hor-waz had assumed he and his band were included in the old man's party, so that the records—once transferred to lovely paper and passed on up to offices in Thebes—would prove very incomplete. But one need not weep for Egypt on that account, nor assume that the land now fell into disorder. In any case, for the Ishmaelites the main thing was that the soldiers of Zel now swung back the iron doors of the portal that opened onto the floating bridge, so that they, their animals and wares could cross over it and enter the wide fields of Hapi.

As the least among them, noticed by no one and left unnamed in Hor-waz's official record, Joseph, son of Jacob, had come to the land of Egypt.

Part Two

THE ENTRANCE INTO SHEOL

Joseph Sees the Land of Goshen and Comes to Per-Sopd

What part of it did he see first? We know that with certainty; circumstances tell us. The road along which the Ishmaelites led him was appointed for them in more than just the one sense; it was also determined by geography, and it is therefore certain, though little noted, that the first section of Egypt through which Joseph passed was a region that does not owe its distinction, if not to say its fame, to any role it plays in the history of Egypt, but rather to the one it played in the story of Joseph and his people. It was the land of Goshen. It was also called Gosem or Gosen—depending on who you were or how your tongue fit around the word—and belonged to the district of Arabia, the twentieth nome of the land of Uto the Serpent, that is, of Lower Egypt. It lay in the eastern part of the Delta, which is why Joseph and those who led him entered it as soon as they had left the brackish lakes and frontier fortifications behind them, and there was certainly nothing all that grand or remarkable about it—Joseph did not see himself in any great danger for now of being helplessly intimidated or of losing his head over the wonders of Mizraim.

Beneath a dull, drizzly sky, wild geese flew above a monotone marshland, home to a few solitary blackthorn or mulberry trees and crisscrossed by ditches and dikes. They followed these dikes that led beside muddy watercourses, where wading birds, storks and ibises, stood among the reeds. Villages with shading fans of doom palms and cone-shaped clay storehouses were mirrored in the waters of greenish duck ponds—no different from villages in his homeland and certainly no feast for the eye after more than seven times seventeen days. Ordinary farmland, with nothing unsettling about it, is what Joseph saw, and nothing even like the great "granary" Keme was said to be; for all that was to be seen here was simple grassland

and pasture, though wet and lush to be sure—and the son of shepherds regarded it with interest. There were some herds grazing on it as well—white-and-red-spotted cattle, some with lyre-shaped horns rising straight up, some with none at all, and sheep, too—and shepherds squatted beside their jackal-eared dogs under reed mats stretched between staffs to protect them against the drizzle.

These animals, the old man instructed his followers, were not local for the most part. Landowners and stewards of temple stables sent their herds here from far upstream—where there were only cultivated fields and cattle had to graze on clover—so that they could enjoy a season in the marshes of the northern Lower Land, feeding on the grass that grew so lush here thanks to this navigable freshwater channel, the main canal that they were now walking beside and that led straight ahead to Per-Sopd, the ancient and holy city of this nome. For it was there that the canal branched off from one of the delta arms of the Hapi, linking the river with the Bitter Lakes, which, so the old man told them, were connected by yet another canal with the Sea of Red Earth or, more succinctly, the Red Sea—an unbroken route, then, from there to the Nile, and one could sail from the city of Amun clear around to Punt, the land of frankincense, as had been dared by the ships of Hatshepsut, the woman who had once been Pharaoh and worn the beard of Osiris.

The old man chattered on in his wise, easygoing way, sharing what tradition said of her. Joseph, however, was not listening closely and had no ear for the deeds of Hatshepsut, the woman whose very nature was altered by her status as king and who wore a beard. Would it be saying too much if one were to include in his story how even now his thoughts built an airy bridge between these meadows here and his clan at home, his father and little Benjamin? Certainly not—given that his way of thinking was not ours, but rather played with a few dream-born motifs that formed the musical substance of his spiritual life, as it were. He could hear one such motif that from the very beginning had been deeply bound up with his dream of being "carried off" and "raised up"—the motif of "sending for others to follow." A countermotif played against it in his thoughts, that of Jacob's revulsion for the land to which he was being carried off; but he reconciled them into a harmonious whole by telling himself that although this peaceful ancient pasture land might be Egypt, it was not yet really that in a fully revolting sense, and that it might well appeal to Jacob, the king of flocks, who could hardly stomach this land when seen from home. He watched the herds that landowners of Upper Egypt had sent here for the good grass, and he was keenly aware, indeed above all else, how the motif of his being carried away would first have to be complemented by that of his being raised up, before the herds of those lords upstream would make way for other flocks in the land of Goshen—that is, before it would be time for the motif of "sending for others to follow." Once again he weighed and gained strength from the idea that if one must go to the West, then at the least one must become the first of those who dwell there.

For now, however, he joined his owners as they moved along the level, clay bank of the blessed canal, at whose edge stood an occasional spindly palm tree and over whose smooth surface a flotilla of boats with very tall sails attached to swaying masts slowly glided toward them, heading east. Following this route they could scarcely miss Per-Sopdu, the holy city, which, once they reached it, proved to be a cramped town with disproportionately high walls and little life inside them, for almost the entire population consisted of the official staff of the Privy Bearer of the King's Commands—who acted as the arbiter of field disputes and bore the fine Syrian title of *rabisu*—and the shorn priests of the local god Sopd, who was called He Who Conquers the Inhabitants of Sinai. As for the rest, people in colorful Asiatic garb and speaking the tongues of Amor and Zahi far outnumbered those marked by the white garments and language of Egypt. The narrow streets of Per-Sopd were so redolent of carnations, or clove pinks, that the odor was pleasant only at first, but soon became disagreeable, for it was the favorite spice in the temple of Sopd and it was added in excess to every offering brought to him—a god so ancient that his own attendants and prophets, who wore lynx skins on their backs and always held their eyes cast down, could no longer say for certain whether his head was actually that of a pig or that of a hippopotamus.

He was a god who had been pushed aside, growing ever more obscure and, to judge by the mood and words of his priests, rather embittered, and it had also been a long time since he had defeated any inhabitants of Sinai. An image of him, only as big as your hand, stood at the very rear of his ancient, squat temple, whose courtyards and antechambers were adorned with equally squat seated statues of the Pharaoh who had built this house in the distant past. In an attempt to lend Sopd's house some semblance of cheerfulness, gilded flagpoles with gaudy banners had been set in the niches of the front gatehouse, whose sloping walls were covered with murals. The temple was poorly endowed, the storehouses and treasuries lining the main court were empty, and not many people came to pay their respects with offerings for Sopdu, the lord—in fact, only the city's Egyptian populace, but no one from outside, for there was no universally observed feast to lure excited crowds downstream and inside the crumbling walls of Per-Sopd.

When, as a business courtesy, the Ishmaelites bought a few bouquets in the open courtyard and laid them and a duck studded with cloves on the offering table in the low temple chamber, the priests, with their shiny skulls, long fingernails, and always lowered eyelids, told them in singsong voices of the sad state of their ancient lord and his city. They blamed the passage of time, which had brought with it great injustice, heaping all power, brilliance, and privilege into one bowl of the scale of the Two Lands, the bowl of the southern Upper Land, and making Wase so great—whereas originally it was the bowl of the northern Lower Land, the land of the Delta, that, in accord with justice, had held that holy weight. For in those just and ancient days when Mempi had been the gleaming capital of kings, the Delta had been the real and true Egypt, whereas the river's upper reaches, including Thebes, had been considered as good as part of wretched Kush and other Negro lands. Back then, the South had been destitute of culture and spiritual light, as well as lacking in beauty of life, and these good things had come from the ancient North and spread fruitfully upriver. Here were the wellsprings of knowledge, civilization, and prosperity, and here the oldest, most venerable gods of the land had been born, as, for instance, Sopd, Lord of the East, in his chapel, whom the shift in weights on the scale had now entirely eclipsed. For nowadays, Amun of Thebes, far up in the vicinity of Negro lands, had set himself up as judge over what was to be considered Egyptian or not—so certain was he that his name was synonymous with the name of Egypt, and its with his. Only recently, the god's embittered attendants said, people from the West, who lived near the Libyans, had petitioned Amun, asserting that it seemed to them they were not Egyptians but Libyans; for they lived outside of the Delta and agreed with the Egyptians in nothing, either in worship of the gods or anything else. They loved, so they said in their petition, to eat the flesh of cows and wanted the freedom to eat the flesh of cows just as Libyans did, of whose race they were. But Amun replied, instructing them that the flesh of cows was out of the question, for Egypt is the land that the Nile makes fertile, upriver and down, and all who live on this side of Elephantine and drink from the river are Egyptians.

So said Amun, and the priests of Sopdu, their lord, raised their long-fingernailed hands in an attempt to make the Ishmaelites understand the arrogance of it. Why this side of Yeb and the first cataract? they asked sardonically. Because Thebes lay just this side of it? Behold that god's generosity of heart! If Sopd, their lord, here in the lower North, in the first and real land of Egypt, were to declare that everyone is Egyptian who drinks from its waters, that would, to be sure, be true generosity and magnanimity of heart. But when Amun—a god who, to put it cautiously, stood under the suspicion of being of Nubian origin and initially a god of the miserable land of Kush, and who had been able to gain popular primacy only by arbitrarily equating himself with Atum-Rê—when Amun said it, one could not take that generosity of heart at full value or confuse it in any way with true magnanimity. . . .

In short, the jealousy and pique aroused in the prophets of Sopd by changing times and the ascendancy of the South was patently clear, and the Ishmaelites, the old man at their head, respected such sensitivities and showed their approval as good businessmen by augmenting their offering with several loaves of bread and jugs of beer in a demonstration of the due esteem in which they held Sopd, the slighted god, before then proceeding to Per-Bastet, which lay close by.

The City of Cats

Here there was such a pungent odor of catnip that it almost turned the stomach of any stranger unaccustomed to it. For it is a smell that disgusts every creature except the holy animal of Bastet, the cat, which is renowned for its voracious love for it. Countless specimens

of these animals were kept in Bastet's holy of holies, the great core of
the city—black, white, and tabby, they prowled with the silent resolve of their charming kind along its walls and between their devotees' feet in its courtyards. And people coaxed them with this foul
herb. But since cats were kept everywhere, in every home in Per-
Bastet, the odor of valerian was so intense that it pervaded everything, flavoring the food and clinging to garments for so long that
even on arrival in On and Mempi, travelers would be singled out and
people would laugh at them and say, "Obviously you've come from
Per-Bastet."

Such laughter, by the way, was directed not only at the smell, but
also at the city of cats itself and the amusing things associated with it.
For Per-Bastet, in contrast to Per-Sopd, which it also far surpassed
in size and population, was a city famed for its humor and merriment, despite the fact that it lay in the heart of the ancient Delta—
merriment that was in fact ancient and crude and at the mere thought
of which all Egypt was seized with laughter. Unlike the house of
Sopd, the city was home to a universally recognized festival, for
which, or so its inhabitants boasted, "millions" (that is, tens of thousands at least) of people traveled downriver, by land or water, everyone already in high spirits, because women in particular—all of them
carrying loud rattles—were supposed to behave wantonly, shouting
out ancient crude profanities from the decks of their boats and making obscene gestures at each town as they passed. But the men were
very merry as well, they whistled, sang, and clapped; and all those
who journeyed to Per-Bastet gathered there in a great throng, camp-
ing in tents for a three-day festival—with sacrifices, dances, and
masquerades, with a market fair, thumping drums, storytellers, jugglers, snake charmers, and more wine than was drunk in Per-Bastet
all the rest of the year, until, so it was said, the crowd was so caught
up in a mood both ancient and primitive that some people even
scourged themselves with whips or rather, more painfully still, with
a kind of spiny club, to the accompaniment of a universal clamor
that was an integral part of the old Feast of Bastet and, indeed, was
the very thing that evoked laugher at the mere thought of it—for the
sound was like screeching cats being visited by tomcats at night.

Boasting of the profitable crowds they entertained once a year,
the inhabitants told the strangers about this annual interruption of
their normally peaceful lives. The old man regretted that business

had prevented him from arriving in time for the festival, which was held at a different season of the year. His young slave Usarsiph listened to these descriptions with apparently respectful eyes, nodding politely and remembering Jacob. He also thought of him and of his forefathers' God who had no temple as he gazed down from a higher spot in the city to the sacred peninsula that lay at its heart below, embraced by the arms of two tree-shaded streams, and to the goddess's residence, its main building surrounded by high walls and hidden within a grove of old sycamores. Resting amid pylons laden with images, courtyards covered with awnings, and colorful arcades whose columns imitated open and closed buds of papyrus, the temple opened toward the east and the stone-paved avenue that had also brought him here along with the Ishmaelites. And he thought of Jacob again when he actually strolled among its columns and gazed at the dark red and sky blue engraved reliefs decorating its walls: Pharaoh burning incense before the cat goddess, while beneath miraculously clear-cut inscriptions made up of birds, eyes, arrows, beetles, and mouths, stood reddish brown divinities—all wearing tails and loincloths and adorned with sparkling bracelets and collar necklaces, with tall crowns on their animal heads and the ring-and-cross, the symbol of life, in their hands—who reached out in friendship to touch their earthly son on the shoulder.

Joseph, a tiny figure among giants, looked up at them all with young but tranquil eyes, for he was a young man confronting the power of age. But an awareness that he stood in marked contrast with it not only because of his years, but also in a larger sense, stiffened his back before its oppressive weight, and when he thought of the primitive screeching with which those who gathered for the feast filled the courts of Bastet by night, he could only shrug.

The Lessons of On

How well we know the road along which the lad who had been carried off was now led! Down or up, however you wish to take it or put it. For just as so many things here conspired to confuse him, so, too, this "up" and "down" was confusing. Seen from his homeland, he, just as Abram before him, thought of it as "going down" to Egypt, but within Egypt you went "up," that is, against the current, which flowed from the south, so that once inside the country, by going southward you no longer "went down" but "up." The confusion seemed deliberate, like the game where you're blindfolded and spun around a few times, so that your head is whirling and you can't tell forward from backward. And even time itself—that is, seasons and the calendar—was not as it should be down here either.

This was the twenty-eighth year of Pharaoh's reign and, as we would put it, the middle of December. The people of Keme said that it was the "first month of the flood," which they called Thoth, as Joseph learned to his delight—or Djehuti, as they pronounced the name of this monkey and friend of the moon. But this dating did not match natural circumstances—the current year almost always conflicted with reality, for it was in flux and only from time to time, at vast intervals, did its New Year's Day once again coincide with the actual, real New Year, when the Dog Star appeared once again in the morning sky and the waters began to rise. The general state of things, however, was a muddled mismatch between the calendar year and the ebb and flow of nature, just as now there could be no question of this being the onset of the flood—at the moment the river had receded so greatly that it was almost confined to its old bed. The land had reemerged, seed had been repeatedly sown, the crop was growing—for the Ishmaelites' downward journey had been so sluggish that half a year had passed since the summer solstice when Joseph had gone down into the pit.

And so, somewhat confused in matters of time and space, he moved from station to station—and what stations were those? We know them well, since circumstances dictate them. For those who led him, the Ishmaelites, took their time now, too, as was their habit, did not worry about time at all, but paid attention only to holding sluggishly to their goal more or less, and, upon leaving Per-Bastet, headed southward with Joseph along one branch of the river toward the point where it joined the main current at the apex of the Delta's triangle. And thus they came to golden On, set at that apex, a most strange city, the largest Joseph had thus far seen—the House of the Sun, made chiefly of gold, or so it seemed to his dazzled eyes. But from there they would one day set out for ancient Mempi, or Menfe as some called it, the former city of kings, where the dead had no need of a watery journey across the river, for the city already lay on its western banks. That much they knew about Mempi even now.

From there, however, they planned to leave land behind them and charter a boat to take them upriver to No-Amun, Pharaoh's city. That was the plan as conceived by the old man, whose counsel determined everything, and following it, they strode on for now, stopping to haggle along the banks of the Yeôr, which here was called the Hapi, its brownish waters now returned to its bed with only a few ponds still left stranded here and there in the fields, which were beginning to turn green as far as fertile soil extended between desert and desert.

Where its banks were steep, men stood beside low-walled wells, lifting fecund water from the river in leather bags attached to a sweep counterweighted with a ball of clay and pouring it into troughs that drained into the ditches below, so that they might have grain when Pharaoh's scribes came to collect it. For this was Egypt's house of bondage, of which Jacob disapproved, and the scribes who collected the grain were accompanied by Nubian bailiffs who bore bundled rods of palm.

The Ishmaelites did business in these peasant villages, trading lamps and resins for necklaces, headrests, and the linen that the farmers' wives wove from the flax of the field and then turned over to tax gatherers—they talked with the people and saw the land of Egypt. Joseph saw it, too, and as they traded and bargained he breathed in its strangely potent vital air, for its beliefs, customs, and usages were almost as pungent as its spices; but one ought not to conclude that everything his mind and senses sampled there was completely new, wild, and strange. As a land between lands, a land of passage, his fatherland—that is, if one wishes to regard the region of the Jordan and its mountains along with the hill country where he grew up as a unified fatherland—was influenced just as much by Egyptian customs and civilization from the south as by the hegemony of Babylon to its east; Pharaoh's campaigns had passed through it, leaving behind garrisons, viceroys, edifices. Joseph had seen Egyptians and their garb; the sight of an Egyptian temple was nothing strange; and all in all he was a child not only of his mountains, but also of a large geographical entity, the Mediterranean Orient, where nothing could seem to him totally mad and unfamiliar. He was, moreover, a child of his time, that now-submerged time in which he moved and into which we have descended, just as Ishtar went down to her son. Together with space, time created a unity and commonality in both the outward aspect and the mind-set of that world. The truly new thing about it that Joseph perceived on his journey was surely this: that he and his kind were not alone in the world, not utterly exceptional, that a great deal of his forefathers' pondering and brooding, their earnest speculations, their constant alertness to God's presence, did not make them so very different, singling them out for preference, as much as this was part of a time and a place, a common realm—aside, of course, from significant differences in the blessing this bestowed and their own aptitude for making use of it.

When Abram, for instance, had held such long and urgent discussions with Malkizedek about the extent to which there might be some unity between his own Adôn and El-Elyon, the Shekemite Baal of the Covenant, it had been a conversation very common to its time and world, both in terms of the problem itself and the significance attached to it with such openly expressed emotion. So then, at the very time of Joseph's arrival in Egypt, the priests of On, the city of Atum-Rê-Horakhte, the Lord of the Sun, had canonized the relationship between their holy bull, Merwer, and the Dweller upon the Horizon in the dogma of "living repetition"—a formula in which the ideas of identity and simultaneity were both paid equal due, which was why it had given rise to lively discussions all through Egypt and had even made a great impression on the royal court. Everyone was talking about it, from commonfolk to nobility, and the Ishmaelites could not trade five debens of labdanum for beer or a good cowhide of the same value without their trading partner's introducing and framing the conversation with something about the new definition of the relationship between Merwer and Atum-Rê and wanting to know what sort of impression it had made on these foreigners—and he could count on their interest if not their approval, for although they came from faraway, this was still the same region, and above all the same time that was common to them all and allowed them to take in such news with a certain amount of excitement.

This then was On, the House of the Sun, that is, the house of him who is Kheper in the morning, Rê at noon, and Atum in the evening, who opens his eyes and there is light, who closes his eyes and there is darkness—of him who had named his name to Eset, his daughter. On, which had stood on this site in Egypt for thousands of years, lay on the Ishmaelites' route toward the south, lay bathed in the glittering rays of the four-sided tip of the huge, brightly polished granite obelisk set on projecting foundations and crowning the great temple of the sun, where lotus-wreathed wine jugs, cakes, bowls of honey, birds, and every fruit of the field covered Rê-Horakhte's alabaster table and his attendants, wearing stiffly starched aprons and panther skins—still with the tail—across their backs, burned incense before Merwer, the Great Bull, the living repetition of the god, with a neck of brass just behind his lyre-shaped horns and powerful dangling testicles. It was indeed a city unlike any Joseph had ever seen before, different not only from other cities of the world, but also from those of Egypt, and even its temple, beside which lay the Ship of the Sun, its high flanks made of gilded bricks, was different in ground plan and appearance from all other Egyptian temples. The whole city glittered and sparkled with the gold of the sun, so much so that it left its inhabitants with inflamed, tearing eyes, while strangers usually pulled their hoods and cloaks over their heads to avoid its radiance. The encircling wall had a roof of gold and was studded with phallic sun-lances whose tips sent golden rays darting and flashing in all directions; the city was filled with golden animals, monuments to the sun in the shape of lions, sphinxes, rams, bulls, eagles, falcons, and kestrels; each of its buildings made of Nile brick, even the poorest of them, shone with a gilt symbol of the sun—a winged disk, a spiked wheel or a wagon, an eye, an ax or a scarab—plus a golden ball or apple on its roof; and as if that were not enough, the same held true for the villages surrounding On, where every residence, warehouse, or granary likewise bore such an emblem—a copper shield, a spiral serpent, a golden shepherd's crook, or a goblet—that glistened with reflected sunlight. For this was the domain of the sun and the precinct of blinking eyes.

Millennial On was a city whose outward appearance made all eyes blink. But it was also a city whose inner nature and spirit did the same. Ancient wise precepts had their home here, and even a stranger could sense them—absorbing them through his pores, as people say. These were precepts that dealt with measurement, with the structure of bodies conceived exactly and purely within three-dimensional space and with the planes that define them, set them off from one another by equal angles, their edges abutting precisely and meeting in a point that has no further extension and occupies no space—and all such holy matters. This passion for pure, conceptual geometry, this interest in theoretical space, which had its home in On and set that ancient city apart, was apparently bound up in its local cult of worshiping the daystar and was evidenced even in its formal arrangement. For located at the tip of the triangular region where the arms of the river parted to empty into the sea, its very buildings and streets formed another equilateral triangle, whose apex (at least theoretically and for the most part actually) coincided with that of the Delta; and from that apex there towered up from the massive rhombus of fiery granite foundations, the four-sided obelisk whose planes as they merged toward the top were covered with gold that flashed with the first rays received from the sun each morning—all of this surrounded by a stone wall that formed the culmination of vast temple precincts extending well out into the triangular city.

Here, just outside the gate to the temple, which was hung with banners and led to passageways adorned with the most delightful paintings depicting the events and gifts of all three seasons, there was an open area planted with trees, where the Ishmaelites would spend almost the entire day; for this was the place where people—blinking residents of On and strangers alike—met and bartered. And the servants of the god likewise came out to the market—eyes watering from too much staring into the sun, shaved heads glistening, bodies clad in the short apron and sacerdotal sash of ages long past—and mixed with the people, for they had nothing against a conversation with anyone who wished to ask them about their wisdom. To that task, it appeared, they were as good as exhorted from on high and could hardly wait to be asked to testify on behalf of their venerable cult and their temple's ancient tradition of scientific wisdom. Our old man, Joseph's master, made use of this unspoken but clearly imparted permission and frequently spoke with these scholars of the sun while Joseph listened.

Contemplation of the god and a gift for handing down doctrinal decrees, so they said, were hereditary within their order. The discerning of holy things had been its possession for ages now. They—their predecessors in office—had first divided and measured time and established the calendar, an accomplishment that, like their instructive talent for pure abstraction, was in essence bound up with the nature of the god, who opened his eyes and it was day. For until then, human beings had lived out their lives in blind timelessness, without measure or awareness; he, however, who made the hours—from which arose the days—had opened men's eyes by the agency of his sages. That they—their predecessors, that is—had invented the sundial was self-evident. It was less certain whether this was true of the apparatus for measuring the hours of the night, the water clock; but presumably it came into being because Sobk, the water god of Ombo who took the form of a crocodile, was—like so many other figures worthy of veneration when one fixed them under one's watery gaze—simply Rê under another name, in token of which he bore the disk arrayed with serpents.

This form of association was, by the way, the work and doctrinal assertion of these shiny-headed priests; they were, by their own account, very good at associating and equating all the divinities who watched over each nome and city along with Atum-Rê-Horakhte of On, who in turn was an association and constellation of what had originally been several independent numina. To make one out of many was their favorite activity, and indeed, in listening to them one learned that there were basically only two great gods: the god of the living, who was Hor in the Mountain of Light, Atum-Rê; and a lord of the dead, Osiris, the Eye Enthroned. But Atum-Rê was also the eye, that is, as the solar disk, and so to a mind of sharpened acuity it was clear that Usir was Lord of the Barque of Night, which, as everyone knew, Rê had to board after setting in order to travel from west to east, spending light on those below. In other words, these two great gods were, strictly speaking, one and the same. And if the acuity of such associations was admirable, no less so was the skill by which these teachers—despite their endeavor to identify all as one—managed to offend no one and left intact the actual multiplicity of Egypt's gods.

This they achieved by means of the science of the triangle. Were their listeners at all conversant, perhaps, with the nature of this splendid symbol, the teachers of On asked. The width of its base corresponded to the many names and forms of the deities invoked by the people and served by priests in the cities of the Two Lands. But above it rose the two sides of this beautiful figure, each striving to join the other, and the unique space that they delimited might be called "associative space," characterized by the property that it grew ever narrower, so that each hypothetical base drawn across the triangle became shorter and shorter, until it had only an extremely narrow width and finally none at all. For the sides met in a point, and this final intersection, beneath which all the widths of the figure existed simultaneously, was the lord of their temple, was Atum-Rê.

This, then, was the theory of the triangle, the beautiful figure of association. The servants of Atum took no little pride in it. They had of late found adherents everywhere, they said, who were now busy associating and equating, but really only as blundering, awkward schoolboys, and not in the true spirit—that is, lacking in spirit and replacing it instead with a cruel clumsiness. Amun, the god rich into cattle, for example, whose home was Thebes in Upper Egypt, had allowed himself to be equated with Rê by his prophets and wished to be called Amun-Rê in his shrine. Fine, but this had not happened in the spirit of the triangle and of reconciliation, but rather as if in some way Amun had conquered and devoured Rê, incorporating him in his own body, as if Rê, so to speak, had had to name his name to him—a brutal implementation of their teachings, narrow-minded presumption contrary to the meaning of the triangle. Atum-Rê, for his part, was not called the Dweller upon the Horizon for nothing; his horizon was wide and all-embracing, and even more all-embracing was the triangular space of his associations. Yes, in his kindness to the world he was as wide as the world—that was the meaning of this ancient god who had long ago matured to a serene mildness. He recognized himself, according to his priests with shaved heads, not only in his own ever-changing forms, which the people worshiped in the nomes and cities of Keme, no, more than that, he was also serenely inclined to join in all-seeing, all-protecting concord with the solar deities of other peoples—just the opposite of young Amun in Thebes, who lacked all talent for speculative thought and whose horizon was in fact so narrow that he not only knew nothing and understood nothing but Egypt, but also could do nothing here, either, but consume and incorporate everything, instead of allowing it to be, being unable, so to speak, to see beyond his own nose.

But, said the bleary-eyed priests, they did not want to remain in conflict with the young Amun in Thebes, for their god's nature and interest was not conflict, but obliging concord. He loved the stranger as himself, which was why, as his servants, they were so happy to speak with these strangers—that is, the old man and his companions. Whatever gods they worshiped and by whatever names they called them, they could go right ahead without fear of betrayal and approach Horakhte's alabaster table to lay, as their resources allowed, a few doves, some bread, fruit, or flowers there. One look at the tenderly smiling face of the Father High Priest as he sat in his golden chair at the foot of the great obelisk, watching over their offerings with serene kindness—a winged solar disk at his back, his white robe spread wide around him, a golden cap covering his shaved head wreathed in flowing white hair—one such look would reveal to them that, along with Atum-Rê, their own local gods would also be receiving these gifts and be satisfied as well, all in accord with the meaning of the triangle.

And the servants of the sun embraced and kissed the old man and those with him, including Joseph, one after the other, in the name of the Father and Great Prophet, then turned to the other visitors in the market to continue their propaganda for Atum-Rê, Lord of the Wide Horizon. The Ishmaelites, however, though agreeably impressed, departed from On at the tip of the triangle and guided their steps ever farther down, or up, into the land of Egypt.

Joseph at the Pyramids

The Nile rolled at its slow pace between low, reedy banks, but the trunk of many a palm tree still stood in reflecting waters left behind by the river's now-receding outpouring, and while many parcels of land in the blessed zone between desert and desert were turning green with sown wheat or barley, there were other fields over which brown men clad in white aprons and waving rods drove cattle and sheep, so that the animals would tread the seed deep into the soft moist soil. Under a sky now bright with sunlight, hovering vultures and white falcons peered down before diving at some village settlement built beside an irrigation canal under the swaying crowns of towering date palms, its houses like buttressed pylons made of mud brick and covered with dung roofs—each stamped by the unique spirit of Egypt, whose sense of form and feeling for its gods pervaded everything, shaping men and objects in its image, a spirit whose manifestation Joseph had sensed at home in its extensions out into the world, the solitary tokens of an edifice here and there, but which now spoke to him with commanding, original force in all things great and small.

In a swirl of poultry destined for slaughter, naked children played beside village landing places, where awnings of woven twigs had been stretched over poles and where people returning home from necessary errands, poling their way along the canal in reed boats with high sweeping sterns, now stepped ashore. For just as the river with its panoply of sails divided the land from north to south into two parts, there were also irrigation canals running athwart it, west and east, dividing it into islands, little green oases beneath shading fans of palm. The roads, however, were dikes that cut their way through ditches, low-lying fields, and groves, and along them the Ishmaelites moved southward, together with the people of the country, riding asses and carts pulled by oxen or mules or trudging along in loincloths, poles across the shoulders, from which dangled ducks and fish for market—a lean, reddish people with no bellies, but square shoulders, harmless enough and ready to laugh, all with small-boned but protruding jaw lines, small noses ending in a broad tip, childlike cheeks, and smooth hair cut evenly across the brow and just below the earlobe, most with a rush blossom clenched in their teeth or stuck behind an ear or into the diagonally folded cinch of a skirt that had been washed many times and was worn higher in the back than in front. Joseph liked these wayfarers; given that these were people from the land of the dead and citizens of Sheol, they were a delight to watch as they laughed at the sight of these Habiritic riders on their dromedaries and greeted them with jokes, for they found anything foreign comical. He privately tried to wrap his tongue around their language and trained himself by listening, so that he might soon be able to speak deftly and easily to them with the playfulness of the vernacular.

Egypt was constricted here, its fertile ribbon narrow. Not far to the east on their left, mountains of the Arabian desert extended southward, and in the west ran the line of Libya's mountains of sand, whose deadly barrenness was transfigured to a beautifully deceptive purple as the sun set behind them. But straight ahead in front of this chain, at the edge of the desert and close to the belt of green, the travelers beheld another line of very peculiar mountains rising up— symmetrical forms made up of triangles whose pure edges were immense diagonal lines that rose to meet at a pointed tip. But what they saw were not Creation's mountains, but man's; these were the great world-famous bastions that the old man had described to Joseph early in their trip, the tombs of Khufu, Chefren, and other kings of long ago, built by hundreds of thousands of gasping slaves toiling beneath the whip during decades of holy drudgery, workers who had hewn out of Arabian quarries millions of granite blocks weighing several tons, which they then dragged to the river, ferried across it, and then, amidst great groans, sledged up ramps to the very edge of the Libyan desert, where, incredibly, they piled them with hoisting tackle to a point as high as a mountain—workers who fell dying beneath the blaze of the desert sun, their tongues lolling from such inhuman exertion, so that the god-king Khufu might rest deep beneath it all, within a chamber barricaded by the weight of seven million tons of heavy stones, a sprig of mimosa over his heart.

It was no human achievement that the children of Keme had accomplished, and yet it was the achievement of these same small people who trotted and trudged along the dike roads, of their bleeding hands, lank muscles, and gasping lungs—a work extorted from human beings, though surpassing anything human, because Khufu was the god-king, the son of the sun. But the sun, which struck down and devoured the builders, might well be satisfied with this superhuman human accomplishment—Rahotep, the satisfied sun; for in their pure abstract figures, as both tombs and monuments to the sun, these great bastions, rising to life above the desert, stood in pictographic relationship to the sun. And their monstrous triangles, polished to a luster from their bases to a shared acme, were turned in pious precision toward the four quarters of heaven.

Joseph gazed ahead wide-eyed at the solid geometry of these tomb mountains, piled high by slaves in the Egyptian house of bondage that Jacob so disapproved of, and he listened to the old man's chatter as he launched into tales about King Khufu—how even nowadays talk about that supernatural builder turned to gloomy anecdotes, a testimony to the bad memories of that terrible king preserved for a thousand years and more by the people of Keme, who had been forced to do the impossible for him. For he was said to have been an evil, selfish god, who first closed all the temples so that no one would steal time from him to offer sacrifices. And afterward he placed everyone, without exception, in harness, to drudge away at building his wondrous tomb, and for thirty years never permitted anyone an hour to live a life of his own. For ten years, then, they had had to chisel and drag, and for two times ten to build, exerting every ounce of strength they possessed, and more. For if one added up all their collective strength, it was still not enough to have built this pyramid. The rest that had been required had come from Khufu's divine status, though they had not thanked him for it. The pyramid had cost great treasures, and when the treasures of his majesty the god were exhausted, he had stripped his own daughter and prostituted her there in his palace to any man who paid the price, so that she might fill his treasury with her whore's wages.

So said the people, according to the old man, and it was quite possible that what they said of Khufu a thousand years after his death was largely a matter of fairy tales and misunderstandings. But this much was clear: The only gratitude they felt toward the deceased was filled with a horror at how he had extorted from them their utmost and more, how he had demanded the impossible.

As the travelers drew nearer, the points of the mountain chain spread out across the sand, and they could see the damaged state of its triangular surfaces, whose polished outer plates had begun to crumble. Desolation lay between the giant tombs, each set off to itself on the bluffs of a sand shelf above the desert floor, and each so massive that time had been unable to gnaw at more than their surface. They alone had proved victors over the dreadful mass of time past, beneath which lay buried the vanished pious splendor that had once divided and filled the area between their monstrous forms. The temples of the dead that had once stood braced against their slopes and in which "eternal" services had been established in honor of those who had died to join the sun, the covered arcades filled with paintings that had once led to them, the wide imposing portals that had once stood to the east at the edge of the green ribbon as the entrance to the final paths into the magic realm of immortality— Joseph no longer saw anything of that even in his day and did not know that in not seeing he was seeing devastation, seeing what was no more. He came upon them really rather early in comparison to us, but was a callow latecomer if the comparison is made in the other direction, and his gaze prodded at these bare remains of titanic mathematics, this vast trash heap of death, the way a foot kicks at debris. Not that he was not also moved with amazement and awe at the sight of these triangular cathedrals—far from it. But the dreadful permanence with which they stood—deserted by their own time and yet left standing in God's presence—lent them, among other things, a gruesome quality that damned them in his eyes, and he thought of the Tower.

The mystery in a head scarf, Hor-em-akhet, the Great Sphinx, was also left standing here, its remains appearing abruptly out of sands that had drifted and covered much of it again, even though Pharaoh's immediate predecessor, Thutmose IV, had freed it, rescued it, from them in obedience to the dream of promise that came to him in a midday nap. The monstrous creature—which had always lain here, so that no man could say when and how it appeared out of the rocks—rested in sand sloping up its chest and covering one of its paws, while the other one, still exposed, was as large as three houses. The king's son had slumbered leaning against its chest, a little doll beneath an immense divine beast, while servants stood off at a distance guarding his hunting chariot, and high above the tiny man rose the enigmatic head—with its stiff neck-covering and eternal brow, its eroded nose, which lent it a kind of wanton air, with its stony vault of an upper lip and broad mouth beneath set in a kind of calm, yet savagely sensual smile and its shrewd, wide-open eyes, intoxicated by a deep draught from time's chalice, gazing forever toward the east.

There it lay now, too, this immemorial chimera—in a present so distant and different from the one it once knew that it was doubtlessly reduced to nothing in its eyes—and in savage, sensual immutability lifted its gaze to far beyond the sunrise and the tiny band of Joseph's masters. An inscribed stone tablet tall as a man was propped against its chest, and in reading it the Minæans felt blessed and their hearts were uplifted, for this recent stone offered them firm temporal ground, like a narrow platform or foothold above the abyss. This was the memorial stone that Pharaoh Thutmose had erected here, in honor of his dream and his having freed the god from the burden of sand. The old man read the tidings of the text to his family: How at the hour when the sun had stood at its zenith, the prince had lain down in the shadow of the monster and been overcome with sleep, and in his dream he had seen the majesty of this splendid god, Harmakhis-Kheper-Atum-Rê, his father, who had spoken to him like a father and called him his beloved son. "It has

been a goodly number of years now," he had said, "that my countenance has been directed toward you and my heart as well. I will give
to you, Thutmose, my kingdom, you shall wear the crowns of both
lands on the throne of Geb, the country shall belong to you in its
length and breadth, as well as everything that is illumined by the
rays of the Universal Lord's eye. The treasures of Egypt and the
great tribute of nations shall be allotted to you. But meanwhile,
though I am to be worshiped, the sand of the desert upon which I
stand oppresses me. My just wish arises from this discomfort. I do
not doubt that you will attend to it as soon as you can. For I know
that you are my son and my deliverer. I, however, will be with you."
And upon awakening, so it is said, Thutmose still knew the words of
this god and kept them with him until his elevation to the throne.
And in that very hour yet, his command went forth that they should
begin at once to remove the sand oppressing Harmakhis, the Great
Sphinx, in the desert near Mempi.

　　These, then, the tidings. And Joseph who listened while the old
man, his master, read them, took care not to append a single word;
for he recalled the old man's admonishment that he hold his tongue
in the land of Egypt and wanted to prove he could, if need be, keep
to himself the sort of thoughts going through his mind. But for
Jacob's sake, he was secretly vexed by this dream of promise and in
his vexation found it very dry and meager. Pharaoh, it seemed to
him, had made far too much fuss with his memorial stone. After all,
what was promised to him? Nothing more than what had been his
destiny from birth, that is, to become king over both lands when his
hour came. The god had confirmed him in this particular prospect—
that is, if Pharaoh would deliver his image from the sands oppressing
him. It only showed how silly it was to make an image for oneself.
The image was threatened by sand, and the god was forced to beg,
"Save me, my son!" and enter into a covenant by which, in return for
a paltry benefaction, he promised what was likely to happen anyway. It was truly absurd. What a different covenant, a much finer
one, had the Lord God concluded with his own forefathers; also out
of need, but mutual need, so that they rescued one another from the
desert sands and were made holy, one in the other. Moreover, the
king's son had become king when his hour came, but the god was already covered again with sand to a great extent. For such temporary

relief, then, a superfluous promise was probably the right sort of repayment, Joseph thought, and also said as much when he was alone with Kedma, the old man's son, who was amazed at such fault-finding.

But although, to honor Jacob, Joseph found fault and mocked, in one way or another the sight of the sphinx really did make a greater impression on him than anything he had seen thus far in the land of Egypt, stirring his young blood with an uneasiness for which mockery was no match and that would not let him sleep. Night had fallen even as they still lingered by these great objects in the desert; and so they set up their tents to sleep and wait for morning to continue on their way to Menfe. Joseph, however, who had been lying beside Kedma, his tentmate, wandered out again under the stars, and as jackals howled in the distance, he approached the giant idol to study it properly again all on his own, by the glimmer of night and without any witnesses, and to examine its appalling enormity.

For this monstrosity of the ages in its royal headdress of stone was enormous not only in size, appalling not only because of the darkness of its origins. What riddle did it speak? But it did not speak at all. Its riddle was its silence, that calm, intoxicated silence, in which the creature directed its shrewd and brutal gaze on past the man who stood there questioning and questioned. And that missing nose had the same effect as someone wearing a cap tugged down over one ear. Yes, if only it had been a riddle like the good old man's about his neighbor Dagantakala's property—then, no matter how deeply hidden and covert the numbers, you still could have shoved what was unknown back and forth and weighed relationships until you not only might have found the solution, but also have been brazen enough to work it into a playful conversation. But this riddle was nothing but silence; and to judge by that nose, the monster was the brazen one; and that human head was not really meant for such a monster, no matter how shrewd that head might be.

For example . . . what was its nature—man or woman? People here called it Hor in the Mountain of Light and, like Thutmose not long before, took it for an image of the sun god. But that was a recent interpretation that had not always been thought true, and even if it was the sun god who proclaimed himself in this crouching image— what did the image itself say as to its sexual nature? That was hidden and covert, for it lay recumbent. If it were to stand up, would it have majestically dangling testicles like Merwer in On—or prove to be female in form, a young lioness? It provided no answer. For even if it had once emerged from stone all by itself, it had nevertheless made itself the way artists make their fraudulent images and pictures—or, better, represent, not make—so that nothing is there that cannot already be seen; and even if you called upon a hundred stonecutters to inquire about its sexual nature with hammers and chisels, it still would have none.

It was a sphinx, which means a riddle and a mystery, and a savage one at that, with the claws of a lion and a thirst for young blood—a threat to any child of God and a snare for any offspring of the promise. Alas for the stone tablet of the king's son! But on this stony breast, between the paws of this dragon-woman, you did not dream dreams of promise—or very meager ones at best. Crouching there in brutal immutability, with a nose eaten away by time and cruel open eyes gazing out at its river, the monster had nothing to do with promises, that was not the nature of its menacing riddle. It would endure drunkenly into the future, and yet that future was brutal and dead, for it was merely endurance and a false eternity, devoid of all expectancy.

Joseph stood there testing his heart against endurance's voluptuously smiling majesty. He stood very close to it . . . might not the monster raise a paw from the sand and snatch him, the boy, to its breast? He armed his heart and thought of Jacob. Sympathetic curiosity is a shallow-rooted weed, nothing more than youth's triumph in its freedom. Eye to eye with what is forbidden, a child knows what spirit has sired him, and holds to his father.

Joseph stood there beneath the stars and before the giant riddle for a long time, his weight on one leg, an elbow propped in one hand and his chin in the other. When he was once again lying beside Kedma in the tent, he dreamt of the sphinx, which said to him, "I love you. Come to me and name your name to me, whatever my nature may be." But he answered, "How can I do this great wickedness and sin against God?"

The House of the Wrapped God

They had traveled along the western bank, the bank on their right as they gazed straight ahead, and it was indeed the right one. For they did not need to cross the river to arrive at the great city of Mempi, which itself lay in the west—the most immense sheepfold for human beings that the eyes of Rachel's firstborn had ever seen, towered over by cliffs from which stone was quarried and in which the city buried its dead.

Mempi was so old that it left a man dizzy and reverent, to the extent the two are compatible. For at the beginning of all memory and the dynasties of kings had stood Meni, the first king, who had fortified the position to intimidate the Lower Land he had forced into his empire; and the mighty House of Ptah, built of eternal stones, was also the work of Meni, the first king, and so it had been standing here much longer than the pyramids beyond its walls, since a time behind which no man could peer.

But it was not as rigid silence that antiquity presented itself to the senses in Mempi, but as a city teeming with life and alert to the present, a vast conglomeration of more than a hundred thousand people, living in various quarters, each with its own name—a tangle of twisting narrow lanes, running uphill and down, each sloped to an open drainage ditch in the middle, each a reeking and roiling swirl of commonfolk caught up in gossip, trade, and toil. There were quarters smiling with wealth, where beautifully gated villas lay serenely set off amid delightful gardens, and constitutive temple compounds beneath fluttering banners, where tall, delicately painted arcades were reflected in sacred pools. There were boulevards of sphinxes, fifty ells wide, and grand tree-lined avenues along which rolled the chariots of the great, drawn by fiery steeds crowned with feathery plumes and preceded by panting footmen who cried out, "*Abrek!* Take hold of your heart! Pay heed!"

Yes, "*Abrek!*" Joseph might well have said that to himself and seen to his own heart if he wanted to avoid being helplessly intimidated by such exquisite refinement. For this was Mempi or Menfe, as the locals called it, a jaunty abbreviation of Men-nefru-Mirê, which meant "The beauty of Mirê abides"—of King Mirê, that is, from the sixth dynasty, who had extended the original temple fortress beyond his royal quarters and nearby built his own pyramid, in which his beauty was to abide. It had been his tomb, in fact, that had been called Men-nefru-Mirê, but finally the entire city that grew up around it called itself by that funereal name: Menfe, the balance scale of the Two Lands, city of the royal tomb.

How strange that Menfe's name was the jauntily abbreviated name of a tomb. Joseph was preoccupied with the idea. It had most assuredly been the commonfolk in those open-ditch lanes who wrapped their tongues so casually around the name, the lean-ribbed people of the crowded quarters of the city, in one of which the Ishmaelites had found lodging at a caravansary crammed with a pot-pourri of the human race—Syrians, Libyans, Nubians, Mitannis, and even Cretans—its filthy courtyard filled with bleating beasts and the squalling and strumming of begging blind musicians. Joseph set out on his own—this was no different from life in the cities of his homeland, merely on a larger scale and in an Egyptian mode. On both sides of the drainage ditch barbers scraped at their customers and cobblers tugged at straps with their teeth. Potters shaped hollow vessels, spinning them rapidly with skilled and clayey hands, all the while singing songs to Khnum the Creator, the goat-headed lord of the potter's wheel. Coffin makers applied their adzes to chests, carving them into human shapes with chin beards, and drunkards staggered out of noisy beer halls, followed by jeering boys whose youthful curls still hung down over their ears. So many people! They all wore the same linen skirt and cut their hair the same way; they all had the same squared shoulders and thin arms and raised their eyebrows in the same naive and impudent way. Their numbers were so great, and similarity in such numbers was the source of their ironic mood. How like them to have merrily simplified the formality of death into "Menfe," and in Joseph's breast the name rekindled familiar emotions, like those he had once explored while looking down from a hilltop at home toward the city of Hebron and the double cave, the inherited grave of his ancestors, and in his heart had felt a mixture of the piety that has its source in death and in the sympathy that the sight of a populous town inspires. It was a delicate and sweet mixture, uniquely appropriate to him and secretly corresponding both to the double blessing whose child he felt himself to be and to his wit, the messenger that moved back and forth between the two. And that was why his wit saw the humor in the popular name of this tomb metropolis, and his heart went out to those who had shortened it, to these lean-ribbed people moving along both sides of the ditches, so that he made it a point to chat with them in their tongue, to laugh with them and raise his eyebrows just as impudently—which was not difficult for him.

He did, by the way, indeed have a sense—one congenial to his soul—that their mockery came not only from there being so many of them, nor was it directed solely outward at others, but that the people of Menfe also made fun of themselves because of what the city had once been and had long since ceased to be. Their wit was the big-city version of that same peevishness that had colored the words of the people of Per-Sopd and its bitter temple attendants—a mood of obsolete antiquity, which here had become a joke, a skeptical mockery of both themselves and the world in general. For the fact was: the royal and thick-walled city of Menfe, the balance scale of the Two Lands, had occupied its throne long ago, in the age of pyramid builders. From Thebes, however, in the land high to the south, a city no one had heard of at a time when Menfe had already been world-renowned for innumerable years—from Thebes and its reigning dynasty of the sun had come a new age, a time of liberation and reunification after a damnable period of confusion and foreign rule, and Wase now wore the double crown and held the scepter, whereas Menfe, though teeming with people and great as always, was an erstwhile queen, the grave of its own greatness, a metropolis with an impertinently abbreviated name of death.

Not that Ptah, the lord in his shrine, had become an impoverished, neglected god like Sopdu to the east. No, his name was great throughout the nomes of Egypt, and this god in human form was rich in foundations, estates, and cattle, as was immediately apparent from the treasuries, granaries, stalls, and barns that made up the complex of his residence. The Lord Ptah, whom no one ever saw, for even when he made his processions in his barque or paid visits to other local divinities, his small image was hidden behind golden curtains and only the priests who served him had ever seen his face— Ptah resided in his temple with his wife, Sakhmet, or the Mighty One, who was depicted on the temple walls with the head of a lion and was said to love war, and their son Nefertêm, whose very name meant beautiful, but who was more obscure than either Ptah, the god in human form, or Sakhmet the Fierce. He was their son, but that was all anyone knew, and Joseph could inquire no further. At most, people knew that Nefertêm, the son, wore a lotus blossom on his head, yes, some believed that in his entirety he was nothing but a blue water rose. Such uncertainty, however, did not prevent the son's being the most beloved person of the triad of Menfe. Since it was at least established that the sky-blue lotus was his favorite flower and the perfect expression of his nature, his chamber was always lavished with bouquets of that beautiful plant, and even the Ishmaelites could not refrain from bringing him blue lotuses and paying homage to his popularity in a gesture of commercial goodwill.

Never before had their captive Joseph wandered amid forbidden things as he did here—that is, to the extent that his tradition's prohibition said "You shall not make for yourself a graven image." It was not for nothing, after all, that Ptah, the god who made works of art, was the patron of sculptors and craftsmen, who were said to realize the plans of his heart and to carry out his thoughts. Ptah's great residence was nothing but images; his house and the courts of his house were filled with figures. Hewn from the hardest stone, but sometimes also from limestone or sandstone, wood or copper, the thoughts of Ptah populated his halls, whose columns shimmered with images and rose, elephant-like, from millstone-shaped bases to capitals crowned with papyrus beneath gold-dusted beams. These statues stood, strode, or sat everywhere—alone or as embracing pairs and trios enthroned on benches, but with the children represented on a much smaller scale: royal images, the pleated front of the skirt spread out over the lap, with crooked staff and a caplike crown or a headscarf that fell down over the shoulders and made the ears stand out; all had refined, reserved faces, delicate chests, and hands pressed flat to their thighs—broad-shouldered, narrow-hipped lords of the ancient past, led by goddesses, who laid dainty but clumsy fingers around the muscular arms of their wards, while a falcon spread its wings behind their necks. King Mirê, who had made the city great, was a figure in copper who strode forth with his staff, his disproportionately small son at his side. His nose and lips were fleshy, and, like all the others, he neglected to lift the sole of his rear foot from the ground—he walked on both soles, standing as he walked, walking as he stood. Heads held high, they strode forth on sturdy legs, as if to leave behind them the stone columns that rose up from the backs of their pedestals, letting their arms dangle from right-angled shoulders and holding short, cylindrical pegs in their closed fists. They sat as scribes with their legs tucked under them, hands busy with the work spread out in their laps, but with clever eyes directed up at those observing them. Knees clenched, they sat together as man and wife, their skin painted in the most natural tones, as were hair and clothing, so that they were like the living dead, like static life. Often Ptah's artists had made eyes for them, eyes most terrible—not of the same stuff as their bodies, but inserted into the sockets, with a black stone set in glass as a pupil and within it, then, a tiny silver pin that flashed with life and gave these images' wide eyes a ghastly flickering stare, so that you did not know how to save yourself before that piercing, twitching gaze and hid your face in your hands.

These, then, were Ptah's static thoughts, residing in his house together with him, the lion mother, and the lotus son. He himself, the god in human form, was represented hundreds of times on his shrine's walls, not an inch of which lacked the magic of his art—in human form, to be sure, but it was an oddly doll-like and, as it were, abstract form, in one-legged profile with an elongated eye, a tightly fitting cap covering the head, and the wedge of a royal beard artificially attached to the chin. Like the fists holding the staff of power before it, the entire figure was strangely underdeveloped and reduced to a general outline; it seemed to be trapped in a sheath, in a narrow, disfiguring cover—or to be frank, seemed to have been wrapped in cloth and embalmed. . . . What was the Lord Ptah about? How did things stand with him? Had the ancient metropolis earned its graveyard name not only from the pyramid from which it was taken or because of its past, but also, and in fact primarily, as the home of its lord? Wherever his masters had led him on the way down to Egypt, Joseph had known he was going to the land Jacob condemned. And he fully recognized that, given his current condition, he belonged here and that what was once forbidden was not forbidden to him now, but aptly appropriate. Had he not at one point on their journey given himself a name that was meant to mark him as belonging to those who were native to this land? And yet he constantly harbored a grudge similar to his father's against his new surroundings and felt an ever-present itch to put the children of this land to the test, to ask them how things stood with their gods and their land of Egypt, so that they might betray it—both to him, who already knew, and to themselves, since they seemed not really to know.

That was how it was with Bata, the master baker of Menfe, whom they met at the sacrificial altar to Apis in the temple of Ptah.

For also living there—and alongside the unformed god, his static thoughts, the lioness, and the indistinct son—was Hapi, the great bull, the "living repetition" of the lord, sired by a ray from heaven in a cow that never again gave birth; and his testicles dangled as powerfully as those of Merwer in On. He lived behind bronze gates at the rear of an arcade open to the sky and adorned with relief tablets of splendid craftsmanship, each topped with a delicate line of molding that ran at half the height of the columns; and the stones of its courtyard were thronged with worshipers whenever Hapi's attendants led him out from the lamplit twilight of his chapel stall so that people might see the god alive and offer him sacrifices.

Joseph and his owners were on hand to watch such a ceremony—a remarkable abomination, but amusing as well, thanks to the good mood of the people of Menfe, men and women with fidgety children: an animated, festive crowd, chatting in expectation of the god, "kissing" (their word for "eating") sycamore figs and onions, letting the juice of melon slices drip down from the corners of their mouths at every bite, and haggling with merchants stationed at the sides of the court and peddling holy bread, sacrificial fowl, beer, incense, honey, and flowers.

A potbellied man in bast sandals was standing next to the Ishmaelites, and when the throng pressed them still closer together, they began to speak to one another. He was wearing a knee-length skirt of coarse linen with a triangular fold draped at the waist, and around his torso and arms he had wound all sorts of ribbons into which he had tied sacred knots. His short hair lay tight against his round skull, and his glassy, cheerful bug-eyes popped out all the more once his well-shaped, clean-shaven mouth began to chatter away. He had been inspecting the old man and his followers from one side for a good while before he spoke and, intrigued by their foreignness, asked them about their whence and whither. He himself was a baker, he explained, which was to say, he did not bake with his own two hands or stick his own head into the oven. He employed a half dozen apprentices and delivery boys, who crisscrossed the city, carrying his very good crescents and twists in baskets on their heads;

and woe to them if they didn't pay attention and forgot to wave an arm above their wares to keep the birds of the heavens from diving to pilfer from their baskets. Any bread carrier guilty of that was "taught a lesson," as Bata the master baker put it. For that was his name. He also owned several fields outside the city, and it was their grain that he baked. But it was never enough, for his was a major enterprise, and he had to buy additional grain. He had come out today to see the god, which was to his advantage inasmuch as it was to his disadvantage to fail to do so. Meanwhile his wife was visiting the Great Mother in her house and offering flowers to Isis, to whom she was especially devoted, whereas he, Bata, found greater satisfaction in this spot. And so, the baker asked, they were traveling through the Two Lands for commercial reasons, were they?

Such was the case, the old man replied. And they had more or less reached their goal in reaching Menfe, grand in its gates, rich in residences and eternal edifices, and could now just as well turn back.

He was very much obliged, the baker said. They could, but presumably would not; for like the rest of the world they probably regarded this old dump of a city as only a tread beneath their feet on the stairway to the splendors of Amun. They would be the first travelers to do otherwise, to have any other goal than Weset, the brand-spanking new city of Pharaoh—may he live a long, healthy life!—to which people and treasures flowed and for which Menfe's weather-beaten name was now only good enough for Pharaoh's courtiers and chief eunuchs to boast of in their titles—just as, for instance, the god's head baker, who supervised the palace bakeries, was called Prince of Menfe, though not entirely without justification, one had to admit, for it was certainly true that fine cakes in the shape of cows and snails had been delivered to the houses of Menfe back when Amun's people had still been content just to gobble down roasted grain.

The old man replied that, yes, well, they would, after a significant sojourn in Menfe, probably also cast a glance at Wase just to see to what extent it had caught up by now in matters of refinement and the embellishment of baked goods—when with a drum roll the rear gate opened and the god was led out into the courtyard, but only a few steps beyond the open doors. And great was the excitement of the crowd. Hopping about on one leg, people shouted, "Hapi! Hapi!" and anyone with enough room threw himself on his face and kissed the ground. Everywhere spines twisted and bent low, and hundreds of throats filled the air with the guttural huffing sound with which the god's name began. It was also the name of the river that had created and still preserved the land. It was the name of this sun-bull, the embodiment of all those powers of fertility on which these people knew they depended, the name of continued existence for both the land and its people, the name of life. Easygoing and talkative these people might be, but they were deeply moved, for their devotions contained all the hope and anxiety with which a precisely limited existence can fill the human breast. Their thoughts were of the flood, which dared not be one ell too high or too low if life was to have stability; of the fitness of their wives and the health of their children; of their own bodies and of those easily jeopardized functions that supplied pleasure and comfort if all went smoothly, but fierce torments when they failed and that had to be safeguarded by employing magic against magic; of the enemies of the land to the south, east, and west; of Pharaoh, whom they likewise called the Strong Bull and who, as they knew, was cherished and preserved in his palace at Thebes as carefully as Hapi was here, for in his transitory person he protected them and established the link between them and that on which all else depended. "Hapi! Hapi!" they cried in anxious jubilation, haunted by the sense of how brief and imperiled their lives were, and stared with hope at the god beast's square brow, iron horns, and stocky neck, running in an unbroken line from spine to skull, and at his sexual organs, the guarantors of fertility. "Security!"—that is what their cries meant. "Protection and permanence!" "Long live the land of Egypt!"

Ptah's living repetition was extraordinarily beautiful—but then, since experts spent years searching for the most beautiful bull between the swamps of the Delta and Elephant Island, he surely ought to have been. He was black; and the scarlet saddlecloth across his back was a splendid, if not to say divine, match for his own blackness. Two bald attendants in pleated skirts of some gold fabric, which left the navel exposed but rose halfway up the back, held him, one on each side, with golden cords, and the attendant on the right lifted the blanket for the crowd to show them a white spot on Hapi's flank that they were to regard as a symbol of the crescent moon. A priest, across whose back was hung a leopard skin, including tail and paws, bowed low and, placing one foot before the other, held out his long-handled censing bowl toward the bull, who lowered his head and sniffed, flaring thick, moist nostrils tickled by the spicy smoke. He gave a mighty sneeze, which only redoubled the crowd's urgent cries and one-legged hops for joy. As accompaniment to the censing ritual, crouching harpists, faces turned heavenward, sang hymns, while behind them other singers clapped in time. Women appeared now as well, temple girls with hair hanging free, one of them naked and adorned only with a cord belt above her wide hips, the other in a long garment delicate as a veil and open to the front, which likewise left the fullness of her youth in plain view. Shaking sistrums and tambourines above their heads, they danced around the spectacle, extending a leg from the hip with each long stride and raising it to an amazing height. A lector priest sat down facing the crowd at the feet of the bull and, rocking his head, began to chant a text from his scroll, with the people joining in at the constant refrain of "Hapi is Ptah. Hapi is Rê. Hapi is Hor, the son of Eset!" This was followed by the entrance, amid waving feathered fans, of an obviously high-ranking attendant in a long and wide batiste skirt with shoulder straps, a proud man with a shaven head who held before him a basin of spices and herbs, which—by skillfully creeping forward, one leg thrust wide behind and the other foot on tiptoe and tucked as far underneath as possible—he now shoved forward with both hands as a gift to the god.

Hapi paid no attention. Accustomed to all this fuss being made on his behalf and to the life of solemn boredom that was his melancholy fate thanks to certain physical hallmarks, he stood with legs spread and let his little, bloodshot bull's eyes sweep in dull cunning beyond those offering sacrifices to him and out into the hopping, leaping throng, who, one hand on their chests, the other stretched out to him, were shouting his holy name. They were so happy to see him bound by golden ropes and to know that he was in the safe custody of the temple, constrained by the guards who served him. He was their god and their prisoner. In reality, it was in honor of his imprisonment and the security it gave them that they made their leaps and called out to him in joy; and perhaps his gaze was so cunning and wicked because he understood that despite all the ceremonial fuss their intentions were not all that good.

Bata the master baker, being a stout man, did not hop about with joy, but, visibly edified by the sight of Hapi, he, too, responded to the lector's chant in a powerful voice and greeted the god over and over by prostrating himself and raising his hands.

"It does one good to see him," he explained to his neighbors. "It strengthens one's vital spirits and helps restore one's confidence. It has been my experience that when I see Hapi, I need nothing more to eat the whole day, for it is as if a hearty meal of beef were coursing through my limbs, and with my belly full I then become drowsy, and after a nap I awaken as if newborn. He is a very great god, the living repetition of Ptah. You should know that his grave awaits him in the West, for the order has been given that upon his death he is to be salted and wrapped, using the finest resins and cloths of royal linen, with no expense spared, and as custom demands be entombed in the eternal house of divine animals in the City of the Dead. It has been so ordered," he said, "and so it will be. Already two Usar-Hapis lie resting in their stony chests in the Eternal House of the West."

The old man cast Joseph a glance that the slave took as encouragement to test this man with a question. "Have this man explain to you," he asked, "why he says that Usar-Hapi's eternal home awaits him in the West, since it is not really in the West at all, but in Menfe itself, a city of the living, which is situated on the west bank, so that the dead are not ferried across the river."

Turning to the baker, the old man told him the lad's question. "Do you care to reply?"

"I spoke as everyone does," the Egyptian answered, "and gave it no thought. For we all speak that way and think nothing of it. The West is simply the West, the City of the Dead in our language. But it is true that the dead of Menfe do not travel across the river as in other places, but that the city of the living is likewise already in the West. According to reason, your lad is right to object. But according to our usage, what I said is correct."

"Then ask him this as well," Joseph said. "If Hapi, the beautiful bull, is the living Ptah in the eyes of the living, what then is Ptah in his shrine?"

"Ptah is great," the baker replied.

"Tell him I do not doubt that," Joseph responded. "But Hapi is called Usar-Hapi once he has died, and by the same token Ptah in his barque is Osiris and is said to have a human form because he has the shape of the bearded chests that the carpenters turn out and appears to be wrapped in cloths. What is he then?"

"Instruct the lad," the baker said, "that the priest enters Ptah's chamber daily to open his mouth with a powerful tool, so that he may drink and eat, and renews the color of life on his cheeks daily as well. That is the service and care he renders."

"Which leads me to ask politely," Joseph replied, "what happens to the dead man at the door to his grave, with Anup standing behind, and what sort of service is it that the priest renders for the mummy?"

"He doesn't know even that?" the baker retorted. "It is quite obvious that he is a sand-dweller, an utter stranger, and a recent arrival in the land. I would have you tell him that this service consists, above all, in the so-called opening of the mouth, which we call that because the attending priest opens the dead man's mouth with a special staff, so that he may again eat and drink and enjoy the nourishing offerings brought to him. Moreover, in token of a return to life in accord with Usir's example, the priest of the dead paints the mummy a rosy hue, which is a comfort to those who mourn him."

"I hear and am grateful," Joseph said. "So that, then, is the difference between the service offered the gods and that offered the dead. But now ask master Bata what materials are used for building in Egypt."

"Your lad," the baker replied, "is pretty, but stupid. For the living, we build with Nile bricks. Whereas both the dwellings of the dead and our temples are of eternal stone."

"I hear this," Joseph said, "with many thanks. But if the same holds true of two things, then the two are the same and one may interchange them with impunity. Egypt's graves are temples, but its temples—"

"Are houses of the gods," the baker finished the thought.

"As you say. Egypt's dead are gods, and your gods, what are they?"

"The gods are great," Bata the baker responded. "That I can tell from the full belly and drowsiness that have come over me at the sight of Hapi. I wish to return home and lie down for my nap of rebirth. My wife will also have returned from serving the Great Mother by now. May you be well, strangers. Rejoice and journey in peace."

And with that, he departed.

But the old man said to Joseph, "The man's god made him weary, and you should not have used me to press him with captious questions."

"But your slave," Joseph said, justifying himself, "must surely inquire about all such things, that he may find his way into the life of Egypt, seeing as you wish to leave him here and should his stay prove permanent. Everything here is strange and new enough in this lad's eyes. For the children of Egypt worship in graves, whether they call them temples or eternal dwellings; at home, however, we follow the custom of our fathers and worship beneath green trees. Do these children not give you pause to think and laugh? For them, Hapi is now Ptah's living form, and, I would say, Ptah can certainly use one since he himself has obviously been wrapped in cloths and is a corpse. But they cannot rest until they have also wrapped his living form and turned him as well into a divine mummy and another Osiris, or else they are not satisfied. But I feel a fondness for Menfe, whose dead need not travel across the water, because it already lies in the West—this great city, so full of people, who have no trouble abbreviating its graveyard name. It is a shame that the house of blessing, the house of Peteprê the fan-bearer, to which you wish to bring me, is not in Menfe, for of all the cities of Egypt it might well suit me."

"You are much too immature," the old man responded, "to decide what is to your benefit. I, however, know that and bestow it upon you as would a father; for I am surely that to you, if we assume that your mother is the pit. At the earliest hour tomorrow we shall board ship and travel through the land of Egypt for nine days, moving upstream toward the south, so that we may set foot upon the shimmering shore of Weset-per-Amun, the royal city."

Part Three

THE ARRIVAL

Journey by River

Sparkling with Speed was the name of the ship up whose gangplank the Ishmaelites strode with their animals, but only after having first secured nine days' worth of provisions at trading booths set up along the river landing. That was its name, written on both sides of a prow decorated with the head of a goose—a name born of the Egyptian love of boasting, for it was the bulkiest freighter to be found anywhere on Menfe's quay, with a big belly for holding more cargo, wooden lattice along its sides, a cabin that was merely a vaulted canopy of mats open to the front, and a single, but very heavy, rudder rising at a sharp angle and attached to a pole at its stern.

The boat's captain was named Thot-nofer, a man from the north, with rings on his ears and white hair on his head and chest, whose acquaintance the old man had made at the inn and with whom he had come to an agreement for a cheap fare. Thot-nofer's boat had already taken on lumber, one bale each of royal and coarse linen, papyrus, cowhides, and ship's rope, twenty sacks of lentils and thirty casks of dried fish. In addition, *Sparkling with Speed* had on board a statue, the likeness of a rich citizen of Thebes, that stood in protective sackcloth and crating far forward at the prow. It had been commissioned for the man's "good house," that is, for his grave on the west side of the river, where, stepping out of a false door, it was to survey its—or better, the grave's occupant's—eternal possessions and the representations of his daily life painted on the walls. The eyes with which it would do this had not yet been inserted, nor had it been tinted with the colors of life, and it lacked the walking stick that would pass through the fist extended at the side of the flaring front of the skirt. But the model had insisted that his double chin and stout legs be executed, at least in the rough, under the eyes of Ptah and by the hand of his artists—final touches could then be added in a workshop in Thebes' City of the Dead.

At noon the crew untied the ship from its moorings and raised the patched brown sail, which immediately filled with a stiff breeze from the north. The helmsman, sitting on the steeply slanted beak of the stern, began to work the rudder with a lever jutting out from under it; a man stationed forward at the goose head tested the channel with a pole, while Thot-nofer, the captain, stood in front of the cabin and, burning some of the resin with which the Ishmaelites had paid their fare, implored the gods to grant them an easy voyage. And so this barque, curved high at both fore and aft and with only the middle of the keel cutting the water, bore Joseph out onto the river, while the old man, who was sitting with his family on the pile of lumber stored behind the cabin, launched into observations on how wise life was, so that its benefits and drawbacks balanced and canceled each other out, establishing a middling perfection between not-all-too-good and not-all-too-bad. So now, he said, they were traveling upstream, against the current, whereas the wind was from the north, as it almost always was here, pushing helpfully at the sail, so that thrust and impediment cooperated for a measured progress. Going downstream was, to be sure, quite amusing, because you could let yourself drift along—except that it was very easy for the motion to get out of hand, leaving the boat athwart the river, and that meant exhausting rowing and steering to keep the journey from turning topsy-turvy. Thus life's benefits were always held in check by its drawbacks, and its drawbacks compensated for by its benefits, so that in purely mathematical terms the result was naught and nothing, but in practical terms, it was the wisdom of balance and of middling perfection—in light of which neither jubilation nor curses were in order, but rather contentment. For perfection did not consist of a one-sided amassing of benefits, just as life would be impossible if it were naught but drawbacks. Instead, life was made up of the mutual cancellation of benefit and drawback, resulting in nothing, which was to say, contentment.

These, then, were the words the old man spoke with raised finger and tilted head, and his followers listened with slack mouths, exchanging the stubborn, sheepish glances of ordinary people offered higher wisdom that they would prefer not to have to listen to. But Joseph, too, was paying scant attention to the old man's distilled wisdom, for he was enjoying this new experience of travel by water—the fresh breeze, the melodic gurgle of the waves striking the bow, the gentle, gliding roll over the vast river, whose flood glittered as it leapt up toward them, the way the earth had once leapt up to greet Eliezer on his journey. Serene, fertile, sacred—the scenery was in constant motion along the banks, often lined with pillared arcades, some furnished with a grove of palms, or, just as frequently, stony galleries hewn by human hand and belonging to city temples. Villages with their tall dovecotes glided past, then verdant fertile land, soon relieved again by the gaudy urban splendor of glittering golden spires of the sun, pennant-hung pylons, and giants seated in pairs beside the river and gazing, hands on knees, in lofty rigidity out across river and countryside to the desert. At times it was all very close—and then far away again, whenever they took to the middle of the river, whose waters could widen into a lake or follow twisting curves, revealing new scenes of Egypt lying hidden behind them. Fine entertainment was also to be found on the sacred avenue itself—the grand highway of Egypt, where wind swelled a panoply of sails, both coarse and elegant, and a multitude of rowers braced themselves against the current. The air was filled with voices carrying easily across the water—of boatsmen hallooing and joking, of pole-men at the beaked prows calling out warnings of eddies and shoals, of captains on the roofs of cabins giving singsong instructions to men at the sails and rudders. There were lots of ordinary boats like Thot-nofer's, but elegant and trim barques sailed by as well, either coming toward *Sparkling with Speed* or passing it—painted blue, with short masts and broad, dove-white sails billowing with the modest tempo, with sterns shaped like a lotus blossom and delicate pavilions instead of cabin huts. There were temple barques with purple sails and large paintings at the bow, and the noble and stylish river craft of the powerful, twelve oarsmen on each side, the cabin built with columns at its entrance and enough room on the roof for the baggage and chariot of its elegant owner, who sat between walls of magnificent tapestries, hands in his lap, and gazed neither to the right or left, as if frozen amid such beauty and wealth. They also met a funeral procession, three ships roped together, one behind the other, and in the last, a white boat without sail or rudder, a brightly painted Osiris lay headfirst on lion-footed trestles, surrounded by his mourners.

Yes, there was much to see, both on the banks and on the river, and for Joseph, sold into slavery, the days passed like hours beneath the smile of his first journey on water—and what a journey it was. How accustomed he would one day become to this mode of travel, and how familiar to him this stretch between Amun's house and the witty graveyard town of Menfe would become! And like those nobles in their tapestried shrines, that is how, by the decree of Providence, he would sit one day in stately immobility—which he would have to learn because the people expected it of their gods and great men. For, under God's care, he was to conduct himself so wisely and with such grace that he became first among those in the West, entitled to sit there looking neither to the right nor to the left. All this had been set aside for him. But for now he still looked right and left as much as he could, soaking up this land and the life of this land with his senses and mind, but always taking care that his curiosity not degenerate into confusion and pointless intimidation, but instead maintain a cheerful reserve in honor of his fathers.

So morning and evening were days, and the days increased in number. Menfe lay behind them now, as did the day on which they had set sail. When the sun sank, the desert beyond turned violet and the Arabian sky to their left softly reflected the extravagant orange glow in the Libyan sky to their right, and then they tied up wherever they happened to be and slept, to continue their journey come morning. The wind was almost always favorable, except for days of calm. Then they had to row, and the slave Usarsiph and the younger Ishmaelites lent a hand, for their boat did not have a large crew and they were falling behind, which upset Thot-nofer, since the statue for the grave had to be delivered on time. But the delay was not serious, because on other days the canvas had billowed all the fuller, and benefits and drawbacks were canceled out to their satisfaction. And on the ninth evening they saw jagged peaks rising in marvelous rose-colored transparency against the distance and looking like red corundum, although everyone knew that they were as parched and dead, as cursed as all the mountains of Egypt. Both the ship's captain and the old man recognized them as the mountains of Amun, the heights of No; and once they had slept and set sail again, even manning the oars in their impatience, it all began—with a flash of gold up ahead, a delicate shimmer of the colors of the rainbow—and soon they were entering Pharaoh's city, the city of fable and renown, as was evident from their boat even before they landed, for the river became a ceremonial boulevard, flowing between rows of celestial edifices set amid the green bliss of gardens, between temples and palaces to the right and left, between the banks of death and life, between colonnades of papyrus and colonnades of lotus, between golden-tipped obelisks, colossal statues, and sphinx-lined avenues that led away from the river and ended at turreted pylons whose doors and flagpoles were covered in gold—which was the source of the flashes of light that left eyes blinking, until what was painted and written on building walls, in cinnamon red, plum purple, emerald green, ocher yellow, and azure blue, blurred to a chaotic sea of color.

"That is Ipet-Isowet, the great House of Amun," the old man said to Joseph, pointing with one finger. "It has a hall fifty ells wide, with two hundred and fifty columns and pillars like tent poles, and the hall, should you have no objection, is paved with silver."

"I certainly have no objection," Joseph replied. "I knew, of course, that Amun is a very wealthy god."

"Those are the god's wharves," the old man resumed, pointing to basins and dry docks to his left, where countless aproned workers, the god's carpenters, busied themselves among ship skeletons with drills, hammers, and pitch. "That is Pharaoh's Temple of the Dead and this is his House of Life," he said, indicating various points in a complex of buildings further inland to the west, its splendor due in part to its immensity, in part to its charm. "That is Amun's Southern House of Women," he said, returning to the other bank, directing his finger to an extensive group of temples at river's edge, their façades dazzling in the sunlight, though with porticos sharply etched by dark shadows, and bustling with industrious men obviously still busy at construction. "Do you see all this beauty? Do you see the Secret Place of the Royal Conception? Do you notice how Pharaoh is building a hall directly in front of that other hall and court, its columns taller than all the rest? My friend, what we see rising before us is Nowet-Amun, the proud. Surely you have caught sight of the Street of the Rams there, leading overland from the Southern House of Women to the Great House? You should know that it is five thousand ells long and lined with nothing but Amun's rams to both right and left, each bearing Pharaoh's image between its legs."

"It's all very nice," Joseph said.

"Nice?" the old man said, flaring up. "What words you choose for me from the storehouse of language—absurdly inept words, I must say, and your responses to the grandeur of Weset give me little satisfaction."

"I said *very* nice," Joseph replied. "As nice as you wish. But where is the house of the fan-bearer that you intend to bring me to? Can you point it out to me?"

"No, it can't be made out from here," the old man rejoined. "There, toward the desert to the east, where the city is not so dense, but opens up into the gardens and villas of the wealthy, that's where it is."

"And will you bring me to that house today yet?"

"You can't wait, can you, for me to bring you there and sell you? Do you know whether the steward of the house will take you and offer me enough for you that I can cover my costs and pocket a small, but fair profit as well? There has been many a change of moon since I delivered you from the well, your mother, and many a day's journey during which you have baked cakes for me and from the storehouse of language selected words with which to wish me good-night. It may well be that the time has grown long for you and you are weary of us and desirous of some new service. But it might equally be true that this same sum of days has become a habit, so that you might find it difficult to take leave of an old Minæan from Ma'on, your midwife, and be content to wait out the hours until he departs and leaves you in the hands of strangers. Those are the two possibilities that can be drawn from the sum of days we have wandered together."

"The latter," Joseph said, "the latter is the reality far outweighing any other. I most certainly am in no haste to be separated from you, my deliverer. My only haste is to arrive where God wishes to have me."

"Be patient," the old man replied. "We shall land and be put to the botheration to which the children of Egypt subject new arrivals, and that takes a long time. After that we shall proceed to the heart of the city, to an inn I know and spend the night. Tomorrow, however, I shall bring you to the house of blessing and offer you for sale to Mont-kaw, its steward and my friend."

As they were speaking they crossed over from the middle of the river and arrived in port, or, better, to the place where they were to tie up, and meanwhile Thot-nofer, their captain, once again burned balsam in front of the cabin in gratitude for their successful journey—and their arrival was subjected to all the tedious formality and time-consuming botheration that any such arrival by ship at any port ever is or has been. For they found themselves amid the hubbub and clamor of the quay and the water before it, where there was a crush of a good many ships, both local and foreign, that had already tied up or were requesting permission to fling their ropes the moment a post was free; and *Sparkling with Speed* was boarded by harbor police and customs agents, who began writing up their report on every man, mouse, and stick of cargo, while on shore the servants of the man who had ordered the statue stood with outstretched arms, shouting for the item they had been awaiting for some time now, and, alongside them, peddlers were trying to sell sandals, caps, and honey cakes to the new arrivals, their loud voices blending with the bleats of herds being unloaded from a nearby ship and the music of jugglers on the quay trying to draw attention to themselves. It was all one great confusion, and Joseph and his fellow travelers sat, silent and helpless, on the pile of lumber in the aft of the ship and waited for the moment when they could disembark and go in search of their inn—though that would take some time yet. For the old man had to appear before customs and register himself and everyone in his party, as well as pay duties on his wares. He knew how to handle these men, how to establish a wise and human, rather than an official, relationship with them, so that they laughed and, in exchange for small gifts, were not all too particular about the traveling merchant's arrival. And a few hours after they had flung their ropes, Joseph's owners were able to lead their camels down the gangplank and, quite unnoticed by a crowd accustomed to every sort of skin color and garb, they worked their way through the motley tumult of the harbor quarter.

Joseph Passes Through Wase

The city whose name the Greeks would later find it easier and more natural to pronounce as "Thebai" was not yet anywhere near the height of its fame when Joseph arrived to live there—although its fame was already evident both from what the Ishmaelite said of it and from the emotions that overcame Joseph when he learned he had arrived at his goal. Since the dark, narrow days of its beginnings, it had been growing for a long time and was well on the road to its full beauty; but it still fell short in many ways of that point where its magnificence would be incapable of further growth or enhancement and it would pause in its perfection as one of the Seven Wonders of the World—both, as was already the case, in its entirety and, more especially, because of one of its parts: the incomparably splendid and spectacularly vast hall of columns that a later Pharaoh, by the name of Ra-messu or The Sun Has Sired Him, added to the north of the complex of buildings of the great temple of Amun at an expense commensurate with that level of importance the god could by then claim to have achieved. Joseph's eyes beheld as little of all that as they had noticed of past ages in the vicinity of the pyramids, but for the opposite reason—that is, because they had not yet attained a present that no one had the courage to imagine. For that to become possible, many other things would first have to be built, which human imagination, in having grown accustomed to them, would find increasingly inadequate and could then surpass—for example, the great silver-paved hall of Ipet-Isowet that was familiar to the old man, who compared its fifty columns to tent poles, and had been built by the third predecessor of the current god; or the hall that the latter was now having built as an extension of Amun's Southern House of Women, surpassing, as Joseph himself had seen, even that beautiful temple beside the river. Such beauty must first be imagined and executed in the belief that it is the ultimate, so that man's insatiable desire may find a foothold there and imagine and realize in its own day what is truly ultimate—utter beauty that can never be enhanced, the wonder of the world, the Hall of Ramses.

Although all of this was not yet known to Joseph or his, that is, our time, but was still under way, as it were, Wase, known also as Nowet-Amun, the capital on the Nile, was, even at this stage, cause for greatest wonder to the far ends of the earth, or at least to those that knew of it, and, indeed, the report of it was exaggerated—for human beings love to collude in celebrating fame, are unanimous and stubbornly insistent about it merely on hearsay and for decorum's sake if nothing else, so that people would have looked askance and more or less ostracized anyone who might have publicly expressed doubts that No in the land of Egypt was great and beautiful beyond measure, the epitome of architectural splendor, or, put simply, a dream of a city. For us, who have descended to it—descended, that is, in a spatial sense, by moving upstream with Joseph, and also in the temporal sense of descending into a past where, even at these relatively moderate depths, the city still seethes, shouts, and shimmers, its temples still crystal-clear reflections in the serene mirrors of sacred ponds—for us, our relationship with Wase is necessarily reminiscent of our relationship with Joseph, who was so idealistically ballyhooed in song and saga and whose ostensibly fantastic beauty, when we first glimpsed it in reality beside the well, we attributed to the human standards of his day, but which, despite rumors that had embellished his beauty quite unnecessarily, still left us with winning charms enough.

So, too, then, with No, the heavenly city. Not that it was built of heavenly stuff, but like any other city, of smoothed brick mixed with straw, and its streets were, as Joseph observed to his relief, as narrow, crooked, filthy, and foul-smelling as the streets of any human settlement, large or small, always has been and will be in these climes—at least that was true of the extensive quarters of the poor, whose numbers, as usual, far exceeded those of the rich, who lived in sweeter, more spacious surroundings. If out in the larger world—on the islands of the sea and still more distant shores—it was said and sung that Wase's "houses were rich in treasure," that applied, apart from the temples where gold was measured by the shovelful, to only a very few that Pharaoh himself had made rich; the great majority had no treasures whatever to hide, but were as poor as the people who lived on islands and distant shores and basked in the legendary glow of Wase's riches.

As for No's size, it was held to be enormous, and so it was, with the qualification that "enormous" is not a self-contained, unambiguous concept, but rather is relative and applicable in one instance or, indeed, another, depending entirely on one's personal and general views. But as regards the chief hallmark of Wase's size in the eyes of the world, the term was the result of an out-and-out misunderstanding, for it was said to be "the city of a hundred gates." On Cyprus-Alashia, on Crete, and elsewhere, it was said that Egypt's capital had a hundred gates, and this title was spoken with mythical awe, for it was said that from each of those one hundred gates, two hundred men with chargers in harness could ride forth to battle. It is quite obvious: these chatterboxes were thinking of an encircling wall of such circumference that it could be broken not by four or five but by a hundred city gates—a childish notion, conceivable only if one had never seen Wase with one's own eyes and knew it only from hearsay and legend. In a certain sense, the concept of a multitude of gates was rightly associated with the city of Amun; it did indeed have many "gates," but these were not sally ports cut through its walls, but engagingly massive pylons, sparkling with the colors of their densely packed magical inscriptions and painted reliefs, with bright pennants fluttering above them on gilded flagpoles—each erected one by one in the course of many jubilees and grand progresses by bearers of the double crown as a supplementary adornment to the shrines of the gods. There were indeed a lot of them, although many more were still to come before the days of Wase's perfect and unrivaled beauty—but never a "hundred," either then or later. A hundred, however, is simply a round number, and as it passes our lips often means no more than "a good many." Ipet-Isowet, Amun's Great House in the North, contained six or seven such "gates" within it even then, and the smaller temples in its vicinity—the houses of Khonsu and Mut, of Mont, Min, and Ipet, who took the form of a hippopotamus—each had a few. The other great temple by the river, Amun's Southern House of Women (also simply called "the Harem"), had several more pylon gates, and others belonged to the dwellings of divinities who, while not truly local, had at least taken up residence here and were supplied with nourishment—the houses of Usir and Eset, of Menfe's Ptah, of Thoth and others.

These temple precincts, surrounded by gardens, groves, and ponds, formed the core of the city; they were in effect the city itself, and its profane part, mere lodgings of human beings, filled up the spaces between them, stretching from the harbor area and Amun's House of Women in the south toward the temple complex in the northeast and traversed lengthwise by the god's great ceremonial road, the boulevard lined with rams and sphinxes that the old man had already pointed out to Joseph from the ship. That was an imposing distance of five thousand ells; and since this processional avenue ran inland, to the northeast and away from the Nile, the residential city not only occupied the area between it and the river on one side, but also extended eastward beyond the avenue toward the desert on the other, where the city opened up into the gardens and villas of the aristocracy—there where "the houses were rich in treasure." Amun was indeed very large, indeed enormous, if you like. It was said that more than a hundred thousand people lived within it; and if one hundred represents a poetic, upward rounding-off of the number of gates, then one hundred thousand as a large number referring to Wase's great population had doubtlessly been rounded off downward. If in our overview we may trust both our and Joseph's estimate, there were not just *more* inhabitants than that, but indeed many more, possibly two or three times as many, especially, indeed certainly, if one were to include the population residing in the City of the Dead to the west, on the far side of the river, which was also referred to as Face-to-Face with Its Lord—not the dead themselves, but the living who resided there for serious professional reasons, because they fulfilled some cultic function or worked as craftsmen in the service of those who had departed and been ferried across the water. These people and their dwellings formed a city unto itself, which, if included in Wase as a whole, made it very great. Pharaoh himself was one of them, since he did not live in the City of the Living; for far to the west, on the edge of the desert and beneath its red cliffs, his palace stood in airy elegance, and there, too, were the pleasure gardens of his palace, with a lake and dancing fountains that had not been there before.

A very great city, then, and great not only in extent and numbers, but truly great as well in the intensity of its inner spirit and diversity, its potpourri of races that lent it the vitality of a market fair—great as the core and focus of the world, of which it considered itself the navel, a presumptuous notion in Joseph's eyes, and debatable on other grounds as well. After all there was still Babel on the Euphrates, which flowed backward, but where people thought just the opposite, that it was Egypt's river that flowed backward, and had no doubt that the rest of the world was arranged in an admiring circle around Bab-ilu, even though it, too, had not yet achieved its full beauty in architectural terms. It was not for nothing, however, that the people of Joseph's homeland liked to say of Amun's city that "her strength lay in Nubians and Egyptians without number and people of Punt and Libyans lent her their aid." Even as he first crossed through the city with the Ishmaelites on the way from the riverbank to the inn, which lay deep within narrow confines, Joseph took in a hundred impressions that confirmed the lines of the song. No one looked at him and his party, for the foreign was the ordinary here, nor were they conspicuously odd enough to attract attention, making it all the easier for him to look about. And if there was some reserve in his glance, that was due at most to a concern that the crush of so great a world might befuddle his spiritual pride and leave him intimidated.

But what all he did see on his way from the harbor to the inn! What a wealth of wares spilled out from under arches, and the streets surged and bustled with every stock and stamp of Adam's children. The entire population of Wase seemed to be out and about, passing from one end of the city to the other on some urgent errand, and then back again; and mixed in with those who had ancient roots here were human types and costumes from the four corners of the earth. On the quay itself there had been a hubbub centered around a group of ebony-black Moors with incredible lips like padded cushions and ostrich feathers in their hair—men and doe-eyed women with breasts like goatskins and comical children in baskets on their backs. They were leading animals on chains, panthers emitting terrifying snarls and baboons walking on all fours; towering above them was a giraffe, tall as a tree at the front, but merely like a horse at the rear, and there were greyhounds, too. The Moors also carried objects hidden under golden veils, their value doubtless worthy of such wrappings—presumably gold and ivory. This was, so Joseph learned, a tribute carried by a delegation from the land of Kush, which lay to the south of the land of Weset, far upriver, but it was only a small tribute, nothing obligatory, but sent on the spur of the moment by the administrator of those southern lands, the viceroy and prince of Kush, to delight and win Pharaoh's heart with a surprise from his prince, so that His Majesty might not take it into his head to recall him and replace him with some lord from his immediate entourage, men who kept dinning his ears about this choice post and castigating its present occupant at levees in the royal morning chamber. The strange thing was that the denizens of the harbor gawking at this delegation—even street urchins making fun of the giraffe and its palm-tree neck—knew exactly what was behind this spectacle, knew about the viceroy's worries and the carping in the royal chamber, and they held forth at length in loud, derogatory phrases about it within earshot of Joseph and the Ishmaelites. What a shame, Joseph thought, that such cold knowledge deprived them of the pure and simple pleasure of enjoying this colorful display. But perhaps they saw it as giving it an added spice; and he, for his part at least, was happy to eavesdrop on what they said, since he considered it useful to learn a little something on the sly about the confidential, private secrets of this world—how the prince of Kush trembled for his office, how courtiers castigated him, how Pharaoh liked to be surprised—for all that strengthened his self-assurance and armed him against intimidation.

Guarded and guided by Egyptian officials, the Negroes were ferried across the river so that they might come before Pharaoh—Joseph watched them go, and he also saw a few others of the same skin color on the way to the inn. He saw skin of every shade, from obsidian black through all the stages of brown and yellow to cheesy white, he even saw yellow hair and azure-colored eyes, faces and garments of every cut—he saw humanity. That was because ships from the foreign lands with which Pharaoh traded quite frequently did not stop in the harbors of the Delta region, but instead chose to set sail upstream before the north wind and unload their cargo, be it tribute or goods to trade, at the very spot where it would all end up anyway, in Pharaoh's storehouse—to the enrichment of both Amun and his friends, so that the former might continue to augment his architectural demands and surpass what already existed, and the latter might add ultimate refinement to their lives, culminating an exquisiteness whose elegance could indeed degenerate into foolishness.

This was how the old man explained it to Joseph, who now noticed that besides Moors from Kush, the populace of Wase included Bedouins from the land of God along the Red Sea; pale-faced Libyans from the oases of the western desert, dressed in bright knitted skirts, their hair in plaited, stiff braids jutting out from their heads; people of Amu and Asia like himself, in colorful woolens, with the beards and noses he knew from home; Chettite men from beyond the Amanus Mountains, who wore close-fitting shirts and bagwigs; merchants from Mitanni in the dignified layers of the fringed garments of Babel; traders and sailors from the islands and from Mycenae, clad in white woolens that fell in pleasing folds, with bronze rings on the arm not hidden under their robes—they were all there, even though out of modesty the old man led his little procession down the poorest streets of the commonfolk, avoiding noble avenues so as not to detract from their beauty. But he couldn't avoid detracting from it entirely. The lovely Avenue of Khonsu, which ran parallel to the god's ceremonial avenue, the Street of the Son, as it was called, because the moon god Khons was the son of Amun and Mut, his Baalat, and was what Nefertêm, the blue lotus, was for Menfe, forming, together with his great parents, the triad of Weset—his street, then, was a main artery, truly an avenue for *abrek,* for constantly taking hold of one's heart. And the Ishmaelites found they had to follow it for a while, despite the danger of being banished from its beauty; and Joseph saw palaces like the one housing the administrative offices for storehouses and granaries or the palace for foreign princes, where the sons of Syrian city kings were educated—marvelous, huge buildings of brick and precious woods, shimmering with color. He watched chariots roll past, covered entirely in hammered gold, in which proud men stood and flicked their whips across the backs of horses charging ahead with rolling eyes, snorting with fiery energy, flinging foam from their mouths. They had the legs of deer and their heads were reared back and crowned with ostrich plumes. He watched sedan chairs hurry past, their poles resting on the shoulders of tall young men in golden skirts, moving in double-time with a cautious, springy gait. The chairs were carved, gilded, and canopied, and inside sat men with hands hidden from sight, lacquered hair pulled back from the forehead to the nape of the neck, and a scant beard adorning their chins; with eyelids lowered, they sat motionless as required by high rank, their backs protected from the wind by a large cane basket hung with painted fabric. Who, one day, would sit there like that, too, and be carried home to a house made opulent by Pharaoh? That lies in the future, and that festive hour in our narrative has not yet come, though it already exists in its proper place, familiar to everyone. For now, Joseph merely saw what he would one day be, gazing at it with eyes as large and estranged as those that would gaze upon him, or wince before him, a strange and great man—Osarsiph, the young slave, the son of the well, stolen and sold to this lower world, standing here in a wretched hooded shirt and with dirty feet, and forced to press up against the wall, when, to the blare of trumpets, a military unit, bristling with lances and armed with shields, bows, and clubs, suddenly came rushing down the Street of the Son in shining, ordered ranks. He took these fierce, interchangeable men to be the soldiers of Pharaoh; but the old man recognized from their standards and the insignia on their shields that they were the armed troops of the god, temple military, Amun's Strength. How could Amun have an army, a combat force, just like Pharaoh, Joseph wondered. It did not please him, and not only because the squad had pinned him to the wall. His jealousy was stirred on behalf of Pharaoh and by the question of who was the highest here. He felt Amun's pride and fame to be oppressively close in any case, and the presence of another highest power, that is, of Pharaoh, seemed to him a salutary counterforce, and it angered him that in maintaining an army, this idol imitated Pharaoh in his own arena; yes, he thought he could guess it angered Pharaoh as well, and he took his side against this overbearing deity.

But they soon left the Street of the Son again to avoid any further disfigurement of it, and, continuing along narrow lanes of less importance, arrived at their inn, called Sippar Court, because its owner and innkeeper was a Chaldean from Sippar on the Euphrates, who preferred to put up Chaldeans, though he took in all sorts of people as well. But it was called a court because it really was nothing more than a courtyard and a well, as full of filth, noise, and stench, of bleating animals, squabbling people, and squawking conjurers as their quarters in Menfe had been—and that same evening the old man opened shop for barter and had a good run of customers. They slept in their cloaks that night and—with the exception of the old man, who was left to sleep the night through—had to take turns keeping an eye out, standing guard to prevent any possibility of their goods and treasures being stolen by the inn's mixed company. And after they had stood at the well for a long time to wash up and had downed the Chaldean morning porridge served here, a thick broth made from sesame and called pappasu, the old man began to speak, but without looking at Joseph.

"Well, my friends, you, Mibsam, my son-in-law, Epher, my nephew, and you, Kedar and Kedma, my sons—we shall now take the goods we have to offer toward the sunrise and the desert, where the city opens up in splendor. I know of customers there and people in great need of our wares, who I hope will be anxious to buy this or that of what we have for their storehouses and to pay us well enough that we shall not merely cover our costs but also pocket a fair profit and gain such riches as are seemly for our role as merchants in this world. So then, load the wares on our beasts and saddle mine that I may lead you."

And so it was done, and they departed from Sippar Court for the east and the gardens of the wealthy. At their head was Joseph, leading the old man's dromedary by a long rein.

Joseph Comes Before Peteprê's House

They set out for the desert and the blazing hills of the desert where Rê appeared in the morning, which was also the direction of God's land, bordering the Sea of Red Earth. They moved along a level road, just as they had once entered the valley of Dothan, except that it was not the thick-lipped boy named Jupa who led the old man's animal, but Joseph. They came to a long wall receding toward the top and enclosing a large area, and visible within its enclosure were tall beautiful trees—sycamores, thorn acacias, date palms, fig and pomegranate trees—as well as the upper stories of buildings, some dazzling white, some painted bright colors. Joseph looked at them and then at his master, hoping to read from his face if this was the fan-bearer's house, for it was obviously a house of blessing. But as they moved along the wall, the old man stared straight ahead, his head tilted, and gave no hint until the wall formed a high portal with a covered gateway. There he stopped.

In the shadow of the gateway was a brick bench, on which some lads in loincloths, four or five of them, were sitting playing a finger game.

The old man looked down at them from his camel for a while, until they began to take notice of him—by dropping their hands, falling silent, and arching their eyebrows with mock surprise in hopes of disconcerting him.

"Health to you," the old man said.

"Joy to you," they replied with a shrug.

"What sort of game was that," he asked, "that you stopped because of my arrival?"

They looked at each other and laughed, one after the other.

"Because of your arrival?" one of them repeated. "We stopped because your gaping face vexed us."

"Do you know no better way to peddle your ignorance, you old desert rabbit," another one called out, "than to ask us about our game?"

"I peddle many things," the old man rejoined, "but not ignorance, however well supplied my stock, for I do not know that commodity, but assume from your vexation that you have an excess of it. Which is probably the source of your need for diversion, which you were satisfying, if I'm not mistaken, with the amusing game of How Many Fingers?"

"Well, then," they said.

"I asked only in passing and by way of introduction," he went on. "So this is the house and garden of the noble Peteprê, Fan-Bearer at the King's Right Hand?"

"And how do you know that?" they asked.

"Memory instructs me," he replied, "and your answer confirms it. You, it would appear, have been set here at the blessed man's gate as guards and to send report when familiar visitors appear, am I right?"

"And what familiar visitors you are!" one of them said. "Cutpurses and highwaymen of the desert. Thanks, but no thanks."

"You are mistaken, my young guardian of the gate and sender of reports," the old man replied, "and your knowledge of the world is as unripe as green figs. We are neither cutpurses nor footpads, but despise their kind and are their exact opposite in the order of things. For we are dealers in goods, who commerce between empires and cultivate fine connections, and as we are well received everywhere, so, too, here, in this house with its many needs. Except that at the moment we are not that as yet, for which your acrimony is to blame. But I would suggest you not bring blame upon yourselves before Mont-kaw, your overseer, who stands over this house and calls me his friend and treasures my treasures. But rather, do the duty granted to you in the order of things and run to report to the steward that familiar traveling traders from Ma'on and Mosar—that is, the Midianite merchants—have arrived yet again with good things for the chambers and sheds of this house."

The guards had exchanged looks when they heard him name the

name of their overseer. Now the one whom he had addressed, a chubby-cheeked lad with slit eyes, said, "And what I am supposed to report to him? Consider that, old man, and go your way. Can I run to him and report: The Midianites of Mosar are here, which is why I have left the gate where the master is to arrive at noon, and now disrupt you? He will call me a son of a dog and grab me by the ear. He is settling accounts in the bakery or consulting with the scribe of the sideboard. He has more to do than to rummage in your rummage wares. So be gone!"

"What a shame, my young watchman," the old man said, "that you set yourself up as a barrier between me and Mont-kaw, my friend of many years, placing yourself there like a river full of crocodiles or a mountain of impassable steeps. Is your name not Sheshi?"

"Ha, ha, Sheshi!" the guard cried. "I'm called Teti!"

"That's what I meant," the old man rejoined. "If I spoke it differently, that's only because of my pronunciation and because I am missing teeth at my age. And so, Chechi—ah, that was no better—do let me see if there is not a dry ford across this river and perhaps a winding road around the mountain steeps. You mistakenly called me a cutpurse, but here," he said, reaching into his robe, "is a bit of real cutting, and a pretty one, too, and it belongs to you if you will hop to it and announce me and bring Mont-kaw back here. There, take it from my hand. It is but a small example of my treasures. Behold, its casing is of hardest wood, beautifully stained, and it has a slot, from which you can pull a cutting blade hard as diamonds, and see how the knife holds fast. But if you push the blade back toward the handle, it snaps into place before you have pushed it all the way and rests secure in its sheath, so that you can conceal it in your apron. So then?"

The lad came forward and examined the clasp knife. "Not bad," he said. "Is it mine?" And he pocketed it. "From the land of Mosar?" he asked. "And from Ma'on? Midianite merchants? Wait here a while!"

And he went inside through the gate.

Smiling and shaking his head, the old man watched him go.

"We overcame the fortress of Zel," he said, "and made short shrift of Pharaoh's border guards and military scribes. We will surely press our way through here as well to my friend Mont-kaw."

And he gave a cluck of the tongue that signaled his animal to lie down so that he could dismount, and Joseph lent him a hand. His other riders got down as well; and they all waited.

After a while Teti returned and said, "You are to enter into the courtyard. The overseer will come."

"Good," the old man replied. "If he attaches importance to seeing us, we shall take the time and comply with his wishes, although we must move on yet."

And led by the young watchman they passed through the echoing, covered gateway and into the courtyard, which was paved with well-trodden clay, and found themselves opposite a set of open doors to a gate flanked by shading palm trees and leading through a brick wall with slits for archers, inside whose quadrangle stood the house itself, with its portal of decorated columns, fine moldings, and triangular west-facing vents on the roof.

It lay in the middle of the estate, bordered on two sides—to the west and south—by the green bands of gardens. The courtyard was spacious, with ample open area between the various south-facing buildings that stood, with no extra walls of their own, in the northern part of the grounds. The most important of them extended away to the right of the new arrivals—a long, airy, graceful structure with its own guards and maidservants who passed in and out of its door bearing bowls of fruit and tall pitchers. Other women were seated up on the roof, spinning and singing. Farther back to the west, set against the north wall, was another building from which steam was rising, while out in front of it people were tending to brewing vats and grain mills. Yet one more building lay still farther to the west behind the orchard, and workmen were busy in front of it as well. At the rear, in the northwest corner of the enclosing wall were barns and granaries with ladders.

An estate of blessing without doubt. Joseph's eyes hastily scanned it, trying to probe it everywhere, but he was not yet permitted to claim it as his own, for he had to help with the task to which his master put them immediately upon entry: to unload the camels, then unpack and set up shop on the courtyard's clay floor, spreading out their wares between the covered gateway and the master's house, so that the steward, or anyone of his staff with an urge to trade, might have an alluring overview of the Ishmaelite's merchandise.

The Dwarves

Indeed this display was soon encircled by a good many of the people who had seen these Asiatics arrive and, though this was hardly a rare event, saw in it a welcome diversion from their labors—or from mere idling about. There were Nubian guards from the women's house and maidservants, their female figures clearly visible, as was the custom in Egypt, under the sheer batiste of their garments; menials from the main house, dressed either in just a loincloth or, depending on their rank in the domestic hierarchy, in a longer skirt worn over that plus a short-sleeved tunic; people from the out-kitchen, some half-plucked item in their hands, stable boys, craftsmen from the servants' quarters, and gardeners—they all came over to look and chatter, bending down to the wares, picking up this or that and asking about its value in trade, expressed in silver and copper weights. Two little people found their way over as well—dwarves; the fan-bearer's household included two of them, but although neither man was more than three feet tall, their comportment showed them to be very different—the one a buffoon, the other a figure of dignity. The latter came over first, from the main house, striding with studied prudence on legs that looked even more stunted than his torso, holding himself so erect that he even leaned back a little, glancing about him from time to time, and rowing with stubby arms, palms turned backwards. He wore a starched skirt that stood out at an angle in front of him. His head bulged out at the back and was large in relationship to the rest of him and covered with short hair that grew low into his brow and temples; the nose was strong, the face bore a steady, indeed determined look.

"Are you the leader of this merchant caravan?" he asked, stepping up to the old man, who was now crouched on his heels beside his merchandise, which the dwarf obviously welcomed, since he wished to speak to him more or less man-to-man. His voice was muffled, he pitched it as low as possible, pushing his chin against his chest and pulling his lower lip down over his front teeth. "Who admitted you? The guards outside? With the permission of the overseer? Then it is all right. You can stay and wait for him, although it is uncertain when he will find time for you. Do you bring useful things, lovely things? Probably all just trumpery, isn't it? Or are items of some value included, serious, seemly, and solid things? I see balsam, I see walking sticks. I could presumably use a walking stick myself, if it were of hardest wood and sensibly fitted out. Above all, do you have trinkets—chains, necklaces, rings? I am the keeper of the master's wardrobe and jewelry, the warden of the dressing room. Dûdu is my name. And I could also bring delight to my wife with a solid piece of jewelry—to Zeset, my wife, in gratitude for her having borne me children. Do you carry items in that department? I see glass, I see gewgaws. What would interest me would be gold, electrum, would be fine gems, lazule, carnelian, crystal . . ."

While the one little man went on talking and demanding in this vein, the other came bounding from the direction of the harem, where he had probably been amusing the ladies with his antics. News of these events had been late in reaching him, it appeared, which was the reason for his childish, eager haste—for he ran as fast as his pudgy little legs would carry him, now and then interrupting his two-legged progress to simply hop on one of them, all the while gasping and shouting in a thin, sharp voice, as if in spasms of joy, "What's up? What's up? What's happening in the world? A hubbub, some great hurly-burly? What's there to see? What's the cause of wonder in our courtyard? Men of commerce—and wild men at that—men of the sand? That's enough to frighten this dwarf, enough to fill him with curiosity, hop, hop, and here he comes running . . ."

With one hand to his shoulder he was steadying a rust-colored meerkat that stared from its perch, neck outstretched, fierce eyes wide with terror. There was something ludicrous about the little fellow's garb, for it was a kind of festive costume that he apparently was fool enough to wear every day, leaving the entire outfit—the finely pleated skirt that fell well below his calves and had tassels at its waistband fold, the transparent camisole with pleated sleeves—looking rumpled and soiled. Around his embryonic wrist he wore golden spiral rings, around his neck was a bedraggled garland of flowers, linked to a few more wreaths that stuck out at his shoulders, and on his little head was a woolen wig of brown curls, topped by a cone for ointment, which instead of containing a fragrant salve, was really just a felt cylinder drenched in perfume. Unlike the dwarf who had first appeared, this one had the face of a childlike old man—of a wrinkled, shriveled mandrake.

Dûdu, the guardian of the wardrobe, had been greeted respectfully by those milling about, but the arrival of his companion in misfortune and brother in brevity evoked a merry response. "The vizier!" they cried—this evidently was his nickname. "Bes-em-heb!" This was the name of an imported comical foreign god, Bes the dwarf—with the added tag of "at the feast" in reference to the little fellow's permanent gala attire.

"Do you want to buy, Bes-em-heb? Look at him take his legs under his arms! Fly, Shepses-Bes, fly!" (That meant "splendid Bes," "glorious Bes.") "Fly and buy, but catch your breath on the sly. Buy yourself a sandal, vizier, and attach little oxen legs to it, that'll make a bed for you to stretch out in, but you'll have to add a step so you can climb up."

Once he had arrived, he replied to their shouts in an asthmatic, cricketlike voice that seemed to come from a distance. "Trying your hand at jokes, are you, my overstretched friends? And they're tolerably successful, are they? The vizier, however, can only yawn at them—huh, huh—for your attempt at wit bores him, as does the world that a god placed him in after first making everything for giants—its wares, its wits, its ways. For if the world had been cut to his size and made his home, then time itself would be cut and trimmed for laughter and there'd be no need for yawning. There'd be speedy short years and brief double hours and swift watches of the night. Tick, tick, tick, the heart would hurtle along, and run out in a twinkling, so that the generations of men would turn over so rapidly that one would barely have time enough to make one good joke on earth, and it would be gone, and another would greet the light. What a lark that little life would be! But left here among the overstretched, all a dwarf can do is yawn. I don't wish to buy your monstrous wares and I'd not accept your thumping wit even as a gift. I simply want to see if anything new in your giant epoch has come to our courtyard—strange men, men of misery and sand, wild nomads, in clothes no man wears . . . phooey!" His chirping suddenly broke off and his gnomelike face gathered into a wrinkled ball of vexation. He had noticed Dûdu, his fellow dwarf, standing in front of the squatting old man and flailing his stubby arms, demanding full value for his money.

"Phooey!" the so-called vizier said. "There's the gossip himself, His Honor the Dwarf! Must I bump into him when trying to satisfy my nosiness for what's new—how unpleasant! There he stands, the warden of the wardrobe, pushing in ahead of me and mincing muffled, but most edifying words . . . Good morning, master Dûdu!" he chirped as he placed one pint-size body beside the other. "A proper good morning to you, Your Stateliness, and my manifold respects to Your Robustness. Might one also inquire as to the health of your wife Zeset, whose arm embraces you, as well as that of your towering offspring, Esesi and Ebebi, those sweet children?"

Dûdu turned to look over his shoulder with great disdain, but evidently without actually fixing his gaze on the other man, but letting it drift somewhere in the vicinity of his feet.

"You mouse," he said, more or less shaking his head over him and tucking in his lower lip, so that the upper stood out like an overhanging roof. "What is all this wriggling and piping? I pay you no more regard than I would a common crab or a hollow nut emitting a puff of dust—that is my regard for you. How dare you ask about my wife Zeset and at the same time conceal your private mockery in the inquiry about her and my high-aspiring children, Esesi and Ebebi? Such an interrogation does not befit you, for it is no business of yours, nor is it suitable, proper, or appropriate for you, a whippersnapper, a fragment . . ."

"Why look at that," replied the dwarf whom they had greeted as Shepses-Bes, and his little face wrinkled up all the more. "Would you rise above me—who knows how high—and make your voice sound as if coming from a barrel full of punctilious pomp, even though you, too, cannot peek over a molehill and cannot measure up to your brood, not to mention to her whose arm embraces you? You are a dwarf for good and all, of a race of dwarves, no matter how respectably you comport yourself, and you rebuke me for politely inquiring as to your family's health because I am not fit to do so. Oh, but it fits you quite well and is a fine match for your figure, this playing husband and family father before full-grown people, taking a woman of stature to wife and denying your own small kind . . ."

The people in the courtyard laughed loudly at these squabbling little men, whose mutual aversion appeared to be a familiar source of merriment, and their shouts egged them on to bicker the more. "Give it to him, Vizier!"—"Make him pay for that, Dûdu, spouse of

Zeset!" But the one they had called Bes-em-heb stopped arguing and suddenly appeared to lose interest in the altercation. He was standing beside the man he despised, who stood facing the crouching old man, next to whom, then, stood Joseph, so that Bes was standing directly across from Rachel's son. And when he became aware of him, his words fell away and, in fixing his gaze on Joseph, his elderly wizened face, at first still full of petty annoyance, smoothed out and took on an expression of bemused scrutiny. His mouth hung open, and the empty space where his eyebrows should have been—for he had none—was drawn up high into his forehead. That was how he looked up at the young Habiru; and the little monkey on his shoulder was as captivated as he, by the way—its neck stretched far forward, its wide eyes staring fiercely up into the face of Abram's grandson.

Joseph held up under the test. He returned the gnome's gaze with a smile, and they both remained frozen like that while Dûdu, the solemn dwarf, went on making his demands of the old man and the attention of the others in the courtyard returned to the foreigners and their wares.

Finally the little man pointed with a dwarf's finger at his own chest and said in a strangely distant voice, "Se'enkh-Wen-nofre-Neteruhotpe-em-per-Amun."

"What did you say?" Joseph asked.

The dwarf intoned his phrase yet again, while continuing to point at his chest. "Name," he declared. "Name of little man. Not vizier, not Shepses-Bes. Se'enkh-Wen-nofre . . ." And he whispered the words a third time, his full name, as long and splendid as he was insignificant in stature. The name meant "May the kindly being (that is, Osiris) preserve the life of the beloved (or the favorite) of the gods in the house of Amun"; and Joseph understood it, too.

"A beautiful name," he said.

"Yes, beautiful, but not true," the dwarf murmured from a distance. "Me not favored, not an heir, only a toad. You favored, *you* Neteruhotpe, so that is both beautiful and true."

"And how do you know that?" Joseph asked with a smile.

"See it!" came the answer as if from under the earth. "See clearly!" and he put a little finger to his eye. "Clever," he added. "Small and clever. You not one of the small ones, but you clever.

Good, beautiful, and clever. You belong to him?" And he pointed to the old man haggling with Dûdu.

"I belong to him," Joseph said.

"From when you were very small?"

"I was born to him."

"So he is your father?"

"He is a father to me."

"What is your name?"

Joseph did not reply at once. He smiled before he answered. "Osarsiph," he said.

The dwarf blinked. He gave the name some thought.

"Were you born of the reeds?" he asked. "Are you an Usir in the reeds? Did your mother wander the marshes and find you there?"

Joseph said nothing. The dwarf went on blinking.

"Mont-kaw is coming!" The word spread among those in the courtyard, and they began to disband, so that he who stood over them would not find them gawking and dawdling. Peering between the men's and women's houses, someone had spotted him in the courtyard that opened up before the buildings that stood in the northwest corner of the estate—there he stood and now began walking, an older man dressed in beautiful white, accompanied by several scribes with reeds behind their ears, slaves who bowed low around him and took down his words on their tablets.

He approached. The staff had scattered from the courtyard. The old man had stood up now. But amid all the commotion Joseph had heard the whisper, like a voice from underground: "Stay with us, young sand man!"

Mont-kaw

The overseer had arrived at the open gate in the crenelated wall around the main house. Turning halfway toward it now, he glanced back over his shoulder at the group of foreigners and their merchandise spread out for sale.

"What is this?" he asked, rather testily. "What men are these?"

It appeared that amid his other duties he had forgotten the report delivered to him, and the old man's displays of obeisance from across the courtyard were of little help. A scribe reminded him, pointing to his tablet, on which the matter had evidently been noted.

"Yes, yes, the traveling merchants from Ma'on or from Mosar," the steward said. "Fine, fine, but I need nothing except time, and that they don't sell." And he approached the old man, who came bustling toward him. "Well, old man, how are you, after the passing of these many days?" Mont-kaw asked. "So we see you at our gate once again, here to swindle us with your odds and ends, are you?"

They laughed. Both had only their lower canines left, which jutted up like two posts. The overseer was a sturdy, stocky man of fifty, with an imposing head and the decisive bearing that came with his position, though softened by goodwill. The bags under his eyes were so prominent that they pressed up under them, making them look swollen and small, almost like slit eyes set beneath the bands of strong, still totally black eyebrows. Deep creases ran from the well-formed if somewhat wide-nostriled nose to each side of the mouth and strongly emphasized the arc of the upper lip, which like his cheeks was shaved clean and shiny. A wedge of a beard speckled with gray set off the chin. His hair had receded far back from the brow and along the sides of the skull, but formed a dense, fan-shaped mass behind ears adorned with gold rings. There was something of both ancient peasant cunning and a sailor's good humor about Mont-kaw's physiognomy, and his dark reddish brown complexion stood out against the snow white of his clothing—made from that incomparable Egyptian linen that could be folded into such exquisite pleats, like those of his apron, which began just below the navel and then fell in a flair almost to the hem of his ankle-length skirt. The wide, half-length sleeves of his tunic, which he wore tucked into the apron, were also pressed into delicate pleats. The outline of his hairy, muscular body was visible beneath the fine batiste.

Dûdu the dwarf had joined him and the old man—approaching with great importance, rowing with his stubby arms; for the two men of reduced stature had taken the liberty of remaining.

"I'm afraid you're wasting your time with these people, overseer," he said with the demeanor of a man of equal rank, though from very far below. "I examined their display. I see gewgaws, I see trumpery. What is lacking are items of higher value, of serious import, things proper for this very exalted estate and house. You will earn scant gratitude by acquiring any of this rubbish."

The old man was saddened. He intimated with gestures how sorry he was that the friendly and highly promising good cheer established by the overseer's words of greeting had now been disrupted by Dûdu's harsh comments.

"But I do have treasures worth treasuring!" he declared. "Perhaps not worth treasuring by senior officials such as you or the master himself, I would not say as to that. But consider the number of servants on this estate, which would include its bakers, roasters, water carriers for the gardens, errand boys, guards, and standabouts—countless as grains of sand, even if not so many as to be enough or too many for one so great as His Grace Peteprê, the friend of Pharaoh, or that their number might not yet be increased by one or another talented and well-fashioned servant, be he native or foreign, if only he is useful. But how I digress and babble on, instead of simply saying that you, great steward, are responsible for this multitude and its needs, and to be of assistance in that task is the business of an old Minæan, a traveling merchant with well-traveled wares. Do but regard these earthenware lamps, prettily painted, from Gilead beyond the Jordan—they cost little, and should I then overprice them for you, my patron? Take a few as gifts and if for that I may bask in your favor, I am a rich man. On the other hand, these small jars of eye paint plus tweezers and spoons of cow horn—their value is substantial, though their price is not. Here are hoes, an indispensable tool—I will give one for two pots of honey. More valuable still are the contents of this little sack, for there are Ashkelon onions inside, from Askuluna, rare and hard to come by, and they lend all dishes a delicate sour taste. The wine in these jugs, however, is eightfold good wine from Khazati in the land of the Phoenicians, as the inscription shows. Behold, I rank my wares, from lower grade to excellent and from there to choice, for that is my well-considered practice. For this balsam here and this frankincense resin, this boxthorn gum, this brownish labdanum—they are the pride of my shop and the stated specialty of my house. We are famous for them in all the world, acclaimed between the rivers for a stronger line of sublimates than that carried by any other merchant, be he a traveler or a man who sits beneath city gates. 'Those are the Ishmaelites of Midian,' people say of us, 'who bring spices, the balsam and myrrh of Gilead, down to the land of Egypt.' It is the talk of every tongue—as if we carried and bore no other goods, whatever we may chance to find, dead or alive, items made by human hand or even the human hand to make them, for we are men who not only provide for a household but who increase it as well. But I will be silent."

"What, you are silent?" the director of the estate marveled. "Are you ill? If you are silent I won't know you, but only when speech spills from your beard in a gentle babble—it still rings in my ears from last time, for it is by your speech that I recognize you."

"Is not speech the glory of man?" the old man replied. "He who knows how to place his words well and can give form to their expression earns nodding approval from the gods and men and finds a favorable hearing. But your servant, I admit, is less well blessed in forms of expression and no master of the storehouse of words, and so must replace fine speech with persistence, with a river of words in the place of felicity. For the merchant must indeed be quick with words, and his tongue must know how to curry a customer's favor, for he would not be able to live otherwise or to dispose of his seven-fold goods . . ."

"Six," came the whispering small voice of Neteruhotpe, as if from a distance, although he stood close by, "for you have offered us sixfold, old man—lamps, ointments, hoes, onions, myrrh, and wine. Where is the seventh?"

The Ishmaelite cupped his ear with his left hand and set his right over his eyes to search. "What was the remark," he asked, "of the medium-sized, festively attired gentleman?"

One of his party repeated the demurral for him.

"Oh my," he rejoined, "there's surely a seventh to be found among all the things we have brought down to Egypt, exceeding even the myrrh that is the talk of every tongue, and for it I shall wag-gle my tongue as well, with persistent, if not felicitous words, so that I may dispose of my goods in this house and make a name for the Ishmaelites from Midian because of all the good things they have brought for sale down into Egypt."

"How kind of you," the overseer now observed. "Do you sup-pose I can stand here chatting with you for all the days of Rê? He is almost at his zenith, have mercy on me! At any moment now the master can return home from the west and arrive here from the palace. Shall I leave it to the menials and take no further care to see that everything—roast ducks, cakes, flowers—is in order in the dining chamber, that the master may find a meal ready for him as he is accustomed, as well as for his spouse and his saintly parents on the upper floor? Make haste or hasten on your way! I must go to the house. Old man, I have little use for you and your sevenfold wares, very little, to be frank—"

"For they are the rubbish of a beggar," Dûdu, the married dwarf, interjected.

The overseer cast a fleeting glance down at the source of this stern remark.

"You need honey, it seems," he said to the old man. "And so I shall give you a few pots in exchange for two of your hoes, so that neither you nor your gods may be offended. Give me five sacks of your spicy onions as well, in the name of the Hidden God, and five measures of your Phoenician wine, in the name of the Mother and the Son. . . . What is your charge for it? But do not, old slow coach, name me a threefold price, so that we have to sit down and haggle, but at most twofold, so that we may arrive more quickly at a just price and I can go into the house. I shall give you writing paper in kind, and some of the estate linen. If you like you can have beer and bread, too. Just see to it that I can be on my way."

"At your service," the old man said, loosening his portable scale from his sash. "You shall be served at once and without ceremony by your servant, who is at your beck and call. What am I saying, without ceremony! Certainly with ceremony, but of a special sort. If I did not have to live, the items would have no price. But I shall suggest one that allows me both to make a scant living and to remain, by a hair, in your good grace, for that is the main thing. Hey There!" he said over his shoulder in Joseph's direction. "Take out that list of wares you made, the items in black, but weight and quantity in red. Take it out and read for us the weight of both the shallots and the wine, figuring the price, however, on the spur of the moment and in measures of the Two Lands, in debens and lots, so that we may know what the items are worth in pounds of copper and the esteemed steward can pay for them in linen and writing paper equal to the same amount of copper. And if you so wish, my good patron, I shall weigh out the goods yet again by way of test and proof."

Joseph had been holding the scroll at the ready and now stepped forward, unrolling it. Next to him stood Master Neteruhotpe, the favored one, who could not come close to getting a peek at the list, but kept his eyes trained upward on the hands unrolling it.

"Does my master wish his slave to give the fair price or double it?" Joseph asked modestly.

"The fair price, of course; what sort of drivel is that?" the old man scolded.

"But the high steward ordered you to name double the price," Joseph replied in the most charming earnestness. "If I name him the fair price, he may well take it to be double the price and offer only one-half—and how can you live from that? It would be better for him to believe double the price to be the fair price, and even if he bargained it down a little, you would still make not all too scant a living."

"Ha, ha," the old man said. "Ha, ha," he repeated and glanced at the overseer to see how he might have taken this. The scribes with the reeds behind their ears laughed. Little Neteruhotpe even slapped a tiny hand against one leg, lifting it high, while hopping on the other. His mandrake face crumpled into a thousand wrinkles of dwarfish delight. Dûdu, to be sure, his brother in brevity, thrust out the roof of his lip with all the more dignity and shook his head.

As for Mont-kaw, who, quite understandably, had paid this clever young reader of lists no attention thus far, he now fixed his eye on him in some surprise, which quickly grew to amazement and soon thereafter to a feeling that, although not so different from amazement, would have deserved a term of incomparably deeper resonance. It is possible—we are merely offering a supposition, not venturing an assertion—that at this very moment, on which so much depended, the planning God of Joseph's fathers went out of His way for Joseph and let fall upon him a ray of light designed to produce the desired effect in the heart of the man gazing upon him. He of whom we speak has indeed granted us vision, hearing, and all our senses to use freely for our own enjoyment of life, but on one condition: that He may also make use of them as a medium and portal for His intentions, as a means for influencing our hearts to serve more or less wide-ranging plans. Which explains why we have left the matter open and are prepared to withdraw our suggestion if so supernatural an element should appear out of place in our very natural story.

Natural and sensible interpretations are especially appropriate here, for Mont-kaw himself was a sensible, natural man, and belonged, moreover, to a world already very different from those in which there was nothing out of the ordinary about the idea of unexpectedly meeting up with a god by the broad light of day and, as it were, in public. Nevertheless, his world did stand closer than ours to such possibilities and expectations, even if it had retreated to a position that was still only half-and-half, no longer totally unambiguous, real, and literal. It came to pass that he looked upon Rachel's son and saw that he was beautiful. For Mont-kaw, however, the idea of beauty that now forced itself upon him visually and arrested his mind was associated, to his way of thinking, with the idea of the moon, which was the star of Djehuti of Khmunu, the heavenly presence of Thoth—master of measure and order, the star of the wise man, magician, and scribe. And here Joseph stood before him, scroll in hand, and, for a slave, even a scribal slave, he spoke clever, roguishly subtle words—and that combination of ideas was unsettling. This young Bedouin and Asiatic did not have the head of an ibis on his shoulders and was, needless to say, a human being, not a god, not Thoth of Khmunu. But he had intellectual connections with that god, and there was something ambiguous about him—just as there is about certain words, about the adjective "divine," for instance, a word that, when compared to the sublime noun to which it refers, has undergone a certain diminution, no longer contains that noun's total reality and majesty, but is simply a reminder of it and thus retains about it something half unreal and figurative, at the same time laying precarious claim to reality, insofar as "divine" implies what is perceptibly real in the manifestation of the god.

Such were the ambiguities that came to mind for Mont-kaw the steward and occupied his attention when he first set eyes upon Joseph. There was a repetitive quality to what was happening here. The same thing or something very like it had happened, and would happen again, to others. But let no one think the man was greatly moved. What he felt was in essence not much more than what we would express in exclaiming "I'll be damned!"

But he did not say that. Instead, he said, "What is this?" He said "what" out of caution and disparagement, which made it easier for the old man to offer his reply.

"This," he answered with a grin, "is number seven."

"It is the custom of barbarians," the Egyptian responded, "to speak in riddles."

"Doesn't my patron like riddles?" the old man replied. "What a shame! I might offer many more. But this one is very simple. It was said that the wares I presented came to only six items and not the seven I may have boasted of—a far lovelier number. Well, this slave specimen here who keeps my lists is the seventh, a Kenanite lad that I have brought down to Egypt along with my highly acclaimed myrrh and that I offer for sale. Not unconditionally, however, and not because he is of no use to me. He can bake and write and has a sharp mind. But to an honored house, a house such as yours, in brief, to you I am offering him for sale, if you will compensate me so that I may make a living, if only a scant one. For I wish him to be well taken care of."

"We have servants enough," the overseer declared with some haste and shook his head. For he was not a man for ambiguities, of either an evil or, for that matter, a higher nature, and spoke as a practical man who deals sensibly with the area of business under his management and tries to prevent any disruption of its usual order by loftier or, as it were, "divine" forces.

"There are no vacancies," he said, "and the house has its full quota of servants. We need neither a baker, nor a scribe, nor a sharp mind, for my mind is sharp enough to keep the house in order. Take your seventh item with you on your way that it may benefit you."

"For it is rubbish and a beggar and a beggar's rubbish!" Dûdu, the spouse of Zeset, added pompously.

But another little voice was heard in response to those muffled tones—the cricket voice of Neteruhotpe, the jester, which whispered, "The seventh is the best. Acquire it, Mont-kaw!"

The old man began again. "The sharper one's own mind, the more vexatious the dullness of others, which one must endure with impatience. A sharp mind at the top needs sharp minds below it. I intended this servant for your house while there was still a great deal of space and time between you and me, and out of friendship I brought him down to your house in order to make you a special offer of this specimen. For the lad is sharp and of most gratifying eloquence, and will select baubles from the storehouse of language to tickle you. He can wish you good-night in a different phrase three hundred and sixty times a year and knows new ones for the five extra days as well. But if he says the same thing even twice, you may return him to me and be refunded what you paid."

"Listen to me, old man," the overseer replied. "That's all well and good. But speaking of impatience—my patience is very near its end. Out of goodwill I am prepared to buy a few trinkets from your oddments, though I don't need them, simply so that I may not insult your gods and may finally go into the house—and right away you try to foist off on me a slave to wish me good-night and act as if he had been destined for the house of Peteprê since the foundation of the land."

At this point a full-throated laugh of mockery could be heard from below, a "Hoho!" coming from Dûdu, the keeper of the wardrobe; and the overseer cast him a hasty, annoyed look.

"Just where did you get it, this piece of eloquence?" he went on and at the same time, without looking, stretched out a hand for the scroll that Joseph had stepped forward to offer him politely. Mont-kaw unrolled it and held it at a good distance from his eyes, for he was already very farsighted.

Meanwhile the old man said, "It is as I said. What a shame that my patron does not like riddles. I know one that would answer the question of where I got the boy."

"A riddle?" the overseer repeated distractedly, for he was examining the list.

"Guess at it if you like," the old man said. "What is this? A barren mother bore him to me. Can you solve the riddle?"

"So he wrote this, did he?" Mont-kaw asked, still inspecting the scroll. "Hm—step back, you! It is executed with devotion and enjoyment and with a sense for ornamentation, I will not deny it. It could indeed decorate a wall and would work as an inscription. Whether it also has any rhyme or reason I cannot say, for it is written in gibberish.—Barren?" he asked, for he had been listening to the old man with one ear. "A barren mother? What are you talking about? A woman is barren, or she bears. How can she be both at once?"

"It is a riddle, my lord," the old man explained. "I took the liberty of cloaking my answer in a jesting riddle. If you like, I will give you its solution. Far, far from here, I happened on a barren well, out of which came whimpering. And into the light of day I pulled what had been in that belly for three days, and I gave it milk. Thus was the well both a mother and barren."

"Hm," the overseer said, "your riddle isn't bad. I can't say it makes one burst into laughter. Any smile would be purely out of politeness."

"Perhaps," the old man responded, concealing his irritation, "you would like the jest better had you solved it yourself."

"Solve another riddle for me," the steward rejoined, "one that is far more difficult—just why is it that I am still standing here chattering with you? And provide me a better solution than the one for your own riddle, for to my knowledge there are no monsters who sire offspring in wells that then give birth. How, then, did this child find its way into the belly and the slave into the well?"

"Hard masters, his previous owners from whom I purchased him," the old man said, "had cast him into it for relatively slight misdemeanors, which in no way reduce his value, for they were merely matters of subtle sophistry, such as the distinction between 'so that' and 'in order that'—it's not worth wasting words over. But I acquired him, because my gift for appraisal between thumb and forefinger told me that the fellow was of fine fiber and grain, despite the murkiness of his origins. He also repented of his misdemeanors while in the well, and the punishment so cleansed him of them that he has been a most valuable servant to me and can not only read and write, but also bake uncommonly tasty flat cakes on stones. One ought not to boast of what one has, but leave it to others to call it extraordinary; but within the storehouse of language there is but one word for the intelligence and skills of this lad who has been cleansed by severe punishment: they are extraordinary. And since your eye has now fallen upon him and I owe you amends for the folly of plaguing you with riddles, accept him as a gift from me for Peteprê and his house, over which you have been set. I know only too well that in recompense you will think of some gift for me from the riches of Peteprê, so that and in order that I may live and provide for, and even increase, your house in the future as well."

The overseer looked Joseph over.

"Is it true," he asked with proper gruffness, "that you are eloquent and know to speak in delightful phrases?"

Jacob's son collected all the Egyptian he knew.

"A servant's speech is no speech," he replied, recalling a popular adage. "That the lesser man falls silent when greater men speak stands at the head of every scroll. The name by which I call myself is likewise a name of silence."

"How's that! What is your name?"

Joseph hesitated. Then he raised his eyes. "Osarsiph," he said.

"Osarsiph?" Mont-kaw repeated. "I do not know the name. It is not foreign, and one can understand it, since Abôdu's god, the Lord of Eternal Silence, appears within it. And yet it is not common usage, and no one in Egypt bears the name, not now, nor did they bear it under kings of yore. But even if you do have a name of silence, Osarsiph, your master says that you can speak pleasant blessings and know a multitude of ways to say good-night at the end of the day. Well, I shall be going to bed this evening myself and lie curled up on my couch in the special chamber of trust. What do you say to me?"

"A gentle rest," Joseph replied with heartfelt sincerity, "after a day of labor. May the soles of your feet, scorched by the heat of the path, wander in bliss over the mosses of peace and your languishing tongue be refreshed by the murmuring springs of night."

"Well, that is, I admit, very touching," the overseer said, tears welling in his eyes. He nodded to the old man, who nodded back, grinning and rubbing his hands. "For a man as plagued by this world as I, who at times does not feel all that splendid when his kidney troubles him, that is downright touching. In the name of Seth," he said, turning back to his scribes, "can we use a young slave—perhaps to light lamps or sprinkle the floors? What do you say, Kha'ma't?" he asked a tall, stoop-shouldered man with several reeds behind each ear. "Do we need one?"

Wavering between yes and no, his scribes assumed a look of indecision, pursing their lips, tucking their heads between their shoulders, and raising their hands halfway in the air.

"What does *need* mean?" the one named Kha'ma't responded. "If need means to lack what is indispensable, then no. But one can use even what one can do without. It would depend on the price of what is offered. If this barbarian wishes to sell a scribal slave, then chase him off, for we are scribes enough and do not need another, nor can we use him. But if he is offering a menial slave for the dogs or the bath, then let him state his price."

"So then, old man," the overseer said, "be hasty about it! What do you want for your son of the well?"

"He is yours!" the Ishmaelite replied. "Simply by our having spoken about him and your having asked me for him, he is yours already. Truly, it is not proper for me to determine the value of the gift that you intend, or so it would seem, to present me in recompense. But since you have commanded it—the baboon sits beside the scales. He who violates weights and measures is convicted by the power of the moon. Given his extraordinary qualities, one must set the value of this servant at two hundred debens of copper. The onions, however, and the wine of Khazati I will throw in as a bonus and as the makeweight of our friendship."

That was a steep price, particularly since the old man had quite rightly included those wild-growing shallots and very ordinary wine from Phoenicia free of charge and was basing his entire demand on the young slave Osarsiph—an audacious sum, even granting that of the traveling merchant's seven items, not even excepting his famous myrrh, only this one had been worth transporting to Egypt, yes, even if regarded from the viewpoint that all the Ishmaelite's wares were a bonus and his sole purpose in life was to bring the boy Joseph down into Egypt so that the grand plan might be fulfilled. We do not venture to suggest that so much as a trace of a hint of such a notion touched the soul of the old Minæan. Such an interpretation was likewise worlds away from the overseer Mont-kaw's view of things, and he would have objected to so extravagant a price himself, if Dûdu, the dignified dwarf, had not interfered and anticipated his response. From beneath the roof of his upper lip his protest emerged at full strength, while stubby arms and little hands gesticulated at his chest.

"That is absurd," he said, "that is utterly and intolerably absurd, good overseer. Turn your back in anger. How shameless of this old vagabond thief to speak to you of friendship, as if there could be any such between you, a man of Egypt who oversees the estate of a great man, and him, a wild creature of the sands. His commerce, however, is a snare and a trap, for he would take as much as two hundred copper debens from you for this lout here"—and he thrust the palm of his hand up at Joseph, beside whom he had taken his position—"for a snot-nose from the desert and a suspicious bit of rubbish. For this specimen is highly suspicious, and, granted, he babbles sweetly about mosses and murmuring springs, but who knows the truth of what irredeemable vice led to his acquaintance with that pit, out of which the old scoundrel claims to have pulled him. It is my opinion, however, that you ought not buy this ninny, and my advice is that I counsel against purchasing him for Peteprê, for he will not thank you for it."

These, the words of Dûdu, guardian of the jewelry chests. But after his voice, another little voice was heard, like a cricket in the grass, the voice of Neteruhotpe in his festive attire, of the "vizier," who was standing on the other side of Joseph—for they had put him between them.

"Buy, Mont-kaw!" he whispered, standing on tiptoe. "Buy the boy of the sands. Of all these seven items buy him alone, for he is the best. Trust your little man, who sees clearly. Good, beautiful, and clever is this Osarsiph. Blessed is he, and he will be a blessing to this house. Heed this fine advice of mine!"

"Accept no inferior advice, but only that of sterling substance!" the other one countered loudly. "How can this dried prune give you advice of substance, when he himself is not to be taken seriously and is as insubstantial and windy as a hollow nut? He has no weight in the world after all and no social status, but floats along like a cork, a gamboler and jester—how can he offer sterling advice and judge in matters of the world, its goods, its humans, its human goods?"

"Ah, you pompous, punctilious dolt, you fusspot!" Bes-em-heb shrieked, and his gnomish face crumpled into a thousand wrinkles of rage. "How will you judge and give fine advice in the smallest matter, you turncoat midget? You have betrayed the wisdom of the small by denying your dwarfhood and taking an overstretched woman to wife, by setting children long as flagpoles into the world, named Esesi and Ebebi, and by playing the stuffy prig. You remain a dwarf in size, it's true, and still can't see over a boundary stone. But your stupidity is full-grown and bollixes any judgment of goods or humans or human goods . . ."

Embittered by this characterization of his mental capacities, Dûdu now flew into an incredible fury at these accusations. His face turned cheesy white, that roof of an upper lip quivered, and he let loose a volley of nasty protest against Neteruhotpe's windiness and insubstantiality, to which the latter was quick to pay him back with more malicious remarks about the surrender of finer intelligence to punctilious pomp; and so, hands on their knees, the two little men bickered and squabbled as they circled Joseph as if he were an inter-vening tree that protected them from one another; and all those gathered around—both Ishmaelites and Egyptians, including the overseer—roared with laughter at the bantam warfare below them. When suddenly everything came to a halt.

Potiphar

Out on the street distant sounds began to swell ever louder: clatter-ing hooves, rolling wheels, and the soft drumming of feet amid a chorus of cries for all to take heed. Approaching at great speed, the clamor was now at the gate.

"Now we're in for it," Mont-kaw said. "The master. And the arrangements in the dining chamber? Great Triad of Thebes, I've frittered away the time with farce. Silence, you menials, or there'll be leather. Kha'ma't, finish this business, I must join the master in the house. Buy these wares at a reasonable price. Health to you, old man. And come back to this house again—in five or seven years."

And he turned away in haste. The watchers at the gate on their brick bench shouted ahead into the courtyard. Servants came run-ning from several directions, anxious to throw themselves on their faces and line both sides of their lord's entry. From under the stony gateway came the rattle of a chariot and the tramping of footmen—Peteprê drove in, with panting heralds before him and panting fan-bearers beside and behind him. Two glistening, high-spirited bays adorned with beautiful trappings and ostrich plumes pulled the little two-wheeled carriage, an elegant sport vehicle with soft, curving lines and standing room for only two, the master and the driver, who stood idly by, however, his position evidently honorary, for Pharaoh's friend was himself the driver, since from both his bearing and attire it was clear that he was the master, with reins and whip in hand: an exceedingly tall, heavyset man with a small mouth, as Joseph noticed at a glance; but what really caught his attention were the fireworks released by bright gemstones embedded in the spokes of the wheels and spinning in the sunlight, a colorful spectacle of whirling sparks that Joseph would have loved for little Benjamin to see and whose beauty was repeated, though not in a whirl, on Pe-teprê's own person in the form of a collar, a magnificent piece of craftsmanship consisting of countless enamelwork plates and precious gems of every color, arranged in rows, narrow side to narrow side, a glittering rainbow of flame beneath the strong white light that the god at his zenith hurled down upon Weset and this spot.

The ribcages of the footmen were heaving. The smartly groomed steeds stood stamping, snorting, and rolling their eyes, and a servant who had grabbed the bridle patted their sweating necks and spoke gentle words to them. The chariot halted by the palm trees, directly between the party of merchants and the gate in the wall that surrounded the main house, where Mont-kaw had taken up his position to greet his master and now stepped forward—smiling and bowing, gesturing his delight and even shaking his head in wonder—to lend his master a hand in stepping down. Peteprê gave reins and whip to the driver, while retaining in his very small hand a short staff of cane and gilt leather rolled together in a knot at one end, a kind of elegant cudgel. "Wipe them down with wine, cover them well, walk them!" he said in a thin voice, gesturing toward the horses with that elegant vestige of a savage weapon that had now become a mere token of commanding authority, and, although he could have stepped down, he waved aside the hand offered him and jumped from the vehicle, a vigorous, nimble man despite his weight.

Joseph could see and hear him quite well, especially after the chariot was slowly driven off toward the stables, leaving the Ishmaelites with a clear view of both master and steward, who watched as it drove off. The exalted man himself was perhaps forty, or maybe thirty-five years old, and truly tall as a tower—Joseph was reminded of Ruben at the sight of the columnlike legs visible under the royal linen of the almost ankle-length robe, which also revealed the folds and dangling ribbons of the skirt beneath it; but the man's bulk was of a very different sort from that of Joseph's heroic brother, for the entire body was fat, fat all over, but especially around the chest, which rose like two hills beneath the fine batiste of his tunic and had jiggled more than a little when he had taken his unnecessarily enterprising leap from the chariot. His head was very small in relation to his height and girth, but nobly proportioned, with short hair, a short, finely arched nose, a delicate mouth, a pleasantly prominent chin, and long-lashed eyes, whose gaze was veiled and proud.

Standing in the shade of the palm trees with his overseer, he watched with satisfaction as his stallions were led away at a walk.

"They are extremely fiery," he could be heard to remark. "Weser-min even more than Wepwawet. They were unruly, tried to bolt on me. But I kept them well in hand."

"As only you can," Mont-kaw responded. "It is amazing. Your driver Neternakht would not dare take them on. No one in this house would dare it with those wild Syrians. They have fire in their veins, not blood. They aren't horses, they're demons. But you can control them. They feel the hand of the master, and their high spirits yield, and they run under the restraint of harness for you. Even after a victorious struggle with their wildness, you, however, are not weary at all, but leap from your wagon, my lord, like a fearless lad."

Peteprê cast him a fleeting smile, tucking the folds at the corners of his small mouth. "It is my intent," he said, "to pay homage to Sebek this afternoon yet and to hunt in the marshes. Make preparations and wake me in time should I fall asleep. There should be throw-sticks in the boat and lances for spearing fish. But see to it that there are harpoons as well, for I have been told that a hippopotamus of great size has strayed into the backwater where I hunt, and that is what interests me above all—I wish to slay it."

"The mistress, Mut-em-enet," the overseer replied with downcast eyes, "will tremble when she hears of it. At least yield to entreaties not to attack the hippopotamus single-handed, but leave the danger and difficulty to servants instead. The mistress . . ."

"There's no pleasure in that for me," Peteprê replied. "I shall throw the spear myself."

"But the mistress will tremble."

"Let her tremble! Surely," he said, turning around suddenly to the overseer, "everything is in order with the house, is it not? No accidents or misfortunes? Nothing? What people are these? Traveling merchants—fine. The mistress is of good cheer? My exalted parents on the upper floor are in good health?"

"Both order and health are perfect," Mont-kaw responded. "Late this morning our gracious mistress ordered she be carried to visit Renenutet, the consort of the Chief Steward of Amun's Bulls, to practice singing hymns with her. She has returned and has sent for Tepem'ankh to read fairy tales to her in the house of seclusion, having also expressed a desire to kiss the sweets that your servant ordered be offered to her. As for the most estimable parents on the upper floor, it pleased them to be ferried across the river to make sacrifices in the Temple of the Dead to Thutmose, father of the god and now reunited with the sun. Having returned from the West, those exalted siblings, Huya and Tuya, have spent the time sitting in the summerhouse by your garden pond, peacefully and piously holding hands and awaiting the hour of your return, when dinner is to be served."

"You may also inform them," the master of the house said, "or have it told them privately in passing that I intend to hunt the hippopotamus yet today. They should know of it."

"Unfortunately," his overseer replied, "that will be a cause of great anxiety to them."

"No matter," Peteprê declared. "Life here this morning," he added, "appears to have been spent to everyone's liking, while I had only the annoyance of court and vexation at Merima't Palace."

"You had what?" Mont-kaw asked in dismay. "How is that possible, for the good god is in the palace and . . ."

"One is Captain of the Guard," the master was heard to say to himself, turning away and shrugging his massive shoulders, "and Chief High Executioner, or one is not. If, however, one is that . . . and then someone comes along . . ." His words faded away. With his steward a few steps behind him—bowing, listening, responding—Peteprê passed between servants, who held hands uplifted, and now strode through the gate toward his house. Joseph, however, had seen Potiphar, as it was his custom to pronounce the name—the great man of Egypt to whom he would be sold.

Joseph Is Sold a Second Time and Throws Himself upon His Face

For that is what happened now. In the name of the overseer, Kha'-ma't, the tall scribe, took care of business with the old man while the dwarves looked on. But Joseph paid scant attention to such matters or to what price he brought, so caught up was he in his musings and preoccupation with first impressions of his new owner's character. That glittering collar and other tributes of gold; his overweight, but proud figure; the way he had jumped down from the chariot and the way Mont-kaw had flattered him, telling him how strong and brave he was at handling horses; his intention of taking on the savage hippopotamus single-handed, heedless that it would make Mut-em-enet, his consort, and Huya and Tuya, his parents, tremble—though "heedless" apparently did not even come close to characterizing his mood; and in contrast, his series of quick questions about the unruffled order in the house and the good cheer of its mistress; even those fragmentary hints about vexation suffered at court that had passed his lips as he departed—it all gave Jacob's son some very urgent things to think about, to test and surmise, as he silently endeavored to fathom, interpret, and augment them, like a man trying to make himself as quickly as possible intellectual master of circumstances and realities in which he finds himself placed by chance and with which he must now deal.

Would he—so his thoughts ran—stand someday beside Potiphar in his chariot as his driver? Would he accompany him on a hunting party to the backwater of the Nile? In fact, believe it or not, he was thinking even this early—having just been brought before this house and taken note of its objects and people in an attentive, quick survey—of how sooner or later, indeed as soon as possible, he might be able to take his position at the side of his master, the highest man in this circle, though not the highest in the land of Egypt—from which latter reservation it becomes clear that even unforeseeable difficulties in achieving his first, still far too distant goal did not prevent him from letting his thoughts play with a connection to even more definitive embodiments of what is highest.

But it was so—we know him well. Would he have achieved as much in the Two Lands as he did, had he demanded any less? He was in the underworld, for which the well had served as the entrance—was no longer Joseph, but Usarsiph, the last of those here below, but that dared not continue for long. His gaze passed swiftly over what stood to his favor and disfavor. Mont-kaw was good. A gentle greeting had brought tears to his eyes, for he often did not feel all that splendid. And Neteruhotpe, the jester, was good and obviously inclined and ordained to help him. Dûdu was an enemy—for as long as he remained so, but perhaps one could get around him. The scribes had displayed jealousy, because he was one of them—he would have to keep that enmity in mind, handle it with care. Thus he weighed his immediate prospects—and it would be a mistake to impugn him for this and think of him as a man of base ambition. Joseph was not that, nor is that a correct judgment of his thoughts. He was thinking and pondering about his higher duty. God had put an end to his life, a life of foolishness, and resurrected him to a new one. God had led him into this land with the help of the Ishmaelites. As with all things, here, too, He doubtless had great purposes. He did nothing that did not bring great things with it, and the important part was to use all the faculties one had been granted and faithfully lend Him a hand, not cripple His intentions with an indolent lack of endeavor. God had sent him dreams that the dreamer should have kept to himself—about sheaves, about stars; and such dreams were not merely a promise but also an injunction. They would be fulfilled, one way or another; only God knew how, but Joseph's being carried off to this land marked the beginning of that fulfillment. This would not happen all on its own—one had to help bring it about. To live by the silent assumption, or conviction, that God has something unique in mind for one's life is not a base motive, ambition is not the right word for it—as ambition on God's behalf, it deserves more pious names.

Joseph, therefore, paid scant attention to the outcome of his second sale, scarcely cared at all what price he was sold for—so preoccupied was he with sorting out his impressions and preparing himself mentally to be master of his circumstances. In order to lower the price, Kha'ma't, the tall scribe with reeds behind his ear—and how amazingly he balanced them, as if they were glued on, so that not one was lost, no matter how he fidgeted as he haggled—stubbornly insisted on differentiating between "need" and being able to "use at best," while the old man kept on advancing his tried and sturdy contention that the value of the gift given in recompense had to allow him to live so that he could continue to serve this house; and he was able to present this prerequisite as so self-evident that the scribe, much to his disadvantage, never thought to dispute it. Kha'-ma't was supported by Dûdu, chamberlain of the wardrobe, who disputed both "need" and "use at best" as regarded all three items—the onions, the wine, and the slave—and the old man by Shepses-Bes, who chirped away, asserting the clarity of his dwarfish eye and demanding Osarsiph be purchased straight-out and without any greedy trifling over the initial price asked for him. And only later and really just in passing did the object of their dispute intervene by suggesting that he considered one hundred fifty debens too low a price for himself and that they really should be able to agree to one hundred sixty at least. He did it out of ambition on God's behalf—and was chastised for it, of course, by the agitated scribe Kha'ma't, who declared it totally impermissible for an object for sale to interfere in the discussion of its price; and Joseph fell silent again and let the matter be.

Finally he saw a spotted young bull being led from the stall on Kha'ma't's order; and he found it strange to be confronted with his own value and worthiness in so external a form as an animal—strange, though not offensive in this land, where most gods recognized themselves in animals and where the congruity between identity and simultaneity was the object of such great intellectual endeavor.

Nor was the young bull the end of things, by the way; its value was not identical to that of Joseph, for the old man refused to value its worth at more than one hundred twenty debens, and so various other goods—a cowhide breastplate, several bales of writing paper and everyday linen, a couple of panther-hide wineskins, a measure of natron for salting down corpses, a string of fishhooks, and several whisk brooms—had to be presented to him before the scales hovered in sacred balance under the eye of the baboon, though all of this was more by common agreement and appraisal with the eye than by pure reckoning, for after a long argument each party had abandoned a deal based purely in numbers and decided to trust his sense of not being swindled all too much. A copper weight between one hundred fifty and one hundred sixty debens was the approximate rate of exchange kept in mind, and for that Rachel's son, along with a few makeweight items, became the property of Peteprê, one of the great men of Egypt.

It was done. The Ishmaelites from Midian had fulfilled their purpose in life, had delivered what they had been appointed to bring down to Egypt and could go their way, vanishing out into the world—they were no longer needed. Their own sense of self-worth, by the by, was unimpaired by this state of affairs; they took themselves as importantly as ever, for in packing up their wares again now, they did not feel the least bit superfluous. And did not the old man's motive—his paternal desire to care for his foundling and find a place for him in the best house he knew—carry its own full weight in dignity within the moral world, even though, viewed in another way, this disposition might also have been merely a means, a tool, a vehicle for goals of which he had not the vaguest? It is striking in itself that he sold Joseph again as if that had to be—though for a profit that, as he said, "let him live" and tolerably soothed his commercial conscience. But he obviously did not do it for the sake of profit, and, if we see it rightly, he would have gladly kept this son of the well to say his good-nights and bake flat cakes for him. He did not act out of selfishness, however great his concern to serve his own interests, at least commercially. But what does selfishness mean here? He was driven to care for Joseph and to find a good place for him in life, and with the fulfillment of that wish he had still served his own ends as well, whatever the source of this overwhelming wish might have been.

And Joseph himself was a lad who recognized the dignity of freedom, which lends a human soul to all that we must do; and when, upon concluding the bargain, the old man spoke to him, saying, "So you see, Hey There, or Usarsiph, as you call yourself, you are no longer mine, you belong to this house, and I have made good on my intention." Joseph repaid him with all due gratitude, repeatedly kissing the hem of his robe and calling him his savior.

"Farewell, my son," the old man said, "and prove worthy of a generous deed. Be wise and obliging in your dealings with everyone and control your tongue when it itches and tickles to take command and attempts to make disagreeable distinctions, such as those between what is honorable and what has merely survived over time—for that will land you in the pit. Your lips have been granted a sweetness and know how to speak tender good-nights and much more as well—hold to that and give delight to others, instead of arousing their disfavor by faultfinding that does no good. In short, farewell! Surely I need not admonish you to avoid the mistakes that brought your life into the pit—culpable trust and blind expectation—for in that regard you are, I think, the wiser. I have not inquired of you as to any further details, nor tried to delve into your affairs, for it suffices for me to know that many a mystery lies hidden within this raucous world, and experience has taught me to believe a great many things possible. If, as your manners and talents have sometimes led me to presume, your circumstances were once fine and you anointed yourself with the oil of gladness before entering

into the belly of the well, then my having sold you into this house is
a lifeline that has been cast your way, a happy prospect now given
you so that you may lift yourself up to a more fitting state. Farewell,
for the third time! For I have said it twice already, and what is said
thrice is binding. I am old and do not know if I shall see you again.
May your god Adôn, who, to my knowledge, is like the setting sun,
guard and preserve your steps that you may not stumble. And blessing upon you."

Joseph knelt on the ground before this father and kissed the hem
of his robe once more, while the old man laid a hand on his head.
The slave also took leave of Mibsam, the son-in-law, thanking him
for lifting him out of the pit; and of Epher, the nephew, and Kedar
and Kedma, the old man's sons, as well as, more informally, of
Ba'almahar, the groom, and Jupa, the thick-lipped lad who was now
holding Joseph's animal equivalent, the young bull, by a rope. And
then the Ishmaelites departed from the courtyard by way of the
same echoing gateway through which they had come, except without Joseph, who stood there watching them go, not without some
pain in his heart at their departure and trepidation in the pit of his
stomach at all the new and uncertain things awaiting him.

When they had vanished and he looked around, he realized that
all the Egyptians had gone their way and he was alone, or almost
alone; for the only one who had remained was Se'enkh-Wen-nofre-
Neteruhotpe-em-per-Amun, the favorite of the gods, the jesting
vizier, who stood beside him, gazing up at him with a wrinkled
smile, his red meerkat still on his shoulder.

"What do I do now, and to whom should I turn?" Joseph asked.

The dwarf did not answer. He just nodded up at him and went
on smiling. Suddenly, however, he flinched and turned his head to
whisper, "Throw yourself on your face."

At the same time he followed his own command, pressing his
brow to the ground, a little heap of humanity crouching on its belly,
with an animal on top, for the meerkat had nimbly handled the
abrupt motion and was now settled on its little master's back instead
of his shoulder and, with uplifted tail and eyes wide in permanent
fear, was staring in the same direction in which Joseph could not
help looking. He had indeed followed Neteruhotpe's example, but

while bent low had kept his brow free between hands raised at the elbow, in order to see to what or to whom he was showing devotion.

It was a procession from the women's house set catercornered to the men's house: at its head five servants in aprons and little linen caps, at the rear five maidservants with flowing hair, and between them, swaying above the naked shoulders of Nubian slaves and leaning back, with feet crossed, into the cushions of a kind of gilt sedan chair adorned with animals with gaping jaws, a lady of Egypt, elegantly dressed, with flashing jewels in her curly hair, gold around her neck, rings on her fingers, and lily-white arms, one of which—it was a very white and delectable arm—she dangled indolently at the side of the chair. And Joseph saw—beneath the jeweled headdress and despite all the tokens of fashion—a matchless and individual profile, so personal, so special, with eyes extended to the temples by cosmetics, a rather flattened nose, rouged hollows beneath the cheeks, and the thin but soft, serpentine line of a mouth meandering sinuously between deep folds at its corners.

This was Mut-em-enet, mistress of the house, on her way to dinner—Peteprê's consort and a woman of great portent.

Part Four

THE HIGHEST

How Long Joseph Remained with Potiphar

There once was a man who had a headstrong cow that refused to wear the yoke necessary for plowing his field and always threw it off. He took her calf away from her and took it to the field that was to be plowed. When the cow heard her calf bellowing, she was easily led to where the calf was and submitted to the yoke.

The calf is out in the field where the man has brought it and does not bellow, but is as still as death, for it first eyes this strange field, which it takes to be a field of death. It senses that it is too soon to let its voice be heard; but this calf, Jehosiph or Osarsiph, has a very good idea of the man's intentions and long-term plans. Knowing the man as it does, it at once surmises, with the clarity of a dream, that it is not for some vague and indefinite purpose that it has been carried off to a field rejected with such headstrong dislike at home, but that this is part of a plan in which one thing follows another. In the calf's intelligent and dreamy soul, where, as sometimes happens, sun and moon stand together at opposite ends of the heavens, the theme of "following" and of "sending for others to follow" is one of several counterthemes; and the leading motif of the moon, whose shimmering path prepares the way for its brothers, the gods of the stars, also plays its role. Joseph, the calf—as he gazed at the shining meadows of the land of Goshen, had he not already thought his own thoughts, though always in accord with the man's designs? Premature thoughts, that skipped ahead far into the future, as he well knew, and that had to remain mute for now. For many other things must first be fulfilled before such thoughts can find fulfillment, and simply being carried off will not of itself bring them about; something else must first occur, something that involves very quiet waiting and childlike secret confidence, though one cannot even guess how it might be initiated and how it will proceed from there. That lies with the man who brought the calf to the field, that lies with God.

No, Joseph did not forget the old man at home, numb with grief.

His silence, the silence of so many years, ought not lead us to such reproach for even a moment—least of all at the point where we have now halted and are experiencing feelings that match his own to a tee, for they are his. If, in fact, we have a sense that we have arrived at this point in our story once before and have told all this once before, if we are deeply stirred by a special sense of recognition, the sense that we have seen and dreamt all this before, and feel the need to give that sensation free rein—our hero was caught up in the very same experience, and such a correspondence surely has a sound basis. What we in our language are tempted to call his bond with his father—a bond all the deeper and more intense since, thanks to all-embracing correspondences and substitutions, it was at the same time a bond with God—proved extraordinarily strong at just this moment; and why should it not have held strong in him, since it held strong to him, both within and beyond him? What he experienced was imitation and succession—for his father had first experienced it before him in a slight variation. And there is a mystery in watching how the components of will and guidance are blended in the phenomenon of succession, so that it becomes impossible to distinguish who or what is actually doing the imitating and attempting to repeat what has been experienced before—the individual or his destiny. What lies within is reflected in the external world and, seemingly without being willed, becomes the reality of events that are bound up in the individual and were always one with him. For we wander in the footsteps of others, and all of life is a pouring of the present into mythic forms.

Joseph played with all sorts of imitations and softly dazzling self-substitutions, knew how to use them to make an impression and to win people over to them if only for the moment. But now he was totally preoccupied with the return and resurrection of his father's story within him. He was Jacob, his father, entering into Laban's realm, carried off to the underworld, intolerable to those at home, fleeing before fraternal hatred, before the red man's snorting jealousy of blessing and birthright—Esau transformed tenfold this time, that was one variant; and Laban looked somewhat different in this present as well, had arrived clad in royal linen and on fire-spending wheels, was Potiphar, tamer of horses, large, fat, and so bold that it set those around him trembling. But it was he, there was no doubt of it, though life might play with ever new forms of the same thing.

Once again, as proclaimed by what once was, Abram's seed was a stranger in a land that did not belong to him, and Joseph would serve this Laban, who in returning now bore the high-flown Egyptian name Gift of the Sun—and how long would he serve him?

We asked the same question in Jacob's day and settled the issue by applying reason. Determined to clear up the matter for good and all this time as well and to bind dreams to reality, we ask it yet again in the case of the son. Objectifying consideration of chronology and age has always been very lax in the case of Joseph's story. Superficial, dreamy fantasy ascribes to his figure the same immutability beyond the touch of time that it had won in Jacob's eyes, who believed him dead and mutilated—and that indeed only death can bestow. But the boy who in his father's mind now belonged to eternity went on living and increasing in years, and it is important to make it clear that the Joseph before whose throne his indigent brothers would one day appear and bow down was by then a forty-year-old, rendered unrecognizable to those petitioning him not only by dignity, rank, and attire, but also by the changes time had wrought on his person.

Twenty-three years had passed since his Esau-brothers had sold him into Egypt—almost as many as Jacob had spent altogether in the Land of No Return; and the land where Abram's seed was a stranger this time might likewise bear that name, indeed even more rightly so than the first, for Joseph did not remain there fourteen plus six plus five years—or seven, plus thirteen and five—but in fact his whole life, and returned home only in death. Fully unclear, however, and a subject to which little thought has been given is the question of how his years in the underworld are to be divided between clearly separated epochs in his blessed life, that is, between the first decisive period of his stay in Potiphar's house and the time spent in the pit, where he found himself yet a second time.

The time encompassed by these two periods comes to a total of thirteen years, the same number that Jacob spent in producing his string of twelve Mesopotamian children—assuming, that is, that Joseph was thirty years old when his head was raised up and he became first among those in the lower world. Granted, his age at the time is recorded nowhere—or at least not there where it ought to be found if it is to be authoritative. And yet it is a generally accepted fact—an axiom that requires no proof but speaks for itself and begets itself like the sun, so to speak, by its own mother—with clearest claim to a simple "so it is." For it is always so. Thirty years is the right age for entering on that stage of life at which Joseph had arrived; at thirty a man steps out of the darkness and wasteland of preparation into active life; it is the time to show oneself, the time of fulfillment. Thirteen years, then, passed between the seventeen-year-old's entrance into the land of Egypt and the day he stood before Pharaoh—that much is certain. But how many of those were spent living in Potiphar's house, and how many, therefore, in the pit? Established tradition leaves the matter open; a few noncommittal phrases are all that can be teased from it that might help us clear up the chronology of our story. Which arrangement should we apply to it? What grouping of years shall we settle upon?

The question appears unseemly. Do we know our story or do we not? Is it fitting and proper to the nature of a story for its teller publicly to account for its dates and facts according to a given set of considerations and deductions? Should the narrator be present as anything other than an anonymous source of what is told or, better, of a story that tells itself, in which everything *is* by virtue of itself, is this way and no other, indisputable and certain? The narrator, or so some find, should be inside his story, one with it, and not outside it, calculating and substantiating it. But how is it then with God, whom Abram thought into being and recognized? He is in the fire, but He is not fire. He is both in it and outside of it. It is, to be sure, a twofold matter: to be something and to observe it. And yet there are planes and spheres where both take place at once—the narrator is in his story, but he is not the story; he is the story's space, but its space is not coequal with his, but rather he is outside of it as well, and by a shift in his nature he puts himself in a position to comment on it. At no point have we intended to awaken the illusion that we are the original source of the story of Joseph. Before anyone could tell it, it happened; it flowed up out of the same spring from which all that happens flows, and in happening it told itself. It has been in the world ever since; everyone knows it or thinks he knows it, for often enough it is merely a superficially dreamy and vague knowledge without much accountability or commitment. It has been told a hundred times and passed through the medium of a hundred tellings. And here today it is passing though another, in which it gains self-contemplation and the specificity of detail by recalling what once actually happened to it, so that it both flows forth and comments on itself.

It comments, for example, on how the thirteen years between Joseph's sale and the raising up of his head were passed. This much at least is certain: that the Joseph who was put in prison was a long way from being the boy the Ishmaelites brought to Peteprê's house; rather, by far the largest part of those thirteen years belonged to his sojourn in that house. We might categorically state that this was so; but we would happily deign to ask how it could have been otherwise. In social terms, Joseph was a complete cipher when he entered the Egyptian's service at age seventeen or barely eighteen, and for the career that he enjoyed in that house he needed the time he actually spent there. It was not on his second or third day there that Potiphar placed this Habiru slave over all that he possessed and put it into Joseph's hands. It took time before he was even aware of him—he and other people who played such a decisive role in the outcome of this significant period in Joseph's life. Moreover, that career, in aspiring to rise to great heights, must necessarily have spanned many years if it was to be the preparatory school in business and administration that it is thought to have been—that is, for a stewardship on the grandest scale that was to follow.

In a word, Joseph remained with Potiphar for ten years, during which he reached the age of twenty-seven and became a Hebrew "man," as it is said of him, though occasionally in some quarters he is also called a "Hebrew servant," which, however, has an insultingly desperate sound to it, since in practical terms he had by then not been a "servant" for a long time. The point at which he ceased to be a servant, both in terms of position and recognized status, cannot be identified or determined with accuracy—no better today than it ever has been. In fact, ultimately and in purely legal terms, Joseph always remained a "servant," a slave, even during the period of his highest sovereignty and to the end of his life. For we do indeed read of his being sold and then sold again, but nowhere do we read of his being redeemed or set free. His extraordinary career silently passed over the legal fact of his status as a slave—and no one inquired about it, then, after his abrupt elevation. But even in Peteprê's house he did not remain a servant in the pejorative sense for long, nor did his blessed rise to Eliezer status as steward of the house take up all his years with Potiphar. Seven years were required for it, that is *one* certainty; and another is that it was only the rest of his decade there that was dominated and overshadowed by confusions that were created by the emotions of an unhappy woman and that led to the end of this period. Despite its general and approximate estimation of the time involved, tradition manages not to leave us with the perception that these confusions occurred simultaneously with or soon after his entrance into the house or were concurrent with the rise of his career, but began only after it had risen to its high point. They began, it says, "after these things"—that is, after its account of Joseph's winning Potiphar's highest confidence. That fateful passion, then, should be regarded as lasting a mere three years—long enough for those involved!—before it foundered in catastrophe.

The result of such a self-imposed examination of our story stands the test. If, on this basis, ten years of Joseph's life are to be assigned to the Potiphar chapter, that leaves three for the following period of imprisonment. No more and no less; and it is surely rare for truth and probability to coincide as convincingly as they do in this instance. What could be more illuminating and fitting than for Joseph, in correspondence to the three days he lay in the grave at Dothan, to lie in that hole for three years, neither more, nor less? One could go so far as to say that he himself suspected as much from the start, indeed knew it and, given his regard for the meaningful, correct, and lovely order of things, could have considered no other possibility—and was confirmed in his belief by a destiny that yielded to pure necessity.

Three years—not merely was it so, it could not have been otherwise. And tradition, exhibiting unusual precision in its chronology, states how these three years were divided up; it declares that Joseph's famous episode with his elegant fellow prisoners—the chief baker and the head butler, whom he was assigned to wait upon—occurred within the first year. "After two full years," it is said, Pharaoh had a dream and Joseph interpreted his dream for him. Two years after what? One could argue the issue. What might be intended is: two years after Pharaoh had become Pharaoh, which is to say, after the ascension to the throne by the particular Pharaoh granted these puzzling dreams. Or it could mean: two years after Joseph had interpreted the dreams of the two gentlemen and after the chief baker, as we know, had been hanged. But it would be a pointless argument, for the statement is supported by both sets of circumstances. Yes, Pharaoh dreamed his dreams two years after the episode with the incriminated courtiers; and at the same time, he dreamed them two years after he had become Pharaoh, for during Joseph's stay in prison, toward the end of his first year, it happened that Amenhotep, the third of that name, was united with the sun—and his son, the dreamer, set the double crown upon his head.

And thus one can see that there is nothing false in our story, that it all fits within these ten plus three years, until Joseph was thirty years old, and is harmoniously resolved in truth and accuracy.

In the Land of the Grandchildren

The game of life, in terms of people's relationships with one another and these same people's total ignorance in regard to the future of such relationships, which at the first exchange of glances could not be more fragile, lightweight, tenuous, strange, and detached, yet are destined, come some unimaginable day, to become a searing entanglement of dreadful, close-breathing intimacy—that game and that ignorance may well be cause for pondering and head-shaking by the forewarned observer.

With knees drawn up beneath him Joseph lay huddled there in the hard clay courtyard beside the favored dwarf called Shepses-Bes and peeked with curiosity between his hands at this precious and thoroughly unfamiliar phenomenon, swaying past him only a few steps away on a golden chair decorated with lions—this piece of underworldly but high civilization, which aroused in him no other emotions than those of respect mixed with very critical disapproval and no other thoughts than something like "Hello! That must be the mistress, Potiphar's wife, who is said to tremble for his safety. Does she belong among the good or the bad? There's no telling from her appearance. A very great lady of Egypt. Father would disapprove of her. I'm more easygoing in my judgments, but I'm not about to be intimidated, either . . ." That was all. And it was even less on her side. As she passed she turned her bejeweled head toward those showing reverence to her. She saw them and did not see them—so vacantly and blindly did her eyes sweep past them. Presumably she recognized the midget, whom she knew, and it may be that for a second the hint of a smile appeared in her eyes with their enameled extensions and slightly deepened the tucked corners of her serpentine mouth—though that might be disputed, too. She did not know the other one, but scarcely took him into account. He was somewhat out of place with that faded Ishmaelite hooded cape he still wore, and his hair was cut in unsuitable fashion. Did she notice? Perhaps. But any such awareness never reached any realm of account-taking in her proud conscious mind. If he did not belong here, then the gods only knew how he came to be here—it was perfectly sufficient if *they* knew; as for her, Mut-em-enet, or Eni as she was called, she considered herself far too precious to think any further about it. Did she see how beautiful and handsome he was? What is the point of such a question! Her seeing was not seeing; she never noticed, it was concealed from her that there was any need here to use her eyes. Neither of these two people was brushed by the palest shadow or hint of a suggestion of where they would find themselves within a few years and what would play out between them. That that unknown heap of reverence over there would someday be her one and all, her rapture and her wrath, her one morbid obsession that excluded all else, crippling her mind, driving her to deeds of madness, destroying all the composure, dignity, and order of her life—the idea never touched her. That she would cause him tears, that she would place his status as a wreath-crowned bride of God in absolute peril, and that by her folly he would, by a mere hair, miss being cut off from his God—the dreamer could not have dreamt any of it, although that lily-white arm dangling from her chair should have given him pause for thought.

The observer who knows this story in all its hours may be forgiven for stopping a moment to shake his head at the ignorance of those who are inside the story and not outside of it as well. But he at once forgoes the meddlesome curiosity that led him to lift the curtain on the future, and holds instead to the festive hour now prevailing. It embraces seven years, the years of Joseph's improbable—or so it seemed initially—rise in Peteprê's house, beginning at the moment when, once the mistress had floated past, Bes-em-heb, the jester, had whispered to him there in the courtyard, "We have to cut your hair and dress you, so that you're like all the rest," and led him to the servants' quarters where the barbers bantered with the little man while cutting Joseph's hair in the Egyptian style, so that he now looked just like the men he had seen tramping along the dikes, and from there to the wardrobe chamber in the same building, where in the room for aprons and loincloths, a scribe issued him Egyptian garments from his inventory, Peteprê's standard garb for work and holiday, so that he looked exactly like a lad of Keme—and perhaps even then his brothers might not have recognized him at first glance.

Seven rounds of the year—an imitation and repetition of a father's years in the life of his son, corresponding to the period of time in which Jacob had gone from a fugitive and beggar to a man weighed down with riches, Laban's indispensable partner in an enterprise bursting with prosperity from the power of his blessing. Now it was Joseph's turn to make himself indispensable—how did that happen, and what did he do? Did he find water as Jacob had? That was totally unnecessary. There was water in abundance on Peteprê's estate, for not only was there a lotus pond in the pleasure garden, but square basins had also been dug among the plants in the orchard and vegetable garden, and though these were not connected to the Great Provider they still nourished the gardens, for they were filled to the brim with groundwater. There was no lack of water; and even if Potiphar's house was not a house of blessing in its interior life—on the contrary, it soon became apparent that, despite its dignity, it was a house of folly and worry, haunted by great sorrow—it was at any rate overflowing with material prosperity, so that it would have been difficult, if not superfluous, to be its "increaser." It would be enough if its owner should one day arrive at the conviction that his estate was in the best of hands with this young foreigner as its manager and that he need not concern himself with anything or put his hand to any problem whatever—as was fitting for a man of his rank and as was his custom in life. The power of the blessing, then, proved itself by creating a sense of all-embracing trust; and a natural aversion to the betrayal of that trust in any regard—and especially in the most ticklish of regards—would powerfully assist Joseph and help him avoid a break with his God.

Yes, it was the Laban period that now commenced for Joseph—and yet it wasn't at all like what had happened to his father in the flesh; things came together very differently for his successor. For every return is a transformation, and just as the same number of colorful splinters keep falling into an ever-changing display in a kaleidoscope, so life as it plays out constantly brings forth something new out of the same components—with the son's constellation made up of the same fragments that had formed the constellation of his father's life. There is much to be learned from playing with a kaleidoscope; how different the pattern of arrangement in the son's splinters and stones from those arrayed in Jacob's life—and in falling into place, how much richer, more intricate, but also more troubling. A later, more delicate "case," this case of Joseph the son—lighter and wittier than that of his father, to be sure, but also more difficult, painful, and interesting, the simple outlines and patterns of the father's earlier life barely recognizable in the shape in which they returned in Joseph's. What, in his case, then becomes of the concept and model of Rachel, that charming and classic basic pattern? A perverse and perilous arabesque! It is surely obvious: events that are about to happen, but which are already present because they were played out even as the story first told itself and are still awaiting their turn now that we have reengaged the laws of time and sequence—what a powerful, mysterious attraction these events have; what a lively curiosity we have about them, and yet what a unique sort of curiosity it is, for it knows everything already and is interested as much in the telling as in the events themselves, and it is that same meddlesome urge that constantly tempts us to rush beyond the festive hour now prevailing. That is what happens when the double sense of the word "once" works its magic; if the future is the past, everything was played out long ago and need only be played out again in a clear-cut present.

What we can do to slacken the reins on our impatience is expand our concept of the present somewhat beyond these narrow confines and arrange larger portions of sequential events to form a unified and liberally treated simultaneity. The span of years during which Joseph served as Peteprê's personal servant and was then promoted to high steward is well suited to such a perspective; yes, it demands it, especially since the circumstances that contributed to his success (although one might think that they ought to have hindered it) were not only spread out over this entire period of time—indeed exercised their influence well beyond it—but also played a definite role at the beginning, so that one cannot speak of beginnings without discussing conditions that permeated everything atmospherically from the start.

Our source, after confirming the fact that Joseph had been sold a second time, asserts above all else that Joseph "was in the house of his master the Egyptian." To be sure, that is where he was. Where else? He was sold into that house, and there he was in the house— our source appears to confirm what is already certain and to repeat it to no purpose. But it must be read correctly. The statement that Joseph *was* in Potiphar's house is meant to instruct us that he *remained* there, which is in no way a confirmation of the sale that preceded it, but is a bit of news worth emphasizing. After having been sold into Peteprê's house itself, Joseph remained there, which means: he escaped, by God's will, the all too obvious danger of being sent to drudge in the Egyptian's fields, where he would have languished by the heat of day, shivered in the chill of night, and might well have ended his days unknown, never to move beyond darkness and privation under the lash of a less civilized overseer.

That sword hovered over him, and we should be amazed it never fell—for it dangled loosely enough. Joseph was a foreigner sold into Egypt, a son of Asia, an Amu lad, a Habiru or Ebrew, and we must first deal with the contempt to which this necessarily exposed him in this most arrogant of all created nations, before moving on to discuss how it was moderated, indeed abrogated by forces that stood in contradiction to it. That for a few seconds the steward Mont-kaw was tempted to take Joseph as more or less a god does not prove that, particularly at that point, he took him for *more* than half a man. For, frankly, he did not. The citizens of Keme, whose ancestors had drunk from the waves of the holy river and over whose incomparable homeland—with its edifices, a script handed down from the ancient past, and a panoply of statues—the Lord of the Sun had himself once been king, reserved the term "human" so expressly for themselves that very little of such an evaluation in any real sense was left over for non-Egyptians, for Negroes of Kush, for instance, or for Libyans with their braids or Asians with lice-infested beards. The concepts of impurity and abomination were in no way inventions of Abram's seed and certainly not the exclusive property of the children of Shem. They and the Egyptians both held some things to be impure: the pig, for example. But in addition, the Ebrews themselves were considered an abomination by the Egyptians, and to such an extent that they felt it beneath their dignity and offensive to pious scruples to break bread with such people—it was a breach of table manners; and some twenty years after the point in time where we have now halted, when, with God's permission, Joseph had totally become an Egyptian in all his habits and general bearing, he looked out upon certain barbarians at his table and ordered them served separately from himself and his Egyptian entourage, both to save face and not to defile himself in the eyes of his servants.

That was how things stood on principle for the people of Amu and Haru in Egypt; it was how things stood for Joseph himself upon his arrival. That he remained in the house and did not have to waste away in the field is a miracle, or at least a cause for wonder; but it was not one of God's miracles in the full sense of the word, since contributing to it were a great many human conventions, matters of fashion and taste—in short, those influences that we said stood in contradiction to this fundamental attitude, moderating and indeed abrogating it. This sort of contempt, for example, was evident in Dûdu, husband of Zeset, he was its champion; he tried to propose that Joseph be sent off to drudge in the fields. For he was not only a person—or little person—of full and sterling substance, but was also an adherent and defender of the strict observance of all ancient and sacred traditions, a fundamentally pious dwarf; and that made him a partisan, a zealot for a school of thought, a movement, a natural and aggressively unified alliance of all sorts of resolute opinions on matters of morality, the state, and religion, which had to take its stand against all other less restrictive, less backward-looking views and whose stronghold on Peteprê's estate was primarily in the women's house, or more precisely, in the personal chambers of Mut-em-enet, its mistress, which were frequented by a man whose austere personage was quite rightly seen as the center and focus of all such endeavors: Beknechons, the First Prophet of Amun.

More of him later. It was some time before Joseph first heard of him and saw him, just as he only gradually gained an insight into the conditions we have sketched here. But he would have had to be less attentive and less quick in evaluating favor and disfavor not to have picked up some of this, indeed its essence, in a very short time—after his first exchange of chitchat with the rest of the house's servants, in fact. He made a practice of pretending he had picked things up ahead of time and already knew as well as anyone about Egypt's mysteries and secrets. Although cautious in his choice of words, he spoke in a very adroit Egyptian that others found rather droll and evidently amusing, so that he was in no special hurry to regularize it, and—deftly making use of a favorite nickname given to Nubian Moors—he would mention the "rubber-eaters" he had seen ferried across the river to a royal audience, adding that the carping of jealous nobles at levees would probably not be able to accomplish much for a while now against the prince-viceroy of Kush, who by delighting Pharaoh's heart with his surprise tribute had known how to pull the rug out from under them. They laughed even harder at this than if he had told them any real news, for they were comfortable with familiar and oft-repeated gossip; and the amusement they took in his foreign accent—in fact, they admired it to some extent and kept their ears open for any makeshift Kenanite words that might find their way into his speech—immediately shed light for him on the issue of favor and disfavor.

Indeed, they used such words themselves as best they could. They tried to intersperse their own conversations with foreign fragments, from Akkadia or Babylonia, as well as from the language of Joseph's world; and he at once sensed, even before finding any real confirmation for it, that this was their way of trying to emulate people of elegance, and that, in turn, even the latter did not speak this way at the prompting of their own folly, but were themselves imitating an even higher realm, that is, the court. As we noted, Joseph grasped these dependencies before he tried his own hand at them. It was really true, and he smiled to himself in discovering it: This little race of people, who took virtually boundless pride in having been raised on Nile water and belonging to the land of human beings, the only land to have truly given birth to the gods; who would have responded not with anger but simply with laughter to the least doubt about the ancient and quite incontrovertible superiority of their civilization over the world set round about them; and who were filled to the brim with the martial glory of their kings, their Ahmoses, Thutmoses, and Amenhoteps, who had conquered earth's disk as far as the backward-running Euphrates and advanced their boundary stones to the remotest northern edge of Retenu and the southernmost lands of desert-dwelling archers—this little race so certain of itself was also weak and childish enough openly to envy him his

Canaanite mother tongue, and in fact, automatically and against all common sense, credited his natural fluency in it as an intellectual merit.

Why? Because anything Canaanite was refined. And why refined? Because it was foreign and exotic. But were not wretchedness and inferiority part of all things foreign? Certainly, but it was refined nonetheless, and in their eyes such illogical esteem was based not on childish weakness but on liberality of spirit—Joseph could sense it. He was the first ever to sense it in this world, for this was that phenomenon's first appearance in the world. It was the liberal spirit of people who themselves had not defeated and subjugated those wretched foreign lands, but had let earlier generations do it for them and now permitted themselves to find refinement in their liberality. The grand and powerful set the tone—that much was evident to Joseph from the house of Peteprê, the fan-bearer, for the more he saw of it the more he was able to convince himself that its treasures were for the most part goods from the harbor—imports produced by foreigners, primarily goods from Joseph's homeland, in both the narrower and wider sense, from Syria and Canaan. He found that flattering, and at the same time soft-headed, for on his leisurely journey from the Delta to the House of Amun he had had ample opportunity to observe the attractive, homegrown enterprise and expertise of Pharaoh's Two Lands. Potiphar had bought horses of Syrian blood—and yes, the best such animals came either from there or Babylonia, those bred in Egypt were less valuable. And his chariots, including the one with the gemstone fireworks on its spokes, were likewise from there; but that he had imported his cattle from the land of the Amorites could only be regarded as an eccentricity of fashion when one considered the agreeable domestic cattle with their lyre-shaped horns—the soft-eyed cows of Hathor, the strong stock of bulls from which Merwer and Hapi were selected. Pharaoh's friend carried an inlaid walking stick from Syria, and the beer and wine he drank came from there as well. The pitchers from which these were served to him were also "from the harbor," as were the weapons and musical instruments that decorated his rooms. The gold of splendid ornamental vessels, which stood almost man-high in painted alcoves in both the northern and western columned halls of his house and also adorned the dining room on both sides of its raised dais, doubtlessly came from Nubian mines, but the vases themselves were from Damascus and Sidon; and in the banquet hall that also served to receive guests and was accessible both through beautiful doors of the entrance hall and of the family dining chamber directly adjoining it, Joseph was shown other vessels—somewhat outlandish in shape and decoration and from the Goat Mountains in the land of Edom of all places, like a greeting from his foreign uncle Esau, who was evidently likewise considered a refined fellow here.

The gods of Amor and Canaan, Baal and Astarte, were regarded as very refined, something Joseph noticed right off from the way Potiphar's servants, assuming they were his gods as well, inquired about them and complimented him on them. That seemed an even more soft-headed piece of religious fanaticism because relationships and the balance of power between peoples and nations were commonly believed to be embodied in their gods, to be simply the external expression of their personal lives. Granted, what was the thing itself and what was its image? What was reality and what was its restatement? Was it merely a turn of phrase to say that Amun had conquered the gods of Asia, proving himself worthy of tribute, whereas it had actually been Pharaoh who had subjugated the kings of Canaan? Or was the latter simply the unreal but earthly expression of the former? Joseph was well aware that no such distinction could be made. The thing and its image, the real and the unreal, formed an inextricably intertwined whole. But that is precisely why the people of Mizraim were in some sense betraying Amun not only in finding Baal and Ashtaroth so refined, but also in larding the language of their gods with transmogrified words taken from Shem's children—saying *"seper"* for "scribe" or *"nehel"* for "river," because the Canaanite words were *"sofer"* and *"nahal."* It was indeed a liberality of spirit upon which such customs, whims, and fashions were based—a liberality directed, in fact, against Egypt's Amun. The result was that the fundamental contempt for all things Semitic and Asiatic was no longer taken very seriously; and in calculating favor and disfavor, Joseph entered that fact in the credit column.

He took note of these drifting differences of opinion, these currents and countercurrents, with which, as we said, he would become truly familiar only as his life merged with the life of the land. Since Potiphar was a courtier, one of the friends of Pharaoh, it was not hard to guess that the source of this hostile attitude toward Amun lay in the West, beyond the *nehel,* in the Great House itself. Might that, Joseph wondered, have something to do with Amun's troops and combat force, the temple militia bristling with lances that had pinned him to the wall on the Street of the Son? With Pharaoh's displeasure that this all too powerful god of the state was competing with him in his own arena of martial enterprise?

A strangely intricate, far-reaching web! Pharaoh's resentment of Amun or the presumptuous strength of his temple was perhaps the ultimate reason why Joseph did not end up in the fields, but instead was allowed to remain in his master's house and have nothing to do with the fields until much later, and then not as a drudging laborer but as an overseer and administrator. The young slave Osarsiph enjoyed the idea of a connection that made him the silent beneficiary of distant, but lofty impulses and bound him from afar, through the agency of his high master, with the highest. But he enjoyed still more the general atmosphere drifting his way from the world to which he had been transplanted and liked sniffing for traces of its favor and disfavor with his pretty, if somewhat thick-nostriled nose—an atmosphere familiar to his nature and in which he felt like a fish in water. This was the air of late autumn, the aura of a society of grandchildren and heirs already far removed from the foundations and patterns of their fathers, whose victories had left them in a position to regard as refined what had once been conquered. All this spoke to Joseph, because he himself was a latecomer, in time and in his soul; his case, too, was that of a son and grandson—light, witty, difficult, and interesting. Which is why he felt like a fish in water here, and was filled with good hope that, with God's help, he would do God honor and go very far in Pharaoh's underworld.

The Courtier

Dûdu, then, the wedded dwarf, acted out of loyalty to the past and as a partisan of the good old days, and was simply acting in Amun's name when with deep voice and stubby arms waving zealously he looked up at Mont-kaw and admonished him to hand this recently acquired Habiru slave over to work in the fields, because he was a child of the enemies of the gods and did not belong in the house. But at first the steward claimed he did not even recall what the dwarf was talking about—whom did he mean? An Amu slave? Bought from

Minæans? Named Osarsiph? Ah, yes! And using his own forgetful-ness as a lesson to his admonisher in the cool indifference with which the matter was to be more properly regarded, he expressed amazement that the keeper of the wardrobe should waste a single thought, let alone words, on it. It was a matter of decorum, Dûdu replied. It was an abomination for the human children of the house to break bread with such a creature. But the overseer denied that they were all that squeamish, and mentioned a Babylonian maidser-vant who worked in the house of seclusion, Ishtarummi, with whom the other women got along well enough. "Amun!" the guardian of the jewel chests said. He spoke the name of the god who preserved all things, and there was insistence, indeed a certain threat in the look he cast up at Mont-kaw. It was for the sake of Amun, he said.

"Amun is great," the overseer replied with a shrug he was unable to conceal entirely. "I may very well send our purchase out into the fields," he went on. "Perhaps I'll send him, perhaps not, but if I do, it will be because I happen to think of it. I do not like having others casting lines for my thoughts so that they may lead them by a string."

In a word, he rebuffed both Zeset's spouse and his admonish-ment—to some degree intentionally, for he really couldn't stand the fellow, for which he had reasons and rationale. The reason for his distaste was the dwarf's sterling pomposity, which annoyed him; his rationale, however, was his own great and genuine devotion to Pe-teprê, his master, to whom such pomposity was an affront and a nui-sance. All of which will become clear in due time. But Mont-kaw's aversion to Dûdu's robust personality was not his only motive for turning a deaf ear. Another was the jester Neteruhotpe, for whom he had a real liking—less on the dwarf's account than as the converse of his attitude toward Dûdu—and he had only just rebuffed him in much the same way for coming to him on Joseph's behalf with the opposite intent. This man of the sand, he had whispered, was beauti-ful, good, and clever, a favorite of the gods—a true Neteruhotpe, as he himself was named, though he was not that—as his unspoiled and keen dwarfish eye had recognized, and the overseer should make certain that Osarsiph be given chores, whether indoors or out, in which he could prove his qualities. But in this instance as well the steward had claimed to have no recollection whatever, and then, peevishly, declined to pursue the issue of how to put to use an inconsequential, superfluous purchase he had chanced to make purely as a favor. There was really no hurry about it, and he, Mont-kaw, had other things to think about.

That was a plausible reply; for an overworked man, whose kidneys gave him occasional trouble besides, it was a perfectly proper answer, and Neteruhotpe could only hold his peace. In reality the overseer did not want to know about Joseph and pretended both to others and to himself that he had forgotten him because he was ashamed of those ambiguous thoughts or impressions that had overcome him, a sensible man, when, upon first beholding the lad offered for sale, he had taken him half and half for a god, for the Lord of the White Ape. He was ashamed of that and wanted neither to be reminded of it nor to accept suggestions that, if carried out, might have represented, in his own eyes, any sort of indulgence of those impressions. He refused either to send the purchased slave to drudgery in the fields or to make sure that he was employed in the house—because he did not want to worry about him in any way, wanted to wash his hands of him. The good man did not notice, and even hid from himself, that his very reticence was an accommodation to his first impressions. It was an affirmation of his fear; and, just between us, it arose from a feeling that lies at the foundation of the world and thus also lay at the foundation of Mont-kaw's own soul: expectation.

And that is why Joseph, now properly trimmed and clad Egyptian-style, idled about with nothing to do for weeks and months, or, what amounted to the same thing, was sporadically employed now here, now there, today at this task, tomorrow at that, wherever needed for easy, basic chores on Peteprê's estate—which no one really noticed, by the way, since given the wealth of this house of blessing there were plenty of idlers and standabouts. And in a certain sense he was pleased and happy that no one paid him any attention—that is, not prematurely, before they would do so in earnest and to his honor. It was important to him that his career not begin with a false and untoward step, with his being summoned, for instance, to a task among the house's common laborers and thus being lost forever to some obscure handiwork. He guarded against that and learned how to make himself scarce at the right moment. He enjoyed sitting down to chat with the watchmen on their brick bench by the gate and mixing in a few Asiatic fragments to make them laugh. But he avoided the bakery, because such exquisite pastries were baked there that he would have impressed no one with his extraordinarily good flat cakes, and he avoided as best he could being seen among the sandal and paper makers, the weavers of colorful palm-fiber mats, the carpenters and potters. An inner voice told him that it would not be wise to play the untutored, clumsy beginner with them—not, at least, with a view to the future.

On the other hand, it was all right to appear now and then in the laundry or at the granaries to set up lists and accounts, for which his knowledge of the local script soon proved adequate. With a flourish he would end them with a note: "Written by the young foreign slave Osarsiph, for Peteprê, his great master, ah, may the Hidden One grant him long life, and for Mont-kaw, overseer of all things, highly skilled in his office, whom Amun is implored to grant ten thousand years of life beyond his present one, on such and such a day, of the third month of Akhet, the season of the flood." He expressed his blessings in these conventional phrases despite their disloyalty to his God, out of the sure and evidently legitimate confidence that, given his situation and his need to make himself well liked, God would not hold it against him. Mont-kaw saw these lists and signed addenda from time to time, but said not a word about them.

Joseph broke bread with the rest of Potiphar's servants in their quarters and drank his beer with them as they chattered away. And when it came to chattering, he soon was as good or better at it than they were, for his talents had more to do with language than with handiwork. He listened to the local idiom and wrapped his tongue around it, at first so that he could chat with them, but later to command them. He learned to say "As true as the king lives!" and "By the great Khnum, Lord of Yeb!" He learned to say "I am in earth's greatest joy," or "He is in the rooms beneath the rooms," meaning "on the ground floor"; or to say of an angry overseer "He was like a leopard of Upper Egypt." When telling a story, he grew accustomed to giving demonstrative pronouns the special attention Egyptians loved to give them, and always to speak like this: "And as we arrived at this impregnable fortress, this good old man said to this officer, 'Behold this letter!' And when this young commanding officer looked at this letter, he said, 'By Amun, let these foreigners pass.'" They liked hearing it told this way.

On holidays, of which there were several each month, both according to the calendar and the actual season—for example, the day when Pharaoh cut a swath of grain at the beginning of harvest, or the anniversary of his ascension to the throne and of the unification of the Two Lands, or the day when a column was erected in honor of Osiris, to the accompaniment of masques and tinkling sistrums, not to mention days of the moon's phases and the great days celebrating the triad of Father, Mother, and Son—on those days roast goose and haunches of beef were served in the servants' quarters; but Neteruhotpe, Joseph's pint-size patron, also brought him from the women's house a variety of other tasty sweets that he had set aside: grapes and figs, cakes shaped like recumbent cows and fruit glazed with honey, and he would whisper to him, "Take it, my young man of the sand, it is better than leeks with your bread, and this dwarf took it for you from the tables after those who live in seclusion had eaten. For they are all growing far too plump from nibbling and nipping, have become cackling fattened geese for whom I dance. Take these provisions that the dwarf brings you, all the way up to your mouth, and may you enjoy them, for the others have nothing like it."

"And has Mont-kaw not yet thought of me and my advancement?" Joseph might then ask, after having first thanked him for what he had brought.

"Not really just yet," little Neteruhotpe would reply, shaking his head. "He is asleep and deaf to your cause and does not like being reminded. But your little one is already busy steering your ship ahead of the wind, let him work his ways. He is pondering just how to bring Osarsiph before Peteprê, and it shall be done."

Joseph had, you see, pressed him to arrange it so that at some point he might somehow come before Potiphar; but that was truly almost impossible, and as anxious as he was to help, Bes-em-heb could only attempt to go about it one step at a time. Tasks with even the remotest connection to the person of the master, and especially anything to do with attending upon him in his chambers, were all too firmly held in jealous hands. It would have been a mistake to put Joseph to work caring for his horses, feeding, currying, harnessing, and unharnessing the Syrians—that was out of the question. He still would not have been allowed to lead the team out, not even to Neternakht the driver, let alone to the master. It might have been a step in the right direction, but the position was not open to him. No, for now it was not possible for him to speak with the master, but only to listen to his servants speak about him, to pump them about him and what was going on in general in the house to which he had been sold, and, whenever possible, to observe them attentively as they went about serving their master—especially the steward Mont-kaw, just as he had first watched him at noontime on the day he was sold.

Again and again, it was the same every time; he saw it and heard it. Mont-kaw flattered the master—polished the apple, one might have said, had the idiom been appropriate in a land without apples—he encouraged him, perhaps that is the better way to put it, clothing the man's life in words, praising the splendor of his wealth and high rank, holding up to him his bold manliness as a leader of the hunt and a tamer of horses, a man who set the world trembling for him; and he did it all, so Joseph came to believe with some certainty, not to curry favor, not out of servility and sycophancy, not for his own sake, but for his master's, for Mont-kaw appeared to be an honest man, neither cruel to those below him nor cringing before those above—rather, if one were to speak of adulation, the word should be used in its basic, unimpeachable sense and those flattering remarks understood simply as the overseer's love for his master and desire to comfort his soul in open and loyal service. That at least was Joseph's impression, and it was underscored by the tender smile, at once both melancholy and triumphant, with which such kindness was received by Pharaoh's friend, this man tall as a tower and yet so unlike Ruben. The more Joseph made the affairs of the house his own over time, the clearer it became to him that the relationship between Mont-kaw and his master was only a variation on the way all the members of the household treated each other. They were all very dignified, showing one another a great deal of reverence, tenderness, and flattering, forbearing consideration, a mutually supportive courtesy, but of a somewhat tense and fretful sort—it was how Potiphar dealt with his consort, the mistress Mut-em-enet, and she with him; how "the saintly parents on the upper floor" treated their son Pe-teprê and he them; and in turn how they responded to their daughter-in-law, Mut, and she to them. Nevertheless, for all these people it was as if dignity—seemingly so greatly favored by external circumstance and also powerfully governing their conduct, for they needed to feel strong in their awareness of it—did not stand on the firmest footing, but seemed hollow and something of a sham, which, then, was the very reason that they all made a point of trying to confirm and strengthen their sense of dignity with gentlest courtesy and loving deference. If there was something fatuous and disconcerting about this house of blessing, this was its source, and if worry haunted it, it was this that hinted at it. It did not name its name, but Joseph thought he could hear it spoken. To him its name was Hollow Dignity.

Peteprê had many titles and honors. Pharaoh had raised his head high and on several occasions had stood at the Window of Presentation and tossed tributes of gold to him in the presence of the royal family and the entire court, while the mob shouted its approval and hopped its ceremonial hops for joy. They told Joseph all about it in the servants' quarters. The master was called Fan-Bearer at the King's Right Hand and Friend of the King. His hope one day to be called Sole Friend of the King (of which there were only a few) was well founded. He was Captain of the Palace Guard and Chief High Executioner and Warden of the Royal Prisons—which is to say, he was called by these names, held these court offices, bore these empty or almost empty titles. In reality—as Joseph learned from the servants—a rough soldier, a colonel named Haremheb, or Hor-em-heb, both commanded the bodyguards and was chief executioner; and although this high officer was to some extent accountable to the titular commander and honorary warden of the prisons, this was really only a formality. It was a good thing, too, that this fat, Ruben-like tower of a man with his soft voice and melancholy smile did not have to make mush of people's backs with five hundred strokes of the rod—or, as it was said, "receive them into the house of torture and execution" and "put the color of the corpse in their faces"—for he would have found it less than suitable and not at all to his taste; and Joseph came to realize that this state of affairs meant that his master often had to put up with vexations and many a gilded humiliation.

The fact was that Potiphar's status as an officer and commander—the refined, but frail symbol of which was that cudgel ending in a pinecone that he held in his small right hand—was an honorary fiction, which in his conscious mind was reinforced hourly not only by Mont-kaw but also by the whole world and its external circumstances, but which, without his actually realizing it, he secretly may have taken for what it was: an unreal and hollow pretense. Just as the ornamental cudgel was the token of his hollow dignity, so, too—it seemed to Joseph—the symbolism might well have reached to deeper roots that had less to do with profession and service and were more a matter of natural human dignity; and, in turn, the hollowness of his offices might well have been symbolic of the hollowness of that more deeply rooted dignity.

Joseph possessed memories outside of his own life that told him how little the acceptance of customs and social arrangements can accomplish against the dark and silent awareness of honor that lies in the depths and will not be deceived by the bright fictions of the day. He thought of his mother—yes, strangely enough, in tracing and considering the circumstances surrounding Peteprê, this man of Egypt, the master who had bought him, his thoughts moved in a broad arc to Rachel, the charming wife, and to her confusion, which he knew about because it was a chapter of his own tradition and prehistory and because Jacob had told about those days many times, recalling how Rachel, his eager wife, had been barren to him according to God's decree and had had to let Bilhah take her place, so that she might give birth on Rachel's knees. Joseph believed he could see with his own eyes the bewildered smile on the face of the wife scorned by God so long ago—the smile of pride in the prestige of motherhood, which gave her honor among men but had no reality or hold in Rachel's flesh and blood—a half happiness, half deception that found makeshift support in custom, but was ultimately hollow and despicable. He used such memories to assist him in exploring his master's circumstances, in pondering the contradiction between the conscience of the flesh and the makeshift honor of custom. Without doubt such support and comfort, such compensations of some theoretical correspondence, were stronger and more productive in Potiphar's case than they had been in the case of Rachel's putative motherhood. His wealth, all the dignified splendor of a life adorned with gemstones and ostrich feathers, the familiar sight of slaves falling prostrate before him, living and guest quarters filled with treasures, overflowing storehouses and pantries, a house of women full of twittering, cackling, fibbing, and nibbling accessories to his lordly life, among whom the lily-armed Mut-em-enet was the first and true wife—all of it proved helpful in buoying up his sense of self-worth. And yet somewhere deep beneath, there where Rachel had felt ashamed of that silent abomination, he must have secretly known that he was not Captain of the Guard in reality, but in name only, precisely because Mont-kaw felt it necessary to "flatter" him.

He was a courtier, a chamberlain and servant of the king, very highly placed, to be sure, and showered with honors and worldly goods, but a courtier from head to toe; and the word had a malicious secondary meaning, or rather, it was made up of two related concepts that had merged into one; it was a word that is no longer used today—or at least not exclusively—in its original sense, but it had an extended meaning, while still preserving its original one, so that in both an honorable and malicious way its application was twofold and it gave rise to a twofold form of flattery: with regard to both honor and dishonor. A conversation that Joseph overheard—and not at all deceitfully, but quite openly and in his capacity as a servant—offered many an explanation for this set of circumstances.

The Task

It was ninety or a hundred days after Joseph had entered this house of honor and excellence that the dwarf Se'enkh-Wen-nofre-Neteruhotpe-em-per-Amun assigned him a happy and easily accomplished task—though it also had its difficult and painful side. For better or worse, he had once again been playing the quietly expectant role of idler and standabout in Potiphar's courtyard, when the little man in his rumpled festive attire, the cone for ointment atop his head, came running up and whispered his announcement that he had something for him, a bit of luck, something fine and lovely to hear, an opportunity for advancement. He had procured it from Mont-kaw, who had not said yes or no, but simply allowed it. No, Joseph was not to stand before Peteprê, not just yet. "But listen, Osarsiph, to what you are to do and to the blossom opening for you at the instigation of this dwarf, who has managed it by always keeping you in mind. Today at the fourth hour after noon, when they have rested from their meal, the saintly parents on the upper floor will go to the cottage in the pleasure garden, to sit there protected from sun and wind and enjoy the cooling water and the peace of old age. They love to sit there hand in hand on two chairs, with no one nearby except a mute servant, who kneels in one corner and holds a tray of refreshment to reinvigorate them from the exhaustion of peacefully sitting there. You are to be the mute servant, Mont-kaw has ordered it or at least not forbidden it, and you shall hold the tray. Except you may not budge, only kneel and hold it out, without so much as a blink of an eye, for otherwise you would disrupt their peace and force your presence upon them. Rather you must be a mute servant from head to toe, like a figure of Ptah—that is what they are accustomed to. Only when those exalted siblings show signs of weariness are you to set yourself in nimble motion, without ever standing up, and, as deftly as possible, offer them refreshment, taking care not to bumble on your knees or put your garb into a state of disarray. And once they have cheered themselves, you must retreat to your corner just as softly and nimbly, all the while staying on your knees and holding your body in control so that you do not pant for air or make yourself present in any inept way, and immediately become a mute servant again. Will you be able to do it?"

"Certainly!" Joseph replied. "Thank you, Neteruhotpe, I shall indeed do it, just as you have told me to, and shall even make my eyes as fixed as if of glass, so that I look like a piece of sculpture and my presence is no more than the space of air my body takes up—so impersonal shall I be. My ears, however, will remain wide open, but not so that those saintly siblings will even notice as they converse before me, allowing the internal affairs of this house to name their names to me, that I may become master of them in my mind."

"Fine enough," the dwarf replied. "But do not imagine it is all that easy to kneel there as a mute servant and figure of Ptah, scurrying back and forth on your knees with refreshment in hand. It would be good if you would practice it on your own first. You are to let the scribe of the sideboard present you with the refreshment, not in the out-kitchen, but in the pantry of the master's house, where it is kept at the ready. Go through the gate into the entrance hall and then turn left where there is a stairway and the special chamber of trust, Mont-kaw's bedroom. Cut through it and open the door on your right, which opens onto a long chamber or hallway full of supplies for the dining room, by which you will recognize the pantry. There you will find the scribe, who will hand you the necessary items, and you will bear them devoutly through the garden and to the cottage, a little ahead of time, so that, no matter what, you are there when the saintly pair arrives. You will be kneeling in the corner and listening. But once you hear them coming, you will stir not another eyelash and breathe only in secret, until signs of their weariness become apparent. Do you understand your task now?"

"Completely," Joseph responded. "There once was a man whose wife turned to a pillar of salt because she turned around to look at the city of desolation. I shall be just like her in my corner with my tray."

"I don't know that story," Neteruhotpe said.

"I shall tell it to you sometime," Joseph replied.

"Do that, Osarsiph," the little man whispered, "by way of thanks that I have procured for you this assignment as a mute servant! Tell me again, too, the story of the snake in the tree and how the unpleasant brother slew the pleasant one and about how the man of foresight built his ship like a box. And I would also like to hear again the story of how the sacrifice of the boy was averted, and the one about the smooth man that his mother made rough with skins and how he lay with the wrong wife in the dark."

"Yes," Joseph said, "our stories are worth hearing. But now I want to practice nimbly moving forward and backward on my knees, and I shall keep an eye on the shadow of the dial so that I may make myself smart in time for my task and fetch refreshment from the pantry and do everything you have told me to do."

Which is what he did, and once he thought he had the knack of it, he anointed himself and donned his holiday attire, putting on a longer skirt transparent enough to reveal the short apron beneath and tucking in his short tunic of darker, unbleached linen; he also made sure to garland his brow and chest with flowers in honor of the task for which he had been chosen. Then glancing at the sundial that stood in the open courtyard enclosed by the master's house, the women's house, the servants' quarters, and the out-kitchen, he stepped through the inner wall and entered the main door to Potiphar's entrance hall, which had seven doors of red wood, their wide lintels exquisitely adorned. Its roof was borne by round columns of the same red wood, polished to a shine, with stone bases and green capitals; on the floor of the hall were depicted heaven's constellations in a hundred shapes: Lion, Hippopotamus, Scorpion,

Snake, Ibex, and Bull formed a circle surrounded by any number of gods and kings, plus the Ram, the Monkey, and the Crowned Falcon.

Joseph moved across this floor and came to the stairway leading to the rooms above the rooms and passed through the door of the special chamber of trust, where Mont-kaw, he who stood over the house, curled up at night to rest. Joseph, who slept in his coat anywhere on the floor with the other menials, surveyed the special chamber, took note of the graceful bed set on animal legs, the blankets of hides, the headboard decorated with images of the divinities who watched over slumber—crook-legged Bes and Epets, the pregnant hippopotamus—the chests, the stoneware washing utensils, the basin for burning charcoal, the lampstands, and he thought of the long climb to the heights of trust that it took to enjoy such special comforts in the land of Egypt. Which is why he made sure he now proceeded with this task and entered the long pantry hall, so narrow that it needed neither columns nor support beams and ran to the back of the house on the west, adjoining not only both the reception hall for guests and the dining room, but also a third columned hall on the west—this latter was in addition to an entrance hall on the east and yet another on the north, so richly and extravagantly was Peteprê's house built. The pantry hall, however, was, as the dwarf had said, full of racks, shelves, and compartments to hold the provisions and dishes for the dining room: fruit, bread, cakes, spice jars, bowls, beer skins, long-necked wine pitchers in lovely stands, and the flowers to wreath them. Here Joseph met up with Kha'ma't, the tall scribe with reeds behind his ears, counting and taking notes as he moved through the chamber.

"Well, you greenhorn and dandy of the desert?" he said to Joseph. "So you've spruced yourself up, have you? So you like it here in the land of human beings and the gods, do you? Yes, you are to wait upon the saintly parents, I've already heard—you're here on my list. Presumably it was Shepses-Bes who arranged it; for, really, how else would you come by it? He wanted to buy you straightaway and ratcheted up your price to a ridiculous sum. So, you calf, you're evidently worth an ox, are you?"

Pay heed to your words before too long, Joseph thought to himself, for someday I will most certainly be set over you in this house. But aloud he said, "Be so kind, Kha'ma't—scholar of the house of

books, reader, writer, and magician—and give this least of petitioners the refreshment for Huya and Tuya, the venerable parents, that
as a mute servant I may have it at the ready for them in their hour of
exhaustion."

"I suppose I must do it," the scribe replied, "since you are on the
list and that fool has managed to put you there. I predict you'll spill
the beverage over the saintly pair's feet, and be hauled off for some
refreshment of your own, until both you and he who delivers it are
exhausted."

"I see it turning out quite differently, thank God," Joseph responded.

"Oh, you do, do you?" tall Kha'ma't asked, and blinked. "As
you please, it really is up to you. The refreshment is here as listed:
the silver tray, the golden pitcher with the blood of pomegranates,
plus the golden goblets, five shells of the sea with grapes, figs, dates,
doom-palm fruit, and almond cakes. You wouldn't steal or nibble,
would you?"

Joseph glared at him.

"Well, I suppose you won't," Kha'ma't said in some confusion.
"All the better for you. I simply asked, though I knew right away
you wouldn't care to have your nose and ears cut off, and it's probably not your habit in any case. It was only because," he went on, for
Joseph was silent, "it's well known, after all, how your previous
owners were forced to decide to favor you with the punishment of
the well for certain mistakes I know nothing of. They may indeed
have been minor, having nothing to do with the difference between
yours and mine, and merely have been matters of sophistry—that I
cannot know. And one has also heard that the punishment cleansed
you thoroughly of them, so that I found my question to be in order
simply by way of general precaution . . ."

What am I going on about, Kha'ma't said to himself, letting my
tongue run in circles like this. I amaze myself, but strangely enough
I have this deep desire to keep on talking and saying all sorts of
things for which there is no pressing need, and yet do it nonetheless.

"My office demanded of me," he said, "that I ask what I asked. It
is my duty to determine the honesty of a servant whom I do not
know, and I cannot avoid doing it for my own sake, for it would be
charged to me if tableware were to be misplaced. But I do not know
you, for your origins are dark, seeing that it is dark inside a well. It

may be brighter beyond that, but the third syllable of the name by which people call you—it is Osarsiph, is it not?—seems to indicate that you are a foundling from the marsh and perhaps drifted about in a reed basket until someone fetching water pulled you out—that sort of thing does happen now and again in this world. All the same, it is possible that your name refers to something else, but I shall let that be. In any case, I asked you what I asked because it was my duty, or if not absolutely my duty, then as a matter of course and in a manner of speaking. For it is the agreed manner of speaking among men that one addresses a young slave as I did, and calls him a calf in the ordinary tone of voice. I did not mean to say that you actually are a calf in reality—how could that even be? But I merely spoke as everyone does by common agreement. Nor is it really my prediction or my expectation that you will spill pomegranate juice on the feet of the saintly couple. I said it merely to be gruff in the ordinary way and lied to some extent. Is it not strange in this world how one usually does not say what one thinks, but what one believes others would say, and so speaks after the pattern of a scroll?"

"Tableware and what remains of the refreshment," Joseph said, "will be returned to you upon completion of my task."

"Fine, Osarsiph. You can go out through this door at the end of the pantry and need not retrace the way through the special chamber of trust. This will lead you directly to the encircling wall and the small gate through it. Go straight ahead, and you are already among trees and flowers and will see the pond and garden cottage smiling upon you."

Joseph departed.

Well, thought Kha'ma't, left behind to himself, God help me, did I ever babble on! There is no way of telling what that Asian may think of me. If only I had spoken like someone else and after the pattern of a scroll instead of following the mood of the moment and saying things very peculiarly close to the truth and speaking rubbish against my own will, so that my cheeks are burning now that it's over. By the aardvark! The next time he shows his face I'll be gruff with him in the most ordinary way.

Huya and Tuya

Meanwhile Joseph stepped through the small gate in the wall and into Potiphar's garden and found himself under the loveliest sycamores, date and doom palms, fig, pomegranate, and persea trees standing in rows on a greensward, with paths of red sand between. Half hidden among the trees was a small mound with a ramp leading to a delicately but colorfully painted summerhouse, which looked out on the rectangular pond that was bordered with papyrus and on whose green surface beautifully marked ducks were swimming. A light boat floated among the lotus blossoms.

Refreshment in hand, Joseph climbed the steps to the cottage. He knew these grounds, which were very grand. From here one could gaze across the pond to an avenue of plane trees, which led to the double-towered gate in the southern flank of the outside wall and allowed direct access to Potiphar's blessed park from that direction. The orchard, with its little basins full of groundwater, extended to the east from the pond, and then came a vineyard. There were beautiful beds of flowers as well, lining the avenue of plane trees and encircling the cottage. It must have cost the children of this Egyptian house of bondage a great deal of sour sweat to have brought the rich topsoil here to make all these things grow in what was originally desert.

With one side open entirely to the pond and flanked by small white columns fluted in red, the little cottage was handsomely furnished as a refined hideaway, intended not only for sheltered, solitary contemplation and enjoyment of the beauties of the garden but also for intimate social occasions, or just for a twosome, as the game board set to one side of a table suggested. Decorating the walls were amusing and natural scenes painted against a white background, partially in floral designs—charming representations of draped and dangling cornflowers, yellow persea blossoms, wild grape, red poppy, and the white petals of the lotus—partially in animated natural scenes taken from life: a herd of asses one could almost hear braying, a frieze of fat-breasted geese, a green-eyed cat among reeds, strutting cranes of a perfect rust color, people slaughtering animals and bearing fowls and haunches of beef to the sacrifice, and other delights for the eye. It was all exquisitely done, revealing the joyful,

ingenious, and softly ironic relationship of the designer to his subject and executed in an audacious and yet devoutly traditional
hand—indeed to such a degree that one was moved to laugh and exclaim, "Yes, yes, oh yes, that precious cat, that arrogant crane!"—
and yet be transfigured to a more austere and cheerful sphere, to a
kind of heaven of elevated taste, for which Joseph, as his eyes passed
over it, knew no name, but knew that he understood it perfectly
well. Culture was smiling down at him here, and Abram's belated
grandchild, Jacob's next to youngest, already somewhat worldly and
inclined to relish curiosity and to triumph in youth's freedom, took
some pleasure in secretly looking back upon his all too spiritual father, who would have disapproved of so much image-making. It is
utterly lovely, he thought, so let it be, old Israel, and do not scorn
what Keme's worldly children have accomplished here, its smiling
tension and high-soaring taste, for it may well be that it pleases God
Himself. Behold, I am its good friend and find it charming, though,
to be sure, always with a silent awareness in my blood that transferring what is on earth to the heaven of refined taste may not be the
most genuine and important thing, and that what is far more urgent
is God's concern for the future.

That is what he said to himself. The furnishings of the little cottage revealed the same heavenly good taste: set on lion's feet, the elegant long couch of ebony and ivory was strewn with down cushions
and draped in hides of panther and lynx; the roomy armchairs, their
backs of artfully stamped gilt leather, were heaped with embroidered
pillows and had overstuffed footstools in front; precious fumes rose
from the bronzed incense stands. And although the interior was a
comfortable domestic refuge, at the same time it functioned as a
chapel and place of worship; for on a raised bench at the back, little
silver teraphim, with crowns of gods on their small heads, stood
amid offerings of bouquets, and the various cult utensils showed
signs of use.

So Joseph knelt down in the corner by the entrance, ready to
serve, but leaving the refreshment on the mat in front of him for now
to rest his arms. But it wasn't long before he hastily picked it up and
froze in position, for here came Huya and Tuya shuffling in beak-
toed sandals through the garden, each supported on one side by a
child servant, two little girls with arms thin as twigs and mouths held
foolishly agape. For the pair of aged siblings desired and allowed no

one else to wait on them and now let the girls prop them up as they climbed the ramp into the cottage. Huya was the brother and Tuya the sister.

"First to our lords," old Huya ordered in a husky voice, "so that we may bow low."

"Quite so, quite so," agreed old Tuya, whose broad oval face was very pale. "To the silver lords first of all, so that we may beg their indulgence before taking our ease on chairs in the peace of the cottage."

And they had the little girls brace them up before the teraphim, where they raised withered hands and bent backs already bent, for age had twisted and buckled both their spines. Huya's head wobbled badly as well, both back and forth and sometimes from side to side. Tuya's neck was still steady. On the other hand, her eyes were strangely hidden in folds, were no more than a pair of blind slits, revealing neither gaze nor color, and her broad face was held under the spell of a fixed smile.

After the parents had prayed, their thin-armed servants led them to the two armchairs standing at the ready for them at the front of the cottage; they carefully lowered the two into place and picked up their feet, placing them on cushions edged in gold cord.

"Ah yes, ah yes, ah yes, yes, yes, yes," Huya said again in a husky whisper, for that was the only voice he had. "Go now, children who serve us, you have carefully done your duty by us, our legs are extended, our limbs are at rest, and all is well. Let it be, let it be, I am seated. Are you seated as well, Tuya, sister who shares my bed? Then all is well, and you two are to depart and withdraw for the present, for we wish to be by ourselves and to enjoy all alone this lovely hour of afternoon and early evening descending upon the reeds and duck pond and the tree-lined paths beyond, as far as the towers of the gate in the wall that defends us. Quite undisturbed and seen by no one, we wish to sit here and exchange the intimate words of old age with no one to hear."

But there was Joseph kneeling nearby in the corner with his tableware, just diagonally opposite to them. He knew quite well, however, that he was only a mute servant, no more present than a thing, and he fixed glassy eyes to stare just past the old people's heads.

"Do it then, maidens, obey that gentle command," said Tuya,

who, in contrast to the hoarseness of her brother and husband, had a soft, but full voice. "Go and keep yourselves just far and near enough away that you may still hear the handclap by which we shall call you. For should we fall faint or death approach to surprise us, we shall clap our hands as a sign that you should assist us and, if need be, allow the bird of the soul to flutter out of our mouths."

The little girls prostrated themselves and then departed. Huya and Tuya sat side by side, their ancient, well-ringed hands joined where the inner arms of the chairs touched. They both wore their ice-gray hair—the color of badly tarnished silver—exactly alike: in thin strands that fell from the sparse crown down over their ears and almost to their shoulders, except that in the case of Tuya, the sister, someone had attempted to braid the ends of every two or three of these strands to form a kind of fringe, which, given her thin hair, could never have worked very well. For his part, Huya wore a little beard of that same murky silver on the underside of his chin. He also wore golden earrings that stuck out through his hair, while Tuya's old head was wreathed in a broad band of black and white enamel worked into a petal pattern—an artfully crafted piece of jewelry one would have wished worn by a less tottering head. For we are jealous of beautiful things on behalf of youth's freshness, and secretly begrudge them to heads already more like skulls.

Peteprê's mother was elegantly dressed in other respects as well. The upper part of her petal-white garment was cut like a pilgrim's collar and the waist was cinched with a costly and colorfully embroidered ribbon whose ends fell in the broad arc of a lyre almost to her feet; a large necklace of the same black and white glass enamel as her headband covered her ancient breast. In her left hand she carried a small bouquet of lotus blossoms that she now passed under her brother's nose.

"Here, my treasure," she said, "let your nose sniff at these holy blossoms, the beauty of the marsh. Refresh yourself with the scent of anise after the wearisome journey from the upper floor to this place of peace."

"Thank you, my twin and bride," said hoarse old Huya, still entirely wrapped in a great cloak of fine white wool. "It is enough, let it be, I have sniffed and been refreshed. I wish you health," he said, bowing his stiff old nobleman's bow.

"And I you," she replied. Then they sat silent for a while,

squinting out into the beauty of the garden and the open view of duck pond, tree-lined avenue, flower beds, and towered gate. When he squinted, by the way, he looked more ancient than she, for the light was spent in his wearied eyes and his toothless jaws chewed away, setting the little beard under his chin bobbing up and down in an even rhythm.

Tuya did not munch with her jaws like that. She held her broad face still, tilted to one side, and the blind slits of her eyes seemed to share in her constant smile. She was evidently accustomed to enlivening her husband's spirit by keeping his mind on present circumstances, for she said, "Ah yes, my little bullfrog, here we sit and take our ease with the indulgence of the silver ones. Those tender young things had to see to it that our venerable selves were settled in the cushions of these lovely chairs and have now slipped away so that we two may be alone, like the divine pair in the womb of their mother. Except that it is not dark in our cavern, but rather we may revel in its comeliness, its pretty pictures, its trimly shaped movables. Do but look, they have placed our feet on soft braided footstools as a reward for their having wandered for so long upon earth, always the four of them. But if we lift our eyes from them, above the entrance to our cavern are spread the bright wings of the beautiful solar disk, defended by hooded serpents—Horus, Lord of the Lotus, son of the dark embrace. A shapely alabaster lamp by the stonecutter Mer-em-opet has been placed on the low bench to our left, and in the corner to our right kneels the mute servant, little dainties in his hands, at the ready for us whenever we are so moved. Are you perhaps so moved already, my booming bittern?"

In a dreadfully hoarse voice, her brother replied, "I am indeed so moved, dearest field mouse, but I suspect that it is only my mind and palate that are moved, and not my stomach, which would fiercely oppose it and rebel within me as cold sweat and mortal terror were I to feed it inopportunely. It would be better if we wait until we are exhausted from sitting and truly need such enhancement."

"Quite so, my little marsh marigold," she responded, and after his voice, hers sounded soft and full. "Moderation is the wiser course, for you will live long yet and our mute servant will not run off with his refreshment. Behold, he is young and handsome. He is as exquisitely pretty as are all the things placed before the eyes of this saintly old pair. He is wreathed with flowers like a pitcher of wine; they are the blossoms of trees, of the reeds, and flowers from their beds. His nice black eyes are looking past your ear, not at where we are sitting, but at this cottage's background, and thus at the future. Do you understand my play of words?"

"It is easily understood," old Huya rasped with some effort. "For your words play upon another usage of this summerhouse, where for some little while the dead of the house are preserved and placed behind us on lovely trestles in front of the silver gods in their shrines—but only after they have been disemboweled and filled with nard and linen by physicians and wrappers and before they are placed upon the ship and escorted downstream to Abôdu, where the god himself lies buried and has prepared for them a most beautiful funeral in the same fashion as that performed for Hapi and Merwer and for Pharaoh, and they are then shut up within that good and eternal house and among its columned rooms, where their life laughs in all its colors from the walls."

"Right you are, my swamp beaver," Tuya replied. "With clarity of mind you have grasped both the play and the goal of my words, just as I also always grasp in a twinkling your goals, however veiled your words, for we are old married siblings experienced in playing all the games of life together, first those of childhood and later those of man and woman—nor is it shameless of your old coney to speak thus, but rather out of intimacy and because we are alone here in our little cottage."

"Well yes, well yes," old Huya said apologetically, "it was life, the life of two from beginning to end. We have seen much of the world and been among the people of the world, for we are nobly born and near the throne. But ultimately we two were always alone in our little cottage, the cottage of brother- and sisterhood, just as in this one here as well: first in our mother's womb, then in the house of childhood and the dark chambers of marriage. Now we gray-hairs sit in the tranquil cottage of our old age, light of frame and built for but a day, a fleeting refuge. But eternal shelter has been prepared for this saintly pair in the columned cavern of the West, which will finally hold us in safekeeping through countless jubilees, and from those walls embraced by night the dreams of life will smile."

"How true, my good spoonbill," Tuya rejoined. "But is it not peculiar how in this hour we are still sitting here on our chairs at the front of this little temple and speaking—and in but a little while we shall be resting back there on lion-footed trestles, in our wrappings, with feet pointing up and faces on the outside once again bearing the god's beard on the chin—Usir Huya, Usir Tuya, while pointy-eared Anup bends down over us?"

"It is most likely very peculiar," Huya wheezed. "Yet I am unable to see it so clearly and am loath to make the effort to do so, for my head is weary, whereas you are still so forceful in your thoughts, and your neck still holds firm. Which gives me pause, for it might be that in your freshness you will not depart with me, but remain upon your chair, while I lie down and am left to walk that narrow path alone."

"Then be of good cheer, my little owl," she replied. "Your little coney will not let you depart alone, and should you render up a last sigh before she does, she will administer to her body a dose of bane that will make life congeal, and we will remain together. For by all means I must be beside you after death, so that I may assist you in thoughts and reasons in our justification and explanation when judgment is held."

"And will there be judgment?" Huya asked uneasily.

"One must assume so," she said. "It is the doctrine. But it is uncertain whether it should still be granted full validity. There are doctrines that are like deserted houses; they still stand and endure, but no one dwells within anymore. I spoke with Beknechons, the Great Prophet of Amun, about it and asked him how it will be in the hall of the goddesses of justice, at the weighing of the heart and the interrogation in the presence of Him Who Is in the West, at whose side sit the forty-two with dreadful names. Beknechons did not speak clearly to me. The doctrine holds true, he replied to your little coney. All things hold eternally true in the land of Egypt, he said, both the old and the new erected alongside it, so that the land is swollen full of images, edifices, and doctrines, of what is dead and what is alive, and one walks among them in propriety. For what is dead is the more holy only for being dead, for being the mummy of truth to be eternally preserved for the people, though it is also wanting in the spirit of those newly instructed. So said Beknechons, the wise. But he is a strong servant of Amun and zealous for his god. He is less concerned with the king below, who holds the crooked staff and the fan, and he cares little for the great god's stories and doctrines. That he calls them a deserted building and mummified truth does not make it more uncertain that we shall have to stand before him as people believe and declare our innocence and let our hearts be weighed, before Thoth can record our absolution of the forty-two sins and the Son can take us by the hand and lead us to the Father. One must assume it is so. That is why your little she-owl must by all means be at your side, just as in life, so, too, in death, that she may speak up in the presence of him who sits enthroned in the hall and of those with dreadful names and explain our deeds, in case you have misplaced our reasons and the justification refuses to occur to you at the decisive moment. For at times twilight reigns in the head of my little bat."

"Do not say it!" Huya burst out even more hoarsely. "For if I am weary and in twilight, then it is only from long and difficult pondering of the reasons and the explanation; but even he who is in twilight may speak of the cause of the twilight. Was it not I who turned our minds to it, enkindling there in the holy darkness the thought of sacrifice and reconciliation? You cannot deny it, for of course it was I, because I am the man and of us two the one who engenders—perhaps a man of the dark as your husband and spouse in the holy cavern of our pairing, but a man nonetheless, to whom the thought came, who enkindled within an ancient and holy house the idea of offering partial payment to what is holy and new."

"Do I deny it?" Tuya rejoined. "No, your aged spouse does not deny that it was the man who joins her in the dark who first broached the idea and began to distinguish between what is holy and what is glorious, that is to say, what is new in the world, perhaps establishing a new order in it, but with uncertain intentions toward us, so that by way of precaution one must offer something to appease it. For your little mouse did not see it," she added, moving her broad face with its slit eyes from side to side as the blind do, "and, reposing in what was holy and old, was incapable of understanding this new order."

"Not so," Huya contradicted her in a croaking voice, "you understood it quite well when I first broached it, for you are the aptest of pupils if not the most inventive; but you very easily grasped the invention of your brother and his uneasiness about the new order and the new eon—why else would you have consented to the sacrifice and payment? But when I say 'consented,' that is surely not yet enough; for it altogether seems to me as if I taught you only my concern about the new eon and its order, but that you first suggested on your own the idea of consecrating the dark son of our holy marriage to the glorious new order and of removing him from the old."

"Well, a fine one you are!" the old woman said primly. "A crafty corncrake is what you are, for now it is presumably I who first broached the idea and in the end you will want to put it off on me when we stand in the lower world before the king and those with dreadful names. What an arrant scoundrel! When at most I simply understood and received it from you, but only after you, the man, proposed it to me, just as I conceived by you our Horus, our dark son, Peteprê the courtier, whom we made a son of light and consecrated to what is glorious at a prompting that came solely from you and that I merely tended and hatched and brought to the light of day as Eset the mother. But now, when it is a matter of justification and it may well be proved before the judge that we acted clumsily and committed a blunder, you do not wish to have been the one, you rascal, and want to claim that I both engendered and bore it myself, entirely on my own."

"Ha, what utter nonsense!" he wheezed in anger. "It is a good thing that we are alone in this cottage and no one may hear the misconception you're cackling. For on my own I gladly admitted that I was the man, that I enkindled the idea in the dark, but you insinuate and falsely impute to me that I meant to say that engendering and birth are fused and made one, which at most is the case in swamps and in the blackness of the river's muck, where seething maternal stuff embraces and impregnates itself in the dark, but is not so here in the higher world, where the male properly visits the female."

He gave a husky cough and chewed with his jaws. His head wobbled the more.

"Might it not be time, dearest toad," he said, "to set our mute servant in motion so that he may present us with refreshment? For it seems to me that your green frog is greatly wearied from these thoughts and his energies are spent from the effort to call to mind his motives and clarify the justification."

Joseph, directing his detached gaze unswervingly on past them, made ready to move nimbly on his knees; but the moment passed and Huya went on to say, "But I believe it is the agitation of those efforts and not true exhaustion that made me think of refreshment, and my agitated stomach would rebuff it. Nothing is more agitating in this world than concern for the eon and the order of the times, for it is the most important of all—at most the fact that a man must eat takes precedence. He must first eat and be sated, true, but as soon as he is sated and free of that care, he is overcome with concern for holy matters and whether they are still holy and not already despised because a new eon has dawned; and he must make haste to keep pace with the newly proclaimed order and appease it with some consecrated offering if he is not to perish. But since we, as married brother and sister, are rich and of noble birth and dine, needless to say, only on what is finest, nothing could be more important, nothing more agitating than this matter, and your old salamander has been wobbling his head for a long time now with agitation, which can easily lead one to make a clumsy blunder simply from trying to do the right thing and to appease . . ."

"Calm yourself, my penguin," Tuya said, "and do not needlessly shorten your life with so much agitation. If there is a judgment and the doctrine proves true, I shall do the talking and speak for us both and will explain with ease the act of appeasement, so that the gods and those with dreadful names will understand and not count it among the forty-two misdeeds, but instead Thoth will record our absolution."

"Yes, it will be good," Huya responded, "if you speak, for you have more presence of mind and are not so agitated, because you have the idea from me and only received and understood it, so that speech will come more easily. As he who engendered, I could easily become confused in my excessive agitation and begin to stammer before judges so that we would lose the venture. You shall be the tongue for us both; for the tongue, as you well know, has a twofold nature in the slippery dark of the cavern and stands for both sexes, just as does the swamp and the seething muck that embraces itself, prior to the higher order of male visiting female."

"You, however, were wont to visit me properly, the male with the female," she said and rocked her broad face back and forth in blind, prim modesty. "You had to do so often and for a long time until the blessing came and your sister became fertile for you in wedlock. For our parents consecrated us to one another early in life, but it required many rounds of the year, twenty surely, before we became fertile and conceived as brother and sister. And I presented the courtier Peteprê to you, our Horus, the beautiful lotus, Pharaoh's friend, on whose upper floor we saintly elders now spend our last days."

"It is true, surely true," Huya confirmed. "That was the course of it, just as you say, with decorum and even holiness, and yet there was a snare to catch silent supposition and the secret concern that pays heed to the eon and wishes to keep pace with the order of the times. For we did indeed engender, as male and female, with higher decorum, but we did so in the dark chamber of sibling marriage and in the embrace of brother and sister—tell me, is that not indeed the self-embrace of the deep and akin to the engendering by seething maternal stuff, despised by the light and the powers of the newer order?"

"Yes, so you once presented it to me as my spouse," she said, "and I took it to heart and yet held it against you in part for wanting to call our beautiful marriage seething stuff, when in fact it was pious and honorable to the point of holiness, in conformity with finest custom, a delight to both the gods and men. Is there anything more pious than imitation of the gods? They all engender from their own blood and are joined in marriage to their mothers and sisters. It is written: 'I am Amun, who impregnated his mother.' And it is said to be so because every morning heavenly Nut gives birth to the radiant one, but at midday when he has become a man, he engenders himself again by his own mother, and is the new god. Is not Eset the sister of Usir, both mother and spouse? Even before birth, the noble siblings embraced in wedlock within the shelter of the mother's womb, where to be sure it was as dark and slippery as in the house of the tongue and the deeps of the swamp. But darkness is holy and marriage after this model highly esteemed in the eyes of men."

"So you have said and rightly so," he responded, straining his husky voice. "But the wrong siblings embraced in darkness as well, Osiris and Nephthys, and it was a grave error. And light, glorious light, took its revenge, for it despises maternal darkness."

"Yes, so you say and said as husband and master," she rejoined, "and you are of course for what is glorious, but I as mother and wife am more for what is holy and for ancient piety, therefore your views were a grievance to me. We are old and noble and near the throne. But the Great Consort, was she not usually Pharaoh's sister, following the divine model, and as his sister destined to be the wife of the god? He whose name is blessing, Men-kheper-Rê-Thutmose—whom should he have embraced as mother of a god if not Hatshepsut, his holy sister? She was born to be his wife, and they were one divine flesh. Male and female should be one flesh, and if they are that from the first, then their marriage is propriety itself and no seething stuff. So was I born in union and for union with you, and our noble parents foreordained us for each other from the day of our birth, because they surely believed that the holy pair had already embraced within the womb."

"I know nothing of that and cannot recall any of it," the old man replied hoarsely. "We might just as easily have quarreled in that cavern and kicked one another, and I would not know that either, for one has no thoughts at that stage. Even outside it we sometimes quarreled, as you well know, though of course never kicking at each other, for we were raised to be noble and highly respectable, a delight to other men, and lived happily in harmony with the most refined customs. And you, my coney, were perfectly content in your soul, much like a holy cow with its contented face, especially after you became fertile for me with Peteprê, our Horus, oh my sister, wife, and mother."

"So it was," she nodded sadly. "I was blissfully content, a coney and meek cow, within the house of our happiness."

"But in the spirit of my strong days," he went on, "and being sufficiently related by lineage to what is glorious in the world, I was man enough not to wish to content myself with what was holy and ancient. For I had enough to eat, and so I thought. Yes, I recall now, my twilight grows brighter, and at this moment I could put it into words before the court of the dead. For we lived according to the pattern of gods and kings, in harmony with pious custom, a delight to other men. And yet as a husband there was a thorn in my side, and concern that the light would take its revenge. For the light is glorious, which is to say, manly, and it despises the seething of maternal darkness, to which our engendering was still quite close, hanging from it by its umbilical cord. Behold, it must be cut, that umbilical cord, so that the calf may be free of its mother cow and become a bull of the light. Which doctrines are still valid, and whether there is even a judgment after we sigh our last sigh, that is not the most important matter. The only important thing is the question concerning the eon and whether the thoughts by which we live are still the order of the times. That alone is of consequence—after eating one's fill. But now there has come into the world, as I have long suspected, the male's desire to rend the umbilical cord between himself and the cow, for he wishes to set himself on the throne of the world as lord over maternal stuff and to found the order of light."

"Yes, so you taught me," Tuya responded. "And though I was content in our holy cavern, I took that teaching to heart nonetheless and bore it for you. For the wife loves her husband, and so loves and receives his thoughts as well, even if they are not the same as hers. What is holy belongs to the wife, but for the sake of her husband and master she loves what is glorious. And that is how we came to the sacrifice and the appeasement."

"That was the path," the old man concurred. "Today I would like to explain it clearly before the king below. Our Horus, whom as brother and sister, Usir and Eset, we engendered in the gloomy deeps—we wished to remove him from that dark realm and consecrate him to the realm of purity. That was our partial payment to the new age, which we agreed upon. And did not ask his opinion, but did to him what we did, and perhaps it was a blunder, but a well-intentioned one."

"If it was," she responded, "then we both are guilty of it, for together we hatched the plan to do this to our little son of darkness; but you had your thoughts the while and I had mine. For as his mother I thought not so much of the light and its conciliation, as of our son's greatness and honor on earth. In so preparing him, I wished to make a courtier and chamberlain of him, a royal official, so that in that state he would be preordained to bear the highest titles and Pharaoh would shower tributes of gold and favor upon a man so consecrated to serve him. Such were, I admit, my thoughts, which appeased my heart to such an appeasement, for it was very hard for me."

"It was only in the order of things," he said, "that you would bear my inspiration in your own way and add to it what was your own, so that it became our deed, which we did out of love to our little son, for he could not yet have an opinion. And I also gladly accepted the advantages that, in accordance with your womanly thoughts, flowed from so preparing this consecrated lad. My thoughts, however, were manly and turned toward the light."

"Ah, dear old brother," she said, "to my mind it is only all too necessary that we should speak of the advantages that have flowed to him, not only when our hearts are tested in the hall below, but also when speaking to our son himself. For however tenderly reverent his conduct toward us and no matter how highly and dearly he places his noble, venerable parents in his household, I nevertheless believe and fear that at times it can be read from his private demeanor that he is secretly somewhat annoyed with us both for cropping him to be a courtier without asking his opinion, passing right over him, inasmuch as he could not lodge a protest."

"That would mean," Huya flared up, despite his hoarse voice, "that he is secretly grumbling against his saintly parents on the upper floor! For he should be appeasing the new eon and be a consecrated son to the order of the times, that is his task, and if he has the most flattering advantages that make up for everything, then he need not pull a long face. Nor will I believe that he does pull a long face or is even against us, for he is a man by nature and in spirit, and thus related to what is glorious, so that I have no doubts that he approves of his parents' act of appeasement and proudly bears his state."

"To be sure, to be sure," she said, nodding. "And yet you yourself, old man, are not certain if the cut with which we cut the umbilical cord between him and the maternal darkness was not perhaps a blunder. For in being so consecrated, has he become a bull of the sun? No, but merely a courtier of the light."

"Do not repeat to me my own scruples," he rebuked her huskily, "for they are of secondary rank. The highest scruple is concern about the eon and the order of the times and about the concession made in appeasement. That it may turn out somewhat clumsily and not resolve itself purely, despite good intentions—that is in the nature of every concession."

"To be sure, to be sure," she said again. "And our Horus undoubtedly does enjoy the most flattering consolation and more than recompense of the most magnificent sort as a chamberlain to the sun and honored official of a glorious court, there is no question of that. But there is also Eni, our daughter-in-law Mut-em-enet, the beautiful, the first wife of the house and Peteprê's consort. As a wife and mother I sometimes have my worries for her sake as well, for despite the endearing and devout consideration she shows us saintly parents, I do suspect that at the bottommost bottom of her soul she, too, nurses a slight annoyance and a secret rebuke for our making a courtier of our son, whereas for her he is not a true Captain of the Guard, but bears only the title. Believe me, our Eni is woman enough to sulk in private because of it, and I am woman enough to read the vexation in her countenance when she is not on her guard."

"Pah!" Huya replied. "It would be ingratitude itself were she to hide such vexation in her sanctified bosom. For she too has as many and more consolations as Peteprê, and I refuse to believe that she is tormented by the worm of envy for earthly things, for she walks with the gods and is called a concubine of Amun by the house of the god's consort in Thebes. Is it nothing, is it a bagatelle to be Hathor, the consort of Rê, and, clad in the clinging dress of the goddess, to dance with others of the order of Amun and sing before him to the tambourine while wearing a golden helmet with the solar disk between its horns? That is neither nothing nor a bagatelle, but rather an exceptional consolation of the most glorious sort, granted to her as consort of our son the courtier, and her family knew well enough what they were doing when they gave her to him in marriage as his first and true wife, even while they were still children and no marriage of the flesh could have taken place between them—which was wise, for it was an honorary marriage and remained so."

"Yes, yes," Tuya replied, "it remained that of necessity. And yet, when I consider it as a wife, it is a hard thing, sparkling with honor by day, and yet a sorrow by night. She is called Mut, our daughter-in-law, Mut in the Valley of the Desert, and bears the name of ancient mothers. But she cannot and dare not become a mother because of our son's official position at court, and I fear she secretly harbors ill will toward us and hides resentment behind the tenderness she bestows on us."

"Let her not be a goose," Huya chided, "nor a bird of the waterlogged earth! For my part, I will have our daughter-in-law told as much if she sulks. It is not good that you should speak to her as mother and wife at our son's expense, I do not hear it gladly. You come close to offending our Horus and, moreover, the nature of woman, for which you intend to speak but instead demean it in the world—as if, try as one might, woman is to be viewed under no other image than that of a hippopotamus great with young. You are, to be sure, but a coney by nature, and it was as a man that I imbued you with thoughts of the new eon and the partial payment. And yet you would not have been able to receive and understand them, would not have agreed to the atoning deed performed on our son, were there no path connecting woman's nature with what is glorious and more pure, nor could woman ever have any portion in such. Is her image and portion always and only to be the black, gravid earth? Not at all; for woman may also appear in full dignity as a chaste priestess of the moon. I will have her told, your Eni, that she is not to be a goose. As our son's first and true wife, she is numbered among the first women of the Two Lands and she has his greatness to thank that she is called a friend of the Queen, of Tiy, wife of the god, even as she herself is a wife of the god by virtue of Amun's Southern House of Women and of the Order of Hathor, at whose head, as matron and first wife of the harem, stands the consort of Beknechons, the Great Prophet. These exceptional spiritual consolations are so great that she is, in short, a goddess with horns and solar disk and a white nun of the moon because of her sanctified state. Is it not, then, splendidly fitting that her earthly marriage is of honorary luster and her husband here below a son of atonement and a courtier of light? Indeed, it exceeds all fitness in my opinion, and you know well what I would have her told should she show a lack of reason in regard to that fitness."

But Tuya shook her head and replied, "I cannot tell her that, my dear old man, for she gives her mother-in-law no cause whatever for such an admonition and would, as they say, be thunderstruck were I to act according to your charge and call her a little goose. She is proud after all, our Eni, proud as Peteprê, her spouse and our son, and they both know nothing but their daylight pride as nun of the moon and chamberlain of the sun. Do they not live happily and worthily in the presence of each day, in harmony with the most re-fined decorum, and are they not a delight to all men? What else should they know but their pride? And if they did know something more as well, they would not admit it or confess it to their soul, but still render only their pride full honor. How can I tell our daughter-in-law for you that she is a goose, when she is not, but haughtily knows that she is a woman set apart for the god and that her whole being carries the austere fragrance of the myrtle? When I speak of sorrow and resentment, it is not the day that I have in mind or the

honors that come with the day, but the silent night and the hushed
darkness of motherhood, to which the rebuke of 'goose' cannot be
applied. And if you once feared the revenge of the light because of
our dark marriage, then I, as a woman, sometimes fear the revenge of
motherhood's darkness."

At this point Huya began to giggle, which startled Joseph somewhat, so that he jarred the refreshment and for a moment lost his detachment as a mute servant. He hastily shifted his gaze from the
background of the cottage to the old people, hoping to discern
whether they had noticed his shocked response; but they had not.
Completely lost in their conversation about the deed they had done
together, they paid him no more attention than they did to his counterpart in the room, that well-shaped alabaster lamp by the stonemason Mer-em-opet. So he let his eyes drift to one side again, his
glassy gaze now fixed on the background just beyond Huya's ear.
But, given all he had heard until now, he still had to catch his breath
a little at the sound of old Huya's senile giggle—he found it eerie.

"Tee-hee," Huya went. "No need to fear, darkness is mute and
does not know if it is even out of sorts. Our son and daughter-in-law
are proud and perceive nothing of their grudge and grievance against
their parents, who long ago did what they did to them by making a
barrow of a little boar, which as yet had no mind of its own, which
could only squirm but not protest. Tee-hee-hee, no need for fear!
Grudge and grievance are surely banished to the darkness, and if
they were ever to peek up into the light, they would be banished yet
again to the realm of pious decorum and acts of tender reverence toward us, their loved ones, who are kept high and holy on the upper
floor, although we once clipped our children's wings for the sake of
appeasement. Tee-hee-hee, doubly banished, twice secured, and
under twofold seal, with nothing to be done against such cozy parents—is that not wry and waggish?"

Taken aback, Tuya had at first seemed unsettled by her brother's
behavior, but allowed herself to be won over by his words and now
giggled as well, squinting the folds of her eyes to blind slits. Hands
clasped over bellies, old heads tucked into hunched shoulders, the
little couple sat on their stately chairs and cackled to themselves.

"Yes, tee-hee-hee, you're right," Tuya cackled. "Your coney understands how waggish it was to clip our children's wings, but resentment is doubly banished and sealed and cannot find fault with

us. Which makes it all truly wry and cozy. And I am glad that my
mole is now cheered and has forgotten his concern about the interrogation in the hall below. But has not weariness perhaps revealed itself in your body, and should I not wave to our mute servant to
bring us refreshment?"

"Not a trace," Huya responded, "not a hint of a trace of exhaustion is to be found in my constitution. Rather, it has been truly refreshed by our time spent chatting. Let us save our appetite for the
supper hour, when the holy clan gathers in the dining chamber and
out of tender consideration offers one another nosegays of lotus to
smell. Tee-hee! But first let us clap for those who serve us, that they
may support us for a brief stroll in the orchard, for I am of a mind to
set my refreshed limbs into motion."

And he clapped. Mouths gaping in eager foolishness, the little
girls came running and offered the old couple twiglike arms to help
them down the ramp and on their way.

Breathing a great sight of relief, Joseph set his burden on the
floor. His arms were almost as cramped and paralyzed as on the day
when the Ishmaelites pulled him out of the well.

What utter fools before the Lord this pair of saintly parents are,
he thought. And what insights I've gained into the painful and hidden affairs of this house of blessing—God have mercy. It only shows
that dwelling in a heaven of exquisite taste is no protection against
foolishness or the most awful blunders. How I would love to tell Father of this heathen ignorance of God. Poor Potiphar!

And he first stretched out on the mat to recover from his task as
a mute servant, easing the ache in his arms and legs before bringing
the refreshment back to Kha'ma't.

Joseph Considers These Things

He was both dismayed and touched by what he had heard while
serving, and for a while it occupied his thoughts a great deal. The
lively revulsion he felt toward these elderly saints was to be banished and held under seal only by wise politeness and displays of respect, but certainly not by oblivious darkness, for neither his anger
at the old couple's irresponsible ignorance of God nor his abhorrence of the cozy way in which they smugly considered themselves

secure against all reproach brought with it any lack of clear self-understanding.

Nor did he fail to recognize the instructive implications of his experience as a mute object, and he would not have been Joseph, grandson of Abram, had he lacked a readiness to profit from them. What he had heard was more apt to broaden his point of view and serve as a warning to the scion and pupil of his fathers against his regarding their narrow spiritual homeland and wrestling with God as something all too unique and incomparable. It was not just Jacob who worried in this world. That occurred everywhere among men, and everywhere men fretted whether they still had an understanding of both the Lord and the times—even though that also led here and there to the most awkward sort of knowledge and even though Jacob's inherited ideas about the Lord provided him with the most refined and exhausting means for testing the worrisome question about the extent to which man's usages and customs could lag behind the will and development of that same Lord.

All the same, how very close at hand error constantly lurked here as well. One need not even think of Laban, left behind in the land of origins, and of how he put his little son in a jar. He had simply lacked any awareness of the problem—for instance, of how custom could become abomination. But an advanced sensitivity to these same changes—how easily that could lead to mistakes! Had not Jacob's melancholy scruples about the feast tempted him utterly to destroy the feast and its customs because of its roots, which might well be nourished by filth far below? His son had had to plead that the Feast of Life Spared be spared itself, for if one were to rip it up by its filthy roots, its shade-spending treetop, which had grown up with the Lord, would also wither and die. Joseph was for sparing, he was not for uprooting. He saw in God, who ultimately had not always been who He now was, a God of sparing and of passing by, who even in the case of the Flood had not done the final deed of ripping humanity out by the root, but had awakened in one wise man the idea of a rescuing ark. To be wise and to spare—for Joseph the two notions seemed like brother and sister, who wore and exchanged one garment and even probably shared a common name: the name of kindness. God had tempted Abram to bring Him his son, but He had not taken the boy, and in order to instruct the father had substituted a ram. The tradition of these people here, though they moved in a high heavenly realm of good taste, was sadly lacking in such wise stories—one could excuse them for many things, however disgusting their giggles at the blunder of having clipped their children's wings. They, too, had received instruction from the spirit of the father in the form of an uncertain but pervasive spiritual rumor, itself still very much a part of the realm of darkness, calling us to move by stages and by custom beyond the old and sacred and into greater light—but they had heard it as an unreasonable demand for sacrifice. But, how like Laban, they had persisted in old customs in the very act of trying to accommodate what was new in the world. For no ram had appeared for them to turn into the gelded ram of light, and instead, being bereft of God, they had gelded Potiphar, their squirming son.

One might well call that a godforsaken act and characterize it as a foolish, clumsy attempt to consecrate something to a glorious and new world. Uprooting things, Joseph thought, was not the way to approach the spirit of the father, and what a great difference there was between the perfection of two sexes united in one and the absence of sexuality in the case of the courtier. Like the image of the Nile with its one female and one male breast, or like the moon, which was the wife of the sun, but male in relation to the earth, for which its ray of seed engendered the bull within the cow—so, too, the male-female that united the power of both sexes within it was divine and its relationship to the world of courtiers was, as Joseph saw it, the same as two to zero.

Poor Potiphar! In all the splendor of his fiery wagon wheels, in all his greatness among the great men of Egypt, he was a cipher. The young slave Usarsiph had a cipher for a master, a tower like Ruben, but without strength or fallibility, a blundered sacrifice neither averted nor accepted, a neither-nor of something outside of humanity and yet not divine, very proud and dignified in the daylight of his respectability, yet well aware of his mutilated nothingness in the night of his being, and in utter need of the flattery and props for his dignity that circumstances in general and the devotion of his servant Mont-kaw in particular bestowed upon him.

In light of what he had heard, Joseph took a new look at that flattering devotion and did not hesitate to consider it worth emulating. The fact is: on the basis of insights gained as a mute servant he decided he would take Mont-kaw as his model and also be "helpful" to his Egyptian master as soon as and in whatever way the opportunity presented itself, but to do so in an even more refined and grateful way. For in this fashion, he told himself, he would be most "helpful" to another master, the Most High, in his attempt to advance as the young slave Usarsiph in this world to which he had been transplanted.

At this point and in the interest of truth, we wish to fend off those accusations of cold calculation that overhasty moralists will not fail to raise against him. Things were not all that easily subject to such moral pronouncements. For Joseph had long since had his eye on Mont-kaw, the house's eldest servant, and thought he recognized in him an honest man whose servile flattery of his master deserved a better name, that of loving service; and from this he further concluded that Peteprê, though a captain in title only, must surely be worthy of such devotion—a conclusion that Joseph's own impressions as to the character of his master confirmed. This great man of Egypt was a noble and worthy man, and as Joseph saw it, a kindly man of gentle soul as well; for one had to make allowances for him as a victim of spiritual illiteracy, even if he did make a point of letting others tremble for his safety—surely, Joseph thought, he should be granted the right to some spitefulness.

From this, one can see that Joseph first served, defended, and sought to help Potiphar in his own mind before he ever dealt with him. Above all the Egyptian was *his* lord, the man to whom he had been sold, the highest in his immediate surroundings; and by nature and by tradition Joseph had always associated the idea of the Lord and the Most High with an element of loving service and forbearance that proved transferable from upper realms to lower and applicable, more or less, to earthly matters and one's immediate surroundings. This must be understood correctly. The concept of the Lord and the Most High created a unified order that favored a certain reciprocity, an equating of the upper with the lower. Reinforcing this tendency was the concept of "helpfulness" and Joseph's realization that he would be most helpful to the provident Lord of his dreams by following Mont-kaw's model and being helpful to his lord, Peteprê. But added to this was the fact that his relationship with the Lord of Heaven colored to some extent his attitude toward his lord of the fiery wheels. He had seen the melancholy, proud, and secretly grateful smile with which Potiphar had responded to the flattery of his steward—the needy loneliness it expressed. It may be childish to say it, but Joseph felt there was a kinship—evoking in him much the same sympathies—between a lonely God the Father outside of the world and this mutilated Ruben, this proud tower of a man decorated with tributes of gold, who stood outside of humanity. Yes, even God the Lord was lonely in His greatness, and in his blood and memory Joseph understood how very much God's being alone, wifeless and childless, helped explain His great jealousy of the covenant He had made with mankind.

He recalled the very special blessing that a servant's forbearing devotion can be to a lonely man—and the very special pain his disloyalty can inflict. Of course he did not fail to see that God's nature was such that He took no part in procreation and death, since He was simultaneously both Baal and Baalat in one; the vast difference between two and nothing did not escape him for a moment. All the same, we are simply helping to put into words an unspoken state of affairs when we say that certain sympathies and forbearance merged for him into a dreamlike unity—which is to say, he decided to be as loyal to this needy cipher as he was accustomed to being to his twofold God of far higher needs.

Joseph Speaks Before Potiphar

And with that we come to Joseph's decisive first meeting and conversation with Potiphar in the orchard, about which in all the many accounts of this story, whether Occidental or Oriental, whether prose or poetry, nothing is ever discussed or so much as noted, no more than all the other countless details, singularities, and corroborative arguments that our version can boast of helping to bring to light and of incorporating into humane letters.

It is certain that once again it was Bes-em-heb, the mock vizier, to whom Joseph owed immediate thanks for the meeting that he had so long yearned for and that would indeed decide his future— though the dwarf was able only to lay the groundwork for it. This consisted in Osarsiph's being promoted to gardener one fine day, after so many days of simply standing about superfluously, gazing here and there—not to head gardener, of course; the head gardener was a certain Khun-Anup, son of Dedi, also nicknamed Firebelly, because he had a strikingly red, sunburned paunch that hung like the setting sun above the apron tied just below his navel—a man of the same age as Mont-kaw, but of lower social standing, though with feet worthily planted in his specialty and calling, of which he was a master: an expert and authority in plants and their lives, not only for purposes of ornamentation and commerce, but also as regarded their toxic and beneficial powers, so that he served the house as its gardener, forester, and florist for its tables, and was also its apothecary and knowledgeable dispenser of decoctions, extracts, salves, laxatives, emetics, and poultices, prepared for both humans and animals in case of illness, though only for the servants among the former, since the masters of the house were attended by an austere professional physician from the temple of the god who ruled over life and death. Khun-Anup's bald head was red as well, for he refused to don a cap; and he made a habit of wearing a lotus blossom behind his ear, the way scribes wore reeds. Various bunches of herbs were always sticking out from his apron—cuttings of roots and sprouts clipped in passing with his garden shears, which clattered against his thigh along with a chisel and a little saw. The stocky man had a ruddy complexion and his face wore a scrunched-up but not unfriendly expression; he had a bulbous nose and a mouth that rose up to meet it in a strange sort of way, though one couldn't rightly say if out of annoyance or contentment, and covering his face was an irregular growth of beard—never-shaven bristles that hung like fibrous roots, giving Firebelly's countenance an even more tellurian look, despite his sunburn and the twinkle in his eye. The stubby, earthy, cinnabar red finger that he raised to admonish any less than diligent underling looked very much like a pulled-up beet.

Neteruhotpe, then, had approached the head gardener about this recently purchased foreigner, who, so he whispered in his ear, had a natural talent for matters of the earth and its gifts that had been schooled since childhood—why, before he was sold, he had cared for his father's olive grove at home in the wretched land of Retenu and had so loved that fruit that he had quarreled with his fellows for having harvested it by throwing stones and pressing it badly. The slave had also been able to persuade him, the dwarf, that he had inherited a magical touch or had received a so-called blessing, indeed of a double nature: from heaven above and from the deep that lies below. That was precisely what a gardener needed, and since the lad was lazing about and doing the estate no good, Khun-Anup should add him to his staff. This, then, was the advice of dwarfish wisdom—and no one as yet had ever regretted acting upon it.

So said the vizier, because he carried in his heart Joseph's wish to stand before their master and knew that employment in the garden offered by far the best prospect for that wish to be fulfilled. For like every other great man of Egypt, the fan-bearer loved his irrigated park—the like of which he also hoped to possess and enjoy just as it was now in the life after life—resting and walking in it at various times of the day, even halting, if the mood struck him, to talk with its caretakers, and not just with Firebelly, its overseer, but also with the laborers, the hoers and water bearers. And it was on that basis that the dwarf constructed his plan—which succeeded perfectly.

And Firebelly did indeed employ Joseph to tend the garden, putting him to work in the orchard, or more precisely, in the palm garden, which extended south from the main house to the duck pond in the east and beyond it to the courtyard where the vineyard began. But the grove of palms was itself a vineyard, for everywhere among its columns topped with feathers were festoons of rambling grapevines, with openings here and there for the paths that led through the little forest. This joining of two fertilities—vines heavy with grape and feathery palms bearing several hundred quarts of dates each year—was like a paradise, a delight to the eye; and it was no wonder, then, that Peteprê was especially fond of his palm garden with its water basins placed here and there and frequently even ordered a couch set up for him, where in the shade of the gentle rustling crowns of palm trees he would have someone read to him or would listen to a report of his scribes.

And so this was where Jacob's son was given employment, and in a painfully pensive way the task reminded him of a precious, but now horrifyingly lost possession from his former life: the veil, the coat of many colors, his and his mother's *ketônet passîm*. Among its embroidered images, there was one that had struck his eye the first time he saw it in Jacob's tent as the shimmering bridal robe hung draped between his father's arms: it depicted a holy tree at whose sides stood two bearded angels facing one another and touching it to impregnate it with the cones of male flowers. Joseph's task was the

same as that performed by these two spirits. The date palm is a dioe-
cious tree, and the pollination of its fruit-bearing trees with the
pollen of those whose flowers lack pistil and stigma and have only
stamens is the work of the wind. But since time out of mind man has
relieved the wind of its task and artificially fertilized the date palm
by cutting off the flowers of a nonbearing tree and brushing them
against the blossoms of those that do bear fruit to pollinate them.
This is the very thing one could see the spirits of the veil doing to the
holy tree, and this was now Joseph's work as well—Firebelly, son of
Dedi, Potiphar's head gardener, had assigned him the task.

He had entrusted it to Joseph because of his youth and the sup-
pleness of his young limbs; for acting in the wind's stead is exacting
work that requires a climber to be both courageous and free of ver-
tigo. With the help of a special padded rope, which is slung around
both his own body and the palm tree, a man carrying a basket or
wooden pail and using old frond stumps or whatever other projec-
tions the scaly trunk offers for footing has to work his way up to the
crown of the pollen-bearing tree, while constantly having to shift
the rope upward on both sides and, in a motion like that of a carriage
driver giving his horses the reins, bring it to the level where he has
now climbed. Upon arriving at the top, he must then cut off the panicles, carefully gather them in his container, and slide back down
again. He now repeats the procedure on the trunk of a fruit-bearing
tree, climbing first one and then another and letting the pollinated
panicles "ride"—which is to say, he dangles them into the ovary-
bearing racemes, so that they are fertilized and soon put forth pale
yellow dates that can then be plucked and eaten, though only those
ripened by the hot months of Paophi and Hathyr are the really tasty
ones.

With his earthy red beet of a forefinger Khun-Anup showed
Joseph the palm trees that bore pollen, of which there were only a
few, since just one can pollinate some thirty of those that bear fruit.
He gave him the rope—a quality Egyptian product, not of hemp but
of reed fibers, wonderfully softened and beaten until supple—and
supervised as Joseph tied it around himself the first time, for this was
his responsibility and he did not care to see this newcomer fall from
the tree and spill out his bowels, with his master taking the loss of
what he had paid for him. After having observed that the lad was
adept at climbing—scarcely needing his halter, but ascending into

the tree's feathery crown with a nimbleness to put a squirrel to shame and going about his business with both care and intelligence—Khun-Anup left Joseph on his own and promised to assign him further chores in the garden, so that in time he might become a real gardener if he accomplished his task here successfully and the fruit-bearing trees put forth a rich crop.

Joseph was not only ambitious for the sake of his God, but he also took delight in this bold and practical task, performing it with great eagerness and in the hope that his speed and precision would so impress the head gardener that he would be taken aback—a reaction Joseph strove to produce in everyone—and he worked all that day and yet another on into evening until, beyond the lotus pond to the west, crimson and tulip pink spread their extravagant daily splendor over city and Nile. The garden had now been deserted by its other caretakers, and he was left alone among his trees or actually up in them, where he used the rest of the rapidly fading light to "ride" them with pollen. Working carefully, he was sitting in the swaying crown of a long-trunked, fruit-bearing palm, when he heard footsteps and whispering and looking down recognized the dwarf Neteruhotpe, no bigger than a mushroom far below, waving up at him with both arms and then cupping his tiny hands to his mouth and whispering with might and main, "Osarsiph! He's coming!" And at once he vanished again.

Joseph hastened to leave his delicate occupation behind and slid more than climbed down the tree, so that once on the ground he could make sure that Potiphar really was coming from the pond through the palms, down the little path that opened up through the grapevines, that it was his master, dressed in white against the red of the sky, who was strolling grandly along, followed by a small entourage—with Mont-kaw the steward close by, only a step or two behind at one side, plus Dûdu, keeper of the jewelry chests, two scribes from the house, and Bes-em-heb, who, after announcing Potiphar, had taken a devious route back to rejoin him. Why, look at that, Joseph thought, gazing ahead at his master, he is walking in the garden in the cool of the day. And when the group had come a little closer, Joseph prostrated himself at the foot of the tree, his forehead touching the ground, with only the palms of his hands raised toward the approaching group.

Glancing down at the hunched spine beside the path, Peteprê halted, and those in his company did the same.

"On your feet," he said briskly, but gently; and Joseph obeyed his command in one swift motion. Pressed against the trunk of the palm tree, he stood there as modestly as possible, hands crossed at his neck, head bent forward. His heart was very alert and ready. The moment had come—he was standing before Potiphar. Potiphar had come to a halt—he dare not move on again all too soon. Above all else, he must be taken aback. What question would he ask? Joseph could only hope it would be one that allowed for an answer that would take him aback. Joseph waited with downcast eyes.

"Are you with the house?" he heard the mild voice inquire curtly.

Well, that offered few possibilities for now. At most the reply could leave an impression by the polish of its how, but hardly by the what of its contents, so that even if it did not take him aback, he might gently prick up his ears and above all be prevented from moving on once he had heard it.

Joseph murmured, "My great lord knows all. Here he sees the least and lowest of his slaves. Happy am I to be counted as the least and lowest of my lord's servants."

Middling, he thought. But surely he won't move on just yet? No, first he will ask why I am still here. And I must provide him with a pretty response.

"Are you one of the gardeners?" he heard the mild voice above him say after a brief pause.

He replied, "Like unto Rê who gave him, my lord knows and sees all. Of his gardeners, I am the lowest."

To which the voice responded, "But what are you still doing in the garden at the hour of departure, when your fellows are enjoying their evening rest and breaking bread?"

Joseph lowered his head even further over his hands.

"You who preside over Pharaoh's hosts, my lord, the greatest among the great of the Two Lands," he entreated, "you are like unto Rê, who moves across the heavens in his barque with his entourage. You are he who steers Egypt, and the boat of the realm moves according to your will. You are next to Thoth, who judges without distinction of person. Bulwark of the poor, may your mercy come over me like the satisfaction that allays hunger. Like a garment that puts an end to nakedness, may your pardon come over me for lingering at my work on your trees until the hour when you walk in the garden and for being a stumbling block in your path."

Silence. It was possible that Peteprê had turned to his companions in response to this cultivated petition, which though it still bore a slightly sand-drifted accent, had nonetheless been fluent and well-spoken—and if a bit formal, then not without sincerity. Joseph could not see if he was looking at the others, but he hoped he was and he waited. Listening closely, he could tell that Pharaoh's friend was smiling gently as he replied:

"The anger of the master is not provoked by zeal in service to his house or extra hours of diligence. You may breathe easy. So you are attentive to your task and love your handiwork, do you?"

Joseph thought this the appropriate moment for him to raise his head and eyes—Rachel's eyes, black and deep, raised fairly high to meet soft and rather sad eyes, brown like a doe's, but proud, veiled by long lashes and yet probing his own with kindness. Potiphar stood before him, tall, fat, and clad in finest linen, one hand on a bracing disk just below the crystal pommel of his long walking stick, the other holding his pine-cone cudgel and a fan for flies. The colorful faience of his necklace collar was set in a floral pattern. Leather gaiters protected his shins. The platform shoes on which he stood were also made of leather, bast, and bronze, with a shaft running between the big and second toe. His elegantly coifed head—with a fresh lotus blossom dangling from the crown into his forehead—was tilted forward to listen to Joseph.

"How could I not love the gardener's art," the latter replied, "and not be zealous in it, my great lord, since it delights both the gods and men, for the work of the hoe surpasses that of the plow in beauty, as it does many other, indeed most occupations? For it honors him who exercises it, including those chosen for it in days of yore. Was not Ishullanu a gardener for a great god, and did not even Sin's daughter cast a friendly eye upon him for bringing bouquets each day to add radiance to her table? I know of a child who was left exposed in a basket of reeds, but the current bore him to Akki, the drawer of water, who taught the boy the fine art of the garden, and Ishtar gave Sharuk-inu, the gardener, both her love and his kingdom. I know of yet another great king, Urraimitti of Isin, who in jest exchanged places with his gardener Ellil-bani and set him upon his throne. But behold, Ellil-bani remained seated there and became king himself."

"Why, look here, look here," Peteprê said, smiling and glancing again at his overseer, Mont-kaw, who shook his head and looked embarrassed. Like him, the scribes—and especially the dwarf Dûdu—also shook their heads, and only Shepses-Bes, the favorite, nodded wrinkled approval with his. "From where do you know all these stories? Are you from Karduniash?" the courtier asked in Akkadian, for that was his name for Babylonia.

"My mother gave birth to me there," Joseph answered, likewise in the language of Babel. "But he who is now your property grew up among his father's herds in the land of Zahi, in one of the valleys of Canaan."

"Oh?" Potiphar was heard to respond fleetingly. He liked conversing in Babylonian, and was captivated—and at the same time disconcerted—by a certain poetic tone in the answer, the vaguely allusive quality in the phrase "among his father's herds." Refined misgivings that he might provoke all too great an intimacy with his questions and hear things of no concern to him stood in conflict with a curiosity and attentiveness that had already been awakened and with a desire to hear more from these lips.

"But you do not speak badly the language of King Kadesh-mankharbe," he said and then, falling back into Egyptian, added, "Who taught you these tales?"

"I read them, my lord, with my father's eldest servant."

"What, you can read?" Peteprê asked, glad he could marvel at this; for he wished to know nothing of a father who had an eldest servant, or any servants at all.

Joseph bowed his head more than he lowered it, as if confessing his guilt.

"And write as well?"

The head sank deeper still.

"What was the work," Potiphar asked after a moment's hesitation, "by which you were lingering?"

"I was 'riding' the blossoms, my lord."

"Oh? And is that a male or a female tree there behind you?"

"It is a fertile tree, my lord, it will bear fruit. Whether such a tree is to be called female or male has not been agreed upon, and people are of differing opinions. In the land of Egypt those that bear fruit are designated male. But I have spoken with people from the islands of the sea, from Alashia and Crete, who call those that bear fruit female and term male those that do not bear fruit but only pollen and are of a bachelor nature."

"So, then, a fruit bearer," the Captain of the Guard said curtly. "And how old is the tree?" he asked, since a conversation such as this could serve only one purpose: to test the expertise of the servant addressed.

"It has been blooming for ten years, my lord," Joseph responded with a smile and a certain enthusiasm, which to some extent came from the heart—for he had a love of trees—but also seemed to him would serve his cause. "And seventeen have passed since it was set out as a seedling. In two or three years it will be at its fullest—or he or she will—and at the peak of productivity. But each year it already bears for you some two hundred hins of the best fruit, of wonderful beauty and size, with a color like amber—that is, of course, if one does not leave the tree's pollination to the wind, but makes sure that it is done by human hand. It is a splendid tree among your many," he said, bursting with excitement, and laid his hand on the slender column of its trunk, "a proud male in its high-towering vigor, so that one is inclined to share the view of the people of Egypt in their designation for it; but then again, female in its lavish generosity, so that one would like to agree with the people of the sea and their term for it. In short, it is a divine tree, if you will permit your servant to unite in one word what is divided by the tongues of nations."

"Why, look here," Peteprê said with covert irony, "you also know how to advise me in things divine? So you pray to trees at home, do you?"

"No, my lord. At most under trees, but not to the trees. We do, to be sure, revere trees, for there is something sacred about them, and it is said that they are older than even earth itself. Your slave has heard of the Tree of Life, in which lay the power to bring forth all that is. Should one, however, call that fruitful vigor male or female? Behold Ptah's artists in Menfe and Pharaoh's master sculptors here, who are fruitful in creative forms and fill the world with beautiful figures: Is the power by which they accomplish this to be called male or female, engendering or bearing? It cannot be determined, for that power is of both kinds, and the Tree of Life must have been of both sexes, a hermaphrodite, as most trees are and as is Kheper, the sun beetle, which engenders itself. Behold, the world is torn asunder in its sex, so that we speak of male and female and yet do not agree in our differentiation, for indeed the nations dispute whether the fruit-bearing tree or the bachelor tree is to be called male. But the Foundation of the World and the Tree of Life are neither male nor female, but both in one. But what does both in one mean? It means neither. They are virginal, like the bearded goddess, and are both father and mother to what has come into being, for they surpass all sexuality, and their generous virtue has nothing to do with being torn asunder."

Potiphar said nothing, but merely braced his towering figure on his beautiful walking stick and stared at the ground beside his examinee's feet. Potiphar felt a warmth in his face, in his chest and in all his limbs, a slight excitation that held him to the spot and would not let him move on—and yet, though he was as a man of the world, he did not know how to proceed with this exchange. Out of refined restraint he had not thought it advisable to hear more of this slave's personal circumstances; now, however, a different restraint seemed to have blocked their conversation in the direction it had taken instead. He could have moved on and left this young foreigner standing beside his tree; but he did not want, did not dare, to do that. He hesitated, and forcing its way into his hesitation was the respectable voice of Dûdu, Zeset's spouse of reduced stature, who thought it good to offer an admonition.

"Might it not be better, my great lord, if you were to resume your walk and direct your steps toward the house? The fires of heaven will soon grow pale and the cold of the desert can descend any moment now, which might leave you with the sniffles, seeing as you are without a coat."

Much to Dûdu's vexation, the fan-bearer paid him no attention, for the warmth in his head closed his ears against the dwarf's sensible words. He said, "You would appear to be a thoughtful gardener, young man of Canaan." And since he had come to a word whose sound and meaning had left an impression on him, he now asked, "Were they great in number—your father's herds?"

"Very great, my lord. The land can scarcely bear them all."

"So your father was a man free of concerns?"

"He had none, my lord, except for his concern for God."

"And what is this concern for God?"

"It is widespread throughout the world, my lord. It is a concern known to all people, with more or less blessing and good fortune. But long ago it was laid especially upon my kinsmen, so that my father, the king of flocks, might also be called a prince of God."

"So you call him both a king and a prince! Did you then spend the days of your childhood in such great prosperity?"

"Your servant," Joseph replied, "may well say of himself that he was anointed with the oil of gladness all the days of his childhood and lived in fine estate. For his father loved him more than his fellows and made him rich with the gifts of his love. And so he presented him with a holy robe in which every sort of light and high symbol was woven—a garment of deception and a robe of substitution, bequeathed from his mother, and he wore it in her place. But it was torn from him by the tooth of jealousy."

Potiphar did not have the feeling that Joseph was lying. The sincerity of his speech spoke against it, as did the lad's eye peering deep into the past. A certain unsettled vagueness in the way he expressed himself might be due to his foreignness, and hidden within was a kernel of detail that could not deceive.

"How was it that you ended up ..." the man of rank began to probe, but he wanted to put his question gently and so he asked, "How did your past become your present?"

"I died the death of my old life," Joseph replied, "and a new one was given me in your service, my lord. Why should I tax your ear with the circumstances of my story and the stations of my progress? I must call myself a man of grief and gladness. For he who received gifts was driven into desolation and misery, he was stolen and sold. After gladness, he drank his fill of woe, adversity was his nourishment. For his brothers sent for him in their hate and laid snares in his path. They dug a pit for his feet and thrust his life into the pit, so that darkness became his dwelling place."

"Are you speaking of yourself?"

"Of the lowest of your servants, my lord. Three days he lay bound in the underworld, so that he truly stank most foully and like a sheep soiled himself with his own filth. And travelers passed by, men of gentle souls, who raised him up out of the goodness of their hearts and released him from that gorge. They nursed the newborn with milk and gave him a robe for his nakedness. But after that they brought him down here before your house, oh Akki, great drawer of water, and out of the goodness of your heart you made him your gardener and an aid to the wind among your trees, so that his new birth is to be called as marvelous as his first."

"As his first?"

"In his confusion your servant has erred and misstated himself. My mouth did not wish to say what it said."

"But you said your birth was marvelous."

"The words slipped from me, my great lord, because I am speaking before you. It was a virgin birth."

"How can that be?"

"My mother was lovely," Joseph said, "sealed with the kiss of loveliness by Hathor. But her body was closed up for many long years, so that she despaired of motherhood and not a man there was who expected to see the fruit of her loveliness. After twelve years, however, she conceived and amid pains beyond what is natural she bore a child just as the constellation of the Virgin was rising in the east."

"And you call that a virgin birth?"

"No, my lord, if it displeases you."

"One cannot say that one's mother gave birth as a virgin simply because it occurred under the sign of the Virgin."

"Not for that reason alone, O my lord. One must take other circumstances into account as well—the seal of loveliness and that the body of God's handmaid had been closed up for so many years. Those things, together with the sign, determined it."

"But that does not make for a virgin birth."

"No, my lord, for you have said so."

"Or does it, in your opinion?"

"Thousands of times over, my lord," Joseph said cheerfully. "It happens thousands of times over in this world torn asunder in its sex, and yet the cosmos is full of conception and birth that surpasses sex. Does not the ray of the moon bless the body of the cow in heat, who then bears Hapi? Does not ancient lore teach us that the bee was created out of the leaves of the tree? And, then again, you have the trees, the wards of your servant's hand, and their secret, in which creation makes sport of sex, placing it together in one sort and separating it in another, just as fancy strikes, and sex is constituted now one way and now another, so that no one knows the order or name of a tree's sex or if it even has one, and the nations dispute the matter. For it often happens that they do not propagate by means of sex, but rather outside of it—not by pollination and conception, but by off-shoots and runners, or they are set out as shoots, for the gardener sets them out as shoots and not as seeds so that he may know whether he is growing a fertile or a bachelor palm tree. And if they do propagate by sex, at times pollen and conception are placed to-gether in their blossoms and at times separated among the blossoms of the same tree, but sometimes on the blossoms of different trees in the garden, those that bear fruit and those that do not; and it is the work of the wind to bear the seed from the blossom with pollen to the blossom that conceives. But when one rightly considers it, is that still an engendering and conceiving by sex? Is not what the wind does akin to the engendering in the cow by the ray of the moon, a halfway thing or already a transition to a higher engendering and a virginal conception?"

"It is not the wind that engenders," Potiphar said.

"Do not say that, O my lord, in all your greatness. Often times, I have heard, the zephyr's sweet breath impregnates birds even be-fore the time for nesting approaches. For it is a breath of God's spirit, and the wind is spirit, and just as Ptah's master sculptors fill the world with beautiful figures without anyone's being able to de-termine if their act is to be called male or female, because it is both and neither, which means virginal and fruitful—so, too, the world is full of impregnation and birth without sex, full of engendering by the breath of the spirit. God is the father and creator of the world and of all things, not because they were brought forth by seeds, but rather He who is unbegotten used another power to place within all matter a fertile cause that changed and transformed it into a multi-plicity of things. For these manifold forms were first in God's thoughts, and His word, borne by the breath of the spirit, engen-dered them."

It was a curious scene, one that had never occurred before in the house or courtyards of the Egyptian. There Potiphar stood leaning on his walking stick and listening. In the delicate features of his face was mirrored a struggle between patient irony, which he decorously tried to interject, and satisfaction so strong that one might have called it joy, even happiness—so strong in fact that one can scarcely speak of grateful satisfaction's struggle with mockery, but only of its evident victory. Next to him was Mont-kaw, the steward of the house with his wedge of a beard and small bloodshot eyes with drooping, swollen bags; in surprise, incredulity, gratitude, and with a certain approval that was more like amazement, he stared into the face of his loquacious purchase, this boy who was doing the same thing that faithful service and love for his noble master had taught him to do—but in a far higher, gentler, and more effective fashion. Behind him, then, stood Dûdu, spouse of Zeset, filled with the most dignified vexation at how his master had been deaf to his words of admonition and at how the attention Peteprê was paying to this young slave now prevented him from interrupting again and ending a conversation in which the puppy was apparently doing very well for himself—at the expense of the wedded dwarf. For it certainly seemed to him as if this slave's brazen and highly inappropriate words—which the master was drinking up like living water—were somehow detrimental to his dwarfish dignity and apt to detract from those things that constituted the life in which he took such sterling pride and from his superiority over certain people, both little and tall. As for little people, there was Neteruhotpe as well, his mandrake face wrinkled with delight at his protégé's success, his whole body swelling with gratification at how well the lad had known to use this moment—proving how rightly and justly he himself had yearned for it. And there stood the two scribes, who had never witnessed anything like this before either and who had swallowed their laughter after diligently observing the faces of master and overseer and taking stock of their own impressions. But there beside his tree stood Joseph, smiling as he enchanted his group of listeners with his peroration. He had long since relaxed the slave's pose that had constrained him at first and stood there now with a pleasant openness, adding the winning gestures of an orator to his words, which flowed fluently and artlessly from his lips in buoyant earnestness as he spoke of a higher conception and the engendering breath of the spirit. Standing there in the dusk of this columned orchard's temple, he looked no different than does an inspired child whose tongue God has loosened that He may be glorified in the child's teachings, much to the amazement of the teachers.

"God is but once," he continued happily, "but there is much of the divine in this world and much of that generous virtue that is neither male nor female, but surpasses all sexuality and has nothing to do with its being torn asunder. Let me sing with nimble tongue, O my lord, of such virtue as I stand here before you. For my eyes were opened in a dream and I saw a house of blessed nature and an estate of prosperity in a far-off land—buildings, granaries, gardens, fields, and workshops, with men and beasts without number. Industry reigned and was rewarded with success, there was sowing and harvesting, the oil mills never rested, and wine flowed from the vats of the wine pressers, and rich milk from udders, and sweet gold from honeycombs. But who roused all this to occur and thrive in its order? Why, the lord at its head, to whom it belonged. For all things were done at his bidding and proceeded as if from the ingoing and outgoing of his breath. If he spoke to one, saying 'Go!' then he went, and if to another he said, 'Do this!' he did it. Without him, however, nothing would have lived, but withered and died. From his fullness all his household was nourished and praised his name. He was both father and mother to his house and its commerce, for the gaze from his eye was like the ray of the moon that impregnates the cow so that it gives birth to the god, the breath of his word like the wind that bears pollen from tree to tree, and from the loins of his presence all beginning and thriving gushed like golden honey from the comb. And so, still far from here, I dreamed a dream of generous virtue and learned that there is engendering and fertility that is not according to its earthly kind and sex, nor of the flesh, but rather divine and spiritual. Behold, the nations dispute whether the fruit-bearing tree or the pollinating tree is to be called male, and are not united in their word for it. And why are they not? Because the word is spirit, and because in the spirit things become open to dispute. I saw a man— dreadful for you to look upon, O my lord, splendid of body and terrible in the power of his flesh, a warrior and a son of Enak, and his soul was of cow's leather. He went out against lions and smote the wild ox, the crocodile, and the rhinoceros, slaying them all. But when he was asked 'Do you have no fear?' he replied, 'What is that, fear?' For he did not know it. But I saw another child of man in the world, who was tender both of soul and of flesh, and was afraid. He took up his shield and spear and said, 'Come forth, my fear!' And he smote the lions, the wild ox, the crocodile, and the rhinoceros. And if, my lord, you were now to test your servant, and it occurred to you to ask him which of these two men was worthier of the name of a man—may God perhaps provide me the answer."

Potiphar stood there, leaning on his long walking stick, bent slightly forward, a pleasant warmth in his head and limbs. It was just such a sense of well-being, so it was said, that people felt when visited by a god in the guise of a wanderer or beggar or of some acquaintance or relative wishing to converse with them. It was from that feeling, so they said, that they had recognized him—or at least it formed the basis of a happy conjecture. The peculiar sense of well-being suffusing these people had been for them a sign that this might indeed be a wanderer or beggar or such and such an acquaintance or relative speaking to them and common sense demanded they take such a reality into account and behave accordingly, but—given the presence of this striking sense of well-being—only while simultaneously considering more far-reaching possibilities. For all things are simultaneous in their nature and being, realities appear in shared disguises, and a beggar is no less a beggar because a god may conceal himself there. Is not the river a god, whose form is that of a bull or a wreathed-crowned male-female with one breast of each, has it not created this land and does it not nourish it? That does not prevent one from treating its water objectively, from being as sober as water itself: one drinks it, travels upon it, washes one's linen in it, and only the sense of well-being that one feels when drinking and bathing can serve to admonish one to take higher points of view. The line between the earthly and the heavenly is fluid, and one need only let one's eye rest upon a single phenomenon and it breaks apart into a double perspective. And there are also intermediary and preliminary stages of the divine—intimations, moieties, transitions. A great deal of what the lad beside the tree had said about his previous life sounded familiar, like teasing memories and reminders that to some degree could be regarded as literary reminiscences, but it was hard to say to what extent they might be based on arbitrary arrangement and assimilation and to what extent grounded in facts—on those traits characteristic of the life of beneficent figures who have merged with the divine, bringing health, consolation, and salvation. The young gardener knew these traits; he had made them spiritually his own and knew how to bring the representation of his life into harmony with them. That could be the work of a witty, allusive mind; but Potiphar's sense of well-being spoke for the fact that such things—both by themselves and through him—at least assisted him as well.

He said, "I have tested you already, my friend, and you have withstood the test not all that badly. But the idea of a virgin birth is out of the question," he added in an amiably instructive, but cautionary tone, "merely because the birth stands under the sign of the Virgin. Take note of that." He said it out of a healthy sense of the practical part of reality now turned to him and, as it were, in order not to let the god know he recognized him. "Enjoy your evening rest with your fellows now," he said, "and resume your work with my trees by the light of the new sun." Smiling and with a flushed face, he now turned to go, but took only two steps before bringing those following close on his heels to a halt again and, to avoid retracing his steps, waved Joseph to him.

"What is your name?" he asked. For he had forgotten to ask that question.

Not without a pause that surely could not have been to gather his thoughts, the lad gazed up in earnest and replied, "Osarsiph."

"Good," the fan-bearer replied quickly and curtly and resumed his walk at a faster pace. And the words he spoke to his steward Mont-kaw also came at a faster pace—and Neteruhotpe heard them and brought tidings of them to Joseph within the hour. What he said was: "That is an uncommonly clever servant whom I questioned just now. I can well believe that work with the trees is in good hands with him. But I do not think one ought to keep him at such chores for very long."

"You have spoken," Mont-kaw responded and knew what he had to do.

Joseph Makes a Covenant

It was not for nothing that we reproduced this conversation—although it is recorded nowhere else—word for word, just as it happened, with all its twists and turns. For it marked the beginning of Joseph's famous career in the house of Potiphar; it was the basis for the Egyptian's making him his personal servant and later placing him over all that was his and giving it into his hands—and like a swift horse, report of it has brought us into the midst of those seven years that led Jacob's son to a new high point in life before plunging him to his death again. For by this test he had proved he understood what was essential in the house of painful blessing into which he had been sold: to provide mutual, flattering assistance and to spare and support its hollow dignity with the service of love. Not only had he understood it, he had also proved that he knew how to perform what was required better and more deftly than anyone else.

This was in fact Mont-kaw's experience, who found that his striving faithfully to serve the soul of his noble master was quite overtrumped by Joseph's incredible deftness at being flatteringly helpful—but, we would expressly like to add, he did so not with jealousy, but with joy, which is a credit both to his honesty and to the significant difference between loving service and servile flattery. Indeed in the wake of his purchase's debut in the orchard, it would not even have required the master's hinted order for the overseer to have resolved to remove Joseph from the dark state of a low menial and open up for him the brighter possibilities of probation. After all, we have known for some time that what had prevented him from doing so before now was nothing but the embarrassing fear that had secretly overcome him at the first sight of the scroll bearer and that was closely related to what had stirred Potiphar himself during the conversation with his garden slave.

Which is why with the light of the next sun, when Joseph had barely finished his morning porridge and resumed his service as an assistant to Khun-Anup and the wind, Mont-kaw had the Ebrew summoned to him so that he might announce drastic changes in his employment, which he thought it good to present as long overdue and to chide Joseph for being more or less responsible for the delay—for that is how people are and how they think they have to twist facts. He played the surly boss in fact and had a peculiar way of announcing to the summoned slave his good fortune, pretending as if it were Joseph's fault that such an untenable state of affairs had lasted so inordinately long.

He received him near the stalls, out in the courtyard defined by the servants' quarters, the out-kitchen, and the women's house.

"There you are!" he said to the slave, who greeted him. "Good thing you come when you're called at least. Do you suppose it can go on like this forever, your lolling about in trees till the end of your days? Well, you think wrong, let me tell you. There'll be another tune sung from now on, and your idling about is at an end. You are to serve in the house, and in very short order. You are to wait upon the master's family in the dining chamber, handing them bowls of food and standing behind the chair of Pharaoh's friend. No one intends to ask you if this suits you. You've played the tomfool and avoided higher duties long enough. Just look at you! Skin and linens covered with the debris of trees and the dust of the garden. Go clean yourself up. Have the supply room provide you with the silver apron of table servers and tell the flower gardeners to give you a proper wreath for your hair—how else did you presume you could stand behind Peteprê's chair?"

"I had not even thought of standing there," Joseph replied softly.

"Yes, well, what you think has nothing to do with it. And be prepared for something else, too. After the meal you are to be tested at reading aloud from the book scrolls for the master, before he falls asleep in the north columned hall where it's cool. Will you be able to do it passably?"

"Thoth will help me," Joseph made bold to answer, trusting that he would be spared and passed over by Him who had carried him off to Egypt—and following the principle of "when in Egypt, do as the Egyptians do." "But who has been permitted to read to the master until now?" he added.

"Until now? It was Amenemuia, apprentice in the house of books. Why do you ask?"

"Because for the sake of the Hidden One I would not wish to trespass on any man's land," Joseph said, "nor infringe on any man's boundary stone by robbing him of the office in which he takes honor."

Mont-kaw was very pleasantly touched by this unexpected discretion. Since yesterday—if only since yesterday—he had a very clear notion that this young man's calling and ability to compete with others for positions extended beyond what even he himself might have conjectured, beyond Amenemuia's post as a reader—well beyond it, in fact. That was why this delicacy pleased him, apart from the fact that he was one of those Ruben-like people who find their soul's happiness and dignity in being "just and fair"—or put another way, in joyfully uniting their own plans with those of higher powers, even if that may mean a certain resignation of self. By nature Mont-kaw was a man who longed to attain such happiness and dignity, perhaps because he was not that well and was often troubled by his kidneys. All the same, let us repeat, Joseph's concern pleased him.

What he said was: "It seems to me you are considerate beyond your circumstances. Let Amenemuia's honor and employment be his concern and mine. And such consideration and meddlesomeness are twigs off the same branch. You have heard your orders."

"Did our most noble lord order it himself?"

"The overseer's order is an order. And what did I order you to do at this moment?"

"To go clean up."

"Then do it."

Joseph bowed and stepped back.

"Osarsiph," the steward said in a milder voice, and at his call Joseph again approached.

Mont-kaw laid a hand on his shoulder. "Do you love our lord?" he asked, and his little eyes with their heavy, drooping bags searched with painful urgency in Joseph's face.

A particularly moving question, fraught with memories and familiar to Joseph since childhood. It was what Jacob had asked whenever he set his favorite on his knee; and his brown eyes with their soft pouches had searched the child's face with that same painful urgency. The slave now instinctively answered with the phrase that befitted this constantly repeated question and that, though a commonplace, did not detract from its inner emotion.

"With all my soul, with all my heart, and with all my mind."

The overseer nodded with satisfaction, just as Jacob had once done.

"And rightly so," he said. "He is good and great. You spoke commendably before him yesterday in the date orchard; not everyone could have done so. I certainly saw that you can do more than say good-night. You did make some mistakes, such as calling a birth virginal merely because it occurred in the sign of the Virgin—well, that can be excused by your youth. The gods gave you subtle thoughts and loosened your tongue to speak them so that they intertwine like bodies in a dance. The master took satisfaction in them, and you are now to stand behind his chair. But you are also to be like a pupil and an apprentice to me when I walk through the estate, so that you may apply yourself in the house, courtyards, and fields and acquire insight into the enterprise and its stocks and gain an overview, so that perhaps with time you will come to be my assistant, for I am greatly plagued by this world and at times do not feel all that splendid. Are you content?"

"If it is certain that I am not infringing on anyone by standing behind the master's chair and at your side," Joseph said, "then I shall indeed be content and grateful, though not without trepidation. For privately I must ask who am I and what can I do? My father, the king of flocks, did indeed allow me to learn to write and speak a little, but as for the rest I was able to anoint myself with the oil of gladness, but not to learn a craft—I cannot cobble or paste paper or throw a pot. How am I then to find courage to walk among those who sit and know what to do, one man this, the other that, while I presume to oversee and supervise them?"

"Do you suppose I can cobble or paste paper?" Mont-kaw replied. "I cannot throw a pot or make chairs and coffins, that is not necessary, and no one demands it of me, least of all those who can. For I am of different birth from them and made of other stuff, with a head for generalities, which is why I became overseer. Those busy in their workshops do not ask what you can do, but who you are, for a different ability is bound up with that, and it is made for supervising. Whoever can speak before the master as you do, and whoever can intertwine subtle thoughts with their words, should not sit stooped over some single task, but walk at my side from time to time. For oversight and governance is in words, not in the hand. Do you find any fault, anything to criticize, in what I have said?"

"No, great steward. I most thankfully find myself in agreement."

"That, Osarsiph, is the word. And it shall be a word between you and me, between young and old, that we wish to agree in our service to and love of our master, the noble Peteprê, Pharaoh's Captain of the Guard, and we shall make a covenant concerning such service, each with the other, that we wish to keep, each until his end, so that even the death of him who is older shall not break this covenant, but the other shall continue to keep it beyond his grave, like a son and successor, who protects and vindicates his father by protecting and vindicating his noble master in his covenant with the dead. Can you see that, and does it sound plausible? Or does it seem to you some bizarre whimsy?"

"Not in the least, my father and overseer," Joseph replied. "Your words are in full accord with my reason and understanding, for I have long understood such a covenant, which one makes with both one's Lord and one another in service to His love, and in my eyes I can imagine nothing more customary and of less bizarre whimsy. By my father's head and by Pharaoh's life, I am yours."

The man who had purchased him still had one hand on Joseph's shoulder, but with the other he now grasped his hand.

"Good, Osarsiph," he said. "Good. Now go and cleanse yourself to serve the master as his reader and personal attendant. When he sends you away, however, then come to me so that I may introduce you to the business of the house and teach you to oversee it."

Part Five

THE MAN OF BLESSING

Joseph as Reader and Personal Servant

We do know, don't we, the smiles and downcast eyes of persons of lower rank when someone from their midst—of whom they least expected it—has his head raised up and is incomprehensibly and apparently quite unjustly called to higher service? During this period Joseph was very much aware of such smiles, exchanged glances followed by downcast eyes—perplexed, spiteful, jealous glances that also expressed indulgence, even some delight in acquiescing to their superiors and the whims of fortune—at first there in the garden when word spread that Mont-kaw wanted to see him of all people, the young climber and pollinator of trees, and then later again and again. For this was the beginning, and his head was raised up in many ways; but as for his becoming the servant closest to Potiphar—who, as the story presents it, then gradually placed the entire household in the Ebrew's hands—all that was already fully prepared for, its seed contained in Mont-kaw's words and in the covenant he made with Joseph, as surely as a tree's slow years of growth already lie within its seed, needing only time for development and fulfillment.

Joseph was given his silver apron and floral wreath, the uniform of those who served in the dining chamber, and, as we hardly need mention, it suited him very nicely. That was how all those permitted to wait upon Peteprê and his family had to look; but there was something about this son of a lovely mother that made him stand out from all the others—a higher brilliance that was not purely lovely, but that by wedding the physical with the spiritual enhanced both.

He was placed behind Peteprê's chair on the raised dais, or rather at first beside the stone platform at the opposite, narrow end of the room, where the wall was tiled with flagstones and a brass ewer and basin were set out. For when the exalted family entered for a meal, whether from the hall to the north or west, they first had to climb a single step to this raised platform and have water poured over their hands; and it was Joseph's task to pour water over Potiphar's small, white hands bejeweled with signet rings and scarabs and to offer him a sweet-scented towel to dry them. But while his master dried his hands, he had to make his way hastily but silently across the room's mats and colorful woven runners to the raised dais at the far end, on which were placed the chairs of the noble family—of the saintly pair from the upper floor as well as those of their son and Mut-em-enet, the mistress of the house. Joseph had to step behind Potiphar's chair, wait there for his master, and serve him the food others in silver aprons first handed to him. For Joseph did not go on running back and forth, fetching things and taking them away, but others passed them to him for him to offer to Pharaoh's friend, so that everything he chose to eat came from Joseph's hands.

The dining chamber was high and bright, although daylight did not enter directly but only from adjoining rooms, especially the hall to the west, with its seven doors to the outside and windows of lovely open-work stone set above them. Augmenting the light, however, were very white walls painted all round with a frieze that abutted an equally white ceiling traversed by sky-blue beams and supported by blue wooden columns with brightly colored capitals and round white bases. These sky-blue wooden columns were a beautiful ornamentation—both ornamental and beautiful—but Potiphar's family dining room was filled with a cheerful abundance of decorative items: the family's chairs of ebony and ivory, trimmed with lion heads and upholstered with embroidered cushions; splendid lamp holders and tripods for incense along the walls; freestanding basins, urns for ointment, and large-handled wine pitchers garlanded in flowers and set in stands; plus all the other sparkling utensils and furnishings required for elegant service. In the middle of the room stood a sizable buffet, like Amun's table of sacrifice piled high with food, which the mediating servants passed on to those who waited directly upon the four exalted figures on the dais—far too much food for them ever to have come close to devouring it: grilled goose, roast duck, and haunches of beef, vegetables, cakes, and breads, plus a bounteous display of cucumbers, melons, and Syrian fruits. A costly centerpiece of gold stood in the midst of the edibles, a New Year's gift from Pharaoh to Peteprê, depicting a temple beneath exotic trees where monkeys scrambled among the branches.

Whenever Peteprê and his family sat down to eat, a hush fell over the hall. The bare soles of the servers' feet were inaudible on the carpeted floor, and any conversation among the exalted personages was kept spare and low out of mutual respect. They bowed considerately to one another, during pauses in the meal one might offer the others a lotus blossom to smell, or they might also hold up tidbits to one another's lips—and the tender circumspection with which each treated the others was alarming. The chairs were placed in pairs, with a narrow space between. Peteprê sat beside her who had given him birth, and next to old Huya sat Mut, the mistress. She did not always look as she had when she first appeared to Joseph in the courtyard, floating past with gold dust in the curls of her own hair. She often wore a wig that fell down over her shoulders—blue, blond, or brown, worked into a multitude of tiny curls ending in a plaited fringe and crowned with a close-fitting woven wreath. Puffing out in a heart-shaped curve above her white forehead, the wig was shaped something like a sphinx's headscarf; and an extra pair of strands or tassels, with one of which the woman occasionally toyed, hung down at her cheeks and framed her unusual face, where eyes and mouth were at war with each other—for the eyes were austere, dark, and slow to move, but the mouth was a serpentine curve tucked strangely deep at the corners. As she busied herself with her meal, the mistress's arms were no less remarkable from up close than from a distance—as if chiseled and polished by Ptah's artists, they were bare and white, one might even say divine.

Though his lips were small, Pharaoh's friend ate large portions of everything offered, for his tower of flesh had to be fed. And at every meal his goblet had to be refilled several times from a long-necked pitcher, for wine apparently warmed his self-esteem and let him believe that, despite an officer named Hor-em-heb, he was still the true and genuine Captain of the Guard. The mistress, however—hovered about by a dainty and very demure personal slave draped in a garment of very thin gossamer, beneath which (and what a good thing that Jacob, Joseph's father, never saw it!) she was as good as naked—Mut-em-enet, then, showed so little appetite that it was as if she attended only out of custom and ceremony. She would accept a roast duck and, scarcely opening her mouth, take a single bite of the breast, then toss the rest into the basin. As for the saintly parents, who were served by the foolish little girls (for they would not suffer adults to serve them), they fretted and fussed over this and that, but likewise came to the table only to be civilized and had had enough after two or three bites from some vegetable or pastry—especially old Huya, who always had to worry that his stomach would rebel against anything more, leaving him in a cold sweat. Sometimes favored Bes-em-heb, the unmarried dwarf, would sit on the steps of the dais at the feet of his masters and nibble away, even though he took his meals at a sort of officers' table, where he ate his fill along with Mont-kaw himself, Dûdu, guardian of the jewelry chests, Firebelly, the head gardener, and a few scribes—the higher-ranking servants of the house, that is, who were soon joined by the Habiru slave Joseph, or Osarsiph as he was called; or the mock vizier in his rumpled finery might perform droll dances around the large buffet table. In one remote corner there was usually crouched an old harpist, who gently plucked his strings with gaunt, crooked fingers and murmured chants no one could understand. He was blind, as was only proper for a bard, and could also prophesy, though only haltingly and vaguely.

This was the daily routine of meals at Peteprê's. Often the chamberlain was with Pharaoh at Merima't Palace on the far side of the river or he joined the god on his royal barque to sail up and down the Nile visiting quarries, mines, or dams and buildings under construction. On those days no meals were served, and the blue hall remained empty. But if the master was present and the midday meal had ended with mutual declarations of tender feeling—after which the saintly parents let themselves be helped upstairs and their daughter-in-law, the nun of the moon, either returned to her drawing room in the main house, which was separated from her spouse's bedroom by the great northern columned hall, or was borne back to the house of seclusion on her lion chair, with footmen before and after—then Joseph had to follow Potiphar to one of the adjoining rooms, airy arcades with painted niches along three walls, but open to a slender-pillared front: either the northern hall extending from dining chamber to reception hall, or the western one, which was even lovelier, since it looked out on the garden, with its trees and elevated summerhouse. The former, however, had the advantage that the

master could gaze from there out to the workshop courtyard, to the
granaries and stables. It was also cooler.

In both halls were many magnificent objects that Joseph regarded with the mixture of admiration and skeptical mockery that
he reserved for the high civilization of Egypt—gifts from a gracious
Pharaoh to his chamberlain and titular captain, of which that golden
marvel in the dining chamber was but one example, arranged on various chests and side tables or hung on the walls: statuettes in silver or
gold, ebony and ivory, that portrayed their royal donor, Neb-maat-
Rê-Amenhotep, a squat, fat man, in various vestments, crowns, and
hairstyles; brass sphinxes, also bearing the head of the god; objets
d'art in the form of animals, such as a running herd of elephants,
squatting baboons, or a gazelle with flowers in its mouth; costly
vases, mirrors, fans, and whips; but, above all, weapons, great numbers of every sort of weaponry of war, including axes, daggers, and
coats of mail, hide-covered shields, bows, and bronze scythelike
swords. It made one wonder why Pharaoh—successor to great con-
querors, yet no man of battle, but a prince of peace with vast riches
and a plethora of building projects—would have showered so many
implements of war upon his courtier, this Ruben-like tower whose
disposition likewise did not appear intent on wreaking bloodbaths
among "rubber-eaters" and "sand-dwellers."

Among the furnishings in both halls were beautiful decorated
bookcases, and while Potiphar stretched out his massive body on an
elegant couch, whose delicacy looked even more fragile beneath
him, Joseph would step over to one such bookcase and offer suggestions for reading. What should he unroll: the adventures of a ship-
wrecked sailor on the island of monsters; the story of King Khufu
and a man named Dedi, who was able to put his head back on after it
had been chopped off; the true and fitting story of how the city of
Joppa was taken by Thuti, great officer of His Majesty Men-kheper-
Rê-Thutmose III, by having sacks and baskets containing five hundred warriors smuggled into the city; the fairy tale of the royal child
whom the priestesses of Hathor predicted would be slain by a crocodile, a serpent, or a dog—or something else? The selection was imposing. Peteprê owned a fine and varied library that he kept in
bookcases in both halls and included amusing fantasies and comical
fables—like "The Battle of the Cats and the Geese"—as well as fascinating works of dialectic, such as the sharply polemical exchange

of correspondence between the scribes Hori and Amenemone, plus religious and magical texts and tracts on wisdom in a dark, elaborate language, as well as lists of kings from the days of the gods down to the alien shepherd kings, along with dates for the reign of each son of the sun and annals of notable historical events, such as extraordinary levies of taxes and important jubilees. Nor did he lack the *Book of Breathing,* works entitled *Striding Through Eternity* and *May the Name Flourish,* or a learned geography of the world beyond.

Potiphar knew them all well. He listened in order to hear something familiar, the way one listens to music. This response to what was offered him was all the more appropriate since for the great majority of these works it was not their contents or the fable that counted, but instead, the important factor was the charm of the style, the rarity and elegance of the rhetoric. With his feet drawn up under him or standing at a kind of liturgical lectern, Joseph made an excellent reader—fluent, precise, without pretensions, moderately dramatic, and so natural in his command of words coming from his lips that even the most difficult formal writing had the sound of conversational palatability and improvised ease. He literally read his way into his listener's heart, and for a better understanding of the simple fact of his well-known rise in the Egyptian's favor, these hours of reading should certainly not go unremarked.

Potiphar, by the way, would often soon doze off as he listened, lulled by the reserved, yet pleasant voice speaking to him so evenly and intelligently. But he would also interrupt the reading sometimes to correct Joseph's pronunciation, to call both his own and his reader's attention to some rhetorical flourish or to offer literary criticism of what he had heard; he might even discuss some obscure passage with Joseph, so taken was he by the lad's keen mind and exegetical talents. Over time the master's personal and emotional bias for certain literary works became evident—for example, his preference for the "Song in Praise of Death by a Man Weary of Life," which he often had Joseph read to him as his days of service wore on and in which a yearning, but steady voice compared death with many good and gentle things: with recuperation from a grave illness, with the fragrance of myrtle and lotus blossoms, with sitting beneath the shelter of an awning on a windy day, a cool drink beside the shore, a path in the rain, the homecoming of a sailor from his battleship, a reunion with family and home after years of captivity, and other such things that we wish for. Just as he awaited all these, said the poet, so too he awaited death; and Potiphar listened to the words as they were carefully shaped on Joseph's lips, the way one listens to music one knows in every detail.

Another literary work that fascinated him and had to be read to him frequently was the dark and dire prophecy of disorder laying waste to the Two Lands, of wild anarchy left in its wake, of a ghastly reversal of all things, so that the rich would become poor and the poor rich, all said to go hand in hand with desolation of the temples and total neglect of the gods. Why it was that Peteprê loved to hear these descriptions remained unclear; perhaps just for the horror of it, which could be pleasant inasmuch as for now the rich were still rich and the poor still poor and would remain so, as long as one shunned disorder and nourished the gods with sacrifices. He said nothing about it, any more than he ever remarked about the "Song of the Man Weary of Life," or about the so-called "Delightful Songs," to whose honeyed words and lovers' plaints he reacted with silence. These romances expressed the sufferings and joys of a love-struck girl, a catcher of birds, who coos for her lad and wants desperately to be a housewife, so that his arm can always lie upon her own. And when he did not come to her at night, she would lament in words sweet as honey, saying she was like someone lying in her grave, for he was health and life. But it was all a misunderstanding, for he, too, lay in his bedchamber, struck down by an illness that mocked the skill of his doctors, the illness of love. But then she found her way to his bed, and they no longer wounded one another's hearts, but each made the other the first person in the world, and with flushed cheeks they wandered hand in hand through the flower garden of their happiness. From time to time Peteprê would have their cooings read to him. His face showed no expression as he listened, his gaze revealing only a cool attentiveness as it wandered slowly back and forth across the room, and he never expressed either his like or dislike of these songs.

But when such days were now past counting, he did indeed ask Joseph whether these "Delightful Songs" appealed to him, and it was the first time that master and servant again brushed up against and warily hovered over the subject of that testing conversation in the palm garden.

"You recite the songs of this bird catcher and her lad very

nicely," Potiphar said, "almost as if with their voices. So you like these songs better than others, do you?"

"My endeavors to win your satisfaction, my great lord," Joseph replied, "are the same with all subjects."

"That may be. But it seems to me that the reader's mind and heart provide greater or less effective support to such endeavors. The subject may be closer to him or, then again, more distant. I do not wish to say that you read this book better than others. But that does not prevent you from preferring to read it over others."

"Before you, my lord," Joseph said, "I am as happy to read one as another."

"Yes, fine. Except I would like to hear your opinion. Do you find these songs beautiful?"

And the air Joseph now assumed was both shrewd and haughtily critical.

"Quite beautiful," he said and pursed his lips. "Beautiful, and with every word, as it were, dipped in honey. Somewhat too simple, perhaps, as a result—a trace too simple."

"Simple? But this work, which is a perfect expression of simplicity and a brilliant model of what happens between the children of men, will stand for countless jubilees yet. Your years demand that you judge whether such words are a model of model speech."

"It seems to me," Joseph replied with detachment, "as if the words of this bird catcher and her bedridden lad convey model simplicity very nicely and fix them for preservation."

"It seems that and nothing more?" the fan-bearer asked. "I was counting on your experience. You are young and yours is a beautiful face. But you speak as if for your part you have never strolled in a flower garden with such a snarer of birds."

"Youth and beauty," Joseph replied, "can also imply a more austere adornment than the wreath such a garden supplies the children of men. Your slave, my lord, knows of an evergreen that is both the symbol of youth and beauty and also an adornment of sacrifice. He who wears it is set apart, and he whom it adorns has been chosen."

"You are speaking of myrtle?"

"Of myrtle, yes. My family and I like to call this herb 'touch-me-not.'"

"And do you wear this herb?"

"My seed and tribe wear it. Our God has betrothed Himself to us and is a bridegroom of the blood and filled with jealousy, for He is lonely and burns for faithfulness. We, however, are like a bride to His faithfulness, consecrated and set apart."

"What, all of you?"

"In principle, all of us, my lord. But from among the friends of God and the heads of our tribe, it is God's custom to select one who is especially betrothed to Him by the adornment of consecrated youth. It is demanded of the father that he offer this son as a whole offering. If he can, he does so. If he cannot, then it is done for him."

"I cannot bear," Potiphar said, tossing back and forth on his couch, "to hear of something being done to someone that he does not wish and cannot do. Speak, Osarsiph, of other things."

"I can at once mitigate what I have said," Joseph replied, "for a certain forbearance and leniency apply to the whole sacrifice. For, you see, what is commanded is also averted and declared a sin, and thus the blood of an animal shall intervene for the blood of the son."

"What was that word you used? It is declared what?"

"A sin, my great lord. It is declared a sin."

"What is that—sin?"

"Just this, my lord—what is demanded and yet averted, what is commanded and yet cursed. We are as good as alone in the world in knowing what sin is."

"That must be a burdensome knowledge, Osarsiph, and, it seems to me, a contradiction full of suffering."

"God also suffers for the sake of our sin, and we suffer with Him."

"And might it be," Potiphar asked, "as I am beginning to surmise, that a stroll in that bird catcher's garden would also be a sin in your mind?"

"It has a strong element of sin about it, my lord. If you ask me—most definitely, yes. I cannot say that we especially love it, though if need be we could also manage to produce songs of similar 'delight.' That garden there—it would not be out-and-out the land of Sheol for us, I would not go that far. It is not an abomination to us, but nonetheless it is a misgiving and a demonic realm full of God's jealousy, where accursed commands run free. Two beasts lie in wait before it: one is named Shame and the other Guilt. And yet a third peers out from among the branches as well, and its name is Mocking Laughter."

"After all this," Peteprê said, "I begin to understand why you called the 'Delightful Songs' simple. Yet I cannot help thinking there is something peculiar and life-threatening about a tribe of men for whom model simplicity is a sin and a cause of mocking laughter."

"It has its own history with us, my lord, taking its place both in time and in stories. It first occurs in model form, and then in a variety of others. There was a man and friend of God, who was as devoted to a lovely woman as he was to God, and there was model simplicity in this story of a father. God in His jealousy, however, took her from him and plunged her into death, out of which she reemerged for the father in a different form—that is, as his young son, in whom he now loved his lovely wife. And so death had made a son of his beloved, in whom she lived on, and the boy lived only by virtue of death. But the father's love for him was a love now altered by the bath of death—love no longer in the form of life, but of death. And thus my lord can see that there is more variety to this story, in all directions, making it less of a model."

"And that young son," Potiphar said with a smile, "was he perhaps the same one about whom you went so far, too far, as to say that his birth was a virgin birth simply because it occurred under the sign of the Virgin?"

"Perhaps in your kindness, my lord," Joseph replied, "you may be inclined to soften your rebuke of what was said, or even graciously to revoke it—who knows? For since the son became a lad only through death, became his mother in the form she took on in death, and is, as it is written, female in the evening, but male in the morning—might one not, upon consideration, speak quite legitimately of a virgin birth? God has chosen my tribe, and all of them bear the betrothed's adornment of sacrifice. But one there is who wears it yet again and is set apart for God's jealousy."

"Let that be as it may be, my friend," said the chamberlain. "Our talk has wandered far afield, from simplicity to variety. If you so beseech and entreat me, then I shall surely soften my rebuke, indeed retract it, with only the smallest vestige left. Read something else for me now. Read to me of the sun's journey by night through the twelve houses of the underworld—I've not heard it for a long time, though, if memory serves, it contains several very beautiful maxims and exquisite words."

And Joseph read about the sun's underworld journey with fine good taste, so that Potiphar was well fed; and that word is in order, for the reader's voice and the excellent text to which he applied it fed the sense of well-being that the previous conversation had left with the listener, fed it the way a flame feeds the sacrificial altar when supplied with fuel below and strewn with good things on top—that same sense of well-being that the Ebrew slave knew how to instill in Pharaoh's friend again and again and that was much like trust, both in his own person and in his servant. The essential thing was the trust that Potiphar put in Joseph in this twofold regard, and the growth of that trust—which is why we have also provided a detailed reconstruction of at least this conversation as well, for in earlier versions of the story it is as little noted as the test in the palm garden.

We cannot provide all the conversations in which this sense of trusting well-being was nourished, until it grew to the level of unconditional partiality that defined Joseph's good fortune. It is enough for us to provide a few striking examples that characterize his method for "flattering" his master and proving "helpful" to him, just as his covenant with the good Mont-kaw stipulated about his service to Potiphar. Yes, with no fear of any sense of coldness being attached to it, we use the word "method" here, because we know that calculation and sincerity in Joseph's artful treatment of his master blended in a truly perfect kinship, just as they did in his relationship to still higher lonely entities. And we would ask as well whether sincerity can ever succeed without the art of calculation, without wise technique, if it is to be set into reality—for example, into creation of a sense of trusting well-being? Trust is a rarity among men; but among men of Potiphar's fleshly stamp—titular men with titular wives at their side—there develops a general and unfocused zealous distrust of all who have not had the same done to them, distrust of the very basis of life itself, so that nothing is more suited for bestowing upon them an unfamiliar and thus all the more gratifying sense of trust than the discovery that one man among all that eager crowd bears in his hair a bitter evergreen that strips his person of the usual disconcerting qualities. It was by calculation, by method, that Joseph provided Potiphar with this discovery. Let those who presume they must take offense at this make good use of their previous knowledge of the story we are telling and, in looking ahead, recall that Joseph did not disappoint the trust he thus created, but rather remained truly faithful to it amid a storm of temptation—just as required by the covenant he had made with Mont-kaw, swearing to it by the head of Jacob and, incidentally, by the life of Pharaoh himself.

Joseph Grows As If Beside a Spring

When he was free of his service as a personal attendant, he would walk the estate with the overseer, whom he already called "father," gaining an overview of things as his pupil and apprentice, the object of other people's smiles and downcast eyes. Usually the steward was joined by a few other officials of the house, like Kha'ma't, the scribe of the sideboard, or a certain Meng-pa-Rê, the scribe of the stalls and kennels. But these were average men who were happy simply to meet the normal demands of their narrow circle and special field and to satisfy the steward by keeping people, animals, tools, and written accounts in good order, but never aiming at anything higher or setting their hearts on it, for that demanded a mind for generalities—lax souls, who were happiest merely writing down what others dictated and to whom it would never have occurred that they were born for oversight and governance, which for that very reason they were not. A man must first happen upon the notion that God has something special in mind for him and that, in turn, he must help Him—then his soul spreads its wings and his reason plucks up its courage to bring things under its control and to step forward as their master, though the tasks be as manifold as those in Peteprê's blessed household in Wase in Upper Egypt.

For they were manifold, and of the twofold services that Joseph rendered to Potiphar as his comforting and indispensable personal attendant and as the man into whose hands he placed his entire household, this second was the incomparably more difficult task to accomplish. Mont-kaw, in whose hands the household stood when Joseph arrived, was surely correct in saying that he was plagued by this world—there were a few too many vexations for a man who often did not feel all that splendid given his kidney trouble, even if he did have a very good head for generalities; and in retrospect one can well understand that Mont-kaw gladly seized this excellent opportunity to take on a young assistant and train him to be his deputy—in fact, he had quietly been looking for one for a good while.

Peteprê, Pharaoh's friend, Captain of the Palace Guard and
Chief High Executioner (in name, at least), was a very rich man—
rich in far grander style than Jacob in Hebron, and was still growing
rapidly richer; for he was not only a highly paid courtier, but a recipient of royal gifts as well, and such emoluments were constantly enriching and nourishing his estate—only a small part of which he had
inherited, whereas the vast majority, particularly his landholdings,
was also the gracious gift of the god—so that the whole of it increased and bore abundantly. But he knew to respond only with acquiescence—applying himself exclusively to maintaining his massive
bulk by eating, his manly self-confidence by hunting in the swamps,
and his intellect by having books read to him; all the rest lay in the
hands of his overseer, to whom, when respectfully compelled to take
a quick, indifferent squint at his ledgers, he would then say, "Fine,
fine, Mont-kaw, old man, it's all in fine order. I know you love me
and do your work as best you can—which is saying a great deal, for
you know to do it well. Is this entry for wheat and spelt correct? Of
course it is, I see that now. I am convinced that you are as true as
gold and devoted to me body and soul. Could it even be otherwise?
It certainly could not, not when one considers your nature and what
an abomination offending me would mean to you. Out of love for
me you make my concerns your own—fine, I let them be yours because you love me, for you would not harm your own cause by carelessness or worse. Besides, the Hidden One would see it, and it
would bring you only torment later. Whatever you submit to me is
surely correct. Take it back with my best thanks. You no longer have
a wife or any children—for whose sake would you wrong me? For
your own? You are not all that well—strong, to be sure, and with a
hairy body, but you are somewhat worm-eaten inside, so that you
often look jaundiced and the bags under your eyes grow larger and
you will presumably not live to a very old age. What would it profit
you to overthrow your love and do me harm? It is my heart's desire,
to be sure, that you will grow old in my service, for I would not
know whom I could trust as I trust you. Is Khun-Anup, the herbalist, satisfied with the state of your health? Does he give you sound
and useful simples and roots? I understand nothing of all that, for I
am healthy, though not so hairy. But if he does not rightly know
what to do or were you to become seriously ill, we shall send to the
temple for a physician. For although your rank is that of a servant

and Firebelly is in fact responsible in case of illness, you are so dear to me that I shall summon a learned physician, from the House of Books, if your body is in need of him. No need to thank me, my friend, I do it for the sake of your love and because your accounts are so obviously correct. Here, take them back and continue to do everything as you have thus far."

This is what Potiphar would say to the overseer of his estate on such occasions. For he concerned himself with nothing—out of refined elegance, out of the inauthenticity of his nature, which made him shy away from life's practical realities, and out of his trust in the love and concern others bore for him, this sacred tower of flesh. It is one thing to say that he was right about this and that Mont-kaw truly was his loving and faithful servant, whose prudence and utterly selfless correctness made Peteprê ever richer. But what if it had been otherwise and the sole administrator of his house had robbed him, plunging him and his family into poverty? Potiphar would have had himself to blame, nor could he have been spared the reproach of indolent blind trust; he presumed and counted upon tender, ardent devotion as the requisite response to his delicate and sacred condition as a courtier of the sun—and we cannot refrain from passing such judgment even at this juncture.

And so he concerned himself with nothing other than what he ate and drank. For Mont-kaw, however, that meant just that much more vexation in the world, for he had his own affairs and these were tied up with those of his master. For the estate's produce he was given in reward for his services—grain, bread, beer, geese, linen, and leather—was, of course, more than he could eat or use on his own and had to be brought to market and exchanged for durable goods that added to his assets. And on the whole it was the same with all the goods of the estate, those it produced and those from outside.

The fan-bearer stood high on the list of Pharaoh's beneficiaries, and there was a steady flow of rewards and exceptional consolations for his inauthentic, titular existence. The good god paid him annually in great quantities of gold, silver, and copper, of garments, yarn, incense, wax, honey, oil, wine, vegetables, grain, and flax, of birds caught by bird catchers, of cattle and geese, even of chairs, chests, mirrors, chariots, and entire wooden boats. Only a portion of all this was needed by his household, and it was no different with what the estate itself produced in handcrafted goods and fruits of the field and garden. For the most part these were traded, sent by boat to markets and merchants up and down the river, in exchange for other goods or for metal in both wrought and unwrought form, all of which filled Potiphar's treasury. This trade, which was intertwined with the actual business of a productive and consuming estate, required a great deal of tallying and bookkeeping and demanded keen oversight.

There was the task of setting aside provisions for the craftsmen and servants and determining their rations: bread, beer, and a porridge of barley and lentils for workdays, geese for holidays. The house of women had its own special arrangements, requiring items to be delivered and accounted for day in and day out. There were the raw materials to be supplied the craftsmen—bakers, sandal makers, papyrus pasters, beer brewers, mat weavers, carpenters, and potters, the women who wove and spun—and their products had to be distributed for daily usage, some directed to storehouses, some to the world outside, as was also the case with the yield of the orchards and vegetable beds. Potiphar's livestock had to be cared for and their numbers replenished: the horses that drew his chariot, the dogs and cats he used for hunting—big, savage dogs for hunting in the desert, and very large, almost jaguarlike cats that accompanied him when he hunted for birds in the marshes. There were also a few cattle on the estate itself; but the majority of Potiphar's herds were out in the field, having been sent upstream toward Dendera and the House of Hathor, to an island in the river that Pharaoh had given him as a token of his love: five hundred square rods of farmland, each yielding twenty sacks of wheat and barley and forty bushels of onions, garlic, melons, artichokes, and gourds—multiply such yields by five hundred and the worry involved is evident. Granted, there was an administrator in charge, a man skilled at his office—scribe of harvest and overseer of barley, filling bushels to overflowing and measuring out wheat for his master. That was the man's smug way of speaking about himself, rather like the style of a tomb inscription; but that was no reason one should ultimately depend on him, for everything rested finally on Mont-kaw, the steward, through whose hands passed all the accounts for sowing and harvesting, as well as for the oil mills, winepresses, larger and smaller animals—in short, for everything a house of blessing produces and consumes, imports and exports. And in the end he also had to see if things were in order in the fields beyond, since in his tender inauthenticity Potiphar, the courtier to whom all this belonged, was not accustomed to seeing after or assuming responsibility for any of it whatever.

And so it happened that Joseph went out to the fields after all, but at the right time and under the right circumstances—not the wrong ones, thank God, at the wrong time. He went out to them not as the drudging slave he would have been had the conservative worldview of Dûdu, the wedded dwarf, prevailed, sending this boy of the sand there straightaway, before he could even speak before Potiphar—no, he went out to them to gain an overview as the steward's companion and apprentice, carrying a tablet and reed pens. He joined Mont-kaw's party on a sailing barque with rowers, heading upstream to Potiphar's island of grain, while the steward sat just as solemnly immobile within his tapestried shrine as those grand travelers Joseph had seen floating past on his first river journey, although he himself sat behind him with the other scribes. Those who encountered them, however, knew this barque well and said to one another: "There goes Mont-kaw, keeper of Peteprê's house, off on an inspection, it would seem. But who is that strange and beautiful lad who stands out from among all those accompanying him?"

Then they disembarked and walked the fertile island, inspecting the sowing or reaping and letting cattle be driven before them, and their keen eyes put fear into him who "filled bushels to overflowing"; and he was likewise amazed at this lad to whom the overseer showed everything—indeed, to whom he himself more or less presented things and bowed by way of precaution. Joseph, however, recalling how easily this man might have become his foreman, his slave driver, had he gone out into the fields at the wrong time, said to him privately, "Just be certain you don't let those bushels overflow to your own advantage, my man. We would notice at once, and you would end on the ash heap."

The phrase "end on the ash heap" was one familiar at home, but not customary here—and was thus all the more frightening to the scribe of the harvest.

When Joseph walked with Mont-kaw among the craftsmen's benches in the courtyard at home, examining their work and listening attentively first to the formal reports that the foremen and scribes in charge gave to the steward and then to further explanations that the latter provided him, he congratulated himself on having successfully preserved his standing among the workers and having avoided betraying his ignorance to them; they would otherwise have found it more difficult to regard him as a man made for an overview and generalities, as a man created to supervise them. But how difficult it is to make of ourselves what we were created to be and to achieve the heights God has intended for us, even if they are only of a middling sort; but God's intentions for Joseph were very great—and Joseph had to follow. He spent a good deal of time sitting and working through the accounts of the household and estate, keeping numbers and entries at his fingertips, but directing his mind's eye to the reality from which they had been extracted. He also worked together with his father, Mont-kaw, in his special chamber of trust, and the steward was amazed at the speed and vigor of Joseph's mind, the ability of such a beautiful head to grasp things and connect relationships—indeed, to make his own suggestions for improvement. Great quantities of the sycamore figs that the garden produced were sold to the city, or more precisely to the City of the Dead in the west, where masses of the fruit were needed for the sacrificial altars of the temples of death and as ceremonial gifts for the dead to eat in their graves, and it occurred to Joseph to have the house's potters produce models or imitations of the fruit in clay, which when painted in natural colors fulfilled their graveside purpose as well as natural fruits. Indeed, since the purpose itself was magical, they fulfilled such magical implications all the better, so that very soon there was a great demand for these magic figs, which cost very little to produce and could be made in whatever quantity needed, with the result that this branch of Potiphar's domestic industry soon began to flourish, employing a great number of workers and enriching their master, if not immensely in relation to all the rest, at least commendably.

Mont-kaw the steward was grateful to his helper for keeping the covenant they had concluded that day for the sake of their noble master, and as he observed his apprentice's clear-headed endeavors and the ingenuity with which his mind gained control of such manifold tasks, he quite often found rising up within him again that peculiar vacillation of ambiguous emotion that had stirred him when Joseph first stood before him, scroll in hand.

And to save himself the trouble, he also very soon began sending his pupil on business trips, to various markets with wares—both downriver, to Abôdu, the resting place of the mutilated god, or even to Menfe, and upriver toward Elephantine to the south, so that Joseph was master of a barque, or of several, which carried Peteprê's goods: beer, wine, vegetables, hides, linen, earthenware utensils, and the oil of the castor bean, to be burned as fuel and, in a finer form, for lubricating the body's interior.

It was not long before those who encountered him began to say: "There goes Mont-kaw's assistant sailing by, from the house of Peteprê, an Asiatic lad, fair of face and engaging of manner. He takes goods to market, for the steward trusts him, and not without reason, for he has a magic in his eyes and speaks the language of humans better than you and I, so that he wins people for his wares by winning them to himself, and sells at prices that must delight Pharaoh's friend."

Such were the words, more or less, of the boatsmen of the Nehel as they sailed past. And there was truth in what they said, for blessing was upon what Joseph did. He had a charming way of dealing with buyers in the markets of villages and cities, and his turns of phrase delighted everyone, so that people crowded around him and his products and he brought profits home to the steward that Mont-kaw himself, or any other agent, could not have realized. And yet it was not all that often that the overseer could send Joseph on such trips, and he had to return from his journeys posthaste—for Peteprê was highly displeased if his servant was missing in the dining chamber, if it was not Joseph who poured water over his hands and passed him his dish and goblet, or if he had to miss being read to while dozing off after his meal. Yes, one can measure the full rigor of the demands made on Joseph's mind and energies during this period, only if one recognizes that his duties as Potiphar's reader and personal attendant continued amidst the many other tasks required for gaining an overview of the workings of the house. But he was young and full of fervor, determined to achieve the heights of God's intentions for him. Already he was no longer the last of those here below; there were many who had begun to bow before him. But things would have to take a still different turn—for the sake of his God he was imbued with this idea. Not just some should bow before him, but all people, with the exception of the highest himself, for he was to serve only him—this was Abraham's grandson's firm conviction and, even with the direction still undefined, it determined his life. How that was to happen and how this turn was to be made, he did not know and could not picture even to himself; but the crucial thing was to follow with goodwill and courage the path that God placed beneath his feet, to see as far down that path as a man is allowed to see, and not to quail if it grew steep, for that indeed pointed to a high goal.

And so he was not discouraged at having to master more and more of the estate and its business; with each day he made himself increasingly indispensable to Mont-kaw, while at the same time holding to the covenant that he had made with the steward in regard to Potiphar, their good master, the highest in this immediate circle, by dedicating himself to him as his personal and spiritual attendant and confirming himself in his trust, just as he had done in the orchard and in their conversation about the bird catcher's garden. It took a great deal of intellect and skill to do this—to assist his master in the depths of his soul, to give him a better sense of warming himself than wine at meals ever could. And if only that had been everything! But to gain some true picture of all the things Jacob's son had to look after in assisting both steward and master, one must also consider that he had to say good-night to Mont-kaw each evening, and always with different words waiting to be extracted from the storehouse of language; for it was for that reason he had originally been purchased, and Mont-kaw had been too pleasantly touched by the initial test to have wished to forgo the pleasure later. He was a poor sleeper besides—the bags that drooped under his eyes and made them smaller attested to that. The demands of a busy day made it difficult for his preoccupied mind to find rest; and his kidneys, which did not function all that splendidly, surely made it all the more difficult for him to find the path to sleep; and so he could indeed use gentle wishes and melodious whispers in that regard at day's end. Which was why Joseph dared not miss appearing before him each evening to trickle a few sedative drops in his ear—words that along with and in the midst of everything else, had to be prepared and given a little thought during the day, for their form had to be eloquent.

"Greetings, my father, for the night," he might say, raising his hands. "Behold, the day has lived its life and, grown weary of itself, has closed its eyes, and silence has come over all the world. Hark, how wonderful! The sound of stamping from the barn, and the bark of a dog, but then the silence is all the deeper, gently suffusing a man's soul as well, lulling him to sleep, while the vigilant lamps of God are lit above courtyard and city, tilled land and desert. Having grown weary, the nations rejoice that evening has come at the right moment and that when they are refreshed day will open its eyes again on the morrow. Truly the ordainments of God deserve our thanks. For let man but consider there would be no night and that the burning road of toil might still lie before him unbroken, in garish monotony as far as eye can see. Would that not be a cause of horror and despair? But God has made the days and set an end to each, that we may assuredly attain it in its hour. It is the grove of night that invites us to holy rest, and with arms outstretched, head sinking backward, lips open, and eyes fluttering with bliss, we enter its precious shade. Do not think, dear master, that you *must* rest upon your bed. Think, rather, that you *may* rest—regard this as a great boon, and peace will be yours. Lie down then, my father, and may sweet sleep descend upon you, over you, filling all your soul with blissful rest, so that free of life's problems and plagues you may breathe sleep upon the breast of the divine."

"Thank you, Osarsiph," the steward would then say, and just as when Joseph had first wished him good-night by broad daylight, he felt his eyes moisten a little. "May you rest well too. Yesterday your words were perhaps a trace more harmonious, but today as well they were consoling and kindred to the poppy, so that I truly believe they will help me do battle with wakefulness. Your distinction that I *may* rather than *must* sleep is strangely pleasing to me; I intend to think about it, it will bear me up. How is it that the words come to you for this magic charm, words that say 'On you, over you, filling all your soul'? You probably cannot say why yourself. And so, good night then, my son."

Amun Looks Askance at Joseph

Thus it was that many and varied demands were made upon Joseph in those days, nor was it enough that he meet them, since he also had to worry that others would hold his good fortune against him; for the smiles and downcast eyes that accompany an ascendancy such as his conceal much ill will, which it is important to appease by cleverness, forbearance, and gentle skill applied in all directions—yet one more demand amidst all the others on a man's prudence and vigilance. It is quite impossible for a person like Joseph, growing as if beside a spring, not to trespass on someone else's land or infringe upon the boundary stones of others; he cannot avoid it, because the diminishment of others is irrevocably bound up with his own existence, and a good portion of his wit must constantly be applied to reconciling those whom his existence has overshadowed and shunted aside. The Joseph of the days before the pit had lacked any regard or finer feeling for such truth; his opinion that everyone loved him more than themselves had left him insensitive to it. In his death and as Osarsiph, he had grown more clever, or shrewder if you like, for as Joseph's earlier life reveals, cleverness does not protect a man from folly; and in his conversation with Mont-kaw the tender consideration he had shown to his predecessor as a reader was directed first of all toward the steward himself, out of an awareness that Mont-kaw would be agreeably touched by it—given the fact that he was also a man who tended to happy resignation. But Joseph also did his best in regard to Amenemuia, went to see him and spoke to him so courteously and modestly that the scribe was completely won over in the end and sincerely willing to accept having been removed from his post as reader simply because his successor was so charming to him. For with hands crossed at his chest, Joseph described in supple words how his soul had been pained by the decision and by their master's whim, which though sacred, he had not knowingly done anything to influence, the best proof of which was his conviction that as a scholar of the house of books Amenemuia read far better than he, being a son of the black earth after all, whereas he, Osarsiph, was an Asian who mangled human speech. But it had simply come about that he had had to speak before the master in the orchard and out of embarrassment had told all sorts of things he chanced to know about trees, bees, and birds—and incredibly enough it had pleased the master so inordinately that, with the swift wit of the great and mighty, he had made his decision, but not to his own advantage, as the master surely realized now himself. For again and again he frequently held up Amenemuia's example to him,

Joseph, and said, "Amenemuia, my previous reader, read it like this, with this emphasis, and if you wish to find favor with me, you must read it the same way, for I have long been spoiled." Then he, Joseph, would attempt it, which meant his life and breath were really those of someone else, of his predecessor. Nevertheless the master had not rescinded his previous decision, because great lords never will or should admit that they have been too hasty in giving an order to their own detriment. Which was why Joseph daily tried to console the master in his unspoken regrets, by saying, "You must give Amenemuia two garments for feast days, my lord, and also assign him a good post as scribe of sweets and revels in the house of seclusion; that will ease your mind, and mine as well, on his account."

For Amenemuia this, of course, was balsam. He had not even known he was such a good reader, for as soon as he had opened his mouth, the master usually dozed off; and since, as he told himself, he had had to be dismissed in order to learn of it, then surely he should be content with his dismissal. And his successor's pangs of conscience and the master's unacknowledged regret did his soul good; and since he had in fact received the two garments for feast days and been appointed master of revels in Peteprê's house of women—which was a very good post and proof that Joseph really had spoken to the master on his behalf—he bore the Kenanite no ill will, but instead was inclined in his favor, seeing as he had treated him so very nicely.

To be sure, it made no difference to Joseph if he could find good positions for others, since with God's help he was aiming for the best one himself and, even if from afar and still at Mont-kaw's side, was preparing himself for the general oversight of things. He did much the same thing for a certain Merab, a household servant who had usually accompanied Peteprê on bird hunts and spearfishing expeditions. For as his companion in these manly pursuits, Potiphar no longer took along Merab, but his favorite, young Osarsiph—which really ought to have driven a thorn, and a very poisonous one at that, into Merab's side. But Joseph took the sting and poison from the thorn by speaking to Merab as he had to Amenemuia and arranging for both a gift of honor and another post, that of supervisor of the brewery, so that instead of making an enemy, he made a real friend of him. And to anyone who would listen Merab would say of him: "He comes, I grant, from the wretched land of Retenu and those gadabouts of the desert, but I must admit he is an elegant fellow all the same, and has the nicest way about him. By all the Holy Three, he still makes mistakes in speaking the language of humans, and yet it's true, no denying it, that if you must make way for him it is a joy to do it, it sets your eyes shining even as you step back. Explain why that is so if you like, but there is no explanation and you will only miss the mark—but your eyes do shine."

Such were the words of Merab, an ordinary Egyptian; and it was Se'enkh-Wen-nofre-et-cetera, the favored dwarf, who whispered to Joseph the news that the dismissed servant spoke of him to people in that fashion. "Well, then that's all to the good," Joseph replied. But he knew quite well that not everyone spoke that way. He had got over his childish delusion that all people ought to love him more than themselves and perfectly understood that his rise in the house of Potiphar was not only annoying to many in and of itself, but was also lent a special opprobrium because he was a foreigner, a "sand-dweller," a man of the Ibrim—all of which demanded the greatest tact on his part. And we are back now to the inner contradiction and partisanship that ruled in the land of the grandchildren and amid which Joseph's career followed its path—back to certain pious and patriotic principles that stood in opposition to his career and almost managed to send him into the fields at the wrong time, but back as well to certain other principles that favored his rise and that one might call freethinking and tolerant, or even fashionable and flimsy. These latter were the beliefs of Mont-kaw, the overseer, simply because they were the beliefs of his master Peteprê, the great courtier. And why were they his? Because they were those of the court, of course; because people there were annoyed by the burdensome weight of the power of Amun's temple, which was the embodiment of patriotic, conservative moral rectitude in these latter days of the Two Lands, and because for that very reason the great men of the court favored and encouraged a different cult—it is easy to guess which. It was the worship of Atum-Rê in On, the tip of the triangle, of a very old and mild god, with whom Amun had equated himself, not in an obliging but in a brutal fashion, so that he was now called Amun-Rê, the imperial god of the sun. Both Rê and Amun were the sun in his barque, but in what dissimilar senses, what different ways!

In conversation with the bleary-eyed priests of Horakhte, Joseph had been offered proofs on the spot of the resourceful and serenely instructive sense in which Rê was a god of the sun; he had learned of the god's desire to expand and of his inclination to join in all-seeing concord with all the solar gods of other nations, with Asia's youthful suns, each of whom emerged like a bridegroom from his chamber, ran his course like a joyful hero, and was mourned as he went down, lamented by women. Much as Abraham in his day had compared his own God to Malkizedek's El-Elyon, Rê, it appeared, wished to admit no great difference between himself and these others. He was called Atum at his setting, in which he was very beautiful and pitiable; but of late the resourceful speculation of his edifying prophets had supplied him a new, similar-sounding name for his entire and universal sunship, not just in his setting, but for morning, noon, and evening—he called himself Atôn, a name whose peculiar suggestiveness was apparent to all. For it brought his name into close proximity with the name of the youth mutilated by the boar, for whom flutes mourned in the groves and ravines of Asia.

This was the resourceful, slightly exotic, and world-embracing tendency of Rê-Horakhte's sunship, and it was of great significance at court. Pharaoh's scholars knew nothing finer than to conjecture about him. Amun-Rê in Karnak, however, Pharaoh's father in his massive house rich in treasures, was the opposite of everything Atum-Rê was. He was unbending and strict, a forbidding enemy of any speculation with a view to universality, ill disposed to all things foreign, rigid in the observation of national customs that brooked no discussion, locked in holy tradition—and all that despite his being much younger than the god in On. Here an ancient god, resourceful and open to the world, there a newer but inflexibly conservative god—a confusing set of circumstances.

But if Amun in Karnak looked askance at the esteem Atum-Rê-Horakhte enjoyed at court, Joseph was quite aware that he also looked askance at him, the foreign personal attendant and reader to the courtier; and in assessing favor and disfavor he soon recognized that the meaning of Rê's sunship was favorable to him, but that of Amun unfavorable, and that such disfavor demanded that he exercise the greatest tact.

The most immediate embodiment of Amun's sunship was Dûdu,

the stuffy prig, the keeper of the jewelry chests. That the man did not love him more than he loved himself, indeed loved him considerably less, was only too clear from the beginning; and over this entire period, indeed for years on end Jacob's son went to untold trouble trying to placate this dwarf of substance, employing the most circumspect courtesy to win over not only him, but also her whose arm embraced him, his wife Zeset, who held a high position in the house of women, and even his tall, but nasty children, Esesi and Ebebi; and he painfully avoided the least infringement of any boundary stones. Given the standing he had with Potiphar thanks to his warming helpfulness, who can doubt that it would have been easy for him to push Dûdu aside and have himself named supervisor of the wardrobe? The master wanted nothing better than to draw Joseph more and more into his personal service, and it is as good as certain that, without ever being asked, he expressly offered him the position of head of the wardrobe, particularly since—as Joseph himself observed, having drawn his own conclusions from the faithful steward's dislike of the arrogant wedded dwarf—Potiphar could not stand the fellow. But Joseph's refusal of the offer was both meek and firm, first because he did not want any more new duties as a personal attendant while still trying to gain an overview of things, and second, as he emphasized, because he could not and would not trespass on the dignified little man's land.

But do you suppose the dwarf thanked him for this? Certainly not—in that regard Joseph had cherished false hopes. The enmity Dûdu had shown toward him from the first day—no, from the first hour by trying to frustrate his purchase—was not to be overcome, or even moderated, by any sort of forbearance or courtesy; but anyone hoping to gain an insight into deeper reasons and motivations behind this entire matter will not be satisfied with the explanation that so stubborn a dislike was based on an Egyptian party man's abhorrence of favor shown a foreigner or of his rise in Potiphar's house. Rather, one must certainly take into account those peculiar magical ways in which Joseph knew to be "helpful" to his master and win him for himself—and of which Dûdu had already seen examples. He found them particularly odious because he thought them prejudicial to his own high status and to those privileges that constituted the pride and sterling superiority of his undersized life.

Joseph also surmised as much. He was perfectly aware that by his orations in the date garden he had wounded the one in the secret depths of his soul while managing to delight those same depths in the other and that, without wishing to, he had nevertheless trespassed in some way upon the wedded dwarf's field. Which was why he treated Dûdu's wife and brood with such great delicacy. But that did not help, for Dûdu showed his disfavor from below in any way he could and enjoyed particular success in stressing venerable moral strictures that declared Joseph, a Habiritic foreigner, unclean. For at meals, when the higher-ranking servants of the house, including Joseph and the steward Mont-kaw, broke bread together, Dûdu stubbornly insisted, all the while letting his upper lip build a dignified roof above his retracted lower lip, that the Egyptians be served separately from the Ebrew; and in fact, when the overseer and the others, as followers of Atum-Rê's sunship, did not prove to be so punctilious, he demonstrated his devotion to Amun and adherence to his decrees by withdrawing from this abomination—and presumably spat in all four directions as well as spun in a circle while casting all sorts of exorcising spells to atone for this defilement, and with such diligence that his intention to offend Joseph was quite obvious.

If only that had been all! But Joseph quickly learned that dignified Dûdu was working explicitly against him and trying to force him out of the house—learned it in detail and piping hot once again by way of his friend Bes-at-the-Feast, who, thanks to his own brevity, was extraordinarily good at spying and eavesdropping, as if created for being secretly present wherever there was something to be overheard, a master at hiding in nooks that full-grown people would never even have considered. Dûdu, likewise of dwarfish lineage and built to the same small scale, should also have been less oafish and defenseless than people of stature. But what Neteruhotpe alleged may well have been true: by marrying into the world of the overstretched, Dûdu had forfeited many of the refinements of the smaller life—though the same sterling qualities that had enabled him to enter into such a marriage probably meant that his portion of dwarfish refinement was imperfect to begin with. In any case, he could be crept up on, unaware that he was being spied upon by his despised little brother, who quickly learned what paths Dûdu took in his attempts to prevent Joseph's ascendancy—they led to the house of seclusion, they led to Mut-em-enet, Potiphar's titular consort. And anything the dwarf told her she in turn discussed, either in his presence or tête-à-tête, with a powerful man who had access to the inner chambers of Peteprê's house of women: Beknechons, First Prophet of Amun.

We know already from the conversation of Potiphar's mischievous parents what a close relationship Joseph's mistress had with the temple of the imposing imperial god, the house of Amun-Rê. Like countless women of her social class—including, for instance, her friend Renenutet, the consort of the Chief Steward of Amun's Bulls—she belonged to the aristocratic Order of Hathor, whose patroness was Pharaoh's Great Consort and whose head was always the wife of the chief attendant to the god at Karnak, who at that time was the pious Beknechons. The order's focal point and spiritual home was the beautiful temple by the river, Amun's Southern House of Women, or "the Harem" as it was called, which was connected by the amazing Street of the Rams with the great dwelling in Karnak that Pharaoh was in the process of enlarging with a columned hall higher than any other. The ceremonial title for the members of the order was "harem wife of Amun," which corresponded to the title First of the Harem Wives conferred on the head of the order, the high priest's wife. But then why were these women called "priestesses of Hathor," since Amun-Rê's great consort was named Mut, or "the mother," and Hathor of the fair countenance and cow eyes belonged instead to Rê-Atum and was the wife of the lord of On. Yes, these were the refinements of the land of Egypt, its politic way of counterbalancing forces. For since it had been politically pleasing to Amun to be equated with Atum-Rê, Mut, the mother of her son, had had herself equated with triumphant Hathor, and Amun's earthly harem wives, the women of Thebes' high society, followed suit: each of them was Hathor, the mistress of love in person, when at great feasts they donned the clinging garment and the golden helmet topped by cow horns with the solar disk between and made music, danced, and sang for Amun—as well as ladies of society can sing; for they were chosen not for the beauty of their voices, but for their wealth and elegance. Mut-em-enet, however, the mistress of Potiphar's house, sang very beautifully and also instructed others, including Renenutet, the chief stewardess of the bulls, in singing; indeed, her standing in the god's house of women was very high in general, so that her place in the order was more or less at the side of its head—whose consort, Beknechons, the great prophet of Amun, went in and out of Mut-em-enet's chamber as a friend and pious confidant.

Beknechons

Joseph had long since come to recognize this austere man on sight; he had seen him on his frequent visits to the estate and its house of women and had been as annoyed as if sharing Pharaoh's soul at the pomp and splendor with which he arrived: the god's militia with spears and clubs ran before his floating sedan chair, its long poles borne on the shoulders of four times four shiny-headed temple attendants. With a second troop following after and bearers of ostrich feathers moving alongside, it was like the barque of Amun himself in festive procession; and in front of the first unit were rod bearers who filled the courtyard with their pretentious, excited cries calling people to assemble and for him who was set over the house, if not Peteprê himself, to receive the great guest at its threshold. It was Potiphar's custom not to be at home on such occasions, but Montkaw was on hand without fail, and Joseph had also stood behind him several times, carefully fixing his eye on this very great man, in whom he saw the highest and most distant embodiment of that hostile doctrine of the sun of which Dûdu was the nearest and smallest representative.

Beknechons was a tall, lanky man and of very proud bearing besides—ribcage thrust upward, shoulders thrown back, chin raised. His egg-shaped head with its smooth-shaven skull was always uncovered and always imposing, and its expression, defined entirely by a deep, permanent crease between the eyes, was never less than stern, even when the man managed a smile—which came in any case as a condescending reward for special obsequiousness. The high priest's face, every bristle of beard carefully removed, was chiseled, regular, and impassive. With high cheekbones and furrows at nostrils and mouth as deep as the one between his eyes, he had a way of looking on past other people and things that was more than haughty and more like a rejection of the current state of the world, a negation and condemnation of the entire direction life had taken for the past few centuries or, for that matter, millennia, just as his attire was very costly and fine, but also old-fashioned, a sacerdotal abstention from the entire present epoch. Clearly visible under his outer robe, which fell from armpits to feet, was a loincloth in the simple, narrow, and short style of the first dynasties of the Old Kingdom; and the priestly leopard hide flung around his shoulders likewise referred to more distant and surely more pious ages—the great cat's head and front paws hanging at his back and its rear paws crossed at his chest, which bore other tokens of high rank: a blue ribbon and an intricate golden brooch of rams' heads.

By the clear light of day, this leopard hide was a presumption, since it was part of the vestments of the First Prophet of Atum-Rê in On and thus unbecoming for servants of Amun. Beknechons, however, was very much a man to decide for whom it was appropriate, and no one, including Joseph, could fail to see why he wore man's primal garb, the pelt of a sacred animal: He wished to proclaim by it that Atum-Rê had been merged into Amun and was a mere manifestation of the great god of Thebes, subject to him to some extent, indeed more than to some extent. For Amun—which is to say, Beknechons—had managed to force Rê's high prophet in On to accept the honorary office of assistant priest of Amun in Thebes, so that the high priest's preeminence over him and his right to wear his insignia were on display here; but also at the seat of Rê, in On itself, this same superiority prevailed. For Beknechons not only called himself Chief Priest of the Priests of All the Gods of Thebes, but had also taken on the title of Chief Priest of the Priests of All the Gods of Upper and Lower Egypt and thus was also the head and first priest of the house of Atum-Rê—why, then, should he not have been allowed to wear the leopard skin? Observing the man in the awareness of all that he represented, one could not help feeling fear; and Joseph was by now enough a part of the life and workings of Egypt that his heart pounded with misgiving at the thought of how Pharaoh was still making this powerful man ever fatter and prouder with endless gifts of goods and treasures, out of the tender notion that it was his own father, Amun, for whom he did these good things, and thus for himself. Joseph, for whom Amun-Rê was merely an idol like any other, though he did not let on that he thought so—half a ram in his chamber, half a doll-like image in his temple shrine, to be taken out on his barque for a sail on the Yeôr, because people did not know any better—Joseph, however, discriminated more finely and freely than Pharaoh; he did not think it good or wise to fatten up this puta-tive father all the more. And so it was with a higher concern that he watched the great priest of Amun vanish into the house of women, a concern that for reasons of statecraft transcended his own well-being, though he was aware that this latter was the subject of dubi-ous discussions within its walls.

He knew from favored Bes, his earliest benefactor in Potiphar's house, that Dûdu had complained to Mut, their mistress, about him several times already—the little fellow had listened in on their dis-cussions from the most unbelievable hiding places and whispered his report of it all in such exact detail that Joseph could see the warden of the wardrobe standing there in his starched apron before his mis-tress, thrusting the dignified roof of his upper lip out over the lower, flailing stubby arms in outrage, and speaking up at her in his deepest possible voice about this offense and nuisance. The slave Osarsiph, as he obscurely and presumably arbitrarily called himself, this Habiru dandy, this puppy of the wretched desert—his rise here in the house was a scandal, Dûdu had said, the favor shown him a dan-gerous cancer, regarded, no doubt, with animosity by the Hidden One. Against his, Dûdu's, sterling advice, he had been bought far too dearly, for one hundred sixty debens, from lowly wandering ped-dlers of the desert, who had stolen him from a well, from a pit of punishment, and had been put to work in Peteprê's house at the urg-ing of that hollow nut, that unmarried buffoon, Shepses-Bes. But in-stead of sending this foreign lout to drudge in the fields, as respectable people had advised the steward, Mont-kaw had let him loiter about the courtyard, and then permitted him to speak before Peteprê in the date garden, an occasion that the gallows bird had used to his benefit in ways for which "shameless" was not a harsh, but all too mild a word. For he had dinned the master's ears with wily quibbles that defamed Amun and blasphemed against the high-est powers of the sun; but these words had dazed the holy master's senses and so culpably bewitched him that he had raised him to be his personal attendant and reader, while Mont-kaw treated him like a son, or better like a son of the house itself, who was now learning its business as if he were its heir, with all the pretenses of a vice-overseer—a mangy Asiatic in an Egyptian house! He, Dûdu, took the humblest liberty of informing his mistress of this abomination, which could easily rouse the wrath of the Hidden One, calling down his revenge on those who tolerated and committed such corrupted freethinking.

"What did the mistress reply?" Joseph asked upon hearing this account. "Tell me exactly, Neteruhotpe, and as best you can, repeat her own words for me."

"Her words," the dwarf responded, "were as follows: 'As you were speaking, overseer of the jewelry chests,' she said, 'I was thinking about whom you might actually mean and what sort of foreign slave you might possibly have in mind in lodging your complaint, for I could not recall the slave in question and searched my memory in vain. You cannot expect me to keep the entire staff of menials in my head and to know whom you mean merely from a reference to one or another of them. But now that you have allowed me time to think, the surmise has grown within me that you mean a servant, still quite young in years, who for some while now has filled the goblet of Peteprê, my consort. If I force my mind, I can vaguely recall that particular silver apron.'"

"Vaguely?" Joseph responded, not without some disappointment. "How can I be so vague in our mistress's memory when I am so close to her and the master at their meal each day and the grace that I have found before him and Mont-kaw cannot have escaped her entirely? I am truly amazed that she had to search so long and hard in her memory before surmising whom the malicious Dûdu meant. What else did she say?"

"She said," the dwarf replied, continuing his report, "she said: 'Why do you bother me with this and tell me about it, keeper of the wardrobe? Indeed, you call up Amun's anger over me as well. For you yourself said that his wrath will come down upon those who tolerate this offense. If I know nothing, I tolerate nothing, and you should have let it stay at that and spared me, instead of making me aware of it and putting me in danger.'"

Joseph laughed on hearing these words and gave them high praise. "What a splendid retort and what a clever rebuke! Tell me more about our mistress, little Bes. Repeat everything for me precisely, for you were paying attention, I hope."

"It was malicious Dûdu," Neteruhotpe replied, "who had more to add. For he justified himself, saying, 'I have announced this abomination to my mistress not so that she may tolerate it, but put an end to it, and out of love I have given her an opportunity to be of service to Amun by speaking to the master, so that this unclean servant may be removed from the house and, seeing as he has been bought, be transferred to toil in the fields, as is only proper, instead of making himself the master here and setting himself impudently over the children of the land.'"

"Very vicious," Joseph said. "Spiteful, nasty words. But the mistress, how did she answer them?"

"She replied," favored Bes reported: "'Ah, my solemn dwarf, only very rarely is the mistress permitted to speak intimately with the master—you need but recall the formality of this house, and do not think our comings and goings with one another are like those between you and her whose arm embraces you, your wife Zeset, with whom you are intimate. She comes to you, I presume, with easy courage and speaks to you, her husband, about whatever concerns her and you, and may well persuade you of this or that. For she is a mother and has borne you two comely children, Esesi and Ebebi, so that you are tied by gratitude to this woman and have every cause to lend an ear to her whose fertility has won her merit and to pay attention to her wishes and admonitions. But what am I to the master, and what reason has he to listen to me? His stubbornness, as you know, is great, his moods are proud and deaf, so that I and my reminders are powerless before him.'"

Joseph said nothing and, lost in thought, gazed on past his little friend, who now propped his worried, wrinkled face on one hand.

"Well, and the wardrobe warden's reply?" Jacob's son probed after a while. "Did he answer her by further sermonizing on the subject?"

But his small friend said that was not the case. In response, Dûdu had lapsed into dignified silence; the mistress had, however, added that she would speak with the Father High Priest about the matter as soon as possible. For since Peteprê had raised up this foreign slave after he had spoken to him about issues of the sun, it was apparent that religious and political affairs were at stake here, and that was of interest to Beknechons, the great priest of Amun, her friend and confessor—he ought to know of it, and much to her relief, she would pour out into his fatherly heart what Dûdu had told her about this offense.

These, then, were the midget's tidings. But Joseph would later

recall how Bes-em-heb had sat a while longer with him that day—
dressed as always in his comical garb, the little cone for ointment
atop his wig—chin propped in one hand and eyes scowling
gloomily.

"What are you frowning about, Beloved of the House of
Amun," he had asked, "and why are you still brooding over these
things?"

In his little cricket voice Bes had replied, "Ah, Osarsiph, this
dwarf is thinking how it is not good for that vicious gossip to speak
about you with Mut, our mistress—not good in any way."

"Of course not," Joseph had responded. "Why bother to tell me
that? I know all on my own that it is not good, and may even be dangerous. But look, I accept it serenely, for I trust in God. Did not the
mistress herself admit she does not have that much power over Peteprê? You may set your mind at ease, for one word or signal from
her will not suffice to send me to drudge in the fields."

"How can I be at ease," Bes had whispered, "when the danger is
just the opposite and comes from another direction—for that gossip
has admonished the mistress and put vagueness into sharp focus
where you are concerned."

"Let him who can understand that, do so," Joseph had cried in
response, "for I do not, and only your drivel seems vague to me. The
opposite danger and from another direction? What dark and vague
words are you whispering?"

"I am whispering, whispering my fear and foreboding," he heard
Neteruhotpe resume, "and murmur the wisdom of dwarfish care,
which cannot yet reach up to an overstretched lad like you. For
Dûdu, that gossip, desires to be vicious, but it may well be that he
does good despite himself, does so much good that it turns to evil,
evil far greater than he intended."

"Well, my little man, do not hold it against me, but no man can
make sense of what makes no sense. Evil, good, so much good and
far greater evil? That is dwarfish fiddle-faddle and midget gibberish—I can make nothing of it try as I may."

"Then why is your countenance flushed and murky, Osarsiph,
and why are you as peevish as you were when I told you the mistress
recalled you only vaguely? Dwarfish wisdom would wish that you
remain vague to her forever, for it is dangerous, doubly dangerous,
more dangerous than danger itself, if in his evil intent that cursed

gossip has opened her eyes. Ah," the little fellow had said, cowering in the clasp of his own tiny arms, "this dwarf is very much afraid and alarmed by the enemy, by the bull whose fiery breath lays waste to the fields."

"But what fields do you mean?" Joseph asked with insistent incomprehension. "And what sort of fiery bull? You're a bit touched in the head today, so there is no way I can touch your fears. Have Firebelly fix you a soothing extract of roots to cool your brain. I am off to work. Can I alter the fact that Dûdu complains of me to our mistress, dangerous as that may be? You, however, can see my trust in God and need not carry on like this. Just go on paying close heed and if possible do not let a single word escape you of what Dûdu says before our mistress—nor especially of what she replies to him—so that you may report it to me in detail. For it is important that I know what's what."

That was the course of their conversation that day, and Joseph later recalled both it and how Neteruhotpe had been so strangely fearful. But was it truly trust in God and nothing more that allowed Joseph to accept with such relative serenity the news of the steps Dûdu had taken against him?

Up to this point, Joseph had been for his mistress if not exactly air, then a tenuous figure, an object in the room, like the mute servant he had been for Huya and Tuya. In his intent to do evil, Dûdu had at least brought about a change in this regard. If at meals her gaze happened to fall on Joseph while he handed the master his food or filled his goblet, it now did so not purely by chance or the way eyes register an object, but rather she watched him with personal interest, as if taking in a phenomenon with its own history and associations that—whether out of cordiality or annoyance—give one pause for thought. In a word, this great lady of Egypt, his mistress, had recently begun to pay him attention. She did so, needless to say, in a very languid and cursory way; it would be too much to say that her eyes rested on him. But for that short duration we might call the flash of an eye, they found their way to him now and again—probably with the thought of reminding herself that she intended to speak to Beknechons about him; and from beneath lowered eyelashes Joseph took note of these flashes, never missed one of them, despite all the attention he had to focus on serving Peteprê, even if it was only once or twice that he allowed the flash to become mutual, so that the flashing eyes of mistress and servant met more or less openly—hers languid, proud, and with ongoing austerity, his respectfully startled and melting into humility as he hastily lowered his eyelashes.

This sort of thing happened once Dûdu had spoken with the mistress. It had not happened before, and, just between us, Joseph did not find it entirely disagreeable. He saw some sort of progress in it and was tempted to be grateful to his adversary, Dûdu, for mentioning him. Nor, the next time he saw Beknechons entering the house of women, did he find the thought unpleasant that he and his rise were the probable topic of discussion—a certain satisfaction, even joy was bound up with the idea, despite whatever gravity and worry it also entailed.

Once again he learned of this discussion from the mock vizier, who had been able to follow it secretly from some nook or niche. First the priest and the lady of the Order of Hathor had exchanged several thoughts on matters of ritual and on social and personal issues—they "made tongues," as the children of Keme put it, though the idiom was actually Babylonian, or in other words, traded the gossip of the metropolis; but when talk moved to Peteprê and his house, the mistress had indeed presented Dûdu's complaint to her spiritual friend and reported about the domestic impropriety of the Ebrew slave whom the courtier and his overseer were favoring with such great and egregious attention. Beknechons had received her report with nods of the head, as if this merely confirmed his general gloomy expectations and reflected only too well the moral state of an age that had forfeited so much piety in comparison with those epochs when aprons were cut as short and tight as the one he, Beknechons, wore. A sobering sign, no doubt, as he put it. It was what came of a spirit of freethinking, of a disdain for national order based on ancient piety, which, though refined and cheering enough at first, inevitably wandered off into the desert and wilderness, shattering the most sacred bonds and enervating the Two Lands, so that there was no longer any awe before the scepter along its coasts and the kingdom fell into ruin. And Amun's chief priest, according to Neteruhotpe's report, immediately dropped the topic and moved on to larger issues of statecraft, to questions of dominion and the preservation of power, pointing his hands in several directions as he expatiated on how Tushratta must be prevented from expanding his

Mitannite kingdom by Suppiluliuma, the great king of the Chetites to his north—but, then again, he dare not be all too successful. For if the bellicose Chetite were to bring Mittani entirely under his sway and then surge forth to the south, he would endanger Pharaoh's Syrian possessions, acquired by the conqueror, Men-kheper-Rê-Thutmose; although, goaded on by his savage gods, he might in any case circumvent Mittani entirely one day and overwhelm the land of Amki by the sea, between the Amanus and Cedar Mountains. In the world's great board game, he was opposed, to be sure, by the figure of Abdasharat the Amorite, who as Pharaoh's vassal ruled the land between Amki and Khanigalbat and whose function it was to act as a bulwark against Suppiluliuma's southward expansion. But the Amorite would be that only as long as his awe for Pharaoh was greater than his fear of the Hetti—otherwise he would without fail come to an agreement with them and betray Amun. For they were all traitors, these kings of the Syrian conquests who were duty-bound to pay tribute—traitors the moment there was a slackening of the awe on which all else depended, for without it the Bedu and nomads of the steppes would, if worse came to worst, invade the fertile land and lay waste to Pharaoh's cities. In short, there were many such worries that admonished the land of Egypt to steel its nerve and maintain its manly virtue—always presuming that it wished to maintain awe for its scepter and a realm for its crowns. Which is why it had to be a pious and moral nation, as in ages past.

"A powerful man," Joseph remarked upon hearing this speech. "Inasmuch as he belongs to his god and as a shiny-headed priest of his lord should be a good father to his children, extending a hand to those that stumble—one can only admire what a fine mind he has for earthly matters and the affairs of state. Just between us, favored Bes, he should leave his worries about the realm and the awe felt by other nations to Pharaoh in his palace, who has been ordained and set in his place for that purpose; for that is doubtless how things stood between temple and palace in those earlier days that he praises. But our mistress, did she have nothing to say in reply?"

"I heard," the dwarf said, "how she answered by saying: 'Ah, my father, is it not true that when Egypt was a nation of pious and strict observance it was small and poor, with no boundary stones set far-off among tribute-paying peoples, either to the south beyond the cataracts in the Negro lands or to the east beside the river that runs backwards. But riches have come from that poverty and a great realm from that confinement. And now the Two Lands and Wase the Great teem with foreigners, overflow with treasures, and everything has become new. Do you not also take delight in the new that has come from the old and is its reward? Pharaoh sacrifices generously to Amun his father from the tribute of other nations, so that the god can build as he pleases and swells up like the river in springtime, when it already stands at flood. Must my father not also applaud the course things have taken since those pious early days?' "

"Perfectly true," Beknechons had responded, according to favored Bes. "My daughter speaks aptly on the question of the Two Lands as it now presents itself. For the question is: The old bore within it the new—that is, the realm and its riches—as its reward, but the reward—that is, the realm and its riches—bears within it this free spirit, and also enervation and loss. What is to be done so that the reward does not become a curse—and good is not ultimately repaid with evil? That is the question that presents itself, and the lord of Karnak, Amun, the god of the realm, answers it as follows: The old must become lord within the new, and steeled nerves and strict observance are to be imposed upon the realm so that the old can steer this free spirit and not be denied its just reward. For these sons of the old are not duly honored with the kingdom, nor are they favored with the crowns—the white, the red, the blue—nor with the crowns of the gods either."

"Strong stuff," Joseph said upon hearing it. "Thanks to your small size, favored Bes, you have heard strong, uncompromising words. I am dismayed by them, if not surprised, for ever since I first saw Amun's troops on the Street of the Son, I have surmised that this was what Amun has in his heart. So our mistress spoke only a few words about me, and Beknechons at once proceeded to such large issues that they both probably forgot all about me. Did they, from what you heard, ever come around to me again?"

They did so only at the very end, Shepses-Bes responded, and in taking his leave Amun's chief priest had agreed to chastise Peteprê as soon as possible and to point out to him with what gravity old, strict observance regarded his favoring a foreign slave.

"Then surely I should tremble," Joseph said, "and be greatly afraid that Amun will put an end to my rise, for if he is against me, how shall I live? This is very bad, little Bes, for if I am to end up now drudging in the field, after the scribe of the harvest has already bowed before me, it will be worse than if I had gone there at once, and I may languish before the heat of day and shiver in the chill of night. But do you think Amun will be given the power to treat me this way?"

"I am not all that stupid," whispered Neteruhotpe in response. "I am after all no wedded dwarf who has squandered away his dwarfish wisdom. True, I grew up—if I may express it in those terms—in fear of Amun. But I have long since come to the conclusion that a god is with you, Osarsiph, who is stronger than Amun and wiser than he, and I no longer believe that he will give you into Amun's hands or allow him in his shrine to set limits to your rise that your god has not already set for it."

"Well then, be of good cheer, Bes-em-heb," Joseph cried, clapping the little fellow on the shoulders, but gently so as not to hurt him, "and of high heart for my sake. After all, I too have the ear of the master and can point out the gravity of this or that to him when we are alone, matters that may also be of some gravity to Pharaoh, his lord. So he shall hear us both, Beknechons and me. The high priest will speak of a slave and the slave of a God, and we shall see to whom he inclines his ear more urgently—or better, as I meant to say, not to whom but to which topic. But remain alert, my friend, and maintain your wise presence in nooks and niches to see if Dûdu complains yet again to our mistress, so that I may hear his words and hers."

And so it turned out. For it is certain that the warden of the wardrobe did not leave it at just *one* complaint to Mut-em-enet but that Dûdu would not let go, returning now and again to protest to her about the glaring favor shown this foreigner from the pit. Favored Bes was at his post, reporting to Joseph and faithfully keeping him abreast of Dûdu's maneuvers. Had he been less vigilant, however, Joseph would have known all the same whenever the wedded dwarf complained of his rise—for each time there were those flashing glances in the dining chamber. Yes, when there had been none for so many days that Joseph was unhappy, the return of the woman's austere gaze, directed at him not as an object but as a person, clearly indicated that Dûdu had once again complained to her, and he said to himself: He has reminded her. How dangerous! But what he also meant was: How wonderful! And in a certain sense he thanked Dûdu for reminding his mistress.

Joseph Visibly Becomes an Egyptian

No longer under his father's eye, but left on his own and very much alive to the here and now, Joseph beheld and roused himself for each Egyptian day, quickly assuming the yoke of its stern demands—whereas as a lad in his first life he had known no duties or strenuous endeavors, but had been able to do as he pleased—and from now on actively strove to reach the heights of God's intentions; his was a head full of business affairs, of numbers, wares, and values, and his life was intertwined with a web of ticklish and problematic human relationships that constantly demanded his careful attention and whose threads ran to Potiphar, to the good Mont-kaw, to the dwarves of the household, to God knows who else in and outside the house—all vital concerns of which people in his former home, where Jacob was and his brothers were, had not the vaguest notion.

That was far away, more than seventeen days away, farther even than Isaak and Rebekah had been from Jacob when he had beheld and roused himself for each Mesopotamian day. Back then they, too, had not known or been able to picture their son's vital concerns and problematic relationships, and he had been estranged from their daily life. Wherever a man is, that is his world—a narrow circle of life, experience, and activity; the rest is fog. To be sure, people had always endeavored to relocate their lives, to let their accustomed world sink into fog and to behold a different day. They had always felt the strong urges of a Naphtali to run into the fog and inform its inhabitants, who know only their own world, of their lives and, in turn, to bring home a few things worth knowing from that other day. In short, there was communication and trade, which had also existed since time out of mind between the far-off cities of Jacob's people here and Potiphar's there. Accustomed to changing his horizon, the ancient wanderer himself had also been in the Land of Mud, if not so far down into it as Joseph now was; and his sister-wife, Joseph's "great-grandmother," had for a time joined the house of women belonging to Pharaoh, who at the time was not yet in Wase, but had shone in his horizon farther to the north, closer to Jacob's own sphere. There had always been relationships between his sphere and the one now enclosing Joseph—for had not the darkly beautiful Ismael taken a daughter of the mud to be his wife, to which mixture the Ishmaelites owed their existence, being half Egyptian and thus called and chosen to bring Joseph down into Egypt? There were many like them who traded back and forth between the rivers; and for a thousand years and more, short-skirted messengers had been traveling the world, carrying in the folds of their skirts letters inscribed on bricks. But although these same urges of a Naphtali had existed early on, how normal, customary, and well-schooled they now were in Joseph's day, when the land to which he had been carried off, the land of his second life, was already very much a land of grandchildren—no longer a people of truly strict observance, looking only piously inward, as Amun still wished them to be, but already so accustomed to the joys of a wider world and so easygoing in their customs that for a chosen lad from Asia it took only a certain cunning ability for saying good-night and the art of making two out of nothing for him to become the personal servant of one of Egypt's great men—and what all else besides.

Oh no, there was no lack of opportunities for communication between the cities of Jacob and those of his favorite; but Joseph, whose responsibility it would have been to make use of them (since he knew the dwelling place of his father, but his father did not know his) and for whom it would have been an easy thing to do, since as the right-hand man of a great steward and already well-schooled in an overview of things, he also had a clear overview of opportunities for sending news—Joseph did not do it, not for many years, for reasons we made clear to ourselves some time ago, for reasons that almost without exception are contained in one word: expectation. The calf did not bellow, it kept deathly still and did not let the cow know to what field the man had taken it, demanding—no doubt with the man's consent—that the cow also live in expectation, however difficult that might be, for she had no choice but to believe her calf dead and mutilated.

It is strange and to some extent confusing to think that Jacob, the old man left behind in the fog, believed his son to be dead all this time—confusing insofar as on the one hand we would like to be happy for him that he was deceived, and on the other we pity him because of that same deception. For the death of a loved one also has, as we know, its consolations for him who loves, though they may be of a rather hollow and bleak nature; and so, when viewed rightly, the result is a twofold pity for the penitent old man at home, first because he believed Joseph to be dead and second because in fact he was not. His paternal heart was cradled—with a thousand aches, but also with a gentle consolation—in the certainty of Joseph's death; it presumed him to be sheltered and safe in death, unchangeable, inviolable, no longer in need of care, immortalized as the seventeen-year-old lad who had ridden off on white Hulda—a complete mistake, not only in terms of the heartaches but also of that certain consolation that gradually prevailed. For meanwhile Joseph lived, exposed to all of life's dangers. Though carried off, he had not been released from time and did not remain a seventeen-year-old, but grew and matured in the place where he now was, turned nineteen and twenty and twenty-one, always still Joseph, to be sure, yet even now his father would not have quite recognized him, not at first glance. The stuff of his life changed, while, of course, still preserving its very felicitous outward stamp; he matured and grew a little firmer and broader, less a boyish youth, and more a young man. A few years more and there would be almost nothing left of the stuff of the Joseph whom Jacob had held in a farewell embrace, as Rebekah had once held him—as little as if his flesh had dissolved into death. Except that, since it was not death that changed him, but life, his form as Joseph remained more or less intact, but less faithfully and perfectly than sheltering death would have kept it in the mind's eye and as it actually, though deceptively, had done in Jacob's mind. But it should still give us pause that, in regard to the content and form of life, the difference between whether it is death or life that removes a person from view is not nearly so important as people would probably like to think.

Moreover, Joseph's life gathered the stuff out of which by turns it gained its form amid all the changes of his maturing from a totally different sphere than it would have done under Jacob's eyes, thereby influencing the stamp of his form as well. He was nourished by the airs and juices of Egypt, he ate Keme's foods; the cells of his body swelled with the thirst-quenching water of the Two Lands, whose sun's rays filled them with warmth; he clothed himself in the linen of its flax and wandered its earth, which sent its ancient energies and silent formative impulses up through him; each day his eyes actively took in realities and hallmarks that human hands had shaped out of these same silently determinative and all-embracing basic impulses; and he spoke the language of the land, which reformed his tongue, lips, and jaw from what they once were, so that Jacob, his father, would very soon have said to him: "Damu, my twig, what is wrong with your mouth? I no longer recognize it."

In short, Joseph was visibly becoming an Egyptian, both in appearance and demeanor, and it all happened swiftly, easily, and unnoticeably, for when he arrived in this land he was already a child of the world, supple both in spirit and stuff, and very young besides; and thus the integration of his person into the style of the land took place all the more readily and comfortably since, first, in physical terms—God knew why—there had always been something about him that tended to the Egyptian, what with his slender limbs and square shoulders, and, second, in psychological terms, living life as a foreigner adapting himself to the "children of the land" was nothing new, but rather as old and familiar as his own tradition, for at home he and his family, Abram's people, had always lived as *gerim* and guests among the children of the land, having long ago settled among them, joining with and adapting to them, yet always with inner reservations and a detached, sober view of the comfortable but cruel rites of Baal practiced by the real children of Canaan. And it was the same again with Joseph in the land of Egypt, for his reservations and ability to adjust cooperated smoothly to aid him in his worldliness; but it was the former that made the latter easier and removed its sting of faithlessness to Him, Elohim, who had brought him to this land and whose dispensation and passing over in forbearance Joseph could count upon if he strove to be an Egyptian in every sense and outwardly became a child of Hapi and a subject of Pharaoh—yet always with the reservation of his own silent reservations. And so his worldliness was something unto itself, for it did indeed allow him to wander as a cheerfully well-adjusted foreigner among the people of Egypt and permitted him to be a good friend of its beautiful civilization; but, conversely, they themselves were the worldly children whom he could silently regard with benevolent indulgence and detachment—with the spiritual mockery of his tribe for the delicate abomination of their national customs.

The Egyptian year took hold of him and spun him round within its circle according to the ebb and flow of its nature and the ring dance of its feasts, of which one or another could be regarded as its beginning: the New Year's Feast at the onset of the inundation, which was a day abounding in hope and incredible tumult—a fatefully significant day for Joseph, by the way, as it will turn out—or the recurrent anniversary of Pharaoh's ascent to the throne, an annual day of renewal for the people's jubilant hopes, which were bound up with the primal day itself, the dawning of a new dominion and age, when justice would drive away injustice and life would be lived in laughter and amazement. But, then again, since the year's cycle always returned upon itself, any day of memorial or celebration might do.

Joseph had entered Egypt's natural cycle at the time of the river's diminishment, when the land had reemerged and seed had been sown. That was when he was sold; and then he moved farther into and around with the year—the time of harvest came, which in name lasted on into the blazing summer and the weeks we call June, when to the devout jubilation of all Egypt's people the now narrow river began to rise again and slowly emerge from its banks under the watchful eye and precise measurements of Pharaoh's officials, for it was of first and final importance that the river rise correctly, not too wild and not too weak, because it governed whether the children of Keme would have bread to eat and Pharaoh a year of bountiful taxes for building. It rose and rose for six weeks, the Great Provider, very quietly, inch by inch, by day and by night—while people slept and believed in it even as they slept. Then, however, around the time of the most blazing sun, which we would date as the second half of July, but which the children of Egypt called Paophi, the second month of their year and its first season, called Akhet, it swelled truly mightily, spreading far over the fields on both sides and covering the land—a peculiar land of unique conditions, a land that was unlike any other in the world and that, much to Joseph's initial amazement and laughter, was now transformed into a single sacred sea, out of which, however, its cities and villages, set on higher ground and joined by causeways, emerged as islands. And the god stood up and lowered his fatness and nourishing muck down over the fields for four weeks, until Peret, the second season and the time of winter, when he began to pull away and return into himself—or as Joseph, out of the depths of admonishment, said privately to himself, when "the waters receded from off the earth"—until, beneath the moon of our January, the river was once again in its old bed, continuing then to diminish and retreat until the summer. These were the seventy-two days, the days of the seventy-two conspirators, the days of winter drought, in which the god declined and died, until the day Pharaoh's wardens of the river announced that he had begun to grow again, until the commencement of a new year of blessing—perhaps middling, perhaps abundant, but at least, Amun forbid, without famine and a poor yield of tax moneys for Pharaoh, so that he might not even be able to build by year's end.

Joseph found that the time passed very quickly from New Year to New Year—or, as he reckoned it, from the moment in the year when he had first entered the land until its return, for he set that as its beginning—passed through its three seasons of inundation, sowing, and harvest, each lasting four months and arrayed with its feasts, in which he, as a child of the world, took part, though with reservations and trusting in a higher indulgence; but take part in them he did and with good grace, if only because most of these idolatrous feasts were bound up with commercial life and as Peteprê's servant and Mont-kaw's business agent he dared not neglect the markets and fairs that were part of these holy proceedings, for commerce bursts from the very soil wherever people gather in great numbers. The steady trade in goods for sacrifices meant that there were always markets and business in the courtyards of Thebes' temples; but up and down the river were many places of pilgrimage, to which boisterous hosts of people came streaming from all directions whenever here or there a god held his feast, adorned his house, was of a mind to speak in oracles, and promised, along with these spiritual refreshments, crowded fairs, amusements, and revels. It was not merely Bastet, the cat down in the Delta, who held her own feast, about which Joseph had heard so many rollicking tales early on. Each year people traveled from near and far to nearby Mendes—or Djedet, as Keme's children called it—for a similar, but far more roistering feast than the one held in Per-Bastet; for Bindidi, the crude and lewd goat, was even closer to the popular heart than Bastet the cat, and at his feast he publicly engaged in intercourse with a local virgin. But we can definitely vouch for the fact that although Joseph traveled downriver to do business at the goat's fair, he did not go looking for that particular diversion, but as his steward's agent was interested solely in marketing his paper, utensils, and vegetables.

There was much in this land and its customs—its festive customs in particular, for the feast is custom's hour of greatness, its self-glorifying pinnacle—for which Joseph, who despite his worldliness was still mindful of Jacob, did not go looking or regarded only with a very cool, detached eye. He did not share the Egyptian's love of drink—memory of Noah thwarted any such sympathies, as did both the deeply embedded model of his soberly reflective father and his own nature, which though bright and joyous, abhorred the befuddlement of intoxication. But the children of Keme, men and women alike, knew nothing better than to get drunk on beer or wine on every occasion. At each feast they were all given more than enough wine, so that they and their wives and children could drink for four days, and be of no use whatever. But there were special drinking days, like the great beer festival in celebration of the old story that told of how mighty Hathor, the lion-headed Sakhmet, had raged against humankind to destroy it, and was prevented from totally annihilating our race only by a lovely ploy in which Rê made her drunk on beer dyed blood red. Which was why the children of Egypt drank beer on this day in truly appalling quantities: dark beer, a beer called *khes*, very strong, honeyed beer, beer both imported from the harbor and brewed locally—primarily in the city of Dendera, Hathor's residence, to which people went on pilgrimages for that very purpose and which, as the home of the goddess of intoxication, was in fact called Seat of Drunkenness.

As a result, Joseph did not go looking about and drank only a few token sips out of courtesy, as much as business and accommodation demanded. For Jacob's sake he also regarded with great detachment popular customs associated with the high feast of Osiris, Lord of the Dead, observed during the period of the shortest day, when the sun died—though he followed the feast itself and its rituals and beliefs with some attentive interest. For they marked the return of the sufferings of the mutilated and buried god who rose again, as presented by both priests and laymen in very beautiful masques depicting both the terrors of his death and his jubilant resurrection, all to the accompaniment of people jumping for joy on one leg and other indigenous foolishness—ancient traditions for which no one had any real explanation, such as very earnest brawls between various groups of men, some representing the "people of the city of Pe" and others the "people of the city of Dep," even though these cities themselves were long forgotten; or a herd of asses driven around outside the city amid loud scornful cries and under equally rough blows from cudgels. In some sense it was a contradiction to mock and beat these creatures, which were symbols of phallic potency, since this festival of the dead and buried god was also a sanctification of the erect male member that had ripped open Usir's mummy wrappings so that Eset, in the form of a female vulture, could conceive the avenging son; and during the days of the feast, village women would carry an ell-long male member about in procession, singing its praises and moving it like a puppet on strings. And so mockery and thrashings contradicted the exaltation of the feast—for the obvious reason that stiffened procreation was on the one hand a matter of sweet life and fruitful continuance, but on the other, and in particular, a matter of death. For Usir was dead when the vulture conceived by him; but all the gods became stiffened for procreation in death—and this was, just between us, the reason why Joseph, despite personal sympathies for the feast of Osiris, the mutilated god, did not go looking for many of its traditional customs and kept an inner detachment from them. What sort of reason was that? Yes, it is difficult to speak about so delicate a subject if one person understands, but the other does not yet see it—which is all the more pardonable since Joseph barely saw it himself and his dark account of it was at best only a half- or three-quarter-way affair. Almost without his being aware of it, the gentle bite of conscience stirred within him because of unfaithfulness—unfaithfulness in fact to his "lord," whether one chooses to set that concept on one level or another. One dare not forget that he regarded himself as dead and as part of the realm of death in which he was now rising, and one must also always keep in mind the name that, out of deliberate presumption, he had assumed there. His presumption, however, was not even all that great, for Mizraim's children had finally prevailed so that each, even the least of them, became Usir when he died and united his name with that of the mutilated god, just as Hapi the bull became Serapis in death—and so the meaning of this unification was "to be dead in the god" or "to be like the god." But precisely this "being the god" and "dead" implied the same procreative state that had ripped open the mummy's wrappings; and that bite of conscience of which Joseph was only partially aware was bound up with his secret realization that certain momentary flashes, for which Dûdu was responsible and that had begun to play a worrisomely delightful role in his life, had some distant and dangerous relationship with divine rigidity in death and thus with unfaithfulness.

So now it is out, expressed in the most lenient words possible, why it was that Joseph did not wish to spend much time looking about for popular customs of the feast of Osiris, or its processions of village women, or its beaten asses. Otherwise, however, during the circuit of the festively adorned Egyptian year, he did indeed look about, both in the cities and in the countryside. Once or twice, as the years went on, he even saw Pharaoh—for there were occasions when the god would appear, not only in his Window of Presentation, when he would toss tributes of gold down to favorites in the presence of a selected audience, but also in moments of splendor, when he left the horizon of his palace and shone in all his radiant glory before the people, who to a man jumped for joy on one leg, as prescribed both by custom and the love in their hearts. Pharaoh was fat and squat, Joseph noticed; the color in his face not the best—at least not the second or third time that Rachel's son beheld him—and his expression was very reminiscent of Mont-kaw's when his kidneys troubled him.

It was during the years of Joseph's rise within Potiphar's house that Amenhotep III, Neb-maat-Rê, actually began to fail, his physical condition revealing—or so said his temple priests skilled in medicine and the magicians from his House of Books—a growing tendency to decline again with the sun. The prophets of healing were in no way equipped to control this tendency, since there was all too great a natural justification for it. In the same year that Joseph witnessed the Egyptian year complete its second round, the divine son of Thutmose IV and Mutemwia the Mitannite, celebrated the jubilee of his reign, called the *hebsed,* which meant that it had been thirty years since—amid innumerable ceremonies, all of which were exactly reproduced on the great day of its anniversary—he had set the double crown upon his head.

Behind him lay a magnificent, regal life, virtually free of war, weighed down, as it were, by the golden robes of hieratic pomp and care for his nation, filled with the joys of the hunt, in commemoration of which he had had scarabs distributed, and arrayed with the building projects he had loved; but his nature was now in decline, even as Joseph's was in ascendancy. In his early years the majesty of the god had suffered occasionally only from toothache, an affliction promoted by his habit of nibbling balsamic sweets, so that not infrequently it was with a swollen cheek that he had had to hold audiences and state receptions in his throne room. Since his *hebsed,* however—when Joseph had seen him drive forth—his physical complaints had had their origins in other, more deeply concealed organs: Pharaoh's heart wavered at times or pounded with far too many beats inside his chest, leaving him short of breath; his excrement contained matter his body should have retained, but could not, for it was in the process of breaking down; and later it was no longer only his cheek that was thick and swollen, but his belly and legs were as well. It was during this time that the god's distant colleague and correspondent of equally divine standing in his own sphere, King Tushratta of the land of Mitanni, son of Shuttarna, the father of Mutemwia, whom Amenhotep called his mother—which is to say, his brother-in-law on the Euphrates (for it was from Shuttarna that he had received Princess Gilu-kheba as a concubine for his house of women)—had sent him a healing image of Ishtar under securest escort from his distant capital city to Thebes, for he had heard of Pharaoh's complaints and had himself had good success with this blessed image for his own less serious ailments. The entire capital, indeed all of Upper and Lower Egypt from the borders of Nubia to the sea, spoke of the arrival of this shipment in Merima't Palace, and it was also almost the sole topic of conversation in Potiphar's house for several days. But there is no doubt that this Ishtar of the Way proved either unable or unwilling to bring anything more than very temporary relief to Pharaoh's shortness of breath and swellings, much to the satisfaction of his local magicians, whose doses of wolfsbane had not accomplished anything much more substantial, simply because the inclination to reunion with the sun was stronger than everything else and was slowly, but inexorably gaining ground.

Joseph beheld Pharaoh at his *hebsed,* when all of Weset came out to see the god drive forth, which was just one of the solemn acts and ceremonies that filled the whole day of jubilee. The entire investiture—the throne ascension, coronation, purifying bath performed by priests in masks of the gods, censing, and other acts of primal symbolism—took place solely before the eyes of the court's and the nation's greats, while the people outside drank and danced, indulging themselves in the idea that henceforth time would be renewed in its foundations, establishing a new era of blessing, justice, peace, laughter, and universal brotherhood. This happy, fervent conviction had played a role in the original change of sovereigns a generation before and had been renewed, though in a weaker and more fleeting form, at the return of this day each year since. But at *hebsed* it arose with full freshness and festal energy in every heart, a triumph of faith over all experience—the cult of expectation that no experience can wrench from the human heart, for it has been planted there by a higher hand. But when, at noon, Pharaoh drove forth to visit the house of Amun and offer sacrifices, he was the object of public display, and crowds of people, including Joseph, awaited him in the West, at the very gate of the palace, while others thronged the road that the royal procession would take through the city on the far side of the river, particularly along the boulevard of ram sphinxes, Amun's ceremonial avenue.

The royal palace, Pharaoh's Great House, from which in fact Pharaoh took his name, for Pharaoh means "great house," even if on the lips of the children of Egypt the word itself sounded somewhat different—about as different as "Peteprê" is from "Potiphar"—the palace, then, lay at desert's edge at the foot of Thebes' colorful cliffs, in the middle of a vast gated and well-guarded circular wall that enclosed both the god's beautiful gardens and, amid flowers and exotic trees, the smiling lake that Amenhotep's word had caused to shine in the east of the gardens, primarily for the pleasure of Tiy, his Great Consort.

Even by stretching their necks, the people outside did not see much of Merima't's shining splendor. They saw palace guards at the gates, with wedge-shaped leather plates at their aprons and feathers on their storm helmets, saw sunlight-bathed foliage flickering in the constant wind, saw ornate roofs hovering above bright, polished columns, saw long ribbons of multicolored pennants fluttering atop golden masts, and they could smell the fragrance of Syria rising from the flower beds of the invisible garden—which accorded very nicely with the idea of Pharaoh's divinity, since sweet fragrance usually attended the gods. But then the expectations of the merry and eager crowd of gossipmongers, lip-smackers, and dust-eaters outside the gate were fulfilled, and at the very moment when Rê's barque reached its zenith, a cry rang out, sentries raised their spears, and the bronze gates between the flagpoles opened to reveal a sphinx-lined avenue strewn with blue sand and leading through the garden—and moving down it came Pharaoh's procession of chariots, emerging now through the main gate and into the crowd, which gave way and fell back, even as it screamed with joy and awe. For men bearing rods waded in among them, clearing the way for chariots and horses and shouting in piercing voices: "Pharaoh! Pharaoh! Hold your heart! Turn your head! He drives forth! Make way, make way, for he drives forth!" And like waves of the sea rolling in a storm, the ecstatic throng parted, hopping on one leg, thrusting skinny arms at Egypt's sun, throwing ardent kisses; the women, however, raised their wailing, kicking urchins into the air or flung back their heads and offered their breasts, holding them in both hands, their cries of exultation and yearning filling the air: "Pharaoh! Pharaoh! Strong Bull of your mother! Tall in feathers! Live a million years! Live for all eternity! Love us! Bless us! We love and bless you deliriously! Golden Falcon! Horus! Horus! You are Rê in all your members! Kheper in your true form! *Hebsed! Hebsed!* Jubilee! Jubilee! Turning point of time! End of toil! Dawn of happiness!"

Such mass jubilation is very thrilling and grips the heart, even of someone whose emotional detachment makes him not quite a part of it. Joseph shouted a little and hopped a little along with the rest of the children of the land, but mainly he watched—and was silently moved. What moved him, however, and what made his watching so urgent was that he was seeing Pharaoh, the highest of all, emerge from his palace like the moon among the stars—and his heart pounded in response, for according to his legacy, though now slightly modified for a child of the world, it was the Most High alone that man should serve. Even when he had still been far from standing before the next highest, before Potiphar, his thoughts, as we noted at the time, were already being directed to a still higher penultimate embodiment of this idea. We shall now see that his audacity did not stop even there.

Pharaoh was a magnificent sight. His chariot was of pure gold and nothing else—its wheels were golden, as were its shaft and sides, which were covered with embossed figures, though what they depicted could not be made out, for in the blinding glare of the noonday sun the chariot sparkled until eyes could scarcely bear it; and since the wheels were enveloped by thick clouds of dust kicked up by the hooves of the steeds before them, it looked as if Pharaoh were passing in smoke and flashing embers—terrible and splendid to behold. One actually expected the horses pulling the chariot, Pharaoh's Great First Team, as people called them, to breath fire from their nostrils, so wildly did these smooth-muscled stallions prance and dance along in their embellished harness, with golden breastplates against which they pulled and at their brows golden lion's heads decorated with tall, colorful bobbing plumes. Pharaoh himself drove; he stood alone in his fiery chariot cloud, holding the reins in his left hand, while in his right he clutched a whip and a crooked black-and-white staff, holding them to his chest at an angle just below his forged collar—a traditional and holy stance. Pharaoh was already a fairly old man, one could see it in the sagging mouth, in the strained look in his eyes, and in the somewhat stooped line of his back beneath the lotus white linen of his robe. His cheekbones were prominent and gaunt, and it looked as if he had rouged them a little. And then there were all the various amulets hanging at his hips under his robe—intricately knotted and looped ribbons and fixed emblems. The blue tiara studded with yellow stars covered his head to behind his ears and the nape of his neck; but at the brow, just above Pharaoh's nose, there reared a poisonous hooded cobra in shimmering enamel, a protective talisman of Rê.

And thus, without glancing either to the right or to the left, the King of Upper and Lower Egypt passed before Joseph's eyes. Tall fans of ostrich feathers waved above him—soldiers of his bodyguard, shield bearers and archers, Egyptians, Asians, and Negroes, bearing standards ran alongside his wheels, and officers followed in chariots whose cabs were upholstered in purple leather. Then the vast crowd began shouting its supplications again, for after these came a single chariot, whose wheels shone golden in the dust, and in it was a boy of eight or nine years old, he too standing beneath ostrich fans and driving with weak, braceleted arms. His face was long and pale, and amidst the pallor were full raspberry lips that smiled with halfhearted benevolence to the shouting throng and eyes that were only partly open, veiling, or so one might think, either pride or sadness. This was Amenhotep, the divine seed and prince, heir to thrones and crowns when he who rode before him should one day decide to reunite with the sun—Pharaoh's only son, a child of his old age, his Joseph. Except for the arm bracelets and a lustrous collar of flowers at the neck, the childishly skinny torso of the boy the crowd acclaimed was bare. His aproned skirt of pleated golden fabric, however, rose high in the back and fell to his calves, while at the front, where the gold-fringed waistband was folded over, it was scooped below the navel, revealing a drumlike belly, like that of a Negro child. Wrapped around the boy's head was a scarf of the same golden fabric, fitted snug to his forehead and, as with his father, bearing a cobra, but gathered at the back as a hair bag; and over one ear, like a broad ribbon of fringe, dangled the braid of childish hair, a mark of the sons of the king.

People shouted at the top of their voices to him, to this engendered but not yet risen sun, the sun below the eastern horizon, the sun of the morrow. "Peace of Amun," they cried. "Long live the god's son! How beautifully you shine in the lighted place of heaven! You are the boy Horus in your child's braid. You are the falcon rich in magic! Protector of the father, protect us!" They had still more reason to shout and supplicate, for behind the company, hurrying past in the wake of tomorrow's sun, came another well-guarded chariot of fire, in which, just behind a driver bent over its front rail, stood Tiy, wife of the god, Pharaoh's Great Consort, the mistress of the Two Lands. She was a small woman of dark complexion; there was a flash in those eyes extended by makeup, a resolute arch to her daintily firm and divine nose, a satisfied smile on her pouting lips. Nothing on earth equaled the beauty of her headdress, for it was the helmet of the vulture, the entire bird made of gold, covering her head with its body and its own outstretched head, while marvelously crafted wings fell down over her cheeks and shoulders. A ring had been worked into the bird's back and from it a few long, rigid feathers thrust upward, turning a helmet into a divine crown; and to cap it all, there at the woman's brow, in addition to the vulture's naked rapacious skull, was yet again the hooded, venomous uraeus. These were more than sufficient tokens of greatness and hallmarks of the divine, so much so that the crowd could only erupt in ecstasy and mindlessly shout: "Eset! Eset! Mut! Heavenly mother cow! Bearer of the god! You who fill the palace with love, sweet Hathor, have mercy!" And they also shouted for the royal daughters, who stood embracing each other behind their chariot's driver, bent far forward to his horses, and likewise for those who now followed: the ladies of the court, who also came in pairs and bore the fan of honor in their arms, and the great men who stood by him and in his trust, Pharaoh's Sole and True Friends who attended his levees. And so the jubilee procession left the House of Merima't and passed overland through the crowd to the river, where colorful barques lay ready, especially Pharaoh's heavenly barque, *Star of the Two Lands,* so that the god and the bearer of gods and their seed and all the royal household could cross to the eastern shore and be pulled by other teams through the City of the Living, where people shouted in narrow streets and from housetops, and on to the House of Amun for the great censing.

And so Joseph had seen Pharaoh, just as once as a slave for sale in the courtyard of the house of blessing, he had first beheld Potiphar, the highest in the immediate vicinity, and had thought how he might most speedily find his way to his side—where he now was, thanks to a clever way with words. But our story claimed that even then he secretly resolved to establish connections with still more distant and definitive manifestations of the Most High, and we credited his temerity with still greater aspirations. But how can that be? Is there something higher still than the Most High? To be sure; when a sense of the future is in one's blood, there is always tomorrow's highest. Standing in the crowd and sharing their exultation with a certain reservation, Joseph had fixed his eye with sufficient zeal on Pharaoh in his fiery chariot. And yet his innermost, ultimate curiosity and concern had been not for the old god, but for the one who came after him, the boy with the braid and that feeble smile on his lips—Pharaoh's Joseph, the sun yet to come. He watched him pass, gazed at his narrow back and golden hair bag and observed how he drove his team with weak, braceleted arms. It was he, not Pharaoh, whom he still saw in his soul when everything was over and the crowd pressed its way to the Nile; he had to keep his mind on the small god, the coming god—and it may well be that in this he was in agreement with the children of Egypt, who had shouted and supplicated even more fervently at the sight of the young Horus than they had as Pharaoh himself drove by. For the future is hope, and out of kindness providence has given man time, so that he may live in expectation. Would Joseph not first have to grow strong in his present place before the thought of standing before, or even at the side, of the highest could gain the least and vaguest prospect of fulfillment? There was good reason, then, why his observations at the Feast of Hebsed should look beyond the present highest, and to the future, to a sun that had not yet risen.

Account of Mont-kaw's Modest Death

The Egyptian year had borne Joseph round in its circuit seven times, the heavenly body that he loved and to which he was related had run through all its phases eighty-four times, and in the course of life's changes, truly nothing was left of the stuff of Jacob's son who had been sent on his way with his father's cares and blessings upon him; the bodily garment that he wore, so to speak, and with which God had now clothed his life was entirely new, not a thread of it belonged to the old one he had worn as a seventeen-year-old, for this was a garment woven of Egyptian fabric, in which Jacob would have recognized him only incredulously—indeed his son would have had to reassure him by saying "I am Joseph." Seven years had passed in sleeping and waking, in thinking and feeling, in acting and being acted upon, the way days always pass, which is to say, neither swiftly nor slowly—they had simply passed, and he was now twenty-four years old, a young man, very beautiful both in figure and face, the son of a lovely woman, a child of love. The routine of work had given his demeanor more substance and firmness, his once demure boyish voice was more resonant when, as master of oversight, he moved among craftsmen and menials of the house and gave them directions or passed on Mont-kaw's orders as the overseer's deputy, or mouth—for he had been that for years now, and one could also have called him his eye, his ear, his right arm. The staff of the house, however, simply called him his "mouth," for that is the Egyptian way of putting it, the term for a master's authorized agent through whom orders are passed; and in Joseph's case the idiom was reinvigorated by a second sense, for the young man spoke like a god, an attribute highly admired, indeed a source of laughter and pleasure for the children of Egypt, and they were well aware that it was with beautiful and clever words, far beyond their ability to employ them, that he had made his way or at least had prepared it both with the master himself and with his steward Mont-kaw.

By now the overseer trusted him in everything—administration, bookkeeping, oversight, and business—and if tradition says that Potiphar left all that he had in Joseph's charge, having no concern for anything but the food he ate, that was actually and ultimately a matter of transference from master to steward and from the latter to the slave whom he had purchased and with whom he had made a covenant to serve their master with love. And both the master and his house could be glad that it was Joseph and no one else who stood at the end of this transference and who truly managed the house's affairs, for he managed them with great skill and loyalty for the sake of the Lord and His far-reaching plans, even as by day and night he looked to the advantage of the house, so that, as in the words of the old Ishmaelite and in accordance with his own name, Joseph not only provided for it but increased it as well.

Why it was that toward the end of this period of seven years, Mont-kaw entrusted Joseph with more and more and finally with all oversight of the house, withdrawing entirely from its affairs and keeping to his special chamber of trust—of all that soon enough, though not just yet. First it should be noted that, despite all his endeavors, wicked Dûdu did not succeed in barring the path that Joseph followed with such happy success and that, well before seven years had passed, had set him above all the other servants, even above the rank and prestige of Potiphar's undersized warden of jewels. Dûdu's post was one of great honor, to be sure, just as it had surely come to him because he was a little man of honor, sterling quality, and dwarfish perfection, and his post kept him close to the person of his master, so that by its very nature it should have carried with it opportunities for exercising confidential influence to Joseph's endangerment. But Potiphar could not endure the wedded dwarf; his dignity and self-importance were repugnant to his soul, and though he did not think this justified relieving him of his post, he kept him at the greatest possible distance by employing lesser intermediaries in his morning chamber and dressing room as a buffer between his person and the guardian of the wardrobe, to whom he left only the task of supervising his jewels, attire, amulets, and decorations of honor, without having to deal with him at length and face-to-face more often than absolutely necessary—so that Dûdu never really got to speak to him in general, let alone to speak those words of petition that he would so have liked to offer against this foreigner and his vexing rise in the household.

Even if circumstances had permitted it, however, he would not have dared to speak—not before the master himself. For he was well aware of the aversion Potiphar felt for him, the solemn dwarf, both because of his veiled arrogance—which he himself could not and would not deny—and because of his partisanship for the supreme powers of Amun's sun, and he could only fear that his words would prove useless before Peteprê. Did he, Dûdu, spouse of Zeset, need to subject himself to such an experience? No, he preferred to follow indirect paths—the one that led to his mistress, to whom he frequently complained and who at least listened to him respectfully; and the one that led to Beknechons, the strong man of Amun, who visited her and whom he could rouse against the tradition-defying favoritism shown the Habiru. He also contrived with Zeset, his full-grown wife who served Mut-em-enet, for her to influence the mistress on behalf of his spiteful cause.

But even the most diligent person can be unsuccessful—as for example, one need only imagine that Zeset had not proved fruitful to her spouse. So, here, too, Dûdu's endeavors met with no success—they bore the good man no fruit. Granted, it is certain that at court one day, in Pharaoh's antechamber, Beknechons, Amun's First Prophet, did, after a fashion, diplomatically chastise Peteprê for the vexation that the pious members of his household had to suffer because of the ascendancy of an unclean foreigner, and remonstrated with him about the matter in a paternal but polite way. But the fan-bearer didn't understand, could scarcely remember, blinked, seemed preoccupied; and, given his larger talents, Beknechons was incapable of sticking for more than a moment to such a trivial domestic detail. He soon moved to matters of import, began to point in all four directions of heaven, to speak of affairs of state and the preserving of power in reference to those foreign kings—Tushratta, Suppiluliuma, and Abd-ashirta—and so the conversation fluttered off into generalities. As for Mut, the mistress, she had not even been able to bring

herself to address the matter with her consort, for she knew his deaf
stubbornness; nor was she accustomed to speaking with him about
everyday matters, but only to exchanging overanxious tender
phrases with him, and she preferred not to make any demands of
him. These were reasons enough for her silent passivity. In our eyes,
however, it is also a sign that even at this point—that is, toward the
end of the seven years—the woman was still indifferent to Joseph's
presence and as yet saw no real reason for having him removed from
the house. The time for wishing him gone, for banishing him from
her eyes, was yet to come for the wife of the Egyptian—but come it
would, simultaneously with her fear of herself, something she was as
yet still too proud to recognize. Strangely enough, two other events
in this regard were to take place concurrently as well, for once the
mistress recognized that it would be better for her if she were no
longer to see Joseph and she in fact interceded with Peteprê for him
to be sent away, at the same time it appeared as if Dûdu had converted to the Habiru's cause and become his advocate. He began to
court him and to play his obliging helper, to such an extent that
dwarf and mistress exchanged roles, so that she appeared to have assumed his hatred, while he praised and extolled the lad before her. It
was only for show in both cases. For at the very moment when the
mistress would come to wish Joseph to be gone, she no longer could
truly wish it and was deceiving herself by seeming to work to remove him. Dûdu, however, who certainly had some glimmering of
this, was merely being cunning, hoping to do greater damage to
Jacob's son by treating him as a comrade.

Of all that soon enough, but not quite yet. The event, however,
that brought about these changes—or at least upon which they followed—was the sad and fatal illness of the steward Mont-kaw,
Joseph's brother in the covenant of loving service to their master—
sad for him, sad for Joseph, who was truly devoted to him and for
whom his suffering and dying were almost a matter of conscience,
and sad for anyone who feels sympathy for this simple but percep-
tive man, even if that sympathy is bound up with the insight that his
demise was a necessary part of a larger plan. For there is definitely
something like a plan behind the fact that Joseph was brought to a
house whose overseer was a child of death, and in some sense the
steward died a sacrificial death. It is only fortunate that he was a man
whose soul tended to resignation, a predisposition that elsewhere we

wished to trace to his old kidney trouble. But it is equally possible that this was only the physical embodiment of a psychological tendency, was indeed the same thing, different only in the way word and thought or symbol and word are different, so that in the book of the steward's life a kidney might well have been the hieroglyph for "resignation."

And why do we care about Mont-kaw? Why do we speak of him with a certain emotion, without being able to say much more about him than that he was an intentionally simple—that is, modest—man, and an honest one, both practical and tender-hearted? A man who walked the earth and the land of Keme in those days, early or late days, depending on one's viewpoint, at a time when life in all its engendering multiplicity happened to bring him forth—but if late, then at least so early that even the smallest particles of his mummy are long since dust scattered to the winds and the universe. He was a sober-minded son of the earth, who did not presume to be better than life itself, and basically wished to know nothing of bold deeds or higher things—not out of meanness of spirit, but out of modesty, even if in his silent, secret heart he was really quite susceptible to promptings from on high, which made it possible for him to play a role, and a not all that unimportant one, in Joseph's life and, in the end, to behave much as tall Ruben had done that day and, metaphorically speaking, likewise to lower his head, take three steps back, and then turn away from him. In and of itself, the role that fate assigned to him obliges us to feel a certain sympathy for his person. But apart from such obligations and speaking solely for ourselves, we have an eye and a heart for the figure of this simple and yet refined man whose life was awash in unassuming melancholy and whom now, thousands of years after he vanished, we recreate in remarks made possible by the sympathetic power of imagination, which he would have called magic.

Mont-kaw was the son of an ordinary clerk in the treasury of the temple of Mentu in Karnak. His father, whose name was Akhmose, consecrated him at the early age of five to Thoth and handed him over to the House of Lessons that was affiliated with the temple administration and where by dint of strict discipline, spare rations, and plenty of beatings—following the maxim that a pupil has ears in his backside and hears when it is beaten—the next generation of officials to serve Mentu, the falcon-headed god of war, was trained. This was not, by the way, the sole purpose of the school, which was attended by children of various origins, from both elegant and modest homes; there they were taught the basics of a literary education: the word of the god—which is to say, writing—the art of the reed, and a good epistolary style, all of these being requirements for a career as either a clerk or a man of learning.

As for Akhmose's son, he did not want to become a man of learning, not because he would have been too stupid for it, but out of modesty and because from the very start he was fully resolved to hold to a respectable middle course and not rise above it for anything in the world. Indeed, it was almost against his will that he did not spend his life like his father as a clerk in the offices of Mentu's temple, and became instead the steward of a great man, because, out of a respect for both his talents and his self-effacement, the school authorities and his teachers recommended him for this fine post and brought him to it without his having to do a thing. At the House of Lessons he had received only the most unavoidable of beatings—which even the best students received in any case, for the betterment of their hearing—and proved that he had a head for generalities by the speed with which he mastered the baboon's great gift, the art of writing, and by the sensible neatness with which he wrote long lines on his learner's scroll of what was presented to him to copy—all those codes of conduct, exemplary letters for shaping one's writing style, and centuries-old teachings taken from didactic poems, hortatory speeches, and tributes to the scholarly life—while at the same time covering the reverse side with calculations about sacks of grain received and stored, but also with notations for business letters. For almost from the start he was likewise put to practical work in the administration of the temple, more by his own desire than his father's, who would gladly have made of him something higher than he was himself—a prophet of god, a magician, or an astrologer—whereas even as a boy Mont-kaw had modestly and resolutely committed himself to life's practical affairs.

There is something peculiar about this kind of native resignation, which expresses itself as both honest diligence and placid tolerance for vicissitudes of life that would bring another man to storm the gods with wailing lamentations. Mont-kaw lost his heart to the daughter of one of his father's colleagues and married her fairly early on. But his wife died giving birth to their first child, and the child

with her. Mont-kaw wept bitterly for her, but was not all that astonished by the blow, did not flail his arms wildly at the gods because
things had turned out this way. He did not attempt to find domestic
happiness again, but remained alone, a widower. One of his sisters
was married to a man who owned a booth in Thebes' bazaar; he visited her on occasion if he had some spare time, though he seldom
made time for himself. Upon finishing school, he first worked in the
administrative offices of Mentu's temple, later became the steward of
the first prophet of that god, and finally attained the highest post in
the lovely house of Peteprê the courtier, where for ten years he had
wielded his office with jovial but firm authority, until the day the
Ishmaelites brought him an excellent assistant in loving service to his
tender master—and his successor.

He had very early surmised that Joseph was marked to be his
successor, for despite his diligent simplicity he was an intuitive man;
and one can say that this simplicity, this tendency to self-renuncia-
tion, to setting limits for himself, was itself a product of his intuition—a premonition of the illness slumbering within his powerful
body; indeed, without its workings, which while silently diminishing his courage for life were also refining his heart, he would scarcely
have been capable of the delicate impressions Joseph had made on
him at first sight. By then he had already learned what his infirmity
was, since Firebelly, the herbalist—upon being told of a certain dull
pressure the steward often felt in his back and the left side of his
groin, of sporadic pain in the region of the heart, of frequent dizziness, sluggishness of the bowels, sleepless nights, and an inordinate
urge to urinate—had told him straight out that he suffered from
wormy kidneys.

The nature of this illness is such that it is often hidden and slow-
working, striking its roots very early in life, but allowing for intervals of apparent health, when it looks as if it is in remission, or even
cured, only to reveal symptoms of its renewed advance. Mont-kaw
recalled having once passed blood in his urine at age twelve, but just
that once, and then not again for many years, so that the alarming
symptom was gradually forgotten. Not until he was twenty did it
reappear, along with the discomforts noted above, including attacks
of dizziness and headache that culminated in a bilious nausea. But
that too passed; since then, however, the calm and diligent life he led
had been a struggle with this intermittent illness, which seemed to

leave him untouched for months, even years, but then overcame him again with greater or lesser virulence. The modesty that came from his illness could often develop into profound exhaustion, listlessness, and despondency of both body and soul, which in his quiet, heroic fashion, Mont-kaw would counter by doing the work of each day and by being bled by men skilled in medicine, or such was their claim. Since his appetite was satisfactory, his tongue clean, his perspiration normal, and his pulse more or less regular, those treating him did not regard his case as all that serious, even when one day his ankles became swollen and pale, releasing a watery fluid when pricked. And indeed, since releasing the fluid brought obvious relief to his vascular system and a strengthening of his heart, the phenomenon was even greeted as a favorable sign, because the disease was leaving the body in a discharge.

It must be admitted that, with the help of Firebelly and his herbal medicine, he had got through the decade prior to Joseph's arrival in the house tolerably enough, though his ability to maintain, with only rare interruptions, his effectiveness as the head of the estate might well be ascribed more to his modest strength of will in keeping the festering illness at bay than to Firebelly's traditional arts. It was almost immediately after purchasing Joseph, however, that he had to surmount his first truly serious attack—with such severe edema of the hands and legs that they had to be wrapped, savagely drumming headache, violent stomach upset, and even clouded vision; yes, the attack was probably coming on even as he was negotiating with the old Ishmaelite and inspecting his wares. That at least is our supposition; for it seems to us as if those receptive surmises at the sight of Joseph and the special way in which he was touched by the slave's trial good-night greeting were already harbingers of the attack, tokens of a sensitivity heightened by illness. But the other medical interpretation is also possible, which says that, on the contrary, those all too gentle words of peace had caused a certain softening of his constitution and his ability to withstand the illness that always lay in wait for it—and in reality we are inclined to fear that Joseph's good-night wishes each evening, however soothing for the steward, were of no particular benefit whatever to his will to live and its instinctive struggle against illness.

Mont-kaw's failure to concern himself with Joseph in any way at the beginning is also largely attributable to that same attack, which paralyzed his sense of initiative. It passed, just as did many later attacks, some weaker, some equally fierce, thanks to Khun-Anup's bleedings, leeches, ingenious mixtures of extracts of both vegetable and animal material, and abdominal compresses of old inscribed papyrus that were first softened in warm oil. Recovery or apparent recovery followed and held sway over long periods of the overseer's life thereafter, even during the time Joseph was in the house and advancing to the position of first assistant and "mouth." In the seventh year of Joseph's presence there, however, Mont-kaw attended the funeral of a relative—it was his brother-in-law, the owner of the booth in the bazaar, who had departed this life—and caught a cold that opened the portals to his undoing and immediately removed him from his post.

"Taking it all too hard," or as people say, "catching one's death," while paying final respects in a drafty cemetery chapel has always been a fairly frequent phenomenon, both then and now. It was summer and very hot, but, as so often in the land of Egypt, very windy as well—a dangerous combination, since the fanning of a steady breeze accelerates the cooling effect of evaporating perspiration. Buried under work, the steward had lingered at home too long and was afraid he might arrive late for the ceremonies. He had had to hurry, had sweated, and even while crossing the river to the West with other mourners behind the funeral barque, he had felt seriously chilled in his light clothes. Next came the gathering before the little grave cut in the rocks, for which the booth's owner, now Usir, had saved his money and before whose modest portal a priest wearing the mask of Anup the dog held the mummy upright, while another priest performed the ceremony of opening the mouth with the mystical calf's foot and the small group of mourners, hands clasped to heads strewn with ashes, observed the magical act—and the draft exuded from the cave was as cold as stone itself and not especially salubrious. Mont-kaw returned home with the sniffles and a bladder catarrh; the next day he complained to Joseph of having strange difficulty moving his arms and legs; a kind of stupor forced him to forgo his domestic activities and take to his bed. And when the head gardener placed leeches at his temples to relieve the unbearable headache that had left him half-blind and nauseated, he was struck with a fit of apoplexy.

Joseph was greatly dismayed when he realized God's intentions.

Human measures designed to work against them were not, he decided, a sinful attempt to subvert His will and its plans, but merely a way of putting it to a necessary test. Which is why he immediately persuaded Potiphar to send to the House of Amun and request a learned physician, before whom Firebelly was forced to retreat—offended, but also relieved of a responsibility whose gravity he was knowledgeable enough to recognize.

The man of medicine from the House of Books proceeded to repudiate most of Firebelly's measures, although in the eyes of the world and in his own as well, the difference between his and the gardener's remedies were not so much medical as social—the latter were for the masses and might well do them some good, the former for higher levels of society, who were cured more elegantly. And so the expert from the temple rejected the old papyrus soaked in oil, with which his predecessor had covered the belly and loins of the patient, and demanded instead poultices of linseed oil and good toweling. He also turned up his nose at Firebelly's popular cure-alls, which were said to have once been invented by the gods for Rê himself when he grew old and sick and which contained from between fourteen and thirty-seven loathsome ingredients, such as lizard blood, crushed pig's tooth, oozings from the ears of the same animal, milk from a woman in childbed, all sorts of dung, including that of antelopes, hedgehogs, and flies, human urine, and many more such items; but also in the recipe were other, less disgusting things that the learned man likewise administered to the steward: honey and wax, henbane, small doses of poppy juice, bitter bark, bearberry, natron, and ipecac. The chewing of the berries of the castor-oil plant mixed with beer, which the gardener held in high regard, also met with the physician's approval, likewise the use of a root rich with resins as a strong purgative. On the other hand, he found drastic bleeding of the patient—which Firebelly had performed almost every day, regarding it as the only way to control the agonizing pounding in the head and the clouded vision—as inappropriate and suggested it be administered with great reservation at best; for given the patient's pallor, he declared, such temporary relief exacted too high a price in those lost constituents of the blood that nourished and stimulated life.

What we have here is probably a dilemma that defies solution; for obviously it was the blood, which, though indispensable, was now deprived of its beneficial components and transporting harmful ones instead, spreading insidious inflammations, and flooding the body with a variety of concurrent illnesses, all of which, however, as both doctors well knew, were indirectly caused by kidneys that had always performed their function poorly. And so regardless of his caretakers' understanding of these ugly phenomena and the names they might give them, Mont-kaw suffered from a series, sometimes concurrently, of inflammations of the chest, peritoneum, lungs, and pericardium; there were also severe symptoms of brain damage— vomiting, blindness, congestion, and cramps. In short, death attacked him from all sides and with all its weapons, and it was almost a miracle that he managed to resist it for weeks yet after taking to his bed, and even recovered from some of these various illnesses. He was a valiant patient; but though he fought the good fight and defended his life—no doubt of it, he was to die.

Joseph realized as much early on, even when Khun-Anup and the learned man of Amun were still hoping to put the steward back on his feet; and he took it very much to heart, not only because he was devoted to this honest man who had treated him with kindness and felt a true fondness for his mixed nature—for it was likewise that of a "man of grief and gladness," the Gilgamesh mixture, a man both favored and stricken—but also and especially because Mont-kaw's suffering and dying pained his conscience; for all this had obviously been arranged for Joseph's own benefit and ascendancy and poor Mont-kaw was a sacrifice to God's plans—he was being shunted aside, and Joseph would have very much liked to speak to the Lord of these plans: "What You are doing here, Lord, is solely according to Your intentions and not mine. I must most emphatically state: I do not wish to have anything to do with it, and that it is happening for my benefit does not mean, I would hope, that I share any guilt in it—and I would close my prayer in all humility." But that did not help. His friend's sacrificial death still pained his conscience, and he was perfectly aware that if guilt was involved here, then it fell upon him, who benefited from all this—for God knew no guilt. That's the nub of it, he thought to himself, God does everything, but has given us the pain of a conscience, so that we may stand guilty before Him, because we are guilty in His stead. Man bears God's guilt, and it would only be fair if someday God were to decide to bear our guilt. It is unclear how He, being both holy and a stranger to guilt, would manage that. But in my opinion He would actually have to become a man to accomplish it.

Over the course of these four or five weeks he never left the bedside of the suffering sacrificial victim, who lay there still holding back death's multiple onslaughts—the suffering pained Joseph's conscience far too much. He faithfully cared for the stricken man day and night, "sacrificing" himself, as people might put it, and here quite rightly so, for his was a sacrifice in repayment for sacrifice, and Joseph performed it without regard to a loss of sleep or weight. He made his bed beside his patient's in the special chamber of trust and did what he could for him, hour after hour: warmed his compresses, gave him his medication, rubbed salves into his skin, had him breathe the vapor of crushed leaves placed on hot stones, just as the doctor had prescribed, and held his limbs when they were knotted with cramps—for in his final days the poor man suffered from them so severely that he would scream each time he was seized in this brutal way by death's laying rough hands upon him, evidently impatient for his surrender. Especially when Mont-kaw tried to sleep, death would interpose with these cramps, almost chasing the man's exhausted body from his bed, as if to say "What, you want to sleep, do you? Get up, get up, and die!" And then Joseph's soothing goodnight wishes were more fitting than ever, and he applied them with great skill, softly murmuring to the steward the thought that he would now certainly find the path to the land of consolation for which he longed, and stride down it unmolested—without being wrenched back in painful torment into the daylight of his suffering by his left arm and leg, now carefully fixed in place with strips of linen.

That was well done and helped to some extent. But Joseph was himself dismayed when he thought he noticed how the sum effect of his coaxing toward peace was far too helpful, and the steward, who had not slept well for so many years, now began to drift into a stupor, to lose himself in the haze of toxins, so that a good path became an evil one and Joseph's worry now was that the wanderer might forget to return. And so he had to go about it differently, and instead of composing lullabies for his friend, he tried to tie him to the here and now by rousing his vital spirits with stories and tales taken from that vast and deeply rooted treasury of history and anecdote that, thanks to the tutoring of Jacob and Eliezer, had been his from boyhood on. For the overseer had always enjoyed hearing about the first life of the slave he had purchased, about his childhood in the land of Canaan, about his lovely mother, who had died beside the road, and his father's grand and despotic tenderness, which he had first shown to her and then to his son, so that the two were one in the festive garment of his love. He had also heard about savage fraternal jealousy and the culpable trust and blind expectation of which Joseph in his childishness had been guilty, and about his mutilation and the well. Moreover, the overseer—and in this he was no different from Potiphar or others in the household—had always regarded Joseph's past and the land of his youth as very remote, a world of dust and destitution, from which quite understandably a man quickly became estranged when the hand of fate removed him to the land of human beings and gods; and so, like everyone else, he had not been at all surprised or put off that the Egyptian Joseph had refrained from any attempt to reestablish his connection with the barbarian world of his childhood. But Mont-kaw had always been happy to hear stories from that world, and during his final illness, it was his favorite and most soothing diversion to lie there with hands folded and listen as his young nurse treated him to memories of his own tribe, recounting them with fascinating charm and solemn good humor, telling him of the rough and smooth twins, who already battled in the womb; of the feast of the cheated blessing and of the smooth man's wanderings in the underworld; of the evil uncle and his children, whom he exchanged on the wedding night, and of how, with his knack for cleverly joining forces with nature, the subtle rogue got the better of the clumsy one. Switching here, there, everywhere—the switching of birthright and blessing, the switching of brides and fortunes, the switching of a son for an animal on the altar of sacrifice, of the animal for the son who resembled him by bleating as he died. All these switches and illusions charmingly roused the listener and tied him to the here and now—for what is more charming than illusion? There was also a play of light and reflection between storyteller and story—the illusory light from the stories, the charm of their illusion, fell back on him who told them, and in turn he also lent them something of his own person, that same person who had exchanged the veiled garment of love with his mother and who in Mont-kaw's eyes had always been a kind of amiable and roguish puzzle that engaged his mind from that first moment when he had stood before him with the scroll and a smile that tempted the steward to confuse him with the ibis-headed god.

Mont-kaw could barely see at all now or name the number of fingers held before his eyes. But he could still listen, and with the help of these strange and foreign stories so cleverly told at his bedside, he could drive away the torpid slumber into which his poison-laden blood tried to lure him. He learned about Eliezer who is always present, who, along with his master, had defeated the kings of the East, and whom the earth had leapt up to greet on his journey to find a bride for the averted sacrifice. About the virgin at the well, who had jumped down from her camel and veiled herself upon seeing him for whom she had been wooed. About the savagely beautiful brother of the desert, who had tried to persuade the cheated hairy red man to slay his father and devour him. About the ancient wanderer, the father of them all, and what had once happened to him and his sister-wife here in the land of Egypt. About his brother Lot, the angels at his door, and the flagrant shamelessness of the Sodomites. About the rain of brimstone, the pillar of salt, and what Lot's daughters had done out of worry for the future of mankind. About Nimrod of Shinar and his tower of presumption. About Noah, the second first man, the arch-clever man, and his ark. About the first man himself, made of clay in the Garden of the East, about the woman made from his rib, and about the serpent. Sitting by the dying man's bed, Joseph spent of his treasure, his heirloom of most marvelous stories, trying to ease his conscience with wit and eloquence and to tie the steward to the here and now for a little longer. But finally, caught up in this epic spirit himself, Mont-kaw began to speak; he had himself propped up in his pillows and, with the look of approaching death on his face, groped to lay his hand on Joseph's, as if he were Yitzchak feeling for his sons' hands in his tent.

"Let me see with seeing hands," he said, his face directed toward the ceiling, "whether you are Osarsiph, my son, for I wish to bless you before my end and am greatly strengthened for blessing by the stories you have so richly fed me. Yes, it is you, I see and know you well in the way blind men do, and there can be no creeping doubt or deception here, for I have only one son to bless, and that is you, Osarsiph, of whom I have grown fond over the course of years, in place of the little boy whom his mother took with her in her labors, suffocating him, for she was built too narrowly. Beside the road? No, she died in childbirth in her chamber at home, and I do not venture to say her torments were beyond nature, but they were terrible and cruel, so that I fell upon my face and begged the gods for her death, which they granted. They also granted the death of the child, though I had not begged for that. But what would the child have been to me without her? She was called Olive Tree, the daughter of Kegboi, a treasury official. Beket was her name, and I was not bold enough to love her the way that man of blessing made bold to love his wife, the lovely woman of Naharina, your mother—I could not presume to do so. But she was lovely too, unforgettably lovely in the adornment of her silken eyelashes, which she would lower whenever I spoke words of the heart to her, words of songs, which I myself would never have presumed to speak, but which became my words in those days, in those beautiful days. Yes, we loved each other, despite the narrowness of her body, and when she died along with the child, I wept for her through many nights, until time and work dried my tears—dried my eyes, and I no longer wept at night, but the heavy bags beneath them and the fact that they are so small comes, I think, from those many nights—I do not know for certain, it may be so, it may not be so, but since I am dying and the light is fading in those eyes that wept for Beket, it will all be one in this world whether it was so or not. But after my eyes had dried, my heart stood empty and bleak; it had also grown small and narrow, like my eyes, and despondent at having loved to no avail, so that it seemed to have room left only for resignation. But the heart must care for something besides resignation and wants to beat for something more tender than its advantage and profit. I was Peteprê's chief steward and oldest servant and knew of nothing except to make his house flourish and blossom in beauty. For he who is resigned is good for service. Behold, it was something that my narrowed heart could care for—service and tender helpfulness to Peteprê, my master. For is there anyone who is more in need of loving service than he? He has no other concern, for all things are foreign to him and he was not made for business. Strange, tender, and proud is he, this titular official, in the face of all human enterprise, moving one to pity and to care for him, for he is a good man. Has he not come to me and visited me in my illness? He took the trouble to come here to my bed, while you were looking after business, and inquired after me, a sick man, out of the goodness of his heart, though it was clearly evident that illness, too, makes him feel strange and shy, for he is never ill, though one would hesitate either to call him healthy or to believe that he will die—I can scarcely believe it myself, for one must be healthy in order to become ill, and live in order to die. But does that diminish one's care for him and the need to be helpful to his tender dignity? On the contrary! My heart has offered such care beyond its own advantage and profit and made a point of serving in love so that I might be able to be helpful to his dignity and humor his pride as well I knew how and was able to do. You, however, Osarsiph, know how to do it incomparably better, for the gods have given your mind subtle refinements and higher charms that mine lacks, whether because it is too dull and dry for them, or because it simply did not presume to trust itself for higher things. Which is why I have made a covenant with you for the sake of such service, which you are to keep when I am dead and am no more; and if I should bless you and bequeath you my office as steward of this house, you must swear to me here at my deathbed that you will not only watch over this house and its affairs for our master as best your wit and eye for business allow, but that you will also faithfully keep our more tender covenant by providing loving service to Peteprê's soul and by shielding and justifying his dignity with all your skill—nor need I even mention that you would never offend that worrisomely delicate dignity or be tempted to disgrace it in word or deed. Will you swear this to me by all that is holy, my son Osarsiph?"

"Gladly and by all that is holy," Joseph replied to these dying words. "You need not worry about that, my father. I swear to you to be helpful to his soul in considerate, faithful service according to our covenant and to remain as loyal as humanly possible to him in his need, and will think of you should I ever be assaulted by the temptation to cause him the special pain that unfaithfulness inflicts upon the lonely—you may depend upon it."

"That is a great comfort to me," Mont-kaw said, "although the sense of death agitates me greatly, which it ought not; for nothing is more common than death, and particularly my own—the death of so simple a man who always made a point of avoiding higher things. And so I shall die no higher sort of death, either, and wish to make no great fuss, no more than I made over my love for Olive Tree, or in presuming that the torment of her labor was beyond nature. But I wish to bless you all the same, Osarsiph, in place of my son, not without solemnity, for it is the blessing that is solemn and not I, and so bow now beneath a blind man's hand. I bequeath this house and estate to you, my true son and successor in the office of steward to Peteprê, the great courtier and my lord, and I resign from it in your favor, which gives my soul great satisfaction—indeed death brings me this joy and, as I now notice, the agitation it causes me is one of joy and nothing more. But my leaving all this to you is in accordance with the will of the master, who has pointed his finger at you among all his servants and has marked you to be his overseer in my place upon my death. For when he recently visited me out of the goodness of his heart and gazed upon me helplessly, I arranged this with him and entreated him to point his finger at you alone and to call you by name when I have become a god, so that I might depart with confidence as to the house and all its affairs. 'Yes,' he said, 'that's fine, Mont-kaw, old man, that's fine. Should you in fact depart, which would grieve me sorely, I will, without hesitation, point to him and no other, that is agreed, and should anyone attempt to meddle, he will learn that my will is of iron and like black granite from the quarries of Rehenu. He himself has said that such is the nature of my will, and I must agree with him. He stirs in me the sense of well-being that comes with trust, even more than you have done in your lifetime, and often I have thought I sensed that a god or several gods are with him, who lend success to everything he puts his hand to. And he is even less likely to go behind my back than you in all your honesty, for he was born knowing what sin is and wears in his hair a kind of sacrificial adornment as an amulet against sin. In short, it is settled, Osarsiph shall follow after you and be set over the house and assume all those affairs that I cannot possibly concern myself with. My finger is pointed at him.' Those were the master's very words—I have kept them faithfully. So I am blessing you now only after he first blessed you, for is it ever done otherwise? One always blesses only him who is blessed and wishes happiness to him who is happy. Even the blind man in his tent blessed his smooth son only because he, and not the rough one, was a man of blessing. One can do no more. So then, be blessed, as you are blessed. You have a joyful heart and boldly presume to deal with higher things and venture to say that your mother's torments were beyond nature and to call your own birth virginal for reasons that are at least disputable—those are the signs of blessing, which I did not have and so cannot bestow upon you, but I can bless you by also wishing you happiness as I die. Incline your head lower still beneath my hand, my son—the head of one who strives higher beneath the hand of a modest man. I bequeath to you house, estate, and fields in the name of Peteprê, for whom I administered them; I give to you their fatness and their purity, that you may preside over the workshops, the provisions in the storehouses, the fruits of the garden, the beasts, large and small, as well as the tilled fields of the island, the ledgers and every act of trade, and I set you over sowing and harvest, kitchen and cellar, the master's table, the needs of his house of women, the oil mills and winepresses, and all the servants. I hope I have forgotten nothing. But likewise do not forget me, Osarsiph, when I have become a god and like unto Osiris. Be my Horus, who shields and justifies his father, and do not let what is inscribed upon my grave grow illegible, but maintain my life. Tell me, will you see to it that Min-neb-mat, the master of wrappings, and his assistants make a very beautiful mummy of me? And not black, but a beautiful yellow, for which I have left behind what is needed, not for them to consume for themselves, but rather that I may be salted with good natron and fine balsam, so that I may live eternally—with storax, juniper wood, cedar resin from the harbor, mastic from the sweet pistachio bush, and soft linens nearest my body. Will you pay heed, my son, that my eternal shell is beautifully painted and covered on the inside with protective words, without gap or breach? Do you promise me to make sure that Imhotep, the priest of the dead in the West, does not distribute among his children the funds I have set aside for my sacrificial provisions of bread, beer, oil, and incense, but that they remain intact so that your father is provided with food and drink on feast days for all eternity? It is good and loving of you to promise me all this in a reverent voice, for though death is common, it is bound up with great cares, and a man must secure himself on many sides. Also place a little grate in my chamber, so that servants may roast haunches of beef for me there. Likewise add an alabaster goose, a wine pitcher carved of wood, and provide me as well with an abundance of your sycamore figs made of clay. It pleases me to hear you agree to all this in calming, pious words. Place a little boat manned by rowers beside my coffin, just in case, and see to it that a few aproned slaves are there inside with me, too, so that they may report in my stead when the god of the West calls me to work in his fertile field, for I had a head for generalities and was good at oversight, but cannot manage plow and sickle. Oh, how many precautions death demands! Have I forgotten any? Promise me you will also think of those that I have forgotten—for instance, that you will see to it that in place of my heart they insert the lovely jasper scarab that Peteprê gave me out of the goodness of his heart and that bears an inscription saying that my heart may not rise up to witness against me upon the scale. It is in the little box of yew wood lying just to the right in the chest, along with both my necklaces, which I bequeath to you. But enough of this, I shall now close my dying words. A man cannot think of everything, and there is left behind much uneasiness, which death itself brings with it, so that there is but an apparent need to take precautions. Even the question and uncertainty of how we shall live after our departure is more a guise of death's uneasiness, the form it takes in our thoughts—but these happen to be my thoughts, thoughts of uneasiness. Shall I sit in the trees as a bird among other birds? Shall I be permitted to be this or that just as I please: a heron in the marshes, a scarab rolling his little ball, a lotus chalice upon the water? Shall I live within my chamber and enjoy the sacrifices from the funds I left behind? Or shall I be there where Rê shines by night and where everything will be just as it is here—both heaven and earth, river, field, and house, and shall I again be Peteprê's oldest servant as has been my custom? I have heard it told one way and the other and both at once, and one way may well stand for another and all of it for our uneasiness, which, however, falls away beneath the rustling of sleep that calls me now. Lay me out upon my bed again, my son, for I am without strength, having spent the last of it in blessings and cares. I will give myself over to sleep, which rustles with a great rustling in my head. But before I give myself over, I would, to be sure, like to know whether in the West, on the far side of the Nile, I shall again meet my Olive Tree that perished. Ah, but above all let my care be that in the last moment as I try to fall asleep, I shall not be wrenched back again by a cramp. Say good-night to me, my son, as you know so well to do, hold my arm and leg and conjure away the cramp with soothing words. Discharge once more this fine office of yours—for the last time. And yet not the last, for if everything along the Nile of the transfigured is just as it is here, then you, too, Osarsiph, will surely be at my side again as my apprentice and will speak evening blessings to me, sweetly reshaped by your gifts for each night. For you are blessed and may spend your blessing, while I can only wish you happiness. . . . I can speak no more, my friend. Here is an end to my dying words. But do not think I do not still hear you."

Joseph laid his right hand on the pale hands of the dying man, and with his left he firmly held his thigh.

"Peace be with you," he said. "A blessed rest, my father, this night. Behold, I wake and watch over your limbs so that you may follow the path of consolation without care or any further worry. Rather, be of good cheer and let your thoughts be of nothing at all. Not of your limbs, nor the affairs of this house, nor even of yourself and what will become of you or how the life after this life may be— for that is the nub, that all this and everything else is not your care or concern and you need not be troubled by any uneasiness, but can let all things be as they are, for since they are, they must be some way or other, conduct themselves in one way or another—they have been taken care of, and your cares are at an end and your bed is one of cares provided for. Is that not gloriously comforting and soothing? Is it not with *must* and *may* today just as always, just as when I took leave of you with my evening blessing, saying you need not think that you must rest, but that you may? Behold, you may! Here is an end to problems and plagues and every vexation. No more bodily pain, no choking constriction, no fear of cramps. No loathsome medicines, no burning poultices or sucking, wriggling worms at your neck. The dungeon pit of your troubles is open wide. You walk out of it and stroll whole and free down the paths of consolation, which with each step lead deeper into consolation. For at first you move through fields you know well, those that received you each evening with the help of my blessing. Yet without your knowing it, there is still some heaviness and shortness of breath in you, in your body, which I hold here in my hands. But soon—you do not even notice the step that leads you across—new meadows of total lightness receive you, where you are not aware, even from afar, of the least distress still clinging, still tugging at you, and of a sudden you are likewise free of every care and nagging doubt as to how it is and how you stand and what will become of you, and are amazed to think you might ever have troubled yourself with such qualms, for everything is as it is and stands at its best, at its most natural and correct, and in happiest harmony with itself and with you, who are Mont-kaw for all eternity. For what is, is, and what was, will be. Do you doubt there in your heaviness that you will find your Olive Tree in the fields beyond? You will laugh at your faint heart, for behold she is beside you—and why should she not be, for she is yours. And I, too, shall be beside you—Osarsiph, the name by which you know the Joseph who died, for the Ishmaelites will bring me to you. You will always be crossing the courtyard with your wedge of a beard, your earrings, and the bags under your eyes, which presumably stayed with you from the nights when in private modesty you wept for Beket, your Olive Tree, and you will ask: 'What is this? What men are these?' And you will say: 'How kind of you. Do you suppose I can stand here chatting with you for all the days of Rê?' For since you are Mont-kaw, you will not fall out of your role and will pretend to the others that you truly believe I am none other than Osarsiph, the foreign slave who is for sale, though in your modest surmising you will secretly know, from the previous time, who I am and the arc I follow, that I prepare the way for the gods, my brothers. Farewell, then, my father and overseer. In light and in lightness we shall meet again."

Here Joseph closed his lips and ceased to say good-night, for he saw that the steward's ribs and belly stood still and that without his noticing he had left the fields and entered the meadows. He took a feather, which he had often held up to Mont-kaw's eyes to discover if he could still see it, and laid it on his lips. But it no longer stirred. He did not need to close the eyes, for they had closed peacefully on their own early in his slumber.

The doctors who tended to corpses came and salted and spiced Mont-kaw's body for forty days, and then he was ready to be wrapped and placed in his coffin, whose dimensions fitted him exactly; and now, a colorful Osiris, he was allowed to rest for a few more days before the silver lords at the back of the garden's summerhouse. But then he still had a journey to make by boat, downstream, to Abôdu's sacred grave, to pay the Lord of the West a visit before he could travel to the cliffs of Thebes and move into the rocky chamber of moderate pomp for which he had saved.

Joseph, however, never thought of this father without a dampness coming to his eyes. And in that moment they were strikingly like the eyes of Rachel when they had welled up with tears of impatience during those years she and Jacob had waited for each other.

Part Six

THE SMITTEN WOMAN

A Misinterpretation

And it came to pass after these things, his master's wife cast her eyes upon Joseph and said—

The whole world knows what Mut-em-enet, Potiphar's titular consort, is supposed to have said after having "cast" her eyes upon Joseph, her husband's young overseer; and we neither wish nor dare to deny that there finally came a day when, in utter confusion, in the highest fever of desperation, she did indeed speak precisely the blunt phrase of terrible directness that tradition has put into her mouth— words so abrupt and wanton in their explicitness as to suggest the proposal came quite naturally to her and at no personal cost, rather than being a final cry of ultimate psychological and physical anguish. To be frank, we are dismayed at the grudging brevity of an account that does so little justice to life's bitter and exacting particularity as our source does here, and seldom have we been more acutely aware than in this instance of how unfair laconic abridgment is to truth. Not that anyone should think we are indifferent to the censure that, whether spoken or perhaps left unspoken out of courtesy, hangs in the air concerning our entire account, our grappling with this story—the upshot of which is that the conciseness one finds in the ancient original cannot be surpassed in any way and that our entire enterprise, already so long in the telling, is labor lost. Since when, however, one might ask, does a commentary compete with its text? And then: is not a discussion of the "how" as worthy and important in life as the transmission of the "that"? Yes, is not life first truly fulfilled in the "how"? It should be remembered, as previously noted, that before a story can even be told it must first tell itself—and, indeed, tell it in the kind of detail of which life alone is the master, detail that lies beyond any narrator's hope or prospects of attaining it. He is able only to approximate such detail by serving the "how" of life more faithfully than the lapidary spirit of the "that" has deigned to do. And if commentary was ever justified, then it is here, in regard to Potiphar's wife and what tradition claims she said point-blank.

The portrait that one is forced or, perhaps, almost inevitably tempted to make of Joseph's mistress on such a basis and that, we fear, is indeed widely made of her, is so erroneous that any conscientious correction can only serve to benefit the ancient text—whether one understands this as it was originally written or, better, as life telling its story. At least this false portrait of unbridled lasciviousness and seduction devoid of all shame accords very poorly with what both we and Joseph heard in the garden cottage from the lips of the, in any case, venerable Tuya in regard to her daughter-in-law, comments that revealed to us a few more precise details about her life. When declaring it impossible to disparage her as a goose, Peteprê's mother called her "proud"; she called her haughty, a nun of the moon, a woman set apart, whose whole being carried the austere fragrance of the myrtle. Would such a woman, then, speak the way tradition has her speak? And yet, she did speak that way, spoke those very words, spoke them repeatedly once her pride had been fully broken by passion—we have already confirmed that. But tradition neglects to add how long a time passed during which she would rather have bitten off her tongue than to have spoken them. It neglects to say that as she sat there in her loneliness, she did indeed literally, physically bite her tongue, before that first time, when, stammering with pain, she brought her lips to utter words that would forever stamp her as a seductress. A seductress? It goes without saying that a woman overcome as she was will be a seductress— but seduction is the exterior and physiognomic manifestation of our common affliction; for it is nature that makes her eyes shimmer more sweetly than any artificial eyedrops she has learned to apply as part of the art of makeup ever can; nature that makes her lips more enticingly bright red than any rouge and swells them to a soulful, suggestive smile; that causes her to dress and adorn herself with innocent and skilled calculation, endows each movement with a sweet purpose, and gives her entire body—to whatever possible extent its structure allows, sometimes even beyond it as well—the stamp of promised bliss. All of this, initially and ultimately, means nothing more than what Joseph's mistress finally said to him. But can we say that the woman within whom all this takes place is responsible for it? Does she do it out of deviltry perhaps? Does she even know of it—that is, other than through the torment of her passion, which then reveals itself in external charms? In short, if she is made to be seductive, does that mean she is a seductress?

Above all, the birthplace and upbringing of a woman so smitten can transform the form and character of seduction in several ways. Speaking against the assumption that, as a smitten woman, Mut-em-enet—or Eni and sometimes Enti, as she was nicknamed—behaved like a harlot, are her childhood years, which were aristocratic beyond all imagining. And what was fair in the case of the honest Mont-kaw must surely be fair in terms of a woman whose influence shaped Joseph's destiny in an entirely different way—that is, that we take note of the essentials of her background.

It will come as no surprise to hear that the consort of Peteprê the fan-bearer was not the daughter of a tavern keeper or a quarry drudge. She was no less and no more than of ancient princely blood, even if it had been some time since her ancestors had held vast landed property and reigned as patriarchal lesser kings in a nome of Middle Egypt. At that time foreign rulers, a race of Asiatic nomads who dwelt in the north of the land, had worn Rê's double crown, and Wase's princes in the south had been these invaders' subjects for centuries. But powerful men had appeared among them, Sekenenre and his son Kamose, who rose up against these nomad kings in a bitter struggle in which the latter's foreign blood had proved an effective war cry in assisting the former in their ambitions. In fact, Kamose's valiant brother, Ahmose, had stormed and taken Avaris, the foreigners' fortified royal capital, driving them completely from the land, liberating it after a fashion by claiming it for himself and his kin, and setting them in the place of the foreign rulers. Not all the lords of the nomes, however, had immediately recognized the hero Ahmose as their liberator or equated his reign with freedom, as he chose to do. Many of them would have been more inclined—and they surely knew why—to stick with the foreigners in Avaris, preferring to remain their vassals than to be liberated by one of their own. Yes, even after the complete expulsion of their rulers of many years, these local kings had resisted liberation, had mutinied against their liberator and, as certain documents put it, "gathered malcontents against him," so that he first had to defeat them in open battle

before freedom was established. It was understood that these insur-
rectionists would of course lose their landed property. But it was
typical of these national liberators from Thebes that they held on to
whatever they took from foreigners, thus initiating a process that
was well advanced, but not yet completed by the time of our story
and would be concluded only in the course of it—which is to say, ex-
propriation of landed property from old, established noble families
and confiscation of their goods for the Theban crown, which increasingly became the sole owner of all land, leasing it or presenting
it as a gift to temples and favorites, just as Pharaoh had given Peteprê
that fertile island in the river. The old princely families of the nomes,
however, were transformed into an aristocracy of officials and officers, who swore allegiance to Pharaoh and assumed high positions in
his army and administration.

Which was also the case with Mut's noble clan. Joseph's mistress
was directly descended from the local prince named Tetian, who had
"gathered malcontents" in his day and first had to be defeated before
he acknowledged his liberation. But Pharaoh bore no malice toward
Tetian's grandchildren and great-grandchildren. Their race remained
one of powerful aristocrats, providing the state with commanding
officers, heads of cabinet, and keepers of the treasury, and the court
itself with high stewards, first charioteers, and guardians of the royal
bath, and, indeed, as administrators of large cities like Menfe or
Tihna, some of those from Tetian's loins even retained the old title of
Prince of the Nome. So it was with Eni's father, Mai-Sakhme, who
held the high office of City Prince of Wase—one of two, for there
was one for the City of the Living and one for the City of the Dead
in the West, and Mai-Sakhme was prince of the western city. As such
he lived, to use Joseph's expression, in high estate and could most
certainly anoint himself with the oil of gladness—he and all his family, including Enti, his fine-limbed child, even if she was no longer a
landed princess of the nome, but a modern civil servant's daughter.
In the decisions her petty-princely parents made concerning her, one
can indeed read the kinds of changes that had occurred in the family
mentality since the days of her ancestors. For the sake of gaining
what was, to be sure, great advantage at court, they had given their
beloved child at a very tender age to be the wife of Peteprê, whom
his parents Huya and Tuya had already prepared for titular officialdom, and by doing so had clearly proved that the virtue of fertility

cherished by an old established family deeply rooted in the soil had been greatly qualified by modern notions.

While still a child, Mut had been treated in much the same way as Potiphar's engenderers had treated their squirming little son by speculating on the future and consecrating him to be a courtier of the light. The claims of her sex, which were thus ignored—claims symbolized by the earth drenched black with water and by the moon-egg, the origin of the very stuff of life—still slumbered mute and embryonic within her, without her even realizing it or raising the softest objection to her parents' loving but life-denying decision. She was light, merry, untroubled, free. She was like a lotus blossom floating on the water's surface, kissed by the smiling sun, untouched by the knowledge that its long stem is rooted deep in dark mire. Back then there had been no contradiction whatever between her eyes and mouth; and instead childish, vague harmony had reigned over both of them, for her saucy little-girl eyes had known nothing then of the austerity that would later darken them and that special serpentine shape of her mouth with its tucked corners had been much less pronounced. The disparity between them had only gradually come about in the course of her years as a nun of the moon and honorary consort of a chamberlain of the sun—apparently in token of the fact that the mouth is a symbol and tool more closely bound and related to lower powers than is the eye.

As for her body, everyone knew its form and all its beauties, for "woven air"—that gentle breath of silken, luxurious gossamer that she wore in accordance with custom—revealed every line of it to her advantage. One might say that what her body expressed was more in harmony with her mouth than with her eyes; her honorary rank had not hindered its blossoming or constrained its swelling; with its small, firm breasts, delicate neck and back, supple shoulders, perfectly sculpted arms, and noble long, firm legs, whose upper lines flowed in a most feminine curve to form the splendid hips and buttocks, it was recognized as the finest female body far and wide. The people of Wase knew none more worthy of praise, and, being who they were, the sight of it stirred in them ancient lovely visions, images of beginnings and a time before beginnings, images related to the moon-egg of all origins, the image of a glorious virgin, which in its depths—its truly moist depths—was the goose of love in the form of a virgin; and nuzzled in her loins was a noble specimen of a swan, flapping its widespread wings, a tender, powerful snow-feathered god, performing upon her, to her virtuous amazement, a fluttering work of its love, that she might bear the egg. . . .

And, truly, such primal images, which had lain in darkness, illuminated the innermost world of Wase's inhabitants at the sight of Mut-em-enet's translucent figure, although they knew of the honorary status in which this chaste moon-woman lived and which could be read in the austere look in her eyes. They knew that those eyes were a more telling testimony to her nature and conduct than the very different message told by her expressive mouth, which might well have smiled indulgently down at the swan's royal pursuits; they knew that her body enjoyed its finest moments, its satisfaction and fulfillment, not in receiving such visits, but solely on those high holidays, when, shaking a rattle, it danced in full ritual extension before Amun-Rê. In short, they spoke no ill of her; there were no ugly rumors or winks exchanged in regard to what her mouth said, but what her eyes rejected as lies. Sharp tongues condemned others whose marriages were more authentic than that of Tetian's granddaughter, but of whom it was said nonetheless that their lives were topsy-turvy when it came to morals—including ladies of the order, members of the god's harem, including, for example, Renenutet, the consort of the Chief Steward of Amun's Bulls, for people knew things about her that the Chief Steward of Amun's Bulls did not know or did not want to know, knew a good many things about her and joked about others. But no one in Thebes knew anything about Peteprê's first and, so to speak, true wife, and they were all convinced that there was nothing to know. Both inside and outside Peteprê's house and court, she was regarded as a saint, as a woman set apart and chosen—and that is saying a great deal given these people's deep-rooted appetites and love of jesting.

Despite what our audience may think, we do not regard it as our task to probe the details of daily life in Mizraim and in particular those of the ladies who made up No-Amun's female world—details and customs whose grossness we long ago heard solemnly described by old Jacob. His knowledge of the world was not devoid of a certain pathos and a penchant for myth that it would be well to discount if one is to avoid exaggeration. But his lofty words were not without a connection to reality, either. Among people who had neither a conception of nor a word for sin and who walked about in clothes made of woven air, people whose worship of animals and death implied and promoted a certain carnal mind-set, there is, from the very start and quite apart from any experience or proof of it, a probable laxity of morals, which Jacob had painted in bold poetic strokes. And experience, then, corresponded to probability—which we note more for the sake of logic than out of malice. It would be mere snooping to examine the life of Wase's women for individual instances of that correspondence. There is little here to be disputed and much to be forgiven. We would need only to let our gaze pass back and forth between Renenutet, the Chief Stewardess of Bulls, and a certain very dapper lieutenant of the Royal Bodyguards—and, indeed, also between that same high-ranking lady and a young, shiny-headed attendant in the temple of Khonsu—in order to suggest the conditions that on the whole justify Jacob's vivid characterizations. It is not up to us to condemn on moral grounds a city like Wase—that great city of more than a hundred thousand people. What cannot be held back or saved, we shall simply let go. But we would put our hand in the fire for one woman—and are prepared to stake our entire reputation as a storyteller upon the blamelessness of her conduct up to a given point in time, when, to be sure, she yielded to divine forces and became a reeling, frenzied maenad—and that one woman is Prince Mai-Sakhme's daughter, Mut-em-enet, Potiphar's wife. That she might have been a harlot on whose lips the proposition imputed to her would have lain ever at the ready, so to speak, and have slipped from them easily and saucily, is so misleading a notion that for the sake of truth we must do everything we can to subvert it. When her badly bitten tongue finally whispered those words, she herself no longer recognized herself; she was more than beside herself, a woman undone by passion, a victim of the scourge-swinging, avenging lust of those base powers to which her mouth was answerable—whereas her eyes had thought they could defy them with cool disdain.

Eyes Are Opened

We know that, in accordance with the well-intentioned agreement between parents, Mut was engaged and married to the son of Huya and Tuya while still a young child, a fact that deserves mention since its natural consequence was that she grew accustomed early on to the formal nature of their marriage, and the moment when her natural fiber could have taught her something was lacking in it, still lay in the flow of darkness. This is not an idle observation, for her loss of virginity had occurred in name only and much too soon, and that is how things remained. Hardly a young woman yet, more a half-grown girl, she found herself the pampered mistress of an elegant house of women, with every luxury at her command—coddled by gently fawning eunuchs and naked Moorish maids of almost fierce servility, the first and true wife among fifteen other local beauties of very mixed origin, all living out their lives in purposeless extravagance and together composing one pure, empty, and honorary luxury. The sham appurtenance of a house of blessing, a royal courtier's superfluous trappings of love, she was queen of these dreaming, chattering women, who hung on her every raised eyebrow, sank into melancholy when she was sad, broke into unbridled cackling when she seemed cheerful, and squabbled mindlessly over every trivial display of favor shown by Peteprê, their master, when, amid sweetmeats and amber liqueur for all, he would join Mut-em-enet for a perfunctory match at some board game. She was the star of the harem—at one and the same time, female head of the household, Potiphar's consort in a narrower and higher sense than any concubine, and the absolute mistress, who under other circumstances would have been the mother of his children and who resided whenever she pleased in her own chambers in the main house. (These lay to the east of the north columned hall, where Joseph served as a reader and which separated the rooms of the spouses.) She also played hostess and housewife, receiving guests at entertainments graced with dance and music, which Potiphar, the friend of Pharaoh, gave in his home for Theban high society, and in turn she joined him in visiting other aristocratic houses, most particularly the royal court, for similar functions.

Hers was an intense life, densely packed with elegant duties—frivolous duties, if you like, but they are no less taxing than significant ones. We know how in every civilization the demands of social life, the culture itself with all its lavish details, completely engages the energies of genteel women, so that, what with all the p's and q's of form, they probably never get to the essentials, to the life of the soul and mind, and a cool emptiness of the heart that knows no hardship—or at least is unaware of it—becomes a routine of life that one cannot even call sad. All times and places have known this barely lukewarm feminine worldliness, and one could go so far as to say that it does not matter much whether the husband at whose side such a grand-lady life is led is a commander of troops in a real or merely titular sense. The ritual of the dressing table, for instance, remains equally demanding, whether its goal is to maintain the vigor of a spouse's desires or is merely an end in itself, practiced purely out of social obligation. Mut, like all the ladies of her social class, devoted hour after hour to it every day. The process involved the meticulously perfected care of her shimmering enameled finger- and toenails; perfumed baths, depilatory procedures, the massages with oils to which she submitted the lovely form of her body; the delicate application of paint and drops to her already beautiful eyes, with their metallic blue irises and mastery of every wink and blink, enhanced now by the high art of cosmetology, by the tracery of pointed brush and other sweet embellishments, until they became veritable jewels and baubles; the dressing of her hair, both her own, a thick half-length mass of shining black curls, often dusted with blue or gold powders, and her wigs, dyed various colors and worked into braids, plaits, tresses, and pearl-drop fringes, during the process of which—as well as later, while gentle fingers fitted her into petal-white garments with embroidered hip sashes perfectly pressed into the shape of lyres and shoulder drapes tucked in tiniest pleats—she selected jewels from those offered by kneeling servants for adorning her head, breast, and arms. Throughout all this, however, the naked Moorish maidens, the eunuch hairdressers, and the wardrobe maids had nothing to laugh about, nor did Mut herself ever laugh, for some bit of carelessness, some minor oversight in these cultural matters would have resulted in a whirl of gossip in high society, a malicious scandal at court.

Then there were visits with women friends of the same social circle, for which she either received them at home or had herself carried to them in her chair. There were her duties as one of the ladies-in-waiting who attended Tiy, the god's wife at Merima't Palace—for she bore a fan just as nicely as Peteprê, her consort, and was required to join evening parties given by the receiver of Amun's seed, water

galas held on the artificial lake that Pharaoh's word had called forth
in the royal gardens and whose beauty was bathed in the splashing
hues of colored torches, themselves a recent invention. There were
also (the name of her who gives birth to the god has reminded us)
those ceremonial obligations of serious piety we have frequently
mentioned, in which elegant society merged with sacerdotal worship
and which more than all others demanded that look of arrogant austerity in her eyes—duties, that is, that stemmed from her member-
ship in the Order of Hathor and participation in Amun's harem as a
bearer of cow horns with the solar disk between them, that is, as a
goddess for a brief space of time. It is strange to note just how much
this aspect or function of Eni's life contributed to enhancing this
great lady's worldly coldness and to keeping her heart empty of
softer dreams. It did so in connection with the titular nature of her
marriage—when there was really no necessary connection at all between them. Amun's House of Women was not in any way a house
of the undefiled. Chastity was far from being a divine attribute of the
Great Mother, who embodied herself on festive occasions in Mut
and her companions. The queen, who made her bed with the god
and bore the next sun, was the patron of the order. Its head, as we
have mentioned now and again, was a married woman, wife of
Amun's important Great Prophet, and like Renenutet, wife of the
Chief Steward of the Bulls—not to mention any further conduct on
her part—the great majority of its members were married. In fact,
the only connection between Mut's temple service and her marriage
was that the former grew out of the social status of the latter. But
quite on her own she achieved within herself what Huya, that
hoarse-voiced old man, had asserted in his conversation with his
aged sister and bed partner: she created a relationship between her
priestly office and the singularity of her marriage, found means and
ways, without actually putting it into words, of showing how fitting
it was—indeed, how fundamentally legitimate for a concubine of the
god—that her earthly consort be a man of Peteprê's nature. She
knew how to suggest and share this interpretation with society, so
that in turn society assisted her in maintaining it by regarding her
position in the circle of Hathor's priestesses as a form of divine
chastity, of being set apart, and thus tacitly lent Mut a superior status—far more than her lovely voice and dancing ever could—more

or less at the side of the head of the order. This was a work of her will, by which an idea took shape in the world, giving her those extra consolations that her mute depths demanded.

A nymph? A loose woman? How truly ridiculous. Mut-em-enet was an elegant saint, a nun of the moon casting cool light on this world, her vital energies partly consumed by a demanding civilization and—as temple property, so to speak—partly dissolving into spiritual pride. That is how she had lived as Potiphar's first and true wife, pampered and catered to, reinforced in her self-indulgence by adorers kneeling all around her, but untouched even in her dreams by certain wishes—by goose wishes, to put it bluntly—from the same realm that manifested itself in the serpentine shape of her mouth. For it is wrong to regard dreams as a playground or hunting preserve, where the taboos of the day may freely emerge to find compensation in running rampant. Those things of which truth has no fundamental knowledge, from which truth itself is barred, are also unknown to dreams. Between these two realms is a shifting, porous, uncertain border that traverses a single psychological space; but conscience and pride regard this space as indivisible, as was immediately evident in the confusion, in the shame and panic, that overcame Mut not just when she awoke, but also during the night when she dreamed her first dream of Joseph.

When did that happen? In her home and largely in accord with the customs of the world of our narrative, life's years were counted rather carelessly, so let us be content with rough estimations as well. Eni was certainly several years younger than her consort, who was a man in his late thirties when we first made his acquaintance at the time of Joseph's purchase and had now added another seven years or so. She was not, therefore, in her mid-forties like him, but a good deal younger; all the same, she was a mature woman, undeniably several years older than Joseph. Yet we sense a certain disinclination to puzzle out just how many—out of moral respect, in fact, for a high civilization whose cosmetics as good as erase any age differences among women, such achievements being so persuasive to our senses as to lay claim to a higher truth than that of sums done with a mere pencil. Since Joseph had first seen his mistress float past on her golden sedan chair, he had—in terms of what engages female sympathy—changed to his advantage, while she had not, at least not for those who had observed her continually since then. Woe to any massaging eunuch or oil-rubbing slave, if the years had been able to prevail against her body! But her face as well—which had never been truly beautiful, given its saddle nose and the unusual shadowy hollows of the cheeks—still maintained the same balance between harmony and the whims of nature, between the stamp of fashion and its own irregular charms, that it had had back then. The gently disconcerting contradiction between eyes and sinuous mouth had clearly become stronger over the years, and if one is inclined to see beauty in what is disconcerting—and that inclination does exist—one might even say that she had grown more beautiful over time.

Conversely, during this same period Joseph's beauty had grown out of that stage of youthful, not yet manly charm to which we had to pay tribute in its day. At twenty-four his beauty still—indeed, quite justly so now—made people gawk, but it had ripened beyond the ambiguous charm of his early years, maintaining its universal attraction, to be sure, but concentrating its emotional efficacy more decisively in one direction, that is, in terms of its appeal to women. But in growing more manly, his beauty had become more noble still. His was no longer the charmingly beguiling physiognomy of that Bedouin lad of old; the face retained traces of it, especially when—although he was not at all nearsighted—he would narrow his Rachel eyes, veiling them in that certain way his mother had done. But it had become fuller, more serious, and darker as well under Egypt's sun, its features even more regular and refined now. We have already noted in passing the changes that had taken place not only in his figure, but also—this the result not just of years, but of the many tasks he had come to master—in his movements and the timbre of his voice. Added to all of which were refinements to his appearance, the work of the culture of the Two Lands, and if we wish to have a clear image of how he looked at the time, these dare not be neglected either. One must imagine him in upper-class Egyptian attire, its white linen transparent to undergarments shimmering beneath, its broad, short sleeves revealing forearms adorned at the wrist with enameled bracelets. Although in casual circumstances he displayed his own smooth hair, on more formal occasions he wore a light artificial wig, something between a head scarf and a periwig that covered the top of the head with very fine, dense parallel strands of finest sheep's wool, much like ribbed silk, and descended as far as the nape of the neck, but then, following a definite diagonal line, the weave changed to small, regular curls that interlocked like roof tiles and fell down over the shoulders. Around his neck, in addition to his colorful collar, he wore a flat necklace of reed and gold, from which a scarab amulet dangled. With an expression lent a strangely hieratic, iconic look by artifices of makeup gladly applied each morning in accordance with custom—a firm accentuation of the brow line, a linear extension of the upper eyelid toward the temples—he would walk the estate, usually setting his long staff before him, as the steward's "mouth," would travel to markets, would stand behind Potiphar's chair at meals, signaling the other servants. This was also how his mistress saw him, either in the dining chamber or when he appeared in the house of women, stepping before her to speak with her in deferential tones and posture about some household matter; indeed, this was how she first really beheld him, for previously, as a purchased nonentity and even during the period when he had learned how to warm Potiphar's heart, she had not noticed him at all—in fact, even as he grew in the household as if beside a spring, it had still always required Dûdu's complaints for her eyes to be opened to his presence.

But this opening of the eyes—performed by the ceremonial calf's foot of Dûdu's tongue—was far from complete, for, having been forced to hear about this slave's offensive rise within the household, she kept an eye out for him solely out of austere curiosity. The dangerous part (and out of respect for her pride, her peace of mind, one must put it that way) was simply that it was Joseph upon whom her eyes rested and whose eyes met hers for a few seconds—a truly momentous state of affairs, which, given his dwarfish wisdom, had immediately sent coursing through Bes a fearful foreboding that malicious Dûdu was contriving something exceeding even his malice and that this opening of the eyes would come to a pernicious conclusion. Inborn terror of those strange powers that he perceived in the image of the fire-snorting bull made him receptive to such premonitions. Joseph, however, out of culpable frivolity (for we are unwilling to spare him in this regard), had not wanted to understand him and had acted as if the vizier were speaking gibberish, despite his being ultimately in agreement with the whispering dwarf. For Joseph, too, placed less value and weight on the meaning of those moments in the dining chamber than on the fact that they occurred at all and in his heart very foolishly prided himself on no longer being a piece of furniture in his mistress's eyes, but rather the object of her personal, if angry, glance. And what about our Eni?

Well, she was no wiser, either. She, too, would not have wanted to understand the dwarf. She found her gazing at Joseph with angry austerity sufficient excuse for gazing at him at all—a total mistake from the very beginning, pardonable before she knew whom she was looking at when she did look, but later an ever increasingly deliberate and culpable mistake. The unhappy woman did not want to notice how the "austere curiosity" with which she kept an eye out for her consort's personal servant gradually lost its austerity and her remaining curiosity soon deserved another fortunately unfortunate name. She believed herself to be stern and businesslike in sharing Dûdu's indignation at Joseph's vexatious rise, felt herself justified and duty-bound to share in it for religious or—what was the same thing—political and partisan reasons, given her commitment to Amun, who surely had to regard the ascendancy of a Habiru slave in her house as an offense, an acquiescing to Atum-Rê's Asiatic proclivities. The gravity of the offense was made to serve as the justification for the pleasure that dealing with it gave her—which she called her concern and zeal. Human capacity for self-deception is astounding. When, relieved of social duties for a brief moment in summer or a longer one in winter, Mut would pause to think, stretching out on her couch beside the square basin set into the floor of the open arcade in the house of women and filled with colorful fish and floating lotus chalices, while crouched against the wall behind her was a small Nubian woman with heavily oiled curly hair, whose task it was to accompany her mistress's thoughts by gently strumming on a harp—in such moments, then, she was convinced that it was her intention to consider the question of how, despite her husband's stubbornness and Beknechon's discursive grandiosity, she might remedy the harm of allowing a slave from the land of Zahi, one of the Ibrim, to rise to such heights in her household; and given the importance of the matter she was not surprised that she delighted in thinking about it, even when she almost knew by now that the sole basis of her delight lay in her intention to think about Joseph. Were it not for a sense of pity, one could be annoyed at such infatuated blindness. The woman did not even notice that she had begun to look forward to meals when she would see Joseph. She assumed that her delight came from the chastising glances she intended to send his way. Deplorable as it sounds, she did not even notice how her serpentine mouth smiled in reverie when she recalled how his gaze vanished in terrified humility beneath lowered eyelids in response to the austerity in her own eyes. If at the same time she simply scowled in displeasure at this household offense, that would suffice, so she thought. And if worried dwarfish wisdom had warned her of the fiery bull and tried to inform her that the structure of her life—artificial as it was—had begun to totter and was about to collapse into a heap, her face, too, might have quickly turned flushed and clouded; but if someone had actually chided her on that account, she would have declared it to be an expression of her anger over such confused gibberish and have outdone herself in gaily stressing her own hypocritically exaggerated incomprehension of such worries. And who is supposed to be deceived by such affected, strained emphasis? The person offering the warning? Ah no, the point is to conceal the path of adventure one's own sweet soul demands be pursued at any cost. Keeping the wool pulled over one's own eyes until it's too late—that's what matters. To be disturbed, awakened, called back to oneself *before* it's too late—that is the very "danger" such lamentable wiles mean to avoid. Lamentable? The kindhearted should take care not to let misplaced sympathy make them look foolish. To put it mildly, there is no proof for the naive, kindhearted assumption that people's deepest concern is for peace and quiet, for making sure that the structure of their lives, built up and secured with such artifice and care, is never shaken or, worse, threatened with collapse. Experience, and in more than just isolated cases, teaches us that people are far more intent on bliss and ruin and have no thanks to spare for anyone who wishes to hold them back from it. In that case—please, go right ahead.

As for Enti, the kindhearted can only note—not without bitterness—how easy she found it to move beyond the moment when it would not have been too late and she would not yet have been lost. A blissfully horrible premonition that she already was came to her in the aforementioned dream she dreamt about Joseph—and, to be sure, it came as a shock. But, of course, she also told herself that she was a woman endowed with reason, and she acted accordingly—which is to say, she imitated a woman endowed with reason and automatically acted *like* one, but not really *as* one. She took steps that in truth she could no longer want to succeed—confused and unworthy steps, to which the kindhearted would do best to close their eyes if they do not wish their pity to be misplaced.

It is almost impossible to tell about dreams and put them into words, because a dream is far less about its narratable substance and almost completely about its aroma and aura, its ineffable meaning, that sense of horror or happiness—or both—pervading it, the effects of which often fill the dreamer's soul for long afterward. Dreams play a decisive role in our story—its hero dreamed grand and child-ish dreams, and there will be others yet who will also dream. But in what predicaments they all landed by trying to share with others some rough sense of that inner experience, how unsatisfactory for them were the results of every such attempt. One need only recall Joseph's dream about the sun, moon, and stars and how incoher-ently the helpless dreamer imparted it. We have some excuse, then, if in telling Mut-em-enet's dream, we should fail to make completely comprehensible the impression it made, and left, on its dreamer. In any case we have alluded to it so often that we cannot be allowed to hold back its contents now.

She dreamed, then, that she was sitting on the dais in the hall of blue columns, eating dinner there on her low stool beside old Huya, amid the tactful silence that always reigned during this routine. But the silence was especially considerate and deep this time, for not only did the four diners refrain from saying a single word, but they also tried to keep every action associated with eating soundless, so that in the hush one could clearly hear the intermingled breathing of the busy servants—so clearly, in fact, that it would have been audible had the silence been less tactful, for it sounded more like panting. Their hurried, soft pants were unsettling; and perhaps because Mut was listening for them, or perhaps for some other reason, she was not paying close attention to what her hands were doing and hurt herself. For she was about to segment a pomegranate with a bronze knife, but was so distracted that the well-honed blade slipped and cut her hand, slicing deep enough into the soft flesh between thumb and four fingers that the wound began to bleed profusely. The blood was as ruby red as pomegranate juice, and as she watched it flow, she felt both shame and concern. Yes, she was ashamed of her own blood, despite its beautiful ruby red, probably also because in-evitably it at once spattered on her petal white attire, but even be-yond that, quite apart from these stains, she felt inordinately ashamed and tried as best she could to conceal her bleeding from the others in the hall; and with success it appeared, or perhaps was meant to appear, for everyone made a great—more or less natural and credible—show of having not noticed Mut's accident, so that no one paid the least attention to her plight, which only added to the wounded woman's distress. In her shame, she did not want to call attention to her bleeding; but she was also truly and profoundly outraged that no one wanted to notice, that no one lifted a finger to help her, but, as if by common agreement, left her to look after herself. Her waitress, the demure slave clad in gossamer, bent down hastily to Mut's little one-legged table as if something there urgently required her setting it to rights. Grabbing a gilt thighbone in his aged hand to spear pieces of ring cake that he then dunked in wine, old Huya at her side munched toothlessly away, waggling his head and acting as if munching were his sole concern. Peteprê, the master, held his goblet up over his shoulder so that his Syrian cup-bearer and personal slave could refill it. And with her broad white face and blind slits for eyes, his mother, old Tuya, even gave the helpless woman an encouraging nod, though it was uncertain just how she meant it and whether she was aware of Eni's distress or not. In her dream, however, Eni went on bleeding shamefully, staining her dress, and feeling silently embittered by this general indifference—but also, quite apart from all that, distressed at the sight of her own bright red blood, for its steadily oozing and bubbling crimson was a source of indescribable regret. How sorry, how very sorry she felt, deeply, unutterably sorry—not for herself or because of her plight, but for the sweet blood flowing out of her like that—and in her sadness she heaved a quick, tearless sob. Then it occurred to her that because of her wound she was neglecting her duty on Amun's behalf to keep a reproachful lookout for the offense to her house, for that Kenanite slave, whose ascendancy was so unseemly; and she scowled and gazed sternly across to the offender behind Peteprê's chair, to young Osarsiph. But as if summoned by the austerity of her glance, he left his post and came toward her, ever nearer. And was now so near that she could feel his nearness. But he had come nearer in order to stanch the flow of blood. For he took her wounded hand and put it to his mouth, so that four fingers lay against one cheek and her thumb against the other, but the wound rested against his lips. And in her rapture, the flow of blood stopped and was stanched. Even as she was healed, however, the mood in the hall turned hostile and fearful. The servants, and there were a good number of them, ran about in a flurry, still on hushed bare feet, to be sure, but panting in random chorus. Peteprê, the master, had veiled his head, while the woman who had borne him groped with splayed hands for his lowered, covered head and rocked her upturned blind face back and forth above him in despair. Eni saw old Huya, however, stand up and threaten her with that gilt thighbone—munched free of its last piece of cake—while his mouth, opening and closing above his tarnished beard, uttered soundless insults. The gods alone knew what ghastly words his toothless mouth and the tongue working inside it were saying, but their meaning was probably the same as the panting of the servants running about helter-skelter. For their breathy chorus now took on whispered shape, repeated over and over: "To the fire, to the river, to the dogs, to the crocodile." Eni's ears were still ringing with this dreadful whisper as she reemerged from her dream, cold with horror, but turning hot again at once in the rapture of healing—and was well aware that she had been struck with the rod of life.

Husband and Wife

Having had her eyes opened, Mut decided to behave like a woman endowed with reason and to take a step she would be proud to show before the seat of reason, since its clear and indisputable purpose was to remove Joseph from her sight. She would do her best to take up the matter of this servant's dismissal with Peteprê, her husband.

She had spent the day after the night of her dream in seclusion, withdrawing from her sisters and refusing to receive visitors. Seated beside the basin in her quarters, she had watched the fish dart about—"staring vacantly" as we say when a person's gaze is lost in the void, floating and fixing on no particular object but itself. In the midst of this floating, fixed stare her eyes had suddenly flared wide as if with horror, yet without freeing themselves from the void, while her mouth opened and hastily sucked air down her throat. Her wide eyes had then abandoned the horror, returned to serenity; but without her realizing it, her mouth had begun to form a smile at its deepening corners and had kept on smiling for several minutes beneath pensive eyes, until she had noticed and pressed her hand in alarm to her vagabond lips, thumb against one cheek, the other four fingers opposite. "Ye gods!" she had murmured. Then it had begun all over again—the dreamy stare, the gasping for air, the unconscious smiling to herself, the dismayed discovery of that smile—until Eni had decided then and there to put an end to all this.

Around sunset, she inquired and learned that master Peteprê was in the house and told her handmaids to adorn her for a visit with him.

The courtier was in the west hall of his house, with its view to the orchard and one side of the cottage set atop its little hill. Falling between the slender, colorful columns of the outer wall, the hues of sunset began to fill the room and enrich the more pastel tones of the wall paintings that an artist's easy hand had flung across the plastered floor, walls, and ceiling—birds fluttering above the marsh, gamboling calves, ponds with ducks, cattle being driven by a herder across a ford in a river, under the eyes of a crocodile peering up out of the water. The frescos on the rear wall, between the doors that opened onto the dining room, depicted the master of the house himself as real as life, portraying his return home, with servants diligently preparing everything for his customary reception. Framing the doors were inset glazed tiles—blue, red, and green hieroglyphics against a camel-colored background—with quotations from fine, old authors and lines from divine hymns. Between the doors ran a kind of gallery or terrace, with a low ledge in front and a back for sitting that projected from the wall, all made of white stuccoed clay, but with colorful inscriptions along the front of the gallery. It served both as a shelf for a variety of objects—works of art, all those gifts that filled the halls of Peteprê's house—and as a bench; and there in the middle is where the man of many honors was now seated on a cushion, his feet placed together, the ledge as his footstool. Arranged to his right and left were rows of beautiful objects—animals, statues of gods, and royal sphinxes of gold, malachite, and ivory—and at his back were owls, falcons, ducks, zigzag lines, and other iconographic inscriptions. He had made himself comfortable, having removed his garments except for his knee-length skirt made of white linen and held by a wide starched drawstring. His outerwear and his walking stick, from which hung his sandals, lay on a lion-footed armchair next to one of the doors. But he had struck a pose that did not allow him to relax; instead, he sat very erect, his little hands—tiny indeed in relation to his massive body—stretched out in his lap and his likewise relatively dainty head, with its elegantly arched small nose and finely chiseled mouth, held just as erect, while he gazed beyond the hall into the reddening sunset from beneath gentle, long-lashed, brown eyes—a fleshy, but composed, noble, and dignified seated statue, its mighty calves like columns, its arms like an obese woman's, its breasts like plumped-up cushions. Despite his corpulence he had no potbelly; his hips in fact were rather narrow. His navel, however, was quite striking, being exceptionally large and so stretched horizontally that it resembled a mouth.

Peteprê sat there quite a long time, his dignified and motionless pose ennobling his idleness. Shrouded perhaps in the darkness of a false door in the grave that awaited him, a lifesize copy of his person would stand—forever—with this same immobile calm, its brown glass eyes gazing at his eternal household, at objects sent with him or painted on the walls for magical effect. He and his standing statue would be one; he anticipated that identity by sitting here and making himself eternal. At his back and on the ledge where his feet rested, the red, blue, and green inscriptions spoke their message; to his right and left stood rows of gifts from Pharaoh; the painted columns of his hall, through which he stared out into the evening, were the epitome of Egypt's sense of form. A surrounding of possessions reinforces one's immobility. One lets them abide in their beauty even as one abides in well-ordered composure in their midst. And mobility is more appropriate to those who are open to the world—conceiving, sowing, spending, and dying as they lose themselves in their seed— than to a man like Peteprê, constituted as a closed existence. In his self-collected poise he sat there with no access to the world, inaccessible to the death that comes with conceiving—eternal, a god in his shrine.

At the periphery of his gaze, a black shadow glided soundlessly closer from between the columns—a mere outline of darkness against the colors of sunset, it crouched very low even as it made its entry and was still silent now as it clasped its hands to its brow and touched it to the floor. He slowly turned his eyes in its direction: it was one of Mut's Moorish handmaids, a small naked animal. He blinked, gathering his thoughts. Then, merely flexing his wrist, he raised one hand from his knee and commanded: "Speak."

She snapped her head up from the floor, rolled her eyes, and in the hoarse voice of the desert blurted out her answer: "The mistress is near to the master and her wish is to be nearer still."

He gathered his thoughts again. Then he replied, "It is granted."

The little animal retreated backwards over the threshold. Peteprê sat there with raised eyebrows. But only for a few moments, and then Mut-em-enet was standing at the same spot where the slave had cowered. With elbows pressed against her body, she spread the palms of her hands as if spreading an offering before him. He saw that she was dressed warmly. Over her tight-fitting, ankle-length undergarment she wore something like a wide-flowing, pleated robe. The shadows of her cheeks were framed by a dark blue wiglike headscarf that fell to the nape of her neck and shoulders and was bound by an embroidered ribbon. Atop her head was a perforated cone for ointment, into which had been inserted a lotus, its stem following the curve of her head at a slight distance, its blossom hovering above her brow. The gemstones of her necklace and bracelets flashed darkly.

Peteprê likewise raised his small hands in greeting and pressed the back of one to his lips for a kiss.

"Flower of the Two Lands," he said in voice of surprise, "whose beautiful face has a place in the house of Amun, who is alone in her comeliness when her pure hands bear the sistrum and when she sings in a voice beloved by all." He maintained this tone of happy surprise as he hastily recited the formulaic phrases. "You who fill this house with beauty and to whose grace all things pay homage, you who are the confidante of the queen—you know how to read my heart in fulfilling its wishes ere they are spoken, fulfilling them by your very coming. Here is a cushion," he said in a more prosaic voice, pulling out one from behind his back and arranging it on the ledge at his feet. "May the gods grant," he added, resuming his courtly tone, "that you, you yourself, have come with a wish that, the greater it may be, the greater may be my joy in fulfilling it."

He had good reason to be curious. Such a visit was most unusual and, in falling outside the customary routine of tactful consideration, it unsettled him. He presumed its purpose was some petition, which left him feeling a certain anxious pleasure. But for now she spoke only the prettiest words.

"What wish could I, your sister, still have of you, my lord and friend?" she said in her mild voice, a melodious alto in which one could hear her training as a singer. "I have breath only through you, but thanks to your greatness all my wishes are fulfilled. If I have a place in the temple, then it is because you tower above all other enhancements of this land. If I am called the queen's friend, then only because you are Pharaoh's friend and manifest yourself as the golden radiance of the sun's favor. Without you I would be dark. But as I am yours, I have light in all its fullness."

"Since this is your opinion, it would be to no avail to contradict you," he said with a smile. "At least let us see to it that what you say of the fullness of light not be marred at the moment." He clapped his hands. "Make light!" he commanded of the aproned servant who now appeared from the dining room.

Eni, however, protested and begged, "Let it be, my husband. It is barely dusk. You sat here delighting in the beautiful light of this hour. You will make me regret having disturbed you."

"No, I insist upon my order," he replied. "Take it, if you like, as confirmation of that for which I am chided by others: that my will is like black granite from the valley of Rehenu. I cannot alter that and am too old to mend my ways. But how could I ever receive in darkness and dusk my dearest and true wife, who visits me and guesses at the most secret wish of my heart. Is it not a cause for celebration that you have come, and does one celebrate in darkness? All four!" he said to the two servants bearing torches, who made haste to light the five-lamped candelabra standing on pedestals in the corners of the hall. "Let them burn high, do you hear."

"Be it according to your will," she said as if in admiration and shrugged obediently. "Truly, I know the steadfastness of your resolve and will leave any chiding of it to such men as take offense at it. Women cannot but treasure inflexibility in a man. Shall I tell you why?"

"I would gladly hear it."

"First, because it lends value to any indulgence shown, making of it a gift that we can be proud to receive."

"How charming," he said and blinked, partly because of the brightness that now filled the hall—for the wicks of twenty lamps floated in a waxy oil that made them burn with a bright, dazzling flame, so that the hall was cradled in the milk of their white light and the blood of red dusk—and partly from pondering the intention of her words. She definitely has some petition in mind, he thought, and no minor matter, for otherwise she would not prepare the way for it like this. It is quite contrary to her customary manner, for she knows how important it is that I, as a special and a holy man, am left in peace and do not have to concern myself with other things. She is usually far too proud to demand anything of me, and thus her hauteur and my comfort unite in marital concord. All the same, it would surely be good and uplifting to do her a favor by which I can demonstrate my power. I am anxiously eager to hear what she wants. It would be best if it were merely to seem great to her, but be nothing to me, so that she might be delighted at no serious expense to my own comfort. There is, I see, a certain contradiction in my breast: between my own justifiable selfishness, which arises from my special and holy nature, so that I find it particularly unwelcome when someone comes too close to me or simply disrupts my peace, and, on the other hand, my desire to prove both loving and powerful to this woman. She is beautiful in her heavy garments, which she wears in my presence for the same reason that I ordered the hall made light— beautiful with those eyes like gemstones and those shadowy cheeks. I love her, to the extent my justifiable selfishness permits; but here is where the real contradiction lies, for I hate her as well, hate her continually somewhat because of the demand that she, of course, does not make of me but that is generally contained within a relationship such as ours. Yet I do not gladly hate her, but would like to be able to love her without hate. If she will now but give me a good opportunity to prove myself loving and powerful, then for once the hate would be removed from my love, and I would be happy. Which is why I am very curious to know what it is she wants, though at the same time anxious about my own comfort.

These, then, were Peteprê's thoughts as he blinked, watching his slaves set the lamps ablaze and then hastily and silently retreat, still holding the torches in their crossed arms.

"You will allow me, then, to sit beside you?" he heard Eni ask with a little laugh, and, roused from his thoughts, he bent down yet again to set the cushion aright while assuring her of the pleasure it would give him. She sat down on the inscribed step at his feet.

"In truth," she said, "it all too rarely happens that one may celebrate such an hour, each offering the other her or his presence simply as a gift, without point or purpose, and 'making tongues' about this, that, or whatever, with no object in mind—for necessity governs an object and the words centering around it, but speech with no object is cheerfully superfluous. Don't you agree?"

He spread his massive feminine arms out across the back of the gallery bench and nodded agreement. But what he thought was: Rarely happens? It never happens, for we members of a noble and holy family, parents and married children alike, live in our separate quarters of the house and avoid one another out of tender consideration, except when we break bread together; and if it is happening today, there must surely be an object and a necessity behind it, about which I remain expectantly and uneasily curious. Might I be mistaken? Might the woman have come just so that we might share our presence with one another, might her heart simply have felt a longing for this hour? I do not know what I should wish for, for indeed I do wish she might have some petition in mind that does not encroach all too greatly on my comfort. But that she might have come simply for the sake of my presence—I almost wish that even more.

But thinking this, he said, "I heartily concur. It is the poor and lowly for whom speech must serve as a means of some meager understanding about necessities. Whereas for us, the rich and noble, our portion is what is beautiful and superfluous, both in general and in the words of our mouth, for beauty and superfluity are one. It is indeed a wonder how words can occasionally ascend, in both dignity and meaning, from their typical dullness to the proud essence of their nature. Does not the pronouncement 'superfluous' imply a shrug, a chastisement, a dull disparagement? But then that word stands up and sets its royal crown upon its head and is no longer a pronouncement, but beauty itself, both in essence and in name, and it is called 'superfluity.' When sitting alone, I often ponder the secrets of words, entertaining my mind in such beautiful and unnecessary fashion."

"I know to thank my lord for allowing me to share in it," she replied. "Your mind is as bright as the lamps that you have ordered set ablaze for our meeting. Were you not Pharaoh's chamberlain, you might also easily be one of the divine scholars who dwell in the courts of temples and pursue words of wisdom."

"Quite possibly," he said. "A man might be many things other than what he has been charged to be or to represent. He is often rather amazed at the farcical role this very charge requires he play, and the mask of life feels tight and hot to him, the way a priest may feel stifled beneath a god's mask at a festival. Do you understand what I'm saying?"

"Quite possibly."

"But perhaps not entirely," he conjectured. "Perhaps you women lack some understanding of these strictures for the simple reason that, through the kindness of the Great Mother, you have been granted a more general dispensation and may be more a woman in the likeness of the Mother and less this or that particular woman, so that you may be not so much Mut-em-enet as I am required by a stricter paternal spirit to be Peteprê. Do you agree with me?"

"The hall is exceedingly bright," she said with lowered head, "from flames that burn at your manly behest. Such thoughts, it seems to me, would be easier to follow were there less light; twilight, I think, would make it easier for me to immerse myself in a wisdom that says I may be more woman, more the likeness of the Mother, than simply Mut-em-enet."

"Forgive me," he hastened to reply. "It was inept of me not to have provided an elegant, idle conversation that knows neither purpose nor object and is better suited to the illumination. I will at once turn it toward what is more in accord with the light I have deemed appropriate for this happy hour. Nor could anything be easier. For I shall provide the bridge that leads us from speaking about matters of the mind and our inner nature to matters of the comprehensible world that light places within our grasp. I know very well how to arrive at that bridge. But first, just in passing, let me take pleasure in the pretty mystery by which the world of things we comprehend is the world we can grasp. For what one can grasp with the hand is easily comprehended by the minds of women, children, and commonfolk, while what cannot be grasped is comprehensible only to the stricter paternal mind. 'Grasp' is the mind's symbol and name for 'comprehend,' and yet the latter can also be represented by a symbol, for we like to say of some easily comprehended intellectual object that we grasp it, with both hands."

"Your observations and idle thoughts are most charming," she said, "and I cannot describe, my husband, how they enliven our marriage for me. You must not think I am in such haste to move from incomprehensible matters to tangible things. On the contrary, I would gladly abide with the former and listen to your superfluous

words, countering them within the limits of my womanly and childish mind. I meant nothing more than that one may converse more
profoundly about things of our inner nature by a less glaring light."

Annoyed now, he first said nothing.

"The mistress of this house," he then remarked with a scolding
shake of his head, "keeps returning to the same point, to a decision
made not entirely according to her will, but according to a stronger
one. That is less than lovely and is not made more lovely by its being
women's usual way not to move beyond such a point, but to have to
poke and prick at it again and again. Allow me to offer the reprimand that, in this regard at least, our Eni should attempt to be less a
woman in general and more the special woman Mut."

"I hear and repent," she muttered.

"And if we were to reproach one another for mutual decisions
and actions," he went on, giving still further vent to his annoyance,
"how easily might I prick at you, my dear friend, and note with regret your having appeared for this visit in a heavily pleated robe,
since it is your friend's wish and joy to be able to follow the contours
of your swanlike body beneath some more amiable fabric."

"How truly this pains me!" she said, lowering her head and
blushing. "I would rather die than to learn I have blundered in my
attire when visiting my lord, my friend. I swear to you that I believed this garment would best serve my beauty in your presence. It
is more costly and more exactingly sewn than most of my others.
Kheti, the seamstress slave, made it without closing her eyes for
sleep and together we shared the worry whether it would find favor
in your eyes; but sharing a worry does not make it half a worry."

"Let it be, my dear," he replied. "Let it be. I did not say that I
wished to chide and prick you, but rather that if you wished to do
so, I could reply in kind. But I do not assume you have any such intent. Let us rather move lightly on in our conversation with no object, as if no jarring note had ever crept into it through the fault of
one or the other of us. For I shall now build my bridge to matters of
the comprehensible world by noting what satisfaction it gives me
that the charge laid upon my life bears the stamp of pointless superfluity rather than of necessity. I said that what is superfluous is royal,
and so it is both in the courts of my home and in the palace of Merima't: that is, as ornament, as form with no object, as the elegant and
elaborate words with which one greets the god. That is the business

of the courtier, and to that extent one can say that the mask a courtier wears in life sits less tightly than the mask of a man who is not at court, but is stifled by so many objects—and that the courtier is closer to women, since he is allowed a more general dispensation. It is true that I am not among those counselors whose opinion Pharaoh solicits in regard to the boring of a well along the desert road to the sea, or the erection of a monument, or how many men are needed to secure a cargo of gold dust taken from the mines of wretched Kush, and it may be that at one time my self-satisfaction was wounded and I was vexed by the man Hor-em-heb, who commands the palace guards and administers the affairs assigned to the Chief High Executioner—and as good as without even asking me, though I bear the titles of these offices. But each time I have quickly overcome the temptation of that baser mood. After all, I am as different from Hor-em-heb as the honorary fan-bearer is from that necessary, but lowly man who actually carries Pharaoh's fan when he drives forth from the palace. That sort of thing is beneath me. But it is my task to stand before Pharaoh at his morning levee and, along with other bearers of titles and high dignitaries of the court, to recite in my finest voice the hymn of greeting to His Divine Majesty, which begins 'You who are as unto Rê,' and to give myself over to purely elaborate embellishments such as 'Your tongue is a balance scale, O Neb-me-Rê, and your lips are truer than the tongue on the scales of Thoth,' or to assure him of some truth beyond truth such as 'If you say unto the waters, "Come, rise up the mountain!" the ocean rises the moment you have spoken'—in just that beautiful fashion, which knows no object and is removed from all necessity. For my concern is pure formality and ornament without purpose, for that is what makes royalty royal. This much, then, in regard to my self-satisfaction."

"How splendidly apt," she replied, "though at the same time it serves in regard to truth as well, as is doubtless the case with all your words, my husband. Except it appears to me that, for the sake of our country's vital concerns, such courtly ornamentation and elaborate speech at morning levees serve to clothe the god's objective cares—wells and edifices and dealings in gold—in a garment of honor and awe, but that provisions made in their regard is what is truly royal about royalty."

In response to these words Peteprê shut his lips tight, refraining from any answer for a while as he played with the embroidered drawstring on his skirt.

"I would be lying," he finally said with a gentle sigh, "were I to claim, my dear, that your rejoinder to my idle conversation reveals a matchless dexterity. For, not without some skill, I have built the bridge to worldly, tangible matters by shifting the topic to Pharaoh and his court. But instead of catching the ball and asking me who it was that Pharaoh, as he was exiting the Hall of the Canopy after his morning levee today, chose to tug by the earlobe as causal proof of his favor, you wander off into tiresome matters and make observations about desert wells and mines, about which, just between us, my dear friend, you of necessity know even less than I myself."

"You are right," she replied and shook her head at her mistake. "Forgive me. My curiosity to hear whose ear Pharaoh tugged was simply too great. So I concealed it beneath inapt remarks. Please understand me rightly: I thought to delay my inquiry, for delay seems to me a lovely and essential part of any ornamental conversation. Who would blurt something out at once, thus betraying what most concerns him? But since you have now opened the way for the question: Was it not you yourself, my husband, whom the god touched as he departed?"

"No," Peteprê said, "it was not I. I have often before been the one, though not today. But what you uttered sounded—I can't say quite how . . . sounded as if you are inclined to believe that Hor-em-heb, the acting troop commander, is greater than I both at court and in the Two Lands . . ."

"In the name of the Hidden One, my spouse and friend!" she said in alarm, laying her hand on his knee, where he regarded it and its rings as if a bird had suddenly alighted there. "My mind would have to be clouded and all my senses muddled, without hope of improvement, if for even a moment I were to . . ."

"But it came out sounding that way," he repeated with a regretful shrug, "even if, as seems likely, contrary to your intention. It would be more or less as if you were to suggest—what example shall I give you? As if you were to suggest a baker in Pharaoh's royal bakery, who actually bakes bread for the god and his house and sticks his head into the oven, were greater than the Grand Overseer of the Royal Bakery, Pharaoh's chief baker, whose title is Prince of Menfe.

Or it would be as if you were to suggest that I, who of course concern myself with nothing, were of less importance in this house than Mont-kaw, my steward or, rather, than his youthful 'mouth,' Osarsiph the Syrian, who oversees its business. These are striking comparisons . . ."

Mut winced.

"Indeed their blows strike me and leave me quivering," she said. "But having seen as much, you in your benevolence will let that be my punishment. I now realize what great confusion my penchant for delay has brought to our conversation. But allay the curiosity that I hoped to conceal, stanch it as one might stanch the flow of blood, and tell me who received that caress in the throne room today."

"It was Nofer-rohu, the Overseer of Salves in the king's storeroom," he answered.

"So that was the prince!" she exclaimed. "Did everyone gather round him?"

"As is the custom at court, people gathered round to congratulate him," he replied. "He is very much in the vanguard of Pharaoh's attention at the moment, and it might well be important if he were seen at the banquet we plan to give at the next quarter moon. It might well be of decisive significance, adding luster to both the meal and my house."

"Without doubt," she confirmed. "You must have a very beautiful invitation written, one that he will truly enjoy reading because of the salutations with which you must address him, something like 'Beloved of his lord,' and 'To him whom his lord has rewarded and consecrated.' And you must select servants to bring it to his home, together with a gift. It is highly unlikely that Nofer-rohu would then refuse you."

"I believe that as well," Peteprê said. "And of course the gift must be carefully selected. I shall have all sorts of things brought to me that I may inspect them, and this very evening I shall have a letter readied with salutations that he will truly enjoy reading. You must know, my child," he went on, "that I wish this banquet to be one of extraordinary beauty, so that it is the talk of the city and its fame reaches other, far more distant cities as well—a banquet with some seventy guests, replete with slaves, flowers, musicians, fine food, and

wine. I have purchased a very pretty cautionary mummy to be carried around the room this time, a fine piece, one and a half ells
long—I shall show it to you if you would like to see it beforehand.
The coffin is gold, but the body is of ebony, with 'Seize the day!'
written across its forehead. Have you heard about the Babylonian
dancers?"

"What dancers are those, my consort?"

"A traveling troupe of these foreigners who are in the city. I have
had them plied with gifts so that they will make an appearance at my
festive banquet. I've been told that these women are of exotic beauty
and accompany their dancing with handbells and little clay hand
drums. They are said to be proficient in new and impressive poses
and that there is a kind of fury in their eyes as they dance and
demonstrate affection. I have great hopes that they will be a sensation and a success at our festive gathering."

Eni appeared to be thinking; she did not raise her eyes.

"Do you also intend," she asked after a period of silence, "to invite Beknechons, Amun's first priest, to your banquet?"

"Unquestionably, absolutely," he replied. "Beknechons? It goes
without saying. Why do you ask?"

"You regard his presence as important, it seems?"

"How could it not be? Beknechons is a great man."

"More important than these young women from Babel?"

"What sort of comparisons and choices are these, my dear?"

"The two are not reconcilable, my husband. I am merely calling
to your attention that you will have to make a choice. Should you
allow these young women from Babel to dance at your banquet before Amun's highest priest, it could well be that the exotic fury in
their eyes would not equal that in Beknechons' heart, that he would
rise up and call his servants and leave the house."

"Impossible!"

"More than probable, my friend. He will not permit the Hidden
One to be insulted before his eyes."

"By women dancing?"

"By foreign women dancing—seeing as Egypt has its own abundance of charms, which it sends to foreign nations."

"Then all the more should it enjoy the fascination of something
new and rare."

"That is not the opinion of strict Beknechons. His aversion to all things foreign is unswerving."

"But it is your opinion, I would hope."

"My opinion is that of my lord and friend," she said, "for how can it be contrary to the honor of our gods?"

"The honor of the gods, the honor of the gods," he repeated, shifting and jerking back his shoulders. "I must admit that your words have begun to darken the mood of my soul, although this cannot be the point and purpose of an ornamental 'making of tongues.'"

"I could only despair," she replied, "if such were the effect of my concerns on your soul. For what would its mood then be if Beknechons were to call his servants in anger and leave your banquet, so that his rebuke would be the talk of the Two Lands."

"He would not be so petty as to take affront at some elegant amusement, nor so bold as to rebuke the friend of Pharaoh."

"He is great enough that for petty causes his thoughts can move on to great things, and he would be more likely to rebuke Pharaoh's friend than Pharaoh himself—that is, as a warning to the latter. Amun hates the freethinking that comes with things foreign, for it shatters all bonds and disdains the national order based on ancient piety, enervating the Two Lands and robbing the kingdom of its scepter. That is Amun's hatred, as we both know, and it is the expression of his will that the nation should steel its nerves for a strict observance that will rule the land of Keme as in days of yore, so that its children may walk in patriotic paths. But you know as well as I that over there"—and Mut-em-enet pointed toward the sunset, in the direction of the Nile and its far bank, where the palace stood— "that over there a different doctrine of the sun reigns and that its freethinking is beloved by Pharaoh's sages—the doctrine of On at the apex of the triangle, Atum-Rê's pliant doctrine, whose tendency is to expand and incorporate and that goes by the name of Atôn, calling up I know not what other enervating associations. Should not Beknechons be angry for Amun, whose son upon earth aids and abets freethinking and allows his inquisitive sages to flirt with things foreign and thus weaken the marrow of the nation's people? He cannot chide Pharaoh. But he will chide him through you and demonstrate Amun's power by turning as angry as a leopard of Upper

Egypt at the sight of these Babylonian women, and he will jump up and call his servants."

"You speak, my dear," he responded, "like a chattering bird from the land of Punt, whose loosened tongue cackles back what it has often heard of matters beyond its own ken. The people's marrow and patriotic custom and foreign freethinking—that is Beknechons' disagreeable list of words that you recite here, much to the noticeable darkening of my soul's mood, for by your coming you opened to me the prospect of an intimate chat with you, not with him."

"I am reminding you," she replied, "of his thoughts, which you know well, in order that I may protect your soul, my husband, from grave unpleasantness. I do not say that Beknechons' thoughts are my thoughts."

"But they are," he retorted. "I hear him when you speak, and it is not true that in telling me his thoughts you speak of something strange in which you do not share, for you have made them your own and are of one mind with that bald-headed priest against me— that is what I find offensive in your conduct. Do I not know that he comes and goes in your rooms, visiting you every quarter moon at least? This occurs much to my silent vexation, for he is not my friend, and I cannot endure him and his obstinate list of words. My nature demands a mild, refined, and tolerant doctrine of the sun, which is why my heart belongs to Atum-Rê, the obliging god, but above all because I belong to Pharaoh and am his courtier, for he allows his sages to inquire and think about this glorious god's gentle and all-seeing doctrine of the sun. You, however, my consort and my sister before the gods and men, how do you conduct yourself in these circumstances? Instead of siding with me, that is with Pharaoh and his court's way of thinking, you side with Amun, the immovable, brazen-browed god, take up with his party against me, and wrap yourself in a blanket of schemes with that disobliging god's highest bald-headed priest, without giving so much as a thought to how particularly offensive it is to slight me by showing such disloyalty."

"You make comparisons, my lord," she said in a thin voice pinched with anger, "lacking in taste—which is surprising, given what you read. For it is without taste or in very bad taste to say that the prophet and I wrap ourselves in a blanket of schemes to show disloyalty to you. That is a lame comparison, I must say, and uncommonly distorted. According to both the doctrine of our fathers and the people's ancient piety, Pharaoh is Amun's son, and therefore it would in no way infringe upon your duties as a courtier if you would accommodate Amun's sacred doctrine of the sun, even if you find it obstinate, and offer him the small sacrifice of your and your guests' curiosity about some dance of disreputable impressiveness. That much is asked of you. I, however, am Amun's, fully and completely and with all my honor and piety, for I am a bride of his temple and of his house of women. I am Hathor and dance before him in the garments of the goddess, that alone is my honor and my desire, and I have no other, my life is dedicated solely to this honorable state. You, however, quarrel with me because I am faithful to my lord, my god, my heavenly spouse, and speak against me in comparisons so distorted that they are shameful." And she took hold of her pleated robe and, bowing low, covered her face with it.

The Captain of the Guard was now more than painfully embarrassed. He shuddered and his body turned cold, for innermost things, things never mentioned out of tact, now threatened to be put into dreadful, life-destroying words. With his arms still outstretched along the edge of the bench, he leaned rigidly even farther away from the weeping woman, staring at her in dismay and guilty confusion. What is happening? he thought. This is bizarre and unprecedented, and my peace is greatly imperiled. I have gone too far. I advanced the cause of my justifiable selfishness, but she has banished it with her own—and not just from our conversation, but from my heart as well, which is overthrown by her words and in which pity and care are mixed with my terror of her tears. Yes, I do love these tears—for, terrible as they are, they allow me to feel, and I want my words to make her feel something as well.

And removing his arms from the ledge and bending down over her—though, of course, without touching her—he now said, not without pain, "As is clear from your own words, dearest flower, you surely see that you have not spoken to me to warn me against the obstinate thoughts of Beknechon the prophet without sharing in them, but in fact these are your words as well. Your heart has joined his in party against me, for candidly and to my face you have announced: 'I am Amun's, fully and completely.' Was my comparison then so false, and can I help it that I, your husband, find the taste bitter?"

She pulled her robe from her face and looked at him.

"Are you jealous of god, of the Hidden One?" she asked, making a wry face. The gemstones of her eyes, where scorn was mixed with tears, were very close to his, staring into them fiercely, so that he took fright and quickly sat up straight. I must pull back, he thought. I have gone too far and must retreat one or two steps for the sake of my own peace and the peace of my house, which all unexpected appear to be in horrible danger. How could it happen that I should suddenly find my peace threatened and that all at once I behold such terrors in this woman's eyes? Everything seemed fine and assured of remaining so. And he recalled the many occasions when, upon returning home from court or from a journey, his first question in response to his steward's greetings had always been "Is everything in order? Is the mistress of good cheer?" For at the bottom of his heart there had always been a secret worry about the peace, dignity, and security of his house, a dim awareness that it stood on weak, imperiled foundations, and in gazing into Eni's fierce, weeping eyes, he understood that such forebodings had always been present and that, to his horror, his silent fears were now somehow in danger of being realized.

"No," he said, "far from it, for what you said in your question—that I might be jealous of the lord Amun—I dismiss out of hand. I know quite well the difference between what you owe to Him Who Is Hidden and to him who is your husband. And since it is my impression that the imagery of the phrase I used to describe your confidential dealings with Beknechons has displeased you to some extent, and since I am always ready and eager to find any occasion for giving you cause for joy, I shall do so by retracting my comparison of being wrapped in a blanket and declare it never to have been said, erasing it from the tablet of my words. Are you content?"

The tears still stood in Mut's eyes, and as if unaware of them, she let them dry there on their own. Her husband had expected a show of gratitude for his retraction, but she offered him none.

"That is the least of it," she said, shaking her head.

She sees me diminished and fearful for the peace of my house, he thought, and yet, in typical female fashion, does her best to use it to her own advantage. She is more a woman in general than she is one special woman and my own, and it is not surprising, though somewhat distressing, to see what is general and commonplace in women artlessly, yet cunningly revealed in one's own wife. What a sorry, almost absurd thing it is, how annoyingly it chafes the mind, to observe and register quite by accident how someone believes herself to be thinking and acting cunningly on her own, without her noticing that it is merely a shameful repetition of a general pattern. But what good does that do me now? Something to think, but not to say. What I have to say, as it were, is the following:

"The least of all else, surely not," he replied, moving on, "but nonetheless the least of what I wished to say. For I had no intention of leaving it at that, but hoped to increase your pleasure still further by revealing how, in the course of our conversation, I have retreated from my idea of employing the dancers from Babel at my banquet. It is not my wish to offend the judgments, which may be regarded as prejudices, of a man of high position so close to you—that is, unless one can eliminate them entirely. My banquet will shine brilliantly without those foreign travelers."

"That, too, is the least of it, Peteprê," she said, calling him by name, which compelled his attention by unsettling him anew.

"What do you mean?" he asked. "That is still the least of it? The least of what?"

"Of what one might wish. Of what one might demand," she answered after heaving a great sigh. "There should be, there must be changes made here in this house, my consort, so that it is not a house of offense to the pious, but a house of example. You are the master of these halls, and who does not bow before your rule? Who would begrudge your soul the gentle refinement of an obliging doctrine of the sun by which you may live and in which your habits of life are sustained? I certainly understand that one cannot desire this great realm and steel-nerved antiquity both at once, for over time the former came from the latter, and one lives differently amid the riches of this realm than in a national order based on ancient piety. You ought not to say that I am no judge of the times and of life's changes. But everything has and must have its limits, and a remnant of that sacred patriarchal discipline that created this realm and its riches must remain forever honored within it, so that it may not be shamefully corrupted and the scepter wrested from the Two Lands. Do you deny this truth, or do Pharaoh's sages deny it in thinking and inquiring after Atum-Rê's pliant doctrine of the sun?"

"One cannot deny the truth," the fan-bearer replied. "And it may be that truth is more precious even than the scepter. You speak of destiny. We are children of our time, and I believe it is far better and more proper for us to live according to the truth out of which we were born, than to attempt to act according to time immemorial and play at being steel-nerved paragons of antiquity by denying our own souls. Pharaoh has many mercenary troops—Asians, Libyans, Nubians, and even Egyptians. Let them guard the scepter as long as fate allows. We, however, shall live sincere lives."

"Sincerity," she said, "is easy, but not noble. What would become of us, if everyone would simply be sincere and claim for his natural desires the merit of truth, refusing entirely to better or curb himself? The thief is sincere as well; so, too, is the drunkard rolling in the gutter, or the adulterer. But would we overlook their deeds were each to lay claim to his own truth? You desire to live a truthful life, my husband, as a child of your time and not according to antiquity. But savage antiquity is found where each man lives according to the truth of his instinct, while a more advanced age demands he place limits upon himself for higher, more pressing reasons."

"And in what way do you demand that I better myself?" he anxiously asked.

"In no way whatever, my consort. You are unchangeable, and I would not think of unsettling the holy and static steadfastness that is in you. Far be it from me as well to chide you for having no concern for this house or estate or for anything in the world except what you eat and drink—for even were that not your nature, it would be in accordance with your rank. The hands of your servants do for you what is yours to do, even as they will do it in your grave. Your sole interest is to order your servants to do it—and not even that, but to order him who is your deputy to order your servants, so that this house may be governed according to your wishes, the house of a great man of Egypt. That is your sole obligation, a matter of the most elegant effortlessness, but of utmost importance. That you not fall short in it, that your finger not point in the wrong direction—that is what matters."

"For more rounds of the year than I care to count," he said, "Mont-kaw has been the steward of my house, an honest man, who loves me as he ought and is filled with a sense of how awful it would be to offend me. From what I can tell from his accounts, he has hardly ever deceived me in any serious manner and has managed the house in a fine style acceptable to me. Has he had the misfortune of incurring your dissatisfaction?"

She smiled disparagingly at this evasion.

"You know," she replied, "as well as I and all of Wase that Mont-kaw is wasting away with wormy kidneys and for some time now concerns himself with these matters no more than you. In his place another man now governs, who is called his mouth and whose ascendancy to such a rank one would never have thought possible. And as if that were not enough, it is also said that upon Mont-kaw's anticipated demise, this so-called mouth will assume his position in full, for good and all, and that everything that is yours will be given into his hands. You praise your steward's faithful regard for your dignity. Permit me to confess that I search in vain for such regard in his actions."

"You are thinking of Osarsiph?"

She bowed her head.

"It is a peculiar way of putting it," she said, "to say that I think of him. If only the Hidden One would grant that he not exist, so that one could not think of him, instead of being shamefully compelled to do so because of your steward's culpability. For that ailing man purchased the youth you have named from traveling peddlers, but instead of keeping him as befits his lowly station and miserable race, he drew him near to him and allowed him to run rampant in the house, placing all the servants under him, yours and mine alike, with the result that you, my lord, speak of this slave with a familiarity that I find disgraceful and that arouses outrage in my heart. For if you had considered and said, 'I believe you mean the Syrian, from the wretched land of Retenu, that Ebrew slave,' that would have been natural and to the point. But by your turn of phrase you reveal how far things have gone, for you speak of him as if he were your cousin, intimately calling him by name and asking me 'Are you thinking of Osarsiph?'"

There, she had spoken his name as well and was secretly overjoyed by the self-control with which she spoke it and that she had worked so hard to school. In uttering those mystic syllables, resonating with death and deification and containing for her all the sweetness of fate itself, she gave a little sob in which she tried to express her outrage and now pulled her garment over her eyes as before.

And once again Potiphar took genuine fright.

"What is it, what is it, my good wife?" he said, spreading his hands above her. "More tears? Let me know their cause. I called the servant by the name he calls himself, the name that everyone calls him. Is not a name the quickest way of coming to agreement about someone? I see that I was correct in my assumption. You have in mind the Kenanite lad who serves as my cup-bearer and reader—and indeed, I do not deny it, much to my satisfaction. Should that not be reason enough for you to think kindly of him? I had nothing to do with his purchase. Mont-kaw, who has full authority to acquire and dismiss servants, bought him years ago from reputable traders. But then it happened that I examined him in conversation as he was riding date blossoms in my orchard, and I found him to be an extraordinarily pleasant young man, whom the gods have endowed with genial gifts of both body and mind, indeed, entwining them in most remarkable fashion. For his beauty appears to be the natural embodiment of the grace of his mind, which, in turn, seems to be a different, invisible expression of his visible self—and I would hope you see that in my word 'remarkable' I have passed a fitting judgment. Nor are his origins such as to make him just anybody—for one might, if one cared to, call his birth virginal—and it is certain at any rate that his sire was a sort of king of flocks and a prince of god and that the boy lived in fine estate, showered with gifts and growing up among his father's herds. To be sure, woe of all sorts later became his daily bread, and there were people who successfully laid snares in his path. But the story of his suffering is likewise remarkable—it has both spirit and sense or, as people say, rhyme and reason, and it is governed by a kind of intertwining very similar to whatever it is that makes his favorable appearance and his mind seem one and the same. For, to be sure, the story has its own reality, but in addition it also appears to be related to some higher preordained order with which it stands in accord, so that it is difficult to separate one from the other, since each mirrors the other—with the result that, taken all in all, there is a charming ambiguity about the lad. Since others noticed that he did not do badly in my examination of him, he was made cup-bearer and reader, not at my behest, but, as is quite understandable, out of love for me, and I admit that he has become indispensable in these matters. And, again not at my behest, he has grown and gained oversight of the various businesses of the estate, literal proof that the Hidden One works through him, lending good fortune to all he undertakes—I can put it no other way. But since he has become indispensable to me and my house, what is it that you would have me do with him?"

And indeed what else could she have wanted or done now that he had spoken? He looked about him, smiling in satisfaction at what he had said. He had secured his position well and taken such precautions that her impending demand could only be declared monstrous, a violation of the love shown him—and that was surely unthinkable. He did not guess, however, that the woman had paid almost no attention to his words as a bulwark and bastion, but instead had secretly sipped them like honeyed wine or that, in her profoundly eager intensity as she huddled there beneath her garment, she had not let a single word of what he had said in praise of Joseph slip past her. This diminished greatly the intended cautionary effect of his words and, oddly enough, did not prevent Mut from faithfully and honestly holding to the reasonable, moral purpose for which she had come.

She sat up straight and said, "I assume, my consort, that you have presented the very best that, with any justice, can be said of this servant. All the same, it is not sufficient, it is futile before the gods of Egypt, and what you have had the goodness to tell me about your slave, about that intertwining within his person and his charming ambiguities, can prevail against neither what is desirable nor the demand that Amun unambiguously wishes to make through my mouth. For I, too, am a mouth, and not just that fellow whom you call indispensable to you and your house—patently without due thought. For how can some casually acquired alien be indispensable in the land of human beings and in Peteprê's house, which was a house of blessing before this peddler's wares began to rise up within it? For his rise should never have been permitted. If the boy was purchased, then he belonged in the fields, to drudge there, instead of being kept in the house and, worse, entrusted with both your cup and your ear in the hall of books—all because of his captivating gifts. Gifts are not the man; one must differentiate between the two. All the worse then, if an inferior has gifts that may ultimately allow his natural inferiority to be forgotten. What gifts can justify the ascendancy of an inferior? That is what Mont-kaw, your steward, should have asked himself before allowing an inferior—not at your behest, as I now learn—to grow like a weed in your house, to the great grief of the pious. Will you allow Mont-kaw to defy the gods even in death and to point his finger at this Habiru as his successor, disgracing this house before all the world and humiliating your native menials beneath the hand of an inferior, leaving them to gnash their teeth?"

"My good wife," the chamberlain said, "how mistaken you are! To judge by your own words, I would say you have not been well instructed, for there can be no talk of gnashing of teeth. My household servants—from highest to lowest, from the scribe of the sideboard to the kennel boy and the lowliest of your handmaids—all love Osarsiph and are not in the least ashamed to obey him. I do not know how you came by your information that there is gnashing of teeth in my house because of his high rank, but you have been falsely informed. On the contrary, they all search out his eyes and are happy to vie among themselves in performing their tasks as he moves among them, and they affably hang on his words when he gives them orders. Yes, even those who had to step aside from their posts to make way for him, even they do not look askance at him, but gaze straight and full into his eyes, for his gifts are irresistible. And why is that? Because they are not at all as you have described them, proving that you have been poorly instructed as to this matter in particular. For it is most certainly not the case that his gifts form some confusing appendage to his person that may be separated from him. Rather they and he are one and inseparable. They are the gifts of a man of blessing, so that one might say he has merited them, if that did not yet again imply an inadmissible division between person and gifts and that one can even speak of merit when dealing with natural gifts. And so it happens that both upon highways and waterways people recognize him from afar, nudge one another, and remark joyfully: 'There comes Osarsiph, Peteprê's personal servant and Mont-kaw's mouth, an excellent young man, who is under way on his master's business, which he will bring to a favorable conclusion, as is his wont.' Moreover, if men's eyes gaze straight and full into his, women cast him sidelong glances from the corners of theirs, which I take to be an equally good sign. And I am told that when he appears in the narrow streets and bazaars of the city, it frequently happens that young women climb atop walls and roofs and toss golden rings from their fingers at him to catch his eye. But his eye is never caught."

Eni listened with indescribable fascination. There are no words for how this glorification of Joseph, the description of his popularity, intoxicated her—joy coursed through her veins over and over again like a river of fire, causing her bosom to rise, her breath to come in short, urgent thrusts much like sobs, her ears to turn red, and what great effort it cost her to ban joy's blissful smile from her lips as she listened to all this. The kindhearted observer can only shake his head at the absurdity of it. This praise of Joseph had to have confirmed the woman in her weakness—if one may use the term—for this foreign slave, had to have vindicated her weakness before her pride, to have sent her plunging deeper still, leaving her incapable of carrying out the purpose of her coming: to save her own life. And was that a cause for joy? Not for joy, but for bliss—a difference to which the kindhearted observer can only reconcile himself with more shakes of the head. And she suffered, too, as is only proper. The report of women casting sidelong glances and rings at Joseph filled her with all-consuming jealousy, reconfirmed her weakness, and at the same time imbued her with a desperate hatred of those who shared it. That these women had failed to catch the eye of their target comforted her somewhat and helped her to persevere in acting like a creature endowed with reason.

She said, "Allow me to overlook, my friend, the indelicacy of your conversing with me about the bad behavior of the young women of Wase, irrespective of the truth of such rumors, which may have been circulated simply by their vain hero himself, or by those whom he was won over with promises so that they now spread his flattering fame." It cost her less than one might think to speak in this way of the man with whom she was hopelessly in love by now. She did it quite mechanically, by giving voice, so to speak, to someone not herself, so that her singer's alto took on a hollow tone that matched the frozen features of her face, the vacancy of her stare, and was itself an acknowledgment of its own mendacity. "My chief point," she went on in this same way, "is that your reproach that I have been falsely instructed about the affairs of the house simply bounces off me and back to you, so that it were better you had not brought it. Your custom of taking no concern in anything, but of gazing upon it all with a distant and detached eye, should cause you some doubt as to your knowledge of what is going on around you. The truth is that the ascendancy of your slave has aroused fierce animosity and spread discontent among your staff. Dûdu, the overseer of your jewelry chests, has spoken to me more than once, indeed frequently, about the matter and complained bitterly of how offensive such unclean dominion is to the pious . . ."

"Well," Peteprê said with a laugh, "you certainly have chosen a stately witness in your cause, my dear flower, a most important fellow, if you'll forgive my saying so. This Dûdu is a runt, a wren, and a would-be giant. He is but a quarter of a man and a ludicrous miniature ninny. How in the world could his word carry weight in this or any other matter!"

"The size of his person," she replied, "is not at issue here. If he is so contemptible and his opinion so insignificant, how is it that you made him the guardian of your wardrobe?"

"That was more in jest," Peteprê said, "and one gives a household dwarf such a fine post merely for a laugh. His little brother, that other buffoon, is even called a vizier, which is surely not to be taken very seriously either."

"I need not call your attention to the difference," she retorted. "You know him well enough but simply do not wish to acknowledge him at the moment. It is rather sad that I must shield your most faithful and worthy servant from your ingratitude. Despite his somewhat diminished stature, Master Dûdu is a worthy, serious, and sterling man, who does not deserve the title of buffoon and whose word and opinion in matters regarding this household and his personal honor carry considerable weight."

"He comes up to here on me," the Captain of the Guard remarked, tracing the edge of his hand across his shin.

Mut was silent for a while.

Then she said with composure, "You must consider that you are especially tall and like a tower, my consort, so that to you Dûdu's stature may well appear smaller than it does to others, to Zeset, for instance, his wife and my servant, and to his children, who are likewise of conventional size and look up in awe to him who sired them."

"Look up? Ha!"

"I chose the word deliberately, in its higher, poetic sense."

"You even take recourse in poetry," Peteprê mocked, "when speaking of your Dûdu. I believe you complained of my choosing poor topics of conversation. I would call your attention to the fact that for some time now you have been conversing with me about a puffed-up fool."

"We can easily abandon the topic," she said obediently, "if you find it embarrassing. I do not need this man who found his way into our conversation as support for my request, which is justified thrice over in and of itself and which I must make of you, nor is there need of his honorable testimony for you to understand that you should grant it."

"You have a request to make of me?" he asked. So it's true after all, he thought, not without bitterness. She has indeed come to me with a more or less inconvenient petition. The hope that it might have been solely for the sake of my presence must be cast aside as erroneous. Given which, I am not all that well disposed to her petition even before she presents it.

He asked, "And what request is that?"

"It is this, my husband. That you should remove this foreign slave, whose name I shall not repeat, from house and estate, inasmuch as wrongful favor and culpable carelessness have allowed him to grow like a weed and make of this house a house of offense, rather than of example."

"Osarsiph? Banned from house and estate? The very idea!"

"It is a good and just idea, my consort. I am thinking of the honor of your house, of the gods of Egypt and of what you owe to them—and not just to them, but to yourself and me as well, your sister and wife, who is consecrated and set apart to wear the Mother's festive garb and strum the sistrum before Amun. I think of these things and have no doubt whatever that I need but remind you of them and your ideas will be as one with mine and you will promptly grant my request."

"To remove Osarsiph . . . My good woman, this cannot be, banish it from your mind as an absurd, totally whimsical request. I cannot allow the idea to join my other thoughts, for it is alien among them and they all rise up against it in greatest indignation."

So there we have it, he thought in furious dismay. So this is the petition for which she came to me at this hour, ostensibly merely for an ornamental "making of tongues." I saw it coming and yet for my part did not really see it until the last moment, for it is so contrary to my justifiable selfishness and, sad to say, far removed from anything that would appear great to her and yet be nothing to me; unfortunately it is just the opposite, for she apparently assumes it to be a small matter easily granted, but for me it is utterly discomforting. It was not for nothing that I felt anxious about my own comfort. But what a shame that she has given me no chance to delight her, for I do not hate her gladly.

"How truly lamentable, my little flower," he said, "is your prejudice against the person of this young man, that it allows you to make such an unsuitable request of me. Apparently all you know about him comes from a motley of curses and slanders told you by those who are disfigured, but not from any personal knowledge of his more favorable qualities, which, young as he is, could in my opinion make him suitable for a still higher position than as the overseer of my estate. Call him a barbarian and a slave—and you are right to do so according to the letter, but is that right enough if it is not also right according to the spirit? Is it the custom of our land, its genuine method, to judge a man by whether he is free or unfree, native or foreign, rather than by whether his mind is darkened and unschooled or illumined by the word and ennobled by its magic powers? Which, then, is practice and ancient usage in this regard in our country? This man's speech, however, is refined and serene, his words well chosen and spoken in a charming voice; he writes in an elegant hand and reads books to you as if he himself were speaking, on his own, impelled by his own mind, so that all the wit and wisdom seems to come from him, belong to him, and you are amazed. My wish is that you would become acquainted with his qualities, graciously associate with him, and win his friendship, which would be far more beneficial to you than that of this arrogant imp . . ."

"I do not wish to make his acquaintance or to associate with him," she said inflexibly. "I see that it was a mistake for me to think that you had finished praising your slave. You had other things to add. But now I await your word granting me my sacred and legitimate request."

"Such a word," he replied, "is not at my disposal inasmuch as your request is born of error. It misses the mark and cannot be granted for more than one reason—the only question is whether I can make that clear to you. And if I cannot, that will not, believe me, make it any more likely to be granted. I have already told you that Osarsiph is not just anybody. He has increased this house and is its invaluable servant—who could possibly bring himself to drive him from it? What foolish robbery of this house, what a crude injustice to him who is free of fault and a young man of refinement, so that to give him notice, to banish him willy-nilly from the estate would be a task of rare discomfort, to which no one would easily bring himself."

"You fear this slave?"

"I fear the gods who are with him, seeing as they allow everything he touches to succeed and make him agreeable to all the world—which gods those are is beyond my ken, but they make their power evident in him, that much is certain. You would swiftly rid yourself of ideas such as casting him into the pit of drudgery or disdainfully selling him to others if only you would cease to refuse to know him better. I am, you see, very certain that you would soon take an interest in him and that your heart would soften toward this young man, for there is more than one point of contact between your life and his, and if I love to have him about me, then, you may rely on it, I do so because he often reminds me of you . . ."

"Peteprê!"

"I say what I say, and what I think is most certainly not without meaning. Are you not consecrated and set aside for the god before whom you dance as one of his holy consorts and do you not proudly wear the sacrificial adornment of your consecration before all men? Well, this young man, as he himself has told me, likewise wears such a sacrificial adornment, as invisible as yours—one needs to imagine, it would seem, a kind of evergreen that is a symbol of consecrated and chosen youth, as is evident from its, I grant, somewhat peculiar name, for they call it the herb touch-me-not. This I heard from him, and not without amazement, for he told me of things new to me. I was, to be sure, aware of the gods of Asia—Attis and Ashirat and the Baals of fruitfulness. He and his family, however, are under a god whom I did not know and whose jealousy surprised me. For this lonely god craves faithfulness and has betrothed himself to them as their bridegroom by blood—which is strange enough. In principle they all wear this herb and are set apart for their god as a bride. But among them he chooses one in particular as his whole offering, that he especially should wear the adornment of consecrated youth and be set aside for this jealous god. And—what do you think—Osarsiph is such a person. He says they know of something they call sin and a garden of sin, and have also invented animals that peer from among the branches of this garden and that are ugly beyond all imagination—three in number, and their names are Shame, Guilt, and Mocking Laughter. But now I would ask you two questions: Can one wish for a better servant and steward than a man born to be faithful and bearing a fear of sin in his bones? And what is more: Did I say too much when I spoke of points of contact between you and this young lad?"

Ah, what terror filled Mut-em-enet at these words! The pain that consumed her to hear that young women tossed their rings to Joseph was nothing, was in fact a pleasure, in comparison with the cold sword that pierced her upon learning the reasons why the daughters of the city had been unable to catch his eye. She was overwhelmed with terrible fear, like a foreboding of what all she would have to suffer for his sake, and the pallor of anguish was clearly painted in her face as she looked up. One need only try to put oneself in her position—which, besides all else, did not lack its absurdity. What was the point of battling and struggling against Potiphar's stubbornness if he was speaking the truth? If the dream of healing that had opened her eyes and brought her here had been a lie? If the man from whom she was struggling to save her life and that of her master, the Captain of the Guard, was himself a whole offering—promised and set apart for a jealous god? In what entanglement had she feared she would entangle herself? She did not have the strength and felt incapable of even covering her eyes with her hand, which stared into the void where she thought she spied the three beasts of the garden: Shame, Guilt, and Mocking Laughter, the last yawping like a hyena. It was unbearable. Away, away with him, she thought, her mind racing—now more than ever, away with this man about whom my healing dreams speak a lie, dreams shameful beyond all shame, for it would be in vain, ah, all in vain, even to cast him the ring from my finger. Yes, I am right to do battle and must continue, now more than ever, if all this is so. But do I believe it, or do I not instead secretly hope with triumphant confidence that my longing for healing will prove stronger than his betrothal and will conquer it, that he will obey my glances, so that he may stanch the flow of blood? Do I not hope and fear this with a power that I ultimately believe irresistible? Well, then, it is clear, still clear as day, that for the sake of my own life he must be banished from my sight and from this house. There my stout-armed husband sits like a tower—Dûdu, the dwarf who sires children, comes up only to his shin. He is Captain of the Guard. It is from him and his protecting arm that I can expect healing and rescue, from him alone!

And as if fleeing for refuge to the man nearest at hand, she now tested the power of her longing for healing on her lethargic husband and began to speak again, replying in her ringing alto voice, "By your leave, I shall not respond to your words, my friend, and counter with arguments to refute them. That would be pointless. What you have told me does not apply to the object of our dispute, indeed, you needn't have told me any of it, but merely to have noted: 'I do not wish this.' All the rest is merely a cloak and a parable for your intractability, and the sole impression it leaves upon me is the iron determination of your resolve, your granite will. Should I then argue against your will with quarrelsome, unavailing words, when as a woman I can only love and tenderly admire it? But now I shall anticipate that which would be nothing without your will, but that becomes glorious and priceless through it—I await your yielding to me in forbearance. In this hour—which is unlike other hours, an hour shared by two and full of the expectation with which I have come to plead with you—your manly will surely will incline to me and satisfy my wish, saying: 'This offense is removed from this house and Osarsiph is expelled, cast out, and sold.' Do I hear it spoken, my lord and husband?"

"You have heard that you cannot hear me speak it, my good wife, despite my best goodwill to please you. I cannot cast Osarsiph out and sell him—that is beyond my ability to want it, the will to do so is not at my command."

"It is beyond your ability to want it? Is, then, your will your master, and not you the master of your will?"

"My child, you are splitting hairs. Can there be any difference between me and my will, so that the one is the master and the other the servant, the one lording it over the other? Try mastering your own will and willing what you find abhorrent and absolutely repulsive."

"I am prepared to do so," she said, tossing her head back, "when it concerns higher things—honor, pride, and the realm."

"None of which is at issue here," he replied, "or rather, what is at issue is the honor of sound reason, the pride of wisdom, and the realm of fairness."

"Think not of those, Peteprê!" she pleaded in a ringing voice. "Think of the hour, this most rare hour and of its expectation, when I have come to you outside of our arrangements and contrary to your comfort. Behold, I clasp my arms about your knee and beg you: Employ your power to satisfy my wish just this once, my husband, and let me depart comforted."

"Though it is pleasing to me to feel your arms, which are beautiful, about my knee," he replied, "I cannot possibly gratify you, and it is due to the gentleness of your arms that there is only gentleness in my rebuke for your having shown so little consideration for my peace and for apparently having no wish whatever to inquire further as to my own well-being. But though you do not inquire, I shall give you some particulars in that regard, between us two, in this rare hour. You should know then," he said in a somewhat mysterious way, "that I must keep Osarsiph not simply for the sake of the house and that he increases it for me or because the lad pleases me by reading the books of wise men as no other can. No, he is terribly important for my well-being for another reason. If I were to say that he instills in me a feeling of confidence, that would not exhaust it, for I mean something more indispensable. His mind is rich in beneficial invention of one sort and another; but above all he knows to speak to me, daily and hourly, about my own person, in words that reveal me to myself in a lovely light, a divine light, and that strengthen my heart when I regard my own person, making me feel . . ."

"Let me do battle with him," she said, clasping his knee all the tighter, "and drive him from the field before you, for it is only by turns of phrase that he knows to instill you with strength and a sense of self. I can do better. I shall give you the opportunity to strengthen your heart with deeds you have done, out of your own power, by fulfilling the expectation of this hour and giving this slave back to the desert. How greatly you will feel that you are yourself, my consort, when you have satisfied my wish and I depart from you comforted."

"Do you think so?" he asked, blinking. "Then hear me! I shall order that upon the demise of my steward Mont-kaw—and it is near—Osarsiph shall not oversee this house as his successor, but someone else, Kha'ma't for instance, the scribe of the sideboard. Osarsiph, however, may remain in the house."

She shook her head.

"That does not serve me, my friend, nor does it strengthen you and your sense of self. For only half or some small part of my wish would be assuaged and my expectation satisfied. Osarsiph must depart this house."

"Then," he quickly replied, "if that does not satisfy you, I retract my offer, and the lad shall be placed in charge of the house."

She loosened her arms.

"Is this your final word that I hear?"

"No other, sad to say, is mine to offer."

"Then I shall depart," she said in a soft, hoarse voice and stood up.

"That you surely must," he said. "It was, taken all in all, a charming hour. I shall send you a present to gladden you, an ointment bowl of elephant ivory, whose carvings depict fish, mice, and eyes."

She turned her back on him and walked toward the columned archway. She paused there for a moment, holding several pleats of her robe in her hand, which she braced against one of the fragile pillars, her brow pressed to her hand, her face hidden in the gathered robe. There was no one to behold Mut's face hidden behind its folds.

Then she clapped her hands and left the hall.

Three Exchanges

Having recorded this conversation, we have now come to a point in our story that we would like to connect with an earlier remark that provisionally anticipated how certain circumstances tumbled together here to form a strange constellation in the kaleidoscope of life. For we noted then that at the same time as Joseph's mistress was apparently making serious attempts to have Joseph removed from Potiphar's house—which until then had, after all, been the work of Dûdu, the wedded dwarf—the guardian of the wardrobe had begun to speak sweet words to Joseph and to play his devoted friend, not only in his presence, but also in that of their mistress, to whom he extolled and praised Osarsiph in every possible way. That is exactly how it was—we previously said not one word too many in this regard. But it came about because Dûdu had noticed how things stood with Mut-em-enet and understood the source of her endeavors to remove the lad Osarsiph from her sight. He discovered all this thanks to a certain sun-related potency that had been granted his dwarfish nature—a potency that, though surprising in such a man, he nevertheless honored and cultivated all the more zealously, so that he was indeed a cunning specialist and expert in the field, with a delicate nose for all occurrences in this sphere—however much this very same significant gift may have deprived him of dwarfish good sense and wisdom.

It did not take long before he realized what his patriotic complaints about Joseph's ascendancy had accomplished, or at least fostered, in his mistress—indeed he was startled to realize it significantly earlier than she herself; for at first he was aided by her own proud lack of insight, which as yet precluded her from taking any precautionary measures, and then later, when even her eyes were opened, by the universal inability of those who are seized with infatuation to conceal their condition. And so Dûdu recognized that his mistress was well on her way to falling—ineluctably, miserably, and with the full seriousness of her nature—in love with this foreigner, her husband's personal servant and reader, and he rubbed his hands at the prospect. For his part, he had not expected or foreseen it, but he realized that it could become a deeper pit for this vagabond than any he could have otherwise dug; and so from one day to the next Dûdu decided to play a role that has often been played since his day, but that he was hardly playing for the first time, coming as he does rather late in human history; and though we are poorly informed as to his predecessors, in applying himself to the role he presumably walked in well-worn tracks. As the wicked patron and postman of a ruinous mutual attraction, the dwarf began to move back and forth between Joseph and Mut-em-enet.

He deftly altered his way of speaking with her, matching it—at first out of conjecture and then out of certainty—with what he knew of her heart. For she summoned him to her in regard to the same matter about which he had first pressed his complaints upon her, and began all on her own to speak of this offense—which he at first took as a sign that he had won her over to his hatred and actively engaged her in its service. But he soon caught the scent of something else, for her mode of speech definitely sounded peculiar to him.

"Overseer," she said—that was, much to his joy, her title for him, although he was merely an assistant in charge of the wardrobe and jewel chests—"overseer, I sent a Nubian slave to inform one of the guards of the house of women to call you to me, for I have waited in vain for you to appear on your own that we might continue urgent deliberations in a matter of import—and I use that term since it is a matter of such significance to you that you have called it to my attention. I must remonstrate with you, though gently—out of consideration both for your services and your dwarfish state—for not having come for that purpose unprompted and of your own volition, but having let me wait in some torment; for waiting is a universal torment, though unbefitting a woman of my rank and thus all the more a torment. That this matter burns in my heart, the matter, that is, of this foreign lad, whose name I have been compelled to take note of, since he has become, so I hear, the steward of the house in place of Osiris Mont-kaw and to the blissful joy of all or to the most of you now walks in all his beauty through its workshops as lord of oversight—that this shame and disgrace burns in my heart should please you, dwarf, for you yourself have instilled it in me with your complaints and have awakened in me a sense of his offense, which I might perhaps have otherwise been spared but which now stands before my eyes day and night. You, however, after making it a matter of import to me, have not come to me on your own to speak to me about it as is surely necessary, but rather have left me alone in my affliction, so that I finally have had to send for you and command you to appear before me to discuss this tiresomely unresolved matter, for nothing is more painful than to be left to deal with such a matter on one's own. That is something that you, my friend, should know yourself, for what could you possibly hope to accomplish without your mistress as an ally against this despised servant, who has gained an advantage over you in every way, so that one could say that you, guardian of the wardrobe, are as good as powerless in your hatred of him, however much I may approve of it. Having ingratiated himself by his wit and magic, the man has ensconced himself in the unshakable favor of your master, who cannot endure you, and his gods allow everything to succeed in his hands. How do they manage it? I do not believe his gods to be so strong—particularly not here in the

Two Lands, where they are alien and are not held in honor—that they are able to accomplish what he has succeeded in accomplishing since first coming among us. The gifts that have assisted him must lie within him, for without them a man cannot grow and rise from the lowest of peddler's wares to become the next steward and overseer in all things; and it is clear that you, dwarf, cannot hold a candle to him either in matters of cleverness or in the favor shown him by others, for his acquired manners and comportment appear generally acceptable to all the world, however difficult that may be for you or me to understand. They all love him and search out his eyes, not merely the menials of the household, but also people upon highways and waterways and in the city—indeed I have been informed that upon his appearance there all sorts of women climb up to the roofs to gape at him and even cast him the rings from their fingers in token of their lust. This is truly the height of abomination, and for that reason I was impatient to speak with you, overseer, and hear your advice as to how to govern such shamelessness or, contrariwise, to let you hear my advice. For, since sleep had deserted me, I spent this past night considering whether one might not command archers to accompany him when he visits the city, that they might shoot arrows into the faces of these misbehaving women, directly into their faces—and came to the conclusion that one should definitely act accordingly and take those very measures; and now that you have finally arrived, I commission you to issue such a decree, upon my accountability, though without actually naming my name, but rather acting as if the idea had sprung from your own head, so that you may array yourself with it. At most you may tell Osarsiph, and him alone, that I, his mistress, wish these women to be shot in the face, and you may hear what he says in reply or how he responds to my measures; after which you are to come before me with what he has said, and I mean on your own and at once, without my having first to send an order for you to appear—not after I have been left all alone to endure the torment of waiting and the worry that comes with so weighty a matter. For it appears that the keeper of my wardrobe has been lax in this matter, while I exert myself in Amun's name. As you and His Excellency Beknechons desired, I have clasped the knee of my husband Peteprê, the Captain of the Guard, and contended with him half the night for an end to be put to this offense, much to the vexation of his comfort and very near to my own humiliation, but foundered on his granite will and departed uncomforted and alone. But for you, dwarf, I have had to send messenger upon messenger, that you might come and offer me some support, as for example, by giving me various reports about this shameful young man, this household weed, and his conduct—whether he gives himself airs in the worthy office he recently connived to obtain and what he has to say about his fellow servants and lords, about me, for example, his mistress, or whatever other remarks about me he might make in passing. If I am to thwart him and impede his rise, I must know him and what he thinks of me when he speaks. In your negligence, however, you leave me uninformed about this, instead of being industrious and adept, inducing him, for instance, to wait upon me and seek my favor, so that I may question him more exactly and ascertain what this magic is by which he deludes people and wins them to his side—for there is a mystery here, and the reason for his victories lies hidden from discovery. Or are you able, polisher of jewels, to see and say what others find in him? It was precisely in order to discuss this that I sent for you, a man of experience, and would have presented you these questions earlier had you come earlier, dwarf. Is he perhaps exceptional in stature and figure? Not at all; he is built on the same human scale as a great many other men are, not so small as you, of course, but then again not even close to being such a strapping figure as Peteprê, my consort. One might say his size is just right, but is that to say anything disconcerting? Or is he so strong that he could carry five bushels of seed corn or more from the granary, which would have to impress other men, not to mention enrapture the women? It is not that either, for his physical strength is quite average, or, once again, merely just right. And when he bends his arm, the manly show of muscle is not crude or pretentious, but is simply displayed in a tastefully moderate way that one could call human, but divine as well. . . . Ah, my friend, so it is. But his sort are to be found by the thousands in this world, and how little does that justify his victories. True, it is the head and countenance that lend a figure its meaning and worth, and one can in fairness concede that his eyes are beautiful in their darkness beneath those brows, beautiful both when they are opened wide to see and when, if he so desires, he narrows them in that way you doubtless know and that one might call cunningly veiled and dreamy. But what is there about his mouth, and how is one to understand its effect upon people, so that, as I have heard, they call him straight-out 'the mouth,' the house's chief mouth? There is no understanding it, and here is a riddle that ought to be fathomed, for his lips are really rather too fleshy and the smile they skillfully offer by way of adornment, revealing his sparkling teeth in between, explains but the least part of everyone's delusion, even when one includes the deft words that have their residence there. I am inclined to the view that the secret of his magic is primarily that of the mouth and that one would need to listen closely in order to be all the more certain of trapping the insolent fellow in his own net. If my servants do not betray me and leave me waiting in torment for their assistance, then I shall probably take it upon myself to catch him in his tricks and ruin him. But if he resists me, then you should know, dwarf, that I will command the archers to turn their weapons about and shoot their arrows into his damnable face, into the darkness of his eyes and into his mouth's ruinous bliss."

These then were the strange words of Dûdu's mistress, to which he listened with great dignity, the roof of his upper lip protruding over the lower and his cupped hand behind his ear in token of his attentiveness, which was in no way feigned; and his own experience in the field of engendering put him in a position to interpret her words. But upon perceiving what was in her heart, he also changed the words he spoke to her—not too abruptly, but gradually, slipping out of one tone into another, speaking differently about Joseph today than he had the day before, while appealing to yesterday's words as if they had been equally favorable (even when they had been, if already somewhat milder, still a great deal more pejorative), and above all striving to reverse everything he had said until now about the young steward into its opposite, to turn gall into honey. Any prudent person would have been disgusted by such crude fakery and have erupted in anger at the disregard for common sense it so blatantly revealed. But that same spirit of engendering taught Dûdu what all can be expected of people in Mut-em-enet's state, and he boldly expected as much of her—and by now her mind was far too bedazzled and stupefied by what was brewing within her for her to have wanted to take offense at such great impudence, indeed she was grateful to the dwarf for being so resourceful.

"Most noble lady," he said, "if your most humble servant did not appear before you yesterday to discuss current and unresolved matters with you—for, as you will at once recall upon my reminder,

I was present the day before yesterday and only the holy zeal with which you likewise pursue this matter enlarges the length of my absence—it was solely because the duties of my office made urgent claims upon me, though without their being able to distract my mind even temporarily from the matter that lies so close to your—and thus also to my—heart and that concerns Osarsiph, the new steward. My obligations as chief master of the wardrobe are—and for this you will not chide me—dear and precious to me, for I have grown fond of them, as happens with all duties and burdens that are such only at the start, but over time become more and more the object of the heart's affection. So, too, with this business, with the earnest prosecution of a matter that has frequently allowed your most humble servant to enjoy the benefit of consulting with you. And how could one not take to heart a concern so indispensable that it brings one, whether summoned or unsummoned, before you, my mistress, for daily or almost daily exchanges of questions and answers? And how could one not transfer one's gratitude for so great a pleasure to the object of that concern and take it to heart as well, if only because it has been raised up in becoming an object of your concern? That is one's only possible response, and happily your servant can recall that he has never thought of that object—that is, the person in question—as anything but worthy of your attention. It would be a painful injustice to suggest that Dûdu has allowed even one hour of highly rewarding service in the dressing chamber to prevent him from pondering and pursuing privately the matter in which his gracious lady has allowed him to participate. For one should do one thing, yet not neglect the other—that has always been my motto, whether regarding matters earthly or divine. Amun is a great god, he could not be greater. But should one therefore refuse honor and nourishment to the other gods of the nation, especially those who are so closely related to him as to be one with him and who have named him their name, such as Atum-Rê-Horakhte at On in Upper Egypt? The last time I was graciously allowed to speak before your ladyship, I attempted to express, though probably clumsily and without success, what a great, wise, and gentle god the latter is, distinguished by inventions such as the clock and time's handbook, without which we would be but animals. Beginning in my youth I have silently asked myself—and of late ask myself aloud—how Amun in his shrine could possibly hold it against us if we were to make a place in our hearts for the mild and magnanimous ideas of this majestic deity, with whose name he has joined his own. Is not His Excellency Beknechons the first prophet of one as well as the other? When at high feasts my mistress shakes the clear-sounding rattle before Amun as one of his consorts, she is no longer called Mut as on other days, but Hathor, who, with disk and horns, is the sister and wife of Atum-Rê, not of Amun. In consideration of which, your most faithful servant has never ceased to pursue this matter so close to his heart by approaching that young man, that blossoming sprout of Asia—who in rising to young steward among us has become the object of your concern—in order to fathom him correctly, so that I might speak of him to you more accurately and better than I succeeded in doing last time, despite my best efforts. All in all, I found him charming—within the limits that the natural order sets for approval by a man such as myself. The females upon the roofs and walls are a different matter, but I found that our young man would have little objection to their being shot at with arrows, and, given that fact, there appears little reason for those weapons to be turned about. For I heard him say something to the effect that only one woman has the right to gaze at him and look him in the eye, and all the while he stared at me very darkly from under his brows, his eyes large and shining at first, but then cunningly veiled in that interesting way of his. Though one might find in his remark some indication of the manner in which he regards you, it nonetheless did not suffice for me; and since I am accustomed to evaluating and judging people by their attitude toward you, I was able to turn the conversation to the charms of women in general and posed him the manly question as to whom he regarded as the most beautiful he knows. 'Mut-em-enet, our mistress,' he said, 'is the most beautiful both here and far and wide. For if one were to cross seven mountains, one would not find a woman more charming.' And as he said it, his countenance took on the redness of Atum, which I can only compare with that which colors your own at the moment, out of joy—or so I flatter myself—at the adept industry of your humble servant in this matter of the heart. And as if that were not enough, I anticipated your wish that the new steward should wait upon you more often and be questioned by you, that you may discover the source of his magic and fathom the secret of his mouth, for which tasks I feel myself unsuited by nature. I urgently exhorted him, coaxing him in his timidity, to approach you, my lady, the more diligently the better, and with his lips to kiss the earth at your feet, for the earth would acquiesce. At which point he fell silent. But the redness of Atum that had meanwhile faded from his countenance swiftly rose to cover it anew, and I took that as a sign of his fear of betraying himself to you, of surrendering his secret to you. Nevertheless, I remain convinced that he will follow my instruction. To be sure, he has, by whatever unknown means, outgrown me in this house and stands at its head; but I am his elder both in years and in residence and I am able to speak frankly and openly with such a youngster as befits the plain man that I am and as which I commend myself to my lady's favor."

And with that Dûdu gave his most proper bow, the stumps of his arms dangling from his shoulders, turned on his heels, and hastened on short legs to Joseph, whom he greeted with the words: "My respects, mouth of the house!"

"Aha, Dûdu," Joseph replied, "you have come to see me to offer your esteemed respects? How does that happen? For only recently you did not want to eat with me and made it apparent in word and deed that you were not particularly well disposed toward me, is that not so?"

"Well disposed?" Zeset's spouse asked, throwing his head back to look up at him. "I have always been more well disposed toward you than many another, who may have so disposed themselves over these seven years, but I did not let it show. I am a reticent, prudent man, who does not bestow his favor and respect right off on just anyone, simply because he has beautiful eyes, but rather I hold myself back, testing and allowing my trust to ripen, perhaps even for seven years. But once it has ripened, then my loyalty can be trusted categorically, and he who was tested may test it."

"Very good," Joseph replied. "I'm pleased to have won your regard without having gone to any great lengths to gain it."

"Great lengths or not," the little man retorted, suppressing his anger, "at any rate, henceforth you may depend on my enthusiastic service, which is dedicated above all to those gods who are manifestly with you. I am a pious man, who holds the opinion of the gods in high esteem and who appraises a man's virtue by his good fortune. The favor of the gods is persuasive. Who would be so headstrong as to oppose it with his own opinion for very long? Dûdu is not that stupid and obstinate, and therefore I have become yours, every inch of me."

"I'm glad to hear it," Joseph said, "and congratulate you on your wisdom in divine matters. And on that note, let us take leave of one another, for duty calls."

"It is my impression," Dûdu insisted, "that our young steward does not yet fully realize the value and meaning of my overture, which is tantamount to a proposal. Otherwise, you would not wish to absent yourself to pursue other duties before having truly examined the meaning and extent of my offer and informing yourself as to the advantages it presents you. For you may trust me and avail yourself of my loyalty and industry in all things, since both in matters of the household and in regard to your person and happiness, you may depend upon the solid experience of Dûdu and his ability to pursue, as a man of the world, certain byways and provide every sort of information, whether as eavesdropper, bearer of both messages and tales, or reporter of matters on a higher level—not to mention his ability to keep secrets with a subtlety and inviolability that is surely without compare on earth. I hope your eyes are starting to open as to what my offer entails."

"They were never blind to it," Joseph assured him. "You have greatly misunderstood me if you believe that I have failed to recognize the full import of your friendship."

"I am encouraged by your words," the dwarf said, "though not so much by the tone in which they are spoken. If my ears do not deceive me, I hear in it a certain stiffness, which in my eyes belongs to a period of time now past and for which there should be no place between you and me, since I, for my part, have put it entirely behind me. I cannot help being pained by the vexing injustice of such a tone on your part, since you have had just as long a time to let your confidence in me ripen as was permitted me for the growth of my own—that is, seven years. Trust for trust. I can see that I will have to do something more and draw you still deeper into mine, so that you may likewise receive me into yours without reticence and reservation. You should know then, Osarsiph," he said, lowering his voice, "that my decision to love you and devote myself entirely to your service has not arisen solely out of my fear of the gods. Also contributing to it—decisively, as I must now admit—are the wishes and instructions of an earthly power, of a person who also stands very near to the gods." He said no more, but only blinked.

"Well, and who might that person be?" Joseph could not refrain from asking.

"You need ask?" Dûdu responded. "Fine, for my answer will draw you into my most tender confidence, so that you can only respond in kind." He stood on tiptoe, cupped his little hand to his mouth, and whispered, "It was the mistress."

"The mistress?" Joseph replied all too quickly and just as softly, bending down to the little man straining up at him. Sad to say, it was true—the dwarf had known the word that would arouse his partner's immediate curiosity and draw him into conversation. Joseph's heart—which Jacob in his faraway homeland had long believed secure in death, but which here in the land of Egypt had continued to beat on and was still exposed to life's dangers—stood still in his breast, ceased to beat for a moment of self-forgetfulness, only to follow the heart's ancient custom and make good on the beats it had missed with still faster ones.

Almost at once, however, he stood up erect again and commanded, "Take your hand from your mouth. You may speak softly, but take that cupped hand away."

He said this so that no one would see that he and the wedded dwarf shared secrets—he was quite prepared to share secrets, of course, but was repelled by the visible gestures that accompany them.

Dûdu obeyed.

"It was Mut, our lady," he confirmed, "the first and true wife. She bade me come before her on your account and spoke to me in these words: 'Overseer'—forgive me, for since Mont-kaw departed to become a god, you are the overseer here and have moved into the special chamber of trust, and as before I am an overseer only in a limited but worthy sense; it is, however, the mistress's way, a pretty piece of flattery, when speaking to me—'Overseer,' she said, 'to come back to the lad Osarsiph, the new steward of the house, about whom we have exchanged thoughts several times now, it seems to me the moment has come for you finally to abandon the manly reticence and testing reservation you have shown for several years, perhaps seven or so, and without further ado to place yourself in his service, which at the bottom of your heart you have long wished to do. I have given serious consideration to the misgivings you have thought it appropriate to present to me now and again concerning his inexorable rise in this house, but have finally cast them aside because of his manifest virtues, and have done so all the more readily and easily inasmuch as, over time, you yourself have grown more and more hesitant and feeble in advancing your objections and are scarcely able or willing to conceal the love for him burgeoning within your bosom. You are not to restrain yourself any longer—such is my will—but to serve him with a well-disposed and faithful heart, for such is the heartfelt wish of your mistress. Few things can so concern my heart as that the best servants of this house should be truly well disposed to one another and should ally themselves for the sake of its welfare. You are to make a covenant with this young steward, Dûdu, and as a man of experience are to be aide, advisor, messenger, and guide to his youth—that is my heart's desire. For he is clever, I grant, and the gods usually bestow success upon whatever he does; in many things, however, his youth is in fact a hindrance and a hazard. And to speak first of the hazard, the fact is that his youth is bound up with considerable beauty, such as is found in his suitable stature, his veiled eyes, and his full- and well-formed mouth, so that one might cross seven mountains without coming upon a lad of equally fine appearance. What I command is that you are to protect his person against insufferable curiosity and for his visits to the city to provide him, if necessary, with a guard of archers, who can mitigate any danger by responding with a flurry of arrows to all troublesome objects thrown from the walls and roofs. But to return now to the matter of hindrance, it appears that his youth still renders him all too shy and timorous, so that I wish to extend your duties in that regard as well, and I charge you to assist him in overcoming his faintheartedness. All too seldom, for example, indeed almost never, does he venture to come before me, his mistress, and to engage me in conversation to discuss current and unresolved matters. I am unhappy to forgo such occasions, for I am in no way like Peteprê, my consort, who on principle concerns himself with nothing, but as mistress would gladly take part in affairs of business and have always regretted that Mont-kaw, the steward who is now a god, excluded me from them so entirely, whether out of misplaced respect or a desire to protect his own authority. In that regard, I had hoped for some improvements with this change in high office, but thus far find my hopes disappointed, and I command you, my friend, to play the delicate role of intermediary between me and this young steward and to induce him to overcome his youthful shyness and come before me frequently for discussions of this and that. And you may in fact regard this as the chief goal and purpose of the covenant that you are to make with him, just as I, Mut-em-enet, shall make one with you. For I bind you by your oath on his account, which one can indeed call a threefold covenant, between you, me, and him.' These, then," Dûdu concluded, "are the words that the mistress addressed to me and with which, by having repeated them, I have drawn you, young steward, into my most tender confidence, so that you may respond in kind. For you surely understand better now what all is entailed in my offer, according to which I place myself blindly in your service and am prepared to travel back and forth along every silent byway for the sake of this threefold covenant."

"Very good," Joseph replied in a voice muted by forced composure. "I have listened to you, keeper of the jewel chests, out of respect both for the mistress who spoke through you, or at least so I am led to believe, and for you, a polished man of the world, to whom the only fitting response is one that is no less smooth and cool. For you see, I am not at all convinced that you have lately decided to be well disposed and devoted to me—to be frank, and please do not take this amiss, I believe it to be worldly artifice and a politic lie. And my love for you, my friend, is likewise not without limits, and as for any enthusiasm I might feel toward your person, I can indeed say that it more or less repulses me. But I am firmly resolved to prove to you that as a man of the world I am no less master of my feelings than you and, out of cold calculation, capable of paying them no mind. A man such as I cannot always follow direct paths; he dare not fear taking a crooked one in some cases. And such a man finds his friends not only in upstanding fellows, but, as a man of the world, must also know how to coolly make use of slickly polished spies and informers. Therefore, far be it from me to reject your offer, master Dûdu, and I am prepared to accept you as my dutiful servant. But let us not speak of a covenant, I am uneasy with that word when applied to you and me, even when the mistress is said to be party to it. But any information you may have from the house or the city, you may always blow my way, and I will attempt to make use of it."

"If you but trust my loyalty," the misshapen man said, "then it does not matter to me whether you consider my motives worldly or affectionate. I do not need love from the world; I have it at home at the side of Zeset, my wife, and my thriving children, Esesi and Ebebi. Nevertheless, our glorious mistress has laid upon my heart the covenant I have with you, to be aide, advisor, messenger, and guide to your youth, and for my part I shall hold to it and be aide, advisor, messenger, and guide to your youth, and shall be content if you will but depend on me, whether it be with your heart or your worldly understanding. Do not forget what I have informed you concerning the mistress's desire to be more intimately acquainted with the business of the house than was the case with Mont-kaw and that you are to engage frequently in conversation with her. Do you perhaps have a message to give me as I retrace my steps?"

"Not that I know of," Joseph replied. "Let it suffice that you have delivered yours and leave it to me to take it into account."

"Just as you wish. I can, however," the dwarf said, "augment the information I have faithfully provided. For the mistress happened to mention that she wished to soothe her lovely temperament by walking in the garden at sunset, where she will ascend the embankment to the cozy summerhouse, to hold a rendezvous there with her thoughts. Whoever might be interested in conversing with her, in making requests and offering news, would do well to make use of this favorable and hardly commonplace opportunity and likewise present himself for an audience in that elegant cottage."

Master Dûdu was simply lying through his teeth. His mistress had said nothing of the kind. But if Joseph rose to the bait, Dûdu wanted to follow through on his lie and contrive a tryst by offering her an invitation from Joseph to join him at the cottage. Nor did he abandon his intention, even when the tempted man showed no sign of shaking hands on it.

Without committing himself as to what use he would make of the information blown his way, Joseph simply received it coolly and turned his back on the superintendent of jewels. But his heart was pounding, and if its beats no longer came as fast as before—for it had long since made good on those it had missed—they were still very strong nonetheless; and history cannot and will not conceal or deny that what he had heard about his mistress left him almost ecstatically happy—as did the opportunity that was his to seize at sunset. It is easy to imagine how urgently the voice in his breast whispered its warning against appearing there; and no one will be surprised to hear that all at once the whisper was outside of him as well—beside him as a familiar cricketlike voice. For after his conversation with Dûdu, as he was returning to the house, where he hoped to ponder all this in the special chamber of trust, it was Se'enkh-Wen-nofre-et-cetera, the little mandrake, it was favored Shepses-Bes in his rumpled finery who slipped in at the door with him and whispered up at him, "Do not take that wicked gossip's advice, Osarsiph, do not ever, ever do it!"

"How is it, my friend, that you are here?" Joseph asked, somewhat disconcerted. And then inquired as to what nook or niche he had been hiding in this time, since he claimed to know what Dûdu had advised.

"Not in any," the little man retorted, "but from afar I saw with keen dwarfish eyes how you forbade him to cup a hand to his mouth, but only after you had hastily bent down to his dissembling words. And with that, dwarfish wisdom knew what name he told you."

"What a devil of a fellow you are!" Joseph replied. "And now you have probably slipped up beside me to congratulate me on what a fine turn of events this is that the mistress herself has sent the same enemy who has complained of me to her for so long with an unambiguous signal that I have finally found favor before her and that she desires to speak to me about business? You must admit it is a splendid turn of events, and rejoice with me that it is up to me whether or not to present myself for an audience in the summerhouse at sunset—for it gives me exceeding happiness to hear it. I am not saying, by the by, that I intend to present myself—I am a long way from deciding that. But the simple fact that it is up to me, that I have the choice of doing so or not, makes me uncommonly happy, and you should congratulate me on it, Hop-o'-My-Thumb."

"Ah, Osarsiph," the little man sighed, "if you wished not to do it, the choice would not make you so happy, and your joy suggests to dwarfish wisdom that your inclination is to present yourself. Should this dwarf congratulate you for that, do you think?"

"It is, rather, dwarfish gibberish," Joseph scolded, "and useless chirping with which you regale me. Do you begrudge a man's son for rejoicing in his own free will, particularly as regards something in which he never would have imagined he might rejoice? Think back in time and recall with me the day and the hour when my father of the well, the old man of Midian, sold me to the master through him who is now a god, or rather through the scribe Kha'ma't in his stead, and we were left alone in the courtyard—me, you, and your monkey. Do you still recall? And you advised this confused boy, 'Throw yourself on the ground!' And borne upon the shoulders of rubber-eaters, there floated high and lofty across the courtyard the strange mistress of the house that had purchased me—her lily-white arm dangling from her chair, as I happened to notice from between my hands. Blind with disregard, she looked at me as if at some object, but the boy, blind with awe, gazed up at her as if to a goddess. But then according to God's wish and disposal, for seven years I grew within this house as if beside a spring and rose up among all its menials, until I succeeded to the office of him who was afflicted in the kidneys, and was placed at its head. And the Lord my God glorified Himself in me. In all of this, my good fortune had but one cloud upon its mirror, but one impurity in its ore: the mistress was against me, with the support of Beknechons, the man of Amun, and Dûdu, the wedded cripple, and I was happy if she merely cast me dark glances—which were better than none. But behold—is this not the consummation of my good fortune, for is it not free at last of its impurity, now that her glances have grown bright and she has given me a sign of her newfound grace toward me and of her desire to discuss business with me in a private audience? And in that hour when you whispered to the boy, 'Throw yourself upon the ground!' who would have imagined that one day it would be up to him whether to present himself to her or not? Allow me to rejoice in this, my friend!"

"Ah, Osarsiph, you may rejoice once you have decided to shun this rendezvous—but not before!"

"You begin each reply with an 'Ah!,' my wizened friend, instead of with an 'Oh!' of happy wonder. Why so gloomy, why this moping, why these cares? I have told you that I am more inclined not to present myself at the cottage. Except that itself is a problem. For in the end it is the mistress who has given me this sign—or one might also say, in the beginning it is she, such is its importance. Worldly understanding is fitting for a man like myself, and cool calculation. Such a man must consider his own advantage and dare not let petty fear prevent him from seizing by the horns an opportunity that promises to make him stronger still. Just think how useful a covenant between the mistress, a closer relationship with her, would be, what inestimable support it would provide. So then—tell me who am I that I should pass judgment on the mistress's wish and instruction with a yes or no, raising myself above her with my own decision? To be sure, I stand over the house, yet belong to it as its purchase and servant. She, however, is the first and true wife here, the woman of the house, and to her I owe obedience. There is no one among the living or the dead who could rebuke me for blindly fulfilling her summons as a faithful servant, indeed, I would call down the rebuke of both living and dead were I to respond otherwise. For if I have not learned so much as to obey, then my advancement to my position of command has obviously come too soon. Which is why I have begun to ask myself whether you might not have been right, my little Bes, in finding fault with my joy in free choice. For perhaps it is not up to me at all, and I must present myself without fail."

"Ah, Osarsiph," the little voice chirped, "how can I not say 'Ah'—ah and alas, when I hear your tongue speaking balderdash. You were good, beautiful, and clever when you came to us as the seventh item and I advocated your purchase against the advice of that wicked gossip, for unclouded dwarfish wisdom recognized your value and blessing at first glance. You are still beautiful and good at heart, but as for the third quality, I'd best be mum. When I think back, is it not pitiful to listen to you now? You were clever until today, gifted with a genuine, unerring cleverness, and your thoughts traveled blithely straight ahead, with head held high, serving only your own spirit. But no sooner has your face been brushed by the breath of the fiery bull that terrifies this dwarf like nothing else in the world, and you are suddenly doltish, god help you, doltish as an ass that one would like to drive with cudgels roundabout the city, and your thoughts trot on all fours with lolling tongue, no longer serving your spirit, but your wicked proclivities. Ah, ah, how disgraceful! Blather and flimflam and false conclusions, that is the sole intent of such degraded thoughts, whose only purpose is to deceive your spirit and indulge your proclivities. And you wish to deceive this little man as well, flattering him with pitiable cunning, saying he may well have been right to find fault with your joy in free choice, because ultimately you have none at all—as if that were not the very source of your joy! Ah, ah, how shameful it is, and wretched beyond all measure!" And Favored Bes began to weep bitterly, his little hands pressed to his wrinkled face.

"Now, now, little Master Tears," Joseph said, taken aback. "Take heart and weep no more. It moves a man to pity and his heart is touched to see you so downcast, and all because of a somewhat falsely drawn conclusion that may have slipped in among his words. You yourself may find it easier always to draw correct conclusions and think clearly according to your spirit. But cheer up, for there's no need to be so wretchedly ashamed of a fallible man whose mind can grow confused on occasion."

"That only shows your goodness," the little man said, still sobbing as he dried his eyes with the rumpled batiste of his festive garb, "the way you take pity on my dwarfish tears. Ah, if only you would pity yourself, dear friend, and latch on with all your might to your cleverness, that it may not desert you at a time when you need it most. Behold, I saw it coming from the beginning, when you did not wish to understand me and turned doltish in response to my anxious whispers—saw still worse things coming than what might come from that wicked gossip's complaints to Mut, our mistress, things more dangerous than that danger. For he intended wickedness, but did more wickedness than he intended by opening the eyes of this poor woman to you, my beautiful and good man. And as for you, do you also wish to close yours to a pit far deeper than the first into which your envious brothers cast you after rending wreath and veil from you, as I've often heard you tell? There is no Ishmaelite from Midian who will pull you from the pit that this odious wedded gossip has dug for you by opening the mistress's eyes to you. And now she, our saint, is making eyes at you, and you are likewise making them at her, and in that terrifying play of glances lies the fiery beast that lays waste to fields, leaving only ashes and darkness."

"You are fearful by nature, my poor little man," Joseph responded, "and torment your small soul with dwarfish phantoms. Tell me straight-out what sort of frailties you imagine are mine simply because the mistress has taken note of me. When I was a boy I assumed that everyone who saw me had to love me more than him-self—that's what a jackanapes I was. It brought me to the pit, but I have moved beyond the pit and beyond such folly. But in the mean-time you appear to have become foolish on my account and are imagining frailties. The only eyes the mistress has made at me are stern, and mine have been only those of respect. If she demands of me an accounting of the business of the house and wishes to ques-tion me—should I interpret that with a conceit that comes from your opinion of me? Yet I am not flattered by your view of me, for apparently it says that I need but extend my little finger to the mis-tress and am lost for good and all. But I have no such fear as regards myself and do not intend to become a child of the pit posthaste. And if it were my desire to challenge your fiery bull, do you suppose I would go out to meet him unarmed and simply pack him by the horns? How truly great you imagine my frailties to be! Go now, dance and jest before the women, and be of good cheer. I probably will not present myself for an audience in the cottage. But as a full-grown man, I must ponder these matters on my own and think how to balance them—how to unite one sort of cleverness with the other, so that I neither offend the mistress nor prove damnably unfaithful to the living or the dead or to . . . But that you cannot understand, Hop-o'-My-Thumb, since for you children here, that third is con-tained within the second. Your dead are gods, and your gods are dead, and you do not know what that is: the living God."

These, then, were Joseph's, quite arrogant, words to the wizened dwarf. But did he not know that he himself was dead and had be-come a god, was Osarsiph, the Joseph who had died? To be frank, he wished to be left alone and undisturbed to ponder this—this and something else irrevocably bound up with it: divine rigidity standing ready to receive the descending vulture-woman.

The Coils of Agony

As we peer back into the past, how brief is our own life compared to the world's great depths of time. And yet, when scanning private and intimate matters, our eye floats dreamily back into youthful distance and loses itself just as it does when directed to the grand scale of human life—for it perceives the unity of one repeated in the other. Like humankind itself, each of us is unable to force our way back to the beginning of our own days, to our birth, to say nothing of beyond it—be the vista grand or small, it all lies in the darkness before the dawn of consciousness and memory. But at the first stirrings of our mind's endeavors—when, just as humanity once did, we enter into civilized life, forming and offering our first tender contribution to it—we encounter, much to our happy amazement, a sympathy and partiality that allows us to sense and perceive that unity, which is always the same: It is the idea of visitation by drunken, ruinous, and destructive powers invading a life of composure that, with all its hopes for dignity and a modicum of happiness, is sworn to that very composure. It is a tale of achieved and seemingly secure peace and of life laughing as it sweeps away that artificial edifice, a tale of mastery and of being overwhelmed, of the arrival of the strange god—as it was in the beginning, so it was in the middle. And in a later age of life, which indulges in a sympathy for earlier humanity, once again— and in token of that unity—we find ourselves caught up in that old fellow feeling.

As for Mut-em-enet, Potiphar's wife, whose voice when she sang was beloved by all (this early and distant figure whom the spirit of narrative cordially allows us to behold from up close), she, too, was visited and overwhelmed, was a maenadic sacrifice to a strange god, and the artificial edifice of her life was quite nicely overthrown by those powers of the lower world that in her ignorance she believed she could mock—whereas it was they who mocked all her consolations and extra consolations. It was easy enough for old Huya to demand that she not be a goose, not be the bird of the black, gravid, waterlogged earth, cackling in moist depths for the overshadowing, engendering power of the swan, but, rather, be a chaste priestess of the moon—which is no less feminine. He himself had lived in swampy sibling darkness and, conscientiously but clumsily interpreting presages of a new world, had maimed his son to turn him into a courtier of the light, depleting him, without so much as asking, making a human cipher of him, and giving him then into the stern bonds of marriage with a woman whose name was that of the primal mother—let them worry, then, about propping up each other's dignity with tactful consideration. It is pointless to deny that human dignity finds its realization in both human sexual variations, in male and female; but if one represents neither, one also stands outside of humanity at the same time—and in that case, where is the source of human dignity? All attempts to prop up such dignity should, to be sure, enjoy every respect, for such endeavors are spiritual and—as one must grant for honor's sake—always and beyond any doubt preeminently human. But truth, however bitter it may be, demands we admit that all things spiritual and intellectual make painfully little headway—and almost never prevail in the long run—against eternal nature. How little both the respectable garb of morality and social convention are able to accomplish against the deep, dark, and silent conscience of the flesh, how difficult it is for the mind and its thoughts to deceive this fleshly conscience—we had to learn that early on in our story, when dealing with Rachel's confusion. But in being bound to a chamberlain of the sun, Mut, Rachel's sister of princely blood from one of the nomes here below, stood apart from her womanly humanity in the same way that Potiphar stood apart from his human manliness; she led a sexual existence as hollow and devoid of fleshly honor as his was; and the divine honor with which she believed she could compensate and overcompensate for her dim awareness of this fact was as spiritually fragile as the satisfactions and extra satisfactions that her plump consort exacted from his pose as a dashing tamer of horses and hunter of hippopotamuses, and with a daring that Joseph, always clever in his flattery, had known to suggest to him was the mark of true manhood—though it also lacked a certain fervor, so that whether in desert or swamps Peteprê constantly longed for the tranquillity of his hall of books, for a pure, rather than an applied spirituality.

But we are speaking here not of Potiphar, but of his Eni, the wife of the god, and of the dilemma in which, to her distress, she now found herself: the choice between honoring the spirit and honoring the flesh. Two black eyes of faraway origin, the eyes of a lovely and all too extravagantly loved woman, had enchanted her, and the thrill they gave her was simply the final or penultimate moment of her budding fear of saving or, better, of achieving her fleshly honor, her womanly humanity, which implied, however, the sacrificial surrender of her spiritual and divine honor, of all the lofty ideals on which she had based her existence for so long.

Let us pause for a moment and consider the issue correctly. Let us consider it with her, for she thought of it day and night with mounting torment and lust. Was hers a genuine dilemma, and can sacrifice ever dishonor or profane? That was the question. Is consecration the same as chastity? Yes and no; for being a bride carries with it certain contradictions that cancel each other out; and the veil, which is the sign of the goddess of love, is both a token of chastity and of its sacrifice, the sign of the nun and of the strumpet. Mut's age and the spirit of its temples knew of the consecrated and unblemished woman, the *kedesha,* who was also an "enticer," which is to say, a street prostitute. To her belonged the veil; and these *kadishtu* were unblemished in the same way as is an animal chosen to be sacrificed to the god at his feast precisely because it is unblemished. Consecrated? The question is, to whom and to what end? If one is consecrated to Ishtar then chastity is but a stage on the way to sacrifice, a veil destined to be ripped to shreds.

We have joined in the thoughts of a woman struggling with her infatuation, and if, despite his fear and dislike of an alien sexuality, Favored Bes had eavesdropped on her, he would probably have wept at the deplorable cunning of thoughts that served natural proclivities and not the spirit. Easy for him to weep—he was but a toad and a dancing fool, who knew nothing of human dignity. But what concerned Mut his mistress was the honor of her flesh, and so she was at the mercy of thoughts that reconciled, as best they could, fleshly and divine honor. She deserved both forbearance and sympathy, despite a certain expediency in her reasoning—for thoughts seldom exist for their own sake. And she was having extraordinary difficulty with hers; for in being awakened to womanhood from a priestly and ladylike slumber of the senses, she was not at all like that ancient and model royal child who, upon beholding the princely majesty of heaven, found her childhood peace summoned to the torment and lust of all-consuming love. Mut's was not the—granted, ruinous—good fortune of falling gloriously in love with someone far above her rank (which may ultimately bring with it celestial jealousy and even acquiescence to being transformed into a cow), but rather the misfortune of having fallen in love far below her station—as she saw it—and of having come to know passion by way of a slave, the son of a nobody, a purchased piece of Asiatic household goods. This was a far bitterer blow to her female pride than our history has thus far known how to report. It prevented her from admitting her feelings for a long time, and when she was finally ready to do so, the happiness love always brings was mingled with an element of humiliation, which, being rooted in deepest cruelty, can become a fearsome goad to desire. The expedient thoughts by which she tried to find a more correct definition of her humiliation played with the notion that a *kedesha,* or temple prostitute, could not chose her lover either, but that her body belonged to whoever tossed the god's wages into her lap. But how incorrect was her correction, what violence she did herself in regarding hers as the passive role. For she was the enterprising party who chose and wooed, even if her choice of a lover had not been entirely her own, but had been steered by Dûdu's complaints—she was that by reason both of her years and of her station as his mistress, which in such a relationship is of course the station that provokes and initiates love—that, however, was all she needed: for that wish, that first decision to have come from her slave and for him to have lifted his eyes to her all on his own, turning her into the obedient follower and her feelings into a humiliating response to his own. Never, never would that be! Her pride was quite willing to assume, as it were, the male role in this enterprise—and yet deep within her she could not quite manage it. For however much she would have liked to try to force things, this young slave, whether aware of his arbitrary power or not, was the one who, by the sheer energy of his existence, had awakened her femininity from beneath its seal of sleep and, without his knowing or willing it, had made himself master of her mistress realm, so that her thoughts served him and her hopes clung to his every glance, fearful that he might notice she wished to be his woman, yet trembling all the while for fear he might return her inadmissible desires. All in all, it was humiliation drenched in a dreadful sweetness. But in order to make it less so and also because love's urges, though in fact never governed by value and worthiness, always burn for some equivalence of value and impute every conceivable worthiness to their object, she tried to lift the slave, whose mistress of love she wished to be, out of his servitude, told herself how his low rank was countered by his good manners, his cleverness, his position in the house; and in yielding to her affections—or "indulging her proclivities," as the mock vizier would have put it—she attempted (under Dûdu's tutelage, by the way) to call religion to her aid by appealing to Atum-Rê of On, the mild, inclusive god who was gracious to foreign nations, instead of to her former lord, the stern patriotic Amun, and by so doing to provide her love the backing of the court, of royal power itself, which, as her conscience subtly reasoned, also had the advantage of bringing her spiritually closer to her husband, a man of the court and Pharaoh's friend, and in a certain sense of gaining as a partisan in her lust the very man she increasingly longed to deceive.

This, then, was how Mut-em-enet battled against the snares of her desire, struggling, so to speak, against a serpent sent by a god, its great coils winding round her, squeezing the breath from her, leaving her gasping for air. When one considers that she had to struggle alone and without help, unable to share any of this with anyone other than Dûdu, and even with him in hints and words that hid her confession—or at least not at first, for later she cast aside all restraint and made the world around her a participant in her madness; when one also considers that the anguish in her blood had led her to choose a man who had to defer to the higher cause of a jealous God and wore in his hair an herb of faithfulness and arrogance—or, in a word, of his chosen state—and that he neither wanted nor was allowed to yield to her temptation; and when one likewise bears in mind that her agony lasted for three years, from the seventh to the tenth year of Joseph's sojourn in Potiphar's house, and that even then her torment was not allayed but simply slain—then one must admit that the fate of "Potiphar's wife" (popularly regarded as a shameless seductress and the honeyed bait of evil) was not an easy one and at least grant her the sympathy arising from the insight that the implements of such a testing carry their own punishment within them, bearing a greater share of it than they deserve, even if we admit the necessity of their function.

The First Year

Three years—in the first she tried to hide her love from him, in the second she let him know of it, in the third she offered it to him.

Three years—and in that time she must or may see him daily, for as members of Potiphar's household they lived in close contact, which is a source of great comfort and great torment and nourishes her folly each day. But *must* and *may* are not so gently entwined in love as they are in slumber—including our final slumber, as when Joseph's soothing words equating *may* with *must* assuaged Mont-kaw. Instead, they form a tangled conflict full of anguish and confusion, rending the soul by damnably fulfilling its wishes, until the lover curses the *must*-see with the same fervor as he ecstatically blesses the *may*-see, and the more he suffers from the consequences of his most recent encounter, the more he yearns for and pursues the next opportunity to fan the fire of his craving—and always at the very moment when it is about to ebb, which should be a solid reason for the lovesick soul to be happy and grateful. For it can indeed happen that an encounter that somehow detracts from the luster of the object of one's love brings with it a certain disappointment, disillusionment, and detachment; and this should be all the more welcome to the lover, since the waning of his own infatuation allows him a greater freedom of mind and, with it, an increasing capacity for conquest and the ability to inflict upon the other party what he suffers himself. His main concern should then be to become lord and master of his passion, rather than its victim; because, in fact, the possibility of winning the other party increases considerably as one's own emotion ebbs. But the lover wishes to know nothing of this, and he regards the benefits of revived health, vigor, and audacity—which are indeed benefits, even in relation to that goal that he holds second to none—as nothing in comparison to the loss that he must suffer as a result of cooling passion. For this leaves him in a state of bleak desolation—perhaps much like that felt by a drug addict deprived of his narcotic—and he employs all his energies in rekindling the fires of experience in order to restore his previous condition.

That is how things stand with *must* and *may* when it comes to the folly of love, which of all follies is the greatest, so that one can best learn from it the nature of folly itself and its relation to its victim. For however much he may sigh beneath the burden of his passion, the lover is not only incapable of not desiring his state, but also incapable of even wishing he were capable of it. He knows quite well that, after a longer period of not-seeing the object of his love, he will over time—in perhaps an embarrassingly short time—be rid of his passion. But it is precisely this forgetting that he despises above all else—and indeed the pain of every farewell is rooted in secret anticipation of inevitable forgetting, for once that has occurred, one will no longer be able to feel any pain at all, and so one weeps in advance. No one beheld Mut-em-enet's face when, after struggling in vain with Peteprê, her husband, for him to banish Joseph, she hid it in the folds of her garment as she leaned against a pillar. But there is good, indeed best reason to suppose that the face she concealed was beaming with joy, because now she might have to go on seeing the man who had awakened her and might not have to forget him.

That had to have been of great importance to her in particular, and her fear of separation, of the forgetting that inevitably follows, of the dying of passion, must have been especially acute, because mature women of her age, whose blood has been awakened late and perhaps might never have been awakened without some extraordinary cause, surrender themselves with more than usual fervor to their emotions, to this first and final emotion, and would rather die than exchange their previous peace—which they now call desolation—for this new life made blissful by suffering. It is all the more admirable then, that, persuaded by reason, earnest Mut had done her best to convince her indolent consort to remove the object of her longings—and could such an act of love ever have been wrenched from him, she would even have sacrificed her feelings. But it had simply not been possible to awaken or move him, for he was an inveterate titular commander; and, to give truth its due, Eni had secretly known as much beforehand, had counted on it, and her honest struggles with her consort had actually been only a performance, so that upon his refusal she might give free rein to her passion and all her inborn destiny.

After their conjugal encounter in the hall that evening, she could indeed consider herself free; and if she bridled her desires for so long afterward, she did so less out of duty than out of pride. There was perfect dignity in her demeanor when, at sunset on the same day of those three conversations, she stepped forward to meet Joseph in the garden, just below the little summerhouse, and only the keenest eye would have detected brief moments of weakness or tenderness shimmering through. Dûdu had, in fact, been very clever and cunning in carrying out his secret plan, and, upon leaving Joseph, had returned to his mistress and informed her that the new steward would be more than happy to give her an account of the business of the estate, but placed great importance upon his doing so undisturbed and tête-à-tête, at whatever time and place she would prefer. Joseph had, moreover, so Dûdu said, announced his intention to visit the little temple in the garden that very day, at dusk, so that he might inspect the condition of its furnishings and murals. Dûdu had offered this second bit of news independently of the first, interjecting a quite different matter between the two and delicately allowing his mistress to make the connection. But seasoned as he was at intrigue, he was only half successful this time, since both parties were content with taking half measures. Joseph had chanced upon a middle course between the alternatives of his free choice, choosing to take a walk around the garden just below the summerhouse but without entering it, a tour he might have made, indeed ought to have made, once again in any case, just to make sure that the trees and flower beds were as they should be; and Mut, his mistress, was likewise not in a mood to climb the embankment, but had seen no reason to let some bit of dwarfish news that had merely brushed her ear spoil her plans—made early that morning as she definitely recalled—to take a brief stroll in Peteprê's garden at the close of day and enjoy heaven's beautiful fire reflected in the duck pond, while accompanied, as usual, by two young maids who followed in her footsteps.

And so that evening the young steward and his mistress met on the red sand of the garden path and what happened in that encounter is as follows:

Upon catching sight of the women, Joseph responded with solemn alarm. Forming his mouth in a reverent "Oh!" and raising his hands, he bowed and began to retreat in an easy crouch. For her part, Mut formed her serpentine lips into a fleeting, gentle smile of vague surprise, a questioning "Ah?," above which her eyes remained austere, indeed grim, and first let him take a few more ceremonial backward steps while she walked on, before signaling with a quick downward motion of one hand for him to halt. She, too, came to a stop now, as did the dark-skinned maids of honor behind her, their artificially lengthened eyes full of the joy with which every servant in the household greeted Joseph, while from beneath the curled fringe of their black, woolly hair flashed the large enameled disks of their earrings.

There the two stood face-to-face, and it was not an encounter to engender sobering disappointment in either of them. The light fell at a flattering angle, drenching the garden scene of cottage and reeds in rich color, lending a still fierier hue to the red path, a soft glow to the flowers, and a lovely shimmer to the rustling foliage of the trees; and its reflected luster in human eyes was exactly like that in the pond, whose ducks, foreign and domestic, seemed more like heavenly than earthly ducks, as if they had been painted and lacquered. And by this light human beings—not just shimmering eyes, but entire bodies— took on that same heavenly look, as if they too were painted, were free of all care and inadequacy; they looked like gods and funerary statues, their makeup enhanced by the grace of light, and as each gazed with shining eyes into the beautifully hued face of the other, surely they took pleasure in the sight.

Mut was enraptured to see the man whom she knew she loved, in so perfect a form; for love is always eager to find justifications, but is so sensitive that it winces at any flaw that might mar the image of the beloved and is triumphantly grateful for every favor granted by illusion; and even though the beloved's glory—guarded and protected by love for the sake of its own honor—causes great pain because it belongs to everyone, is visible to everyone, and is a constant cause of much uneasiness, since the whole world is now a suitor, that same pain is more precious than anything; and love presses its sharp blade to its heart, with but one worry: that its keen edge may be blunted by some darkening or blurring of the image. And in seeing Joseph so enhanced, Eni rejoiced to think she might be as well and hoped that she, too, looked glorious to him, even if by ordinary, more direct light things might no longer appear as they had in the bloom of youth. She was aware, was she not, that the long, open cloak of white wool—for winter was approaching—cast over her shoulders and held by an agraffe just above her wide necklace made her look even more majestic? That her breasts were thrust with youthful firmness against the batiste of her close-fitting gown that ended in a hem of red glass beads just above her feet? Look at that gown, Osarsiph! It fell from ribboned clasps at her shoulders, and how very aware she was that it not only left her perfectly groomed, virtually chiseled arms free, but also distinctly revealed the long, stately outline of each wonderful leg. Was that not reason enough for her to hold her head high out of love? She did it. But out of pride she acted as if she found it difficult to raise her eyelids, as if she must lay her head back to gaze out from under them. She knew, and it frightened her to know, that her face—framed this time by a golden brown headscarf held in place at her brow by a broad gem-studded clasp that did not quite encircle her head—was no longer the youngest and how very strange and arbitrary its shadowy cheeks, saddle nose, and deeply tucked mouth must look. But the thought of how precious her painted, jewellike eyes must appear against the ivory pallor of her face gave her confident hope that her countenance would not be an outright impediment to the effect of her arms, legs, and breasts.

Mindful, out of both pride and fear, of her beauty, she gazed at his—at the beauty of Rachel's son in Egyptian finery, which, though it was a work of highest civilization, was cut for a comfortable walk in the garden. All the same, his head had been carefully dressed in a black ribbed-silk headscarf, which ended in curls to show that it was meant to symbolize a wig, and there was something especially smart about the way one corner of his white linen cap, neat and tidy as always, peeked out just from below one small ear. But except for his wig and a matched enameled set of collar and bracelets, plus that flat necklace of reed and gold from which his scarab hung, he wore nothing but a, granted, elegantly cut, knee-length double skirt around his narrow hips, its petal white contrasting charmingly with the skin color of his ornamented upper body, its bronze deepened now in the slanting light—a young man's gently powerful, just rightly formed body, which in the cool breeze and colorful light seemed to belong not to the world of the flesh, but to the purer world of Ptah's thoughts executed in stone, its spirit enhanced by the head and intelligent eyes to which it belonged. And together, head and body were the realization of a unity of beauty and wisdom to gladden both him and everyone who looked upon him.

In her proudly fearful self-awareness, Potiphar's wife gazed across to him, to his dark facial features—large in comparison with her own—and into the cordial night of Rachel's eyes, made even more expressive by the masculine enhancement of the son's heightened understanding; with one glance her eyes took in the golden bronze sheen of his shoulders, the moderate but manly bulge of muscle in his trim arm, crooked for holding his walking staff in one hand—and welling up from within her, feminine anguish intensified maternal tenderness and admiration to an overwhelming, desperate ardor that released from her deepest depths a gasp so violent that her breasts visibly heaved beneath the delicate taut fabric; her one hope was that her majestic demeanor made such a gasp seem so improbable that, however obvious, it would go unnoticed.

Given the circumstances, she knew she ought to speak, but it demanded such effort that she was ashamed of the heroic courage it cost her.

"It is, as I now see," she said in a cool voice, "a most inappropriate hour for idle women to stroll along this path, for they obstruct the official rounds of him who stands over this house."

"Only you, my mistress," he replied at once, "stand over this house, as its morning and evening star, which is called Ishtar in the land of my mother and which like all things divine is indeed idle, yet it is to its tranquil rays that we who toil look up for refreshment."

She thanked him with a wave of her hand and a smile of obliging agreement. She was both delighted and offended by the self-indulgence of a compliment that referred straightway to his mother, a woman totally unknown to her, and was gnawed by jealousy of the mother who had borne him, nursed him, guided his steps, called him by name, brushed the hair from his brow, and kissed him as only pure love allows.

"We shall step aside," she said, "I and my servants, who are accompanying me today as always, so that we may not impede the overseer, who doubtless wishes to determine before dark whether Peteprê's gardens are in proper condition and wishes perhaps even to visit the little cottage upon the embankment."

"The garden and its temple," Joseph replied, "are of little concern to me so long as I am standing before my mistress."

"It seems to me that they ought to concern you at all times and enjoy your services above all else," she responded—and how terribly sweet and daring it was simply to speak with him, to say "me" and "you," "you" and "I," to address him and, by sending the breath of words across the two short steps that separated their bodies, to establish a relationship and a commonality. "For it is well known that they are the source of your good fortune. I have heard it said that you were first permitted to offer your services as a mute servant in the cottage and that you first captured Peteprê's eye in the orchard, where you were 'riding' palm trees."

"So it was," he said with a laugh, and his laugh was a knife whose levity pierced her heart. "Just as you have said, so it was, my gracious lady. I was performing the task of the wind high in Peteprê's palm trees, as instructed by the herbalist, the man they call—but I cannot remember or would prefer not to repeat the name, for it is absurdly vulgar and nothing for my mistress's ear . . ." She stared at the jocular youth, but did not smile. It was a good thing—indeed essential, though also very painful—that he evidently had no idea that she was not in any mood for jests, or why; let him assume that her earnestness in rejecting them was a remnant of her hostility to his rise in the house—but she wanted him to notice it. "As instructed by the gardener," he said, "I was assisting the wind here in the garden, when Pharaoh's friend came past and bade me speak, and because I found favor before him, many things have had their origin in that hour."

"People," she added, "have lived and died on your behalf."

"The Hidden One accomplishes all things," he replied, making use of a term for the Most High that would not offend. "May His name be glorified! But I often ask myself whether I have not been favored by His aid beyond what I deserve, and I have private fears that such an office has been bestowed upon me at so tender an age and that I walk about as an overseer, as the eldest servant of this house, and yet cannot be all that much more than twenty. I speak openly before you, great mistress, though it is not only you who hear me, for you obviously did not come to the garden alone but are accompanied by maids of honor, as befits your rank. They too hear me and for good or ill have learned how the steward indicts his youth and expresses doubt as to his maturity for such high service. Let them hear! I must chance their presence, for I will not allow it to constrain your trust in me, mistress of my head and heart, of my hands and feet."

There are, after all, advantages to falling in love with someone of lower rank, who must submit to us, for his status requires those turns of phrase that make us happy, even when they may mean next to nothing to him.

"It goes without saying," she replied, assuming a still more majestic pose, "that I do not stroll about unescorted—that can never happen. Speak, however, without care of compromising yourself before Hezes and Me'et, my handmaids, for their ears are my ears—what did you wish to say?"

"Only this, my mistress—my authority is greater than my years, and it would not surprise your servant, indeed he would have had to pronounce it fair and just, if his rapid ascendancy to stewardship in this house were accompanied not only with approval but perhaps also with displeasure and some opposition. I had a father, Usir Mont-kaw, who raised me out of the goodness of his heart, and would that, by the grace of the Hidden One, he were still alive. For I was much the better then in my young years and could speak of my good fortune, was still his mouth and his right hand, before he entered through the secret gates and into the splendid places of the lords of eternity, leaving me alone now with more duties and cares than I number in years; and in my immaturity I have no one in the world whom I may ask for advice, who might help me bear a burden beneath which I am bent low. Long may Peteprê, our great master, live, whole and healthy, but it is widely known that he has no concern for anything but what he eats and drinks and boldly to prevail against the hippopotamus, and when I come to him with accounts and records, he is sure to say, 'Fine, fine, Osarsiph, my friend, it is all in fine order. Your entries appear to be correct as far as I can see, and I assume that you intend me no harm, for you know what sin is and you have a sense of how monstrous it would be to cause me injury. Therefore do not weary me with this now.' Such are the words of our lord in his greatness. May blessing be upon his head." He looked to see if she had smiled at his imitation. It was a very small betrayal, done with great love and respect to be sure, a gentle attempt at winning her amused agreement to join him in going over the head of the master. He believed he might risk that much without violating his covenant. He went on believing that he might go that far and perhaps farther without any danger. There was no smile of agreement, however. He was glad of that, and at the same time slightly embarrassed.

"I am young and alone," he continued, "with so many questions and responsibilities that arise from questions of production and trade, of increasing, or of merely sustaining the estate. You saw me walking toward you just now, great lady, with a head full of worries about the sowing. For the river is in retreat and the beautiful feast of mourning approaches, when we dig the earth and bury the god in darkness and plow for barley and wheat. And the question that is now running through your servant's head is a proposal for innovation: that is, whether we ought not to plant a good deal more sorghum in Potiphar's fields, especially on the island in the river, instead of the barley we have planted until now—I mean kaffir corn, the white sorghum grown by Negroes, for we already grow sufficient brown sorghum as fodder, and it satisfies the horses and fattens the cattle; but the change at issue is whether we ought not to plant a greater quantity of the white, plowing more acreage to provide food for humans, so that the servants may be nourished with good bread instead of with barley and lentil porridge and thereby grow stronger for service. For the kernels within the awn are rich in flour and fat with the fatness of the earth, so that the workers need less of it than of barley or lentils and we can sate them quicker and better. I cannot tell you how this keeps running through my head, and when I saw you, mistress, approaching with your escort through the evening garden, I took counsel in my soul and said to myself as if to another, 'Behold, in your immaturity you are alone with the cares of this house and have no one with whom to share them, for the master has no concern for anything. But here the mistress comes in all her beauty, followed by two handmaids, as befits her rank. Why should you not confide in her and speak with her about this innovation, about the matter of kaffir corn, and you will sound out her opinion and her fine counsel will assist you in your youth.'"

Eni blushed, in part with delight, in part out of embarrassment, for she knew nothing of white sorghum and had no idea whether it would be good to plant more. In some confusion she said, "The question is worthy of discussion, that is plain as day. I shall consider it. Is the soil of the island favorable to such an innovation?"

"What experience my mistress displays in her question," Joseph replied, "knowing at once to touch upon the pulse of every matter. The soil is rich enough, and yet one must temper one's heart against initial failure. For the field hands do not rightly know how to plant white sorghum for human food, but only the brown, its sole purpose being animal fodder. What does my mistress suppose it costs to teach the workers to cultivate the earth with a hoe as finely as is required for white sorghum, or to bring them to understand that it cannot tolerate weeds as the brown can? And if they do not carefully trim the runners it prospers poorly, and though there is fodder, there is no food."

"It must be difficult indeed to deal with laborers who lack understanding," she said, turning now red, now white in her uneasiness, since she knew nothing about such things and found herself hard-pressed to find an intelligent answer, although it was she who had wanted him to speak with her about affairs of business. Her conscience left her feeling deeply ashamed before her servant, utterly humiliated, for he spoke to her of such honest and seemly matters as the cultivation of food, whereas she wanted and knew only one thing: that she was in love with him and desired him.

"Difficult indeed," she repeated, concealing her trembling. "But everyone says that you know how to compel such people to do their duty and offer good service. And so presumably you will be successful at instructing them about this innovation."

His gaze went blank, for he was not listening to her babble, and she was glad, though terribly hurt at the same time. He stood there lost in true concern for affairs of business.

"The panicles of this grain," he said, "are very sturdy and pliant. One can make good brushes and brooms from them and so still have something useful both for household and trade if a harvest fails."

She fell silent, painfully offended, for she realized he no longer was thinking of her, but talking to himself about brooms, which, to be sure, were more respectable than her love. He at least noticed, however, that she was silent, and in alarm smiled the smile that won everyone to him and said, "Forgive me, mistress, for this low topic of conversation. I am to blame for wearying you. It comes of my immaturity, of my being alone with my responsibilities, and because I was so very tempted to consult with you."

"There is nothing to forgive," she replied. "It is an important matter, and the prospect of making brooms lessens the risk. That was my immediate response when you spoke to me of this innovation, and I wish to take the matter under further consideration."

She could not stand still, she had to get away from here, away from his nearness, which was dearer to her than all else. For lovers, it is an old conflict, this seeking out and fleeing the nearness of the other. But equally ancient are lies spoken about honest matters with contorted lips and dishonest eyes that seek out and flee. The fear he might realize that in talking about grain and brooms she had but one thing in mind: to caress his brow with her hand and kiss him like a possessive mother; the terrifying wish that he might realize as much and not despise her for it, but share her wish; this and her great uncertainty about things like fodder and food, the topic of a conversation that for her was talk of love and lies—but how can one lie if one is ignorant of the ostensible topic of one's pretense and condemned to fumbling helplessly for words?—it all left her unutterably shamed and unnerved, sending hot and cold flashes over her, urging her to panicked flight.

Her feet twitched to be on their way, but her heart held to the spot—it is the ancient quandary of every lover. She tugged her cloak more tightly around her shoulders and said in a choked voice, "We shall have to continue this at another time and place, steward. Night is falling and I seem to have shivered just now in the chill." And indeed she was subject to little fits of shivering and, having no hope of hiding them entirely, had to find some external cause to explain them. "You have my promise that I shall take counsel with myself about this innovation, and you have my permission to speak with your mistress about this matter again soon, should you feel all too alone in your youth . . ." She should not have attempted to speak this last word; it stuck in her throat, for the word spoke of him and him alone; it was a stronger synonym for that "you" that had threaded its way through their conversation of lies and constituted its truth, was the word of its magic and of her maternal possessiveness, laden with tenderness and pain, so that it overwhelmed her and faded to a whisper. "Farewell," she managed yet in a last whisper and took flight, moving ahead of her handmaids and passing by her steward, whose knees were bent in respectful salutation.

One cannot stop to wonder too long at the fragility of love, at its rare and peculiar nature—that is, if one does not regard it as a banal commonplace, but looks with fresh eyes at how new, unprecedented, and unique each occurrence is, down to the present day. Such a great lady—elegant, lofty, arrogant, and worldly, coolly wrapped up until now in the egotism of her religious conceit—suddenly smitten by a "you" absolutely unworthy of her from her standpoint, but smitten all the same and feeling so fragile that her very status as his mistress disintegrated until she was scarcely capable of even maintaining her role as the mistress of love, as the provocative agent of emotion, and instead realized that she was already slave to this "you" who was her slave, and blindly fled from him on wobbly knees—shivering, thoughts fluttering, mumbled words fluttering, oblivious of the handmaids she had purposely, proudly brought with her to her tryst.

"Lost, lost, betrayed, betrayed, I am lost, I have betrayed myself to him, he saw it all—the lie in my eyes, my fidgeting feet, my shivers—he saw it all, he despises me, it is over, and I must die. One should plant more kaffir corn, keep its runners trimmed, the panicles make good brooms. And how did I reply? With babble that betrayed me, he laughed at me, how horrible, I will have to kill myself. Was I at least beautiful? If I was beautiful there in the light, it may all be only half so bad, and I won't have to kill myself. The golden bronze of his shoulders . . . Oh, Amun in your shrine! 'Mistress of my head and heart, of my hands and feet' . . . Oh, Osarsiph! Do not speak to me like that with your lips, making fun of me in your heart, of my stammering and my trembling knees. I hope, I hope . . . even if all is lost and I must die after this misfortune, yet do I hope and do not despair, for not all is unfavorable, there is favor as well, indeed much favor, for I am your mistress, boy, and you must speak to me as sweetly as when you said 'Mistress of my head and heart,' even if it is only a turn of phrase and hollow courtesy. But words are strong, words are not spoken with impunity, they leave traces in the heart, even if spoken without feeling they speak to the feelings of him who speaks them, though you may lie with them, their magic shapes you according to their meaning, so that what you have said is no longer entirely a lie. That is very favorable and laden with hope, for the words that you must speak to me, your mistress, cultivate your emotions, my little slave, and make them rich and fine soil for the seed of my beauty, if I am lucky enough to appear beautiful to you in the light, and together my beauty and the servility of your words will become salvation and bliss from you to me, and they are the germ of an adoration that awaits only encouragement to become desire, for it is a certainty, my little boy, that adoration encouraged becomes desire . . . Oh, what a depraved woman I am! Shame on me for my serpent's thoughts! Shame upon my head and heart! Osarsiph, forgive me, my young master and savior, morning and evening star of my life! Why did things have to go so wrong today because of my fidgeting feet, so that all seems lost now? But I will not kill myself just yet or send for a venomous asp to apply to my breast, for there is much hope and favor left still. Tomorrow, tomorrow, and each day thereafter. He will remain with us, remain over the house,

Peteprê refused my request to have him sold, I shall have to see him, always, and each day will dawn with favor and hope. 'We shall have to continue this at another time, steward. I will consider the matter and you have my permission to offer your petition again soon.' That was good, that was taking care of next time. Ah yes, you were at least prudent enough, Eni, despite all your madness, to provide for a sequel. He will have to come again, and if he tarries out of shyness, I shall send Dûdu the dwarf to him, to admonish him. And then how I shall improve on everything that went wrong today, and I shall greet him with a calm grace, with feet in total repose, allowing, if I so please, only a little mild encouragement of his adoration to show through. And soon, perhaps this very next time, he may appear less beautiful to me, so that my heart will be cooled toward him and I can smile and jest with a free spirit and enflame his heart for me, while I suffer not at all . . . No, ah no, Osarsiph, that is not how it will be, those are serpent's thoughts, and I will gladly suffer for you, my master and my salvation, for your glory is like that of a firstborn bull . . ."

These fluttering words, some of which Hezes and Me'et, her handmaids, overheard to their astonishment, were only a few of many, of hundreds of soliloquies that escaped her during the year when she still tried to conceal her love from Joseph; and the preceding dialogue about kaffir corn is also representative of countless others like it, carried on at various times of day and at various locations: in the garden just as before, in the fountain courtyard of the house of women, even in the little temple on its hill, to which, however, Eni never came without her escort, just as Joseph was likely to have in his train one or two scribes carrying scrolls containing the accounts, plans, and documents he would present to her. For it was always affairs of business about which they spoke: rations, the tilling of fields, commerce, and various crafts, records of which the young steward would present to his mistress, instructing her and expressing his need for her advice. These were in fact the spurious topics of their conversations, and it should be acknowledged—though with a skeptical smile—that Joseph made a point of turning this pretense into substance, of involving the woman in practical concerns and seeking her honest interest in them—even on the basis, if need be, of her fondness for his person.

It was a kind of cure—and young Joseph enjoyed playing the

role of instructor. His intention was—or so he thought—to divert his mistress's mind from personal to practical matters, from his eyes to his cares, and in the process to cool, disenchant, and heal her, so that he might enjoy the honor, advantage, and fine pleasure of associating with her as the object of her favor, but without any danger of plunging into that pit with which overanxious Bes had threatened him. One cannot help discerning a certain presumption in the youthful steward's healing regimen, by which he thought to hobble the soul of his mistress, of a woman like Mut-em-enet. A far more certain course for seriously banning the pit's dangers would have been to avoid his mistress and stay out of her sight, instead of holding pedagogical sessions with her. That Jacob's son preferred the latter arouses the suspicion that his cure was balderdash and this his idea of turning pretense into honorable substance was itself a pretense that served a mind no longer thinking pure thoughts but indulging in other proclivities.

This was at least the suspicion, or rather keen dwarfish conclusion, of Favored Bes, the gnome; and he made no bones about telling Joseph as much and, wringing his hands, begged him almost daily not to debase himself with blather and flimflam, but to be as clever as he was good and beautiful and to flee the hot breath of the fiery bull that lays waste to everything. But all in vain—his full-size friend, the young steward, knew better. For anyone justly accustomed to trusting his good sense will find, if that good sense should grow clouded, that such trust is itself a great danger.

Dûdu, that robust dwarf, was by now likewise playing his role according to the script: the role of the cunning go-between, of the informer betting on ruin, moving back and forth between two people who would like to sin, blinking and winking here, squinting and pointing there, popping up before you with a wry face and, without so much as parting his lips, turning a corner of his mouth into a pouch that gushes the panderer's insidious words. He played his role without any knowledge of those who had preceded or would follow him in it, as the first and only player, so to speak—just as everyone likes to see his role in life, as if it were his own invention, his personal handiwork—yet with a dignity and self-assurance that belongs to any player who has just stepped out into the spotlight, a dignity that is his not because, as he presumes, his role is unique and unprecedented, but, on the contrary, because he is drawing on a deeper consciousness in order to present once again something basic and legitimate and to conduct himself as a paragon of his kind, no matter how disgusting his kind may be.

In those days Dûdu had not yet traveled a certain byway that also belonged to his role, branching off from the one he diligently trod back and forth and leading to a third party—in this case, to Potiphar, his gentle master, so that he might prick him and trickle into his ear suspicions concerning certain pedagogical sessions. That was yet to come, but for now it seemed to him that things were not yet ripe for him to take that well-trodden path. He was not pleased that—despite all his diligent scheming to create opportunities and all the semicontrived messages that gushed from his mouth's pouch at both ends of the path—the young steward and the mistress were as good as never alone and almost without exception spoke to one another while under an escort of honor. And what they said displeased him as well: Joseph's healing regimen was not to his taste; it annoyed him, even though, just as his pure-minded cousin had, he recognized it to be balderdash in the service of certain proclivities. These exchanges about economic issues appeared to him to delay hoped-for developments, and he also worried that Joseph's method might prove successful and might actually purify and objectify the mistress's thoughts, diverting them from essential matters. For she would often also speak to him, her upstanding dwarf, about business affairs: production and trade, the price of oil and wax, problems of rations and storage; and though it did not escape his sun-inspired wit that she was simply cloaking her real thoughts, all the while secretly speaking about Joseph, her instructor, he felt vexed nonetheless as he passed back and forth, pouring out his cheering messages to both parties, the substance of which at one end was: How the youthful steward was often quite saddened because, although graciously allowed to be with his mistress at the end or in the midst of the day's labors and to bask his soul in her beauty, he was permitted to speak with her only about the tiresome business of the house, instead of being able to mention more refreshing, more personal matters. At the other end, it was: How the mistress had complained and ordered him, Dûdu, to express her bitterness to the young steward that he seemed to lack any appreciation for the favor of her audiences, speaking to her only about economics, without ever talking about himself and quenching her thirst to know about his person, his previous life, his wretched homeland, and his mother, about how it was that his birth might be called virginal and how he had descended into hell and risen again. It was, so Dûdu said, perfectly natural that a woman like Mut-em-enet would find such things far more fascinating than lectures on papermaking and setting up looms; and if the steward wished to make progress in his sessions with Mut—progress toward a highest goal, one higher and more glorious than all others he had thus far achieved in the house—he should pluck up his courage and speak in a less hidebound fashion.

"Let that be my concern, both the goals and the means," Joseph replied sullenly. "You, too, might speak directly instead of out the side of your mouth; for it repels me, and I would wish that you, spouse of Zeset, might hold to more objective topics. Do not forget that our relation is one of worldly understanding and not of the heart. You may report to me whatever you happen to hear in the house and city. But I have not encouraged you to offer friendly advice."

"By the heads of my children," Dûdu swore, "I bring you in accord with our covenant what I have heard of our mistress's bitter sighs about your hidebound lectures. This advice comes not from Dûdu, but from her and her sighs for a few fascinating topics."

This was, however, more than half a lie. For he had remonstrated with Mut-em-enet that if she wanted to learn of the steward's magic and ruin him, she must first get closer to his person, instead of allowing him to barricade himself behind his office and duties. But her response to his admonition had been:

"I find pleasure and some tranquillity of the soul in hearing what he is doing when I do not see him."

A very characteristic answer—even a touching one, if you like, for it reveals the envy that a woman in love feels toward the full life of a man, the jealousy that a creature who is pure emotion feels toward a factual state of affairs that lays claim to such large portions of her beloved's life and leaves her, as the suffering and idle party, with a life dedicated solely to feeling. This jealousy is usually the source of a woman's attempt to participate in the components of a man's life, even if they are not of a practical or economic nature, but intellectual.

Mut-em-enet, then, "found pleasure" in letting Joseph introduce her to these matters, even if under the excuse and pretense that he wished to solicit her advice because of his youth. And it is truly irrelevant what a lover's words are about, for it is his voice that embodies them—his lips shape them, his lovely gaze lends them meaning, and his nearness drenches even the coldest, driest words in moist warmth, just as sun and water warm and moisten the realm of earth. This turns each exchange of words into a conversation of love—which could never be carried on in its pure form, since it would consist only of the syllables "you" and "I" and would surely perish from its own great monotony, which is why it must always take recourse in other makeshift words. Moreover, as was evident from her ingenuous answer, Eni treasured the content of their conversations, it was food for her soul on those bleak and sadly indolent days stripped of hope when Joseph was traveling on business, upstream or down, and there was neither the necessity nor the possibility of "flashing glances" at meals or his visits to the house of women or any of the other encounters she awaited with such anxious desire. For then she would feed on these topics, exalting them in her heart, and, despite her misery as a woman of idle emotions, would find great consolation in knowing what business took her beloved from her to this or that city and its villages, to this fair or that market, and in being able at least to list the practical affairs that filled his manly days. Nor was she able to keep from boasting of her knowledge both to Peteprê's other chattering wives and her female attendants, or to Dûdu whenever he waited on her.

"The young steward," she said, "is on his way down the great waterway to Nekheb, the city of the Feast of Nekhbet, and is towing behind him two boatloads of doom palm and balanite fruits, figs and onions, garlic, melons, lemon cucumbers, and castor beans, which he wishes to trade beneath the pinions of the goddess for wood and sandal leather, because Peteprê is in need of them for his workshops. In consultation with me, the steward has chosen to ship these goods at a moment when, because of demand, the price for vegetables is high, but that of leather and wood is not."

And there was such a peculiar ringing lilt to her voice when she said these things that Dûdu would cup a little hand to one ear and wonder whether he might not soon be able to take that byway that led to Potiphar and to prick his interest.

What else should we say about this year, when out of pride and shame Mut was still trying to disguise her infatuation from Joseph and to hide it, or so she thought, from the outside world? The fierce battle with her feelings toward her slave—that is, her battle with herself—continued for a while, but was in fact over, had been decided, much to her happy misfortune, in favor of her feelings. Her only battle now was to keep her passion hidden from other people and her beloved; in her soul, however, she now gave herself over to this novelty with even less reserve and all the more delight and, one might say, all the more simplicity, precisely because her passion had been unknown to her for so long, because it had taken so long for her—an elegant saint, a nun of the moon casting cool light on this world—to realize the thrill of its awakening, and because it was with ever growing estrangement that she now recalled a previous life still unblessed by passion, into whose rigidity and sterility she could barely transport herself in her mind, for every ounce of her femininity, awakened now from its slumber, loathed the idea of ever being transported back to it again. The bewitching enhancement that the fullness of love brings to a life like hers is as familiar as it is ineffable; but gratitude for these blessings of delight and torment seeks a goal and finds it only in the object from which all else proceeds, or seems to proceed. Is it any wonder, then, that such a fullness of love, augmented by gratitude, becomes idolatry? We have observed on several occasions how for a few, brief, uncertain moments some people took Joseph to be half man, half—perhaps more than half—god. But should such fascination, such a momentary seizure, be called idolatry? What determination, what dynamic rapture there is in that word, at least according to the logic of love—a logic as bold as it is strange. Whoever has done such a thing to my life, it reasons, whoever has sent to me, who was once dead, these fires and frosts, these jubilant cries and tears, must be a god, there is no other possibility. But that person has done nothing at all, and everything comes from the one who is smitten. Except that she cannot believe it, but in her rapture, amid prayers of gratitude, makes a divinity of him. "Oh, ethereal days of vibrant emotion! You have made my life rich—it blossoms!" That was one of Mut-em-enet's prayers of thanksgiving, or a fragment of one, directed to Joseph, stammered in the rapture of bliss as she knelt at the foot of her bed, for no one saw her there. Why then, if her life was blossoming so richly, had she more than once come close to sending her Nubian slave for an asp that she might apply it to her breast? Yes, why had she actually once given such an order, so that the viper lay close at hand in its wicker basket and Mut abandoned her intention only at the last moment? Well, because she believed that she had ruined everything at their last meeting and had not only appeared ugly to her beloved, but also by staring and trembling, instead of receiving him with tranquil grace, had betrayed her love to him—the love of an old and ugly woman. After that, death was her only recourse—as punishment for both herself and her beloved, who from her death might read the secret she had kept so poorly that it had cost her her life.

This is the blossoming, confused logic of love, and so familiar as to be hardly worth recounting—for it is ancient, was ancient long before the days of Potiphar's wife, and appears terribly new only to someone like her, whose turn it is to experience it as the first and only person ever to be so overwhelmed. She whispered: "Oh hark, sweet music! . . . It rings upon my ear, and showers all its bliss." That is familiar, too—ears deceived by a receptive ecstasy that now and then visits both lovers and those ravished by a god, and this blurring of boundaries is a mark of how closely related the two conditions are—the one mingled with the divine, the other with much that is human. We also know (and thus can spare ourselves the full details) those feverish nights of love spent in a series of brief dreams in which the beloved is always present, but seems cold and suspicious, turns away in disdain—a chain of fatal and pernicious encounters with his image, each unflaggingly accepted by the slumbering soul and repeatedly interrupted by a sudden awakening, when, still fighting for air, she sits up and lights a candle, saying: "Ye gods, ye gods, how is it possible! How is such torment possible!" But does she curse him who is the cause of these nights? Certainly not. When morning releases her from her agony and she sits exhausted at the edge of her bed, this is the whisper that she sends from her chamber to his: "I thank you, my salvation, my happiness, my star!"

The kindhearted shake their heads at such a response to horrible suffering; they are baffled and feel that she has to some extent ridiculed their pity. But when the authorship of torment is understood not as human but divine, her sort of response is plausible and natural. And why is it so understood? Because it is a special authorship, which is divided between the "I" and the "you," remaining bound to the latter, to be sure, but also having its home in the former: it is the binding and intertwining of outer and inner, of image and soul—which is to say, a marriage out of which gods have indeed emerged, their manifestations being declared, not without reason, divine. A being whom we bless for the great torments that it inflicts on us must surely be divine and not human, otherwise we would curse it. There's no denying a certain logic here. A creature on whom the happiness and misery of our days in large measure depend, as is the case with love, gets nudged into the ranks of the divine, that is clear enough; for dependency always has been and always will be the source of our consciousness of God. But has anyone ever cursed his god? Quite possibly he has tried—but then the curse took exception to itself and sounded word for word like Eni's whisper.

This by way of explanation to the kindhearted, if not to their satisfaction. Did our Eni not have another special reason, by the way, to make a god of her beloved? She certainly did—particularly since her idolizing him canceled out her sense of debasement, which otherwise would have been inherent in the weakness for this foreign slave that she had had to struggle against for so long. A god descended from on high and in the form of a servant, recognizable only by his unconcealable beauty and the golden bronze of his shoulders—she was aware of that image somewhere within her conceptual world; it was her good fortune to be aware of it, for it explained and justified her infatuation. The hope that her dream of salvation would ever be fulfilled, however, opening her eyes and stanching the flow of blood—that hope took its nourishment from a more distant image, from other tidings, which she likewise found within her, though who knows from where: the image and tidings of mortals overshadowed by a god. It may well be that in reaching for this notion and its otherness, she was concealing from herself something of the fear that had overcome her upon hearing her husband's revelations about Joseph's consecration, how he was set apart and wore an adorning wreath upon his head.

The Second Year

And when the second year had come, something within Mut-em-enet's soul gave way and yielded, so that she began to reveal her love to Joseph. She could no longer help it; she loved him all too much. In giving way, she also began to confess her emotional state to a few people closest to her—but not to Dûdu; first, because, as she well knew, his sun-inspired wit had long since made that unnecessary, and second, because, despite her having yielded, it would have injured her pride to have confided in him. Instead they continued to maintain the convention that they must expose Joseph's magic in order to "ruin" him—the term had established itself between them, and no matter who spoke it, the meaning grew less and less ambiguous from day to day. Though she had never before had a confidante, she suddenly confided in two women of her entourage, each independently and much to the elevation of their positions: the concubine Meh-en-wesekht, a small cheerful woman who let her hair flow free and wore transparent garments; and an old "rubber-eater," a slave named Tabubu, who attended her in her chamber as guardian of the rouge pots, a woman with gray hair, black skin, and breasts like leather bags. In hushed tones, Eni opened her heart to both, but only after having encouraged their coaxing questions by her own behavior—by sighing, by smiling to herself, obviously lost in deepest thought, by refusing to say a word—so that these two women, the one beside the courtyard pool, the other at the dressing table, pressed her, pleaded with her, to confide in them the reason for her emotional state, to which she first responded with twists and turns and coy demurrals, but then, all atremble, whispered exuberantly into the ears of her likewise trembling confidantes the confession of her infatuation.

Although they surely had put two and two together before now, each first clapped her hands, only to hide her face in them, then kissed Eni's hands, and her feet as well; and both began to emit smothered coos and gurgles—a mixture of solemn excitement, sympathy, and tender concern, much as if Mut had told them that she was in the family way. And in fact this is exactly how these women greeted the grand, the sensational item of feminine news that Mut, their mistress, was in the throes of love. They both began bustling about, chatting away, comforting and congratulating the woman on her happy state, stroking her body as if it had become a vessel containing something precious and perilous, and showed in a thousand ways their nervous delight at this great and decisive turn of events, at this onset of feminine jubilation full of the secrecy, sweet deception, and intrigue that would enhance their daily routine. Tabubu, the black slave, who knew all sorts of wicked magic practiced in Negro lands and could conjure with nefarious and nameless divinities, wanted to begin her sorcery at once, to bait the lad with her arts and cast him before her mistress's feet as blissful prey. But at this point the daughter of Mai-Sakhme, prince of the nome, still rejected this idea in horror—thereby loftily displaying not only a higher level of civilization than the woman from Kush, but also the propriety of her feelings, however dubious they might in fact be. The concubine Meh, however, gave not a thought to the ploys of magic, because she for her part did not believe them at all necessary and considered the matter, apart from its danger, to be very simple.

"Why these sighs, blessed one?" she asked. "Is not the beautiful lad a purchased slave of the household, even if he stands at its head, and your obedient property from the first? If you like him, you need only signal as much by raising an eyebrow, and he will deem it the highest honor to place his head and feet alongside yours, and all will be well for you."

"In the name of the Hidden One, Meh!" Mut whispered, covering her face, "do not put it so directly, for you do not know what you say, and it rends my soul."

She felt no need to be angry with the young thing, for, although envious, Mut knew Meh to be pure, to be innocent of love and consuming guilt, and credited her with a good conscience, which can blithely speak of heads and feet lying side by side—however unbearably discomfiting she personally might find it.

"It is obvious," Mut continued, "that you were never in such a state, my child, such a thing having never been befallen or bedeviled you, but instead have chatted and nibbled alongside your sisters in Peteprê's house of women. Otherwise you would not say that I need only signal him by raising an eyebrow, but would know that the status of slave and mistress are quite canceled out because of my affections, that is, if they are not indeed reversed, so that it is I instead who tremble and dote upon his splendidly traced brows, watching to see if smooth cordiality reigns between them or if, disconcerted, they gather into a scowl of suspicion directed at me. Behold, you are no better than base Tabubu, who proposes I practice black arts with her, so that as the prey of her magic the young man's flesh might become mine without his knowing how. You should be ashamed that in your ignorance you plunge a sword into my heart with your proposals, then twist it in the wound. For you prattle and propose as if he were a body and not a soul and a mind besides—against which raised eyebrows are no better than the lure of magic, for both have power over the body only and would bring me only that, a warm corpse. If he once was obedient to me and the commands of my brows, my infatuation has now granted him his freedom, complete freedom, foolish Meh, and as a result I have been blissfully relieved of my role as mistress and bear his yoke, am subservient, in both joy and torment, to the freedom of his living soul. That is the truth, and I suffer quite enough from its not being exposed to the day, for by the light of day he is still falsely seen as the servant and I as his mistress. So that when he calls me mistress of his head and heart, of his hands and feet, I do not know whether he says so as my servant, aping a phrase, or as perhaps a living soul. I hope it is the latter, but then despair of it again at once. Heed my words! If it were only his mouth, then one might possibly listen to what you two say about imperious brows and magic, for the mouth is part of the body. But then there are his eyes and their beautiful night, filled with freedom and soul. Ah, but I have an especial fear of the freedom they contain, for it is, you see, freedom from the longing that holds me, a lost soul, in its dusky bonds and makes merry mockery—not of me directly, no, but of my longing, so that it shames and slays me, since my admiration of his freedom only heightens my longing and thereby coils me in still duskier bonds. Do you understand, Meh? And as if that were not enough, I must also fear the anger of his eyes and their condemnation, because what I feel for him is a deception and betrayal of Peteprê, the courtier, who is both his master and mine, and in whom he awakens the sense of well-being that comes with trust—and yet I would demand of him that he disgrace his master with me, upon my heart. His eyes threaten me with all this, and so now you see that I must deal not only with his mouth and the fact that he is not just a body. For a mere body is not caught up in circumstances and dependencies such as those that shape him and complicate our relationship to him by encumbering it with considerations and consequences and making it a matter of precept, honor, and moral stricture, clipping the wings of our desire and leaving it crouched upon the ground. How I have pondered these things, Meh, pondered them by day and by night. For a body is free and independent, without respect to all else, and there should be only bodies for love, so that they may float free and alone in empty space and embrace without consideration or consequence, eyes closed and mouth to mouth. That would be bliss—and yet a bliss that I reject. For can I possibly want a lover who would be only an indifferent body, a corpse, but no person? I cannot, for I love not only his mouth, but his eyes as well, them above all, and for that reason your proposals repel me, both yours and Tabubu's, and I impatiently reject them."

"I do not understand," said Meh the concubine, "your ticklish scruples in this regard. I merely meant that since you like him it is plainly a matter of putting your feet and heads together, so that all will be well with you."

As if that were not ultimately the goal for which Mut-em-enet, beautiful Mutemône, likewise yearned. The thought that her feet, which could only fidget when she was with Joseph, might lie nestled against his—it was this very notion that thrilled and excited her to the marrow, and Meh-en-wesekht's having lent her such direct words for it—though, to be sure, without its meaning for her anything remotely like what it meant for Mut—only encouraged Mut's inner yielding, one token of which had been her willingness to communicate with these women, so that in both word and deed she now began to offer the young steward intimations of her weakness and infatuation.

As for the deeds, these were childish and rather touching hints, little acts of attentiveness of a mistress for her servant, in response to weighty symbolism of which the latter found it difficult to put on a proper face. One day, for example—and often thereafter—she received him for their business conference in an Asiatic dress that her seamstress, the slave Kheti, had sewn for her with great diligence and the rich fabric for which she had ordered from a bearded Syrian in the bazaar of the City of the Living. It was far gaudier than any Egyptian garment, appeared to be made of two intertwined pieces of embroidered wool, one red and one blue, and was trimmed not only with needlework but also colorful braiding at the sleeves and hem—all very extravagant and exotic. The shoulders were covered by wide straps cut in authentic style, and the dress was set off by an equally brightly embroidered headband—called a *sânip* in the homeland of this fashion—over which Eni had tossed the obligatory veil, which fell to below her hips. And decked out in this garb, she gazed at

Joseph, her eyes widened both by the applied galena and by anxious, mischievous expectation.

"How strange and glorious you appear before me today, my mistress," he said with a chagrined smile, for he had understood her insinuation.

"Strange?" she asked—and her smile was forced, tender, confused. "Rather familiar, I would say, for in this garment, which I donned today for variety's sake, I thought to appear as one of the daughters of your own land—if that was the point of your comment."

"The garment and the cut of it are indeed familiar," he said with lowered eyes, "but it still looks rather strange on you."

"So you don't think it suits me or works to my advantage?" she asked, faltering even as she dared the question.

"There is yet to be a fabric woven," he replied guardedly, "or a garment fashioned, even if it were of sackcloth, that would not enhance your beauty, my mistress."

"Well, then, if it's all the same to you and of no importance what I wear," she responded, "the effort that went into this garment was labor lost. But I have put it on in honor of your visit by way of reciprocation. For you, though a youth from Retenu, dress in Egyptian style among us, out of courtesy for our customs. And I thought I ought not be left behind and, for my part, requite the favor by appearing before you in your mother's garb. And so we have exchanged garments as if for a feast. For since days of yore there has been something festive and godly about such exchanges, when men go about in the clothes of women and the woman in the garb of the man, and differences fall away."

"Might I remark in that regard," he replied, "that such usages and rites do not make me feel especially at home. For there is about them a giddiness and a falling away from godly sobriety that did not please my fathers."

"So I have failed in my purpose," she said. "What news do you bring of the household?"

She was deeply hurt because he did not seem to understand (though he understood quite well) what a sacrifice of feeling it had been for her—a child of Amun, a harem wife of the mighty god, a partisan of his rigor—to pay homage to things foreign and wear this dress because her beloved was a foreigner. Her sacrifice had been sweet, she had thought it bliss to divest herself of patriotic spirit for his sake; and she was now very unhappy because his response had been so feeble. She was happier on another occasion, although its symbolic act required that she divest even more of herself.

Her living quarters, a chamber looking out onto the desert in the house of women to which she preferred to withdraw, was a small portico—an apt term, since its wooden-framed doors were wide open and the verandah beyond was divided by two pillars, which had simple rounded capitals and squared architraves beneath their cornices, but stood without pedestals flush to the threshold. The view was to a courtyard and on the right was a set of low white buildings, beneath whose flat roofs were the apartments of the concubines and which butted up against a tall pylonlike structure with columns. Running at an angle from this was a shoulder-high clay wall, so that only sky, but no land was visible beyond. The little hall was elegant and simple, its ceiling not especially high; long black shadows from the pillars stretched across the floor; the walls were plastered in a modest lemon color, as was the ceiling, beneath which, as the only ornament, ran a band of pastel colors. The room contained little more than a graceful couch at the far end, with cushions strewn over it and pelts scattered before it. It was here that Mut-em-enet often waited for Joseph.

It was his custom to appear in the courtyard and, clamping his scrolls of accounts under one arm, to raise his hands, palms exposed, toward the chamber where the lady lay resting. Then she would grant him permission to approach and speak before her; but one day he immediately realized something had changed in the hall, as was evident from the look in her eyes, which met his with the same happy discomfiture as on the day she had worn the Syrian dress; but he pretended to notice nothing, greeted her with a few well-chosen words, and began to speak of business.

Until she admonished him, saying, "Look about you, Osarsiph. What do you see that is new here?"

New was a very fitting word for what he saw. It was hard to believe: at the rear of the room stood an altar spread with a knitted cloth, and on it was a shrine, opened to reveal a gilded statue of Atum-Rê.

The Lord of the Horizon was unmistakable—he looked like his

hieroglyph. He sat on a small square pedestal, his knees drawn up, a falcon head set atop his shoulders, and atop it a superfluous, elongated solar disk, with the full raised hood and curled tail of the uraeus extending from front and back. On a tripod beside the altar lay long-handled incense pans, as well as a bowl with incense pellets and tools for making fire.

Astounding, almost incredible! But touching as well—what a childishly daring way for her to express the longing of her heart. The mistress Mut, from the harem of the god rich in cattle, who sang and danced for him, the ram-browed god of the empire; a confidante of his cleverly politic and shiny-headed chief priest; a partisan of his solar doctrine that preserved popular piety and morals—she had created within her most private world a shrine to the Lord of the Wide Horizon, to the object of conjecture by Pharaoh's sages, to the god of obliging, all-seeing concord, to the brother and friend of foreign, Asian sun gods, to Rê-Horakhte-Atôn of On at the tip of the triangle. This was how she expressed her love, by fleeing into this language—the language of a space and time that, as Egyptian woman and Hebrew lad, they both shared. How could he not have understood her? He had understood for a long time now, and he deserves praise for how touched he was by this moment—for what he felt was joy mixed with alarm and concern. And it caused him to bow his head.

"I see your devotions, mistress," he said softly. "They alarm me somewhat. For what if Beknechons, the great priest, were to visit you and see what I see?"

"I do not fear Beknechons," she replied, trembling in triumph. "Pharaoh is greater!"

"May he live, whole and healthy," he muttered mechanically. "You, however," he added, still very softly, "belong to the Lord of Ipet-Isowet."

"Pharaoh is his son upon earth," she replied so quickly that it was evident she had prepared herself well. "I surely should be allowed to serve the god whom he loves and whom he commands his sages to fathom. Where is there an older, greater god in the Two Lands? He is like Amun, and Amun is like him. Amun has called himself by his name and said, 'He who serves me, serves Rê.' And so in serving him, I serve Amun as well."

"Whatever you say," he answered softly.

"Let us burn incense to him," she said, "before turning to the affairs of the house."

And she took him by the hand and led him to the statue and the tripod with its sacrificial utensils.

"Place the incense upon it," she said—she actually said *"senter neter,"* which means "divine smell" in the language of Egypt—"and light it, if you would be so kind." But he hesitated.

"It is not good, mistress," he said, "for me to burn incense before an image. It is forbidden among my people."

She stared at him, in such mute, undisguised pain that he took alarm yet again, for written in her eyes were the words: "So you will not join me in burning incense to him who allows me to love you?"

But he recalled On at the tip of the Delta, the gentle doctrine of its scholars, and its Father High Priest, whose smile implied that whoever sacrifices to Horakhte is sacrificing to his own god in accord with meaning of the triangle.

And so in reply to her stare, he said, "I will gladly assist, will place the incense in the pan and light it and officiate at your sacrifice."

And he placed one of the pellets of terebinth resin in the pan and, striking a flame, set it alight, then shifted the handle to her hand so that she could cense the statue. And as she let the fragrant smoke rise before Atum's nose, he raised his hands and worshiped that tolerant god—though with reservation and in hopes that this would be charitably overlooked. But all during the domestic lecture that followed, Eni's breast swelled at the thought of this symbolic act.

Such were the deeds with which she confessed her desire to him; but the poor woman could not dispense with words any longer, either. Yes, once her soul had given way, her longing to let her beloved know precisely what, in a life-and-death struggle, she had tried so long to hide from him gained the upper hand; and since, moreover, she was constantly advised and urged by Dûdu, as he traveled back and forth, to turn their conversation from practical to personal matters so that she might catch the scoundrel in his tricks and "ruin" him, she was forever scratching with feverish hands at the commercial husk of their conversations, at its fig leaf, so that she might strip it away, uncovering the truth and nakedness of "you" and "I"— without ever suspecting what frightening notions Joseph associated with the idea of uncovering nakedness: Canaanite associations, fraught with warnings against what was forbidden and every sort of drunken shamelessness, which could be traced back to the place of beginnings, where the all-pervading encounter between nakedness and knowledge had first occurred, giving rise to the distinction between good and evil. Oblivious of such a tradition and, despite her fine sense of honor and shame, of any deeper understanding of the idea of sin, for which she did not even have a word in her vocabulary and, what was more, which she was not at all accustomed to associating with nakedness, Mut could know nothing of the inborn, impersonal terror of Baal that the thought of exposing their naked conversation stirred within this young man's blood. Every time he would try to reclothe it in the robe of objectivity, she would pull it off and force him to abandon matters of domestic economy and speak of himself, of his current and previous life, would ask him about his mother, whom he had mentioned to her before, and listen as he told of her legendary loveliness. From there it was but a short step to the topic of his inherited personal share in her handsome beauty, a beauty that she would remark upon with a few smiling words, but then could no longer refrain from noting and praising in ever more fervent and passionate tones.

"It is seldom," she said—leaning back in a wide armchair that stood at the tail end of a lion skin, while the head of the ravenous beast gaped its jaws at Joseph's feet—"seldom" she said—replying to a previous remark of his and with forced composure crossing her feet on the padded footstool—"very seldom indeed that we hear tell of someone and listen to her description, even as the illustrative image of that description stands visible before us. It is strange, indeed curious for me to be told about and simultaneously to behold the eyes of that lovely woman, of that mother sheep, directed at me in all their cordial night, the very eyes from which the man from the west, your father, kissed away tears of impatience during that long period of waiting. For it was not without purpose that you have said you are so like the woman he waited for, in the same way that she lived in you after her death and that your father mistakenly loved you both together, mother and son. Yes, you gaze at me with her eyes, Osarsiph, even as you describe her to me as extraordinarily beautiful. Yet I did not know for such a long time from where you have these eyes, which, from all I hear, win the hearts of men on highway and waterway alike. Until now they were a phenomenon without context, if I may put it that way. But it is pleasant and gratifying, if not to say comforting, to learn of the origin and history of a phenomenon that speaks to our soul."

One ought not be astonished at the anguish contained in such words. Love is an illness, though perhaps more like pregnancy and the labors of childbirth, and thus, so to speak, a healthy illness, even if, like them, it is not without its dangers. The woman's mind was dazed, and although as an educated Egyptian she could express herself with literary and, after her own fashion, reasonable eloquence, her ability to differentiate between what was permissible and impermissible was greatly diminished and blurred. What made things more difficult, and indeed pardonable, was her unrestricted power as mistress of the house, which left her thoroughly accustomed to saying whatever she wished, in the certainty that anything she desired to say could by its very nature never violate aristocratic good taste—a certainty on which she surely could also have depended in a time of health. But she failed now to take into account her condition, which was entirely new to her, and dealt with it in her accustomed, unrestricted mode of speech, with necessarily awkward results. There is also no doubt that Joseph found it awkward, indeed insulting, not only because she exposed herself in this way, but also because he took personal offense at it. The least of it was watching as his instructive and healing regimen, embodied in the scrolls of accounts he held clamped under his arm, was foundering more and more. What truly upset him was how his mistress applied her proud, unrestricted freedom of speech to this new state of affairs and spoke to him about his eyes in the beguiling, pretty words that a lover speaks to his lass. It is worth noting that "mistress," as the feminine form of the word "master," still retains by and large its original masculine element. A mistress is, in physical terms, a master in female form; in psychological terms, however, she is a woman of masterful character, which means that the title of mistress never lacks a certain twofold nature, in which the idea of the masculine, however, definitely dominates. On the other hand, beauty is a passive, feminine quality, inasmuch as it arouses longing and transfers the active, manly impulses of admiration, desire, and pursuit to the breast of the male gazing upon it, which can therefore result, by the reverse process, in that same twofold nature, though in this case under the dominance of the female. Now Joseph certainly felt at home with such concepts of duality. His mind easily grasped how a virgin and a virginal man could be united in the person of Ishtar and how that same phenomenon was repeated in her brother, son, and husband, in Tammuz the shepherd, who exchanged the veil with her—so that together they actually made four in all. And though these were only remote and foreign memories now, something for the mind to play with, facts taken from Joseph's immediate sphere and reality taught the same lesson. In terms of its larger meaning, his father's spiritual name of Israel likewise carried the twofold sense of male and female, of a virgin betrothed as both bride and bridegroom to the Lord his God. And what about Him, the lonely and jealous God? Was He not both father and mother of the world in one, a God of two faces, the first that of a man turned toward the daylight, the second, however, that of a woman gazing into the darkness? Yes, was not this double nature the first principle of God, by which both Israel's twofold sexual relationship with Him, and, in particular, Joseph's personal relationship—with its strong components of the female and the bride—were defined?

Quite right, quite true. But it will not have escaped the attentive reader that over time certain changes had taken place in Joseph's sense of himself—changes that made him uncomfortable with serving as an object of admiration, desire, and pursuit for a mistress who paid him the same compliments a man pays a woman. This did not suit him, and his natural growth into manhood—the consequence not only of his twenty-five years but also of his official position and success at bringing a major piece of Egyptian economic life under his oversight and control—easily explains why it could no longer suit him. And yet easily explained is not entirely explained; there were other reasons for his discomfort—reasons that associated Joseph's growth from boyhood into manhood with the image of the dead Osiris' being awakened by the vulture-woman hovering above him and conceiving Horus by him. Need we call attention to the strong correspondence between this image and real circumstances—to the fact, for example, that when dancing before Amun as one of the god's wives, Mut also wore a vulture headdress? There is no doubt that the smitten woman herself was the cause for his increasing

manliness, which had begun to lay its own claim to desire and pursuit and found it unsuitable to be paid compliments by a masterful
mistress.

Which is why on such occasions Joseph would fall silent and
simply stare at the woman with those eyes she had praised, before
turning to the scrolls under his arm and inquiring if they might not
move from this digression about his person to a discussion of business. Mut, however, bolstered in her aversion to such matters by
Dûdu's promptings, ignored his request and persevered in her desire
to disclose her love to him. We are not speaking here of a single incident, but of countless, very similar events over the course of this second year of love. Dazed and free of all restriction, she went into
raptures not only about his eyes, but also about his manly frame, his
voice, his hair—always beginning with his mother, that lovely
woman, and then marveling at the twists and turns of inheritance, by
which excellent qualities that had once assumed feminine shape and
stamp had been passed on in manly form and timbre to the son.
What was he to do? We must acknowledge that he was cordial and
good to her and tried to persuade her with kindly words; and we can
even observe him trying to disenchant her by taking refuge in sensible remarks about the poor quality of those things she so admired.

"Let it be, my mistress," he said, "and do not speak in this way.
These outward shows that enjoy your respect and regard—what are
they really? Nothing but sorry things. One would indeed do well to
recall—and to remind those who smile upon them—what everyone
knows in any case, but tends to forget in his weakness: of what poor
stuff it all is made, and not even that, for, God help us, it is not made
to endure. Do but consider that in a short while this hair will fall out,
as will these now white teeth. These eyes are but a jelly of blood and
water that will ooze away, just as all the rest of this sham is doomed
to shrivel and come to a contemptible end. As you see, I deem it
proper not to keep these rational considerations to myself, but to
place them at your disposal as well, should you find they could be of
use to you."

But she did not find them useful, and her condition made them
quite unserviceable as pedagogical material. Not that she was angry
at him for his penitential homily—she was far too happy that the
topic was not kaffir corn and other such oppressively respectable
subjects, but that their conversation centered on issues in which she

felt competent as a woman, so that there was no need for her feet to take flight.

"How strangely you speak, Osarsiph," she replied, her lips caressing the name. "Your words are cruel and false—that is, false in their cruelty; for though their rational content is true and indisputable, they do not apply at all to the heart and temperament, and to these are truly no better than a tinkling cymbal. For you err greatly in saying that the transience of such stuff is one reason less to admire its form—indeed, it is one reason more, because mixed with our admiration is a touching sympathy that is totally lacking in our regard for the enduring material beauty of brass and stone. How incomparably more vigorous is our fondness for the beautiful living figure than for the enduring beauty of images from Ptah's workshops—and would you instruct the heart that the stuff of life is baser and more contemptible than the enduring stuff of its imitations? The heart will never, ever learn or accept that. For endurance is dead, and only death endures. And though Ptah's diligent students may place sparks in the eyes of those images, so that they appear to gaze out, they do not see you, only you see them; their existence is not that of a 'you' responding to you, not that of an 'I' partaking of its own kind. We feel a sympathy only for beauty of our own kind. Who would ever be tempted to lay a hand upon the brow of some enduring figure from a workshop, to kiss it upon the lips? From which you can see how much more vigorous and touching is our fondness for the—granted—transient living form. Transience! Why and for what purpose do you speak to me of it, Osarsiph, admonishing me in its name? Does one carry a mummy through the banquet hall as an admonition to end the feast because all is transient? No, just the opposite. For upon its brow is written: 'Seize the day!'"

A fine, a truly excellent answer—that is, of its kind, that is, given the dazed state that must serve as the alluring garment for cleverness left over from healthy days. Joseph merely sighed and said nothing more in rebuttal. He felt that he had done his part and ceased to insist upon the deeper cruelty of all superficial flesh, for he was well aware that a dazed mind ignores it and that "heart and temperament" wish to hear nothing about it. He had better things to do than to explain to this woman how life, like the beauty of corruptible human flesh, is as much a sham as are the images of a workshop, or how there is a truth in which life and beauty are solid and do not deceive, but that it belongs to another order and that we would do better to direct our minds to it alone. For instance, he had more than enough to do just fending off the presents she had been trying to shower upon him of late—moved, as she was, by that ancient and forever lively desire of those who love, which is rooted in feelings of dependency upon the person whom they have made into a god, to offer sacrifices, to glorify and adorn them, to woo them with bribes. And that is not all. The lover's gift also acts as a means of claiming and seizing possession, it serves to brand the person loved before the rest of the world with a protective symbol of ownership, to clothe him in a livery that says he is no longer available. If you wear my gift, you are mine. The finest gift of love is the ring—whoever gives it knows perfectly well what he wants and whoever takes it surely knows what is happening to him, for the ring is a visible link in an invisible chain. And so, ostensibly to thank him for his services and having initiated her in the affairs of business, a dazed-looking Eni presented Joseph a very costly ring with an engraved scarab, and as time went on other jewels as well: golden clasps for his wrist, a colorful collar of gemstones, and even an entire festive outfit of the finest handiwork. Which is to say, she wanted to "give" him all these things and attempted to force them upon him each time with innocent words. But he, after having respectfully accepted one or two, refused the rest—at first with tender and pleading words, but then with brief and blunt ones. And it was these very words that made his situation clear to him, for he recognized them.

In fending off the immoderate gift of a festive garb, he said to her curtly: "My cloak and my shirt are sufficient"—and suddenly he was aware of the game being played. He had inadvertently responded as had Gilgamesh when Ishtar besieged him because of his beauty and solicited him, saying: "Come then, Gilgamesh, you shall pair with me and impart your fruit to me," while holding out to him the splendor of many gifts should he comply with her wish. Such a recognition is both calming and terrifying. "There it is again!" a man says, and feels it to be guarded by myth, established and abiding, something more than reality, to be, that is, the truth of what is happening—and the effect is calming. And yet he is also seized by terror to find himself miming a role in a festive masque, to be the present embodiment of a divine story as it is played out in one way or another, and he feels as if he is in a dream. I see, I see, Joseph thought as he gazed upon poor Mut. Inside your truth you are Anu's wanton daughter and yet ultimately you do not know it. I shall curse you and reproach you for the many lovers you have assaulted with your love, transforming one into a bat, another into a colorful bird, a third into a wild dog, so that, though he was himself the shepherd of his flock, he was chased away by shepherd boys and his own dogs bit into his hide. And the words that I have been given to say are: "It will happen to me as to them." Why did Gilgamesh speak those words and offend you, so that in your rage you ran to Anu and convinced him to send out the fire-snorting bull of heaven against this disobedient man? I now know why, for I understand myself in him, as I understand him through myself. He spoke those words out of discomfort that you, his mistress, had paid him masterful compliments, and he flaunted his virginal state before you—Ishtar who wears a beard!—and girded himself with his chastity against your pursuit and your gifts.

Joseph's Chastity

Having observed Joseph, the reader of stone tablets, unite his thoughts with those of his predecessor, we find he has provided us with a catchword for an analysis that is both a reckoning and a summary and that is best inserted here, for we are convinced that we owe as much to humane letters. That catchword is chastity. This concept has been inseparably joined with the figure of Joseph for millennia now; it provides the classical sobriquet for his name, "chaste Joseph"; and sometimes, when applied symbolically to others, "a chaste Joseph." That is the charming but prudish formula by which his memory lives on among a humanity separated from him by such deep abysses of time; and we would not have done our best, we think, in presenting a detailed and trustworthy version of his story had we not gathered together into one place the various allusions to his motives, all the motley and checkered constituent parts of his renowned chastity, and presented them as comprehensively and impressively as possible to the reader, who, out of understandable sympathy for Mut-em-enet's suffering, may well be annoyed by Joseph's stubbornness.

Needless to say, chastity cannot exist where there is no free ability to exercise it—for instance, among titular commanders and mutilated chamberlains of the sun. One obvious prerequisite is that Joseph was an intact and alive human being. We know, by the way, that during his mature years he entered into an Egyptian marriage under royal patronage, from which came two boys, Ephraim and Manasseh (who will be presented in due time). As a grown man he no longer maintained his chastity, but only during his years as a youth—itself a concept that for him was inseparably bound up in some special way with the idea of chastity. It is clear that he preserved his virginity—which surely applies to men as well as women—only as long as its surrender carried the connotation of something forbidden, of temptation and ruin. Later, when it no longer made any difference, so to speak, he let go of his chastity without a thought, so that the classical sobriquet does not apply to him for his entire life but only for a certain portion of it.

Which leaves us to refute the misunderstanding that his was the chastity of a country bumpkin and block-headed bungler in matters of love—that it came from a kind of idiotic clumsiness that a more enterprising temperament all too easily imagines to be linked with chastity. That the darling of Jacob's worries was a ninny, a deadwood, in regard to more risqué matters is an assumption that would not coincide very well with the image that was first presented to us at the very beginning and that we observed through the anxious eyes of his father: the image, that is, of a seventeen-year-old beside a well, dandling with the beautiful moon and making himself beautiful for it. His famed chastity was in fact so far from being due to a lack of talent that it was more like the exact opposite—it was based in a loving spirit that penetrated the entire world and his shifting relationships with it, a universal love, which fully deserved that adjective, because it did not stop at the limits of this earth, but was present as an aura, a gentle infusion, a subtle force, an unspoken substratum in every regard, including what was most terrifyingly holy. It was this love that was the source of his chastity.

Early on we tried to deal with the phenomenon of God's living jealousy, describing unambiguous, passionate visitations by that former desert demon—despite a far more advanced stage of mutual sanctification in covenant with the human spirit—when persecuting examples of unbridled emotional despotism and idolatry, about which Rachel could have written a book. We said in advance even then that Joseph, her son, had a better understanding of God's living reality and would prove more supple in dealing with it than Jacob, the man of feeling who had sired him. So then, Joseph's chastity was above all the expression of this understanding and caution. Of course he had understood that his suffering and dying, whatever other far-reaching purposes they might have had, had been the punishment for Jacob's arrogance of emotion, his imitation of a majestic selectivity and preference, which had no longer been tolerated—an act of utmost jealousy, directed against the poor old man. To that extent, God's visitation upon Joseph had been intended for his father and was nothing more than a continuation of what had been done to Rachel, whom Jacob had never ceased to love all too much—in the form of her son. But jealousy has a double meaning, a twofold reference. One can be jealous of a person because someone to whose feelings one lays total claim loves that other person all too much; or one can be jealous of the person one loves, because in the enormity of having chosen him, one covets his entire feelings for oneself. A third possibility is that these two can join to form perfect jealousy—and Joseph was not so fundamentally wrong to presume such perfection in his case. It was his opinion that he had been mutilated and carried off not simply, not even primarily, as a means for punishing Jacob—or, then again, perhaps the predominant purpose had been such punishment, precisely because he, Joseph, had been the object of an overwhelming selectivity, an all-powerful covetousness, a jealous preemption, and on a scale about which an anxious Jacob might have had his conjectures, but that was still very remote from his own sedate paternalism, which did not even approach such an advanced level of cunning. We are quite aware that modern sensibilities may be deeply confused and wounded by ideas such as these, by this emphasis on the relationship between Creator and creature, for we are no more comfortable with it than with dogged paternalism. But it has its place in time and historical development, and in psychological terms there is no doubt that more than one of the fertile conversations that tradition tells us were held under the cover of a cloud between the Unseeable (whatever name He might bear) and His disciple and darling had about them something so monstrously provocative that it ultimately justifies Joseph's view of things—its probability resting simply upon his own personal merit, which we have no desire to dispute.

"I keep myself pure" were words that little Benjamin had heard that day in the garden of Adoni from the lips of the brother he admired, and they referred both to the purity of his face, whose special, seventeen-year-old beauty would have been undone by a beard, and to his relationship to the outside world, which had been and still remained one of an abstinence far removed from that of a ninny. It meant nothing more than caution, devout cleverness, and holy discretion, in which the experience of that horrible rape—the tearing to shreds of wreath and veil—could only have greatly strengthened him; one must suppose that it was associated with a haughtiness that stripped it of any sense of self-denying gloom. We are not speaking of some dark and painful mortification, in whose haggard image chastity is almost inevitably pictured by modern understanding. Yet even the modern world will have to admit that chastity can also be serene, even high-spirited; and, given that he was predisposed for it by his own bright and jaunty personality, Joseph needed only the added delight he took in his lofty status as a devout bride to find it easy to do what for others is a grim hardship. In her conversation with the concubine Meh-en-wesekht, Mut, his mistress, had made plaintive mention of the merry mockery she claimed to have found in the young steward's eyes—mockery of the dusky bonds of the longing that shamed her. That was a very good observation on her part; for of the three beasts—Shame, Guilt, and Mocking Laughter—that Joseph said stood guard in the garden of the girl who caught birds, he was most familiar with the last, but not in a passive sense, as the beast's victim, as his story implied, but as someone who laughed in mockery, which was exactly what those women on the lookout upon the roofs and walls found in his eyes. There is no disputing that such an attitude toward the world of infatuated lust does occur; it may come from the awareness of a higher bond, of having been chosen out of love. But all those who would see this as arrogance toward our common humanity and think it culpable to view passion in a comic light, should know that our tale is approaching the hour when Joseph's laughter will die within him and that the second catastrophe of his life, his renewed descent into the depths, was caused by the same power to which in his youthful pride he had believed he could refuse to pay tribute.

This was the first reason why Joseph rejected the lustful desires of Potiphar's wife: He was betrothed to God, was cleverly discreet, took into account the special pain that unfaithfulness inflicts upon the lonely. His second motive was closely linked to the first, it was really only its reflection, its repetition, so to speak, in earthly, bourgeois form. This was his loyalty—enshrined in his covenant with the departed Mont-kaw—to Potiphar, to his delicate master, to the highest in his immediate vicinity.

This equation of what is absolutely Most High with what is only locally and relatively the highest, the confusion of those two within the mind of Abram's grandson, cannot help appearing absurd, even crude, to our modern understanding. It must nevertheless be assumed and accepted if one wishes to know how things looked inside the mind of a man from these early (but, then again, actually late) times, a man who thought his thoughts with the same dignity of reason, composure, and self-evidency as we do ours. There is no denying that to Joseph's dreamy mind this plump, though noble courtier of the sun, this titular husband of Mut, appeared, in all his melancholy selfishness, to be the earthly equivalent and fleshly repetition of the wifeless, childless, lonely, and jealous God of his fathers, and it was this man whom he had most earnestly resolved—on the basis of a kind of playful analogue that was not without an element of speculation as to its usefulness—to serve in considerate faithfulness. If one bears in mind the holy oath Joseph had sworn to Mont-kaw in his hour of death—to shield Potiphar's tender dignity with all his skill and never allow it to be disgraced—one can understand all the better how the now scarcely concealed wishes of poor Mut must have seemed to him a serpentlike temptation to learn the meaning of good and evil and repeat Adam's folly. This was his second reason.

For the third, it surely suffices to mention how his awakened manliness did not like being reduced to passive femininity by a mistress's masterful pursuit, wanted to be not the target but the arrow of desire—that's to be understood. And the fourth follows easily enough, since it likewise concerns his pride, his spiritual pride.

Joseph shuddered at the thought of what Mut, an Egyptian woman, embodied in his eyes and of how a proud tradition of laws of purity warned him against mixing his blood with hers. She was the antiquity of the land into which he had been sold, a bleak and immutable expanse of time that stared out into a brutal, dead future devoid of expectation and yet seemed about to raise a paw to snatch to its breast the child of promise standing musing before it, and, whatever its own sexual nature, to make him name his name. For what was ancient and without promise was also lewd, lusting after young blood—particularly blood young not only in years, but also and especially in its having been chosen for the future. Joseph had never forgotten his exclusive rank since the day he had arrived in this land as a nothing, a nobody, a slave from the wretched desert, and despite all his obliging worldliness—both that native to him and that which he had taken on among the children of the mud in hope of great advancement—he had kept his distance and inner reserve, knowing full well that in the end he was not allowed to make common cause with these forbidden people, aware ultimately of what spirit had sired him and who his father was.

His father! That was the fifth—if not the first and overriding—reason. Having grown accustomed to the mournful belief that death safely held his child, the despondent old man had no idea where Joseph now lived, or that he walked about clad in very strange garb. Had he found out, he would have fallen back in a faint, paralyzed with worry, that much is certain. When Joseph thought of the third of his three motifs—of being carried off, raised up, and sending for others to follow—he never denied to himself the resistance it would encounter from Jacob; for he knew the melodramatic prejudices the dignified man held against Mizraim, knew the fatherly and childish abhorrence he felt toward the land of Hagar, toward monkey-faced Egypt. The good man quite falsely traced the meaning of the word "Keme"—which was derived from the black, fruitful soil—back to Ham, who had shamed his father and shamefully bared his own nakedness; and when it came to the cruel folly of Keme's children in matters of morals and modesty, Jacob held quite extravagant notions, which Joseph had always suspected were one-sided and, having lived here, had since learned to smile at as fanciful legends. For the lust of its children was no worse than the lust of other people, and where were these gasping, overtaxed, drudging peasants and systematically flogged water carriers—whom Joseph had known now for nine years—supposed to find the lusty energy to carry on like denizens of Sodom? In short, the old man solemnly imagined all sorts of silly things about the conduct of the people of Egypt—as if their mode of life would have had to leave the sons of God in wanton shock.

All the same, Joseph was the last person to conceal from himself the kernel of truth within Jacob's moral rebuff of a land whose inhabitants worshiped animals and corpses, and during this same period his head was filled with many a pious and harsh word that the worried old man had spoken to him about people who placed their beds beside those of a neighbor and exchanged wives whenever they liked; about women who, when they went to the market and saw a lad after whom they lusted, would lie with him without further ado or any notion of sin. Joseph was familiar with the world from which his father took these ominous images: it was the world of Canaan and its gruesome convulsions of worship contrary to all understanding of God, the world of the madness of Molech, of chanting and dancing, of self-surrender and *aulasaukaula*, where, caught up in solemn coupling fury, people whored before and after fertility idols. Joseph, Jacob's son, did not want to whore after Baals—that was the fifth of the seven reasons why he withheld of himself. The sixth lies close at hand. Out of sympathy for poor Mut, however, it is only appropriate that we note in passing the sad fate that doomed her yearnings for love—which is to say, the man on whom late in life she had hung her hopes saw her in just such a light, misunderstood her according to the myths of his father, and so inevitably had to hear within her cry of tenderness vile seductions that were scarcely there at all. The weakness of Eni's heart for Joseph had little do with the madness of Baal and *aulasaukaula*; its pain was a deeper and more honest longing for his beauty and youth, a sincere desire for them, as decent and indecent as any other, no more lewd than is love itself. If she later grew depraved and lost her reason, the blame lay solely in her grief at encountering his sevenfold rationale for withholding himself from her. It was her misfortune that what decided the fate of her love was not she herself, but what she meant for Joseph—and the sixth of his reasons was her "covenant with Sheol."

We need to understand this correctly. According to Joseph's basic spiritual view of a situation in which he wanted to conduct himself wisely and courteously, without compromising himself or doing harm, the babbling madness of Baal worship, which was a hostile and seductive Canaanite idea, was connected to and greatly weighed down by something particularly Egyptian—the cult of death and the dead, which was simply the local version of whoring after Baal; and it was Mut's misfortune that in Joseph's eyes its chief representative was his own wooing mistress. One cannot take too seriously the primal warning, the original and fundamental "no" that Joseph believed was attached to this mongrel hybrid of death and debauchery, to the idea of allying oneself with the lower world and its inhabitants; to transgress against this prohibition, to "sin" here, to blunder in this sinister matter would in fact mean to undo everything. His way of thinking, together with the serious constraints that it placed upon him, probably seems rather eccentric and remote to more modern, reasonable minds; it is our wish, however, to win them over as allies, to initiate them in his mode of thought. To his mind it was reason itself—or reason as refined by his father—that stood in opposition to the temptation of shameless unreason. It is certainly not the case that Joseph had no feeling or understanding for what is unreasonable—the worries of that old man at home tell us better. But doesn't a person have to understand something about sin in order to be able to sin? Sinning requires understanding; indeed, when rightly regarded, all spiritual understanding is nothing but a sense of sin.

The God of Joseph's fathers was a God of spiritual understanding, at least in terms of the goal toward which He was moving and for the sake of which He had entered into a covenant with men; in uniting man's will with His own will to sanctify, He had never had anything to do with the lower world and death, with any sort of unreason dwelling in the dark realm of fertility. In and through men, He had come to realize that all this was an abomination to Him, just as man had come to realize the same thing in and through Him. In saying good-night to the dying Mont-kaw, Joseph had, to be sure, become involved in the steward's concerns about dying, had sought to comfort him and allay his fears by discussing how it would be after this life and telling him that they would be together forever because their stories were intertwined. But this had been a cordial concession to man's uneasiness, a bit of charitable freethinking, a momentary disregard for what was actually binding and fixed: the rigorous and strict rejection of any sort of peering into the beyond, a doctrine by means of which his fathers—and the God who was becoming holy in them—divorced themselves as clearly as possible from their neighbors' cadaver gods, lying rigid in death within their temple graves. For only by comparisons can a man differentiate himself and learn what he is in order to become all that he should be. And so the fabled and admired chastity of Joseph, future husband

and father, was not fundamentally a self-scourging renunciation of the world of love and procreation—which would have corresponded very poorly with the promise to the primal father that his seed would be as numberless as kernels of dust upon the earth; instead, it was the ordinance inherited in his blood to preserve God's reason in these matters and to keep at a distance horned madness and *aulasaukaula,* which for him constituted an inseparable spiritual and logical unity with worship of the dead. It was Mut's misfortune, however, that Joseph saw her wooing of him as death and indecency united in temptation, the temptation of Sheol, which would have meant total destruction were he to yield and bare his nakedness.

Here we have the seventh and final reason—final also in the sense that it combines all the others, for ultimately they were all focused on this one fear: the fear of "baring his nakedness." We first caught a glimpse of this motive in Mut's desire to remove the fig leaf of practical pretense from their conversation, but we must once again examine it here in terms of its far-reaching consequences and the impressive multiplicity of its sensual connotations.

Strange things happen when the meaning and definition of a word is refracted in the mind in the same way a single ray of light is broken into the colors of the rainbow by a cloud. For if just one of these fragments ends up unluckily associated with some evil memory and becomes a curse, that can suffice for the word in all its meanings to be discredited and become an abomination in every sense, useful only for describing abominable things and condemned to serve as the name for every sort of abomination—much as if, because red is an evil color, the color of the desert and the North Star, its curse were to blot out the serene innocence of the entire, unrefracted light of heaven. The idea of baring one's nakedness was not originally lacking in innocence and serenity; there was nothing red about it, no curse tied to it. But ever since that damnable episode in the tent between Noah and Ham—and Canaan, Ham's evil son—it had been fractured for good, so to speak, and in being fractured had become red and disreputable, so that it blushed red all over; there was no choice but to use the term to designate all things abominable—just as every, or almost every, abomination cried out in its name and saw itself in it. Jacob's behavior beside the well, the concern he showed that day, almost nine years ago now, when he sternly rebuked his son for baring his nakedness in an attempt to respond to the beautiful moon—Jacob's behavior could have served nicely as a case study of the fatal eclipse of an idea that in and of itself was as gladdening as the sight of a naked boy beside a well. At first there had been nothing at all dubious about baring one's nakedness in the simple, literal, physical sense; it was as neutral as heaven's light; the concept began to blush only because of its extended meaning as part of Baal's madness and as fatal, incestuous gazing upon a naked close relative. But what happened was that the red glow of the extended meaning reflected on the innocent literal sense, and, as the light shifted back and forth, it, too, finally turned so red that it could become the term for every sort of incest, whether actually perpetrated or simply realized in glances and wishes, until in the end "baring one's nakedness" was the name for everything forbidden and cursed in terms of sensual lust and fleshly intercourse, but especially—with reference once again to the sacrilege against Noah—for a son's transgression against the rights of his father. And as if that were not enough, a new equation or merger of terms took place when Ruben's lapse, that is, the violation by a son of his father's bed, began to stand for all the rest and everything forbidden in terms of glances, wishes, and deeds was considered, in perception and even in name, tantamount to a violation of the father.

This was how things looked inside Joseph's mind—we must simply accept that. It seemed to him that what the sphinx of this land of death demanded was that he bare his father's nakedness. And was that not the case if one considers what awful things the Land of Mud represented for the old man at home and the worry it would have caused him to learn that his child was not eternally safe but walked amid such temptation? How could Joseph commit this shameful act with those eyes—brown, strained by worry, with soft sagging pouches beneath them—resting upon him? How could he crudely forget himself, as Ruben had in his gushing blunder, so that the blessing was taken from him? Since then, that blessing had rested upon Joseph, and should he now forfeit it by committing a crudely gushing blunder of his own, by sporting with that dubious pawed beast the way Ruben had once sported with Bilhah? Is it any wonder, then, that his innermost answer to this question was: "Not for anything!" Who, we repeat—once he takes into account how complex and laden with identifications was Joseph's understanding of both fatherhood and the offenses against it—would wonder at this?

Can even the most vigorous person, someone highly responsive to matters of love, declare as incredible a "chastity" rooted in a decision, demanded by the most basic religious prudence, to avoid an error more egregious and injurious to Joseph's future than any other he might commit?

These were the seven reasons why Joseph did not wish to follow the call of his mistress's blood—not for anything. We have them now at full count, feel their full weight, and can regard them with a certain composure—though the latter is hardly fitting, given the festal hour of the events we commemorate here, since Joseph still hangs in the balance of full temptation and, as the story originally told itself, it had not yet been determined at this point if he would be able to emerge unscathed. He just barely managed it, he came away with a black eye—we know that. But why did he risk going so far? Why did he ignore the whispered warnings of his true little friend, who already saw the pit gaping wide to receive him, and instead keep company with the phallic dwarf who poured deceiving panderer's words from his pouch of a mouth? In a word: why, after all, did he not choose to avoid his mistress, instead of allowing things to come to the pass between them to which, as we know, they did indeed come? Yes, well, there was his flirtation with the world, a curiosity and sympathy for what was forbidden; there was also a certain intellectual fascination with his own death-ridden name and the divine status it implied; moreover there was some self-assured cockiness, the confidence that he could venture far into danger—and always return if need be; and, as the more praiseworthy reverse of all this, there was a will to demand the impossible of himself, a proud desire to take the hard knocks, to not spare himself, to push things to their limits in order to emerge from temptation all the more triumphant—to be a virtuoso of virtue and more precious in his father's eyes than a cautious, less risky testing would have left him. Perhaps there was even a secret knowledge of his path and its winding course, a premonition that it wanted to complete another smaller loop and for the second time lead him into the pit that could not be avoided if all things written in the book of plans were to be fulfilled.

Part Seven

THE PIT

Billets-doux

As we have said and shall see, in the third year of her smitten state, the tenth of Joseph's sojourn in the chamberlain's house, Potiphar's wife began to offer her love to Jacob's son, and with ever increasing vehemence. In reality, there is no great difference between the "letting him know" of the second year and the "offering" of the third; the latter was already contained in the former—the border between them is fluid. But it does exist, and crossing it, moving from mere adoration and devouring glances (though these, to be sure, had implied pursuit) to actual demands cost the woman almost as much effort as it would for her to have overcome her weakness and renounce her desire for her slave—though not quite as much, really; for otherwise she would obviously have rather made the other effort.

She did not; instead of overcoming her love, she overcame her pride and her shame, which was difficult enough, though somewhat easier—a bit easier also because she was not left entirely alone in her effort, as would have been the case with overcoming her desire, but found help in Dûdu, the propagating dwarf, who passed back and forth with dignity between her and Jacob's son, as the first and only man, or so he thought, to play the role of mischievous patron, counselor, and ambassador, all the while puffing his cheeks full and blowing to fan both fires. For there were indeed two fires here and not just one. The instructive, healing regimen with which Joseph attempted to justify the fact that he did not avoid his mistress, but stood before her almost daily, was outright asinine balderdash, because in fact, whether knowingly or not, he had long since achieved divine status, with mummy's wrappings ripped open wide—and Dûdu understood all this, of course, no less than quivering Favored Bes, for in this regard his wit and expertise did not merely match those of his little cousin, they surpassed them.

"Young steward," he said at Joseph's end of his path, "until now you have known to make your fortune, as even envy—though I know it not—must admit. Despite your doubtlessly respectable, though modest origins, you have shunted aside those over you. You sleep in the special chamber of trust, and the perquisites of grain, bread, beer, geese, linen, and leather that Usir Mont-kaw once enjoyed are now yours to enjoy. You bring them to market inasmuch as you cannot possibly consume them all; you increase your wealth and appear to be a made man. But as is often said, what goes up must come down, what is made can be unmade if a man knows not how to hold fast to his good fortune, to fortify it with underpinnings and unshakable foundations, so that it may endure like a temple of the dead. Again and again, it has been known to happen that a man may lack only some little something to crown his good fortune, to perfect it and make it unshakable, and he need only reach out his hand to grab it. But be it out of fear or bewilderment, be it out of indolence or even arrogance, the fool refrains from doing so, hides his hand in his robe, and for the life of him stubbornly refuses to reach out for that last bit of good fortune, neglects it, disdains it, casts it to the wind. And the outcome? The sad outcome is that all his fortune and all his gains collapse and are razed to the ground, so that the place where he was knows him no more—and all because of one act of disdain. For by it he provoked those powers that wished to join in his good fortune and proposed to add their lovely favor as the last and highest portion of his good fortune, so that it might endure forever; but once disdained and offended, they rage like the seas, so that their eyes shoot flames of fire and their hearts bring forth sandstorms like those from the mountains of the East, and they do not merely turn away from the man's good fortune, but turn against it in great wrath and destroy it to its foundations—which costs them nothing at all. I do not doubt that you recognize what great concern I, as an honest man, have for your good fortune, though not only for yours, but also and equally for that of the person to whom my words—unmistakably, or so I would hope—allude. But they are one and the same: her good fortune is yours—and yours, hers. That union has long since become happy truth, and all that matters now is that it be luxuriously perfected in reality. For when I think and picture in my soul what luxury that union would surely have to provide you, even I, stalwart as I am, grow giddy. I do not speak of fleshly luxury, first out of modesty and second because it would, but of course, be so very great because of said person's silken skin and the exquisite composition of her frame. The luxury of which I speak is that of the soul, by which that of the flesh would surely be exalted beyond measure, and it consists in the thought that you—being as you are of certainly honorable, but really quite modest and foreign origins—will embrace the most beautiful and noble woman of the Two Lands in your arms and evoke from her the finest sighs on your behalf, in token as it were that you, a lad of the wretched sands, have subdued the land of Egypt, which lies sighing beneath you. And how do you pay for this twofold bliss, of which the one form would necessarily prick the other to quite unheard-of heights? You do not pay a thing, but are rewarded—by the irreversible and unshakable perpetuation of your good fortune, inasmuch as you would truly rise up to become lord and master of this house. For whoever possesses its mistress," Dûdu said, "is truly its master." And he raised his stubby arms just as he did before Potiphar and blew a kiss to the earth, as if to suggest that he was already kissing it before Joseph's feet.

Joseph had listened in disgust, it's true, to this seasoned panderer's very vulgar words—but he had listened, so that the haughtiness of his reply did not quite become him.

"I would prefer, dwarf, if you did not delight in speaking for yourself so much and in spinning out all on your own peculiar ideas that are little to the purpose, but that you would confine yourself to your post as messenger and informer. If you have anything to reveal and deliver from a higher party, then do so. If not, I would prefer you toddle off."

"It would be culpable of me," Dûdu responded, "were I to toddle off prematurely, before having delivered my message. For I have something to transmit and offer to you. Surely a ranking messenger should be allowed some personal trimming, decorating, and elucidating of his message."

"And what is it?" Joseph asked.

And the gnome handed something up to him, a papyrus note, a small slip, long and very narrow, on which Mut, the mistress, had painted a few words . . .

For at the other end of his path, this jack-of-all-mischief had spoken as follows:

"If your most faithful servant, by which I mean myself, may speak to the depths of your soul, great mistress, he finds he has grown weary of the pace at which your affairs and concerns move forward and progress, for it is sluggish and stagnant. This pinches your servant to the core with vexation and worry for your sake, for your beauty could suffer from it. Not that one sees it suffer at present—heaven forbid—for it flourishes at the zenith of its bloom and will enjoy all manner of increase yet, so that it could even diminish a great deal and still radiantly exceed the humanly commonplace. So far, so good. But your honor, if not your beauty, suffers—and mine with it as well—under conditions and circumstances pertaining to this young man who stands over the house, who calls himself Usarsiph, but whom I would like to call Nefernefru, for he is assuredly the most beautiful of the beautiful . . . The name pleases you, does it not? I devised it for your use—or, no, did not devise, but heard and snatched it up so that I might place it at your disposal; for he is frequently called that, whether in the house or upon highways and waterways or in the city; indeed, it is his special name among the women upon its roofs and walls, against whose behavior, sad to say, it has as yet proved impossible to take serious countermeasures. . . . But allow me to continue with my well-considered words. For the sake of your honor, your most humble servant is rankled to his liver by how very slowly you are nearing your goal with this Nefernefru—that being, as we both know, to discover his magic and bring him to ruin and for him to name you his name. It is true that I have arranged for and seen to it that my mistress and her servant no longer approach one another under escort of scribes and handmaids, so that wherever they chance to meet they may converse without constraint and onerous formalities, tête-à-tête and mouth to mouth. That improves prospects that he will at last tell you his name in some sweetest, most quiet hour, when you will faint away with the joy of your triumph over him, that wicked man, and over all those whom his mouth and eye have bewitched. For you will seal up his mouth in such fashion that his beguiling speech will fail him and you will cause the eye that enchants everyone to grow dim in the bliss of defeat. But the difficulty is that the lad resists his defeat and does not want to be brought to his ruin by you, his mistress, which to my eyes is sedition so shamefaced that Dûdu does not shrink to brand it as shameless. For how is it? What is this? You wish to conquer him and call him to his defeat—you, the child of Amun, the blossom of his Southern House of Women. And he, a Habiru from Amu, a foreign slave and son of low rank, proves fractious, does not want what you want, hides from you behind chitchat and household accounts? That is not to be tolerated. It is insurrection and saucy contempt by the gods of Asia, who owe tribute to Amun, the lord in his shrine. Thus the vexation of the house has changed its aspect and content, which at first consisted only in the rise of a slave within the house. But it has now become open rebellion by the gods of Asia, who do not wish to offer the tribute they owe to Amun, payable in the form of the defeat of this lad before you, Amun's child. For it has to come to that. I offered timely warning. But the just man cannot wash you entirely clean, either, great lady, or exonerate you of all guilt in the abomination that prevents progress in this matter, so that it is stagnant. For you do not push it forward and out of maidenly delicacy allow the lad to play his game with Amun, the king of the gods, and, by feints and subterfuges, prove more fractious with each new moon. This is most dreadful indeed. But it can be traced to your maidenly reserve, which falters for lack of full vigor and mature experience in such affairs. Forgive your sterling servant such a remark, but, in truth, from where else are you to gain what you lack? What you should do without hesitation is call this artful dodger before you and demand outright his tribute and defeat, so that he cannot slip from your grasp. If, in your maidenly reserve, you cannot do so in spoken words, behold, there are always written ones—the path of the billet-doux, so that, willy-nilly, he will understand when he reads something such as 'Do you wish to triumph over me today in a game? Let us play, the two of us, upon the board.' That is what is called a billet-doux, for in it vigorous maturity speaks with clarity, but in words of maidenly indirection. Let me place the utensils before you, and you can write as I dictate, so that I may deliver it to him and the affair may at last progress to the glory of Amun."

These, then, were the words of Dûdu, the stalwart dwarf. In her dazed state and out of maidenly submission to his own fractious authority in these matters, Eni actually did prepare the note according to his direction; but as Joseph read it now, he could not hide the red of Atum that rose to his face, and in anger at his own reaction he roughly chased the letter carrier off without a word of thanks. Despite all the anxious whispers from the opposing side advising him not to accept this treacherous challenge, he accepted it nonetheless and played a game with his mistress—just the two of them, beneath the image of Rê-Horakhte in the columned portico—during which he "forced her into the water" at one point, but then let himself be forced into it as well, so that victory and defeat canceled each other out and the score of their encounter was a zero—much to Dûdu's disappointment, who regarded the affair as still stagnant.

Which is why he took yet another step and went for the prize, arranging things so that he could once again speak to Joseph from that pouch at one side of his mouth.

"I have something to present to you from a special party."

"What is it?" Joseph asked.

And the dwarf handed up to him a narrow slip that one might well say advanced matters with one desperate jolt, because it clearly and unmistakably contained a word that we previously said has been misinterpreted, because it came not from a harlot but from a woman who had been overwhelmed—a word expressed, however, in the roundabout way that the written word allows in all things, particularly the Egyptian written word (which of course was what the writer of the note used), an ornamental but concise script that allows vowels to remain mute, but by scattering symbols throughout to help indicate the conceptual category evoked by purely consonantal sounds, always retains about it something of a magic rebus, of a florid game of hide-and-seek, of a witty, logographic masquerade, so that it truly seems made for composing billets-doux, lending even the most straightforward statement an ingenious grace. The crucial passage in Mut-em-enet's message—what we would call the point of it—consisted of three phonic symbols, preceded by several other equally pretty ones and concluding with the swiftly sketched outline of a lion-headed couch with a mummy lying upon it. The rebus looked like this:

and it meant "to lie" or, indeed, "to sleep," for those two are a single word in the language of Keme; "to lie" and "to sleep" are the same in its script; and the entire line on the narrow slip, signed with the symbol of a vulture—which is what "Mut" means—clearly and bluntly said: "Come, that we may sleep together for an hour."

What a document! Precious as gold, so honorable and touching, but also by its very nature dangerous, depressing, and wicked. Here in its basic, original version—in the form that Egypt's language

stamped upon it—we have the insistent proposal that tradition says
Potiphar's wife made to Joseph. It was in this written form that she
first made it to him, under the influence of Dûdu, the propagating
dwarf, who had dictated it to her from his pouch of a mouth. But if
we are moved by the sight, what must have been Joseph's shock
when he deciphered it. Pale with dismay, he hid the note, crumpling
it up in his hand and chasing Dûdu off with the handle of his flyswatter. But the message—that sweet demand, that eager and promising call of love's mistress—had been delivered, and though in all
honesty Joseph should hardly have been surprised, it came as a terrible shock and set his blood in such turmoil that if one did not know
their outcome, one might be so caught up in the solemn events com-
memorated here as to fear for the power of his seven reasons to resist. Joseph, however, to whom these events happened just as they
originally told themselves, was actually living in the immediate present of their solemn festal hour, was unable to see beyond it, and
could not at all be certain of the outcome. At the point where we
have paused to stop, his story still trembled in the balance and when
the decisive moment came, it would hang by a hair whether Joseph's
seven reasons would be overthrown and he would fall into sin—for
things might just as easily have gone as badly amiss as they barely
managed to go at all. Certainly Joseph knew that he was determined
not to make this great mistake—not at any price would he destroy
his relationship with God. But wizened Favored Bes had indeed
been right in wanting to view his friend's delight in his freedom to
choose between good and evil as something like a delight in evil itself
and not just in the freedom to chose; above all, however, such an unacknowledged inclination toward evil, expressed as relishing one's
own free choice, also includes an inclination to let evil pull the wool
over one's eyes and cloud reason to the point where one is even willing to see some good in it. God had such wonderful plans for
Joseph—could He actually be of a mind to begrudge him the proud
and sweet delight offered him, perhaps offered by God Himself?
Was this delight not perhaps the planned means for his being raised
up—in the expectation of which he had lived since having been carried off—inasmuch as his advancement in the house had already
raised him up so far that his mistress had now cast her eyes upon
him, and by telling him her own sweet name, the name that comprised all the land of Egypt, did she not wish to make him, as it were,

lord of the world? What young man does not equate his lover's giving herself to him with his being raised up to be lord of the world? And was it not precisely this, to make him lord of the world, that God had in mind for Joseph?

One can see the temptation to which his no longer unclouded reason was subjected. He was well on his way to making a muddle of good and evil; there were moments when he was tempted to give evil the meaning of good. And even though the mummy that was part of the symbol that came after "to lie" ought to have opened his eyes to see from what realm this temptation had arisen and that his succumbing to it would be an unforgivable slap in the face of Him who was not a mummified god enduring forever without promise, but the God of the future—Joseph nevertheless had every cause to mistrust his seven reasons and the course that future solemn festal events might take, every reason for not lending an ear to his little friend, whose whispers pleaded with him not to see his mistress again, not to accept another narrow slip of papyrus from his wicked cousin, and to fear the fiery bull whose breath was very close to transforming a laughing meadow into a field of ashes. There is no denying that avoiding his mistress was easier said than done, and when she called, he had to come. But how gladly a man leaves open the choice for evil, basks in his freedom to make it, and plays with fire—be it out of overconfident courage, which falsely assumes it can grab the bull by the horns, or be it out of recklessness and secret lust. And who can tell the difference?

The Painful Tongue (A Play with Epilogue)

There came a night during that third year, when Mut-em-enet, Potiphar's wife, bit her tongue because it imperiously demanded that she say aloud to her titular spouse's young steward what she had written to him in her rebus, and yet, out of pride and shame, she wanted to prevent her tongue from speaking to him that way and from offering her slave her blood that he might stanch it. For this conflict was part of her role as mistress, so that on the one hand it was dreadful to speak to him that way and to offer her flesh and blood to him in exchange for his, but on the other, she had every right to take the initiative as the manly and, so to speak, bearded lover. Which was why she bit her tongue that night, bit both top and bottom, bit it almost clear through, so that on the next day the pain of the wound left her lisping like a little child.

For several days after having sent him her billet-doux, she had not wanted to see Joseph and had refused to show her face to him, for she did not want to gaze into his after having demanded in writing that he accept defeat. But depriving herself of his nearness made her ripe for saying with her mouth what she had already said in magical script; her longing for his presence took the form of a longing to say words it was forbidden him to say as a slave of love, so that if she was ever to learn whether those same words were spoken from his soul, she had no choice but to speak them herself, as his mistress, and to take the words from his mouth by offering him her flesh and blood in the fervent hope that this corresponded to his own secret wishes. Her role as mistress condemned her to shamelessness; but she had punished herself in advance that night by biting her tongue, so that she might now at least say what was absolutely necessary—as best she could after her punishment, that is, in a lisping, childish way, which was itself a refuge, lending innocence and helplessness to drastic words and a touching air to something crude.

Through Dûdu she had sent for Joseph to join her for a business discussion and a board game afterward, saying she would receive him in the Atum portico an hour after dinner, as soon as the steward had finished his service as a reader in Potiphar's hall. She came to him out of the room where she slept, and as she stepped before him, for the very first time he was aware, or consciously aware, of something we have refrained from noting before now: that is, that she had changed during the period of her infatuation and, we can only conclude, because of it.

It was a peculiar change, so that in describing and characterizing it one runs the risk of either putting others off or being misunderstood, and once it was apparent to Joseph, it gave him cause for considerable puzzlement and profound reflection. For life is profound not only in the spirit, but also in the flesh. Not that the woman had aged during this time—love had prevented that. Had she grown more beautiful? Yes and no. But more no than yes. Indeed, definitely no, if one understands beauty to be purely admirable, its perfection as something that gladdens the heart, a glorious image that surely it would be heaven to embrace, but that does not ask to be embraced, and instead retreats from the very notion, because its appeal is to the brightest of the senses, the eye, and not to the mouth and hand—to the extent that it intentionally appeals to anything at all. For all the fullness of its sensuality, beauty retains about it something abstract and spiritual, asserts its independence and the priority of idea over manifestation; it is not the product and tool of sexuality, but rather just the opposite: sexuality is both its stuff and its instrument. Female beauty—it can be beauty embodied in the feminine, the feminine as a means for expressing the beautiful. But what if the relationship between spirit and stuff is reversed and instead of female beauty one would do better to speak of beautiful femininity, because the feminine has become the starting point and controlling idea, with beauty as its attribute instead of the feminine as the attribute of beauty—what then? What, we ask, happens if sexuality treats beauty as the stuff in which to embody itself, so that beauty serves and works as the means for expressing the feminine? It is clear that this will result in an entirely different sort of beauty from that which we celebrated just now—a dubious, indeed eerie beauty, that may even approach ugliness, all the while exercising the attraction and emotional effectiveness of beauty, but by virtue of the sexuality that replaces it, espouses its cause, and usurps its name. In such a case there is no longer a spiritually honest beauty revealed in femininity, but only a beauty in which the feminine reveals itself—an eruption of sexuality, the beauty of the witch.

That word, however appalling, has proved indispensable for characterizing the change in Mut-em-enet's body that had come with the years. It was a change both touching and exciting, sad and thrilling—a change that made her witchlike. It goes without saying that in internally picturing this concept one must set aside any sense of the hag—one must, we repeat, set it aside, though it would be best not to do away with it entirely. A witch is certainly not necessarily a hag. And yet one cannot help observing a slight trace of something haglike about even the most charming witch—it is inescapably part of the image. Mut's new body was the body of a witch, a body of sexuality and love, and thus from a distance somehow haglike, although that element manifested itself at most in a clash between its voluptuousness and its gauntness. Tabubu, the guardian of the rouge pots, was, for instance, a hag of the first water, with breasts like leather bags. Under the influence of her own emotional state, Mut's breasts, once dainty and virginal, had developed into great, robust, splendid fruits of love, whose protruding exuberance took on something haglike only because of how they contrasted with her thin, indeed emaciated and fragile shoulder blades. The shoulders themselves looked small, delicate, touchingly childlike, and the arms had lost a great deal of their fullness, had become almost skinny. But it was just the opposite with her thighs, which were unduly large and sturdy, their development having been, one may say, almost illicit in comparison to her upper extremities, so much so that one might picture a broomstick clamped between them, on which the woman now rose on high, holding tight with her weak arms, her thin back bent forward, her breasts protruding—an impression that seemed not merely to suggest itself, but indeed to force itself upon the observer. And this was intensified by her face in its frame of black curly hair— that saddle-nosed, hollow-cheeked face in which contradiction had long reigned, but that only now seemed to have found its true name and won its purest expression: the truly witchlike contradiction between the austere, indeed menacingly sinister look of the eyes and the daring serpentine shape of the mouth tucked deep at its corners, a poignant contradiction that, having now reached its peak, lent her face an abnormal, masklike tension, which was probably reinforced by the searing pain of her injured tongue. In point of fact, however, one of the reasons she had bitten it so hard was that she knew it would make her lisp like an innocent child, and that her childish lisping would perhaps varnish over and hide what she was fully aware was the witchlike look of her new body.

One can imagine the uneasiness that the sight of these changes stirred in the man who had caused them. What first welled up in him that day was an understanding of how foolishly he had acted in casting the pleas of his pure friend to the wind and instead of avoiding his mistress had let things come to a point where a virginal swan was now a witch. He became aware of the absurdity of his instructive, healing regimen, and for the first time it may have dawned on him that his behavior in his new life was no less culpable than his conduct toward his brothers had once been. This insight, which would ripen from surmise to full realization, explains much of what will happen later.

For now, however, his bad conscience and agitated awareness that his mistress had changed into a hag of love were hidden behind the special respect, indeed reverence, with which he greeted her and spoke before her, continuing to pursue, for better or worse, his culpably absurd healing regimen; and with the assistance of the scrolls of accounts he had brought with him, he now held forth on the consumption and delivery of foodstuffs and sweetmeats to the house of women and also offered a partial list of those servants who had been dismissed and those newly employed. This prevented him from noticing right off the injury to her tongue; for she merely listened to him with an overanxious air and said almost nothing. But when they sat down to their board game on two sides of a beautifully carved gaming table—she on her couch of ebony and ivory, he on an oxen-legged taboret—and had placed their pieces, in the shape of recumbent lions, and had agreed upon the rules, he found that, much to his increased uneasiness, he could not help noticing her stammering; having observed it a few times, he was no longer in any doubt of it and so allowed himself a gentle inquiry by saying:

"What is it I hear, mistress, and how can this be? It seems to me there is a slight stammer in your speech."

And was compelled to hear in reply that the lady's tongue was "cauthing her thome pain"; she had hurd herthelf during the nighd, had bidd'n her tongue, and the thteward should pay it no mind.

That is how she spoke—we record the pained elisions and childishness of her speech in our language rather than theirs, but it sounded much the same in the latter; and in great alarm Joseph pulled back from the game and would not touch another piece until she tended to her injury and applied to her tongue a balsam that Khun-Anup, the herbalist, would have to prepare at once. But she would not hear of it and mockingly accused him of making excuses and trying to slip away from their game, which after the opening move was already going very badly for him, so that he would soon be forced into the water—that was why he was trying to save himself by breaking off their game and appealing to the apothecary. In short, she kept him firmly in his seat with her pained childish speech and agonized teasing, for she instinctively matched her turns of phrase to the helplessness of her tongue and in every sense was now speaking like a little girl and trying to add an expression of foolish charm to her tense, suffering air. We shall not continue to mimic the way she stammered words like "pietheth" and "ecthutheth," for fear it might look as if we wanted to ridicule her, since she did indeed have death in her heart and was on the verge of casting aside all pride and spiritual honor out of an overpowering desire to do honor to her flesh by fulfilling the dream of healing she had once dreamt.

The man who had instilled this desire in her likewise felt death squeezing his heart, and rightly so. He pursed his lips and did not dare look up from the board, for his conscience spoke against him. He played a sensible game nonetheless, he could not do otherwise, and it would have been difficult to say whether reason mastered him or vice versa. She, too, moved her pieces, picking them up and setting them down, but in such distraction that very soon she was defeated straight-out, with no route of escape, yet had not even noticed and so kept on making even more inane moves, until his refusal to respond brought her back to her senses and she now stared down at the muddle of her ruin with an anxious smile. Under the delusion that he could bring healing and order to this abnormal situation, Joseph tried to save it with reasonably measured and polite words.

Which is why he said in deliberate tones, "We must begin again, my mistress, either now or at some other time, for our game has gone amiss, most likely because I opened so clumsily and now cannot make another move, as you can well see; nor can you, because I cannot, and I cannot because you—the game is blocked on both sides, so that one would truly be wasting words to speak of victory or defeat, since it is both for both players . . ."

These last words were halting and toneless by now, for although he could not stop once he had started, neither could he hope to save the situation by discussion, for it had already happened—her head and face had fallen forward onto his arm, which lay beside the game board, so that her gold- and silver-powdered hair pushed the recumbent lions from the board and he could feel against his arm the hot breath of her feverish stammers and futile lisps, whose sickly childishness we shall not mimic out of respect for her distress. The sense and nonsense of them, however, was as follows:

"Yes, yes, no further, we can go no further, the game is blocked and our only recourse is defeat for both, Osarsiph, my beautiful god from far away, my swan and bull, for whom my love is hot and high and eternal, so that now we can die together and descend into the night of desperate bliss. You may speak, speak out and speak freely, for you cannot behold my face since it is lying upon your arm, upon your arm at last, and my vanquished lips brush your flesh and blood, while pleading and begging with you that you freely confess, without looking into my eyes, whether or not you received the billet-doux I wrote you before I bit my tongue so that I might not have to say what I wrote, but must say nonetheless, because I am your mistress and it is for me to speak the word that you may not speak, that you dare not make bold to speak for reasons long since devoid of any meaning. But I do not know how gladly you may say it—that is my great sorrow, for if I knew that you would speak it eagerly and gladly if only you might, then I would blissfully take the word out of your mouth and speak it as your mistress, even if as a lisping whisper, my face hidden upon your arm. Tell me, did you receive from the dwarf the letter that I wrote, and did you read it? Were you happy to see the symbols I painted and did your blood crash in a wave of happiness against the shore of your soul? Do you love me, Osarsiph, my god in servant's form, my heavenly falcon, as I love you, have loved you for so long, so long in rapture and torment, and does your blood burn for mine as I burn for you, so that after much struggle I had to write that little note, enthralled as I am by your golden shoulders and by how everyone loves you, but above all by your godlike glance, which has changed my body and made my breasts grow to be fruits of love? Sleep—with—me! Give to me, give to me of your youth and glory, and I will give to you raptures of which you cannot dream—I know whereof I speak. Let us put our heads and feet together, so that all may be well for us beyond all bounds and we may die, each in the other, for I can no longer bear that we live as two, you there, I here."

These, then, the words of the fully enthralled woman; but we have not imitated what her pleas sounded like in reality as she lisped with a split tongue, each syllable a sharp pain, and yet all of it stammered upon his arm in an unbroken flow, for women can bear a great deal of pain. But one should know, imagine, and keep in mind from here on that her misinterpreted words, those lapidary words of tradition, were spoken not as an adult with tongue intact, but amid pain that cut like knives and in the language of small children, so that she stammered: "Thleep with me!" For she had done harm to her tongue so that it might sound like that.

And Joseph? He sat there, reviewing his seven reasons, reviewing them forward and backward. We would not want to claim that his blood did not crash upon the shore of his soul in a great wave, but the reasons standing in its way were sevenfold and they held. It should be said to his credit that he did not strike back at her and treat her with contempt as a witch who had tempted him to break with his God, but was gentle and kind to her and sought to comfort her with loving reverence, although, as any insightful person will admit, therein lay great danger for him—for where is the end of comforting in such a case? He did not even pull his arm back roughly, despite the damp heat of her lisped words and the touch of her lips thrusting against it, but casually let it lie where it was, until she had stammered her way to the end, and even for a while longer, during which he said:

"My mistress, for God's sake, what is your face doing there and what words do you speak in the fever of your injury—come to your senses, I implore you, for you have forgotten yourself and me. Above all—your chamber is open, do but recall that someone, be it dwarf or man of full stature, might see us and catch sight of where you have your head. Forgive me, I dare not allow it, and with your permission must now withdraw my arm and look to see whether from outside there might . . ."

He did as he said. But she likewise lifted her head, and with ferocity, from where his arm no longer was, and sitting very erect, with flashing eyes and a suddenly ringing voice, she called out words that might have taught him with whom he was dealing and what he might expect from someone who had just pleaded like a broken woman but now seemed to bare her claws like a lioness and was not even lisping at the moment; for if she wanted and was willing to bear the pain, she could force her tongue to speak correctly.

And with savage precision she now cried out, "Leave the portico open, leave the view open for the whole world to see me and you, my beloved. Are you afraid? I fear neither gods, nor dwarves, nor men, nor that they may see me with you and spy out our company together. Let them come, let them come in throngs to see us! I shall cast my modesty and propriety as trash before their feet, for they are no more than that to me—trash and paltry rubbish in comparison to what is between you and me and to the distress of my soul, which has forgotten the rest of this world. Am I afraid? I alone am fear-inspiring in my love. I am Isis and whoever is watching us together will see me whirl around to him and cast him such a fearful look that he will turn pale with death on the spot."

That was Mut the lioness, totally unaware of her wound and the pain that cut like knives with each forceful word she spoke.

Joseph, however, closed the room by pulling the curtains between the pillars and said, "Let me practice prudence in your stead, for I have the gift to foresee what would happen were someone to spy on us, and I hold sacred what you wish to cast away to the world, which is not worthy of it, not even worthy to die under the fury of your glance."

But once he had cloaked the view and returned to her in the shadows of the room, she was no longer a lioness, but once again the lisping child—but as subtle as a serpent, turning what he had done around and stammering in her beguiling voice, "Have you locked us in, you evil man, and wrapped us in shadows, away from the world, so that it can no longer protect me against your wickedness? Ah, how wicked it was of you, Osarsiph, to have done this to me without naming your name, changing me body and soul, so that I no longer even recognize myself. What would your mother say if she knew what you do to people, how you treat them so that they no longer recognize themselves? If only my own son were so beautiful and so evil. Must I see him in you—see in you my beautiful, evil son, a child of the sun, whom I bore and who puts his head and feet together with those of his mother at noon so that he may engender himself by her anew? Osarsiph, do you love in heaven as upon earth? Did I picture your soul as well when I painted those symbols on the note I sent you, sending shudders to your very core when you read it, just as I shuddered with infinite desire and shame as I wrote it? When you delude me with your lips by calling me the mistress of your head and heart, just how do you mean it? Tell me, is it because it is the proper phrase, or is it an expression of ardor? Confess to me here in the shadows. After so many nights in the torment of doubt, lying here alone without you, while my blood cried out for you in its helplessness, I demand you heal me, be my healer and salvation, by admitting that you were speaking the language of pretty lies in order to tell me the truth—that you love me."

Joseph: "Not like that, most noble lady . . . yes, like that, just as you say—yet spare yourself, if I am to believe that you regard me with favor, spare yourself and me, I beg you, for it pains my heart unbearably to hear you force your injured tongue to speak words, instead of soothing it in balsam—to speak cruel words. How could I

not love you, my mistress? I fall to my knees in love and beg you
upon my knees that you ought not cruelly to fathom the love I bear
for you, to probe its humility and ardor, its devotion and sweetness,
but rather graciously let it be in all its components, which form a
tender and precious whole that does not deserve to be cut off and
unraveled by probing cruelty, for what a pity that would be. No, be
patient yet and let me speak to you. . . . You are usually happy to listen when I speak before you about one matter or the other, and so
kindly hear me in this matter as well. For a good servant loves his
master, if he be in any way noble—that is as it should be. But if the
name of his master is changed to that of a mistress and a dear lady,
the change imbues a servant with sweetness and gracious ardor, and
his love infuses this gracious emotion as well—it is humility and
sweetness, which is to say, the adoring tenderness that is called
'ardor.' And may the heart's curse be upon him who is so cruel as to
approach too near with his probing and unraveling and an evil look
in his eye—may he find no profit in it. If I call you the mistress of
my head and heart, then to be sure it is because custom would have
it so and because it is only fitting as a formal phrase. But how sweet
I find that phrase, and how fortunate for my head and heart that it is
fitting, for it is a matter of delicate discretion and a secret. Is it then
gracious and in any way wise of you to ask me indiscreetly how I
mean it and to leave me with but the one choice between lie and sin?
That is a false and cruel choice, and I do not wish to own it. And
upon my knees I plead with you that you would show grace and
kindness to the life of the heart."

The Woman: "Oh, Osarsiph, you are terrible in your articulate
beauty, which makes men regard you as divine, rendering them
amenable, but which by its deftness plummets me into despair. What
terrible divinity there is in that deftness, in that child of wit and
beauty—but for the unhappily loving heart, it is fatal ravishment!
You call my fervent question indiscreet, yet how indiscreet you are
in your eloquent reply—saying that what is beautiful should keep silence and refrain from speaking for the sake of the heart, that silence
should surround beauty as it surrounds the holy grave at Abôdu, because love, like death, wishes silence—indeed, in silence they are
alike and the spoken word wounds them. You ask that the life of the
heart be spared by clever kindness and would seem to side with that
kindness against me and my unraveling examination. But that is to

turn the world upside down, for in my plight I am she who fights for life by urgently probing it. What else am I to do, beloved, how else am I to help myself? I am a mistress to you, who are the master and healer for whom I burn, and I cannot spare your heart or let your love be, for what a pity that would be. I must assail it with probing cruelty, like the bearded man who assails the tender virgin ignorant of her own heart, who must seize love's ardor from her humility, love's desire from her devotion, so that she may be bold enough to be herself and capable of grasping the idea of your sleeping next to me, for in that, in your doing that with me, is found all the healing of the world—it is a question of bliss or the torment of hell. It has become a tormenting hell for me that our limbs are separated, lie here and there, and when you speak of your knees, from where you would beg me for I know not what, I am seized by an unutterable jealousy of your knees, that they are yours and not mine as well, but must be next to me as you lie with me, or I shall perish and die."

Joseph: "Dearest child, that cannot be, your slave implores you to reconsider and not to entrench yourself in this idea, for it is surely born of evil. You lay undue, indeed morbid weight upon this act by which dust may lie with dust, for though it would indeed be sweet in the moment, it only seems to you in your delusion, in your feverish judgment before the deed, that it would make up for all the evil consequences and all the remorse to follow. Behold, it is not good and cannot appear good in anyone's eyes for you to assail me like a bearded man and as a mistress to court the passion of my love; there is something of the abomination about it and it does not suit our times. For I have not been a slave all that long, and all on my own I can indeed form the same idea that you suggest to me—can form it only too well, I assure you, but we simply dare not act upon it, for more than one reason, for many more than one, for a whole cluster of reasons, like that cluster of seven stars within the Bull. Understand me rightly—I dare not take a bite of the lovely apple you offer me, that we may eat of wrongdoing and ruin everything. Which is why I speak and am indiscreet. And yet do regard me kindly, my child, for if I may not keep silence with you, then I must speak and choose words of comfort, for my greatest concern, dear mistress, is that you be comforted."

The Woman: "Too late, Osarsiph, it is already too late for you and for us both! You cannot go back, and neither can I, we have already melted together. Have you not drawn the curtains, enclosing us in the shadows of the room and shutting us off from the world, so that we two are one? Do you not say 'we' and 'us' and 'someone could see us,' drawing both yourself and me together in sweet unity within those little words, which are a code for all the bliss that I suggest to you and that is already consummated in them, so that the act itself creates nothing new at all once the word 'we' is spoken, for we already share that secret before the whole world and together have drawn apart from it with our secret, so that we are left with no choice but to act upon it . . ."

Joseph: "No, hear me, my child, that is not right, and you distort things, so that I must contradict you. In forgetting yourself you force me to shut off the room for the sake of your honor, so that no one in the courtyard can see where you have laid your head—and you turn that around until it makes no difference at all, as if it had happened already, because we have now shared a secret and have had to lock ourselves away? That is most unfair, for I have no secret whatever, I am merely protecting yours, and only in that sense can there be any meaning in 'we' and 'us,' and nothing whatever has happened, just as nothing may happen in the future, for as many reasons as there are stars in that cluster."

The Woman: "Osarsiph, my sweet liar! You do not wish to acknowledge our union and our secret, even though you yourself admitted just now that you find it only too easy to suggest to yourself what I suggest in wooing you? And you call that not hiding a secret with me from the world, you evil man? Do you not think of me as I think of you? But how would you then think of me and of lying with me if you knew what passion awaited you in the arms of your heavenly goddess, my golden lad of the sun? Let me proclaim to you what awaits you—speak the promise into your ear, here in the shadows, as our secret from the world. For I have never loved, never received a man in my womb, never given up the least treasure of my love and bliss; this entire treasure has been reserved for you instead, and it will make you rich beyond all bounds, beyond your every dream. Listen to my whispers: My body has changed and been transformed for you, Osarsiph, and has become a body of love, from tip to toe, so that when you lie with me and give to me your youth and glory, you will not believe you are with an earthly woman, but will, I give you my word, restore the passion of the gods with mother, spouse, and sister—for behold, I am she! I am the oil that craves your salt so that the lamp may flare up in the feast of night. I am the field that in its thirst cries out for you, O rolling flood of manhood, bull of your mother, that you may swell and burst over it, and wed yourself with me, before leaving me, my beautiful god, and forgetting your crown of lotus still lying in my moistened soil. Listen, do but listen, to what I whisper to you. For with each of my words I draw you deeper into the secret that we share with one another and from which you are no longer able to escape, for by now we are lost in the deepest secret together, so that there is no purpose in your refusing what I suggest to you . . ."

Joseph: "Oh but there is, my dear child! Forgive me for calling you that, yet there is no doubt that we are indeed caught up in a secret together because of your distraction, which was why I had to shut off the room; but there is still good purpose, sevenfold purpose, in my having to reject what you have so enticingly suggested to me, for it is swampy ground onto which you would entice me, where at best hollow reeds grow wild, but no grain, and you wish to make of me an adulterous ass and of yourself a roving bitch—how, then, can I not shield you from yourself, and protect myself against such a vile transformation? Have you thought what would happen to us were our crime to catch up with us and descend upon our heads? Should I let it come to that, for us to be strangled and your body of love cast before the dogs or your nose cut off? One cannot bear even the thought. But the ass's portion would be beating upon beating, a thousand cudgel blows for its dumb depravity, that is if it is not left to the crocodile. Such are the lessons that threaten us should our deed take possession of us."

The Woman: "Ah, cowardly boy, if you would but allow yourself to dream what accumulated passion awaits you beside me, you would not think beyond it and would laugh at any punishment, which, however meted out, could bear no comparison to what you have enjoyed with me."

"There, my dear friend," he said, "you can see how your distraction demeans you and sets you below the level of human beings; for our merit, the portion of our honor, is precisely that we think beyond the moment and consider what is yet to come. Nor do I fear in the least . . ."

They were standing close together in the middle of the shadowy room, speaking to one another in low but urgent tones, like people debating a matter of greatest import, with raised eyebrows and faces flushed with emotion.

"Nor do I fear in the least"—he was saying—"any sort of punishment for you and me, that is the least of it. Rather I fear Peteprê, our master, the man himself and not his punishment, just as one fears God for His own sake, out of the fear of God, and not because of what hurt He may inflict. It is from him that all my light comes, and whatever I am in this house and this land, I have him to thank for it—how, then, after having lain with you, would I dare come before him and gaze into his gentle eye, even if there were no punishment whatever to fear from him? Hear me, Eni, and, in God's name, collect your faculties for what I wish to say to you, for my words shall abide, and when our story is revealed and spoken among men, this will be how they are recited. For everything that happens can become a story and fine discourse, and it may well be that we are caught up in a story. Therefore you, too, should beware and show some regard for your own tale, lest you become a monster and the mother of sin. I could say a great many complicated things to oppose your and my own desire; but for the mouths of others, should these words ever be passed on to them, I will say what is most simple and binding, so that any child can understand, and therefore I say: *My master has entrusted everything to me and there is nothing in his house so great that he has kept it from me, except yourself, because you are his wife. How then can I do this great wickedness and sin against God?* These are the words that I say to you for all time to come, in opposition to the desire that we have for one another. For we are not alone in the world that each may simply enjoy the flesh and blood of the other, but there is also Peteprê, our great master in his loneliness, to whose soul we are to provide loving service and whom we dare not offend by such a deed, disgracing his tender dignity and breaking the bond of loyalty. He stands in the way of our bliss, and there's an end to it."

"Osarsiph," she lisped, whispering close to his ear and girding herself to make her proposal. "Osarsiph, my beloved, with whom I have long shared our secret, listen now and understand your Eni correctly. . . . I can, after all, can I not . . ."

This was the moment in which it became perfectly clear why and to what end Mut-em-enet had actually bitten her tongue and what carefully prepared answer, held at the ready for so long, she wanted to render under the guise of touching helplessness and pained charm that her injury made possible—for the reason she had done it and left herself in a condition where she would speak like a child was not, first and last, in order to suggest that he sleep with her, but rather, if not first, then last and ultimately, for the sake of the proposal she made at this moment, placing the beautiful work of art that was her blue-veined, ring-adorned hand on his shoulder, pressing her cheek to it, and stammering with sweet, pursed lips:

"I can thlay him."

He jerked back—the sheer daintiness of it was too much for him, and he would never have thought it, never have expected it of this woman, although just now he had seen her as a lioness with bared claws and had heard her pant: "I alone am fear-inspiring!"

"We thall thlay him," she coaxed, nestling closer even as he pulled away, "thimply kill him and get him out of the way. What is there to it, my falcon? There's nothing to it at all. Do you suppose that at one wink from me Tabubu would not prepare some clear broth or little crystalline residue of most mysterious power that I could place in your hand and you could pour into the wine he drinks to warm his flesh—let him drink it, however, and all at once he turns cold, and thanks to the culinary skills of Negro lands, no one suspects a thing, and he is sent on a boat to the West and is gone from this world and no longer stands in the way of our bliss. Do let me do this, beloved, and do not resist so innocent a measure. Is his flesh not already dead in life, and is it good for anything, or does its useless mass not simply grow more and more rank? I cannot tell you how I have loathed his indolent flesh ever since my love for you has rent my heart and made a body of love of my own flesh. I can only scream it! Which is why, sweet Osarsiph, we must do away with him, there's really nothing to it. Or does it matter to you if you take a stick and knock down an empty puffball, some bursting vile fungus? It is not some great deed, but merely good riddance. . . . But once he is in his grave, and the house is rid of him, then we are free and alone and, rid of contingency and circumstance, are blissful bodies of love that may embrace without a second thought or regard for consequence, mouth to mouth. For you are correct, my divine boy, in saying that he stands in the way of our raptures and that we dare not subject him to them—I approve of your scruples. But surely you see, for that very reason we must slay him and remove him from the world, putting an end to such scruples, for our embraces will no longer matter to him. Don't you underthtand, my thweet boy! Just picture it, our happiness, and how it will be when that fungus is knocked down and tossed aside and we are alone in the house—but you, still in your youth, will be its master. You will be master because I am mistress, and whoever sleeps with the mistress is the master. And we shall drink bliss by night, and by day as well we shall rest upon purple cushions amid the fragrance of spikenard, while girls and boys, their heads bound in wreaths, strum lutes and strike elegant poses, and as we watch and listen we shall dream of the night that was and of the one that will be. For I shall hand you your goblet, and we shall drink from the same spot on its golden rim, and as we drink our eyes will meet, sharing pleasures tasted the night before and planned for the night ahead, and shall nestle our feet together . . ."

"No, listen to me, Mut in the Valley of the Desert!" he said in reply. "I truly must implore you . . . for that is what people say, though here perhaps it would be better not to say 'implore' but in truth to say I 'conjure' you, or rather the demon that speaks from within you and by whom you are evidently possessed—for that is surely the case. You show your own tale little regard, I must admit, and make of yourself a woman whose name for all time will be Mother of Sin. Do consider the possibility, indeed the probability, that we are in a story, and collect yourself a bit. As you can see, I have to collect myself as well to repel your rapturous onslaught, though I find it easier to do so now because of the horror aroused in me by your mad proposal to murder Peteprê, my master and your noble husband. It is indeed ghastly! All that is lacking is for you to say that we now share the secret together because you have drawn me into your thoughts and it is, alas, my secret now as well. But that it remains in your thoughts and that we do not make a story of it—I will see to that. Dear Mut! I find nothing at all pleasing in the manner of life you would demand of me here in this house, once we have murdered and dispatched its master so that we may revel in one another. When I picture it, how I would reside as a slave of your love in a house of murder, live as its master because I sleep with its mistress, I feel only contempt for myself. Should I not perhaps don a woman's garment made of byssus, so that each night you may demand pleasure of me, the master seduced into murdering the father so that he may sleep with the mother? For that is exactly how it would be for me: Potiphar, my master, is like a father to me, and were I to live with you in the house of his murder, it would be as if I were living with my mother. Therefore my dear, good child, I implore and conjure you with kindest words to be comforted and not to demand this great wickedness of me."

"Fool! Childish fool!" she replied in her resounding alto. "You are a little boy responding out of a fear of love, but as a wooing mistress I will break down your fear. Every man sleeps with his mother—did you not know that? The female is the Mother of the World; her son is her husband, and each man begets with his mother—must I tell you the most basic things? I am Isis, the Great Mother, and I wear the vulture's cap. Mut is my name as the Mother, and you shall tell me your name, dearest son, there in the world's sweet engendering night . . ."

"No, not so, not so!" Joseph dissented fervently. "What you believe and proclaim is not right—I must correct your views. The Father of the World is the son of no mother, and He is not its master at the bidding of a mistress. I belong to Him and walk before Him, am the son of a Father, and once and for all I tell you: I will not sin against God, the Lord and Master to whom I belong, by disgracing and murdering the father and coupling with the mother like a shameless hippopotamus. And with that, my child, I now depart. Dear mistress, I beg you, let me take my leave. I do not wish to forsake you in your distraction, most definitely not. I wish to comfort you with words and to advise you as best I can, for I owe that much to you. But now I must take my leave and go, that I may look after my master's house."

He left her.

But she called after him, "Do you think you will escape me? Do you think we can flee from one another? I know, I know all about your jealous god, to whom you are betrothed and whose wreath you wear. But I do not fear this foreigner and I will rip that wreath from you yet, whatever it be made of, and crown you instead with ivy and tendrils of the grape for the Mother's feast of our love. Stay, my darling! Stay, most beautiful of the beautiful, Osarsiph, stay!" And she fell to the floor and wept.

He separated the curtains with his arms and hastily went his way. But where he had flung the curtains aside, a dwarf now stood wrapped in each fold to right and left—one named Dûdu, the other favored Shepses-Bes. Stealing up from either direction, they had found each other here, had stood side by side at the break in the curtains, eager to eavesdrop—the first out of malice, the second in trembling fear—each with one little hand braced on a knee, the other held to an ear; from time to time each had threatened the other with his little fist, gnashing his teeth and gesturing for the other to go, which increased the difficulty of eavesdropping not a little, but neither had yielded.

But now behind Joseph's back, as they unwrapped themselves from the folds, they struck out at each other, hissing, clenching fists to their temples, and scolding with choked rage—both as peevish as spiders, as one little man to the other, but also because they were so different in nature.

"What are you doing here?" the first one, Dûdu, spouse of Zeset, snarled. "You runt, you mite, you undergrown snippet! Did you have to come sneaking up to the curtain flap, where I alone have rightful duties, and never budge from the spot, despite all my many signals that you should make yourself scarce, you tadpole, you sad little zany. I will knock the stuffing out of you so that you never move from here again, you dandiprat, you small fry, you feeble little worm! Has to come sniffing and prying, the gimcrack does, and playing lookout for his master and great friend—that pretty face, that bastard of the reeds he brought into the house, so that a bit of trash goods might abuse and lord over it, much to the disgrace of the Two Lands, and finally even make a strumpet of the mistress . . ."

"Oh, oh, you blackguard, you scapegrace, you spiteful fiend!" the other chirped, his little face shattering into a thousand wrinkles of fury, the cone of ointment askew on his head. "Who is lurking and listening here so that he may spy out what he himself brought about with his slips of paper and tinderbox, and now stands at the curtain flap reveling in the torments and sweet pain of great people, so that they may be ruined according to his own shameful plan—who but you, odious brazenface, blowhard, knight of the turnspit—ah, ah! and oh, oh!—you scarecrow and whippersnapper, you monstrosity, all of it dwarfish except for one giant thing, you walking tool of manhood, you contemptible knave of the bed . . ."

"Just wait!" the other yelped back. "Just wait, you nil, you hole in the world, Sir Lack-It-All, Sir Come-Up-Short, you useless ninny. If you do not abscond at once from here, where Dûdu watches and guards the honor of this house, I will shame you on the spot with my manly weapon, you miserable milksop, so that you will not soon forget it. But, when I go now to Peteprê and prick him with the proceedings that occurred here in these shadows and tell him of words whispered by the steward to the mistress in this curtained chamber, the shame that will then be yours, you vermin, is inscribed on a special scroll—and you will read it soon enough. For you brought the good-for-nothing into this house and there was no end to your wise babblings to the departed steward in praise of your keen dwarfish eye for men and goods and human goods, until he bought the scoundrel from those other scoundrels despite my warnings and placed him in this house that he might abuse the mistress and make a cuckold of Pharaoh's gelded friend. You are to blame for this mess, you above all, you from the very beginning! You are due to appear on the crocodile's menu, will be fed to him as a tidbit, a last little treat, after he's been served up your bosom friend, once they have bound and beaten him."

"Ah, you foulmouth," Favored Bes wailed, quivering and wrinkled with rage, "the words on your smutty tongue come not from your reason, but rise up from elsewhere and are slavering filth. Should you dare touch me and venture the least attempt to shame my poor wizened person, you will feel my fingernails in your runtish face and in the sockets of your eyes, for they are sharp, and the pure have likewise been given weapons to deal with the miscreant. . . . To blame, I, little I, am to blame for the torment and distress in there? The blame lies with the evil force, with the greedy affliction in which you take such swaggering pride and that, out of envy and hate, you have devilishly put to your service, so that it will become a pit dug to snare Osarsiph, my friend. But do you not see, you goatish mouse, that it has missed its mark and left no mark upon my beautiful friend? Since you had to eavesdrop, could you not determine that he was as resolute as an initiate into the mysteries and held fast like a hero to his own story? Did you hear anything at all at the flap? What witness can you bear to what was said, seeing as you lack all dwarfish subtlety and your cock-of-the-walk antics have turned your wits all lumpish? I would like to know what you can possibly hope to prick the master with in regard to Osarsiph, for your dull ears certainly snatched up nothing of value at their listening post . . ."

"Oho!" Dûdu cried. "Zeset's spouse is prepared to match his fine ears and delicate hearing with yours, you milksop, especially concerning a matter in which he is well versed but of which you understand not a whit, you chirping insufficiency. Were they not cooing and flirting in there, that fine little pair, prancing and preening at each tickle of love? I know all about that and was easily able to determine that the slave called his mistress 'dear child' and 'darling,' and that in her sweetest voice she named him 'falcon' and 'bull' and that they arranged in every detail how to enjoy each other's flesh and blood. So you see, Dûdu can hold his own as a hearing witness, can't he? But the most precious item I heard there at the flap is that in their rutting they have conspired to bring about Peteprê's death, agreeing to knock him down with a stick . . ."

"You lie! You lie! You see, you understood only the sheerest nonsense there at your listening post and would carry back to Peteprê the crudest misconception about both of them. For my youngster called the mistress child and friend only out of pure kindness and gentleness, trying to comfort her in her distraction, and dutifully rebuked and rebuffed her for even wanting to knock down a puffball with a stick. His conduct was nothing short of wonderful for his years, and as yet he has not let his story be marred by the slightest stain, despite such rapturous importuning . . ."

"And so, dupe that you are," Dûdu barked at him, "you think I therefore cannot accuse him to the master and ruin him? There's the subtle twist, my trump card in a game of which a puppet like you understands not one damn whit—it makes no difference how the rascal conducts himself, a bit more respectably, a bit more wantonly, for what matters is that the mistress is smitten, in love with him up over her ears and knows nothing finer in the world than to bill and coo with him—that alone is his ruin, and it is not up to him to save himself. The slave with whom the mistress is infatuated is headed straight for the crocodile in any case, there lies the trick and trap of it. For if he is willing to bill and coo with her, I have him. But if he resists, he only goads her in her madness and makes things worse, so that either way he is headed for the crocodile, or at least the barber's knife, and that will put an end to billing and cooing and his deprivation will heal the mistress of her madness . . ."

"Ah, you villain, you monster," Favored Bes screeched. "It's plain as day, your person is proof for good and all of what abominations creep forth and waddle upon earth when someone of the dwarfish race is not pious and proper as befits a dwarf, but endowed with full-grown dignity—he's sure to be a rogue and eyesore like you, Sir Breeding Stall."

To which Dûdu retorted that once the barber's knife did its work, Osarsiph would be all the more suitable a match for a hollow puppet like him. And so Masters Piddling and Piffling went at one another with bitter rejoinders several more times, until they drew a crowd from the courtyard. They then went their separate ways, the one to accuse Joseph before his master, the other to warn him that he must, if at all possible and as best he could, guard against the gaping pit.

Dûdu's Accusation

As everyone knows, Potiphar could not endure Dûdu, for he considered him arrogant, which was why the sight of the sterling little man had always annoyed Usir Mont-kaw as well. It has also previously been noted that the courtier kept the guardian of his jewelry chests at the greatest possible distance, hardly ever receiving him and employing intermediaries in his dressing chamber as a buffer between himself and Dûdu—grown men who, first, for reasons of stature were better suited to place jewels and garments on his tower of flesh, whereas Dûdu would have had to use a ladder, and, second, because, being full-grown, they put less weight on certain natural gifts and powers of the sun and made them less a matter of dignity than did Dûdu, for whom they were a lifelong marvel and a matter of consequential, self-defining pride.

Which was why it was not all that easy for this stump of a man to achieve his goal along the byway that he had finally decided to take after so many diligent trips between the young steward and his mistress—the goal, that is, of lighting a light for his master. He certainly did not manage it immediately after his quarrel with the mock vizier outside the curtained chamber, but had to wait and keep announcing himself not for days, but for weeks, before finally receiving an audience—he, the guardian of the chamber, had to bribe and sometimes threaten slaves, saying he simply would not hand over some article of jewelry or clothing but keep it under lock and key, thereby putting them in danger of arousing the master's displeasure, unless they repeatedly and urgently reported to him that Dûdu wished to, indeed had to speak before him about a weighty domestic concern. And so for a full quarter of the moon he had to engage in such labors—begging, conniving, stamping his feet—before gaining the favor that he itched all the more to achieve because he believed that if he attained and made good use of it this time, it would never again present such difficulties, for the service he intended to render would surely bring him his master's eternal love and grace.

The stalwart fellow's gifts had at last softened up two slaves of the bath, so that with each pitcher of water that they poured over the chest and back of their snorting master they alternated in crying out, "Master, remember Dûdu!" and kept repeating this reminder as the dripping tower of flesh emerged from the sunken basin and stepped out onto the limestone-tiled floor to be dried with perfumed towels—for even then they took turns saying "Master, remember Dûdu, who still waits!" until Potiphar testily commanded: "Let him come and speak." With that they gave a signal to the slaves in charge of salves and massages, who were waiting in the bedchamber and had likewise been bribed, and they called the dwarf from the western hall, where he had almost perished with impatience, and admitted him into the room with its bed alcove. Dûdu first raised the palms of his little hands high in the direction of the kneading bench, where Pharaoh's friend had stretched out to give his flesh over to the hands of massaging servants, and then, letting his dwarfish head hang humbly to one side between his raised arms, he waited for a syllable from Peteprê's mouth, a glance from his eyes; but neither the one nor the other followed, for the chamberlain lay groaning softly under the bold grip of servants working oil of nard into his shoulders, hips, and thighs, his plump womanish arms and his corpulent torso; and shifting on his leather pillow, he even turned the small and noble head atop this mass of flesh in the other direction, away from Dûdu's greeting—much to the dwarf's indignation. But for the sake of his promising cause, he was not about to be robbed of courage, did not dare allow for defeat.

"May your destiny last ten thousand years," he said, "you who stand at the pinnacle of mankind, our sovereign's great warrior! May there be four jars for your entrails and a coffin of alabaster for your enduring form!"

"Thanks," Peteprê replied. He said it in Babylonian, the way we might say "merci," and then added, "Does the fellow intend to speak at length?"

"The fellow" was bitter. But Dûdu's cause was far too promising; he did not let his courage falter.

"Not at length, master, sun of our day," he answered, "but rather, succinctly and to the point."

And at a sign from Peteprê's small hand he set one foot forward, crossed his stubby arms behind his back, and, tucking in his lower lip to let the other form a dignified roof above it, began his speech, which he knew very well he would not have to complete in the presence of the two masseurs, for Peteprê would very soon dismiss them in order to listen to him in private.

One might have called the strategy of his speech clever, had it only been more tenderhearted. He began with praise for Min, the god of the harvest, who was honored in several places as a special form of the sun's fiercest power, but who had also had to name his name to Amun-Rê and together with him made up the god Amun-Min or Min-Amun-Rê, so that Pharaoh found it just as easy to speak of "my father Min" as of "my father Amun"—particularly at the festivals of coronation and harvest, when the Min nature of Amun was in evidence and he became that fertile god, protector of desert travelers, tall in feathers and mighty in engendering power, the ithyphallic sun. And so with great dignity Dûdu invoked Min as a means of imploring his master to approve of how, as a highly placed member of the household and scribe of the master's wardrobe chests, he had not limited his zeal for service, his concern for domestic affairs, to more narrowly defined duties, but, as a spouse and father, the author of two well-proportioned children, who bore such and such names and to which, if signs did not deceive, there would indeed soon be added, as his wife Zeset had confessed to him upon his breast, a third— which was to say, to approve of how, as one who himself had increased the number of those dwelling in the house and who felt an especial devotion toward the majesty of Min, or rather of Amun in his Min qualities, he had kept his eye upon the larger whole, particularly in respect to human fertility and propagation, just as he had assumed oversight, guidance, and record keeping for everything pertaining to marriage and its issue, to such happy events as nuptials, the seeding of the womb, and childbirth, advising other members of the household about these matters, encouraging them, and providing in his own person a model of assiduousness and established order. For much in this regard depended on examples from on high, Dûdu said—not from the highest authority, of course, where quite understandably one neither wished nor was able to concern oneself with anything at all, including this matter. It was all the more important and necessary, then, that by taking precautions at the right moment everything be avoided that might disturb the sacred peace of this zenith high above all example—and that might even have the power to supplant such dignity with its opposite. Those standing next to the highest, however, were, in the opinion of the dwarf, duty-bound to take the lead by offering a good example to those beneath them, both in terms of assiduousness and order. And the speaker now asked if, up to this point, he had the approval of his master, the sun of his day.

Peteprê shrugged and turned over onto his stomach to offer his massive backside for the masseurs to deal with, but then raised his dainty head and asked what the reference to disruption of peace might mean, and those remarks about dignity and its opposite.

"Your highly placed servant will get to that in a moment," Dûdu replied. He now spoke of the late steward Mont-kaw, who had striven to lead an honest life and had at one time brought home a civil servant's daughter, through whom he had become a father or would have become one had things not taken a bad course and his resolve not been undone by fate, so that, discouraged, he had ended his days as a widower, after having shown such goodwill in the cause. But enough of him. Dûdu wished now to speak of the beautiful present, beautiful insofar as the departed steward had found a man of equal rank—or if not equal rank, since he was after all a foreigner, then a man who was his equal in intellectual gifts—and as the head of the household one now encountered a young man of the most impressive sort, and though, to be sure, his name was a bit unusual, he was of winning countenance, well-spoken and clever, in short, an individual of obvious merits.

"Idiot," Peteprê muttered into his crossed arms, for nothing seems more stupid than praise of an object whose true appreciation we prefer to reserve entirely to ourselves.

Dûdu ignored this. It could be that his master had said "idiot," but he chose not to take notice of it, for he had to keep up his courage and good spirits.

He could not emphasize enough his praise for the captivating and dazzling and—for some—disconcerting qualities of the lad in question, for they in fact lent real weight to concerns one necessarily had about him in regard to the stability and welfare of the house, at whose head he stood thanks to those same qualities.

"What is the fellow babbling about?" Peteprê said, turning and raising his head slightly as if asking his masseurs. "The overseer's qualities threaten the stability of the house?"

"Babble" was bitter, as bitter as another "fellow." But the dwarf was not about to be deterred.

"Under circumstances other than those that unfortunately exist," he responded, "they need not have done so, but could have served this house as purest blessing, were they subject or, better, had they earlier been subject to the limitations and lawful amelioration that qualities such as his—that inviting countenance, the astuteness, the eloquence—require if they are not to spread uneasiness, turmoil, and disruption in their immediate vicinity." And Dûdu lamented the fact that the house's young overseer, whose religious affiliations were, to be sure, quite opaque, refrained from paying due tribute to the majesty of Min, that as a man of high position he was still unmarried, that he had not deigned to enter into a conjugal relationship commensurate with his origins—for instance with the Babylonian slave Ishtarummi in the house of women—and so bless the estate with an increase of children. That was regrettable and troublesome; it was serious; it was dangerous. For it wasn't merely that it detracted from the prestige of the house and that the higher example of assiduousness and order was also neglected, but that, thirdly and in particularly, it also meant that those same seductive qualities, which no one denied the young steward possessed, lacked the restriction and rectification they so needed—had needed for so long now—to prevent them from inflaming hearts, turning heads, clouding minds, or, in short, from wreaking mischief on all sides, and not just on all immediate sides, but also beyond and above to loftier levels.

A pause followed. Peteprê let himself be rubbed down and did not reply. It was either-or, Dûdu declared. A young man of this sort should either be married off, so that his qualities could not spread their wild and ruinous flames in all directions, but be restricted to the safe harbor of marriage and rectified with the world—or it would be better to let the razor do its work, allow it to produce its salutary rectification, thereby preventing any disturbance of highest personages and having their dignity and honor subverted.

Another long silence. Peteprê suddenly turned over on his back—leaving the masseurs who had been busy with it standing helpless for a moment, their hands in the air—and lifted his head toward the dwarf. He measured him from top to bottom and back again—which did not take his eyes long—and glanced fleetingly across to a chair where his clothes and sandals, his fan and other utensils were lying. Then he rolled over again, pressing his brow to his folded arms.

He was filled with an anger that brought with it a cold shudder, a sense of outrage and fear at having his peace disrupted by this nasty manikin. This vain, misbegotten fellow knew something and wanted to inform him of it, something that, if it was true, he, Peteprê, really ought to know, but that he also found it grossly uncharitable to be informed of. "Everything is in order with the house, is it not? No misfortunes? The mistress is of good cheer?" That was evidently what this was about, and evidently someone, without even being asked, wanted to give him an unwelcome answer. He hated him— him above all; leaving aside the question of truth, he was not really inclined to hate anyone else. And so he should probably send away his masseurs and be left alone to speak with this valiant guardian of honor here so that his own sense of honor might be aroused—by truth or empty slander. Honor—one need only stop and consider what that means in terms of what was doubtlessly happening here. It is sexual honor, the rooster's honor, which consists in a wife's being faithful to her spouse to symbolize that he is the cock of the walk, who lacks nothing and gives her such lovely satisfaction that she would never think of having anything to do with another man, with the advances of some third party who could never even tempt a woman so splendidly provided for. But if it does happen, if she does carry on with another man, it is a symbol of just the opposite—the result is sexual dishonor, the cock of the walk becomes a cuckold, a capon; a gentle pair of hands places a ridiculous set of horns atop his head, and if he is to save what can be saved he must challenge and run a sword through the man whom his wife believes to be more splendid than he, though it is best to slay her as well—an even more impressive bloody deed for restoring regard for his virility, both in his own eyes and in those of the world.

Honor. Peteprê had no honor at all. He lacked it in the flesh, for in his condition he was no judge of cock-of-the-walk privileges, and it horrified him whenever others—such as, evidently, this pompous runt—tried to make him into a grand paragon of honor. Instead, he had a heart—a heart, that is, for justice, which is to say, a heart mindful of the rights of others; but it was a vulnerable heart as well, which hoped those others would show him devoted consideration, indeed love, a heart made to suffer bitterly from any disloyalty. During this pause—while the masseurs had gone back to work on his massive backside and he kept his face buried in his plump womanish arms—a great many things swiftly passed through his mind in regard to two people upon whom he pinned such fervent hope for love and loyalty that one might well say he loved them. The one was Mut, his first and true wife, whom, granted, he also hated a little because of the reproach that she could not possibly make and yet simply by her very existence did make, but to whom he also would gladly, sincerely have shown his love and strength, and not merely for his own sake. The other was Joseph, that genial young man, who knew how to make him feel better than wine ever could and for whose sake he had, much to his regret, been unwilling and unable to show himself loving and strong in response to the demand his wife had made in the columned hall that evening. Peteprê did not lack some insight into what he had refused her that day; just between us, even during their conjugal discussion he had not lacked a hint of that same insight: that the reasons she gave for requesting Joseph's banishment were mere pretexts and excuses and that her demand had been made for the sake of his own honor. But since he lacked that honor, her fear had been less important to him than ownership of the lad who gave him strength. He had preferred the latter and, by surrendering his wife to her feelings, had invited the two of them to prefer each other to him and to betray him.

He understood that. It hurt, for he had a heart. But he understood it, because his heart inclined to justice—also, perhaps, because that was more comfortable and because justice relieves one of rage and the need to avenge one's honor. He probably also sensed that it is dignity's surest refuge. It looked as if this nasty guardian of honor here wanted to inform him that his honor was in danger of betrayal. As if, he thought, dignity ceased to be dignity if it has to hide its head in the agony of being betrayed. As if the one betrayed does not possess more dignity than his betrayer. But if he does not, because he is to blame and has provoked the betrayal, then there is still justice, so that through it dignity can admit both its own blame and the rights of others and thereby reestablish itself.

And so Peteprê the eunuch strove for justice, both immediately and in anticipation of whatever information was supposed to rouse his honor. Justice is spiritual, unlike the honor of the flesh—and since he lacked the latter, he knew he had no recourse but the former. He had likewise relied on spiritual qualities in dealing with the two people who—or so this mischief maker and show-off apparently wanted to inform him, without ever being asked—had proved unfaithful to him. A strong spiritual safeguard had, as far as he knew, held their flesh under its spell, for they were both called and chosen, united in their spirituality: the woman, who was more than consoled as Amun's consort, a bride of his temple, dancing in her clinging garment before the goddess; and the young lad, who was loved by a jealous god and in his hair wore a wreath that set him apart, the boy Touch-Me-Not. Had the flesh mastered them? The thought sent a cold shudder through him, for although he possessed flesh in great abundance, it was his enemy, and whenever he had asked upon returning home "Everything is in order with the house, is it not? No misfortunes?" it had always been his subconscious worry that in his absence the flesh might have caused ghastly disruption by somehow becoming master over that considerate, but unreliable, safeguard, over the spiritual spell cast upon his house. But his cold shudder was accompanied by anger—did he have to know this, could he not be left in peace all the same? If that consecrated pair had been overcome by the flesh behind his back and had secrets they kept from him, there was still enough considerate love in their secrecy, in their deception, that he was prepared to thank them. Whereas he had only unutterably bad things to say about this pompous wretch here, this arrogant little guardian of honor, who, without being asked, wanted to force knowledge upon him, was planning a vile attack on his peace and quiet.

"Are you almost finished?" he asked. This was directed to the masseurs, whom he had to dismiss, but did not want to dismiss, because the reason for doing so came from this tattletale scoundrel—yet send them away he must. They were, to be sure, very stupid fellows, who had more or less consciously cultivated their stupidity so that its magnitude might truly correspond to what was proverbially said of their profession: "dumb as masseurs." But though they had certainly not understood anything until now and would not easily grasp anything that might yet be said, Peteprê could not evade his tormentor's implicit demand that he wished to speak with him tête-à-tête. Which only made him more angry at him.

"You are not to go before you've finished," he said, "and don't be all too hasty about it. But if you are finished, then give me a towel and, in due time, be on your way."

They had still not understood that they were to leave even if they were not finished. But since they were in fact finished, they spread a linen sheet over the mass of their master's flesh, all the way up to his neck, bowed so low that their two-finger-wide brows touched the floor, and with arms akimbo exited at a sort of steady waddle that all by itself was convincing proof of their self-willed and total stupidity.

"Come nearer, my friend," the chamberlain said. "Come as near as you like and think fitting for what you wish me to learn, for it appears to be something for which it would be advisable that you not stand so far from me that you would have to shout—to be instead a matter that charges us both with a more muted intimacy, which I count to its credit whatever its nature may be. You are a valuable servant to me, small to be sure, far below average and in that regard a silly creature, but you have dignity and substance and certain qualities that justify your going beyond your duties in my chamber, keeping an eye to larger affairs of the house and setting yourself up as master of its orderly fertility. Not that I can recall having appointed and installed you in that office—no, I do not. But I confirm you in it now after the fact, for I cannot help acknowledging it as your calling. If I understood correctly, love and duty demand that you report to me concerning disturbing observations you have made in that field in which you have oversight and keep records, certain incidents that may kindle disorder."

"Most definitely!" Joseph's antagonist responded emphatically to the words addressed to him, swallowing certain insulting elements for the sake of their otherwise encouraging nature. "The loyalty of a concerned servant brings me before your presence, master, sun of our days, to warn you of a danger that may be of such urgency that you should have admitted me long before now, as I requested, for all too easily, indeed at any moment now, my warning may come too late."

"You frighten me."

"I am sorry for that. But then again, it is very much my intention to frighten you, for danger is imminent, and despite all the ingenuity I bring to the task, your servant cannot say definitively if it is not already too late and your disgrace an accomplished fact. In that conceivable case it would not yet be too late only insofar as you are still alive."

"Do I face the threat of death?"

"Both, ignominy and death."

"I would welcome the one if I could not avoid the other," Peteprê said loftily. "And from whence arise these dreadful things that threaten me?"

"My intimations as to the source of danger," Dûdu countered, "have already been as good as unambiguous. Only fear of understanding them would explain your not having understood me."

"Just how dreadful my situation is," Peteprê responded, "is clear from your impudence, which evidently corresponds to my own misery, and I have no choice but to praise the zealous loyalty from which it flows. I admit that my fear of understanding is insurmountable. Help me to surmount it, my friend, and tell me the truth so straightforwardly that my fear is robbed of any chance to hide from it."

"Fine, then," the dwarf replied, putting his other foot forward now and setting one fist to his hip. "Your situation is that the ungratified and wildly incendiary qualities of the steward Osarsiph have kindled a fire in the bosom of my mistress Mut-em-enet, your consort, and the smoking, crackling flames are already licking at the roof beams of your honor, which threaten to collapse and bury your life beneath them."

Peteprê pulled the linen sheet covering him higher still, over his chin and mouth, up to his nose.

"You wish to say," he asked from under the sheet, "that the mistress and the steward have not only cast eyes at one another, but also seek to end my life?"

"Most definitely!" the dwarf replied, shifting his position by vigorously thrusting his other fist against his other hip. "That is the situation in which a man who but a moment ago stood as tall as you now finds himself."

"And what proof," the captain asked in a muffled voice, the sheet moving with his lips, "do you have for such a dreadful accusation?"

"My watchfulness," was Dûdu's answer, "my eyes and ears, the acuity that my zeal for the honor of this house has lent my observations—may these be witnesses, my pitiable master, for the sad and awful truth of my revelation. Who can say which of the two—and one must speak of 'the two' of them, despite the infinite difference in their rank—which of them first cast his eyes upon the other? Their eyes met and were illicitly immersed in each other's depths—and there you have it. We must be clear, my great master, that Mut-in-the-Valley-of-the-Desert is a woman who lies in a lonely bed; and as for the steward, well, he is simply incendiary. What slave would wait for such a mistress to signal twice? That would presume a love and loyalty to the master of the mistress that evidently is not to be found at the highest level of steward but at the next highest level of oversight. . . . And guilt? What good would it do to inquire who first raised his eyes to the other and in whose mind the crime first sprouted? The young steward's guilt does not lie primarily in what he did, but in his existence and in his presence in this house, where his qualities are free to set fires, are gratified neither by marriage bed nor razor; and if the mistress catches fire for her servant, the blame lies in his very existence and upon his head, and in terms of his guilt it is the same as if he had vilely assaulted this pure woman—that is how he is to be dealt with. So that is how things stand. Alas, it has come to this: the two are in most voluptuous concord. Billets-doux—which I have seen with my own eyes, so that I can testify to their sultriness—have passed between them. Under the pretext of discussing household matters they meet together, now here, now there—in the women's chambers, where to please her slave the mistress has set up an image of Horakhte, in the garden and in the cottage upon the embankment there, yes, even in the mistress's room here in your house—the pair secretly meets together in all these places, and as for respectable matters, they long ago ceased to speak of them, and it is all vain billing and cooing and hot lisping. How things may have proceeded, and whether it has now gone so far that they have already enjoyed each other's flesh and blood, so that it would be too late for any preventative measures and only revenge remains—that I cannot say with complete and absolute certainty. But what I can swear—at my own peril before every god and before you, my humiliated master—to be certain truth, because I heard it with my own ears at the flap in the curtain, is that in their cooings they have agreed to beat you about the head with sticks until you are dead, and once they have dispatched you, intend to pursue their lust as master and mistress upon a garlanded bed here in this house."

At these words, Peteprê pulled the sheet completely over his head, so that nothing more of him was visible. He remained like that for some time, until the pause began to seem overlong to Dûdu, though he had been happy to observe how at first his master had lain there like an amorphous mass, covered in his own shame and vanishing beneath it. Suddenly, however, Peteprê threw the sheet back as far as his hips, sat up halfway and, propping his little head in a little hand, turned to the dwarf.

"I must offer you my earnest thanks," he said, "guardian of my chests, for your revealments"—"revealment" was a borrowed Babylonian word—"in the cause of saving my honor, or even for the determination that it is already lost and that I have only my naked life left to save, which I must strive to save not for its own sake, but for the revenge that my life must serve in terrible devotion from this moment forward. Caught up in thoughts of punishment I run the danger of neglecting the equally important thanks and reward that I owe you for your discoveries. The horror and rage they cause me is equal to my amazement at your own feats of love and loyalty. Indeed, I admit to you my surprise—which I should moderate, I know; for how often is not some humble person—to whom one has not exactly shown the respect and trust he deserves—a source of finest things. All the same, I cannot refrain from a certain incredulous amazement. You are a deformed mooncalf, a queer dwarfish buffoon, to whom, far more out of amusement than in earnest, I assigned duties in my chamber—a half-ridiculous, half-disgusting sort of fellow, both halves heightened all the more by your pomposity. Under such circumstances does it not border on the incredible, or perhaps even cross that line, that you should have succeeded in penetrating the secret life of persons who, apart from me, stand highest in this house and, for example, in reading billets-doux that, according to your charge, have found their way between the young steward and the mistress? Must I or should I not doubt the very existence of these papers, as long as it seems inconceivable to me that you could ever have managed to read them? For that, my dear man, you would have had to worm your way into the trust of the confidential person commissioned to carry such letters, and how can that seem even somewhat probable given the undeniable nastiness of your person?"

"Fear of having to believe your own shame and lamentable abasement," Dûdu replied, "allows you, poor master, to look for other reasons to mistrust me. You are content with very flimsy reasons—so great is your quaking fear of the truth, though, granted, the mockingly wretched face it presents you makes your quaking understandable. Hear, then, how feeble your doubts are! I did not have to steal my way into the trust of the confidential person chosen to carry those lush letters, for I myself was the person chosen."

"Stupendous!" Peteprê exclaimed. "You, a little and funny man like you, carried the letters? My respect for you has begun to grow swiftly in simple response to your statement; but it still must grow a good deal more before I also actually believe what you say. So you are so intimate with the mistress, are on such friendly footing with her that she would deliver herself, her happiness and her guilt, into your hands?"

"Most definitely!" Dûdu riposted, boldly shifting his weight to his other leg and his other hand to his hip. "And it is not just that she gave me these letters to carry, but I also dictated what her reed should write. For she knew nothing of billets-doux and first had to be instructed in that tender art by me, a man of the world."

"Who would have thought it!" the chamberlain marveled. "I realize more and more how greatly I have underestimated you, and my respect has begun its swift, unstoppable ascent. You did that, I assume, in order to push matters to the brink and to see how far the mistress would be willing to go in this offense."

"But of course," Dûdu confirmed. "I acted out of love and loyalty to you, my humbled master. Would I be standing here otherwise, pricking you to take your revenge?"

"But how," Potiphar wanted to know, "being the scurrilous and odious fellow you at first appear to be, did you gain the intimate friendship of the mistress and make yourself master of her secret?"

"They occurred at the same time," the dwarf replied, "both at once. For as any good person would be, I was grieved and angered for Amun's sake by this foreigner's cunning ascendancy in the house, and I nursed a mistrust of both him and the deceit in his heart—not unjustly, as you will now admit, since he has miserably cheated you and violated your bed of honor, so that, after having received kindness upon kindness from you, he makes you the laughingstock of the capital and soon, most probably, of the Two Lands. In my grief and suspicion, then, I complained before Mut, your wife, about this offense and injustice and pointed out this wretched person to her, calling her attention to him. For at first she claimed not to know which servant I meant. But then she entertained my bitter complaints in a strikingly tangled fashion, babbled on in curiously slippery words, which, under a pretext of concern, became ever more wanton, so that I realized her loins merely lusted after the slave, that she was as infatuated with him as any kitchen maid—that is what, by his guilty presence, he brought this proud woman to. And if a man such as I had not taken on the matter, cleverly associating myself with it, so that I might burst the scheme wide open at the right moment, your honor would have been undone. That is why, once I spied your wife's thoughts slinking off down dark paths, I slunk right behind them as one would slink behind a thief in the night in hope of nabbing him in the act, instructed her in billetsdoux—both to tempt her and to see how far gone she already was and to learn what she was capable of—and found my every expectation and worry exceeded; for with the help of the blind trust she placed in me because she believed that I, as a resourceful man of the world, was ready to serve her in her lust, I realized to my horror that this wicked, incendiary young steward had made this noble lady capable of truly anything and that not only your dignity, but your life as well are in imminent danger."

"I see, I see," Peteprê said, "you called her attention to him and prompted her—I understand. So much, then, for the mistress. But I simply cannot as yet accept, absolutely cannot believe that a man with your imperfections could have also won the trust of the steward."

"Your incredulity, my stricken master," Dûdu rejoined, "must capitulate before the facts. I attribute it to your fear of the truth, and also to your sacred, special condition, to which one must ascribe, as

I'm sure you'll admit, this entire misfortune, for it makes you incapable of appreciating and understanding other people—how very much their opinion of a fellow man, their fondness for him, be he of short or moderate stature, is conditioned by his willingness to satisfy their desires and lusts. I needed only to give myself the air of such willingness and in my best polished fashion offer him my services, as a worldly, discreet go-between for his lust and that of our lady—and with that the ninny fell into my trap and I stood on such tender footing with him that he no longer concealed anything from me; and from then on I could not only observe and follow every detail of the game this traitorous pair was playing, but could also promote and abet it with my seeming patronage, so that I might observe how far they would go and to what point of culpability they might be willing to advance, in order that I might nab them at the very brink. That is the method of the guardians of established order, among whom I am a model. For by patiently slinking after them I also succeeded in exposing a conviction they both share, a most remarkable aspect that forms the basis of their game: that whoever lies with the mistress is the master. That, you should know, my poor master, is their lewd, murderous hypothesis, which they discuss daily and from which, as I have heard from their own lips, they derive the right and higher legitimacy to fell you with a stick and rid the house of you, so that, its slain master dispatched, they may celebrate their feast of roses together—as mistress and master of love. But when as her confidant I had brought them to this brink, had heard their lips admit it, the boil seemed ripe for lancing, and I came to you, my disgraced master, to whom I am faithful in your misery, that I may prick you and we can nab them."

"Let us do so," Peteprê said. "Let us come down upon them in terror—you, dear dwarf, and I, and their crime shall catch up with them. What do you think we should do with them, what punishments seem to you painful and awful enough for us to inflict upon them?"

"I am of a gentle mind," Dûdu replied, "at least in regard to our Mut, the beautiful sinner, for her lonely bed excuses much, and although her lapse has left you in a bad way, it would not—just between us—be seemly for you to raise a great cry. And as I said: if the mistress becomes infatuated with a slave, one should look to the slave, for by his mere presence he is to blame for this misfortune and should suffer for it. But I am also of a gentle mind on his behalf and do not even demand he be bound and left to the crocodiles, as he deserves on the basis of both his fortune and misfortune. For Dûdu is not inclined to revenge, but rather to security measures to douse the enkindling flames, and the man should be bound merely so that the razor can do its work, thereby eliminating the danger at its root and putting an end to the possibility of his ever being with Mut-em-enet or of his beautiful form having any meaning in the woman's eyes. And if he is properly bound beforehand, I myself am prepared to perform the pacifying deed."

"I find it worthy of you," Peteprê said, "that you offer yourself for this task as well, after all you have done for me. Do you not think, my little fellow, that the act would reestablish justice in the world, insofar as this precaution would, you see, give you an advantage over the docked young man, precedence that would offer you, who are so oddly built, redress for his fair form?"

"There is something to that," Dûdu responded. "I would not deny that it is worth mention in passing." And with that he crossed his short arms, thrust one shoulder forward, began letting the leg he had boldly set before him wave in the air, and rocked his head to and fro amid jaunty glances and ever increasing merriment.

"And where does that lead, do you think?" Peteprê continued. "One really cannot leave the man at the head of the household, can one—not after you have made him pay in full by performing such a procedure?"

"Most definitely not!" Dûdu laughed, still carrying on as before. "The head of a household in command of all its servants should not be a pacified culprit, but a competent man with all his capacities intact, who can represent his master in every business dealing and in every situation with which he cannot or does not wish to concern himself."

"So then I also know," the captain added, "the promotion with which to reward you, my stalwart fellow, in gratitude for your loyal service as a spy and for having pricked me in order to save me from ignominy and death."

"I would hope so!" Dûdu cried, his arrogance now veering out of control. "I would certainly hope that you know where Dûdu belongs, and have a clear sense of gratitude and rightful succession. For it is not too much to say that I am protecting you from ignominy and death, and our beautiful sinner as well. But she ought to know that I pleaded her case with you on account of her lonely bed and that I have granted her life, so that she has breath only by virtue of my favor and grace. For if I so choose and she responds to me with ingratitude, I can, just as I please and at any time, trumpet her crime throughout city and realm, so that you would be compelled to strangle her after all and turn her fine body to ashes, or at least, with nose and ears docked, send her back to her family. So let her be prudent, the poor murderous flirt, and turn her gemstone eyes from a pleasant but now meaningless form to Dûdu, ingenious comforter, master of his mistress, doughty little steward of the house."

As he spoke Dûdu cast still jauntier sidelong glances into nowhere, gyrated his shoulders and groin, pranced on his little feet, and behaved very much like a courting cock in a tree, blind and deaf in its frenzy, completely absorbed in its own allurements. But the same thing happened to him as happens to the cock when the hunter leaps up to grab him. For suddenly Peteprê, his master, was out from under the sheet and on his feet in a single bound, quite naked, a tower of flesh with a little head—and with the second bound reached the chair where his things lay, and was now swinging his cudgel of office. We have seen this handsome piece, this emblem of command or one like it, in his hand before: a cylindrical, gilded leather staff wreathed in golden leaves and ending in a pine cone, a symbol of power—and probably a fetish and cult object for women as well. Suddenly the master was swinging it, flailing Dûdu's shoulders and back with it, thrashing away at him until the dwarf was soon deaf and blind, but for other reasons than before, and was squealing like a pig.

"Ow, ow!" he cried, buckling at the hip. "Oh that hurts! The pain, I'm dying, I'm bleeding, my little bones are broken, have mercy on your faithful servant!" But there was no mercy, for Peteprê drove him from corner to corner of the bedchamber with relentless blows and cries of "There, there! That's for you, you buffoon and shameful runt, you arrant knave, who has confessed to me all his treachery!" Until the loyal dwarf found the door and, bending beneath his bruises, took to his heels.

The Threat

Our story reports that Potiphar's wife addressed such "words" to Joseph day after day, begging him to lie by her or be with her. Does that mean he gave her opportunity to do so? That even after that day of the painful tongue he did not avoid her company, but continued to join her at various places and various times of day? He did. Surely he had to, for she was his mistress, his female master, and could summon him and command he appear whenever she liked. Besides which, he had promised her that he would not forsake her in her distraction, but comfort her with words as best he could, because he owed her that much. He realized that. He was bound to her by an awareness of his own guilt, and in his heart he admitted that he had foolishly stood by as things came to this pass and that his healing regimen had been culpable balderdash, the consequences of which he must now bear and ameliorate if possible, however dangerous and difficult, if not indeed pointless, that task may have become. Should one also praise him for not withdrawing from the sight of the afflicted woman, but exposing himself "daily"—or let us say, almost daily—to the breath of the fiery bull, daring over and over to confront one of the strongest temptations that has ever laid siege to a lad in the history of the world? Perhaps, in a certain sense and in some part. Among his motives some were praiseworthy, one can credit him for that. The feelings of guilt and obligation that motivated him deserved praise; as did the courage that allowed him in his plight to trust in his God and his own seven reasons; also, if you like, even the defiance that had begun to determine his conduct and demand of him that he match the woman's madness with the power of his reason—for she had threatened him and pledged herself to ripping from his brow the wreath that he wore for the sake of his God and to crown him with her own instead. He found that shameless, and it should be noted here and now that there were several other things about it all that made him feel this was a matter between his God and the gods of Egypt—just as over time Amun had become a motive behind her desires, or had been turned into one by others; and so one can understand, indeed condone him for regarding backing off as impermissible and for considering it necessary to see the matter through and let it redound to God's honor in the end.

Good enough. But not quite unalloyed good, for there was another reason why he obeyed her, met with her, visited her, but one that, as he himself well knew, was not laudable. One may call it curiosity and frivolity, call it an aversion to finally giving up the possible choice of evil, the wish to keep the choice between good and evil still open, though with no intention whatever of siding with evil. . . . Did he, despite the seriousness and danger of his situation, also take pleasure in dealing with his mistress tête-à-tête and calling her "my child," in which he felt fully justified by her passion and forlornness? A banal conjecture, but one that is certainly warranted alongside other more pious, more profoundly dreamy explanations of his behavior—which is to say, the far too playful but profoundly exciting idea of his having died and become the god Usarsiph and of the sacred state of readiness that this implied, but over which, to be sure, there also hovered the curse of the adulterous ass.

But enough—he met with his mistress. He stuck with her. He survived her constant barrage of such "words," her entreaties that he lie with her, saying "Sleep with me!" He survived it, we say—for it was no joke, no bagatelle to persevere in the presence of this woman of dreadful desires, to offer kind advice and, for his part, always to keep those seven opposing reasons in mind at their full intensity as a defense against her demands, which, after all, corresponded so nicely with certain feelings arising from his own dead and deified state. Indeed, one is inclined to overlook the less laudable motives behind the conduct of Jacob's son when one considers the trouble the unhappy woman caused him with her daily importuning, until he had moments when he understood why in his rage and distress, Gilgamesh had finally ripped off the bull's penis and cast it in Ishtar's face.

For the woman was growing worse, becoming ever less particular about her methods of laying siege to him so that they might put heads and feet together. She did not, however, return to her suggestion that they murder the master and rid the house of him so that they might live a life of bliss there as the mistress and master of love clad in beautiful raiment and flowers, for she saw only too well that he found the idea perfectly repulsive and could only fear that in repeating it she would alienate him beyond repair. Her own state of elated melancholy did not prevent her, however, from realizing that his absolute refusal to entertain this savage idea was naturally, obvi-

ously right and that it was entirely in order to reject an outrageous
demand that it would have been very difficult even for her to have
repeated once her tongue had healed and she no longer lisped like a
child. But she bombarded him again and again with her argument
that there was no point in his resisting her, that they shared a secret
they might as well bring to blissful fruition—as well as with promises of the unutterable rapture he would find in her loving arms,
for she had saved it all for him alone. But when he insisted on responding to such sweet wooing by simply declaring, "My child, we
dare not," she moved on to provoking him by casting doubt on his
manliness.

Not that she was especially serious about it—that was hardly
possible. But she had a certain formal and reasonable right to mock
his behavior in this way. Joseph could not really submit to her his
seven reasons; she would have found most of them incomprehensible; and what he offered instead must have sounded mundane and
lame to her—if not outright invention. What was she to do in her
passion and plight with the moral maxim like the one he had given
her as his final answer—to be put in other people's mouths just in
case these events became a story: that his master had entrusted
everything to him and that there was nothing in his house that he
had kept from him, except herself, because she was his wife, and that
he therefore could not do this wickedness and sin with her? That
was threadbare stuff, of no use to her plight or passion, for even if
they were in a story, Mut-em-enet was convinced that in all times
and places the world would find such a pair as she and Joseph justified in putting heads and feet together despite some Captain of the
Guard and honorary husband—that everyone would take far more
delight in that than in some moral maxim.

What else did he say? He would say, for instance: "You want for
me to come to you by night and to sleep with you. But it was by
night that our God, whom you do not know, usually revealed Himself to my fathers. If He wished to reveal Himself to me by night and
found me like that—what then would become of me?"

That was childish, really. Or he would say: "I'm afraid because
of Adam, who was driven from the garden for so small a sin. What
then would be my punishment?"

She thought that as shabby an answer as when he said: "You
don't know how it is. Because of his gushing ways my brother

Ruben lost his birthright, which father then gave to me. He would take it from me again were he to hear that you had made an ass of me."

That had to sound very feeble, indeed ragged to her ears, and he ought not to have been amazed when she broke into tears of pain and anger at such far-fetched excuses and insinuated that she was beginning to believe, really had no choice but to surmise, that the wreath he wore was simply the straw wreath of impotence. Once again: she did not and surely could not have meant what she said. It was more a desperate provocation of his fleshly honor, and the look with which he replied equally shamed and enflamed her, for its message was clearer and more stirring than the one Joseph put into words:

"Do you think so?" he said bitterly. "Then desist! But if it were as you think you've guessed, I would have it easy, and temptation would not be like a dragon and a roaring lion. Believe me, my lady, I have certainly thought about ending your suffering and mine by adopting the condition that you mistakenly suggest, and to do as that lad in one of your stories, who, in order to demonstrate his innocence, wounded himself with the sharp leaf of a bulrush and flung the impugned member into the river for the fish to eat. But I may not act in that fashion—the sin would be as great as if I were to succumb, and I would no longer be of any worth to God, either. For He wishes that I remain healthy and whole."

"How horrible!" she cried. "What were you thinking, Osarsiph? Do not do it, my beloved, my glorious lad, what a dreadful shame that would be. I could never mean what I said. You love me, you love me, your punishing glance betrays you to me, as does your monstrous purpose. Oh sweet man, come and save me, stanch my flowing blood, for what a pity it is to waste it."

But he replied, "It dare not be."

At that she flew into a rage, threatening him with torture and death. That was how far she had come, and it was this that was weighing on our mind when we said that the methods with which she assailed him were increasingly beyond her will to choose. He now learned whom he was dealing with and what had been the real meaning of her resounding cry: "I alone am fear-inspiring in my love!" The giant cat raised its paw, menacingly extended its claws from their velvet sheaths in order to tear his flesh to pieces. If he did not obey her will, she told him, and did not give her his god's wreath in exchange for the wreath of her bliss, she must and would destroy him. She urgently begged him to take her words seriously and not as hollow jangle, for she was, just as he saw her here, capable of anything, prepared for anything. She would charge him before Peteprê with doing what he refused to do for her and accuse him of a rapacious assault upon her virtue. She would charge him with having forced himself upon her, and would take greatest pleasure in her accusation, would know how to play the ravished and sullied woman, so that no one would doubt her statement. Her word and her oath, of that he could be certain, would be worth more in this house than his, and his denial would be to no avail. Besides which, she was convinced that he would not deny it, but silently take the guilt upon himself; for he was to blame that things had come to this pass and had left her in such furious desperation, he and his eyes and his mouth, his golden shoulders and his rejection of love; and he would realize that it made no difference in what charge guilt was clothed, for every accusation would be true because of the truth of his guilt, and he must be prepared to suffer death for it. But it would be a death that would surely give him cause to repent his silence and perhaps even his cruel rejection of her love. For men like Peteprê were especially inventive in the ways of revenge, and the death in store for a libertine who overpowered his mistress would leave nothing to be desired in its exquisiteness.

And now she announced to him the death he would die because of her accusation, painted it for him in her resounding alto—but bending close to his ear now and then, she also spoke in a murmur that might have been taken for the tender whispers of love.

"Do not hope," she whispered, "that they will make short work of you by pushing you off a cliff or hanging you upside down so that the blood swiftly rushes to your brain and you die a gentle death. Things will not proceed so mercifully, once cudgels rip your back to shreds after Peteprê has spoken his sentence. For like the mountains of the east, his heart will bring forth a sandstorm when I charge you with violating me and his taunting wrath will know no bounds. It is ghastly to be left to the crocodile and to lie bound and defenseless among the reeds as the ravenous beast approaches in its hunger and rolls up on you with its wet belly, beginning its meal with your thighs or shoulder, so that your wild shrieks mix with its grunts of greedy pleasure, for no one hears or wants to hear you in your abandonment. The same thing has happened to others—one is aware of it and of a superficial sense of sympathy, but not of any responsibility, and it passes, for it does not concern one's own flesh. But now it is you and your flesh that the greedy beast is attacking, beginning here or there—and even if you are still fully conscious, withhold the inhuman shrieks ripping your chest apart, do not scream, my beloved, for me, who wished to kiss you there where that wet-bellied monster now buries its grisly teeth. But perhaps they will be different kisses. Perhaps you will be stretched out on the ground on your back, your hands and feet held in iron clamps, while flammable material is piled up over you, which is then ignited and your flesh is slowly charred by the flame, amid agonies for which there is no name, that you alone experience, breathlessly wailing and begging as others simply look on. That, my beloved, is how it may be, or perhaps they will seal you alive, along with two large dogs, in a pit, covering it with beams and earth, and once again no one can imagine—not even you yourself, not as long as what awaits you is not yet reality—what will happen over time among the three of you there underground. And do you recall the door to the hall and its peg? And once I have leveled my charge, you will be the man who begs in loud, wailing cries of lamentation, because that peg has been rammed into his eye and the door crushes his head each time his avenger chooses to pass through. These are but a few of the punishments that will certainly be yours when I utter my accusations against you, which I am resolved to do should I be driven to final desperation. You, however, will not be able to paint yourself white after my sworn testimony. Out of pity for yourself, Osarsiph, give me your wreath."

"My mistress and friend," he answered her, "you are right, I cannot be made white again if you wish to blacken me in this way before my master. But Peteprê will have to choose among the punishments with which you threaten me; he cannot impose them all, but only one, and that in itself sets bounds to his revenge and my suffering. And even beyond those bounds, my suffering will be limited by what humans are capable of, and whether one chooses to call that limit narrow or very wide, suffering cannot move past it, for it is finite. Desire and suffering, you paint both as unbounded, but you exaggerate, for both very quickly come up against the limits of human capacity. The only thing one can call unbounded would be the mistake I would make in breaking with the Lord my God, whom you do not know, so that you cannot know what that is, what that means: God-forsaken. Which is why, my child, I cannot comply with your wishes."

"Cursed be your cleverness!" she cried in her alto voice. "Let it be cursed! As for me, I am not clever. I lack cleverness because of my unbounded desire for your flesh and blood, but I will do what I say. I am the loving Isis, and my gaze is death. Beware, beware, Osarsiph!"

A Gathering of Ladies

Ah, how grand she must have appeared, our Mut, as she stood before him, threatening him in her bell-like voice. And yet she was as weak and helpless as a child, devoid of all sympathy for her own dignity and story, and by now had begun to confide to the whole world both her passion and the anguish the young man caused her. It had come to that: not only Tabubu the "rubber-eater" and Meh-en-we-sekht the concubine were now initiates in her love and suffering, but also Renenutet, wife of the Chief Steward of Amun's Bulls, and Neit-em-hêt, consort of Pharaoh's Chief Bather, and Akhwêre, spouse of Kakabu, the Scribe of the Silver Houses, from the king's House of Silver—in short, all her female friends, the entire court, half the city. This was a definite sign of how much worse off she was as the third year of her love drew to a close; without shame or inhibition she told everyone things she had at first kept proudly and shyly within her bosom and would have rather died than confess to her beloved or anyone else, but now recklessly made the concern of the whole world. Yes, not only Dûdu, the dignified dwarf, degenerates in the course of our tale, but Mut the mistress as well, to the point of fully losing control of herself, of her civilized self. She was afflicted and deeply smitten, had left herself behind, no longer belonged to the civilized world, was estranged from its standards, a glassy-eyed woman running wild in the mountains, willing to offer her breast to every wild beast, gasping, exultant, crowned with a savage crown and swinging the thyrsus. And to what all did this not finally lead? Just between us—and a bit ahead of ourselves—let it be noted that it led to her demeaning herself by engaging in magic with black Tabubu. But this is not yet the place for that. At this point we can only regard with wonder and pity how she chattered away with anyone who would listen about her love and ungratified longings, unable to keep this to herself, whether in the presence of the highborn or the lowly, so that it was not long before her suffering was the talk of the household, and whether it was cooks busy stirring and plucking or guards on their brick bench at the gate, they all said:

"The mistress is hot for the young steward, but he spurns her. What a shindy!"

For that is the shape such an affair assumes in the heads and on the tongues of people—the result of the sorry contradiction between blind passion's sacredly earnest, painfully beautiful awareness of itself and the impression it makes upon the level-headed, for whom weak-willed passion, in its inability to conceal itself, becomes an object of scandal and mockery, like a drunk reeling in the streets.

All versions of our story (with the exception, of course, of the shortest but most cherished)—both the seventeen Persian songs that speak of it and the Koran, both the poem to which Firdousi the Disillusioned devoted his old age and Jami's later polished rendering—all of them, plus countless depictions in brush or pencil, tell of a gathering of ladies for a party given at this juncture by Potiphar's first and true wife for her friends, the ladies of No-Amun's highest society, so that she might reveal her sufferings to them, might gain her sisters' understanding and arouse their sympathy, and envy. For love, however ungratified, is not only a curse and a scourge, but also a great treasure that one does not gladly conceal. These songs and poems slip into many an error and are guilty of numerous digressions and variant adornments, whereby the sweetness and charm to which they give such free play come at the cost of strict truth. In regard to this gathering of ladies, however, they are correct; and if here, too, for the sake of sweet effect, they also deviate from the way in which the story originally told itself—indeed, variations in each reveal the fabrications of the others—these balladeers did not fabricate this event, but rather it was the story itself that devised it, or rather, on a personal level, Potiphar's wife, poor Eni did, who cun-

ningly planned it and saw it to fruition—and it stands in the
strangest, but true-to-life contradiction to her own dazed state.

Those of us who know about the eye-opening dream that Mut-
em-enet dreamt at the start of these three years of love can see quite
clearly the connection between dream and plan, can follow the train
of thought that lead her to this poignantly ingenious idea of opening
her friends' eyes; and for us the reality of her dream—which obviously bears all the marks of authenticity—is the best proof for both
the historicity of this gathering of ladies and why it is only out of laconic economy that the venerable tradition closest to us remains
silent about it.

In prelude to this gathering of ladies, Mut-em-enet fell ill. Although familiar to us in merely rough outline, it was the illness that
in so many tales befalls princes and princesses when they love in vain
and that invariably "mocks the skill of the most famous physicians."
Mut fell victim to it first of all because such tales require it, because it
was the fitting and timely thing to do, and it is hard to resist what is
fitting and timely; and secondly, because her one great concern
(which also consistently seems to be a principal reason behind the
maladies of princes and princesses in those other stories) was to create a stir, to set the world into an uproar, and to be *questioned*—to be
urgently asked universal, life-and-death questions, even though the
changes that had altered her appearance for a good while now had
previously given rise to isolated and more or less sincerely worried
inquiries. She grew ill out of a compelling desire to involve the world
in her own affliction, in the happiness and torment of her love for
Joseph. That, in terms of rigorous science, there was not all that
much to her illness is evident from how, when it came time to give
her party for the ladies, Mut was perfectly capable of rising from her
bed and playing hostess—and no wonder, since the gathering had
been part of the plan of her illness from the beginning.

Mut, then, became seriously ill, though for rather indeterminate
reasons, and took to her bed. Two elegant physicians, the doctor
from Amun's House of Books, who had been called in once before
to treat the old steward Mont-kaw, and another temple scholar, attended her; her sisters from the house of seclusion, Peteprê's concubines, cared for her; and her friends from the high Order of Hathor
and Amun's Southern House of Women visited her. The ladies Re-

nenutet, Neit-em-hêt, Akhwêre, and many others came in their
sedan chairs to look in on her—as did Nes-ba-met, head of the order
and consort of the great Beknechons, Chief Priest of the Priests of
All the Gods of Upper and Lower Egypt. And all of them, whether
they came singly or in twos and threes, sat at the stricken woman's
bedside, pitied and questioned her in a great flood of words, partly
from their hearts, partly with cold calculation, out of pure convention and even schadenfreude.

"Eni, whose voice is beloved by all when you sing," they said,
"in the name of the Hidden One, what is wrong with you and what
is this anguish you cause us, you wicked thing? As surely as the king
lives, you have not been what you were for a long time now, and all
of us who hold you dear have seen the signs of exhaustion and other
changes, which, needless to say, have proved incapable of detracting
from your beauty, but which nevertheless have aroused our tender
concern. May no glance of the evil eye be upon you! We have all seen
and remarked to one another amid hot tears how exhaustion has resulted in a loss of weight, which did not, however, affect all parts of
your body—rather, some now have a fuller bloom, while others
have indeed become too lean: your cheeks for example, have become
gaunt, and your eyes have also begun to take on a glassy look, and
torment has settled upon that renowned meandering mouth of
yours. We, who love you, saw all this, and wept as we spoke of it.
But your exhaustion is now so far advanced that you have taken to
your bed, you do not eat or drink, and your illness mocks the skill of
the physicians. Indeed, when we heard of it we no longer knew
where we stood upon the earth, so great was our alarm. We have
stormed the wise men of the House of Books, Te-Hor and Pete-
Bastet, your physicians, with our questions, and they have replied
that their wisdom is near its end and they are verging on helplessness. They say they know of only a few nostrums yet that might
promise some result, for your exhaustion has baffled all the others
thus far employed. It must be some great sorrow that gnaws and
consumes you like a mouse gnawing at the roots of a tree and making it ill. In Amun's name, my dear, is that true, do you have some
gnawing sorrow? Tell it to us, who love you, before that cursed sorrow attacks sweet life itself."

"Presuming," Eni answered in a faint voice, "I had one, what

would it profit me to name it to you? All your goodness and sympathy still could not rid me of it, and apparently all that is left for me is
to die of it."

"So then it is true," they cried, "and it is indeed such a sorrow that has exhausted you?" And in their loftiest tones the ladies
marveled at how that could be possible. A woman like her—from
the cream of society, rich, enchantingly beautiful, the envy of the
women of the kingdom! What could she lack? What wish must she
deny herself? Mut's friends could not understand it. They pelted her
with questions—some sincerely, but some out of curiosity, schadenfreude, and a love of excitement—and for a long time the exhausted
woman evaded them, refusing in a dull and hopeless voice to give an
answer, since that could not help her in any case. Finally, however—
well, all right—she declared she would give them an answer, all at
once, all together, on the occasion of a small, informal reception, a
ladies' party, to which she would soon be inviting them one and all.
For if, though she had no appetite, she could eat a little something,
the liver of a fowl and a bit of vegetable, she would, she hoped, find
the strength to rise from her bed for the purpose of disclosing to her
friends the cause behind these changes and her exhaustion.

No sooner said than done. At the very next quarter of the
moon—only a short time before New Year's Day and the great Feast
of Opet, when decisive events were to take place in Potiphar's
house—Eni did in fact invite the ladies to assemble within the walls
of Potiphar's house of women for a gathering that has been celebrated often, but not always accurately: an afternoon affair on a
rather grand scale, to which the presence of Nes-ba-met, the consort
of Beknechons and first among the women of the harem, lent a still
greater brilliance, and which lacked for nothing, not flowers, or
ointments, or cooling drinks, some intoxicating, some merely refreshing, or all sorts of pastries, preserved fruits, and sugar-spun
sweets, served by young women in delightfully scanty attire, with
black braids falling to their necks and veils at their cheeks—a nuance
that had never been seen before and found great approval. A charming orchestra of harps, lutes, and double flutes—all played by
women in diaphanous, wide-cut, flowing garments, the embroidered
sashes round their waists visible beneath them—played in the fountain court, where the great majority of the ladies were either seated
in casual groupings on chairs and stools placed among the heavily

laden tables or had knelt down on brightly colored mats. But they also occupied the familiar porticoed chamber—from which, by the way, the statue of Atum-Rê had been removed.

Mut's friends were a gracious and exquisite sight to behold. Fragrant oils set atop their heads melted to anoint their hair, whose wide tresses ended in a twisted fringe and through which the rims of the golden disks at their ears could be seen; their limbs were deliciously brown, their shining eyes had been extended to their temples, their little noses suggested nothing but pride and haughtiness, and the patterned faience and gemstones of their collars and bracelets, the gossamer fabric that was draped across their sweet breasts and seemed woven of the sun's gold or of moonshine, were all of the latest fashion. They sniffed at lotus blossoms, they passed each other delicacies to sample, and chatted away not only in high chirping voices but also in the deep, rasping tones that are likewise to be heard among women in these latitudes—Nes-ba-met, for example, Beknechons' spouse, had such a voice. They spoke of the coming Feast of Opet, of the great procession of the Holy Triad in their barques, of their shrines, both on land and water, and of the reception to be prepared for the god in the Southern House of Women, where as Amun's consorts they would have to dance, shake their rattles, and sing in beloved voices before him. It was an important and fascinating topic; and yet it was only a pretext, a way of keeping tongues wagging for now, of filling time until the eagerly awaited hour arrived and Mut-em-enet, their hostess, would answer their question and excite them by naming the reason behind her exhaustion.

She was sitting among them, a figure of suffering beside the basin, a feeble smile on her anguished serpentine mouth as she waited for her moment. She had gone about making her arrangements for instructing her friends as if in a dream, had patterned them after her dream, and was likewise dreamily certain that the proceedings would have to be a success. Her moment came at the high point of the banquet. Splendid fruit stood at the ready in garlanded baskets: fragrant orbs of gold, that concealed an abundance of refreshing juice beneath their bumpy skins, so-called blood oranges, China oranges, a great rarity, were now served, and lying at the ready beside them for peeling were charming little knives with inlaid lapis lazuli handles and highly polished bronze blades, to which the lady of the house had paid particular attention. For she had had them whetted and honed very sharp—indeed so sharp that probably never before in history had little knives known such sharpness. The things had been whetted so thin and razor-sharp that a man could easily have used one to shave his beard, no matter how dense and wiry— though he needed to be advised to be extremely careful, for if he jiggled or lost himself in dreams for only a moment, it was certain to inflict the nastiest wound. Such was the edge these knives had been given—an absolutely dangerous edge; one had the feeling that one needed only to bring the tip of a finger close to the blade and blood would start spurting. And was that the end of her preparations? Certainly not. There was also a costly wine from the harbor, Cypriot wine, which with its sweet fire was well-suited for desserts and would be served with the oranges; and for embracing it, beautiful goblets made of hammered gold and pewter-glazed, painted earthenware were the first items to be dispensed throughout both the fountain court and porticoed chamber, on a signal from the hostess to dainty waitresses who wore nothing but colorful sashes about their hips. Who, however, was to pour the island wine into the goblets? The same dainty girls? No, that, the hostess had decided, would not give due honor either to her hospitality or to those to whom it was extended—Mut had decreed it be done differently.

She signaled again, and the golden oranges and the charming little knives were distributed. Both were a cause for delighted chitchat: the women praised the fruit, praised the elegant utensils—though only for their elegance, since no one was aware of their special property. And they all at once began peeling to get at the sweet flesh—but almost immediately were diverted from what they were doing and lifted up their eyes.

Mut-em-enet had given another signal, and the person who now appeared upon the scene was the cup-bearer—it was Joseph. Yes, the woman who loved him had ordered him to perform this service, had demanded he pour the Cypriot wine for her friends, without disclosing to him any of the other arrangements she had made, so that he did not know the instructive purpose he was to serve. It had pained her, that we do know, to hoodwink him by this deception and to misuse his image for her purposes; but she was far too intent upon instructing her friends and explaining her heart to them. That is why she had demanded this of him, but also because once again he had, with all due deference, refused to lie with her.

"Will you then at least do me a favor, Osarsiph," she had said, "and pour the ninefold good wine from Alashia at my party for the ladies the day after tomorrow, as a token of its quality, and further as a token that you at least love me a little, and finally as a token that I am of some importance in this house, so that he who stands at its head waits upon me and my guests?"

"But of course, mistress," he had answered. "I will do it gladly and will pour the wine with greatest pleasure, if that is your wish. For I am at your service, body and soul, and am at your disposal in all things, except sin."

And thus, dressed in his finest white holiday attire, Rachel's son, Peteprê's young steward, made his unexpected appearance in the fountain court; carrying in his arm a colorful Mycenaean wine jug, he wandered among the ladies still peeling their fruit and, bowing to each, began to fill their goblets. At the sight of him, however, all the ladies—both those who had previously chanced to see him and those who did not yet know him—not only forgot what they were doing, but also forgot themselves, so to speak, and could think of nothing but of gazing upon this cup-bearer, with the result that those cunning little knives did their work and, one and all, the ladies cut their fingers terribly—without being in the least aware of their gory misfortune right off, since one hardly even feels a cut from a blade sharpened to such keenness, particularly if one is as thoroughly distracted as Eni's friends were at that moment.

This frequently described scene has been judged by some as apocryphal, as not belonging to the story as it happened. They are wrong, for it is true and every probability speaks for it. When one considers that on the one hand we are dealing with the most beautiful young man of his time and place, and on the other with the sharpest knives the world had probably ever seen, it is clear that events could not possibly have proceeded any differently—that is, less bloodily—and that Mut's dreamy certainty of how they would turn out had been fully justified. With a face full of long-suffering, a mask of serpentine gloom, she watched the mischief she had wrought, the silently unfolding bloodbath that she alone noticed at first, for the eyes of the ladies followed the young man with lascivious rapture as he slowly moved off in the direction of the porticoed chamber, where, as Mut was convinced, and rightly so, the exact same scene would be played out. Only after her beloved had vanished from sight did she break the silence, asking in a voice of malicious concern, "My dears, what is this, what have you done? Look how your blood is flowing."

It was a horrible sight. In some cases the nimble little knives had skidded an inch deep, so that blood was not just seeping but gushing and streaming; little hands and golden apples were inundated and smeared with the red liquid that soaked into the petal-white fabric covering the ladies' laps, dying it red, forming little puddles, dripping down onto their small feet and the floor. What wails of woe, what lamentations, what a screeching and rolling of eyes there was once Mut-em-enet's remark of insincere amazement made them realize what was happening. Some of those who could not stand the sight of blood, especially their own, were close to fainting and were kept barely conscious only by vials of zedoary and pepper oil carried by dainty serving girls who leapt about among them. Emergency measures in general were now taken, and the dainty maidens were soon dashing about with basins of water, cloths, vinegar, lint, and linen bandages as well, so that at this point the gathering looked like a field hospital, a station for the wounded—both in the court and in the porticoed chamber, to which Mut-em-enet withdrew for a moment to make certain that everything was swimming in blood there as well. Renenutet, the spouse of the Chief Steward of the Bulls, was among the most seriously wounded, and in order to stop the flow of blood her pale yellowish hand had to be more or less deadened by brutally tying it off from the flow of life for a while. Nes-ba-met, Beknechons' deep-voiced consort, had also wounded herself badly. Her gown was ruined, and she scolded away loudly at whoever was to blame, while two maidens—one black, one white—dressed only in sashes comforted her as they attended to her.

"Dearest head of our order and all my darlings," Mut-em-enet said sanctimoniously when something like peace and order had been restored, "how could it happen, how can it be that you did yourselves such harm in my home and that this crimson misfortune has disgraced my party? Your hostess finds it almost unbearably painful that this could happen to you in her home—but how was it possible?

There are surely occasions when one or two people may cut themselves when peeling fruit—but all of you at once and some to the bone? That has never happened before, from what I know of the world, and will probably remain unique in the social history of the Two Lands—at least one must hope so. But comfort me, my sweet friends, and tell me how this could possibly have happened."

"Never mind," Nes-ba-met replied in her bass voice on behalf of the rest of them. "Never mind, Eni, for things seem to be all right now, even if red Seth has ruined our afternoon gowns and some of us are still pale from the bloodletting. But do not fret. We assume you meant well, and your reception is fashionable in every detail. But you did manage a serious piece of thoughtlessness in the midst of it, my dear—I speak frankly here for all of us. Put yourself in our place. You invite us in order to reveal to us the reason for your exhaustion, which has mocked the skill of the physicians, and keep us waiting for the revelation, so that we are already nervous as it is and hide our curiosity behind idle talk. As you see, I am presenting the whole affair in the name of us all, frankly and in accordance with simple truth, without any prudishness. You serve these golden apples— very good, very splendid, even Pharaoh does not enjoy them every day. But just as we are about to peel them, you arrange for this cupbearer to appear here in our susceptible ranks—whoever he is, though I assume he is your young steward, whom people upon highways and waterways call Nefernefru, and it is humiliating enough for a lady to be forced to agree with the judgment and taste of people upon the dikes and canals. The issue here, however, is not one of taste and contention, for he is indeed a heavenly young man, both in countenance and form; but since it is, in and of itself, a veritable shock for a young man suddenly to appear among so many already anxious women, even were he somewhat less charming—how could you think it would not strike a person to the quick and cause tears to well in her eyes when such a divine scamp comes into view and bends low with his jug over her goblet? You cannot demand that one pay attention to the business at hand and prevent one's fingers from looming disaster. We have caused you embarrassment and considerable bother with our bleeding, but I cannot refrain from the charge that you yourself, Eni with the beloved voice, are to blame for this vexation because of the shocking arrangements you made."

"That is so," cried Renenutet, the chief stewardess of bulls. "You must accept the rebuke, dearest, for having played a trick on us with your orchestration of things, which we shall all remember—and if not in anger, then only because in not being affected by it you surely thought nothing of it. But that is the problem, my darling, that you completely failed to give it careful consideration and, if you are just, you must assume the blame yourself for this crimson calamity. Is it not clear that the aggregate femininity in a gathering of so many ladies has, in turn, its effect on the feminine nature of each individual, raising it to a level of highest sensitivity? In such a circle, then, you suddenly allow a male person to appear—and at what moment? At the very moment we are peeling oranges! My good woman, how could that not result in blood—judge for yourself. And then who was it but this cup-bearer, your young steward, a truly divine scamp. The mere sight of him made me feel so odd—I'm telling you exactly how it is and am not mincing words, for this is a moment and a situation when one's heart and mouth overflow and one feels permitted to say everything quite candidly and all at once. I am a woman with much regard for men, and since all of you know it in any case, I will merely mention that besides my own consort, the Steward of Bulls, who is himself a man in his best years, my house is also visited by both an officer of the bodyguards and an attendant from the house of Khonsu—but everyone knows that already. But that does not prevent me from being on the alert, so to speak, for male persons at all times or from allowing them to easily charm me—but I have an especial weakness for cup-bearers. There's always something divine about a cup-bearer, or the favor of the divine, though I don't why I find it so—it has to do with the office and the demeanor. But then here's this Refertēm, this blue lotus, this honeyed youth with his jug—it was all over with me, good ladies. I most definitely thought I beheld a god and in my pious delight did not know where I stood upon the earth. I was all eyes, and while eyeing him, I sawed into my flesh and bone with this peeling knife, ignored how my blood was flowing in streams, was not even aware of it, that's how odd I felt. But that is not the entire calamity, of that I am certain. The moment I start peeling fruit in the future, the image of your damned scamp of a cup-bearer will reappear to me, and in my reverie I will saw into my bones again, so that I will never again dare let myself be served fruit that must be peeled, though I am passionately fond of it—that is what you have accomplished, my darling, with your unconsidered arrangements!"

"Yes, yes!" all the ladies cried, including those in the porticoed chamber, who had come out during Nes-ba-met's and Renenutet's speeches. "Yes, yes!" they cried all at once in voices high and low. "So it is, so it was, those who have spoken have spoken well, we all almost committed bloody suicide in the sudden confusion that the sight of this cup-bearer caused us, and instead of telling us the reason for your exhaustion, as you intended in inviting us, Eni, you have played us this trick."

But then Mut-em-enet lifted her voice in its full alto power and cried out, "Fools! I have not simply told you it—I have shown it to you, the reason for my deathly exhaustion and all my misery. And so have an eye to me as well, since you were all eyes for him. You saw him for only a few heartbeats and injured yourselves in your reverie, so that you are all still pale from the red distress into which the sight of him plunged you. Whereas I must and may see him daily and hourly—where do I turn, then, in my unending distress? I ask you: Where shall I flee? Ah, blind women, whom I have made to see but all in vain, this boy is my spouse's steward and cup-bearer—he is my plight and my death, he has injured me fatally with his eye and mouth, my sisters, so that my red blood spills only in my anguish for him, and I shall die if he does not stanch it. For you merely cut yourselves in the finger at the sight of him, but love for his beauty has slashed my heart and I am bleeding to death." This was the song that Mut sang in a choked voice, and sobbing madly she fell back into her chair.

One can imagine the festive feminine excitement this revelation aroused among the chorus of her friends. They behaved very much as Tabubu and Meh-en-wesekht before them had responded upon hearing the great news that Mut found herself in the throes of love, and they reacted to her affliction on a grand scale, just as those two had: encircling her, stroking her, and speaking together in a babble of many thrilled voices, congratulating her and sympathizing with her. The glances they secretly exchanged, however, the words they whispered to one another, told of something very different from tender compassion: malicious disappointment that it was nothing more than this, that her entire ostentatious distress came simply from common infatuation with a servant; plus silent envy and general jealousy on account of the male involved; but above all self-satisfied schadenfreude that it was Mut, proud and pure Mut, bride of Amun, chaste as the moon, who had been so smitten at her advanced age, was afflicted in the most common way, was left languishing for a pretty servant, and did not even understand that she should keep this to herself, but had helplessly betrayed to everyone an abasement common to all women, wailing: "Where shall I flee?" This flattered her friends, though they did not fail to notice that her public announcement and betrayal of herself revealed the same old arrogance, which desired to make an unprecedented event, a world-shaking affair out of something so common, simply because it was Mut's affair—and that added to her friends' anger as well.

But even while all this was being expressed in the ladies' exchanged glances, the festive delight they took in this sensational, lovely social scandal was great enough to arouse their feminine solidarity and heartfelt compassion for their sister's affliction, so that they crowded around her, took her in their arms, celebrated her in a comforting, babbling rush of words, and exclaimed how fortunate the young man was to have the honor of awakening such feelings in the bosom of his mistress.

"Yes, sweet Eni," they cried, "you have instructed us, and we understand perfectly that it is no bagatelle for a woman's heart to have to behold such a divine scamp every day—no wonder that you, too, finally lost your heart! What a lucky fellow! What no man has succeeded in doing all these many years, he in his youth has managed, and, saint though you are, he has stirred your senses. It was hardly foretold him at his birth, but that only shows how unbiased is the human heart, for it inquires not after rank or status. He is certainly not the son of a prince of a nome, neither officer nor state councilor, but merely your husband's steward; yet he has softened your senses, that is his rank and title. And that he is a foreigner, a lad from Asia, a so-called Habiru, only adds spice to the affair, lends it a certain cachet. My dear, how glad we are and how relieved to the depths of our souls that your sorrow and exhaustion are nothing more than your having set your mind on this lovely lad. Forgive us for ceasing to fear for you and beginning instead to fear for him; surely the only real reason for concern now is that he may go mad at the honor of it all—otherwise the matter seems very simple to us."

"Ah," Mut sobbed, "if you only knew. But you know nothing,

and I knew that you could not begin to know or understand, even after I had opened your eyes to it. For you have no idea what he is like or what the jealousy of his god is like, the god to whom he belongs and whose wreath he wears, so that his soul has no ear for all my cries and he considers himself far too good to stanch the blood of an Egyptian woman. Ah, how much better it would be, my sisters, for you not to worry about him and his sense of being too greatly honored, but to summon all your worries for me, for I am doomed by his stubborn godliness."

And her friends besieged her now in their wish to learn the details and circumstances of this stubbornness, for they could not believe their ears that the servant had not burst with pride at the honor of it all, but had refused his mistress. The glances they exchanged also suggested some malice based on the conjecture that their Eni really was too old for the beautiful lad and that he had told her pious fibs because he felt no desire for her—with one or another flattering herself that he would surely feel more desire for her; but honest indignation at this foreign slave's recalcitrance prevailed in their responses, particular that of Nes-ba-met, the head of the order, who now interposed in her bass voice to declare the affair, seen from this angle, to be scandalous and intolerable.

"As a woman," she said, "I am on your side, my dear, and shall make your sorrow my own. But in my opinion the matter is also political, a concern of both temple and state, for beyond a doubt the rebuttal of this snot-nosed boy—forgive me, but though you love him, I call him that out of honest anger, not as an insult to your feelings—his unwillingness to pay you the tribute of his youth represents outright insubordination, an endangerment to the realm that is tantamount to some local Baal of Retenu or Phoenicia deciding to oppose Amun and to deny him the payment owed him, against whom then a punitive expedition would of course be marshaled to uphold Amun's honor, even if its costs should exceed the value of the tribute. I see your sorrow in that light, my love, and no sooner shall I have returned home than I shall discuss this gross instance of Kenanite insurrection with my consort, the head priest of all the gods of Upper and Lower Egypt, and ask him what measures he considers appropriate for dealing with this disturbance."

This then, amidst heated chitchat, was the outcome of this now famous gathering of ladies—the true and actual course of its events having finally been presented here—and it now broke up. It served as the principal means by which Mut-em-enet managed to make her unhappy passion the talk of the town—and occasionally, in clearer moments, she might well have suddenly been horrified at her success, even though, as her condition continued to worsen, it was also a source of elated satisfaction; for most people in love are reluctant to believe that their feelings have been adequately honored until the whole world—even if it is only in mockery and scorn—concerns itself with them: the news must be blazoned abroad. And her friends continued, singly or in small groups, to pay frequent visits to her sickbed, to inquire after the state of her anguish, to comfort her and offer advice that foolishly missed the point of her very special circumstances, so that the suffering woman could only shrug and reply: "Ah, children, you babble away giving me advice and yet do not understand a thing about my particular case." This only rekindled the anger of Wase's ladies, who would say to one another: "If she thinks the matter is too lofty for us and has about it something so special that it is beyond our counsel, then let her hold her tongue and not involve us in her affair."

The other person who visited her personally and had his chair carried to Potiphar's house of women, with footmen running before and after, was the great Beknechons, Amun's high priest, who had been informed of the story by his wife and was unwilling simply to shrug it off, but rather was determined to see it in the light of far larger interests. Dressed in his usurped leopard skin, the powerful, shiny-headed statesman of his god paced back and forth before her lion-footed couch, taking long strides, ribs thrust forward and chin held high, while he explained to her that every personal and even moral aspect was to be set aside when judging this incident, which, to be sure, was lamentable both in terms of moral principle and social order, but once begun must now be brought to its conclusion with a view to more important considerations. As priest, counselor, and guardian of pious discipline, and not least also as a friend and peer of the good Peteprê at court, he could only censure the attention Mut paid to this young man and protest the feelings that he aroused in her. But the recalcitrance this foreigner had showed in regard to them and his refusal to pay tribute were intolerable to the temple, which could only insist the matter be settled as quickly as possible to the glory of Amun. Therefore, irrespective of what was personally desirable or damnable, he, Beknechons, had to reprimand Mut, his daughter, and peremptorily demand that she do everything, indeed her utmost, to bring this willful man to submission, not only for her own satisfaction, were she—very much without his approval—to derive such from it, but for the satisfaction of the temple; and if need be the dawdler should be brought to compliance by means of public coercion.

That Mut's soul was gladdened by this spiritual instruction, that she was capable of seeing this higher authorization to commit a moral offense as a strengthening of her position over against her beloved, is a sad but clear indication of just how far Mut had come— the same woman who only shortly before had, in accord with her civilized status, declared her happiness and misery dependent on the freedom of Joseph's living soul, but whose sense of helplessness had now sunk to such depths that she took a certain desperate and twisted delight in the thought of the object of her hot desire being publicly coerced by temple police. Yes, she was ripe for joining Tabubu in her magic.

Nor did Joseph remain ignorant of the position Amun's temple had taken in the matter; for no curtain flap or door crack was too narrow for his faithful Bes-em-heb not to find a sequestered spot for being secretly present at the visit the great Beknechons had paid to Mut-em-enet, for catching with his refined dwarfish ear the instructions the priest gave her, so that he might bring them piping hot to his protégé. Joseph listened and found this an extraordinary reinforcement of his own view that what was at issue here was a test of strength between the power of Amun and the Lord his God, and that in no case, and at no price, and no matter how poorly this imperative might accord with the desires of Adam, did the Lord his God dare come off second-best.

The Bitch

And so it came to pass that, in the course of her degeneration, proud Mut-em-enet was so distraught by the anguish of love that she stooped to taking an action for which only recently she had proved far too refined; she sank to the level of civilization of Tabubu the Kushite and agreed to join her in squalid mysteries—that is, to bait her love with magic by sacrificing to some ghastly deity of the netherworld, whose name she did not know and did not wish to know. Tabubu simply called it "The Bitch," and that sufficed.

This nocturnal spook was, so it appeared, a wicked ghoul and fury, and the black woman promised to use her charms to dispose it to serve the wishes of Mut her mistress; and in the end Mut was satisfied with that, a sign that she had renounced her lover's soul and would be happy simply to hold his body, or better, his warm corpse, in her arms—or if it did not make her happy, it would at least leave her sad but sated. For, of course, magic charms and sorcery can lure only the body, the corpse, and deliver only it into someone's arms, but not the soul as well, and one must be highly disconsolate to be consoled by that, by the thought that it is primarily the body that is needed to satisfy love and that, for heaven's sake, one can always do more easily without the soul than vice versa, though the satisfaction provided by a corpse may be of a rather sad sort.

That Mut finally agreed to the "rubber-eater's" degraded proposals and was prepared to practice witchcraft with her, was, by the way, bound up with the state of her body and its witchlike nature, of which, as we have seen, she was well aware—those striking hallmarks that, so she felt, sufficed to make her part of the coven and more or less enjoined her to act in accordance with her physique. One dare not forget that her new body was love's creation, love's product, which is to say: a painfully yearning accentuation of Mut's femininity—just as in general a witch's nature is nothing more than exaggerated femininity carried to illicitly stimulating extremes. From which it follows that not only has witchcraft always primarily, indeed almost exclusively, been the concern and business of women, with male warlocks playing hardly any role, but also its nature is such that love has always played a significant part, has at all times stood at the center of witchcraft, and that magic in the service of love is quite rightly considered the epitome of magic, its naturally preferred object.

The slightly haglike element in Mut's physical nature, which we have likewise been forced to remark upon with all due delicacy, might have contributed to a feeling that inclined, indeed more or less ordained, her to engage in witchcraft and to allow Tabubu to set in motion certain dubious rituals of magical sacrifice; for the divinity at which they were aimed was, according to the black woman, the personification of the hag, a divine hag, a hag goddess, in whom one had to envision a higher, more concentrated realization of all the repulsive ideas that can possibly be associated with the word "hag," a monster of the most sordid habits: the arch-hag. There are, there must be such divinities, for the world has sides that, though they are covered in loathsome and bloody filth and seemingly hardly fit to be deified, nevertheless require, just as do the world's more engaging sides, eternal representation and preeminence, spiritual embodiment, so to speak, or personal spiritualization. And so it can happen that the name and nature of the divine are merged in the monstrous, with bitch and mistress becoming one, for we are dealing after all with the arch-bitch, to which all the characteristics of the mistress inherently belong—just as Tabubu, when invoking the assistance of this epitome of all filthy debauchery, would speak of her as "Our Gracious Lady Bitch."

The black woman thought that she should prepare Mut for the proceedings she had planned, for their unusual style would be a radical departure from social customs with which the grand lady was familiar. Tabubu apologized ahead of time for any offense to her refinement and begged her, for the sake of the issue and purpose at hand, to reconcile herself just this once with the vulgar tone that simply had to prevail because Our Gracious Lady Bitch knew and understood no other and without certain shameless words there was no dealing with her. It was not a very tidy ritual, she announced by way of precaution, for some of its ingredients were very unappetizing, and it also had to include considerable bombast and imprecation; the mistress should be prepared for that and not be offended when the time came, or, if she was, at least not let it be noticed. It was in its violence, insolence, and hideousness that a rite of coercion differed from the normal worship to which she was accustomed. It was conducted not primarily for man and according to man's taste, but instead simply revealed the shameless nature of the deity whom they invoked and whose presence was conjured up—that is, of the mistress bitch, worship of whom could only be indecent and whose nature as the arch-hag necessarily determined the crude level of decorum. But in the end, Tabubu suggested, an especially refined tone was hardly appropriate for a ritual whose purpose was to coerce a young man into complying purely physically with the act of love.

Upon hearing these words, Mut turned pale and bit her lips, partly out of shock as a civilized woman, partly out of loathing for this slattern, who had urged and forced the coercion of the lad upon her and now that she, Mut, had agreed to participate was insultingly informing her what a contemptible decision it was. It is an ancient human experience that once seducers—especially those that lead people to depths below their rank—have successfully dragged a person down, they terrify and mock him by the vile words with which they suddenly begin to describe these new, still unfamiliar environs. Pride demands that one not allow one's fear and confusion to be noticed, but that one reply: "Let whatever happens here happen just as usual—I knew what I was doing when I decided to follow you." And that is more or less what Mut said in defiantly standing by her original decision—foreign as it was to her nature—to bait her lover with magic.

She had to be patient for several days: first, because the black priestess had to make preparations and not all the ingredients were on hand—not only weird things that could not be supplied from one day to the next, such as the rudder of a wrecked ship, lumber from a gallows, rotting meat, and various body parts from an executed criminal, but also, and above all, some hair from Joseph's head, which Tabubu first had to procure from the house's barbershop by cunning and bribery; second, however, because one had to wait for the moon to grow round in order to operate with more certain hope of success by using the full potency of that ambiguous heavenly body, which is female in relation to the sun, but male in relation to the earth, a double nature that conceals within it a certain unity of the universe, thus making it efficacious as an intermediary between the mortal and the immortal. Besides Tabubu as sacrificing priestess, the participants in this act of coercion were to be her client, Mut the mistress, another Moorish girl as her attendant, and the concubine Meh-en-wesekht as witness. The flat roof atop the women's house had been chosen as the site for the sacrifice.

Whether feared or longed for, or fearfully longed for with impatient shame, each day arrives at last and becomes a day of life, bringing with it what was once only a prospect. And so it was with this day filled with hope and abasement for Mut-em-enet, when out of bitter anguish she betrayed her own rank and consented to actions unworthy of her. She had waited through the hours of the day, just as she had grappled with each previous day, one after the other. But when the sun had vanished and its glory had slowly faded and the earth was wrapped in darkness and an incredibly large moon had risen above the desert, its borrowed luster taking the place of the proud true light that had departed and supplanting glaring day with the wavering gossamer web of its pale and painful magic; when, slowly growing smaller, it had floated to the top of the world; when life had gone to rest and everyone in Potiphar's house lay with drawn-up knees and tranquil faces as they suckled at the breasts of sleep—the hour had come for the four women, who alone were still awake and whose plans for the night were mysterious and feminine, to gather upon the roof, where Tabubu and her helper had prepared everything for the sacrifice.

With a white cloak around her shoulders and a burning torch in hand, Mut-em-enet hurried up the stairs—first the flight leading from the fountain court to the low upper story, and then the narrower one that led to the roof—moving so swiftly that the concubine Meh, who was also carrying a white-flamed torch, could scarcely keep up. Eni had broken into a run the moment she left her bedchamber; clutching her garment in her right hand and holding her fiery torch high, she flung back her head, with eyes staring and mouth agape.

"Why are you running, dearest?" Meh whispered. "You'll be out of breath, and I'm afraid you'll stumble. Stop, be careful with your torch."

Peteprê's first and true wife's reply came in disjointed phrases: "I must run, must run, can only make this climb by running, by storming it breathlessly—do not hinder me, the spirit commands me, Meh, and it must be so, we must run."

Panting these words and with eyes staring wide, she waved the torch above her head, scattering a few fiery sparks of flax soaked in pitch, so that her winded companion made a grab for the wobbling handle, to wrench it from her—but Mut refused to let go, which only heightened the danger. This happened on the second stairway to the roof, and in the scuffle Mut tripped and actually would have

fallen had Meh not held her tight in her arms; and so, still embracing
and waving their torches, the two women stumbled up over the narrow door's threshold and out into the night of the dark roof.

They were received by the wind and the gruff voice of the priestess, who, having taken charge here, was now their spokeswoman.
And she spoke continuously, never once falling silent, spoke in a
boastful, dictatorial, crude bombast that was mixed from time to
time with the howling of jackals from the bleached desert to the east
and even with the more distant, low trembling roar of a prowling
lion. The wind was blowing from the west, from the sleeping city
and the river—where the moon dabbled in silver flashes from on
high—from the shore that belonged to the dead and from its mountains. Puffing and spitting, the wind got tangled in roof vents that
opened in that direction, little plank awnings designed to divert cool
air down into the house. There were also a few cone-shaped granaries on the flat roof, but today there were other items, other arrangements besides these usual ones—the apparatus of their intended
ritual, including some things that profited from the breeze, for both
in tripods and on the roof itself were long strips of bluish, rotting
meat that otherwise would have stunk, and immediately did whenever the wind fell. What else was there, lying at the ready for the
grim ritual, would have been evident even to a blind man, who
would have seen it in his mind's eye—or to someone who did not
want to see it and did not look around, someone like Mut-em-enet,
who both now and later kept staring with eyes askance up into the
void, her mouth half open, its corners pulled down. For while the
wind rummaged in the tufts of her gray hair, Tabubu stood there
black and naked to the waist, a goatskin cinched beneath her hag's
breasts—her helper was dressed in the same way—and listed everything that was there, her loosely flapping mouth revealing two
lonely snaggleteeth as she cried out like a peddler the name and use
of each item.

"There you are, woman!" she said, busily gesturing and pointing
about as her mistress staggered onto the roof. "Welcome, you who
are scorned, languishing, and seeking protection, welcome, mortar
denied its pestle, infatuated minx, come to the hearth. Take what you
are offered. Take grains of salt in your hand and hang this laurel at
your ear, then crouch down beside the fire, whose flame in this wind

blazes up out of its hole, blazes on your behalf, pitiful wretch, so that you may find help within certain limits.

"I speak. I was speaking as priestess in charge here before you ever came. Now I shall go on speaking, in loud and vulgar words, for it is no use to be squeamish here, not as long as one grapples with these things, which must be called by their names without shame, and that is why, seeker of protection, I now call you a lovesick rag and a disdained slut. Are you seated now, the salt in your hand, the laurel at your ear? Does your companion have hers as well and is she crouching beside the altar? Then let us begin the sacrifice as priestess and attendant. For all is readied for the meal, all the trappings and impeccable gifts.

"Where is the sacrificial table? It is where it is, facing the hearth, properly adorned with leaves and twigs, with the ivy twigs and leafy grain that she loves, our invited guest who now approaches—dark husks, their mealy kernels locked inside. That is why they garland the table and adorn the tripods with their tempting, stinking repast. Is the rotted rudder propped against the table? It is propped. And what else is there to see? A beam is there, taken from a cross on which criminals are hoisted—and in your honor, O vile one, you who gladly cling to villains, it is propped against the table to excite you. But what about some piece of the hanged man himself, an ear, a finger—is nothing offered for your pleasure? Oh, but indeed! The table is adorned with his putrid finger, there among the lovely clumps of pitch, as well as a gristly ear from the scoundrel's head, waxy and sticky with trickling blood, just to your taste, and to bait you, monster. But as for those bunches of hair there on the table, shiny and alike in color, they do not come from that rogue, but from different heads, far and near, for we have prettily gathered the near and the far together here that the fragrance may please you, if you will help us, you who came from the night, whom we invoke.

"So hush now, let no one utter a peep! You who sit at the hearth, gaze at me and nowhere else, for one does not know from which side she will come slinking. I command the silence of the sacrifice. Put out that torch, wench! That's right. Where is the two-edged blade? Here. And that cur of a dog? He is still lying on the floor, like a young hyena, his paws bound, his muzzle tied, that moist muzzle that would so gladly rip into any sort of filth. First give me pitch.

The strapping priestess throws black chips of it into the flames, so that the fumes of its leaden smoke may rise as musty sacrificial incense to greet you, bitch from below. The drink offerings now, each vase in proper sequence: water, cow's milk, and beer—I pour them, splash them, let them flow. My black feet are standing now here in the puddle, in the pool, in the blistering pond, for I shall sacrifice the dog, a revolting act, but it is not we humans who have chosen it for you—we know, you like nothing better.

"Here to me with that sniffling, disgusting beast, and now let its throat be slit open. The belly is rent wide and hands are immersed in the hot entrails, which steam up to you now in the coolness of the moonlit night. Smeared with blood, dripping with guts, I lift them up to you, my sacrificial hands, for I have made them in your likeness. And so I greet you and piously, properly invite you to your sacrificial meal, mistress of all people of the night. Politely, for now, and solemnly we beg you to take part in this meal and our impeccable gifts. Are you pleased to gratify our wishes? If not, then know that your priestess will strengthen herself to rise up against you, will grab hold of you more tightly and apply expertly measured force. Come near! Whether you have just slipped your noose, have been tormenting a woman in childbirth or cuddling with suicides— whether you join us smeared with blood, come strolling our way from your haunting and gnawing in a field of corpses, or come to us sullied from a three-forked crossroads where, consumed by morbid lust, you embraced your criminal.

"Do I know you, and do you know yourself in my words? And in grappling with you do I now strike better and closer? Have you noticed that I know all your doings, your indescribable habits, your unspeakable foods and drinks, and all your abysmal lusts? Or should my hands take a more knowing, more exacting hold of you yet? Should my mouth put aside niceties for good and all, give a name to your most swinish nature? I curse you as a spook, a she-wolf and whore, you pus-eyed nightmare! Tainted toadstool, greasy hag from hell, at home in slaughterhouses, where you crawl and claw and gnaw, slavering over carrion bones. You who ease the last lust of the hanged man as he croaks, your wet womb fornicating with despair—horrible, enfeebled, and enervated by vice, shuddering at every gust of wind, baffled by ghosts, cowardly prey to the creatures of the night. Bestial atrocity! Do I know you? Do I name your name? Do I have hold of you? Do I perceive you? Yes, it is she! She has used the moon's darkening in a patch of cloud. Her coming is heard in the loud baying of the dog before the house. The flame blazes up from the hearth. Behold, a fit has seized the companion of this suppliant here. In what direction does she roll her eyes? For there where her eyes roll, from there the goddess will approach.

"Mistress, we greet you. Be content. We have given to you as best we know how. If this impure meal and these impeccably vile gifts please you, then help! Help her who languishes here, help her who has been rejected. She groans for a lad who does not want her. Help her as best you can—you must, for I have you within my charmed circle. Torment his body to come this way, torment that stubborn boy to join her in her bed, he knows not how, that he may nestle his neck beneath her hands, that for once she may delight in what she aches for, that sweet acrid odor of young male.

"Now the shaven hair, wench, be quick! I shall perform the sacrifice of love, the magic burnt offering, in the presence of the goddess. Ah, what pretty locks, from heads far and near, lustrous and soft. Waste of the body, samples of its stuff—I, the priestess, twist, tangle, knot, and wed them, again and again, with fervent, bloody sacrificial hands, and let them fall into the crackling flame that devours them swiftly. . . . What is this that wrenches your face with pain and disgust, my suppliant? I believe you are sickened by the foul odor of burning hair? That is his and your stuff, my fine lady, the vapor of bodies aflame—the smell of love. Enough of this!" she said in her usual voice. "The rite has been performed perfectly. May you relish his taste and enjoy him, your beautiful lad. The mistress bitch has consecrated him to you, thanks to Tabubu's arts, which are worth their wages."

And stepping back, the baseborn woman laid aside her arrogance; her task completed, she wiped her nose with the back of her hand and then plunged both hands, still sullied by the sacrifice, into a basin of water. The moon stood clear in the heavens. The concubine Meh had recovered from having fainted in terror.

"Is she still here?" she asked, still trembling.

"Who?" Tabubu asked, washing her black hands like a doctor after bloody surgery. "The Bitch? Calm yourself, concubine, she has already vanished. She did not come at all gladly and was obedient to me only because I treated her insolently and know precisely how to encircle her nature with words. And she cannot do anything here except carry out what I have forced upon her, for beneath the threshold I buried a threefold charm against evil. But she will carry out her task, there is no question of that. For she accepted the sacrifice and is also bound by the magical offering of woven hair."

At this point they heard Mut-em-enet, the mistress, heave a deep sigh and saw her stand up from where she had been crouching by the hearth. Still in her white robe and with laurel at her ear, she stood facing the carcass of the dog, her hands clasped together beneath her raised chin. Ever since she had smelled the odor of burning hair, hers mixed with Joseph's, the corners of her half-open, masklike mouth, had been drawn further down in bitterness, as if heavy weights were tugging at them, and what a mournful sight it was when she began to speak with that mouth, the lips touching and parting stiffly and sadly as she lifted up her alto voice in lamentation:

"Hear me, you purer spirits, whom I would have been so happy to see smile upon my great love for the Ebrew lad Osarsiph, hear and behold the pain I feel in my abasement, how sick unto dying is my heart at this horrible and heavy loss, which I have chosen, for good or evil—because, Osarsiph, my sweet falcon, your mistress in her deep despair had no other choice. Ah, you purer spirits, how heavy the disgrace of this loss, this renunciation, weighs upon me. For I have renounced his soul, because I saw myself forced at last to accept the seduction of magic. I renounced your soul, Osarsiph, my beloved—and how grievous and harsh for my love is that loss. I have abandoned any claim to your eyes, so great was the pain, I could not do otherwise, I had no choice in my helplessness. Your eyes will be closed and dead when we embrace, and only the swelling lips of your mouth will be mine—and abased by my bliss I shall kiss it again and again. The soft breath of your mouth means more to me than anything, that is true—and yet beyond that, beyond all else, the gaze of your soul would have meant still more. This is my deep lament rising up within me. Hearken to it, you purer spirits! I send it up to you out of deepest bitterness, here beside the hearth of this black woman's magic. Behold how I, a woman of high rank, was forced to sink beneath myself for love, how I had to forgo happiness for lust, in order to have that at least—for if I am not to know the happiness of his eyes, I would know the lust of his mouth. But how grieved and sickened I am by this loss—the daughter of a prince cannot conceal that from you, purer spirits. I must raise my loud lament before atoning for lust attained by the artifice of magic, before delighting in the soulless bliss of his sweet corpse. Leave me some hope in my abasement, good spirits, some innermost secret hope that lust and happiness may not in the end be so precisely separated and kept apart, that happiness may blossom from lust, if only it is deep enough, and that amid my irresistible kisses the dead boy may yet open his eyes to grant me the gaze of his soul—that by some means or other the strictures of magic may be deceived and undone. You purer spirits to whom I lift my lament, allow me this silent secret even in my abasement, do not begrudge me the hope of this deception, this one small deception . . ."

And Mut-em-enet raised her arms and, continuing to sob violently, threw herself around the neck of her companion, Meh the concubine, who led her down from the roof.

New Year's Day

The audience's impatience to be told what everyone already knows has doubtless reached its peak by now. The hour for satisfying it has come—a great solemn festal hour and a turning point in our story, an hour established the moment it came into the world and first told its own story: the hour and the day when Joseph—Potiphar's steward of three years, his property for ten—barely avoided the crassest mistake that he could ever have made and just managed to escape from burning temptation with nothing more than a black eye, though to be sure his life would complete yet another loop, leading him into the pit a second time, the fault for which, as he surely realized, was his own, since it came as punishment for behavior that in its defiant recklessness, if not to say its frivolous wickedness, was only all too similar to his conduct in his previous life.

There is good justification for establishing parallels between his offense against this woman and his earlier offense against his brothers. In his wish to "take people aback," he had once again taken things too far, had once again allowed the effects of his amiable charm—which he certainly had every right to enjoy and to use to further the greater glory of God—to run wild, to degenerate dangerously, to get out of hand. In his first life these effects had taken the

negative form of hatred, this time they had become excessively positive, only to grow, then, into pernicious, passionate love. In his
blindness he had encouraged both the former and the latter and, misled by his own responses to the woman's emotions as they ran riot,
he had also wanted to play the instructor—he, who was still in such
obvious need of instruction himself. There is no denying that this
cried out for punishment, though, to be sure, one cannot help remarking with a quiet smile that the chastisement justly rushing toward him had been so well arranged that it would serve his future
good fortune, until it was greater and more brilliant than what was
destroyed. What amuses us in all this is our ability to peer into that
most exalted mind that permitted this course of events. It has long
been presumed—and the supposition reaches back into our story's
preludes and preparatory stages—that the imperfection of the creature has always been greeted with pointed satisfaction on the part of
certain higher realms, where hovering on the lips of many is the ancient reproach, "What is man that You are mindful of him?";
whereas that same imperfection has been an embarrassment to the
Creator, who is then forced to remit His creatures to the Realm of
Sternness and to let chastising justice reign, acting evidently less in
accord with His own wishes and more in accord with certain moral
pressures that He cannot easily evade. Our charming example here
teaches us that Highest Goodness and Kindness understands how to
yield to this pressure with great dignity and at the same time to
hoodwink that petulant Realm of Sternness by practicing the art of
healing even as He chastises and by turning misfortune into a fertile
field for renewed happiness.

The day of decision, the turning point, was the great festival of
Amun-Rê's visit to his Southern House of Women, the day when the
Nile began to rise, the official Egyptian New Year. The official, let it
be noted; for it was a long way from coinciding with the natural
New Year, the day when the sacred cycle actually flowed back into
itself, when the Dog Star reappeared and the waters began to rise—
in this regard disorder almost always reigned in Egypt, a land where
disorder was viewed with great revulsion. It had happened in the
course of the ages, during the life of men and dynasties, that the natural New Year matched the date on the calendar for once; but the re-
occurrence of this lovely instance of harmony required another one

thousand four hundred sixty years, a period of approximately forty-eight human generations destined not to experience it—for which they gladly made allowances, given their many other worries. The century in which Joseph spent his life in Egypt was likewise not called upon to behold this beautiful unity of reality and officialdom, and the children of Keme who wept and laughed beneath the sun in those days knew nothing more than that the two simply did not match—it was the least of their concerns. Nor was it the case that they had to celebrate Akhet, the New Year, the beginning of flooding, at the exact same time as the harvest season of Shemu; but they did find themselves in the season of winter, called Peret, also known as the season of sowing; and although the children of Keme made nothing of it, because disorder that would last another thousand years was necessarily regarded as order, Joseph, as a man who felt an inner detachment from the customs of Egypt, found each such occurrence rather ridiculous and observed the unnatural New Year only in the same sense that he took part generally in the life and ways of people here below: with reservations and out of a conviction that his worldly participation was viewed with forbearance from on high. As a matter deserving our recognition and perhaps even wonder, it should also be noted in passing that a man who kept such a critical distance from the world into which he had been conveyed, the behavior of whose children he regarded as basically foolish, was still able to muster the sort of seriousness about life necessary to advance as far among these children as Joseph did and to achieve for them those praiseworthy things he was destined to achieve.

But whether taken seriously by a detached mind or not, the day of the official swelling of the Nile was celebrated in all the land of Egypt, and most especially in Nowet-Amun, Wase of the Hundred Gates, with a gala solemnity that one can imagine only if one keeps in mind our own greatest and most tumultuous national, popular, and patriotic holidays. The entire city was out and about from earliest morning on, and the huge population—far exceeding a hundred thousand, as we know—was vastly increased by swarms of country folk from both upriver and down, who streamed in through the gates to join in the celebration of Amun's great day in the city where the imperial god resided, and who now mixed with the city people to hop on one leg and gaze with mouths agape at glorious and majestic spectacles presented by the state to an overtaxed and overworked peasantry in compensation for a whole year's gray penury and as a means of strengthening them in their patriotism for the drudgery of the year now dawning. As part of a great sweating crowd, their noses filled with the aroma of burning fat and mountains of flowers, they thronged temples provisioned for the holiday with immense quantities of food and drink and filled those radiantly colorful forecourts plastered with alabaster, covered by awnings and tents, and echoing with pious hymns, where they could stuff their bellies for once at the expense of the god—or, actually, of those higher powers who oppressed and swindled them all the rest of the year, but today smiled upon them with prodigal beneficence—and thus, against their better judgment, be lulled in the belief that it would always be so, that with this turning point of celebration and delight, the golden age of free beer and roasted goose had dawned and they would never again be visited by scribes demanding payment and accompanied by Nubians armed with bundled rods of palm, but that every day of life would now be lived as if in Amun-Rê's temple itself, where one could see a drunken woman with hair flowing free, who squandered her days feasting because she carried the king of the gods within her.

In fact all of Wase was so drunk by sunset that it was a scene of bawling, blindly staggering, public mischief. But for the beautiful wonders of the early morning and forenoon, when Pharaoh came forth "to receive the honor of his fathers," to use the official phrase, and Amun embarked on his famous festive procession on the Nile to Opet Resit, his Southern House of Women—for this the populace was still dewy-eyed and ready for merrymaking, receptive as jubilant worshipers and pious spectators for the national and religious pomp unfolding before them, the point of which was to provide the hearts of the city's children and guests with a new supply of quotidian patience and proud but intimidated devotion to the fatherland, in which purpose these ceremonies were almost as successful as the triumphs of earlier kings, who had returned to the city laden with the booty of Nubian and Asian campaigns and whose victories were eternalized in reliefs on temple walls and had made the land of Egypt great, though it was with them that the harsh subjugation of the peasantry had really first begun.

On such high days of the calendar, Pharaoh came forth wearing his crown and gloves, emerged as brilliant as the rising sun from his palace, and took his place in his high canopied sedan chair, from where, fanned by ostrich feathers and enveloped in clouds of heavy aromatic smoke wafted up at him by incense-bearers who preceded him while walking backwards with faces turned toward the good god, he floated past on his way to visit the house of his father and behold his beauty. The voices of the chanting priests were drowned out by the jubilation of the hopping throngs. Drummers and trumpeters marched noisily at the head of the procession, while royal relatives, dignitaries, the king's Sole and True Friends, as well as some real friends, walked in separate parties and soldiers with standards, throw-sticks, and battle-axes brought up the rear. "May you live as long as Rê, may Amun's peace be with you!" But where should one stand and swallow dust, strain one's neck and bug out one's eyes— here or in Karnak, at Amun's house with its fluttering banners, where all this would ultimately conclude? For the god would also come forth today, would leave his holiest dark chamber at the far rear of his gigantic tomb—far beyond all the forecourts, courts, and corridors, each more hushed and narrow than the last—and as a strangely shapeless seated puppet hidden in his veiled shrine proceed through rooms that grew increasingly high-ceilinged and bright with color, his barque adorned with ram's heads and borne on long poles that rested on the shoulders of twenty-four shiny-headed priests in starched aprons—he too surrounded by fans and incense as he moved through light and tumult toward his son.

It was a matter of great urgency to observe the "flight of the geese," a rite practiced since time out of mind and performed at the beautiful Place of the Encounter, that is, in the square before the temple. And what a beautiful and joy-filled place it was! Colorful flags fluttered on golden masts crowned with the head ornaments of the god. Mountains of flowers and fruits had been piled on the tables of sacrifice before the shrines of the Holy Triad—father, mother, and son—and statues of Pharaoh's ancestors, the kings of Upper and Lower Egypt, had been brought here and set up as columns by four different units from the crew of the *Barque of the Sun*. Atop golden pedestals high above the crowd stood priests, variously facing east, west, north, and south, who released the wild birds to the four corners of the heavens, so that each might bring to the gods the news that Hor, son of Usir and Eset, had set both the white and the red crown upon his head. For this was the mode of proclamation he who was born out of death had first used upon ascending the throne of the Two Lands, and through countless jubilees the festive rite had been repeated; for from the flight of these messengers, the scholar and the common man, each employing his own methods, drew all sorts of conclusions about destiny, both general and individual.

What lovely mysteries and rites Pharaoh would then perform in this same place after the geese had flown. He sacrificed before the images of the primal kings. With a golden sickle he cut a sheaf of spelt handed him by a priest and then laid the grain, as an offering of gratitude and petition, before his father. As readers and singers chanted psalms from their scrolls, he offered up to him divine fragrance from a long-handled pan. Then the majesty of the god sat down upon his chair and, holding his rigid pose, accepted the court's good wishes, which were clad in rare and lofty words and often took the form of ingenious letters of congratulation read aloud to him because their authors were those officials unable to be in attendance— a special delight for all who heard them.

This was only the first act of the feast, whose beauty steadily increased. For now the Holy Triad were taken to the Nile, each of their barques floating high on the shoulders of twenty-four shiny-headed priests; and, as a modest son, Pharaoh walked as a man on foot behind the barque of Amun, his father.

The entire crowd moved toward the river, pressing around the procession of the three gods, which was led by horns and drums and, behind them, by Beknechons, First Attendant of Amun, dressed in his leopard hide. Hymns ascended, incense billowed, fan-bearers fanned. Upon arriving at the riverbank, the barques were loaded on three ships—each long and wide, each as radiantly beautiful as the other, but Amun's ship was beyond description, for it was made of cedar that had been felled in the Cedar Mountains by order of Retenu's princes, who, so it was said, had had to drag the wood over the mountains themselves; it was covered in silver, but the great canopied throne in the middle was of gold, as were the flagpoles and obelisks set before it; crowns guarded by serpents adorned its bow and stern, and it was fitted out with all sorts of figurines representing souls and other images of religious importance, most of which people had long ago ceased to recognize, nor could they have explained what they were, so terribly ancient was the tradition behind these symbols, though this did not diminish, but only added to the reverence people showed them and the joy they took in them.

The magnificent ships of the Holy Triad were barges without rowers; they were pulled instead by light galiots and a crew of men hauling on a rope from the bank and towing them up the Nile toward the Southern House of Women. It was a great honor to be part of that crew, for it brought a man practical benefits throughout the coming year. All of Wase, except for the deathly ill and the frailest of the elderly—babies were carried on their mothers' backs or at their breasts—rolled in a vast throng along the bank with the towing crew, becoming part of the parade escorting the procession of divine boats. They were led by a hymn-singing chorus of Amun's priests; the god's soldiers followed with shields and throw-sticks; after them came brightly costumed Negroes, who were greeted with salvos of laughter as they danced to drums, pulled faces, and made lewd jokes—for they knew they were disdained and so played the fool, even if that was not their nature, in order to flatter the grotesque expectations the populace had of them—and then came rows of temple attendants of both sexes, musicians playing castanets and thrumming sistrums, garlanded sacrificial animals, war chariots, standard-bearers, lute players, high-ranking priests with their minions, who were then joined by citizens of town and field rhythmically clapping their hands.

And so with gladness and jubilation they moved toward the columned building by the river, where the divine boats docked; the sacred barques were shouldered again and, to the sound of long trumpets and drums, carried in yet another procession into the splendid House of Birth, where they were received by Amun's earthly concubines, by the ladies of the high Order of Hathor in their flimsy gowns, who curtsied and, writhing their bodies and fanning with their fronds, danced before their exalted consort—that is, before the mummified seated puppet in its veiled shrine—as they beat their hand drums and sang in voices beloved by all. It was Amun's grand New Year's visit to his harem, celebrated with sumptuous hospitality, with heaped piles of offered food and drink, with endless reverences and elegant formalities—most of which no one understood any longer—in the inner courts, the inner chambers and antechambers, of the House of Embracing and Birth, with its apartments filled with bright-colored reliefs and painted runes, its pink granite arcades of papyrus columns, its tented halls paved in silver, and its statue-lined courtyards open to the public. When one keeps in mind that toward evening the god's procession returned—still just as jubilant, just as brilliant—by water and land to Karnak; when one also considers that all day long the temples played host to feasting without end, to market fairs, popular entertainments, and theatricals—with priests in head masks presenting the stories of the gods—one has some idea of the beauty of New Year's Day. By evening the metropolis was swimming in careless abandon and beer-sotted faith in the golden age. The divine towing crew, crowned with wreaths, anointed with oil, and now very drunk, roamed the city doing more or less whatever they pleased.

The Empty House

This account, if only in roughest outline, of the events of the Feast of Opet and the official day of the rising Nile was necessary for acquainting our audience with the larger public context in which the crucial moments of our story, the private and real story, took place. A grand overview of that context suffices for an understanding of how very busy the courtier Peteprê was on that day. He was after all in the immediate retinue of His Majesty Hor-in-His-Palace, who on no day or holiday had so many pontifical duties to fulfill as on this one—and by immediate retinue we mean among the Sole Friends of the king. For on that very New Year's morning his elevation to that special rank at court had become a reality—his advancement accompanied by speeches he truly enjoyed reading. The titular captain had been absent all day from his house—which, like all houses of the capital, was emptied of its residents; for, as previously noted, only those near death or paralyzed cripples had remained behind at home. Among the former one must include the saintly parents on the upper floor, Huya and Tuya—under the best of circumstances their path now led no further than the embankment in the garden and the summerhouse atop it, and even that far only rarely. It bordered on the unnatural that they were still alive at all; for ten rounds of the year now, they had reckoned hourly with their own demise, but had just kept doddering along—field mouse and swamp beaver, her with her blind slits for eyes, him with his tarnished silver beard, together in the dark chamber of their sibling marriage—whether simply because some old people just keep on living and, too weak to die, cannot find death or because their blundering act of appeasement had left them in fear of the king below and of the forty with dreadful names.

So the two of them had remained at home on the upper floor, along with their childish servants, two foolish little girls who had replaced their predecessors, whom time had rendered less docile; but otherwise the house and estate were as deserted as all the others. Were they really? One must allow for one other slight, but important qualification of that claim: Mut-em-enet, Potiphar's first and true wife, had likewise stayed at home.

How puzzling that must be for anyone familiar with the day's larger context. She did not take part in the beautiful worship service of her sisters, Amun's concubines. She did not sway in their dance, clad in Hathor's clinging garment, with horns and solar disk upon her head, did not raise that voice beloved by all as she shook her silver rattle. She had sent her regrets to the head of the order and had offered apologies to the order's highest protector, to Tiy, the wife of the god, and with the same excuse that Rachel had used to defend herself when she sat atop the teraphim hidden under the camel's straw and refused to stand up for Laban. She had informed them that unfortunately on that very day she was indisposed, in the discreet sense of the word; and those great ladies had shown more understanding for her difficulty than had Potiphar, whom she also told, but, lacking any feeling for human frailty, he showed the same obtuseness as coarse Laban had in his day. "Indisposed in what way? Do you have a toothache or the vapors?" he had asked, employing high society's silly medical term for any ill humor that might affect a person's general health. And when she had finally made the matter clear enough for him, he had refused to accept it as a valid excuse. "That doesn't count," he had said, just as Laban had, if you will recall. "It is not an illness worth mentioning and for which one may excuse oneself from the god's feast. Many would drag themselves there half dead so as not to miss it, but you want to stay away on account of a matter so normal and regular."

"There need not be something unnatural about an illness, my friend, for it to afflict us," she had responded and had then presented him with the choice of dispensing with her services either at the public feast or at the private reception for a small circle of guests that was to mark the conclusion of New Year's Day here in the house, in celebration of the chamberlain's having been named a Sole Friend. She could not possibly manage both, she declared. If she were to dance for the god in her present state, she would be a broken woman by evening and would have to forgo the entertainment at home.

In the end he had reluctantly allowed her to rest during the day so that she could play hostess come evening—reluctantly because he was filled with misgivings, that much we can certainly say. He did not feel right about it, did not trust his wife's remaining home alone because she was ostensibly feeling qualmish—he did not like the look of it, regarded it with general foreboding, both in terms of his own peace of mind and of the spiritual safeguard that enfolded the house in peace. And so he would return home from the god's feast earlier than was really necessary for his party that evening with his standard, confident, though ultimately fearful, question on his lips— "Everything is in order with the house, is it not? The mistress is of good cheer?"—this time to receive at last the terrible answer he had so long secretly expected.

With these words we anticipate events that, to use the phrase of Renenutet, chief stewardess of the bulls, everyone knows already, events that can leave no one in suspense as to details. Nor will it come as a surprise to anyone that Peteprê's reluctance and uneasiness included thoughts of Joseph, and that, reflecting on his wife's indisposition and resolve to stay at home, he made a mental note as to his whereabouts. Which we shall also do, by inquiring, not without some worry as to the power of his seven reasons to hold up, whether he might perhaps have stayed at home as well?

He had not; it would have been quite unfeasible for him to do so and would have stood in obvious and extraordinary contradiction to his usual habits and principles. We know that by age twenty-seven the Egyptian Joseph, removed to this land of death for ten years now, had become an inveterate Egyptian—in the civil if not spiritual sense—and for the last three of them had been clad in a very Egyptian bodily garment, so that his Joseph form was now protected and informed by Egyptian stuff; we also know that, although always keeping an inner distance, he had conformed and become Egypt's child, sharing in Egypt's year, celebrating its freakish customs and the feasts of its idols in an amiable, worldly fashion, though always with moderation and no little irony, confident that the man who had brought his calf to this field would close one eye. More than all other festivals, the New Year, the great day of Amun, was cause to be amiable, to live and let live; Jacob's son observed it just like anyone else here below, setting out in holiday garb early that morning and even—by way of honoring popular custom and being part of it all—having a drop too much to drink. But only later in the day, for first he had official duties to perform. As steward of a bearer of titles, he was part of the retinue in the royal procession from the western House of the Horizon to Amun's Great Dwelling and rode in the river parade from there to the temple of Opet. The divine family's return journey no longer held to quite the correctness of the boat ride upriver; one could sneak away if one wanted, and Joseph spent the day, as did thousands of others, strolling and watching with curiosity all sorts of temple ceremonies, sacrificial feasts, and divine theatricals—while always keeping in mind that he had to return home punctually by evening, or actually late afternoon, *before* all the other servants, in order, as a responsible overseer, to fulfill his duties as head of domestic affairs and to make sure that both the long pantry (where he had once received refreshment for Huya and Tuya from the scribe of the sideboard) and the hall for receiving guests stood ready for the party celebrating the New Year and Potiphar's promotion.

In his mind he attached great importance to these intentions, to examining and checking everything on his own in the empty house before the rest of the personnel, the scribes and servants below him, had returned home from the feast. That was, Joseph decided, the proper thing to do, and as solid reasons for propping up his decision he reflected on moral maxims that did not actually exist but that he invented on his own for the occasion, pretending they were bits of standard folk wisdom—for example: "High position, golden mission," or "Honor ordains greater pains," or "Last at his post, duty uppermost," and other similar golden rules. He came up with them and began rehearsing them only after learning, while still on the river, that his mistress had excused herself from participating in the dance of Hathor because of an indisposition and would be remaining home alone—for before learning this he hadn't given a thought to little rhymes or convinced himself that they were popular adages, had been quite unaware of what he now recognized all the more clearly: that proverbial wisdom and decorum demanded he return home to the empty house as its first servant to see if things were in order there.

He used that very phrase, "to see if things are in order," even though it sounded somewhat ominous to him and an inner voice advised him it was a danger to be avoided. As an honest young man, Joseph did not try to hoodwink himself about the great, soul-shattering danger inherent in his following rhymed maxims—soul-shattering, however, not only as a danger, but also in the happier sense of a great opportunity. An opportunity for what? An opportunity, little Favored Bes, to bring a matter that has become a matter of honor between God and Amun to its conclusion, one way or the other, to take the bull by the horns, and, in God's name, to chance everything. *This,* trembling little friend, is the great, soul-shattering opportunity, and all the rest is dribble. "When people are wont to rest, the master does his mightiest"—the young steward Joseph clung to such pithy, venerable adages, nor was he about to be confused by useless dwarfish chirping or the awkward fact that his mistress was home alone.

One should have gathered enough from his train of thought to realize that there is no reason to bask in certitude on his behalf. If one did not know how the story ends because it told itself to the end in its own time, did not know that this is only a festive repetition and recounting of it, a kind of temple theatrical, as it were, there would be good reason to worry about him, for drops of sweat to appear on the brow. But what does "repetition" mean? Repetition in the feast is the abrogation of the difference between "was" and "is"; and there is no more reason for flippant nonchalance here and now than when the story first told itself, when no one could be assured at this turn of events whether the hero would come away with only a black eye or ruin everything instead by breaking with God. The lament of the women who bury the beautiful god in the cave sounds no less shrill because the hour approaches when he will rise again. Because for now he is dead and mutilated, and every festive hour of the event deserves the full honor and dignity of its present grief and gladness, gladness and grief. Did not Esau also celebrate his hour of honor, swelling with pride and kicking his legs high so that his boasting was both a calamity and a joke? For the story had not yet advanced far enough for him to have howled and wept. So too, for us, in following Joseph's train of thought and golden couplets, things are not yet advanced far enough to prevent those worried beads of sweat from appearing on our brows.

And a glance into Potiphar's deserted house will make them bead up all the more. His wife, who has stayed behind alone and whose role it is to play the Mother of Sins—is she not filled with the most glowing confidence in her festive hour? Does anyone believe that she is less determined than Jacob's son to let things come to a head, and does she not have every reason to be certain of the bitterly blissful triumph of her passion—not have the best of causes for her shadowy fervent hope of soon being able to embrace her young man and lie beside him? Her desire not only knows that it is authorized by the highest spiritual power, that it stands under the solar aegis of Amun's honor and might, but it also sees its fulfillment guaranteed from below with the help of hell's ghastly coercion, for which this daughter of a prince of a nome had, to be sure, descended beneath her rank, but whose humiliating stipulations she most sincerely hoped to deceive and undo, for in her female cunning she wondered whether body and soul could be so easily separated in love and whether in sweet physical embrace she might not succeed in winning the young man's soul as well, in uniting happiness and lust. Since the story is happening again in our words, Potiphar's wife is as bound up in these events here and now as she was then (a "then" that has become a "now") and cannot know what is coming. But that Joseph will be coming to her in the empty house, that much she knows— she is ardently certain of that. The mistress bitch will "torment" him to join her—which is to say: he will learn under way that Mut is not taking part in the feast, that she has remained behind, alone in the quiet house, and the thought will grow powerful within him, indeed overpower him, so that he will change the hour of his return home to a time when that significant and extraordinary state of affairs is still in force. And will it be the exclusive work of The Bitch if this thought gains power over him and directs his steps? Joseph, so the woman thinks in her longing, knows nothing of The Bitch and

Tabubu's vile handiwork; he will think that the compelling idea of visiting Mut in the empty house came from himself, and if that is his opinion, if he believes the idea to be his own and is convinced he is acting of his own volition—will that deception not become a reality in his soul and will not the arch-hag herself be deceived in this regard? "I am driven to act," someone is likely to say, but what lies behind such a distinction? How can he place the responsibility for his actions on something that is not himself, but that "drives" him? It most certainly is himself—what "drives" him is only himself, together with his own demands. Is there any difference between saying "I want to" or "something in me wants to"? Does one even need to say "I want to" in order to act? Does action come from our will, or does not will first reveal itself in action instead? Joseph will come, and in coming he will realize that he wanted to come, and why. But if he comes, if he hears the call of some great opportunity and seizes it, then everything is already decided, then Mut has triumphed and will crown his head with a wreath of ivy and tendrils of grape.

These then are the too keenly sharpened thoughts of Potiphar's wife. Her eyes are unnaturally large and equally excessive in their luster, for she has applied a great deal of antimony to her brows and lashes with an ivory rod. The luster of those eyes is dark and wild, but her mouth reveals a fixed sinuous smile of triumphant confidence. But all the while her lips are in barely perceptible motion, sucking and chewing, as she lets little balls of pulverized frankincense mixed with honey melt in her mouth to sweeten her breath. She has put on a dress of flimsiest royal linen, whose transparency reveals all the contours of her bewitched and loving limbs and from whose pleats wafts the same delicate cypress perfume she wears in her hair. Her quarters are the lady's chamber in the master's house, the room reserved for her there, where one interior wall adjoins the entrance hall with its seven doors and zodiac floor and another is shared with Peteprê's north columned hall, where he customarily reads books with Joseph. One corner of the room abuts the reception and dining hall for guests, which leads then to the family dining chamber and is the site of the banquet to be held this evening in celebration of Peteprê's new rank at court. Mut keeps the door between her room and the north hall open, and one of the two doors that leads from there to the reception hall is open as well. Expectant and confident, she moves about these rooms, alone in the house except for those two old people, sitting in the upper story, awaiting their demise. As their daughter-in-law Eni paces back and forth, whenever her gemstone eyes, dark with excessive luster, happen now and again to glance up at the painted ceiling, she thinks of these saintly parents. She frequently returns from the hall and dining chamber to the twilight of her own room, into which light falls from high-set, open-work stone windows, and she then stretches out on her couch inlayed with greenstone, burying her face in its pillows. Cinnamon bark and myrrh resin burn in the room's incense stands, and the aromatic fumes from the embers drift through the open doors and into the dining chamber and reception hall.

So much, then, for Mut, the sorceress.

To return now to the son who was dead to his father Jacob: he came home before all the other servants—that we know already. He came and may have been aware that he wanted to come, or that he had been driven to come—whichever. Circumstances had not been able to divert him from duty, from his belief that it was his responsibility to cut his pleasures short before anyone else and shift his attention to the house that had been placed in his charge. All the same, he had hesitated and postponed fulfilling those duties, which had been marked and verified by so much proverbial wisdom, for longer than one might have expected. He came back to the still-empty house, it is true, but it would not be all that long before the others returned home as well—that is, all those who had not been given leave to stay in the city, but whose service was needed in the house that evening—perhaps only one short winter hour before, or not even that, always bearing in mind that in these climes winter hours are much shorter than those of summer.

He had spent his day very differently from the waiting woman—amid sunshine and hubbub, caught up in the colorful bustle of the idol's feast. Still imprinted behind his eyelashes were the many images of splendid processions and spectacles, of teeming masses of people. His Rachel nose still carried the scent of burnt sacrifices, of flowers, of the perspiration of so many people still overheated from hopping for joy and excited by this banquet for the senses. The sound of drums, trumpets, and rhythmic clapping, the cries of fervent and hopeful rapture still filled his ears. He had eaten and drunk, and without any exaggeration as to his state of mind, it is perhaps best described as that of a young man who, in the face of a danger that is also an opportunity, is ready to see more opportunity than danger. He had a blue wreath of lotus in his hair and another blossom in his mouth. With a flick of the wrist he brushed his shoulders with the white horsehair of his colorful flyswatter, all the while singing to himself: "Let the servant run scot-free, his master chooses drudgery"—in the belief this was some ancient traditional maxim and only the tune was his invention. And so as day drew to a close, he arrived at his master's estate, opened the house door of cast bronze, crossed the zodiac mosaic of the entrance hall, and stepped into the beautiful banquet hall with its raised dais, where everything was arranged with luxurious elegance for Peteprê's evening party.

Joseph, the young steward, had come to see if everything was at the ready, if Kha'ma't, the scribe of the sideboard, might not deserve a reprimand. He walked about the columned hall, among its chairs and tables, the wine amphorae in their stands, the buffets laden with pyramids of fruits and pastries. He checked the lamps and banquet table with its wreaths, flower necklaces, and dinner ointment boxes, and listened to the chime of the golden goblets as he rearranged them on the buffets. And when he had looked about for a while with a masterly eye, even letting the goblets chime once or twice more, he pulled back, startled—for he heard a voice calling him from a distance, a singer's voice with a resonant timbre, calling out his name, the name he had adopted in this land:

"Osarsiph!"

He never forgot that moment his whole life long, the sound of his name falling on his ear from somewhere far-off in the empty house. He stood there, his fan under his arm, in each hand a golden goblet, whose polish he had just examined, at most letting them chime just a little as he held them—and listened, for it seemed to him, or so he thought, that he had not heard rightly. But it only seemed that way as he stood there motionless, listening, goblets in hand, for there was not another call for a good long time. Finally, however, its song came ringing through the rooms again:

"Osarsiph!"

"Here I am," he answered. But his hoarse voice faltered, so that he cleared his throat and repeated, "I'm listening."

It was hushed for a while again—and he stood there waiting,

motionless. But then the song rang out to him: "Is that you, Osarsiph, whom I hear in the hall? Have you returned from the feast to this empty house before the others?"

"As you say, mistress," he replied, setting the goblets back in place and stepping through the door into Peteprê's north columned hall so that he could be better heard in the adjoining room on the right.

"Yes, that's right, I am here to see if things are in order. 'To weigh and measure is to forgo pleasure.' You surely know the proverb, but since my master has set me over this house and does not concern himself about anything other than the meals he eats—for he has entrusted everything into my hands and there is nothing he has kept from me and has expressly desired to be no greater than I am in his house—I have not begrudged the menials a little more time to taste those good things, but found it only proper for me to forgo the rest of the day's amusements so that I myself might return home in good time, following the adage: 'To others be kind, to your own joy blind.' Yet I do not wish to praise myself before you, for I do not precede the others by all that much, and my head start is hardly worth mentioning—there's not all that much for me to do with it and they could come streaming in any moment now, and soon Peteprê himself may be home, the Sole Friend of the god, your consort and my noble master . . ."

"And me?" the voice called out from its twilit chamber. "Since you are looking after everything else in the house, do you not want to look after me, Osarsiph, and have you not heard I remained behind, alone and suffering? Cross the threshold, come to me."

"I would gladly do so," Joseph replied, "would gladly cross your threshold to visit you, mistress, if several details in the reception room were not in total disarray and did not demand my immediate attention."

But the voice rang out: "Step in here to me. Your mistress commands it."

And Joseph crossed the threshold into her room.

The Countenance of the Father

Here our story falls silent. Which is to say: it falls silent in its current version as a festive presentation, for in the original, just as it happened and told itself, it was not at all silent, but continued there inside the twilit chamber in a lively exchange or even as a dialogue, in the sense that both participants spoke at once—over all of which, however, we shall throw the veil of tact and humane consideration. It came to pass back then all on its own and without witnesses, whereas it is unfolding here and now before a large audience—a crucial difference in terms of tact, as no one can deny. In particular it was Joseph who was not the least bit silent, nor dared to be, but who kept up an incredible flow of polished words as if all in one breath, setting all the charm and cleverness of his spirit against the woman's desires, trying to talk her out of them. And that is the very reason for our own reticence. For he got himself tangled up in a contradiction—or, better, there arose a contradiction that human emotion finds very troubling and embarrassing: the contradiction between spirit and flesh. Yes, when faced with the woman's responses, both spoken and silent, his flesh stood up in revolt against his spirit, making an ass of him, despite his most fluent and clever words; and what a shocking contradiction it is, what forbearance it demands of a narrator: eloquent wisdom revealed as a terrible lie by the flesh, wisdom in the image of the ass.

He fled (and everyone knows he managed to flee) in the same state as the dead god, which for the woman was a cause of despair and frustrated rage; for her desire had found him in a state of manly readiness, and the cry of woe and exaltation that accompanied her paroxysms of ecstatic pain as she caressed and abused the garment he left behind in her hands (and everyone knows he left a piece of clothing behind), the cry the Egyptian woman shouted over and over again was "*Me'eni nachtef!*"—"I have seen his strength!"

Something enabled him to tear himself away, however, and flee from her at the last, desperate moment—Joseph saw the countenance of his father; all the more detailed versions of the story report this, and its truth is confirmed here. The fact is that when, despite all his eloquence, he was about to be undone, the image of his father appeared to him. That is to say Jacob's image? Certainly, his. But it was not an image with fixed personal features that he saw somewhere in the room. He saw it rather in his mind and with his spirit: It was both a memory and an admonition, the image of the father in a broader, more general sense—Jacob's features were blended with the paternal traits of Potiphar, in other ways it shared a resemblance with Mont-kaw, who had died a modest death, and beyond all these similarities it also bore far more powerful features. Those bright brown paternal eyes, with soft pouches beneath them, gazed anxiously at Joseph.

That saved him; or rather—for we want to be reasonable in our judgments and ascribe his steadfastness to his own merit and not some ghostly phenomenon—he saved himself by calling that cautionary image to mind. In a state that can only be called very advanced and bordering on defeat, he tore himself away (much to the unbearable sorrow of the woman, as one must add if one is to divide one's sympathies fairly), and it was his good fortune that his eloquence was matched by physical agility, which enabled him to slip— one, two, three!—out of the jacket (or "robe," or "outer garment") by which in her desperate plight as a lover she tried to hold on to him, and so managed, though in less than a stewardly state, to gain the columned hall, the reception room, and then the entryway.

He left behind him raging, disappointed love, love half blessed— "*Me'eni nachtef!*"—and yet unbearably deceived. She did terrible things with the still-warm garment left in her hands. She covered it with kisses, drowned it with her tears, tore it with her teeth, stomped it with her feet, for it was both odious and sweet, and what she did to it was hardly any different from what his brothers had once done to the son's veil in the valley of Dothan. "Beloved!" she cried out. "Where have you gone? Stay! O, blessed boy! O, shameless slave! Curse you! Death! Treachery! Violence! Stop the brute! He has slain my honor! Help me! Help your mistress! A fiend has assaulted me!"

There we have it. Her thoughts—if one can speak of thoughts where there was only a whirlwind of anger and tears—merged with the accusation with which she had threatened Joseph more than once, whenever she had grown vicious in her demands and raised her lioness's paw against him: the deadly accusation of a monstrous loss of self-control and violation of his mistress. The savage memory rose up within the woman, pouncing upon her, so that she screamed with all her might, just as people always hope excessive volume will lend truth to untruth; and in our fairly divided sympathies, let us be glad that the aggrieved woman's pain found this outlet, that some means of expression offered itself, which, though false, was by its nature so appalling that it horrified everyone, turning them into partisans panting to avenge the offense done to her. Her screams rang out.

There were already people in the entrance hall. The sun was setting and the majority of Peteprê's staff had returned to the house and estate. So it was a good thing that as he fled, Joseph had time and space to collect himself before reaching the entryway. The servants stood there listening, spellbound with fear, for the screams of their mistress carried well; and although the young steward entered the ceremonial hall with measured steps and walked across it with a composed demeanor, it was nearly impossible for them not to make some connection between his less than fully clothed state and the screams coming from the private chamber. Joseph had hoped to reach his own room, the special chamber of trust off to the right, in time to pull himself together; but the servants stood in his way and, what was more, a need to get out of the house and into the open air gained the upper hand, so that he crossed the hall and passed through the open bronze door into the courtyard, where the bustle of homecoming reigned, for arriving now at the harem were the sedan chairs of the chattering concubines, who had likewise been permitted to watch the day's spectacles under the supervision of Nubian eunuchs and the scribes of the house of seclusion and were now being returned to their special cage.

Where was he headed, our fugitive with a black eye? Out the main gate through which he had once entered? But where to from there? He did not know himself and was happy to have before him an open courtyard that he could walk across as if going somewhere. He felt a tug at his clothes—it was Favored Bes, that little shriveled man, his face wrinkled with grief, who chirped up at him: "The fields lie in waste, scorched by the bull! Ashes! Ashes! Ah, Osarsiph!" This occurred about halfway between the main house and the gate through the outer wall. With the little man hanging at his skirt, Joseph turned around. The voice of the woman, of the mistress, now caught up with him, for her white figure was standing at the top of the steps outside the door to the house, amid a press of people who swarmed out of the entrance hall behind her. She stretched out her arm toward him, and ahead of its extension and running toward him were men with their arms outstretched. They grabbed him and led him back to the people who had now assembled in the courtyard before the house: craftsmen, door- and gatekeepers, grooms from the stalls, gardeners, kitchen help, and the silver-skirted men who waited table. Still clinging to his skirt, the blubbering dwarf was dragged along with him.

And with the servants of her titular consort gathered behind her in the house and before her in the courtyard, Potiphar's wife now gave the well-known speech that has always met with humanity's disapproval, and that we, too, are forced to censure, despite all we have done for Mut-em-enet's cause and story—not because her account, which might have served to disguise the truth, was untrue, but because in her frenzy she did not disdain demagoguery.

"Egyptians!" she cried. "Children of Keme! Sons of the river and black earth!" What was this? Those to whom she now turned were ordinary people and, what was more, almost all of them were tipsy at the moment. Being a genuine child of Hapi (to the extent that they in fact were, since there were also Moors from Kush and servants with Chaldean names among them) was a merit granted by nature and nothing they could help or that was of the least advantage if they failed in their service to the house—their backs would then be efficiently flogged and left nicely welted with no regard to the distinction of birth. But suddenly a thing that had always remained very much in the background and served no practical purpose in their individual lives had been flatteringly emphasized and called to their attention because someone could make good use of their sense of honor, of their snorting communal pride, in order to deal with a man who had to be destroyed. The appeal sounded odd to them, but did not fail to have its effect, particularly since the spirit of barley beer enhanced their receptivity.

"Egyptian brothers!"—Suddenly it was "brothers"! This thrilled them through and through, gave them great pleasure.—"Do you see me, your mistress and mother, Peteprê's first and true wife? Do you see me at the threshold of the house and do we know one another, you and I?"—"We" and "one another"! That went down smoothly, common folk were doing well today.—"And do you also know this Habiru youth, who on the great day of our calendar stands here half naked, because he is missing his outer garment, because I am holding it here in my hand. . . . Do you recognize him, who was set over you, children of the nation, as your steward—over the house of a great man of the Two Lands? Behold, he came from his wretched home down to Egypt, to the beautiful garden of Usir, the throne of Rê, the horizon of the gentle spirit. They brought this alien to us, into our house here"—"us"! yet again—"so that he might play fast and loose with us and insult us. For something hideous has happened. I was sitting alone in my parlor, alone in the house, for I had been excused from service to Amun on account of illness and was tending the empty house by myself. And the villain made use of it for his own devices, and the Habiru monster came to me in order to do with me as he pleased and to insult me—the slave wanted to lie with his mistress," she shrieked, "to force her to lie with him! But as he was about to do this and violate me according to his slavish lust, I cried out in my loudest voice—and now I ask you, Egyptian brothers, if you heard me cry at the top of my voice, as proof that I resisted and defended myself most fiercely, as the law demands? You heard it! But when he also heard it, when the brute heard me crying out and screaming, his wanton courage failed him and he wriggled free from his outer garment, which I hold here in evidence, for I wanted to hold him fast by it so that you might seize him, and he fled from me, his wicked purpose unachieved, so that, thanks to my outcry, I stand before you still pure. But he, who stood over all of you and over this house, he stands there disgraced, for his deed will lay hold of him and judgment will come upon him as soon as the master, my husband, returns home. Place the manacle on him!"

This then was Mut's speech—which was not only untrue, but, sad to say, demagogic as well. And Potiphar's household stood there dumbstruck and helpless, their heads already muddled by the temple's free beer and now even more so by what they had just heard. Hadn't they heard, didn't they all know that the woman was infatuated with their beautiful steward, but that he had refused her? And now suddenly it turned out that he had laid hands upon her and tried to force himself upon her? Their heads were spinning, from beer and from this story, for it made no sense, and they all were very fond of the young steward. Nevertheless, the true wife had screamed; they had all heard it, and they all knew the law, which said a woman proved her innocence by screaming loudly during an attack on her honor. Besides which, she was holding the steward's outer garment in her hand, which certainly looked as if he had forfeited it to her in trying to escape; he, however, stood there with his head sunk on his chest, and said not a word.

"Why do you hesitate?" a respectable manly voice called out— the voice of Dûdu, the little master, who had arrived on the spot in his best stiffly starched, flared skirt. "Have you not heard our mistress, who has been cruelly insulted and almost disgraced, give instructions to manacle the Ebrew rascal? Here it is, I have brought it with me. For when I heard her lawful screams, I knew at once what we had here and what hour had come and swiftly fetched the manacle from the whipping room, so that we would have it. Here! Enough gaping, now bind the wanton hands of this villain, who contrary to sterling counsel was purchased on the hollowest advice and has played the master over those of us of genuine birth long enough. By the obelisk! He shall be delivered into the house of torture and execution."

This was Dûdu's finest hour, and the wedded dwarf savored it. And two menials were happy to take the wooden vice from him and clamp it on Joseph—and people really couldn't help laughing at Shepses-Bes's constant whimpers. It was a spindle-shaped block of wood split in the center so that it opened and closed, and once the culprit's hands were clamped tightly together in the opening he was helpless and weighed down by the wood.

"Throw him in the dog kennel!" Mut commanded with a dreadful sob. And then she crouched down on the ground, right where she stood at the open house door, and laid Joseph's garment beside her.

"Here I shall sit," she said, her lilting voice drifting across the darkening courtyard, "on the threshold of the house, the incriminating garment at my side. Step back from me, all of you, and let no one advise me to return into the house, for fear that in my delicate apparel I might take a chill as evening falls. I would be deaf to such advice, for here I shall sit with the forfeited evidence until Peteprê arrives and I receive retribution for this most monstrous of insults."

The Judgment

The hours of the feast are great, each according to its kind, whether proud or wretched. When Esau was able to boast and kick his legs high, things were certainly going well for him, it was his hour of glory. But when he burst out of the tent, crying "Damn! Damn!"

and sat down on the ground to let his tears roll, big as hazelnuts—was *that* hour any less great and solemn for the hairy man? Pay close attention now! This is Peteprê's most painful and solemn festal hour, one that he had always expected at any moment, by the way: whether hunting in the desert or in the marshes for birds and hippopotamuses or reading fine old authors, he had always been vaguely prepared for just such an hour, ignorant only of its details, which would, however, depend largely upon him when the time came—and behold, he fashioned them nobly.

He arrived between torches, in a chariot driven by Neter-nakht—returning earlier, as noted, than was absolutely necessary for his evening party, because of his forebodings. It was a homecoming like many others, when each time his heart had dreaded some evil, and now the hour had in fact come. "Everything is in order with the house, is it not? The mistress is of good cheer?" No, indeed she is not. The mistress is sitting tragically on the threshold of your house, and the cup-bearer who provides you such well-being is lying manacled in the kennel.

So then, this is the form reality has taken. Let us deal with it then! He had noticed even from a distance that Mut, his wife, was seated in some horrible pose at the door of his house. All the same, as he stepped down from his elegant sport vehicle, he threw out his usual questions, which this time remained unanswered. Those assisting him hung their heads and said nothing. So, then, it was exactly as he had always expected it would be, despite certain details of this hour that might differ from what he had anticipated. While his team was led away and people in the torchlit courtyard held back, keeping their distance, this gentle, Ruben-like tower of a man, his fan and cudgel of office in one hand, walked up the steps to the crouching woman.

"What should I think, dear friend," he asked with guarded courtesy, "of this scene? You sit here in light attire at this busy passageway and have something there beside you that I fail to understand."

"So it is!" she replied. "You describe it with dull, feeble words, yet this scene is far more powerful and horrible than you have depicted it, my consort. But your observation is correct in its essentials: I am sitting here and have beside me something about which you shall soon gain a most ghastly understanding."

"Help me to do so," he replied.

"I sit here," she said, "awaiting your judgment against the most awful wickedness that the Two Lands and probably all the realms of other nations have ever seen."

He made a gesture with his fingers to ward off evil and waited calmly.

"The Habiru slave," she sang in her alto voice, "whom you brought in among us, came to me and wanted to play fast and loose with me. Embracing your knee, I begged you there in the hall that evening to drive away this foreigner whom you brought into this house, for I had misgivings about him. But in vain, the slave was too dear to you, and you sent me away uncomforted. Now the villain has come upon me and has attempted to inflict his lust upon me in your empty house, and stood in manly readiness to do so. You do not believe me and cannot conceive of this horror? Then behold this token and interpret it for yourself! This token is stronger than the word, it leaves no room for quibbling or doubting, for it speaks the incorruptible language of things. Look! Is this garment your slave's garment? Inspect it carefully, for I am made pure before you by this token. When I cried out as the monster pressed upon me, he took fright and fled from me, but I held him by his garment, and in his fear he left it behind in my hand. The proof of his abominable guilt—I hold it before your eyes, proof of his flight and proof of my outcry. For if he did not flee, then I did not hold his garment; but if I did not cry out, then he did not flee. All of your household is witness to my having cried out—ask them."

Peteprê stood silent, his head lowered. Then he sighed and said, "That is a very sad tale."

"Sad?" she repeated menacingly.

"I said: very sad," he rejoined. "It is indeed horrifying, and I would search for a still more grievous term had I not been able to gather from your words that, thanks to your presence of mind and knowledge of the law, things turned out well enough and the worst did not happen."

"And you do not search for a term to describe your infamous slave?"

"He is an infamous slave. Since the entire matter concerns his behavior, the term 'very sad' naturally applies to that first and foremost. To think this dreadful thing should happen to me this evening of all evenings—on the evening of the lovely day of my advancement

to Sole Friend, just as I am returning home for a small party in celebration of Pharaoh's love and grace, with guests arriving at any moment. You must admit that is hard."

"Peteprê! Is there a human heart in your breast?"

"Why do you inquire?"

"Because in this unspeakable hour you can speak of your new
title at court and of how you wish to celebrate it."

"I did it only to place the unspeakableness of this hour in glaring
contrast to the glory of the day, thereby emphasizing just how unspeakable it is. It is obvious that what is unspeakable cannot be spoken about, but that one must speak of something else instead in
order to express its meaning."

"No, Peteprê, you have no human heart."

"I shall tell you something, my dear: There are circumstances
when one indeed ought to welcome a certain insufficiency of the
human heart—in interest both of the person concerned and of the
circumstances, which can perhaps be mastered more successfully
without all too much intervention by the human heart. What must
now be done about this very sad and dreadful affair that blemishes
my day of honor? It must be dealt with and settled without delay,
for, first of all, I understand completely that you do not wish to rise
from what is by its nature an impossible position before something
is done about the unutterable unpleasantness you have encountered.
Second, however, I must set this entire affair in order before my
guests arrive, which will be very soon. I must therefore hold a
household court at once, which, the Hidden One be thanked, will be
a matter of summary justice, since your word alone, my friend, will
be binding and no weight given to any other, so that the sentence can
be spoken quickly. Where is Osarsiph?"

"In the kennel."

"I thought so. Have him brought to me. Let my saintly parents
be called from the upper story, even if they may be sleeping. The
household servants are to gather before my seat of authority, which
I would have placed here where the mistress is sitting, that she may
rise only after I have passed judgment."

These orders were hastily carried out, the only difficulty arising
from the initial refusal of the parental siblings, Huya and Tuya, to
appear. For they had been told about the disturbance by their

docile servants. With little funnel-shaped mouths, the twig-armed girls had informed them of these events, which, like their son of atonement and courtier of light, the old couple had always been secretly expecting; and now they were afraid and did not want to come down because any investigation of these matters promised to be a foretaste of their own judgment before the king below and they both knew themselves to be too weak in the head to muster arguments to justify their actions, knew that they would be unable to manage anything more than "we meant well." Which was why they sent word that they were shortly before their demise and no longer up to the rigors of a household court. But their son, the master, grew angry, even stamped his feet, and demanded that they have someone help them downstairs just as they were; for if their demise was imminent, the place where Mut, their daughter-in-law, sat lamenting and demanding justice was a very suitable spot for it.

And so they came downstairs to the gate, supported by their child attendants—old Huya, his little silver beard quivering, his head shaking terribly; old Tuya with a halfhearted smile and those blind slits in her broad white face shifting back and forth as if in search of something. They were made to stand beside Peteprê's chair of judgment, and at first both of them could only excitedly stammer "We meant well," but they then calmed down. Mut the mistress sat with her forfeited token beside a footstool in front of the chair, behind which a red-robed Moor kept tall fans in motion, while men bearing torches were stationed around the group. But the courtyard was also brightened by torchlight wherever servants still on leave for the day had gathered; and Joseph was led forward to the stairs, manacled and accompanied by Se'enkh-Wen-nofre-et-cetera, for the little man refused to let go of his skirt; just as Dûdu, in certain hope that his finest hour could only become finer still, also took his dignified place—so that the two men of reduced stature now stood next to the delinquent, one on each side.

Peteprê was quick to speak, invoking legal formulas in his high voice: "Judgment will now be rendered here, but we are in haste. I call upon you of the ibis-head, who wrote the laws of mankind, upon you, white ape beside the scales; and upon you, Mistress Ma'at, whose charge is truth and whose adornment is ostrich feathers. The sacrifices we supplicants owe you will be offered afterward, that is my pledge and they are as good as performed. But time presses. I shall speak justice over this house, which is mine, and this is what I speak."

Having said this with uplifted hands, he now took a more comfortable position in one corner of his chair of authority, and, bracing one elbow and casually letting his little hand dangle over the armrest, he now went on:

"Despite the host of precautions this house has taken against evil and in defiance of an impenetrable wall of charms and good words to ward off evil, sorrow has succeeded in forcing its way in and breaking for now the spell of peace and tender consideration in which this house rested. A very sad and horrible state of affairs, all the more so since this evil became manifest on the very day that Pharaoh's love and grace deigned to adorn me with the ring and splendid title of Sole Friend, on a day, that is, when one would expect finest courtesy and salutary congratulations from one's fellow men, not, however, to be met with the horror of tottering order. Be that as it may, this sorrow long ago penetrated the defenses of this house and has been gnawing at its lovely order and working toward its collapse, for such is its threat and so it is written: the rich shall be poor, the poor rich, and the temples shall be desolated. For a long time now, I say, this evil has been eating away in silence, hidden from most, but not hidden from the eye of its master, who is both father and mother to this house, for his eye is like the ray of the moon that impregnates the cow and the breath of his word like the wind that bears pollen from tree to tree in token of divine fertility. And since from the loins of his presence all beginning and thriving gushes like golden honey from the comb, nothing escapes his view, and though it be hidden from most, it lies open before his gaze. Learn this, then, from this occasion of such destruction. For I know very well the saying attached to my name, that is, that I concern myself with nothing on earth except the meals I take. But this is only idle chatter and misses the point. Let it be known, then, that I know all; and so if there emerges a fear of the master and a dread of his penetrating eye from this disruption over which I now sit here in judgment, it will then be said of it that despite its being a great sadness it has had its good side as well."

He grasped a malachite flacon of perfume that hung from a chain down over his collar and put it to his nose, and having refreshed himself with it, he continued as follows:

"And so I have long been familiar with the paths this invading sorrow has followed within my house. But also open to my gaze were the paths of those who abetted it with arrogant cunning and prepared a way for it out of envy and hate—and not only that, but also first divulged those points where it might slip through all good protective charms and gain entrance to this house. The traitor stands before my chair in the dwarfish person of the erstwhile guardian of my jewels and chests, and his name is Dûdu. He was forced to admit all his wickedness to me, how he opened the door to greedy evil and showed it the way. Let judgment be spoken against him! Far be it from me to rob him of the potency that the lord of the sun was once disposed to unite with his shrunken form—I will not touch it. But let the traitor's tongue be cut out."

"Half his tongue," he corrected himself and gave a wave of his hand in disgust when Dûdu let out a loud wail of anguish. "But since I am accustomed," he added, "to having my gemstones and clothing kept in the care of a dwarf and it is not my wish that my customary ways should suffer from any confusion, I herewith name the other dwarf of my house, Se'enkh-Wen-nofre-Neteruhotpe-em-per-Amun, to be scribe of the wardrobe chamber—may he have charge over my chests from henceforth."

Favored Bes—that little nose in that wrinkled face now cinnabar red from weeping for Joseph—gave a leap of joy.

Mistress Mut, however, lifted her head to look up at Peteprê's chair and whispered between her teeth, "What judgments are these that you render, my consort? They deal with only marginal affairs and are quite irrelevant. What are people to think of you as a judge, and how shall I rise again from this place if such are your judgments?"

"Patience," he replied just as softly, bending down to her from his chair. "For little by little justice and judgment shall be meted out to each and the evildoer will be overtaken by his offense. Just sit still. You will soon be able to rise again as gratified as if you yourself were judge. For I judge for you, my dear, but without intervention by all too much human heart—and be glad of that. For if the heart were to speak in its impetuosity, it might well fall prey to eternal remorse."

And having softly spoken these words to her, he sat up straight again and said, "Muster all your courage, Osarsiph, my erstwhile steward, for I now come to you, and you shall hear your judgment, which you have perhaps anxiously awaited for some time—I have intentionally prolonged your wait in order to magnify your punishment. For I intend to deal roughly with you and impose harsh punishment upon you—quite apart from that which arises from within your own soul, for those three beasts with ugly names are now hot on your heels. Their names, if I recall correctly, are Shame, Guilt, and Mocking Laughter. It is they who understandably cause you to sink your head and stand before my chair with lowered eyes, which I notice not for the first time; for I have not lifted my secret gaze from you during the long torment of the wait I have demanded of you. You stand manacled, your head sunk deep, and are silent, and how could you not be silent, for no questions will be asked you as to your justification and it is the mistress who has witnessed against you with her unimpeachable word, which of itself would suffice for my decision, but in addition to which there also lies before me the shameful evidence of your outer garment, speaking the irrefutable language of things and telling of your insolence, which finally went so far that you rose up against your mistress and, when she attempted to call you to account, you had to leave your garment in her hand. I ask you: What point would there be in your offering anything in your defense against the word of the mistress and the language of things?"

Joseph was silent and hung his head lower still.

"Apparently none," Peteprê answered for his part. "You must be dumb as the lamb is dumb before its shearers—you have no other choice here today, however quick and indeed pleasant your speech may otherwise have been. But thank the god of your clan, your Baal or Adon, who is probably like the setting sun, that he guarded you in your insolence and did not allow your rising up against her to come to the worst, but stripped you of your garment—thank him, I say, for otherwise this would be the hour of the crocodile, or your portion were slow death by fire, if not the peg in the door to the hall. But there can indeed be no question of such punishments—for since you were protected from the worst, I am in no position to impose them. But do not doubt that it is nonetheless my will to deal roughly

with you, and now hear your judgment after your intentionally prolonged wait. I cast you into the prison where the king's prisoners
lie—Zawi-Rê, the island fortress in the river; for you no longer belong to me, but to Pharaoh and are a slave of the king. I give you into
the hand of the jailer, a man who is not to be trifled with and who,
one can assume, is not a man to be easily misled by your seemingly
beneficial ways, so that you will have it very hard in prison, at least
at first. Moreover, I shall particularly inform the warden about you
in a letter that I shall send with you and in which I intend to describe
you in a fashion befitting you. Tomorrow you will be taken by boat
to that place of atonement, which knows no laughter, and will no
longer behold my countenance, after having been near me for a succession of many cordial years, with permission to fill my goblet and
to read to me from good authors. This may indeed pain you, and I
would not be amazed to find your lowered eyes filled now with
tears. Be that as it may, tomorrow you shall be taken to that very
hard place. You need not return now to the kennel. You have served
out that punishment, and it is rather Dûdu who may spend the night
there, until his tongue is cropped in the morning. You, however, may
sleep where you normally sleep, in the special chamber of trust,
which for this night, however, should bear the name of special chamber of custody. Furthermore, since you are manacled, justice demands that Dûdu should be fitted with a manacle as well, that is, if
there is another. But if there is none, then let Dûdu wear it. I have
spoken. The household court is ended. Let each man return to his
post to receive our guests."

No one will be surprised to learn that upon hearing these judgments all those in the courtyard fell upon their faces, raising their
hands and calling out the name of their gentle and wise master. And
Joseph, too, fell upon his face in gratitude, as did Huya and Tuya,
who, supported by their child attendants, bent low to honor their
son—and were you to ask about Mut-em-enet, the mistress, you
would hear that she was no exception. One saw her bend low across
the footstool that stood before the judge's chair and hide her brow in
her consort's feet.

"No need to thank me, my friend," he said. "I would be happy if
I have succeeded in satisfying you in this affliction and in having
proved my kindness with my power. We can now enter the reception

hall, that we may celebrate my day of honor. For since you wisely tended the house during the day, you have spared yourself for the evening."

And so Joseph descended into the pit and into prison a second time. How he rose up again from that hole to a higher life, let that be the subject of future songs.

JOSEPH THE PROVIDER

PRELUDE IN
HIGHER ECHELONS

In higher circles and echelons there reigned at that time, as always under similar circumstances, a gentle but pointed satisfaction, a tip-toeing schadenfreude, revealed in every encounter by glances exchanged with demurely lowered lashes and lips pulled down into little pursed rounds. Once again the cup was brimful, mercy exhausted, justice overdue. In a complete reversal of plans and wishes—the result of pressure from the Realm of Sternness (before which the world, to be sure, could not even stand; indeed that realm could never have built it upon those all too soft foundations of compassion and mercy)—One had been compelled, in all the majesty of One's sorrow, to intervene and set matters aright, to overthrow, to destroy, and, yet once again, to level the whole—just as in the time of the Flood, or on that day of raining brimstone when those wicked cities were engulfed by the caustic sea.

Granted, this concession to justice was not of that style or on that scale, not of such ferocity as when that great fit of remorse resulted in wholesale drowning—or when two of us, thanks to the depraved aesthetics of the people of Sodom, almost had an unspeakable city tax extorted from them. This was an instance not simply of humankind's landing in the pit, in the cesspool, or even of some human group whose corrupt ways cried out to heaven, but of one particularly saucy and arrogant individual specimen of the race, a man especially burdened with predilection, zeal, and far-reaching plans, who had been thrust in our faces—the result of a whimsical train of thought only too familiar to these circles and echelons and long a source of bitterness, though also of the not unfounded expectation that that same bitterness would soon be the portion of the One who had initiated the offensive scheme and set it into motion. "The angels," the scheme said, "were created in Our image, yet are not fruitful. Whereas, behold the beasts are fruitful, yet are not after Our likeness. We will create man—in the image of the angels, and yet fruitful!"

How absurd. Worse than gratuitous, injurious in fact, eccentric, and gravid with remorse and bitterness. We were not "fruitful"— certainly not. We were, one and all, chamberlains of light and serene courtiers, and the tale of our having once gone in to the daughters of men was baseless worldly gossip. But all in all, no matter what interesting corollaries, beyond mere bestiality, may be inherent in that bestial advantage and quality of "fruitfulness," we, though "unfruitful," at least did not drink iniquity like water; and One will see just how far One gets with One's fruitful race of angels—perhaps even so far as the insight that, for One's own peace of mind, an omnipotence informed by self-control and prudent foresight might well have rested eternally content with just our respectable existence.

An omnipotence that knows no boundaries in inventiveness and in calling things into being with a mere "Let there be" carried, needless to say, its own risks—even omniscience may not have been completely up to the task, may have been insufficient to prevent the blunders and highly egregious, otiose effects of exercising such absolute attributes. Out of pure restlessness, out of a pure need to act and a pure urge for "if one thing, why not another," for "after angels and beasts, why not an angelic beast as well," One became entangled in imprudence, created something flagrantly precarious and embarrassing—on which, given One's venerable obstinacy, One then, precisely because it was an undeniably botched creation, hung One's heart all the more and attended to it with a zeal insulting to all heaven.

Did One come up with the idea of calling this unpleasantness into being all on One's own, solely of One's own accord? Certain confidential and clandestine surmises suggesting the contrary circulated through the ranks of the hierarchy—surmises that although unverifiable were definitely based on the probability that the entire matter could be traced to the promptings of the great Sammael, who at the time, before his effulgent fall, had still stood very close to the Throne. Such whispered promptings were very like him—and why? Because his chief concern had been to initiate and make a reality of evil, which, although no one else entertained or cultivated such an idea, was his innermost thought, and because there had been no other means by which to enrich the world's repertoire with that same evil than through the establishment of man. There could be no question of evil—Sammael's great innovation—among the fruitful beasts, let alone among us unfruitful images of God. In order that it might come into the world, one creature was needed, and in all probability Sammael suggested that it be introduced there: something like unto God, but at the same time fruitful, which is to say man. Not that this had required any deception of creative omnipotence, by the by, inasmuch as Sammael, in a display of his customary grandeur, presumably did not even conceal the consequence of his recommended creature—to wit: the birth of evil—but had instead fiercely and straightforwardly proclaimed it, though always, or so the hierarchy surmised, with an appeal to the significant growth in vitality that the Creator's own nature would experience through it. One needed only to think of the exercise of grace and mercy, of judgment and correction, of the emergence of merit and guilt, of reward and punishment—or, better, quite simply of the establishment of *good,* which was bound up with that of evil, since in fact the former had to lie in the womb of possibilities, awaiting its opposite, before it could come into existence; and in its essence creation itself was founded upon division, had begun in the moment of the dividing of light from darkness, so that the logical consequence would be for omnipotence to proceed from this purely external division to its establishment in the moral world.

The opinion that these had been the arguments with which the great Sammael had cajoled the Throne and won it over to his suggestions was widespread among the circles and echelons—very sly suggestions indeed, sly enough to set them giggling, for it was a trap despite all its fierce candor, the latter itself merely the cloak for a cunning and malice that did not meet with a total lack of sympathy among the echelons. Sammael's malice, however, consisted of the following: If those beasts for which the gift of fruitfulness was intended were not made after God's likeness, then neither, to be precise, were we courtiers made in His image, for, thank God, we enjoyed a tidy lack of fruitfulness. The qualities portioned out between them and us—godliness and fruitfulness—had originally been united within the Creator Himself, and only the creature suggested by Sammael would be truly created in His image, only in it was that union likewise to be found. With this creature, however—that is, with man—evil came into the world.

Was that not a jest to set off giggles? Precisely the creature that, if one wished to put it that way, was most like the Creator brought evil with it. Upon the advice of Sammael, God created for Himself a mirror that was not very flattering, anything but, and that out of anger and chagrin He frequently set about to smash to smithereens, though without ever taking the final step, perhaps because He could not bring Himself to thrust what He had once called into being back into nonbeing, because He felt a greater fondness for His failure than for His success; perhaps also because He did not want to admit that anything that He had created explicitly after His own likeness could itself be a total failure; and last of all, perhaps because a mirror is a means for self-recognition and because He would then see the consciousness of that ambivalent creature reflected in one son of man, in a certain Abirâm or Abraham—see it as a means for His own self-awareness.

Judging from which, man was the product of God's curiosity about Himself—which Sammael shrewdly presumed and exploited with his advice. Anger and chagrin were the inevitable and ongoing consequences—especially in those hardly rare cases in which evil was joined with cheeky intelligence, logic, and truculence, as in the case of Cain, the founder of fratricide, whose conversation with the Creator after the deed was fairly well known and bandied about in our circles. One had not exactly cut a very dignified figure in the question One put to this son of Eve: "What have you done? The voice of your brother cries out to Me from the earth, which has opened its mouth to receive his blood from your hand." For Cain had answered: "To be sure I slew my brother, and that is sad enough. But Who created me as I am, jealous to the point that on occasion my conduct becomes so dissembling that I no longer know what I am doing? Are You not a jealous God, and did You not create me after Your likeness? Who put the evil impulse in me to do the deed that I have undeniably done? You say that You alone bear the burden of the whole world, and will You not also bear our sins?" Not bad, that. Exactly as if Cain, or Kayin, had taken counsel with Sammael beforehand, though perhaps the crafty hothead had no need to do so. Any rebuttal would have been difficult, which left only a crushing blow or indignant amusement. "Begone!" came the answer. "Go your way. You shall be a fugitive and a vagabond, but I will set upon you a mark that you belong to me so that no one may slay you." In short, thanks to his logic, Kayin was let off lightly to say the least; this cannot be called punishment. Even talk about being a fugitive and a vagabond was not in earnest, for in fact Cain settled in the land of Nod, east of Eden, and quietly set about siring children, a work for which he was urgently needed as well.

On other, well-known, occasions, punishment was meted out and, always in majestic sorrow, terrible measures taken against the compromising behavior of that "most similar" creature—just as there were rewards, terrible rewards, which is to say, exaggerated, extravagant, and outrageous rewards. Do but recall Enoch, or Hanok, and the incredible—indeed one must, in a whispered aside, say irresponsible—rewards bestowed on the fellow. In our circles the prevalent opinion, shared to be sure with greatest caution, was that not everything was on the up-and-up when it came to rewards and punishments down below and that the moral world established upon Sammael's advice was not treated with requisite seriousness. It would not have taken much, indeed at times nothing at all, for our circles to have come to the conclusion that Sammael took the moral world more seriously than He.

It could not be hidden, even had there been a desire to hide and disguise, that the rewards—being in so many cases quite dispropor-tionate—served as a moral cloak, as pretexts for blessings that were in truth explicable only as fundamental favor, a predilection that had scarcely anything to do with the moral world. And the punish-ments? Here, for example, punishment was meted out, the field lev-eled, in the land of Egypt—apparently with regret and sorrow, apparently out of respect for the moral world. Someone—a favorite, a piece of conceit, a dreamer of dreams, a little fruit from the tree of him who had first hit upon the notion of being a means of self-awareness—had fallen into the pit, into the dungeon, into the hole, and for the second time now, because his stupidity had run wild, be-cause he had let love, just as he had once let hate, run wildly out of control; and how pleasant that was to observe. But were we of the entourage perhaps deceiving ourselves now by taking satisfaction in this new version of brimstone?

Just between us: We did *not* let ourselves be deceived, not for a moment actually. We knew precisely, or at least presumed to the point of certainty, that this was merely sternness feigned out of re-spect for the Realm of Sternness, that One was making use of pun-ishment, that fixture of the moral world, as a means for opening up a cul-de-sac whose only access to light was through an exit in the underworld; that One, begging your pardon, was misusing punishment as a means to show more favor and raise up higher still. If we, in brushing past one another in silence, kept our radiant lashes lowered and pulled our lips down so expressively in little pursed rounds, we did so out of that insight. Punishment as an instrument to even greater greatness—that jest by the Almighty also shed light back upon the mistakes and impudence that had been the cause of punishment and "forced" Him to act, a light that had not exactly come from the moral world; for those very mistakes, that impudence, prompted by whomever, by God knows whom, had already become the means, the vehicle for being extravagantly raised up anew.

The circles of the entourage believed they more or less knew what these stratagems were all about—thanks to their, albeit limited, share in omniscience, which out of respect was used of course only with considerable precaution, indeed self-abnegation and dissimulation. And it must be added, in as low a voice as possible, that they believed they knew even more about other matters and steps taken—about enterprises, intentions, machinations, secrets of a wide-ranging nature—which it would have been a mistake to dismiss as court gossip, but to which, to be sure, it was absolutely forbidden to give voice, for they could scarcely be mentioned even in a whisper, so that the means of discussing or conferring about them verged on silence itself: a gentle flutter of the lips, those softly, maliciously pursed lips. And what sort of matters, rumors, and plans were these?

They were bound up with that peculiar, and though of course irreproachable, patently obvious treatment of rewards and punishments, with its entire nexus of favoritism, preference, election that called into question the moral world (itself the consequence of evil, and thus of good, having been called into being) or, in short, the creation of humankind. This in turn was further bound up with not definitively proved, but well-supported tidings—borne on barely fluttering lips—that Sammael's suggestion or whispered proposal to create a "similar" creature—that is, man—had not been the final such notion that the Throne had allowed to be brought before it; that relations between the Throne and the overthrown angel had not been completely severed or had at some point been resumed—though just how was not known. It was also not known whether, behind the backs of the entourage, a journey had been undertaken to the cesspool, where ideas had been exchanged, or whether the banned exile had on his own found an opportunity, perhaps on repeated occasions, to leave his abode and speak once again before the Throne.

In any case he had been able to augment and enhance his erstwhile witty and intentionally compromising suggestion, although it took the form—probably no differently from on that first occasion—of provoking and stimulating thoughts and wishes that may have already been embryonically, tentatively present and needing only additional encouragement.

In order to understand what was in progress and at work here, it is necessary to recall certain information and facts found in the premise and prelude to our current story. The reference here is to none other than the "romance of the soul" briefly recounted now in the terms available there: how, like unformed matter, primal man's soul was one of the originally posited principles and how its "Fall" created the prerequisite basis for all narratable events. One can indeed speak here in terms of Creation. For did not the Fall occur because the soul—out of a kind of melancholy sensuality surprised and shocked by a primal principle dwelling in the higher world—allowed itself to be overwhelmed by a desire lovingly to penetrate formless matter still clinging very stubbornly to its formlessness, in order to generate out of matter forms by which it could achieve its physical desires? And was it not the Most High Himself who came to the soul's assistance in a struggle far beyond its own powers and created for it the narratable world of events, the world of forms and of death? He did so out of sympathy for the plight of His errant concomitant—a compassion that allows one to conclude a certain constitutional and emotional kinship of the two; and where one can conclude a thing one must do so, even if that conclusion may sound bold or blasphemous, given the fact that one is speaking of errancy in the same breath.

Is the concept of error to be connected with Him in any way? The only possible answer to such a question is no, a resounding no, and that would have been the answer of all the choirs of the entourage—followed, however, by a discreet pursing and pulling down of lips. It would doubtlessly be going too far to make the rash claim that mercifully creative and supportive participation in another's errancy is to be regarded as personal error. It would be rash inasmuch as the creation of the finite life-and-death world of forms still did not inflict even the slightest injury—or perhaps only very minor injury—to the dignity, spirituality, majesty, and absoluteness of the God who stood before and outside all worlds, so that *up to this point* there can be no serious talk of errancy in the true sense of the word. But it is a different matter with those ideas, plans, and wishes that *now* hung in the air, if only as surmises, and formed the object of secret dialogues with Sammael, during which the latter surely put on the air of someone who believed he was personally bearing a new idea to the Throne, whereas presumably he knew very well that One was already silently, provisionally contemplating that same idea. Evidently Sammael was counting on the universality of the error that says when two are taken by the same idea, that idea must surely be good.

It is pointless to beat about the bush, to talk all around the matter, any longer. What the great Sammael suggested—one hand to his chin, the other stretched out toward the Throne in peroration—was the embodiment of the Most High in some not yet extant, but moldable chosen people, after the pattern of the earth's other national and tribal divinities with all their magical powers and fleshly vitality. It was not by chance that the word "vitality" was introduced, for the cesspool's chief argument (just as it had been when the creation of man was suggested) was the increase in vitality that the spiritual God, existing beyond and above the world, would experience—though in a far more drastic and thus fleshly sense—by following such advice. Let it be noted: the chief argument. For the clever cesspool had many, and he assumed, more or less correctly, that in any case they had all been secretly at work in the place where he now introduced them and needed only be brought to a white heat.

The emotional realm on which they now focused was that of ambition—which of necessity was an ambition for diminution, an ambition directed downward; for in the Highest Instance, where any upward-directed ambition is unthinkable, all that is left is its downward expression: an ambition for adaptation and "wanting to be as others are," an ambition to renounce the extraordinary. The cesspool found it easy to appeal here to a certain mood of stale, flat, demeaning abstractness and universality that inevitably had to color any comparison the spiritual, supraworldly God might make between Himself and the magical sensuality of national and tribal gods, thereby awakening an ambition for vigorous diminution and limitation, for the addition of a more sensual spice to His form of life. To surrender the somewhat anemic loftiness of spiritual omni-efficacy for full-blooded, fleshly existence as the divine body of a nation and to be what other gods were—that was the Almighty's secret aspiration, his tentative deliberation, to which Sammael appealed with his cunning advice. And, in order to understand this temptation and the willingness to yield to it, ought one not then be permitted to introduce the romance of the soul, its love affair with matter and the "melancholy sensuality" that inspired it, in short, to introduce the *Fall* as a kind of parallel? In truth there is nothing to be introduced here—the parallel forces itself upon us, particularly in light of the sympathetically creative assistance granted to the errant soul on that occasion, from all of which, then, the great Sammael most assuredly drew malicious courage for his counsel.

Malice and the fervent desire to cause embarrassment were, needless to say, the innermost meaning of this counsel; for if man had been a general—and thereby a source of constant—embarrassment for the Creator, then His fleshly union with a given tribe of men, by assuming a vitality tantamount to biological existence, would have to bring things to a pinnacle of distastefulness. The cesspool knew only too well that such a downward ambition, the attempt to be like other gods (which is to say, to be a tribal god, the divine body of a nation), through the union of the cosmic God with one tribe, could never ever come to a good end—or at best might come to a good end only after lengthy detours, after much embarrassment, disappointment, and embitterment. He knew only too well what his Advisee doubtless also knew in advance: that after a perilous episode of biological vitality as the divine body of a tribe, after the dubious, if also full-blooded pleasures of a reduced earthly existence, of residing within the life force of a national entity, of being served, coddled, and enkindled by magic ritual, of being sustained by its energies, there would necessarily follow that universal moment of contrite reversal and self-reflection, the repudiation of all such dynamic limitations, the swinging of the pendulum of the beyond back to the beyond, the reclaiming of omnipotence and spiritual omni-efficacy. But what Sammael—and he alone—nourished in his heart was the thought that even this return, this homecoming equivalent to a cosmic turnaround, would of necessity—and much to the delight of his own primal malice—be accompanied by a certain humiliation.

By chance, or not by chance, the character of the tribe chosen and molded to be His national embodiment was such that on the one hand, the cosmic God, by becoming its body and its God, not only forfeited His dominion over the earth's other national gods and became *like* one of them, but also ended up considerably *below* them in terms of power and glory—also to the delight of the cesspool. On the other hand, however, the condescension of becoming a national god, the entire experiment of enjoying biological life, took place against the better judgment and deeper insights of the chosen tribe itself, so that without its intensive spiritual assistance that reversal and self-reflection, that restoration in the beyond of dominion over the other gods of this world, would not have been possible. This was what tickled Sammael's malice. To serve as the divine body of this peculiar tribe was on the one hand no particular pleasure—as such one could not, as they say, cut a very dashing figure among the other national gods. One inevitably ended up taking a back seat. But on the other hand and in this same regard, the universal capacity of the human creature for being an instrument for God's own self-awareness grew particularly prominent in this tribe. An urgent, worried striving to determine the nature of God was innate to it; from the very beginning there stirred within it a seed of insight into the Creator's extraworldy nature, His totality and spirituality—that is, that He was the space of the world, but the world was not His space (much as the narrator is the space of his story, but the story is not his, which then offers him the possibility of commenting on it)—a seed capable of development and destined over time and by means of strenuous effort to grow into full knowledge of God's true nature. Dare one assume that this is precisely why such a "choice" was made? That the outcome of this biological adventure was as fully known to the Advisee as it was to his astute counselor? That He Himself knowingly created His so-called humiliation and edification? Perhaps duty requires that assumption. In Sammael's eyes at any rate, the droll point of this process lay in how from the very start the chosen tribe knew better, so to speak (at least in the form of that hidden seed), than did its own national God and employed all the energies of its maturing reason to help Him out of a state inappropriate to Him and return to a beyond of spiritual omni-efficacy—

whereby it remains the cesspool's unproved assertion that the path leading back from the Fall to a home and position of honor was possible only with the help of humanity's exertions, that left to His own devices He would never had found His way.

The foreknowledge of the circles in the entourage scarcely reached so far ahead, reached only as far as whispered rumors about secret meetings with Sammael and what was discussed there; but it sufficed to hone general angelic displeasure in regard to that "most similar" of creatures into a special petulance directed against the chosen tribe now in the process of being molded; sufficed, moreover, for cautious schadenfreude at that small-scale Flood and brimstone shower that One, to One's sorrow, had been compelled to inflict upon a scion of that same tribe, who had been the object of special and far-reaching plans—though to be sure with the poorly disguised intent of turning punishment into their instrument.

All this was expressed in lips pursed and pulled down and in the almost imperceptible jerks of their heads by which the choristers gestured to one another, directing an ear toward the river of Egypt, toward an oared sailboat in which that same scion, with arms bound behind his back, was being transported to prison.

Part One

THE SECOND PIT

Joseph Recognizes His Tears

Obeying the law of correspondence between above and below, Joseph, too, was thinking of the Flood. These thoughts met or, if you like, moved side by side, separated by a vast distance—except that here below on the waves of the Yeôr, the human scion, burdened by the spiritual weight of hard experience, thought of that primal episode, that pattern for all inflicted punishment, with far more urgency and associative energy than those delicate gossipmongers, knowing neither suffering nor experience, could ever have managed.

More of that in a moment. The convicted man lay, quite uncomfortably, in the plank shed that served as both cabin and storeroom on a smaller freighter that was made of acacia wood and had a caulked deck: a so-called oxen boat, the same sort on which he himself had probably once moved up and down the river, bringing his house's goods to market and learning oversight as a future steward. It was manned by four rowers, who, when the wind was adverse or fell away and the swaying double mast was lowered, had to stand at the deck railings near the bow and put their weight to the oars, plus a helmsman at the stern, and two of Peteprê's menials who served as escorts, but also as sailors, handling lines and observing the current. Over them all was Kha'ma't, the scribe of the sideboard, who had been entrusted with the command of the boat and transport of the prisoner to the island fortress of Zawi-Rê. He carried on his person a sealed letter that his master had written about his reprehensible steward to the warden of the prison, a captain of troops and "commissioned scribe of the victorious army," whose name was Mai-Sakhme.

The journey was long and wearisome—Joseph could not help thinking of that other, earlier one, when, some seven plus three years before, he had traveled these waters the first time, together with the old man who had bought him, and with Mibsam, the old man's son-in-law, Epher, his nephew, and Kedar and Kedma, his sons—a nine-day boat trip from Menfe, the city of the wrapped god, to No-Amun, the royal city. But this return journey downriver was taking him far beyond Menfe, even beyond the golden city of On and Per-Bastet, the city of cats; for Zawi-Rê, their grim goal, lay deep in the land of Seth and the red crown, which is to say in Lower Egypt, in the Delta in fact, in the middle of a branch of the river that ran through the nome of Mendes, which was here called Djedet; and the idea that he was being brought to the nome of that loathsome goat only added to his uneasiness, to the general depression and gloom that overshadowed him, but that was also accompanied by a lofty awareness of destiny and a meditative play of thought.

For the son of Jacob and his true wife had been unable to resist such play his whole life long, no more as a grown man, whose years were now counted at twenty-seven, than as a callow lad. But for him the dearest and sweetest form of play was allusion, and whenever events in his carefully monitored life grew rich with allusion and circumstances proved transparent for a higher correspondence, then he was happy, for transparent circumstances can never be entirely gloomy.

And his present circumstances were gloomy indeed; in a mood of pensive sadness and with elbows bound together, he regarded them as he lay on his mat in the cabin shed, its roof piled high with the crew's provisions for the journey: melons, ears of corn, and bread. It was the return of a frighteningly familiar situation: once more he lay helpless in his bonds, just as he had once lain for three ghastly black-mooned days in the round depths of a well, sharing that hole with crickets and cellar denizens, and like a sheep had soiled himself with his own filth; and although his situation was milder and not as straitened as then, since his fetters had been applied only for the sake of appearances and good form—out of consideration and instinctive leniency they had tied the piece of warp rope they had used fairly loosely—nevertheless, the fall itself was no less deep and numbing, this change in life no less abrupt and incredible. That first time his father's favorite, the coddled pet, who had always anointed himself only with the oil of gladness, had been mistreated in ways that he never could have dreamt or thought possible; and now it was Osarsiph—who had risen so high in the land of the dead, who as the master of oversight and resident of the special chamber of trust had grown accustomed to refinement, charming culture, and clothes of pleated royal linen—who was being ill used. And he, too, was thunderstruck.

There was no question now of pleated refinement, of a fashionable apron and expensive sleeved jacket (like the one that had served as "proof" against him)—a slave's loincloth no different from what the crew wore was all that had been allowed him. There was no question now of wigged elegance, nor of enameled collars, bracelets, and a necklace of reed and gold. That entire beautiful civilization had melted away, and the only paltry ornament left him was an amulet bag hung on a bronzed cord around his neck, the same one he had worn in the land of his fathers and had taken with him into the pit as a seventeen-year-old. The rest had been "removed"—Joseph himself used that evocative word, a word rich with allusion, just as the thing itself was an allusion, a thing of sorrowful order and correspondence. It would have been entirely wrong of him to travel where he was traveling still wearing necklaces and bracelets; for the hour of unveiling and the removal of ornaments was at hand, the hour of the descent into hell. One cycle had come around, one small cycle, often repeated, but also a larger, rarer one that restored what was, for these cycles shared a center and moved each within the other.

One little year was turning back on itself, the sun's year—in the sense, that is, that the water had deposited its mud and receded once more and (not according to the calendar, but in practical reality) it was now the time of sowing, the time of hoe and plow, of ripping the earth open. When Joseph got up from his mat, as Kha'ma't, his guardian, occasionally had to permit, he would stand on the caulked deck, his hands at his back as if held there voluntarily, moving with the river through the bright echoing air filled with calls and cries, or he might sit on a coil of rope, watching the farmers along the fertile banks go about the serious, dangerous business of tilling and sowing, each task with its attendant rules of precaution and atonement—and a mournful business as well, for seed time is a time of mourning, a time for burying the god of grain, for Usir's interment in darkness, a time of only distant hope. It is a time of weeping—and Joseph wept a little as well at the sight of peasants burying their grain, for he too was about to be buried in darkness again, with any hope still very distant—as a sign that another great year has come round again, bringing with it repetition, renewal of life, a journey into the abyss.

It was the abyss into which the True Son descends: Etura, the subterranean sheepcote, Aralla, the realm of the dead. He had arrived, by way of the well's pit, in the underworld, the land of death that turned rigid; and now his path led down there again, into the *bôr* and prison, into Lower Egypt—it could go no deeper. Days of the dark moon returned, great days that would become years, and during that time the underworld had power over the Beautiful One. He waned and died; after three days, however, he would rise to wax again. As the evening star, Attar-Tammuz likewise sank into the well; but as the morning star he was certain to rise again. This is called hope, and it is a sweet gift. But there is something forbidden about it as well, for it diminishes the value of the sacred moment and anticipates those festal hours of the cycle that have not yet come. Each hour enjoys its own honor, and the man who cannot despair does not live his life rightly. Joseph shared this view. His hope was indeed a most certain knowledge; but he was a child of the moment, and he wept.

He recognized his tears. Gilgamesh had wept them in rejecting Ishtar's demands, for she had "prepared tears" for him. He was truly exhausted from the trouble he had been through—the woman's importuning, the grave crisis in which it had culminated, the upheaval that had changed his life entirely; and during the first few days he had not even asked Kha'ma't for permission to stroll on deck to watch the colorful, bustling traffic on Egypt's highway, but had kept to himself in the shed, lying on his mat and weaving dreamy thoughts. He dreamed of verses on a tablet:

In her rage Ishtar soared up to Anu, king of the gods, demanded revenge. "You shall make the bull of heaven, and he shall trample the world, scorch the earth with the fiery breath of his nostrils, withering and destroying its fields!"

"I will make the bull of heaven, Lady Ashirta, for you have been sorely offended. But years of chaff shall follow, seven in number, years of famine because of his trampling and scorching. Have you made provision for sustenance, piled up foodstuffs with which to counter the years of want?"

"I have made provision for sustenance, have piled up foodstuffs."

"Then will I make the bull of heaven and send him forth, for you have been sorely offended, Lady Ashirta."

What strange behavior! If Asherah wanted to destroy the earth because of Gilgamesh's prudery and burned to have her bull of heaven, it made little sense for her to pile up foodstuffs in anticipation of the seven years of chaff that were to be his work. All the same, that is what she had done, replied that she had indeed done it, so great was her burning desire for her bull of revenge. What Joseph liked about the whole story, what preoccupied him, was precisely that, if she was to have her fiery bull, the goddess had had to worry about taking precautions, even in her rage. Precaution, foresight, had always been a familiar and important idea for the dreamer—even if in his childish way he had sinned against it often enough. Moreover, it came close to being the primary maxim of life in the land where he had grown as if beside a spring, in the land of Egypt, an anxious nation, incessantly concerned, in things both great and small, to secure every step, every action with magic signs and charms to counter any possible evil lying in wait; and because he had been an Egyptian himself for so long now, because both his flesh and bodily garment were of pure Egyptian stuff, that nation's idea of precaution and foresight was fixed deep in his own soul, where, though for different reasons, it had always had a home. For its roots were equally deep in his own original tradition—where sin was nearly the same thing as a failure to exercise precaution, which was folly and absurd clumsiness in one's dealings with God, whereas foresight and precautionary safeguards were wisdom. Noah-Utnapishtim—was he not the arch-clever man because he had seen the Flood coming and taken measures, that is, built his ark? The ark, the great chest, the *arôn* in which creation survived a time of curses, was for Joseph an early example, a primal model of all wisdom—that is, of all wise precaution. And thus—by way of Ishtar's embitterment, her scorching, trampling beast, and her piles of foodstuffs as a safeguard against want—his thoughts, in requisite parallel to higher trains of thought, had arrived at the great Flood; and with tears in his eyes he also thought of the smaller one that had swept over him, for even though he had not been so foolish as to betray God and totally destroy his relationship with Him, he had certainly proved culpable in his lack of foresight.

Just as he had done in that first pit, one great year ago, he confessed his guilt and repented, and the hurt he felt was for his father, it was a hurt for Jacob's sake, and he was bitterly ashamed before him because he had managed once again to bring himself into the pit, here in the land to which he had been carried off. What a beautiful raising-up had resulted from his being carried off, and now it had been destroyed and laid low out of a lack of wisdom, so that the third motif of sending for others to follow appeared to have been delayed beyond all reckoning. Alone, Joseph was truly contrite of heart and begged the forgiveness of the "father" whose image had saved him from the worst at the last moment. But when dealing with his guard Kha'ma't, the scribe of the sideboard, who partly out of boredom, partly out of the delight he took in the downfall of someone who had once risen far above him in the household, often sat down to talk with him—when dealing with him, Joseph was very cocky and confident, refusing to allow even a hint of despondency to show. In fact, after only a few days of travel, simply by his way of presenting things, he was able, as we shall see, to convince his guard to remove his fetters and allow him to walk about freely—despite Kha'ma't's fear that doing so might be a gross violation of his duties.

"By the life of Pharaoh!" Kha'ma't said sitting down beside Joseph's mat in the cabin shed, "what has become of you, ex-steward! How you have sunk beneath all those of us whom you once climbed over so nimbly. It's hard to believe, and a man can only shake his head at the sight of you. There you lie like a Libyan prisoner of war or maybe one from the wretched land of Kush, elbows tied together, when only just recently you scrambled your way to head of the household, and have now been cast, so to speak, before the devourer, before the dog of Amente. May Atum, the lord of On, have mercy! How you've managed to end up on the ash heap—to use a figure of speech from wretched Syria that we managed to pick up from you. By Khons! we won't be picking fine things up from you from here on. Why, you've come so low that a dog wouldn't accept a piece of bread from you now. And why is that? Because of pure folly and lechery. Wanted to play the great man in a household like ours and couldn't even tame the gaping hunger of your lust. To think you made our holy mistress, of all people, the object of your gluttony and lechery, when here she's almost as sacred as Hathor herself. What enormous brazenness! I'll never forget you standing there before the master at the household court, and just hanging your head because you couldn't find one word of excuse, hadn't the least idea how to cleanse yourself of your guilt. And how could you, what with the loud and clear testimony against you of that garment you left behind crumpled in the mistress's hand, after first trying in vain to overpower and violate her—and evidently went about it very clumsily besides. What a sorry mess in every regard! Do you remember when you first came to me in the pantry to fetch the refreshment for the old couple from the upper floor? You turned arrogant right off when I warned you not to spill the beverage on the old ones, and you threw me into some confusion by pretending that sort of thing could never happen to you. Well, now you've spilled it over your own feet, till they're so sticky you can't move. Oh my! I knew that in the long run you wouldn't be able to hold the serving tray. And why not? Because you're a barbarian! Because you're nothing but a sand rabbit, as dissolute as every other wretched Zahi, lacking all moderation, ignorant of the wisdom of the land of human beings. You were incapable of taking our moral precepts to heart, for they teach that a man may indeed take his pleasures in this world, but not with married women, for that can cost him his life. But in your blind lust and lack of reason, your threw yourself on the mistress herself, and you can be very glad you weren't turned into a pallid corpse on the spot—though that's the only thing left to gladden your heart."

"Do me the favor, Kha'ma't, scholar of the house of books," Joseph said, "of not speaking about matters you do not understand. It is a terrible thing when a delicate and difficult subject that is far too subtle for the great masses becomes public knowledge, so that everyone whets his tongue on it and speaks purest bilge. It is almost intolerable and odious, less for the persons involved than for the matter itself, for it is far too good for that. Your addressing me in this way is foolish and crude and no testimony to Egypt's culture—not because until only yesterday I was your overseer before whom you bowed low, I leave that aside. But you need to consider that in the matter between myself and the mistress I must surely know what is what far better than you, who can have heard only the most superficial gossip. What right have you to lecture to me? It is moreover rather ridiculous of you to make a false comparison between the raw gaping hunger of my flesh and the moderation of Egypt—which has earned a very sultry reputation everywhere in the world; and when you spoke of 'violation' and did not hesitate to apply that word to me, you were surely thinking instead of the goat, toward whose

realm we are sailing and to whom the daughters of Egypt give themselves at his feast. Now I call that moderation and reason indeed! I
shall tell you something: It may well happen that in the future people will talk of me as one who preserved his purity among a people
whose rutting was like the rutting of the ass and the stallion—it may
well be. It could be that the maidens of this world will one day weep
for me on the eve of their wedding, offering me locks of their hair
and lifting up a lament in which they bewail my youth and tell the
story of a young lad who, though he stood firm against the feverish
importuning of a woman, lost both his reputation and life all the
same. Lying here and reflecting on it all, I can imagine such customs
arising on my behalf. On that basis, then, judge how petty your in-
vective directed against my fate and situation must sound! Why are
you so amazed, and also a bit delighted, at my misfortune? I was Peteprê's slave, purchased by him. Now, by his decree, I am Pharaoh's
slave. Why then, surely I've become more than I was—I have increased! Why this simpleton's laughter? All right, then, I am on my
way down at the moment. Is descent not without its own honor and
solemnity, and does this oxen boat not remind you of the barque of
Usir and his journey by night, when he goes down to bring light to
the subterranean sheepcote and to greet those who live in caves? It
seems strikingly that way to me, let me tell you. You may be right in
thinking that I am departing the land of the living. But who says that
my nose will not sniff the herb of life, that I will not rise up over the
rim of the world come the morrow, like a bridegroom emerging
from his chamber so radiant that those dull eyes of yours will sting?"

"Oh, ex-steward, I see that you are still the same, even in your
misery. The trouble is that no one knows what 'the same' means
with you. For it's much like those colorful balls that dancers throw
in the air and catch again in their hands, and yet no one can tell one
ball from the other because they form a flashing arc in the air. Where
you get your arrogance, despite your fate and situation, is known
only to the gods with whom you commune, so that a pious man can
just smile and shudder at the same time, leaving his skin as bumpy as
the skin of a goose. You have no qualms at babbling on about brides
who will someday dedicate their hair in your honor, the way they do
only for a god, and you compare this barge, which is the barge of
your shame, with Usir's barque of evening—in the Hidden One's

name, would that were your only comparison! But you weave the word 'striking' into it—it's a 'strikingly' good comparison between barge and barque—knowing full well that for a simple soul that has to arouse the suspicion that it really is the case and that you may actually be Rê when he is called Atum and boards the barque of night—that's where those goose bumps come from. But let me tell you, they also come not just from smiles and shudders, but from anger, too, they come from indignation and resentment, and above all from your arrogance, and the presumption with which you see yourself reflected in the highest and mistake yourself for it, as if you were the same thing, and make of yourself a flashing arc in the air to dazzle vexed and blinking eyes. Anybody could come along and do that, but a respectable person doesn't, he just worships and adores. I sat down here beside you partly out of sympathy, partly out of boredom, just to chat a while with you, but if you're trying to tell me that you are Atum-Rê and the great Usir in his barque, then I'll leave you to yourself, for your blasphemy makes my blood boil."

"Take it however you must, Kha'ma't of the house of books and the pantry. I did not beg you to sit down beside me, for I am just as happy alone, perhaps even a bit happier, and know how to entertain myself without you, as you yourself have noticed. But if you knew how to entertain yourself as I do, then you wouldn't have sat down beside me—but then you also would not look so askance at the diversions I allow myself, but that you begrudge me. Ostensibly it is out of piety that you begrudge me them, but in fact it is simply out of ill will, and your piety is but a fig leaf to clothe your ill will—begging your pardon for what to you must be an obscure comparison. That a man can entertain himself and not spend his life like some dumb beast is really the point after all, and the heights to which he can bring his diversion are what matter. You're not quite correct in saying that anybody could come along and do what I do, because not just anybody could—not because respectability prohibits him, but because he lacks all harmony with what is Most High and has been denied a tender affinity with it—his is not the gift of a flowery life in the heavens, just as we say someone doesn't possess the gift of flowery speech. He sees in the Most High something very different from himself, and rightly so, and can only serve Him with a tedious hallelujah. But if he hears of a more intimate kind of praise, he turns green with envy and approaches the altar of the Most High weeping sham tears: 'O Highest of the High, forgive this blasphemer!' What a silly way to behave that is, Kha'ma't of the pantry—and you shouldn't do it, either. Give me my noonday meal instead, for the hour has come and I am hungry."

"I suppose I must if the hour has come for it," the scribe replied. "I can't let you starve. I have to deliver you alive to Zawi-Rê."

Since Joseph was in fact bound by the elbows and had no use of his hands, Kha'ma't, as his guard, had to feed him—there was no other choice. He had to squat down and with his own hands put the bread into Joseph's mouth and set the cup of beer to his lips. Joseph made it his habit to add comments of his own at every meal.

"Yes, there you squat, gangly Kha'ma't, feeding me," he said. "It's very cordial of you, despite that abashed look on your face. You obviously don't like it. I drink to your health, though I cannot help thinking how you've come down in the world that you have to nurse me and feed me my pap. You never had to do it when I was your overseer and you bowed before me, did you? You're forced to serve me in ways you never did before, and it really does appear as if I have increased, and you have dwindled. Here we have the old question of who's greater and more important, the guard or the one guarded. Without doubt it is the latter. For is not a king also watched over by his servants, and is it not said of the just man: 'He has given His angels charge over you to keep you in all your ways'?"

"Let me tell you something," Kha'ma't replied at last, a few days later, "I am fed up with having to feed you your fill, of your gaping your mouth like a jackdaw chick in its nest, for you gape it wide for your infuriating words besides, which disgust me all the more. I'm simply going to remove your fetters so that you're not so helpless and I no longer have to play your servant and angel, which is not a scribe's task. Once we draw near to your final abode, I shall, as is only fitting, put them on again and deliver you in bonds to the warden there, to Mai-Sakhme, a captain of troops. You must swear to me, however, not to tell the warden that you were freed of them during the journey or that I have neglected my duty by showing leniency—otherwise I shall end up on the ash heap."

"On the contrary. I will tell him that you were a cruel guard who punished me daily with scorpions."

"Nonsense, that's going too far again! All you know how to do is tease people. I don't even know what's in that sealed letter I carry on my person and have no idea what the plan is for you. That's the worst part—no one ever knows what the plan is for you. But you shall tell the head of the prison that I have treated you with all due, though humane, severity and harshness."

"That I will do," Joseph said, and was given use of his arms until they had traveled deep into the Land of Uto the Serpent, had followed the seven-armed river into the nome of Djedet, and were approaching the island fortress of Zawi-Rê—where Kha'ma't bound them again with rope.

The Warden of the Prison

Joseph's house of punishment, his second pit, which he reached after a journey of some seventeen days and where, according to his own sense of the correspondence of things, he would have to spend three years before his head would be raised up again, was a place of dismal buildings whose irregular shapes occupied almost the entirety of the island that rose up out of Mendes' arm of the Nile: a collection of cubelike barracks, stalls, storehouses, and casemates, grouped around courts and passageways and towered over at one corner by a *migdal*-like citadel, where the prison warden, Mai-Sakhme (a "commissioned scribe of the victorious army," who served both as bailiff of the prison and commander of its garrison), was said to reside and in the middle of which there stood, just in front of the pylon, a temple to Wepwawet, whose pennants were the sole bright spot amidst all the bleakness—all of it surrounded by a circular wall made of unbaked bricks and roughly twenty ells high, with jagged projecting bastions and bayed defensive platforms. The landing and portal, behind whose breastworks guards were posted, were located off to one side somewhere, and, standing at the high prow of the oxen boat, Kha'ma't started waving his letter in the direction of the soldiers while still a good way off. As they sailed in under the portal, he called out that he was bringing a prisoner whom he had been charged to hand over personally to the captain and head of the prison.

Ne'arin (a military term adapted, for lack of a native one, from the Semitic), young mercenary lance-bearers, with heart-shaped leather protectors as aprons and shields at their backs, opened the gates for the transport and let it in—and Joseph felt as if once again, together with the Ishmaelites who had bought him, he were being admitted through the walled gate of the frontier fortress of Zel. He had been a boy then, intimidated by Egypt's wonders and abominations. Now he was as familiar with those wonders and abominations as any man, an Egyptian from head to toe—always keeping in mind, of course, that in regard to the follies of this land to which he had been carried off, he held deep private reservations, some of which had been passed on from boyhood to manhood. But now he was being led by a rope like Hapi, the living repetition of Ptah in his temple court in Menfe, as much a captive of the land of Egypt as that divine bull; for two of Peteprê's menials, holding the ends of the ropes bound to his arms, shoved him along before them, directly behind Kha'ma't, who was first interrogated under the portal by a subaltern bearing a staff—he had apparently given the order granting entry—who then directed him to a mace-bearing officer of higher rank now crossing the courtyard toward them. This man took his letter, promised he would try to bring it to the captain himself, and told them to wait.

So they waited in a small square courtyard, under the curious eyes of the soldiers and the meager shade provided by two or three wispy palm trees with green fringe only at the very top and reddish pellets of fruit scattered among the roots at their base. Jacob's son was deep in thought. He thought of what Peteprê had said about the jailer into whose hand he planned to deliver him: that he was a man not to be trifled with. He was understandably worried and anxious to meet the man, but he assumed the titular captain probably didn't even know him and had concluded he was no trifler simply because he was a warden of a prison—at best a probable, though not necessarily binding, conclusion. Joseph consoled himself in his worries with the notion that he would at any rate be dealing with a real human being, and in his eyes that somehow implied a sense of civil approachability and sociability whatever the circumstances—that is, in God's name, however suited by nature to be a prison warden, however hard the office may have made him, surely the man could be approached from some angle, opened up by some means or other, however trifling.

And Joseph knew his children of Egypt, which although a land of death that turned rigid and of entombed gods, was nonetheless, even against that gloomy background, filled with a childlike, harmless gaiety that was easy to live with. There was, moreover, that letter the bailiff was reading now, in which Potiphar informed him about the character of the man he had banned, describing him "in a fashion befitting him." Joseph was confident that the description would not be all too heinous, that its intent was not to arouse the warden's grimmest qualities against him. As is usually the case with children of blessing, however, this personal and universal confidence was not projected from within toward the world outside, but rather directed back at himself and at the happy secrets of his nature. Not that he had remained stuck at the boyish stage of blind expectation, when he had believed that people surely loved him more than they loved themselves. What he had continued to believe, however, was that he had been granted power to convince the world and its people to turn their best and brightest face toward him—which, as one can see, was a trust more in himself than in the world. To be sure, in his view these two, self and world, were bound up with one another and in some sense were one and the same, so that the world was not simply the other, turned in on itself, but in fact *his* world, which thus could be molded into something good and amiable. Circumstance was powerful; but Joseph believed in its pliability under the force of personality, in the determining force of individual destiny over the general determining power of circumstance. When, just as Gilgamesh had done, he called himself a man of grief and gladness, he did so in the sense that he knew that what determined his nature for gladness was susceptible to much grief; but on the other hand he did not believe in any grief black and opaque enough to prevent some ray of his innermost light, or the light of God within him, from shining through.

Such was the nature of Joseph's confidence—or, to call a spade a spade, his trust in God. And with it he now armed himself so that he might gaze into the face of Mai-Sakhme, his new taskmaster; and for that he and his keepers did not have long to wait, for they were now led through a low-ceilinged passageway to the foot of the citadel tower, to its defiant portal manned by other guards with embossed helmets. No sooner had they approached than its grating opened to reveal the captain in person.

He was accompanied by the high priest of Wepwawet, a gaunt baldheaded man, with whom he had been playing a board game. He himself was a stocky man, roughly forty years of age, wearing a jacket of mail—which he had probably donned just now for the occasion and onto which little metal images of lions were sewn like scales—and a brown wig, beneath which were round brown eyes, very thick black eyebrows, and a little mouth in a ruddy-brown face, darkened by a fresh growth of beard, just as his forearms were dark with hair. The expression on the face was one of peculiar calm, even sleepiness, but for all that of cleverness, and the captain's voice sounded calm too, even monotone, as he stepped out through the portal, still conversing with the prophet of that bellicose god, evidently about certain moves in their game, for the end of which the newcomers had had to wait. In one hand he held the fan-bearer's scroll, the seal now broken.

He stopped to unroll and scan it once more, and when he lifted his countenance again it seemed to Joseph to be more than just a man's countenance, to be in fact the image of gloomy circumstance through which the light of God shines, the very same countenance that life shows to the man of grief and gladness—for his black eyebrows were knitted menacingly, but at the same time a little smile played about the mouth. But he at once erased both smile and gloom from his face.

"You were in charge of the boat that brought you here from Wase?" he asked, looking about from under arched eyebrows and addressing the scribe Kha'ma't in an offhand, monotone voice.

Kha'ma't confirmed this, and Mai-Sakhme then looked at Joseph.

"You are the former steward of Peteprê, the great courtier?" he asked.

"I am he," Joseph answered in all simplicity.

And yet it was a rather strong answer, too. He could have replied with a "so you have said," or "my lord knows the truth," or even a more flowery "Ma'at speaks from your mouth." But "I am he," spoken plainly to be sure, but with an earnest smile was, first off, slightly impolite—for one did not speak in the first person to a superior, but said, "Your servant," or, in true abasement, "This servant here"; but worse still, the "I" itself played an alarming role, for in connection with the "he" it raised a vague suspicion implying more than merely the household position one was asked to confirm, so that question and answer did not seem quite congruent, as if the latter went beyond the former, as if there were a temptation to ask in return: "What are you?" or even "And who are *you*?" ... In short, "I am he" was an old, familiar phrase with popular appeal and far-reaching echoes, the formula for announcing oneself, a proclamation beloved from ancient times as part of narratives that told of men and gods, which carried with it all by itself the idea of a series of effects and consequences of the same nature, from downcast eyes to a thundered cry of "Fall on your knees!"

Mai-Sakhme's calm face, the face of a man who is not easily shocked, also displayed slight confusion and discomfort, turning the tip of his small, but nicely arched nose a shade of white.

"So, so, you are he, are you," he said; and if for the moment he didn't exactly know what he actually meant by this "he," a contributing factor to his forgetful reverie may have been that the man standing before him was the handsomest twenty-seven-year-old in the Two Lands. Beauty's stamp is impressive; it unfailingly awakens a special sort of mild apprehension in even the calmest soul quite unaccustomed to apprehension and is apt to lend a dreamy hue to the meaning of an "I am he" spoken with an earnest smile.

"You appear to be a frivolous sort of bird," the captain went on, "so foolish and rash that it's fallen out of its nest. You were living up there in Pharaoh's city, a very interesting place, and could have led a life like a never-ending feast, but for no earthly reason whatever you've managed to get yourself sent down here into utter boredom. For it is utter boredom that reigns here," he said and again knitted his eyebrows menacingly for a moment, even while, as if they belonged together, that half smile played about his lips. "Didn't you know," he went on, "that one should not cast one's eyes after women in the house of a stranger? Have you not read the maxims in the Book of the Dead, or the precepts and warnings of holy Imhotep?"

"I am familiar with them," Joseph replied, "for I have read them aloud and to myself countless times."

But the captain, although he had asked for an answer, paid no attention.

"What a man he was," he said, turning to the priest at his side, "a good companion through life, Imhotep the Wise! Physician, architect, priest, and scribe—he was all those, Tut-ankh-djehuti, the living image of Thoth. I revere the man, I must say, and if I were a man to be shocked—though I am not, perhaps I should say unfortunately not, inclined to that, for I'm much too calm—I would presumably fall back in awe before such an amassed wealth of knowledge. He has been dead now for years beyond counting, Imhotep the Divine has—men of his sort existed only in earliest times, in the morning of the Two Lands. His sovereign was the ancient king Djoser, whose eternal abode he most assuredly built, a stepped pyramid near Menfe, six stories high, a good hundred and twenty ells. But the limestone is poor; that taken by our convicts from the quarry across the way is not as poor—the master simply had nothing better at hand. Architecture, however, was but a minor part of his wisdom and art, for he knew all locks and keys to the temple of Thoth. He was a skilled healer besides and an adept of nature, expert in all things solid and liquid, whose soothing hand gave rest and repose to all who tossed and turned. For he himself must have been very calm and not easy to shock. Moreover he was a reed in god's hand, a writer of wisdom—uniting the two, not a physician today and a scribe tomorrow, but each in the other and both at once, something to be emphasized, for in my opinion it is a virtue of exceeding worth. Healing and writing lend their light one to the other, and each is the better for walking hand in hand. A physician inspired by written wisdom knows better how to comfort those who toss and turn; a scribe, however, who understands the body's pleasures and pains, its fluids and functions, toxins and talents, will have advantage over him who knows nothing of them. Imhotep the Wise was such a physician and such a scribe. A divine man, to whom incense should be burned. I believe once he is dead a while longer, that will happen. To be sure, he lived in Menfe, a very stimulating city."

"You need not blush before him, Captain," replied the high priest, to whom he had addressed all this. "For without the least detriment to your military duties, you too study the art of healing, benefiting those who toss and turn, and also write very engagingly, in terms both of form and content, while calmly uniting all these fields in one."

"Calm alone does not suffice," Mai-Sakhme rejoined, and the composure in his face with its round, clever eyes took on a certain pensiveness. "Perhaps a shocking bolt of lightning would do me good. But where might that bolt come from here? And you fellows?" he suddenly said, arching his eyebrows and shaking his head in the direction of Peteprê's two slaves, who were still holding tight to the ends of Joseph's ropes.

"What are you doing there? Do you intend to plow a field with him or play horsy like little boys? I suppose your steward can do hard labor here with his limbs bound like an ox for the slaughter? Untie him, you idiots! Pharaoh is served here by hard work, in the quarry or new construction, not by being left lying about bound and helpless. What stupidity! These people," he said, turning again to explain to the god's attendant, "have the notion that prison is a place where men lie in fetters. They take everything literally, for that is how they are, clinging to each phrase like children. If it is said that a man is to be put in prison where the king's prisoners lie, they firmly believe he's actually going to be dumped into a hole filled with starving rats and rattling chains, to lie there robbing Rê of his days. I have observed that such a confusion of speech and reality is a primary characteristic of ignorance and lowest rank. I've often found it among the rubber-eaters of wretched Kush, but also among peasants in our own fields, yet not so much in cities. There is undeniably a certain poetry in the literalness of such speech, the poetry of simplicity and fairy tales. There are, as I see it, two kinds of poetry: one born of the simplicity of the masses and one born of the spirit of the written word. The latter is indubitably the loftier, but in my opinion it cannot exist except in friendly association with the former and requires its fertile ground, just as all the beauty of a higher life, even the splendor of Pharaoh himself, needs the topsoil of a vast, indigent population in order to flower above it and set the world in amazement."

"As a scholar of the house of books," Kha'ma't, the scribe of the sideboard, remarked, after first hurrying over to free Joseph's elbows himself, "I do not share at all in that confusion of speech and reality, and it was only for the sake of momentary propriety that I thought the prisoner should be delivered to you bound, Captain. He himself might confirm for me that I spared him the rope for the greater part of the journey."

"That was no more than reasonable," Mai-Sakhme replied, "especially since one must discriminate among crimes, since murder, thievery, the moving of boundary stones, evasion of taxes or embezzlement by their collector are to be regarded with different eyes than mistakes that involve a woman and therefore demand to be treated with discretion."

He unrolled the letter halfway again and glanced at it.

"What we have here," he said, "is, as I see, another tale involving a female, and I would not be an officer and student of the Royal Stables were I to lump together such an affair with the dishonest deeds of the rabble. Literal-mindedness and an inability to discriminate between speech and reality are, to be sure, tokens of childish ignorance, but now and then such a confusion is also unavoidable among the better classes; for although it is written that one should not cast one's eyes after a woman in the house of a stranger, for it is dangerous to do so, men do it nonetheless, because wisdom is one thing and life another; and it is precisely the danger involved that adds an element of honor to the mix. And indeed it takes two for any love affair, which always leaves the question of guilt rather opaque, and although its resolution may appear quite clear to the outside world—because one party, the man of course, takes the entire guilt upon himself—it may also be advisable yet again to discriminate in private between speech and reality. When I hear of a woman's being seduced by a man, I chuckle to myself, for I find it rather droll, and think: 'Oh great Triad! One knows all too well who has been charged with the art of seduction since the days of the god—and most assuredly 'twas not us stupid men.' Do you know 'The Tale of the Two Brothers'?" he asked Joseph directly, gazing up at him with round brown eyes, for he was considerably shorter, as well as stouter. His thick brown eyebrows were also raised as high as he could raise them, as if that might help even things out.

"I know it well, my captain," Joseph replied. "Not only did I have to read it aloud to my master and Pharaoh's friend—I had to copy it out for him in finest calligraphy, with black and red ink."

"And it will be copied many times yet," the commandant said. "It's an excellent piece of fiction and a model not merely in its style, which is convincing, despite the fact that its events, when calmly considered, are unbelievable—as for instance the episode where the queen is impregnated by a splinter of persea wood that flies into her mouth, which is far too great a contradiction to medical experience to be accepted just at face value. Nevertheless it is a model tale and like a mold into which life is poured, so that, when the wife of Anup presses against the lad Bata because she has found him strong and says to him: 'Come, let us take delight in one another for a while. I shall also make two festal garments for you,' Bata then calls out to his brother, 'Woe is me, she has perverted everything!' and before his eyes uses the leaf of a bulrush to cut off his manhood, giving it to the fish to eat—that is very moving. Later the alleged episodes degenerate into the incredible, but all the same it is uplifting when Bata transforms himself into Hapi the bull and says: 'I shall be a marvel of a Hapi and all the land will exult over me,' and then reveals himself and says: 'I am Bata! Behold, I still live and am god's holy bull.' These are, to be sure, bizarre inventions; but into what strange molds shaped by formative imagination does not supple life sometimes cast itself."

He fell silent for a while, and his calm face, the little mouth slightly agape, stared intently into space. Then he read a little more of the letter.

"You can imagine, good father," he said raising his head to look at the shiny-headed priest, "that an occurrence such as this represents a certain stimulating change for me amidst the monotony of this stolid place, where a man who is already calm by nature runs the risk of losing himself in sleep. It is hardly likely to lessen the risk that what are usually brought before me—whether already under sentence or for temporary detention while the scales of justice hang in the balance and a trial is still pending—are all sorts of grave-robbers, highwaymen, and cutpurses. By comparison, a case where the offense belongs to the domain of love is significantly, stimulatingly different. There's surely no doubt of that, and as far as I know foreign nations of even the most divergent mentality likewise agree that this domain is among the most stimulating, subtle, and mysterious segments of human life. Who has not had his own surprising, thought-provoking experiences in the domain of Hathor? Have I ever told you about my first love, who at the same time was also my second?"

"Never, Captain," the priest said. "The first and yet the second as well? I cannot imagine how such a thing can be."

"Or the second was still the first," the commandant responded. "However you like. Still or once again or forever—who can be certain of the right word for it? But that doesn't really matter."

And there before Joseph and his guards, before the priest of

Wepwawet and a number of soldiers who had been standing nearby and now stepped closer, and with a relaxed, indeed sleepy air—arms crossed, the scroll thrust into one armpit, head tilted to one side, heavy brows raised slightly above the brown orbs of his eyes, rounded lips moving at a measured, earnest pace—Mai-Sakhme began to tell his tale in the steadiest of voices:

"I was twelve years old and a pupil in the house of instruction within the scribal school of the Royal Stables. I was rather short and plump, just as I am today, for such is the stature and state given my life both before and after death. But my heart and mind were impressionable. One day I noticed a girl bringing her brother, a fellow student of mine, his midday bread and beer, for his mother was ill. His name was Imesib, son of Amenmose, a civil servant. He called his sister who brought him his rations—three small loaves of bread and two jugs of beer—Beti, from which I surmised that her name was Nekhbet, which Imesib, in response to my question, confirmed. For the name interested me because she interested me, and I could not take my eyes from her as long as she was still there: not from her braids, her small eyes, or the bow of her mouth, and especially not from her arms, left bare by her dress and so beautiful in their slender fullness—they made the most profound impression on me. But all that day I did not know how great an impression Beti had left on me, and discovered it only that night as I lay in the dormitory with my comrades, my clothes and sandals beside me and my sack of writing tools and books beneath my head as a pillow, just as regulations prescribed. For by pressing against them, we would then not forget our books in our dreams either. But I forgot them nonetheless, and all on their own my dreams knew to free themselves from this pressure. For in true and vivid detail I dreamed that I was betrothed to Nekhbet, daughter of Amenmose; our fathers and mothers had spoken with one another, and she was soon to be my sister-bride and wife, so that her arm would be lying on mine. I rejoiced beyond measure, as I had never rejoiced in all my life. My bowels rose up within me for joy at this arrangement, which was then sealed when our parents ordered us to put our noses close together, and how delightful that was. But this dream had about it something so lifelike and natural that in its way it was no less than real to me and, remarkably, was still able to conceal its unreality from me after night had passed, after I had awakened and washed. This had never happened to me before, nor has it since, that a dream has held me under its vivid sway after awakening, so that I continued to believe in it in a waking state. For several hours that morning I was fondly and firmly convinced that I was betrothed to this girl Beti, and only slowly, as I sat in the scriptorium and the teacher roused me with blows to my back, did that bliss depart from my bowels. Halfway to total disenchantment, the idea came to me that, although the agreement and our almost touching noses had indeed been a dream, nothing stood in the way of their being realized immediately, that I needed only to approach my parents and ask them to come to an agreement with Beti's parents on our behalf; thus for a while my one thought was that, in the wake of such a dream, this was a perfectly natural demand that could astonish no one. Only later, quite gradually and much to my chilled disappointment, did I also disabuse myself of the notion that the fulfillment of what had truly seemed so real to me was a vain hope, a total impossibility given the state of things. For I was a mere schoolboy, daily thrashed like papyrus, only at the start of my career as a scribe and officer, much too short and fat of constitution, both in this life and the next; and as my blissful dream melted away, my betrothal to Nechbet—who was probably three years older than I, and could betroth herself at any time to a man far superior to me in rank and dignity—proved to be a complete absurdity."

"And so I abandoned an idea," the warden calmly continued his story, "that never would have come to me had it not come as a dream's lovely reality, and continued my schooling in the stable's house of instruction, repeatedly admonished by blows to my backside. Twenty years later, long after I had advanced to the rank of commissioned scribe of our victorious army, I was sent with three companions on a journey to Syria, to the wretched land of Her, to levy and inspect a tribute of horses, which were to be sent by cargo ship to Pharaoh's stables. Departing the harbor at Khazati, I arrived first in the defeated city of Sekmem and then a city that, if I recall correctly, is named Per-Shean, where there was a posting of one of our garrisons, whose commanding office threw a party for both locals and the scribes in charge of remount horses, an evening affair with wine and wreaths held in his home of many beautiful doors. There were Egyptians there, along with the city nobility, both men and women. And there I saw a girl, who was a relative of this Egyptian house on the wife's side, she and the girl's mother being sisters, and who had come to visit, accompanied by male and female servants, from faraway Upper Egypt, where her parents lived in the vicinity of the first cataract. For her father was a very rich trader from Suenêt, who filled the markets of Egypt with the wares of wretched Kasi—ivory, leopard skins, and ebony. And when I beheld this girl, the ivory merchant's daughter, in all her youth, what had happened to me so many years before in the boys' house of instruction happened to me a second time: I could not take my eyes from her because of the extraordinary impression she made on my heart, and the bliss I had tasted in that long-faded dream of betrothal returned in all its amazing familiarity, so that at the sight of her my bowels rose up for joy in exactly the same way. But I shied away from her, although a soldier should never be shy, and for quite a while I was even too shy to inquire about her, to learn her name and who she was.

"But when I did, I discovered that she was the daughter of Nechbet, the daughter of Amenmose, who, only a very short time after I had seen her and been betrothed to her in my dream, had become the wife of the ivory merchant from Suenêt. The girl Nofrurê, however—for that was her name—bore no resemblance to her mother, either in her features or in the color of her braids and skin, indeed she was of a decidedly darker complexion. At most her charming figure was similar to Nekhbet's; but how many are the young ladies who share such a form. Nonetheless the sight of her instantly stirred within me the same profound emotions I had rehearsed that first time, but had not known since, so that one might very well say that I had loved her already in her mother, just as I loved her mother again in her. I even consider it possible and more or less expect that when, after another twenty years, I chance to meet Nofrurê's daughter, without knowing who she is, my heart will unhesitatingly be hers once again, just as it had been her mother's and grandmother's, and it will be one and the same love for all eternity."

"That is a truly remarkable instance of the heart's affection," the god's attendant said, considerately ignoring, as it were, how peculiar it was for the captain to have favored them with his tale here and now, even if it was in that calm monotone of his. "But if the daughter of the ivory merchant were ever to have a daughter herself, how regrettable if she were not your child as well, for even if your boyhood dream upon your pillow of books could not become reality, with the return of Nekhbet or, better, the return of your affection for her, that reality might well come into its own."

"Not really," Mai-Sakhme replied, shaking his head. "Such a wealthy and beautiful girl and a stoutly constituted scribe for remount horses, what sense does that make? She has since married the baron of a nome or a man who stands at Pharaoh's feet, an overseer of the treasury with a collar of golden tribute around his neck—but we'll leave that aside. Do not forget, either, that one stands in a kind of paternal relationship with a girl whose mother one has once loved, so that certain inner scruples are arrayed against any marital bond. Besides, such thoughts as those you've suggested would be pushed into the background by what you have called the remarkable nature of the incident. Consideration of how remarkable it was prevented me from any decision that would have resulted in a child of mine that was also the grandchild of my first love. And would that have even been desirable? It would have deprived me of the expectation in which I now live—that one day, without ever knowing it, I shall meet Nofrurê's daughter, Nekhbet's granddaughter, and that she too will make that same wonderful impression on me. Thus I may be left with something to hope for in my old age, whereas in the other case this sequence of repeated experiences of the heart's affection would perhaps be broken off prematurely."

"That may be," the god's guardian hesitantly agreed. "But the least you could do would be to bring this story of mother and daughter or, rather, the story of your encounter with them to paper, and by the reed give it a charming form to enrich our already gratifying literature. The third appearance of that figure and your love for her could, as I see it, be added as a free invention and presented as if it had likewise already happened."

"Sketches," the captain replied placidly, "have been made, and my ability to provide such a flowing account of the incident can be explained by the fact that it has been preceded by preliminary drafts. The only difficulty I am having is that by including Beti's granddaughter, I must shift the setting of my story to the future and thereby make an old man of myself, which is an effort before which I recoil, although as a soldier one should not recoil before any task. Primarily, however, I worry whether I am not too calm to incorporate within my story certain exciting effects, such as those that are found, for example, in that model story of the two brothers. The story is far too dear to me, however, for me to chance the reproach of bungling it. But at the moment," he said, breaking off his self-censure, "the issue is one of delivering and receiving. How many beasts of burden," he asked, turning to Joseph as superciliously as he could manage, "does it take, in your estimation, to bring provisions to five hundred hewers and draggers of stone in a quarry, including the officers and guards over them?"

"Twelve oxen and fifty asses," Joseph replied, "might be a good number for the task."

"It might well be. And how many men would you order to man the rope for dragging a block four ells long by two ells wide and one ell high, five miles to the river?"

"Including those needed to prepare the way and bear water to moisten the path under the sledges and to carry the roller that must be inserted again and again," Joseph responded, "I would employ a good hundred men."

"Why so many?"

"It is a cumbersome slab," Joseph replied, "and if one chooses not to span oxen to the task, but men, because they are cheaper, one should employ a sufficient number of them so that along the way one gang of draggers can replace another at the ropes, and thereby avoid deaths resulting from a failure to sweat, or simply keep some from overexerting their innards and having the wind knocked out of them, leaving you with exhausted men tossing and turning in agony."

"It is better to avoid that to be sure. But you forget that we have not just a choice between oxen and men, but that we also have at our disposal here vast numbers of barbarians who dwell in the red sand of the desert, from Libya, Punt, and Syria."

"He who has been given into your hand," Joseph replied in a measured voice, "is of a similar origin, for he is a child of a king of flocks in Upper Retenu, which is called Canaan, and is here in the land of Egypt only because he was stolen away."

"Why do you tell me this? It is here in the letter. And why do you call yourself a child, instead of saying a son? It sounds to me like a man coddling or wooing himself, which is not fitting for a man who has been sentenced, even if his offense is not one that touches his honor but is of a more delicate nature. You appear to be afraid that because you are originally from the wretched land of Zahi, I will yoke you to the heaviest slabs of stone, until your sweat fails and you die a dry death. That is an attempt, as impertinent as it is clumsy, to think my thoughts. I would be a poor prison warden if I did not place and make use of each according to his talents and experiences. Your answers do indeed reveal that you were once in charge of the house of a great man and understand something about industry. Nor is it exactly contrary to my own wishes that you would do your best to avoid overtaxing men, even when they are not the children— I mean, the sons—of Hapi and the Black Earth, for that gives evidence of economic thinking. I shall employ you as the overseer of a gang of convicts in the quarry or put you to work inside, in the office; for it is certain that you are faster than others at reckoning how many bushels of spelt will fit into a storeroom of such and such dimensions, or the amount of grain needed to brew a certain amount of beer or bake a given number of loaves of bread, so that one can then know the value of both in trade, and so on. I would truly welcome," he added by way of explanation to the opener of Wepwawet's mouth, "some relief in those areas, so that I would not have to concern myself with everything and could have more leisure for my attempts to put to paper in a gratifying and perhaps even exciting fashion 'The Adventure of Three Loves That Are One and the Same.'"

"You people of Wase," he said to Joseph's escorts, "can now be on your way again, sailing against the current, but with a north wind. But do take your rope with you, along with my respects to your master and Pharaoh's friend. Memi," he ordered in conclusion, addressing the mace-bearer who had led the visitors here, "show this royal slave who is to do hard labor as an administrative clerk a cell to himself and give him an outer garment and a staff for his hand in token of his office as an overseer. Though he once stood very high, he has let himself be brought down here to us and will have to accommodate himself to the iron regimen of Zawi-Rê. But what he has brought with him from his high estate we shall ruthlessly exploit, just as we know to exploit the bodies and energies of those of low standing. For such things no longer belong to him, but to Pharaoh. Give him something to eat. Till the next time, good father," he said, taking leave of the god's attendant and turning back toward his tower.

And this was Joseph's first meeting with Mai-Sakhme, the warden of the prison.

Of Goodness and Cleverness

And so, like Joseph, you are now reassured as to the particular qualities of the jailer into whose hand his master had delivered him. His even temperament made him an especially engaging man, and the foregoing episode of this narrative, in its attempt to illuminate all things, quite intentionally was in no hurry to shift the spotlight away from his eternally stout figure, but instead let it rest on him long enough for you to have time to imprint his essential humanity—previously as good as unknown to you—on your minds; for a not insignificant supporting role—likewise practically unknown—had been reserved for him in the story unfolding here anew with the same accuracy of detail in which it came to pass in reality. In fact, after those few years in which Mai-Sakhme served over Joseph as his taskmaster, he would stand at his side for a far longer period, sharing in the solemn management of certain grand and cheering events, for a worthy and precise description of which may the muse lend us strength.

This simply by way of introduction. But since tradition uses the same formula for the prison warden that it applies to Potiphar in saying that he "had no concern for anything," until very soon whatever happened in that hole had to happen through Joseph, some explanation is in order, for the phrase carries a very different sense from what it did in the case of that courtier of the sun and consecrated tower of flesh, who did not concern himself with anything because in his titular inauthenticity he stood outside of humanity and in his perpetually closed existence was a stranger to all that was real, his sole concern being pure formality. In contrast Mai-Sakhme was a thoroughly responsible man, who took a warm, if quite unruffled concern in a great many things, and especially in people. For he was a very dedicated physician, who arose early every day in order to examine what had been passed from the rectums of the ailing soldiers and convicts quartered in the infirmary shed, and his office, a well-secured room in the citadel tower of Zawi-Rê, was a regular laboratory where, surrounded by his apparatus—a herbarium, utensils for grinding and grating, vials and crucibles, goatskins, distilling flasks, and evaporation basins—the captain would get that same sleepy but clever look in his eyes with which he had told his story of the three loves on the day of Joseph's reception and then proceed to prepare his agent for flushing the stomach, his decoctions, pills, and poultices for combatting retention of urine, tumors on the neck, stiffening of the spine, and burning in the heart, for some of which remedies he would consult the work *For the Benefit of Man* or other such tried and true manuals; but where he also would read and think of more general, overarching issues beyond individual cases, such as whether the number of paired blood vessels that ran from the heart to the various members of the human body and were so very susceptible to hardening, occlusions, and inflammations often resistant to any medicine, were really only twenty-two in number, or if in fact, as he was more and more inclined to believe, they came to a total of forty-six, or would ponder whether worms in the body, which he had tried to kill with several different electuaries, were the cause of certain illnesses or should more correctly be understood as their consequence, inasmuch as the blockage of one or several blood vessels led to tumorous growths, which, because they permitted no outlet for drainage would then putrefy and, as could only be expected, transform themselves into worms.

It was a good thing that the captain devoted himself to these matters, for although officially they were less his concern as a soldier and more the business of his opponent at board games, the priest of Wepwawet, the latter's knowledge in regard to the nature of the body did not go much beyond the inspection of sacrificial animals slaughtered to oblige his god, and his therapeutic methods were always far too one-sidedly oriented toward the world of magic and charms—a necessary element, to be sure, inasmuch as a malady affecting an organ, be it spleen or spine, could unarguably be attributed to whether its tutelary divinity had departed from that body part, willingly or otherwise, leaving the field clear for some hostile demon, which then went about its destructive work and had to be forced to depart by the appropriate exorcism. The god's attendant did, however, have a cobra he kept in a basket, and by applying pressure to its neck he could turn it into a magic wand, a feat that persuaded Mai-Sakhme to borrow the animal from him on occasion.

But on the whole it was the warden's conviction, based on experience, that magic employed by itself and for its own ends rarely accomplished much, and instead required the material support of profane knowledge and remedies, so that it might enter and penetrate them and thereby achieve its effect. For instance, when it came to the excess of fleas that afflicted everyone at Zawi-Rê, the charms of the god's guardian had never been of much help, or the relief so temporary that it might have been merely an illusion; and only after Mai-Sakhme—though, to be sure, with the aid of charms—had ordered natron water sprinkled and a mixture of charcoal and a pulverized form of the plant *bebet* strewn about, did the plague abate. He was likewise the one who had had the lids on food supplies in the storerooms smeared with cat fat—to ward off the mice, which were almost as numerous as the fleas. Upon calm reflection, he had concluded that the mice would think they smelled the cats themselves and out of fear would leave the supplies alone, which proved true.

The fortress's infirmary shed always had plenty of injured and sick patients, for labor in the quarry five miles inland from the river was truly hard labor, as Joseph soon learned, since on numerous occasions he had to spend several weeks out there supervising a detachment of soldiers and convicts as they hacked, cleaved, hewed, and dragged. The soldiers had things no better than the others, and those members of the garrison of Zawi-Rê, both native Egyptians and foreigners, not on guard duty were put to the same use as the convicts, were urged on with the same blows of the rod. At best, injuries or instances of exhaustion or failure to sweat were more readily recognized in their case, orders for them to return to the fortress hospital given somewhat sooner than for men under sentence, who had to keep on giving their utmost—that is, until they collapsed, and then only the third time, for on principle a first or second collapse was held to be a sham.

In this regard, by the way, there was some easing of conditions under Joseph's supervision—at first only in his own work gang. Later, however, when, as recorded, it had come to pass that the warden committed into his hand all the prisoners that were in the prison, and he would come out to the quarry, now as a kind of chief inspector and immediate deputy of the commandant, conditions were eased in general. Joseph remembered Jacob, his distant father, for whom he was dead, and how he had always disapproved of the Egyptian house of bondage, and so he introduced the rule that a man be pulled out and brought back to the island at the second collapse, for the first was still held to be a sham—that is, unless death immediately followed.

And so the infirmary shed was never empty of those who tossed and turned—whether it was a man who had broken a bone or could "no longer look down at his own belly," or whose body was covered with swollen stings from flies and gnats that were like leprous sores, or whose stomach, if one placed one's fingers on it, shifted back and forth like oil in a goatskin, or whose eyes were inflamed and festering from the dust of the quarry; and the captain took charge of all these cases, never shrinking from any of them, and knew some remedy for each—that is, if it was not death itself with which he had to contend. He splinted broken bones with planks and tried to alleviate the problem of a man's being unable to see his own belly with mild mushy poultices; he treated those leprous stings with goose fat mixed with a soothing vegetable powder, ordered the patient with that nasty shifting around of the stomach to chew castor beans washed down with beer, and for the great many cases of inflamed eyes he had a fine salve from Byblos. But some magic was always involved as well, lending support to medicine and playing its role in vexing whatever demon had sneaked its way in; but the magic came not so much in the form of spoken charms or the patient's being touched with the stiffened cobra, as in the power that emanated from Mai-Sakhme personally, a calm that flowed from him and spread through the patient, soothing him until he no longer felt afraid of his illness, which could only be harmful, and instead stopped tossing and turning and automatically adopted the captain's own facial expression—the rounded lips slightly open, the eyebrows raised in knowing composure. His patients would lie there like that and, armed with his calm, gaze ahead to recuperation or to death— for Mai-Sakhme's influence taught them not to fear the latter either; and even when a man's face had taken on the pallor of a corpse, he would lie with hands and mouth at rest, still imitating the composed expression of his physician, and from under wise raised brows gaze steadily ahead to the life after life.

And so it happened that Joseph would enter this infirmary, pervaded by calm and a lack of fear, as the warden's right-hand man, sometimes even lending him a hand. For Mai-Sakhme soon called him back from oversight at the quarry to work inside the fortress; and the statement that he committed all the prisoners that were in the prison into Joseph's hand and that whatever was done there Joseph was the doer of it, should be taken to mean that Potiphar's former steward very quickly, within six months after being sent there, rose—as if as a matter of course and without any special appointment—to the post of chief administrator and supervisor of provisions for the entire fortress, so that, much to the relief of those who had previously dealt with such matters, there passed through his hands all the correspondence and accounts (of which, as everywhere in Egypt, there was an endless stream) dealing with purchases of grain, oil, barley, and cattle and their distribution among the guards and convicts, with the operations of Zawi-Rê's brewery and bakery, even with the income and expenditures of Wepwawet's temple, as well as with the delivery of hewn stone and so forth. He alone was required to render an account of these things to the fortress's commandant, to the calm man with whom his relationship had been friendly from the start and over time came to be very cordial.

For in all this Mai-Sakhme found confirmed what Joseph had said to him at that first interrogation by announcing himself in that primal and dramatic phrase that for once had ruffled the commandant's composure and in some very broad and vague way had so alarmed him that even he was aware of the tip of his nose turning a shade of white; and the captain was in some sense grateful to the man who had helped to shock him, for at its most fundamental level his composure demanded such a shock, which in his clever modesty he felt he had never given its due and so had stood in wait for it, just as he awaited the reappearance of the girl Nekhbet in her granddaughter and being stirred by her yet a third time. His sense of the truth embedded in the words with which Joseph had announced himself was equally broad and vague, nor would he have been able to say what meaning he ought to impute to the "he" in that always shocking phrase "I am he"—indeed it never even dawned on him that he would not have known what to say, for he was not the sort of man who would have thought it necessary or desirable to account for it. That is the difference between his obligations and our own. Mai-Sakhme, living in that earlier, if also already much later, day, was totally exempted from rendering such an account and, with all due calmness, if also a fair amount of shock, could confine himself to surmises and faith. Our ancient document puts it this way: that the Lord showed Joseph steadfast love *and* gave him favor in the sight of the keeper of the prison. That "and" might be read to imply that the steadfast love God showed to Rachel's son consisted in his taskmaster's finding favor in his heart for him. That, however, would somewhat misrepresent the relationship between the steadfast love and the favor. It was not that God showed Joseph His steadfast love by causing the captain to feel favorable toward him, but that instead the sympathy and trust—in a word, the faith—that Joseph's appearance and conduct instilled in him came from the unerring instinct a good man has for divine steadfast love, which is to say, for the divine power that was with this prisoner—just as it is the way, indeed the mark, of every good man that he is clever enough to perceive the divine with reverence, a state of affairs that closely links goodness and cleverness, and in fact makes them appear to be one and the same.

What, then, did Mai-Sakhme take Joseph for? For something right and true, for the right and long-awaited one, the bringer of a new age, though for now only in the modest sense of the man who had been banished for very interesting reasons to this boring place—where the captain had been ordered to serve for a such a long time now, and for who knew how much longer—and had brought with him a certain interruption in its rampant monotony. If the commandant of Zawi-Rê was so fierce in his condemnation of the confusion of speech and reality, rejecting it as base ignorance, that may well have come from his laboring so mightily under the same confusion and, if he did not pay close attention, from poor skill at distinguishing between metaphor and actuality. Put another way: even the gentlest traces, memories, and hints in the traits of some phenomenon were sufficient for him to see in it the fullness and reality of what was merely hinted at—and in Joseph's case that was the figure of the long-expected bringer of salvation, who comes to put an end to all that is old and boring and, amid the jubilation of all mankind, to establish a new epoch. About such a figure, of which Joseph showed some traces, there hovers the nimbus of the divine—and that is just one more notion that carries with it the temptation to confuse the metaphorical with the actual, the particular with something from which all particularity has been removed. And is that such a misleading temptation? Where the divine is, there God is—there, as Mai-Sakhme would have said (if he had said anything at all and not simply let surmises and faith prevail), is *a* god, though at most wrapped in a disguise that needs to be respected outwardly and, what's more, in one's mind, even when that disguise, given its naturally beautiful and handsome appearance, is inadequate or, so to speak, not quite successful. Mai-Sakhme would not have been a child of the Black Earth had he not known that there are images of god, breathing divine images, that are to be seen as fundamentally different from those without life or breath and are to be worshiped as images of god—like Hapi, the bull of Menfe, and like Pharaoh himself in the horizon of his palace. That he was familiar with this fact helped more than a little in forming the surmises he cherished in regard to Joseph's nature and appearance—and of course we know that Joseph himself was not exactly anxious to curb such surmises but, on the contrary, loved to take people aback.

Joseph's appearance proved a true blessing for the fortress's office and archives; for however unjust the slander that the captain had no concern for anything, office organization—so important in the eyes of his superiors in Thebes—had in fact, as he well knew, suffered because of his calm private passion for medicine and literature, imperiling his official reputation and resulting on occasion in polite, if distressingly oblique, letters of rebuke from the capital. And in precisely this area Joseph proved himself to be Mai-Sakhme's long-awaited bringer of change, the man of the "I am he." It was he who brought order to the records, who taught Mai-Sakhme's clerks—great devotees of bowling and the game of mora—that their commandant's loftier distraction was no reason for them to allow their work to be buried under dust, but on the contrary, an incentive for them to be all the more diligent; and he saw to it that the ledgers and reports sent off to the capital would gladly be read by higher-ups there. In his hand an overseer's staff was like a cobra stiffened into a magic wand; for merely by tapping it against a storeroom's conical bin, he could make the impromptu announcement "This will hold forty sacks of emmer"; and when the issue was how many bricks were needed for building a ramp, he only had to touch his brow with the staff in order to declare "Fifty thousand bricks will be needed." In the former instance, he was right, in the latter not exactly. But since the prediction on that first occasion had proved so startlingly true, it cast its glow over the imprecision of the second, so that it seemed to people as if it were right as well.

In short, in saying "I am he," Joseph had not lied to the captain—nor did it prove prejudicial either to the fortress's business or bookkeeping, despite the fact that, to cap it all off, Mai-Sakhme often requested Joseph's presence in the tower for literary and apothecarial pursuits. For he wanted to have him around and not only enjoyed discussing with Joseph such questions as the number of blood vessels or whether worms were the cause or consequence of illness, but also put him to work making a deluxe copy on fine papyrus in black and red ink of "The Tale of the Two Brothers," just as Joseph had once done for his former master, a task for which the warden found him particularly suitable not only because of his neat hand, but also because of his personality and fate. For Mai-Sakhme was particularly interested in this newcomer as a student of love, a field for which—inasmuch as it is the primary playground for all gratifying literature—the commandant felt a warm and deep, if also unruffled, sympathy. And the amount of time Jacob's son had to spare from administrative chores, though never to their detriment, in order to satisfy Mai-Sakhme's private interests is evident in his long hours of conference with the warden on how best to approach the story of his three-in-one love affair, how to put to paper in some gratifying and if possible exciting, if not to say shocking, manner a tale that was partly one of expectation—whereby the chief difficulty, and a topic of much discussion, lay in the fact that in order to anticipate and incorporate that expectation it would have to be told in the spirit of an old man of at least sixty years, which in turn threatened to diminish the desired element of excitement, already endangered by his own natural calm.

In addition, Joseph's own adventure, which had landed him in prison, his tale of the chamberlain's wife, was an object of Mai-Sakhme's literary sympathies, and Joseph told it to him with every tender consideration for the smitten woman, while showing no consideration whatever for the mistakes he had made in the course of it, presenting them as analogous to the offenses he had previously committed against his brothers, and thus against his father, the king of flocks—all of which led him then step by step back to the story of his youth and origins and permitted the captain's clever round eyes a

peculiar and tellingly blurred view of what lay behind the phenomenon of his assistant, Osarsiph the convict, whose curious name,
obviously built upon allusion, he was willing to accept and pronounced with all the tenderness of a good man, though he never believed it was the newcomer's real name, but only a pseudonym, an
alias, simply a paraphrase for "I am he."

He would have liked to put the story of Potiphar's wife to paper
in the style of gratifying literature and often discussed with Joseph
the best methods and strategies for doing so. But whenever he tried
to write it, he ended up following the model of "The Tale of Two
Brothers" and producing another version of it, which put an end to
his attempts.

And so after these days, many more passed, and almost a year
had come round since Rachel's firstborn came to Zawi-Rê, when an
event occurred in the prison that was only a partial manifestation of
important events in the larger world and that, although not immediately, but a little later, would bring about extraordinary changes for
both Joseph and Mai-Sakhme, his friend and taskmaster.

The Gentlemen

One day, then, at the usual early hour, Joseph appeared in the warden's tower residence bringing papers that awaited Mai-Sakhme's
approval, although affairs were conducted here very much as they
had been between Peteprê and his old steward Mont-kaw and normally ended in a "Fine, fine, my good man"; but this time the warden did not even look at the accounts, but waved them off with one
hand, and from the way he raised his brows exceptionally high and
held his rounded lips farther apart than usual, it was immediately apparent that he was preoccupied with some extraordinary incident
that, given the limits of his customary calm, had agitated him.

"Some other time, Osarsiph," he said in reference to the paper-
work. "This is not the moment. You should know that not everything in my prison is as it was yesterday and the day before.
Something has happened, something took place before daybreak,
very quietly and under special and confidential orders. Know, then,
that we have had a delivery—a delicate delivery. Two people arrived
under the cover of night, to be held under safeguard in provisional

custody—people who are out of the ordinary, that is, highly placed personages, by which I mean to say, formerly highly placed until just now, personages who have toppled from their perches and landed in hot water. You yourself have taken a fall, but theirs has been much nastier, for they stood far higher. Pay heed to what I have told you, and you'd do better not to ask for details."

"But who are they?" Joseph asked all the same.

"Their names are Mesedsu-Rê and Bin-em-Wêse," the warden answered diffidently.

"Come, come!" Joseph cried. "What kind of names are those? People aren't called by such names."

He had good reason to be astounded, because Mesedsu-Rê meant "Hated by the Sun God," and Bin-em-Wêse "Wicked in Thebes." It would have taken peculiar parents to have given their sons such names.

The captain busied himself with some decoction or other, rather than look at Joseph.

"I thought you knew," he responded, "that a man's name is not necessarily the one by which he calls himself or may be temporarily called. Circumstances alter names. Rê himself changes his according to his state. The gentlemen bear the names I used in their papers and in the orders given me concerning them. They are the names used in documents being kept in the legal action that has been initiated, and they use those names themselves as circumstance demands. You don't want to know any different."

Joseph quickly considered this. He thought of the spinning sphere, of how what is on top returns and rises again with each rotation; thought of how one thing is exchanged for its opposite, thought of reversals. "Hated by the God," that was the same as Mersu-Rê, "The God Loves Him," and "Wicked in Thebes" had been Nefer-em-Wêse, "Good in Thebes." From his friendship with Potiphar he knew enough about Pharaoh's court and those in favor with the palace at Merima't to recall that Mersu-Rê and Nefer-em-Wêse—hidden beneath their honorary titles, of course—were the names of Pharaoh's chief baker, the man in charge of his pastries, whose title was Prince of Menfe, and of his chief butler, the supervisor of the scribes of the sideboard, who was called Count of Abôdu.

"The true names," he said, "of those given into your hands are surely more like 'What does my lord eat?' and 'What does my lord drink?'"

"Well now, well now," the captain responded, "give you the tip of a sleeve and you'll soon have the whole coat—or think you have it. Well then, know what you know, and don't ask for details."

"What can have happened?" Joseph asked all the same.

"Enough!" Mai-Sakhme retorted. "Word is," he said, looking away, "pieces of chalk were found in Pharaoh's bread and flies in the good god's wine. As you can see yourself, something like that sticks to those in positions of highest responsibility and they've had to be placed in detention pending trial under names appropriate to the situation."

"Chalk? Flies?" Joseph repeated.

"They were brought here under heavy escort at daybreak," the captain went on, "on a ship bearing the symbol of suspicion on its bow and sail, and were handed over to me to be held in strict custody, commensurate with their status, until their guilt or innocence is established—a delicate matter, an awful responsibility. I have had them placed in the Vulture Cabin—you know, you take a right from here, then back along the rear wall, has that vulture with outspread wings on the roof—it's been standing empty, definitely empty given the furnishings they're accustomed to. There they've been since early this morning, each sitting on a standard camp stool over a little bitter beer—those are all the comforts the Vulture Cabin has to offer. It's a touchy situation with them, and no one can say how things will turn out, whether they'll soon take on the pallor of corpses or if His Majesty the good god may not perhaps raise their heads again. We have to handle it in the light of such uncertainty, but to some extent we also need to keep in mind their former rank, and, by the by, our own resources as well. I'm appointing you their guard, you see, whose job it is to check once or twice a day to see if things are in order and inquire as to their wishes, if only as a formality. Such gentlemen require formalities. They'll feel better simply for being *asked* about their wishes, and then it's less important whether their wishes are granted. You have the good manners," he said, "and the *savoir-vivre*"—though this was a phrase borrowed from the Akkadian—"for speaking with them and treating them in terms of both their elegant rank and suspect status. My lieutenants here would be either too rough or too subservient. When the important thing is to keep a happy medium. Respect tinged with gloom would be about right, in my opinion."

"I'm not much of a master of gloom," Joseph said. "Perhaps one could lend the respect a tinge of irony."

"That might be good, too," the captain replied, "for when you inquire about their wishes, they'll notice at once that it's asked more in jest and that of course they can't have things here the way they're accustomed to—or only very roughly. All the same, they can't go on sitting on those camp stools in that bare cabin. They'll have to be furnished with two beds with headrests and, if not two, then at least one armchair with cushions for the feet, so that they can at least take turns sitting in it. Moreover, you'll have to play vizier What-Does-My-Lord-Eat and vizier What-Does-My-Lord-Drink for them, and meet their demands halfway. If they demand roast goose, give them an occasional roast stork. If they demand cake, give them sweetened bread. And if they ask for wine, then at least let them have a little grape juice. In all such things you are to make moderate concessions, giving them some indication that they are being tended to. Go visit them at once and pay them your respects, tinged with whatever you like. From tomorrow on, then, you may do so once each morning and evening."

"I hear and obey," Joseph said and, leaving the tower, he followed the wall to the Vulture Cabin.

The guards at its door saluted him with daggers and broad grins on their peasant faces, for they were partial to him. Then they pushed back the heavy wooden bolt, and Joseph stepped into the bare cubicle to find the gentlemen sitting on their stools, bent low at their stomachs, their hands clasped over their heads. He extended them an elegant greeting, not as elaborate as the one he had once seen Hor-waz, scribe of the Great Gate, offer, but fashionable, with one arm raised toward them and a smile to accompany formulaic good wishes that they might enjoy a life as long as Rê's.

They had leapt to their feet the moment they caught sight of him and now showered him with questions and complaints.

"Who are you, young man?" they cried. "Have you come for good or ill? At least you have come. At least someone has come! Your manners show good breeding, so that one may conclude that you have some sensitivity for the impossible, intolerable, untenable situation in which we find ourselves. Do you know who we are? Has anyone informed you? We are Prince of Menfe, Count of Abôdu, Pharaoh's Chief Inspector of Pastries and he who is First Scribe of His Sideboard, General Master of His Wine Cellar, who proffers him his cup on the finest occasions—his baker of bakers, his butler of butlers and Master of the Grape Adorned with the Vine. Is that clear to you? Have you come with that in mind? Do you have any idea how we have lived—in pavilions where everything was covered in lapis and malachite, and where we slept on down while select servants scratched the soles of our feet? What shall become of us in this pit? They have put us into a bare room, where we have been sitting since before daybreak behind bolted doors, and no one pays us any attention. The heart's curse upon Zawi-Rê! There is nothing, nothing, nothing here. We have no mirror, we have no razor, we have no rouge box, we have no bath, we have no privy where we can tend to our necessities, so that we must hold them inside us, despite their being made more urgent by our agitation, until we are in pain—we, the Chief Baker, the Master of the Vine! Do you have a soul that can respond to our state, for it cries out to high heaven? Have you come to rescue us and raise up our heads? Or have you come merely to see whether our misery has reached its extremity?"

"Noble sirs," Joseph replied, "calm yourselves. I have come for good, for I am the warden's mouth and adjutant, whom he has entrusted with oversight. He has appointed me your servant, who is to hear your commands, and since my lord is a good and calm man, you may judge my own sentiments from his having chosen me. I cannot raise up your heads, only Pharaoh can do that, as soon as your innocence is established, which out of respect I must assume exists and can be established."

Here he paused and waited a little. They both were staring directly at him—the one with plucky little eyes that loved wine but were now floating in sadness, the other with wide-gaping, glassy eyes, in which fear and lies were in hot pursuit of one another.

One might have expected the baker to be a sack of flour, the butler to be thin as a grapevine—but that was not the case. On the contrary, it was the butler who was portly—he was short and stout, with a red face set between the wings of a headscarf stretched tight across his brow, the corkscrew ears studded with gemstones and sticking out on either side. One could tell that his chubby cheeks, though regrettably covered now with a stubble of beard, could, when shaved and oiled, glisten with mirth—just as present tribulation and distress could not entirely erase the basic merriment from his sommelier's face. By contrast, the chief baker was a tall, though stoop-shouldered man; his face looked sallow, but again that might only have been a matter of contrast, and also because it was framed by a deep black wig, peeping out from which were broad gold earrings. But there was no mistaking the explicitly underworldly traits in the baker's face—the long nose ran slightly askew, the mouth also grew thicker and longer where it drooped awkwardly to one side. A sense of some curse sat sinister and urgent between his brows.

One ought not think, however, that Joseph would have registered the contrasting impressions left by the physiognomies of his wards with a shallow preference for the serenity of the one and an equally shallow dislike of the more disagreeable characteristics of the other. Both training and piety prompted him to observe the traits of merriment or pensiveness with respect for the destinies they revealed—indeed, had conditioned him to extend even greater politeness to the man whose appearance bore the mark of underworldly pensiveness than to the man of joviality.

The gentlemen were dressed, by the by, in beautifully pleated courtier's garb richly trimmed with colorful knotted ribbons, but now dirty and rumpled from their journey; each of them, however, still wore the insignia of high office: the butler a collar of golden grapevine, the baker a brooch of golden ears of grain, bent in the shape of a sickle.

"I am not the one," Joseph repeated, "who can raise up your heads, nor is the warden. All that we can do is to allay a bit—perhaps with some success, perhaps not—the discomfort that has fallen to your lot due to some dark providence, and you must realize that a beginning has been made in the very fact that you have lacked for everything in these first hours. For from now on you will not lack for at least some few things, and after such complete deprivation this will seem to you more pleasant than all those things that you had when you were still anointed with the oil of gladness and that this dismal place can never provide you. You see, then, my lords, Count of Abôdu and Prince of Menfe, what good intentions lay behind your having been in temporarily straitened circumstances. Within the hour, two—granted, simple—beds will be set up for you here. An easy chair, which you may use by turn, will join these stools. A razor, unfortunately probably only of stone—for which I must apologize beforehand—will be made available, as will some very good eye makeup, black, but with a greenish cast, which the commandant himself prepares and some small quantity of which, upon my recommendation, he will gladly and calmly supply you. As for a mirror, it was again only with the best of intentions that you had none to begin with, for it is far better that it first reveal a tidied-up image rather than your present one. Your servant, by which I mean myself, owns a reasonably clear copper mirror, and I would be happy to lend it to you for the duration of your stay, which one way or the other can only be brief. It will please you that its frame and handle are in the shape of the symbol of life. Moreover on the right side of the cabin I shall post two guards who will assist you in bathing with water twice daily, and on the left side you can take care of your bodily needs, which at the moment is probably the most pressing matter."

"Splendid," the butler said. "Splendid for the moment and in light of the circumstances. My lad, you come like dawn after the night and like cooling shade after the blaze of the sun. To your health and happiness, long may you live! Accept the greetings of the Master of the Vine! Lead us to the left side."

"But what did you mean," the baker asked, "by 'one way or the other' when speaking of our stay and its 'brief duration'?"

"I meant," Joseph answered, "'in any case,' 'definitely,' or 'most certainly.' I meant to be reassuring."

And for now he took his leave from these gentlemen, bowing somewhat more respectfully to the baker than to the butler.

Later that day he returned, bringing with him a game board for their amusement, and inquired how they had dined, to which they responded to the effect of "Well, if you can call it that!" and with a demand for roast goose, whereupon he promised them something similar, a roasted waterfowl, as well as the version of cake that this dismal place produced. They were, moreover, to be allowed to leave the Vulture Cabin, though always under guard, for an hour of target practice or bowling whenever they liked. They thanked him profusely, but also asked him to thank the warden for these lenient arrangements, for these few hints of comfort that they now found so pleasant after such total barrenness at the start; and, having come to place great confidence in him, they kept Joseph with them as long as possible, for conversation and registering their complaints, both that day and on those that followed, each time he stopped by to inquire about their health and receive their orders—except that, for all their talkativeness, they preserved the same diffident reserve and taciturnity concerning the reasons for their being here that had characterized the warden's initial announcement of their arrival.

Most of all they suffered under their criminal aliases and never ceased to beg him to believe that these were not even remotely their real names.

"It is very considerate of you, Usarsiph, my dear lad," they said, "that you do not call us by those absurd names that have been attached to us and that are used here while we are in custody. But it is not enough that you do not let them pass your lips; you dare not call us by them even in your heart and to yourself, but rather you must feel certain that we would never be called such disreputable names, quite the contrary. That would be a great help in and of itself, for we fear the danger that these unseemly names—which have been written in indelible ink in our papers and in the trial documents of the Book of Truth—will gradually take on the truth, so that we shall be called by them for all eternity."

"Not to worry, noble gentlemen," Joseph replied. "This will pass, and ultimately it is tantamount to thoughtfulness that pseudonyms have been applied to you during these preliminary stages, so that your true names are not compromised in the Book of Truth. Thus in a certain sense you are not the men who are recorded in the documents and indictments, are hardly even those who are sitting here—and instead it is Hated by God and Scum of Thebes who suffer these hardships and not you."

"Ah, but we are the ones who must suffer them, even if incognito," they wailed inconsolably in protest. "After all, out of delicacy you likewise address us with the embellishment of those lovely honorary titles that adorned us at court—His Excellency of Menfe, the Prince of Bread, is what you call us out of politeness, and His Solemn Eminence the Great Presser of the Blood of the Grape. Know then, if you do not already know it, that we were stripped of all these names before being brought here for safekeeping, and that we stand here practically naked, much as when the soldiers pour water over us at the right side of the cabin. All that is still left of us at present are the names Dross and Despisal—that is what makes it so horrible."

And they wept.

"How is it possible," Joseph asked, looking away, just as the captain had done when first diffidently broaching the subject, "how is it even possible, how in the world could it have happened that Pharaoh was roused against you like an Upper Egyptian leopard or the raging sea, so that, like the mountains of the East, his heart brought forth a sandstorm and overnight you fell from your stations of honor, were carried off down here to us to be held under suspicion?"

"Flies," sobbed the butler.

"Chalk," said the chief baker.

And they, too, looked away diffidently, each in a different direction. But there was not that much refuge in the cabin for three pairs of eyes, and so inadvertently their glances met and fled again, only inadvertently to meet yet another pair of eyes in their new place of refuge—an agonizing game, which Joseph hoped to bring to an end by departing, for he could tell that he would get no more out of them beyond "flies" and "chalk." But they did not want him to leave and held on tight to him with words intended to convince him of the untenableness of any suspicion of guilt cast upon them and of the absurdity of calling them Mesedsu-Rê and Bin-em-Wêse.

"I beg you, most excellent lad of Canaan, dear Ibrim," the butler said, "to listen and behold. How could that be, how could I, Good-and-Merry-in-Thebes, have anything to do with such an affair? It's ludicrous and contradicts the order of things; the very nature of the charges cries out that it's slander, a misunderstanding. I am in charge of the vine of life and bear its tendriled staff before Pharaoh as he strides into the banquet hall where the blood of Osiris flows. I am the herald who cries out, 'Health and Prosperity and Salutation,' as I swing my staff above my head. I am the man of the wreath, of the wreath around the head, of the wreath around the foaming cup. Just look at my cheeks, now that they are shaved smooth, even if with a shoddy razor. Are they not like berries about to burst when the sun brews the holy juice within them? I live and let live, crying my cries of 'Health!' and 'Long Life!' Do I look like a man who measures the coffin for the god? Do I bear any resemblance to the ass of Seth? That beast is not yoked to the plow with the ox, nor are wool and flax woven in the same garment, the grapevine does not bear figs, and what does not go together, will never go together in this world. I beg you, judge with your sound reason, which knows what is and what stands in opposition to it, knows one thing and what is completely different, the possible and the impossible—judge whether I can share in the guilt of this offense and partake in what one cannot partake in."

"I can see," Prince Mersu-Rê, the chief baker, then said, looking to one side, "that the count's words did not fail to make an impression on you, man of Zahi and gifted lad, for compelling words they are, and your judgment will of necessity be in his favor. Which is why I now likewise appeal to your fairness, convinced as I am that you will show no less common sense in judging my case as well. Since you realize that the suspicion under which we noble gentlemen stand cannot be reconciled with the sacred office of the Cup-bearer of Cup-bearers, you will also have to admit that it is equally, if not to say all the more, incompatible with the sacredness of my own position, which, if that is possible, is even greater. It is the oldest, earliest, most spiritual of offices—there are higher perhaps, but none of deeper meaning. It is a paragon, just as anything is a paragon when it is aptly described by the adjective derived from it—it is a holy office and holiest of holies. It is a grotto and a ravine into which one drives the swine of sacrifice and hurls torches from above to keep alive the primal flame that burns there, bringing warmth and fertility. Thus I bear a torch before Pharaoh, yet do not swing it above my head, but carry it with priestly solemnity before me and him when he goes in to dine, to eat the flesh of the buried god who sprouts up to greet the sickle from below, from depths that welcome our oaths."

The baker looked alarmed, and his wide-staring eyes suddenly jerked even farther to one side, so that his eyes were locked at the corners, one in the outermost, the other in the innermost. It was not unusual for him to be alarmed by his own words, but in trying to take them back or revise them, he would only talk himself deeper into difficulty. For his words were directed to the depths below, and he could not turn them around.

"Pardon, that's not what I wanted to say," he started afresh. "I didn't want to put it that way and fervently hope that you do not misunderstand me, my clever boy, to whose common sense we appeal on behalf of our innocence. I speak, but when I listen to my own words, I fear they may sound as if, in countering suspicions against me, I am invoking a sacredness so great and deep that it carries implications that are, so to speak, grave and precarious, a sacredness that is thus no longer suitable for refuting such suspicions. I beg you summon all your reason and do not be misled into thinking that a proof can be so strong that it is condemned to ineffectiveness as a proof or, worse, proves its opposite. That would be a terrible imperiling of the soundness of your judgment were you to think such things. Look at me—even if I do not look at you but look in search of my proofs. I—I am guilty? I am involved in such an affair? Am I not the Lord of Bread, the servant of the roaming mother? Of her who searches for her daughter with the torch, the bringer of fertility, the great giver of all that is warm and green, who refused the stupefying blood, preferring instead the drink from grain, who brought to men the seed of the wheat, the seed of the barley, and who first broke the soil with the curved plow so that from a gentler nourishment might come gentler customs—for prior to her, men ate the bulbs of bulrushes or even one another. I belong to her and take my holy stance for her who winnows kernels and chaff upon the windy threshing floor, separates the honorable from the dishonorable, who is the giver of laws, who establishes justice and rebukes tyranny. Consider these things with reason, asking yourself if I could have become involved in such a darkling affair. Speak your judgment on the basis of this incongruity, which results not so much from its being a darkling affair—for justice, like bread, comes from the dark and is bound up with the womb that lies below where the goddesses of revenge dwell, so that one might indeed call sacred law the watchdog of the goddess, all the more so since the dog is in fact sacred to her, and from that perspective one might also call me, who am consecrated to her, a dog as well . . ."

Here he took dreadful alarm again, and casting his eyes to opposing corners he assured them he had not meant to say that or at least not in that way. But Joseph soothed them both, saying they should really let it be, that they needn't go to such lengths on his account. He was honored, and valued their having presented their account of the affair, or if not of the affair, then the reasons why it could not have been their affair. But it was even less his affair to set himself up as their judge, for he was appointed only as their attendant, who asked them for orders, just as they were accustomed to. True, they were also used to having their orders carried out, which he, much to his regret, was usually not in a position to do. But at least in this way they were being granted half of what they were accustomed to. And he asked if he had the pleasure of taking some other order with him on his way.

No, they said sadly, they knew of nothing; they could no longer think of a single order now that they knew that it would have no consequences. Oh, but why did he want to go so soon? Instead he should tell them how long he thought the investigation of their affair was likely to drag on, and how long they would have to endure living in this hole.

He would obligingly tell them at once, he replied, if he knew. But as was only understandable he did not know, and he could only venture a rough guess—his, in no way binding, conclusion was that, taken all in all, it would probably be at most or at least thirty and ten days before their fate was decided.

"Oh, that long!" the butler wailed.

"Oh, that short!" the baker cried, but was immediately and terribly alarmed by his cry and assured them that he also had intended to say "That long!" But the butler thought a moment and then remarked that Joseph's rough guess and calculation had something to it; for counting from the day of their arrival, it was thirty and seven and three days until Pharaoh's wonderful birthday, well known to be a day of mercy and judgment, on which in all probability their own sentences would be spoken.

"As far as I know I hadn't thought of that," Joseph replied, "and my calculation was not based on it, but was simply an inspiration of the moment. But now that it turns out that Pharaoh's Great Birthday will occur on that same day, you can see that what I said is already beginning to be fulfilled."

The Sting of the Serpent

With that he departed, shaking his head over his two wards and their "affair," about which he already knew more than he was permitted to let on. For no one in the Two Lands dared give an inkling that he knew more about it than was considered good for him; all the same—however thick the cloud of circumlocutions and euphemisms, of "flies" and "chalk," of camouflaged names like Hated by God and Scum of Wase that higher-ups might wrap it in—there had been no way to prevent this dangerous matter from soon becoming the talk of the entire nation far and wide, so that very shortly everyone, even if he might use the prescribed turns of phrase, knew what lay behind the belittling and whitewashing: a story, which, despite all the horror it evoked, did not lack a certain popular appeal, if not to say festive solemnity, for it had the look of repetition and return, in short, of the present embodiment of events familiar from and based in the ancient past.

To put it bluntly, there had been a plot against Pharaoh's life—even though the days of this old god's majesty were obviously numbered in any case and, as you know, his inclination to reunite with the sun could not be prevented either by the advice of his magicians and experts on the body from his House of Books or even by the Ishtar of the Way that out of solicitude his brother and brother-in-law on the Euphrates, Tushratta, king over the land of Khanigalbat or Mittaniland, had sent to him. But just because the Great House, Si-Rê, Son of the Sun and Lord of the Diadem, Neb-maat-Rê-Amenhotep, was ill and could barely get his breath, was no reason why harm should not come to him, but was rather, if one was of that mind, a very good reason *for* it—irrespective, of course, of how heinous such an enterprise was.

It was universally known that originally Rê himself, the sun god, had been king of the Two Lands or, better still, ruler over the earth and all humankind and had governed them with his most glorious and radiant blessing, as long as he was still young in years, and on into his full and later manhood, indeed for a considerable period of his early and increasing old age. Only when he had become terribly old and the painful complaints and frailties of old age, though to be sure in a rarified form, had encroached upon the majesty of this god did he deem it a good idea to abdicate from the earth and withdraw into the upper sphere. For gradually his bones had become silver, his flesh gold, his hair, however, the purest lapis lazuli—a very beautiful form of senescence, but nonetheless accompanied by all manner of pain and illness, which the gods themselves had striven to counter with a thousand medicines, but all in vain, for no herb grows that can cure the silvering, the gilding, the lapidifying of advanced old age. But even in this state, the aged Rê had continued to cling to his sovereignty over earth, although he should have realized that it had begun to free itself from his old and enfeebled grip and that fearlessness, indeed insolence, was gaining the upper hand on all sides.

Isis in particular, Eset, the great goddess of the island, more cunning than millions of other beings, believed her hour had come. Like Rê, the superannuated king, she possessed knowledge that encompassed both heaven and earth. There was only one thing she did not know, and having no command over it limited her scope—this was Rê's last and most secret name, his ultimate name, and in gaining knowledge of it one gained power over him. For he had a great many names, each more secret than the last, yet none that investigation could not ultimately reveal. It was only this final and most powerful name that he would not yield up; but whoever forced him to name the name would weaken him and, vaulting on high, would tower above him through wisdom's power.

That is why Eset devised and created a serpent to sting Rê in his golden flesh, so that the unbearable pain that the sting caused him—and from which only the serpent's creator could relieve him—would force him to name his name to the great Eset. And as it was devised so was it realized. Old Rê was stung and in the throes of agony from the sting had no choice but to reveal his hidden names, one after the other, always in the hope that the goddess would be content with one of his carefully concealed names. But she was not, and kept battering him with her queries until he had named to her the most secret name of all—and now the power of her knowledge over him was complete. After which it cost her nothing to heal the sting; but his was a sickly convalescence, limited by the recuperative powers of an old being, and soon thereafter he chose to retire to the heavens.

This then was the ancient lore, familiar to every child in Keme and suggesting that harm might be done to Pharaoh, since by now his condition was only too reminiscent of—indeed was almost identical with—that of the exhausted god. But the person who had taken those long-ago events especially and personally to heart was a certain resident within Pharaoh's House of Women, the sealed and closely guarded pavilion that was attached in ornate splendor to the palace of Merima't and to which Pharaoh would sometimes still have himself carried—though of course only to chuck the chin of one or another of the graceful ladies kept there, or perhaps to defeat her in a game on the board with thirty squares while being entertained by the perfumed corps of the others as they danced, sang, and played the lute. In fact he often enjoyed a game with the very woman who took the story of Isis and Rê so personally that she was inspired to try to reenact it in the present. No narrative, even those claiming to be familiar with every detail of the story, has ever been able to name her name. It has been erased, chiseled away, from every version; it is cloaked under the night of eternal oblivion. Yet this woman had on occasion been one of Pharaoh's favored concubines and, some twelve or thirteen years before, in the days when now and then he still deigned to sire children, had borne him a son named Noferka-Ptah (that name has been preserved), who as fruit of the divine seed was raised in finest style and whose existence gave her, the favored concubine, the right to wear the vulture helmet—not one as wonderful as that worn by Tiy, the Great Royal Consort, but a golden vulture helmet all the same. This and a mother's weakness for Noferka-Ptah, the divine seed, doomed the woman to her fate. For the helmet seduced her to confuse herself with cunning Eset; and interwoven with those traditional patterns of thought was her own ambitious, doting love for her precious semi-scion, so that befuddled by ancient lore, her narrow, but shrewd mind decided to have Pharaoh stung by a serpent, to precipitate a palace coup, and in place of the rightful successor, the—granted, sickly—Horus-Amenhotep, to place the fruit of her womb, Noferka-Ptah, upon the throne of the Two Lands.

Indeed preparations for this coup—whose goals were to topple a dynasty, initiate a new age, and elevate the never-named concubine to the position of Goddess-Mother—were well advanced. Pharaoh's House of Women was its breeding ground; but with the assistance of several officials of the harem and officers guarding its gate and hungry for something new and different, connections were established: first, to the palace itself, where a number of sympathizers, some of them highly placed—a Lead Driver of the Royal Chariot, the Administrator of the God's Fruit Pantry, the Chief of Gendarmes, the Supervisor of the Cattle Herds, the Overseer of Salves in the Treasury of the Lord of the Two Lands, and others—were won over to the enterprise; and, second, to the world of the capital city outside, where with the help of those officers' wives, male relatives of Pharaoh's graceful ladies were drawn into the conspiracy and urged to spread malicious rumors to incite Wase's population against the old Rê, who was now nothing but gold, silver, and lapis lazuli.

In all there were seventy-two conspirators who backed the secret plan—a promising number dictated by tradition, for there had once been seventy-two conspirators to help red Seth lure Usir into the chest, and they in turn had had good cosmic reasons for setting their number at no more and no less than seventy-two. For that is the number of five-day weeks that make up the three hundred and sixty days of the year, leaving aside the extra days; and the lean fifth of the year, when the water level of the Provider is at its lowest and the god sinks into his grave, also lasts seventy-two days. So then, wherever a conspiracy takes place in this world, it is customary, indeed necessary for the conspirators to be seventy-two in number. And if the coup fails, one can be certain that had that number not been adhered to, the failure would have been far worse.

The current plot had now failed, although it was inspired by the best models and all the preparations had been made with greatest caution. The Overseer of Salves had in fact managed to pilfer a magic text from Pharaoh's library and, following its instructions, had formed certain wax figures that were smuggled here, there, and everywhere into the palace, spreading magical confusion and bewilderment that surely had to assist the cause. It was decided to poison Pharaoh's bread or wine or both at once and to use the ensuing turmoil for an armed coup inside the palace, which, in conjunction with an uprising in the city across the river, would have led to the proclamation of the new age and the elevation of the bastard Noferka-Ptah to the throne of the Two Lands. And then everything fell to pieces. Whether it was because at the last moment one of the seventy-two saw better chances for his career and was seduced by the promise of lovely inscriptions for his grave if he chose to remain loyal, or because a police decoy had wormed his way into their schemes from the start—however it came about, a list was placed in Pharaoh's hands, and painful reading it was, for it included a number of those who were truly close friends of the god, participants in his morning levees. Though not entirely free of blunders and mistaken identities, the list was largely correct, and countermeasures had been swift, silent, and thorough. The Isis of the House of Women was promptly strangled by eunuchs, her young son exiled to remotest Nubia, and while a secret committee was formed to investigate both the plan as a whole and matters of individual guilt, those who were now compromised were labeled "Execration of the Land" and in addition, under cruelly distorted names, banished under custody to various locations, where they awaited their fate under conditions very different from those to which they were accustomed.

That is how Pharaoh's chief baker and butler had landed in the prison where Joseph himself was imprisoned.

Joseph Assists as an Interpreter

It was the thirty-and-seventh day those two gentlemen had spent there, and when Joseph, as always, obliged them with his morning visit to ask them how they had slept and if they had any orders to give, he found them both in a frame of mind that might be called excited, depressed, and angry all in one. By now they had begun to adjust to their simplified situation and had ceased to whine; for it is not necessary for a man to live as they had amid lapis and malachite and with servants to scratch the soles of his feet, he can in the end make do quite well with a bath to his right and a latrine to his left and an occasional opportunity for target practice and a game of ninepins instead of a fashionable bird hunt. But today they had completely reverted to their coddled habits and no sooner had Joseph entered than they launched into their old bitter complaints of how they lacked everything, even the most necessary items, and how their life here, despite their honest attempts to reconcile themselves to it, still continued to be a dog's life.

They had dreamt that night, they said in reply to Joseph's sympathetic inquiry, both at the same time, but each his own dream; and these had been dreams of the most eloquent vividness, very forceful, unforgettable, leaving behind a most peculiar taste in the soul—highly meaningful dreams with the words "Understand me rightly" printed on their brows, for they were literally crying out for interpretation. At home each had had his own interpreter of dreams, knowledgeable experts on the whole monstrous brood of the night, with an eye for any detail in such a vision that manifestly carried some meaning or premonition, and also in the possession of the best dream catalogues and case histories, both Babylonian and Egyptian, which they needed only to consult when they ran out of ideas of their own. If necessary, in cases that were very inscrutable or without precedent, these gentlemen could call together a council of temple prophets and scholars whose concerted efforts were sure to get to the bottom of the matter. In short, they had in every instance been provided prompt, dependable, and elegant service. But here and now? They had dreamt—each his own special, very strikingly accentuated, and peculiarly spiced dream, with which his soul was still overflowing—and there was no one in this cursed pit who could interpret the dreams and provide them their accustomed service. This was a hardship far worse than a lack of down, roast goose, or bird hunting, and the awareness of such intolerably straitened circumstances left them on the verge of tears.

Joseph listened, thrusting his lips up a little.

"Gentlemen," he said, "if it be of any initial comfort to you that someone commiserates with you in your sorrow, then know that in me you find such a person. Beyond that, however, some help just might be available to make up for this lack that so oppresses and offends you. I have been appointed your servant and caretaker and am, as it were, your all-purpose attendant, so then why not in the matter of dreams as well? I am not entirely inexperienced in the field and might even boast a certain familiarity with dreams—and please don't take that amiss, but simply as an apt way of stating that my family and clan have always dreamt a good many highly suggestive dreams. At one particular place in the course of his travels, my father, the king of flocks, had a first-rate dream that imbued his entire personality with dignity, and to hear him tell of it was an extraordinary pleasure. And I myself in my previous life was so involved with dreams that among my brothers I was known by a nickname that jocularly alluded to that fact. You've become so accomplished in taking potluck thus far, why not take it with me and tell me your dreams, so that I may try to interpret them?"

"Well now," they said. "Fine, fine. You're an amiable lad and when you speak of dreams you stare off into space with a veiled look in those handsome, even beautiful eyes of yours, so that we are tempted to trust in your ability to assist us. But all the same, *dreaming* is one thing and *interpreting dreams* quite another."

"Do not say that," he replied. "Do not say it without a second thought. It may well be that there is a wholeness to dreaming, that it is a circle to which both the dream and its interpretation belong and that dreamer and interpreter only seem to be two entirely separate things, but in reality are interchangeable and actually one and the same, for together they make up the whole. Whoever dreams interprets as well, and he who would interpret must first have dreamt. My lord Prince of Bread, Your Excellency the Chief Cup-bearer, you have both lived in very luxurious circumstances where there is an excessive division of labor, so that you dreamt the dream and left its interpretation to your private prophets. But ultimately and by nature every man is the interpreter of his own dream and so has his dream interpreted only for the sake of elegance. I wish to reveal to you the secret behind our dreaming: the interpretation precedes the dream and what we dream issues from the interpretation. How else could it be that a person knows perfectly well if an interpretation is false and cries out: 'Begone, you bungler! I want a different interpreter, one who will tell me the truth.' So then, try it with me, and if I bungle it and do not interpret according to what you already know, then chase me off with curses and contumely."

"I do not wish to tell mine," the chief baker said. "I am accustomed to better things and I prefer to do without in this matter as in everything else, rather than use an unprofessional interpreter like you."

"I wish to tell mine," the butler said. "For in fact I am so eager to hear an interpretation that I'm willing to take the first that comes along, especially when the interpreter has that veiled look in his eye so full of promise and has demonstrated some familiarity with dreams. So prepare yourself, my lad, to hear and interpret, but pull yourself together just as I must do my best to pull myself together to find the right words for my dream and not take its life by telling it. For it was so terribly lifelike and clear, the spice of it so unique—and alas, we know too well how once a dream is wrapped in words it is only just a mummy, the gaunt swaddled image of what it was as we dreamt. Yet it budded, blossomed, and bore fruit, just like the grapevine that stood before me in this dream of mine, which, it seems, I have already begun to tell. For I saw myself with Pharaoh in his vineyard, under the arching branches of his vineyard, where my lord lay resting. And before me was a vine, I can still see it, it was a peculiar vine and had three branches. Understand me—it was green and had leaves like human hands, but although the rest of the vine-yard was hung heavy with grapes, this vine had not yet blossomed or borne fruit, for that took place only now as I watched. Behold—it grew before my eyes and began to blossom, shooting tender clusters of petals out from among the leaves, and the three clusters brought forth grapes, which ripened, swift as the wind, before my eyes, and their purple berries were as plump as my cheeks, filled to bursting like no other berries all around. And I was delighted and picked the grapes with my right hand, for in my left I was holding Pharaoh's cup, half filled with cool water. And I lovingly pressed the juice of the grapes into it—while recalling, I believe, that you, my lad, some-times press a little grape juice into the water when we order wine—and placed the cup into Pharaoh's hand. And that was all," he concluded crestfallen, disappointed by his own words.

"That was quite a lot," Joseph replied, opening his eyes, which he had kept shut while bending an ear to listen. "There was the cup, and there was clear water in it, and with your own hand you pressed the juice of the grapes from the vine that had the three branches and gave it to the Lord of the Two Crowns. That was a pure gift and there were no flies in it. Shall I interpret it for you?"

"Yes, do!" the butler cried. "I can hardly wait."

"This is the interpretation," Joseph said. "The three branches are three days. And in three days you will receive the water of life, and Pharaoh will raise up your head and take your name of shame from you, so that you will be called Honorable in Thebes just as before, and he will restore you to your office, so that you will place the cup in his hand as you used to do as his butler. And that is all."

"Excellent," the fat man cried. "That is a sweet, excellent, exem-plary interpretation. You have served me better than I have ever been served in my life, my sweet lad—have provided a service to my soul beyond all telling. Three branches—three days! The way you say it right out, you clever boy! And to be Honorable in Thebes again and in the same way and Pharaoh's friend once more! Thank you, my darling lad, thank you so very, very much."

And there he sat and wept for joy.

Joseph, however, said to him, "Count of Abôdu, Nefer-em-Wêse! I have prophesied according to your dream—it was easily and gladly done. I take joy in having been able to offer you a joyful in-terpretation. And, cleansed of guilt, you soon will be surrounded by

friends. But here in these narrow confines let me be the first to congratulate you. I have been your servant and steward for thirty-seven
days; and for another three yet, so the captain has commanded, I
shall ask about your orders and provide you some hints of comfort,
to the extent circumstances allow. I have come to you here in the
Vulture Cabin each morning and evening and have been like an angel
of God to you, if I may put it that way, into whose heart you could
pour out your woe, and who comforted you in these unaccustomed
straits. You, however, have not asked me much about myself. And
yet I was not born to live in this hole, either, nor have I chosen it for
my habitation, but rather ended up here, I know not how, and have
been put away here as a convict and royal slave for a crime that is
only a misrepresentation before God. Your souls were too full of
your own sorrow for you to have given mine much thought and to
have asked me questions. But do not forget me and my service,
Count Chief Butler, but rather remember me when you are restored
to your former glory. Mention me to Pharaoh and call his attention
to how I sit here purely because of a misrepresentation, and plead
for me that he might graciously release me from this prison, where I
do not gladly reside. For as boy I was stolen, literally stolen from my
homeland and brought down to the land of Egypt, and stolen again
and put into this pit—and am like the moon, when a hateful spirit arrested him in his course so that he could not continue along his shining path, at the head of the gods, his brothers. Will you do that for
me, Count Chief Butler, will you mention me there?"

"Why yes, a thousand times yes!" the fat man cried. "I promise
you that once I stand before Pharaoh again, I will mention you at the
first opportunity and will remind him on succeeding occasions if his
mind does not seize upon it at once. I would be but a grubbing aardvark were I not to remember you and not want to mention you to
best advantage, for it makes no difference to me whether you have
stolen or were stolen, you shall be mentioned, mentioned and pardoned, my honey-sweet lad."

And he embraced Joseph and kissed him on the mouth and on
both cheeks.

"That I had a dream too," the tall man said, "appears to have
been completely forgotten here. I did not know, Ibrim, that you are
such a clever interpreter, otherwise I would not have refused your
assistance. But now I am inclined to tell you my dream as well, to the

extent that is possible in words, and you shall interpret it for me. Make yourself ready to listen."

"I'm listening," Joseph replied.

"What I dreamt," the baker began, "was this, and was the following. I dreamt—but here you can see how ludicrous my dream was, for how did it happen that I, Prince of Menfe, who most certainly never stick my head in the oven, how did it happen that like some baker's apprentice or delivery boy with crescents and twists—but enough, you see, I was strolling about in my dream, carrying on my head three baskets of fine cakes, one basket atop the other, the flat kind that fit neatly into one another, and each was filled with all sorts of pastries from the palace bakery, and in the top one were baked goods for Pharaoh, waffles and pretzels. Then three birds flew down, beating their wings, with their talons tucked back in flight and necks outstretched and beady eyes glaring, and they shrieked as they came. And these birds had the audacity to swoop down and eat the food on my head. I wanted to raise my free hand and wave it over the baskets and shoo the vermin away, but I couldn't do it, my hand hung limply at my side. And they hacked away and as they beat their wings there was the sour, foul stench of bird all around me . . ." Here the baker got his usual alarmed look, blanched, and tried to smile with the drooping corner of his mouth. "That is to say," he said, "you shouldn't picture the birds with their foul stench or their beaks and beady eyes as all too ghastly. They were birds like any others and when I say they hacked—I don't recall exactly if I said that, but I might have—I chose a rather vivid word in an attempt to make my dream more understandable. I should have said they pecked. The little birds pecked at my basket, since they probably thought I wanted to feed them, because the top basket on my head wasn't covered and had no cloth spread over it—in short, everything in my dream happened very naturally, with the exception that it was I, Prince of Menfe, who was carrying baked goods on my head, and then perhaps also that I found it impossible to wave my hand, but maybe I didn't want to, because I was enjoying playing host to the little birds. And that was all."

"Shall I now interpret it for you?" Joseph asked.

"As you like," the baker responded.

"The three baskets," Joseph said, "are three days. In three days Pharaoh will lead you out of this house and will raise up your head by binding you to a crossbar and to an upright post, and the birds of the heaven will eat the flesh from your body. And that, unfortunately, is all."

"What are you saying!" the baker cried, then sat down and hid his face in his hands, while tears flowed out from between his heavily ringed fingers.

But Joseph comforted him and said, "Do not weep so very hard, Your Excellency and Chief Baker, nor should you melt into tears of joy, Master of the Wreath. Rather, both of you should bear this with dignity, because that is how things are and how you are and how things will happen. There is also a wholeness to the circle of the world and it has its top and its bottom, its good and evil; yet one should not make too much fuss over that duality, for in the end the ox is like the ass and they are interchangeable and together they make up the whole. You can see from the tears you both weep that the difference between you two gentlemen is not all that great. You, my esteemed Crier of Good Cheer, have no reason for conceit, for you are good only after a manner of speaking, and I believe your innocence consists in your not having even been approached in this evil matter because you are a chatterbox and you were not to be trusted, and so you never heard about the evil. Nor will you remember me when you come into your kingdom, although you have promised—I am telling you this beforehand. Or you will do so only much later, after you bump your nose against the memory of me. When you remember me, remember also that I told you beforehand that you would not remember me. As for you, Master Baker, do not despair. For I believe you conspired with evil because you thought it was dedicated to an honorable cause and you confused it with good, as can very easily happen. Behold, you belong to the god when he is below and your companion belongs to the god when he is above. But you are both God's, and the raising up of the head is the raising up of the head, even if it is on the post and crossbar of Usir, on which an ass is sometimes seen as well, as a sign that Seth and Osiris are the same."

These were the words Jacob's son addressed to the two gentlemen. Three days after he had interpreted their dreams, however, they were removed from the prison, and both had their heads raised up, the butler in honor, the baker in shame, for he was bound to the crossbar. The butler, however, forgot Joseph entirely, for he did not like to think of the prison and so not of Joseph either.

Part Two

THE SUMMONS

Neb-nef-nezem

After these events Joseph remained in prison, in his second pit, for another two years, in order that he might reach the age of thirty before being removed from there in great, indeed breathless haste—but this time it was Pharaoh himself who had dreamt. For two years later Pharaoh had a dream. He had *two* dreams, yet since they essentially came to the same thing, one can also say that Pharaoh had *a* dream, but that is of no real importance and the least of it—the main thing, the point to be emphasized is, rather, that when we speak of "Pharaoh" here, the word no longer (in a personal sense, that is) has the same meaning it had at the time when the baker and butler dreamt their dreams of truth. Pharaoh is always the same word, and Pharaoh is always Pharaoh; but at the same time he comes and goes, just as the sun is always the sun, but likewise goes and comes. But in the meantime, that is, very soon after Joseph's wards, those two gentlemen, had had their heads raised up in very different ways, Pharaoh had indeed gone and come; and with that we allude to all the things that Joseph missed while he lay in the *bôr* (that is, in his pit and prison), or concerning which only a feeble echo found its way down to him: a change of sovereigns, a mournful farewell to one day in this world and the jubilant dawn of a new age, from which people expected a turn for the better, toward happiness, even if the previous age had been, within earthly limits, a quite happy one, and in which they trusted injustice would be driven out by justice and "the moon would come right" (as if it had not "come right" before); in short, that they would live in laughter and amazement—reason enough for the whole nation to hop on one leg and drink for weeks, that is, after a time of mourning in sackcloth and ashes, which was in no way a mere hypocritical convention, but can be attributed to genuine sorrow at the departure of the old age. For man is always a muddled creature.

Amun's son—the son of Thutmose and of a child of the king of

Mittaniland—Neb-ma-Rê-Amenhotep III–Nimmuria had sat enthroned, building and ruling in pomp, for as many years as his chief butler and the general-superintendent of his bakery had spent days at Zawi-Rê, that is forty; whereupon he died and was united with the sun, shortly after his sad experience with the seventy-two conspirators who had wanted to lure him into his coffin. He now lay in his coffin anyway—in a, needless to say, marvelous coffin studded with nails of pure gold—was placed in it after first being salted and bitumened, made to last for eternity with juniper wood, turpentine, cedar resin, storax, and mastic, and wrapped in four hundred ells of linen. Preparations took seventy days before the Osiris was ready to be placed upon a golden sledge that was pulled by oxen and atop which stood the oared galley bearing the lion-pawed bier shaded by a baldachin, and then—preceded by priests waving censers and sprinkling water and accompanied by a train of mourners evidently crushed with grief—brought to its Eternal Dwelling in the cliffs, a multichambered tomb furnished with every comfort, before whose door divine rites were held and the "opening of the mouth" with the foot of the Horus calf was performed.

The queen and the court were no longer sealed with the dead man inside his multichambered dwelling, to starve and rot there; the time when that was considered necessary or simply proper was long past, the custom had fallen into general disuse and been forgotten—and why? What had been the objection to it and why was it far removed from every mind? These people certainly indulged in endless ancient practices and diligently performed all sorts of magic, stuffed all the openings of the exalted cadaver with protective amulets and employed that calf-footed instrument with undeviating ceremony. But to seal the entire court inside—no, none of that, that was no longer done; not because they shrank from doing it and no longer regarded as a good idea something that had once been held in reverence—they didn't even want to acknowledge that the custom had ever been observed or thought a good idea; and neither those who once would have been sealed inside nor those who would have sealed them in gave the matter a single thought. Obviously the idea no longer bore up under the light of day, whether that day be termed early or late—and that is very remarkable. Many people might regard as remarkable the old observance itself—being buried alive inside those walls. Except that it is far more remarkable that one day, by common, tacit, and perhaps even unthinking agreement, it was simply no longer considered.

The members of the court sat with their heads upon their knees, and the entire nation mourned. But then the land rose up, from the borders of Negro lands to the river's many mouths, from desert to desert, to hail the new era, which would no longer know injustice and in which the moon would "come right"; it rose up to greet with jubilation the sun that had risen in succession—a charmingly unattractive boy, who, if they had counted correctly, was only fifteen years old, which was why Tiy, Goddess-Widow and Mother of Horus, would hold the reins of power for him for a while yet—rose up to enjoy the great feasts of his enthronement and crowning with the crowns of Upper and Lower Egypt, celebrated with ponderous circumstance both in the Palace of the West in Thebes and, for the most sacred rites, at Per-Mont, city of coronations, to which young Pharaoh and his mother, both tall in feathers, traveled a short distance upstream in splendid retinue on the heavenly barque *Star of the Two Lands,* amid cheers from both banks. When he returned, he bore these titles: Strong Warrior Bull, Favorite of Both Goddesses, Great of Kingship at Karnak; Golden Falcon Who Lifted the Crowns at Per-Mont; King of Upper and Lower Egypt; Nefer-khe-peru-Rê-Wanrê, which means "beautiful in form is he who is unique and him to whom he is unique"; Son of the Sun, Amenhotep; Divine Ruler of Thebes, Great in Permanence, Living in All Eternity, Beloved of Amun-Rê, Lord of the Heavens; High Priest in the Horizon of Him Who Rejoices by Virtue of His Name "Fire that is Atôn."

Those were the names of young Pharaoh after his coronation, and this combination was, as Joseph and Mai-Sakhme agreed, the painfully balanced product of long and dogged negotiations between the court, which was inclined to Atum-Rê's obliging doctrine of the sun, and the zealous and oppressive power of Amun's temple, the result of which had been a few deep bows before the Lord of tradition, but only in recompense for certain clearly transparent concessions made to the Lord of On at the tip of the triangle, which is to say, the royal lad had in fact consecrated himself to the Power of the Seeing of Rê-Horakhte, and, what was more, woven the antitraditional and didactic name of Atôn into his long train of titles—despite all of which his mother, the Goddess-Widow, when addressing her

Strong Warrior Bull, to which he bore not the least resemblance, simply called him Meni. The people, however, so Joseph heard, had another name for him, a tender and delicate name. They called him Neb-nef-nezem, "Lord of Sweet Breath"—though no one knew why for sure. Perhaps because it was known that he loved the flowers in his garden and liked to bury his little nose in their fragrance.

There in his hole, Joseph missed all this and the joyful tumult that had accompanied it, and the only echo of these events to find its way down to his prison was the three-day carousal that Mai-Sakhme's soldiers were permitted. He was not there to witness them, was not present on earth, so to speak, for the change of day, when tomorrow became today and with it, tomorrow's highest today's highest. He only knew that it had happened, and from down here in his pit he took notice of the highest. He knew that Neb-nef-nezem's sister-wife, another princess from Mitanniland, whom his father had wooed and won for him in correspondence with King Tushratta, had disappeared into the West more or less upon her arrival in the land to which she had been sent—but then, Meni, the Strong Warrior Bull, was used to such disappearances. There had always been a good deal of dying around him. All his siblings had died, some of them before his birth, some during his lifetime, including a brother; and only a late-born sister was left, though she likewise displayed such a strong inclination for the West that she was rarely ever seen. Nor, to judge by the sandstone and limestone images that the disciples of Ptah sculpted of him, did he himself look like someone who would live for ever and ever. But since it was crucial that the line of the sun should be propagated before he too might depart this life, he had been married yet again, while Neb-maat-Rê-Amenhotep was still alive: to a child of the Egyptian nobility named Nefertiti, who had now become his Great Consort and Mistress of the Two Lands and on whom he had bestowed the radiant second name of Nefernefru-atôn, "Beautiful Beyond All Beauty Is the Atôn."

Joseph had also missed these marriage festivities, with their accompanying jubilation on both banks; but he knew of them and took notice of this young highest. For instance, he heard from his captain Mai-Sakhme, who learned many things through official channels, that immediately after he had lifted the crowns at Per-Mont, Pharaoh, with the permission of his mother, had issued an order that greatest haste be made at Karnak to complete the house for Rê-Horakhte-Atôn that his father had commissioned before his departure to the West, and decreed that first of all there be erected in the temple's open court an exceptionally huge obelisk of hewn stone set upon a high pedestal—representing a doctrine of the sun adapted from tenets taught in On at the tip of the Delta and apparently intended as a direct challenge to Amun. Not that Amun would on principle have had anything against having other gods in his neighborhood. All around his great presence in Karnak there were a good many houses and shrines—for Ptah, the wrapped god; for rigid, erect Min; for Montu, the falcon; and for many others—and Amun not only benevolently tolerated their worship in his vicinity, but believed the multiplicity of Egypt's gods was of implicit value and importance for his own conservative views—always presupposing that he, in all his gravity, was king over everything, king of all the gods, and that from time to time they would wait upon him, in return for which he was even prepared to repay them with a visit on appropriate occasions. But being waited upon was out of the question here, for no image would be present in this great shrine, this House of the Sun now under construction, but only the obelisk, which threatened to be so presumptuously tall that it might seem as if one were still living in the days of the pyramid builders, when Amun had been small and Rê very great in all his horizons, as if since then Amun had not absorbed Rê into himself to become Amun-Rê, the god of the empire and king of the gods, beneath whom Rê-Atum might at most meanwhile continue to exist on his own after his fashion, or rather, *should* continue to exist for the sake of preserving tradition, but not in this presumptuous way and not as a new god named Atôn making the sort of philosophical fuss over himself that was befitting only to Amun-Rê—or, more precisely, not even to him, since thinking was uncalled-for and must come to a halt before the fact that Amun was king over all the traditional multiplicity of Egypt's gods.

Even under King Neb-maat-Rê, the court had seen a good deal of fashionable thinking and wild speculation, and this appeared now to be on the verge of running rampant. In honor of the obelisk's erection, the young Pharaoh had issued a decree to be chiseled into stone as a testimony to a sophisticated attempt to provide a new and antitraditional definition of the nature of the solar divinity, a definition so incisive that it could not help suffering from its own tortuousness: "There lives," the definition read, "Rê-Hor of both horizons and he rejoices on the horizon in his name of Shu, who is the Atôn."

That was obscure, although it spoke of clarity and brightness and wanted to be very clear. It was complicated, although it aimed at simplification and unification. Rê-Horakhte, a god among the gods of Egypt, was threefold in form: animal, human, and heavenly. His image was a man with a falcon's head, above which stood the solar disk. But as a heavenly body he was also threefold: in his birth out of night, in the zenith of his manliness, and in his death in the west. He lived a life of birth, of death, and of regeneration, a life that stared at death. He who had ears to hear and eyes to read the inscription in stone understood that Pharaoh's doctrinal message did not want the god's life to be viewed in that same way, not as a coming and going, a becoming, perishing, and becoming again, not as life attuned to death and therefore phallic, indeed not as life at all, inasmuch as life is attuned to death, but rather as pure being, as the changeless source of light subject to neither rise nor fall, from whose image both the human and the bird were henceforth to be removed, so that only the pure, life-radiating solar disk remained, and its name was Atôn.

This was understood, or not understood, but in any case was a topic of lively discussion in city and country, both among those qualified to comment on it and among those who lacked all qualifications and therefore simply chattered. Such chatter even found its way down into Joseph's pit; Mai-Sakhme's soldiers chattered away about it, as did convicts in the quarry once they could catch their breath, and they all understood that at the least this was an offense to Amun-Rê, just as were the great obelisk that had been set before his nose and Pharaoh's other far-reaching decrees tied to this philosophic definition of the name—and those did indeed reach very far. The quarter of the city in which the new House of the Sun was being erected was to bear the name Radiance of the Great Atôn; yes, it was also rumored that Thebes itself, Weset, the city of Amun, was to be called City of the Radiance of Atôn, and there was no end of chatter about that. Even those who lay dying in Mai-Sakhme's infirmary shed summoned their last energies to talk about it—not to mention those who suffered only from leprous stings and eye irritation—the result of which was a serious challenge to the captain's system of organized calm.

The Lord of Sweet Breath, it appeared, could not do enough in this regard and continued to pursue the matter—the matter, that is, of his beloved doctrinal god and the construction of his temple—with such great haste and urgency that every stonemason from Jebu, the Elephant Isle, down to the Delta was set to work at it. And yet even this vast enterprise did not suffice to provide the House of Atôn with the kind of structure befitting his eternal residence. Pharaoh was in such a hurry and so driven by his own impatience that he dispensed with those great blocks used for building the tombs of gods, for they required careful hewing and were difficult to transport, and gave the order that the temple of changeless light be constructed of small stones that could be tossed from man to man, which in turn meant a great deal of mortar and cement had to be applied for the walls to be smooth enough for the dazzling painted bas-reliefs that were to adorn them. Amun simply sneered at this, so it was generally reported.

The repercussion from these events likewise found its way down to the world of Jacob's son, though he was not on hand to witness them, if only because of the heavy demands Pharaoh's hasty construction methods placed on those drudging in Mai-Sakhme's quarry; and Joseph, bearing his staff of authority, had to spend a good deal of time there, making sure that pickaxes and spikes were in constant use, so that the warden would not receive any unpleasant letters containing nasty veiled threats from higher-ups. But otherwise, there at the side of his calm captain, he continued to lead a tolerable convict's life at Zawi-Rê, and though it was as monotone as the captain's speech, it was nourished by expectation. For there was a great deal to be expected, from both near and far—but first, the near. Time passed for him as it tends to pass at its familiar pace, which can be called neither fast nor slow; for it passes slowly, especially if one lives in expectation, but when one looks back, it has passed very quickly. He lived there until, without his paying much attention, he had turned thirty. Then came the day of breathlessness and a winged messenger, a day that would almost have taught Mai-Sakhme what shock is had he not always expected great things for Joseph.

The Courier

A barque arrived, its stern swung like a lotus petal, its sails dyed purple—and propelled by five oarsmen on each side, it was so light that it flew. It bore the symbol of royalty—an express boat from Pharaoh's personal flotilla. It docked with elegance at the landing of Zawi-Rê, and a man sprang forward, a young man, as light and trim as the barque that had borne him, with a lean face and long, sinewy legs. His chest was heaving under the linen, he was out of breath or appeared to be—in other words, he pretended to be. For there was no real reason to be out of breath, since after all he had traveled by boat, not run all the way here; his was a simulated, demonstratively dutiful breathlessness. To be sure, he now ran and flew at great speed through the portal and courts of Zawi-Rê, fending off every attempt to stop him with short, though hardly loud cries that left the guards standing there in frozen dismay, and having cleared his own path demanded to see the captain at once, no ifs, ands, or buts—which is to say, he ran or flew so swiftly toward the citadel, to which the guards pointed, that despite his slender frame the breathlessness he had feigned may well have been genuine now. For, of course, the little pairs of gold-foil wings at the heels of his sandals and on his cap could not have been of any real help to his progress, but were merely external badges of his alacrity.

Joseph, who had been busy in the office, was well aware of this arrival, of the running and commotion, but paid it no mind, even when it was called to his attention. He went on sorting papers with the chief clerk until a mercenary came running up—he, too, out of breath—and gave him the message to drop everything, no matter how important, and report to the captain at once.

"I shall do so," he said, but first finished his discussion with the clerk about the paper he still held in his hand, before proceeding to the captain in his tower—not, of course, at an ambling pace, but not in any rush either, perhaps because of some premonition that very soon any rash or hasty movement would no longer become him at all.

As Joseph entered the apothecary chamber, the tip of Mai-Sakhme's nose was already a shade of white, his strong eyebrows were arched higher than usual, and his rounded lips well separated.

"There you are," he said, lowering his voice to Joseph. "You should have been here before now. Hear your instructions!" And he waved a hand at the winged messenger standing nearby—or not standing, really, not standing there calmly, but moving arms, head, shoulders, and legs as if running to and fro in place, trying to keep himself busy, or better, breathless. Now and then he would rise up on tiptoes as if about to take flight.

"Your name is Usarsiph?" he asked in a soft, hurried voice and cast a glance at Joseph with hasty, close-set eyes. "The captain's assistant and supervisor, who was placed in charge of certain residents in the Vulture Cabin here two years ago?"

"I am he," Joseph said.

"Then you must come with me just as you are," the man replied, accelerating the motion of his limbs. "I am Pharaoh's First Runner, his express courier, and I have come by express boat. You must board it with me immediately, so that I may take you to the court, for you are to stand before Pharaoh."

"Me?" Joseph asked. "How can that be? I am too lowly for that."

"Lowly or not, it is Pharaoh's beautiful wish and command. Breathlessly have I brought it to your captain, and breathlessly must you now obey the summons."

"I was placed in this prison," Joseph replied, "though to be sure due to a misrepresentation, after having been stolen, so to speak, and brought down here. But here I lie as a slave condemned to hard labor, and though my chains may not be visible, they are there. How then could I depart with you through these walls and gates to board your express boat?"

"That," the runner hurriedly replied, "has not the least to do with this beautiful command. In a twinkling it lets all such things vanish into thin air and instantly breaks your chains. Nothing stands before Pharaoh's beautiful will. But calm yourself, it is more than likely that you will not withstand the test before him and more than likely that you will be brought back here to hard labor posthaste. You will not be cleverer than Pharaoh's greatest experts and magicians from his House of Books and will not put to shame the seers, prophets, and interpreters of the House of Rê-Horakhte, who invented the solar year."

"That rests with God, and whether He is with me or not," Joseph replied. "Has Pharaoh had a dream perhaps?"

"Yours is not to ask, but to answer," the courier said, "and woe to you if you cannot do it. For then you presumably will fall far deeper than simply back to this prison."

"Why am I to be tested in this way," Joseph asked, "and how does Pharaoh know about me, that he should send forth his beautiful command down here to summon me?"

"You were named and mentioned and remarked upon due to a dilemma," the man responded. "You shall learn more of it under way at the earliest. Now you must follow me breathlessly, so that you may stand before Pharaoh at once."

"Wase is far," Joseph said, "and Merima't, the palace, a great distance away. However swift your express boat may be, my express courier, Pharaoh will have to wait until I can fulfill his will and stand before him to be tested, so that before I arrive he may perhaps have forgotten his beautiful command and indeed no longer find it beautiful."

"Pharaoh is near," the runner riposted. "It has pleased the world's Beautiful Sun to shine at On at the tip of the triangle; he has proceeded there aboard his barque *Star of the Two Lands*. In but a few hours my express boat will fly and flit with us both to its goal. Arise, and not one word more."

"But I must have my hair cut and put on better clothes first, if I am to stand before Pharaoh and withstand the test," Joseph said. For while in prison he had let his own hair grow and his garb was only the most common linen of coarser weave.

The runner, however, replied, "That can be done aboard ship while we flit and fly. All this has been taken care of. If you believe that one pressing matter can delay another instead of being packed together in the same time to save time, then you know nothing of what breathlessness is before Pharaoh's beautiful command."

Now the summoned prisoner turned to say farewell to the warden, calling him "my friend."

"You can see, my friend," he said, "how things stand with me and what is being done with me after three years. They are hastily releasing me from this hole and pulling me from the well according to an old pattern. This courier thinks that I shall fall back down to you here, but I do not believe it, and if I do not believe it, it will not be so. And so farewell and receive my thanks for how in your good and calm way you have made this stagnation of my life, this penitence and darkness, bearable, and for allowing me to be your brother in expectation. For you still await the third appearance of your Nekhbet, just as I awaited what must become of me. This is farewell, but not for long. After a long forgetting, someone remembered me when he bumped his nose on the memory of me. But I will remember you without forgetting, and if my father's God is with me, which I do not doubt, lest I offend Him, you shall also be removed from this cave and boredom. There are three beautiful things, three tokens your servant has always kept in mind; they are called 'carried off,' 'raised up,' and 'sending for others to follow.' If God raises me up—and I fear I would offend Him were I not to expect it with certainty—then I promise you that I will send for you to follow, so that you may share in more stimulating circumstances, where your calm runs no risk of degenerating into sleepiness and the chances of that third appearance will also be improved. Shall that be a word of promise between you and me?"

"My thanks whatever happens," Mai-Sakhme said and embraced him, which he had not been permitted to do before—and he had some vague sense that it might not be appropriate again in the future either, but for just the opposite reason. But this, the hour of leave-taking, was the moment for it. "For an instant," he said, "when this messenger came running up, I thought I might be shocked. But I am not shocked, my heart is beating calmly, for how can a man be rattled by something he is already prepared for? Calm is nothing more than being prepared for anything, and so when it does come there's no shock at all. Though being touched is a different matter—there is always room for that even when one is prepared, and I am very touched by your desire to remember me when you come into your kingdom. May the wisdom of Lord Khmunu be with you! Farewell!"

Hopping from one foot to the other, the courier barely let the captain speak his final words, and now took Joseph by the hand and, making a show of breathlessness, ran with him from the tower and through the courts and corridors of Zawi-Rê to the express boat, into which they leaped, flitting away on it now at incredible speed.

As they swept along Joseph was not only shorn, made up, and dressed anew while he sat beneath the roof of the little cabin pavilion on its quarterdeck, but also, during the process, was informed by the winged messenger about some of what had happened in On, the city of the sun, and why he had been sent for: Pharaoh had indeed dreamt an extremely important dream, but had been left fully in the lurch by the prophets he had called upon for interpretation, resulting in both their disgrace and a great dilemma, until finally Nefer-em-Wêse, the Chief Butler, had spoken before Pharaoh and mentioned him, that is Joseph, saying that if anyone could help Pharaoh out of his dilemma it might very well be Joseph and that one ought at least to try to fetch him. The courier could provide only a muddled and distorted account of what it was that Pharaoh had actually dreamt— a version that had seeped to Pharaoh's courtiers from the council chamber where the experts had gone down in defeat. The Majesty of the God, so it was said, had dreamt first of seven cows eating seven ears of grain, and on a second occasion of seven cows being eaten by seven ears of grain—in short, the kind of stuff that would never occur to anyone, not even in a dream, but that nevertheless was somewhat helpful to Joseph during the journey, and his thoughts played with images of nourishment, famine, and precaution.

Light and Darkness

What had actually happened that led to Joseph's being summoned was this:

A year before—toward the end of the second year that Joseph had spent in prison—Amenhotep, the fourth of that name, had turned sixteen and thus come of age, bringing to an end the regency of Tiy, his mother, and automatically transferring rule over the Two Lands to the successor of Neb-maat-Rê the Magnificent. With that a situation had come to an end that both people in general and those more closely concerned had regarded as symbolized by the early morning sun recently born out of night, whereby the radiant son is more son than man, still attached to his mother, a fledgling under her wings, waiting to rise to the zenith of his full powers. Then Eset, the mother, steps back and renounces her sovereignty, although she still retains all the dignity of having given birth and of being the first-born, for she is the source of all life and power and the man is always her son. She yields power to him; but he exercises it for her, just as she has exercised it for him.

Tiy, the Mother-Goddess, who had in fact ruled and nourished the life of the Two Lands during the years when her spouse had declined into the senescence of Rê, removed the braided beard of Usir, which like Hatshepsut, the Pharaoh with breasts, she had worn on her chin, and gave it to the young, male son of the sun, on whom a beard looked only a little less peculiar than on her when he donned it for certain occasions of high solemnity—such as those that also demanded he wear a tail, or better, tie a jackal's tail to the back of his apron, an animal attribute that, for some sacred, primal reason now forgotten but still preserved in darkness, belonged by ancient and strict tradition to his ceremonial vestments, despite the fact, as the court well knew, that the young Pharaoh detested it, since wearing this primal tail did not agree with his stomach and tended to arouse nausea in His Majesty, making him turn very pale, even greenish, although, given the state of his health, he was subject to such attacks all on his own, without any help from his primal tail.

Unless all records are in error, the transfer of royal power from mother to son must have been accompanied by doubts as to whether it might not be better to delay it or forgo it entirely and to leave the young sun beneath those protecting wings for good and all. The god's mother herself entertained such doubts, as did her highest advisors, and one of the most powerful of them, a man we already know, did his best to foster them: Beknechons, the stern Great Prophet and Chief Priest of Amun. Not that he was a servant of the crown or, like several of his predecessors, jointly held the offices of high priest and chief vizier in charge of administering the Two Lands. King Neb-maat-Rê, Amenhotep the Third, had felt it his duty to separate religious and civil power and had installed secular men as viziers of both North and South. But as the mouth of the imperial god, Beknechons had a right to the ear of the queen regent, and with all due courtesy she allowed him to use it, even though she surely knew that she was lending her ear to the voice of a political rival. She had played a crucial role in her spouse's decision to remove such a threat by separating what had once been united; she felt that it was necessary to restrain the power of this troublesome Council of Karnak and to preclude a predominance whose threat had arisen not just yesterday—for the need to defend against it was an ancient royal tradition. Meni's grandfather, Thutmose, who had dreamt his dream of promise at the foot of the Great Sphinx and freed it from sand, had claimed that huge primal image's lord, Harmakhis-Kheper-Atum-Rê, to be his own father, saying it was to him that he owed his crown; and, as everyone understood—as Joseph himself had surely come to understand—this was nothing but a hieroglyphic euphemism for the defensive strategy of providing religious underpinnings for political self-assertion. And no one failed to notice that the advancement of the new celestial god Atôn—which was the object of his grandson's loving thoughts and efforts, but the beginnings of which were to be found as early as the court of Thutmose's son—had as its goal to wrench Amun-Rê out of the cruelly imposed union with the sun to which he owed his universal legitimacy and to reduce his superior position to the rank of a local power as the city god of Wase, which was what he had been prior to his own political gambit.

One fails to recognize the unity of the world if one considers religion and politics as two fundamentally different things that neither have nor should have anything to do with one another, so that the one is debased and exposed as lacking in authenticity if it can be proved to contain the slightest hint of the other. In truth they exchange garments, just as Ishtar and Tammuz wear their veiled garment by turns, and it is the world in its wholeness that speaks when one of them speaks the language of the other. But the world speaks in other languages as well, for example through the works of Ptah, those manifestations of taste, skill, and worldly ornamentation that it would be equally foolish to regard as self-contained, as something that has fallen away from the world's unity and has nothing to do with religion or politics. Joseph knew quite well that the young Pharaoh—all on his own and without any advice from his mother—had made the pictorial ornamentation of the world the object of his eager, indeed zealous attention, had done so, in fact, in complete accord with the efforts he expended in conceiving and advancing the god Atôn in all his truth and purity. Joseph also knew that Pharaoh was devoted to certain changes, to a remarkable easing of ancient traditions in this regard, which in his opinion corresponded to the wishes and attitudes of his beloved god. This was quite obviously dear to his heart, something he did for its own sake, out of a personal conviction of what was true and delightful in the world of images.

But did it therefore have nothing to do with religion and politics? Since time out of mind, or, as the children of Keme liked to say, for millions of years, the world of images had been subjected to sacred, obligatory, and, if you like, rather rigid laws, whose patron and conserver was Amun-Rê in his shrine, or, in his stead, his grave priesthood. To ease the restrictions on such images—or, indeed, to want to remove them entirely for the sake of some new truth and delight that the god Atôn had revealed to Pharaoh—was a direct blow to Amun-Rê, the lord of a religion, and to a political structure that was irrevocably bound up with certain sanctified pictorial understandings. In Pharaoh's theories for relaxing the rules of how images are to be created, the world in its wholeness was speaking the language of aesthetics, one language among the many in which it expresses itself. For wherever he turns, man is always dealing with the unity of the world as a whole, whether he knows it or not.

For Amenhotep, however, the royal boy who actually wanted to know, the world in its wholeness was evidently a bit too much at the moment; his energies seemed too frail for it, he had trouble dealing with it. He was often pale and greenish, even when that animal tail was not forced on him, and was subject to agonizing headaches when he could not open his eyes and had to vomit over and over. Then he would have to lie in the dark for days on end—he, whose one love was the light, the golden link between heaven and earth, the rays of his father Atôn, ending in caressing and life-spending hands. Of course it gave pause for thought that at any moment such attacks might keep a sovereign from fulfilling his official duties, from sacrificial rites and consecrations, or even from receiving great men and councilors to advise him. But, unfortunately, there was worse. One never knew what might suddenly happen to His Majesty in the midst of fulfilling his duties, in the presence of great men and councilors or even of an assembled throng of commonfolk. For there were occasions when Pharaoh would clasp his fingers tightly around his thumbs, roll his eyes back under half-lowered lids, and fall into an eerie oblivion, which, granted, did not last long, but all the same came as a disconcerting interruption in the proceedings or discussion. He himself explained these attacks as an instant visitation by his father, the god, and rather than fearing them, looked forward to them with eager expectation—because he returned out of them and back into the light of day enriched with authentic doctrines and revelations concerning the beautiful and true nature of the Atôn.

It should therefore be a cause for neither wonder nor doubt that serious consideration was given to the idea of leaving the young sun in his morning state, of keeping him beneath the shadow of night's wings even after he had come of age. The idea, however, never ripened to maturity, and despite the arguments of Amun, it had at last been dismissed. The reasons against it ultimately outweighed those for it. It was not prudent to admit to the world that Pharaoh was ill or so frail that he could not exercise his sovereignty—that ran counter to the interest of the sun's reigning hereditary dynasty and might have entailed dangerous misunderstanding throughout the empire and those regions required to pay tribute to it. Moreover, Pharaoh's infirmity was of such a nature that it provided no valid reasons for his being permanently kept under tutelage—was, in fact, of a sacred nature that was more likely to contribute to his popularity than to detract from it, and that it would be better to use not as the basis for denying him his majority but for countering Amun instead, whose secret desire to unite the double crown with his own feathered headdress and to establish his own dynasty lurked behind everything he did.

That was why, then, maternal night had ceded to her son the full and sovereign authority of his noonday manliness. Closer examination, however, reveals that Amenhotep himself greeted the event with some ambiguity, that he felt not only pride and joy, but also apprehension, and all in all would perhaps have preferred to remain under those wings. For one particular reason he had even looked ahead to the day of his coming of age with horror: Tradition demanded that at the beginning of his reign Pharaoh, in his capacity as commander in chief, personally undertake a campaign of war and plunder against Asiatic or Negro lands, at the glorious conclusion of which he would be solemnly received at the border and upon his return to the capital would not only have to sacrifice a large portion of the booty to mighty Amun-Rê—who had, after all, brought these princes of Zahi and Kush under his feet within their own lands—but also to slay with his own hand a half dozen prisoners of as high a rank as possible, or, if need be, those promoted for the occasion.

The Lord of Sweet Breath, however, felt totally incapable of performing such formalities and at their mere mention—or if he simply thought of them himself—his face would become contorted and immediately turn pale and green. He abhorred war, which might be of interest to Amun, but was not even remotely a concern of "my father Atôn," who had instead expressly revealed himself to his son, in one of his states of sacred, ominous oblivion, as a "Lord of Peace." Meni could not take to the field with steed and chariot, or pillage, or shower Amun with booty, or slay princely—or ostensibly princely—prisoners for him. He could not and would not do it, not even indirectly or in pretense, and he refused to be depicted on temple walls and pylons as standing high in his chariot, shooting arrows at the terrified enemy, or holding a pack of them by the hair with one hand and brandishing a murderous club above them with the other. All that was intolerable and impossible for him, which is to say for his god and thus for him. The court and the nation needed to understand that under no circumstance would there be an initial campaign of pillage—and ultimately this could be got round with a few good words. One could proclaim, for instance, that the lands of the earth lay in such submission and in such numbers at Pharaoh's feet, and their tribute flowed in such timely abundance, that any war campaign would be superfluous and that Pharaoh wished to glorify the inauguration of his reign precisely by engaging in no such thing. And that is what happened.

But though he was spared in that regard, Meni's feelings at entering upon his noonday glory remained mixed. He could not disguise from himself that as sole ruler he had to deal directly with the world as a whole and in all its dimensions, in all its languages and idioms, whereas until now he had had the luxury of contemplating it from only one particular viewpoint, the religious perspective he so ardently preferred. Free of all the claims of earthly affairs, he had been allowed to wander among the flowers and exotic trees of his garden and dream of his loving god, to conceive and advance him, and to ponder how his nature was best comprehended in a name and suggested in an image. Those had been taxing responsibilities enough, but he loved them and gladly endured the headaches they caused him. But now he had to act and think in ways that left him with headaches for which he felt no fondness whatever. Every morning, while sleep still lay in his head and limbs, there would appear before him a man named Ramose, the Vizier of the South, a tall man with a little goatee and two golden necklaces; and after first greeting him in a litany of very flowery and long-winded formulas, Ramose would then unroll his marvelously inscribed scrolls and pester him for several hours with the current affairs of state—with court decisions, tax rolls, plans for new canals, foundations to be laid, questions about the lumber supply for construction, the opening of quarries and mines in the desert, and so forth, all the while informing Pharaoh just what his beautiful will was in all these matters, only then to raise his hands and marvel at the beauty of that will. It was Pharaoh's beautiful will to travel this or that desert road in order to determine appropriate places for wells and way stations that had previously been established by others who knew far more about such things. It was his admirably beautiful will to bid the count of the city of El-Kab to come before his countenance that he might interrogate him as to why the payment of his official taxes in gold, silver, cattle, and linen had arrived at the treasury in Thebes so unpunctually and, what was more, in less than full measure. It was also his lofty will to depart the day after tomorrow for wretched Nubia in order to participate in the solemn founding or opening of a temple that was primarily dedicated to Amun-Rê and thus, to his way of feeling, in no way worth the exhaustion and headaches such an arduous journey inflicted on him.

In general, obligatory ceremonies, the ponderous rituals of the imperial god, laid claim to a major part of his time and energies. Outwardly this had to be his beautiful will, but inwardly it most definitely was not, since it prevented him from thinking of the Atôn and, what was more, demanded he keep company with Beknechons, Amun's man of strict observance, whom he could not stand. He had tried in vain to bestow the name City of the Radiance of Atôn on his capital, but the name never won the hearts of the people, because the priests never allowed it to be mentioned; and so Wase was and remained Nowet-Amun, the city of the Great Ram, who by the arm of his royal sons had overthrown foreign lands and made Egypt rich. Even then Pharaoh was secretly toying with the idea of moving his residence away from Thebes, where the image of Amun-Rê gleamed on every wall, pylon, column, and obelisk, offending his eye. He had not yet thought, however, of founding a new city of his own, dedicated solely to the Atôn, but was merely contemplating resettling the court at On at the tip of the Delta, where he himself felt much more comfortable. He had a pleasant palace there very near the Temple of the Sun, nothing so magnificent as Merima't to the west of Thebes, but one equipped with all the comforts that his delicate nature demanded; and court chroniclers had to record the good god's frequent journeys, both by ship and chariot, down to the city of On. True, this was also the residence of the Vizier of the North, who oversaw the administration and the justice system of all the nomes between Asyut and the mouths of the river and who also was quick to give him headaches. But here Meni was at least spared having to waft incense in Amun's direction under the watchful eye of Beknechons, and he took great pleasure in conversing with the learned baldheaded priests from the house of Atum-Rê-Horakhte about the nature of their splendid god, his father, and about that god's inner life, which despite his vast age remained fresh and active, rendering him capable of the loveliest transformations, refinements, and developments, so that, with the aid of human reasoning, from an old god, if one might put it that way, there was slowly emerging a new, increasingly more perfect, ineffably more beautiful god—which is to say, the marvelous Atôn who illuminated the universe.

If only one could have given oneself over entirely to him, have been nothing except his son, midwife, herald, and confessor, instead of having also to be King of Egypt, the successor of those who had set Keme's boundary stones at great distances and made of it a world empire. One was indebted to them and their deeds, one was under obligation to them and their deeds; and it was reasonable to presume that one could not stand Beknechons, the man of Amun, who constantly emphasized all this, because he was right in emphasizing it. Which is to say: the young Pharaoh himself presumed as much, it was a suspicion of his innermost conscience. He suspected that not only was it one thing to found a world empire and quite another to help bring a universal god to life, but that also this second activity very possibly stood in some sort of contradiction to his royal responsibility to preserve and maintain the creation he had inherited. The headaches that made him close his eyes when the Viziers of the South and North pestered him with imperial business were also linked to suspicions that implied—or, if not definitively implied, at least tended in that direction—that those headaches resulted not so much from fatigue and boredom, but rather from that vague, but disquieting awareness of the contradiction between his devotion to the theology of his beloved Atôn and the responsibilities of a King of Egypt. Or put another way: they were headaches of conscience and conflict, and were, moreover, understood to be just that, which did not make them better, but only worse and reinforced his nostalgia for his former state as a morning sun shaded by the wings of maternal night.

Without doubt, not only he but the nation itself as well was in better hands back then. For the prosperity of a nation of this earth is always better tended to by the mother, even if its transcendental affairs are better left to the thoughts of the son. This was Amenhotep's secret conviction, and he was surely inspired to it by the spirit of the land of Egypt itself, by the creed of Isis of the Black Earth. In his mind he differentiated between the world's material, earthly, natural prosperity and its spiritual, psychological well-being, though always with the vague fear that these two concerns might not only not coincide, but instead might also stand in basic conflict, so that to be entrusted with both at once, to be both king and priest, was an awful burden that ended in headaches. Well-being and prosperity were the concern of the king; or, rather, it was far better for them to be the concern and business of a queen, the concern and business of the mother, of the Great Cow—so that her son the priest could spin his solar thoughts and freely pursue the issue of spiritual well-being with no responsibility for matters of material prosperity. The royal responsibility for material concerns weighed heavily on the young Pharaoh. For him, the very idea of his kingdom was bound up in the notion of that black Egyptian loam that lay between desert and desert—black and fertile with the impregnating flood. But his passion was for pure light, for the golden youth of the sun at its zenith—and it left him with an uneasy conscience. Ramose, the Vizier of the South—to whom everything was reported, including the rising of the Dog Star, which presages the first swelling of the waters—kept him constantly informed about the current state of the river and its prospects for flooding, for fertilization and harvest; but to Meni, no matter how attentively, indeed anxiously, he listened, it seemed as if it would be better for the man to turn, as before, to his mother, the Isis Queen, who was more familiar with these things and into whose care they were better entrusted. Nevertheless, both for him and the land as a whole everything depended on the blessed regularity of the black workings of fertility, that they never falter or fail; if that sort of thing were to happen, he would be blamed. It was not for nothing that the nation had a king who was god's son, who thus surely represented a safeguard, in god's name, against any wavering in these sacred and necessary processes, over which no one had any influence otherwise. Any failure and general distress in the Realm of the Black Earth necessarily meant that the people would be disappointed in him whose mere existence should have prevented such a thing—and that would bring with it a severe decline in the prestige he sorely needed to assist in the triumph of his beautiful doctrine, the creed of Atôn, whose nature was heavenly light.

This was the source of his quandary and qualms. He had no connection to the black below, but loved only the light above. But if things did not go smoothly and well with that nourishing blackness, it would be the undoing of his authority as a teacher of light. That was why the young Pharaoh's feelings were so divided when maternal night removed its sheltering wing and ceded the kingdom to him.

Pharaoh's Dreams

And so Pharaoh had journeyed once again to edifying On out of an insuperable desire to escape the precincts of Amun and to converse with the shiny-headed priests of the House of the Sun concerning Harmakhis-Kheper-Atum-Rê, the Atôn. Bending low and pursing their lips, the court chroniclers had delicately recorded how His Majesty had announced his beautiful decision, whereupon he had boarded a great chariot made of electrum, together with Nefertiti, whose name was Nefernefruatôn, Queen of the Two Lands, whose womb was now fertile and who flung her arm around him, and how in a blaze of radiance he had flown off down his beautiful path, followed by other chariots—by Tiy, the mother of the god, by Nezemmut, the queen's sister, by Baketatôn, his own sister, and by a host of chamberlains and ladies of the women's court, fans of ostrich feathers at their backs. The barque *Star of the Two Lands* had also been used for parts of the journey; and the chroniclers likewise described how, sitting beneath the baldachin, Pharaoh had consumed a roast pigeon, holding out to the queen the little drumstick on which she had dined and inserting confections into her mouth after first dipping them in wine.

At On, Amenhotep had entered his palace in the temple district and, exhausted from the journey, had slept there that first night without dreaming. He had begun the following day with a sacrifice to Rê-Horakhte of bread and beer, wine, birds, and incense, had then held an audience for the Vizier of the North, who spoke with him at length, and thereupon, despite the headache this had caused him, had devoted the rest of his day to those conversations with the god's attendants that he had so longed for. The chief topic of their consultations, a subject to which Amenhotep had been giving much deep thought, was the bird Bennu, also called Offspring of Fire, because it was said that it was both motherless and in fact its own father, that for it dying and genesis were one and the same, since it burned itself alive in its nest made of myrrh only to be reborn from the ashes as the young Bennu. This occurred, so several teachers claimed, every five hundred years, and in fact occurred within the sun temple of On, for the golden-purple bird, said to resemble a heronlike eagle, came there expressly for that purpose from somewhere in the east, from Arabia or India. Others asserted that it brought with it an egg made of myrrh, as large as it was able to carry, and, having sealed its own deceased father—meaning actually itself—inside, placed it upon the sun's altar. These two statements could coexist side by side—so many things can coexist and, though different, be equally true and thus merely different ways of expressing the same truth. But what Pharaoh first wanted to know or at least wished to discuss was what part of that period of five hundred years between the birth of the Offspring of Fire and its depositing of the egg had already passed, and where they now stood between its last appearance on the one hand and its next arrival on the other—in short, at what point in the phoenix year were they? The great majority of the priests were of the opinion that they must be somewhere in the middle of the time span; for if they stood close to its beginning then there would still have to be some memory of Bennu's most recent appearance, which was not the case. But if they were close to the end and new beginning of the cycle, then they would have to expect the bird's return very soon or perhaps even momentarily. But they did not expect to have such an experience in their own lifetime, leaving the midway point as the only possible conclusion. Yes, a few of them went so far as to conjecture one would always be left hovering in the middle, and that the true mystery was that the interval between the phoenix's most recent return and its next one was always the same and always at midpoint. But this mystery was not Pharaoh's chief concern, the object of his burning interest. The point he had come to discuss above all others and that he then spent half the day discussing with these shiny-headed priests was the doctrine stating that the myrrh egg of the fiery bird, in which it sealed the body of its father, did *not become heavier* in the process. For the bird had made it so large and heavy that it could just barely carry it, but if it could still carry it after sealing its father inside, then it was obvious that the egg's weight was not increased by the body.

To the young Pharaoh's eyes, this was an exciting, a ravishing fact of universal importance that demanded the most urgent discussion. If one added one body to another and it did not become any heavier, that meant that there were immaterial bodies—or to put it another, better way: disembodied realities, as immaterial as sunlight itself. Or to put it yet another, even better way: there was such a thing as spiritual reality, and this spiritual reality was ethereally embodied in Bennu's father. But in accepting that Bennu body, the myrrh egg's own character was changed in the most exciting and significant way. An egg was definitely a thing of female specificity, only female birds laid eggs, and nothing could be more maternally feminine than the great egg from which the world had once emerged. Bennu, however, the bird of the sun, was motherless and its own father; it made an egg of itself, a rival world egg, a male egg, a father egg, and laid it as a proclamation of paternity, spirit, and light on the alabaster table of the sun divinity.

Surrounded by these men of the solar calendar in the temple of Rê, Pharaoh could not get enough of discussing this subject and the significance it had for further understanding of the nature of the Atôn. He talked about it with them until deep into the night, talked to the point of excess, he luxuriated in golden immateriality and paternal spirituality, and even after the god's attendants were worn out and their shiny heads were nodding, he still had not had enough and could not bring himself to dismiss them, as if afraid to be left alone. Nevertheless he finally granted the nodding, tottering priests leave to go and sought out his own bedchamber, where the slave who

dressed and undressed him—an older man, who had been assigned
to him when Meni was a little boy and who still called him "Meni,"
though he showed him all other formal demonstrations of respect—
had long been waiting in the lamplight. He quickly and tenderly
made him comfortable for the night, bowed low, pressing his forehead to the floor, and withdrew to sleep just outside on the threshold. Nestled in the pillows of his artfully crafted bed—which stood
on a platform in the middle of the room, its headboard ornamented
with the most delicate ivory carvings of jackals, ibexes, and figures
of the god Bes—Pharaoh fell almost at once into an exhausted sleep,
but only for a short time. For after a few hours of heavy stupor, he
began to dream—topsy-turvy, alarming, and absurdly vivid dreams
of a kind he had known only as a child with a fever and a sore throat.
He did not dream, however, of Bennu's weightless father or the sun's
immaterial rays, but of quite the opposite.

In his dream he was standing at a lonely spot, a place of swamp
and reeds, along the banks of Hapi, the Provider. He was wearing his
red cap, the crown of Upper Egypt, and his beard was tied on and
the animal tail dangled from his upper garment. He was standing all
alone at this spot, his heart heavy, his crooked staff clutched in his
arm. Then he heard splashing not very far from the bank, and out of
the flood seven shapes emerged—climbing on land were seven cows
that must have been lying in the river the way water buffalo cows do,
and they walked past, one after the other in single file, seven of them,
but without a bull. There was no bull, but just the seven cows.
Splendid cows—white, black with a paler back, gray with a paler
belly, and two dappled ones, splotched with markings—such beautiful, sleek, fat cows, with bulging udders and the heavily lashed eyes
of Hathor and tall, curving lyre-shaped horns; and they began to
graze contentedly among the reed grass. The king had never seen
such magnificent cattle, not in all the land; what a great show of
sheer prosperity their bodies were, and Meni's heart wanted to rejoice at the sight, but could not, and instead felt heavy and anxious—
and was very quickly filled now with fear and dread. For the line of
cattle did not end with these first seven. More cows emerged from
the water, and there was no break between the one group and the
next. Seven more cows climbed on land, likewise without a bull—
but what bull would have wanted them? Pharaoh shuddered at these
cattle, they were the ugliest, leanest, gauntest cows he had ever seen

in his life—their bones stuck out from under their wrinkled hide, their udders were empty sacks with teats like cord; the sight was terrifying and thoroughly demoralizing, for the miserable creatures seemed scarcely able to stay on their feet; but their behavior was shamelessly impudent, viciously hostile, quite out of keeping with their frailty, yet somehow only too appropriate to it as well, for it was the savagery of starvation. As Pharaoh watches the wretched herd attack the sleek one: the hideous cows climb onto the beautiful ones, the way cows do when they play bull; then the wretched animals devour the splendid ones, wolf them down, simply wipe the meadow clean of them—but afterward stand there as emaciated as before, showing no sign whatever of having eaten their fill.

With that the dream ended, and Pharaoh started from his sleep bathed in the sweat of anxiety. His heart pounding, he sat up, looked around the softly lit chamber, and realized it had been a dream, but a dream so eloquent and immediate that it seemed as hostile as those starved cows from the river, and its icy grip lingered in the dreamer's bones. He did not want to stay in bed, but stood up, pulled on his white woolen nightshirt and paced the room, thinking about his vicious, absurd, but palpably clear dream. He would have liked to awaken his valet, to tell him his dream, or rather, to find out if what he had beheld could be put into words. But he was too tenderhearted to disturb the old man, whom he had kept waiting until late into the night, and so sat down in the cow-legged armchair that stood beside his bed, wrapped his nightshirt, its wool soft as moonlight, tighter around him and, snuggling into one corner of the chair, his feet resting on a footstool, dozed off again.

But no sooner had he fallen sleep than he began to dream again—he could not help it, once more, or perhaps still, he is standing on the riverbank with his crown and tail, and there lies a tilled patch of field with its black soil. And he watches as the fertile earth ripples and rolls a little, and a stalk grows from it, on which seven ears of grain sprout, one after the other, all on one stalk, fat, plump ears of grain, bursting with richness and nodding in the golden fullness of their yield. And his heart tries to rejoice, but cannot, for what follows is more sprouting from the stalk—another seven ears of grain emerge, miserable ears, barren, dead, and sere, blighted by the east wind, blackened by smut and rust, and as they emerge in their shabbiness below the fat ones, these then dwindle, as if vanishing into the others, and it's as if the blighted ears are devouring the plump ones, just as before the wretched cows devoured the sleek ones, and this time, too, grow no fatter and fuller than before. Pharaoh saw it all palpable before his eyes, started up in his chair, and found that once again it had been a dream.

Another absurdly topsy-turvy dream, silent in its frenzy, but with a hostility that spoke almost directly to his heart, as both warning and instruction, so that Pharaoh could no longer sleep at all until dawn, which fortunately was near now, nor did he want to sleep, but instead he constantly shifted between bed and armchair, pondering the clarity of this pair of dreams grown from one stalk and crying out for interpretation; and now he firmly resolved that in no case would he keep such dreams to himself and allow them to fade into silence, but that he would make an issue of them and sound an alarm on their behalf. In them he had been wearing crown, crooked staff, and tail, which beyond any doubt made them royal dreams of imperial significance, highly peculiar dreams drenched in care. He had no choice but to make them public and exert every effort to come to grips with them and to get to the bottom of their obviously menacing import. Meni was in fact outraged at his dreams and increasingly despised them with each passing moment. A king could not put up with such dreams—although, on the other hand, they could only have come to a king. Under his reign, under Nefer-khe-peru-Rê-Wanrê-Amenhotep, this sort of thing dared not happen—ghastly cows eating up fat ones and miserable smut-ridden ears of grain devouring plump, golden ones—nothing dared occur in the realm of real events that corresponded to anything like those ghost-ridden images. For he would be blamed, his prestige would suffer a severe decline, ears and hearts would be closed to the message of the Atôn, and Amun would be the one to profit. Light was endangered by a threat from the blackness, weightless spirituality menaced by danger from the material world—there was no doubt of it. His distress was very great; it assumed the form of an anger that steadily gathered into a determination that this danger first had to be recognized and exposed so that one could then meet it head-on.

The first person to whom he told his dream, as well as it could be put into words, was the old man who had slept at his threshold and now dressed him, fixing his hair and binding it in a scarf. He had only shaken his head in amazement and remarked that that was what happened when the Good God went to bed so late after having heated his brain with endless "speculating"—as he put it in his foolish, commonplace way. Actually it is likely he automatically considered these worrisome dreams to be a kind of punishment for Meni's having made his old servant stay up waiting for him so long. "Oh, you old muttonhead!" Pharaoh had replied, smiling in annoyance and lightly slapping the old man's brow with the palm of his hand, and had then gone to the queen, who was feeling sick because of her pregnancy and so paid scant attention. Whereupon he sought out Tiy, the divine mother, and found her being tended to by her chambermaids at her dressing table. He had told her his dreams as well, discovering that as time went on they were not easier to tell, but only made his foul mood worse with each telling—nor did he find much consolation or encouragement from her. Tiy always scoffed a little when he came to her with his royal cares—but he was certain that this was something for a king to worry about and had said so right off, and in response her maternal face had at once taken on that mocking smile. Although, after much deliberation, King Neb-maat-Rê's widow had voluntarily relinquished her regency and ceded to her son the full sovereignty of his noonday zenith, she could not conceal her jealousy of that sovereignty; and what pained Meni was that he was aware of this—it did not escape him that he evoked just such demonstrations of bitterness whenever he attempted to mollify her with a childlike request for assistance and advice.

"Why does Your Majesty come to me, the abdicated queen?" was Tiy's usual response. "You are Pharaoh; then be it and stand on your two feet, instead of on mine. Hold fast to your servants, the Viziers of North and South, if you do not know what to do, and let them tell you what your will is, if you are unsure of it, but do not turn to me, for I am old and have retired."

She had responded to his dreams now in much the same way. "I have been weaned from power and responsibility, my friend," she had replied with a smile, "and so cannot judge whether you are correct in placing so much weight on these events. 'Darkness,' so it is written, 'lies hidden if there is abundant light.' Allow your mother to hide herself. Allow me likewise to hide my opinion whether these dreams are worthy dreams and suitable to your position. Devoured? Wolfed down? One group of cows ate another? Blighted ears of grain ate plump ones? These are no real dream visions, for one cannot see them or picture them, either waking or, in my opinion, sleeping. Presumably Your Majesty dreamt something quite different, which you have forgotten and have now replaced with this nonsensical image of impossible gluttony."

It was to no avail that Meni had tried to assure her that this and not something else was what he had really and clearly beheld with the eyes of his dream, and that this clarity was full of a significance that cried out for interpretation. It was to no avail that he spoke to her of his deep-felt fear of the damage that "his teachings"—that is, the Atôn—would suffer if these dreams were to interpret themselves without hindrance, by which he meant were to be fulfilled and take the shape of the reality of which they had been only the prophetic disguise. He had once again learned the lesson that ultimately his mother had no heart for his god, and that her partisanship was purely intellectual, a matter of political and dynastic concerns. She had always supported her son in his tender love, his spiritual passion for the Atôn; but today, yet again, he saw, as he had long since come to see—just as, unfortunately, thanks to his sensitive nature, he saw everything—that she did so only out of calculation, that she was exploiting his heart as a woman who saw the whole world solely from the viewpoint of political expediency and not, like himself, from that of religion above all else. This offended Meni and hurt him. He left his mother, though only after first being told that if he truly thought his cow and grain visions were of national importance he should approach Ptahemheb, the Vizier of the North, about them during his morning audience. Besides, there was no lack of interpreters of dreams around here.

He had already sent for interpreters some time before and was impatiently awaiting them. But their audience was preceded by that of the great official, who arrived with the intention of informing Pharaoh about certain concerns of the Red House, that is, of the treasury of Lower Egypt, but was interrupted right after his hymn of greeting and forced to listen to the story of the dreams—told in a pinched, anxious voice that faltered in its search for words—followed by the demand that he answer two questions: first, whether he, like his lord, considered this of imperial significance, and, second, if yes, in what regard and to what extent. Ptahemheb had not known what to say, or rather, had said in a flood of very carefully chosen words that he was incapable of saying anything and knew not the first thing about such dreams, and then concluded by trying to return to matters of the treasury. But, apparently impatient and incapable of speaking about or listening to anything else, Amenhotep had made him stick to dreams and kept trying to make it clear to him how eloquently urgent or urgently eloquent they had been—and still had not abandoned the topic when the experts and prophets were announced.

Filled or, better, obsessed as he was with his experience of the night before, the king made a ceremony of the first rank out of their reception—which then, in terms of its substance, turned out miserably. Not only had he commanded Ptahemheb to remain behind for it, but he had also decreed that all the dignitaries of the court who had accompanied him to On attend this audience of interpretation. There were about a dozen very elegant gentlemen: the Great Steward, the Steward of the Royal Garments, the Palace's Chief Launderer and Bleacher, the so-called Sandal Bearer to the King (a very respectable office), the Supervisor of the God's Wigs (who was also the Protector of the Magic Empires, meaning that he was the keeper of the two crowns and the councilor in charge of royal jewels), the Supervisor of All Pharaoh's Horses, the new Chief Baker and Prince of Menfe (whose name was Amenemopet), the Supervisor of the Stewards of the Sideboard (Nefer-em-Wêse, who for a while had been called Bin-em-Wêse), and a few Fan-Bearers at the King's Right Hand. They had all had to find their way to the Hall of Council and Interrogation and now gathered in two equal groups on either side of Pharaoh's beautiful throne, which stood one step higher under a baldachin borne by slender, ribboned columns. The prophets and dream specialists were led before it, six in number, all of whom had some more or less intimate relationship with the temple of Him Who Dwells on the Horizons, and a couple of them had even taken part in yesterday's phoenix discussions. People such as these no longer, as had long ago been the custom, threw themselves upon their belly to kiss the ground before the throne. Apart from a few more ornaments and figures than it had had in those ancient days, it was still the same throne as the one used in the days of the pyramid builders and even before that: a boxlike chair with a low back, before which lay a cushion. But although the throne had become slightly more magnificent and Pharaoh much more omnipotent, one no longer kissed the ground before them—that was no longer done. Its status was much like that of the practice of burying the court alive in the royal grave—it was simply no longer the fashionable thing to do. These magicians merely raised their arms in adoration and, in a rather unrhythmical muddle, murmured a long formula of pious greeting in which they assured the king that his form was like that of his father Rê and that both of the Two Lands were illuminated by his beauty. For the rays of His Majesty pierced darkest caves, and no place was removed from the penetrating gaze of his eyes, nor was there anywhere that the delicate hearing of his million ears did not reach—he heard and saw everything, and whatever came from his mouth was like the words of Horus in his horizon, for his tongue was the balance scale of the world and his lips truer than the tongue on the just scales of Thoth. He was Rê in all his limbs, they said in a jumble of louder and softer voices, and Kheper in his true form, the living image of his father Atum of On in Lower Egypt—"Oh Nefer-khe-peru-Rê-Wanrê, Lord of Beauty, through whom we breathe!"

A few were finished before the others. Then they all fell silent and listened. Amenhotep thanked them, told them first in general the reason why he had called them, and then, before this assemblage of roughly twenty, some quite elegant, some quite learned, men, began to tell his peculiar dreams—for the fourth time. He found it painful, he blushed and stuttered through his narrative. An all-pervading sense of the menacing significance of his dreams had moved him to make them public. But now he repented this, for he could not help noticing that what had been of such high seriousness and was still a matter of innermost seriousness, looked ridiculous to the world at large. And indeed, how could such beautiful and strong cows allow themselves to be devoured by such weak and wretched ones? And how and by what means could one ear of grain devour another? But that, and not some other way, is how he had dreamt it. The dreams had still been fresh, natural, and impressive by night; by day and put into words they looked like poorly prepared mummies with distorted faces—one couldn't be seen in their company. He was ashamed and finished his story only with some effort. Then he gazed in shy expectation at his dream experts.

They had all nodded their heads solemnly; but gradually, one after the other, their thoughtful nods had changed into the side-to-side motion of heads shaken in amazement. These were queer, virtually unprecedented dreams, the eldest explained on their behalf, any interpretation would be difficult. Not that they doubted there was one—the dreams were yet to be dreamt that they could not expound. They did, however, need time for consideration and begged Pharaoh's gracious leave to withdraw for a conference. They also needed to send for certain compendia that had to be consulted. No man was so learned that he had a purview of all dream case histories. Being learned, if they might be so free to remark, did not mean having all knowledge in one's head—there was not room enough in a man's head for that; but rather it meant possessing the books in which such knowledge stood written. And those they possessed.

Amenhotep had granted them permission for their conference. The court had been given orders to stand at the ready. The king had spent a full two hours—for that is how long the consultation lasted—in great uneasiness. Then the assembly was reconvened.

"May Pharaoh live a million years, beloved of Ma'at, mistress of truth, in return for his love for her, for she is without falsehood." She, so they said, was standing at their side, personally at the side of these experts as they now proclaimed the outcome and offered their interpretation to Pharaoh, Guardian of Truth. First: The seven beautiful cows were seven princesses to which, over time, Nefernefruatôn–Nefertiti, Queen of the Two Lands, would give birth. But that the fat cattle were devoured by the decrepit ones meant that all seven daughters would die during Pharaoh's lifetime. That did not mean, they hastened to add, that the king's daughters would die in their youth. For Pharaoh would be granted a life of such duration that he would outlive all his children, no matter how old they grew to be.

Amenhotep stared at them, his mouth agape. What were they talking about? he asked, lowering his voice. They responded that they had been granted the privilege of offering their interpretation of the first dream. But this interpretation, he replied, his voice still faint, had no relationship whatever to his dream, had nothing to do with it at all. He had not asked whether the queen would bear him a son and successor to the throne or a daughter and still more daughters. He had asked them the meaning of the sleek and ugly cows. But the daughters, they responded, were the meaning. He ought not to expect to find cows again in the interpretation of his cow dream. In the interpretation the cows were transformed into royal daughters.

Pharaoh's mouth was no longer agape; he had in fact closed it quite tightly and opened it again only just the least bit to demand that they move on to the second dream.

As for the second, they said, the seven plump ears of grain were seven flourishing cities that Pharaoh would build; the seven sere and scrubby ones were their ruins. To be sure, they hastened to explain, all cities inevitably fall into ruin over time. Pharaoh, however, would live so long that he would see the ruins of the cities he himself had built.

With that Meni's patience was at an end. He had not had enough sleep, it had been an embarrassment to repeat dreams that withered as he told them, the two-hour wait for the verdict of these learned doctors had unnerved him. And now he was so imbued with the idea that these were botched interpretations, missing the mark of his vision's true meaning by many ells, that he was no longer master of his anger. He asked if what his wise men had told him was found in their books? But when they replied that their presentation was a sound combination of what was in their books and deductions derived from their own joint efforts, he sprang from his chair—something unprecedented during an audience, so that the courtiers raised their shoulders high and covered their mouths with their hands—and with tears in his voice, he called his dreadfully frightened prophets bunglers and ignoramuses.

"Begone!" he cried almost with a sob. "And take with you Pharaoh's disfavor rather than a wealth of golden tribute that My Majesty would have bestowed upon you had truth come from your mouths. Your interpretations are fraud and falsehood. Pharaoh knows that, because it was Pharaoh who dreamt, and even if he does not know the interpretation he still knows how to distinguish between a true interpretation and one so mediocre. Out of my sight!"

The pale scholars were led out by two palace guards. Meni, however, without even taking his seat again, had declared to the court that this fiasco had in no way convinced him to let the matter rest. His courtiers had unfortunately been witness to a shameful failure, but, by his scepter! he would call other dream experts to him on the morrow, this time from the house of Djehuti, of Thoth, the Scribe of Ninefold Greatness, the Lord of Khmunu. From priests consecrated

to the white baboon one could expect a worthier and truer interpretation of what an inner voice told him must be interpreted.

The new consultation had taken place the next day under the
same circumstances. But the outcome was even worse than on the
day before. Once again, despite his inner struggle and faltering
tongue, Pharaoh had publicly displayed his dream mummies, and
once again there had been much nodding and head-shaking among
these luminaries. The king and his court had had to wait not two, but
three long hours for the result of the secret consultations that the
sons of Thoth had likewise requested; and even then these experts
could come to no agreement among themselves, but had been divided in their opinions about the dreams. There were, their eldest
announced, two interpretations for each, although these were the
only ones worth considering and others were unthinkable. According to one theory, the seven fat cows were seven kings from the seed
of Pharaoh, the seven ugly ones, however, seven princes of wretched
lands that would rise up against them. But this lay far in the future.
On the other hand, the beautiful cows might also be a group of
queens that either Pharaoh himself or one of his distant successors
would bring into his house of women, and who—as suggested by
the seven emaciated cows—would unfortunately die one after the
other.

And the ears of grain?

The seven golden ears meant, or so some of them were convinced, seven heroes of Egypt, who would be slain in some future
war by seven warriors, even though, as indicated by the blighted ears
of grain, they were less powerful. The others firmly believed the
seven plump and seven withered ears were fourteen children that
would be born to Pharaoh by those foreign queens. Except that
strife would break out among them and, by their superior wiles, the
seven weaker children would murder the seven stronger ones.

This time Amenhotep did not even leap up from his throne of
presence. He remained sitting there, hunched over, his face hidden in
his hands, and the courtiers to the right and left of the baldachin had
to cock their ears to hear what he murmured into his hands. "Charlatans, charlatans!" he had whispered over and over, and then gestured to the Vizier of the North, who stood nearby, to bend down to
him and receive his barely audible command. Ptahemheb carried out

the order by proclaiming to the experts in a loud voice that Pharaoh wanted to know if they were not ashamed of themselves.

They had done their best, they answered.

Then the vizier had bent down to the king again and this time it turned out that he had been given an order to tell these sorcerers to vacate the hall. In great confusion and amid exchanged sidelong glances, as if each were asking the other if he had ever experienced anything like this, the men withdrew. The courtiers left behind stood there in anxious puzzlement, for Pharaoh was still sitting bent over in his chair, his hands covering his eyes. When he finally took them away and sat up, his face was lined with sorrow and his chin was quivering. He told his courtiers that he would gladly have spared them and only with reluctance had plunged them into such pain and sadness, but he could not conceal from them the fact that their lord and king was most unhappy. His dreams had undeniably borne the stamp of imperial significance, and their interpretation was a matter of life and death. The explanations they had received, however, were flimsy stuff; they did not match his dreams in any way, nor had they recognized themselves in them the way that dream and interpretation must recognize one another. After the failure of these two grand attempts, he had no choice but to doubt if he would ever receive an interpretation that would correspond to the truth and be immediately recognized as such. But that meant one was forced to leave it to the dreams to interpret themselves and, barring any preventative measures, to realize their own sad fulfillment—possibly resulting in gravest injury to both state and religion. The Two Lands were in danger; but Pharaoh, to whom this was apparent, was now left alone on his throne, without advice or assistance.

The apprehensive silence that followed these words lasted only a moment. Then it was that Nefer-em-Wêse, the Chief Butler, after much struggle with himself, had stepped forward from among the king's assembled friends and requested the favor of speaking before Pharaoh. "I remember my faults this day"—with these words, according to tradition, he began his address; that statement hangs in the air, one can still hear it even now. The Chief Wine Steward was not, however, speaking of sins he had not committed, for he had been wrongly imprisoned and had not been party to the plan to have the aged Rê bitten by Eset's serpent. He meant another fault—that is, that he had firmly promised someone that he would mention him, but had not kept his word, for he had forgotten that someone. But now he remembered him and spoke of him before the royal baldachin. He reminded Pharaoh, who scarcely remembered it, of the "ennui"—as he put it, borrowing a foreign euphemism—of his experience from two years before, when he was still butler under Nebmaat-Rê, and by mistake had ended up at the island fortress of Zawi-Rê, along with someone it would be better not to name, a man despised by god, whose body and soul had both been destroyed. Upon their arrival there, a young lad, the captain's aide, had been appointed to wait upon them, a Habiru from Asia, with the odd name of Osarsiph, the son of a king of flocks and friend of a god in the East, borne to him by a lovely wife, which was certainly evident from the look of the lad. This Osarsiph had been given the greatest talent in the field of dream exegesis that he, Excellent in Thebes, had ever encountered in all his life. For both his guilty comrade and he, the innocent man, had dreamt on the same night—very difficult, momentous dreams, each for himself—and had been terribly hard-pressed to find a correct interpretation. This Usarsiph, however, who had never made an issue of his talent before, had interpreted their dreams easily and quite on his own, and had told the baker that he would end up hanged on the crossbar, whereas he himself, on account of his radiant purity, would be received into favor again and restored to his office. It had happened exactly that way, and today he, Nefer, remembered his faults—that is, that during all this time he had not called attention to this talent still living in shadows and pointed a finger to him. He did not hesitate to state his conviction that if anyone might be able to interpret Pharaoh's important dreams, it was presumably this lad still vegetating at Zawi-Rê.

A stir among the friends of the king, and something stirred in Pharaoh's face and form as well. There followed a few questions and answers exchanged between the king and his fat butler—and the beautiful order was issued for the First Express Runner and Winged Messenger to set out by express boat for Zawi-Rê and, wasting as little time as possible, to bring this prophetic foreigner before Pharaoh's face at On.

Part Three

THE CRETAN LOGGIA

The Introduction

When Joseph arrived in the millennial city of blinking eyes it was the time of sowing, of the burial of the god, just as it had been back then, when for the second time he had fallen into the pit, where he had spent three great days under tolerable conditions with Mai-Sakhme, the calm captain. This was as it should be: exactly three years had passed and, just as then, the same point in the great cycle had come round and the children of Egypt had again erected the god's spine in celebration of the Festival of the Ripped-Open Earth—it was the week between the twenty-second and last day of the month of Khoiak.

Joseph was delighted to see Golden On again, through which once, now three and ten years ago, he had traveled as a boy, following the route along which the Ishmaelites had led him and together with them had been instructed by the servants of the sun about the beautiful figure of the triangle and the gentle nature of Rê-Horakhte, Lord of the Wide Horizon. Once again he passed through the triangular district of this edifying city with its many glistening symbols of the sun, this time at the side of a courier, and sped toward its tip—that is, toward the endpoint where its lateral sides intersected and where the topmost slanted planes of the great obelisk, their gold outshining all else, greeted them from afar.

Jacob's son, who had spent so long gazing at nothing but prison walls, had no time to use his eyes and enjoy the sights of a busy city and its people—his guide, the winged messenger, who had not a minute to spare and was still pushing ahead with breathless haste, did not allow him to take in the outside world; nor was he himself in a mood for leisurely observation. For another cycle was repeating itself, and another return was about to take place: he would once again be standing before the highest. Back then it had been Peteprê, the highest in the vicinity, before whom he had been permitted to speak there in the palm garden, and that had meant everything. Now it was Pharaoh himself, the highest of all here below, before whom he was to speak, and this time it meant the highest of everything. What it also meant was that he had to be helpful to the Lord in His plans and not clumsily thwart them, which would be great folly, a scorning of the course of the world out of a lack of faith. Only a wavering in his faith that God wanted to raise him high could lead him to be inept and to fail to seize the opportunity arranged for him; and so Joseph was filled with suspense as to what was to come and had no eyes for the hustle and bustle of the city—he was confident in an expectation that knew no fear, for he was certain in his faith, itself the source of all pious proficiency, that God had joyful, loving, and significant things in store for him.

We, who share in the suspense of expectation with him, even though we know how it all turned out, do not wish to reproach him for his confidence, but accept him as he was, and as we have come to know him over so long a time. There are those who are chosen who in despairing humility and self-castigation are never able to believe in their election, who dismiss it with anger and self-abasement, never trusting their own senses, and to some extent even feel their lack of faith has been insulted when, despite everything, they are raised up at last. And then there are the others, for whom nothing in the world is more self-evident than their being chosen—those who are aware that they are God's favorites, who marvel at nothing when they are raised up and crowned with the crown of life. Whichever race of the elect one may prefer, the one haunted by disbelief or the one filled with presumption—Joseph belonged to the second. We should nonetheless be glad that at least he did not belong to a third, which also exists: these are the hypocrites before God and man, who feign their unworthiness even to themselves, but in whose mouth the word "grace" sounds more arrogant than all the blissful self-confidence of those who are never amazed by it.

Pharaoh's stopgap quarters at On lay to the east of the temple of the sun and were connected to it by a boulevard of sphinxes and sycamores, the same path the god took whenever he wanted to burn incense to his father. The residence itself was a light and cheerful improvisation, which like all residences was constructed of brick and wood—but without any stone, which is appropriate only for Eternal Dwellings—and, of course, as charmingly and finely ornamented as

anything Keme's luxurious high culture might dream of; it lay enclosed and protected amidst its gardens by a dazzling white wall, before whose lofty entrance stood gilded flagpoles with colorful
pennants fluttering in the breeze.

It was now past noon, the midday meal was over. Although the
express boat had not put up for the night, it had still required the
morning hours to reach On. In the square outside a gate in the wall a
throng had gathered, for many of the city's people had come simply
to stand about and wait for some spectacle; but a troop of military
police, gate guards, and charioteers—who stood chatting away beside their snorting, pawing, and sometimes even loudly whinnying
steeds—now blocked the way, which was likewise filled with peddlers and vendors offering brightly colored candies, fritters, souvenir scarabs, and inch-high statuettes of the king and queen. The
courier and the man he had brought made their way through all this
only with difficulty. "A decree! A decree! A guest, a guest!" he
shouted over and over, trying to frighten the crowd with his professional breathlessness, which he had not displayed during their journey until now. Once inside the palace courts he continued to shout
these words to servants who had run out to meet them, but now
raised their eyebrows and gladly fell back; he brought Joseph to the
foot of a stairway leading up to the entrance of a pavilion set on a
high platform, where a palace official, evidently some substeward or
other, had planted himself and stared down at them with dulled eyes.
Calling up the stairs, the courier announced in hurried words that he
was bringing the soothsayer of Zawi-Rê, whom he had been commanded to fetch in greatest haste; whereupon the man measured
Joseph from head to toe with the same dulled gaze, as if in the wake
of this announcement it was up to him whether to admit him—and
then signaled to him, once again leaving the impression that this was
his own decision, that if he liked he could also refuse him entrance.
The courier hastily enjoined Joseph that he, too, should breathe in
rapid gasps when he came before Pharaoh, since this would leave the
lovely impression that he had run the whole way without rest to appear before his countenance—instructions that Joseph, however, did
not take seriously. He thanked his long-legged companion for fetching and escorting him and now climbed the stairs to the official, who
responded to his greeting not with a nod, but a shake of his head,
and then ordered him to follow.

They strode through a portico painted with bright colorful scenes and borne by four columns wound with ribbons and now entered a fountain court shimmering with the precious woods of more round columns and opening to the front and sides onto broad pillared passageways. Here armed men stood guard. The man led Joseph straight ahead into an antechamber with three deep doors, one beside the other, and escorted him through the middle one. With that they entered into a very large hall that was supported by perhaps twelve columns and whose sky blue ceiling was decorated with birds in flight. An openwork cottage done in red and gold, much like a garden gazebo, stood in the middle; inside it was a table surrounded by armchairs with colorful cushions. Apron-clad servants were sprinkling and sweeping the floor here; they were clearing away trays of fruit, plumping up cushions, tending to the incense bowls and lamps on tripods that alternated with broad-handled alabaster vases, and arranging gold-embossed goblets on the buffet tables. It was obvious that Pharaoh had just dined here and had now retreated to some place of rest, to the gardens or deeper into the building. All of this was somewhat less new and amazing to Joseph than was probably presumed by his guide, who from time to time cast him appraising sidelong glances.

"Do you know how to conduct yourself?" he asked as they left the hall, turning to the right and entering a courtyard of flowers with four basins set in its ornamented pavement.

"In a pinch, perhaps," Joseph responded with a smile.

"Well, the pinch is probably here," the man replied. "Do you know at least how to greet the god first off?"

"I wish I did not," Joseph riposted, "for how delightful it must be to learn that from you."

The official maintained his seriousness for a moment, then burst into laughter—one would never have expected it of him; but then his wide-beaming face immediately turned dour and earnest again.

"You would appear to be a kind of jester and buffoon," he said, "a rascal and cattle thief, whose antics can only provoke laughter. I assume therefore that your prophecy and interpretations are mere roguery as well, the market cries of a quack peddling nostrums."

"Oh, I haven't much to say about prophecy and interpretation," Joseph replied. "For it is not up to me and not my doing, it just happens to come to me at times. But I've never made much of it until now. But since Pharaoh has called me to him in such haste, I've begun to think of it more highly myself."

"In saying which you intend to teach me a lesson, I suppose?" the steward asked. "Pharaoh is gentle and young and full of kindness. That the sun shines upon a man is no proof that he's not a rogue."

"It not only shines upon us, but allows us to shine as well," Joseph answered as they walked on, "some in one way, some in another. May you be pleased with yourself in its light."

The man cast him a sidelong glance, several in fact—in between he would stare straight ahead—but then with a certain haste, as if he had forgotten to look to something or had to make a quick double check as to what he had seen, he turned his head to the man he was escorting, until finally Joseph had no choice but to repay his sidelong glances. He did it with a smile and a nod that seemed to say "Yes, yes, that's how it is, you needn't be so amazed, you've seen rightly." As if taking fright, the man quickly turned his head to look forward again.

Leaving the court of flowers they entered a corridor lighted from above, one wall of which was painted with scenes of harvest and sacrifice, while the other was a series of pillared doorways that looked into various chambers, including the Hall of Counsel and Interrogation with its baldachin, whose purpose the steward explained to Joseph as they passed. He had grown more talkative. He even told his companion where Pharaoh was to be found at the moment.

"After lunch they proceeded to the Cretan garden room," he said. "Cretan, because a foreign artist from those shores ornamented it. The chief royal sculptors Bek and Auta are in attendance as well, receiving instructions. The Great Mother is there too. I will hand you over to the chamberlain on duty in the antechamber, who will announce your arrival."

"Yes, let's do it that way," Joseph said, and there was nothing more than that to what he said. But as they walked along the man at his side, after giving another shake of his head, suddenly broke into soundless, unstoppable giggles, a laughing fit that shook his belly with quick, short, visible spasms and that he had not yet quite mastered when they entered the antechamber at the end of the corridor, where a short, stooped courtier, whose apron had a marvelous waist-band fold and who carried a fan under his arm, stepped out from the flap in a bee-embroidered portière, where he had apparently been listening. The steward's voice was still quivering with the peculiar distress of his suppressed giggles as he explained to the chamberlain, who came flouncing and mincing toward them, who it was he had brought.

"Ah our long-awaited, much-sought-after know-it-all," the little man said in a lisping high voice, "who knows more than the experts of the House of Books. Fine, fine, ex-qui-site!" All the while he remained as stooped as before, perhaps because he was born that way and could not stand up straight, perhaps merely because elegant service at court had accustomed him to this posture. "I shall announce you, announce you at once, and why shouldn't I? The entire court awaits you. Pharaoh is, to be sure, busy at the moment, but I shall announce you posthaste all the same. I shall interrupt Pharaoh, cut him short on your account, right in the middle of his instructions to his artists and report your arrival to him. One would hope that surprises you somewhat. But let us also hope your surprise does not lead to confusion, so that you then utter something foolish—for which perhaps no confusion is required. I call to your attention beforehand that Pharaoh is exceptionally short-tempered when it comes to saying anything foolish about his dreams. My congratulations. And your name would be?"

"My name was Osarsiph," came the answer.

"It is your name, you mean, it is what you are called. Strange enough, I grant, always to have to answer to that name. I shall now go in to announce you by it. *Merci,* my friend," he said with a shrug to the steward, who now withdrew, and slipped with a stooping gait through the curtain flap.

One could hear muted voices inside, especially a soft, youthful, prim voice that then fell silent again. Evidently the hunchback had flounced his way forward to lisp into Pharaoh's ear.

He returned now, his eyebrows drawn high, and whispered, "Pharaoh summons you!"

Joseph stepped inside.

He found himself in a loggia, not large enough to actually deserve the name "garden room" that had been applied to it, but of rare beauty all the same. With a floor whose squares depicted octopuses and children riding dolphins, and a ceiling supported by two columns inlaid with colored glass and sparkling gemstones and entwined with grapevines painted so naturally they appeared real, the room looked out onto gardens through three large windows that drew the fullness of the gardens' charm inside. One could see lustrous tulip beds, the marvelous blossoms of exotic shrubs, and paths strewn with gold dust and leading to lotus ponds. The eye ranged far out into a vista of islands, bridges, and gazebos and caught the flash of enameled tiles with which the distant summerhouse was decorated. The hall of the verandah itself gleamed with color. Its walls were covered with frescoes that departed from any style known to Egypt. Strange peoples and customs were portrayed there, evidently those of the Islands of the Sea. Women sat and walked in stiff, colorful formal skirts, their breasts bared above tight-fitting midriffs, their hair piled in curls above headbands, then falling in long braids to their shoulders. Pages, in a dainty livery no one had ever seen before, waited upon them with tapered pitchers in their hands. Crowned with bright feathers atop his curly head, a little prince with a wasp-waist jacket, two-colored trousers, and lambskin boots strolled smugly between fantastically blossoming grasses and shot arrows at fleeing game, painted so that they flew freely over ground their hooves never touched. In another place acrobats did somersaults across the backs of raging bulls—a diversion for ladies and gentlemen gazing down on them from pillared windows and balconies.

The same exotic taste defined the objets d'art and handcrafted utensils that adorned the chamber: earthenware vases glazed in shimmering hues and inlaid with ivory reliefs set in gold, splendid embossed goblets, a black onyx bull's head with golden horns and rock-crystal eyes. As he entered the room with hands raised, Joseph took in the scene, casting an earnest but modest glance around the group of people to whom his presence had been announced.

Amenhotep-Neb-maat-Rê's widow sat on her throne, a tall chair with a high footstool, directly opposite him, framed against the light coming through the arch of the middle deep-set window, so that her bronzed complexion, already contrasted against her attire, was darkened even more by shadows. All the same Joseph recognized the unusual facial features he had seen on various occasions when the royal family drove forth: the daintily arched nose, the pouted lips set between furrows left by bitter knowledge of this world, the eyebrows traced by a brush above small, black, sparkling eyes that gazed with a cool attentiveness. The god's mother was not wearing the golden vulture helmet that Jacob's son had seen her wear in public. Her hair—surely gray by now, since she had to be in her late fifties—was wrapped in a silver cloth bag that left room for the golden band of a clasp running from temple to temple across her brow, while slithering down onto her forehead were two equally golden, sinuously erect royal serpents—two of them: as if she had appropriated the one that belonged to her spouse who had now merged with the god. Her ears were adorned with round disks of the same bright gemstones from which her necklace was made. Her small, vigorous body sat very straight, very upright and poised, in the old, hieratic style, as it were—forearms on the arms of the chair, feet placed tightly together on the high footstool. Her shrewd eyes met those of the reverential new arrival, but then, out of an inborn, perfectly understandable indifference, she let them swiftly glide down over his form and immediately turned back to her son—but those bitter furrows at her pouting lips formed a mocking smile in response to the excited, boyish curiosity with which this long-expected and highly recommended newcomer greeted her.

To the left and backed by a muraled wall, Egypt's king sat on a lion-pawed armchair with an ample supply of soft cushions and a slanted back—which he was not resting against, but was bent energetically forward, his feet thrust back under the chair, his slender hands adorned with scarab rings grasping the chair's arms. One must also add that the pouncelike pose of eager attentiveness from which Amenhotep—turning to his right and opening his gray, veiled eyes as wide as possible—viewed his newly arrived interpreter of dreams did not take shape all at once, but formed by starts and stages over the course of a minute—it took that long—until it finally reached a point where Pharaoh had actually risen from his chair somewhat and shifted his weight entirely to his clasping hands, the strain clearly visible in the working of his knuckles. As he did so, an object that had been lying in his lap, a kind of lyre, fell to the floor with a gentle, reverberating tinkle—and was quickly picked up and presented to him by one of the men who stood before him, one of the sculptors he was instructing. The man had to hold it out to him for a while before he accepted it, closing his eyes, sinking back into the cushions of his chair, and returning to the same pose he had evidently assumed while conversing with his master craftsmen—an extraordinarily relaxed, soft, and all too comfortable pose, for the seat of the chair was hollowed out for a cushion that yielded until Pharaoh could not help sinking into it and thus sat not only at a long angle but also very low, while dangling one hand down over the arm of his chair, strumming the thumb of his other hand softly against the strings of the improbably small harp lying in his lap, and pulling up his legs to cross one knee over the other beneath his linen skirt, which left one foot jiggling rather high in the air. The golden shaft of his sandal emerged from between his big and second toe.

The Child of the Cave

At the time Nefer-khe-peru-Rê-Amenhotep was as old as Joseph—who now stood before him as a thirty-year-old man—had been when he tended the flock together with his brothers and coaxed his colorful garment from his father; that is, Pharaoh was seventeen. Yet he looked older, not only because in this clime people age more quickly, and not solely due to his precarious health either, but also because early on he had committed himself to the world as a whole—with a multiplicity of impressions storming his soul from all the quarters of heaven—and had labored with zealous enthusiasm in the cause of the divine. In describing his face—beneath the round blue wig with its royal serpent that he wore today over a linen cap—we should not be discouraged by intervening millennia from making the apt comparison that he looked like a young, aristocratic Englishman of rather faded stock: tall, arrogant, and weary, with a large drooping chin that one could not call receding but that was nevertheless weak; a nose whose narrow, somewhat indented bridge made his broad, sensitive nostrils all the more striking; and deep-set, dreamily veiled eyes from which he was never able to raise the lids entirely and whose dull luster stood in bewildering contrast to the unhealthy, flushed red of very full lips, a hue that came not from rouge but from nature. The face was thus a mixture of sensuality and painfully convoluted spirituality—but still at a boyish stage and presumably even with something of a boy's playful recklessness. It was anything but handsome and beautiful, and yet it held a disquieting attraction—it was not surprising that Egypt's people felt a tenderness for him and gave him flowery names.

Nor was there anything beautiful about Pharaoh's body—which was of scarcely medium height and to some extent rather oddly misshapen, as was clearly evident beneath his light, though to be sure exquisitely luxurious attire and from the way he draped it over the cushions with a casualness indicative not of bad manners but of an oppositional style of life: a long neck, a narrow and weak chest half covered now with a marvelous collar garland of gemstones, thin arms with embossed golden bracelets, and a slightly protruding stomach that he had had since birth and that was now exposed by a skirt hanging from well below the navel but rising high in the back, its elegant front fold adorned with fringed ribbons and images of the uraeus. Moreover the legs were not only too short, but also lacking all proportion, since the thighs were decidedly too full, while the calves were almost as skinny as chicken legs. Not only did Amenhotep urge his sculptors not to disguise this peculiarity, but he also even directed them to exaggerate it for the sake of precious truth. In contrast his hands and feet were of a very beautiful and noble shape, especially his long-fingered and elegantly sensitive hands, in the beds of whose nails still lay traces of scented oils. How odd that the ruling passion of this coddled lad—who obviously accepted the luxury of his birth as a matter of course—was said to be a longing to know the Most High; and as he stood there off to one side, Abraham's great-grandson was amazed at how this concern for God could appear on earth among members of the human race so terribly different, so remote and so strange each to the other.

Amenhotep had now turned back to bid farewell to his two master sculptors—simple, robust men, one of whom busied himself wrapping a damp cloth around a still-unfinished clay statuette set atop a pedestal, which he had just been showing to his patron.

"Do that, my good Auta," Joseph heard the soft, prim voice say—the same voice he had heard from outside, which though rather too high also had a certain solemn cadence that at times alternated with a more hurried rhythm—"do it as Pharaoh has instructed you, make it charming, lively, and beautiful, the way my father in the heavens desires it. There are still errors in your work—not errors of craftsmanship, for you are very competent, but errors of the spirit.

My Majesty has demonstrated that to you, and you will correct it. You have depicted my sister, Sweet Princess Baketatôn, all too much in the old, dead style that is repugnant to my father, whose will I know. Make her charming and light, make her according to the truth that is the light and that lives in Pharaoh, for he has placed it deep inside himself. Let her one hand be putting a garden fruit, a pomegranate, to her lips, and let the other hang free, not with the rigid palm facing her body, but with the palm curved toward the back—that is the will of the god who is in my heart and whom I know as no one else knows, because I have come from him."

"Your servant," Auta replied, wrapping the clay figure with one hand and raising the other to his king, "will do it exactly as, much to my good fortune, it has been commanded and taught me by Pharaoh, the sole son of Rê, the beautiful child of the Atôn."

"Thank you, Auta, my warm and cordial thanks to you. It is important, you do understand, don't you? For as the father is in me and I in him, so shall all be one in us, that is the goal. Your work, however, if executed in the right spirit, can perhaps contribute a little toward all becoming one in him and me. And now as for you, my good Bek—"

"Remember Auta," the almost manly deep voice of the Goddess-Widow could be heard to remark from her high throne, "always remember that it is not easy for Pharaoh to make himself understood, and that therefore he probably says more than he means so that our understanding can follow his intention. What he means is not that Sweet Princess Baketatôn should be depicted eating, biting directly into the fruit; rather you should merely place the pomegranate in her hand and let her lift her arm slightly so that one may presume she might perhaps put the fruit to her lips—that will be sufficiently new and is the meaning to which Pharaoh wishes to bring you when he says you should let her eat of it. You must also subtract something from what His Majesty has said about the hanging hand, so that the rounded palm should not be turned completely toward the back. Just turn it away from her body slightly, only halfway, that is the meaning intended and will bring both praise and censure enough. This by way of improving your understanding."

Her son was silent for a moment.

"Have you understood?" he then asked.

"I have," Auta replied.

"And so you will also have understood," Amenhotep said, staring down at the lyrelike instrument in his lap, "that in attempting to soften my words, the Great Mother says, of course, something rather less than she intends. You can place the hand with the fruit fairly close to the mouth, and as for the free hand, it is to be sure only half a turn from the body when you rotate the palm toward the back, for no one turns the palm completely to the outside, and you would be violating the shining truth were you to do it that way. And thus you can see how prudently my mother has softened my words."

With a mischievous smile he looked up from the instrument, revealing small, but too pale and transparent teeth between his full lips, and then glanced across to Joseph, who returned his smile. The queen was smiling as well, by the way, as were the two master craftsmen.

"And you, my good Bek," he went on, "shall travel as I have decreed. Travel to Yebu, travel to the land of the elephants, and fetch the red granite that grows there, a large quantity of it, of the very finest sort, which is shot through with quartz and sparkling black— you know the sort that my heart hangs upon. Behold, Pharaoh wishes to adorn the house of his father at Karnak, so that it may surpass the house of Amun, if not in size then in the preciousness of its stone, and the name Radiance of the Great Atôn may be adopted ever more generally for that quarter, as a transition perhaps to a time when it will be common usage for people to call the entire city of Wase itself 'City of the Radiance of the Atôn.' You know my thoughts, and I place my trust in your love of them. Travel, my good man, travel at once! Pharaoh will sit here on his cushions, and you shall travel far upstream and bear the burden that comes with winning this red stone and dragging great quantities of it over land and shipping it by boat to Thebes. So it is, and so let it be as well. When do you depart?"

"Tomorrow morning," Bek answered, "after I have seen to my wife and household. And love for our sweet lord, for the beautiful child of the Atôn, will make my journey and difficulties so light it will be as if I were seated on the softest of cushions."

"Fine, fine, and now go, my good men. Pack up and go, each to his own work. Pharaoh has important business; only outwardly does he rest on his cushions, inwardly he is most anxious, eager, and full of care. Your cares are lovely, to be sure, but tiny in comparison with his. Farewell and be gone!"

He waited till the masters had respectfully withdrawn—and meanwhile eyed Joseph.

"Step closer, friend," he said once he saw the bee-embroidered curtain close behind them. "Step closer, my dear Habiru from Retenu, do not be afraid and do not take fright at your own steps, but approach very close. This is the mother of the god, Tiy, who lives millions of years. And I am Pharaoh. But do not think further of that, lest you be afraid. Pharaoh is god and man, but he places as much weight on the second as on the first—yes, he rejoices, at times rejoices to the point of defiance, even scorn, to reveal that he is human and insist that he is a man like all others, when seen from one side; he rejoices to snap his fingers at those spoilsports who would have him conduct himself unvaryingly as god."

And with that he actually snapped his slender fingers in the air.

"But I see that you do not fear me," he went on, "and take no fright at your steps, but step toward me with an easy charm. That is agreeable, for many there are whose soul vanishes when they must stand before Pharaoh, their heart departs from them, their knees give way, and they cannot tell the difference between life and death. But you are not struck by dizziness, are you?"

Joseph smiled and shook his head.

"There can be three reasons for that," the royal lad said. "Either it is the case because you are of noble lineage after your fashion, or because you see the man in Pharaoh, as he likes to be seen, if it is also done under the proviso of his divinity—or, however, because you feel that some reflection of divinity lies upon you yourself, for you are as beautiful and wondrously handsome as a picture. My Majesty noticed it at once when you entered, and though it did not surprise me—for it was told me that you are the son of a lovely wife—it nevertheless caught my attention. It is evidence that you are loved by him who gives beauty its form through himself alone, who by his own beauty gives life to the eye and vision to behold his beauty. One can call those who are beautiful the darlings of his light."

Tilting his head, he gazed at Joseph with pleasure.

"Is he not as wondrously handsome and beautiful as a god of light, Mama?" he asked Tiy, who was resting her cheek against three fingers of a small, dark hand sparkling with jewels.

"You have summoned him before you because of the wisdom and powers of interpretation for which he is reputed," she replied, gazing into space.

"They are related," Amenhotep said, hastily and eagerly breaking in. "Pharaoh has pondered much about this and heard of it in speaking with the emissaries that frequently visit him from foreign lands—magicians, priests, and initiates, who have brought him tidings from east and west concerning the thoughts of men. For what all must he not hear and to what must he not pay heed in order to test, to choose, and to use what is useful for the perfecting of his doctrine and the establishment of the image of truth according to the will of his father in the heavens. Beauty, dear Mama—and you, my dear Amu—is related to wisdom, through the medium of light. For light is the medium and the midpoint, from which the relationship radiates in three directions: to beauty, to love, and to the knowledge of truth. They are one in it, and light is a triune unity. Strangers brought me the doctrine of an initial god, born of flames, of a beautiful god of light and of love, and his name was Firstborn Radiance. That is a glorious, useful contribution, for it is a verification of the unity of love and light. Light, however, is beauty just as it is truth and knowledge, and if you would know the medium of truth, learn then that it is love. It is said of you that when you hear a dream you know to interpret it, is that so?" he asked Joseph, blushing, for he felt embarrassed and confused by his own words of visionary enthusiasm.

"Let there be no talk of me, my lord, in this regard," Joseph replied. "I can do nothing. God alone can do it, and He does it at times through me. Everything has its season, both dreams and their interpretation. When I was a boy, I dreamt, and my hostile brothers scolded me as a dreamer. Now that I am a man, the season of interpretation has come. My dreams interpret themselves for me, and at most it is God who gives me the gift to interpret them for others."

"So, you are a prophetic young man then, a so-called inspired lamb?" Amenhotep inquired. "It appears one should assign you to those ranks. Will you then topple over dead with your last words, once you have fallen into ecstasy and proclaimed the future to the king, so that he may then solemnly inter you and have your prophecies written down to be handed on to posterity?"

"It is not easy," Joseph replied, "to answer the question of the Great House, either with yes or with no, but at most with both. Your servant marvels and is touched to the quick that you have deigned to see in him a lamb, and an inspired one at that. For as a child I grew accustomed to that name, since my father, a friend of God, used to call me 'the lamb,' because my lovely mother, for whom he served in Shinar beyond the river that flows backwards, the maid of the stars, who bore me in the sign of the Virgin, was named Rachel, which means 'mother sheep.' But this does not justify my agreeing unconditionally, Great Lord, with your assumption so that I may say 'I am he'; for I am and I am not, precisely because it is *I*—which is to say, because the general and its form undergo variations when they are fulfilled in the particular, that is, when the unknown becomes the known and one does not recognize it. Do not expect, because it is held to be appropriate, for me to fall down dead with my last words. Your servant, whom you have called from the pit, does not expect it, for it is only a matter of form, and has nothing to do with me, in whom the form is varied. But if God gives me the gift to prophesy before Pharaoh, I shall not foam at the mouth in ecstasy, after the pattern of the prophetic young man. When I was a boy, I was indeed transported and caused my father great worry by rolling my eyes like those who babble oracles and run about naked wearing horns. His son has put that away since he has become somewhat more adult, and he holds to divine reason even when he interprets. Interpretation is transport enough; one need not drool at the same time. Interpretation is clear and intelligible, not some *aulasaukaulala.* "

He had not looked at the god's mother while he talked, but from the corner of his eye he could see her sitting on her lofty throne and nodding in agreement now. She could even be heard to say, in that almost manly deep and energetic voice that came from her dainty body: "The stranger speaks things before Pharaoh that are worth hearing and taking to heart."

And with that Joseph could now continue, for the king fell momentarily silent, his head drooping with the sulky look of a child who has been gently scolded.

"In the opinion of this lowly servant, however," he went on in

the wake of her praise, "composure while interpreting and prophesying is connected with the fact that it is an I, a single particularity,
through which form and tradition are fulfilled—which, in my view,
provides them with the seal of divine reason. For the pattern of tradition comes from the deep that lie below, and is what binds us. But
the I is from God and is a child of the spirit, which is free. This,
however, is civilized life—that the binding pattern from the depths is
fulfilled in the divine freedom of the I, and there is no human civilization without either the one or the other."

Raising his eyebrows, Amenhotep nodded to his mother and
now applauded, holding one hand erect and tapping the palm with
two fingers of the other.

"Did you hear, Mama?" he said. "This is a highly talented young
man full of insight, whom I have summoned before My Majesty.
Please bear in mind that it was my own decision to call him to court.
Pharaoh is also very talented and advanced for his years, but it is uncertain whether he would have known how to discern and order this
matter of the binding pattern of the depths and the dignity that
comes from above. So, then, you are not bound to the binding pattern of the lamb foaming at the mouth," he asked, "and you will not
crush Pharaoh's heart with a traditional announcement of some
ghastly misery that is yet to come, of the invasion of foreign nations,
when what is at the bottom will be swept to the top?" He shuddered.
"One is familiar with that," he said, his lips turning pale. "But My
Majesty must show himself some little forbearance, for he does not
bear up well under such savagery, but needs love and gentleness. The
land has fallen into ruin, lives in upheaval, Bedouins move over it,
poor and rich have exchanged places, all law has ceased, the son slays
his father and is slain by his brother, the beasts of the desert drink
from the watercourses, people laugh the laugh of death, Rê has
turned away, and no one knows when it is noon, for no one can read
the shadow of the sundial, the beggars eat the sacrificial offerings,
the king is captured and dragged away, and the only consolation is
that afterward things will improve through the power of a savior.
And so Pharaoh will not have to hear that song? May he hope that
the reshaping of the traditional by the particular will spare him such
horrors?"

Joseph smiled. It was here that he spoke the recorded answer
that has often been praised for its diplomacy and courtesy:

"God shall give Pharaoh an answer of peace."

"You say 'god,'" Amenhotep probed. "You've said it several times now. Which god do you mean? Since you are from Zahi and from Amu, I assume that you mean the bull of the field that in the East is called the lord Baal."

Joseph suppressed a smile. He shook his head.

"My fathers, who dreamt of God," he said, "made their covenant with another Lord."

"That can only be Adonai, the bridegroom," the king quickly replied, "for whom the flute wails in the ravines and who rises again. You see, Pharaoh knows his way around among the gods of mankind. He must know all this and test it, and like a gold washer sluice his kernel of truth out of all the absurdity, in order to perfect the creed of his revered father. Pharaoh's life is hard, but also good, very good, and that makes it royal. Thanks to my talents I have come to know that. Whoever has things hard, should also have it good— but only he. For merely to have things good is repulsive; but to have them only hard is not fair either. Just as at the great Feast of Tribute, My Majesty sits in the lovely Pavilion of Decision beside his Sweet Consort, and the ambassadors of the nations—Moors, Libyans, and Asians—pass by in an unending train before me with payments of gold bars and rings, ivory, silver in the shape of vases, ostrich feathers, cattle, byssus, leopards, and elephants—so, too, the Lord of the Two Crowns simply sits in the beauty of his palace in the center of the world and, surrounded by the comfort due him, receives in tribute the thoughts of the inhabited earth. For as I already had the pleasure to mention, the singers and seers of strange gods file by me one after the other, they come to my court from all regions of the earth—from Persia, celebrated for its gardens, where it is believed that one day the earth will be made plain and level and all men will live life in the same fashion, with one law and language; from India, the land where frankincense grows, from Babel, land of astronomers, and from the Islands of the Sea. They all visit me, they pass by my throne, and My Majesty converses with them, just as he converses now with you, the special lamb. They report to me of matters early and late, old and new. Sometimes they leave behind strange souvenirs and divine tokens. Do you see this toy here?" And he lifted up the curved, stringed item in his lap and showed it to Joseph.

"A lyre," the latter declared. "It is only appropriate that Pharaoh holds a token of charm and goodness in his hands." He said this, however, because the lyre is the hieroglyph for the Egyptian word "*nofert*," which means both charm and goodness.

"I see," the king responded, "that you also understand the arts of Thoth and are a scribe. I think that has to do with the dignity of the same I in which the binding pattern of the depths fulfills itself. But this item is a token of something besides charm and goodness— that is, of the mischievousness of a foreign god, who may be a brother of the ibis-headed god or even his second self and who as a child invented this toy during an encounter with an animal. Do you recognize the shell?"

"It's a tortoiseshell," Joseph declared.

"Right you are," Amenhotep confirmed. "That wise animal encountered this crafty child god, who was born in a grotto, and it fell victim to his quick wit. For he impudently stole its hollow shell and stretched strings across it and also attached a pair of little horns, as you can see: and the result was a lyre. I am not saying that this is the same toy that that rascal god made. Nor was that the claim of the man who brought it and gave it to me, a seafarer from Crete. It is probably only fashioned after it, as a pious and amusing memento, and was meant as an enhancement to the several anecdotes the Cretan told Pharaoh about this swaddled child in his cave. For the little fellow kept leaving his grotto and swaddling clothes behind just to play tricks. For instance, though it's hard to believe, he stole the cattle of the sun god, his elder brother, from the hill where they were grazing, once the sun had set. He took fifty of them and drove them here and there, making a muddle of their tracks; and he disguised his own by binding to his feet monstrous sandals made of woven twigs—thus leaving behind a giant's tracks, or really none at all. Which was probably the right thing to do, for he was a child, but a god as well, and so tracks of vaguely gigantic size were well suited to a divine childhood. He drove the cattle off and hid them in a cave— a different one from where he had been born; there are many of them there—but not without having first slaughtered two of them under way beside the river and roasting them over a huge fire. He ate them all up, this suckling god did—a childish gigantic meal to match his gigantic tracks."

"Having done all this," Amenhotep continued from his far too comfortable pose, "the thievish child slipped back into its maternal cave and swaddling clothes. But when the sun god had risen again and saw his cattle missing, he became his own oracle, for he was a god with prophetic powers, and learned that only his newborn brother could have done this. Burning with fury, he entered the cave. The thief, however, who had heard him coming, was all snuggled up in his divinely fragrant swaddling clothes, feigning the slumber of innocence—his invention, the lyre, under his arm. And how naturally lies came to the dissembler when his sun-god brother, who was not taken in by his wiles, threatened and accused him of theft. 'My cares are quite different,' he stammered, 'from those you assume— they are sweet sleep and mother's milk and swaddling clothes around my shoulders and warm baths.' And then, according to the seafarer, he even swore a great oath, saying he knew nothing about the cows. But am I not boring you, Mama?" he asked, interrupting himself and turning to the enthroned goddess.

"Ever since I have been freed of the cares of governing the Two Lands," she answered, "I have a great deal of time to spare. I might just as well spend it listening to tales of foreign gods as with any-thing else. But it does seem an upside-down world to me—usually it is the king who is told stories. But Your Majesty tells them himself."

"Why shouldn't I?" Amenhotep riposted. "Pharaoh must teach. And what he has learned he at once feels compelled to pass on to others. What my mother is actually objecting to," he went on, point-ing a couple of fingers at her as if to explain her own words to her, "is, most certainly, that Pharaoh has failed to tell his dreams to this sensibly inspired lamb, so that he might at last hear the truth about them. For I shall receive a true interpretation from him—his pleas-ing person and several of his statements have almost convinced me of that. Nor is My Majesty afraid of truth, for the man has promised me that he will not prophesy after the model of a youth foaming at the mouth or terrify me with predictions of beggars eating the sacri-ficial offerings. But do you not know or understand that strange turn of temperament whereby, when a man has finally arrived at the fulfillment of his most-longed-for wish, he voluntarily refrains from that fulfillment yet a while? 'It's here in any case,' he's likely to say, 'and it is simply up to me for it to happen; so I can just as well post-pone it a bit, for in some way I have grown fond of both the longing and the wishing, and it's something of a pity to let them go.' That is a very human thing to do, and since Pharaoh attaches great importance to his humanity, he shall do it as well."

Tiy smiled.

"Whatever Your Dear Majesty chooses to do," she said, "we shall call it beautiful. But since this soothsayer may not ask you, I shall ask you myself—did this naughty babe succeed in his perjury, or what did happen next?"

"This," Amenhotep replied, "this—according to my informant: The sun god bound his brother the thief and brought him before their father, the great god, so that the babe might confess and be punished. But there as well the rascal lied with greatest cunning and spoke sanctimonious words. 'I hold the sun in high honor,' he lisped, 'and the other gods as well, and I love you, but I fear this god here. You, then, should protect the younger son, and help poor little me.' And so he played the hypocrite and slyly emphasized his lovely nature as the younger, all the while winking at his father, who had to laugh out loud at this prodigy and merely ordered him to show his brother where the cattle were and return the stolen goods, to which the sun god agreed as well. But when the elder realized that two of the cows had been slaughtered, his fury was enkindled anew. And while he scolded and threatened, the little god played on his instrument—this lyre here—and the accompaniment made his song sound so lovely that the scolding died away and the sun god had only one thing on his mind: to have that lyre. And it became his; for the two of them came to an agreement: the cattle remained with the thief and the brother departed with the stringed instrument—that he now retains forever."

He fell silent and gazed down with a smile at the souvenir in his lap.

"What a truly informative way," his mother said, "Pharaoh has for delaying yet a while the fulfillment of his most-longed-for wish."

"Informative it is," the king replied, "for it informs us that divine children merely disguise themselves as children—they do it out of pure roguery. As soon as he liked, he stepped out of his cave as a jaunty, wily young lad, full of ideas and never at a loss for useful advice, a helper of gods and men. And what all he invented, or so people there believe, that had not existed before: writing and numbers for reckoning, plus the cultivation of the olive, and clever, persuasive speech that does not shy from deceit, though it deceives with charm. My informant, the seafarer, reveres him as his patron. For he is a god of good fortune, so he says, and of happy discovery, a spender of blessing and prosperity, of both what is honestly and perhaps a bit fraudulently won, just as life allows; a monitor and guide who leads men through this world's twists and turns, smiling back at them with upraised staff in hand. He even leads the dead, so the man said, to their realm of the moon, and directs dreams as well, for he is lord of sleep along with all the rest, who closes men's eyes with his staff—and in the end is a gentle magician, for all his cunning."

Pharaoh's glance fell on Joseph—who was standing before him with his handsome and beautiful head tilted back and slightly to one shoulder, looking up to the mural at his side with an easy, bemused smile that said he really had no need to hear all this.

"Are you acquainted with these stories of the divine rascal, my prophet?" Amenhotep asked.

Joseph swiftly changed his pose. He had, quite against his wont, behaved impolitely and demonstrated that he was aware of the fact—but in a rather exaggerated way so that Pharaoh, who always noticed everything, had the impression that this startled recollection of what was proper was not only a pretense but was also intended to create that very impression. He let his question hang in the air by opening his veiled gray eyes as wide as possible and staring at Joseph.

"Acquainted with them, highest lord?" came the reply. "Yes and no—if your servant may be permitted the liberty of a double answer."

"You request such liberty rather often," the king remarked. "Or rather, you take it. Your every word is trimmed to 'yes' and at the same time to 'no.' Should I be pleased by that? You are the young man foaming at the mouth and yet are not, simply because it is *you*. You are acquainted with this trickster god and yet are not, simply because—of what? Are you acquainted with him or not?"

"In a certain sense," Joseph replied, "you, Lord of the Crowns, have been acquainted with him for a long time yourself, since you called him a distant brother, even a second self, of the ibis-headed god, of Djehuti, the scribe who is the friend of the moon. Were you then acquainted with him or not? He was familiar to you. That is more than obvious, and in familiarity my yes and no are canceled out as well and become one and the same. No, I did not know this child of the grotto, this master of tricks. Never did wise Eliezer, my father's oldest servant and my teacher, who could claim that the earth leapt up to greet him on his journey to woo a bride for the averted sacrifice, my father's father—but forgive me! This leads us far afield—your servant cannot narrate the whole world to you in this one hour. And yet the words of the Sublime Mother pursue him and ring in his ears: it is the custom of this world for the king to be told stories, not for him to tell them. I might tell of several tricks that would prove to you and to the Great Wife that the spirit of this rascal god has always had a home among my people and is familiar to me as well."

Amenhotep glanced across to his mother with a jesting motion of his head that said "My my, can you believe this?"

"The goddess," he then responded, "will permit you to tell of one or two such tricks if you believe it would amuse us, as a prelude to your interpretation."

"One's breath comes from you," Joseph said, bowing. "I shall use it to divert you."

And with arms crossed—though for the sake of description he often raised one hand from its folded position—he spoke before Pharaoh, saying:

"Esau, my uncle the mountain goat, was rough and as my father's twin had forced his way first at their birth—red with tufted hair he was, the oaf, but his brother was smooth and delicate, keeping to his tent, the son of his mother, wise in God, a shepherd, for Esau was a hunter. Jacob had always been blessed, long e'er the hour when my forebear, the father of both, resolved to bestow the inherited blessing, for he was declining toward death. The old man was blind, his old eyes no longer wished to obey, but refused, and he saw only with hands, groping instead of seeing. He called the red man to him, his eldest son, whom he had ever loved. 'Go, my honest shaggy son, my firstborn,' he said, 'and shoot me game with your bow, and cook me a spiced dish from the quarry that I may eat of it and bless you, after the meal has strengthened me mightily for blessing.' And Esau went and hunted. But meanwhile his mother wrapped her younger son in a goat kid's hide because of his smooth limbs and gave him a dish from the flesh of the kid, tastily spiced. He took it to his lord in his tent and said: 'My father, here I am again, Esau, your Rough Hide, who has hunted and cooked for you; now eat of it and bless your firstborn.' 'Let me behold you with seeing hands,' the blind man said, 'to see if you are truly Esau, my Rough Hide, for anyone can make that claim.' And he fingered him and felt the hide—wherever there was no garment it was rough, like Esau, though not red—his hands could not see that, and his eyes refused. 'Yes, no doubt, it is you,' the old man said. 'I know it clearly from your fleece. Rough or smooth, so it is, and how good that one needs no eyes to tell the difference. The hands suffice. You are Esau, so feed me, that I may bless you.' And he smelled and ate and gave the wrong son, who was the right son, the fullness of his unalterable blessing. And Jacob took it with him. And then came Esau from his huntsman's work, swollen with pride and boasting in his great hour. He cooked and spiced his dish of game for all to see, and bore it to his father. But the duped son did not fare well inside the tent, and as an imposter he was received, the wrong right son—for aided by a mother's guile the right wrong son had long since come before him. His was only a curse, a desert ban, for nothing else was left after the blessing was bestowed. What jesting, what laughter, when he sat down in the dust, blubbering loudly, tongue lolling, thick tears rolling down, the overthrown dolt, skinned by the quick and nimble mind of a deft and ready brother."

The son and the woman who given him birth laughed—the one in a sonorous alto, the other in a bright, almost falsetto voice. Both shook their heads as they laughed.

"No, what a bizarre story!" Amenhotep cried. "A barbaric farce—excellent in its way, if also somewhat depressing, so that one doesn't know what sort of face to put on and is torn between laughter and pity. The wrong right son, you say—and the wrong son, who was the right one? That's not bad—both bewildering and witty. May a higher kindness preserve every man from being right and yet wrong, so that in the end he may not be left sitting there blubbering, his tears rolling down into the dust. How did you like the mother, Mama? Goat hides to cover smoothness—that's how she helped the old man and his seeing hands, so that he might bless the right son, that is, the wrong one. So tell me—have I not summoned a most original lamb? My Majesty allows you, Habiru, yet another tale of tricks, so that I may see whether the first was good merely by chance and whether that deft and ready spirit is more than just known among you, but indeed familiar. Let us hear!"

"Pharaoh commands," Joseph said, "and it is done. The blessed son had to flee before the wrath of the duped son, had to journey and journeyed to Naharayim in the land of Shinar, where kindred dwelled: Laban, the clod of earth, a gloomy man of business, and his daughters, one red of eye, the other more lovely than a star, who, next to God, became the son's one and all. But his taskmaster made him serve seven years for his virgin of the stars, years that passed as seven days do, and when he had served them, the uncle slipped the one daughter, whom he did not want, in the place of the other by dark, but then later, to be sure, gave the right wife as well, Rachel, the mother sheep, who bore me with pain that went beyond nature, and they called me Dumuzi, the true son. This but in passing. When the virgin of the stars had healed from me, my father wished to depart with me and the ten whom his wrong wife and handmaids had borne him—or he pretended that wish before his uncle, who was not pleased, for Jacob's blessing made him fruitful. 'Give me all the speckled sheep born in your herd,' he said to his uncle. 'They shall be mine, but all that are of one color are yours—that is my modest proposal.' And they came to an agreement. But what did Jacob do? He split rods from tree and bush and peeled white streaks in their bark, leaving them spotted. He laid them in the troughs where the sheep drank and after drinking mated and conceived. And as they went about this business, he let them see only what was speckled, and this enchanted them through their eyes, and they bore speckled young, which he took for his own. And so he grew rich beyond measure, and Laban was the worse for it, was left in a pickle by the spirit of the artful God."

Again Mother and son were greatly delighted and shook their heads. When the king laughed, a vein swelled unhealthily on his brow and tears glistened in his half-veiled eyes.

"Mama, Mama," he said, "My Majesty is highly amused. He split rods, peeled them spotted, and enchanted the sheep through their eyes. Is it not said that an exceptionally good tale of tricks leaves a man splitting with laughter, his face spotted with delight? As Pharaoh's now is. Does he still live, your father? What a prodigy he was! And so you are the son of a rascal and a lovely woman?"

"The lovely wife was also a rascal and a thief," Joseph added.

"Her loveliness was no stranger to tricks. She stole in fact, out of love for her husband, the idols of her gloomy father, hid them in the camels' straw, sat upon them, and said in a sweet voice, 'I am indisposed and suffering from my period, and cannot stand up.' Laban, however, searched himself half sick."

"One after the other!" Amenhotep cried, his voice breaking into laughter. "No, no, Mama, you owe me an answer: Have I not summoned a truly original lamb before me, a beautiful and amusing lamb? . . . This is the moment," he suddenly declared. "Pharaoh is now disposed to hear from this sensible lad the interpretation of his difficult dreams. I will hear it before the tears of this merry diversion are dried from my eyes. For as long as my eyes are still damp from such unaccustomed laughter, I will not fear my dreams, or their interpretation, whatever it is. This son of a rascal will not prophesy such stupid or fearful things as did those pedants from the House of Books. And even if the truth he speaks is bad, it will not sound that way coming from his merry mouth, will not suddenly turn the happy tears in my eyes to their opposite. Soothsayer, do you need any utensils or tools for your work? A kettle, perhaps, that can receive the dreams, and from which their interpretation then rises?"

"Nothing at all," Joseph replied. "I need nothing between heaven and earth to perform my task. I interpret dreams extemporaneously, for better or worse, just as the spirit moves me. Pharaoh need only tell them."

And the king cleared his throat, cast his mother a somewhat embarrassed look, and with a small bow apologized to her for making her listen to his dreams yet again. Then, with damp eyes still sparkling, for his tears of laughter dried only slowly, he painstakingly told his now stale visions for the sixth time—both number one and number two.

Pharaoh Prophesies

Joseph listened in a respectful pose devoid of all affectation. His eyes were closed, but that was the only indication he gave of an intensification and profound concentration of his being on the content of Pharaoh's description—plus one other thing: he kept them closed for a while after Amenhotep finished and sat waiting with bated breath. He even went so far as to keep him waiting, kept them closed even while he knew the king's own eyes were directed at him in pure expectation. It was very still in the Cretan loggia. The only sounds were a sonorous cough by the Goddess-Mother and the rattling of her jewelry.

"Are you asleep, lamb?" Amenhotep finally and hesitantly asked.

"No, here I am," Joseph replied, opening his eyes before Pharaoh, but in no great haste. It was, in fact, more as if he were seeing through him rather than looking at him, or better: his introspective glance broke on the person of the king and returned into itself—which only enhanced his black Rachel eyes.

"And what do you say to my dreams?"

"Your dreams?" Joseph responded. "Your dream, you mean. To dream twice does not mean to have two dreams. You dreamt one and the same dream. That you dreamt it twice, first in one form and then in another, is merely meant as a guarantee that your dream will most certainly be fulfilled, and very soon. Moreover, the second form is only an explanation and closer definition of what the first one meant."

"Exactly what My Majesty thought at once!" Amenhotep cried. "Mother, that was my first thought, what the lamb has just said, that both dreams were basically only one. I dreamt of the thriving and loathsome cattle, and then it was as if someone said: 'Did you understand me correctly? This is what I meant!' And after that I dreamt of the ears of grain, the plump and blighted ones. Surely when someone speaks he also tries to express himself and then tries again: 'In other words,' he says, 'it's like this.' Mama, that is a good beginning for the interpretation that the prophetic young man has made, with no foaming of the mouth. Such a beginning was missing with those bunglers from the House of Books, and so nothing good could come after either. Well then, continue, prophet, and interpret. What is the one meaning of my double royal dream?"

"The meaning is one, just as the Two Lands are one, and the dream is double, as is your crown," Joseph responded. "Is that not what you wished to say by your latest words—saying it only approximately, but not accidentally? What you meant was betrayed in the phrase 'royal dream.' You were wearing your crown and tail in your dream—in the dark, I heard you say that. You were not Amen-hotep, but Nefer-khe-peru-Rê, the king. God spoke to the king through his dreams. He revealed to Pharaoh what He intends in the future, so that Pharaoh might know it and take measures appropriate to such instruction."

"Absolutely!" Amenhotep cried again. "Nothing could have been clearer to me. Mother, there was nothing of which My Majesty was more certain at the very start than what this special lamb says: that it was not I who was dreaming, but the king—to the extent the two can be separated and insofar as it was necessary for me to dream so that the king might dream. Did not Pharaoh know and swear to you that morning that the double dream was of imperial significance and therefore absolutely had to be interpreted? But it was sent to the king, not in his capacity as the father, but in his capacity as the mother of the Two Lands—for the king's sexuality is twofold. My dream was concerned with the Black Earth and matters of dire necessity—I knew and I know it. But I know nothing more," he suddenly reflected. "How can that be, that My Majesty completely forgets that it knows nothing more at all and that the interpretation is yet to come? You have a way," he said, turning to Joseph, "of making it happily appear as if things had all been most beautifully solved and taken care of already, and yet all you have said thus far was what I knew in any case. But what does my dream mean and what was it trying to tell me?"

"Pharaoh is mistaken," Joseph replied, "if he thinks he did not know it. Your servant is capable of no more than offering him in prophecy what he already knows. Did you not see the cows climbing up out of the flood, one after the other in single file, hot on each other's heels, first the fat ones, then the lean, with no break in their rank, but all in one line? What rises out of the vessel of eternity, one after the other, not side by side, but in single file, with no gap between what is departing and arriving, with no break in rank?"

"Years!" Amenhotep cried, thrusting his fingers forward and snapping them.

"But of course," Joseph said. "There's no need for that to rise up out of a kettle—no need for a foaming mouth and rolling eyes to know that the cows are years, seven and seven. And the ears of grain that grew afterward, one after the other, in equal numbers, are they likely to be something totally different, something terribly difficult to guess?"

"No!" Pharaoh cried and snapped his fingers again. "They too are years."

"In the light of divine reason, of course," Joseph answered, "for to it honor is surely due in every regard. But that the cows became ears of grain in the second version of your dream, seven yielding fullness and seven barren—surely we must bring in a kettle big as the moon for that connection to rise up before us. And as for what closer relationship might exist between the beauty of the seven cows that came first and the ugliness of those that followed—may Pharaoh be so gracious as to call at once for a kettle on a tripod."

"Oh, enough of your kettles!" the king cried again. "Is this a moment to be talking about kettles, and do we really have any need of one? The connection is patently obvious and is as transparent as a gemstone of purest water. The beauty and ugliness of the cows is connected to the ears of grain, connected to their growth and failure to grow." He paused and stared wide-eyed into space. "Seven fat years will come," he said, taken aback, "and seven of scarcity."

"Certainly and without delay," Joseph said, "for it was announced to you twice."

Pharaoh looked directly at him.

"You did not topple over dead after your prophecy," he said with some amazement.

"Were it not too horrible and criminal," Joseph replied, "one would also have to say that it is astonishing that Pharaoh himself did not fall over dead, for he has prophesied."

"No, you're just saying that," Amenhotep contradicted, "and, as the son of a rascal, let it seem to me as if I myself have prophesied and interpreted my dreams. Why could I not do it before now, before you came, and only knew what was wrong, but not what was right? For this interpretation is right, there is not the least shadow of a doubt in my soul of that, and my own dream recognizes itself precisely in its interpretation. You are truly an inspired lamb, but an extraordinarily peculiar one. For you are no slave to the binding pattern of the deep and did not predict first a season of curse and then a season of blessing, but rather the other way round, first the blessing and then the ordeal—that is what is so original!"

"It was you, Lord of the Two Lands," Joseph answered, "and

it depended on you. For you dreamt it that way, first the fat cows and ears of grain and then the miserable ones, and you alone are original."

Amenhotep worked his way up and out of the hollow of his chair and leapt to his feet. With a few quick strides of his strangely thick and thin legs, his thighs visible through the linen batiste, he stepped before his mother's throne.

"Mother," he said, "there we have it, my royal dreams have been interpreted for me, and I now know the truth. When I think of that learned trash they wanted to sell as truth to My Majesty, about daughters, cities, kings, and fourteen children, it makes me laugh, whereas its inadequacy previously drove me to despair; but I can laugh at it now that I know the truth, thanks to this prophetic young man. The truth, however, is serious. It has been declared to My Majesty that seven years of plenty will come to all of the land of Egypt, and after that seven lean years will follow, so lean that the previous fullness will be completely forgotten, and scarcity will devour the land, just as the lean cows devoured the fat ones and the blighted ears of grain the golden ones, for that, too, was proclaimed: that no one will remember the fullness of the land in the days of scarcity that will follow after and whose severity will devour all memory of plenty. That is what was revealed to Pharaoh through his dreams, which were one dream, and it was provided to him as the mother of the land. I find it hard to understand how it could have remained obscure to me until this hour. But now it has been brought to light with the help of this genuine, but peculiar lamb. For just as I was necessary for the king to dream, so he was necessary for the lamb to prophesy, and our being is but the juncture of not-being and always-being, and our existence in time merely the agent of the eternal. But there is more to it than that! For the question is, the problem that I would like to present to the great thinkers of my father's house is: whether what is singular and particular within time receives more value and dignity from eternity—or vice versa. That is one of those beautiful questions that does not yield to solution, so that there is no end to contemplating them from dusk to dawn . . ."

But here he noticed Tiy shaking her head, and he broke off.

"Meni," she said, "Your Majesty is incorrigible. You have pestered us with your dreams, which you held to be of imperial significance and absolutely had to have interpreted, so that they would not interpret themselves without hindrance. But now that you have the interpretation or believe you have it, you act as if that were an end of it, you forget the message even as you declare it and lose yourself in unsolvable questions and in the remotest abstractions. Is that motherly? I would scarcely wish to call it fatherly, and I cannot wait until this man here has returned to whence he came and we are alone to admonish you angrily from the mother's high throne. It is possible that this prophet knows his craft, and that what he declares may happen. It has happened that in the course of alternating years of abundant and passable harvest the Provider has failed entirely, denying the fields his blessing several times in a row, so that famine and scarcity coiled themselves around the Two Lands; it has truly happened, indeed seven times in a row, as the annals of former dynasties have recorded. It could happen again, and that is why you dreamt it. But perhaps you dreamt it because it is going to happen again. If this is your opinion, my child, then your mother can only be astonished that you rejoice at having this interpretation and thus know something that you in some sense produced yourself, but then instead of assembling your advisors and great men for a crown council in order to consider those measures by which one might counter this ominous evil, you at once drift off into luxurious considerations such as the juncture of not-being and always-being."

"But Mama, we have time!" Amenhotep cried, gesticulating. "When there is no time, one cannot, to be sure, take one's time, but we can, for a time of abundance lies before us. Seven years! That is what is so excellent about it, why a man would like to dance and rub his hands, because this most individual of lambs was not bound to some sorry scheme and did not prophesy a season of curse before a season of blessing, but the season of blessing first, an entire seven years. You would be right in scolding me if dearth and the day of wrinkled cows were to begin tomorrow. Then there would be not a moment to lose for considering expedients and preventative measures—although I must admit My Majesty cannot imagine any adequate measures for countering a failure of harvest. But since we have been permitted seven years of abundance in our Realm of Black Earth, during which the people's love for Pharaoh's motherliness will grow like a tree beneath which he can sit and teach his father's doctrine, I do not see why suddenly on this very first day . . . Your eyes are saying something, prophet," he interrupted himself, "and you gaze ahead with such urgency. Have you anything to add to our mutual interpretation?"

"Nothing," Joseph answered, "except a request that you would now release your servant to return to whence he came, to his prison of hard labor and to the pit out of which you pulled him for the sake of your dreams. For his task is ended, and his presence is no longer fitting in this place of greatness. He shall dwell in his hole and live from the memory of the golden hour when he stood before Pharaoh, the beautiful sun of the Two Lands, and before the Great Mother, whom I name second only because of the inadequacy of words, which belong to time and can only deal with one thing after the other, unlike images which enjoy the luxury of being side by side. But since naming names must obey time, the first is due to the king, and yet the second is not the second, for the mother was before the son. But enough of this sequence. In that place to which your lowly servant now returns, I shall continue within my mind this conversation of the great, since it would be culpable of me to intrude into its reality. 'Pharaoh was probably right,' I shall say silently to myself, 'to delight in this reversal and in the beautiful period that precedes the season of curse and the years of want. But how could the mother who preceded him not be right as well in her opinion and admonishment that from the very first day of blessing, indeed from the day of interpretation, there must be consultation and advisement concerning this coming evil, not to prevent it—one cannot prevent God's decrees—but to think and plan ahead with the power of foresight. For the period of blessing that has been promised us not only means a reprieve, a time for catching one's breath in order to bear up under the ordeal, but also allows room for precaution and is the only means for perhaps clipping the wings of the crow of calamity and warding off the coming evil, for working against it and, if possible, not merely holding it in check, but perhaps even extracting some blessing from it as well.' This or something like it I shall say to myself in my dungeon, for it would be worse than unseemly of me to insert my words into the conversation of the great. 'What a great and wonderful thing,' I shall softly cry out, 'is precaution, which in the end is even capable of turning disaster into blessing. And how gracious is God that he permits the king this view far ahead into time through his dreams—not just seven years ahead, but fourteen—for in that lies both the dispensation and dictate of precaution. For fourteen is *one* unit of time, just as it is two times seven, and it begins not in the middle but at its beginning, which is today, and today is the day for viewing the whole. But to have such a view is to take wise precaution.'"

"It is truly astounding," Amenhotep remarked. "Did you speak just now or not? You have spoken not by speaking, but by simply allowing us to listen in on your thoughts—thoughts, however, that you are only thinking of thinking. And yet it is as good as if you had spoken. It seems to me as if you have invented a rascal's invention and introduced something that has never been before."

"There is a first time for everything," Joseph replied. "But wise precaution and knowledgeable use of limited time have long been with us. Had God set the season of curse before the season of blessing and it were to begin on the morrow, there would be no help for it and nothing to be done, and what those years of chaff wrought among men could likewise not be made good again by the plenty to follow. But now it is just the opposite, and there is time—not to squander, but to make up for scarcity with plenty, to create a balance between plenty and scarcity by saving from the plenty in order to provide for the scarcity. That is the message that lies in the sequence by which the fat cows climb out first and then the lean ones, and he who is master of the overview is called and directed to be the provider amid scarcity."

"You mean someone should pile up provisions and gather them in barns?" Amenhotep asked.

"On the grandest scale," Joseph said resolutely. "On a scale totally different from any that has ever been seen since the birth of the Two Lands. The master of the overview would be the taskmaster of plenty. He would deal with it sternly and, as long as it lasts, take from it bit by bit whatever he needs to remain master of scarcity afterward as well. Pharaoh is the source of plenty, and his people's love will find it easy to tolerate his managing the plenty with a stern and heavy hand. But if he can distribute provisions during famine, how the faithful love of his people will then grow, so that he may sit in its shade and teach. The master of the overview would create shade for his king."

Having said this, Joseph's eyes accidentally met those of the

Great Mother, who was still sitting there on her lofty throne—small, dark, erect, and divinely posed, with her feet set close together—met the clever, piercing gaze of her eyes sparkling darkly in the darkness and directed at him, while the furrows around her pouting mouth formed a mocking smile. He gravely lowered his gaze before her, but not without first demurely lowering his eyelids.

"If I have heard you rightly," Amenhotep said, "it is your opinion, which you share with my mother, that I should without delay summon my great men and advisors to assemble so that they may determine how to discipline plenty in order to master scarcity?"

"Pharaoh," Joseph responded, "did not have all that much luck with assemblies when it was a matter of interpreting his double royal dream. He interpreted it himself—and found the truth. To him alone was the message sent and the overview given—it is up to him alone to manage that overview and discipline the plenty that shall precede the famine. Measures on an uncommon, unprecedented scale must be taken, whereas it is the wont of assemblies to come up with only the usual middling steps. *One man* dreamt and interpreted—*one man* should make the decisions and execute them."

"Pharaoh does not execute the decisions he makes," Tiy could be heard to remark coolly as she let her gaze slip between Joseph and her son. "That is an ignorant notion. But presuming he would decide on his own what is to be decided in light of his dreams—which, in fact, presupposes that one should make decisions in light of those dreams—their execution would be left in the hands of the great men appointed to accomplish it: the two Viziers of the North and South, the Administrator of Granaries and Cattle Yards, and the Controller of the Treasury."

"That is exactly," Joseph said in amazement, "what I had planned to tell myself in my cave, in the continuation of my thoughts about the conversation of the greats; I had intended to speak those very words, including every jot and tittle of the charge of 'ignorant notion' and put them in the mouth of the Great Mother to punish myself. It makes me think a great deal of myself to hear her say verbatim what I would have had her say to me there alone in my pit. I shall take her words with me, and once I am dwelling there, feeding off this sublime hour, I shall want to reply in my own mind and say: 'All my notions are ignorant, with one exception: that is, the notion that Pharaoh, the beautiful sun of the Two Lands, should execute his own decisions and not leave their execution to tried and true servants, and he does so simply by saying "I am Pharaoh! You are to be like me and it is from me that you have authority in this matter for which I have tested you, and you shall be an intermediary between me and the people, as the moon is the intermediary between sun and earth, by applying what I have decreed as a blessing both for me and the Two Lands"—no, my ignorance is not so vast as to permit that exception, and in my mind I hear Pharaoh speaking those very words, not to several men, but to one.' And if there were someone to hear me, I would likewise say: 'Several men are not good in such a case; let it be but *one,* just as the moon, who is *one* among the stars, mediates between above and below and knows the dreams of the sun. Those extraordinary measures must first begin with the choice of him who will put them into action—otherwise they will not be extraordinary, but only the usual middling and unsatisfactory steps. And why? Because they will not be executed out of firm belief and wise precaution. Tell those several men your dreams—they will believe and not believe, each will be but one portion of belief, one portion of precaution, and all the portions together will not make up the totality of belief and complete precaution that is needed and can be found only in *one.* That is why Pharaoh must search out a discreet and wise man, in whom the spirit of his dreams lives, the spirit of the overview and the spirit of precaution, and place him over all the land of Egypt with these words: "Be as I am," so that it will then be said of him as in the song: "He it was who saw all things unto the borders of the land" and disciplined the plenty with unprecedented measures, giving shade to the king in days of want.' These are my future words, which I shall speak to myself in the pit, since it would be mere crude impudence to speak them here before the gods. Will Pharaoh now let his servant depart from before his countenance, so that he may leave the sun and enter his own shadow?"

And Joseph turned around toward the bee-embroidered curtain with a gesture of his arm that asked if he might pass through it. He intentionally did not look to see the piercing gaze of the Goddess-Mother directed at him or how those worldly-wise furrows deepened into a mocking smile.

"I Do Not Believe in It"

"Stay," Amenhotep said. "Tarry a while, my friend. You have been quite adept at strumming your invention, which allows one to speak without speaking, or not to speak and yet speak, by letting others listen in on your thoughts, and, in addition to having supplied My Majesty with the interpretation of crowned dreams, you have delighted me with this novelty. Pharaoh cannot let you depart unrewarded, surely you don't think that. The only question is: how should he reward you—My Majesty still has no clear idea as to that; for if I were, for example, to present you with just this tortoise lyre, the invention of the master of tricks, that would be too little in my opinion and surely in yours as well. But take it in any case for now, my friend, clasp it in your arm, it indeed becomes you. The wily babe gave it to his soothsaying brother, and you are a soothsayer yourself, and wily as well, by the way. Moreover I am also thinking of keeping you here at my court, if you'd like, and of establishing a grand title for you, perhaps the King's First Interpreter of Dreams or the like, something splendid that will mask your true name so that it is completely forgotten. What is your name actually? Ben-ezne probably, or Nekatiya, I presume?"

"The name I am called," Joseph replied, "is not my name, and neither my mother, the virgin of the stars, nor my father, the friend of God, called me by it. But ever since my hostile brothers cast me into the pit and I died to my father by being stolen and brought down to this land, what I am has taken on another name: it is now Osarsiph."

"That is interesting," Amenhotep declared, settling back again into the cushions of his all too comfortable chair, while Joseph stood before him, the seafarer's present under his arm. "So you are of the opinion that one should not always have the same name, but one that suits one's circumstances, something appropriate to how one feels and what one will become? What do you say to that, Mama? I believe that pleases My Majesty, for I take pleasure in surprising views that leave the mouths of all those others—who know only outworn ideas—gaping, the sort whose views, to be sure, leave one's own mouth gaping as well, with yawns. Pharaoh himself has been called by his name far too long now, and for some time his name has been out of keeping with what he is and how he feels, so that for a good while now he has been silently playing with the idea of adding a new and more correct name and setting aside the old, confusing one. I've never spoken of this intention before, Mama, because I would have found it awkward to reveal it to you just between us. But in the presence of this soothsayer Osarsiph, who once had a different name, I am revealing it to you—it seems a good opportunity. Certainly I will do nothing rash, it does not have to happen tomorrow. But it must happen someday soon, for my name is daily becoming more and more a lie and an offense to my father in the heavens. It is a scandal that cannot continue, for my name bears the name of Amun, who stole the throne and pretends to have swallowed up Rê-Horakhte, the lord of On and the forebear of kings of Egypt, and now reigns over the empire as the god Amun-Rê. You must understand, Mama, that with time it has become a great burden to My Majesty to carry this name instead of one that is pleasing to the Atôn; for I have proceeded from him in whom are united what was and what will be. Behold, my present name belongs to Amun, but what was and what will be belong to my father, and we are both young and old at the same time, both from of yore and in the time yet to come. Pharaoh is a stranger in the world, for his home is in that ancient time when kings raised their arms to Rê, their father, the days of Hor-em-akhet, of the Great Sphinx. And he is at home in the time that is yet to come and that he proclaims, when all men will look up to the sun, the only god, their kindly father, just as it is taught by his son, who is in possession of his precepts, for he proceeded from the father, whose blood flows in his veins. Look at me," he said to Joseph, "come close and look!" And he pulled the batiste from his skinny arm and showed him the blue veins on the inside of his forearm. "That is the blood of the sun!"

The arm was trembling noticeably, although Amenhotep was bracing it with his other hand. But the hand was trembling as well. Joseph regarded what he was shown with respect and then retreated a little from the royal throne.

The Goddess-Mother said, "You are exciting yourself, Meni, and it is not good for Your Majesty's health. After this business of interpretation and this exchange of ideas, you should rest and take some time from the time given you to let your decisions ripen, both as regards the measures to be taken against what may possibly lie ahead and the very serious matter of the change of name you are considering, but also, by the way, as regards a suitable reward for this soothsayer. Retire to take your rest."

Except that the king did not want to. "Mama," he cried, "I beg you kindly and affectionately do not demand that of me now, not when things are proceeding so promisingly for me. I assure you, My Majesty is perfectly robust, and I have noticed no trace of fatigue. I am excited from feeling so well, the excitement does me good. You are speaking exactly like the nursemaids of my youth—when I was at my merriest, they would say, 'You have overtired yourself, heir of the Two Lands, and must go to bed.' That could make me mad as a hornet, I would stomp with fury. But now I am grown, and so I shall thank you respectfully for your concern. But I have a very clear sense that this reception can lead to still other lovely results, and that my decisions will ripen far better in conversation with this wily soothsayer than in bed, for I am already grateful to him simply for giving me the opportunity to inform you of my intention of assuming a more truthful name, one that contains the name of the only god—the name Ikhnatôn, in fact—so that what I am called may be pleasing to my father. Everything should be named after him and not after Amun, and when the mistress of the Two Lands, who fills the palace with her beauty, my sweet Titi, happily gives birth soon, the royal child, be it prince or princess, shall be called Merytatôn, so that it will be loved by him who is love—no matter if that does mean I shall be received ungraciously by the great man of Karnak, who will come before me to complain and tediously threaten me with the anger of the ram. I can endure that. I will gladly endure anything for the love of my father in the heavens."

"Pharaoh," his mother said, "you forget that we are not alone and these things, which must be handled with cleverness and moderation, are best not discussed before the ears of this common soothsayer."

"Enough of this, Mama!" Amenhotep rejoined. "In his own way he is of noble lineage, he has told us that himself—the son of a rascal and a lovely wife, and for me there is something utterly attractive about that, and it also attests to a certain elegance that as a child he was called the lamb. Children from the lower classes are not called by such names. Moreover, I have the impression that he is capable of understanding and providing answers to a great many things; but especially that he loves me and is prepared to help me, just as he has helped me to interpret my dreams and is of the original opinion that one should name oneself in the light of circumstances and one's feelings. How lovely and fine all this would be if only the name by which he calls himself pleased me better. . . . I do not wish to seem unfriendly or to grieve you," he said turning to Joseph, "but it grieves me to hear the name you have taken for yourself—Osarsiph, that is a dead name, in the same way that the dead bull is called Osar-Hapi, and it contains the name of the Lord of the Dead, of Usir, the dreadful god, who sits upon his throne of judgment, scales in hand, who is not only just, but merciless, and before whose verdict every fearful soul trembles. That old faith, which is itself dead, is all about fear and trembling, an Osar-faith, and my father's son does not believe in it."

"Pharaoh!" the voice of his mother was again heard to say, "I must appeal to you once more and remind you to be cautious, nor do I hesitate to do so in the presence of this foreign interpreter of dreams, inasmuch as you have honored him with such a lengthy reception and would regard as a badge of higher origins his claim to have been called 'the lamb' as a child. Then let him hear me admonish you to moderation and wisdom. It is enough that you are trying wherever possible to lessen the power of Amun and to set yourself against the universality of his sway by depriving him, step by step, of his unity with Rê, who dwells upon the horizon, who is the Atôn—for that requires all the political astuteness in the world, and a cool head as well, since all hot-headed haste comes from evil. But let Your Majesty beware of also offending the people's faith in Usir, the king of the world below, of whom they are fonder than of any other divinity, because all are equal before him and each man hopes to be merged with his name. Show forbearance toward the affections of the many, for what you give to the Atôn by diminishing Amun, you will take away from him again in doing harm to Usir."

"Oh, I assure you, Mama, the people only imagine that they are so fond of Usir," Amenhotep cried. "How can they be fond of the notion that the soul, on its way to the throne of judgment, must pass through seven times seven fields of horror, surrounded by demons who dog its every step and cross-examine it to hear all three hundred and sixty charms that are so difficult to remember—and the poor soul must be able to rattle them off by heart, reciting each at just the right point, otherwise it will not get through and will be devoured before it ever gets to the throne, where, however, everyone has a fair chance of being devoured if his heart is found to be too light upon the scales, and in that case is handed over to the monster, to the dog of Amente. I beg you, what is there to be fond of in that—it is contrary to all the loving-kindness of my father in the heavens! Before Usir, god of the lower world, they are all equal—yes, equal in fear. But before my father they shall all be equal in joy. And it is the same with the universality of Amun and the Atôn. With the help of Rê, Amun claims to be universal and to unite the world in devotion to him. The two are of one mind in that. But Amun wants to make the world one in the service of rigid terror, which is a false and darkling unity that my father does not want, for he wants to unite his children in joy and tenderness."

"Meni," his mother said in a low voice, "it would be better if you were to spare yourself and not speak so much about joy and tenderness. It is has been my experience that these are dangerous words for you, that they upset you."

"I am merely talking about belief and unbelief, Mama," Amenhotep replied, working himself up out of his cushions again and getting to his feet. "That is what I am talking about, and my own talents tell me that unbelief is almost more important than belief. Belief requires a great deal of unbelief, for how can anyone believe what is true as long as he believes nonsense? If I wish to teach the people what is true, I have to take from them some of the beliefs of which they are fond—that is perhaps cruel, but cruel out of love, and my father in the heavens will forgive me for it. Yes, which is more splendid, belief or unbelief, and which must come first? Belief is great bliss for the soul. And yet unbelief is almost more blissful than belief—I have discovered that, My Majesty has experienced it, and I do not believe in those fields of horror, in the demons and in Usiri, in his companions of the dreadful names and his great devourer down below. I don't believe in it! I don't believe in it! Don't believe! Don't believe!" Pharaoh sang and twittered, turning about on his odd legs in a little dance and snapping his fingers at the ends of both outstretched arms.

After that he was out of breath.

"Why did you give yourself such a dead name?" he asked, coming to a panting halt beside Joseph. "Though your father believes you dead, you are not."

"I must keep silent before him," Joseph answered, "and have consecrated myself to silence with my name. And he who is holy and set apart belongs to those below. You cannot separate what is below from what is holy and consecrated—they belong together—and that is precisely why the radiance from above shines upon him who is holy. Every sacrifice is made to the powers below, but that is the mystery: that in so doing one is offering it to the powers above. For God is the unified whole."

"He is light and the sweet solar disk," Amenhotep said with emotion, "whose rays embrace the Two Lands and bind them with love—he allows his hands to grow weak with love, and only those who are wicked, whose belief descends to the depths, have strong hands. Ah, how much more a world of love and kindness this would be were it not for belief in what is below and in the devourer with her grinding teeth. No one can persuade Pharaoh otherwise—that men would not do a great many things, or regard what they do with satisfaction, were their belief not directed downward. You surely know that my earthly father's grandfather, King Akheperurê, had very strong hands and with them could string a bow that no one else in all the land could string. And he went forth to defeat the kings of Asia and captured seven of them alive—he hung them by their heels at the bow of his ship, their heads hanging down—their hair waved below them and they all glared at the world with upside-down, bloody eyes. But that was only the beginning of all that he did with them, and though I do not tell it, he did it nonetheless. It was the first story that my tutors told me as a child, to instill a kingly spirit in me—but I awoke from sleep screaming with what had been instilled in me, and the physicians from the House of Books had to instill me with something else, with an antidote. Do you think, however, that Akheperurê would have done all those things with his foes had he not believed in the fields of horror and their spooks and Usir's companions of the dreadful names and the dog of Amente? Let me tell you: Human beings are a helpless lot. They do not know how to do anything on their own, and if left to themselves not the least notion ever occurs to them. They are always merely imitating the gods, and as they picture them, so they act. Purify the idea of god and you purify mankind."

Joseph did not reply to this speech until he had first glanced at the mother and read in her eyes, which were directed at him, that she would appreciate a response on his part.

"It is more difficult than difficult," he then said, "to reply to Pharaoh, for he is talented beyond measure, and what he says is true, so that one can only nod and mutter 'quite right, quite right,' or fall completely silent, letting all speech pass into slumber before the truth he utters. And yet one knows that Pharaoh does not like conversation to end in slumber and to falter before the truth, but instead wishes it to rouse itself and move on, beyond even what is true, thus leading perhaps to a more distant truth. For what is true is not the truth. That lies endlessly far off, and all conversation is endless. It is a wandering into eternity and at every station of the truth—after only a brief rest, after each impatient 'quite right, quite right'—it moves on restlessly, just as the moon moves on from each station in its eternal wanderings. But this necessarily brings me, whether I will or no, be it permissible or quite out of place, to my own earthly father's grandfather, whom at home we always called by the not entirely earthly name of moon-wanderer, though we knew full well that in reality his name had been Abirâm, which means 'my father is exalted,' or perhaps also 'father of the exalted,' and that he had come from Ur of the Chaldees, the land of the Tower, where he was not happy and could not endure it—though he could not endure it anywhere, which is why we gave him the name we did."

"You see, Mama," the king interrupted, "my soothsayer is of fine lineage after his fashion, isn't he? Not only was he himself called 'the lamb,' but he also had a great-grandfather who was given celestial names. People of the lower classes, from the great masses, do not usually even know their great-grandfathers. And so he was a wanderer in search of truth, this great-grandfather of yours?"

"And of such doughty vigor," Joseph replied, "that in the end he discovered God and made a covenant with Him, that they would be holy, each in the other. But he was vigorous in other ways, a man of strong hands, and when the robber kings from the East attacked, burning and plundering, and led his brother Lot away captive, he went forth in a brief and determined assault against them with three hundred and eighteen men and Eliezer, his eldest servant, making three hundred and nineteen, and defeated their forces, driving them beyond Damashki and freeing Lot, his brother, from out of their hands."

The mother nodded, and Pharaoh lowered his eyes.

"Did he take to the battlefield," he asked, "before he discovered god or after?"

"In the midst of discovery," Joseph answered. "In the midst of laboring at it and in no way weakened by it. What can you do with robber kings who burn and pillage? You cannot teach them the peace of God, they are too stupid and wicked for that. Only by striking them can you teach them so that they feel it—feel that the peace of God has strong hands. For it is your responsibility before God to see that things on earth occur halfway according to His will and not entirely according to the intentions of incendiary murderers."

"I can see," Amenhotep said with boyish annoyance, "that if you had been one of my tutors when I was a child, you would have also told me stories about hair dangling down and upside-down eyes filled with blood."

"Can it be," Joseph asked, addressing his question to himself, "that Pharaoh is mistaken and entertains erroneous thoughts despite his extraordinary talents and precocity? One is loath to believe it, and yet it appears error can creep in, as a reminder that he has a human side as well as a divine. For those who troubled him with tales of glory," he continued, still talking to himself, "stood unconditionally on the side of war and the lust of the sword for its own sake; his soothsayer, however, the moon-wanderer's latter-day grandchild, is attempting to bring to war tidings of the peace of God and to speak to peace on behalf of doughty vigor as an agent between the spheres, as an intermediary between what is above and below. The sword is stupid, but I would not wish to call meekness wise. Wise is the intermediary who advises meekness to be vigorous, so that in the end it does not stand there stupidly before God and man. If only I might say to Pharaoh what it is I think."

"I have heard," Amenhotep said, "what you have said to yourself. But this is just another trick and one of your inventions, speaking to yourself and acting as if others had no ears. You hold the seafarer's gift in your arm—it may be that these pranks come from that, and that something of the spirit of the rascal god has crept into your words from it."

"That may be," Joseph responded. "Pharaoh speaks the word of the hour. It may be, it is possible, it cannot be dismissed outright, one must assume that the wily god is present and wishes to remind Pharaoh that it was he who brought him his dreams, drawing them up from below to his royal bed, and that despite his jauntiness he is also the guide into the depths, a friend to the moon and to the dead. He puts in a friendly word with what is above for what lies below, and vice versa; he is the obliging intermediary between heaven and earth. For all things abrupt and unmediated are abhorrent to him, and he has knowledge of one thing that sets him apart from all other beings, and it is this: that something can be right and yet wrong as well."

"Are you referring again to your uncle," Amenhotep asked, "the wrong right son, whose thick tears rolled down into the dust amid the world's laughter? Let that story be. It is amusing, but depressing. It may be that what is amusing is always depressing and that free and blissful breathing comes only from what is golden in its seriousness."

"Pharaoh has said it," Joseph replied, "and may he be the right one to say it. Earnest and strong are both the light and the power that reaches up to the light in its purity—but that power must be true and manly, not merely tender, for otherwise it comes out wrong and too soon, and will end in tears."

He did not look over to the mother as he spoke these words, not directly, but he did glance just enough her way to see if she was nodding approval or not. She did not nod, but he thought he saw that she was staring steadfastly at him, which was perhaps even better than a nod.

Amenhotep had not been listening. He was leaning back in his chair in one of those all too relaxed poses that were tendentiously directed against the old style and Amun's rigor—one elbow set against the back of his chair, the other hand braced at the hip of the leg on which his weight rested, the tip of the other foot extended—and mused on his own words.

"I believe," he said, "that My Majesty's talents expressed something very good, very much worth lending an ear to—about what is amusing and earnest, about what depresses and makes us happy.

There is something amusing but also spooky and uncanny about the moon's mediation between heaven and earth. But the rays of Atôn, which bind them in truth, are of golden seriousness, have nothing wrong about them, and end in the kindly hands with which the father caresses his creation. God alone is the solar orb that floods the world with truth and unswerving love."

"All the world lends its ear to Pharaoh," Joseph replied, "and no one fails to hear a single word he says when he teaches. That may happen to others—even when, by way of exception, their words should be as worth taking to heart as are his own—but never to the Lord of the Two Crowns. His golden speech reminds me of another of our stories, the one about Adam and Eve, the first humans, who were terrified by the first night. They actually believed that the earth would become formless and void again. For it is light that separates things and establishes each in its place, creating space and time; but night brings back the disorder, the muddle, the *tohu-bohu*. They were both seized with indescribable fear as day died in the red of sunset and darkness came creeping in from all sides. And they threw themselves on their faces. But God gave them two stones: one of deep darkness and one of deathly shade. He rubbed them together for them, and behold, fire sprang from them, the fire of the womb, the innermost primal fire, young as lightning and older than Rê, which fed on what was dry and went on burning, making order of their night for them."

"Very lovely, very fine," the king said. "I can see that you don't only have stories about rascals. What a shame you have not also told of the delight those first humans took in the new morning, when the fullness of god beamed upon them again and drove the dark monster from their world, for the comfort they found must have been indescribable. Light, light!" he cried, leaving his dangling pose and, now with hesitation, now with hasty steps, he began to move back and forth in the room, raising his ornamented arms above his head and sometimes clutching both hands to his heart.

"Blessed brightness that created the eye that it might greet you, both that which sees and all that is seen, the world as it comes to itself, that knows itself only through you, O light, O loving discernment. Oh, Mama, and you my good soothsayer, how splendid beyond all splendor, how singular in all that exists is the Atôn, my father, and how my pulse pounds with pride and emotion because I have proceeded from him and he permitted me, before all others, to understand his beauty and love. For he is singular in greatness and goodness, as I am singular in my love for him, his son, to whom he has entrusted his precepts. When he rises in the flood of heaven and ascends from the divine land in the east, crowned with radiance as king of the gods, all creatures rejoice, the baboons pray with uplifted hands and all wild game praises him, leaping and running. For every day is a season of blessing and a feast of joy after the curse of night, when he turns himself away and the world sinks into oblivion. It is terrible when the world forgets itself, though it may also be needful for the sake of its refreshment. Men lie in their chambers, their heads covered, they breathe through their mouths, and one eye does not see the other. They do not notice the thief who steals their goods from under their heads, lions are prowling, and all the serpents sting. But he comes and closes the mouths of men, he removes the lids from their pupils and sets them on their feet, so that they may wash and reach for their garments and go to their work. Bright is the earth, the ships sail up the river and down, and every road lies open in his light. In the sea the fish dart before him, for his rays penetrate down to them as well. Distant he is—ah, immeasurable that distance—but his rays are nonetheless upon both earth and sea and bind all creatures with his love. For were he not so high and distant, how would he be over all and everywhere in his world, which he has divided and spread out in manifold beauty: the lands of Syria and Nubia and Punt and the land of Egypt; those foreign lands, where the Nile is set in the heavens, so that it may fall down upon your people and like the sea may beat its waves against mountains and water the fields among the cities, so that it swells up out of the earth for us and makes fertile the desert, that we may eat. Yes, how manifold, O lord, are your works. You have made the seasons and populated space and time with millions of forms, so that they live in you and perfect the season of life that you have given them, in cities, villages, and settlements, upon the highways and upon the rivers. You differentiated them and gave them a multitude of tongues, so that each speaks his special words amidst diverse customs, yet all are held in your embrace. Some are brown, others red, and others again are black, and still others like milk and blood—and in their many hues they reveal themselves in you and are your revelation. They have crooked noses and flat ones as well, and even those that stick straight out from the face; they clad themselves in bright colors and white, in wool or flax, each according to what they know and think; yet none of this is reason for them to laugh at one another, or to be hateful, but is merely interesting and solely a basis of love and worship. You fundamentally kind god, how full of joy and health is all that you have created and provide for, and what heart-uplifting rapture for it you have instilled in Pharaoh, in your beloved son, who proclaims you. You have made seed in men and you give breath to the boy in the body of the woman. You soothe him that he may not weep, you good nursemaid and innermost wet nurse. You create that from which the gnats live, as do the fleas, the worm and the offspring of the worm. It would gratify the heart, and almost overwhelm it, to know that the cattle are content in your pastures, that trees and plants are rich in sap and send forth blossoms in thankfulness and praise, while countless birds flutter in devotion above the marshes. But when I think of the little mouse in its hole, where you supply it with its needs—there it sits with little beady eyes, cleaning its nose with both paws—then my eyes well up with tears. And I cannot even think of the chick already peeping inside its shell, from which it breaks forth once he has perfected it—it comes forth from its egg and peeps with all its might while running around before him on little feet in great and nimble haste. This I dare not call to mind most especially, else I must dry my face with finest batiste, for it is flooded with tears of love. . . . I would like to kiss the queen," he suddenly cried and stood still, his faced upturned. "Let the call go out at once for Nefertiti, who fills the palace with beauty, the mistress of the Two Lands, my sweet consort."

All Too Blissful

Jacob's son was almost as weary from standing before Pharaoh as he had once been when he had had to play the mute servant for the old couple in the garden cottage. But young Pharaoh—despite all his tender feelings for gnats, chicks, the little mouse, and the son of the worm—apparently had no sense of this particular problem, for his was a royal and rather forgetful tenderness. Neither he nor the Mother-Goddess on her high throne even considered—were in fact probably incapable of considering—asking him to take a seat, however much his legs might feel like it and despite several charmingly inviting taborets with which the Cretan loggia was furnished. It was taxing, but when one knows what is at stake, one gladly puts up with a good many things and stands one's ground—a phrase that has rarely or perhaps never been more apt than on this long-ago occasion.

The Goddess-Widow took it upon herself to clap her hands the moment her son announced his wish. From his vestibule, the stooped chamberlain came gliding and gesturing sweetly through the bee-embroidered curtain. He rolled his eyes when Tiy tossed him the command, "Pharaoh has called for the Great Consort"— and then vanished. Amenhotep was standing with his back to the room before one of the great arched windows and gazed out across the gardens, his chest and body still heaving rapidly from his hymn to the sun's creation. His mother was turned toward him, watching him with concern. Only a few minutes passed before the woman he had asked for appeared; she could not have been far away. A little door that had previously been invisible opened now in the middle of the images of the mural on the right, two female servants prostrated themselves at its threshold, and between them there floated with careful steps the queen of the Two Lands, the bearer of the sun's own fruit—a wan smile on her lips, her eyelids lowered, her long neck thrust forward with an anxious grace. She said not a word as she made her hasty entrance. Wearing a blue cap, a circular extension at the back of her head that covered her hair and was framed by her large, thin, and finely formed ears, and clad in the ethereal pleats of a flowing robe transparent to both navel and thighs, though her breasts were hidden beneath a shoulder drapery and a glittering floral collar—she hesitantly approached her young husband, who was still panting slightly as he turned toward her with a touching gesture of affection.

"There you are, my golden dove, the sweet sister of my bed," he said in a quivering voice, then embraced and kissed her on the eyes and mouth, so that the serpents at both their brows kissed as well. "I had to see you and show my love for you if only fleetingly, it just came over me in the midst of conversation. My call was not too demanding, was it? You are not feeling sick at the moment from your holy condition? My Majesty is perhaps wrong to ask such a question, for in doing so I touch upon your inner state, which in being

thus reminded might be roused to nausea. You see with what subtlety the king understands everything. I would have been so grateful
to my father had you been able to hold down our exquisite breakfast
this morning. But no more of that. . . . You see the Eternal Mother
there upon her throne, and this man with the lyre is a foreign magician and soothsayer, who has interpreted my dreams of imperial significance and knows such roguish stories that I may well keep him
here at court in some higher position. He has been lying in prison,
by mistake apparently, as can happen. Nefer-em-Wêse, my butler,
also lay in prison by mistake, whereas his comrade, the deceased
Prince of Pastries, was guilty. Of any two men who lie in prison, it
appears one is always innocent, and of any three, two. I say that as a
man. As a god and king, however, I say that prisons are necessary
nonetheless. And as a man I now kiss you, my holy darling, repeatedly on the eyes, cheeks, and mouth, and you should not be surprised that I do so in the presence not only of my mother but of this
soothsaying foreigner as well, for you know that Pharaoh loves to
explicitly present his human side. I intend to go further still in that
regard. You do not know of it yet, nor does Mama—which is why I
now take the opportunity to announce it to you. I have been toying
with the idea of scheduling a pleasure trip on the royal barque *Star of
the Two Lands,* for which the people on both shores, in part out of
curiosity, in part on command, will stream forth to greet us. And,
without having first asked Amun's chief priest, I shall sit beneath the
baldachin with you, my holy treasure, and hold you on my knees
and kiss you, ardently and frequently, before all the people. That
will annoy the man from Karnak, but it will rouse the people to jubilation and teach them a lovely lesson not only about our happiness, but also, and this is main thing, about the nature, spirit, and
goodness of my father in the heavens. I am glad I have now spoken
of my intention. But do not think that it was for that reason I called
you here. This announcement simply leapt to my mind. But I called
you solely out of a sudden, overpowering desire to prove my tenderness to you. That has been done. Go now, my crowned treasure.
Pharaoh is exceedingly busy and has to take counsel concerning
things of great moment with his dear, immortal mama and with this
young man here, who, you should know, comes from the stock of
the inspired lamb. Go, and carefully guard against every alarm and
jolt. Let yourself be entertained with dancing and lute playing. And

when you have happily given birth, the name will be Merytatôn, no matter what—if that is fine with you. I can see that it is. What Pharaoh suggests is always fine with you. If only the whole world would find what he thinks and teaches to be fine, it would be far better off. Adieu, my swan throat; adieu, my little morning cloud edged in gold—until later!"

The queen floated away again. The muraled door closed behind her, leaving a seamless wall. Embarrassed by his emotions, Amenhotep turned back to his cushioned chair.

"Happy the lands," he said, "that have been granted such a mistress, and a Pharaoh whom she makes so happy. Am I right in saying so, Mama? Do you agree with me, soothsayer? If you remain at my court as the King's Interpreter of Dreams, I shall have you wed to someone, that is my decision. I shall choose the bride for you myself, someone of higher status, befitting your office. You do not know how agreeable it is to be wed. For My Majesty it is—as is apparent from my plan concerning a public pleasure trip—a manifest expression and image of my human side, of which I am fonder than I can ever say. For behold, Pharaoh is not arrogant—and if not he, who else in all the world should be? Sad to say, I do sense, despite otherwise pleasant manners, a kind of arrogance in you, my friend— I repeat, a kind, for I do not know your arrogance, but assume that it is connected with what you indicated to us about being set apart in some fashion and consecrated, to silence and the lower world, that is, as if a sacrificial wreath of some evergreen named 'touch-me-not' lay across your brow, which is the very reason why the thought came to me to have you wed."

"I am in the hand of the Most High," Joseph answered. "Whatever He does with me will be to my benefit. Pharaoh does not know how necessary arrogance was for me, how it protected me from the evil deed. I am set aside for God alone, who is the bridegroom of my tribe, and we are His bride. But as it is said of the star, 'female in the evening, but male in the morning,' so it may also be true that the suitor will emerge from the bride."

"Such a double nature may well suit the son of a rascal and a lovely wife," the king said in a show of worldliness. "In any case," he added, "let us speak earnestly and not lightly of most serious matters. Your god—who is he and of what sort is he? You have neglected, or avoided, to provide me clear information about him. Your father's grandfather, you say, discovered him? That sounds as if he had found the one true god. Can it be that, at so great a distance and so long before me, a man discerned that the one true god is the solar disk, the creator of that which sees and all that is seen, my eternal father in the heavens?"

"No, Pharaoh," Joseph replied with a smile. "He did not stop at the solar disk. He was a wanderer, and even the sun was but a way station on his arduous journey. He was restless and insatiable—call it arrogance on his part, and you will be enhancing that word of censure with the token of honor and necessity. For the man's arrogance was his belief that man should serve only the Most High. That is why his striving went beyond the sun."

Amenhotep had blanched. He sat bent forward—even his head in its blue wig was stretched forward—and was squeezing his chin in his fingertips.

"Pay attention now, Mama. For the love of all you hold dear, pay attention," he exclaimed in a soft voice, without turning his head toward his mother, but instead keeping his gray eyes fixed rigidly and unblinkingly on Joseph—eyes so intense it was as if he was trying to rend the veil that lay over them.

"Go on!" he said. "Wait! Wait; no, go on ! He did not stop. He forged his way beyond the sun? Speak! Or I shall speak myself, though I do not know what I shall say."

"He made things difficult for himself out of necessary arrogance," Joseph said, "and for that he was anointed. He prevailed over many temptations to worship, for he wanted to worship, but only what was highest, the Most High alone, nothing else seemed proper to him. Earth, our mother, tempted him, for she brings forth fruits and sustains life. But he saw her neediness, which only the heavens can assuage, and so he turned his eyes on high. He was tempted by roiling clouds, the storm's tumult, pelting rain, the blue lightning as it thrusts through the damp, the thunder's rumbling voice. But he shook his head at their demands, for his soul instructed him that they were all of merely second rank. They were no better, or so his soul said, than he himself—perhaps even poorer, despite their power. But he was powerful in his own way too, he thought, perhaps more powerful, and if they were above him, then only in space, not in spirit. To worship them, he found, would be to pray to what was too near and too low, and better not to pray at all, he said to himself, than to pray to what was near and low, for that is an abomination."

"Good," Amenhotep said, almost without any voice, still kneading at his chin. "Good, stop; no, go on! Mother, pay attention!"

"Yes, what great phenomena did not tempt my forebear," Joseph went on, "the starry host among them, the shepherd and his sheep. They were indeed distant and high and great in their passage. And yet they scattered before the beacon of the morning star—which to be sure was beautiful and of a twofold nature and rich with stories, yet too weak, too weak for what it heralded, before which it then turned pale and vanished. Poor morning star!"

"Spare your pity," Amenhotep commanded. "For here now is triumph. For before whom did it turn pale and who appeared just as it had announced?" he asked as proudly and menacingly as he knew how.

"Why, the sun, but of course," Joseph responded. "What a temptation for a man eager to worship. All round the earth people bent low before its goodness and cruelty. How good, what a beneficial rest, to join one's own devotions with theirs and bend low together with them. Except that my forebear's caution knew no limits, his reservations were inexhaustible. It is not, he said, a question of the benefit of rest, but solely of how to avoid the great peril to man's honor that comes from bending low too soon and not before what is ultimately the Most High. 'You are powerful,' he said to Shamash–Maruduk–Baal, 'and terrible is the power of your blessing and curse. And yet, worm that I am, there is something within me that exceeds you and that warns me not to confuse the witness with that to which it bears witness. The greater the witness, the greater the fault if I allow myself to be seduced to worship it instead of that to which it witnesses. The witness is godlike, but not God. In my pondering and striving I am likewise a witness who reaches beyond the sun to that to which it more powerfully bears witness than does the sun itself, and its fire is greater than the sun's fire.'"

"Mother," Amenhotep whispered, never taking his eyes off Joseph, "what did I say? No, no, I didn't say it, I only knew it, it was said to me. When it seized hold of me most recently and there was revealed to me an improvement in doctrine—for it is not perfected, I have never claimed that it is finished—I heard my father's voice, which said to me: 'I am the fire of the Atôn, which is within him. But

I could feed millions of suns with my fires. When you call me by the name of the Atôn, you should know that the name is in need of improvement, and that you are not calling me by my final name. My final name, however, is the Lord of the Atôn.' That is what Pharaoh, his father's beloved child, heard, and he brought it with him out of his seizure. But he kept silent about it and in keeping silent forgot it. Pharaoh has set truth in his heart, for his father is the truth. But he is responsible for the triumph of the doctrine, for its acceptance by everyone, yet he is afraid that improving and purifying the doctrine until it is nothing but purest truth might result in its being made unteachable. That is an onerous fear, a dilemma that one cannot explain to those who do not bear the burden of responsibility that Pharaoh does, and it is easy for them to say: 'It is not truth that you have set in your heart, but doctrine.' But the doctrine is the only means for bringing people closer to the truth. It should be improved upon; but if one does that to the point that it finally becomes useless as a means of truth—I ask the father and both of you: Is not that in fact proof of the truth of the accusation that one has sealed the doctrine in one's heart to the detriment of the truth? Behold, Pharaoh has shown mankind the image of his venerable father, as executed by his artists: the golden disk, from which rays descend to his creation, each ending in a sweet hand that caresses his creation. 'Worship!' Pharaoh says. 'This is the Atôn, my father, whose blood courses in me, and who has revealed himself to me, but who wishes to be father to you all, so that you will become beautiful and good in him.' And then he adds: 'Forgive me, dear people, for being so stern about your thoughts. I would gladly be lenient toward your simplicity. But this must be. Which is why I say to you: In worshiping the image, you should not worship it, nor in singing, sing hymns to it, but rather worship that of which it is the image—do you understand?—the true solar disk, my father there in the heavens above, who is the Atôn, for the image is not yet him.' That is already hard; it is a heavy demand upon mankind, and of a hundred men, twelve understand it. But if the teacher now says: 'For the sake of truth I must require you to make an effort even beyond this, however sorry I feel for you in your simplicity. For the image is the image of the image, and bears witness to a witness. When you burn incense to the image and sing its praise, it is not the actual solar disk high in the heavens that you mean—not that either, but rather the Lord of the Atôn, who is the fire in him, and who directs his course.' That is going too far and is too much for any doctrine—and of those twelve, not one will understand it. Only Pharaoh himself, who is beyond all numbers, understands it and yet he is supposed to teach it to numberless people. Your ancient father, soothsayer, had it easy, although he made it difficult for himself. He could make it difficult just as he pleased and could strive for truth for his own sake and the sake of his pride, for he was only a wanderer. I, however, am a king and teacher, and dare not think what I cannot teach. And such a king soon learns not even to think what he cannot teach."

Here Tiy, his mother, cleared her throat, rattled her jewelry, and gazing up into space, she said, "Pharaoh is to be praised for his diplomacy in matters of faith and for his leniency toward the simplicity of the people. That is why I warned him not to offend the popular fondness for Usiri, the king below. And there is no contradiction between leniency and knowledge, and instruction need not suppress knowledge. Priests have never taught the masses all they themselves know. They have shared whatever is wholesome for the masses and prudently restricted to their holy precincts anything not beneficial to the masses. Thus both knowledge and wisdom, truth and leniency, were in the world at the same time. Your mother recommends that it remain so."

"Thank you, Mama," Amenhotep said, with a modest bow her way. "Thank you for your contribution. It is very valuable and will be held in honor for all eternity. Except we are speaking of different things. My Majesty is speaking of the bonds that are laid upon the teaching of ideas about god. Your Majesty, however, speaks of priestly diplomacy that distinguishes between doctrine and knowledge. Pharaoh, however, does not wish to be arrogant, and there is no greater arrogance than such a distinction. No, no arrogance in the world is like that which divides the father's children into the initiate and uninitiate and teaches twice: prudently for the masses and knowingly within its own precincts. We should speak what we know and witness to what we have seen. Pharaoh wants nothing more than to improve the doctrine, but that is made difficult by his having to teach it. And yet it has been said to me: 'Do not call me the Atôn, for that name is in need of improvement. Call me the Lord of the Atôn!' But in my silence I forgot it. Yet behold, what does the father do for his beloved son? He sends him a messenger and interpreter of dreams—who interprets his dreams, dreams from below and dreams from above, dreams of imperial and heavenly significance—that he might awaken within Pharaoh what he already knows and interpret for him what has been said to him. Yes, how great is the father's love for his child, the king who came from him, for he has sent down to him a soothsayer who knows from long tradition that it is fitting for man to strive for what is ultimately the Most High."

"To my knowledge," Tiy remarked coolly, "the soothsayer came from below, from that hole of a prison, and not from above."

"Ah, in my opinion it is out of sheer roguishness that he came from below," Amenhotep cried. "And besides, above and below mean little to the father, who descends in order to make what is below part of what is above, for where he shines is the realm of the above. Which is why his messengers interpret dreams from below and above with equal skill. Go on, soothsayer. Did I say stop? I said go on. And if I said stop, I meant go on. That wanderer from the East, from whom you are descended, did not stop at the sun, but forged beyond it?"

"Yes, in spirit," Joseph answered with a smile. "For in the flesh he was but a worm upon earth, weaker than most of those beside and above him. And yet he refused to bow low and worship even one of these phenomena, for they were handiwork and witness just as he was. All that is, he said, is handiwork, and before handiwork comes the spirit to which it witnesses. How could I commit such great folly and burn incense to a piece of handiwork, however powerful? For I who know that I am merely a witness, whereas the others are that as well, yet do not know it. Is there not something in me of that to which all this bears witness, of the being of the Being that is greater than all His works and is outside them? He is outside the world, and He is the space of the world, and so the world is surely not His space. The sun is distant, probably three hundred and sixty thousand miles distant, and yet its rays are here among us. But Whoever directed their course is more distant than distant and yet near in the same degree—nearer than near. Distant or near, it applies equally to Him, for He has neither space nor time, and though the world is in Him, He is surely not in the world, but in heaven."

"Did you hear that, Mama?" Amenhotep asked in a small voice, with tears in his eyes. "Did you hear the message that my heavenly father has sent through this young man, whom I saw had something about him the moment he entered, and who interpreted my dreams for me? For I merely want to say that I have not said everything that was said to me in my seizure, but in keeping silent, I forgot it. But when I heard 'You shall not call me Atôn, but the Lord of the Atôn,' I heard this as well: 'Do not call me your father in *the heavens,* that is in need of improvement. You should call me your father in *heaven.*' That is what I heard and I sealed it up within me, because I feared the truth on account of the doctrine. But he whom I have pulled from his prison now opens the prison of truth, that it may step out into beauty and light, so that doctrine and truth may embrace, just as I shall now embrace him."

And again he worked his way out of the depths of his chair, and with eyelashes moist with tears he embraced Joseph and kissed him.

"Yes," he cried, as he once again clutched his heart in his hands and began to run to and fro in the Cretan loggia, from the bee-embroidered curtain to the windows and back again. "Yes, yes, in heaven and not in the heavens, more distant than distant, nearer than near, the being of being, that does not look death in the eye, that neither becomes nor dies, but rather is, the abiding light that neither rises nor sets, the immutable fount from which all life, light, beauty, and truth flow—that is the Father as He has revealed himself to Pharaoh, His son, who lies on His bosom and to whom He shows everything that He has made. For He has made all things, and His love is in the world, and the world knows Him not. Pharaoh, however, is a witness and bears witness to His light and His love, so that through him all men may be blessed and believe, though they still love the darkness more than the light that shines in it. For they do not understand it, and therefore their deeds are wicked. But the son, who came from the Father, will teach them. The light is golden spirit, the Father's spirit, and the power of the maternal depths works its way on high to Him, so that it may be purified in His flames and become spirit in the Father. God is immaterial, as is His sunshine, He is spirit, and Pharaoh shall teach you to worship Him in the spirit and in truth. For the son knows the Father, as the Father knows him, and he will royally reward those who love Him and believe in Him and keep His precepts—he will make them great and golden at his court, because they love the Father in the son who came from

Him. For my words are not my words, but the words of my Father
Who sent me, so that all may become one in light and in love, just as
I and the Father are one . . ."

He now smiled an all too blissful smile and at the same time
turned pale as death, and placing his hands behind his back, he
leaned against the muraled wall, closed his eyes, and remained that
way, standing erect but obviously no longer present.

The Wise and Discreet Man

Tiy, his mother, stepped down from her chair into the room and in
several quick, short strides was now beside the son who had been
snatched away. She gazed at him for a moment, passed the backs of
her fingers over his cheek in a fleeting caress—which he evidently
did not notice—and then turned to Joseph.

"He will raise you up," she said with a bitter smile. But her
mouth with its pouted lips and furrows could probably never have
offered anything but a bitter smile.

Joseph was staring in alarm at Amenhotep.

"No need to worry," she said, "he cannot hear us. His sacred affliction absents him from us, but it is not serious. I knew that it
would come to this, for he was talking at length about joy and tenderness. It always ends up like this, and sometimes the holy state is
worse. When he spoke of the little mouse and the chick I suspected it
would happen, but was certain of it when he kissed you. You must
take that in the light of his holy infirmity."

"Pharaoh loves to kiss," Joseph remarked.

"Yes, too much," she replied. "I believe that you are clever
enough to understand that it is a danger for the realm, which has
within its borders an all too powerful god and beyond them those
who envy it, yet must pay tribute, and lie in wait, plotting rebellion.
That was why I approved of your speaking to him about the
doughty vigor of your forebear, who was not weakened by thinking
about god."

"I am not a man of war," Joseph said, "and even my forebear was
so only when sorely pressed. My father kept to his tent and was
given to deep pondering, and I am his son by his true wife. To be

sure, among my brothers, who sold me, are several who have shown themselves capable of considerable brutality. The twins—we call them that, even though they are a year apart—were war heroes. Yet even Gaddiel, the son of a concubine, went about, in my day at least, more or less in full armor."

Tiy shook her head.

"You have a way," she said, "of speaking of your clan—as a mother, I'm inclined to call it pampered. All in all you think rather highly of yourself, it would seem, and feel yourself equal to any raising up of your state, don't you?"

"Let me put it this way, Great Mistress—" Joseph replied, "nothing in that regard would surprise me."

"All the better for you," she rejoined. "I am telling you that he will raise you up, presumably quite inordinately. He does not yet know it, but he will when he returns."

"Pharaoh has raised me up," Joseph answered, "by honoring me with conversation about God."

"Balderdash," she said impatiently. "You planned it that way and insinuated yourself from the very first word. You needn't play the child with me—or the lamb, as you were called by those who pampered you. I am a political woman; it does not pay to put on innocent airs with me. 'Sweet sleep and mother's milk,' am I right? 'Swaddling clothes and warm baths'—those are your concerns. Don't even try it! I have nothing against politics, I value them highly and am not rebuking you for making the most of your hour. Your talk about god was also talk about the gods, and you weren't bad at telling about that rascal god, the thievishly cunning child of the world, the lord of taking advantage."

"Beg your pardon, Great Mother," Joseph said, "it was Pharaoh who told of him."

"Pharaoh is sensitive and receptive," she riposted. "Whatever he said was suggested by your presence. He received you and spoke of his god."

"I was without guile in my dealings with him, my queen," Joseph said, "and so it will remain, whatever he may decide about me. By Pharaoh's life, I will never betray his kiss. It is a long time since I received my last kiss. It was in the valley of Dothan, my brother Jehuda kissed me before the eyes of the children of Ismael, who purchased me, to show them how much he valued his wares. Your dear son has erased that kiss with his own. And ever since, my heart has been filled with the wish to serve him and to help him in whatever way I can and to the extent that he empowers me to do so."

"Yes, serve and help him," she said, stepping forward to place her small, sturdy figure very close to him and laying her hand on his shoulder. "Do you promise his mother you will? You should know that the child is a source of high and anxious concern—but you do know. You are painfully clever and even spoke of the wrong right son, attributing to the deft and ready brother the idea that a man can be right and yet wrong as well."

"People did not recognize or know it before then," Joseph replied. "It is a founding principle of fate that one can be on the right road, but not the right man for the road. That was not so until today, but will be so, ever and again, from now on. Every founding principle should be shown due respect. And shown love as well, when it is as worthy of love as is your gracious son."

A sigh came from Pharaoh's direction, and his mother turned to him. He stirred, blinked, pulled his back away from the wall; natural color returned to his lips and cheeks.

"Decisions," he was heard to say. "Decisions need to be made here. My Majesty insisted that I had no more time to stay there and had to return immediately to make royal decisions. Forgive my absence," he said with a smile, allowing himself to be led to his chair by his mother and sinking down into its cushions. "Forgive me, Mama, and you as well, my good soothsayer. Pharaoh," he remarked with a smile after further consideration, "need not apologize, for he is absolute—besides he did not leave, but was taken away. But he apologizes all the same, out of cordiality. But now to business. We have time, but none to lose. Take your seat, Eternal Mother, if I may respectfully request it of you. It is not fitting that you are still on your feet while your son rests. Only this young man with the name from below may stand a while yet before Pharaoh as he pursues business that has been enforced upon us by his dreams. They, too, came from below, came from concern for what is above—but it seems to me that this soothsayer has been blessed both up from below and down from above. And so you are of the opinion, Osarsiph," he asked, "that one must discipline the plenty for the benefit of the scarcity to follow, and must gather vast provisions into barns in order to be able to distribute them in the years of want, so that what is above may not suffer along with what is below?"

"Precisely, my dear lord," Joseph replied—a totally false form of address according to etiquette, but one that at once brought glistening tears to Pharaoh's eyes. "That is the silent instruction of your dreams. There cannot be enough barns and granaries—there are many in the land, but too few. New ones must be built everywhere, until their number is like the stars in the sky. And officials must be installed everywhere who will discipline the plenty and exact payments—not according to arbitrary estimates, which are subject to bribery by gifts, but according to a firm and sacred formula; and they will store up bread in Pharaoh's granaries until it is like the sand upon the seashore, as a supply for the cities; they must guard over it so that food may be at the ready in the years of want and the land does not perish with hunger to the advantage of Amun, who would misrepresent Pharaoh before his people, saying: 'The king is to blame, and this is the punishment for novel doctrine and worship.' But when I say distribute, I do not mean to do so once and for all, but that food should be distributed among the commonfolk and the poor and sold to the great and rich. For a time of chaff is a time of scarcity, and if the Nile is low, prices will be high, and one should sell to the wealthy at a high price so that one may humble their wealth and humble everything in the land that still considers itself great beside Pharaoh—only he shall be rich in the land of Egypt, and become gold and silver."

"Who shall do the selling?" Amenhotep cried in alarm. "God's son, the king?"

But Joseph responded, "Certainly not. For I am thinking here of the wise and discreet man whom Pharaoh must choose from among his servants, of a man who is filled with the spirit of precaution, the master of the overview, who sees everything to the borders of the land and beyond, because the borders of the land are not his borders. Pharaoh will install him and set him over the land of Egypt with these words: 'Be as I am,' so that he may discipline the plenty as long is it lasts, and provide for the scarcity when it comes. Let him be the moon between Pharaoh, our beautiful sun, and the earth below. He shall erect the barns, supervise the host of officials, and set the formula for collection. He shall measure and determine when to distribute and when to sell, shall see to it that the commonfolk eat and listen to Pharaoh's teaching, and he shall milk the mighty to the benefit of the two crowns, so that Pharaoh will become silver and gold beyond all measure."

The Goddess-Mother on her throne gave a little laugh.

"You laugh, Mama," Amenhotep said, "but My Majesty finds what this prophet prophesies truly interesting. Pharaoh gazes down from on high at these lower things, but he takes a high degree of interest in whatever comical stratagems the moon deploys on earth. Tell me more, soothsayer, since we are taking counsel, about this middleman, this jaunty, deft young man and how, in your opinion, he should move and manage things once I have installed him."

"I am not a child of Keme, nor a son of the Yeôr," Joseph answered, "but come from far away. But the garment of my body has long since been made of Egyptian stuff, for I came down here at seventeen with Midianites, the guides whom God had appointed for me, and arrived in No-Amun, your capital. Although I am from far away, I know this and that about the circumstances of the land, about the history of how things came to be and how its nomes became an empire and the new emerged from the old, whereby the old that once was still defiantly maintains certain remnants, inconsistent with the time's passage. For Pharaoh's fathers, the princes of Weset, who defeated the foreign kings and drove them out and made crown lands of the Black Earth, had to reward petty kings and lords of the nomes, who had helped them in that struggle, with gifts of land and lofty titles, so that even to this day some still call themselves kings concurrently with Pharaoh and sit insolently upon their estates, which despite time's passage are not Pharaoh's. Since these conditions and history are not unknown to me, I can easily prophesy how Pharaoh's agent, as master of oversight and prices, will manage things and what use he will make of this opportunity. He will set prices for these lords of the nome and outdated local kings during those seven years of chaff, when they have neither bread nor seed, but he has an abundance of both—fancy prices that will bring tears to their eyes and strip the last garment from their backs, so that the land will at last fall to the crown, as is only proper, and these insolent petty kings will be made crofters."

"Good!" the Goddess-Mother said briskly in her deep voice.

Pharaoh was exhilarated.

"What a rascal your young middleman and moon is, my magician," he said with a laugh. "My Majesty would never have thought of it, but finds it superb all the same. But do you have nothing to prophesy about this man, my deputy, in regard to the temples that have grown too rich and fat for the land, about how in his rascally way he might likewise milk and strip them as they deserve? Above all I would like to see Amun's fatness milked and have my agent immediately exact payments according to the general formula from him, who has never had to pay tribute."

"If the man is exceedingly discreet, as I anticipate," Joseph responded, "he will spare the temples and leave the gods of Egypt alone when it comes to payments in the days of plenty, since it is ancient usage that the gods' holdings are not taxed. Above all, Amun ought not be provoked against the work of precaution, so that he agitates among the people against the piling up of provisions and they believe all this is directed against the gods. But come the time of scarcity, the temples will have to pay the price set by the master of prices, that will suffice, and they will receive none of the blessing of the crown's enterprise, so that Pharaoh shall become heavier and more golden than all of them—that is, if his agent understands his office even halfway."

"Wise," the Mother-Goddess said with a nod.

"If I am not mistaken as to the man," Joseph continued, "—and how could I be, since Pharaoh will choose him—he will likewise direct his attention beyond the borders of the Two Lands and see to it that disloyalty is smothered and that vacillation is bound to Pharaoh's throne. When Abram, my forebear, came down to Egypt with his wife Sarai (which, in fact, means heroine and queen), at the time of their departure there was famine at home and scarcity in the lands of Retenu, Amor, and Zahi. In Egypt, however, it was a time of plenty. And must it be different every time? If it is a time of lean cows for us here, who can say whether it might not also be a time of chaff in those lands? The warning in Pharaoh's dreams was so strong that it may well be that their meaning applies to the whole earth, that it would be a situation much like the Flood. Then these nations would make their pilgrimage down to the land of Egypt to acquire bread and seed, for Pharaoh will have amassed them. People will come, people from everywhere and from who knows where, even such as have never been seen here before; they will come, driven by famine, and step before the master of the overview, your agent, and say to him: 'Sell to us, otherwise we are sold and betrayed, for we and our children die of starvation and no longer know how we shall live unless you sell to us what is in your barns.' Then the seller will give his answer and deal with them according to what sort of people they are. How he will deal with this or that city king of Syria or the land of Phenice, I can venture to prophesy. For I know well that one or two of them do not love Pharaoh, his lord, as he should, and wobbles in his loyalty to him, so that he carries water on both shoulders and indeed feigns obedience to Pharaoh, but at the same time flirts with the Hetti and makes pacts to his own advantage. If things turn out as I see them, the man will make those sorts tractable with his dealings. For not only will he make them pay in silver and wood for bread and seed, but also, if they wish to live, they will have to deliver up their sons and daughters to Egypt in payment or as security, and thus will they be bound to Pharaoh's throne, so that henceforth one can rely on their loyalty."

Like a little boy, Amenhotep bounced in his chair with delight.

"Mama," he cried, "do you recall Milkili, the king of Ashdod, who more than wobbles and whose attitude is so vile that he does not love Pharaoh with all his soul, but plots treachery and defection, as I have learned from letters? I've been reminded of him the whole time. Everyone wants me to send troops out against Milkili and to dye my sword red—Hor-em-heb, my commander in chief, demands it twice a day. But I do not want to, for the Lord of the Atôn does not desire blood. But have you heard how this man here, this son of a rascal, prophesies to us that we may soon coerce the loyalty of such wicked kings and be able to bind them to Pharaoh's throne without any bloodshed whatever, simply in the course of business? Superb, superb!" he cried, repeatedly slapping his hand on the arm of his chair. Suddenly he turned serious and stood up solemnly, but then, seized by some scruple, at once sat down again.

"There is a difficulty, Mama," he said peevishly, "with the office and rank that I wish to confer upon my friend, the mediator, the man who will have the overview and be in charge of distribution. For where is there a place for him in government? Unfortunately, the government is fully staffed, and all its finest offices are occupied. We have the two viziers and we have the Overseers of Granaries and Cattle Herds, plus the Great Scribe of the Treasury and all that. Where is the office for my friend, to which I can appoint him and confer on him a title that befits him?"

"That would be the least of it," his mother replied coolly, turning her head away as if out of indifference. "There is a tradition that was often employed in early times and in later ones as well and that could be resumed at any time, if Your Majesty so wishes, by which a mediator, a Supreme Mouth, stands between Pharaoh and the great men of his government—a chief of all chiefs, an overseer of all overseers, through which the king's words must pass, the god's deputy. A Supreme Mouth is quite customary. One need not see difficulties where there are none," she said, turning her head still farther aside.

"That's true too!" Amenhotep cried. "I knew it and had merely forgotten, for there has not been a Supreme Mouth for a long time now and no moon between heaven and earth, and the Viziers of the South and North were the highest officials. My warmest and most cordial thanks to you, Mama."

And assuming a very solemn face, he stood up from his chair once more.

"Approach the king," he said, "Usarsiph, messenger and friend. Step close before me that I may speak to you. Good Pharaoh fears he may shock you. Therefore I beg you, compose yourself for what Pharaoh has to say to you. Compose yourself in advance, before you have heard my words so that you do not fall down in a faint, feeling as if you are being borne to heaven on a winged bull. Have you composed yourself? Then hear: *You are this man!* You yourself and no other, whom I choose and raise up at my side to be master of the overview, into whose hands highest authority is given, that you may discipline the plenty and provide for the Two Lands in the years of want. Can you be amazed at this, can my decision have come as a complete surprise to you? You interpreted my dreams from below without book or kettle, exactly as I felt they must be interpreted, and you did not fall over dead after prophesying, as is the wont of inspired lambs, which is a sign to me that you have been set apart to institute the measures that, as you clearly recognized, follow from the interpretation. You also interpreted my dreams from above, exactly according to the truth my heart knew, and have explained why my father said to me that he does not wish to be called the Atôn, but rather the Lord of the Atôn, and you have clarified for my soul the doctrinal difference between a father in the heavens and a father in heaven. But you are not only a wise man, but a rascal as well, and have prophesied to me how the years of want can be used to strip naked those lords of the nomes who no longer fit the times and to bind the wobbling city kings of Syria to Pharaoh's throne. Because god has made known all this to you, there is no one so discreet and wise as you, and there is no reason why I should search for any other, near or far. You shall be over my house, and all my people shall obey your word. Are you terribly shocked?"

"I lived for a long time," Joseph replied, "at the side of a man who knew how not to be shocked, because he was calm personified—he was my taskmaster in the dungeon. He taught me that calm is nothing more than being prepared for anything. And so I am not especially shocked. I am in Pharaoh's hand."

"And the Two Lands shall be in your hand and before the people you shall be as I am," Amenhotep said with emotion. "Take this as a first token," he said, nervously twisting and turning a ring over the knuckle of his finger and putting it on Joseph's hand. In its high, oval setting was a lapis lazuli of exceptional beauty that shimmered like a sunlit sky, and engraved in the stone was the royal cartouche with the name of Atôn inside. "Let this be the sign," Meni said excitedly, turning very pale again, "of your plenary power and deputyship, and whoever sees it, let him tremble and know that every word you speak to any of my servants, be it the highest or lowest, is as my own word. Whoever has a request of Pharaoh, let him first come before you and speak with you, for you shall be my Supreme Mouth, and let your words be kept and followed, because wisdom and reason stand at your side. I am Pharaoh! I set you over all the land of Egypt, and except you will it, no one in the Two Lands shall lift up hand or foot. I wish to be higher than you only by the height of the royal throne, and I will invest you with the sovereignty and splendor of my throne. You shall ride in my second chariot, directly behind mine, and runners shall run alongside and call about before you: 'Pay heed, take hold of your heart, this is the Father of the Land!' You shall stand before my throne and have the power of the keys, without limitation. . . . I can see you shaking your head, Mama, and you turn aside to mutter something about 'exaggeration.' But at times there is something splendid about exaggeration, and Pharaoh wishes to exaggerate for once. A title shall be established for you, lamb of god, such as has never been heard before in Egypt, and in which your name of death will vanish for good and all. For we do indeed have the two viziers, but I shall create for you the unprecedented title of Grand Vizier. But that is not enough, not by a long way, you shall also be called Friend of the God's Harvest and Provider of Egypt and Spender of Shade to the King, and Father of Pharaoh besides, and whatever else occurs to me—but in my happy excitement nothing more does occur to me at the moment. Do not shake your head, Mama, allow me this pleasure for once, for this time my exaggeration is intentional and deliberate. It really is splendid that it shall all be just as in the foreign song that says:

> 'Father Inlil has named his name Lord of the Lands,
> he shall rule over the vast domain of my authority,
> shall assume all my responsibilities.
> His land shall flourish, and he himself will prosper.
> His word stands firm, nor shall his orders be altered.
> No god shall change the word of his mouth.'

Just as the song says, just as that foreign hymn puts it, that is how it will be—what endless pleasure it gives me. At your investiture you shall be called Prince of the Interior and Vice-God. . . . We cannot undertake your golden investiture here, there is not even a proper treasure house here from which I can honor you with gold, with necklaces and collars. We shall have to return to Wase at once, only there can it be done, in the palace at Merima't, in the courtyard beneath the balcony. And a wife must be found for you as well, from the most refined society—that is, a great number of wives, but above all the first and true one. For I insist that you shall be wed. You will see how agreeable that is."

With a boy's exuberant eagerness he clapped his hands.

"Eiy," he called, still short of breath, to the stooped chamberlain as he entered, "we are departing. Pharaoh and the entire court are returning today to Nowet-Amun. Make haste, this is my beautiful command. Make my barque *Star of the Two Lands* ready, for on it shall I journey with my Eternal Mother, my Sweet Consort, and the chosen one, the Adôn of my house, who will henceforth be as I am in the land of Egypt. Tell the others. There shall be a great golden investiture."

The hunchback had, of course, been glued to the curtain, listening, and still did not want to believe his ears. But now he had to believe them. And that he now melted away, slinking like a cat and kissing all the tips of his fingers in delight—that is easy to imagine.

Part Four

THE TIME OF PERMISSIONS AND LIBERTIES

Seven or Five

What a fine thing that the exchange between Pharaoh and Joseph that led to the raising up of the man who had been dead and to making him great in the West, that this famous and yet almost unknown conversation—which the Great Mother, who was present at it, not inaptly called a conversation about God and the gods—has been restored from beginning to end, with every twist, turn, and conversational incident, and is preserved forever in all its accuracy, so that anyone can now follow the development it took back then and, if he has forgotten some point of it, need only open this book and read what has slipped his mind. The laconic nature of what has been passed down of it until now verges on venerable improbability. The idea that upon hearing Joseph's interpretation of his royal dreams and the advice that he seek out a wise and discreet man, a man of precaution, Pharaoh replied without further ado, "None is so wise and discreet as you, I shall set you over all the land of Egypt," and then showered him with honors and tributes in a truly enthusiastic, one might even say intemperate fashion—that version has always seemed to us to be excessive in its abbreviation, deletion, and shrinkage, has seemed to us an eviscerated, salted, and embalmed remnant of truth, not truth's living form; it has seemed to us that it lacked too many of the links in the chain of reason for Pharaoh's enthusiasm and exuberant grace. And when we first overcame our own reservations of the flesh and made ourselves strong for the descent into hell, for the journey down through the abyss of the centuries, to the well and meadow of Joseph's own present, we resolved above all else to listen in on this conversation and to bring it back up in all its segments, just as it actually occurred that day in On in Lower Egypt.

Let there be no misunderstanding—we have nothing against deletion. It is beneficial and necessary, for in the long run it is completely impossible to tell life just as it once told itself. Where would that get us? It leads to infinity, overtaxes human capability. Whoever took that into his head would not only never finish the job, but would also suffocate in its initial stages, entangled in a web of crazed accuracy. At the beautiful feast of narrative and reawakening, deletion plays an important and indispensable role. We prudently practice it at every step; for it is our reasonable intention to finish a presentation that, as it is, bears some distant resemblance to an attempt to drink the sea dry, but that dare not be taken to the absurd extreme of our actually, literally trying to drink dry the sea of accuracy.

Without such deletion what would have become of us when Jacob was serving that devil Laban for seven and thirteen and five years, that is, for a quarter century—of which every tiny element of time was filled with details of life ultimately worth narrating? And what would become of us now that the steady current of narration has driven our skiff to where it hovers trembling at the brink of a cataract of time—those prophesied seven plus seven years? First off, and just between us, let it be said that those numbers were neither so very bad nor so very beautiful as the prophecy predicted. It was fulfilled—of that there is certainly no doubt. But it was fulfilled with a lively imprecision rather than counted off in literal numbers. Life and reality always maintain a certain independence, sometimes to such an extent that one can scarcely or just barely recognize a prophecy in them. It goes without saying that life is bound to prophecy; but it moves freely within those bonds and in such a way that it is almost always a matter of goodwill whether one should consider a prophecy as fulfilled or not. We, however, are dealing with a time and with people who in all regards were inspired by the best will to recognize fulfillment in imprecision as well, and, for the sake of fulfillment, to let two and two make five, if that turn of phrase is appropriate in a situation where it was more important to consider that odd sum of five to be a somewhat higher odd number—which was not difficult, inasmuch as it is at least as respectable a number as seven and no reasonable man would even think to regard the substitution of a five for a seven as any sort of inaccuracy.

In fact and in reality the prophesied seven looked more like five. But versatile life committed itself unconditionally to neither the one nor the other, since, you see, the years of plenty and scarcity did not arise from time's womb with the same accuracy, did not offset one another with the same incontestable precision, as the fat and lean cows in Pharaoh's dream. The years of plenty and scarcity that did come were, like life itself, not equally fat and lean. Among the fat ones were one or two that one certainly could not call lean, but, if one were critically inclined, might possibly have been termed no more than middling fat. The lean ones were indeed all lean enough, five of them certainly, if not seven; but among them were a couple that did not reach the ultimate degree of misery, but came halfway close to being tolerable, so that, had it not been for the prophecy, one might not have recognized them as years of chaff and curse. But in this case, out of goodwill, they were included.

Does all this then speak against the prophecy's fulfillment? It does not. The fulfillment is unimpeachable, for the facts lie before us—the facts of our story that make up our story, without which our story would never be in this world and without which the carrying-off and the raising-up would never have been followed by the sending-for-others-to-follow. Things were certainly fat and lean enough in the land of Egypt and adjoining regions—years of plenty and years of more or less scarcity; and Joseph had ample opportunity to discipline the plenty and to distribute to the egregious scarcity and proved himself to be Utnapishtim-Atrahasis, to be Noah, that arch-clever man of foresight and precaution, whose ark rocks gently upon the waves of the Flood. Joseph did all this as a faithful servant of the Most High, as its minister, and his enterprise enriched Pharaoh with gold heaped upon gold.

The Golden Ceremony

First, however, he himself was enriched with gold, for "to become a man of gold" was a phrase the children of Egypt had for exactly what now happened to him when, obeying Pharaoh's beautiful command and joining the god, his Great Mother, the Sweet Consort, and the princesses Nezemmut and Baketatôn, on the royal barque *Star of the Two Lands,* he had made the return journey upstream—amid jubilation from both banks of the river—to Wase, the capital city, where together with the sun's family he had entered Merima't, the Palace of the West, set amidst gardens and beside the lake of its gardens at the foot of the colorful desert cliffs. There he was given chambers, servants, raiment, and every amenity, and already on his second day there the ceremony of gold was held, though only after Pharaoh had solemnly driven forth in the company of his court, with the purchased slave indeed riding in Pharaoh's second chariot, right behind the king himself, surrounded by the same Syrian and Nubian bodyguards and fan-bearers and separated from the god's vehicle only by a troop of runners who cried *"Abrek!* Pay heed!" and "Grand Vizier!" and, "Behold, the Father of the Land!"—so that the people in the streets might have some notion of what was happening before their eyes, of who that was in the second chariot. And they saw and understood that at the least Pharaoh had made someone very great, for which he surely had his reasons, even if they were only those of his own beautiful mood and whim—that sufficed entirely. But since such an elevation and golden investiture also somehow always carried with it the idea that a new age was beginning, that all things would now be better, Wase's population cheered lustily from the rooftops and hopped on one leg along the avenues. They shouted, "Pharaoh! Pharaoh!" and "Neb-nef-nezem!" and "Great is the Atôn!" and, upon closer hearing, many of them were calling out that name with a softer consonant, saying "Adôn, Adôn!" which was doubtless intended for Joseph. For it had surely leaked out that he was of Asian origins, and so it was thought fitting—particularly the women thought it fitting—to call out to him the name of the Syrian "lord" and bridegroom, especially since this man who had been raised up was so beautiful and young. It should also be added here that this same name would, among all his titles, be the one that stuck to him in particular, and throughout Egypt for the rest of his life, whether people spoke of him or to him, he was called Adôn.

After this beautiful procession, they were ferried across the river and now returned to the western shore and the palace, where the ceremony of gold—a wonderful ritual, and on this occasion particularly irresistible to eye and heart—took place. It unfolded more or less as follows. Pharaoh and She Who Filled the Palace with Love, Queen Nefernefruatôn, appeared at the so-called Window of Presentation, which in fact was not a window at all, but a kind of balcony that adjoined the Great Reception Hall and looked out on the palace's interior courtyard—a columned gallery of lapis and malachite richly ornamented with bronze cobras, it was extended at the front by a set of charming lotus pillars that were flagged with pennants and connected by a colorfully upholstered balustrade. It was on this that Their Majesties braced themselves as they tossed gifts of gold—which came in every form and were handed to them by treasury officials—to the recipient who stood beneath the balcony, in this case Jacob's son. With all its frills and furbelows, it was a scene that remained unforgettable to anyone who ever attended it. Everything was bathed in color and splendor, in a most generous bounty and pious rapture. The openwork magnificence of the architecture, the enchantingly gilded and brightly painted pillars with their pennants fluttering in the wind beneath a sunny sky; the courtyard filled with ranking officials clad in billowing skirts and bearing large and small fans in blue and red, who bowed low, shouted jubilant greetings, adored; women tapping tambourines and boys with the special braid of childhood, who were brought here for the sole purpose of turning ceaseless cartwheels; the host of scribes who stood in a demure posture and registered everything with their reeds; the view through the three open gates into the outer courtyard filled with chariots and prancing horses, heads held high and sporting colorful plumes, behind whom their drivers likewise lifted arms high while bowing low with respect in the direction of the ceremony; gazing down on all this, the red and yellow cliffs of Thebes, their rocky clefts lost in dark blue and violet shadows; and there on the raised glorious platform, the divine pair, their heads adorned with high caplike crowns with cloths that fell down over their necks, smiling tenderly and gazing ahead with languid superiority, dipping with visible delight into a never-ending wealth of riches and showering precious blessings on their favorite: necklaces of linked beads of gold, gold in the shape of lions, golden bracelets, golden daggers, headbands, collars, scepters, vases, and axes, all of purest gold, which the recipient could not catch all by himself, of course, and so had been given a pair of slaves who did it for him and heaped the hoard of gold, flashing in the radiant sun, on the pavement before him, to the crowd's cries of wonder—it was the prettiest scene one could ever behold, and if it were not for the implacable law of deletion, there would now follow a still more detailed description of the event.

While serving the devil Laban, Jacob had once assembled riches in the Land of No Return; and that is also what his darling did on this day, in the happy land of death, down into which he had been sold and there had died. For, to be sure, only in the underworld is there so much gold, and, simply from this golden tribute, Joseph became a wealthy man on the spot. Foreign kings who approached Pharaoh to trade for gold were accustomed to say that it was well known that in the land of Egypt this metal was no more precious than the dust of its roads. But it is indeed an economic error to believe that gold can ever exist in such great quantities as to decrease its value.

Yes, it was a day of beautiful significance, full of worldly blessing for him who had been carried off, separated from his family; and one could only have wished that Jacob, his old father, could have observed it all—though to be sure with a mixture of reservation and pride, in which surely pride would have prevailed. Joseph wished that as well; for later he would say "Tell my father of my glory!" He also received a letter from Pharaoh, which the latter of course had not written himself, but had dictated to his True Scribe, his Secretary of the Privy Cabinet, and though somewhat stiff in expression, it was very gracious in content and as a calligraphic product absolutely exquisite. It read:

> Decree of the King to Osarsiph, Overseer of All That Heaven Gives, That Earth Yields, and That the Nile Brings Forth, Overseer of Everything in All the Land, and True Overseer of Pharaoh's Orders. My Majesty was very glad to hear the words that you spoke a few days before today in a conversation it pleased the King to hold with you at On in Lower Egypt. On that beautiful day you truly delighted the heart of Nefer-kheperu-Rê with such things as he truly loves. My Majesty was extraordinarily glad to hear the words you spoke, for in them you joined the heavenly with the earthly, thereby showing not only your concern for the latter but your great concern for the former as well and contributing moreover to an improvement in the doctrine of My Father in Heaven. Verily, you understand to say those things of which My Majesty is exceptionally fond, and what you say makes My Heart laugh. My Majesty also knows that you say all such things of which My Majesty is fond. O Usarsiph, I say to you, times without number: Beloved of His Lord! Rewarded by His Lord! Darling and Initiate of

His Lord! Verily, the Lord of the Atôn loves me, for he has given you to me. As surely as Nefer-kheperu-Rê lives eternally: whenever you express a wish, be it in writing or orally, to My Majesty, it shall be granted by My Majesty upon the instant.

And in anticipation of one such wish, the most urgent possible wish as people in the Two Lands saw things, the letter concluded with the announcement that Pharaoh had given instructions for the excavation and architectural and decorative ornamentation of Joseph's eternal dwelling—which is to say, work on a tomb for Joseph in the western cliffs was to begin at once.

After the man who had been raised up had read this letter, the court then assembled in the great columned hall that lay behind the Window of Presentation for the grand formalities of his investiture, during which Pharaoh—in addition to the ring of authority he had already bestowed on him and all the gold he had just showered on him—draped an especially heavy gold necklace of favor over Joseph's immaculate court raiment, which of course was not of silk, as someone ignorant of the situation might brag, but rather of finest royal linen; and then Pharaoh had his Vizier of the South read the prodigious list of titles that he had established for Joseph and under which his name of death would henceforth be concealed. We know most of these gilded phrases from Pharaoh's own expressly announced intentions and from the formal letter he had written, making official those such as Overseer of All That Heaven Gives, etc. Among the others, surely the most impressive were Spender of Shade to the King, Friend of the God's Harvest, and Food of Egypt—*Ka-ne-Kême* in the language of the realm. Grand Vizier, although unprecedented, and Unique Friend of the King—in contradistinction to Sole Friend—seemed almost pallid by comparison. But that did not end the matter, for Pharaoh wished to exaggerate. Joseph was called Adôn of the Royal House and Adôn over All the Land of Egypt. He was named Supreme Mouth, Prince of Mediation, Augmenter of Doctrine, Good Shepherd of the People, the King's Double, and Vice-Horus. There had never been anything whatever like it before, nor did the future ever repeat it—surely it could only have happened during the reign of such an impulsive young ruler with a penchant for visionary pronouncements. There was yet one more title, though it was more a personal name, whose purpose was not so much to conceal Joseph's name of death as to replace it. Posterity has speculated much over it, and even the most venerable tradition supplies an inadequate, indeed erroneous translation. It says that Pharaoh called Joseph his Privy Councilor. That is an uninformed transcription. In our alphabet the name would have been spelled something like Dje-p-nute-ef-ônkh, which the nimble mouths of the children of Egypt would have pronounced as "Djepnuteefonekh," with a guttural *kh* sound at the end. The most prominent component of this grouping is "*ônkh*" or "*onekh*," the word whose icon is the looped or ansate cross, which signifies "life" and which the gods held under the noses of human beings, especially their sons, the kings, so that they might have breath. The name that Joseph received along with his titles was a name of life. It meant "The god"—Atôn, one did not have to name the name—"speaks: 'May life be with you!'" Even that was not yet its complete meaning. Every ear that heard it in those days took this to signify not only "May you yourself live," but also "May you be a bringer of life, may you spread life and provide life's nourishment to the many." In a word, it was a name of satiety and sufficiency; for above all else, Joseph was raised up to be the Lord of Fullness. All his titles and names, to the extent that they did not refer directly to his personal relationship with Pharaoh, contained in one form or another this notion of the preservation of life, of feeding the Two Lands, and all of them, including this much disputed and excellent personal name, could be summarized in a single title: the Provider.

The Sunken Treasure

After Jacob's son had been draped with this garland of names, he was at once surrounded, of course, and we shall leave it to you to imagine just how saccharine the congratulatory adulation of these sycophants was. Human beings have a tendency to wax enthusiastic, indeed ecstatic, over the whims of arbitrary power and incomprehensible election, over the monstrous "I favor whom I favor" that is totally exempt from all accountability and that even undoes envy and actually lends sincerity to toadying. As to Pharaoh's reasons for this stupendous raising up and investiture of this young foreigner, no one had any real insight into that, but all were happy to abandon any effort to gain it. To be sure, the art of prophecy was held in honor, and some things were explained by Joseph's having been lucky enough to excel and defeat the best domestic efforts in this field. Moreover, people knew Pharaoh's weakness for those who "hearkened to his words," which is to say, who were happy to entertain his theological ideas and knew to show themselves receptive to his "doctrine"—it was common knowledge that Pharaoh always responded with tenderest gratitude toward such understanding, feigned or not. And in that regard as well this boy wonder must have been lucky enough to have had the benefit of some inherited wisdom and previous schooling. But one way or the other, it was clear that above all else he must have kept his wits about him when dealing with their lord in order to soar right past them all in an instant; and people bowed low before such successful shrewdness, not to mention great arbitrary power; and as they encircled Joseph, they toadied and courted, kissed hands, scraped feet, fawned, and flattered to a fare-thee-well. A poet among the king's friends had even written a hymn of praise in his honor, which he recited to the soft accompaniment of a harp; and it went like this:

> "You live, you are hale, you are healthy.
> You are not poor, you are not wretched.
> You endure like the hours of the day.
> Your plans endure, your life is long.
> Your words are well chosen.
> Your eyes see what is good.
> You hear what is pleasant.
> You see the good, you hear the pleasant.
> You are praised among the councilors.
> You stand firm and your foe falls.
> Whoever speaks against you is no more."

We find this mediocre stuff. But as the achievement of one of their own, the courtiers found it quite good.

Joseph accepted all this as someone who is not surprised by any elevation, responding with an earnest cordiality that was just distracted enough to be slightly embarrassing. For his thoughts were not here in Pharaoh's great hall. They were on distant heights, in a tent made of felt, in the nearby grove of the Lord, with his little brother in his helmet of hair, his nearest and truest brother, to whom he told his dreams; they wandered to a harvest field, to companions resting beneath the shade of an awning, to whom he had also related the dreams he had dreamt; and to the valley of Dothan and a well and a landing that was anything but gentle. In his distraction he almost failed to notice the flash of an eye, a wink, directed at him from out of the encirclement—and had he avoided it, it would have caused the man offering it great anxiety.

Among the congratulants, in fact, was Nefer-em-Wêse—who had once been named just the opposite—the Master of the Vine. One can sympathize with this fat man in his bewilderment and confusion at the tricks life plays even as, under incredibly altered circumstances, he now found himself congratulating his young attendant from those terrible days. He had reason to hope that the new favorite would be well disposed toward him and not "speak against him," since it was he, Nefer, whom he had to thank for his being summoned and given this great opportunity. But this hope was somewhat qualified by his awareness that he had pointed a very belated finger at him and, just as Joseph had prophesied, had thought of him only when he had bumped his nose against the memory of him. Besides, he was not certain whether this man might not be as loath to be reminded of prison as he himself was; and so along with his congratulations he confined himself to a wink of cautious intimacy that could have meant almost anything—and was gratified to see this Adôn wink back.

Here now, on the occasion of an encounter that might lead one to think of another potential and indeed more highly charged meeting, one can only confirm and declare as fully justified a silence that not every version and account of Joseph's story has been wise enough to maintain. We are speaking here of Potiphar or Putiphera, or more correctly Peteprê, the great eunuch, Joseph's former owner, the lord and judge who magnanimously cast him into prison. Was he also present for this golden investiture, at this encirclement, and did he, too, pay homage to Joseph at court—perhaps by expressing to him the respects of a man who, lacking command of a thing himself, knows the value of its having been renounced by someone who might very well have commanded it? It would be fascinating to describe such an encounter; but there is nothing to describe here, for nothing of the sort took place. The agonizingly beautiful motif of reunion plays a triumphant role in our story, and many wonderful things in that regard still lie ahead—we can scarcely await them. But here the same motif is wrapped in silence, and the silence maintained in this part of the story by the standard version accepted in the West, the silence concerning the chamberlain of the sun and especially concerning his honorary and pitiable wife Mut-em-enet—this silence is not a deletion, or only to the extent that it deletes a negative: the explicit statement that something did *not* happen, which is to say, that after his removal from the courtier's household Joseph never again met either his lord or his mistress.

People—and, being an all too obliging breed, the writers who wish to please them—have spun out various versions of the tale of Joseph and Potiphar's wife, which was but one episode, though a very momentous one, in the life of Jacob's son; they have provided poignant sequels to an affair that had ended conclusively in catastrophe, and thus have lent it a dominant position within the whole of Joseph's story, which, under their hands, is then turned into a cloyingly sweet romance with a happy ending. If it were up to these poetic fictions, the temptress—who usually bears the name Zuleika, and what can one do but shrug at that—repented having sent Joseph to prison and retreated to a "hut," her sole purpose in life now being to atone for her sins, in the course of which atonement her husband died and she was left a widow. But when Yussuf (by which they mean Joseph) was about to be released from prison, he refused to let them remove "his chains" until all the elegant ladies of the land had first testified to his innocence before Pharaoh's throne. According to this version, then, the entire female aristocracy of Egypt actually had to assemble before the throne—including Zuleika, who left her penitent's hut to join them. The whole bevy of ladies unanimously proclaimed Joseph a prince of innocence, a paragon of purity. But then Zuleika took the floor and, humbling herself, publicly admitted that she had been the sinner, but that this man was an angel. Hers was the ignominious crime, she candidly confessed, but now she had been purified and would willingly bear the shame and disgrace. This she continued to do in her hut for many years after Joseph's elevation, growing old and gray in the process. Not until the festive day when Father Jacob made his purportedly magnificent entrance into the land of Egypt—that is, at a point in time when in reality Joseph already had two sons—did the pair meet again. Joseph forgave the old woman, and in reward the powers of heaven restored her former seductive beauty, whereupon Joseph joined with her in sweetest wedlock, so that at last she gained her wish and their "heads and feet lay together."

All that is pure Persian rosewater and musk. It has nothing whatever to do with the facts. First off, Potiphar did not die that soon. Why should a man have died prematurely who, given his peculiar constitution, was spared any squandering of his energies, who lived within himself and for his most private interests and could often refresh himself with bird hunting? History's silence as to his person after the day he held household court does indeed imply that he vanished from the scene, but not necessarily as a consequence of his death. One dare not forget that a change of sovereigns had occurred during Joseph's imprisonment and that such an event usually goes hand in hand with changes at court. Following the interment of Neb-maat-Rê the Magnificent—service to whom, had, as we know, caused some annoyance to a titular commander of troops without any real authority—Petreprê retired to private life with the title and rank of Sole Friend. He no longer attended court, or at least did not need to, and evidently out of the sense of tact that most certainly distinguished him he avoided doing so on the occasion of Joseph's golden investiture. If he did not encounter him again later either, the reason was in part that Joseph, as master of precautionary measures and supplies, did not, as we shall see, maintain his residence in Thebes, but in Memphis, and in part that Peteprê once again exercised this same tactful avoidance. But if such an encounter did occur at some festivity or other over the course of the years, one can be certain that it took place without the bat of an eyelash, with total discretion and sovereign disregard of the past—it is, in fact, this very conduct that is reflected in the silence of the standard version of tradition.

This silence applies to Mut-em-enet as well, and for equally good reasons. That Joseph never saw her again is really quite certain, but it is likewise certain that she did not move to some penitential hut or publicly upbraid herself for her shamelessness—which would have been a lie besides. After the failure of her desperate attempt to escape from an honorary into a truly human life, this great lady, the instrument of Joseph's testing—a testing that he did not stand up to with any particular brilliance, indeed barely stood up to at all—was forced to return for good and all to the only form of life that before her affliction she had regarded as perfectly natural: yes, she fortified herself in it more rigidly and proudly than ever. As a result of the splendid wisdom that Potiphar had displayed at the time of the catastrophe, her relationship with him had not so much suffered as it had taken on a certain warmth. He had passed judgment like a god who stands above the concerns of the human heart—and for that she knew to be grateful and from that day forward was a blameless and obedient titular consort. She did not curse the man she loved because of the suffering he had caused her, or that she had caused herself on his account, for the pains of love are special pains that no one has ever repented having endured. "You have made my life rich—it blossoms!" Those were the words of Eni's prayer in the midst of her anguish, and one can see in them the special nature of love's torments, which can even emerge as a prayer of thanksgiving. In any case, she had lived and loved—loved unhappily, to be sure, but is there really such a thing and should not every sense of pity here be dismissed as silly and officious? Eni demanded none and was far too proud for self-pity. The blossom of her life, however, had faded, and there was finality and austerity in her resignation. The forms of her body, which had temporarily been those of the body of a witch of love, were quickly restored—not to the swanlike beauty that had characterized her youth, but to those of a nun. Yes, henceforth Mut-em-enet was a cool nun of the moon with chastely restored breasts, unapproachably elegant and—one must add—extremely bigoted. We all still recall how at one time, during the period of the painful blossoming of love, she had joined with her beloved to burn incense to all-seeing, all-embracing Atum-Rê at On, the Lord of the Wide Horizon, whom she expected would favor her passion. This was now past. Her horizon had contracted again, to a narrow, rigid, patriotic piety; more than ever her full devotion was given to the conservative sunship of the lord of Ipet-Isowet, rich in cattle, her mind open solely to the spiritual advice of the great Beknechons, that god's bald-headed high priest, who despised every innovation and forbade every form of speculation; and this alone would have alienated her from the court of Amenhotep IV, where the fashionable trend was a religion of tender, all-embracing rapture, which in her eyes had nothing to do with piety. When, clad in the clinging garb of Hathor, she shook her rattle before Amun and joined the chorus of noble concubines to dance in measured step and to lead them in singing (though from a flat chest now) with a voice beloved by all, she celebrated sacred constancy, the eternal balance of the scales, the stony stare of endurance. And yet at the bottom of her soul lay a treasure in which she secretly took greater pride than in all her spiritual and worldly honors, and which, whether she admitted it or not, she would not have surrendered for anything in the world. A sunken treasure in the depths—but it still silently sent its light up into the murky days of her renunciation. And however much it represented her defeat it also lent to her spiritual and worldly pride an indispensable element of essential humanity—a pride in life. It was a memory—not so much of him, whom she heard had now become lord over Egypt; he was merely an instrument, just as she, Mut-em-enet, had been an instrument. But rather—almost independently of him—it was a recognition of her justification, the awareness that she had blossomed and burned, had loved and suffered.

Lord over Egypt

Lord over Egypt—we use the term in the spirit of a convention that can never get enough of this apotheosis and in the sense of beautiful exaggeration that, after all, Pharaoh had once allowed himself for the benefit of the interpreter of his dreams. But we do not use it without having put it to the test or with the reckless abandon of fables, but rather with the proviso of reason enjoined upon us by reality. For there is no bragging here, only narration, which in any case are two very different things—whichever of the two one may prefer. For rodomontade will always leave the momentarily stronger effect; but in fact an audience truly profits only from narrative based in prudent investigation.

Joseph became a great lord at court and in the land, there can be no question of that, and the personal position of trust that had bound him to the monarch since their conversation in the Cretan garden room, that is, his status as a favorite, meant that the limits of his authority were blurred and vague. But he was never actually Lord over Egypt or even Regent of the Two Lands, as it is sometimes put in story and saga. His elevation, which was dreamlike enough, and his extravagant list of titles did not alter the fact that vast branches of the administration of the land to which he had been carried off remained in the hands of the crown's officials, some of whom had been entrusted with them since the days of Neb-maat-Rê; and only out of pure exuberance could one assume that, for instance, the justice system, which since earliest days had been the province of the high judge and the vizier (at present of the two viziers) or the conduct of foreign policy had been put into the hands of Jacob's son—although had Joseph assumed such powers, it would most probably have resulted in a happier course of events than those familiar to historians. One dare not forget that, however much of an Egyptian he was in his outward conduct, the glory of the empire was ultimately of no concern to him and that, however beneficial the measures he energetically enacted for the populace, however sensibly he served the public good, his inner eye was always still directed toward private spiritual matters, family matters of world-shaking significance, toward the advancement of plans and intentions that had little to do with the weal or woe of Mizraim. One can be certain that he immediately saw a connection between what was foreboded in Pharaoh's dreams and those same plans and intentions, his expectations of preparing a way. Indeed one cannot deny that his behavior before Pharaoh's throne had about it a resoluteness of purpose that might have a chilling or damaging effect on the sympathy that we have likewise wanted to preserve for Rachel's child—or might if our audience did not keep in mind that Joseph regarded it as his duty to encourage such plans and to assist God in their prosecution as best he knew how.

He was appointed, whatever else his titles might say, to be Minister of Provisions and Agriculture and in this capacity he instituted important reforms, of which his land-rent law in particular left an impression on history. But he never overstepped the boundaries of his administrative capacities; and even when one considers that the concerns of the treasury and supervision of the granaries were too closely related to his own official duties for his authority not to have extended into such matters as well, the terms Lord or Regent over Egypt still remain fantastical embellishments on the real state of affairs. To be sure, there is something else to be considered here. Given the conditions that dominated the first crucial ten to fourteen years of his tenure in office—conditions in anticipation of which he had been installed—there had to have been an extraordinary increase in the importance of his office, and indeed it put all others in the shade. The famine that broke out both in Egypt and neighboring lands five to seven (but more like five) years after he was raised up made the man who had predicted it—who had taken precautions and knew how to help people get through it tolerably well—practically the most important figure in the empire and gave to his decrees a life-and-death significance unlike those of any others. It may well be that any critique, if it is rigorous enough, finally ends up endorsing popular opinion, and so we shall let it be and simply say that Joseph's position, at least for a good number of years, was indeed tantamount to that of a Lord over Egypt, without whose consent no one in the Two Lands might lift up hand or foot.

First of all, immediately after being granted plenary powers, he undertook an inspection tour of the entire land of Egypt, by ship and by chariot and in the company of a large staff of scribes whom he had selected himself, the great majority of them young men not yet fossilized by bureaucratic routine, his intent being to gain first-hand knowledge of all matters concerning the Black Earth and, before taking measures, to make himself the true master of oversight. Property rights at these levels were peculiarly vague and muddled. Theoretically, as with everything else, every parcel and plot belonged to Pharaoh. All land, including provinces that had been conquered or that paid tribute, as far as "the wretched land of Nubia" and to the borders of Mittaniland, were ultimately his private property. In reality, however, the true state domains, the "estates of Pharaoh," existed as special crown lands quite separate from both the latifundia that earlier kings had given as gifts to their great men and the estates of minor nobles and farmers, which were treated as the personal property of their managers, even though, strictly speaking, these were tenant arrangements subject to rents, albeit the property itself was inheritable. The only exceptions here were, first, temple lands, in particular the fields of Amun, which were true freeholds and exempt from all taxes; and, second, vestiges of a far older organization of land in a patchwork of special rights, properties belonging to individual princes of the nomes who had remained strong or at least made a show of independence, inherited estates that stood out here and there like islands of an obsolete feudalism and whose owners, like the priesthood of Amun, demanded that these lands be regarded as their unencumbered property. But whereas Joseph's administration left the temple lands in peace, he rode roughshod over these stubborn barons, incorporating their properties from the very start and without further ado into his system of duties and reserves and, over time, managing to expropriate them outright for the crown. It is not correct to say that the so-called New Kingdom's peculiar agrarian conditions, a phenomenon so striking in the eyes of other nations—that is, that in the land of the Nile every bit of soil, except that of the priests, belonged to the king—were created by measures instituted by Jacob's son. In reality he merely completed a process already far advanced, by solidifying conditions that had existed before him, by lending them legal status and clarity in people's minds.

Although his journey did not include the lands of the Negroes, nor extend as far as Syrian and Kenanite regions, to which he sent out his agents, the inspection required between two and three times seventeen days, for there was much to be recorded and brought under his oversight. Then he returned to the capital, where he and his staff occupied a government building in the Street of the Son; and it was from there that in Pharaoh's name the famous land law was issued in time for that year's harvest, and then proclaimed throughout the kingdom: a universal duty of one-fifth of the total, to be imposed upon the fruits of the field, without regard to person or size of harvest and delivered punctually and without reminder—and if not without reminder, then with a very energetic reminder—to the royal storehouses. At the same time the children of Egypt could observe how throughout the nation, in the immediate vicinity of cities both large and small, these depots were being enlarged and augmented with the help of troops of laborers levied in unprecedented numbers—a glut of depots, one would think, for many of them necessarily stood empty at the beginning. More and more were being built nonetheless, for their surplus was based on a surplus of grain that, so it was said, the new Adôn in charge of storage, the god's Friend of the Harvest, had prophesied. Wherever one went, there they stood, packed row on row, or sometimes set in great rectangles around courtyards: tall, cone-shaped granaries, with hatches at the top for filling and locked doors at the bottom for emptying; and they were built especially sturdy, with terracelike platforms of pounded clay to protect them from the earth's damp and raids by mice. There was also a goodly number of underground pits for storing cereal grains—each well lined and provided with virtually invisible entrances, which were nevertheless kept under close police watch.

We are happy to say that both measures, the tax law and the erection of large depots, were overwhelmingly popular. There had, needless to say, always been taxes, in a variety of forms. It was not for nothing that old Jacob—who had never been there himself, but had his emotionally charged image of the place—liked to speak of the "Egyptian house of bondage," even if his disapproval made too few allowances for special conditions in the land down under. The labor of Keme's children belonged to their king, that was a given, and, to be sure, it was used for building monstrous tombs and incredibly ostentatious palaces—for those too. But above all it was needed for establishing the system of hoists and trenches so essential for a flourishing harvest in this truly exceptional land of oases, for keeping waterways functioning, for digging ditches and canals, for reinforcing dams, and manning sluices—and the maintenance of such things on which the public welfare depended could not be left to the imperfect insight and inconsistent diligence of Pharaoh's individual subjects. Which was why the state required that its children drudge for it. But once work was done, they also had to pay taxes on what they had accomplished. They had to pay taxes on the canals, lakes, and ditches they used, for the machinery and leather bags of the irrigation system that served them, even on the sycamores that grew on their fertilized soil. They paid taxes on house and farm and on everything house and farm produced. They paid with skins and copper, with wood, ropes, paper, linen, and, of course, with grain. But these duties were levied at the very erratic whim of nome administrators and village officials, depending on whether the Provider, that is to say Hapi, the river, had been great or small—a reasonable enough system in one sense, it is true; but there were also excessive demands on the one hand and unfair privileges on the other, plus every sort of bribery and nepotism to complain about. One can say that from its first day Joseph's administration both tightened the reins in one regard and slackened them in another—which is say, it placed all the emphasis on the grain tax, but regarded other obligations with a very mild eye. People were allowed to keep their linen of first, second, and third quality, their oil, copper, and paper, if only they conscientiously paid the royal assessment, in grain, of one-fifth of their cereal harvest. This tax rate, being both universal and reassuringly clear, could not be considered onerous in a land with a fertility yielding on average a thirtyfold harvest of seed sown. Besides which, this quota had a certain spiritual beauty and mythical appeal, since it was wisely and deliberately based on the sacred epagomenal number: the five extra days added to the year's three hundred and sixty. And, finally, people were pleased that Joseph unhesitatingly applied it as well to those nome barons with their claims of absolute independence and, what was more, demanded that for the good of the nation they bring their estates up to contemporary standards. For the spirit of defiant backwardness that prevailed among them was likewise expressed in the fact that the irrigation systems on these estates were outdated and inadequate, and not merely out of laziness, but on tendentiously reactionary principle, so that the soil did not yield all that it could. Joseph expressly ordered these gentlemen to improve their systems of canals and wells—and he recalled how Eliezer had told him that Sheleph, a grandson of Eber, was the first to "to turn brooks onto his land" and was considered the inventor of irrigation.

But as for those extraordinary measures for piling up grain in storehouses, any explanation for why this decree of Joseph's likewise pleased the children of Keme must again take its cue from the Egyptian national belief in foresight and precautionary safeguards. Joseph's own personal tradition of the Flood and the clever idea of building an ark to save the human race and the animals after their kind from perishing entirely, was joined here with an old and vulnerable civilization's instinct for security and defense, for it had grown old under precarious conditions. Its children were even inclined to see something magical in Joseph's storehouses; for they were accustomed to protecting themselves against the invasions of demonic evil, which always lay in wait, by weaving as impenetrable a web as possible of magical symbols and charms—which was why in their minds the notions of "precaution" and "magic" were interchangeable and such sober safeguards as Joseph's granaries could appear in a magical light.

In a word: it was the general impression that Pharaoh, young as he was, had scored a success in appointing this young Father of the Harvest, this Spender of Shade. His authority would surely grow over the course of years, but it benefited here and now from the fact that the Nile had grown very large this year, so that under the new administration a well-above-mediocre harvest—particularly of wheat, spelt, and barley—had been brought in and an abundance of sorghum could be gleaned from the stalk. We doubt that it is legitimate to include as part of Joseph's prophecy a year whose prosperity was already decided even as he was standing before Pharaoh and to count it as a year of the fat cows. But that is what happened later in the attempt to bring the number of years of blessing to a total of seven—even if this did not prove completely successful. In any case it was to Joseph's benefit that he took over the enterprise under conditions of rejoicing and abundance. There has always been something venerably absurd about popular opinion—and there still is. It is perfectly capable of concluding that a minister of agriculture appointed in a year of fruitful harvest has to be a good minister of agriculture.

That is why when Jacob's son drove through the streets of Wase, the public greeted him with uplifted hands, crying, "Adôn! Adôn! Ka-ne-Kême! Eternal life to the Friend of the God's Harvest!" And many even cried out, "Hapi! Hapi!" and then pressed thumb and forefinger of their right hand together and set them to their lips— which was going a bit far and must be attributed largely to their childish enthusiasm for someone of such beauty.

He did not drive out into public often, however, for he was very busy.

Urim and Thummim

The deeds and decisions of our lives are determined by proclivities, sympathies, fundamental attitudes, and critical experiences of the soul, which color our existence, tingeing all our actions and providing a far more genuine explanation for them than any of the rational reasons we put forward not only for others' actions, but for our own as well. That only a short time after taking office, Joseph—very much contrary to Pharaoh's wishes, who would have liked to have him always nearby for discussions of his father in heaven and for assistance in his labors at improving his doctrine—that very soon the king's Supreme Mouth and Lord of Provisions moved his residence and all his offices from the capital of Nowet-Amun to Menfe in the north, to the House of the Wrapped God, was based on the honest and certainly superficially justifiable reason that Menfe of the thick walls was the balance scale of the Two Lands, its midpoint, the symbol of Egypt's equilibrium, more or less predestined to be the place of oversight, the most comfortable and serviceable home imaginable for the Lord of Oversight. Granted, what was said about its being the balance scale and Egypt's equilibrium was not quite correct, for Mempi lay well to the north, close to On, the city of blinking eyes, and to the cities of the river's seven mouths, and even if one thought of Egypt as extending only as far as Elephant Island and the Island of Pi-lak and did not include the land of the Negroes, the city of King Mirê, the place where his beauty lay interred, was in no sense the balance point of the Two Lands, but rather lay as far to its north as Thebes lay to its south. But ancient Menfe nonetheless enjoyed its reputation as the midpoint of Egypt, the city that held it in equilibrium; that it provided a commanding view in both directions, upstream and down, was an axiom on which the Egyptian Joseph based his decision, and Pharaoh himself could not refute his contention that commerce with maritime Syrian cities who sent their ships down to fetch grain from their "granary"—for that was how they viewed the Land of Black Earth—could be better implemented if he were located in Menfe rather than in Per-Amun.

This was all perfectly correct, and yet these were only the rational reasons for Joseph's decision to ask for Pharaoh's permission to live in Menfe. The real reasons lay more deeply determinative in his soul. And they were so all-embracing that they included his relationship to life and death. One can put it this way: They were reasons of cordiality set against a dark background.

It has been a long time now, but we all still recall how once as a boy he stood, alone and saddened by a misunderstanding with his brothers, on a hill near Kiriath-Arba and gazed down on the moon-whitened town in the valley and on Machpelah, the double cave, the rocky tomb that Abram had bought and where the bones of his ancestors lay. We remember in detail what a strange mixture of emotions formed in his soul that night, created by the sight of both the grave and the populous town that lay slumbering there—emotions of piety, which is a reverence for death and the past, were united in him with those of a half mocking, half genuinely cordial affection for the "city" and all the teeming tribe that filled the crooked streets of Hebron with humanity's smell and clamor and now lay with knees drawn up, snoring in chambers inside houses. To establish a connection between that early welling up of emotion in his breast—which ultimately was a matter of a few moments spent gazing—with his present actions may seem rather daring and arbitrary, and to trace such actions directly back to it even more so. And yet we have proof in hand that we are correct in establishing this connection in words spoken by Joseph on a day between then and now, spoken to the old man who had purchased him when they were together in Menfe, the tomb metropolis. He had casually remarked that he felt a fondness for this city, whose dead need not travel over the water because it already lay to the west of the river, that of all the cities of Egypt it might well suit him—and that had been so truly characteristic of Rachel's eldest, more than he himself might have realized. And the pleasure he took in how the people there, whose similarity in such great numbers was the source of their ironic mood, had jauntily abbreviated the ancient funereal name Men-nefru-Mirê to Menfe— that pleasure was close to being Joseph's essence, for it revealed the deepest depths of his nature, something very deep in every deed and moment, although the name by which it is designated is simply one of rather tame serenity: sympathy. For sympathy is a meeting of death and life; and genuine sympathy arises only when the sense for the one holds the sense for the other in balance. By itself a sense for death creates rigidity and gloom; by itself a sense for life creates a banal vulgarity devoid of wit. Wit, then, and sympathy arise only where a reverence for death is colored and warmed by a cordial regard for life, while the latter is made more profound and valuable by the former. This was the case for Joseph—this the source of his wit and his cordiality. This was his blessing—the double blessing with which he was blessed, from heaven above and from the deep that lies below, the blessing upon which Jacob his father expanded on his deathbed, acting almost as if he were spending and bestowing it, when in fact he was merely stating it.

In examining the moral world, which is a complicated world, one cannot do without some basic erudition. It had always been said of Jacob that he was *tâm*—that is, an "upright" man who lived in tents. But *tâm* is a strangely equivocal word for which "upright" is a very poor translation, for its meaning includes both the positive and the negative, the yes and the no, light and dark, life and death. This root word is found again in the curious formula "Urim and Thummim," where, in contrast to the bright, affirmative Urim, it evidently stands for the world's dark aspects shadowed by death. *Tâm* or Thummim is the light and the dark, what is above and what is below the world, both at once and interchangeably—and Urim is merely what is joyous, separated out in its purity. Thus Urim and Thummim is not actually a statement of opposites, but instead allows us to perceive the mysterious fact that when one separates one part from the whole of the moral world, the whole still stands in contradistinction to the part. It is not all that easy to make sense of the moral world, especially since its sunny component very often suggests what is underworldly. Esau, for example, the red man, the man of the hunt and the plain, was definitely a man of both the sun and the underworld. But although Jacob, his younger twin, is contrasted to him as a gentle shepherd of the moon, one should not forget that he spent a major portion of his life in the underworld with Laban and that the term "upright" is a more than imprecise designation for the means by which he was turned into a man of silver and gold there. He was most certainly not Urim, but in fact *tâm,* that is a man of grief and gladness, like Gilgamesh. And so, too, was Joseph, whose rapid adjustment to the sunny underworld of Egypt likewise does not suggest a pure Urim-nature. Urim and Thummim should be translated as something like "Yes—yes, no," that is, with a yes and no prefixed by the coefficient of another yes. In purely mathematical terms that means of course that, since a yes and a no cancel one another out, only the additional yes is left over; but such pure reckoning has no color and this sort of mathematics disregards the dark coloring of the yes that evidently remains as an aftereffect of the canceled no. It is, as noted, all very complicated. The best we can do is to repeat that in Joseph life and death met, resulting in a sympathy that was the deeper reason why he obtained permission from Pharaoh to live in Menfe, the witty metropolis of tombs.

The king, whose first concern had been an eternal dwelling for his Unique Friend—and it was already under construction—presented him with a bright, sunny residence in the city's most elegant quarter; it had a garden, a reception hall, a fountain court, and all the amenities of those late early times, not to mention a host of Nubian and Egyptian servants for the kitchen, antechamber, stable, and salon, who swept, sprinkled, and cleaned the villa, placing flowers everywhere—and who were under the supervising stewardship of whom? Even the least enlightened and slowest thinker in our audience can surely guess that. For Joseph was a man who kept his word more faithfully and punctually than Nefer-em-Wêse the butler had kept his; he promptly made good on a farewell promise he had given someone: that, if he should be raised up, he would send for him to follow and employ him; and even while he was still in Thebes, immediately after returning from his inspection tour, he had, with Pharaoh's approval, written to Mai-Sakhme, the commander of Zawi-Rê, and invited him to be his majordomo, to stand over his house and concern himself with all those things with which a man like Joseph could not possibly concern himself. Yes, the same man who had once succeeded to the office of steward and been charged with overseeing Peteprê's household and was now charged with a task of far greater oversight, now had in turn a man who oversaw everything that was his—his chariots and horses, his pantries, table, and menials—and that man was the imperturbable Mai-Sakhme, who was not at all shocked when he received this letter from the slave who had drudged for him, simply because he was not a man to be shocked, and, without even waiting for the newly designated warden to arrive, set off on the overland journey for Menfe, a somewhat old-fashioned city now surpassed by Thebes in Upper Egypt, but in comparison to Zawi-Rê still a tremendously stimulating place, where the versatile Imhotep the Wise had once lived and worked and from where a very lovely job now beckoned his admirer. And he at once took up his position at the head of Joseph's household, assembled the servants, and made purchases to equip the house, so that when Joseph arrived from Wase and Mai-Sakhme greeted him at the beautiful gate to his villa, he found his residence prepared in finest fashion as befits the home of a great man. He even found an infirmary had been set up for those who might twist and turn in pain, and also a little pharmacy, where his steward could pestle and putter to heart's content.

The reunion was very cordial, although of course there was no embrace in the presence of the staff that had assembled to greet their master. That had taken place for good and all on the day of their farewell, at the only proper moment for it, when Joseph was no longer Mai-Sakhme's servant and Mai-Sakhme had not yet become his.

The steward, however, said, "Welcome, Adôn, behold—your house. Pharaoh gave it, and he whom you appointed has appointed it in every detail. You need only go to your bath, be anointed with oils, and take your seat for dinner. I thank you most warmly for having thought of me and removing me from boredom as soon as you found yourself seated in glory, once everything had happened just as your servant always felt it would happen, and for allowing me to share in such a stimulating environment—for all of which I shall earnestly strive to prove worthy every day."

And Joseph replied, "My thanks in turn to you, my good man, for having answered my summons and wishing to be my steward in this new life. Things happened as they happened because I did not offend my father's God by entertaining the smallest doubt that He would be with me. But do not call yourself my servant, for we shall be friends as we were before, when I served under your feet, and together we shall endure the good and bad times in life, the calm and exciting times—and I shall need you especially for the exciting times that may yet come. And for your painstaking service I thank you in advance. But it should not consume you to the extent that you do not find leisure to put reed to paper in your study as you enjoy doing and in time find a gratifying form for the story of three loves. Literature is a great thing. But greater still, to be sure, is when the life one lives is a story—and that we are in a story together, a most excellent one at that, I am more and more convinced with time. You, however, are part of it because I took you into my story, and when in the future people hear and read of the steward who was with me and lent a helping hand in exciting hours, then they shall know that this steward was you, Mai-Sakhme, the man of calm."

The Maiden

In the beginning God once caused a deep sleep to fall over the man that he had set in the Garden of the East, and while the man slept, God took one of his ribs and closed up its place with flesh. And from the rib He made a woman, for it seemed to Him that it was not good that the man should be alone, and he needed her to be human, that she might be with him as company and helpmate. And the intention was very good.

Scholars have provided quite marvelous descriptions of this presentation—it happened, they say, in this way or that, and act as if they must know—and it may be that they truly do know. God washed the woman, so they assure us, He washed her clean (for, as an erstwhile rib, she was probably still somewhat sticky), anointed her, rouged her face, curled her hair, and in response to her fervent urging adorned her head, neck, and arms with pearls and precious stones, including sard, topaz, diamond, jasper, turquoise, amethyst, emerald, and onyx. And escorted by thousands of angels singing hymns and playing lutes, He presented her in her adornment to Adam, in order to entrust her to the man. There was a feast and a banquet—which is to say a festive banquet, in which, it would seem, God Himself affably took part; and the planets danced in a circle to their own music.

This was the first wedding feast, but we are not told that it was also a marriage right off. God had made the woman to be Adam's helpmate, simply as company for him, and had evidently thought nothing further about it. That she would know pain in giving birth to children was a curse that He did not lay upon her until she and Adam had eaten from the tree and both had had their eyes opened. Between the Feast of Presentation and the feast when Adam first knew his wife and she bore him a tiller of the soil and a shepherd, in whose footsteps Esau and Jacob would walk—in between these two first comes the story of the tree and the fruit and the serpent and the knowledge of good and evil, and they came first for Joseph as well. He too did not know a woman until after he had first learned what good and evil are—from a serpent who for the life of her would have loved to teach him what is very, very good, but evil as well. He, however, resisted her and knew the art of waiting until it was good and no longer evil.

One cannot help thinking of that poor serpent now as well, when the sundial points to the hour of Joseph's marriage to someone else with whom he will lay head and feet together, instead of with her. In order to preclude any general melancholy, we quite intentionally spoke of her previously at an appropriate point and let it be known that she had again become a cool nun of the moon for whom all this was of no importance. The proud bigotry to which she again devoted herself may help minimize a certain bitterness that we all might otherwise feel for her sake. It was also good for the peace of her soul that it was not in nearby Thebes but in Menfe that Joseph's marriage took place, for which Pharaoh himself, who had eagerly encouraged the matter from the start, made the journey downriver in order to take part personally in the wedding feast and the dance of the planets. Strictly speaking, he played the role of God in this matter, beginning with the idea that it was not good for the man to be alone; for he had proclaimed to Joseph at the start how pleasant it was to be married—though to be sure he, unlike God, was speaking from experience, for he had his Nefertiti, his dawn cloud edged in gold. God, however, had always been alone, his sole concern being mankind. But in much the same way, Pharaoh was concerned about Joseph and, as soon as he had raised him up, he began to look around for a state alliance for him, which any such marriage had to be—that is to say, one that was politically astute and distinguished, yet invigorating as well, a combination not easily managed. But as God had done for Adam, Pharaoh furnished his creature with a bride, led her to him to the music of harps and cymbals, and took part in the wedding himself.

Who was this bride, Joseph's consort, what was her name? Everyone knows that, which in no way diminishes the pleasure we take in providing it, nor do we have the least worry that this might detract from the joy our audience takes in learning it again. Besides which, many have probably forgotten it and no longer realize they know it and would be at a loss to answer the question. The maiden's name was Asenath, daughter of the priest of the sun at On.

Pharaoh had reached that high for his choice—he could not have reached higher. Marriage to the daughter of the High Priest of Rê-Horakhte was almost a scandal bordering on sacrilege—although, of course, the girl was also destined to be a wife and mother and no one wished for her to remain unmarried, her womb closed. Nevertheless, whoever took her to wife was in some sense her abductor—his deed, however necessary, and even desirable, regarded as sinister and tantamount to a crime. She was not given to him, but abducted—that was the general view and interpretation of her case, even when everything was done in proper order and by elegant prearrangement; and never in this world has another set of parents made such a to-do of placing their child in the hands of a husband. Her mother in particular was quite beside herself, or at least feigned total despair. She could not emphasize enough how incomprehensible she found the event; she wrung her hands and put on airs as if she herself had been or was about to be raped, which explained why among her comments on this occasion some—granted, more out of ceremony than in earnest—were oaths of vengeance.

All this was because the maidenhood of this daughter of the sun was protected by a special shield of holiness, was clad in a garment of inviolability—one ultimately meant to be violated. Girded with virginity like no other, she was the virgin of virgins, the maiden per se, the epitome of maidenhood. The name designating her status was more or less her personal name: she was named and called "Maiden" her whole life long, and the violator of this maiden, the husband who robbed her of her virginity, was, by common agreement, committing a sacred crime—whereby the adjective mitigated, ennobled, and to some extent canceled out the noun. And yet relations between the son-in-law and the girl's parents, especially the hand-wringing mother, always remained strained in public, though in private they could be quite cordial. In a certain sense they never consented to their daughter's belonging to a husband, and included in the wedding contract was a standard clause stating that their child should not dwell continually at the side of this sinister violator, but for a certain portion of the year, and not all that brief a portion either, return to her sun parents and live again with them as a virgin—a condition that, if not in a literal, then at most in a metaphorical sense was observed in the form of visits paid by the wife to her parental home, something perfectly common in most other marriages as well.

If a high priest and his wife had several daughters, all this applied chiefly to the firstborn and only in a lesser degree to the younger ones. Sixteen-year-old Asenath, however, was their only daughter—and one can well imagine what a sacred crime and violation it was to marry her. Her father, the Great Prophet of Horakhte, was, of course, no longer the same gentle old man who, on the occasion of Joseph's first visit to On in the company of the Ishmaelites, had occupied the golden chair at the foot of the great obelisk, the winged solar disk at his back. This was his chosen successor, likewise a kindly, good, serene man—the office demanded that of this high ser-

vant of Atum-Rê, and if he was not that by nature, requisite dissembling helped him make it his nature. Purely by chance the man bore,
as is well known, the same name as Joseph's former owner, the
courtier of light—that is, Potiphera or Peteprê. And what better
name could a man in his position have had than The Sun Has Given
Him? His name speaks for the fact that he was born to this office and
predestined for it. Presumably he was the son of the old man in the
golden cap, whose granddaughter, then, was Asenath. As for her
name, which was written as "Ns-nt," it was related to the goddess
Neith of Sais in the Delta and meant "she who belongs to Neith";
and so Maiden stood under the special protection of this armed goddess, whose emblem was a shield with two crossed arrows attached,
and in her human form she also bore a bundle of arrows atop her
head. Which Asenath did as well. Her hair or, better, the stylized wig
she wore over it—though Egyptian fashion in such items leaves it
uncertain whether these should be called headscarves or hair-
pieces—was always adorned with arrows, either inserted into it or
fastened on top; and as for the shield, the fitting symbol of her exceptional virginity and impenetrability, it was frequently repeated,
along with crossed arrows, in the jewelry at her throat or waist or on
her arms.

Despite all these defenses and this manifest readiness to sting,
Asenath was as charming as she was exceptionally kind, gentle, and
docile, a child obedient to the will of her highborn parents, of
Pharaoh, and finally of her husband, even to the point of renouncing
any will of her own; and the hallmark of Asenath's character was
precisely this union of a holy aloofness kept under seal and an evident willingness to go along with whatever happened to her, a forbearing acceptance of her lot as a woman. The form of her face was
typically Egyptian, fine-boned, with a somewhat prominent chin,
yet not without its own personal stamp. The cheeks were still childishly plump, the lips were full as well, with a delicate indentation between mouth and chin; the brow was clear, the little nose likewise a
bit too fleshy perhaps; her large, beautifully madeup eyes had a peculiarly fixed, attentive look, something like that of a deaf person,
though there was nothing whatever of the mute about her, for her
glance revealed an inner expectancy, an anticipation of some order
about to be given perhaps, a darkly attentive readiness to hear the

call of destiny. As if in apologetic contrast, a little dimple would show in one cheek whenever she spoke—and the whole effect had its own unique charm.

Charming and in a certain sense unique as well were the lines of her body, which could be seen through the gossamer of her garments and were marked by an exceptionally small waist with a wasplike tuck, set above correspondingly full hips and a long abdomen—a childbearing womb. Bold, firm breasts and slender well-proportioned arms that she liked to hold fully extended completed this amber-hued image of maidenhood.

Surrounded by flowers, Asenath the Maiden lived a flowerlike existence until she was abducted. Her favorite haunt was the shore of the holy lake within the precincts of her father's temple, where there was a rolling meadow covered with flowers, a kind of carpet of narcissi and anemones; and she loved nothing better than to join her playmates, the daughters of other priests and nobles of On, and stroll through these fields beside the mirroring waters, to sit in the grass and make wreaths of plucked flowers, her attentive eyes beneath raised brows gazing out into the distance, that little dimple forming in her cheek, as she waited for whatever things might come. And come they did; for one day Pharaoh's messengers were there, demanding of Potiphera her father, who nodded gravely, and her fully uncomprehending mother, who wrung her hands, that this virgin of the shield become the wife of Djepnuteefonekh, the Vice-Horus, the Spender of Shade to the King. She herself, under the influence of the model of her life, raised her arms heavenward, pleading for help, as if someone had grabbed her about her narrow waist to snatch her up and abduct her.

It was all a masquerade, behavior dictated by convention; for not only were the wishes and courtship of Pharaoh a command, but marriage to his favorite, to the king's Supreme Mouth, was also honorable and desirable; the parents could not have reached higher for their child than Pharaoh had reached for Joseph, and there was no reason whatever for despair, or even for any sort of worry beyond the natural sorrow parents feel when letting go an only child so that she may marry. All the same, as much fuss as possible had to be made over Asenath's maidenhood and her abduction and the bridegroom depicted as a very sinister figure, even though the parents who sired her should have been delighted with him and probably really were—for Pharaoh had expressly let it be known that in this case virginity was to be joined with virginity and that the bridegroom himself was a kind of virgin, one who for many years had been jealously set aside as a bride only to emerge now as a suitor. For this even to occur, he had first had to settle with the god of his fathers, the bridegroom of his tribe, whose jealousy he had long treated with consideration but would do so no longer now, or only insofar as he was entering into a special and exemplarily virginal marriage—if that was any sort of excuse. There is really no point in our worrying about this, despite all the implications such a step involved—for Joseph was indeed making an Egyptian marriage, a marriage with Sheol, an Ismael marriage, not lacking in precedent, then, but a dubious precedent nonetheless, one requiring the indulgence that he, so it seems, confidentially felt he had been granted. Scholars and interpreters have taken great offense at this and have tried to sweep the facts under the rug. In the interest of purity they have presented it as if Asenath was not really the child of Potiphera and his wife, but rather a foundling, indeed a child abandoned by Jacob's disowned daughter Dinah and found floating in a basket, which would mean that Joseph married his own niece, though that would hardly improve matters much, since half of the flesh and blood of this niece was that of fidgety Sichem, a Baal-worshiping Canaanite. Moreover, respect for these scholars should not prevent us from calling the story of Dinah's child of the bulrushes what it is: an interpolation and pious fib. Asenath, the Maiden, was the true daughter of Potiphera and his wife, of pure Egyptian blood, and the sons that she would bear to Joseph, his heirs, Ephraim and Manasseh, were for better or worse half-Egyptian by blood—and let people think whatever they choose about that. But this was not all. By marrying this daughter of the sun, Israel's son entered into a close relationship with the temple of Atum-Rê, a priestly relationship, which had also been one of Pharaoh's goals in arranging this marriage. It was almost unthinkable that a high-ranking official such as Joseph would not also fulfill a higher priestly function at the same time and receive temple income, both of which Joseph did as Asenath's husband—and one can make of that whatever one likes. He drew income from the benefice, if one were to put it crudely, of an idol. From now on his official wardrobe included the priest's leopard skin, and on certain occasions, he would find himself having to burn incense before an idol, the falcon Horakhte with the solar disk atop his head.

Only a very few people since then have realized just what all this means, and to hear it stated outright may come as a shock to some. But Joseph had obviously arrived at a time of permissions and liberties, and one can be certain that he knew how to square all this with Him who had separated him from his family, transplanted him to Egypt, and let him become great there. Perhaps Joseph assumed his God would agree with the philosophy of the triangle, according to which a sacrifice at the alabaster table of the tolerant Horakhte did not imply robbing some other divinity. Ultimately it was not a matter of just any temple, but that of the temple of the Lord of the Wide Horizon, and Joseph may well have told himself that it would be a mistake, indeed folly—which is to say, a sin—to ascribe to the God of his fathers a narrower horizon than that of Atum-Rê. And finally, one dare not forget that from this same god there had only recently emerged the Atôn, whom, as Joseph and Pharaoh had agreed, one rightly invoked not as the Atôn but as the *Lord* of the Atôn, calling him "our Father in heaven," and not "our father in the heavens." These may have been the thoughts of a man who from the beginning had been set apart and called to become great in a foreign land, but who on certain, not necessarily frequent, occasions now donned his leopard skin to go forth and burn incense.

There was something very unusual about Rachel's firstborn, Jacob's expatriate darling. The indulgence granted him made allowances for the things of this world, which in turn prevented there ever being a "tribe of Joseph," even though there was a tribe of Issakhar, of Dan, and of Gad. His role and task in the plan was, as we shall see, that of someone sent out into the larger world to be the preserver, provider, and savior of his family, and everything argues for his having been aware of that mission, or at least having sensed it—that he understood his worldly, expatriate life to be not that of an outcast, but rather of someone set aside for special purposes, and that therefore he could trust in the forbearance of the Lord of Plans.

Joseph Marries

And so Asenath, the Maiden, was sent up to Menfe with twenty-four selected slaves, for a virginal wedding in Joseph's house, and her sacerdotal parents, still crushed by this incomprehensible abduction, likewise traveled upriver from On, just as Pharaoh himself came downriver from Nowet-Amun in order to take part in these nuptial mysteries, to give this rare bride into the hands of his favorite and, as an experienced husband, to assure him once more of the pleasures the wedded state brought with it. It should be noted that twelve of the young, beautiful slave girls who came with Asenath and now passed along with her into the possession of her dark bridegroom—automatically reminding one of the retinue that at one time was buried alive in the tomb of the king—that twelve of these twenty-four were there to celebrate, strew flowers, and make music, the other twelve, however, to raise lamentation and beat their breasts. For the wedding ceremonies conducted in Joseph's honorary residence, especially those performed in the torchlit quadrangle of its fountain court, around which all the other rooms were arranged, had something very funereal about them, and if we do not describe them down to the last detail it is out of a kind of consideration for old Jacob at home, who quite mistakenly still believed his darling to be preserved in death forever as a seventeen-year-old and would have clapped his hands above his head at much of what took place here at his wedding. Jacob's venerable prejudices against Mizraim, the Land of Mud, would have been confirmed, and it is more or less out of a respect for them that we prefer not to provide a detailed account of the ceremonies, which would look very much like a stamp of approval.

Behind his back one can admit, however, that there is a certain similarity between wedding and death, bridal chamber and grave, robbing a virgin of her virginity and murder—which is also why one cannot entirely separate the bridegroom from his role as a god of death engaged in violent abduction. Certainly the similarity between the fate of a girl crossing the threshold between maidenhood and womanhood as a veiled sacrifice and that of a seed of grain lowered into the depths to rot there and return to the light as the same grain, yet virginally new—that similarity must be granted; and the ear of

grain mowed down by the sickle is a painful metaphor for a daughter being torn from the arms of her mother—who herself, by the
way, was once virgin and sacrifice, who was also mowed down by
the sickle and relives her own fate in that of her daughter. And thus
the sickles with which the steward Mai-Sakhme had ordered the ceremonial rooms decorated, in particular the fountain court lined with
columns, played a significant—indeed, one could say meaningful—
role, just as did the seed corn, the grain, the cereal that was offered to
the wedding guests in ceremonies before and after the nuptial banquet: men strewed it on the tiled floor and, uttering formulaic cries,
watered it from jugs they carried; women bore vessels on their
heads, one part filled with seeds, but with a lamp burning in a separate compartment. For these ceremonies took place in the evening,
so that it was only natural that there were torches throughout the
rooms, which were draped with colorful tapestries and adorned with
myrtle everywhere. But there was such an intentionally excessive
use of torches that one almost inevitably associates this with the notion that they are meant to light chambers into which daylight cannot penetrate—so many torches beyond any practical purpose that
it was obvious they were meant to stir such associations. The bride's
mother, Potiphar's wife—if one may call her that without causing
confusion—presented a tragic figure wrapped in a robe of dark violet and carried either two torches in one hand or, at other times, one
torch in each, just as everyone else, men and women alike, carried
torches as they moved in the grand procession that was the central
rite of these solemnities, passing through every room in the house
and then emptying into the fountain court—where Pharaoh as the
highest-ranking guest sat in a relaxed pose between Joseph and Asenath, likewise veiled in violet—there to unfold or, rather, to entangle
itself into an elaborate and truly remarkable torch dance. For the
lines of the smoky, blazing procession now moved to the left in a
ninefold spiral with the fountain at its midpoint; and the red cord
that was threaded through the hands of the dancers, following every
coil of their twisting labyrinth, did not prevent them from crowning
their performance with a skillful play of lights, a veritable firework
in which the torches were tossed about in exchange, in all directions
at once, often from the innermost spiral to the outermost rim—and
not one flying arc of fire missed its goal and fell to the floor.

Had you seen it, you could not help sharing our temptation to report about it more extensively than might be commensurable with our declared intent to maintain a certain reserve in our description of Joseph's wedding—out of consideration for the old man, who, had he been present, would have been shocked by much of what took place. But, then, he was far away and secure in the idea of Joseph the eternal seventeen-year-old. He would surely also have been amused by these skillful fireworks as purely visual entertainment, if not by other things. His was a paternal mind, and he would have disapproved (to use a temperate word) of the maternal nature of his son's wedding ceremonies, in which the maiden Asenath's raging, threatening mother—herself once ostensibly abducted and now robbed of her daughter—played such a predominant role. The maternal was also evident in, among other things, the fact that men and boys, or at least a majority of those who took part in the grand procession and spiral dance, were dressed as women, indeed just like the bride's mother—which of course would have been an abomination of Baal in pious Jacob's eyes. Apparently they regarded themselves as her, had merged their personalities with hers; for the same violet veiled robe that the sullen woman wore billowed down over them as well, and they too frequently proclaimed their own resentment, holding the torch in their left hand and shaking menacing right fists, which was all the more terrifying since the masks they wore over their faces bore no resemblance to the matronly countenance of Potiphera's wife, but instead wore an expression of rage and sorrow so horrible it could curdle the blood—and all the while they shook their fists. In addition, many of them had stuffed their robes of mourning so that they looked as if they were in an advanced stage of pregnancy—were playing the role of the mother as she had once borne the sacrificial maiden below her heart, or was still bearing her there, or bearing yet another such sacrifice. They themselves could not have given an exact answer as to that.

Men and boys with distended bodies—that would certainly have been nothing for Yaaqov ben Yitzchak, nor would we wish our extensive description to be taken without second thought for approbation. But for Joseph, who had been set apart for a worldly life, a time for license had come; his wedding itself was a great exercise of liberty, and in the spirit of permission and indulgence that defines that hour, we shall report the details.

These were in part merry and boisterous, in part funereal, just as myrtle, with which all the participants, and not just the rooms, were adorned—some even carried whole bundles of it in their hands—is sacred both to the gods of love and to the dead. In the grand procession there were as many people who exulted with cries of joy while banging cymbals and tambourines as there were those who displayed all the prescribed expressions of grief and lamentation of people following behind a corpse. One must add, however, that the joy and mourning of the celebrants was observed in various stages. As for the mourning, certain groups found pleasure in merely wandering about, hinting at their confusion by mimicking travelers shouldering satchels hung from walking sticks and groping about disconsolately as they passed by the royal throne, the wedding couple, and sacerdotal parents, but without raising their voices in lament or forcing tears. In the same way one could observe various degrees in expressions of mirth. Some had considerable dignity and it was amusing to watch various groups of people place lovely earthenware jugs before the seats of honor and solemnly tip them over to the east and to the west, while repeating in chorus things like "Spill, spill!" or "Receive the blessing!" So far, so good. But very often—and with increasing frequency in the course of the evening—the mirth and laughter betrayed a different mood, one in which the premise of the wedding feast, the idea of what nature had in store, became crudely evident, and one might say that the undercurrent of vile abduction and murder intersected that of fertility at the point of bawdy, so that the air was full of innuendo, broad winks, smutty insinuation, and loud laughter at sotto voce obscenities. Several animals were led about in procession as well: a swan and a horse, at the sight of which the bride's mother wrapped herself deeper in the folds of her purple veil. But what can one say about the inclusion of a gravid sow in the parade, and, what is more, with someone riding it—a fat, half-naked old woman who pulled lewd faces and let out a stream of vulgar jokes? This obnoxious old woman straddling the sow played a familiar, important, and well-loved role throughout the ceremonies, and even prior to them, for she had come with Asenath's mother from On and during the journey had whispered lascivious jests in her ear to cheer up the grieving woman. This was her office, her prescribed role. She was called the "comforter"—a name shouted in high spirits to her from all sides, to which she responded with crude gestures. During the entire celebration she rarely left the side of the woman who on principle was not to be comforted; there was no deterring her—that is, she kept trying to make the bride's mother laugh by muttering filthy jokes, of which she had an inexhaustible supply. And she succeeded, too, because she was supposed to succeed—in response to her whispers, the offended mother, despite her rage and despair, would actually laugh into the folds of her robe from time to time, and when this happened the entire festive crowd would laugh along and applaud the "comforter." But since the mother's grief and anger were based primarily in convention and merely feigned, one can assume that her giggles were likewise only a concession to custom, whereas had it been up to her, she would have simply been disgusted by the "comforter's" furtive remarks. At best her amusement was perhaps no more or less a pretense than was the natural sorrow a mother feels, without any mythical exaggerations, in losing her daughter to a husband.

In any case, after all this our audience can understand why we had intended not to go into too great detail about Joseph's wedding feast. If we have infringed upon that intent, it in no way implies approval. The young couple themselves, who sat holding hands across Pharaoh's knees, were likewise almost unmoved by the entire spectacle and preferred to gaze at one another rather than at the inevitable rituals of the feast. Joseph and Asenath were very taken with one another from the first moment and each was a delight to the other. It goes without saying that in the case of a state marriage arranged by others love does not come before all else; it has to find itself and will find itself over time between people of goodwill. A simple awareness that they now belong together is helpful in preparing the way for love, but in this case the circumstances for its promotion were exceptionally favorable. Even beyond her natural tendency patiently to submit to the will of others, Asenath, the Maiden, acquiesced to her lot in life, which is to say, to the person of the abductor and murderer of her virginity, who had grabbed her about a narrow waist made for just such a purpose and dragged her off to his realm. This darkly beautiful, clever, and amiable favorite of Pharaoh filled her with a delight she had no doubt was capable of developing into a more sincere attachment, and the thought that he was to be the father of her children was like a shell inside which the pearl of love grows. And it was no different for Joseph, a man who had been set aside and now enjoyed a state of exceptional liberty. He was

amazed at God's magnanimous, worldly lack of prejudice in granting it, as if Eternal Wisdom had done more than having simply taken
his own worldliness into account—and Joseph left to Him the ticklish question of how to work out the relation between His chosen
tribe at home and the children of Sheol who might result from this
arrangement. But one cannot blame this suitor now emerging from a
virginal bridal state for directing his thoughts not so much to future
children who would be a mixture of God and the world, but instead
to those totally new—and previously forbidden—things to which
they would owe their existence. What had once been evil and dared
not happen, was now to be good. But simply gaze at this creature
through whom evil will become good, gaze at it, especially when it
has such attentive eyes and such a charmingly amber figure as Asenath, the Maiden, and you will sense that you will love her—yes, that
you already do.

Pharaoh stepped between them, for the ceremony was drawing
to an end; all the guests had formed a new torchlight procession
and—amid cries of joy and woe, while some strewed myrtle and
some in maternal masks shook their fists—set out for the bridal
chamber, where the newlyweds were placed upon a bed covered in
flowers and finest linen. While the parents stood at the threshold
muttering charms and taking their leave of Asenath, the Maiden, the
woman on the sow stood off to one side behind the wife of the priest
of the sun and now whispered remarks over the shoulder of the
angry, despairing mother, so that she had to laugh amid tears. And
are we not also left laughing and weeping at the scheme physical nature has contrived for humankind by which to seal its love, or, in the
case of a state marriage, to learn to love? The ridiculous and the sublime wavered in a play of shadows and torchlight on this wedding
night as well, when virginity met virginity and wreath and veil were
rent—and a difficult rending it was. For it was a maiden of the shield
who was embraced by dark arms, an obstinate virgin, who bore the
name "Maiden," and Joseph's firstborn was conceived amid blood
and pain, and was named Manasseh, which means "God has made
me forget all my bonds and my father's house."

Clouds Gather

It was Year One of the fat cows and plump ears of grain—usually the years were counted from the god's ascension to the throne, but now the children of Egypt began reckoning them concurrently by this second method. The fulfillment had, in its way, preceded the prophecy—so that the so-called first year had begun things in a convincing fashion, but the rich blessings of the year that followed far exceeded those of the previous, merely above-average year and proved to be one of splendor, jubilee, and miracles, of extravagant fertility in every sense. For the Nile had been very large and beautiful—not too large and wild, which would have stripped the farmer of his fields, but instead covering the plains not one mark of measurement below its best and silently spreading its dung over the fields, so that one could only laugh at how fine the land looked toward the end of the season of sowing and at the thought of what plenty would be harvested in the third season. The following year was not quite as prosperous, it was close to average, more or less, it was satisfactory, indeed praiseworthy, though not astonishing. But when the next year almost approached the second and was at least as good as the first had been, and when the fourth turned out to deserve a rating of "excellent" if not better, one can imagine how Joseph's reputation as Overseer of All That Heaven Gives grew among the people and with what eager, joyful punctuality his land-rent law, with its duty based on the beautiful number five, was carried out not only by his officials but by those subject to it. "He stored up," so it is said, "in every city the food from the fields around it"—which means that, year in, year out, the payments in grain streamed from the surrounding land into those cone-shaped depots of magical precaution that the Adôn had had built in every city and on its periphery, and not an excessive number of them as it turned out; they were filled up, and new ones kept having to be built, so great was the flow of taxes and so generous was Hapi, the Provider, in regard to his land in those days. The stored grain was indeed like the sand upon the seashore, song and saga are correct in their description. But when they add that people ceased to measure it because there was too much to measure, that is overenthusiastic exaggeration. The children of Egypt never ceased to measure, to write down numbers and keep accounts; that was their nature, they could not do otherwise. And if the plenty that came from precaution was like the sand upon the seashore, that proved merely the loveliest of reasons for worshipers of the white baboon to happily fill paper with dense columns of addition—and as for the accurate ledgers that Joseph demanded of his collectors and storehouse supervisors, he most certainly received them.

The date was now Year Five of such plenty—a few people, indeed a great many, however, dated it as Year Seven. It is pointless to argue this discrepancy. One group of observers held to five, basing this perhaps on the way it tallied with the holy number of extra days in the year and the corresponding figure Joseph had set as his tax quota. On the other hand five years of plenty in one swoop is something so worthy of celebration that someone might not hesitate to glorify them with the number seven. It is possible, then, that people let "five" stand for seven, but it is a whit more possible that they called five "seven"—the narrator frankly admits his uncertainty in this regard, for it is not his style to pretend to know something he really does not know for sure. In any case, his confession also includes the admission that is not absolutely certain whether Joseph was thirty-seven or thirty-nine years old at a given point in time during the following period of famine. All that is certain is that he was thirty when he stood before Pharaoh—we are certain of it and can record it as fact. Whether he himself could have provided so exact a figure is doubtful; and whether at a later, exciting point in time he was in his late thirties or perhaps already as good as forty—as a child of those climes, he was sure to have kept a very casual account of that, perhaps none at all, which reconciles us somewhat with our own lack of knowledge.

However that may be, he was in the prime of life at this point, and when stolen as a child, had he been taken to Babylon instead of Egypt, he would long since have grown a black, curly, nicely oiled beard—a bit of drapery that might have been of some use in the game of hide-and-seek yet to come. Nevertheless, let us thank Egyptian custom for keeping his Rachel countenance free of a beard. That he succeeded at his game for so long indicates what changes had been worked on the enduring stamp of his features by the chisel of time, the exchange of life's stuff, and the sun of his adopted land.

Until he was lifted from his second pit to stand before Pharaoh,

Joseph's appearance had remained more or less that of a young man. But at about the time of his marriage—during those years of plenty when God made him fruitful in Asenath, the Maiden, and she bore him first Manasseh and then Ephraim, there in the women's wing of his house in Menfe—he put on a little weight, at most giving his figure some heft, though one ought not think of him as plump: he was a tall enough man for the added weight to be distributed well. But his continued commanding presence—softened by the mirthful cunning in his eyes and the same winning expression in the calm smile with lips set together that he shared with Laban's child—was all that was needed for the abiding opinion: An exceptionally handsome man! Perhaps a trace too heavy, but absolutely superb.

His personal gain in weight accords well with the epoch's successive years of prosperity, when a tendency for life to increase in amazing ways was apparent on all sides. It occurred among the livestock, where there was a powerful upsurge in fertility, so that educated people were reminded of the words of an old song: "Your goats shall bear double their young, and your sheep twins." But even the women of Egypt, both in city and country, gave birth more frequently—apparently simply as a result of an increased availability of food. To be sure, nature—assisted in part by the carelessness of overburdened mothers and in part by a number of newly imported childhood diseases—countered with an increase in infant mortality and thus prevented any overpopulation. Birthrates, however, were manifestly higher.

Pharaoh, too, became a father—the Mistress of the Two Lands had already been expecting on the day his dreams were interpreted, but people were inclined to attribute her delivery of a healthy child to the fulfillment of prophecy. It was Sweet Princess Merytatôn who came into the world—for aesthetic purposes the doctors extended her still pliable skull almost too far to the rear. Jubilation in both the palace and throughout the land was all the louder in an attempt to hide the disappointment that no heir to the throne had appeared. Nor was one to appear later after this fashion. His whole life long, Pharaoh was presented with nothing but daughters, six in all. No one knows the law that determines the sex of a creature—whether it depends upon the seed or if the balance scale wavers and then dips to one side or the other somewhat later; and we have nothing definitive to say on that score, which should not be all that surprising, since even the wise men of Babel and On could provide no information about it, not even in private. But there is no arguing with the feeling that Amenhotep's fathering of daughters exclusively was not a matter of pure chance but somehow characteristic of this appealing ruler.

This could not help resulting in a mild though unacknowledged clouding over of his marital happiness, although, needless to say, tenderest consideration was observed on both sides, since in fact each could have said to the other what Jacob once said to his innocent Rachel: "Am I in the place of God, who has withheld what you desire?" It was out of such tenderness that one of the Sweet Princesses, the fourth, was even given as her own name the sobriquet of the Queen of the Two Lands, Nefernefruatôn. But it also reveals a certain flagging in invention that the fifth was given a name almost exactly like it, Nefernefrurê. We could likewise recite by heart the names of the others, some still products of very loving ingenuity; but since we, too, are slightly irritated by this monotonous chain of femininity, we have no real desire to list them.

When one considers that Tiy, the Great Mother, still stood at the zenith of the house of the sun, that Queen Nefertiti had a sister Nezemmut, that the king still had a living sister, Sweet Princess Baketatôn, and that over the course of years six royal daughters were added, one after the other, one begins to see a veritable court of women where Meni was patently the only cock among all these hens—a strange contradiction to his phoenix dream of an immaterial, paternal spirit of light. One automatically thinks of Joseph's statement during the Great Conversation, one of his better ones in fact: that the power that reaches up to the light in its purity must be a power that is true and manly, and not merely tender.

And so, because they were not granted a son, a slight shadow lay over the royal happiness of Amenhotep and his "golden dove," the Sweet Mistress of the Two Lands. The marriage of Joseph the Abductor and Asenath the Maiden was also a happy and thoroughly harmonious one—with one contrasting qualification. They were granted only sons: first one, then a second, then more later, upon whom history casts no light. But there were only sons, and since that came as a bitter disappointment to the abducted bride, how could it not also disappoint her husband, who would gladly have created a daughter for her, at least *one*? Except that it will always be so: man can beget, but not create. Asenath was absolutely obsessed with the idea of a daughter, and not just one, she would have preferred nothing but daughters. For she was eager to give birth to another maiden of the shield, just as she herself had been; there was nothing she longed for more ardently than for a maiden to rise up out of the death of her own virginity, and since she was constantly and insistently supported in this desire by a mother still angry at having been robbed, how could this not have resulted in a slight but persistent disharmony in their marriage—though, of course, always kept within bounds by mutual consideration and affection?

This was perhaps at its worst at the very start, when Joseph's eldest son was born—the disappointment was indescribable, one can quite justifiably call it exaggerated, and it appears that something of the anger at the reproach Joseph had to bear found its way into the name that he gave the boy. "I have forgotten," he may have wanted to say, "all that lies behind me, and my father's house. You, however, and your sulking mother, act as if not only everything has gone wrong for you, but also as if I am to blame." That may represent something of the meaning of the puzzling name "Manasseh"; but one would do well to add that this name and what it represented were not meant in all that great earnest. If God had let Joseph forget everything that bound him to the past and his father's house, how could it be that this same Joseph would give his sons, born in Egypt, Hebrew names? Because he assumed that in this foolish land of the grandchildren such names would be considered elegant? No! But because Jacob's son, though the garment of his flesh may have long since become totally Egyptian, had forgotten nothing, and indeed constantly bore in mind what he claimed to have forgotten. The name Manasseh was merely a flourish, revealing the same courtesy and tact that were the very opposite of folly and that Joseph had successfully displayed his whole life. It was his audible admission that God had ordained for him to be carried away, transplanted, and set apart for a worldly life—for all of which there was a twofold reason. The first was His jealousy, the other a plan of salvation. Joseph could have only conjectures as to the second; but the first was completely apparent to his shrewd mind, which was even capable of seeing through both reasons and recognizing that the first was the only real one, that the second had merely offered a means by which to unite passion and wisdom. The phrase "to see through" may seem offensive—given the object seen through. But is there a more religious practice than the study of the psychology of God? To anticipate the policies of the Most High with earthly policies is indispensable if one wishes to get through life. If Joseph had kept silent before his father all these years like a dead man—no, *as* a dead man—it was well-considered policy, intelligent insight into that psychology, that made it possible for him to do so; and it was no different with the name of his firstborn. "If I am supposed to forget," is what this name is trying to say—"behold, I have forgotten!" But he had not.

In the third year of plenty Ephraim came into the world. His mother Maiden did not even want to look at him at first, and Joseph's mother-in-law was more than irritated. But Joseph calmly went ahead and gave him a name that means "God has made me to increase in the land of my exile." He might well say that. Accompanied by runners and glorified by Menfe's populace with the name of Adôn, he drove back and forth in a light chariot between his splendid villa overseen by Mai-Sakhme and his office in the center of the city, where three hundred scribes labored—and he gathered in his storehouses an abundance of grain they could barely keep track of. He was a Great Man and the Unique Friend of the Great King. As for Amenhotep IV, who by then had already laid aside his Amun name, much to the fierce displeasure of the temple at Karnak, assuming in its place the name Ikh-n-Atôn, which means "It is pleasing to Atôn," and already toying with the idea of leaving Thebes behind entirely and founding a new city, built with his own hands and dedicated solely to Atôn, where he planned to reside—as for Pharaoh, then, he wanted to see the man who spent shade for his doctrine as often as possible, in order to speak with him about things above and below. And just as Joseph, the high official, could not avoid traveling several times a year up to Nowet-Amun, either by waterway or highway, to lay his reports before Hor in his palace and spend long hours in intimate conversation with him, so, too, Pharaoh—whenever he journeyed to golden On or drove forth to seek a suitable site for his new city, the City of the Horizon—would stop in Menfe and drop in on Joseph, which was always a source of considerable vexation for his steward Mai-Sakhme, though it could never disrupt his calm.

The friendship between this tender descendant of the pyramid builders and Jacob's son, foundations for which had been laid that day in the Cretan loggia, solidified during these years to one of such comfortable cordiality that the young Pharaoh came to call Joseph his "little uncle" and would clap him on the back when they embraced. This god was an enthusiast of all things informal, after all, and it was Joseph who, out of his native reserve, preserved the tension of polite distance in their relationship—indeed, the formality he maintained in the midst of familiarity often made the king laugh. Their bad luck as fathers—that the one had been given only daughters, the other only sons—provided the basis for many a conversation. But the discontent of his shield maiden and her angry mother did little to dampen the joy Joseph took in Jacob's grandsons flourishing here in this worldly foreign land; and in the same way the failure as yet to produce an heir to the throne rarely darkened Pharaoh's cheerful mood at this point. Indeed his prestige as the teacher of fatherly light was now strengthened by how splendidly things were going in the maternal Kingdom of Blackness, and he was allowed to sit in the shade of prosperity and proclaim the god to whom his soul clung and whom he constantly strove to advance in ever better ways, both when alone and in conversation.

His discussions with Joseph, then, in which he defined and compared the sublime qualities of his father Atôn, are perhaps reminiscent of those divine diplomatic negotiations once held at Salem between Abraham and Malkizedek, the priest of El-Elyon, the highest or also the only god, with the result that this El proved to be the exact, or almost exact, same person as Abraham's God. It was obvious, however, that whenever the conversation began to verge on such agreement, the courtly stiffness that never entirely left Joseph in his dealings with his high friend would emerge most clearly.

Part Five

TAMAR

The Fourth Son

A woman was seated at the feet of Jacob, the man rich in stories, in the grove of Mamre at or near Hebron, the great city in the land of Canaan. They often sat like this, whether in the tent of felt, close to its entrance, at the same spot where the father had once sat with his favorite and let himself be coaxed out of that colorful garment, or under the oracle tree or at the edge of the well that adjoined it, where we first met that clever lad by moonlight and his father leaned on his staff to gaze in concern at him. How is it that this woman is sitting with him now, be it in one place or the other, her face upraised to listen to his words? Where does she come from, this young and earnest woman whom one finds sitting at his feet quite often, and what sort of woman is she?

Her name was Tamar. We look around our audience and see a light of recognition on only a very few scattered faces. Apparently the vast majority of those who have gathered here to learn the precise circumstances of this story do not recall, are not even aware of some of its basic facts. We ought to take exception to this—that is, if such general ignorance were not just what the narrator wanted and can only be of use to him by increasing the value of his work. So you really no longer know, have never known as best you recall, who Tamar was? A Canaanite woman, to begin with, a child of the land and nothing more; then, however, the wife of the son of Jacob's son Jehuda, his fourth son, the man of blessing's granddaughter-in-law, so to speak; above all, however, she was his admirer, his student in matters of the world and of God, who hung on his words and gazed up into his solemn countenance with such devotion that the heart of the bereaved old man opened up to her entirely—and he was even a little in love with her.

Tamar's nature was a peculiar mixture that only made life more difficult for her: one part austerity and spiritual ambition (for which in due time we shall have a stronger name) and one part the mystery of Astarte, with its own psychological and physical attraction—and we know how receptive to the latter a heart given to tender and worthy emotions can be, even at an advanced age.

Jacob's personal majesty had only increased since Joseph's death—or, better, as a result of that heartrending and at first seemingly quite unacceptable event. But once he had grown more accustomed to it, once his bickering with God had exhausted itself, the cruel dispensation of that same God had found its way into a heart seized tight against it and came to be an enrichment to his life, one more weighty story for it to carry, making his pondering, whenever he fell to pondering, an all the more impressive, more picturesquely perfect kind of pondering than it had ever been, leaving people with a sense of sacred apprehension, so that they would whisper to one another: "Behold, Israel is pondering his stories!" Expression leaves an impression—no doubt of it. The two have always belonged together, and the former always tends to keep one eye cocked to the latter, though that is nothing to laugh about when one discovers that the expression is not hollow humbug, but the real weight of stories, a life truly lived. Then, at most, a respectful smile is in order.

Tamar, the child of the land, did not know even that smile. She was deeply impressed by Jacob's grandeur from the moment she first joined his circle, which did not come about by way of Judah, Leah's fourth son, but by way of his sons, two of whom married her, one after the other. That story is well known, along with the mysterious and partly enigmatic circumstances surrounding it and leading to the ruin of both of Judah's sons. But what is not well known, what the chronicle passes over, is Tamar's relation to Jacob, although it is really the essential premise of this episode, of these strange peripheral events that we interpolate here in our story, though not without reminding ourselves that our story, the story of Joseph and his brothers—which one might well term seductive, since it has seduced us into telling it in such precise detail—is itself only a charming interpolation in an epic of an incomparably vaster scale.

Did Tamar, this child of the land, a simple Baal-worshiping farmer's daughter living in an episode within an episode, have any idea of this fact? Our answer is: She definitely did. The proof is found in her own behavior—simultaneously shocking and glorious, but based in a profound seriousness. It is not without good reason that we have repeatedly and with a certain obstinacy used the word "interpolation." It is the watchword of the hour. It was Tamar's watchword as well. She wanted to interpolate herself—and did so with astonishing determination—into the grand story, into the vast play of events, about which she had learned by way of Jacob's instruction, and she was not to be left out of it at any price. Did not the world "seduction" also come to mind just now? It had its reasons. It is likewise a watchword. For it was by means of seduction that Tamar interpolated herself into that grand story of which our story is but an interpolation; she played the fascinating seductress, the harlot by the road, in order not to be left out, ruthlessly debasing herself in order to raise herself up. And how did that come about?

No one knows exactly when and by what prosaic chance Tamar first found her way to Jacob, the friend of God, and became his devoted pupil—it may have been before Joseph's death, it may have been quite apart from any action of Jacob's that she was received into the clan and given as a wife to young Er, Judah's firstborn. But whatever the case, her relationship with the old man grew to the intimacy of daily contact only after that gruesome blow and Jacob's long, reluctant recovery from it, when his pillaged heart secretly began to look about for new emotions. Only then did he become aware of Tamar and draw her to him in response to her admiration for him.

At the time his sons, the eleven, were almost all married—the older ones for some time, the younger more recently, and had children by their wives. Even Benjamin–Benoni, the Little Son of Death, soon had his turn—some seven years after he had lost his true brother, when he was barely no longer a whelp and had only just matured into young manhood, Jacob wooed and provided for him first Mahalia, the daughter of a certain Aram, of whom it is said that he was a "grandson of Terah," and so in some fashion a descendant of Abram or one of his brothers; and then to the maid Arbath, the daughter of a man named Shimron, who is explicitly called a "son of Abraham," which surely must mean that he came from the seed of one concubine or another. In the matter of the genealogy of Jacob's daughters-in-law a great deal has been glossed over or invented in a halfhearted effort to maintain the blood kinship of the entire spiritual tribe, though any real basis for it is rather weak and such efforts were made only in some cases. Levi's and Issakhar's wives were believed to be "granddaughters of Eber"—perhaps they were; for that they needed merely to have come from Assyria or Elam. Following the example of their father, Gad and fleet-footed Naphtali had fetched wives from Haran in Mesopotamia, who surely never claimed they were actually great-granddaughters of Nahor, Abraham's uncle—that is merely ascribed to them. Sweet-toothed Asher took as his wife a brown child of the tribe of Ismael—well, she was kin, if rather dubious kin. Zebulun, whom one would have expected to wed a Phoenician wife, actually married a Midianite—an acceptable marriage only insofar as Midian had been a son of Keturah, Abraham's second wife. But had not big Ruben, for good or ill, already married a Canaanite woman? Judah did the same, we know that, and so did Shimeon, who abducted his Bunah from Shechem. As for Dan, Bilhah's son, the one called a serpent and an adder, it was well known that his wife was a Moabite, that is, a daughter of the tribe of Moab, whom Lot's eldest daughter had borne to her father as her own sibling. There was something a bit iffy about that, too, nor did it have anything to do with purity of the blood, since Lot was not Abram's "brother," but had only been his proselyte. To be sure, he too had descended from Adam, perhaps even from Shem, since he had come from the land between the two rivers. One can always prove kinship by blood if one expands the perimeters wide enough.

His sons, then, "brought their wives to their father's house," or so we are told, which means: the clan's camp in the grove of Mamre, close to Kiriath-Arba and their ancestral tomb, where they gathered around Jacob's tent of felt, increasing as the days themselves increased until, as had been promised, their progeny teemed about Jacob's knee whenever the exalted old man allowed it—and from time to time, out of kindness, he did allow it and caressed his grandchildren. In particular he caressed Benjamin's children, for Turturra, a sturdy fellow who still had the same trusting gray eyes and that thick metallic helmet of hair, became the father of five sons in rapid succession by his Aramaic wife, and of several other children borne him by Shimron's daughter—and Rachel's grandchildren were Jacob's favorites. But despite their presence and Benoni's status as a father, Jacob still treated his youngest son like a child, kept him on a toddler's leading-strings and allowed him almost no freedom of movement, so that no misfortune might befall him. He scarcely permitted this sole pledge of Rachel's love still left him to walk to the city, to Hebron, or even into the fields, let alone to journey cross-country, though he loved him not nearly as much as he had loved Joseph and thus there was no real reason to fear a higher jealousy. All the same, ever since Jacob's beautiful son had been slain by the tusk of a boar, Benjamin had been the sole treasure of his father's worry and mistrust, which was why he never let him out of his eye, why there was not an hour when he did not want to know where he was and what he was doing. Although such supervision hardly enhanced his prestige as a husband, Benjamin was gloomily obedient and, following Jacob's eccentric orders, reported in to his father several times a day; for if he did not, the old man, halt in one hip and leaning on his long staff, would walk over to look in on him—and all that, even though, as Benjamin knew quite well from the old man's erratic treatment of him, Jacob's feelings toward him were really very divided, a strange mixture of a desire to hold on to what he had and profound resentment, for ultimately he had never stopped regarding him as his mother's murderer, the instrument God had used to take Rachel from him.

Granted, Benoni had one decisive advantage over all his living brothers, beyond being the youngest; and in Jacob's dreamily associative mind this advantage was one reason more always to keep him at home: he had been at home when Joseph was slain out there in the world. We know Jacob well enough to state that this equation of innocence and being at home, of having had no part in the awful deed that had happened out there, became symbolically fixed in his mind, so that Benjamin always had to remain at home as a token and continuing proof of his innocence and of the fact that he alone, as the youngest, was never an object of the constant, gnawing suspicion that Jacob quite rightly, if not correctly in all its details, still nursed—as the others were only too well aware he did. This was his suspicion that the boar that had mutilated Joseph had been a beast with ten heads; and Benjamin had to remain "at home" as a sign that it had most definitely not had eleven.

Perhaps not ten either—God knew, but let Him keep that to Himself—and over time, as the days and years multiplied, the question lost its critical importance. It did so above all because Jacob, once he had ceased to bicker with God, had gradually come to the viewpoint that God had not forcefully imposed this Isaak-like sacrifice on him, but that he had made it of his own free will. As long as the initial pain still raged, the idea had been totally out of the question; he had simply felt himself cruelly mistreated. But as pain receded, as habit set in and death asserted its benefits—that is, keeping Joseph safe in its protective womb as an eternal seventeen-year-old—his tender, passionate soul had seriously begun to imagine itself capable of Abraham's sacrificial act. This flight of imagination was in God's honor, and his own. God had not ravaged him like a monster and cunningly stolen what he held most dear, but had merely accepted what was knowingly and courageously offered Him: his dearest possession. Believe it or not, Jacob convinced himself of this and for the sake of his own pride swore to himself that in that hour when he had dispatched Joseph on his journey to Shechem, he had willingly performed his Isaak-sacrifice and out of love for God had surrendered what he loved all too well. He did not always believe it—at times he admitted in contrition and with tears flowing yet again that he would never ever have been capable, even for the love of God, of tearing from his heart what he held dearest. But the wish to believe triumphed—and did that wish not make it more or less irrelevant who had mutilated Joseph?

The suspicion—certainly it was there, it gnawed away at him, though gently and not hourly; in later years it sometimes dozed off, and then that was that. The brothers had imagined living under suspicion, or under half a suspicion, to be more wretched than it actually turned out. Their father was on good terms with them, there was no other way to put it. He spoke with them and broke bread with them; he shared in their business interests and in the joys and sorrows of their tents. He would gaze at them and only occasionally, only rarely at great intervals, would the smoldering duplicity and sullenness of suspicion cloud his aged eyes—and they would lower their own and words would fail them. But what did that imply? A man will lower his eyes simply because he knows that someone nurses a suspicion. It does not have to be an acknowledgment of guilt; it can even express chaste innocence and a sympathy with the person troubled by mistrust. And so at last a man grows weary of his own suspicion.

He finally lets it be, especially when confirmation of it can change nothing—not just as regards what has happened, but also in terms of the future and the promise, of all that is and is yet to be. The brothers may have been ten-headed Cain, may have been fratricides—but they were what they were, Jacob's sons, the sons he had been given and who, one had to assume, were Israel. Jacob, you see, had decided to make it his habit not to apply just to himself individually the name he had wrested for himself at the Jabbok at the cost of being left halt in one hip, but to give it broader and grander meaning. Why not? Since it was his name, wrested with great effort at dawn, he could do with it as he pleased. Israel—it was no longer a name to be applied to him personally, but to everything that belonged to him, the man of blessing, from the next down to the latest but never last member in every branch of every collateral kinship: the clan, the tribe, the people, whose number was to be countless as the stars and the sand upon the seashore. The children who were sometimes permitted to play at Jacob's knee, they were Israel, he could call them that collectively all at once—much to his relief, for he could not remember all their names; he had particular trouble recalling the names of the children of the Ishmaelite and unequivocally Canaanite wives. But these women were "Yizrael" as well, including the Moabite and the slave from Shechem; but first and foremost and above all their husbands were "Yizrael," the eleven, deprived of their zodiacal number as a result both of an enduring fraternal strife that had begun early on and of his own heroic willingness to sacrifice— but still an imposing number all in all, Jacob's sons, the progenitors of that countless number, to whom they would give their tribal names: mighty men before the Lord, each just as he was created and despite whatever that lowering of the eyes in the face of suspicion might mean. Was that not the same as their remaining "Yizrael" no matter what? For Jacob knew this much, long before it was ever written—and it only stands written because he knew it: Yizrael, even when it has sinned, will always be Israel.

Within Israel, however, within the eleven-headed lion, there was *one* head, the inheritor of the blessing before all others, just as Jacob had been before Esau—and Joseph was dead. Once Jacob conferred the blessing, its promise then rested, or would rest, on one of them: from him would come the salvation to which his father had long sought to put a name—and Jacob had in fact found a provisional name, though no one knew it except the young woman who sat at his feet. But who from among the brothers was to be the chosen one from which the promise would come? Who would be the man of blessing, though no longer chosen on the basis of love—for love was dead? Not Ruben, the eldest, who was like boiling, gushing water and had played the hippopotamus. Not Shimeon and Levi, who were personally nothing more than slippery louts and likewise had unforgettable deeds chalked up against them, for they had behaved like savage heathens at Shechem and acted like demons of the field in Hemor's city. These three were cursed to the extent that Israel could be cursed; they had been cast aside. And so it had to be the fourth son who came after them, Judah—it was he.

Ashtaroth

Did he know it was he? He could count it off on his fingers, and he frequently literally did just that, but never without taking alarm at being chosen as the heir, without plunging into painful doubt as to his worthiness and fear that he would ruin it. We know Jehuda; we have seen his anguished lionlike head with its stag's eyes among the heads of his brothers, and we also kept an eye on him during Joseph's downfall. All in all, he did not come off badly in that affair—not so well, of course, as Benjamin, who had been at home, but almost as well as Ruben, who had never wanted the boy's death, but saw to it that he was cast into the pit so that he could steal him from it. It had also been Judah's wish and proposal that they pull him from the pit and grant him his life, for it had been he who had suggested they sell their brother, seeing as they had really not known how in their own day to emulate Lamech of the ancient song. That excuse was irrelevant and a mere pretext, as most excuses are. Jehuda was fully aware that letting the boy perish in that hole was not one whit better than shedding his blood, and had wanted to save him. That he was too late with his suggestion, inasmuch as the Ishmaelites had already done their work and freed Joseph, was not his fault—he could well claim that, comparatively speaking, he deserved some praise in that cursed affair, since he had wanted the boy to escape.

No matter, the crime pursued him far worse than it did the others, who could have offered nothing for their own exculpation—but how could it not? Only dulled souls should commit crimes; they're not bothered, they live each new day with nothing pursuing them.

Evil is for dulled souls. But whoever displays even a trace of tenderness should keep his hand from crime if he possibly can, for he will have to pay for it and it doesn't matter if he can prove to have had some conscience in the matter—he will be punished precisely for having a conscience.

Judah was terribly grieved by the deed done to Joseph and his father. He suffered from it, for he was given to suffering, as those stag's eyes and something in the delicate nostrils and full lips led us to surmise right off; and the deed laid upon him a great curse and chastisement—or rather, whatever curse and chastisement he suffered, he attributed to it and saw as retribution for what had been done, for his share in it. And that in turn is evidence of a strange pride of conscience. For he could certainly see that the others—Dan or Gaddiel or Zebulun, not to mention the savage twins—walked about freely and quite unscathed, with nothing to repent of, which could have led him to entertain the idea that his torments, both his own and those inflicted by his sons, might be quite independent of what had been done, or of his share in it, might have emerged on their own, purely out of himself. But no, he wanted to suffer punishment all alone and gazed disdainfully on those whose thick skins left them untormented. And that is the strange pride of conscience.

The torments he endured all bore the sign of Ashtaroth, and he should not have been amazed that they came from that corner of the world, for he had always been tormented by his Mistress—or better, had been her slave without loving her. Judah believed in the God of his fathers, El-Elyon, the Most High, Shaddai, the Mighty One of Jacob, his rock and shepherd, Yahweh, from whose nose steam came when He was angry, and destroying fire that came forth from His mouth as lightning. He burned sweet-smelling offerings to Him, sacrificed bullocks and suckling lambs to Him whenever it seemed fitting. In addition, however, he also believed in the elohim of the nations—and there could be no great objection to that, as long as he did not serve them. When one observes how late in time, how far from their beginnings, Jacob's descendants would still have to be admonished with curses by their leaders to put away strange gods, both Baalim and Ashtaroth, and not share in the sacrificial feasts of the Moabites, one has the impression of a serious lack of steadfastness, a tendency down to the last generation to relapse and fall away;

one ought not therefore be surprised that someone at this early stage, a figure so near to the source as Yehuda ben Yaaqov, believed in Ashtaroth, who was a very popular goddess worshiped everywhere under a variety of names. She was his Mistress, and he bore her yoke, that was the vexing reality—vexing to both his spirit and his being chosen. But how could he not have believed in her? He did not sacrifice to her—not in a narrower sense of the word, that is, did not burn bullocks and suckling lambs to her. But her cruel spear pricked him to make more vexing, more passionate sacrifices to her, which he did not make gladly, not with a willing heart, but under the coercion of his Mistress; for his spirit was at odds with his lust, and he never emerged from the embrace of one of her hierodules without hiding his head in shame and doubting in awful anguish his fitness to be the chosen heir.

From the day they had joined to remove Joseph from the world, Judah began to regard Astarte's torments as a punishment for his crime; for they increased, besieging him from without and pinching him from within; and the only way to put it is that since that day, the man had done penance in hell—in one the many hells that exist, the hell of sex.

Many will think: That can't be the worst fate. But whoever thinks that does not know the thirst for purity without which, to be sure, there can be no hell, neither this or any other. Hell is for the pure; that is the law of the moral world. It is for the sinner, and one can sin only against one's purity. If a man is a beast, he cannot sin and is unaware of any hell. That is how things are arranged, and it is quite certain that hell is populated by the better sort, which is not just—but, then, what is our justice!

The story of Judah's marriage and those of his sons, of the ruin to which those marriages brought them, is extremely strange and eerie and really quite obscure, which explains why it is not merely out of delicacy that they can be spoken of only sotto voce. We know that Leah's fourth son was married early on—a step taken out of a love for purity, so that he might commit and restrict himself and find peace, but in vain; it was a calculation made without his Mistress and her spear. His wife, whose name has not been handed down—perhaps she was seldom called by name, but was simply the daughter of Shuah the Canaanite, whom Judah had come to know through his friend Hirah, the head shepherd of the village of Addulam—this woman, then, had good reason to weep over him and much to forgive him, a burden eased somewhat because she at least tasted the joy of motherhood three times, albeit a fleeting joy, for the boys she bore to Judah were nice only at the start, but then turned nasty, though that applied least to the youngest, Shelah, who was born a good while after the other two, since he was merely sickly, whereas his older brothers, Er and Onan, were nasty as well, sickly in a nasty way and nasty in a sick way, likewise both pretty and impertinent— in short, an affliction in Israel.

Boys such as these two—sickly and hardened, but nice for all that—are an anachronism at this place, a premature act of nature, which isn't quite herself for a moment and forgets just where she is. Er and Onan would have belonged more properly in late antiquity, in a senescent world of mocking descendants—let us say: in monkey-faced Egypt. They were out of place so close to the origins of a process aimed at a larger dimension, were born at the wrong time, and had to be destroyed. Judah, their father, should have grasped that and accused no one but himself for having begotten them. He chose instead to shift the guilt for their wickedness to Shuah's daughter, their mother, and blamed himself only inasmuch as he believed he had committed folly in taking a Baal-dazed wife. And he blamed their ruin on the woman to whom he gave them in marriage, one after the other, and whom he accused of being an Ishtar figure, who destroys her lovers by having them die of her love. That was unjust—both to his wife, who soon died of grief over all this, and certainly unjust in large measure to Tamar.

Tamar Learns About the World

Tamar, it was she. Deeply impressed by Jacob's expression, she had been sitting at his feet for some time now, listening to the teachings of Israel. She never leaned back, but always sat bolt upright, on a footstool, on a step of the well, on an extended root of the oracle tree, her back arched, her neck stretched forward, two creases of tension between her velvet eyebrows. She came from a hamlet on the sunny slope of a mountain in the vicinity of Hebron, where people made their living in wine and a little livestock. There stood the house of her parents, small farmers who sent the girl to Jacob with sheaves of grain and fresh cheese, but also lentils and groats, which he purchased with copper. And so she came to him, found her way to him that first time for ordinary reasons, though in reality urged on by a higher need.

She was beautiful in her way, indeed not pretty and beautiful, but simply beautiful in an austere and off-putting way—that is, she seemed angered by her own beauty, and rightly so, for there was something bewitching about it that left men no rest, and to counter such unrest she had set those creases between her eyebrows. She was tall and almost thin, but her thinness was the source of a still greater unrest than any ample flesh would have caused, so that the unrest was really not one of the flesh but must be called demonic. She had remarkably beautiful brown eyes that spoke with great urgency, almost circular nostrils, and a proud mouth.

What wonder, then, that Jacob was taken with her and set her at his side as a reward for her wonderment? He was an old man fond of his own feelings and simply waiting to be able to feel something once again; but in order to awaken emotion in us old men, or at least some gentle and veiled reminiscence of the emotions of our youth, something special must come along to strengthen us even as we marvel at it—combining the quality of Astarte and a spiritual eagerness to hear our wisdom.

Tamar was a seeker. The creases between her eyebrows expressed not only anger at her own beauty, but also a strained effort to find truth and salvation. Is there anywhere in this world that one does not encounter a concern for God? It is found on royal thrones and in the most wretched mountain hamlets. Tamar was one of those who live with it, and the unrest she caused others disturbed and angered her because of a higher unrest she bore within her. One might have thought this country village girl's religious concerns were taken care of. But even before she heard Jacob speak, traditional worship of forest and meadow and nature had not satisfied her urgent needs. She simply could not make do with the Baalim and gods of fertility, for her soul guessed that there was something else far superior in the world, and she strained to track it down. There are such souls: something new that changes things needs only to come into the world and their solitary sensitivity is touched and seized by it and they have to set out to find it. Their unrest is not of the highest order, like that of the wanderer from Ur, which drove him into a void where nothing was, so that he had to create the new out of himself. That is not the way with these souls. But once the new thing is there and in the world, even if at a great distance, their sensitivity leaves them no rest, they must make their pilgrimage in pursuit of it.

Tamar's pilgrimage did not take her far. Bringing wares to Jacob in his tent to exchange for weighed copper was surely only a ploy of her mind, a pretext born of unrest. She found her way to him, and now often, very often sat at the feet of the solemn old man weighed down with stories—sat bolt upright, her urgent, wide eyes directed up at him, so spellbound and motionless that the silver earrings dangling at her lean cheeks never swayed, while he told her about the world, that is, told her his stories, told of a family tree with many branches flung wide, the history of a family that had grown from God and was tended by Him, and, as a bold pedagogue, he presented it all as the history of the world.

He taught about the beginning, about *tohu* and *bohu* and how they were divided by God's word; the work of six days and how at God's command the sea was filled with fishes, and then how the space beneath the firmament of heaven, where the lights were placed, was filled with feathered fowl and the greening earth with cattle, creeping things, and all manner of beasts. He let her hear God's sturdy and blithely plural invitation to Himself, His enterprising resolution: "Let Us make man!" And it seemed to her as if it had been Jacob who had said it, or at least as if God—who was always simply and straightforwardly called "God," which you heard nowhere else in the world—as if He, in doing this, must have looked just like Jacob, which certainly matched the additional statement: "An image that is like Us." She heard about the garden toward the dawn and of the trees in it, the Tree of Life and the Tree of Knowledge, of the seduction and God's first fit of jealousy; how He feared that man, who now knew what good and evil were, might eat of the Tree of Life and become completely like "Us." And We made haste, drove man away and placed a sword-brandishing cherub outside the garden. But to man He gave toil and death, so that he was an image like Us, true enough, but not all too like, merely somewhat more like than fishes, fowl, and cattle, but all the same, despite Our jealousy, given the secret task of becoming, whenever possible, more like Us.

That is how she heard it. It was not very clear-cut, but mysterious instead, and yet as grand as Jacob himself in the telling of it. She heard about brothers as enemies, and the murder out in the field. About the children of Cain and their descendants, how they were divided into three types over the earth: those who dwell in tents and raise cattle; those who are artificers of metal and make themselves shine with it; and finally those who merely fiddle and pipe. This was a temporary division. But from Seth, born as Abel's replacement, came a great many generations, on down to Noah, the arch-clever man. To him God—circumventing Himself and His all-destroying wrath—gave the task of saving Creation, so that he would survive the Flood with his sons Shem, Ham, and Japheth, in whom the world divided itself anew, for each of these three sent forth countless generations; and Jacob knew them all—the names of peoples and their settlements upon earth simply flowed from his instructive lips and into Tamar's ears; and wide was his overview of this teeming brood and their landscapes. But suddenly it all came together in one chosen family. For Shem was the father of Eber in the third generation, who was the father of Terah in the fifth, and so they came to Abram, one of three, but he was the one!

For His own sake, God put unrest in Abram's heart, that he might tirelessly work on God, shape Him in his thoughts and make a name for Him, make of Him his benefactor, who in return gave the benefit of vast promises to the creature who created the Creator in his mind. He concluded a covenant with him to their mutual advantage, that each might become ever more holy in the other, and bestowed on him the right of choosing an heir, the power of blessing and curse, that he might bless the blessed and speak curses upon those he cursed. He threw open vast futures before him, in which nations were cradled, and his name was to be a blessing to them all. And promised him boundless fatherhood, for indeed in his eighty-sixth year Abram was still unfruitful in Sarai.

So he took his Egyptian handmaid and sired with her a son and named him Ismael. But what he had sired was a detour, leading not to the road of salvation, but belonging to the desert, and the primal father did not believe God's assurances that he would also still have a son named Isaak by his true wife, but fell upon his face laughing at God's word, for he was already one hundred and Sarah's life was no longer after the manner of women. But nonetheless this laughter was reshaped in her, so that Yitzchak, the averted sacrifice, appeared, of whom it was said from on high that he would sire twelve princes—which was not quite correct. God misspoke Himself at times and did not mean precisely what He said. It was not Isaak who sired the twelve, or only indirectly. Actually he had done it, the solemn teller of stories himself, on whose lips the country girl hung—Jacob, brother of the Red Man, had sired them by four women while serving that devil Laban in Shinar.

Then Tamar learned yet again about brothers who were enemies, about the red hunter, the gentle shepherd; she heard of the deception that set the blessing right and of the flight of its thief—of how under way and for the sake of his own dignity, a cautious covenant had been made with Eliphaz, the overthrown man's son. Here and in another matter Jacob's words tended to be cautious and reticent, particularly in regard to Rachel's loveliness and his love for her. In terms of Eliphaz he was cautious about himself and for aesthetic reasons presented his humiliation before the boy in less than strongest colors. But when it came to Rachel, his reticence was for Tamar's sake; for he was a little in love with her and his feelings told him one should not praise one woman's loveliness all too liberally before another.

In contrast, his pupil learned of the great dream of the ladder—dreamt at Luz by the thief who stole the blessing—in all its grandeur and splendor, even though such a splendid raising up of his head was not quite explicable without the deep abasement that had preceded it. She heard the heir tell of it, gazing all eyes and ears at the man who bore the blessing of Abraham and had the power to bestow it upon another, who would then be the lord over his brothers and before whose feet his mother's children would have to fall. And she heard him speak the word: "And by you and your seed all the families of earth shall be blessed." And did not stir.

Yes, what all she heard in those hours, told her so expressively—all the stories! The fourteen years of service in the land of filth and gold were spread out before her, together with the extra years, which made twenty-five in all; and thanks to the false wife and the true one and their handmaids, the eleven were assembled, including the charming son. She heard about their flight, about Laban's pursuit and his search. About the ox-eyed man and Jacob's wrestling match that lasted till dawn and for the rest of his life left him halt in the hip like a blacksmith. About Shechem and its abominations, where the savage twins strangled men and maimed oxen, and were more or less cursed for it. About how Rachel had died, only a little way across the fields from the inn, giving birth to the Little Son of Death. About Ruben's irresponsible gushing, and how he too had been cursed, as much as Israel can be cursed. And then the story of Joseph, whom his father had loved too much, but, being a hero of God, had sent on his way, his strong soul knowingly giving in sacrifice what was most dear to him.

This "once upon a time" was still very fresh, and Jacob's voice quavered as he spoke, whereas he had been relaxed in telling the grand epic of earlier and earliest "onces" now covered by time, had worn an expression of solemn joy even for what was grim and heavy, for they were all God's stories, and their telling was holy. But it is quite certain, it could not have been otherwise, and it must be noted that Tamar's listening soul was nourished in her instruction by more than the "once" that lay covered beneath time and history, the holy "once upon a time." "Once" is an unlimited word and has two faces; it looks back, far back, into sublimely dusky distances, and it looks ahead, far ahead into distances no less sublime for being what is yet to come than those others are for having been. Some will deny this, for them only the "once" of the past is sublime, that of the future contemptible. They display piousness not piety, are fools and gloomy souls—Jacob did not sit in their church. If to future's "once" one does not honor pay, one has to the "once" of the past no further words to say, and likewise one surely stands athwart the "now" of today. This is our doctrinal opinion, if we may interpolate it into the doctrines that Yaaqov ben Yitzchak shared with Tamar and that were filled with a twofold "once"—and how could they not be, since he was telling her about the world, and the world's word is in fact "once," both as tidings and as promise? She might well say to him in gratitude, indeed did say it: "My lord, you have paid too little attention to telling me tidings about what has happened, and have spoken instead to your handmaid about tidings of a distant future." For he did so quite automatically, since in all his stories an element of promise was present from the very beginning, so that one could not give tidings of one without the other.

And what did he tell her about? He told her about Shiloh.

It is a completely false assumption to believe that Jacob first

spoke at length about the hero Shiloh when prompted by his imminent end on his deathbed. He had no promptings whatever that day,
but simply solemnly announced what he had prepared long before,
thoughts that he had been setting in order for half his life and to
which his hour of death was made to lend its consecration. This is
true not only of the words of blessing and judgment—some close to
curses—spoken to his sons, but also of his mention of a figure of
promise, whom he called Shiloh and concerning whom his mind had
long since begun to busy itself in the days of Tamar, even if he spoke
of him to no one but her, out of gratitude for her great attentiveness
and because that remnant of feeling still left to him was a little in love
with her. And whom or what did he mean by Shiloh?

My, what he had contrived here!—it was very strange. First off,
Shiloh was nothing but a place-name, the name of a walled town farther north, where the children of the land would come together to
share booty taken in war after making war—not a particularly holy
place. It was called the place of quiet and rest—for that is what
"*shiloh*" means; it means peace and breathing with happy relief after
bloody battle and is a word of blessing, as useful for a personal name
as for the name of a place. Therefore, just as Sichem, the princeling,
bore the same name as his city, Shiloh could likewise serve as the
name of a man and son of man, a bearer and bringer of peace. In
Jacob's mind he was the man of expectation, promised to mankind
early on and ever again in new solemn oaths and intimations, promised in the womb of the Woman, promised in Noah's blessing of
Shem, promised to Abraham, through whose seed all families of
earth should be blessed: the Prince of Peace, the Anointed One, who
would rule from sea to sea and from the river to the ends of the
earth, whom all nations would adore and before whom all kings
would bow down—the hero, who once would be awakened out of
the chosen seed, and the throne of whose kingdom would be established for ever and ever.

He called him who was to come Shiloh—and now it is our urgent task to imagine and picture as best we can how Jacob, a man of
rich expression and impression, spoke in this hour of instruction of
Shiloh as the connecting link between earliest beginnings and farthest future. It was significant, it was momentous; Tamar, the
woman who alone had been honored to hear it, sat immobile; even
upon closest inspection, one could not have noticed the slightest

sway of her earrings. She was listening to the world, and promise lay hidden in it, both early and late, a vast, multibranched history filled with stories through which the purple thread of assurance and expectation ran from once to once, from the most ancient once to the most future, when in a cosmic catastrophe of salvation two stars, blazing at each other in enmity, the Star of Power and the Star of Justice, would collide with a thunderclap that would fill the universe, and become one, a star whose gentle, powerful radiance would henceforth shine above the heads of men: the Star of Peace. This was the star of Shiloh, the Son of Man, the son of election of whom it was promised to the seed of woman that he would bruise the head of the serpent. Tamar, however, was a woman, was *Woman*, for every woman is Woman, the instrument of the Fall and the womb of salvation, Astarte and the Mother of God; and she was sitting at the feet of Man the Father, on whom, by that strange twist that orders all things, the blessing had come and who would bestow it throughout history on someone in Israel. Who was that? Above whose brow would the father lift his horn to anoint his heir? Tamar had fingers for counting. Three were cursed, the favorite, however, the son of the true wife, was dead. The line of inheritance would not be guided by love, and where love has been taken away, only justice remains. Justice was the horn from which the oil of election would drip upon the brow of the fourth son. Judah, he was the heir.

A Resolute Woman

From then on those unvarying creases between Tamar's eyebrows assumed a third meaning as well. They spoke not only of anger at her own beauty and of the strain of her search, but also of resolve. Consider it substantiated here: Tamar was firmly resolved, cost what it might, to interpolate herself with the help of her womanhood into the history of the world. She was that ambitious. All her spiritual strivings had flowed into this inexorable and almost sinister—for the inexorable has something sinister about it—resolve. In certain natures instruction at once turns into wants, indeed such natures seek out instruction to nourish their wants and give them a goal. Tamar had needed only to be instructed about the world and how it strives toward a goal, in order to reach her unconditional conclusion to bind her womanhood to that striving and become a part of world history.

Granted—everyone stands within the history of the world. One need only be born into the world for one's life story to contribute its widow's mite—one way or another, for good or ill—to the whole of the world's enterprise. Most people, however, swarm modestly far off at the periphery, unaware of its central event, taking no part in it, and fundamentally glad not to belong to its illustrious personnel. For them Tamar felt only disdain. No sooner had she been instructed, than she wanted—or better, she had received instruction in order to learn what she did and did not want. She did not want to swarm there on the sidelines. This country girl wanted to put herself on the right course, the course of promise. She wanted to be part of the family, to interpolate herself and her womb into the chain of generations that in due time would lead to salvation. She was Woman, and the prophecy had been made to her seed. She wanted to be an ancestral mother of Shiloh.

No more and no less. The creases stood firmly between her velvet eyebrows. They already had three meanings—how could they not take on a fourth as well: that of angry, envious disdain for Shuah's daughter, Jehuda's wife? That hussy, who stood in the chain, in a privileged position, without merit and knowledge or wants (for Tamar counted knowledge and wants as merit), that cipher honored by history—Tamar bore her no goodwill, indeed hated her in the most womanly way, nor did she hide the fact from herself, and even would have wanted her dead (again without disguising her wish to herself) had there been any point in that. But there was none, for she had already borne Judah three sons, so Tamar would have had to wish those three dead as well for a situation to be created that would truly leave a place free for her at the side of the heir. It was as an heir that she loved Judah and desired him—it was ambition's love. Never—or at least not until then—had a woman so completely wanted a man not for himself, yet loved and desired him, as Tamar loved Judah, entirely for an idea. It was a new basis for love, the first time it ever happened—love arising not from the flesh, but the spirit; one might well call it demonic, just like the unrest that Tamar, quite apart from the form of her flesh, awakened in men.

She would gladly and willingly have let the Astarte part of her, which she otherwise scorned, make its play for Judah, and knew too well what a slave he was to his Mistress not to be certain of victory. But it was too late—which always means, too late in time. She had arrived too late, her ambitious love was at the wrong place in time. She could no longer put herself upon the right course, insert herself in the chain at this point. Therefore she had to take a step forward or backward in time and its generations, had to change generations and direct her resolute desire to some point where she might want to be a mother—which was not hard to imagine, since on a higher level, mother and beloved have always been one. In short, she had to direct her eye away from Judah, the heir as son, and at his sons, the heirs as grandsons—whom she had almost wished dead—so that she might bear more, and better heirs herself; she directed her eye, needless to say, first and solely at the eldest, the boy Er, for he was the heir.

Her own position in time would have made it quite easy for her to descend in time. She would not have been too young for Judah and was not all that old for Er. All the same, she did not take the step gladly. The objectionable nature of this generation—sickly in its corruption, however nice it seemed—made her hesitate. But her ambition was resourceful—it knew it had to be, otherwise she would have been very dissatisfied with it. It told her that the promise need not always follow promising or even appropriate paths; that it can take a dubious, less worthy, even corrupt course and still not wither; that sickness must not always come from sickness, but rather tempered and improved life can emerge from it and continue on its way to health, especially when assisted by the improving energy of a resolve such as Tamar could call her own. And these scions of Judah were, after all, only degenerate men. But what counted was the Woman, the right woman interpolating herself here at the weakest point. The first promise was to the womb of Woman. What did men matter?

And so to arrive now at her goal she had to ascend through time to the third link—there was no other way. And indeed she let the Astarte part of her make its play for the young man, but his response was both childish and lascivious. Er only wanted to sport with her, and when she reacted with a darkened frown, he fell away, proved incapable of anything serious. A certain delicacy prevented her from going higher and seeking refuge in Judah, for it had been he that she had really desired or would have desired; and if he did not know it, she at least did and was ashamed of begging him for the son that she would gladly have borne to him herself. Which is why she sought refuge in Jacob, the head of the clan, her teacher, and in his dignified weakness for her—which was quite obvious to her and which she found more flattering than offensive—by asking to be received into the family and begging for his grandson to be her husband. She did this in the same place inside the tent where Joseph had once coaxed the colorful garment from the old man—but she had an easier time of it with her petition than he had had.

"Master and lord," she said, "my little father, both dear and great, hearken now to your handmaid and incline your ear, please, to her plea and to her most earnest and anxious request. Behold, you have chosen me and made me great before all the daughters of the land, have instructed me in the world and in God, who alone is the Most High, have opened my eyes which were blind and formed me so that I am as you would have me. How can this have been my portion, that I have found favor before your eyes and you have comforted me and spoken kindly to your handmaid—may the Lord recompense you for it and a full reward be given you by the God of Israel, to whom I have been led by your hand, that I might take refuge under His wings. For I shall take heed and keep my soul diligently, that I may not forget the stories you have let me see, that they do not depart from my heart all my life long. I shall tell them to my children and my children's children, if God grant me such, so that they may not perish by making any image like to a man or woman or beast of the earth or bird of the sky or creeping thing or fish; nor lift up their eyes and see the sun, the moon, and the stars, the great host of them, and fall away and serve them. Your people shall be my people and your God my God. Therefore, if He give me children, they should not come to me from a man whose people know a strange god—that can never be. Someone from your house, my lord, can surely take a daughter of the land, such as I was, and lead her to God. But I, being as I am, newborn and formed as you have formed me, cannot be the bride of an uninstructed man, of someone who prays to images of wood and stone that are made by the hand of an artisan and that can neither see, nor hear, nor smell. Behold, my father and lord, what you have done in educating me, and you have made me delicate and tender of soul, so that I cannot live like the throng of the ignorant and cannot wed the first man to woo me or give my womanhood to a dolt before God, which in the simplicity of my heart I surely would have done otherwise—such are the disadvantages of refinement and the difficulties that enhancement brings. Therefore do not think it rash of your daughter and handmaid when she reminds you of the responsibility you have taken upon yourself in educating her, that you are now in her debt almost as much as she is in yours, for you must now defray the cost of her refinement."

"What you say, my daughter," he responded, "is full of energy and not without rhyme and reason; it can be heard with approval. Tell me, however, what your purpose is, for I do not yet see it, and confide in me the goal of your thoughts, for it is dark to me."

"I am of one spirit," she said, "with your people, so my womanhood can only be of one flesh with your people. You have opened my eyes—let me now open yours. A sprout grows from your stalk, Er, your fourth son's firstborn, and he is like a palm tree beside a brook and like a slender reed in the marsh. Therefore speak with Judah, your lion, that he might give me to Er as a wife."

Jacob was as surprised as he could be.

"So that is your purpose," he replied, "and that is your goal? Truly, truly, I would not have thought it. You have told me of the responsibility that I have taken upon myself in educating you, and have now taken me very much aback on account of it. Of course I can speak with my lion and bring my word to bear on him, but can I justify it? You are welcome in my household, it raises its hands high with joy to receive you. But shall I have formed you for God for you to be unhappy? I do not gladly speak ill of anyone in Israel, but the sons of the daughter of Shuah are an unsatisfactory lot and ne'er-do-wells before the Lord, and I prefer not to look upon them. Truly, I am most hesitant to consent to your wishes, for by my lights those boys are not fit for marriage, at least not with you."

"With me," she said firmly, "if with no one else—do stop and consider my father and lord. It was decreed that Jehuda should of necessity have sons. Well, they are what they are, the core is good at any rate, for the seed of Israel is in them, and they cannot be passed over or left behind, unless they leave themselves behind by not standing up to the test of life. And they in turn must of necessity have sons, one son at least, one of them must at least, Er, the first-born, that palm tree by the brook. I love him and will build him up with my love to be a hero in Israel."

"You, my daughter," he replied, "are a heroine yourself, and I trust you to do it."

And so he promised her he would bring his word to bear on Judah, the lion, but his heart was filled with several conflicting emotions. For he loved the woman with strong remnants of feeling and rejoiced to bestow on her a manliness that came from himself. And yet he regretted and was offended in his honor that there should be no better manliness. And, thirdly, he knew not why, the whole affair made him shudder a little.

"Not Through Us!"

Judah no longer resided with his brothers in the grove of Mamre near his father, but, having become good friends with the man named Hirah, now pastured his flocks more toward the plain, on the meadows of Adullam, and there Er, his eldest, and Tamar were wed at the bidding of Jacob, who had summoned his fourth son and brought his word to bear on him. Why should Judah have kicked against that word? His demeanor when he consented was somewhat gloomy, but consent he did, without any fuss, and so Tamar became the wife of Er.

It would not be proper for us to peek behind the curtain of this marriage. Even at the time no one wished to do so, and mankind's remarks as to the facts have always been blunt and brief, free of both sympathy and blame, since allotting them accurately has apparently been too much of a bother. The elements of the mishap were on the one hand historical ambition combined with qualities associated with Astarte and on the other a youthful enervation that was no match for life's first tests. One does best to follow the example of tradition and merely state bluntly and briefly that Judah's Er died very soon after the wedding, or, as tradition puts it, the Lord slew him—well, the Lord does everything and everything that happens can be regarded as his doing. The young man died in Tamar's arms of a hemorrhage that probably would have killed him even if he had not choked to death on his own blood; and many may also find it comforting that at least he did not die all alone like a dog, but in the arms of his wife, though, then again, it is distressing to think of her stained by the lifeblood of her dying husband. She stood up with a darkened frown, washed herself clean, and demanded Onan, Judah's second son, for a husband.

The resolve this woman displayed has always been rather astonishing. She returned upcountry to Jacob and poured out her troubles to him, more or less accusing God before him, causing the old man some embarrassment on Yah's behalf.

"My husband has died," she said, "Er, your grandson, at one blow and in an instant. Who can understand it? How can God do such a thing?"

"He can do anything," he replied. "Humble yourself. He does the most terrible things when it suits Him, for being able to do everything is, when one thinks about it, a great temptation. These are vestiges of the desert, try to understand it that way. He comes upon a man sometimes and slays him, willy-nilly, without explanation. One must accept it."

"I accept it," she replied, "for the sake of God, but not for my part, for I do not acknowledge my widowhood—I cannot, I dare not. If one man has fallen away, then the next must take his place at once, so that the spark left in me does not burn out and there is no name or anything else left on earth of my husband. I am not speaking for myself alone or for him who was slain, I am speaking universally and for all time. You, lord and father, must bring your word to bear in Israel and make it an ordinance that when there are brothers and one of them dies without child, his wife shall not take a stranger from outside, but her brother-in-law shall step into the breach and wed her. The first son that she bears, however, he shall certify in the name of her dead brother, that his name may not be blotted out of Israel."

"But what if the man does not wish to wed his sister-in-law?" Jacob objected.

"In that case, she shall step forward," Tamar said firmly, "and say before everyone, 'My husband's brother refuses to raise up his brother's name in Israel and will not marry me.' Then shall he be summoned and spoken to. If, however, he persists, saying, 'I do not wish to take her,' she shall go up to him before all the people and pull one shoe from his feet and spit upon him and shall answer and say,

'So shall it be done to any man who does not build up his brother's house. And his name shall be Barefoot.' "

"That would give him pause for thought, to be sure," Jacob said. "And you are right, my daughter, inasmuch as it would be easier for me to bring my word to bear on Judah that he should give Onan to you as a husband if I make it universal and can appeal to an ordinance that I have made public beneath the oracle tree."

This was the institution of levirate marriage, founded at Tamar's instigation, a fact of history. This country girl had a flair for things historical. Avoiding widowhood, she was given the boy Onan as a husband, though Judah showed scant enthusiasm for this compromise of collateral marriage, and the man in question even less. When summoned by his father from the pastures of Adullam, Jehuda kicked somewhat longer against the suggestion and disputed the advisability of repeating with his second son what had ended so unhappily with his first. Besides, Onan had just turned twenty and, if meant for marriage at all, he was certainly not yet mature enough for it, was neither inclined nor disposed to it.

"But she will pull off his shoe and the rest of it if he refuses to build up his brother's house, and he will be called Barefoot all his life."

"You act, Israel," Judah said, "as if that were in fact so, even though you have only just introduced the practice—and I know upon whose advice."

"God speaks through this maiden," Jacob replied. "He led her to me so that I might make Him known to her and He might speak through her."

And Judah kicked no more and arranged for the wedding.

The role of bedroom snoop is beneath the dignity of this narrator. So then, to be blunt and brief: Judah's second son, pretty and nice enough in his way, that is in a dubious way, was, likewise in his way, a character—which is to say, in the sense of a deeply rooted contrariness that was tantamount to his speaking a judgment against himself and negating the life within him. Not his personal life exactly—for he had a great love of himself and was very fond of the adornments and makeup of the dandy—but of all continuation of life after and through him, to this he said an intensely personal no. It is claimed that he was angry at having to step into the breach as an ersatz husband and awaken seed not for himself, but for his brother.

That is probably true; to the extent that words and even thoughts are at issue here, he might have articulated it that way to himself. In reality, for which thoughts and words are a mere paraphrase, this entire line of Judah had an inborn sense that it was a cul-de-sac and that life, whatever paths it might choose to take, should not, would not, could not, dare not lead by way of these three boys. "Not through us!" they said with one voice, and were right in their way. Life and procreation could do as they liked—they didn't care a fig! In particular Onan did not, and his prettiness and niceness were simply an expression of a self-love beyond which there is nothing else.

Forced into marriage, he resolved to make a fool of the womb. But he had not counted on Tamar's ambition being armed with the arts of Astarte, which confronted his contrariness the way one thundercloud confronts another, ending in a deadly bolt of lightning. He died in her arms, from one instant to the next, of sudden paralysis of life. His brain stood still, and he was dead.

Tamar rose up and demanded posthaste that she be given Shelah, Judah's youngest, a lad of barely sixteen years, to be her husband. If someone were to call her the most astonishing person in this entire story, we would not venture to contradict him.

This time she did not get her way. Even Jacob was very tentative, if only in expectation of Judah's emphatic objection, which was not long in coming. He was indeed called a lion, but he stood there like a lioness defending her last cub, whatever the boy may or may not have been worth, and would not consent.

"Never!" he said. "So that he may perish on me as well, is that it? Die a bloody death like the first or bloodless like the second? God forbid, it shall not happen. I have been obedient to your summons, Israel, and have hastened here from Chezib in the plains, where Shuah's daughter bore this son to me, and where she now lies ill. For she is ill and near death, and if Shelah were to die as well, I would be stripped bare. Let there be no talk of refusal to obey, for you obviously do not wish to command me, but rather present this as a doubtful suggestion. I, however, have no doubt, but say no and never, both for you and myself. What does this woman think—that I should give her this sheep to wolf down as well? She is an Ishtar who slays those she loves. She is a devourer of young men, and her hunger is insatiable. Moreover, he is but a child, still a minor, and this lamb is not meant for the sheepfold of her arms."

And one truly could not picture Shelah, at least for now, as a married man. He looked more like an angel than a son of man—smug and useless, still lacking beard or bass voice.

"But then there's the problem of the shoe and the rest of it," Jacob hesitantly reminded him, "if the boy refuses to build up his brother's house."

"I have something to say in reply to that, my lord," Judah said. "If this devourer of men does not go and put on mourning clothes and mourn in her father's house as a respectable widow whose two husbands have died, and behave in modest fashion, as sure as I am the fourth son, I will pull off her shoe before everyone and do all the rest as well and indict her publicly as a vampire, that she may be stoned or burned."

"You go too far," Jacob said in great discomfort, "in your aversion to my suggestion."

"I go too far, do I? And how far would you go if someone wanted to take Benjamin from you, wanted to send him perhaps on a most dangerous journey, though he is not your last son, but merely your youngest? You protect him with your staff and keep him close to you so that he, too, may not get lost—he scarcely dares walk the road. Well, Shelah is my Benjamin, and I will resist, everything in me rises up to resist handing him over."

"I shall make you a fair offer," Jacob said, who was sorely grieved by this argument, "for the purpose of winning time and yet of not offering too great an offense to the maiden, your daughter-in-law. For we do not wish to refuse her demand, but merely to wean her of it. Go to her and say, 'My son Shelah is still too young and immature even for his years. Remain a widow in your father's house until the boy grows up, then I shall give him to you that he may awaken his brother's seed.' And thus we shall silence her demand for a few years before she can make it anew. But perhaps she will become accustomed to widowhood and will not renew it. Or, if she does, we shall console her and explain with more or less justification that your son is still not yet grown up."

"However you like," Judah said. "It makes no difference to me what you say, just so long as I do not have to lay his tender conceit in the fiery embrace of this Moloch."

The Sheepshearing

And it was done according to Jacob's instructions. Tamar received her father-in-law's decision with a darkened frown and gazed deep into his eyes. But she acquiesced. As a widow and woman in mourning, she remained in her father's house and nothing more was heard of her, for one year, then two, and even a third. After the second year she had every right to renew her demand; but she intentionally waited yet a third in order not to be told that Shelah was still too young. This woman's patience was as substantial as her resolve. But resolve and patience are probably one and the same.

Now when Shelah was nineteen and thus at the highpoint of whatever manliness he might achieve, she came before Judah and said, "The prescribed period is over, and the time has come for you to give me as a wife to your son and him to me as my husband, so that he may raise up his brother's name and seed. Remember our binding agreement."

Judah, however, had himself become a widower before her first year of waiting had passed; Shuah's daughter had died of the grief that came with his bondage to Ashtaroth, the loss of her sons, and the charge that she was to blame for it all. He had only Shelah now and was less inclined than ever to send him on a dangerous journey.

He therefore replied, "Binding agreement? My dear friend, there was no such thing. Do I mean by that to say that I will not hold to the words spoken by my mouth? I do not mean that. But I had not thought that you would insist on this after so long a time, for my words were words of consolation. If you would have more of those, I shall give them, but they should not be necessary, you should have consoled yourself by now. It is true that Shelah is older, but only by a little, and you are still farther ahead of him than you were when my words consoled you. You could almost be his mother."

"Oh, could I?" she asked. "You've shown me my place, I see."

"Your place," he said, "in my opinion, is in your father's house, that you may remain a widow there and a woman in mourning for her two husbands."

She bowed and left. But now here it comes.

This woman was not easily pushed aside or brought from her course—and our astonishment grows the longer we observe her. She dealt freely with time and her position in it. She had descended into time to join grandchildren she now cursed for having stood in the way of those to whom she would have given birth—and she now decided to change generations again and to climb back up, maneuvering around the last member of the third generation, whom they did not want to give her out of fear that if he did not bring her back on course he would die. For her spark dared not be put out, nor would she allow them to blot her out of God's inheritance.

For Judah, Jacob's son, the affair played out as follows. Only a few days after the day the lion had once again become a lioness and defended her cub, the year came round to the time of sheepshearing, the Feast of the Wool Harvest, when the region's shepherds and herders gathered to make sacrifices, to drink and eat, always at a different place; and this year the chosen spot was a town in the mountains named Timnah, to which shepherds and owners of flocks now came up or down to shear their sheep and have a good time. Judah, however, went up together with Hirah of Adullam, his friend the head shepherd, the same man who had introduced him to Shuah's daughter; and they too wanted to shear sheep and have a good time—or at least Hirah did, for Judah was not in the mood for a good time, he never was. He lived in his own hell, punishing himself for his share in past crimes, and his private hell was closely related to the way in which his sons had lost their lives. His election as heir left him miserable, and he would have preferred the year never came round to any sort of feast or good times; for if one is a denizen of hell, all festivities take on the character of hell and can only end in one's sullying both one's election and one's inheritance. But what was he to do? Only those who are sick in body are excused from life. But if one is simply sick in spirit—that does not matter, no one understands, and one must participate in life and observe its seasons with others. And so Judah had spent three days at the sheepshearing at Timnah, sacrificing and feasting.

He made the return trip home alone; he liked best to travel alone. We know he was on foot because he had with him a good knobbed staff of some value, the kind one does not need for riding but for walking. With it he strode the paths downhill, among vineyards and hamlets, by the fading red radiance of day's departure. He knew these trails and byways well; here was Enam, the village of

Enaim at the foot of the hills, through which he had to pass on his
way to Chezib and Adullam, its houses, mud walls, and gate bathed
now in the purple of a festive sky. A figure was crouching beside the
gate; as he drew nearer he saw that she was shrouded in a *ketônet
paspasim*, the veiled garment of enthrallment.

His first thought was: I am alone. His second: I shall pass by. His
third: To hell with her! Does this *kedeshe*, this priestess of pleasure,
have to sit here on my peaceful path homeward? It always happens
to me. But I will pay no attention, for I am two men at once—the
one to whom this sort of thing happens and the one who passes by in
bitterness, angrily denying himself. The same old song. But must it
be sung over and over? The same song chained galley slaves groan as
they drudge away. I sang it up there, groaned it with a dancing girl,
and should be sated for a while. As if hell were ever sated! Disgraceful curiosity, how absurd, insipid a hundred times over. What will
she say, how will she behave? Let whoever comes after me taste it. I
shall pass by.

And he stopped.

"Greetings in the Mistress's name," he said.

"May she strengthen you," she whispered.

The angel of lust had already grabbed hold of him and her whispers left him shuddering with curiosity about this woman.

"You lie in wait, whispering," he said, his lips trembling, "but
waiting for whom?"

"I am waiting," she replied, "for a lusty man of lust who will
share the mysteries of the goddess with me."

"Then I am half the right man," he said, "for I am a man of lust,
though not a lusty man. I have no lust for lust, but it lusts for me. In
your line of work one is not very lusty for lust either, I would think,
and must be glad if others lust."

"We give our gifts," she replied. "But if the right person comes
along, we know how to receive as well. Do you lust after me?"

He touched her.

"But what will you give me?" she asked, stopping him.

He laughed. "As a token," he said, "that I am a man of lust with
a touch of lustiness, I will give you a billy goat from my herd to remember me by."

"But you do not have it with you."

"I will send it to you."

"A man says that easy enough beforehand. Afterward, he's a different man, who no longer recalls what he said. I must have a pledge."

"Name it."

"Give me the ring from your finger, the knotted cord at your neck, and the knobbed staff in your hand."

"You know how to look after the Mistress," he said. "Here, take them!"

And he sang the song with her beside the road in the dusk, and she vanished behind the wall. But he went on home and the next morning said to Hirah, his shepherd, "By the way, this way or that, you know how it goes. It was at the gate to Enaim, the town of Enam, a temple harlot, whose eyes under her *ketônet* had something about them—in short, no need for a lot of words between men. Be so good as to take her the billy goat I promised her, so that I may get back some things I had to leave with her—my ring, staff, and cord. Take her a good, sturdy billy goat of some value, I don't want to look shabby before a shabby harlot. She may be sitting at the gate again; if not, ask the townspeople."

Hirah chose a splendid, devilishly ugly billy goat with spiral horns, cloven nose, and long beard and led it to the gate at Enaim, but no one was there. "The whore," he asked inside, "who sat by the road out there? Where is she? You surely know your whore?"

But they answered, saying, "There was and is no whore here. We don't allow them. We're a decent little town. Look elsewhere for a nanny for your billy, or stones will fly."

Hirah reported this to Judah, who simply shrugged. "If she can't be found," he said, "it's her fault. We offered our payment, and no one can blame us. I'm out my possessions of course. My staff had a crystal knob. Take the goat back to the herd."

And with that he forgot all about it. Three months later, however, it was obvious that Tamar was with child.

It was a scandal such as the region had not known for some time. She had been living as a widow in mourning at her parents' home, and now it was evident and could no longer be hidden that she had done a shameful deed deserving of death. The men grumbled gloomily, the women screeched scorn and malediction. For Tamar had always treated them arrogantly, as if she were something better.

And at once the hue and cry came to Judah: "Do you know, do you know? Tamar, your daughter-in-law, has behaved in ways she can no longer hide. She is with child from harlotry."

Judah turned pale. His stag's eyes bugged out, his nostrils quivered. Sinners can be terribly touchy about sin in this world; moreover his blood was roused against the woman because she had devoured two of his sons, and also because he had broken his word to her concerning the third.

"She has done wickedness," he said. "May the heavens over her be brass and the earth under her be iron. Let her be burned in the fire. She has long been deserving of the stake, but now it lies open to all that she has committed an abomination in Israel and has sullied her mourning garments. Let her be led out before the gate of her father's house and burned to ashes. Her blood be upon her own head."

And taking long strides, he set off with the tattletales trailing behind, who waved their arms and gathered new arm-wavers from villages all along the way, so that a voracious crowd gathered behind Judah at the widow's house, jeering and whistling. The sighs and sobs of Tamar's parents could be heard from inside, but there was no sign of her.

Three men were appointed to go inside and bring the harlot out. With squared shoulders, stiff arms, chins set to chests, and fists at the ready, they went to fetch Tamar so that she could be charged with her shame and then burned. After a while they came back out, without Tamar, but holding items in their hands. One held a ring between two fingers, splaying the other three. Another had grasped a staff by the middle and held it out before him. A purple cord dangled from the hand of the third.

They brought these items before Jehuda, who stood at the head of the crowd, and said, "We have been instructed by Tamar, your daughter-in-law, to say, 'By the man whose pledges these are, I bear my pledge of the future. Do you know them? Then behold: I am the woman who shall not be blotted out, nor shall her son, from God's inheritance.'"

Judah, the lion, gazed at the items as the crowd pressed in around him, peering into his face, and whereas he had been pale with rage the whole time, he now slowly turned red as blood, to the roots of his hair and into the whites of his eyes. And said nothing. Then a woman began to laugh and then another, and then a man, and then a great many men and women, and finally the whole pack was roaring with unstoppable laughter, until they had to crouch down with laughter, their mouths gaping toward heaven, and cried: "Judah, you're the one! Judah and his whore have an heir! Ha ha, ho ho, and ha ha!"

And Leah's fourth son? With the crowd clamoring around him, he softly said, "She is more righteous than I." And bowing his head he departed from their midst.

But when Tamar's hour came, six months later, she bore twin boys, who were very manly men. By ascending through time, she had blotted two sons out of Israel, and now, by descending again, delivered two incomparably better ones in their stead. In particular, Perez, the first to arrive, was a very manly man and procreated into history and the world with a vengeance. For at the seventh remove he fathered a man who was manliness itself, a man named Boaz, the husband of a lovely wife. They became great in Ephrathah and were praised in Bethlehem, for their grandson was Jesse of Bethlehem, a father of seven sons, the youngest of whom tended sheep, had brown hair and beautiful eyes. He was very good at playing the harp and using his sling and brought down the giant—and even then had silently been anointed king.

But all that lies far ahead in a still open future and belongs to the great story of which Joseph's story is but an interpolation. But into it has been interpolated for good and all the story of the woman who was not to be left out of it at any price, but put herself on the right course with astonishing resolve. There she stands, tall and almost sinister, on a slope of her native hills, gazing, with one hand pressed to her body and the other shading her eyes, out across tilled fields, above which in the distance light breaks through the towering clouds in a great flood of radiant glory.

Part Six

THE HOLY GAME

Of Water and Waters

As for the nature of their divine Provider, that side or aspect of the divinity that Abram's people called El Shaddai, the god of nourishment, but that in the Land of Black Earth was called Hapi, he who swelled and overflowed; as for the nature of the river that had created their peculiar land of oases between deserts and that fed their very existence, a life lived in happy reverence toward death—as for the Nile, then, the children of Egypt, every one, even the best educated, even its wise men, entertained the most infantile notions. They believed and taught generation after generation of their children that it emerged from the underworld—the god himself knew where and how—in order to wend its way to the "Great Green," that is to say, the immeasurable ocean (which they took the Mediterranean to be), and that the shrinkage that followed its fertile overflowing was much like a return to the underworld. In short, in this regard superstitious ignorance reigned among them, and it was only because at the time all the world around them was no more enlightened than they—and some of it even less so—that they managed to get through life even though they understood so little. It is true that despite their ignorance they built a magnificent and mighty empire that is universally admired and that defied several millennia; they produced many beautiful things and in particular were quite ingenious at managing the object of their ignorance, that is, the Nile. Nonetheless we, who know so much better, indeed know exactly what is what, can only regret that none of us was on hand at the time to shed light on these minds in their darkness and provide them illuminating information about the true nature of Egypt's great river. What a stir in that nation's seminaries and learned societies would have been created by news that Hapi, far from originating in the underworld—a locale that itself can only be dismissed as superstition—is nothing more than the discharge from great lakes in tropical Africa and that for the nourishing god to become what he is, he must

first nourish himself by consuming all the waters that pour westward from those Ethiopian Alps. In the rainy season, mountain
streams, rich with finely pulverized gravel, gush down from the
mountains and gather in two tributaries that form the future river's
prenatal state so to speak: the Blue Nile and the Atbara, which only
later at Khartoum and Berber, go to bed together, geographically
speaking, and become the Nile per se, that great fecund river. For toward the middle of summer this single bed gradually fills up with
such masses of water filled with dissolved sludge that the river
spreads out beyond its banks, which is why it bore the name Over-
abundance; and it takes months for it to return, just as gradually, to
within its boundaries. That layer of sludge, however, the residue of
its abundance, becomes, as even those seminarians knew, the fertile
soil of Keme.

They would have been amazed—and perhaps might even have
regarded heralds of such truth with some bitterness—to hear that
the Nile did not come from below, but from on high, from the same
heights, in fact, as the rain that plays the fertilizing role in other less
peculiar lands. They liked to say that there, in those wretched foreign lands, the Nile was set in the heavens—by which they meant
rain. And one must admit that surprising insight, bordering on enlightenment, is expressed in that flowery phrase: to wit, that all the
world's water and waters are interconnected. The Nile's flood depends on abundant rainfall in the mountains of Abyssinia; this rainfall, however, comes from swollen clouds that form over the
Mediterranean and are driven to those regions by the winds. In the
same way that Egypt's prosperity is dependent on the Nile's rising to
a favorable level, so, too, that of Canaan—the land of Kenana or
Upper Retenu, as it was called back then, or Palestine, which is our
enlightened geographical term for the homeland of Joseph and his
fathers—is dependent on rain that falls, under normal circumstances, twice a year, the early rain in late autumn, the late rain early
in the year. For there is a dearth of springs there, and little can be
done with the water of its rivers that run in deep gorges. And so
everything comes from the rains, especially the late rain, whose waters men began to collect in earliest times. If they fail, if instead of
moisture-bearing winds from the west, winds from the deserts to the
east and south hold sway, the harvest is ruined, its growth stunted,
drought and famine prevail—and not just there. For if it does not

rain in Canaan, there are no downpours in the mountains of
Ethiopia either and no gushing mountain streams, the two tributaries of the Provider are not sufficiently nourished for it to become
"great," as the children of Egypt said, and fill the canals that bear the
water to higher-lying fields; then failed harvests and scarcity also
beset the land where the Nile is not in the heavens, but on earth—for
such is the interconnection of all the watery things of this world.

But if one has been enlightened about such matters, even in the
most general way, there is nothing miraculous—though there is
much that is frightening—about a phenomenon by which there is simultaneous scarcity "in all lands," not just in the Land of Mud, but
in Syria, in the land of the Philistines, in Canaan, even in the lands of
the Red Sea, and probably in Mesopotamia and Babylon as well, a
scarcity that is "sore in all lands." Yes, if worse comes to worst, one
year of disruption, of irregular and failed rains, can follow another in
an ill-tempered series, extending the string of misfortune over several years—and then the ordeal assumes fairy-tale-like dimensions,
lasts for seven years, or merely five, which is bad enough.

Joseph Enjoys Life

Everything—wind, water, welfare—had gone so splendidly for five
years that in gratitude people made seven of those five—and they
fully deserved it. But now the tide turned, just as Pharaoh, in his maternal concern for the Realm of Blackness, had previously dreamt in
unclear dreams that Joseph had dared to interpret clearly: the Nile
failed at the same time that the winter rains and especially the late
rains failed in Canaan, failed once, which was a cause of mourning;
failed a second time, and there was great lamentation; failed a third
time, and there was only wringing of hands and deathly pallor—and
if it kept on failing for as many years yet, people might just as well
call it seven years of drought and want.

We human beings always deal with such extraordinary acts of
nature in the same way: at first, being creatures of the quotidian, we
deceive ourselves about the character of the events, do not understand where all this is going. We happily take it for an incident of the
usual moderate sort, but once we have gradually become accustomed to the idea that it is an extravagant affliction, a calamity of the

first order that we never thought could happen to us in our lifetime, we then find it strange to look back at our blindness, at our lack of understanding. It was the same with the children of Egypt. It was a good while before they realized that the phenomenon that had befallen them could be called "seven lean years," like those that had surely happened in days of old and still played a terrible role in their written legends, but that they had never thought to experience themselves. Yet such obtuseness in their case as to what had begun to occur is surely not as easily excused as normal nearsightedness would be. For Pharaoh had dreamt and Joseph had interpreted. Was not the fact that the prophesied seven years of plenty had actually occurred tantamount to proof that seven lean years would follow as well? But the children of Egypt had banished those from their minds during the seven years of plenty, just as we always forget the bill we owe the devil. But now the bill had come due—the providing Nile had been wretchedly low a second and third time—they had to admit it; and the manifest result of that realization was an enormous increase in Joseph's reputation.

And if people's view of him had been very favorable when the years of abundance arrived, how must his fame have been enhanced when it turned out that the lean years had come as well and the precautionary measures he had taken were revealed as inspired wisdom of the highest order. A minister of agriculture surely has a difficult time of it during years of scarcity and hunger, for the great masses, never known for their reason and fairness, will always tend to react emotionally and blame the man in the position of greatest responsibility in the Land of Black Earth for natural disasters. But it is quite different if he has predicted the ordeal; and something even more than that—which is to say, deserving of greatest celebrity and respect—if he has previously taken magical preventative measures against the calamity, so that even if it retains its power to cause great upheavals, it is robbed of its catastrophic character.

The impulses and psychological traits of a people are often displayed in stronger and more exemplary fashion in immigrant sons from foreign lands than in the native population. Over the twenty years Joseph had spent adopting the ways of the land to which he had been carried off and set apart, the typically characteristic Egyptian idea of carefully protecting oneself and warding off evil had entered his flesh and bone, but in such a way that even as he acted upon it, it was never without his being aware of it and maintaining some distance from this determinative idea; and in the end, even while personally guided by that idea, he could still smile at its general popularity and adjust his actions accordingly—a combination of authenticity and humor that has more charm than any authenticity without distance and a smile.

It was the time for harvesting the seed he had sown in managing plenty by taxing it—that is, the time for distribution and dealings in grain so grand and profitable they were unlike any a son of Rê had known since the time of the god himself. For as it is written in the book and celebrated in song: "There was famine in all lands, but in the land of Egypt there was bread." Needless to say, this does not mean that there was not scarcity in the land of Egypt as well; and it is easy for anyone with even the vaguest awareness of economic laws to imagine the price of grain when the need is so great. He may blanch at the thought, but should also remember that this scarcity was being managed just as the plenty before it had been, and managed by the same cordial and subtle man. For the scarcity lay in his hands and he could do with it whatever he pleased: he loyally made the best of it for Pharaoh, and at the same time for all those who were least able to cope with it, the commonfolk. For them he turned it into a scarcity free of charge.

He did it with a system that combined exploitation of the economic situation with benevolence, official usury with a fiscal solicitude unlike any people had ever known, so that everyone, even those hard hit by exploitation, saw something heroic and divine in his mixing of severity and cordiality—for the divine behaves and expresses itself in just this ambiguous fashion, so that one never knows whether to call it cruel or kind.

One cannot be too extravagant in imagining the situation. The dream of the seven scorched ears of grain provided such a perfect metaphor for the state of agriculture that it was no longer a metaphor, but withered reality. The dreamt ears of grain had been scorched by the east wind, that is by the *khamsin,* a searing southeaster—and it now blew almost uninterruptedly through summer and the season of harvest, called Shemu, from February till June, often as an oven-hot gale, filling the air with fine dust that covered plants with its ash, so that whatever might have grown with the meager assistance of the undernourished Provider was now charred by the breath of the desert. Seven ears of grain? Yes, one might well put it that way—there were no more than that. In other words, there were no ears of grain and no harvest. But there was something else, in uncounted—no, actually in very carefully counted and recorded—quantities: that was the grain itself, of every sort, for both seed and bread; and it was found in royal warehouses and pits, in every city and its environs, upriver and down, throughout the land of Egypt and *only* in Egypt; for no precautions had been taken elsewhere, no ark built in anticipation of the Flood. Yes, in all the land of Egypt, and only here, there was bread—in the hands of the state, in the hands of Joseph, the Overseer of All That Heaven Gives; and now he himself was like heaven in its giving, and like the Nile that nourishes and provides. He opened his supply depots—not flinging their doors wide, but acting prudently and closing the doors again from time to time—opened them and gave bread and seed to all who needed it, and they all did: both Egyptians and foreigners who journeyed here to fetch grain from Pharaoh's land, which now more aptly than ever was called a granary, the granary of the world. He gave—which is to say, he sold to those who could pay, at prices not they but he set, commensurate with the unprecedented economic situation, so that Pharaoh made gold and silver. But at the same time he could give in a different way, to the lean-ribbed commonfolk—he ordered grain distributed to them, even if only at the level of that basic necessity for which they cried, gave to peasants and to those who lived in the open-ditch lanes of cities, gave bread and seed, that they might live and not die.

That was divine, and it was a praiseworthy model of what is human as well. There had always been good civil servants, who with justifiable emotion had had the walls of their graves inscribed to tell how they had provided for the king's subjects in times of famine, given to widows, and shown favor to neither high nor low, and afterward, when the Nile had grown great again, "did not take the peasant's arrears," meaning they had not insisted on back taxes or payment in advance. Joseph's managerial methods reminded people of these inscriptions. But since the days of Seth no civil servant had proved so proficient, had dealt on so grand a scale, had been vested with such plenary powers and exercised them so divinely. His commerce in grain, staffed by ten thousand scribes and assistant scribes, extended over all of Upper and Lower Egypt, but every thread led to Menfe, to the palatial office of the Spender of Shade and Unique Friend, and there was no final decision about a sale, a loan, or a gift that he did not leave open for himself to make. The rich came before him, those with great estates, and they cried to him for seed grain—which he sold to them for their silver and gold, but never without conditions, stipulating that they bring their irrigation systems up-to-date and refusing to allow them to continue to bungle along in feudal backwardness—and in this he demonstrated his loyalty to the highest, to Pharaoh, into whose treasury flowed the silver and gold of the rich. And there likewise came before him the cries of the poor for bread, to whom he ordered it distributed from the storehouses for nothing, absolutely gratis, so that they might eat and not starve—and in this he demonstrated his sympathy, that fundamental trait of his character, the nature of which we previously described in excellent detail and so need not return to it here. That it also had something to do with wit—to that we could briefly return nonetheless. And there truly was something witty about his system of exploitation and solicitude, so that during this period, despite a heavy burden of work, he was always in good spirits, and when at home with Asenath, his wife, the daughter of the sun, he would repeatedly remark: "Maiden, I enjoy life."

He also sold to foreigners at inflated prices, as we know, and read reports of grain sold to "the nobles of the wretched land of Retenu." For many of Canaan's city kings, including those of Megiddo and Sharuhen, had sent to him for grain, and the ambassador of Askuluna came and cried to him for his city and received a delivery, though it did not come cheap. But even here, too, the rigor of profit was balanced by cordiality, and he allowed starving sand rabbits, shepherd tribes from Syria and the Lebanon—those "barbarians who do not know how to live," as the scribes put it—to enter with their herds through Egypt's closely guarded portals and, if they promised not to stray beyond the region assigned them, to make a life for themselves east of the river, in the direction of stony Arabia, in the well-watered pastures of Zoan along the Tanitic arm of the Nile.

And so he read frontier reports of this sort: "We have let the Bedouins from Edom pass through the fortress of Merneptah and on to the lakes of Merneptah, that they might provide for themselves and their cattle on the great pasture of Pharaoh, the Beautiful Sun of the Nations."

He would read them carefully. He read all frontier reports very carefully, and they had to be absolutely accurate, just as he had ordered. He had meticulously tightened regulations and by his decree an account had to be kept at all barriers in the east of every person allowed to enter wealthy Egypt, which had now become so much wealthier still, of everyone who came from those wretched lands to fetch grain from Pharaoh's granary; and all frontier officers of the caliber of lieutenant Hor-waz at the fortress of Zel, the scribe of the great gate who had once allowed Joseph himself into the land in the company of the Ishmaelites, had been ordered to exercise great care in keeping their records and to list all immigrants not only by homeland, profession, and name, but also by the names of their father and father's father, and punctually to send these lists each day, by express, to Menfe, to the great office of the Spender of Shade.

There another clean copy was made on deluxe papyrus, in red and black ink, and this was then presented to the Provider. And though he had more than enough to keep him busy, he read all these reports daily, from beginning to end, and with the same care with which they had been prepared.

"They Are Coming!"

It was in the second year of lean cows, on a day in the middle of Epiphi, the month of May by our reckoning, and a dreadfully hot day it was—for though it is, of course, hot in the land of Egypt during summer's third of the year, it was hotter than usual. The sun fell like fire from heaven, we would have measured at least forty degrees in the shade; the dusty wind was blowing, aggravating inflamed eyes with desert sand whipped up from Menfe's streets. There were too many flies and the people were as listless as they. The rich would have given lots of gold for a half hour of a northwest breeze and even have been willing to let the poor have some share in its enjoyment.

Returning home at noon from his palatial office, Joseph, however, the king's Supreme Mouth, appeared—despite a sweat-dampened, sandy face—very animated, his limbs very nimble, if such words are applicable to his seated state. It was not long before his sedan chair, followed by the vehicles of a few great men of his ministry who were to dine with him that noon, turned off from the splendid boulevard and, as was the Vice-God's habit, which even today he did not set aside, bore him through several open-ditch lanes filled with lean-ribbed commonfolk, where he was greeted with hearty and enthusiastic familiarity. "Djepnuteefonekh!" people cried, and blew kisses to him. "Hapi! Hapi! Provider, may your destiny last ten thousand years!" And those who would merely be wrapped in a mat before being carried out into the desert wished him: "Four excellent jars for your entrails and a coffin of alabaster for your mummy!" This was their way of expressing sympathy, in response to his.

Now he was carried through the painted portal of the villa Pharaoh had given him and into its front garden, where—along with the colorful papyrus columns of the house's projecting terrace—olive, pepper, and fig trees, shading cypresses and palm fronds were reflected in the rectangle of a low-walled lotus pond. The driveway, a wide sandy path, led around it, and since Joseph's bearers had now come to a halt, his runners offered their knees and necks for him first to place his foot upon before it touched the ground. On the terrace, or better, at the head of the open stairway leading up one side of it, Mai-Sakhme, his steward, stood waiting with perfect calm, together with two greyhounds named Hepi and Hezes from the land of Punt, terribly elegant dogs adorned with golden collars and trembling with nervousness. Pharaoh's friend bounded up the wide stairs in greater haste than usual—in a haste actually inappropriate for a great man of Egypt to display in front of others. He did not look around to those in his retinue.

"Mai," he said hurriedly in a choked voice as he patted the heads of the dogs, who had placed their paws on his chest to greet him, "I must speak to you alone at once, come along with me to my chambers and let these people wait, there is no rush with the meal, though as for me I won't be able to eat. There are far more urgent matters, concerning the scroll here in my hand, or rather, the scroll concerns more urgent matters—I shall explain what I'm talking about if you will come along with me at once to my chambers, where we can be alone . . ."

"Just keep calm," Mai-Sakhme replied. "What is wrong, Adôn?

You're trembling, aren't you? And as for not being able to eat—I didn't hear that. Not from you, who give food to eat to so many. Do you not want to be cleansed of sweat with running water? One should not let sweat grow old in one's pores and body cavities. It is a caustic and irritant, especially when mixed with gritty dust."

"That later, too, Mai. Washing and eating are not urgent, comparatively speaking, for you need to know what I know, what I have learned from this scroll, which was brought to my office just before I left, and that in fact it has come to pass, or rather that they have come, which is one and the same thing—it has come, that is, they have come, and now the question is what should be done and how we are to set about it, and what shall I do, for I am so terribly excited."

"And why is that, Adôn? Just keep calm. If you say of something that 'it has come,' then you were prepared for it, and whatever one is prepared for cannot come as a shock. If you would be so kind as to tell me who and what has come, I shall prove to you that there is no reason to be shocked, but that only absolute calm is in order."

They exchanged these words while moving with rapid strides—that the composed man tried to slow down—across the peristyle, which opened onto the fountain court. But Joseph and Mai-Sakhme, accompanied by Hepi and Hezes, stepped into a room off to the right, with a malachite lintel above the door, a brightly painted ceiling, and two cheerful friezes, one high, one low, along its walls. The room served as Joseph's library and divided the house's great reception hall from his bedchamber and was furnished with Egypt's finest grace and elegance: an encrusted couch, covered with hides and cushions; charming chests, set on legs and decorated with inlay work, carvings, and inscriptions, in which scrolls were kept; lion-pawed chairs with cane seats and backs of pressed, gilt leather; tables for flowers and stands with faience vases and iridescent glass vessels. Bouncing lightly on the balls of his feet, Joseph gave his steward's arm a squeeze. His eyes were moist.

"Mai," he cried with suppressed jubilation—or something like jubilation, an anxious but merry glee—in his voice, "they are coming, they are here, they are in the land, they have passed the fortress of Zel—I knew it, I've been waiting for it, and yet I still cannot believe it, my heart is pounding in my throat, and in my excitement I don't know where I stand upon the earth . . ."

"Kindly do not dance about with a man of composure like myself, Adôn, but instead explain things more clearly, if you would, please. Who has come?"

"My brothers, Mai, my brothers!" Joseph cried, and bounced some more.

"Your brothers? Those rapacious men who ripped your garment to pieces and threw you into the pit and sold you into the world?" asked the warden, to whom his master had long ago confided all this.

"But yes! Yes! The men I have to thank for all my happiness and glory here below!"

"Well, Adôn, I'd say that is turning matters rather vigorously in their favor."

"God has turned them, my good steward. God has shaped them to the good and to everyone's favor, and one must look to the result at which He was aiming. Before the result has made itself known, there is only the deed, and it may appear evil. But once it is known, then the deed must be judged by its consequences."

"But that still remains an open question, my gracious lord. Imhotep the Wise might perhaps have been of a different opinion. And they also represented the blood of an animal as your own to your father."

"Yes, that was horrible. He is certain to have fallen back in a faint. But it surely had to be, my friend, there was no other way, because it couldn't have gone on like that back then. There was my father, whose heart is great and tender—and then me, what a jackanapes I was! An unspeakable jackanapes, full of culpable trust and blind expectation. It's a scandal how some people mature so late. Assuming that I'm mature now. Perhaps maturity takes an entire lifetime."

"It could be, Adôn, that you still have a great deal of the boy in you. And are you certain that these are indeed your brothers?"

"Certain? There cannot be the shadow of a doubt. Was it for nothing that I gave such strict orders in regard to lists and reports? It was not for nothing, and as for Manasseh, as for the name we gave our eldest son, that was, you must know, simply a matter of form— I most definitely have not forgotten my father's house, ah, not in the least. I have thought of it every day and every hour of all those countless years since I promised Benjamin, my little brother, there in the maze of the mutilated god, that I would send for them all to follow once I was raised up and given power over the keys. . . . Certain that it is they? Here, it's right here, it came by express messenger and so precedes them by a day or even two. The sons of Jacob, the son of Yitzchak, from the grove of Mamre, which is near Hebron: Ruben, Shimeon, Levi, Judah, Dan, Naphtali . . . for the purpose of purchasing grain. And you can speak of doubt? It is they, ten in all. They have come with other new arrivals, in a caravan of buyers. The scribes had no idea what they were recording. And they themselves, they have no notion, haven't the slightest idea of who it is they shall be led before, and who keeps the market as the king's Supreme Mouth in this land. If you only knew what I am feeling, Mai. But I don't even know it myself, everything within me is *tohu* and *bohu,* if you know what that means. And yet I have known it and expected it and have waited for it for all these years. I knew it even as I was standing before Pharaoh and prophesying for him, for I was prophesying for myself what God was aiming at and how He is guiding this story. And what a story we are in, Mai! It is one of the best. And now it all depends on us, it is incumbent on us to shape it well and fine, to make of it something truly delightful and place all our wits at God's disposal. How do we begin to do justice to such a story? That is what I find so exciting. . . . Do you think they will recognize me?"

"How should I know, Adôn? But no, I don't think so. You have matured considerably since they mutilated you. And above all, the fact that they suspect nothing will blind their eyes, so that the idea will never occur to them and they will not believe their eyes. To recognize and to know that you recognize—there's quite a distance between the two."

"Right, right. All the same, my heart is pounding for fear they will recognize me."

"Don't you want them to?"

"Not right away, Mai, by no means right away. For it to be drawn out and for it to dawn on them only very slowly before I speak the word and say, 'It is I'—all that is necessary, first as embellishment, as a way of giving shape to God's story, and second, there is so much that must first be tested and discovered, so much to be sounded out, above all as regards Benjamin . . ."

"Is Benjamin with them?"

"That's just it, he's not. I've told you there are ten of them, not eleven. But we were twelve! There are the red-eyed ones, and the sons of the handmaids, but not my mother's son, the little one. Do you know what that means? You are so composed, you're slow to grasp it all. That Ben is not with them may mean one of two things. It may be, and may this prove the true interpretation, that my father is still alive—just think, the sublime old man still alive!—and is watching over his youngest, so that he has forbidden him to take this journey, has not compelled him to take it for fear that he might meet with an accident under way. His Rachel died while on a journey, I died on a journey—why shouldn't he be prejudiced against journeys and retain for himself the last token of his lovely wife still left to him? It can mean that. But it can also mean that he is dead, my father is dead, and that they have nastily abused defenseless Benjamin, have thrust him aside and denied him their company as brothers, because he is the son of the true wife, the poor little fellow . . ."

"You keep calling him little, Adôn, and apparently are not taking into account that your nearest and truest brother has to have matured as well in the meantime. Clear reason says he must be a man in the prime of life."

"Quite possibly, yes, it's true. But he will always be the youngest, my friend, the youngest of twelve, how can one not call him little? There's always something special and dear about the youngest, there is such a grace and a magic about him in this world that it almost of necessity gives rise to ill-will and treachery among those who are older."

"But when one stops to consider your story, my dear master, one might think that you are in fact the youngest."

"That's just it. I won't deny it, there may be some truth to your remark. Perhaps the story plays loose with things, is a bit off-center. That bothers me and it's why I am determined that the littlest brother shall receive his share of honor as the youngest, and if the ten have thrust him aside and been nasty to him, if—I dare not think of it!—they have mistreated him the way they once did me, then may the Elohim preserve them, for they'll get an unpleasant reception from me. I won't even reveal myself to them. The beautiful words, 'It is I,' will never be spoken. And if they do recognize me, I shall say, 'No, I am not he, you villains!' and all they will have in me is a stern stranger as their judge."

"Why, look at you, Adôn! You've put on quite a different face now, are strumming a different tune on your lyre. Your mind is not occupied with idle generosity and mild reconciliation, and instead you're thinking of how they mistreated you, and seem to me a man who can indeed distinguish between a deed and its consequences."

"I don't know what sort of man I am, Mai. A man never knows beforehand how he will behave in his own story; that is revealed only when the time comes and he finds out who he is. I am curious about myself and about what I shall say to them, for I have no idea what it will be. That's what leaves me trembling—I wasn't anywhere near so agitated when I was to stand before Pharaoh. They're only my brothers, after all. But that's just it. Everything's topsy-turvy in my heart, as I've told you—what a muddle of joy, curiosity, and fear, it's quite indescribable. You can't imagine how shocked I was when I read their names on the list, even though I knew it would happen and had most definitely expected it—but then there's no shocking you. Was I afraid for them or for myself? I don't know. But that for their part they ought to have good reason to be frightened to the bottom of their souls—never mind about that, that's as it should be. For it was no small thing they did that day—however long ago now, it still has not become a small thing. That I told them I had come to see if things were in order with them was flagrantly immature, I admit it—I admit it all, and especially that I should not have told them my dreams, and also that of course I would have told father everything had they pardoned me and released me from the well—they had to leave me there. And yet, and yet, that they were deaf to my cries from the depths as I lay there bound and bruised, wailing and imploring them not to do this to father by letting me perish in that hole and then showing him the blood of some animal—my friend, despite everything it was a hard, hard thing, not so much for me, I'll not speak of that, but for my father. If he died of grief and went down to Sheol in his sorrow—will I be able to deal kindly with them then, too? I don't know, I don't know who I shall be if it comes to that, but I fear who I am, I fear I shall not be able to deal kindly with them. If by breaking his heart, they brought his gray head down into the pit—that would *also* be one of the consequences. Indeed it would be the main one, and would cast a great shadow over the light that other consequences shed on their deed. In any case, it

remains a deed that deserves to be confronted with all its consequences, eye to eye, so that in seeing the good that has resulted they
may perhaps be ashamed of their wickedness."

"What do you intend to do with them?"

"How do I know? I don't know how to proceed with them and
wanted to ask you for advice and support—you, my steward, whom
I have taken into this story so that you may lend me your calm in the
midst of my agitation. You have too much of it already, you can give
me a bit of it; you're all too calm, just standing there with your eyebrows raised and making that little mouth of yours, for there is simply no shocking you—which is why no ideas occur to you now. But
this is a story that should give a man a great many ideas—we owe it
that much. For the encounter of deed and consequence is a feast of a
special sort and needs to be celebrated and adorned with all sorts of
trimmings and holy mischief, so that the world can laugh and cry
over it for five thousand years and more."

"Agitation and shock, Adôn, are less productive than calm. I
shall at once go mix you something to dampen the nerves. I pour a
powder into water, and all is quiet. But if I add a certain other powder to it, the combination fizzes up, and drinking the foaming brew
calms the heart."

"I shall gladly drink it later, Mai, at the right moment, when it's
most needed. But listen now to what I have done so far. I have sent
orders by express messengers that they be set apart from the other
new arrivals with whom they are traveling and not be provided grain
at a frontier city, but be directed down here to Menfe, to the main office. I have ordered that an eye be kept on them during their trip
through the land, that they and their animals be quartered at good
inns and be inconspicuously looked after here in a foreign land that
will seem so strange and peculiar to them, just as it did to me when I
died and came down here at age seventeen. I was a supple youth, but
they, now that I think of it, are all in their late forties or not far short
of it, with the exception of Benjamin, that is; but he is not with them,
and all I know is that he must be brought here—first, so that I can
see him, and second, because once he is here, Mai, then father will
come as well. In short, I have directed that our people discreetly bear
my brothers up on their hands, so that they do not dash their feet
against a stone, if that turn of phrase says anything to you. Once

they are here, however, they are to be brought to me at the ministry, to the hall where I hold audience."

"Not to your house?"

"No, not yet. First quite officially to the ministry. Just between us, the reception room there is also larger and more impressive."

"And what do you intend to do with them?"

"Yes, that will be probably be the moment when I shall drink your foaming brew, for when I stop to think that they will not know what to do once I speak the word and say 'It is I,' then I really have no idea how to proceed. But at least I shall not be so clumsy or inept at adorning the feast that I shall fling the door wide and simply blurt out my 'It is I,' but shall sit pretty behind the door for a while yet and treat them as strangers."

"You mean as enemies?"

"I mean somewhere between strangers and enemies. For I don't think, Mai, that I shall be able to manage the role of stranger without pushing ahead to that of enemy. That's easier. I'll have to come up with some reason for speaking harshly and taking them to task. I must act as if their case seems very suspicious and sinister to me, as if serious investigation is first required in order to bring clarity to the circumstances—or something of this or that sort."

"Will you speak with them in their language?"

"That is the first helpful word that your composure has managed, Mai!" Joseph cried, clapping his hand to his brow. "I definitely needed to be reminded of it, because all this time I've been speaking Canaanite with them in my mind—what an idiot I am. How am I supposed to be able to speak Canaanite? That would be a terrible faux pas. Even though I speak it with my own children—though I think they're picking up an Egyptian accent from me. Well, that's the least of my worries. Here I am chattering away, it seems—going on about things hardly worth noting even under much more tranquil circumstances, and certainly not now. But of course I dare not understand Canaanite, I must speak with them through an interpreter. I'll have to bring in a interpreter, I'll give the order to the ministry for one—a first-rate fellow equally skilled in both languages, so that he can convey to them what I say very precisely, without smoothing it over or crudely coarsening it. As for what they have to say, big Ruben for instance—ah, Ruben, my God, he was at the empty hole, he wanted to rescue me, I know that from the watchman, I don't think I've told you about that, I'll have to tell you some other time—but as for what they say, I shall understand that well enough, but don't dare let them notice that I understand, carelessly responding at once, for example, instead of waiting until that tedious fussbudget between us has translated for me."

"Once you've taken your place, Adôn, you'll do fine. And then I would suggest that you act as if you take them for spies trying to scout out the weaknesses of the land."

"I beg you, Mai, spare yourself such suggestions. How does it happen that suddenly you gaze at me with kind, round eyes and offer suggestions?"

"I thought I was supposed to offer them, my lord."

"I originally thought so myself, my friend. But now I realize that in this high and festive matter no one can or ought to advise me, but that I must shape it all on my own, just as my heart tells me. Think of how you adorn your story of the three loves in a most gratifying and exciting way, and then let me adorn mine as well. How do you know I might not have come up with the idea of pretending to think they were spies all on my own?"

"Then we both came up with the same idea."

"Of course, because it is the only right one and might as well already be written down. This whole story has already been written, Mai, in God's book, and we shall read it together amid laughter and tears. For you do intend to be part of it yourself, don't you? To join me at the office when they arrive, tomorrow or the day after, and are brought before me in the Hall of the Provider, whose walls are filled with Hapi's image? You are part of my entourage, of course. I must have a grand entourage for the reception. . . . Ah, Mai," the man who had been raised up so high now exclaimed, covering his face with his hands, the same hands that that whelp Benoni had once watched weave a wreath of myrtle in the grove of the god and one of which now bore Pharaoh's ring of sky blue lapis that read "Be as I am"—"I shall see them, my family, my own, for they were always that, no matter how bad things were between us for a while, for which we all share the blame. I shall speak with them, with the sons of Jacob, my brothers, I shall hear whether my father is still alive, before whom I had to remain silent in death for so long, and whether he can still hear that I am alive and that God has accepted the animal in place of the son. I shall hear it all and learn from them—how Benjamin lives and whether they have treated him as a brother. And they shall have to bring him to me, and Father as well. Oh, my good taskmaster, who is now my steward, it is all too exciting and festive. And the feast is to be observed with every high delight and amusement. For high delight, my friend, and the subtle jest are the best that God gave us, and the profoundest knowledge we have of this complicated, equivocal life. God gave it to our spirits so that we might make this stern life laugh. That my brothers mutilated me and threw me into the pit and that they shall now be standing before me—that is life. And life is also the question of whether one should judge the deed by its consequences and so call what is evil good, because it was necessary for a good result. Those are the questions that life poses. One cannot answer them with a long face. The human spirit can rise above them only in serene delight, so that in its own profound amusement over what is unanswerable, it may move God Himself, the great unanswering God, to laughter."

The Interrogation

When he sat in his chair on a raised dais in the Hall of the Provider—flanked to the right and left by lance-bearers of the office guard standing at attention and surrounded by the chief scribes of the ministry, extraordinarily haughty magistrates—sat there beneath white ostrich fans thrust into embossed gold shields and held over him by aproned lads with pageboy haircuts, Joseph was indeed "as Pharaoh." Two double rows of elaborately inscribed orange columns with white bases and green lotus capitals stretched ahead of him toward distant entrance doors with enameled lintels; and above the frieze running along the base of the high sidewalls were depictions of Hapi, the Inundator, in human form but with sexual organs hidden, one breast male, the other female, the royal beard at his chin, marsh plants on his head, and a sacrificial tray with swamp blossoms and slender water jugs held on his upturned palms. Between the repeated images of the god, however, other scenes of life were portrayed in sweeping lines and cheerful colors dancing in the shafts of light that fell through the open stonework of the high windows: farmers sowing and threshing, Pharaoh himself plowing with oxen and cutting the first swath of golden grain with a sickle, as well as the seven cows of Osiris, plus the bull whose name he alone knew, all striding one after the other—each scene accompanied by splendidly arranged inscriptions, such as "Oh, that the Nile may bring me food and nourishment, each growing thing in its season."

This, then, was the hall of audience, where the Vice-Horus listened to those cries for seed grain and bread about which he reserved the decision for himself. And it was here he sat on the third day after his conversation with Mai-Sakhme, his steward—who now stood behind him, after having first prepared that foaming brew for him—and had just dealt with some pigtailed and bearded gentlemen in pointed shoes, a delegation from the land of the great King Murshili, that is from Hetti, where drought likewise reigned, and had treated them, as everyone noticed, in a very absentminded and offhand sort of way, dictating to his "true scribe" that these Hettite mayors be granted more wheat, spelt, rice, and sorghum at a lower price than they themselves had proposed. A few people assumed it was for reasons of state and that, who knew why, perhaps the moment had come on the world's political stage to pay attention to King Murshili; but others attributed it to a slight ailment of the Unique Friend, for he had explained at the start of the session that the dust had given him a catarrh and he now kept a handkerchief held to his mouth.

He gazed wide-eyed over it out into the hall as the Hettites departed and a group of Asiatic men who were next in line were led in: one of them towered above the others, one had the head of a melancholy lion, one was sturdy and vigorous, another had long nimble legs, two of them could not hide their rough combativeness, one shot fierce glances, another had noticeably moist eyes and lips, one was remarkable for his strikingly bony build, another for his curly hair, full beard, and the rich reds and blues of the purple dye in his garment. Each, then, had some distinguishing trait. Somewhere in the middle of the hall they decided it was time to kiss the floor, and the Unique Friend had to wait until they were on their feet again to signal with his fan for them to draw closer. They approached and fell on their faces again.

"So many?" he asked in a muffled voice, which, God knew why, he lowered almost to a growl. "Ten at once? Why not eleven then? Repeater, ask them why there aren't eleven of them, or for that matter twelve. Or do you men understand Egyptian?"

"Not as well as we would wish, my lord and our refuge," one of them replied in his own language, the one with legs for running, who evidently had a nimble tongue as well. "You are as Pharaoh. You are like the moon, the merciful father, who sweeps along in majestic robes. You, *moshel,* sovereign, are like a firstling bullock in his adornment. Our hearts unite in praise of him who keeps the market, the Provider of the Two Lands, the Food of the World, without whom no one would have breath, and we wish him as many years of life as the year has days. But, begging your pardon, Adôn, your servants do not understand your tongue sufficiently to engage in commerce in it."

"You are as Pharaoh," they repeated in chorus.

While the interpreter quickly translated Naphtali's statement in a businesslike monotone, Joseph's eyes devoured the men standing before him. He recognized them all, had little difficulty telling one from the other, despite what time may have done to them. There was big Ruben, his hair already completely gray, his legs like columns, the strong muscles of his face drawn in a surly scowl. O God of dispensations, they were all here, every one, this starved wolf pack that in its hatred had pounced upon him crying "Off! Off!," no matter how hard he begged "Don't rip it!," the same enraged men who had dragged him to his grave with a heigh! and a ho!, despite his uncomprehending cry to them, to himself, to heaven: "Oh, oh, what's happening to me!," who had sold him as Hey There the kennel boy to the Ishmaelites for twenty pieces of silver and had dragged the tatters of his garment through a slaughtered kid's blood before his eyes. They were here, his brothers in Jacob, reemerging out of time—his murderers because of dreams, led to him here by dreams, and all of it like a dream. Here were the six sons of the red-eyed wife, and the four of the handmaidens: Bilhah's adder and her gossipmonger, Zilpah's stout firstborn in his battle coat, outspoken Gad, and his sweet-toothed brother. He was the youngest, except for Issakhar, the beast of burden, and pitch-stained Zebulun—and he too had wrinkles and creases in his face and a great deal of silver in his beard and smooth, oiled hair. Eternal God, how old they had all become. How moving it all was—just as life is moving. But he was shocked by the sight, too, for if they were this old it was almost unthinkable that their father might still be alive.

With a heart full of laughing and weeping and anxiety, he gazed at them and recognized them all under their beards, which some of them had not even had in his day. But they, gazing at him in return, did not even think of recognizing him, and their eyes, though seeing, were blind to the possibility that it could be he. They had once sold a shameless blood brother into the world, to the far horizon, to foreign lands lost in mist—they had always known that, they knew it now. But this elegant heathen here on his throne beneath those fans, dressed in pure white, against which the deep brown of his brow and arms stood out in a very Egyptian way—this ruler of the state and keeper of the market here, to whom they had come in their need, this man with his necklace of royal favor, an incredible work of the goldsmith's art, in which was set a large brooch of equal craftsmanship, a design of perfect taste combining falcons, sun beetles, and crosses of life—this man here with his fancy flyswatter, an ornamental silver mace in his sash, and an elaborate headscarf whose stiff wings fell to his shoulders as was the peculiar fashion here—that this could be the Dreamer of Dreams, the brother they had got rid of and whom their father had finally ceased to mourn, that life-giving idea was closed and barred, concealed from them. And that the man constantly held his handkerchief before his mouth and chin certainly could not alter the fact.

He now spoke again, and whenever he paused the interpreter beside him would echo him, rattling off in a Canaanite monotone what he had said.

"Whether commerce is to be engaged in here and a delivery arranged," he said ill-temperedly, "remains to be seen and is unresolved—quite possibly it may resolve itself very differently. That you do not speak the language of human beings is the least of the difficulties. I feel sorry for you, by the way, if you expected you would be able to converse with Pharaoh's Supreme Mouth in your local gibberish. A man such as I speaks Babel's language, he also speaks Chetite, but is loath to deal with Habiritic or any such *aulasaukaula*, and if he ever did know it he would hasten to forget it."

Pause and translation.

"You stare at me," he continued without waiting for an answer, "you regard me in the indiscreet manner of barbarians and silently take note that I am protecting myself with a cloth, from which you privately conclude that I am probably not feeling well. That is cor-

rect, I am slightly ill—but what reason is that for staring, for reconnoitering, and drawing conclusions? I have caught a catarrh from the
dust—even a man such as I is not immune to these things. My physicians will cure me. Medical knowledge is well advanced in the land
of Egypt. My own steward, the overseer of my private palace, is a
physician himself. So you can see that he will cure me. But to those
people—however remote they may be from me—who have been
forced to embark on a journey, indeed a journey through the desert,
under these abnormal and foul weather conditions, my heart responds with sympathy and concern, given what they must have endured in their travels. From where do you come?"

"From Hebron, great Adôn, from Kiriath-Arba, the Fourfold
City, and from the terebinths of Mamre in the land of Canaan, in
order to buy food in the land of Egypt. We are all . . ."

"Stop! Who speaks there? Who is the little fellow with the shiny
lips speaking there? Why does he speak and not, for example, that
tower of a man there—for he is indeed built like a tower in a pasture—who appears to me to be the oldest and wisest of your crew?"

"By your leave, my lord, it is Asher who answers. Asher is your
servant's name, one brother among brothers. For we are all brothers
and sons of one man, united by fraternal bonds, and when a matter
concerns us as a whole and we are together, it is customarily Asher,
your obedient servant, who states our cause."

"So, you are the group chatterbox and platitudinarian. Fine. But
in taking a good look at you, my keen eye has not failed to note that,
despite your fraternal bonds, you are clearly different people, that
this one belongs with that, but others have something else in common. The group spokesman, who responds to our questions, appears to resemble the fellow there in the short coat, to which plates
of brass have been sewn, and that man there, with the eyes of a serpent, has a certain something in common with the man next to him,
who keeps shifting from one lean leg to the other. But still others can
be grouped by the fact that their eyelids are all red and inflamed."

It was Re'uben who took it upon himself to reply.

"Truly, you see all things, my lord," Joseph heard him say. "Let
me explain. The similarities and disparities among us come from our
having different mothers, four of us from two and six from one. But
we are all sons of one man, of Jacob, your servant, who sired us and
has sent us to you to buy food."

"He sent you to me?" Joseph repeated, pushing his handkerchief up to cover his entire face. Then he peered out over it again.

"My man, you surprise me by the thinness of the voice that comes from a body built like a tower, but I am even more astonished by the content of your words. Time has silvered the hair and beards of you all, and the eldest who wears no beard is all the more frosted on top. You get tangled up in your own words, which I do not find credible, for you do not appear to me to be men whose father is still alive."

"By the light of your countenance, he lives, my lord," Judah now said. "Allow me to confirm my brother's word. We deal in truth. Our father, your servant, lives in high estate and is not all that old, eighty years in all or perhaps closer to ninety, which is nothing special in our tribe. For our great-grandfather was a hundred years old when by his true and genuine wife he sired a son, who sired our father."

"What barbarism!" Joseph said, his voice breaking. He looked around for his steward, but then turned back and said not a word for a while, so that everyone grew uneasy.

"You could," he said at last, "be more precise and avoid digressing into nonessentials when answering my questions. What I asked you was how you withstood the adverse conditions of your journey, whether you suffered greatly from the drought, whether your water held out, whether you were attacked by a pack of robbers or a dust Abubu, whether anyone suffered heatstroke—that is what I wanted to know."

"We managed tolerably, Adôn, and we thank you for your kind inquiry. Our caravan was secure against robbers, we were well supplied with water, we lost scarcely an ass and all remained healthy. A moderately unpleasant dust Abubu was all that we had to endure."

"All the better. My inquiry was not kind, it was purely objective. There is certainly nothing unusual about a journey such as yours. There is a great deal of travel in this world; journeys of seventeen days, even seven times seventeen, are quite routine and must be accomplished step by step, for it is hardly likely that the earth will leap up to greet one. Merchants from Gilead travel the road that leads from Beizan by way of Yenin through the valley of—wait, I did know that, yes, I recall it now—through the valley of Dothan, where they then join the great caravan road from Damashki to Lejun and

Ramleh and the harbor at Khazati. You had it easier. You came from Hebron down to Gaza, and then proceeded, I presume, quite simply along the coast to this land?"

"As you say, *moshel*. You know everything."

"I know a great deal. Partly as a result of a naturally keen mind, partly by other means at the command of a man such as myself. In Gaza, however, where I presume you joined your caravan, the worst part of the journey began. One must survive a city of iron and a cursed seabed covered with skeletons."

"We did not look at them and God brought us through that horror."

"I am glad to hear that. Did a pillar of fire also lead you perhaps?"

"It went before us part of the way. It collapsed, and then came the moderately unpleasant dust Abubu."

"You apparently do not wish to boast of its terrors. It could easily have proved fatal. It concerns me that travelers are subjected to such atrocities on their journey down to Egypt. I say that strictly as an objective observation. And so you probably considered yourself fortunate when you came into the territory of our bastions and watchtowers?"

"We exclaimed our good fortune aloud and thanked the Lord for sparing us."

"Were you frightened by the fortress of Zel and its armed hosts?"

"We were frightened of it in that we stood in awe of it."

"And what happened to you there?"

"We were not prevented from passing through, since we declared that we had come as buyers of grain, which we wished to take from this great granary so that our wives and children might live and not die. But we were set apart from the others."

"That is what I wanted to hear. Are you surprised at this measure taken for setting you apart? Presumably you had never witnessed such a measure taken before, let alone that you should be the cause of it? In any case they kept the lot of you intact and at full count, all ten, if one can say that ten is full count—but none of you was set apart again, you simply parted ways with the other new arrivals?"

"So it was, my lord. We were told we would not be permitted to use our money to buy bread anywhere else in the land except at Mempi, the balance scale of the Two Lands, and from you personally, the Lord of Food, the Friend of the God's Harvest."

"Correct. You were guided on your way? You had a good journey from the border down to the city of the wrapped god?"

"A very good one, Adôn. They kept an eye on us. Men who came and then disappeared again directed us and our animals to inns and places of rest, and if we attempted to pay come morning, the landlord would not hear of it."

"Free board and room are given two sorts of people: the honored guest and the prisoner. How do you like the land of Egypt?"

"It is a wondrous land, great vizier. Its power and splendor are like those of Nimrod, it is magnificent in both ornament and form, whether towering or spread wide. Its temples are overwhelming, and its tombs touch the sky. Our eyes often welled with tears."

"Not to the point, I would hope, that you neglected your task and mission, so that it prevented you from spying, from reconnoitering and drawing secret conclusions."

"What you say, my lord, is dark to us."

"So you pretend not to know why you were set apart from the other new arrivals, why an eye has been kept on you and you were brought before my countenance?"

"We would love to know it, your grace, but we do not."

"You put on faces as if you hadn't the vaguest—yet does your conscience not whisper to you that you stand suspect, that a suspicion has come to rest upon you, so heavy and dark that it is already more than a suspicion, that your villainy lies open before our eyes?"

"What are you saying, my lord! You are as Pharaoh. What suspicion?"

"That you are spies!" Joseph exclaimed, slamming a hand on the arm of his lion-pawed chair and standing up. He had used the Akkadian word for spy, *daialu*, a very insulting word, and now stood waving his flyswatter in their faces.

"*Daialu*," the interpreter echoed in a hollow voice.

As *one* man, they recoiled, thunderstruck, horrified.

"What are you saying!" they repeated in a chorus of murmurs.

"What I said is what I said! You are spies, come to see the weakness of the land, which it keeps secret, that you may discover it and find an opening by which to invade and plunder. That is my conviction. If you can refute it, do so."

Ruben spoke now, since the others were nodding eagerly in unison for him to vindicate them. He slowly shook his head and said, "What, my lord, is there to refute? It would be a waste of words—except it is you who have said this, otherwise it could simply be dismissed with a shrug. Even great men can err. Your suspicion is mistaken. We do not lower our eyes before it, but as you can see, we all look back freely and honestly at you, indeed even in polite reproach that you can so misjudge us. For we recognize you in your greatness, but you do not recognize us in our honesty. Look upon us and let your eyes be opened at the sight of us. We are all the sons of one man, an excellent man, in the land of Canaan, a king of flocks and friend of God. We deal in truth. We arrived along with the other new arrivals to buy food in exchange for good rings of silver that you may weigh upon exacting scales, food for our wives and children. That is what we desire. By the God of gods, your servants have never been *daialu*."

"Oh but you are!" Joseph answered and stamped his sandaled foot. "If a man such as I sets it into his head, it remains so. You have come to discover the nakedness of the land, so that it may be harmed with a stroke of the sickle. It is my conviction that you ten have been sent on this mission by the evil kings of the East, and it rests upon you to refute it. But far from having weakened my conviction, this tower here has instead simply made the vacuous claim that it is not so. That is no vindication to satisfy a man such as I."

"But, my lord, consider in your mercy," one of them said, "that it rests more upon you to prove such an indictment, than upon us to refute it."

"Who is it that speaks so subtly there from your midst and gazes so fiercely? I've been aware for some time now of your serpent's eyes. What is your name?"

"Dan, by your leave, Adôn. I am called Dan, born of a handmaid on her mistress's knees."

"My pleasure. And so, master Dan, to judge by the subtlety of your words, you fancy yourself to be a judge, and in your own cause no less, is that right? But here it is I who establishes justice, and he who is under suspicion must exculpate himself before me. Do you denizens of the sand and sons of wretchedness have any idea of the vulnerable opulence of this highly refined land over which I have been set and for whose well-being I am answerable to the god's son in his palace? It is under constant threat from the wanton greed of desert brutes who spy to discover its weakness—Bedu, Mentiu, Antiu, and Peztiu. Are the Habiru then to run riot here as they have from time to time out in Pharaoh's provinces? I know of cities that they have fallen upon like madmen and strangled people in their fury and maimed oxen for barbarian sport. You see, I know more than you thought I did. Two or three of you, though I shall not say all, certainly look to me as if they were perfectly capable of such tricks. And I am supposed to believe you simply at your word that you intend no evil and have no designs on the secrets of this land?"

Shifting and jostling, they took counsel with excited gestures. In the end it was Judah who was given the nod to reply and espouse their cause. He did it with the dignity of a man who has been tested.

"My lord," he said, "let me speak before you and present to you our circumstances in accordance with the exact truth, that you may recognize that we deal in truth. Behold, we, your servants, are twelve brothers, all sons of one man in the land of . . ."

"Stop! How is that?" cried Joseph, who had sat back down, but here almost sprang to his feet again. "Now you are twelve all of a sudden? So you were not dealing with truth when you claimed to be ten?"

". . . in the land of Canaan," Judah completed his statement firmly, with an expression that verged on saying it was impolite and overhasty to interrupt him now that he was about to tell everything and make a clean breast of it. "We, your servants, are twelve sons, or rather we were—we have never pretended that as we stand here before your eyes we are at full count, but simply stated that we ten were all sons of one man. We are twelve by birth, but our youngest brother, born to none of our mothers, but rather to a fourth, who has been dead for as many years as he has known life, remained behind with our father, and one of us is no more."

"What does that mean, 'is no more'?"

"He got lost, my lord, at an early age, lost beyond the reach of our father's and our hand. He got lost in the world."

"He must have been quite an adventurous fellow. But what concern is he to me? The little one, however, your youngest brother, has not been lost? Your hand has not—he is not beyond your reach but still at hand?"

"He is at home, my lord, always at home at our father's right hand."

"By which I am to conclude that this aged father of yours is alive and well?"

"By your leave, Adôn, you asked that question once before, and we said yes."

"Certainly not! It may be that I previously inquired whether your father was alive, but this is the first time that I have inquired whether he is well."

"Your servant, our father," Judah replied, "is very well given the circumstances. These, however, have been very difficult for a year and a day in the world out there, as my lord knows. For since heaven has denied us the blessing of water once and now twice, the scarcity has grown worse with time, oppressing us as it oppresses every land. And to speak of scarcity is to mitigate the evil, for no grain is to be had, not at any price, neither for seed nor for food. Our father is rich, he lives in very comfortable style . . ."

"To what extent rich and comfortable? Does he have a family tomb, for example?"

"As you say, my lord. Machpelah, the double cave. Our forebears lie at rest there."

"Does he live in such style, for example, that he has an eldest servant, a house steward, such as I have, who is likewise a physician?"

"So it is, your grace. He had a wise chief servant of much experience, Eliezer by name. Sheol covers him; he bowed his head and died. But he left behind two sons, Damasek and Elinos, and the elder, Damasek has assumed the deceased steward's place. He is now called Eliezer."

"You don't say," Joseph responded. "You don't say." And for a while his gaze grew hazy as he stared vacantly over their heads out into the great hall.

"But why, man with the lion's head, have you interrupted your attempt to vindicate your cause?" he then asked. "Do you have nothing more to add?"

Judah gave a forbearing smile. He did not say outright that it was not he who was constantly interrupting.

"It was and is your servant's intent," he replied, "faithfully to present to you, my lord, both our circumstances and the events of our journey in a coherent fashion, that you may see we deal in the truth. Our house is countless—and if not exactly like the sand upon the seashore, great in number nonetheless. There are close to seventy of us, for we are all heads of families under our father's head, all are married and have been blessed with . . ."

"All ten of you are married?"

"All eleven, my lord, and blessed with . . ."

"What, even your youngest is the married head of a family?"

"Just as you say, my lord. He has eight children by his two wives."

"That's impossible!" Joseph cried without waiting for a translation, then burst into loud laughter and slapped his hand on the arm of his lion chair. And the Egyptian officials behind him laughed along obsequiously. The brothers broke into anxious smiles. Mai-Sakhme, his steward, gave him a secret poke from behind.

"You nodded," Joseph said, drying his eyes, "which led me to believe that your youngest is also married and a father. That is indeed splendid. I laugh simply because it is so splendid—enough to make a man laugh. For one tends to picture a youngest son as a mere whelp, a tot of a fellow, not, however, as a husband and head of a family. It was that picture that aroused my laughter, which as you see has quickly come to an end. This matter is far too serious and suspicious for laughter. And I find it an ominous sign, man with the lion's head, that you once again hesitate in your defense."

"By your leave," Judah replied, "I shall continue it without hesitation and in coherent fashion. For the scarcity—which, given its horrors, one would do better to call a famine, for there is nothing left even to be scarce—this calamity oppressed our land, our flocks perished and our ears had to listen to our children's cries for bread, which, my lord, is the most bitter and intolerable sound a man can ever hear, except perhaps for the complaints of a holy old man deprived of daily needs and the dignity of accustomed comfort; for we heard our father say that it would not take much for his lamp to go out, leaving him to sleep in the dark."

"Outrageous," Joseph said. "That is a scandal, if not to say an abomination. Have you let it come to that? No precaution, no anticipation, no measures taken in advance to counter this affliction that is part of the world and can always assume a presence in it? No powers of imagination, no fear and no supplies in reserve? Living from day to day like innocent beasts and aware of nothing more than what is happening at the moment, until finally your father must do without his accustomed comfort in his old age? Shame on you! Have you no learning, no stories? Do you not know that under certain circumstances all sprouting lies in fetters and all blossoming in chains, for the fields bear only salt and no herb comes forth, and indeed no grain grows? That life is then frozen in sadness, and the bull no longer covers the cow, nor the ass its jenny? Have you never heard of the waters that flooded the earth and drowned it, which only the clever man survived by making himself an ark that he might float upon the primal flood that had now returned? Must all that, which had merely been turned aside, first come to pass and become the present before you take care, leaving worthiest old age to do without oil for its lamp?"

They hung their heads.

"Go on," he said. "let the one who was speaking go on. But I do not wish to hear anything further about how your father is sleeping in the dark."

"It is but a figure of speech, Adonai, and simply means that he too is afflicted by the calamity and has no sacrificial cakes. We saw many gird themselves to set out for this land that they might buy from Pharaoh's storehouses and bring home food, for only in Egypt is there grain and a market. But for a long time we did not want to come to our father with a proposal that we too should gird ourselves and come down here to do business and buy."

"Why did you not want to do it?"

"He has his own mind at his age, my lord, and preconceived notions about things, including about the land of your gods—he is obstinate in this thinking about Mizraim and has one or two prejudices as regards its customs."

"One must wink an eye at such things, but not so that he notices."

"He would probably not have permitted us to come down here if we had asked him. Therefore we thought the wiser course was to wait until need brought him to the idea himself."

"One ought perhaps not take counsel that way about one's father, either, and deal deviously with him, for it has all the appearance of toying with him."

"We had no choice. And we could also see his sidelong glances and how he would hold his mouth half open to speak, but then close it again. Finally he said to us, 'Why do you look at one another and gaze in all directions? Behold, I have heard, the rumor has found its way to me, that in the land below grain is to be had cheap and there is a market for it there. So up, don't sit there on your backsides while we perish! Draw lots for one or two of you, and whoever draws the lot, be it Shimeon or Dan, let him gird himself and journey down with the other travelers and buy food for your wives and children, that we may live and not die.' 'Fine,' we brothers replied to him, 'but it will not do for just two to go, for there will be questions as to need. We must all go and present ourselves at full count so that the children of Egypt will recognize that we need grain not by the ephah but by the homer.' He said, 'Then let ten of you go!' 'It would be better,' we responded, 'if we all went and showed that we are eleven households within your house, otherwise we shall be shorted in our delivery.' But he answered, saying, 'Have you lost your minds? I see that you want to leave me childless. Do you not know that Benjamin must remain at home and at my right hand? Just imagine if an accident were to happen to him on the journey? Ten of you shall go, or we shall sleep in the dark.' And so we departed."

"Is this your vindication?" Joseph asked.

"My lord," Judah replied, "if my faithful testimony does not outweigh your suspicion and you do not recognize that we are harmless people who deal in the truth, then we must despair of any vindication."

"I fear it will come to that," Joseph said. "For as to your harmlessness, I have my own ideas about that. But as regards the suspicion under which you now stand and my as yet unshakable charge that you are spies and nothing else—fine, I shall now test you. I should, so you say, recognize from the faithfulness of your deposition that you deal in truth and are not rogues. I say, fine! Produce this youngest brother of whom you speak. Place him here before my countenance that I may see and by observation convince myself that these details are correct and that one may rely on the particularities of your story—then I can begin to doubt my suspicions and slowly waver in making my charge. But if you do not, then by the life of Pharaoh—and one hopes that you know no higher oath can be sworn in our land—not only will there be no delivery, whether by the ephah or the homer, but it will also be proved for good and all that you are *daialu,* and you should have considered how such people are dealt with before taking up the profession."

Their faces had turned pale and splotched, and they stood there helpless.

"You wish, my lord," they had the interpreter ask, "for us to make the journey home, of nine or seventeen days—for the earth does not leap up to greet us—and return here again before your countenance with our youngest brother?"

"Now wouldn't that be nice?" he riposted. "No, most decidedly not! Do you suppose a man such as I would let a band of spies like you simply go its way? You are prisoners. I shall set you apart in separate chambers of this building and keep you there for three days, by which I mean today, tomorrow, and part of the day after. Until then you may choose one of your number by lot or agreement who shall make the journey and fetch the lad to be tested. The others, however, will remain prisoner, until he is placed before me, for by the life of Pharaoh, you shall not see my face again without him."

They looked at their feet and chewed their lips.

"My lord," said the eldest, "what you have commanded is practicable until the moment when the messenger arrives at home again and tells our father that before food can be delivered, we shall have to bring our youngest brother here. You cannot know how that will be received, for our father is very much of his own mind and most especially in the matter of our little brother's staying at home and never traveling. You see, he is the nestling and the pet . . ."

"But that is simply absurd!" Joseph cried. "Upon calm reflection, one must conclude that he has long since ceased having to play nestling and is no longer a whelp, even if the youngest. That is a prejudice one should cease to coddle. If one's elder brothers are already well on in years, then one can be ten times the youngest and still a man in the prime of life capable of traveling. Do you believe your father will leave you here as captive spies rather than allow your youngest brother to make a journey for your sake?"

They discussed this for a while, exchanging glances and shrugs, and finally Ruben replied, "We think it possible, my lord."

"Well then," Joseph said, taking to his feet, "I do *not* think it possible. No one can slip that over on a man such as I. And as for my words, they stand. Place your youngest brother before me, that is my unyielding demand of you. For by the life of Pharaoh, if you do not, you will be convicted as spies."

He waved to the officer of the guards, who gave the order, and the lance-bearers stepped to the sides of the frightened men and led them out of the hall.

"It Is Required!"

They were not cast into prison, not banned to a hole, but simply confined to an out-of-the-way chamber to which a few steps descended and that with its blossom-headed pillars appeared to be an unused office or archive for old documents. It offered adequate room for ten men and had benches that ran all around it. For tent-dwelling shepherds, these quarters came close to being rather grand. That the openings for light were barred meant nothing really, since such apertures almost always have latticework of some sort. Granted, sentries were pacing back and forth outside the door.

Jacob's sons squatted on their heels to discuss matters. They had plenty of time—until the day after tomorrow, in fact—to choose the man who was to journey home and present their father with this outrageous demand. Which was why they first discussed their situation in general, the mess they had got themselves into—with worried faces they unanimously declared it very serious and threatening. By some demon of misfortune they had come under suspicion—yet no one knew how. They blamed one another for not having seen this calamity coming: they had been set apart at the border, ordered to appear in Menfe, a close eye was kept on them the entire journey—all of which, they now said, had been suspicious enough, suspicious in terms of their being under suspicion, even if it had all felt more cordial at the start. There was a general mixture of cordiality and danger here that they could make no sense of, that disturbed them and yet at the same time left them with a peculiar feeling of happiness beneath all the serious worry and vexation. They could make no sense of this man before whom they had stood and who nursed this wretched suspicion against such sterling men as themselves, leaving its refutation up to them—a banal, incredibly capricious suspicion from their perspective: that they, men of tenfold innocence and harmlessness in matters of business, had come as spies to discover the weakness of the land. But he had taken it into his head, and even beyond its being an extremely dangerous situation, a matter of life and death, this grieved the brothers in their very souls, for they liked this man, this great man of Egypt, this marketeer; and quite apart from their lives being at stake, it pained them that he should think such evil of them.

A striking man. One could call him handsome and beautiful, and it was scarcely going too far to compare him to a firstling bullock in its adornment. And he was cordial after his fashion. But that was just it, concentrated in his person was that same mixture of cordiality and peril that characterized their situation. He was *tâm,* the brothers were agreed in this description. He was ambiguous, a man of two faces, of both/and—both beautiful and powerful, reassuring and frightening, kind and dangerous. There was no making sense of him, just as one could not make sense of the nature of *tâm,* in which the worlds above and below meet. He could be sympathetic, and had been concerned about the rigors of their journey. He had thought it worth inquiring whether their father was both alive and well, and he had laughed aloud in the hall at their youngest brother's being married. But then, as if he had wanted only to lull them into a cordial feeling of security, he had cast in their faces the peculiarly arbitrary and life-threatening charge of spying and had ruthlessly taken them hostage until such time as they would bring him the eleventh of their number—as if that would provide any genuine exculpation. *Tâm*—there was no other word for it. A man of the solstice, of shifting qualities, who was at home both above and below. A man of business as well—and there is always a trace of thievery in commercial dealings, which fit right in with his ambiguity.

But what help were such remarks, what good did it do to complain that this attractive man was being so nasty to them? It did not change the mess they were in, a dilemma which each admitted to the other was more perilous than anything they had ever encountered. And the moment came when the unreasonable suspicion under which they stood met up with a different, but very reasonable suspicion of their own—that is, that it might have something to do with the suspicion under which they had grown accustomed to living at home. In short, that their ordeal was meant as retribution for former guilt.

It would be a mistake, you see, to conclude on the basis of the texts that they first discussed this conjecture within Joseph's earshot during their second conversation with him. No, already here, in their confinement, it insisted on being spoken—and they spoke about Joseph. It was strange enough: the way was totally blocked for associations of even the vaguest sort between the person of this marketeer and their buried and sold brother—and yet they now spoke about their brother. This development was not purely moral; they did not first move from one to the other by way of suspicion leading to suspicion, from guilt to punishment. It was a matter of intimate contact.

In his composure Mai-Sakhme had surely been correct in saying that several steps lie between recognizing and knowing that one recognizes. One does not come into contact with a blood brother without recognizing it, especially if one has spilled that blood in the past. But acknowledging this is quite another matter. If someone were to claim that Jacob's sons had by this time already recognized their brother in this marketeer, he would be putting it very clumsily and would rightly meet with determined opposition—for what then would be the source of their boundless amazement once he revealed himself to them? They hadn't the vaguest! Which is to say, they hadn't any idea of why Joseph's image and their old guilt rose up in their souls in the wake of, or indeed during, their first contact with this attractively dangerous potentate.

This time it was not Asher who, in his sweet-toothed way, put into words the shared feelings that united them, but rather Judah, the man of conscience. The former decided he was not man enough for the task, the latter that it was his duty.

"Brothers in Jacob," he said, "we are in great peril. Strangers here, we have stepped into a snare, have fallen into a pit of implausible yet ruinous suspicion. If Israel refuses to give Benjamin to our messenger—which I fear he will do—then we are either dead men, who will be admitted into the house of torture and execution, as the children of Egypt put it, or sold into slavery, to build tombs or wash for gold at some horrible place, shall never see our children again, and the lash of the Egyptian house of bondage will leave its welts on our backs. How has this happened? Consider, brothers, why this has happened to us, and know God. For the God of our fathers is a God of vengeance, and has not forgotten us. Nor has He allowed us to forget, but He Himself forgets least of all. Why did He not snort in His rage back then, and instead let lifetimes pass, let the repast of chastisement grow cold, until He prepared this meal for us? That you must ask Him, not me. For we were boys when we did it and our brother himself was a little boy—this punishment is now meted out to very different people. But I tell you this: we share the guilt of what we did to our brother, for we saw the terror in his soul when he cried to us from below and we did not want to hear him. That is why this affliction has come over us now."

One and all they nodded their heads gravely, for he had spoken what each was thinking, and they muttered, "Shaddai, Yahu, Eloah."

Re'uben, however—his white-haired head between his fists, his face red with anguish, swollen veins standing out on his brow—erupted, saying, "Yes, yes, think of it, go ahead, mutter and sigh. Did I not tell you? Did I not tell you that day, when I warned you and said 'Do not lay violent hands on the boy!'? But you were the sort who did not want to hear. And so now you have it—his blood is required of us!"

Actually good Ruben had not expressed himself in quite those terms that day. All the same, he had prevented much, prevented them from shedding Joseph's blood, or spilling even more than had gushed when beauty was superficially wounded. And so it was not exactly correct to say that his blood was now required of them. Or did Ruben mean the blood of the goat kid that had to take the place of Joseph's blood before their father? In any case it seemed to the others as if he had warned them that day and prophesied requital for their deed, and they nodded some more and muttered, "True, true, it is required of us."

They were given food, very good food by the way—bread twists and beer, which accorded well with that mixture of cordiality and danger that reigned here, and they slept the night on the benches, which even came with neck supports for raising their heads. The next day their task was to choose the messenger whom this man demanded must return to fetch their youngest brother—and who would perhaps never come back if Jacob said no. It actually did take the whole day, for they did not want to leave the matter to the chance of lots, but preferred to call upon reason for so serious a question, which needed to be judged from various angles. Who among them did they think would have the most influence in persuading their father? Whom could they most easily do without here in their plight? Who was most indispensable to the tribe, who had to survive if the others perished? That all had to be settled, the various answers squared with one another, and by evening they were still not on the verge of a decision. Since those that had been cursed or semicursed could not be recommended, there was much that spoke for Judah. True, they would not have gladly let him go, but he might be the right man to win their father over, and that his tribe was indispensable, they all agreed as to that—with the exception, that is, of Judah himself, and that thwarted the decision. He shook his lion's head and said that he was a sinner and a slave, neither worthy nor willing to survive.

But whom, then, should they name, to whom should the finger point? To Dan for his subtlety? To Gaddiel for his vigor? To Asher, because he was happy to let his moist lips and tongue speak for them all—seeing as Zebulun and Issakhar themselves said that there was as good as nothing that spoke for them? But finally it had to come down to Naphtali, Bilhah's son: his instincts as a messenger demanded he take on the task, his runner's legs itched, his tongue ran ahead of him—except he did not appear spiritually important enough to his brothers, or to himself for that matter, to be suited for the role in other than a superficially mythical way. Which is why until the third morning the finger had still not been pointed clearly and decisively to any one of them; but in a pinch it would probably have remained directed at Naphtali had not their next audience revealed that they had racked their brains to no purpose, for the stern marketeer had decided on something else.

Once the reception ended, Joseph had no sooner dismissed his great men in order to be left alone with Mai-Sakhme, his steward, than, his face still flushed, he had pounced upon him and exultantly inquired, "Did you hear, Mai, did you hear that? He's still alive, Jacob is alive, he can still hear that I am alive and have not died, he can hear it—and Benjamin is a married man and has a troop of children!"

"That was a bad slip, Adôn, your laughing out loud right off, without a translation."

"Let's not think about that! I glossed over it. One cannot remain sober-minded every moment in such an exciting situation. But otherwise, how was it? How did I do? Did I manage passably well? Did I embellish God's story in proper fashion? Did I provide the festive details?"

"You managed it quite prettily, Adôn, as prettily as can be. But it was also a most gratifying task."

"Yes, gratifying. But what is not so gratifying is you yourself. You are imperturbable, the way you just make those round eyes of yours. When I stood up and accused them, was that not most impressive? I had prepared the way for it, one ought to have seen it coming, and yet it was impressive. And the way big Ruben said: 'We recognize you in your greatness, but you do not recognize us in our innocence'—was that not gold and silver?"

"You had nothing to do with his saying that, Adôn."

"But I had aimed at it! And on the whole I am responsible for all the details of this feast. No, Mai, you are ungrateful, and there is no arguing with you because there is no shocking you. But now *I* shall tell you something else, that I am not at all as satisfied as I seem, for I went about it very stupidly."

"How is that, Adôn? You pulled it off most charmingly."

"I was stupid about one crucial thing and noticed it myself the very next moment. But for now there's no correcting it. That I decided to keep nine of them hostage and send one on his way to fetch my little brother was downright inept of me and a far worse slip than bursting into laughter. That must be changed. What am I supposed to do with nine of them here, since I cannot advance God's cause so long as Benoni is not here? And yet I cannot even see them meanwhile, since I have banned them from my sight until they bring him before me. That is purest bungling. Are they to lie here helplessly as captives in their hole, when there is no bread at home and Father has no sacrificial cakes? No, it should be arranged just the opposite: one of them remains prisoner here as security, one of whom Father is less fond, let's say one of the twins—and just between us, they were the roughest of all in tearing me to pieces—but the others should return, taking home what is necessary to fend off hunger, which of course they shall have to pay for. If I were simply to give it to them it would be very suspicious. That they will leave the hostage in the lurch and admit they are all spies by sacrificing him and not returning with the youngest—I don't believe that for a moment."

"But all that can take a long time, my dear master. I foresee your father's not allowing that young husband to travel with them until the bread you sell them has been eaten and their lamp threatens to go out once more. You're taking time for your story."

"Yes, Mai, why shouldn't a man take his time for God's story, why not demand patience for its careful embellishment. And if it takes a whole year until they return with Benjamin, that won't be too long for me. For what is a year in this grand story. After all, I included you in it precisely because you are the soul of calmness and so that you would lend me your composure when I grow fidgety."

"I am happy to do it, Adôn. I am honored to be part of it. I can even guess in advance some of the things by which you plan to shape it. I am thinking that you intend to let them pay for the food that you will deliver to them, but before they depart secretly hide the silver in their fodder sacks, right on top, so that when they go to feed their animals they will discover the money they have paid—that will be a puzzling poke in the ribs."

Joseph looked at him with big eyes.

"Mai," he said, "that's excellent! That's silver and gold! You have guessed something there, reminded me of a detail that I surely would have come up with myself, for it's such a natural part of the story—though I almost passed over it. I never would have thought that someone who cannot be shocked could come up with such a wonderfully shocking idea."

"I would not be shocked, my lord; but they will."

"Yes, in a most puzzlingly foreboding sort of way. And they will sense that there is someone who regards them cordially, but who is toying with them. Take care that it's done carefully, it's as good as written. I charge you with the task: slip the money nicely into their fodder sacks, so that each will find it when they feed their animals and so be all the more obliged, quite apart from the hostage, to return. So now, until the day after tomorrow. We'll manage to live until then, when I shall tell them and make my correction. But a year and a day, a day and a year—what is that in this grand story?"

The Money in the Sacks

And on the third day the brothers were again standing before Joseph's throne in the Hall of the Provider—or rather, were lying, their foreheads pressed to the floor—and now stood up halfway to bend low with upraised palms and murmur in chorus, "You are as Pharaoh. Your servants are without blame before you."

"Yes, you are a sheaf of deaf ears of grain," he said, "and want to bribe me with your scraping and bending low. Interpreter, repeat for them what I have said they are—a sheaf of hollow ears of grain. By hollow, however, I mean the sham and whitewash that does not deceive me. For a man such as I is not blinded by politeness and bows, nor is my mistrust lulled to sleep by a curtsy. Until you have brought the lad to be examined—your youngest brother, of whom you speak—and placed him here before me, until then in my eyes you are rogues who do not fear God. But I fear Him. And so I shall tell you what has been decreed. I do not wish for your children to go hungry or your old father to sleep in the dark. You shall be delivered grain according to your number at the price that scarcity has set and the current market mercilessly dictates—for surely you did not think that I would give you the bread free of charge simply because you are whoever you are, the sons of one man and actually twelve in all. Those are no reasons for a man such as I not to exploit a business situation to the full, especially when he is in all probability dealing with spies. You are to be delivered grain for ten households, if you can match its weight in silver. But I shall allow only nine of you to take it home; one of you shall remain in his bonds as surety and lie in confinement here until you have returned and washed yourselves clean by presenting me with eleven sons, of the erstwhile twelve. And let him be surety whom I choose on the spur of the moment— let it be *him*."

And he pointed his fan at Shimeon, who gaped defiantly and pretended it made no difference to him.

He was bound, and while the soldiers knotted the ropes his brothers surrounded him and spoke to him. And this was when they came back to what they had spoken of before and said things not meant for Joseph's ears, but that he understood.

"Shimeon," they said, "take heart! So it is you—he wants you and you must bear it as the man you are, a stalwart man, a Lamech. We will do everything we can to return and free you. Take heart, you will not have things all too bad in the meantime, nothing that will exceed your considerable powers. The man is only half evil, for he is good in part and will not send you to the mines without trial and conviction. Do but recall—he had roast goose served to us even though we are his hostages. He is unpredictable, but not the worst sort, and perhaps you won't be kept in fetters the whole time, but even if you are, that's better than washing for gold. Nevertheless, you are truly to be pitied—you're the target of the man's moods, so what can you do? It could have been any one of us, and God knows we've all been hit hard, but at least you won't have to stand before Jacob and confess: 'We have forfeited one of your sons, and are supposed to take your youngest away'—you've been spared that. The whole thing is a visitation and an affliction, sent to us by the God of vengeance. For recall what Judah said when he spoke from the heart for all of us and reminded us how our brother once cried to us from the depths, yet we remained deaf to his sobs, begging us not to let father fall back in a faint. But you can't deny that the two of you, Levi and you, were especially vigorous that day, both when it came to thrashing and lowering into the pit."

And Ruben added, "Take heart, twin, your children will have food to eat. This has been served up to us all, because no one wanted to hear that day when I warned 'Do not lay hands on the boy!' But no, there was no holding you back, and when I came to the pit it was empty and the child was removed from the world. And now God is asking us, 'Where is your brother Abel?' "

Joseph heard this. He felt a tickle in his nose, he had to sniff a little from the pressure, and his eyes suddenly welled with tears, so that he turned to one side in his chair and Mai-Sakhme had to prod him—which was no immediate help. For when he turned back to them, he was still blinking and his nose was stuffy as he spoke.

"I will not ask of you," he said haltingly, "the highest price that scarcity demands and the current market allows for a bushel or an ass-load. You shall not say upon returning to your father that Pharaoh's friend fleeced you. You shall receive delivery of what you can carry and what your sacks can hold, I shall order it given you. I shall order wheat and barley for you. Would you like barley from Upper or Lower Egypt? I recommend that from the land of Uto the

Serpent, it is the better of the two. I further advise that you use the grain for bread and risk very little as seed. The drought may well continue—it will continue, and the grain would be wasted. Farewell! I bid you farewell as I would honest men, for you have not yet been convicted, though you are still gravely suspect. But if you do come before me as eleven, I shall believe you and not take you for eleven monsters of chaos, but as the eleven holy brothers of the zodiac— but where is the twelfth? The sun has hidden him. Shall it be so, my men? Bon voyage! You are a peculiar and suspect people. Take care on your journey as you depart, and even more so when you return. For now you bear only the food you need, which is precious enough, but when you return you will be bringing the youngest son. May the God of your fathers be your shield and your buckler. And do not forget the land of Egypt, where Usir was locked in the coffin and hacked to pieces, but became the first in the realm of the dead and brought light to the subterranean sheepcote."

And with that he left his seat of audience and departed from them under a canopy of fans. The nine, however, were led to one of the ministerial offices and given vouchers with a set price for each bushel, chaldron, or ass-load of grain, and when they fetched their animals from the courtyard of their inn—both those for riding and packing—sworn agents weighed their payment on scales, ten silver rings from each, in order to provide holy warrant that payment and official weights corresponded; and then pouring out of the hatches came wheat and barley with which they filled their sacks to bursting, large double sacks that bulged from the flanks of their slow-moving pack animals. The sacks for fodder, however, were hung at the front of their riding animals' saddles. So as not to lose any time they wanted to move out at once and cover at least some ground between Menfe and the border today yet, but first, while their animals waited in the courtyard, the officials prepared a free meal to strengthen them—joint of lamb and beer soup with raisins—and to top it off they were given food for the first few days' journey, nicely packed to keep it fresh. It was the custom, they were told, to include such supplies in the purchase price, for this was the land of Egypt, the land of the gods, a land that could afford to be generous.

It was Mai-Sakhme, the marketeer's steward, who told them this and who carefully watched over the entire distribution with round eyes beneath arched thick, black eyebrows. They were very taken by the man and his calm manner, especially since he consoled them in regard to Shimeon's fate, saying that in his opinion it would be relatively tolerable. His having been bound before their eyes had merely been more a token of his status as a hostage; presumably it would not continue. Except, of course, if they were to sneak off, leaving him in the lurch, and not reappear with their littlest brother within the year, then, to be sure, he, Mai, could not vouch for anything. For his master was a man who ruled as he pleased—cordial, true enough, but also ruthless when he took certain notions into his head. He considered it possible that Shimeon might come to a very unpleasant end if they did not fulfill the charge his master had laid upon them, and then their little host would be thinned by two—which certainly could not be their old father's intention.

"Oh no!" they said. And they would do everything they could. But it was hard to live between two such obstinate personages. No offense intended, but as for his master, he was *tâm*, a man of the solstice, with something divine about both his goodness and terribleness.

"You may well say that," he replied. "Have you eaten your fill? Then bon voyage! And remember what I have said."

And so they departed from the city, mainly in silence, for they were disheartened both by Shimeon's fate and by the problem of how they would tell their father that they had forfeited him and there was only one way to redeem him. But it was still a long way home to their father, and they talked as well. They remarked that they had enjoyed the Egyptian beer soup, that although they had met with adversity, it had been relatively easy to purchase food at a good price, which would please Jacob. They talked about the stocky steward and what a pleasantly phlegmatic man he was—not *tâm*, but out-and-out cordial, without any thorns. But who knew how he would behave if he were not simply the eldest servant, but himself master and marketeer. Simple people are subject to fewer temptations and find it easier to be goodhearted, for greatness and unlimited power are almost by definition moody and unpredictable—indeed, there was the example of the Most Mighty, whose enormity was often difficult to understand. The *moshel*, by the way, had been almost out-and-out cordial himself today, except for having made a fettered hostage of Shimeon. He had given them advice, blessed them, and compared them in an almost solemn way with the beasts of the zodiac, one of which was hidden. He knew his stars, more than likely, could even read and interpret them perhaps. He had dropped a hint that he did not lack for higher means to enhance his keen mind. It would not surprise them if he was an astrologer. But if the stars had persuaded him that they were spies, then he had read serious nonsense in them.

They conversed about these and similar things and before day's end had made good progress on the road to the Bitter Lakes. But as dusk fell they chose a spot to rest for the night, a pretty and inviting spot, half enclosed by a clayey crag from which a palm tree jutted out on a slant and then grew upright. There was a well there, likewise a shed for shelter, and the black earth before it attested to fire having been made here, to this being a place used occasionally as a campsite. Since this spot will play a further role in our story, we shall mark it by its palm tree, well, and shed. The nine made themselves comfortable. They unloaded the asses and laid the packs together. Others drew water and stacked kindling for a fire. One of them, however, Issakhar, busied himself at once with feeding his animals, for since he was often called a raw-boned ass, he felt a special sympathy for these creatures, and the animal he was riding had already let out several plaintive, labored brays for its dinner.

Leah's son opens his fodder sack and lets out a loud cry.

"Hey!" he calls. "Look! Look what's happened to me! Brothers in Jacob, come here, and see what I've found."

They come from all sides, stretch their necks, and look. What Issakhar has found in his fodder sack, right on top, is money: ten silver rings, the purchase price for his share of grain.

They stand there amazed, shake their heads, make signs to ward off evil.

"Yes, bony brother, what has happened to you?"

Suddenly they scatter, each to his own fodder sack. Each searches, but with no real need to search: the money he spent for grain lies on top.

They sat down on the ground, each man right where he had been standing. What was this? Their payment had been in holy accord with the stone weights—and here it was theirs again. It was incomprehensible—enough to make one's heart fail. What in the world could it mean? Finding one's money next to the wares it bought is a source of pleasure, even of laughter, but it is uncanny as well, in fact primarily uncanny if one already stands accused—it's a suspicious kind of pleasure, suspicious in both directions, both in terms of the intention behind it and one's own intentions, which are then cast in an even worse light. And so it had something both amusing and malevolent about it—who could make any sense of it and who would venture to say why God had done this to them?

"Do you know why God has done this to us?" big Ruben asked, nodding at them, the muscles of his face drawn taut.

They knew very well what he meant. He was referring to the old story, was adding this perplexing find to the threads of misfortune coiling around them now because, despite his warning (had he actually warned them?) they had laid hands on the boy. They understood because their own vague misgivings spoke of more or less the same connection. Simply having brought God into the matter and asking one another why He had done this was proof that they were playing with the same thoughts. But it seemed to them that the thought itself sufficed, that Ruben needn't have nodded like that as well. This incident would make it more difficult than ever to come before their father—here was one more confession to make. Shimeon, Benjamin, and now this bizarre event—they would not exactly be returning home with heads held high. Grain for nothing—that might give Jacob something to chuckle about, but it would also seriously offend his sense of honor in business, and even in his eyes they would now be cast in a rather bizarre light.

At one point they all leapt up together to run to their asses—they would take the money back at once. Then, all together again, they decided against it, went slack, gave up, and sat back down. "It makes no sense," they said, by which they meant that there was as little sense, perhaps even less, in their returning the money as there was in its having been returned to them.

They shook their heads. And went on shaking them in their sleep, first one, then another, and occasionally several at the same time. They sighed in their sleep—there was probably not one of them who did not unconsciously heave two or three great sighs that night. Now and then, moreover, a smile would play across the lips of one slumbering face or the other—in fact, it even happened that several of them smiled happily in concert.

Less Than Full Number

Good news! Jacob heard the announcement that his sons had returned—they were approaching their father's tent with their pack animals, with asses trudging slowly beneath the weight of Mizraim's grain. Those who brought him the news had not noticed that there were only nine, instead of the ten who had departed. Nine is a large group, especially with all those asses; nine makes as respectable a show as ten; that there should be one more is something the moderately attentive eye does not even notice. Benjamin, who was standing beside his father before the tent of felt—and the old man held the hand of Mahalia and Arbath's husband as if he were a little boy—did not notice either; he saw neither nine nor ten, but simply his brothers returning in imposing numbers. Only Jacob realized it at once.

Amazing—the patriarch was approaching ninety, and one would no longer have expected anything like keen vision from his blinking brown eyes, dulled by age, with those soft, sagging pouches beneath them. And for unimportant things—and at his age what all has not become unimportant!—his eye was not keen. But the decrepitude of old age is far more a matter of the mind than of the body—the senses have seen and heard enough, let them grow dim. But there are things to which they can respond with the surprising acuity of the hunter, or the shepherd's making a swift count of his flock. And Jacob could see better than anyone else when it came to making a tally of Israel.

"There are only nine," he said with a resolute and yet slightly quavering voice and pointed in the distance. After a brief a pause he added, "Shimeon is missing."

"Right, Shimeon isn't with them," Benoni responded after searching for a bit. "I don't see him either. He's sure to follow soon."

"Let us hope," the old man said very resolutely and again grabbed the hand of his youngest. And that is how he waited for them to approach.

He did not smile at them, said not a word of greeting. He simply asked, "Where is Shimeon?"

There they had it. Yet again it was evidently his intention to make things as difficult as possible for them.

"More about Shimeon later," Judah responded. "Greetings, Father. We'll speak of him in a moment, but just this much for now—

you need not worry about him. Behold, we have returned from our journey and are again with our lord and father."

"But not all of you," he said adamantly. "My greetings to you as well. But where is Shimeon?"

"Well, yes, he's been delayed somewhat," they replied, "and for the moment not yet at hand. It all has to do with our business transaction and the whims of that man there . . ."

"Have you sold my son for grain perhaps?" he asked.

"Certainly not. But we do bring grain, as our father can see, a great deal of grain, enough at least for a while—and very good grain, wheat and first-rate barley from Lower Egypt, and you will have sacrificial cakes. That is the first thing we have to report."

"And the second?"

"The second may sound rather strange, one could almost say marvelous, or, if you like, even bizarre. But we thought it might please you all the same. We got all this good grain for nothing. Which is to say, not right off for nothing—we did pay for it, and our silver stood in holy accord with the weights of that land. But when we stopped for our first rest, Issakhar found what he had given in payment in his fodder sack, and behold, we all found our payment again, so that we have brought home the grain and the silver, which we assume will meet with your approval."

"Except that you have not brought my son Shimeon back to me. It seems more or less clear that you have traded him for common food."

"What can our lord be thinking—and for the second time now. We are not the sort of men for such business. Shall we not just sit down here so that we may calmly assure you concerning our brother—perhaps, however, we might first let you run some of this golden fruit through your fingers to test it and show you the money, how we have brought both gold and silver home."

"I wish to be informed about my son Shimeon at once," he said.

They sat down with him in a circle, along with Benjamin, and gave their account: How they had been set apart upon entering the land and ordered to proceed to Mempi, a great bustling city. How they had been led through rows of crouching human beasts and into the great palatial office, to a hall of overpowering beauty and before the chair of the man who was lord over that land and was as Pharaoh, that is, the marketeer to whom the whole world came—a strange man, spoiled by greatness, charming but peculiar. How they had bent low and bowed before this man, Pharaoh's Friend, the Provider, and had requested that he do business with them; how he had proved to be a man of two faces, friendly and fierce, speaking to them cordially in part, but then suddenly very roughly, and had claimed—one scarcely wanted to repeat it—that they were spies who had come to scout out the land's secret weakness. Ten upright men such as they! What a blow it had been to their hearts, for they had told him who in fact they were—had solemnly sworn that they were all the sons of *one* man, a friend of God in the land of Canaan, and actually not just ten, but an imposing twelve; how one of them had been lost early on, but that the youngest was still at home at his father's right hand. How that man there, the lord of the land, had not wanted to believe that their father was still alive merely because they themselves were no longer all that young—he had to be reassured twice as to that, for in the land of Egypt they apparently do not know a length of life such as that manifested by their dear lord and father, since evidently people there die early of their monkeylike excesses.

"Enough of that," he said. "Where is my son Shimeon?"

They were just coming to him, they answered, or would get to him very soon. But first, for better or worse, they had to speak of someone else, and it was too bad that he had not joined them on their journey, as had been their wish and suggestion; had that been the case, they would in all probability have returned at full count today, for they would have had with them the very witness that the suspicious man had demanded. Not for one moment had he let go of his whimsical notion that they were rogues and spies, or been willing to accept their solemn word concerning their impressive origins, but had demanded as proof of their innocence that they bring their youngest brother before him—if not, then they were spies.

Benjamin laughed.

"Take me to him!" he said. "I'm curious about this curious man."

"You will be silent, Benoni," Jacob rebuked him sternly, "and stop your childish babbling. Does a whelp like you take part in such counsels? I still have heard nothing about my son Shimeon."

"But you have," they said, "for if you wanted to, my lord, rather than forcing us to tell every painful detail, you would already know all that by now." For it was clear that given the suspicion they were under, given the demand stipulated, they could not have simply departed—and with grain to boot. They had had to offer some surety. The man had originally wanted to detain them all and send only one to arrange for their exculpation; but by their skills in the art of persuasion they had succeeded in changing the man's mind, so that he had detained only one, Shimeon, and let them depart for now with the food.

"And so your brother, my son Shimeon, has been sold for debt as a slave into the Egyptian house of bondage," Jacob said with menacing restraint.

The steward of that man in Egypt, they replied, a good, calm man, had assured them that the detainee would be comfortable enough given the circumstances and would lie in his fetters only temporarily.

"I now know," he said, "better than ever, why I hesitated to give you permission for this journey. You din my ears with your itch to go down to Egypt, and when I finally consent, you take advantage of my forbearance by returning at less than full number and leaving the best of you behind in the claws of this tyrant."

"You did not always speak so favorably of Shimeon."

"Lord of Heaven," he said, looking upward, "they accuse me of having neither a heart nor good intentions for Leah's second, that valiant hero. They act as if *I* had sold him for a measure of grain and cast him into the jaws of the leviathan for rations for their children— I and not they! How grateful I am to You that You at least strengthened my heart against their assault and made me strong against their mischief when they wanted to journey as eleven and take my youngest away as well. They would have been perfectly capable of returning to me without him and telling me 'You weren't really all that fond of him.'"

"Just the opposite, Father! If only all eleven of us had made the journey, if only we had had with us the youngest to have placed before the countenance of that man, the lord of that land, as he demanded, we would all have come back. But nothing has been lost, for we need only take Benjamin along and place him before the man, Pharaoh's marketeer, there in the Hall of the Provider, and Shimeon is free and you have both again, the child and the hero."

"In other words, since you have squandered away Shimeon, you now want to tear Benjamin from my hand as well and deliver him to where Shimeon is."

"We want to do it because of the whimsical notions of that man there, to exculpate ourselves and with our witness free the brother we left as surety."

"You have the hearts of wolves! You rob me of my children and all your thought is how to decimate Israel. Joseph is no more, Shimeon is no more, and now you want to take Benjamin away as well. You have made this bed and I am supposed to lie in it—and all this has come upon me."

"No, my lord, that is not a correct portrayal. Benjamin is not to be surrendered along with Shimeon, but both are to be returned to you if we place the youngest before the man and he realizes that we deal in truth. We humbly beseech you to let Benjamin journey with us, so that we may free Shimeon and Israel may again be at its full number."

"Full number? And where is Joseph? In plain words you demand of me that I should send this son here down that same path to join Joseph. Your wish is denied."

At this Ruben, the eldest, became exasperated and, churning like boiling water, he said, "Father, listen to me now! Listen to me alone, who stand at the head of all of us. You ought not give the boy to them for this journey, but to me alone. If I do not bring him back to you, may you do this to me and more. If I do not bring him back to you, you may strangle my two sons, Hanoch and Pallu. Strangle them, I say—before my eyes with your own hands, and I will not bat an eyelash—if I have not kept my word and redeemed what we left as surety."

"Yes, gush, gush away!" Jacob told him. "Where were you when the boar trampled my beautiful son, and did you perhaps know how to protect Joseph? What good are your sons to me, and am I the Destroyer that I should strangle them and decimate Israel with my own hands? I shall continue to deny any proposal that my son go down there with you, for his brother is dead, and only he is left to me. If harm should befall him on the way, the world would then behold how my gray hairs are brought down to the pit in sorrow."

They looked at one another, lips pressed tightly together. That certainly was lovely, the way he called Benjamin "his son," not their brother, and said that only he was left to him.

"And Shimeon, your hero?" they asked.

"I shall sit here alone," he answered, "and mourn for him. Begone!"

"Your children thank you for this discussion and dismissal," they said and left him. Benjamin went with them as well and patted the arm of one or two with his short-fingered hand.

"Do not let what he has said vex you," he begged, "and hold no bitterness against his worthy soul. Do you suppose I am flattered and take pride in his calling me the only one left to him and in his having refused to allow me to go with you? I know only too well that he has never forgotten that Rachel died giving me life, and it is a sad sort of protection under which I live. Think how long it took until he could bring himself to let you make your journey without me—by which you can see how precious you are to him. And now it will take but a little while until he yields and sends me with you down to that man, for he will not, he cannot, leave our brother in heathen hands. And besides, how long do you suppose the food will last that you were so clever to get for nothing. So be comforted. Little as I am, I shall make my journey yet. But now tell me more about that marketeer there, that stern man who accused you so roughly and made the whimsical demand to see your youngest brother. I could almost take pride in his determination to see and hear me as a witness. Tell me about him. The highest man among those in that land below, did you say? And raised up above them all? What did he look like and how did he speak? It's no wonder I'm curious about a man who is so curious about me."

Jacob Wrestles at the Jabbok

Yes, what is a year within this story, and who would begrudge a tale the time and patience it requires? Joseph showed patience, for he had to go on living meanwhile, playing the statesman and businessman in the land of Egypt. Like it or not, his brothers showed patience with Jacob's stubbornness, and so did Benjamin in restraining his curiosity about their journey and that curious marketeer. We are better off than any of them—but not because we already know how it all turned out. Indeed, those who live within the story and experience it in person have the advantage of us there, since we have to create a lively curiosity where by rights there can be none. Yet we have the advantage over them because we have been given power over the dimension of time and can expand or contract it at will. We don't have to put up with one year of waiting and all its quotidian details the way Jacob once had to put up with seven in Mesopotamia. With narrative flair, we can simply say: A year passed—and behold, it has come round and Jacob has been worn down.

For as everyone knows, the watery things of the world were not yet in order by a long shot and drought continued to oppress the lands that lie in and around our story. Oh, the devilish sequences that can occur in this world! And what can ail chance, which normally loves change, loves leaping back and forth between good and bad, that it suddenly goes mad and, giggling demonically, allows the same thing to happen over and over again! Ultimately chance will have to make that leap—for to have things go on like this would mean doing away with itself. But it can do crazy things, and for it to do them seven times in a row—if one is being generous in one's counting—is no great rarity.

In explaining the traffic among clouds moving between the sea and the Alps in the land of the Moors, where the waters of the Nile rise, we presented, to be honest, only the "how" but not the "why" of the situation. For once you address the "why" of things, there is never an end to it. The causes behind every event are like a backdrop of dunes at the shore: each is always positioned overlapping another, and the "because" where one might come to rest lies somewhere in infinity. The Provider did not become great and did not spill over because there was no rain up there in the land of the Moors. It did not do so because no rain had fallen in Canaan, either, and the reason for that was that the sea had not given birth to clouds, for seven, or at least five, years. Why? That "why" has a hierarchy of causes, leading to cosmic questions, to heavenly bodies that doubtless rule our wind and weather. First, there are sunspots—a cause that is certainly remote enough. But every child knows that the sun is not what is last and highest, and if Abram refused to worship it as the final cause, we should surely be ashamed to rest there ourselves. There are hierarchies in the universe that abrogate the sun's royal status as a resting place, reducing it to one of subordinate movement, and even those very influential spots on its disk are themselves a "why"—and one cannot assume that this "why's" final "because," that place where

one might come to rest, lies in such hierarchies, or in systems that
may be ranged higher still. The final "because" evidently lies or sits
enthroned in a place so remote that it is already near again—for in it
remote and near, cause and effect, are one; it is where we find ourselves by losing ourselves, and where we suspect a design that on occasion may also do away with such things as sacrificial cakes for the
sake of its own goals.

Drought and scarcity were oppressive, and it did not even take a
year before Jacob was worn down. The food his sons had acquired—
gratifyingly, though mysteriously, for nothing—had been eaten;
there had not been all that much for so many mouths, and more was
not to be had locally at any price. And so a few months earlier than
he had the year before, Israel initiated the conversation for which the
brothers had been waiting.

"What do you think?" he said. "Is there not a gaping contradiction, a preposterous incongruity between my prosperity, which I
have maintained and enlarged since I first broke the dusty bars of
Laban's realm, and this calamity by which we must once again do
without seed corn and baked goods, so that your children cry for
bread?"

Yes, they suggested, that all came with the times.

"And strange times they are," he said, "when a man has adult
sons, a whole crew of them, whom, with God's help, he did not fail
to sire, and yet they sit about on their backsides and do not lift a finger to deal with this scarcity."

"That is easy to say, Father. But what can a man do!"

"Do? There is grain for sale in Egypt, or so I have heard from
several quarters. How would it be if you would risk the journey and
go down to buy us a little food?"

"That would be fine, Father, we would already be on our way.
But you fail to note that the man down there made an unyielding demand concerning Benjamin: that we shall not see his face unless our
brother is with us, our youngest, whom we were unable to present
to him to testify for our truthfulness. The man's an astrologer, it
would appear. He said that of us twelve one was hidden behind the
sun, but not that two are to be hidden at once, and that the eleventh
must be presented to him before he would see us again. Give us Benjamin, and we shall go."

Jacob sighed.

"I knew," he said, "this would come up, that you would torture me again about the child."

But now he rebuked them in a loud voice. "Thoughtless wretches! Why did you have to babble and chatter before the man, foolishly unpacking everything about yourselves, so that he now knows you have another brother, my son, and could demand him of me? Had you had the dignity to stick with matters of business, instead of gossiping, he would know nothing about Benjamin and could not set my heart's blood as the price for bread flour. What you all deserve is my curse!"

"Do not do that, my lord," Judah said, "for what would then become of Israel? Consider rather what straits we were in and how we were forced to make a clean breast of things, since he pressed us hard with his suspicions and interrogated us about our friends and family. For he questioned us very carefully and wanted to know: 'Is your father still alive?' 'Do you have another brother?' 'Is your father well?' And when we told him that you were not as well as you should by rights be, he grew angry and rebuked us loudly for having let it come to that."

"Hm," Jacob said, stroking his beard.

"We were frightened," Judah continued, "by his stern manner and yet taken by his sympathy. For it is truly no small thing to be shown such kind and zealous regard by one of the great men of this world, on whom everything depends in that moment. That might well open a man's heart and make him share his thoughts, though not gossip." And how could they have possibly foreseen, Jehuda also asked, that the man would then demand their brother and command them: "Bring him down here!"

It was he, the tried and tested man, who was their chief spokesman today. They had agreed upon this in case Jacob were to show any sign of wearing down; for Re'uben, after having very clumsily and rather tastelessly gushed on about his two sons and how Jacob could strangle them, had been rejected; and Levi, although hard hit by the loss of his twin and only half a man ever since, could not be put forward because of Shechem. Judah, however, was an excellent speaker, whose words carried a persuasive, manly warmth.

"Israel," he said, "you must conquer your reluctance and wrestle with yourself until dawn, as you once did with someone else. This is the hour of the Jabbok—that is, if you want to come forth from it as a hero of God. Behold, the mind of that man down there is fixed. We cannot see him unless Benjamin is with us—and Leah's third will remain in thrall to that house of bondage, nor can there be any thought of bread. I, your lion, know how bitter it is for you to send Rachel's token on this journey, for he is to be always at home and this is, moreover, a journey down to the Land of Mud with its dead gods. Nor do you probably trust this man, the lord of that land, and you fear that he is setting a trap for us and will not give back either your youngest or the son left there as surety—and perhaps none of us at all. But as one who knows people and does not expect much good from either high or low, I say to you: The man is not like that. I know him well enough and shall lay my hand in the fire—he will not lure us into a trap, that is not what the man has in mind. He is indeed strange and uncanny, but also engaging, and though full of error, a man without guile. I, Judah, will go surety for him, just as I go surety for this your son, our youngest brother. Let him travel at my side and I will be father and mother to him, just as you are, both under way and in the land below, so that his foot may not dash against a stone or the vices of Egypt sully his soul. Give him into my hand so that we may be on our way at last and may live and not die—we, you, and our children. For you may require him of my hand, and if I do not bring him back to you and set him before your eyes, I shall bear the blame all my life. As you have him now, so shall you have him, and could have had him again long before now, except that you still have him, for had we not delayed so long we could have returned twice, together with the son left as surety, the son who is witness, and bread."

"Give me time to think," Jacob replied, "until dawn."

And by morning he had yielded and consented within himself to send Benjamin on the journey, not to Shechem a few days away, but far into the land below, a distance of seventeen days or more. His eyes were still red and he made sure that his expression told just how hard this coerced decision had been for his soul. But he had truly wrestled hard with necessity—it was no pretense, but something he expressed with grand suffering and dignity, so that everyone was deeply impressed and moved, and they said: "Behold, Israel has conquered himself this night."

Tilting his head to one shoulder, he said, "If indeed it must be so and it has been written in brass that all shall depart from me, so then take him and do this and go forth, I consent. Take some of the best fruits for which our land is celebrated in your pack, as a present for that man and to soften his heart: balm, tragacanth from the goat thorn, grape honey such as is boiled down to thick syrup for me, that he may sip it with water or sweeten his dessert with it, and also pistachio nuts and fruits of the terebinth—and say that it is but a little. Moreover, take double the money with you, for both new wares and old, since I recall that your silver was found again at the top of your sacks the first time—it may have been an oversight. And take Benjamin—yes, yes, you have heard me right, take him and lead him down to your man, that he may stand before him, I give my consent. I see dismay traced in your faces at my decision, but it has been made, and Israel prepares himself to be like a man bereft of all his children. But may El Shaddai," he exclaimed, raising his hands toward heaven, "grant you mercy before the man, that he send back your other brother and Benjamin. Lord, it is only as a loan to be returned that I give him to You for this journey. Let there be no misunderstanding between You and me. I am not sacrificing him, that You may devour him like my other child—I want him back! Think of the covenant, Lord, and how man's heart is to become fine and holy in You, and You in him. Do not, in Your might, fall short of the tender feelings of the human heart, so that You defraud me of the boy on his journey and cast him before the Monster, but restrain Yourself, I beg You. Return this loan to me with honesty, and I will serve You, bending low before You and burning such things as will delight Your nose—the very best parts."

He sent his prayers on high and then together with Eliezer (actually Damasek) set about making preparations to send his Son of Death on his journey, caring for him like a mother. For the very next morning the brothers would set out for Gaza in order not to miss the caravan assembling down there; and that suited Benoni's happy impatience, for he was overjoyed that he would see the world and be freed at last from his symbolic confinement, from this "always at home" that meant innocence. He did not jump about before Jacob or kick up his heels—because he was no longer seventeen, as Joseph had been that day long ago, but almost thirty, and he did not want to offend that passionate heart with his joy at escaping; and also because a life hung with matricidal crepe did not allow him such leaps, and he dared not fall out of his role. But he boasted not a little before his wives and children of his new freedom and that he would be traveling to Mizraim and by appearing there would liberate Shimeon, for he alone had such power over the lord of that land.

One could make rather short work of the preparations, however, since the travelers would not buy what they needed for their desert journey until they came to Gaza. The bulk of their baggage—all of it items that the young Eliezer had furnished from their storehouses—consisted for now of presents for Shimeon's jailer and Egypt's marketeer: aromatic drops of grape syrup, myrrh resin, nuts and fruits. A single ass was put into service to bear these presents, for which the land was celebrated.

By the light of dawn the brothers departed on their second journey, the same number of them as had set forth the first time, for they were missing one and had added one. The people in the camp stood in a circle surrounding the ten who held their animals by the bridle. But at the very center stood Jacob, holding on to the one thing left to him from his early love. Indeed people had come to hear how Jacob would say farewell to the son he protected and to be edified by worthiest expressions of the pain of separation. He held to his youngest son for a long time, hung his own amulet around Benjamin's neck, and murmured close to his cheek with eyes upraised. But the brothers cast their eyes toward the ground, smiling bitterly forbearing smiles.

"Judah, it is you," he finally said for all to hear. "You have gone surety for my son and said that I may require him of your hand. Hearken, however: You are relieved of that surety. For can a man go surety for God as well? I will not trust in you, for what can you do against God's wrath? Rather I will trust in Him alone, my rock and my shepherd, that He will restore to me what I have entrusted to Him in faith. Hearken all of you: He is no fiend who mocks the hearts of men, stamping them in the dust like a brute. He is a great God, purified and enlightened, a God of the covenant and of trustworthiness, and if a man should go surety for Him, then I have no need of you, my lion, for I myself will go surety for His faithfulness and that He will not commit the wrong of letting that surety be dashed to pieces. Go forth," he said, pushing Benjamin away from him, "in the name of God, the merciful and faithful! But you are to keep an eye on him all the same," he added with a faltering voice and turned back to his tent.

The Silver Cup

This time, as Joseph, the Provider, returned home from his office with the news in his heart that the ten people from Canaan had passed the border, Mai-Sakhme, his steward, could read it all in his face and asked, "Well then, Adôn, so it really has happened, and the wait is over?"

"It has happened," Joseph replied, "and the wait is over. It has come to pass as it had to come, and they have come. They will be here three days from today—with the little one," he said. "With the little one! This story of God's stood still for a while, and we have had to wait. But things have kept on happening, even when there seemed to be no story, for the sun's line of shade is gentle in its passing. One need but calmly put one's trust in time and scarcely worry about it at all—as the Ishmaelites I traveled with once taught me—for it ripens and brings forth everything on its own."

"A great many things," Mai-Sakhme said, "must now be considered about how best to arrange for the continuation of our game. Are suggestions welcome?"

"Ah, Mai, as if I had not long ago considered and arranged, sparing no cares in my inventions. It will be played out as if it already stood written and were being played out to the letter. There are no surprises here, only the thrill of the present taking on the look of familiarity. I am not at all agitated this time either, but merely in a high and festive mood as we stride ahead, and at most my 'it is I' sets my heart pounding—that is, I fear for *them* on that account. You had best have your foaming drink at the ready for them."

"It shall be done, Adôn. But though you wish no advice I shall advise you all the same: watch out for the little one. He shares not just half your blood, but is your full brother, and, if I know you, you will not be able to leave well enough alone, but will set his nose on the scent. Besides, the youngest is always the slyest, and it could easily happen that he will trump your 'it is I' with an 'it is you' and spoil your whole game."

"What if he does, Mai! I would not object all that much to such an alteration. There would be hearty laughter, just as children shout for joy when they set a tower they've made tumbling. But I don't believe in your worries. A little whelp—and he is to say right to the face of Pharaoh's friend, the Vice-Horus and great man of commerce: 'Pooh, you're nothing more than my brother Joseph!' That would truly be brazen! No, the declaration of my role, that I am I, is surely reserved for me."

"Do you want to receive them in the central office again?"

"No, this time here. I shall break noonday bread with them, they shall be invited to join in my meal. Slaughter whatever necessary, my steward, and arrange for eleven more guests than planned three days hence. Who has been invited for the day after tomorrow?"

"A few dignitaries from the city," Mai-Sakhme said, consulting his list. "His honor Ptahhotpe, priest and chief reader of the house of Ptah; our sovereign's warrior, Colonel Entef-oker, from the god's permanent garrison; Pa-neshe, the surveyor and setter of boundary stones, who has a tomb in the rocks where the lord lies; and a couple of bookkeepers from the main Office of Provisions."

"Good. They'll find it rather extraordinary to dine with these foreigners."

"All too extraordinary I fear, Adôn. For, just by way of warning, there is an unfortunate difficulty of certain proscriptions, of rules for dining decorum. It may be an offense to some of them to break bread with these Ibrim."

"Oh, none of that, Mai—you're talking like a Dûdu, a dwarf I once knew, a man of pious principle. Don't try to teach me about my Egyptians—as if they would still be horrified. They would then also have to be horrified to eat with me, for none of them is unaware that I did not drink Nile water as a child. And there is Pharaoh's ring: 'Be as I am'—that trumps everything. That will hold for whomever I eat with, even at mealtime. Besides, there is Pharaoh's doctrine, admired by all who wish to please the court, which states that all men are the dear children of his father. As for the rest, the only special arrangement should be for the sake of maintaining good form: the Egyptians are to eat by themselves, these men by themselves, and I by myself. But you shall seat my brothers in a row according to their age—big Ruben at the head and Benoni last. Make no mistakes—let me tell you the order once again and you can enter it on your tablet."

"Fine, fine, Adôn. But this is dangerous. Why should they not be surprised that you know the sequence in their ages?"

"In addition you shall set my cup before me, the one in which I read things—you know, the silver showpiece."

"I see, I see, the cup. Are you planning to play prophet and read their sequence of birth from it?"

"It could be used for that as well."

"I wish, Adôn, that it could serve me for prophesying too, so that things would stand out like pieces of gold or polished stones in pure water, from which I could then read the plans that you've invented for this story and by which you will lead them to your word of self-disclosure. I fear I shall serve you poorly if I do not know them; and certainly I must serve you and be helpful to you if I'm not just to stand around in this story that you've been kind enough to include me in."

"You certainly must not do that, my steward. That wouldn't be right. But first set out my cup, the one from which I sometimes read and prophesy for fun."

"The cup, yes, yes, the cup," Mai-Sakhme said, with eyes that looked as if he were struggling to remember. "And so they are bringing you Benjamin now and you will see your little brother among your brothers. But when you have dined with them and have filled their sacks a second time, they will take the youngest away with them and return home to your father—and you will be left the loser."

"You must read the cup better, Mai, and see what becomes clear in its water. They shall surely depart, but what if they have forgotten something, so that they must turn back again?"

The captain shook his head.

"Or if they have something with them," Joseph said, "that we find missing, and pursue them for that something and bring them back?"

Mai-Sakhme stared at him with round eyes, his black brows arched above them—and behold! his little mouth slowly broke into a smile. When a man has such a little mouth with which to smile, no matter how stout and portly his constitution, the smile is a woman's smile, and despite the black stubble of his beard his smile was lady-like, delicate, almost sweet. The man must indeed have read from the cup himself, for he nodded to Joseph with a mischievous, knowing look, and Joseph nodded back, raised a hand, and gave Mai the laudatory endorsement of a clap on the shoulder; and in turn his steward, however improperly—though after all Joseph had once drudged for him as a convict in his prison—raised his hand as well to give his master a clap on the shoulder. And so the two stood there nodding at one another and exchanging claps on the shoulder for a good while, in perfect agreement as to how this festive story was to proceed.

The Fragrance of Myrtle; or, The Meal with the Brothers

It did indeed proceed, playing itself out in each of its hours as follows: Jacob's sons arrived in Menfe, the home of Ptah, and put up at the same inn as before, happy to have brought Benjamin here safely, whom they had tended and waited upon and handled like a raw egg for the entire journey of nearly seventeen days—both out of fear for Jacob's feelings and because he was more important than all else, for he was the witness demanded by this ambiguous marketeer and without him they would neither see the man's face nor get Shimeon back. That would have been reason enough to regard their little brother as the apple of their eye, always providing him with the best of everything and protecting him like precious water itself—their primary fear being this man here, but lurking behind it, fear of their father as well. Far in the background stood a third unspoken motive for their carefulness: a wish to atone with Benjamin for their sin against Joseph. For after so long a time, thought of him and of their crime had been reawakened by their first journey down here, with all its attendant circumstances; the thought had risen up out of the rubble of time as if only yesterday they had sold their brother, blotting a name out of Israel. It lay in the air like retribution delayed, felt like a hand trying to drag them to account; and it seemed to them that paying zealous attention to Rachel's other son was the best way to remove that hand and scatter these avenging spirits.

For his presentation to the man who was lord of this land, they clad him in a lovely, gaudy tunic with fringes, tucks, and folds, oiled down his cap of otter fur so that not a hair stuck out, making it truly a shiny helmet, and lengthened his eyes with a pointed brush. But when they appeared at the Central Office for Permits and Deliveries and were turned away and told to report to the Provider's home, they took fright, for anything unexpected, anything that didn't happen as they had imagined, was frightening to them, seemed to threaten new complications and mysteries. What was this now, and why were they being set apart so particularly that they were to report to his home? Did this portend good or ill? It might have something to do with the money from before and its murky reappearance—and was that murky event now to be used against them, had a snare been laid in their path, were they all to be taken prisoner and sold into slavery for fraudulent payment? They had that murky money with them, as well as new metal for new purchases—but that did little to calm their fears. Instead they were sorely tempted to turn tail and, without ever showing their faces to the man, seek refuge in flight—primarily out of worry over Benjamin, who, however, reassured them and boldly insisted that they lead him to this marketeer, for he had now been anointed and adorned and saw no reason to hide himself from this man. And, he went on, they had no reason either, since that money had turned up again due to some oversight and one ought not to act guilty when one was not.

Guilty, guilty, they said, a person always felt a little guilt just in general, even without any particular cause, which was why one didn't feel all that good even in a situation like this where one was downright innocent. Besides, it was easy for him, their little brother, to talk; he had always been innocent at home and had never been in a situation where he found murky money in his sack, whereas they had constantly been out and about in the world where one couldn't avoid all sorts of guilt.

As for guilt in general, Benoni said, the man would be understanding enough—he was a man of the world after all. And as for the money, everything there was in order, even if murky, and they had come, among other reasons, to return it. Moreover, Shimeon had to be ransomed, they knew that as well as he did, and they also needed new grain. There could be no thought of turning tail and fleeing, for by doing that they would leave behind the belief that they were not just thieves but spies as well—and would be their brother's murderer besides.

They really knew all that as well as he—they definitely had to risk it despite the danger of being enslaved one and all. The fact that they had brought lovely bribes with them—Jacob's presents, samples of the celebrated products of their land—cheered them up a bit, and they now decided that first off they should speak with that stout but unambiguously kindhearted steward if they could find him.

That was easily done. For upon arriving at the villa Pharaoh had graciously provided the marketeer in this elegant neighborhood, they had dismounted from their asses beneath the gate in its wall and were leading their beasts past the reflecting pool and toward the house itself when the man who inspired their trust descended from the terrace to welcome them, praising them for keeping their word, though with some little delay, and at once had them present their youngest brother to him, whom he gazed upon with round eyes, saying, "Fine fellow, fine fellow." He had his people take the animals back around the house to the courtyard, ordered others to carry into the house the packs filled with Canaan's fame, and now led the brothers up the open staircase—and all the while they anxiously bombarded him about the money.

Some had started in about it the moment they saw him, even at a good distance away—they simply couldn't wait.

"Good sir, majordomo," they said, "worthy steward"—it was this way or perhaps that way, totally incomprehensible, but it had happened, and here was double the money, they were honest men. Found, they had found the silver rings they had paid, first one had and then all of them had, in their fodder sacks when they stopped to rest, and that murky discovery had left them oppressed the entire time. But here it was again, in full weight, along with more money for new supplies. Surely his master, Pharaoh's friend, would not blame them for this or, worse, pass sentence against them?

They talked all at once, gesticulating wildly, and in their worry some even tugged at him and swore they would not enter that beautiful door to the house unless he for his part would swear to them that his master had not woven a snare for them out of this earlier vexing episode and would not charge them with it.

He, however, was the soul of calmness, soothing them as he said, "My good men, rest assured and fear not, everything is in order. Or, if a bit out of order, it's just an amiable miracle. We received our money, that should suffice for us, and there's nothing here for us to weave a snare from. In light of what you have told me I can only assume that your God and the God of your fathers has had His little joke and left a treasure in your sacks for you—reason offers me no other explanation. Presumably you are His pious and zealous servants, and for once He wanted to show that He's aware of it—understandable enough on His part. But you seem very agitated to me, which is not good. I shall have footbaths prepared for you, first as a token of hospitality—for you are our guests and shall dine with Pharaoh's friend today at noon—but also because it pulls the blood from the head and calms the mind. But do enter now and, above all, behold who awaits you in the hall."

And there in the hall stood their brother Shimeon, a free man, not in the least hollow-eyed and wasted away, but as rugged and rowdy as ever; for he had had things good, as he happily told those now encircling him, and for a hostage had spent quite tolerable days in a chamber in the Central Office, even if he had not seen the *moshel*'s face again and had worried the whole time whether they would ever return—though always buoyed up by good food and drink. They apologized to Leah's second son for having delayed their return so long—due, as he could well understand, to Jacob's stubbornness; and he understood and was happy to be with them, especially with his brother Levi, for one ruffian had missed the other, and though no hugs and kisses were exchanged, each kept punching the other hard in the shoulder.

And now the brothers sat down together to wash their feet. Then the steward led them into the hall where their meal had been set, resplendent with centerpieces of flowers and fruit and beautiful tableware, and helped them spread out their gifts—the delicacies of honey, fruits, and nuts they had brought—on a long sideboard against one wall, making a pretty display of them to delight the eye of his master. In the midst of this, however, Mai-Sakhme had to hurry off, for people were arriving outside—Joseph was returning home at noon along with the Egyptian gentlemen he had invited to break bread with him today: the prophet of Ptah, the warrior of their sovereign, the head surveyor, and the chief bookkeepers.

Joseph now entered with them, saying, "Greetings, my good men." But they all fell upon their faces as if mown down.

He stood there a while, tracing his brow with his fingertips.

Then he repeated, "Greetings, my friends. But do stand on your feet before me and let me see your faces that I may recognize them. For you recognize me, as I can tell, and you see that I am Egypt's marketeer, who had to treat you roughly for the sake of the opulence of this land. But now you have appeased and reassured me by returning in proper number, so that all the brothers are gathered under one roof and in one chamber. That is indeed lovely. Have you noticed that I am speaking to you in your language? Yes, I can do so now. The last time you were here it struck me that I could understand no Ebrew, and that annoyed me. Which is why I learned it in the meantime. A man such as I learns these things in a wink. But how are you, how are things? And above all: Is your old father of whom you spoke still alive, and is he well?"

"Your servant and our father," they replied, "is quite well and still living in high estate. He would be very touched by your kind inquiry."

And they fell on their faces yet again, pressing their brows to the floor.

"Enough bending and bowing," he said, "too much in fact! Let me see you. Is that your youngest brother of whom you spoke to me?" he asked in somewhat clumsy Canaanite—for he had indeed forgotten it a bit—and stepped toward Benjamin. The well-dressed husband reverently raised to him gray eyes filled with a gentle and clear sadness.

"God be with you, my son," Joseph said, laying a hand to his shoulder. "Have you always had such kind eyes and such a lovely shiny helmet of hair on your head, even when you were a little man and ran about like a whelp in the world, in the greenwood?" He swallowed hard. "I shall be back in a moment," he said. "I just have to—" And he quickly left the room—for his own chambers presumably, for his bedroom, but soon returned after having washed his eyes.

"I am neglecting all my duties," he said, "and have not even introduced the guests of my house to one another. Gentlemen, these are buyers of grain from Canaan, whose origins are of high estate, all the sons of one important man."

And he recited for the Egyptians the names of Jacob's sons, in precise order by age, so that they flowed like a poem, with a slight hesitation after every third name—and with the omission of his own, of course, making a brief pause after Zebulun and then ending with, "and Benjamin." They were astonished, however, that he knew their names in order, and looked at one another in bewilderment.

Then he named for them the names of the Egyptian dignitaries, who responded quite stiffly. He smiled at this. "Let the meal be served," he said, rubbing his hands like someone ready to sit down to the table. But his steward pointed to the presents that had been spread out, and he now admired them with heartfelt courtesy.

"From your father, the old man?" he asked. "This is a touching gesture. Would you please offer him my deepest thanks."

It is but a small thing, they declared, from the bounty of their land.

"It is a great deal," he disagreed. "And above all it is very beautiful. I have never seen such fine tragacanth. And such pistachio nuts, with that rich oily fragrance one notices even from a distance—such things are to be had only in your homeland. I can scarcely take my eyes off them. But now the time has come to eat our lunch."

And Mai-Sakhme directed them all to their places, giving the brothers cause for astonishment yet again, for they were seated exactly according to their age, though from the viewpoint of the master of the house in reverse order, so that the youngest sat closest to him, followed by Zebulun, Issakhar, and Asher, on down to big Ruben. Surrounded by the columns of this Egyptian hall were buffets spread with food and arranged in an open triangle, at the tip of which was the table of their host. To his right were tables for the local gentlemen and slanting away to his left were those for the Asiatic strangers, so that he sat at the head of both rows, with the prophet of Ptah to his right and Benjamin on his left. With warm hospitality he reminded them all to set heartily to work and spare neither food nor wine.

This meal is famous for its good cheer, before which the initial stiffness of the Egyptian dignitaries was soon put to rout, for they thawed out and completely forgot that on principle it was an abomination for them to break bread with these Ebrews. Their sovereign's warrior, Colonel Entef-oker, was the first to begin to enjoy himself, the result of a good deal of Syrian wine, and in a booming voice conversed from table to table across the triangular space with outspoken Gad, who of all these denizens of the sand pleased him best.

It should come as no surprise that tradition makes no mention here of Joseph's wife, Asenath, the daughter of the priest of the sun, and insists on leaving the impression that this was a banquet for men only, though by Egyptian custom married couples dined together, nor was the woman of the house absent on festive occasions either. But the accuracy of the old version is hereby confirmed—not by the explanation that perhaps the Maiden, in accord with her marital contract, was spending time with her parents (though that might easily have been possible), but rather by reference to Joseph's daily agenda and lifestyle, for his exalted position usually precluded his even seeing his wife and children during the day. This—to be sure very lively—meal with his brothers and local dignitaries was not a formal banquet, but a business luncheon of the sort that Pharaoh's friend had to host almost daily, so that he usually did not dine with his spouse until evening—and then, in the villa's women's wing and only after first having spent some time with Manasseh and Ephraim, his charming half-breed progeny. At noon, however, he broke bread in the company of men, whether it was with the higher and highest officials of the Great House of Provision or with notables of the Two Lands passing through Menfe or with foreign ambassadors and plenipotentiaries; and this was just such a luncheon with the Friend of the God's Harvest—which is to say, on the face of it, since for now at least all the guests taking part were kept in the dark as to just what stirring events were unfolding here within the framework of God's marvelous and festive story or why their exalted host was in such infectious high spirits.

All those taking part? Should that inclusive statement be allowed to stand? Mai-Sakhme, who stood stoutly at the open end of the triangle and with eyebrows raised high and a white baton in hand was directing bearers of wines and meats as they scurried here and there—he would be one exception. He knew what was going on, but he was not actually a guest. Was there among the diners someone for whom this darkness had a kind of dreadful, delicious, uncanny, unadmitted semitransparency? From our tentative question—best left as a question—it is apparent that it is Turturra–Benoni, the youngest of those on the host's left, whom we have in mind. What he was feeling is indescribable. It has never been described, and neither does this narrative presume to put into words what has never been attempted before—to describe, that is, an intuition that, with all its attendant sweetly terrifying emotions, was a long way from even

trusting itself to be an intuition and instead risked no more than registering gentle, dreamlike spasms of memory and strange evocation
that made the heart tremble as it discerned certain relationships between two very different and widely separated phenomena, one submerged since the days of childhood and one alive and present. Just
imagine what that was like.

They were seated on very comfortable low chairs, a table set at
an angle to one side of each and heavily, happily laden with foods
both substantial and dainty, a delight to the eye: fruits, vegetables,
cakes, pies, cucumbers and squashes, cornucopias filled with flowers
and spun sugar; and to the other side stood both a graceful wash-
stand, which held a pretty amphora, and a copper basin for the
meal's refuse. This was true for each of them. Under the personal direction of the sommelier, aproned servants kept wine cups full; the
steward of the sideboard handed others the main dishes—veal, mutton, fish, poultry, game—to be placed before the guests, who, however, given their host's high rank, did not enjoy precedence over him.
Instead the Adôn was not only served first, but also served the best,
and in greater quantity—though, to be sure, only to redistribute it,
so that, as it is written, "portions were taken to them from Joseph's
table." Which is to say: Along with his warmest greetings he would
send—now to one, now to another, here to an Egyptian and there to
one of the foreigners—a roast duckling, some quince jelly, or a
gilded bone ringed with tasty fritters; but to the youngest of the
Asians, that is, to his neighbor on the left, he personally offered
items from his own plate, again and again. Such demonstrations of
favor implied a great deal and were observed by the Egyptians, who
kept close count and compared and discussed their tallies afterward—and that is why we are told that the little Bedouin's portion
was in fact five times as much as anyone else received from the master's table.

Benjamin was embarrassed, begged to be spared from all these
gifts, and looked about in apology to both the Egyptians and his
brothers. He could not possibly have eaten everything he received,
even had he been of a mind to eat—but his was a dazed and anxious
mind, that sought, found, lost, and suddenly, indisputably found
again, setting his heart racing in fierce beats. He gazed at his host's
beardless face framed in its hieratic, winged headdress, at the man
who had demanded he be a witness, at this great Egyptian, a fairly

hefty man clad in white, with shimmering pendants at his chest; gazed at the lively mouth as it moved in smiling conversation, at those black eyes sparkling with good humor whenever they met his, but then seeming to retreat again, turning earnest, sometimes even closing to shut him out, especially when they met his own, widened with fearful and unbelieving joy; gazed at the shape of that hand, adorned with the engraved stone of the heavens, whenever it offered him food or raised a cup—and it seemed to him as he if smelled the fragrance of childhood, a harsh, warm, peppery perfume, the essence of all admiration and loving confidentiality, of bewildering intuition, of all his childlike failure to understand even though he did understand, of all his credulousness and tender anxiety: the fragrance of myrtle. This scent of memory was inseparably bound up with his innermost struggle to solve this lovely puzzle, with his apprehensively proud and deferential exploration of the frightening oneness now intimating itself, with his agonizing, yet blissful attempt to guess in what way this friendly present reality was identical with something much higher and divine—that was why Turturra's small, sturdy nose thought it whiffed the spicy fragrance of childhood, for everything was the same again, except the other way round. And what a turn-around it was! Here, in this high and strange present, something familiar was trying to be recognized, assuming a transparency that from one moment to the next would set his heart pounding.

The Lord of Grain chatted away with Benjamin over their meal—five times as much with him as with the Egyptian dignitary to his right. He asked about his life at home, about his father, about his wives and children—the eldest of which was named Bela, the currently youngest Muppim. "Muppim!" the Lord of Grain said. "Give him a kiss for me when you return home—how enchanting that the youngest son now has a youngest of his own. But who is the one closest to being youngest? He's named Rosh? Bravo! Is he by the same mother as the other? Yes? And do they do a lot of wandering about together in the world, in the greenwood? Let's hope the older one doesn't frighten the smaller one, who's just a whelp yet, with God knows what all—inappropriate tales, grand fancies, and stories of God. Be careful there, father Benjamin!" And he told him about his own sons, borne him by the daughter of the sun, Manasseh and Ephraim—and did he like those names? "Very much," Benjamin said and was on the verge of asking why they had been given such striking names, but faltered at the threshold of his question and sat there wide-eyed. But not for long; for his neighbor, this prince in the land of Egypt, told him funny stories about Manasseh and Ephraim, about the silly chatter of the one and the mischief the other had got into—which brought Benoni round to similar stories about his own children, and the two could be seen buckling over with laughter as they exchanged tales.

At one point Benjamin summoned his courage and ventured to ask, "Would Your Excellency answer a question for me, solve a riddle for your guest?"

"As best I can," the man replied.

"It's merely," the little brother said, "so that you might calm an uneasiness, resolve my amazement at your knowledge of something you said and at a certain precision evidenced in your arrangements. You are able to rattle off our names, my brothers' and mine, by heart, and in order of age, so that without hesitation or mistake you are able to list them in the same way that, or so our father says, children throughout the world will someday have to learn them, because we are a divinely chosen family. How do you know this and how is it that your unruffled steward could show us to our places, to the firstborn according to his primacy, to the youngest according to his youth?"

"Ah," the marketeer replied, "so you have all been wondering about that? It's very simple. For there is this cup here, you see?—silver, with a cuneiform inscription, which provides me with both drink and prophecy. I am a man of some intelligence, which may even be above average, since I am who I am, and Pharaoh wished to be higher than me by no more than the height of his royal throne; and yet I would scarcely know how to get along without my cup. The king of Babel gave it as a gift to Pharaoh's father, by which I do not mean myself—since I do not bear the title of Father of Pharaoh, though Pharaoh himself likes to call me 'little uncle'—but rather his real father, which is to say, however, not his divine, but his earthly father, Pharaoh's predecessor, King Neb-maat-Rê. It was sent to him as a present, and so it came to my lord, who deigned to surprise me with it. A thing that I can truly use, since it has most helpful qualities. For when I read from it, it shows me both past and future, allows me to penetrate the mysteries of the world and lays its relationships open before me, as for example the order of your birth, which I read effortlessly from it. A good portion of my cleverness, more or less all of it that exceeds the average, comes from this cup. I don't divulge this, of course, to just anyone, but since you are my guest and my neighbor at table, I am confiding it to you. You won't believe it, but if I handle it correctly, this thing allows me to see pictures of faraway places, as well as what has happened there. Shall I describe your mother's grave to you?"

"You know that she's dead?"

"Your brothers told me that, how she departed for the West early on, a lovely woman whose cheek smelled like a rose petal. I make no pretense of having heard these tidings by supernatural means. But now I need only set this cup of visions to my brow—like this, you see—with the intention of seeing your mother's grave, and I see it instantly and with such clarity that it amazes even me. But the clarity comes with the morning sun illuminating the scene, and there are mountains here and at the top of one mountain a town bathed in the light of dawn—not far away at all, only a short path across the fields. There are small orchards among the boulders and vineyards on the hills to the right and, along the front, a wall of loose stones without mortar. A mulberry tree grows beside the wall, an old tree now and partly hollow, its trunk propped up by a pile of stones. No one has ever seen a tree more clearly than I see this mulberry tree and how the morning wind plays in its leaves. Next to the tree, however, is a grave and a stone to commemorate it. But look, someone is kneeling at the spot and has laid provisions there, water and sweetened bread; he must have traveled on the ass waiting under the tree—such a nice creature, white, with eloquent ears and a forelock growing down over its friendly eyes. I wouldn't have believed it myself, would never have thought the cup capable of showing me this so clearly. Is this your mother's grave or not?"

"Yes, it's hers," Benjamin answered. "But I beg you, my lord, do you see only the ass in such detail, but not the rider?"

"I can, if need be, see him even more clearly," the man replied, "but what is there to see? He's more of a dandy, seventeen at most, kneeling there and offering his sacrifice. He's wrapped himself in some colorful garb, the ninny, with images woven into it, and he's a fool besides, for he thinks he's just out for a ride, but the ride will lead to his ruin, and only a few days' journey from this grave his own awaits him."

"That's my brother Joseph," Benjamin said, and his gray eyes spilled over with tears.

"Oh, forgive me," his neighbor said in alarm and set the cup down. "I would not have spoken so disparagingly of him had I known this is your lost brother. And what I said about the grave, about his that is, you should not take all too earnestly, nor exaggerate its seriousness. The grave, is to be sure, serious enough, a hole, deep and dark; but its power to hold things is not so very great. You should know that it is empty by nature—this cave is empty, lying in wait for its prey, and if you arrive after it has taken the prey in, you'll find it empty again—the stone rolled away. I'm not saying that it does not deserve our tears, this pit, indeed we should raise shrill lamentation in its honor, for it is there—a serious, grievously sad feature of the world and of the festive story in all its hours. I shall go so far as to say that out of reverence for this hole we should not let on that we know it to be empty by nature and powerless to hold its prey. That would be rude, seeing as it is such a serious feature of the world. We should weep and wail in shrill voices—for only as a confidential aside are we reassured that nothing descends into it without subsequently rising again. What a mere fragment, what a half-told festive story that would be, if it only went as far as the pit, and knew nothing more to say. No, the world is not just half, but whole, and the feast, too, is whole, and there is consolation, inviolable consolation, in that wholeness. And so do not let yourself be troubled any further by what I said about your brother's grave, but be consoled."

And with that he took hold of Benjamin's wrist, raised it a little, and fanned the air with the limp hand, setting up a light breeze.

And now the little brother was completely terrified. His emotional state was at the peak of indescribability—it was now certain that no one would ever be able to describe it. He could not catch his breath, his eyes welled up with tears, and through his tears he stared with a fierce scowl into the face of the Prince of Grain (and what an indescribable expression that is—tears beneath a scowl), and his mouth stood open as if for a scream, which never came. Instead Benoni tilted his head to one side a little, closed his mouth, relaxed the scowl, and his tear-filled gaze was now only one great, fervent plea—before which the black eyes opposite retreated behind their lids, shutting him out, it's true, and yet, had one dared to risk it, one might have beheld in those lowered eyelids something like secret, confidential affirmation.

Just let someone try to describe what was happening now in Benjamin's heart—in a human heart so very close to belief!

"I shall now proclaim our meal over," he heard the prince say. "Did you enjoy it? I do hope everyone enjoyed it, but I must now return to my office until evening. I presume that tomorrow morning you and your brothers will be wending your way homeward, once you have received the wares I wish to assign you: food for twelve houses this time, your father's house and your own. I will gladly take your money in return and put it in Pharaoh's treasury—what do you expect? I take good care of the god's business. In case I do not see you again, farewell! But just in passing and as an expression of goodwill—why, in fact, don't you open your hearts and exchange your land for this one by settling in Egypt—father, sons, wives, and grandchildren, all seventy of you, or however many there are—and earn your livelihood from Pharaoh's pastures? That is my proposal for you, so do think it over, it wouldn't be the most foolish thing to do. You would be assigned suitable pastures—but one word and it is done, for my word counts for everything here. I know well enough that Canaan means much to you, but, in the end, the land of Egypt is the great world, and Canaan but a little corner where people really have no idea how to live at all. But you're a mobile sort of people, not citizens trapped inside walls. So why not move down here! It's a good life here and you may trade and deal freely in this land. Such, then, is my advice—heed it or heed it not. But I must make haste, that I may listen to the cries of those who have taken no precautions."

With such worldly words, spoken while a servant poured water over his hands, he took his leave of his little brother. Then he stood up, extended greetings to all, and declared an end to this meal—at which, so it has been said, he and his brothers got drunk. But they were only in high spirits; even the savage twins would not have dared get drunk. Only Benjamin was drunk—but not on wine.

The Imprisoned Cry

In a far better mood than the first time, the brothers now set out from Menfe for home by way of the Bitter Lakes and the fortified border. Everything had gone so well it could not have gone better. The lord of the land had proved unambiguously charming, Benjamin was safe, Shimeon ransomed, and they had been honorably exonerated of any suspicion of espionage—indeed, they had even shared a noonday meal with the powerful man and his nobles. This had put them in a very merry mood, had made their hearts light and proud; for that is the nature of man—when he has been found innocent in one matter, has been praised and confirmed to be beyond reproach in that one regard, it seems to him that he is innocent in general and he quite forgets that there are still one or two things chalked up against him. One must forgive these brothers. They had automatically associated the misfortune of being suspected as spies with an older guilt; no wonder, then, that upon being acquitted of the first charge they also assumed that there was nothing more to the second matter either.

They would soon learn that they had not got off that cheaply and were not marching away scot-free, with sacks bursting with food for twelve houses, but dragging a chain that would pull them back into new troubles. For now, however, they were in fine fettle and could have burst into song at their acknowledged and rewarded innocence. They had been treated to yet another meal at the House of Deliveries, again under Mai-Sakhme's calm supervision, and been sent on their way with friendly mementoes. Provided now with everything they needed to stand with high hearts before their father, they went their way: with Benjamin, with Shimeon, and with food— whereby the food they had received from the great marketeer in some sense represented the twelfth of their number who, after all, was still no more. But at least they had brought the total to eleven again—thanks to their innocence.

That is how things looked in the hearts of the brothers, which is to say in those of Leah's sons and the sons of the handmaids—no trouble describing it. But the state of the soul of Rachel's son remains indescribable—and what no one has ventured for several thousand years, we had truly best leave aside ourselves. Suffice it to say the little brother had scarcely slept at all that night at the inn, and what little sleep he found was full of confused and crazy dreams that had gone without a name for some time now. Which is to say, they had a name, a lovely and beautiful and indeed totally crazy name: and it was "Joseph." Benoni had seen a man in whom Joseph was. How can anyone possibly describe that? Men have been known to meet up with gods whom they believed to be disguised as a familiar acquaintance and who acted as expected, but did not wish to be spoken to. This was just the opposite. This was not a case of what is humanly familiar being transparent for the divine, but of the high and divine being transparent for something familiar from one's most intimate childhood—yet, disguised in its strange majesty, it did not wish to be spoken to, but retreated, shutting itself off behind closed eyelids. Granted: The disguised figure is not he in whom he is disguised and from whose eyes it gazes. These are two different things. To recognize the one in the other does not mean making one out of two and unburdening one's heart with the cry of "It is he!" It is impossible to produce this "he," however hard the mind writhes and struggles to give it form. Banished within Benjamin's heart, which he almost hoped would burst, that cry was not really present, was only an unrealized cry with no unified object to name—that was what was indescribable. This unrealized cry filling his heart had no choice but to dissolve into confused and crazy dreams by night. But when morning came and it had solidified again into its oppressive semi-existence, it found just enough of something to put a name to the fact that Benjamin could not grasp how anyone could think of departing now, of simply leaving "all this" behind. "In the name of the Eternal, we simply can't leave now!" he cried to himself. "We really must stay, and let our eyes take it all in—this man, this Vice-God, Pharaoh's Great Marketeer! It is time for a cry that does not yet exist, and we simply cannot return to our father with this cry in our hearts and go on living as before, not when the cry is on the verge of entering into the world, of filling the whole world. It is immense enough for that—no wonder, then, that it's trying to burst open the prison of my heart."

And in his distress he turned to big Ruben and asked him wide-eyed if he really thought they ought to depart and return home, if it did not perhaps seem to him that they were not quite finished here, or better, not finished at all, and if, given such a sound reason, they ought not stay here?

"What's this, little one?" Ruben asked in return. "And what do you mean by 'sound'? Has not everything been taken care of and managed to the best, and did not the man dismiss us with good grace once we had presented you? What matters now is to return posthaste to our father, who is waiting in fear for your sake, and to bring him what we have purchased so that he may have his sacrificial cakes. Don't you recall how angry the man was when he learned of Jacob's complaint that his lamp was going out and that he would have to sleep in the dark?"

"Yes," Benjamin said, "I recall it." And he gazed urgently up into his big brother's gruff face, its strong, clean-shaven muscles drawn taut as usual. Suddenly he saw—or was his mind playing tricks?—those reddened Leah eyes retreat before his gaze behind blinking eyelids, as if both shutting him out and agreeing with him, just as he had seen other eyes do the day before.

He said nothing more. It could be that he had merely imagined he knew that signal because he had seen it yesterday and then constantly in his dreams. The decision held, they set out—there were no words that could have enforced his proposal that they remain behind—but for Benjamin it meant great pain. That the man himself had dismissed them with good grace—that was his pain. That he had let them go, simply go their way—that was his great anguish. They couldn't just depart, not for all the world—and yet, if the man had let them go, then they could and must go. And they departed.

Benjamin rode with Ruben, at his side, and rightly so, for in many ways they formed a pair: not only as the eldest and youngest, as Big John and Tom Thumb, but also psychologically, in their relationship to a brother who was no more and to what his being no more meant. We have observed the gruff weakness Ruben had always felt for his father's lamb and were witnesses to his singular behavior—which singled him out from among his brothers—on the occasion of Joseph's mutilation and burial. To all appearances he had participated fully in the deed and had shared in that binding oath, the gruesome words that bound the ten never with a wink, blink, or twitch of the eye to betray the fact that the tattered garment sent ahead to their father had been stained not with the boy's blood but with an animal's. But Ruben had not participated in his sale; he had not been present for that, but elsewhere, and so his understanding of Joseph's being no more was even vaguer than that of his brothers, which was vague enough, foggy enough—and yet in another sense not sufficiently so. They knew that they had sold the boy to traveling merchants, and so they knew a bit too much. Ruben had the advantage of not knowing it; the place where he had lingered while they were selling Joseph had been the empty grave, and an empty grave produces a different relationship to someone's being no more than does the sale of the victim into endless horizons and faraway mists.

In short, big Ruben, whether he knew it himself or not, had kept and nourished the seed of expectation all these years, and that bound him—in contradistinction to all his brothers—with innocent Benjamin, who had not participated in any of it and for whom the fact that the brother he admired was no more had never been anything but a source of hope. Do we not hear his childish voice, though it is so long ago now, saying to the broken old man: "He will come back. Or he will send for us to come." It is a good twenty years ago now, but that expectation was still as present in his heart as his words are in our ears—though he knew nothing of either the sale (as did the nine who had made it) or the empty pit from which the man interred there might very well have been stolen. He knew only what his father knew, nothing more: that Joseph was dead—which really leaves no room for hope. And yet hope seems to best find a home where there is no room for it.

Benjamin rode with Ruben; on the way Ruben asked him what all the man had said to him during the meal—as the oldest he had been sitting too far from them to hear.

"All manner of things," the youngest replied. "He and I exchanged funny stories about our children."

"Yes, I saw you laughing," Ruben said. "Everyone saw how you were both buckled over with laughter. I think it astonished the Egyptians."

"They know he's a charming man," his little brother responded, "and can amuse almost anyone, until you forget yourself and laugh along with him."

"We've learned," Ruben replied, "that he can also be quite different and very disagreeable."

"True enough," Benjamin said. "You could all tell a tale about that. And yet he means well by us, and I could tell a tale of my own there. Because the last thing he said is still ringing in my ears—a piece of advice, an invitation issued through me to us all, no matter how many we are, to settle in Egypt, to bring Father down here and graze on these pastures."

"Did he actually say that?" Ruben asked. "Yes indeed, the man knows us and our father so very well—him in particular. Why, it's as if he knows him personally, knows exactly what he's going to do. First he forces him to send you on this journey to exonerate us and buy bread, and now he invites him to come to Egypt, the Land of Mud. There's no denying he understands a thing or two about Jacob."

"Are you making fun of him," Benjamin rejoined, "or of Father? Mocking either one doesn't suit your little brother. For it pains me so, Ruben—listen to what I'm saying, Ruben—it pains my heart so that we are leaving."

"Yes," Ruben said, "one can't have lunch and jest with the lord of Egypt every day. That's the exception to the rule. But now you need to remember you're not a child, but the head of your tents, and your children are crying for bread."

It's with Benjamin!

They soon came to a spot where they decided to take their noonday rest and wait until it would be cooler to travel. The previous time they did not make it here until evening, now they had arrived at noon. We need only mention palm tree, well, and shed to mark the place, for it to rise up in the reader's mind as clearly as the man had seen the grave of Benjamin's mother with the help of his magic cup. They were pleased to find this cozy spot again, though, to be sure, it was also associated with memories of the fright certain puzzling events had given them here. But that was all behind them, had melted away in harmony and tranquillity, they could rest easy in the shade of these rocks without a care.

They are still standing there, looking around, have not yet seen to their baggage or begun to set up camp, when they hear a noise growing louder and louder behind them, from the direction they have come, and shouts ring out: "Hey! Ho!" and "Halt!" Are these meant for them? They stand rooted to the spot, listening to this tumult, so startled they don't even turn around. Only one of them turns around—it's Benjamin. What's wrong with Benjamin? He flings his arms and stubby hands into the air and erupts in a cry—a single cry! Then, to be sure, he falls silent—and for a long time.

It is Mai-Sakhme who has charged down on them with steed and chariot, with several chariots. In them are armed men. They leap down and close off the rockbound area. The steward strides stolidly up to the brothers.

His face was very grim. His heavy eyebrows were drawn together in a scowl and one corner of his mouth, only one, was pinched tight—this made the effect especially grim.

He said, "So I have found you and caught up with you, have I? I have chased after you with steed and chariot on my master's order and have caught you here in your camp, where you hoped to hide. What must it feel like to see me here, I wonder?"

"We don't know what it feels like," the baffled brothers replied, sensing that it was all happening again, that the hand had reached out again to drag them to judgment, that all that harmony just now was collapsing into muddled discord. "We really don't know. We're happy to see you again so soon, though we had not hoped to do so."

"If you did not hope for it," he said, "you may well have feared it. Why have you returned good for evil, that we must chase after you and arrest you? My men, you are in very serious trouble."

"Explain yourself," they said. "What are you talking about?"

"You may very well ask!" he replied. "Is this not about that from which my master drinks and with which he prophesies? It is missing. The master had it at his table yesterday. It has been stolen."

"Are you talking about a cup?"

"I am. About Pharaoh's silver cup, and now my master's own. He drank from it yesterday noon. It is gone. Obviously it has been pilfered. Someone has taken it with him. But who? Unfortunately, there can be no doubt. My men, you have indeed done wrong."

They were silent.

"Are you suggesting," Judah, Leah's son, asked with a slight quiver in his voice, "do you intend by these words to say that we have defrauded your master of this table utensil and have taken it with us like thieves?"

"Sad to say, there can hardly be any other name for your conduct. The piece has been missing since yesterday, and it has obviously been filched. And who can have taken it with them? Alas, there is but one answer. I can only repeat that you are in very serious trouble, for you have done wrong."

They were silent again, setting arms akimbo and puffing air from their lips.

"Hear me, my lord," Judah spoke again. "How would it be if you would look to your words and consider what you say before saying it? This is indeed outrageous. We must ask you politely, yet earnestly: What do you think we are? Do we leave the impression of being vagabonds and brigands? But then what sort of impression can it be, that you come here implying we have removed some precious article from the marketeer's table, a cup, it would appear, and have proved all too light-fingered? That is what I, in the name of all eleven, call outrageous. For together we are solemnly, imposingly sons of one man, and indeed are twelve in all. Except that one is no more, otherwise I would call it outrageous in his name as well. You say that we have done wrong. Well then, I shall not boast or sanctimoniously praise us brothers by saying that we have never done wrong and have come through this harsh life without a wicked deed. I do not say we are innocent, that would itself be wicked. But guilt has its own dignity, its own self-respect, more perhaps even than does innocence, and it is not of a mind to pilfer silver cups. My lord, we have been exonerated before your master and by bringing the eleventh of our number have proved to him that we deal in truth. We have exonerated ourselves before you by bringing back to you from the land of Canaan the money we paid but then found at the top of our sacks, offered it to you with open palms—but you did not want it. After such experiences, then, should you not scruple and hesitate before coming here and accusing us of having removed silver or gold from the table of your master?"

Ruben, however, was boiling over now and added, "Why do you have no answer, steward, for the excellent words of my brother Jehuda, and instead simply pinch the corner of your mouth tighter still in that insufferable way? Here we are. Search among us! And with whomever this wretched silver gewgaw, this cup, is found, let him die. Moreover, if you find it, the rest of us, to a man, shall be your slaves for life."

"Ruben," Judah said, "stop gushing away! Inasmuch as we are completely pure in this matter, there is no need for such oaths."

Mai-Sakhme, however, responded, "Quite right, why seethe like this? We know how to exercise moderation. With whomever I find this cup, he shall be our slave and remain in our hands. But the others shall be blameless. Open, if you please, your sacks."

Which they did. They practically ran to their baggage, could not bring it back from their asses fast enough, and ripped their fodder sacks wide open. "Laban!" they cried with a laugh. "Laban, searching there on that mountain in Gilead. Ha, ha! Just let him sweat and ransack himself half to death. Come here, master steward! Come search me first!"

"Just keep calm," Mai-Sakhme said. "Everything in due time and in the proper sequence, just as my lord knew to name you by your names. I shall begin with this big hothead here."

And while they mocked him—ever more certain of victory the farther he went, laughing loudly and constantly calling him Laban, that sweating, searching clod of earth—he moved from one to the other according to their ages and rummaged in their belongings, stood there bent over, hands on hips, eyeing what was in their sacks, and before proceeding to the next was sure first to shake his head or shrug his shoulders when he found nothing despite all his rummaging and digging. And so he came to Asher, to Issakhar, came to Zebulun. There were no stolen goods. He was nearing the end of his search. Only Benjamin was left.

And now they jeered all the louder.

"He's searching Benjamin now!" they cried. "He's sure to be lucky there. He's searching the most innocent of all, innocent not just in this matter, but innocent in general, hasn't been guilty of a wicked deed in all his life. Pay attention now, this is worth watching, how he searches as he gets close to the end, and we're curious just what he'll have to say when he's done searching and has to speak words of—"

All of a sudden they fell silent. They saw it glinting in the steward's hand. From Benjamin's fodder sack, and from not all that deep in the grain, he had pulled out the silver cup.

"Here it is," he said. "Found it with the littlest brother. Had I gone about it the other way round, I would have spared myself a good deal of effort and mockery. So young and yet so thievish. Of course I'm happy to have rounded up the item; but my joy is seriously soured to learn of such ingratitude and such corruption at so early an age. Young man, you are now in extraordinarily serious trouble."

And the others? They clasped their heads in their hands, their eyes bugged out, staring at the cup. They let out a hiss through puffed-out lips—puffed out so far that they couldn't form the words "What's this!" but could manage only the sibilants.

"Benoni!" they cried, their voices filled with tears and exasperation. "Defend yourself! Open your mouth, if you please! How did you come by this cup?"

But Benjamin was silent. He dropped his chin to his chest so that no one could see into his eyes, and said nothing.

They rent their clothes. Several actually grabbed their tunics by the hem and with one hard tug ripped them all the way to the chest.

"We are disgraced!" they wailed. "Disgraced by our youngest! Benjamin, for the last time, open your mouth! Vindicate yourself!"

But Benjamin was silent. He did not raise his head, and he said not a word. His was an indescribable silence.

"He cried out just before," Dan, Bilhah's son, shouted. "Now I remember that he gave an indescribable cry as these men were approaching. Fear tore that cry from his heart. He knew why they were chasing us."

They pounced upon Benjamin with a loud curse and pummeled him with pinches and opprobrium and called him a villainous thief—called him "a son of a thief," and asked, "Did his mother not steal her father's teraphim? It's inherited, it's in his blood. Oh you bloody thief, did you have to put your inheritance to use here, so that you've brought this shameless shame on us, brought your whole tribe to the ash heap, your father, all of us and our children?"

"Now you're exaggerating," Mai-Sakhme said. "That's not the case at all. Besides, you have been exonerated and are blameless. We do not accept your sharing in his guilt, but find instead that your little brother has pilfered all on his own. As free men you may now return home to your honest father. Only he who took the cup is now ours to keep."

But Judah answered him and said, "Not one word more of that. Not a word, steward, for I wish to have some words with your master, and he shall hear the words Judah has resolved to speak. We will all return with you to appear before his face, and he shall judge us all. For we are all liable in this matter and are as one in regard to this incident. Behold, our youngest was innocent his whole life long, for he was always at home. But we others were out in the world, and we became guilty there. We have no intention of pretending purity and leaving him in the lurch now that he has become guilty on this journey, while we have remained innocent in this matter at least. Come, lead us all together with him before the marketeer's throne."

"Fine with me," Mai-Sakhme said, "just as you please."

And under the guard of lance-bearers, they turned back toward the city, following the same road they had traveled without a care. And Benjamin still said not one word.

"It Is I!"

It was late afternoon when they arrived before Joseph's house again; for, as it is written, it was there that the steward took them, and not to the Central Office, where they had first bent low and bowed before him—he was not to be found there, he was at home.

"For he was yet there," or so the story says, and is correct insofar as Pharaoh's friend had returned to his office after yesterday's merry luncheon, but since early morning today had not wanted to leave the house. He knew that the captain, his steward, was hard at work, and he was on tenterhooks. The holy game was nearing its climax, and it was up to the ten whether they would be present at the scene of its unfolding or merely hear of it. Would they let their youngest brother return alone with Mai-Sakhme or would they join him?—Joseph's nervousness knew no bounds. To a large extent this would determine his future conduct toward them. We, on the other hand, are exempted from all such suspense, because we can recite by heart each of the stages of the story being told here, particularly since our own account has established what Joseph was still so anxiously waiting to learn, and we already know that the brothers were unwilling to leave Benjamin alone with his guilt. Knowing what we know, we can smile at Joseph and his expectant anxiety as he paces through his house, from library to reception hall, from there to the hall of bread, then retraces his steps to his bedchamber, where with a trembling hand he touches up this or that in his makeup. His conduct reminds us of a costumed actor running about backstage as he waits for the show to begin.

He also strode to the women's wing to pay a visit to his wife, Asenath, the stolen bride, joined her to watch Manasseh and Ephraim at play. But all the while he chatted with her, he was unable to conceal his own tension and stage fright.

"Husband," she said, "dear master and abductor—what is wrong? You are not relaxed, your ears are pricked, you shuffle your feet. Is something on your mind? Shall we sit down for a game at the board to divert you, or should a few of my handmaids perform a charming dance for you?"

But he responded, "No, Maiden, thanks, but not now. I have other moves on my mind than those of a board game and cannot play the spectator for a dance by handmaids, but must juggle the balls myself and play my own game, whose spectators shall be God and the world. I must return to the vicinity of the reception hall, for that is where it is to be staged. But I know something better to occupy your handmaids than dancing, for I came in fact to order them to make you more beautiful than you already are and clad you in your finest, and to tell the nursemaids to wash Manasseh's and Ephraim's hands and dress them in embroidered shirts, for I am awaiting most extraordinary visitors, whom I wish to introduce to you as my family, once the word is spoken as to who it is whose family you are. Yes, what big eyes you make, my shield-maiden with the dainty waist. But comply with my wishes and make yourselves fine; you will hear from me soon."

Then he ran off, ran back to the men's wing, but could not simply bask in pure expectation and suspense, which is all he really wanted to do, but had to report to the library, along with his reader and true scribe, to receive important agents from the Office of Provisions, who had come on business—certain accounts awaiting his approval—and to spoil the joy of pure expectation, for which he roundly cursed them. And yet they were also welcome, for he needed supernumeraries.

The sun had already begun its decline when, keeping an ear

cocked over his papers, he heard muffled noises at the front of the house and knew that the hour had come, that his brothers' caravan had arrived. Mai-Sakhme entered—that one corner of his mouth pinched more tightly than ever—bearing the cup, which he handed over. "With the youngest," he said. "After a long search. They are in the hall awaiting your verdict."

"All of them?" he asked.

"All of them," the stout man replied.

"You can see I am seriously engaged here," Joseph said. "These gentlemen have not come to see me for fun, but to deal with the business of grain. You have held the position of steward with me long enough to be able to tell whether I am free for such petty private matters or am fully occupied with more urgent obligations. You and your men can wait."

And he bent back down over the scroll that an official held rolled out in front of him. But after a while, since he saw nothing of what was written on it, he said, "We might just as well take care of this bagatelle, a legal matter concerning a crime of ingratitude. Follow me, gentlemen, across to my reception hall, where these miscreants await my sentence."

And they grouped around him as he took the three steps up from the library and, passing through a tapestry, stepped out on the dais where his chair stood; he sat down, the cup in his hand. The moment he took his seat, fans were instantly above him—his attendants were not about to leave him unprotected and unfanned. Between the columns and sphinxes, crouching lions of red stone with Pharaoh's head, a beam of light full of dancing dust fell at an angle from one of the high windows on the left, casting its light on this group of sinners who had thrown themselves on their faces a few feet before the throne. At both sides tall spears were planted. Curious members of the household staff—cooks and chamber servants, those who sprinkled floors or were in charge of flowers for the tables—now crowded the doorways.

"Brothers, stand up!" Joseph said. "I truly had not thought I would see you before me again so soon and for such cause. There are several things I would not have thought. I would not have thought you, whom I received as gentlemen, could do to me what you have done. As happy as I am to have my cup again, from which I both drink and prophesy, you see me saddened, my soul stricken, by your crass treatment of me. I find it incomprehensible. How could you presume to repay good with evil in such crude fashion and offend a man such as I in his daily habits by robbing him of the cup of which he is so fond, and then simply beating a retreat? Your action was almost as ill-considered as it was ugly, for would you not have had to say among yourselves that a man such as I would immediately miss such a precious item and at once deduce the entire matter? Did you really think that, robbed of my cup, I would be unable to prophesy your whereabouts? And now? I assume you admit your guilt?"

It was Judah who answered. Indeed, he spoke on behalf of them all here and now, for it was he who had endured the most in life, who best understood guilt, and so was called to speak. For guilt creates an active spirit—and vice versa, for without an active spirit there is no guilt. On the way here he had won authorization to speak for the others and prepared his words. He stood there among his brothers in his rent garments and said:

"What shall we say to my lord, and what point would there be in attempting to defend ourselves before him? We are guilty before you, my lord—guilty in the sense that your cup was found among us, that is to say, with one of us, and thus with us. How the item came to be in the sack of our youngest brother, the innocent who always stayed at home—I do not know. We do not know. We are powerless to offer even surmises before the throne of my lord. You are a mighty man and are both good and evil, you raise up and you cast down. We belong to you. No justification is of any value before you, and what a fool the sinner would be to insist upon present innocence if the Destroyer demands payment for old iniquities. It was not for nothing that our father, the old man, lamented that we would leave him childless. Behold, he is proved right. We and he with whom the cup was found have become my lord's slaves."

In these first words, which were in no way the entire speech for which Judah is famous, there was a hint of many things Joseph chose not to pursue, but wisely ignored. He restricted his reply to the offer of elevenfold slavery, by rejecting it.

"No, not like that," he said. "Far be it from me to act so. There is no conduct so bad that it can turn such a man as I into a monster. You have bought food for your father, the old man, here in the land of Egypt, and he is waiting for it. I am the agent of Pharaoh; let no one say that I used your sin to keep money, wares, and their purchasers. Whether you all sinned together or only one of you I do not wish to inquire. During the pleasant time we spent together at table, I confided to your youngest the virtues of my precious cup and prophesied to him concerning his mother's grave. It may be that he tattled about it to you all; it may be that together you forged this plan of ingratitude to rob me of my treasure—not for the sake of its silver, I assume. You wanted to control its magic powers, possibly in order to find out what became of your brother who is no more and beyond the reach of your hands—what do I know? Your curiosity would be understandable. On the other hand, it may be that your little brother sinned all on his own, told you nothing, and took the cup. I do not wish to know and shall not probe the matter. The stolen property was found with this little fellow. He has become mine. You, however, may depart in peace for your home and your father, the old man, that he may have food to eat and not be childless."

So spoke this exalted man, and there was silence for a little while. But then out from the chorus of brothers stepped long-suffering Judah, the one they had named to be their spokesman. Stepping toward the throne, he approached Joseph, took a deep breath, and said, "Hearken to me, my lord, for I wish to speak a word in your ears and present to you in my speech how all this came about and what you have done and how things stand with me and with all us brothers. My words shall prove to you in finest detail that you cannot and dare not set our youngest apart and keep him for yourself. Thereupon, I shall declare how we others and most especially I, Judah, who am fourth among us—how we cannot possibly, can never return home to our father without our youngest, never, ever. Thirdly, however, I wish to make my lord an offer and propose to you how your rights may be served by means that are possible rather than impossible. That is the sequence of my speech. Therefore do not let your anger burn against your servant, and, if you please, do not interrupt the words I shall speak as my spirit, and guilt, move me. You are as Pharaoh. I shall begin, however, with how it began and how you began it, for it was as follows:

"When we came down here—for our father sent us that we might procure food from this granary as a thousand had before us—we did not fare as had that thousand, but were set apart and treated strangely and were led down to your city and before the face of my lord. And the strangeness abided, for my lord was strange as well, that is, both rough and gracious, which is to say, double in his dealings, and posed peculiar questions as to our circle of acquaintance. 'Do you perhaps,' my lord asked, 'have a father or brother still at home?' And we replied, 'We do have a father, an old man, and a brother besides, his late-born youngest son, whom he shepherds with his staff, holding fast to his hand, for his brother is no more and is thought dead, so that he alone is left to our father from their mother, which is why he loves him so dearly.' But my lord answered, 'Bring him down to me. Not one hair on his head shall be harmed.' 'This cannot come to pass,' we replied, 'for the reasons stated. And if his youngest son were to be ripped from him, he would die.' Whereupon you responded harshly to your servants, 'By the life of Pharaoh! Unless you come down with your youngest brother, the one who is still left from his lovely mother, you shall see my face no more.' "

And Judah continued, saying, "I ask my lord if that was how it was and began, or if it was not so and began otherwise than by my lord asking for the boy and insisting upon his coming against our protest. For it pleased our lord to present the matter as if by bringing him with us, we might exonerate ourselves of the suspicion of espionage and thereby confirm that we deal in the truth. But what sort of exoneration, what sort of suspicion is that? No one can believe us to be spies, we brothers in Jacob do not look like spies, and if anyone believes it nonetheless, then our providing our youngest brother is no exculpation, but purely a peculiarity and comes merely from my lord wanting to see our brother with his own eyes—and why? As to that I must be silent, God alone knows."

And proceeding with his speech, Jehuda raised his lion's head, stretched out one hand, and said, "Behold, this your servant believes in the God of his fathers and that all knowledge is with Him. But what he does not believe is that this God smuggles treasures into the packs of His servants so that they have both their wares and the money they paid to purchase them—that has never been before and there is no tradition in this regard: neither Abraham, nor Isaak, nor our father Jacob ever found divine silver in his pack, concealed there by the Lord. What is not, is not, and is but a sheer peculiarity and its source in all cases is one and the same mystery.

"Can you then, my lord—can you, seeing that with the help of famine we persuaded our father and borrowed our little brother for this journey—can you, who implacably forced him to come and without whose strange demands he would never have set foot in the land—can you, who indeed said, 'No harm shall come to him here below'—can you now hold him as a slave because they found your cup in his pack?

"That you cannot.

"But for our part we—and particularly your servant Judah whose words these are—cannot come before our father's face without our youngest brother, never ever. We can no more do it than we could have come before your face without him—and not for reasons of peculiarity, but for the most powerful of reasons. For when your servant, our father, admonished us and said, 'Go again to that land and buy us a little food,' we answered, 'We cannot unless you give us your youngest son, for that man down there, who is lord of that land, is unyielding in his demand that we bring him or we shall not see his face'—and behold, the old man raised up a lamentation, known to all, that pierces the heart like the flute sobbing in the ravine, for he broke into song and lamented:

"'Rachel, lovely and eager, for whom I gave to Laban, that black moon, seven years of my youth, Rachel, heart of my heart, who died by the roadside, but a short path from the inn, she was my wife and willingly bore me two sons: one in life and one in death, Dumuzi–Apsu, the lamb, Joseph, my handsome son, who knew how to deal with me so that I gave him everything, and Benoni, the little Son of Death at my hand, who is still left to me. The one departed from me, for I demanded it of him, and a cry filled all the universe: He is mutilated, the beautiful son is torn to pieces! And I fell back in a faint and have been rigid and numb ever since. But with my numb hand I hold fast to him who is all I have, for mutilated, mutilated is my one and only. If you also take from me all I have left and he is then trampled by a boar perhaps, you will bring my gray hairs down to the pit in such sorrow that it would be too much for the world, for it could not endure it. It is filled to its farthest rim with a constant cry: "Mutilated is the beloved son." And were this son to be added, the world must burst into nothing.'

"Has my lord now heard the lament of the flute and the song of the father? Then let him judge in his own mind whether we brothers can come before the old man without his youngest, the little man,

and confess: 'We have forfeited him, he is no more.' Whether we
could endure all that before his soul, which clings to this young soul,
and before the world, which is full of grief and can bear no more, for
this would undo it. Whether, above all, I, who now speak, Judah by
name, his fourth, can come before him—that is now for you to
judge. For my lord does not yet know everything, not by a long way,
and your servant's heart feels his words rising up to address something quite different in this hour of distress. Yes, it feels that the
mystery from which all this peculiarity comes can be brought to
light only by the revelation of another mystery."

Here a murmur of uneasiness stirred among the band of brothers, but Judah, the lion, raised his voice to counter it and continued,
saying, "I assumed surety for our little brother before my father and
offered myself to him as surety; for just as I now stand before you,
near to your throne that I may speak these words, so I stood near to
my father and swore an oath and said: 'Give him into my hand, I
shall be liable for him, and if I do not bring him back to you, I shall
bear the blame before you for all eternity.' This, then, is my liability.
And now judge, peculiar man, whether I can go back up to my father
without our little brother, and there behold a calamity that is too
much for me and for the world. Accept my offer. You shall keep me
to be your slave in his stead, so that you may have a possible atonement and not an impossible one. For I wish to make atonement,
atonement for all. Here before you, peculiar man, I take hold of the
oath we brothers swore, the gruesome oath by which we bound ourselves together—I take hold of it with both hands and break it in two
over my knee. Our eleventh, our father's lamb, the first son of the
true wife—no animal mutilated him, but rather we, his brothers,
sold him out into the world."

With these and no other words Judah ended his famous speech.
He stood there, swaying on his feet, and his brothers were ashen
pale, yet profoundly relieved that their secret was out. That does indeed happen: ashen pale relief. But two cries rang out—they came
from the biggest and smallest brothers. Ruben shouted: "What's this
I hear!" And Benjamin did exactly as he had done before: he flung
his arms into the air and burst into an indescribable cry. And Joseph?
He had risen from his chair, tears sparkling as they ran down his
cheeks. For the slanting shaft of light that had previously fallen on
his huddled brothers had silently wandered to the last opening at the

end of the hall, directly opposite him—that is why the tears running down his cheeks sparkled like gemstones.

"Let all Egyptians go out from here," he said, "everyone out. For I invited God and the world to be guests at my game, but now God alone shall be its spectator."

With reluctance they obeyed. After first giving a wink to the scribes on the dais, Mai-Sakhme put his hands to their backs and politely helped them on their way; and the servants cleared the doorways as well—not that we could convince anyone they moved all that far off. Instead they stood a little outside the hall—and some inside the library, each leaning forward on one leg in the direction of the scene now unfolding, a hand cupped to one ear.

There, however, Joseph, ignoring the gemstones on his cheeks, spread his arms wide and made himself known. He had made himself known often before this, setting people aback by letting them see that something higher than he was revealed in him, so that this higher power was then merged in a dreamy, seductive way with his own person. Now he simply said—and despite outspread arms, even said it with a little modest laugh—"Children, it is I. I truly am your brother Joseph."

"But of course he is!" Benjamin cried almost choking with elation, and dashing forward up the steps of the dais, he fell on his knees and passionately embraced the legs of the brother who was found again.

"Yashub, Joseph-el, Jehosiph!" he sobbed, looking up at him with his head thrown back. "It's you, it's you, but of course it's you, it has to be! You are not dead, you have toppled the great dwelling place of the shadow of death, you have ascended to the seventh level and been invested as Metatron and Innermost Prince—I knew it, I knew it, you have been raised up very high, and the Lord has made for you a throne like His own. But you still know me, your mother's son, and you waved my hand in the breeze."

"Little brother," Joseph said. "Little brother," he said, lifting Benjamin up and putting their heads together. "Do not speak, it is not that great and not that far removed, and my glory is not of that sort, and the main thing is that we are twelve again."

"Do Not Quarrel!"

And he threw his arm around his shoulder and stepped down with him to his brothers—yes, and how did things stand with them and how were they standing there? A few stood with legs spread, their arms hanging a great deal longer than usual, it seemed, almost to their knees, and with mouths agape they stared into space, searching. Others held both fists pressed to chests that heaved up and down with their rapid breathing. They had all turned pale at Judah's confession, but now their faces were dark red, red as a pine tree trunk, red as they had been as they sat squatting on their heels and Joseph came walking up in his coat of many colors. Had Benoni's great rapture and his "But of course!" not set a seal upon the man's declaration, they would have understood none of it and believed none of it. But now as Rachel's sons came down to them with arms entwined, their poor heads were set the task of turning mere association into identification, of recognizing in this man—who, granted, had long had something to do with Joseph in their minds—the brother they had done away with. Was there any wonder it crackled inside their brains? No sooner had these fidgeting, foot-shuffling fellows managed to think of this lord here and their victim, that boy there, as one, than the unity fell apart again—not only because it was so difficult for them to hold it together, but they were also in a difficult position because it was so utterly embarrassing and terrifying.

"Come near to me," Joseph said, even as he stepped toward them. "Yes, yes, it is I. I am Joseph, your brother, whom you sold into Egypt—but never mind, that was all right. Tell me, is my father still alive? Speak a few words with me and do not be distressed. Judah, what a powerful speech that was! You delivered it for all eternity. Here my fervent embrace by way of congratulations and of welcome, and a kiss for your lion's head. You see, it is the kiss you gave me before the Minæans—and I give it back to you today, my brother, and it has been blotted out. And in that one kiss I kiss you all, for surely you do not think I am angry with you for having sold me to this place! It all had to be this way, and God did it, not you. El Shaddai set me apart from our father's house early on and made a stranger of me according to His plan. He sent me down here before you, to be your provider—and has arranged a lovely rescue, by which I feed Israel along with other nations in a time of famine. This is important for people's physical needs, to be sure, but a simple, practical matter and deserving no special hosanna. For your brother is no divine hero, no messenger of spiritual salvation, but merely a man of business, and that your sheaves bent low to mine in the dream I babbled on to you about or that the stars bowed to me— that was not meant to express an overblown grandeur, but only that my father and brothers would know how to thank me for providing a physical benefit. For bread one says, 'Thank you very much,' but not 'Hosanna.' For indeed that must be—bread. Bread comes first and then the hosanna. And now that you understand how simple were the Lord's intentions, do you not want to believe that I still live? You know yourselves that the grave did not hold me, but that the children of Ismael pulled me from it, and that you sold me to them. Just raise your hands and grab hold of me, so that you can see that I live as your brother Joseph."

Two or three of them actually touched him, too, gingerly stroking a hand along his garment and grinning timidly.

"And so it was all but a jest and you just pretended to be a prince?" Issakhar asked, "but are actually only our brother Joseph?"

"Only?" he replied. "That is surely the most of what I am. But you must understand me rightly: I am both, I am Joseph whom the Lord has made to be Pharaoh's father and prince in all of the land of Egypt. Joseph I am, arrayed in the splendor of this world."

"Granted," Zebulun said, "one surely cannot say that you are only the one and not the other, but instead must say that you are both in one. We had a feeling it was so, too. And it's a good thing that you are not the thoroughgoing marketeer, things would have gone badly for us otherwise. For under your robes you are our brother Joseph, who will protect us from the marketeer's wrath. But you must understand, my lord—"

"Foolish man, would you please stop this 'lord, lord'? There is to be no more of that."

"But you must understand that we also would like the marketeer to protect us from our brother, for we treated him badly in times past."

"You certainly did!" Ruben said, setting the muscles of his face grimly taut. "I am outraged, Jehosiph, by what I have had to learn on this occasion. For they sold you behind my back and gave me no hint of it and all this time I did not know that they got rid of you for money . . ."

"Enough of that, Ruben," Bilhah's son Dan said. "You did a few things behind our back as well and visited the grave on the sly so that you could steal the boy. And as for the purchase price, no one got rich on that, as His Excellency Joseph very well knows—twenty Phoenician shekels, that was all, thanks to that old man's tough bargaining. And we can settle the account as to your share any time you like."

"Do not quarrel, men!" Joseph said. "Do not bicker among yourselves about such things, what one did that the other knew nothing about. For God has turned it all to the right. I thank you, Ruben, my big brother, that you came to the pit with your rope-work to pull me out and return me to our father. But I was no longer there, and that was good, for it was not to be and would not have been right. But now it is right. And let us all think of nothing but our father . . ."

"Yes, yes," Naphtali said, giving his tongue free rein, with head nodding and legs twitching. "That's it, that's it. Our exalted brother is quite right, for it is totally intolerable for Jacob to be sitting in—or in front of—his house of felt without the least notion of what has taken place here: that Joseph is alive, has risen high in the world and assumed a resplendent position among the heathen. Just think, he is sitting there wrapped in ignorance, while here we stand exchanging words with his vanished son, touching his garment, so that we may palpably grasp that it was all a misunderstanding, all false tidings that turn to naught our father's grievous grief, turn to naught the worm that has rankled inside us all our lives. It is so exciting one would like to jump through the roof for joy, and there is something excruciatingly askew in this world that we here know all this, but he does not, simply because there is too much distance between him and us, a great dull and dreary expanse that separates us and in which truth advances a few paces, then lies down and can go no farther. Oh, if only a man could cup his hands to his mouth and shout across seventeen days: 'Father! Halloo! Joseph is alive and is as Pharaoh in the land of Egypt, that's the latest news!' But no matter how loud the shout, he sits there unmoved and cannot hear it. Oh, if only a man could send out a dove that has the speed of lightning, with 'Know this,' written beneath its wings, so that there would be an end to what is askew in this world and everyone would know the same thing, both here and there. No, I can stand here no longer, I cannot stand it. Send me, send me! I wish to handle this myself. I shall vie with the stag and bring our father beautiful words. For can there be any more beautiful words than those that bear the latest news?"

Joseph, however, calmed him in his eagerness and said, "Enough, Naphtali, no need to tumble head over heels, for you shall not run alone and no one should have precedence in telling our father what I wish to have him told, for I have given this much thought as I lay upon my back at night, pondering this story. You shall rest here with me for seven days and share in all my honors. I wish to introduce you to my wife, the maiden of the sun, and I shall bid my sons to bend low before you. But then you shall pack your animals and all of you go back up with Benjamin to my father and announce to him: Joseph, your son, is not dead, but is alive and these are the words his mouth speaks to you: 'God has given me preeminence among these foreigners, and a people I did not know are subject to me. Come down to me, do not tarry and have no fear, dear father, of this land of tombs, to which Abraham once came during a famine. For this scarcity, with neither plowing nor harvest, has been in the world for two years now, and will surely continue for three or five years yet, but I wish to provide for you and you shall settle here in rich pastures. Should you ask if Pharaoh permits it, my answer is: Your son has him wound round his finger. And I shall ask His Majesty to let you settle in the region of Goshen and on the fields of Zoan in the direction of Arabia, and there I will provide for you, for you and your children and your children's children, for your flocks and herds, for all that is yours. Long ago I chose the land of Gosen or Gosem, but also called Goshen, as the place for you to come after me, because it is not yet truly the land of Egypt, not yet markedly so, and there you can live from fish at the river's mouth and from the fat of the land, a pretty life, in which you will not have to deal much with the precocious children of Egypt to the detriment of your originality. Yet you would be near to me.' That is what you shall say to my father in my name, men, speaking cleverly and deftly, gently announcing to him in his rigid old age, first, that I am alive, and then that he should come down here with all of you. Ah, if only I could go up with you myself and coax him into it, I would surely go. But I cannot, for I cannot spare a single day. And so in my stead, you must persuade him in fine style and with love's cunning that I live and he must come. Do not say at once: 'Joseph is alive,' but first ask, 'How would it be and how would our lord feel should it turn out that Joseph still lives?' Let him try it that way first. And do not say to him outright: 'You are to settle in the land below, among the corpses of gods,' but employ a prettier word, saying 'in the land of Goshen.' Will you do it in that way, with sly love and without me? I shall instruct you in this better over the next few days. But now I wish to introduce you to my wife, the maiden of the sun, and show you my boys, Manasseh and Ephraim. And all twelve of us shall eat and drink and be merry and remember old times, though not too precisely. But lest I forget: when you go back up to our father, tell him all that you have seen, and do not skimp in describing my splendor here below. For his heart was treated badly—but now it shall be treated to the sweet music of his son's glory."

Pharaoh Writes to Joseph

Nothing would be more regrettable if, in the wake of these events, the majority of our audience were to begin to wander off and scatter, thinking to themselves: "So that was it, the lovely 'It is I' has been spoken, and it can't get any lovelier than that. That was the high point, and now the rest will just be played out, and we already know how, so there's nothing exciting left." Take my advice and do stick around! The author of this story—whom we should understand to be He who is the author of all events—has provided it with many high points and knows how the effect of each is heightened by the others. For Him the motto is: The best is yet to come. He always plans it so that we have something to look forward to. When Joseph learned that his father was still alive, that was surely a delightful moment; but when that springtime song telling of his son's life is sung for Jacob, a man numbed by grief, and when he journeys down to embrace him—that's not supposed to be the least bit exciting? Whoever goes home now can ask the others who stayed to hear the ending whether it was exciting or not. And then he will be overcome with remorse and for the rest of his life will feel he has been left out because he wasn't there when Jacob blessed his Egyptian grandchildren with a crisscross blessing, or when he celebrated the solemn

hour of his death. "We know all that!"—what a foolish thing to say.
Anyone can know the story. But to be present at it—that's the thing.
It appears, however, that our admonition was unnecessary—not a
soul has budged from the spot.

Now that Joseph had spoken with the eleven and they with
him—and now that together they all left the hall where he had made
himself known to them, to join Asenath the Maiden, his wife, so that
they could bend low before her and greet their nephews with their
Egyptian-style children's braid—a happy commotion and joyful
laughter reigned throughout the villa. For all the household staff had
eavesdropped, and Joseph needed to make no announcement, issue
no explanation, for everyone knew at once and called out to one another with a laugh that the Provider's brothers had come and his father's sons had found their way here from the land of Zahi—which
was great fun for all, especially since they could be certain of cakes
and beer in celebration of the event. The scribes from the House of
Provisions and Distribution, however, had also listened in and now
spread the word in the city; and it would have comforted fleet-
footed Naphtali to learn how this latest news ran through Menfe like
wildfire, so that everyone soon shared the same information: the
happy knowledge that the band of brothers had come to visit the
Unique Friend, which resulted then in a great deal of leaping for joy
in the streets and in a crowd gathered before Joseph's house in the elegant suburb, where with loud hurrahs they demanded to see him in
the circle of his Asiatic clan, a request that in the end was granted
when the twelve stepped out on the terrace before the eager
throng—and only we would think it a pity that the people of Menfe
had just the lenses of their eyes but no notion of how to play with
light as we do and so could not capture the group in a photograph.
They were ignorant of all that, however, and did not miss it precisely
because they had never even thought of it.

Nor was the charming news contained for long within the walls
of this tomb metropolis, but flew off like a dove across the land, and
the hullabaloo found its way most quickly to Pharaoh, who, along
with his entire court, was greatly amused by it. Pharaoh, who by
now was called Ikh-n-atôn—for, as announced, he had set aside his
oppressive Amun name and chosen in its place one that bore the
name of his father in heaven—Pharaoh, then, had some years before
relocated his residence closer to that of his favorite minister, moving

it from Thebes, the house of Amun-Rê, to a site that lay farther north in the Upper Egyptian nome of the Rabbit and that after a long search he had found suitable for building a new city dedicated to his beloved godhead. It was a little to the south of Khmunu, the house of Thoth, at a spot where a small island—one that simply cried out for the erection of elegant pleasure pavilions—emerged from the river and the cliffs of its eastern bank drew back in a wide arc, offering ample room for the construction of temples, palaces, and riverside gardens suitable for a theologian whose life is hard but who should also have things good. The Lord of Sweet Breath now had a place after his own heart, had listened to no other advice than that of his heart and of him who dwelt within it and to whom alone hymns of praise would resound here. And so His Majesty's beautiful decree had gone out to his artists and stonemasons for them to build here, and with greatest possible speed, a city, Akhet-Atôn, the city of his father, the city of the horizon—which, first, was a severe blow for Nowet-Amun, for Thebes, "city of a hundred gates," for with the departure of the court it ran the risk of sinking to the level of a provincial town, and, second, served brutal notice to the imperial god at Karnak, with whose dictatorial priesthood—even during the years of plenty—had stood in increasingly severe conflict even with Pharaoh's tender fervor for his loving and all-uniting father.

Pharaoh's delicate constitution did not hold up well under those constant clashes with the power of this warlike god armed with national tradition; given the contradiction between his soul's peaceable disposition and the necessity of defending his discovery of a higher divinity against such bellicose omnipotence—indeed of launching attacks against it—his health steadily declined; and so, upon realizing that in his case flight would be the best method for inflicting severest damage to his foe, he decided, at least as regarded his sacred person, to shake the dust of Wase from his sandals, even if Mama— partly for the purpose of keeping an eye on Amun and partly out a fondness for the palace of her husband, the former king Neb-maat-Rê—did wish to remain in the old capital. For two years Ikhnatôn had had to master his impatience to escape Amun's domination, for that is how long, despite ruthless conscription of a flogged work-force, it had taken to construct even the basic elements of his new city, which at the time the king took up residence—in a high ceremony of ritual sacrifices of bread, beer, horned and unhorned bul-

locks, goats and sheep, birds, wine, incense, and every sort of fine
herb—was not really a city yet, but only an improvised camp for the
court, its half-finished luxury consisting of a palace that provided
barely adequate sleeping quarters for him, his Great Consort Nefernefruatôn–Nefertiti, and the royal princesses, but was scarcely ready
for real living yet, with plasterers, artists, and decorators still hard at
work everywhere; a temple for God the Lord, whose seven courts,
magnificent pylons, and splendid columned halls floated in great
serenity amid fluttering red pennants and the fragrance of flowers;
amazing parks and nature preserves with artificial ponds and shrubs
and trees that had been transplanted, root balls and all, to the desert
from the fertile banks of the Nile; white quays glistening along the
river; a dozen brand-new apartment buildings for the king's entourage of Atôn devotees; and a row of supremely comfortable
tombs that had been carved into the rock of the surrounding cliffs
and that, more than all the rest, were ready for occupation.

There was at present no more than that to Akhet-Atôn, though
of course it was expected that the court would bring a growing population in its wake and that further embellishment would be diligently carried out even while Pharaoh reigned from here, serving his
heavenly father, celebrating feasts of tribute, and siring daughters to
augment his royal household of women. The third, Ankhsenpaatôn,
had recently arrived.

By the time Joseph's express letter—officially informing the god
of the advent of his brothers, from whom he had been separated
since early youth—arrived at the palace, the same news had already
been loudly bandied about in those halls still smelling of fresh paint;
and Pharaoh had excitedly discussed it at length with Queen Nefertiti, her sister Nezemmut, his own sister Baketatôn, even with his
artists and courtiers. He answered the letter at once, dictating as follows:

Command to the Overseer of All That Heaven Gives,
True Overseer of My Mandate, Spender of Shade to the King
and His Unique Friend, My Uncle:
Know that My Majesty regards your letter as one that he
reads with true gladness. Behold, Pharaoh wept greatly at
the news that he received from you, and the Great Consort
Nefernefruatôn, as well as the Sweet Princesses Baketatôn

and Nezemmut, mixed tears of their own joy with those of the dear son of my Father in Heaven. Everything you announce to me is extraordinarily beautiful, and what you have reported to me makes my heart leap. The words you have written me, that your brothers have come to you and that your father still lives, are a delight to heaven, earth rejoices, and the hearts of good men exult to hear them, and without doubt even the hearts of the wicked are softened by them. Be apprised that as a result of your letter, the beautiful child of the Atôn, Nefer-khe-peru-Rê, the Lord of the Two Lands, finds himself in an exceptionally gracious mood. The wishes that you included with your salutations were granted before you ever set them down. It is my beautiful will and in accord with my consenting agreement that all your family, however many they be, should come to the land of Egypt, where you are as I, and the assignment to them of a land of settlement, from whose marrow they shall be nourished, is left to your discretion. Tell your brothers: "Do this, and this is the order of Pharaoh, in whose heart is the love of his father Atôn. Load your beasts and from the royal warehouses take with you wagons for your little ones and your wives, and take your father and come to me. Give no thought to your goods, for you shall be provided in this land with all that you need. Pharaoh is well aware that your culture does not stand so high and that your requirements are easily met. And when you come to this land, bring your father and his servants and his entire household down to me, that you may graze in the nearness of your brother, the Overseer of All Things in the entire land, for the land shall lie open to you." These, then, are Pharaoh's orders to your brothers, given amidst tears. If a great number of important duties did not detain me in Akhet-Atôn, the sole capital of the Two Lands and my residence, I would mount my great chariot of electron and hasten to Men-nefru-Mirê, that I might behold you amid your family and you might present your brothers to me. When, however, your brothers have returned, then you shall present them to me, though not all, for that might prove too tiring for Pharaoh, but a selection thereof, and you shall also present your father, the old man, to me, that I may magnanimously favor him with my conversation and he may live in honor inasmuch as Pharaoh has spoken to him. Farewell!

The letter was delivered to Joseph at his house in Menfe by express courier, and he showed it to all eleven, who kissed their fingertips. They remained with him at his home for a quarter moon; since for twenty years now their father had believed Joseph dead and mutilated, the exact day when he learned that he was still alive no longer mattered. And Joseph's menials served them, and his wife, the daughter of the sun, spoke friendly words to them, and they chatted with their nephews—looking elegant in their special children's locks—with Manasseh and Ephraim, who could speak their language. Of the two, the younger, Ephraim, looked more like Joseph—and thus like Rachel—than did Manasseh, who took entirely after his maternal Egyptian side, so that Judah said, "You'll see, Jacob will favor Ephraim and when he speaks they will not be Manasseh and Ephraim, but Ephraim and Manasseh." He advised Joseph, however, that before Jacob's arrival he cut off that Egyptian braid each wore over one ear, for the old man would take offense at it.

Then, as the week drew to a close, they packed and readied themselves for their journey. A royal commercial caravan was about to depart from Menfe, the balance scale of the Two Lands, traveling by way of Canaan to Mitanniland, and they were to join it with wagons from the royal warehouses, some with two wheels, some with four, which had been handed over to them along with mules and drivers. When one includes ten asses laden with all sorts of baubles and luxuries from the land of Egypt—choice knickknacks of civilization, examples of the finest taste, that Joseph was sending along as presents for Jacob—plus ten she-asses, likewise intended for Jacob and burdened with grain, wine, preserves, smoked meats, and salves, one can well understand that by themselves they formed a grand caravan of their own, especially since the personal property of each had been increased by gifts their exalted brother had lavished on them. For it is well known that he gave them each a festal garment; to Benjamin, however, he gave three hundred debens of silver and no less than five festal garments, in accord with the extra days of the year. So he had good reason for saying as he took leave of them:

"Do not quarrel on the way!" But he meant it more in the sense that they should not bring up matters from the past and accuse one another of what one had done that another knew nothing about. For the notion that they might be hard on Benjamin because as the nearest and truest brother he had been more richly rewarded—that never entered Joseph's mind, just as it was the farthest thing from theirs. They were like lambs and found everything exactly as it should be. As impetuous young men they had risen up in violence against injustice, but now, as things had turned out, they found themselves fundamentally reconciled with injustice and for all time would have no objection to the great "I show favor to whom I show favor, and mercy to whom I show mercy."

How Do We Begin?

How remarkable, how it tickles one's fancy, to note how events in this story are ordered in such lovely correspondence and one piece finds its fulfillment in its counterpart. Long ago, seven days after Jacob received the bloody token, the brothers had returned home from the valley of Dothan to mourn with their father over Joseph's death, yet were sick with dread about what state they might find him in and how they could live with him under the half-false and yet sufficiently accurate suspicion that they had murdered the boy. Now, with hair turning white, they were returning home to Hebron with the no less devastating news up their sleeves: that Joseph had not been dead all this time and was not now, either, but that he lived, lived in glory; and the task of telling this to the old man left them almost equally full of dread. For devastating is devastating and overwhelming is overwhelming—whether it concerns life or death; and they greatly feared that Jacob would fall back in a faint, just as he had then, but that this time, now twenty years older, he would die of "joy," that is of shock, of sheer terror at his good fortune, so that Joseph's life would be the cause of his death and his eyes would never again behold his son alive, nor his son's eyes him. It was, moreover, almost inevitable that at the same time it would be revealed that, although they had not murdered Joseph as a boy—as Jacob had half believed all this time—they had halfway committed that crime and only by accident had not finished the deed, thanks to the Ishmaelites who found him and took him with them to Egypt. This contributed not a little to their throes of both joy and fear, and they found partial relief only in the thought that the grace God had shown them in turning them away from true murder by sending His Midianite emissaries would have to impress Jacob and prevent him from cursing and raking over the coals people so blessed by God.

These, then, were the topics of conversation during the entire seventeen-day journey, which, despite their impatience to complete it, seemed on the other hand far too short for their discussions to reach a conclusion about how best tactfully to tell Jacob of all this and how they would stand before him once they told him.

"Children," they said to one another—for ever since Joseph had said, "Children, it is I," they often addressed one another as "children," which had previously not at all been the case—"Children, you shall see, he will fall back in a faint when we tell him, that is, unless we slip it to him very delicately and gently. But whether delicate or crude—do you think he will believe what we tell him? In all probability he will not want to believe a word we say, for after so many years the idea of death establishes itself in a man's heart and head and is not easily overturned or exchanged for the idea of life—ultimately the soul does not welcome it, but holds fast to old habits. Our brother Joseph thinks it will give the old man great joy, and it will, of course—tremendous joy—but let us hope it does not overwhelm his strength. For how can a man know what to do with joy right off, after feeding upon bitterness for a jubilee of years, and is he glad to learn that he has spent his life in delusion and his days in error? For bitterness was his life, and now it's all gone up in smoke. It will be more than strange having to talk him out of what we once talked him into with that bloody garment to which he still clings. And in the end he will be more embittered with us for having taken this woe from him than for having first inflicted it upon him. He is certain to resist and not believe us—but then again, that is good and necessary. He should and dare not believe us for a while, for if he believed at once, it would slay him. Yes, how to tell him so that the joy is not too abrupt and the disappointment over his bitterness not too great? It would be best if we did not need to say anything, but could lead him back down to the land of Egypt and present him to his son Joseph, so that he might see him with his own eyes and all words would be superfluous. But it will be difficult enough to bring him to

Mizraim and its rich pastures even after he has learned that Joseph is alive there; which is why he'll have to know beforehand, for he won't go otherwise. But truth, after all, has not just words, but tokens as well, and those include our exalted brother's gifts and Pharaoh's wagons transporting us—we will show him those first perhaps, before all words, and then explain the tokens to him. And from the tokens he will realize how friendly are this exalted man's intentions toward us and how we are of one heart and one mind with the brother we sold, so that once everything is revealed the old man can no longer be angry with us, or curse us. Besides, can he curse Israel, ten of the twelve? He certainly cannot, for that would mean kicking against the counsel of God, who sent Joseph before us as quartermaster in the land of Egypt. So then, children, let us not be all too fearful. The hour will come, and the moment itself will whisper to us how to wiggle our way through. First we shall spread the presents before him, the wares of Egypt, and ask: 'From where and from whom do you suppose all this comes, father? Guess! Yes indeed, it comes from that great marketeer down there, he has sent it to you. But since he has sent it, he must surely love you very much, don't you think? Must love you almost as much as a son loves his father?' And once we have arrived at the little word 'son,' we're halfway there, have the worst behind us. And then we'll ring the changes on that word for a while and gradually move from saying, 'The marketeer has sent it to you,' to 'Your son has sent it to you, because, you see, he is alive and is lord over all the land of Egypt!'"

That is how they planned it, all eleven, discussing it by day and within their tent at night; but given their worries, they were soon, almost too soon, near the end of a now familiar journey: up from Menfe to the fortified frontier and through the horrid expanse that led to the land of the Philistines and Gaza, the harbor of Khazati by the sea, where they parted company with the commercial caravan they had joined and now headed inland toward the mountains and Hebron, moving in short day marches or, better still, night marches. For spring was in bloom as they arrived, and the nights were lovely now, silvered by an almost full beautiful moon; and since it was difficult to travel with a convoy now swollen to such a size—with its Egyptian wagons, mules and drivers, and a herd of almost fifty asses—that it aroused curiosity and drew gawking crowds everywhere, they usually found a quiet place to stop by day and advanced by night toward home, toward the terebinths of the grove of Mamre, where their father's house of felt stood and most of them had their tents as well.

The last day, of course, they set out early in the morning and by the fifth hour of the afternoon found themselves nearing their goal, even if from the present slope they could not yet see their clan's camp still lying hidden behind familiar hills. They had left their supply train a little distance behind and now rode ahead on their asses, eleven men lost in thought and not saying a word, for their hearts were pounding and despite all their discussions none of them was sure any longer just how to begin, how to break the news to their father without undoing him. And now that they were so close to him, everything they had intended to say displeased them; they found it all foolish and improper, particularly silliness like "Guess!" and "Who else?" seemed hideously banal and totally inapt for the situation. Each rejected and derided it in his heart, and at the last moment a few tried replacing it with something else: Maybe they should send someone, fleet-footed Naphtali, so that he could tell Jacob that they were approaching with Benjamin and also brought great, incredible tidings—incredible in one sense because one *could* not believe them, but perhaps even in another as well because they were so contrary to one's habits of thought that one might not *want* to believe—and yet it was God's living truth. A herald to precede the others—perhaps, one or two of them thought, that was the best way to soften and prepare their father's heart to receive the news. They rode at a slow walk.

Annunciation

The slope the animals were crossing was rough and stony, but blanketed now with the blossoms of spring. Larger boulders lay all about, and the ground was strewn with rocks and pebbles; but wherever there was soft soil and, or so it seemed, even growing from the stones themselves, exuberant wildflowers ran riot—flowers far and wide, white, yellow, sky blue, pink and purple, heaps of flowers, clusters and pillows of flowers, a glut of pied beauty. Spring had called them and they had bloomed, each in its own hour, and when the rains of winter failed, just morning dew evidently sufficed for them to burst into a fleeting, quickly withering splendor. Even the shrubs scattered here and there in these broad fields blossomed white and pink, for it was their hour as well. Only puffs of high clouds dotted the blue of the sky.

On one boulder jutting up like a cliff amid foaming waves of flowers, sat a figure like another flower in the distance, which soon proved to be a tender young maiden—all alone beneath the sky, clad in a red tunic, marguerites in her hair, and in her arms a zither that she strummed with dainty tanned fingers. It was Serah, Asher's child.

Still a good way off, her father recognized her before all the others and said with delight, "It's Serah there on that boulder, my little girl, plunking out a tune on her strings. That's just like her, the urchin, she sits there all by herself, practicing on her psaltery. She's from the tribe of fiddlers and whistlers, sweet thing. God knows where she got it from; since the day she was born she's had to sing psalms and strum her psaltery. She can make those strings ring with melody, but the voice that blends with her songs of praise is much fuller than you'd ever expect from that little cricket's body—she'll be famous in Israel someday, the hoyden. Look, she's seen us now, has flung her arms up and is running toward us. Halloo, Serah, it's your father Asher, home with your uncles!"

And the child was already near—she ran barefoot between boulders and through the flowers, the silver rings at her wrists and ankles tinkling softly and the yellow and white wreath atop a head of black hair bouncing askew. Panting, she laughed for joy at this reunion and, still short of breath, called out quick words of greeting; yet even her gasps and breathlessness rang with a melody so rich that it was hard to understand how it could come from such a frail little body.

She was indeed what the world calls a maiden—no longer a girl, but not yet a young woman, twelve years old at most. Asher's wife was held to be a great-granddaughter of Ismael—was there something in Serah's blood from Isaac's beautiful and savage half brother that made her sing? Or—since a person's traits can undergo the strangest transformations in his descendants—had the sweet lips and moist eyes of her father Asher, his curiosity and his love of a unity of emotion and opinion become musicality in little Serah? You may find it all too bold, too far-fetched, to trace a child's love of song and art back to her father's sweet tooth, but a man must try as best he can to explain a curious talent for the psaltery like the one Serah had found in her cradle.

The eleven looked down from their long-legged asses to this maiden, they greeted and petted her—and their eyes took on a certain thoughtfulness. Most of them dismounted from their asses and encircled Serah, hands at their backs, nodding and rocking their heads, saying "So, so," and "My, my," and "Look at you!" and "Well, little songstress, there you were sitting and strumming your zither as usual, and now it seems you've come running our way before everyone else, doesn't it?"

Finally, however, Dan, who was called a serpent and an adder, said, "Children, listen to me, I can see it in your eyes that we all have the same thing in mind, and actually it would be up to Asher to say what I have to say now, but it hasn't occurred to him because he is her father. But I have proved often enough that I have the makings of a judge, and my native subtlety has inspired me to say the following: It is not by chance that this maiden here, Serah, the songbird, was the first of our whole tribe to cross our path. God has sent her to us to give us a message, to instruct us as to what we should do. The plan we devised for telling the news to our father, for slipping it to him without slaying him—that was all clumsy stuff and nonsense. Serah—she shall slip it to him in her fashion, so that the truth comes to him in the form of a song, which is always a gentler way to learn a thing, whether it bring bitterness or bliss, or both. Serah shall precede us and sing it to him, and even if he does not believe her song to be the truth, we shall still have softened the soil of his soul and made it ready for the seed of truth, for the moment when we come to him with words and tokens and he will be forced to realize that song and truth are one, just as we were forced to realize, difficult as it was, that Pharaoh's marketeer and our brother Joseph were one and the same. Well? Have I spoken correctly, given solid footing to what was hovering there in your minds as your eyes moved thoughtfully from Serah's foolish little head and out into space?"

Yes, they said, he had, he had judged rightly. That's how it should be, it was a message from heaven and a great relief. And now they began to instruct the child and impress upon her what this was all about—but it wasn't easy, because they all tried to talk at once and seldom let just one speak for all, so that Serah's alarmed but amused eyes shifted from one to the other, staring at excited faces and mouths, at gesticulating hands.

"Serah," they said, "it is like this. Believe it or not—but sing it, and then we shall come after and prove it. But it's better if you do believe it, for then you'll sing it better, for it is true, as unbelievable as it sounds—surely you believe your own father and all your uncles. So now see here—you did not know your uncle Jehosiph, who got lost, the son of the true wife, the son of Rachel, who was called the virgin of the stars, but he was called Dumuzi . . . Ah yes, ah yes! . . . And to your grandfather Jacob, he was dead, because long before you were born, the world swallowed him up, so that he was no more and was dead in Jacob's heart all these years. But now it has turned out, incredibly enough, that it all has been turned about—"

> "A miracle, for now it has turned out,
>   that everything is turned roundabout,"

impatient Serah began to sing with such rich, laughing exultation that she drowned out all the gruff voices around her.

"Hush, you prodigy!" they cried. "You cannot start singing away before you know what's what and we have given you the whole picture. First learn, then warble! Learn this: Your uncle Joseph is risen again, in other words, he was never dead, but is alive, not only alive, but alive in such and such a fashion. He lives in Mizraim, as such and such a man. It was all a mistake, do you understand, and the bloody garment was a mistake, and God has carried it through beyond all expectation. Have you understood? We were with him in the land of Egypt, and he made himself known to us, beyond any doubt, with the words 'It is I!' and has said this and that to us, and that he wants all of us to follow after him—you as well. Have you got that into your head so that you can present it in the form of a song? For you are to sing it to Jacob. Our Serah is a clever child and she can do it. So now take your zither and go across country ahead of us, let your song that Joseph lives ring out. You shall pass between those hills there, making directly for Israel's camp, and look neither right nor left, but just keep on singing. If you should meet anyone and they ask what this means and what your strumming and rhyming are all about, you won't answer any questions, but just keep walking on and singing 'He's alive!' And when you get to your grandfather Jacob, you shall sit down at his feet and sing as sweetly as you know how: 'Joseph is not dead, but alive.' And he, too, will ask you what that means and what is this you've dared put into song. But don't answer him, either, just keep plucking and singing. Then the eleven of us will come after you and offer him a reasonable explanation. So will you now be a proper little songbird and do it just like that?"

"I'll be happy to," Serah replied in a ringing voice. "I never before had words like these to put to the music of my strings, and a person would really like to show what she can do! There are many songsters in town and country, but I've been given a theme to sing before any of them and with it I shall sing them all from the field."

And with that she picked up her lute from the stone where she had been sitting, cradled it in her arm, spread her tapered brown fingers—the thumb here, the other four there—and, setting out across the flowers with an unswerving stride, though its rhythm might vary, she sang her psalm:

"Sing, O my soul, a new song while homeward I'm coming!
My heart tells a verse on eight strings that I'm strumming.
For full is my heart with a song that demands to be told,
and its worth far outweighs fine silver and gold;
sweet is its taste like the honeycomb,
for spring's glad tidings I now bring home.

Listen, you people, and hear my tune's air!
Heed the good word that I may now declare!
For the lot is cast so sweet and unexpected,
and of all earth's daughters I have been elected
to spread the finest wonder of a wondrous story
e'er to lend a poet fame and glory.
This I may sing, with eight strings' assistance,
and to grandfather bear great news from a distance.

By sweet music we're persuaded
that its balm can heal our woe;
but all the more when high silence is aided
by the telling word that man should know.

Word and music, once united,
make the voice of reason strong!
Let us praise with hearts excited
Psalter's verse and finest song!"

Singing these words she strode across the pasture toward the hills
and the gap between them, strumming and plucking her strings till
they thumped and chirped, and sang anew:

"Word and tune have but one duty:
be the song for which I strive,
share its message, share its beauty,
and it says: The boy's alive!

Yes, Endless Goodness, what have I learned lately
and what has surprised my young ears now so greatly!
With mouth agape, the fair news that I pondered
comes from these men who in Egypt have wandered!
Which is to say, both my uncles and him I call father.
They gave me the news worth a rhymer's best bother.
They've offered me the finest of tales for my wonder,
for whom did they meet in that country down under?
Grandfather, 'twill be beyond understanding,
but accept it you must that notwithstanding.
Like to a dream it seems merely fanciful,
yet is as real as it's wonderful.

What a bird of rarest feather,
when these two at last agree:
truth and beauty joined together,
life as purest poetry!
Here for once the soul succeeded,
learned how both can best survive.
Let this grand refrain be heeded:
Truth is beauty! Your boy's alive!

Yet for now perhaps 'tis better
that you think it only beauty. Self-restraint
should assist your pounding heart to fetter
lest at once you fall back in a faint,
as you did that day they brought the bloody token.

Silently they lied, a grievous fault,
left your weary soul in night, and though unbroken
like a pillar made of salt.
You, in agony and sorrow,
thought you'd see him nevermore,
dead he was for every morrow.
Now he rises in your heart on morrow's shore!"

Here a man, who had been standing further up the hill, a shepherd in his sunshade hat, tried to ask her something. He had been gazing down at her for a long while and listening in astonishment; now he descended to her, matched his stride with hers, and asked, "Miss, what are you singing there as you march? It sounds so unusual. I've often heard your songs of joy, and it's no news to me that you can strum the strings brightly, but I've never heard anything so topsy-turvy, never such insinuations as these. And all the while you're marching straight ahead. Are you on your way to Jacob, our lord, and is it for him that you sing? It seems to me it is. But what is this story for which you've been elected? What is as real as it is wonderful? And what is that refrain supposed to mean: 'The boy's alive'?"

But striding straight ahead, she did not even look his way, merely shook her head with a smile and lifted her hand from her strings for a moment to lay a finger to her lips. But then she resumed her chanting:

"Sing now Serah, Asher's child, this happy tiding
from eleven who in Egypt were abiding!
Sing of God's kindness, His grand dispensation,
tell of the man that they met in that nation.
And who is this man? It is Joseph, I say,
it is my uncle, the man of the day.
Behold, old man, it's your own dear son,
Pharaoh alone is greater by comparison.
He is named the Lord of Two Lands,
foreign folk he also commands,
and before kings men sing his praise,
for he serves his land in most noble ways.
The domain of his power is vast and unbounded,
every nation and tribe is astounded,
for from thousands of barns he furnishes bread

to a world in hunger and dread.
For he took precaution, he had a plan,
and is the world's most well-loved man.
His robes laid in aloe and myrrh are sweet-smelling,
ivory palaces are his dwelling,
from where he comes like a bridegroom fair.
Old man, see what your lamb's become down there!"

The shepherd, who was still walking beside her, listened with ever-growing amazement. Whenever he saw anyone, maid or man, he would beckon with one arm for them to come here and listen to this. And so Serah was soon accompanied by a small attentive band of men, women, and children that grew as it approached the family camp. The children skipped, the adults strode in step, and they all turned their faces to her as she sang:

"You have long thought he was torn into pieces,
The flow of your tears never ebbs, never ceases.
Twenty years have passed and still you're mourning,
as if ashes your gray head were adorning.
Look, old man, behold it and see:
after His lash God gives healing.
Ah, how wonderful are the works that He
to His children is revealing!
Far beyond our ken the reach of His rule,
great each deed His breath enkindles,
grandly did He make you a fool.
With what majesty he swindles.
The whole of creation is filled with heavenly glee,
Tabor and Hermon delight in His comedy.
He took from your heart what you most treasure,
but returns him now just for good measure.
In your pain you turned and twisted,
in sad certainty persisted.
And now He gives him back in turnabout,
a beauty still, if perhaps a little stout.
You will not know him,
not know his name or how to show him
proper respect, afraid to blunder
as to who should fall before whom in wonder.

And so it's God that we must thank
for having played such a lovely prank."

By now, together with her escort, she was very near her family's dwellings beneath the terebinths of Mamre and could see Jacob, the venerable man of blessing, seated on a mat before the curtain to his house. And so she took her instrument more firmly in hand, held it higher, and whereas the tones she had just plucked from it had been skillful dissonances to underscore the joke, she now coaxed from it a full surge of harmony and from her breast and throat came purest tones of song for her verses:

> "Hear the word of lasting beauty
> that my song must now revive,
> lovely tones shall do their duty,
> speak that word: The boy's alive.
>> Sing, my soul, in exultation,
>> to my strings fair golden hue.
>> For the grave's made restoration,
>> in your heart, he rises new.
> Heart, rejoice, be glad, and soften,
> 'tis the son they put away,
> whom they lured into his coffin,
> whom the boar's tusk tried to slay.
>> Ah, he lay in death's dark prison,
>> and the fields were left to grieve.
>> Hear the word: He is arisen.
>> Father Jacob, please believe.
> Like a god he strides in power,
> radiant birds wheel into view,
> as from fields that burst in flower,
> he comes forth to welcome you.
>> Winter's grief and death's dark sorrow
>> flee before each word he speaks;
>> God's fair blessing for the morrow
>> lies upon his lips and cheeks.
> Read it in his rascal glances:
> This was God's eternal jest.
> Greet him now as he advances,
> take him to your heart and breast."

Jacob had long since seen his granddaughter, the songstress, coming and had listened with pleasure to her voice. As she approached, he had been gracious enough to tap his hands together in soft accompaniment, the way audiences enjoy clapping in rhythm to songs and verses. Once she arrived, the maiden had sat down on the mat beside him, not saying a word, but continuing to sing, while the band of locals she had attracted came to a halt at a polite distance from the two of them. The old man listened and slowly dropped his hands. And what had been a gentle rocking of his head gradually became a puzzled shaking.

When she had finished, he said, "Well and sweetly done, my grandchild. How considerate of you to have come this way, Serah, to provide this little treat for a bereft old man's ears. You see, I even know your name, though not that of all my grandchildren—there are too many. You, however, are remarkable among the others because the talent for song with which you were born lends prominence to your person, and your name is easily recalled. But you should know, my talented child, that I listened with some thought, and not without concerns of the spirit. For poetry, my dear little girl, always has its own dangerous and flattering allure. Melody is, sad to say, not far from malady, and the first tends to revert to the second, a precarious deviation if left unbridled by a concern for godly things. The play of the mind is lovely, but the mind itself is holy. Poetry is the mind at play, and when my heart is touched I join in by clapping my hands—that is, if the mind holds to godly concerns and is not compromised by the play. But what have you been warbling there for me, and what should I think of someone who comes strolling across flowering fields with a rascal look in his eye and summer birds wheeling round him? That would seem to me to be a dubious god of the meadows, evidently one that local people call 'lord,' much to the confusion of my family and the deception of the children of Abraham. For we, too, speak of the Lord, but mean something different, and there is no end to my having to keep a close watch on Israel's soul and to my preaching beneath the oracle tree that this 'lord' is not the Lord, for the people are always on the verge of confusing them and lustily reverting to this meadow god. For God is hard work, but the gods are a pleasure. Can it be right and good, my dear child, that you have let your talent slip into carelessness and sing to me the psalms of the country folk?"

Serah just shook her head with a smile, however, and did not respond in words, but plucked her strings again and sang:

> "Who is this man that I sing of? It is Joseph, I say!
> It is my uncle, the man of the day.
> Behold, old man, it's your own dear son,
> Pharaoh alone is greater by comparison.
> Grandfather, 'twill be beyond understanding,
> but accept it you must, that notwithstanding.
> > Word and tune have this one duty:
> > be the song for which I strive,
> > share its message, share its beauty,
> > and it says: The boy's alive!"

"Child," Jacob said, deeply touched, "it is indeed sweet and polite of you to come here and sing to me about Joseph, my son, whom you never knew, and to dedicate your talent to him in order to bring me joy. But your song sounds confused, and although your rhymes ring true, you sing without rhyme or reason. I cannot allow it, for how can you possibly sing 'the boy's alive'? That cannot give me joy, for it is a pretty but empty melody. Joseph died long ago. He is torn apart, mutilated."

And Serah replied, strumming with all her might:

> "Sing, my soul, in exultation,
> to my strings' fair golden hue,
> that the grave's made restoration;
> in your heart, he rises new.
> > Long he lay in death's dark prison,
> > while the fields were left to grieve.
> > Hear the word: He is arisen.
> > Father Jacob, please believe.
> To all the nations he supplies bread,
> to a world of hunger and dread.
> For much like Noah, he had a plan,
> and is the world's most well-loved man.
> His robes laid in aloe and myrrh are sweet-smelling,
> ivory palaces are his dwelling,
> from where he comes like a bridegroom fair.
> Old man, see what your lamb's become down there!"

"Serah, my grandchild, you wayward songstress," Jacob said with urgency, "what am I to think of you? Except in psalms and songs it would hardly be polite for you to call me 'old man.' I would let it pass as poetic license if it were the only presumption in your song! But it consists of nothing but impertinences and mad illusions, with which, it would appear, you would like to delight me—but delight in what is null and void is delusion and cannot profit the soul. Can poetry presume as much, and is it not a misuse of talent to announce things that have no relation to reality? A little reason must accompany beauty, or it is only mockery of the heart."

"Behold," Sarah sang,

> "Behold this bird of rarest feather,
>   in which two at last agree:
>   beauty and pure truth together,
>   life as God's great poetry!
>   Yes, for once the soul's succeeded,
>   knows how both can best survive,
>   thus this song's what you have needed:
>   Truth is beauty: Your boy's alive!"

"Child," Jacob said, his head trembling now. "Dear child . . ."
But she rejoiced with verses that took wing to tones that leapt and soared:

> "Look, old man, don't you now see?
>   After His lash God gives healing.
>   Ah, how wonderful are the works that He
>   to His children is revealing!
>   He took from your heart the son you most treasure,
>   and returns him now just for good measure.
>
>   In your pain you turned and twisted,
>   through the years you have persisted;
>   and now He gives him back to you,
>   a beauty still, though plumper, true.
>   And so it's God that we must thank
>   for having played His lovely prank."

Turning aside, he thrust a hand toward her, as if to stop her, his weary brown eyes filled with tears. "Child," he kept saying, "child . . ." And he likewise paid no attention to the commotion that had now arisen nearby or the glad tidings someone told him. For now the band of curiosity seekers who had come with Serah were joined by others who announced the happy homecoming, and as people from the camp came running from all sides, two men hurried to precede them, proclaiming: "Israel, the eleven have returned from Egypt, your sons with servants and wagons and far more asses than they left with."

But here they were now. They dismounted and approached, and in their midst was Benjamin, all the other ten holding on to him in one way or another, for each wanted to be the one to bring him back to their father.

"Peace and good health," they said, "to our father and lord. Here is Benjamin. We have kept him for you in sacred trust, even though for a time we were in tight straits with him, but now you may put him back on the leash. Here is Shimeon again as well, your hero. Besides which we bring food and ample gifts from the Lord of Bread. Behold, we are happily returned—in fact, 'happily' is not even close to the right word for it."

"Boys," Jacob replied, having risen to his feet. "Boys, I do indeed bid you welcome."

As if claiming his property, he laid an arm around his youngest, without even realizing what he had done. He looked dazed.

"You are here again," he said, "are all back together from your perilous journey—that would be a great moment under any other circumstances, and would doubtless fill my soul entirely were it not already preoccupied. Yes, you greet me here in a highly preoccupied state, and it is because of this young maiden—your child, Asher—who sat down beside me, babbling in sweet song her mad tales about my son Joseph, until I do not know how to preserve my reason in her presence, and have therefore greeted your arrival primarily in the expectation that you will protect me from this child and the delusions of her harp, for surely you will not allow my gray head to be mocked."

"We will never allow that," Judah responded, "if we can prevent it in any way. But in the opinion of us all, father—and a well-founded opinion it is—you would do better to entertain the possibility, if only a remote one to begin with, that there might be some truth in the song of her harp."

"Some truth?" the old man repeated, and pulled himself up erect. "Do you dare come to me with such feeble ideas and suggest Israel accept truth half-and-half? Where would we be, where would God be, if we had ever let ourselves be put off with such ifs and maybes? The truth is one and indivisible. Three times your child sang: 'The boy's alive!' There can be nothing true about those words, unless they be the truth. So, what is it?"

"The truth," the eleven said in chorus, each man raising his hands to show his palms.

And a cry of jubilant amazement burst from the crowd gathered behind them. "The truth!" the voices of children, women, and men echoed exultantly. "She sang the truth!"

"My dear papa," Benjamin said, embracing Jacob, "you hear and understand this just as we had to understand it—the one sooner, the other later. That man down there, who asked about me and asked so many things about you—'Is your father still alive?'—he is Joseph, he and Joseph are one and the same. He was never dead, my mother's son. Travelers tore him from the claws of that beast and led him to Egypt, where he grew as if beside a spring and has become the first among men down there. The sons of that foreign land flatter him, for they would perish without his wisdom. Would you like to see to-kens of this wonder? Behold the train that follows us. He has sent you twenty asses, whose burden is food, the reward of Egypt, and those wagons there come from Pharaoh's warehouse and are in-tended to bring us all down to your son. For that you should come—that was his purpose from the start, but I saw through it. And he wants us to graze our flocks in rich pastures near him—though not where it is all too Egyptian, but in the land of Goshen."

Jacob had maintained his upright, almost rigid posture.

"God will decide as to that," he said with a firm voice, "for only from Him does Israel take instruction, not from the great men of this world." And then from his lips came "My Damu, my child!" Hands clasped to his chest, he lifted his brow to the clouds and slowly shook his old head at them.

"Boys," he said, lowering it again, "this young maiden, whom I bless and who, if God hears my prayer, shall not taste of death, but living enter the kingdom of heaven—she sang to me that the Lord had restored Rachel's firstborn to me, but also that though he is in-deed still beautiful, he is now somewhat stout. Does she mean then to say that over time he has unavoidably grown rather fat from the fleshpots of Egypt?"

"Not very, dear father, not very," Judah replied, trying to set his mind at rest. "Only in a stately sort of way. You must recall that it is not death that restores him to you, but life. Were such a thing possible, death would give him back to you as he was; but since it is from the hands of life that you receive him, he is no longer the fawn of former days, but has become a great stag, with all its ornament. You must also be prepared for his seeming somewhat strange to you in his worldly customs, and he wears pleated byssus cloth, whiter than the snows of Mount Hermon."

"I will go and see him before I die," Jacob said. "Had he not lived, he would not now live. The name of the Lord be praised."

"Praised!" the crowd cried and pressed forward to congratulate him and join the brothers in kissing the hem of his robe. He did not look down at their heads; his eyes had turned toward heaven again, and he kept on shaking his head at it. Serah, however, the songstress, took her seat on his mat and sang:

> "Read it in his rascal glances,
> all was God's eternal jest;
> and, though late, in happy trances,
> take him to your father's breast."

Part Seven

RESTORATION

I Will Go and See Him

And so the headstrong cow heard the voice of her child, her calf, which the shrewd farmer had brought to the field that was to be plowed so that the cow would yield to his wishes; and the cow submitted to her yoke and followed. It was still quite difficult for her nonetheless, given her distinct aversion to the field, which she believed to be a field of death. And for Jacob as well his declared decision remained a dubious matter, and he was glad that at least he had time to deal with his doubts; for the execution of the decision to move the entire clan to the land below meant abandoning deep-rooted custom—it both demanded and permitted him time. The sons of Israel were not the sort of people simply to leave everything behind, to take Pharaoh's instruction literally and give no thought to their household goods, inasmuch as they would be provided with everything in the land of Goshen. At most "to give no thought to" meant not to take every last item—not every tool and utensil, or even every sheep, goat, or cow—for that was impracticable; but that most certainly did not mean leaving whatever would encumber their move to whoever might be willing to take it. There was much to be sold, and those sales could not be hurried, but had to be done with all the usual ceremony of leisurely hard-bargaining. But that Jacob allowed these sales to proceed indicated that he was holding fast to his decision in all parts, even though the way he spoke about it had been open to interpretation.

"I will go and see him"—hearing that, one might take it to mean at most "I will go visit him, see his face again before I die, and then return." But as everyone, including Jacob himself, was aware, it could never actually mean that. Had it been only a matter of a visit after which he would return home again, then, if we may say so, it would have been His Excellency and Importancy Joseph who owed his old father a visit, if only to spare him the great inconvenience of a journey to Mizraim. But that ran counter to the motif of sending for others to follow, which, as even Jacob fully understood, determined this fateful hour. Joseph had not been set apart and carried off for that, nor had Jacob's face been swollen from weeping for him so that they might pay one another a visit, but rather so that Israel might follow after. Jacob was far too skilled at reading the ways of God not to realize that the theft of his beautiful son, his glorification in the land below, the persistent drought that had forced the brothers to go to Egypt—that all these arrangements were part of a farseeing plan that it would have been crude folly to ignore.

One might say that it was presumptuous and all too egotistical of Jacob to regard such a vast calamity as this ongoing drought, which afflicted so many nations and resulted in great economic upheavals, as nothing more than a measure taken to guide and advance the history of his own house—it evidently being his opinion that when it came to himself and his family the rest of the world simply had to make the best of it. But presumption and egotism are only pejorative terms applied to beneficial conduct worthy of highest commendation—a far lovelier term for it is piety. Is there a virtue that does not leave itself open to terms of censure or in which certain contradictions, such as humility and arrogance, are not inherent? Piety is the privatization of the world as the story of one's self and one's salvation, and without the, yes, sometimes offensive conviction that one is the object of God's special, and indeed exclusive care, without the rearrangement that places oneself and one's salvation at the center of all things, there is no piety—that is, in fact, what defines this very powerful virtue. Its opposite is neglect of the self, its banishment to the indifferent periphery, from where no benefit for the world can come either. The man who does not think highly of himself will soon perish. Whoever thinks something of himself—as Abram did when he decided that he, and in him humankind, should serve only what is Most High—proves himself to be a demanding sort of person, true, but with that demand comes a blessing for many. This demonstrates the connection between the dignity of the self and the dignity of humankind. The demands of the human ego are of central importance as a precondition for the discovery of God, and only if—by failing to take itself seriously—humankind were utterly to perish, could both discoveries be lost together.

This proposition can be developed as follows: Privatization does not mean reduction, and placing a high value on the self in no way implies its isolation, that it cuts itself off and hardens itself against the universal, against what is outside and above a person, in short, against everything that extends beyond the self, but in which it solemnly celebrates its recognition of itself. If, in fact, piety is the unshakable certainty of the importance of the self, then solemn celebration is its extension, the means by which it flows into what is eternal, which then returns through it and in which it recognizes itself—which results in a loss of the self's closed-off singularity that not only does not detract from its dignity, not only is compatible with that dignity, but also enhances, indeed consecrates it.

We therefore cannot overemphasize the solemnity of Jacob's mood during the time prior to his departure—even as his sons were settling business affairs associated with it. He was about to carry out in actuality what he had dreamt about in his days of his most extreme grief and had feverishly babbled into Eliezer's ear: that is, a descent to his dead son in the underworld. This was a fateful course of action, and whenever the self opens up to the cosmos, losing itself there and identifying itself with it, how can one possibly speak of isolation or of cutting oneself off? The very thought of departure was filled with momentous, self-expanding elements of eternity and of return, elevating the moment beyond any paltry singularity and particularity. Jacob the old man was once again Jacob the youth departing from Beersheba for Naharaim after having set things to rights by deceit. He was Jacob the grown man, who with his wives and flocks had left Haran behind after a sojourn of twenty-five years. But he was not only himself, in whom at various ages in the spiral of his life departure repeatedly rediscovered itself. He was also Isaak, who was journeying to Abimelek, to Gerar in the land of the Philistines. Still farther back, still deeper in time, he saw the return of the primal departure: Abram, the wanderer, leaving Ur of the Chaldees—and even this was not really the primal departure, but only an earthly reflection and imitation of a heavenly wanderlust, that of the moon in its course, of Bel-Charran, the Lord of the Way, passing through one station after the other. And since Abram, the earthly primal wanderer, had himself sojourned at Haran, it was clear that this, then, had to be represented by Beersheba, which would be Jacob's first station of the moon on this journey.

He was greatly consoled by the thought of Abram and how during a different famine he had traveled to Egypt to live there as a stranger—and Jacob was in great need of consolation. Granted, ahead lay reunion with all its painful bliss, after which he would be able to die in peace, for no joy afterward would be worth knowing; granted, the right to immigrate to Egypt and graze his flocks on Pharaoh's pastures was a great boon that many sought in vain and for which many envied him and his house. And yet Jacob found it difficult to reconcile himself with God's decree that he shun the land of his fathers and exchange it for the offensive land of animal gods, the Land of Mud, the land of the children of Ham. He had settled in the land to which Abram had once wandered in much the same loose, provisional fashion as his fathers had—like them, always half a stranger. But he had thought he would die here as they had, and as for the promise that Abram had heard—that his seed would be a stranger in a land not theirs—he had assumed he might apply that to this land here, where he had been born and where his dead rested. Now it had turned out that this prophecy—which not without good reason had always been associated with certain terrors and great darkness—went further still, that its apparent goal was the land to which he would now emigrate: Mizraim, the Egyptian house of bondage. That was what Jacob had always disapprovingly called that strictly governed land down there, never imagining it might become the house of bondage for his own seed—as had now become painfully clear to him. His departure was burdened with the insight that the ominous continuation of God's prophecy—"and they shall serve there and be oppressed for four hundred years"—referred to the land for which he was now departing; in all probability it was a bondage of many generations into which he was leading his house. And even if it was for the benefit of all those included in God's plan of salvation, even if good and bad fortune might cancel one another out in the grand view of fate and the future, it was most assuredly a fateful departure to which Jacob had committed himself in God.

Despite his reservations, he was going to the land of tombs; and yet tombs were what he found it most difficult to leave behind: the grave of Rachel beside the road and Machpelah, the double cave that Abram had bought from Ephron the Hettite, along with the field that it was in, for four hundred shekels of silver according to weights current at the time, that it might serve as a hereditary burial place.

Israel was mobile, as shepherds are wont to be; and yet it did own real estate: this field with its caves—and this would remain Israel's property. The emigrants disposed of many movables, but what was immovable, this field and its grave, could not be disposed of. For Jacob they were the guarantee of his return. For despite however many generations might rot in Egyptian soil while his house increased there, he himself was determined that once he had lived out his life, both God and man should be obliged to bring him home to the one permanent home that he, a man who carried his house with him, had on earth, where he might then lie, where his fathers and the mothers of his sons already lay—except for his beloved wife, who was set apart and lay off to the side of the road, the mother of his beloved son who had been taken away, but who now summoned him.

Was it not a good thing that Jacob had time to ponder his departure for the land of the son who had been stolen from him? What a difficult task it was trying to understand the peculiar role God had assigned to this favorite by setting him apart. We shall learn from Jacob himself what conclusions he reached in that regard. When he spoke of Joseph now, he referred to him exclusively as "his lordship my son." "I intend," he might remark, "to journey to Egypt, to his lordship my son. His is a position of high rank." The people to whom he said such things might smile—behind the old man's back, of course—and make fun of a father's vanity, but they had no idea how much earnest aloofness, renunciation, and stern resolve were expressed in those words.

Seventy in All

Blossoming spring had become late summer before Israel concluded its final transactions and could undertake to depart from the groves of Mamre which are at Hebron. The first goal was Beersheba, and several days of pious devotions were planned for that frontier town, the place where both Jacob and his father had been born and where Rebekah, that resolute mother, had once readied the thief of the blessing for his journey to Mesopotamia.

Jacob freed himself from his ties to those groves and set out with his goods and cattle, his sons and sons' sons, his daughters and daughters' sons. Or as it is also said: He departed with his wives, daughters, and sons and the wives of his sons—a reciprocal count, since here "wives" means the wives of his sons, but "daughters" means the same thing, plus perhaps the daughters of his sons, for example Serah the songstress. They set out with seventy souls—which is to say: they regarded themselves as seventy in all; this was no numbered count, but more an emotional count by considered agreement—that is, determined by a moonlit accuracy that, as we well know, is no longer suitable for our own era, but was perfectly justifiable and held to be correct in theirs. Seventy was the number of nations of the world listed in God's tables, and therefore as the number of progeny to emerge from patriarchal loins it was subject to no recount by the light of day. But since it is Jacob's loins we are dealing with here, the wives of his sons should not have been included in the count, should they? But they weren't. If there's no counting to begin with, nothing can be included in the count, and given a result based on the lovely bias of sacred foregone conclusions, the question of what is or is not included in the count is moot. It is not even certain whether Jacob himself was counted, whether the others included him as part of their number, that is seventy, or excluded him as the seventy-first. We must simply accept the fact that this era allowed for both possibilities at once. Much later, for example, a descendant of Judah—more precisely, of his son Perez, whom Tamar so purposefully bore him—this descendant, then, whose name was Jesse, had seven sons *and* a youngest, a keeper of sheep, above whose head the horn of anointment was raised. But what does that "and" mean? Was the youngest included among the seven, or did Jesse have eight sons? The former is the more likely, for it is much more beautiful and appropriate to have seven sons rather than eight. But it is more than probable, which is to say certain, that the count of seven for Jesse's sons did not change, when, for instance, the youngest was added to it, and that he managed to be included in it even when he exceeded the count. On another occasion a man had a grand total of seventy sons, for he had many wives. A son of one of these mothers slew all his brothers, the man's seventy sons, all upon one and the same stone. By our prosaic sense of things he could, as their brother, have slain only sixty-nine, or more correctly still, only sixty-eight, for to cap it all, another brother, whose name, Jotham, is expressly provided, was left alive. It is hard to accept this, but here we have one man of seventy who slays all seventy, and yet besides himself leaves another of them alive—a solid and instructive example for being both excluded and included at the same time.

Jacob, then, when viewed correctly, was the seventy-first of the seventy wanderers—to the extent that this number can hold up in the light of day. It was, to be prosaically truthful, both lower and higher—a new contradiction, but it cannot be seen or put in any other way. Jacob, the father, was the seventieth and not the seventy-first inasmuch as the male members of the tribe came to a total of sixty-nine souls. But it did so only if one included Joseph, who was in Egypt, and his two sons, who were in fact born there. Since these three members of the tribe were not part of the caravan, they must, though they are included in it, be subtracted from its number. This does not, however, put an end to the requisite subtractions, for the simple reason that it is obvious that souls were included in the count who at the time of their departure had not yet been brought into the world. One might discuss the justifiability of this in the case of Jochebed, a daughter of Levi, with whom her mother was pregnant at the time and who was born "between the walls" (presumably, those of the frontier fortress) upon their arrival in Egypt. But it is clear that included in the sum of travelers were grandchildren and great-grandchildren of Jacob that had been neither born nor conceived—that is to say, were only anticipated, but not yet present. They came to Egypt, as pious erudition puts it, *in lumbis patrum,* and were members of the caravan only in a most spiritual sense.

So much for the necessary subtractions. But there is also no lack of compelling reasons for adding to the total of sixty-nine. This was in fact only the tally of Jacob's male seed; but if—or better, since—the entirety of his direct descendants are to be accounted for, one must include, if not the wives of his sons, then at least their daughters, Serah, for example, to name but one, though certainly with all due emphasis. It would have been quite impermissible not to have counted the maiden who first brought to Joseph's father news that he was alive. She was held in high regard in Israel, and there was never any doubt that the blessing Jacob had spoken over her out of gratitude would be fulfilled—that is, that she would not taste death but living enter the kingdom of heaven. Indeed, no one knows when

she is supposed to have died; her life has every appearance of continuing unbounded. It is said of her that generations later she helped
the man Moses as he wandered aimlessly in search of Joseph's grave
and showed him the spot: that is, in the flood of the Nile; and it is
even said that a vast number of years later her presence moved
among Abram's people under the name of the Wise Woman. Be that
as it may, whether this same Serah was actually alive at such disparate points in time or whether other maidens assumed the sentient
nature of this little messenger and announcer of glad tidings—no
one can ever cast doubt on the fact that she is to be counted among
the seventy wanderers, whatever "seventy" may mean here.

Not even in regard to the wives of Jacob's sons, that is, the mothers of his grandchildren, can one be absolutely certain that they
ought not be included in the count. We speak of "mothers," and not
just of "wives," because we are thinking of Tamar, who, in accordance with the words "Where you go I will go," was part of the procession, along with those two manly sons of Judah. She traveled on
foot for the most part, with a long staff and, for a woman, very long
strides—tall, dark, with a proud mouth, circular nostrils, and eyes
fixed, in that peculiar way of hers, on some distant point. And this
resolute woman who had not let herself be left out—is she not to be
counted as well? It was a somewhat different case with her two husbands, Er and Onan—they could not be counted by either moonlight or daylight, for they were dead, and though Israel included in
its tally future members, surely not dead ones. Shelah, however, the
husband she had not been given, but whom she also no longer
needed—having now presented him with excellent half brothers—
was part of the caravan and counted among the number of Leah's
grandchildren, which came to thirty-two.

"Carry Him!"

Having agreed that they were seventy in all, Israel departed from the
grove of Mamre, the Amorite. Counting everyone not included in
the count—shepherds, herders, slaves, drivers for both pack and riding animals—it was a procession of a good hundred people or more,
a colorful, noisy convoy, a nomadic tribe wrapped in clouds of dust

and ponderous with herds. The mode of transportation varied—just between us, the fleet of Egyptian wagons that Joseph had sent were of little use. This does not apply to the two-wheeled freight wagons called *agolt,* usually pulled by oxen, whose value for transporting household goods, goatskins of water, and fodder (as well as women with small children) requires our grateful acknowledgment. The actual passenger carriages of the *merkobt* type, lightweight, sometimes very luxuriously equipped vehicles, often nothing more than a curved gilt wooden frame, with a pair of mules or horses pulling a dainty coach upholstered in pressed purple leather open to the rear—these toy chariots, despite the good intentions of Joseph and his royal master, turned out to be quite impractical and most of them were returned to the land of Egypt as empty as they had come. It did no one any good that the hubs of their wheels were beautifully ornamented with the heads of Moors, or that some of them were covered inside and out with bas-reliefs in stucco on canvas that vividly depicted court and peasant life. Only two people—or three, if they squeezed close together—could stand upright in one, which, given rough roads and the lack of any suspension, proved extremely tiring over time; or the rider had to sit on the floor of the coach with his back to the team and feet dangling—which very few wanted to do. Like Tamar, many people preferred that exemplary and most ancient form of travel: striding on foot with a staff. Most, both men and women, rode: on wide-hoofed camels, bony mules, white and gray asses, whose saddlecloths were embroidered with big glass beads and decorated with mullein tassels. These were the animals that kicked up the dust of the road, and on them, obeying the summons of Joseph to follow after, rode Jacob's people: a colorful clan in woven wool, the bearded men often clad in the twill cloaks of the desert, their headscarves held in place by felt rings; the women with braided black hair down to their shoulders, silver and brass chains jingling at their wrists, coins hung at their brows, red henna painted on their nails, and in their arms babies swathed in great, soft cloths edged in brocade. Nibbling at roasted onions, sour bread, and olives, they rode along, keeping for the most part to the mountainous ridge and the road that led from Urusalim and the heights of Hebron down to the lower lands in the south, to Negeb, the "dry land," to Kiriath-Sepher, the city of books, and to Beersheba.

Our chief concern, needless to say, is the comfort of Jacob, the father. What was his mode of conveyance? In sending wagons, had Joseph meant for this very old man to stand in one of the bas-relief coaches and spend the entire trip behind a golden railing? He had not. It had not occurred even to Pharaoh, his lord, to demand that. The orders that the beautiful child of the Atôn had decreed from his new palace still smelling of fresh paint had been as follows: "Take your father and *carry* him." The patriarch was to be carried, as if in triumph, that was the idea; and among those generally unusable vehicles that Joseph had sent there was one mode of transport of a very different kind intended for just this solemn purpose, for carrying Jacob: an Egyptian sedan chair, of the sort that Keme's upper class used in the streets of its cities and on journeys, indeed an especially elegant model of this convenience, for the back of its chair was of fine canework, its sides bore dainty inscriptions, and it came with rich curtains, bronzed carrying-poles, and even a light, brightly painted wooden screen at the rear as a protection against wind and dust. The chair could be carried by young men, but it also came provided with poles that could be laid crossways on the backs of two asses or mules, and Jacob felt very much at ease in it—once he resolved to use it. But he did not use it until after Beersheba, which as he saw it marked the border between home and alien territory. Until his arrival there he was borne by a clever dromedary with languid eyes and a sunshade attached to its saddle.

The old man was a very beautiful and dignified sight to behold, and he knew it, too, as, surrounded by his sons, he sat there on his high perch, cradled in the rocking gait of the wise beast. The fine woolen muslin of his *kofia* lay scalloped across his brow, was wound in folds around his head and shoulders, and fell down over his dark, reddish brown robe that opened here and there to reveal an embroidered undergarment. Breezes played in his silver beard. His gentle shepherd's eyes were turned inward, a look that announced he was pondering his stories, both past and future, and that no one dare disturb him—at most someone might respectfully inquire as to his well-being. Above all he was thinking of how he would once again behold the holy tree that Abraham had planted there at Beersheba and of his intention to sacrifice, teach, and sleep beneath it.

Jacob Teaches and Dreams

Shading a primitive stone table and an upright stone column, or *massebah,* the giant tamarisk stood atop a low hill a little apart from the populated settlement of Beersheba, which our wanderers never even entered; and closer inspection revealed that it had probably not been planted by Jacob's father's father, but was a divine tree, an *êlon môreh,* this is, an oracle tree, that had once served the children of the land as a shrine to Baal, but that he had taken and reinterpreted as the focal point of a site sacred to his highest and only God. Jacob may even have been aware of this without being shaken in his belief that Abram had planted the tree. He had planted it in a spiritual sense in any case, and the patriarchal way of thinking was gentler and broader than our own, which knows only an either-or and raps the table, insisting, "If it was already a tree of Baal, then Abraham didn't plant it!" Such zealotry in pursuit of truth is more testy and disruptive than wise, and far more dignity is to be found in silently uniting both aspects in the way Jacob did.

The forms by which Israel honored the God of all ages under this tree were almost no different from the rites practiced by the children of Canaan—with the exception, to be sure, of all the mischief and scandalous sport into which the worship of those children inevitably tended to degenerate. Tents were pitched at the foot of the sacred hill, all the way around it, and immediately preparations were made for the slaughtering that was to take place on the dolmen, that ancient stone table, and for the sacrificial meal to be shared by everyone afterward. Had the children of Baal done anything different? Had they not also let the blood of lambs and kids run out over the altar and then smeared it over its blood-caked posts? Of course they had; but the children of Israel did it in a different spirit, out of a more civilized piety, which found its chief expression in their not sporting with one another after the divine meal—or at least not publicly.

Jacob instructed them about God under the tree as well, which they did not find the least bit boring, and even the teenagers thought it highly diverting and important, for they were all more or less gifted in this way and took delight in grasping even the niceties. He taught them the difference between the multiple names of Baal and the name of the God of their fathers, the highest and only God. The former did in fact imply a multiplicity, for there was no Baal, there were only baals, that is, proprietors, owners, and guardians of cultic sites, groves, localities, wells, trees—a multitude of gods of the field and house, who operated individually, each bound to one spot, but collectively had no face, no person, no personal name and at best, if they were of a sort like the one in Tyre, were called *melkart,* king of the city. One was called Baal Peôr, after his location, or Baal Hermon or Baal Meôn; one was indeed called Baal of the Covenant, which had proved useful in Abram's own work with God; one even bore the ridiculous name Dance Baal—there was little dignity and certainly no overall majesty in that. The multiplicity of names the God of their fathers bore was, by contrast, a very different matter, for it did not detract in the least from His personal oneness. He was called El-Elyon, God most high, El-Ro'i, the God who sees me, El-Olâm, God of the ages, and, ever since Jacob's great vision born of his humiliation, El-Bêtêl, the God of Luz. But those were all just different terms for one and the same person of God in His highest state, who was never tied to a given locality, like the scattered multiplicity of the baals of field and town, but existent in all those things to which they were assigned individual proprietorship. The fertility they bestowed, the wells they guarded, the trees in which they lived and whispered, the thunderstorms in which they raged, the engendering springtime, the withering east wind—He was all those things that were merely individual to them; it was all His property, for He was the universal God, it all came from Him, and in saying "I" He comprised it all, was the Being of all being, Elohim, the many as one.

Jacob expatiated captivatingly on the name Elohim—the seventy found this exciting and not without subtlety. One could see where Dan, his fifth son, got his subtlety, which was merely a lesser filial offshoot of the old man's higher version. The question that Jacob discussed was whether one should think of Elohim as singular or plural, whether one should say "Elohim wills it," or "Elohim will it." Given the importance of expressing things correctly, a decision was necessary here, and Jacob apparently had made it, for he advocated the singular. God was one, and those who regarded *elohim* as a plural form of *el,* that is, "god," were caught up in a maze of error. That plural should be formed as *elim.* Elohim was something quite different. It no more meant a multiplicity than did the name Abraham. The man from Ur had been called Abram, and then his name had been honored by being expanded to Abraham. It was the same with Elohim. It was a majestic, honorific expansion, nothing more—and most definitely it did not mean what one could only have rebuked as polytheism. His pupils imprinted this on their minds: Elohim was one. But then it turned out that he was more than one, perhaps three. Three men had come to Abraham in the grove of Mamre as he sat at the door of his tent in the heat of the day. And the three men were, as Abraham realized in hastening to greet them, God the Lord. "Lord," he had said, bowing low to the ground before them, "Lord," and "You." But at other times he said "Lords" and "Ye." And he begged them to sit in the shade and to strengthen themselves with milk and the meat of a calf. And they ate. And then they said, "I will return to you within a year." That was God. He was one, but He was manifestly three as well. He himself practiced polytheism, though on principle he said only "I" the entire time, whereas Abraham alternated between "You" and "Ye." The use of the name Elohim as a plural, they heard Jacob add, had something to it, despite his having previously imprinted the opposite on their minds. Yes, glimmering through what he now went on to say was a sense that his own experience of God, like Abram's, had been threefold, that it, too, had been made up of three men, three independent and yet coincident persons who spoke as one "I." Jacob spoke first of a father God, or God the Father; second of a Good Shepherd, who tends us, his sheep; and third of a God whom he called the Angel—and the seventy had the impression that He overshadowed us with the wings of a dove. They constituted Elohim, a threefold unity.

I don't know if any of this touches you, but for Jacob's audience beneath the tree it was most diverting and exciting—they were gifted in that regard. As they dispersed now and then later as they sat in their camps before going to sleep, they eagerly discussed at length what they had heard about honorific expansion and Abraham's threefold guests of honor, about the obligation to avoid polytheism despite a divinity whose multiple existence carried with it a certain temptation in that direction, which in fact was merely a test of our talent for the divine—a test that even the teenagers among Jacob's people rejoiced to feel themselves equal to.

Their head and chief had them make camp for him under the sacred tree all three nights he spent at Beersheba. He did not dream the first two nights, but the third brought him the dream that had been the purpose of his sleep and whose consolation and strength he sorely needed. He was afraid of the land of Egypt and was in urgent need of assurance that he need not be afraid to journey down to it—for the simple reason that the God of his fathers was not bound to one place and would also be with him even in this underworld, just as He had been with him in Laban's realm. He fervently needed confirmation that God would not only go down with him, but would also lead him—or at least his tribe, having first made of it a great multitude of people—back to the land of his fathers, which lay between these two realms of Nimrod and was itself a land of ignorance, full of foolish first inhabitants, but not a realm of Nimrod, so that one could serve a spiritual God there better than elsewhere. In short, what his soul needed was reassurance that by departing from here the promises of the great dream of ramps that had come to him at the *gilgal* of Beth-el had not been canceled, but that God the King stood by the words He had called out above the harps that night. Jacob slept in order that he might learn this, and he learned it in his sleep. God comforted him in the holy voice his soul needed to hear, and His sweetest word was "Joseph shall put his hands on your eyes"—an intimately ambiguous message: it might mean that his son, a mighty man of the world, would protect and care for him in his old age among the heathen, but also that his favorite would one day close his eyes in death—a dream that the dreamer had long since not dared to dream.

But now he dared to dream it, dream both messages, and his sleeping eyes were moist beneath their lids. But when he awoke he felt strengthened and reassured, ready to leave this way station and proceed with all seventy. He now boarded his fine, wind-screened Egyptian sedan chair, which was slung across the backs of two white asses with mullein tassels—and looked even more dignified and beautiful in it than he had atop his camel.

Love That Must Deny

A commercial road ran from the northeast of the Delta to the dry southlands of Canaan, then on to Hebron by way of Beersheba. The children of Israel took it, and thus followed a different route from the one the brothers had taken on their trips to buy food. The region through which it led was well populated at first, with numerous settlements, most small, some larger. Then, as the days grew in number, it did, to be sure, take them through utterly accursed stretches without a blade of grass and where the only thing they saw were vagabonds, villains intent on mischief, darting about in the distance. The able-bodied men of their caravan made sure they kept their bows at the ready. Even at the worst, in those horrifying moments when it seemed there was no comfort except in God alone, civilization did not desert them entirely, but accompanied them, just as God did, in the form of protected desert wells, markers—placed there and preserved in the spirit of commerce—lookout towers, and resting places, all the way to their goal, which for now meant as far as the region in which the opulent land of Egypt had posted its forward defenses and guards some distance out into this wretched wilderness and well before one arrived at its invincible border and its rigorous entrance, the walls of the fortress of Zel.

They reached it after seventeen days—or perhaps more? They counted their journey as having taken seventeen days, but would not have argued with someone with a different count or tally. By its very character it was a seventeen-day journey, regardless if the count itself was higher or lower—it could easily have been a few days more, especially if one included the sojourn at Beersheba; for summer was still at full force, and out of consideration for Jacob, their father, they had used only the early and late hours of the day for traveling. Yes, it had been a good seventeen days since they had set out from Mamre on their journey—that is, for some time now they had given themselves over to a nomadic life, pitching their tents at various spots. But the days had now brought them before the fortress of Zel, which opened onto Joseph's kingdom.

Does anyone have the least worry about this grim fortified passageway and whether difficulties might ensure for our wanderers there? Don't make us laugh. Good God!—they had writs, passes, credentials. No one from those wretched lands who had ever knocked at the gates of Egypt had carried the like with them—portals and walls and bars did not exist for them, the bulwarks and bastions of Zel were so much vapor and air for them, and the usual rigor exercised by its officers was now only service with a smile. When it came to these people here, Pharaoh's pass controllers definitely had instructions that softened their demeanor. These children of Jacob had been invited into the land by no less a personage than the Lord of Bread in Menfe, the Spender of Shade to the King, Djepnuteefonekh, Pharaoh's Unique Friend—invited to graze and to settle. Worry? Difficulties? The sedan chair in which they carried their old chieftain spoke for itself, and for its owner, for it was adorned with the uraeus and came from Pharaoh's own warehouse. And as for the man sitting in it, looking solemnly weary and mild, they were after all carrying him to a rendezvous, to be held not far from here with his son, a rather high-placed man, who could turn into a pallid corpse anyone who so much as asked a question to delay these children.

In short, one cannot imagine sweeter, more charmingly obsequious officers—the iron grate swung wide, and as hands were raised in greeting on both sides, Jacob's people crossed the floating bridge with lumbering wagons and trotting herds and moved out onto Pharaoh's fields, into a mixed landscape of marshes and pastures, with copses of trees, dikes, canals, and hamlets at intervals along the road. This was Gosen—also called Kosen, Kesem, Gosem, and Goshen.

The pronunciation varied with the dialect of the people who worked fields enclosed by reedy ditches to both sides of the causeway and to whom they addressed their inquiries to make sure they were on the right road. A short day's journey westward would bring the travelers to Per-Bastet's arm of the Nile, and to the city itself, the home of the cat. But closer still lay the nourishing town of Pa-Kôs, which apparently served as market and seat of government for this nome here, which presumably bore the same name. Gazing out across the land with its meadows and bulrushes, reflecting ponds, islands of shrubbery, and lush fields, they could see the pylon of Pa-Kôs's temple outlined against the horizon by the morning sun. For it was early morning as Israel arrived, since they had spent the night at the border fortress; but after traveling only a few hours in the direction of the edifice there on the horizon, they halted, and Jacob's sedan chair was taken from the backs of the asses and set on the ground, where he would wait; for not far from here, near the market town of Pa-Kôs, was the spot Joseph had chosen for their rendezvous—and he would, so he had announced, come out to this place of meeting to greet his family.

We are willing to swear that this was how things were ordered and arranged, and though it is written with perfect truth "He sent Judah before him to Joseph, to show him the way to Goshen," it would be wrong to read that as if it meant Judah now left his father and traveled all the way to the city of the wrapped god and only then did Joseph have his chariot made ready for his journey to meet his father in Goshen. No, the exalted man had been in the vicinity for some time—since yesterday, or the day before—and Judah was sent out into the neighborhood to search for him and lead him to where his father was, so that they might meet. "Here Israel shall wait for his lordship my son," Jacob said. "Set me down. And you, Jehuda, my son, take three servants and ride forth from here to find your brother, Rachel's firstborn, and announce to him our location." And Judah obeyed.

We can assure our readers that he was not gone long, an hour or two at most, and then returned with news of success; for that he did not arrive with Joseph, but returned prior to his appearing before their father, is clear from the question that Jacob put to him as Joseph approached—as we shall hear in a moment.

The spot where Jacob waited was very charming: his chair was shaded by three palm trees that grew as if from one root, and he was cooled by a little pond with a tall stand of papyrus and pink and blue lotus blossoms. There he sat, surrounded by his sons, ten of them, and very soon eleven again upon Judah's return; and before him, beneath a sky of birds in flight, lay an open land of sheepfolds and pastures, so that his old eyes could gaze out to where the twelfth now appeared.

And that is how it happened; first those eyes saw Judah trotting back with his three servants, saw him nod and point without a word behind him across the fields. And those eyes looked past him into the distance. There was some commotion, still small and far-off, a glimmer, a flash, a sparkle, a whirl of color that sped ever closer and became chariots pulled by horses in dazzling harness and colorful plumes, with runners ahead and between, runners behind and alongside—who turned their heads to gaze at the lead chariot with its fans set atop poles. Here it came, growing ever larger, and to the eyes of those watching its shapes now separated. Jacob, however, who was gazing with one aged hand above his eyes, called to one of his sons, who now stood beside him again, and said, "Judah!"

"Here I am," he answered.

"Who is that rather stout man there," Jacob asked, "clad in all the elegance of this world, who now steps down from his chariot and from the golden coach of his chariot, and whose necklace is like the rainbow and whose garment is very like the light of heaven?"

"That is your son Joseph, father," Judah replied.

"If it is he," Jacob said, "I will rise and go out to greet him."

And although Benjamin and the others first tried to stop him before then helping him, he rose from his sedan chair with dignified effort and—limping worse than usual, for he intentionally exaggerated the lameness in his hip, his badge of honor—walked all alone toward the man, who now hastened his own steps to shorten the distance the old man had to go. The smile on the man's lips formed the word "Father," and he held his arms wide. Jacob, however, extended his before him, the way a groping blind man might, and waved his hands as if both beckoning him and yet somehow warding him off; so that when they met Jacob did not let Joseph embrace him and bury his face in his shoulder as he had wanted to do, but held him at a little distance by both shoulders. He tilted his head to one side and, in pain and love, his tired eyes examined and searched long and urgently in the face of this Egyptian, and he did not know him. But now those eyes gazing at him slowly welled over with tears—and that blackness swimming there, behold, these were Rachel's eyes, from which Jacob had kissed away tears in some distant dream of life, and he knew him, let his head sink on this foreigner's shoulder, and wept bitterly.

They stood by themselves alone in the open, for the brothers shyly held back from their meeting, and Joseph's entourage—his marshal, the drivers of his chariots, his runners and fan-bearers, as well as all the curious bystanders who had joined them from the nearby town—kept its distance as well.

"Father, can you forgive me?" his son asked. And what all was not contained in that question: all the tricks he had played, all the trouble he had caused, the arrogance and hopeless impudence of the favorite, culpable trust and blind expectation, a hundred follies, for which he had atoned with the silence of the dead while he had gone on living behind the back of the old man who shared in his atonement. "Father, can you forgive me?"

Regaining his composure, Jacob took his head from Joseph's

shoulder and stood up straight. "God has forgiven us," he answered. "You can see that yourself, for He has given you back to me and Israel may die in peace now that you have appeared to me."

"And you to me," Joseph said, "my dear papa—may I call you that again?"

"If you would not mind, my son," Jacob replied formally and, as old and as dignified as he was, even made a little bow to the young man, "I would prefer that you simply call me 'Father.' That our heart may retain its seriousness and not jest."

Joseph understood perfectly.

"I hear and obey," he said, and likewise bowed. "But not another word about dying!" he added cheerfully. "Life, Father, is what we wish to share with one another now that penance has been done and our long period of waiting is ended."

"It was bitterly long," the old man said with a nod, "for His wrath is fierce and His anger is the anger of a mighty God. Behold, He is so great and mighty that He can nurse only such wrath and none smaller, and punishes us weaklings until our groanings are poured out like water."

"It is conceivable," Joseph said, feeling talkative now, "that in His greatness He may be unable to gauge things and, having nothing like Himself, unable to put Himself in our place. It may be. He has a somewhat heavy hand, so that His touch is like a crushing blow, even when He does not mean it to be and wants only to prick or prod us."

Jacob could not resist a little smile.

"I see," he replied, "that even among strange gods, my son has preserved his charmingly keen understanding of God from days past. There may be some truth in what it has pleased you to say. Abraham often rebuked Him for His impetuosity, and I also have said to Him in something like admonition: 'Gently, Lord, not so fierce!' But He is as He is, and cannot be more temperate for the sake of our tender hearts."

"All the same," Joseph responded, "a friendly reminder from those whom He loves cannot hurt. But now let us praise His mercy and His compassion, though it did take a long time. For His greatness is matched only by His wisdom, which is to say the fullness of His thoughts and the rich meaning of His deeds. For His decrees fulfill many functions, that is what is makes them so marvelous. If

He punishes, He means to punish, and the punishment carries its own serious purpose and yet is also a means for advancing some greater event. He seized you roughly, my father, and me as well, rending us apart, so that I died to you. He meant it and He did it. But at the same time He meant to send me here before you in order to save you, that I might provide for you, for you and my brothers and all your house in this famine, which He designed for many purposes, and which for its part was a means to many things, and above all, that we might be reunited. That is what is most marvelous about how He wisely intertwines all things. We are hot or cold, but His passion is providence, and His anger farseeing goodness. Has your son expressed himself in somewhat suitable words concerning the God of his fathers?"

"Somewhat," Jacob confirmed. "He is the God of life, and, of course, one speaks of life only in approximate terms. This by way of praising and excusing you. But you have no need of my praise, for you are praised by kings. May the life that you have led since being carried off not need to be excused all too much."

As he said this he let his worried gaze drift down over Joseph's Egyptian façade, from the green and yellow stripes of his headdress, across the shimmering jewels, the costly, strangely cut garment, the little items of luxury at his belt and in his hand, down to the golden buckles of his sandals.

"Child," he said with urgency, "have you preserved your purity among a people whose lust is like that of an ass and whose rut is that of a stallion?"

"O my dear papa—I mean, Father," Joseph replied in some embarrassment, "the worries my dear lord has. Let that be—the children of Egypt are like other children, not essentially better or worse. Believe me, only Sodom was especially exceptional at wickedness in its day. Ever since it was swallowed up in pitch and brimstone, things are pretty much the same everywhere in that regard—six of one, half dozen of the other. You once admonished God and said to Him, 'Not so fierce, Lord.' And so it will be no sin if I, your child, likewise admonish you and lovingly suggest, now that you are here: do not let the people of the Two Lands notice what you think of them, or chide them when describing their conduct, as you may be inclined to do in your spiritual fashion, but always keep in mind that we are strangers here and *gerim,* that Pharaoh has made me great among these children, and so, following God's decree, take up your position among them."

"I know, my son, I know," Jacob replied with another little bow. "Do not doubt my respect for the world. They say you have sons?" he added as a question.

"Yes indeed, Father. By my Maiden, the daughter of the sun, a woman of great nobility. Their names are . . ."

"Maiden? Daughter of the sun? That does not upset me. I have grandchildren from Shechem and grandchildren from Moab and have grandchildren from Midian. Why not grandchildren by a daughter of On as well? After all, it is I from whom they come. What are the boys' names?"

"Manasseh, father, and Ephraim."

"Ephraim and Manasseh. It is good, my son, my lamb, it is very good that you have sons, two of them, and have faithfully called them by such names. I wish to see them. You must present them to me as soon as possible, if you please."

"Your wish is my command," Joseph said.

"And do you also know, my dear child," Jacob continued softly, eyes moist with tears, "why this is so good and so very fitting before the Lord?" He put an arm around Joseph's neck and spoke into his ear, so that in bending closer to his mouth, his son had to turn his face aside.

"Jehosiph, I once gave you the coat of many colors and bequeathed it to you when you begged for it. You know, do you not, that it does not mean the inheritance, the right of the firstborn?"

"I know that," Joseph responded just as softly.

"But I meant it so, I suppose, or halfway so, in my heart," Jacob said now, "for my heart loved you and will always love you, whether you are dead or alive, more than your fellows. But God rent your garment and chastised my heart with His mighty hand, for one cannot kick against His hand. He chose you and set you apart from my house; He took the sprout from the stem and planted it out in the world—I have no choice but obedience. An obedience of action and decision, for the heart is not subject to obedience. He cannot take my heart and its partiality unless He take my life. Even if it does not act and decide, this heart of mine, according to its love, that is still obedience. Do you understand?"

Joseph turned his head toward him and nodded. He saw tears in those old brown eyes, and his own grew moist again as well.

"I hear and know," he whispered, inclining his ear once more.

"God gave you and took you away," Jacob whispered, "and has given you back again, but not entirely. He has also kept you for Himself. He did indeed let the blood of the animal stand for the blood of the son, and yet you are not like Isaak, an averted sacrifice. You spoke to me of the fullness of His thoughts and of the lofty but double meaning of His counsels—you spoke cleverly. For wisdom belongs to Him, and to man is left the cleverness to find his worried way into that wisdom. He raised you up and cast you aside, both in one. I speak this into your ear, my beloved child, and you are clever enough to be able to hear. He has raised you up above your brothers just as you dreamt—I have, my darling, always kept your dreams in my heart. But He raised you up over them in worldly fashion, not according to His salvation and the inheritance of the blessing—you do not bear that salvation, the inheritance has been barred to you. You know that, don't you?"

"I hear and know," Joseph repeated, taking his ear away for a moment and turning instead toward the whispering mouth.

"You are blessed, my dear," Jacob continued, "blessed from heaven above and from the deep that lies below, blessed with high delight and with destiny, with wit and with dreams. And yet it is a worldly blessing and not a spiritual one. Have you ever heard the voice of love that must deny? So hear it now in your ear, spoken in obedience. God loves you as well, my child, though He denies you the inheritance and has punished me for secretly intending it for you. You are the firstborn in earthly things and a benefactor, both to strangers and to your father and brothers. But salvation shall not come to the nations through you, and its guidance has been withheld from you. You know that, don't you?"

"I know," Joseph answered.

"That is good," Jacob said. "It is a good thing to view destiny with high delight and admiring serenity, one's own destiny as well. But I shall do as God has, who has showed favor to you by with-holding from you. You are the one set apart. You have been sepa-rated from your stem, your tribe, and shall not be a stem and tribe. But I will raise you up to the rank of the fathers, for your sons, your firstborn, shall be as my sons. Those whom you still retain shall be yours, these two, however, are mine, for I will accept them in the place of my son. You are not like your fathers, my child, for you are not a prince of the spirit, but of the world. Nonetheless you shall sit at my side, at the side of the tribal patriarch, as a father of tribes. Are you content?"

"I fall before your feet in gratitude," Joseph said softly, once again offering not his ear but his mouth. And Israel released him from his embrace.

The Reception

Those who stood off at a distance, Joseph's retinue here, Jacob's people there, had observed with awe the two in intimate conversation. Now they saw that it was ended and that Pharaoh's friend had invited his father to depart from here. He turned toward his brothers and approached to welcome them; but they hastened ahead to greet him, all bowing before him, and he hugged Benjamin, his mother's son.

"Now I wish to see your wives and your children, Turturra," he said to the little man. "I want to see the wives and children of all of you and make their acquaintance. You are to present them to me and to Father, at whose side I intend to sit. Not far from here I have had a tent set up for your reception. It was there that my brother Judah found me, and from there I have come. Pick up our father again and carry him, dear sirs. Let everyone mount up and follow me. I shall drive ahead in my chariot. If anyone wishes to ride with me—Judah, for example, who was so kind as to summon me—there is room enough in the chariot for him as well as for me and my driver. Judah, you are the one whom I invite. Are you coming with me?"

And Judah thanked him and did indeed climb with him into the chariot, which pulled forward when Joseph waved for it. He rode in the exalted man's chariot and stood beside him in the golden coach of his chariot pulled by spirited horses adorned with colorful plumes and purple harness. Joseph's retainers followed, then the children of Israel—at their head, Jacob in his swaying sedan chair. Off to one side, however, ran the people from the market town of Pa-Kôs who wanted to witness all this.

And so they arrived at a brightly painted and carpeted tent—a beautiful and spacious tent with a full complement of servants, where garlanded pitchers of wine in elegant cane holders lined the walls, cushions had been spread, and drinking bowls, water basins, and all sorts of pastries and fruit stood at the ready. Joseph invited his father and brothers inside, greeted them once again, and with the help of his steward, whom the eleven already knew, offered them refreshment. In high spirits he drank with them from golden cups, into which servers poured wine through cloth sieves. But then afterward he and his father Jacob seated themselves on two camp stools at the entrance to the tent, and there passed before them Jacob's "wives, daughters, and sons, and the wives of his sons"—which is to say, the wives of Joseph's brothers and their offspring or, in short, Israel—so that he might see them and make their acquaintance. Ruben, his eldest brother, named their names for him, and Joseph had a friendly word for each. Jacob, however, was reminded out of the depths of time of another such scene of presentation: how, after the night of wrestling at Peni-el, he had introduced his family to Esau, the tufted man—his handmaids first with their four sons, then Leah with her six, and finally Rachel, along with him who now sat beside him and whose head had been raised up in so worldly a fashion.

"There are seventy in all," he said to him with great dignity, pointing to his people, and Joseph did not ask whether that was seventy with or without Jacob, with or without himself; he did not ask and did not count, but simply let this people pass before his delighted gaze, pulled Benjamin's youngest sons, Muppim and Rosh, to his knees to stand beside him, and was very interested and pleased when Serah, Asher's child, was presented to him and he learned it had been she who had first sung to Jacob the news that his son was alive. He thanked the young maiden and said that soon, as soon as he could find the time, she would have to sing her song on eight strings for him as well, for he wanted to hear it. Among the wives of his brothers Tamar also passed by, with the offspring of Judah, and Ruben, the namer of names, could not explain right there in extemporaneous haste what she and they were all about—that was left for a more opportune occasion. Tall and dark, Tamar strode past, a son on each hand, and she bowed proudly before the Spender of Shade, for in her heart she thought, "I am on the course of promise, and you, however brightly you sparkle, are not."

When all of them had been introduced, the wives and daughters of the sons and the daughters of the wives were served refreshment inside the tent. Joseph, however, gathered his father and the heads of houses around him, instructed them, and with worldly prudence presented his decisions in detail.

"You are now in the land of Goshen, Pharaoh's beautiful mead-owland," he said, "and I will arrange it so that you may remain here, where it is not yet all too Egyptian, and you shall live here as *gerim*, as easy and free to come and go as before in the land of Canaan. You need only drive your flocks onto these pastures, set up your tents, and feed yourselves. Father, I have readied a tent for you, in careful imitation of your old one in Mamre, that you may find everything just as you're used to—it has been set up a little way from here, closer to the market of Pa-Kôs; for it is best to be in the open but not too far from a town, which was also our fathers' custom, dwelling under trees and not between walls, but near Beersheba and Hebron. In Pa-Kôs, Per-Sopd, and Per-Bastet, along the arm of the river, you may trade your wares—Pharaoh, my lord, will be pleased to let you pasture, trade, and move about. For I will arrange an audience with His Majesty and speak before him on your behalf. I will report to him that you are in Goshen and that there is much to recommend your remaining here, since you have always been herders of sheep and goats, as were your fathers before you. Indeed I must tell you, the Egyptians have always had something against shepherds—not so much as against swineherds, no, but they do have a slight distaste for keepers of sheep, at which you ought to take no offense, but on the contrary, we shall make use of it so that you may remain here, yet set apart from the Egyptians, for shepherds belong in the land of Goshen. Indeed, Pharaoh's own flocks graze in this landscape, the sheep and goats of the god. Therefore, my brothers, since you are experienced shepherds and breeders, the idea suggests itself and I shall suggest it to His Majesty—but so that he stumbles upon it on his own—that he appoint you, or at least several of you, to be in charge of his flocks here. He is a very sweet and tractable man, and you already know that he has ordered me to select a group from among you—for all of you would be too many for him—to present to him, so that he may ask questions and you may answer. If he asks you about how you earn your bread, however, and your occupation, you should know, men, that he does so only formally and is well informed as to your livelihood, and that I have already suggested to him that he put you in charge of his sheep. That will be the idea behind his formal question. Which is why you have only to endorse my proposition heartily and say: 'Your servants have been keepers of sheep from our youth, as our fathers were also.' Then he will first order that your dwelling shall be in Goshen, in the lowlands, and second reveal to you that it would be best if I set you, or the most able among you, over his flocks. But as to who is most able, that you may decide among yourselves, or our father, our dear lord, may determine it. When everything has been so ordered, I shall arrange a private audience with the god's son for you, my father; for it is only proper that he behold you in all the dignity and weight of your stories, and that you behold him, who so tenderly strives to pursue the right path, even if he may not be the right man for it. He has also decreed in a letter that he wishes to see you and to ask questions of you. I cannot say how much I look forward to presenting you to him, so that he may see you, Abraham's grandson, the man of blessing, in all your solemn splendor. He knows of you already and even some of your stories—the one about the peeled rods, for example. But when you stand before him, you will, I am sure, do me the favor of recalling that I hold a position among the children of Egypt and so will not censure Pharaoh, the king of these children, with such descriptions of their customs as may hover before your spiritual eye— that would be out of place."

"Certainly not, no need to worry, your lordship my son, my dear child," Jacob responded. "Your old father knows very well to show tender consideration to what is great in this world, for it, too, comes from God. My thanks for the tent and dwelling you have thoughtfully prepared for me in the land of Goshen. Israel will now betake himself there and ponder all these things that he may include them in the treasure trove of his stories."

Jacob Stands Before Pharaoh

We are astonished to note that this story is moving toward its end— who would have thought it could ever run dry and come to an end? But ultimately it no more has an end than it actually had a beginning, and instead, since it cannot possibly go on forever like this, it must at some point excuse itself and simply cease its narration. It must, if reason is to prevail, come to a conclusion because it has none; for in the face of what is endless, conclusion is an act of reason, since, proverbially at least, reason knows when to yield.

Our story, then—as proof that it does have the good sense to achieve its goal by moderate means, despite having manifested immoderacy in its day—stands before its own demise and sets its eye on its final hour, just as Jacob did when the seventeen years he still had to live drew to a close and he went about setting his house in order. Seventeen years, that is also the amount of time still allowed to our story, or that out of a sense of moderation and reason it allows itself. Even at its most enterprising, it never intended to live longer than Jacob—or at most only so much longer as to be able to tell of his death. Its measurements of space and time are patriarchal enough. Old and sated with life, relieved that everything has its limits, our story will put its feet together and fall silent.

But as long as it does last it will not shrink from making good use of its time by at once bravely announcing what everyone already knows, that Joseph kept his word and presented to Pharaoh first a select group of his brothers, five in all, and then formally introduced Jacob, his father, to the beautiful child of the Atôn, on which occasion the patriarch conducted himself with great dignity, if perhaps, by worldly standards, somewhat too arrogantly—details of which in a moment. Joseph personally requested these audiences of the Lord of Sweet Breath, and it is worth noting how the traditional account's familiarity with Egyptian circumstances is revealed in its use of the directions "up" and "down." One traveled "down" to the land of Egypt; the children of Israel had traveled "down" to the fields of Goshen. But if one then kept going in the same direction, one traveled "up," that is, upriver, toward Upper Egypt; and so it is correctly stated that Joseph went "up" to Akhet-Atôn, the city of the horizon in the nome of the Rabbit, the sole capital of the Two Lands, to announce to Horus in his palace that his brothers and his father's house had come to him and to plant the idea in Pharaoh's mind that the cleverest thing one could possibly do would be to put these experienced shepherds to work tending the royal flocks in the land of Goshen. Pharaoh was indeed pleased to have come up with this idea, and when the five brothers stood before him, he told them of it and appointed them his shepherds.

This happened not all too long after the arrival of Israel in Egypt, as soon, that is, as Pharaoh paid another visit to On, the city he loved, to shine in the horizon of his palace there, just as he had done when Joseph was first brought before him so that he might interpret his dreams. They had all waited until then out of consideration for Jacob, now well on in years, so that he would not have too long a journey to come before Pharaoh's throne. But at that point he was in Joseph's house in Menfe, along with the five sons selected for presentation—that is, two of Leah's offspring, Ruben and Judah; one of Bilhah's, Naphtali; one of Zilpah's, Gaddiel; and Rachel's second, Benoni–Benjamin. They had accompanied their father up to the city of the wrapped god on the west bank and to the house of their exalted brother, where Asenath, the Maiden, greeted her abductor's father, and his Egyptian grandchildren were brought before him for examination and blessing. The old man was deeply moved. "The Lord is overwhelming in His kindness," he said. "He has let me see your face, my son, which I would not have thought possible, and behold, He now lets me see your seed as well." And he asked the bigger boy his name.

"Manasseh," he replied.

"And what's yours?" he then asked the smaller one.

"Ephraim," was the answer.

"Ephraim and Manasseh," the old man repeated, naming first the name he had heard last. Then he set Ephraim on his right knee and had Manasseh lean against his left, caressed them and corrected their Hebrew pronunciation.

"How often have I told you, Manasseh and Ephraim," Joseph scolded, "that you say it like this, not like that."

"Ephraim and Manasseh," the old man said, "cannot help it. Your mouth, my lordship and son, is somewhat askew as well. Would you like to become a multitude of nations in your father's name?" he asked them both.

"We'd like that very much," replied Ephraim, who had noticed that he was the favored one, and Jacob then gave them his blessing for the time being.

It was now reported that Pharaoh had come to On, to the house of Rê-Horakhte, and Joseph rode down to him, followed by the five selected sons. Jacob, however, was carried. If someone were to ask why he, the man of venerable dignity, was not received first, but, as is clearly stated, the brothers were first in line instead, the answer is: to heighten the effect. It is rare on festive occasions for the best to step forward first, but rather those of lesser rank are in the lead, followed by the somewhat better, and only then does what is most venerable come tottering in, as applause and jubilation swell to a high point. The debate about precedence is an old one, but in terms of ceremony it has always been a moot question. The man of lesser rank always goes first, and one should yield with a smile to the ambition that insists on that position.

The reception for the brothers, moreover, had a practical—one might say "commercial"—purpose, and that matter had to be clarified first. In contrast, Jacob's brief conversation with the youthful idol was purely a pretty formality, so that in addressing him a discomfited Pharaoh could think of nothing better to ask the patriarch than how old he was. His exchange with the sons had more rhyme and reason to it, although, like almost all of the king's conversations, its particulars had been fixed beforehand by his ministers.

Fawning chamberlains conducted the five into the Hall of Counsel and Interrogation, where young Pharaoh, surrounded by supernumerary palace officials, sat beneath the ribboned baldachin, with crook, scourge, and a golden symbol of life in hand. Although his carved chair was an archaic piece of furniture, as uncomfortable as it was old-fashioned, Ikhnatôn managed to sit in it with exaggerated casualness, since the hieratic pose did not fit with his notion of his god's loving naturalness. His Supreme Mouth, the Lord of Bread, Djepnuteefonekh, the Provider, stood at the right front post of the exquisite enclosure and saw to it that the conversation, which was conducted through an interpreter, went according to plan.

After first establishing contact between their brows and the floor of the hall, the immigrants murmured a not excessively long hymn of praise that their brother had practiced with them and had known how to formulate so that it met court protocol without offending their own beliefs. As a standard embellishment, it did not, by the way, even make it to translation, for Pharaoh thanked them at once in his prim boyish voice and added that His Majesty was genuinely pleased to see the worthy kin of his True Spender of Shade and uncle before his throne. "How do you earn your bread?" he then asked.

It was Judah, who answered that they were shepherds, as their fathers had been, that they were thoroughly versed in the breeding of all kinds of animals. They had come to this land because they had not had pasture enough for their flocks, for the famine was very severe in the land of Canaan, and if they might venture a request before Pharaoh's countenance it was that they might remain in Goshen, where their tents were presently pitched.

Ikhnatôn could not help contorting his sensitive face a little as the translator spoke the word "shepherd." He turned toward Joseph to utter the prescribed words: "Your family has come to you. The Two Lands stand open before you and so before them as well. Let them settle in the best of the land and let them dwell in the land of Goshen, which would greatly gratify My Majesty." And prompted by Joseph's glance, he added, "Moreover, my father in heaven has provided My Majesty an idea that Pharaoh's heart finds very beautiful. You, my friend, know your brothers best and their ability. Set them according to that ability over my flocks down there, and make the ablest of them overseers of the king's herds. My Majesty commands you with much grace and cordiality to set in writing their installation in these offices. It has been my great pleasure."

And then came Jacob.

His entrance was solemn and very labored. He deliberately exaggerated the sum of his years in order to offset the majesty of a Nimrod with the dignity of his own impressive age and thereby avoid compromising God in his presence. All the same he was quite aware that his courtly son was somewhat disconcerted by his conduct and worried that he might behave arrogantly toward Pharaoh, might even start in about the goat Bindidi, in regard to which Joseph had previously admonished him as if he were a child. Jacob did not intend to touch on the matter, but he was nonetheless determined not to compromise anything and so was shielding himself with his awe-inspiring age. Not only had he been relieved, by the way, from the duty of prostrating himself, since he was no longer believed capable of the necessary agility, but it had also been decided that the audience should be as brief as possible so that the old man would not be kept standing too long.

They observed one another in silence for a while: Atôn's visionary, luxury's latecomer within his elegant gilt shrine, who out of curiosity had stirred a little from his elaborately comfortable pose; and Yitzchak's son, the father of the twelve. They gazed at one another, enveloped in this same moment and yet ages apart: the boy crowned by antiquity and devoted to his frail attempt to distill, like an attar of roses, a tenderly ecstatic religion of love from layer upon layer of thousands of years of divine erudition; and this old man, rich in experience, who stood at the source of far-reaching forces in the process of becoming. Pharaoh quickly felt embarrassed. He was not accustomed to speak the first word to those who stood before him, but always waited for the official hymn of greeting by which one introduced oneself to him. And we are also assured that Jacob did not entirely neglect his formal duty. Both upon entering and leaving, it is said, he "blessed" Pharaoh. That is to be taken quite literally; the patriarch spoke a word of blessing in the place of the obligatory singsong of glorification. He did not raise both hands, as if before God, but only his right hand, extending it with a very dignified tremor toward Pharaoh as if raising it paternally, even at this distance, over the young man's head.

"May the Lord bless you, king in the land of Egypt," he said in the voice of very old age.

Pharaoh was quite impressed. "And how old might you be, grandfather?" he asked in amazement.

And now Jacob exaggerated again. We are told that he gave the sum of his years as one hundred and thirty—a completely arbitrary figure. First, he did not know all that precisely how old he was—in his part of the world, even to this day, people tend to be somewhat unclear about this. We, moreover, know that he would live to be one hundred and six years old—an age within the realm of nature's possibilities, if at their more extreme limits. Going by which, he would not yet have been ninety at the time and was very vigorous for a man of his age besides. All the same, this gave him a means by which to wrap himself in the greatest solemnity before Pharaoh. His gestures were those of a blind seer, the cadence of his voice very deliberate. "The days of my pilgrimage are a hundred and thirty years," he said; and then he added, "Few and evil have been the days of my life and they have not attained the days of my fathers in their pilgrimage."

Pharaoh shuddered. Doomed to an early death—to which his sensitive nature had also given its consent—he was absolutely horrified by such life spans.

"Good heavens!" he said with a kind of despondency. "Have

you always lived at Hebron, grandfather, in the wretched land of Retenu?"

"For the most part, my child," Jacob answered, sending pleated officials on both sides of the baldachin into near apoplexy, and Joseph shook his head at his father, admonishing him. Jacob saw this well enough, but pretended not to see, and stubbornly stuck to the depressing topic of age, by adding, "According to the wise men, Hebron's years are two thousand three hundred, and Mempi, the city of tombs, does not approach its age."

Joseph gave another quick shake of his head in the old man's direction, but he paid not the least attention to him, and Pharaoh proved very indulgent as well.

"It may be, grandfather, it may be," he hastened to say. "But how can you possibly call the days of your life evil when you sired a son whom Pharaoh loves as the apple of his eye, so that there is none greater in the Two Lands except the Lord of the Double Crown?"

"I sired *twelve* sons," Jacob replied, "and this is but one of their number. And among them there is curse as there is blessing, and blessing as there is curse. Several have been cast out and yet remain chosen. Just as one has been chosen, yet remains an outcast in love. Because I had lost him, I was to find him again, and because I found him, he has been lost to me. He stepped out of the circle of those I sired and ascended a pedestal, but in his place now step those that he sired for me, and one ahead of the other."

Pharaoh listened with mouth agape to these sibylline words, which grew only darker in translation. In search of help, he glanced toward Joseph, who just kept his eyes lowered.

"Yes, yes," he said, "but of course, grandfather, that is clear. Well and wisely said, just as Pharaoh truly loves to hear it. But now you needn't exert yourself by standing before My Majesty any longer. Go in peace and live as long as it gives you joy, countless years beyond your hundred and thirty."

Jacob, however, raised his hand to bless Pharaoh yet again at the end and now departed from him with high and labored solemnity and without having compromised himself in the least.

The Rascal Servant

It is time to make room for a trustworthy clarification of Joseph's actions as an administrator, so that for good and all this may put an end to poorly informed rumors that have circulated over these many years, frequently degenerating into slurs and slander. The primary blame for such misunderstandings, often ending in the condemnation of Joseph's conduct in office as downright "atrocious," rests— and there is no getting round the charge—on the earliest recorded version, which is so laconic that it cannot come close to the story as it originally told itself, that is, to reality as it once happened.

This earliest record of the actions taken by Pharaoh's great commercial agent is based on the kind of hard and dry facts that neither provide any sense of the universal admiration they originally aroused, nor explain that admiration, which frequently verged on Joseph's being idolized and led to his titles, such as "Provider" and "Lord of Bread," being taken so literally that great masses of people dreamily regarded him as a kind of Nile divinity, indeed, as the incarnation of Hapi himself, the preserver and spender of all life.

The mythical popularity that Joseph acquired and that it had probably always been his nature to acquire was based above all on the shimmering mixed character and ambiguity—mirrored by the laughter in his eyes—of his measures, which functioned, as it were, in two directions at once, combining in a thoroughly personal way his various purposes and goals with a kind of magical wit. We speak of wit because this principle has its place in the little cosmos of our story and early on the statement was made that wit is by nature a messenger who goes back and forth, a nimble ambassador between two opposing spheres and influences—for example, between the forces of the sun and moon, the father's legacy and the mother's legacy, between the blessing of the day and the blessing of the night—indeed, to put it in direct and all-inclusive terms, between life and death. Such mediation, so slender and agile as it merrily goes about reconciliation, had never found real expression in any divinity in the land where Joseph was a guest, in the Land of Black Earth. Thoth, the scribe and guide for the dead, the inventor of so many clever things, came closest to such a figure. Only Pharaoh, before whom all divine matters were brought from far and wide, had knowledge of a more perfected version of this divine character, and the grace that Joseph had found before him was due primarily to the fact that Pharaoh recognized in him the traits of that rascal child of the cave, that lord of tricks, and had quite rightly told himself that a king could wish for nothing better than to have as his minister such a manifestation and incarnation of this profitable divine idea.

The children of Egypt became acquainted with this winged figure through Joseph, and if they did not include him in their pantheon it was only because that place was already taken by Djehuti, the white monkey. All the same, the experience meant an enhancement of their religion, especially because of the delightful change it brought to the concept of magic—and this alone was sufficient to evoke the mythical amazement of these children. For them magic had always had something worrisome and frighteningly serious about it; for them the point of all magic was to build the most solid, impenetrable barrier possible against evil, which is why Joseph's grand hoarding of grain and his countless cone-shaped storehouses had appeared to them in a magical light. But what seemed truly magical to them was the encounter between foresight and evil here— which is to say, the way in which the Spender of Shade led evil around by the nose, used his measures to both his advantage and profit, making them serve purposes about which this stupid dragon, bent only on destruction, could never have had the remotest notion. This was unexpectedly good-humored magic that simply made them laugh.

And among the people there was indeed a great deal of laughter—admiring laughter—at how Joseph, by coolly exploiting every rise in price when dealing with the great and rich, provided for his lord, for Horus in his palace, making Pharaoh a man of gold and silver by directing into his treasury the vast flow of sums he demanded the great landowners pay for grain. In all of this he proved a deft and loyal servant of a divinity who is the epitome of service dedicated to passing on profits. Hand in hand with this, however, went the free distribution of grain among the starving commonfolk of the cities in the name of their young Pharaoh dreaming of his god—who now profited as much if not more from this as he did from being showered with gold. This union of crown politics with concern for the people's welfare was very innovative, its effect exhilarating, and to have any idea of its true appeal when reading the first account of this story, one must be very well versed in its style and able to read between the lines. That report's relationship to its own original version, that is, to the story that told itself as it happened, is hinted at by certain rough and yet utterly comical turns of phrase that sound like remnants of some popular farce through which the character of the original event still glimmers. When, for instance, the starving come to Joseph crying: "Give us bread! Why should we die before your eyes? Our money is gone"—a very rudimentary manner of speech found nowhere else in the Pentateuch—Joseph answers in the same style, that is, in these words: "Here! Give me your cattle! I will give you food in exchange." Pharaoh's great marketeer and the needy did not, it goes without saying, deal with one in that tone of voice. But these turns of phrase sound very much like a recollection of the people's mood as they experienced these events—a comedic mood devoid of all moralistic, whining self-pity.

The venerable narrator was nevertheless unable to prevent reproaches of Joseph's conduct as exploitative and harsh, and instead has elicited cries of condemnation from those inclined to take moral matters very seriously. That is understandable. We learn from them that in the course of those years of desperation Joseph first gathered up all the money to be found in the land, which is say, brought it into Pharaoh's treasury, that he then took people's cattle in security and finally expropriated their fields, drove them from house and farm, resettling them wherever he pleased on strange soil, to have them drudge there as slaves of the state. That is not pleasant to hear, but the reality looked very different, as is clear from certain other turns of phrase the report once again culled from old memories. One reads: "He gave them bread for their horses, flocks, herds, and asses, and he fed them with bread in exchange for all their cattle that year." Except the translation is inexact and leaves out a certain allusion that the original whispers very intentionally. We find there, instead of "fed," a word that means "to lead"; "and he led them," it says, "with bread in exchange for all their possessions that year"—a peculiar expression and very carefully chosen, for it is taken from the language of shepherds and means "to tend," "to pasture," means conscientious and gentle care for helpless creatures, and in particular of an easily confused herd of sheep. And to the mythically trained ear this salient and formulaic word ascribes to Jacob's son the role and character of a good shepherd who tends his people, who grazes them in green pastures and leads them to fresh water. Here, as in those previous farcical turns of phrase, the colors of the original event show through; the strange verb "to lead," which has, so to speak, crept out of reality and into this text's account, betrays in what light the people regarded Pharaoh's great favorite—they saw him quite differently from the way modern political moralists feel compelled to judge him. For tending, pasturing, and leading is the work of a god familiar as the "lord of the subterranean sheepcote."

The factual statements of the text stand firm and unshakable. Joseph sold grain to those who had wealth, that is, to barons of the nomes and great landowners who thought themselves equal to kings, at whatever brazen price the market allowed and brought "money," that is, bartered goods, into the royal coffers, so that very soon there was no longer any "money" in the narrower sense left among the people, that is, in the form of precious metals—for there was no such thing as money in the form of minted coins, and assets offered in exchange for grain were necessarily all sorts of cattle. This did not happen in sequence as need escalated, and any depiction that leaves the impression that Joseph exploited people by first stripping them of their money in order then to take their horses, cattle, and sheep is anything but accurate. Cattle is also money; it is even money in a very particular sense, as can be seen in our modern word "pecuniary"; and even before the well-to-do paid in the form of ornamental vases of gold and silver, they paid with cattle and sheep—which is not to say that every last cow ended up in Pharaoh's stalls and pens. Joseph did not build stalls and pens for seven years, but cone-shaped storehouses, and he had neither room nor use for all this cattle-money. Those who have never heard of the economic practices of the money changers of Lombardy cannot, to be sure, follow a story such as this. Cattle were lent or pawned—one may choose whichever term one prefers. For the most part they remained on the same farms and estates, but had ceased to be owned, in the original sense of the word, by their owners. That is, these things were their property and yet were it no longer, were it only conditionally, as encumbered goods. And if the first account is in any way inadequate, it is because it fails to awaken an impression on which so much else depends: that Joseph's conduct was aimed entirely at casting a magic spell over the idea of property, at leaving it hovering between ownership and nonownership, in a state of conditional or feudal tenure.

For as years of drought and a wretchedly low flood level followed one after the other, as the queen of the harvest continued to turn her breast away, as grass did not sprout and grain did not grow, as the womb remained closed and allowed no child of earth to flourish—what ensued then was indeed very much in accordance with our text, for great portions of the Black Earth previously in private hands became property of the crown, or as the text puts it: "So Joseph bought all the land of Egypt for Pharaoh, for all the Egyptians sold their fields." For what? For seed corn. The scholars are in agreement that this must have been toward the end of the cycle of hunger, when the chains of infertility had begun to loosen somewhat, when watery things had returned to something like normal, and the fields could have yielded a harvest if they had been sown. Which explains the words of the supplicants: "Why should we die before your eyes, both we and our land? Buy us and our land for food, and we with our land will be serfs to Pharaoh; and give us seed, that we may live and not die, and that the land may not be desolate." Who is speaking here? These are spoken words, not an outcry from the people. It is a proposal, an offer, made by individuals, by a group belonging to a previously intractable if not rebellious class of men, the owners of great latifundia and princes of the nomes, to whom early in the dynasty Pharaoh Akhmose had been forced to cede vast independent tracts of land and to grant such grand titles as First Royal Son of the Goddess Nekhbet—old-fashioned, defiant feudal lords, whose reactionary mode of life was of no benefit to the general welfare and had long been a thorn in the side of the new state. As a statesman, Joseph used this opportunity to coerce these lords to join the times. They were the primary targets of the expropriations and resettlements we are told about, for what this wise and resolute minister accomplished was to break up whatever large estates still existed and resettle smaller ones with tenant farmers whom the state held responsible for applying up-to-date farming methods and installing irrigation systems. This resulted therefore in both land's being distributed more equably among the people and an improved agriculture under supervision by the crown. Many a First Royal Son became just another tenant farmer or moved to the city; many a large farmer was banished to one of these new farms within smaller boundaries, while the fields he had previously owned were transferred to other hands. And if other forms of relocation were also practiced, if, as we are told, the Lord of Bread "dispersed" people by whole cities—that is, sent them out into districts surrounding population centers, moving them from one tilled field to another—such measures were based on a well-thought-out plan for educating them in this transformed concept of property, by which it was both abolished and preserved.

This essential precondition for all delivery of seed corn by the state was nothing more than the continuation of the duty based on the beautiful number five, of that same tax by which Joseph had amassed these magical supplies during the years of plenty and into which he now dipped—it was the explication of that tax in permanence, its consolidation for all time. One should note, however, that this levy, even without the aforementioned resettlements, would have been the only form by which the "sale" of the land along with its owners—for they had included themselves in their proposal—could have been effected. Joseph—who never uttered the words "slavery" or "serfdom" himself, terms for which he understandably had no fondness—has never been sufficiently honored for having taken only token advantage of the landowners' joint decision to sell themselves as a means of preventing their ruin; instead, he put the fact that the land and people were no longer "free" in the old sense to no more exacting use than this inviolable tax of one-fifth, the upshot of which was: that those who were lent seed corn no longer worked exclusively for themselves, but in part for Pharaoh, which is to say for the state, for the public coffers. To that extent, their work was the villeinage of serfs—and every friend of humanity and citizen of humane modernity is free to call it that as long as he is prepared, as logic demands, to apply it to himself as well.

Such a term, however, is an exaggeration when one examines the degree of servitude Joseph imposed upon these people. Had he exacted from them three-quarters or even only half of what they produced, they would have been more sensibly aware that they and their fields no longer belonged to them. But twenty from one hundred—malice itself must concede that this is a limited sort of exploitation. Four-fifths of their harvest was left to them as seed to sow and grain for them and their little ones to consume—and if we look both edict and estimation squarely in the eye, even to hint that this was slavery would be going too far. The words of gratitude with which those put under this yoke greeted their oppressor resound down through the millennia: "You have saved our lives; let us find grace in the sight of my lord and we will be slaves to Pharaoh." What more can one want? And should anyone want more, then he should know that Jacob himself, with whom Joseph repeatedly discussed these matters, expressly approved of this tax—that is, in terms of the rate imposed if not of the person to whom it was due. Had he already become a multitude of people, he said, upon whom a polity would have to be imposed, the people of the land would likewise have to regard themselves as no more than custodians of the soil and pay one-fifth in tax—but not to some Horus in his palace, but to Yahweh, for He alone was King and Lord, to Him all fields belonged, and He merely lent us all that we possess. But he indeed recognized that his lordship and son, who had been set apart to rule a heathen world, had to deal with these matters in his own way. And Joseph smiled.

As a concept in the conscious minds of those on whom it was imposed, however, this immutable feudal tax was incongruent with their remaining in their traditional homes and fields. So mild a tax was incapable of awakening in them an understanding of their new situation, of making it self-evident. That was the reason for the re-settlement measures—they formed a desirable addition to the duty already imposed, which by itself proved inadequate as a material symbol for convincing the farmers that their property had been "sold" and impressing upon them this new state of affairs. A farmer who remained on the same soil he had always worked would find it easy to hold on to outdated conceptions, and in his forgetfulness he might one day rise up against the claims of the crown. If instead he was required to leave his estate and received another in its place from Pharaoh's own hand, the feudal nature of the property he held was made far more concrete.

But the remarkable thing was that property still remained property. The mark of freely held personal property is the right to sell and to inherit, and these provisions Joseph let stand. From now on all land in the whole of Egypt belonged to Pharaoh and nonetheless could be sold and inherited. It was not for nothing that we spoke of the magic spell that Joseph's measures cast over the idea of property; for whenever people tried to direct an inner eye on the notion of "property," the concept hovered there and shattered into ambiguities that left them staring. What they were trying to fix their eye upon had not been destroyed and canceled, but appeared in a twilight state of yes and no that seemed to melt away and yet abide, that kept them blinking until their minds grew accustomed to it. Joseph's economic system was a surprising combination of collectivization and individual property rights, a rascal mixture that was perceived as a manifestation of a crafty, mediating deity.

Tradition emphasizes that these reforms did not apply to the land held by the temples; the priestly caste endowed by the state with countless shrines, and especially the estates of Amun-Rê, were left untouched and untaxed. "Only the land of the priests," it says, "he did not buy." That, too, was wise—if wisdom is a rascal's cleverness that knows how to harm its opponent while demonstrating the formality of respect. Forbearance in dealing with Amun and lesser local numina was certainly not what Pharaoh had in mind. He would have been happy to see the god of Karnak plucked and milked, and in his boyish way he argued over this with his Spender of Shade, who, however, had the support of Mama, the god's mother. With her approval Joseph held to his plan of indulging the common man's devotion to the old gods of the land, a piety that Pharaoh would have gladly destroyed root and branch in favor of the doctrine of his father in heaven and indeed tried to destroy by other means that Joseph could not prevent; for in his zeal Pharaoh was incapable of grasping the notion that the people would prove much more amenable to purification by the new if at the same time they were permitted to hold to their traditional faith and familiar rituals. When it came to Amun, Joseph would have considered it a mistake to give the ram-headed god the impression that the entire agrarian reform was directed against him with the intention to belittle him, rousing him to stir up the people against it. It was far better to hold him in check by gestures of polite consideration. The events of all these years—the abundance, the precautionary measures, the rescue of the people—weighed more than enough in favor of Pharaoh and his spiritual prestige; and the riches from sale of grain that Joseph

had passed on and continued to pass on to the Great House were indirectly such a heavy loss for the imperial god that any little reverence paid to his sacred and traditional freedom from taxation verged
on pure irony—and indeed put that laughter in their shepherd's eyes
that people noticed accompanied all his actions.

Even those tools of propaganda offered to the stern god of Karnak by Pharaoh's unconditional pacifism and total rejection of war
were taken from his hand or at least lost their effectiveness as a result
of Joseph's system of supply and mortgage, which for a while at least
was able to restrain the audacity always evoked in humankind by
power that has turned gentle and renounced violence. The sweet disposition of a late heir to the empire of Thutmose the Conqueror
brought with it great dangers, for word quickly spread among nations round about that in the land of Egypt the tone was no longer
being set by Amun-Rê, but by a tender-hearted divinity of blossoms
and twittering birds, who was unwilling, no matter what, to dye the
imperial sword red—and it would have been an offense to universal
common sense not to lead a god like that around by the nose. A taste
for impudence, defection, and betrayal began to spread. The eastern
provinces that owed tribute—from the land of Seïr to Mount
Carmel—were in turmoil. There was an unmistakable move toward
independence among the princes of Syrian cities, who were relying
on the Hetti's warlike incursions to the south, and at the same time
the Bedouin savages to the east and south were pillaging Pharaoh's
cities and, having likewise heard that kindness now reigned, took
outright possession of some of them. Amun's daily call for the vigorous deployment of power—although intended primarily to apply to
domestic politics and directed against the "doctrine"—was only too
justified in terms of foreign affairs, proved a vexingly persuasive appeal by the heroic old god to resist this refined new one, and was a
source of great worry about his father in heaven to Pharaoh. The
famine and Joseph, however, came to his aid; they robbed Amun's
appeal of much of its force by holding the wobbling petty kings of
Asia in economic restraints; and such rigor, though perhaps not carried out with the mildness of Atôn but with purposeful ruthlessness,
can be regarded as minor considering that it spared Pharaoh from
dyeing his sword red. The cries of pain of those bound to Pharaoh's
throne with golden chains of this sort were often shrill enough to

have found their way down to us today, but all in all are not likely to leave us melting with sympathy. Granted, they had to send not only silver and wood down to Egypt in exchange for grain, but also young family members as hostages and security—a hardship to be sure, but not one to break our hearts, since we know that these Asiatic royal children received excellent care at elegant boarding schools in Thebes and Menfe and benefited from a better education there than they would have enjoyed at home. "To that land," the lament was, and still is, heard, "are gone their sons, their daughters, and the wooden furnishings of their houses." But about whom is this said? About Milkili, for example, the ruler of the city of Ashdod; and we know a thing or two about him indicating that his love for Pharaoh was not the most reliable and might very well have needed to be reinforced by the presence of his wife and children in Egypt.

In short, we cannot bring ourselves to see in any of these things marks of some special cruelty, which was not part of Joseph's character, but are much more inclined, as were the people he "led," to recognize in them the tricks of a clever servant, of a versatile divinity with a laughing eye. Even far beyond Egypt's borders, this was the general opinion of Joseph's administration. It was a source of laughter and admiration—and what better reward can a man earn among his fellows than admiration, which by binding their souls together frees them at the same time for high delight.

Obedience

For what remains to be told, one needs to be a realist and to keep in mind the relative ages of the persons involved in these events—concerning which poetry and painting have largely encouraged false views among the broader public. This does not apply, to be sure, to Jacob, who is always depicted on his deathbed as an almost blind old man of very advanced years. (Indeed, in the final years of his life his eyesight obviously deteriorated; to some extent Jacob made a point of the fact and, following the pattern of Isaak, the blind bestower of blessing, exploited it to enhance his look of solemnity.) But as regards Joseph and his brothers, who were also Jacob's sons, public imagination is inclined to preserve them at a certain age and ascribe to them all an abiding youthfulness that totally skews the relation between the age of their generation and the burden of years borne by their father's head.

It is our duty to intervene here with a correction, to permit no fairy-tale vagueness, and to point out that only death (which is the opposite of events as they tell themselves) can guarantee permanence and brings things to a halt, and that no one can be the subject of a narrative and belong in a story who does not rapidly grow older in the course of it. Indeed, as we have been unfolding this story, we have grown a good bit older ourselves—just one more reason to maintain clarity in this matter. We, too, preferred telling of a charming seventeen-year-old or even a thirty-year-old Joseph to having to speak now of a man who is a good fifty-five; and yet we owe it both to life and its ongoing process to insist upon your taking note of the truth. Even as Jacob—honored and well tended by his children and children's children in the district of Goshen—was adding those last seventeen years by which he would achieve the extremely venerable, but still natural age of one hundred and six, his favorite, who had been set apart as Pharaoh's Unique Friend, had ceased to be a mature man and become an aging one, whose hair (had it not been shorn and covered by an expensive wig) and beard (had he not been clean-shaven, as was the local custom) would have revealed a great deal of white against a dark background. One may also add, however, that those black Rachel eyes had preserved the cordial sparkle that had always delighted people, and that in general, though with the appropriate changes, the Tammuz attribute of beauty had remained faithful to him, thanks to the twofold blessing whose child he had always been held to be—a blessing not only from above and by virtue of his wit, but also a blessing from the deep that lies below and sends the vigor of maternal favor up into the external form. Indeed, it is not unusual for such natures to experience a second youth that to some degree takes their image back to an earlier stage of life; and if many of the artistic representations of Joseph beside Jacob's deathbed portray him in a still youthful state, they are not entirely mistaken, inasmuch as Rachel's firstborn had in fact been a good deal heavier and stouter a few lustrums earlier, but had become decidedly thinner by this time and looked more like his twenty-year-old than his forty-year-old self.

But irresponsible and unthinking are the only terms for certain phantasmagoria of the artist's brush that present us Joseph's sons, the young gentlemen Manasseh and Ephraim, in the moment of being blessed by their dying grandfather, as curly-headed lads of seven or eight. It is of course obvious that they were princely cavaliers in their early twenties, dressed in the braided and ribboned garb of court dandies, with peak-toed sandals and chamberlain's fans. The otherwise incomprehensible carelessness of such depictions is at best excusable as a result of a few starry-eyed turns of phrase in the earliest text, to the effect that Jacob took them on his lap or, better, that Joseph took them from there after the old man had "kissed and embraced them." Such treatment would have been quite embarrassing for these young men, and it is very regrettable that this first report is guilty of that same tendency to make time stand still for most of the persons in the story and allow only Jacob to grow exaggeratedly old—one hundred and forty-seven years old!—and thus lends its aid to such preposterous notions.

We will very soon describe what happened during that visit, the second of three that Joseph paid to his father in his final stage of life. But first let us cast just a brief glance at the preceding seventeen years, during which the children of Israel settled down in the land of Goshen—pasturing their herds, shearing, milking, trading and trafficking, presenting Jacob with great-grandchildren—and so set about to become a multitude of people. It will never be possible to say with complete confidence how many of these seventeen years were actually part of the seven lean years, because it has never been determined with certainty whether there were seven or "only" five of them. (We have set that "only" in ironic quotation marks because in terms of its beautiful significance five is in no way inferior to seven.) As reported, variations in the degree of that ongoing calamity resulted in some uncertainty in the count. During the sacred season of the sixth year, the Provider swelled to no less than fifteen ells at Menfe, his color alternating between red and green, which is as it should be when he is doing well, and deposited a layer of fecund muck—only yet once again to prove totally undernourished and feeble the next year, so that it remained a matter of debate whether or not these two were to be counted as numbers six and seven along with their five lean-ribbed predecessors. At any rate, by the time this question was being discussed in every temple and street, Joseph's agrarian reform was completed, and on that basis he now continued to rule as Pharaoh's Supreme Mouth and tended his sheep, leaving the wool of the fifth year over their eyes.

One cannot say that he saw his father and brothers frequently during this time. Their tents were pitched closer to his in comparison to earlier days, but it was still a good distance between his home in the city of the wrapped god and their place of residence, and he was swamped with administrative affairs and duties at court. He maintained far looser contact with them than those three final visits paid to his father in quick succession might lead one to believe, and no one took offense at this in Jacob's household—it met with silent approval, and the silence said a great deal and expressed more than just an understanding for the external obstacles involved. Those who listened with an attentive ear to the whispered conversation between Jacob and Rachel's firstborn at their reunion, when they stood there between the seventy and Joseph's entourage, will know to assign to the reserve expressed on both sides—for it was indeed mutual—the austere and tenderly sad meaning it deserves: obedience and renunciation. Joseph was the man set apart, who in being exalted had stepped back, was now separated from his tribe, and could not be a tribe himself. The fate of his lovely mother, whose name had been "eagerness rejected," had reappeared transformed in him under a different motto, which read "love that must deny." This was understood and accepted, and, far more than distance and pressing business it was the real reason for his reserve.

If one listens closely to the phrase Jacob used in making a certain request of Joseph, to the polite formula "If now I have found favor in your sight," one has an embarrassing and almost chilling example of the accentuated distance that had established itself between father and son, between Joseph and Israel, and one is reminded, as was Jacob, of an earlier dream, dreamt on the threshing floor, where not only eleven *kokabim* but the sun and moon as well had bent low and bowed before the dreamer. These dreams had roused in his brothers a deadly spite and hatred, had inspired them to the crime that had proved a heavy burden. But how strange to realize what they silently realized themselves, that their crime had fulfilled its purpose and that they had achieved their goal by it. For although things had turned out contrary to all expectation and they had lain upon their bellies before the man who had become first among those here below, they had nevertheless not sold him in vain—that is, had not merely sold him out into the world, but to the world, for he was now lost to it and the inheritance that the man of tender feeling had arbitrarily intended for him was now denied him, had been transferred from the beloved Rachel to the disdained Leah. Was that not worth a little bowing and bending low?

"If now I have found favor in your sight"—it was during the first of the three visits that Jacob said these words to this beloved stranger, at about the time, that is, when he felt life, well into its final quarter, waning, dragging itself, red and weary, belatedly over the horizon before the onset of total darkness. He was not ill at the time and knew that the end was not approaching in great haste. For he still had firm control over his life and energies, could accurately assess how much of them was left, and knew that he still had time, but also that it was time to lay upon the heart of the person who alone could fulfill it a wish that lay upon his own heart and concerned him most personally.

Which is why he sent someone to Joseph to have him summoned. Whom did he send? Why, Naphtali, of course, Bilhah's fleet-footed son; for Naphtali was still fleet of foot and nimble of tongue despite his years—which needs to be noted, since tradition has likewise cast a veil of carelessness over the age of the brothers. A clear-eyed view says that at the time they were all between the ages of forty-seven and seventy-eight, with Benjamin, the little man, no fewer than twenty-one years behind Zebulun, the third youngest after Joseph. This is mentioned here so that come the day that Jacob gathers his sons to curse and bless them in his last hour, you will not be under the illusion that the tent was full of young folk. All the same, we repeat that Naphtali at seventy-five still retained, almost unimpaired, a sinewy command over his long legs and a babbling agility of the tongue—as well as his need to balance out the earth's knowledge and pass back and forth with its messages.

"My boy," Jacob said to this vigorous old man, "go down from here to the great city where my son, Pharaoh's friend, lives and speak with him, saying, 'Jacob, our father, wishes to speak to your grace about an important matter.' You are not to alarm him so that he thinks I am already dying. But rather you shall say to him, 'Given the sum of his many years, our father, the old man, is well in Goshen and has no intention of departing this life. But he deems that the hour has come to speak with you about something that concerns himself, though it lies beyond his life. Therefore be so kind as to find your way to the house that you prepared for him and to his bed, to which he now generally keeps, though sitting up.' Depart, my boy, bound ahead, and tell him that."

Naphtali swiftly repeated his charge and took to his heels. Had it not taken him several days, for he went on foot, Joseph would have been there at once. For he came by chariot, with a small entourage and Mai-Sakhme, his steward, who put far too much importance in his being in this story to have been kept from accompanying his master. But he waited outside with the other members of the household staff, while Joseph was alone with his father in the tent, in its well-furnished living and sleeping quarters, the stage to which the usually wide-ranging expanse of our story has now contracted. For there, in and around his bed at the rear of this space Jacob spent his last days of life, waited on by Damasek, Eliezer's son (who was himself now called Eliezer), a man dressed in a white belted tunic, who despite youthful features had a bald head wreathed in gray hair.

When viewed by full light of day, the man was actually Jacob's nephew, since Joseph's teacher, Eliezer, was the son of a handmaid and a half brother to the man of blessing. His position, however, was that of a servant, though of one elevated above the rest of the household staff; like his father he called himself Jacob's eldest servant and stood over his house in the same way that Joseph stood over Pharaoh's and Captain Mai-Sakhme over Joseph's. After announcing his son to the father, he stepped outside to join the captain and converse with him as his equal.

Entering the chamber, Egypt's viceroy knelt down and touched his forehead to the felt and carpet of the floor.

"Not like that, my son, not like that," demurred Jacob, who, with a blanket of hides over his knees, was sitting up in his bed at the rear of the tent, lit by two clay lamps on wooden consoles, one at each side. "We are in this world, and a pious old man has too high a regard for its greatness to consent to your gesture. Welcome—this frail old man bids you welcome, but caution excuses him from stepping forward out of paternal respect, my exalted lamb. Take a seat on a stool beside me here, my dear—Eliezer, my eldest servant, could have drawn one over for you when he let you in. He is not what his father was, that wooer of a bride whom the earth leapt up to greet, nor would he have meant as much to me as his father did at the time of my bloody tears. And what time do I mean? The time when you were no more. Back then he wiped my face with a moistened cloth and lovingly rebuked me for many a headstrong outburst against God. But you were alive. . . . I thank you for asking, I am well. Naphtali, Bilhah's boy, was charged with assuring you that I was not summoning you to my deathbed—which is to say, it will be my deathbed, this spot here, and is gradually taking on that character, but has not assumed it entirely just yet, for there is still some vital strength left in me, and I have no intention of departing immediately from this life, so that before I die you shall find it easy to return once or twice from here to your Egyptian house and the affairs of state. Granted, I am forced as well as willing to husband very carefully what energies are left to me and to manage them with moderation and frugality, for there will be occasions when I shall need them, especially the last of all, and so I must be chary of both my movements and my words. That is why, my son, this conversation of ours will be brief and limited to the most necessary and important business, for it would be contrary to God's will to exhaust myself in superfluous words. It may well be that I have already spoken a few that were not needed. Once I have said what alone is important and presented it to you in the form of an urgent petition, you may then, if you have time, sit quietly beside me yet a little while, here beside my future deathbed, simply that we may be together here without my having to spend my energies in speech. In silence I shall lean my head on your shoulder and think that it is you, and how in Mesopotamia my one true wife bore you to me in pains beyond nature, how I lost you and in some sense won you back through God's extraordinary kindness. But when you were born as the sun reached its zenith and you lay suspended in your cradle at the side of the virgin as she gasped her song of exhaustion, there was about you a luster of all that is pleasing, which I knew to recognize for what it was, and your eyes, when you opened them to me at my touch, were blue then with the light of heaven and only later black, with that rascal's sparkle there in the black—it was to blame for my bequeathing to you that wedding garment of images here in this tent, a little farther to the front there. I shall want to speak of that at the very end perhaps—but that is probably superfluous now and contrary to frugality. It is very difficult for the heart to discriminate between what is necessary and unnecessary when husbanding its words. . . . Look there, you give me a

kind caress in token of your love and faithfulness. Let that be my reminder—I wish to base the request I shall make of you on your love
and faithfulness, building upon them in the practical petition that I
wish to submit while avoiding every superfluous word. For, Joseph-
el, my exalted lamb, the time is drawing near when I shall die, and
though I am not on the verge of dying, Jacob nonetheless approaches his time of death and the time of testamentary words. But
when I have put my feet together and am gathered to my fathers, I
do not wish to be buried in Egypt—do not take it amiss, but I do not
wish it. Even to lie here where we are now, in the land of Goshen,
which is not all too Egyptian, would not accord with my wishes. I
know well that when a man is dead he can have no more wishes and
it does not matter to him where he lies. But as long as he lives and
wishes, then it is of importance to him that what happens to the dead
be according to wishes of the living. I likewise know well that a good
many of us, numbering in the thousands, will be buried in Egypt,
whether they were born here or born in the land of our fathers.
I, however, the father of them all and of you, cannot bring myself
to serve as example to them in this matter. I have come with them to
your realm and the land of your king, for God sent you before us to
open the way; but in death it is my wish to part ways with them. If I
have found favor in your sight, then put your hand under my thigh,
as Eliezer did with Abram, and swear to me that you will prove your
love and faithfulness to me and not bury me in the land of the dead.
For I wish to lie with my fathers and to be gathered to them. Therefore you shall carry my bones out of Egypt and inter them in their
burying place, which is called Machpelah or the twofold cave at Hebron in the land of Canaan. Abraham lies there, who has been enlarged in splendor and who was suckled in the cave of his birth by an
angel in the form of a goat; beside him lies Sarai, the heroine and
heaven's highest daughter. The averted sacrifice lies there, Yitzchak,
conceived so late, along with Rebekah, Jacob and Esau's clever and
resolute mother, who set everything to rights. And Leah lies there as
well, the first wife that I knew, the mother of the six. I wish to lie beside them all and I see that with childish devotion and ready obedience you accept my wish, though a shadow of doubt and a silent
question brushes your brow. My eyes are no longer the best, for I
am approaching my time of death, and my gaze is clouded with
darkness. But that shadow cast over your face, I can see it clearly, for

indeed I knew that it would be there. For how could I not? There is a grave beside the road, only a little way toward Ephrat, which they now call Bethlehem, where I laid to rest what was dearest to me on God's earth. Do I not then wish to lie at her side when you faithfully bring me home, to lie set apart with her there beside the road? No, my son, I do not. I loved her, I loved her too much, but this is not a matter of emotions and of the heart's voluptuous tenderness, but of greatness and obedience. It is not proper that I should lie beside the road, rather Jacob wishes to lie with his fathers, and beside Leah, his first wife, from whom the heir has come. Behold, your black eyes now stand filled with tears, I see that clearly as well, and they are completely, deceptively, like the eyes of her whom I loved so much. It is a beautiful thing, my child, that you are so much like her, even as you favor me now by putting your hand beneath my thigh, swearing that you will bury me in Machpelah, the double cave, in accordance with greatness and obedience."

Joseph swore this to him. And after he had sworn, Jacob bent down at the head of the bed for a prayer of thanksgiving. After that the son who had been set apart sat quietly for an hour or so with his father, beside him on his deathbed, and in silence the old man leaned his head on Joseph's shoulder so that he might save his energies for the future.

Ephraim and Manasseh

A few weeks later he fell ill. A light fever flushed his hundred-year-old cheeks, he was short of breath and kept to his bed, half sitting, propped against pillows so that he could breath more easily. It was not necessary for Naphtali to run to inform Joseph, for the viceroy had set up a dispatch service between Goshen and his own city, by which he received news of the old man's health once, sometimes twice a day.

When it was reported to him "Behold, your father has fallen ill with a light fever," he summoned his two sons before him and said to them in the Canaanite tongue, "Make ready, we shall drive down to the lowlands to visit your grandfather on my side."

They replied, "But we made a date to hunt gazelles in the desert, our lord and father."

"Did you hear what I said," he asked in Egyptian, "or did you not?"

"We are very much looking forward to paying grandfather a visit," they replied, and informed their friends, the wealthy dandies of Menfe, that for family reasons they would not be joining the hunt. They were dandies themselves, children of a high civilization, manicured, coiffed, perfumed, and painted, with toenails like mother-of-pearl, with waists tightly cinched, and flowing colorful ribbons at the front, sides, and back of their skirts. They were not bad fellows, either of them, and one cannot chide them for being dandies, which was a perfectly natural outgrowth of their society. Except, however, that Manasseh, the older of the two, was very arrogant and prided himself even more on the blood of the priesthood of the sun on his mother's side than on the fame of his father. In contrast, Ephraim, the younger lad with Rachel's eyes, should be thought of as innocently merry and rather modest, that is, to the extent that modesty results from merriment—for arrogance does not laugh easily.

Embracing one another at the shoulders with braceleted arms to steady their stance in the bounding chariot, they drove behind their father toward the north, down to the region of the Delta. Mai-Sakhme accompanied them, in the hope that his medical knowledge might be of some use to the patient.

Jacob was dozing on his pillows when Damasek–Eliezer announced the approach of his son Joseph. The old man pulled himself together at once and had his perennial chief steward sit him up in bed—his sudden presence of mind was extraordinary. "If we have found favor," he said, "before the face his lordship my son, that he now visits us, we dare not slacken due to a slight fever." And he fluffed his silver beard and arranged it on his chest.

"The young lords are with him as well," Eliezer said.

"Fine, fine, that's good," Jacob replied and sat upright, ready to receive them.

It was not long before Joseph entered with the princes, who stayed behind at the entrance, greeting politely, while he approached the bed and lovingly took the old man's pale hands in his.

"My dear sainted papa," he said, "I have come with these two because I was told you have been taken slightly ill."

"It is a slight and frail illness," Jacob replied, "as is usually the

case in old age. Severe and flourishing illnesses are for youth and robust manhood. They attack them with violence and carry them in a
rollicking dance to the grave, which would not be suitable for the
elderly. Feeble illness merely touches old age with its withered finger
to extinguish it. But I have not been extinguished yet, my son, not
this time either. This illness is more withered than I; it has let itself be
deceived by my many years and is inadequate. You will return home
once again from your second visit to my deathbed without its having
become the bed of my corpse. That first time I summoned you that
you might appear before me. This time you have come on your own.
But I shall summon you once more, for a third and final visit, in celebration of my dying."

"May that be far off and may many a year of jubilee yet await
my lord."

"How can that be, my child? It is enough that its hour, the hour
of assembly, has not come at the moment. It is courtly decorum that
speaks for you, but I am in the time of my dying, to which pretty
flourishes are not suited, but only rigor and truth—they will soon be
all that is present at the proceedings of that assembly—I tell you that
beforehand."

Joseph bowed.

"Are things well with you, my child, before the Lord and before
the gods of this land?" Jacob asked. "You see, the illness is so much
weaker than I that I can allow myself to ask after the health of others. To be sure, only of those whom I love. Are you still diligently
collecting that fifth in taxes from the children of the land? This is not
just, Jehosiph. That fifth should belong only to the Lord and not to
a king. But I know, my exalted son, I know it well. And I suppose
you also still burn incense before the sun and the stars on occasion,
as your position requires?"

"Dear father—"

"I know, my lamb that was carried off, I know only too well.
And how lovely it is of you to come between the first and third
times without being summoned and all on your own to see an old
man, despite the claims of your affairs and your many incense-burn-
ing duties. I wish to take advantage of your visit to advance a matter
about which we have not spoken since you first reappeared to me in
the pasture, after being so sorely missed, when I whispered in your

ear, my beloved son, that I wish to apportion you within Jacob and disperse you in Israel, and will divide you into the tribes of my grandsons, that the sons of the sons of the true wife may be like Leah's sons, but you shall be like one of us and rise to the rank of the fathers so that the word may be fulfilled: He is the exalted one."

Joseph bowed his head.

"Behold, there is a place in Canaan," Jacob began to proclaim with uplifted eyes, inspired by fever and very grateful to it for the enhancement it lent his blood, "a place, once called Luz, where a wonderful blue is prepared for dyeing wool. But the place is no longer called Luz, but is named Beth-el and Esagila, the House of the Raising of the Head. For there Almighty God appeared to me in a dream as I slept within the *gilgal,* my head raised up by a stone. High on the ramp, the cord that joins heaven and earth and on which the starry angels swirled up and down to the sound of harmony, He appeared in royal estate, blessed me with the Sign of Life, and called out extravagant consolation above the harps, for He promised me His powerful favor and that he would make me fruitful and multiply me to become a multitude of people and countless children of his favor. Therefore, Jehosiph, your two sons, who were born in the land of Egypt before I came here to you, Ephraim and Manasseh, shall be mine, as Ruben and Shimeon are, and shall be called by my name; those that you will have sired after them shall be yours and yet be called after their brothers' names, so that they are as sons to them. For you have been removed from your seat in the circle of twelve, but with so much love that a fourth is prepared for you alongside those other three of most solemn importance."

At this point Joseph was just about to present the princes to him, when the old man began talking about Rachel yet once more—how, as he was coming from Mesopotamia, she had died in the land of Canaan, beside the road, when there was only just a little way to go to Ephrat, and how he had buried her there on the road to Ephrat, which was now called Bethlehem. He said this more or less in passing; it did not have much connection with the concerns of the moment, unless, that is, he wanted to invoke the shade of his one true wife, that she might be present in this hour, but perhaps he wanted to assign to Rachel's descendants a grave of their own, for them alone, since the double cave at Machpelah was to be a place of pilgrimage for the others. And also, perhaps, he wanted to justify in advance a certain trick, a switch, that he was planning, indeed had long had in mind. Scholarly opinion about his intention in mentioning her is divided, but we are inclined to think that he had none at all and was speaking of his lovely wife because he was caught up in solemn words and deep in his stories and took endless delight in speaking of Rachel, even without any immediate connection, just as he liked to speak about God, and also because he was afraid that he would not have another chance to speak about her and was determined to do so just once more.

Then, after he had buried her beside the road one last time, he looked about, put his hand to his eyes, and asked, "And who are these?"

For he pretended not to have noticed his two grandsons at all until now, and greatly exaggerated his inability to see.

"Those are my sons, my dear sainted papa," Joseph replied, "who are familiar to you and whom God has given me here in this land."

"If it is they," the aged man said, "then bring them to me that I may bless them."

What was there to bring? The princes approached with supple strides all on their own and bowed with exaggerated good manners.

Clicking his tongue softly, the old man rocked his head.

"Lovely boys, as best I can see," he said. "Fine and lovely before God, both of them. Bend down to me here, my treasures, that I may caress the young blood of your cheeks with these hundred-year-old lips. Is this Ephraim whom I am caressing, or Manasseh? Well, whichever. If it was Manasseh, then this is Ephraim whom I am now kissing on the cheeks and eyes. Behold, I have seen your face once more," he said turning to his son, while still holding Ephraim in his embrace, "which I never thought I would; and as if that were not enough, God has also let me see your seed. Is it saying too much to call Him the source of everlasting goodness?"

"Surely not," Joseph replied absentmindedly, for he was busy making sure his boys were in their proper places before Jacob, who made it apparent that he could not tell the difference between them.

"Manasseh," Joseph said softly to his older son, "pay attention. Stand here. Get in the proper order, Ephraim, you're there."

With his right hand he took his younger son and shoved him toward Israel's left hand, and with his left he took Manasseh and placed him opposite Jacob's right hand, so that everything would be as it should be. But what did he see to his astonishment, annoyance, and silent high delight? This is what he saw: His father, raising his face and gazing blindly into space, laid his left hand on Manasseh's bowed head and, crossing his arms, his right on Ephraim's, and before Joseph could intervene, began at once to speak and to bless. He invoked his threefold God—Father, Shepherd, and Angel—that He might bless these lads and might name them after his name, Jacob, and the names of his fathers, asked that they might multiply until they teemed like fishes in their fullness. "Yes, yes, so be it. Stream, holy blessing, stream, holy gift, out of my heart, on through my hands, onto your heads, into your flesh, into your blood. Amen."

It was quite impossible for Joseph to interrupt the blessing, and his sons did not even notice what was happening with them. They were not paying all that much attention and were still rather angry—especially Manasseh—at having to miss their gazelle hunt in the desert for the sake of this ceremony. All the same, each felt a hand of blessing on his head, and if they could have seen that the hands were crossed, with the right on the younger's head and the left on the older's, they would have thought nothing of it, but presumed it was supposed to be that way, was some tribal custom of their foreign grandfather. And they would not have been all that wrong. For Jacob, the brother of the hairy man, was, of course, repeating and imitating. He was imitating the blind man in his tent, his father, who had blessed him instead of his red brother. To his mind the blessing would not work without deception. It had to be switched—so at least he could switch hands, with his right resting on the younger, making him the rightfully blessed. Ephraim had Rachel's eyes and was obviously the more pleasant of the two—that played a role. But the main thing was that he was the younger brother, just as he himself, Jacob, had been when he was switched with the help of hides and of pelts. While his hands switched the two, he heard humming in his ears the charms that his able mother had muttered while preparing him and that resounded with ancient beginnings, out of an even more distant past than his own switched blessing. "I swaddle the child, I swaddle the stone, that the lord he may touch, that the father may eat, brothers of the deep will now have to serve you."

Joseph was, as noted, upset and delighted, both at once. He had a fine sense for rascal tricks, but as a statesman he felt it was his duty to save what good and right order might still be saved. And so, as soon as the old man had finished blessing, he said, "Father, forgive me, but not like that! I placed the boys correctly before you. Had I known that you were going to cross your hands, I would have placed them differently. Might I bring to your attention that you placed your left hand on Manasseh, my older son, and your right on Ephraim, who was born after him? The bad light here is to blame for your—begging your pardon—having blessed rather badly. Do you not wish quickly to correct it, to switch your hands to the right position and perhaps just say 'Amen' once more? For your right hand is not the right one for Ephraim; that honor is due Manasseh."

As he spoke he even took hold of the old man's hands, still resting on the boy's heads, with the intention of reverently putting them to rights. But Jacob held them fast in place.

"I know, my son, I know it well," he said. "And you are to let it be. You rule in the land of Egypt and take your fifth in taxes, but in these things I rule and know what I am doing. Do not fret. This one"—and he raised his left hand a bit—"will also increase and become a great people; but his little brother will be greater than he and his seed will be a multitude of nations. What I have done, I have done, and indeed it is my will that it become a proverb and saying in Israel, so that whenever someone wishes to bless, he shall say, 'God make you as Ephraim and Manasseh.' Let Israel take note."

"As you have commanded," Joseph said.

The young men, however, pulled their heads out from under the hands of blessing, tugged the cinches at their waists to rights, smoothed their hair, and were glad to be able to stand up straight again. They were not affected much by the switch—and rightly so inasmuch as the holy fiction that they were made sons of Jacob and equal to the offspring of Leah made no difference in their personal fate. They lived out their lives as Egyptian noblemen, and only their children or, more precisely, a few of their grandchildren would—by association, religious practice, and marriage—become more and more a part of the Ebrew nation, so that certain groups within that larger clan who would one day leave Keme to return to Canaan traced their origins to Ephraim and Manasseh. But even in regard to the future and the effects of Jacob's laying on of hands, the indifference of these young men was not unjustified, at least in terms of the numbers of people who would later name themselves after them.

For our researches have revealed that at the height of their growth, the count of Manasseh's people exceeded that of Ephraim's by a good twenty thousand souls. But Jacob had blessed and had his little deception.

He was quite exhausted after the ceremony and his mind no longer quite clear. Although Joseph begged him to lie down, he remained sitting up in bed and told his favorite about a parcel of land that he was bequeathing to him separately from his brothers and that he had taken from the Amorites with "sword and bow." The only parcel this could have been was the bit of cropland outside Shechem that Jacob had once purchased beneath that city's gates for one hundred shekels of silver from gout-ridden Khamor or Hemor—and he certainly had not conquered it with sword and bow. How is it that Jacob, who dwelt quietly in his tent, came to speak of sword and bow? He had never loved nor wielded such weapons and had never ceased to condemn his sons for having wielded them savagely at Shechem long ago—as a result of which it was very doubtful that the purchase of the land was still valid and whether Jacob still had any right to dispose of this ornament.

In his state of weakness, in any case, he had it, and, pressing his brow to his father's hands, Joseph thanked him for this special bequest; he was touched by this evidence of love, but also by the strange way in which the old man's weakness left him so confused that he saw himself in the role of a heroic warrior. Joseph concluded that this was a sign of the approaching end and decided not to return to Menfe for now, but to wait in nearby Pa-Kôs for the summons to the last assembly.

Assembled for Death

"Assemble, you children of Jacob! Come together in your hosts and gather around your father Israel, that he may tell you who you are and what shall befall you in days to come."

That was the call Jacob had issued from his tent to his sons, when at last he decided the hour had come for his deathbed speech. For he had his life in his hands and knew exactly what energies were left for him to expend in final words and then to die. He sent out the call by way of his chief steward, Eliezer, that old young man; he recited it for him and had him repeat it several times so that Damasek would know the words not just more or less, but by heart. "It's not 'come hither,' " he said, "but 'come together,' and not 'draw 'round' but 'gather around' Israel. Now repeat the whole thing once more and don't forget that double phrase, 'who you are and what shall befall you.' . . . Good, at last! I fear I have spent too much of my energy instructing you. Now make haste!"

And Damasek tucked his robe up under his belt and ran in all directions, so quickly that the earth seemed to leap up to greet him; he cupped his hands to his mouth and shouted: "Gather together, sons of Israel, and assemble your hosts, just as you are, that good things may befall you from day to day." He ran to the settlements, to the fields, and to the royal pastures over which the five had been set, and to the others, ran here and there through bogs and puddles, the murky water splashing his skinny legs; for it was the time of the ebbing flood, the fifth day of the first month of the winter season, which we call the beginning of October, and after an extended late heat spell it had rained heavily in the Delta. He kept shouting through his cupped hands across the land and into dwellings: "Whoever you are, assemble, sons of Jacob, and meet in hosts around him for the days to come!" He also ran to nearby Pa-Kôs, where Joseph was staying at the home of the mayor, who had posted guards outside, and with disgraceful imprecision he shouted the words that Jacob had carefully chosen and ordered for the ages. But despite his garbling them they had their effect and found dismayed obedience everywhere. Pharaoh's friend likewise hastened to his father's house, along with Mai-Sakhme, his majordomo, as well as a good many curious folk in the street, who had heard the call and decided to loiter as bystanders.

The eleven were waiting for their brother at the curtained entrance. He greeted them with a suitably somber and serious air, kissed Benjamin, the little man of forty-seven, and stood outside speaking softly with them about their father's condition and his evident intention of speaking his dying words and departing. They replied with lowered eyes and rather pinched mouths, for, as usual, they were afraid of the old man's powers of expression and of their tyrannical father's stern rigor in the solemn hour of death, for presumably he would spare them nothing, and each mulled over in his own mind a very human thought: "Heavens, this is not going to be easy!" The muscles in Re'uben's face—that tower in the pasture was now a seventy-eight-year-old man—were drawn taut in a surly scowl. He had had his gushing way with Bilhah, and in the course of these ceremonies he would most definitely hear about it in most expressive terms—and he was arming himself against it. There were Shimeon and Levi; as young men they had barbarically ravaged Shechem on account of their sister—an eternity ago now, but they could be certain it would be served up to them on a solemn plate, and they were arming themselves as well. There was Jehuda, who had accidentally slept with his own daughter-in-law—he had no doubt whatever that the old man would be cruel and rigorous enough in death to reproach him for it, especially since he had been a little in love with her himself. There they all were—and, except for Benjamin, always on his leash, they had all joined in selling Dumuzi that day. Jacob was perfectly capable of putting song and words to that for the occasion as well—they expected as much and expectation left them all sullen. The sons of Leah were especially sullen, for none of them had ever forgiven their father for having taken Bilhah, Rachel's handmaid, instead of their mother to be his dearest and true wife after Rachel's death. Jacob had his failings, too, and had given arbitrary rein to his tender feelings all his life. And as for the affair with Joseph, they thought defiantly, the old man was as guilty as they, and he should think about that before making grand use of the occasion of his death to take them to task for it. In short, the fear of this scene had wrapped them in sullenness. Given what awaited them, every face wore a look of hurt in advance.

Joseph saw this and spoke kind words to them, moving from one to the other, touching each with a cordial hand, and saying, "Let us go inside to him, brothers, and in humility hear the judgment our dear father will speak to us, to each man his own. We shall listen, if necessary, with forbearance. For forbearance should flow down from God to man and from father to child, but if it does not, the child should show reverent forbearance for the greater man's inability when it comes to forgiveness. Let us go in, he will judge us out of his sense of truth and we shall all receive our due share—including me, believe me."

They gingerly entered the tent, their Egyptian brother Joseph with them, but certainly not at their head, although they had wanted him to go first; but together with Benjamin he followed behind the sons of Leah and preceded only the children of the handmaids. Mai-Sakhme, his steward, went in with them, partly with the justification that he had long been in this story and had played a role in its embellishment, but partly as well because the assembly was to a large extent public and, as it turned out, open to almost anyone really. It was very full in the deathbed chamber once the twelve were inside, for along with the herald, Damasek–Eliezer, a good number of servants who personally attended Jacob were standing about the old man's bed, and many of his descendants were standing or lying on their faces in the farther reaches of the room. Even women with children, some with babes nursing at their breasts, were there. Boys sat on chests set against the walls and were not always on their best behavior, although every naughtiness was quickly suppressed. The entrance flaps had been pulled far back as well, so that those crowded outside the tent—people of the household and onlookers from the town of Pa-Kôs, a large throng—had a clear view inside and were, so to speak, included in the assembly. The setting sun outlined figures in the crowd outside against the orange hues of an evening sky, making shadows of them, so that it was not easy to discern individual faces. But the opposing light from the two oil lamps flickering on high stands at the foot and head of the deathbed allows us to distinguish very clearly one arresting figure out there: a gaunt matron in black, standing between two strikingly broad-shouldered men, her gray hair covered by a veil. Without a doubt it was Tamar, that resolute woman, with her manly sons. She had not come inside, but stayed just outside in case Jacob's dying words might also happen to mention Judah's sin with her. But she was present—indeed she was present. For Jacob would be passing on the blessing to the man with whom she had played the harlot and thereby put herself on the right course. Even without lamplight from here inside we would not have failed to make out her proud outline against an evening sky whose colors half promised rain.

The man who had once instructed her about the world and the great story into which she had interpolated herself, the man who had summoned those assembled for his death, Yaaqov ben Yitzchak, who had been blessed instead of Esau, lay there at the rear of the tent on his bed, propped on pillows and covered by a sheepskin, with just as much strength left as he needed. The waxen pallor of his countenance was delicately tinted by twilight hues and the glow of a basin of coals nearby. His gaze was both mild and grand. A band of white cloth he usually wore when making sacrifices was bound across his brow. Curling out at the sides from under it, the white hair at his temples fell at the same breadth down across his chest in a patriarchal beard that was thick and white beneath his chin, but grew grayer and sparser further down, and within it were traced the fine lines of a spiritual, if somewhat bitter, mouth. Without turning his head, he directed the gaze of his tender eyes, with pouches sagging beneath them, to one side, leaving a good deal of the yellowish white of the eyeball exposed. His eyes followed the entrance of his sons, all twelve of them, before whom a passage to his bed quickly opened. Damasek and the servants who tended him stepped back; those who had been sired beyond the Euphrates and the little one whose birth had slain his mother in Abraham's land bowed down, pressing their brows to the floor, and then stood up to group themselves around their father's head. Total silence had descended, and all eyes were turned to Jacob's pale lips.

They opened tentatively several times before words formed and with great effort his speech began very softly. In time his voice freed itself and gained its full timbre; only at the very end, at the blessing of Benjamin, did it fade feebly away again.

"Welcome, Israel," he said, "girding the world with the zone of your wandering, a sturdy causeway of the heavens ordered in a sacred array of signs. Behold, you came obediently in your hosts and have gathered bravely about the bed of my demise, that I may judge you according to truth and prophesy out of the wisdom of the last hour. Praise be yours, circle of sons, for your ready compliance and commendation for your stoutheartedness. Blessing from the hand of this dying man be upon you all and benediction to you in your entirety. You are blessed with eternal benediction by energies carefully husbanded. Note well that what I have to say to you, each for himself and one after the other, is said under this general blessing."

Here his voice failed and only his lips moved for a while, all on their own without a sound. But then his features regained their courage, and his forehead wrinkled as he set his eyebrows in defiance of his weakness.

"Re'uben!" came the call from his lips.

The tower in the pasture stepped forward on columns of legs

laced in leather, but with an old man's white head and a smooth-shaven red face wrenched like a little boy's on the verge of tears as he waits to be scolded. His eyes, with their inflamed lids, blinked rapidly beneath white eyebrows, and the corners of his mouth were pulled down in such fierce bitterness that a large bulge of muscle formed at each side. And he knelt beside the bed and bowed across it.

"Ruben, my eldest son," Jacob commenced, "you are my first strength and the firstling of my manhood, yours was the privilege and mighty preeminence, within the circle you were the highest, the closest to the sacrifice, the closest to kingly power. It was a mistake. In open country this was once revealed to me in a dream by an idol, a pungent beast of the desert, a dog-boy, with a beautiful leg and seated upon a stone, conceived by mistake, conceived with the wrong wife in the blindness of night, to whom nothing makes any difference and who knows no distinctions in love. And so I sired you, my preeminent son, in the drafty darkness with the wrong wife, the fit and able wife, sired you in delusion and gave her the flower, for a switch had been made, the veil was switched, and day revealed to me that I had merely sired where I had thought to love—and my heart and bowels turned over, and I despaired for my soul."

They understood nothing more of what he said for a while—with soundless lips he just went on speaking to himself again for a long time. Then his voice returned, stronger than before, and at times he was no longer talking to Ruben, but about him, on past him, in the third person.

"He gushed like unstable water," he said. "Like seething water he boiled over out of the pot. He shall not have preeminence nor shall he be the peg that supports the tent, he shall have no privilege. He went up to his father's bed and in going up to my couch defiled it. He uncovered his father's private parts and mocked him, he approached his father with the sickle and performed great wantonness with his mother. He is Ham, black of face, who goes naked with private parts exposed, for he behaved like the dragon of chaos and in the manner of the hippopotamus. Do you hear, my first strength, what I say about you? You are cursed, my son, cursed under the cover of blessing. The privilege is taken from you, the priesthood removed and the kingship revoked. For you are not worthy of leadership, and your firstborn rights are repudiated. You shall dwell beyond the Salt Sea and border on Moab. Your deeds are feeble and your fruits of no importance. Thank you, my eldest, that you came with the hosts and have bravely faced your judgment. You are like a tower in the pasture and stride about on legs like the columns of a temple because I spilled my first strength and manhood so mightily, there in the delusion of night. Receive a father's curse and farewell."

He fell silent and the aged Ruben stepped back into the group, all the muscles of his face taut with grim dignity, and lowered his eyelids the way his mother had done when she wanted to conceal her crossed eyes.

"The brothers!" Jacob ordered now. "The twins, inseparable in the heavens!"

And Shimeon and Levi bent low. They too were now seventy-six and seventy-seven years old (for they were never twins at all, but only inseparable), but had kept up ruffian appearances as best they knew how.

"Oh, oh, my violent sons, with bodies scarred and dyed red!" their father said, pulling back with the pretense of fear. "They kiss weapons of violence, about which I wish to know nothing. I do not love violence, you savage pair. May my soul not come into their counsels, nor my honor be joined to their company. Their anger has slain a man and their wantonness has maimed the ox, for which the curse of the offended was spoken against them and their downfall proclaimed. What did I say to them? Cursed be their anger, for it is so fierce, and their wrath, for it is so cruel. That is what I have said to them. You are cursed, my dear sons, cursed under the cover of blessing. You shall be divided and separated one from the other, so that you may not commit mischief together for ever and ever. Be scattered among Jacob, my Levi! You shall receive your portion and your land, strong Shimeon, but I see that it will not stand on its own and will dissolve into Israel. You shall be set in the background, twin stars, according to the clear vision of him who blesses as he dies. Step back!"

Which they did, more or less unshaken by this judgment. They had long known all about it and had expected nothing better. Even that it had been spoken yet again for all to hear in a public ceremony did not concern them, for everyone already knew what was what, and they would remain "Israel" in any case—the condemnation had taken place under a general blessing. Moreover, they, along with the entire audience, were convinced that the outcast was a role like any other and had its own dignity. Any status is a status of honor—that was not just their opinion, but the view of everyone else as well. Besides which, it was patently obvious that to some extent their father had spoken not about them, but about the constellation of the twins. Partly out of an innate fondness for larger meaning, partly out of the confusion that came with his frailty and to which he solemnly yielded out of that same love for larger meaning, he had got them all mixed up with Gemini and also included certain Babylonian memories familiar to everyone, even to the little boys sitting on the chests. He had evidently and deliberately confused them at times with Gilgamesh and Eabani in the saga, who had been so fierce and angry on their sister's account that they had dismembered the heavenly bull and were cursed by Ishtar for this sacrilege. At Shechem, at the city of Sichem—where, to be sure, they had run amok—they had paid no special attention to oxen and could not recall having lamed one; Jacob, however, had been obsessed with oxen from the very start and never failed to mention them whenever he brought the episode up. But can one be cursed any more honorably than to be confused with the Dioscuri and with the sun and the moon? That is an outcast status in which one can take pleasure even before a large audience, and one need take it only half personally—the other half is merely the dreamy mind game of a dying man.

It is best to note right here that astronomical meanings and allusions were repeatedly mixed in with Jacob's message to his sons, and while enhancing it, they created at the same time a certain very human inaccuracy. This was both on purpose and out of weakness, and a purposeful use of weakness. Even with Ruben there had been some hint of Aquarius. Judah, whose turn it was now and for whose powerful and decisive blessing the old man taxed himself greatly—so that later he had to call upon God's help at one point out of fear that he might not complete the task and might not make it to Joseph in particular—Judah, then, had always been called a lion, but the dying words dedicated to him were so persistent in their use of this title, were so purposefully aimed at turning tormented Jehuda into a leonine figure that no one could fail to recognize the zodiacal allusion. A great deal of Cancer glimmered through with Issakhar—within it lie the stars of the two Little Asses, which were now brought into cosmic association with his sobriquet of "raw-boned ass." With Dan everyone recognized Libra, the sign of justice and judgment, though the sign of the venomous horned viper codetermined his description as well; and for most people Naphtali's form as a stag or hind clearly moved in the direction of Aries the Ram. Joseph himself proved no exception—on the contrary, such astral enhancement was doubly applicable to him, since Virgo and Taurus the Bull alternated in his characterization. That of Benjamin, when it came his turn at last, seemed determined by Scorpio, for the good little fellow was celebrated as a ravenous wolf simply because Lupus stands just to the south, near the sting in its tail.

Here we have the clearest example of the depersonalization that an air of astral mythology brings with it and that made it so much easier for the bellicose twins to accept their verdict with such equanimity. They lived in an early time, which was likewise a later time, and had considerable experience in a great many things, including in the hardly infallible trustworthiness of deathbed visions and prophecies. The view that the departing have into the future is impressive and worthy of respect; one may have a good deal of faith in it, but not too much, for it does not always hold true in its entirety, and evidently the already extraterrestrial state that produces this view must at the same time be credited as a source of error. Jacob likewise committed some mistakes—along with those things he saw that were right on the mark. Ruben's descendants never really amounted to much, and Shimeon's tribe always remained in need of support and finally lost itself in Judah. But that the blood of Levi would in time achieve the highest honors and the permanent prerogative of priesthood—something we happen to know inasmuch as we are both in this story and outside of it—that fact was evidently hidden from Jacob's departing gaze. In that particular matter—and in others as well—his deathbed prophecy was a venerable failure. He said that Zebulun would dwell at the shore of the sea and become a haven for ships; his border was to be at Sidon. That was obvious enough, since his son's fondness for the sea and the smell of pitch was known to all. But the future territory of Zebulun's tribe most definitely did not extend to the Great Green, nor did it ever border on Sidon. It lay between those waters and the Sea of Galilee, separated from the latter by Naphtali and from the former by Asher.

Such mistakes are of great value to us. For what about those clever fellows who claim that Jacob's blessings were written after the time of Joshua and are to be read as "predictions after the event"? One can only shrug one's shoulders at that—not only because we are present at the dying patriarch's bedside and can hear his words with our own ears, but also because prophecies made on the basis of reported history, backdated prophecies, find it very easy to avoid mistakes. The surest proof for the authenticity of a prophecy will always be its inaccuracy.

And so Jacob called Judah forward—it was a powerful moment, and deep silence reigned both among those beyond the tent and those of us here inside. Only very rarely does such a large assembly of people find itself spellbound in so deep, breathless, and motionless a silence.

The ancient man raised a wan hand toward his fourth son, who out of deepest shame had already bowed his seventy-five-year-old head—he raised a finger to point at him and said, "Judah, you are the one!"

Yes, he was the one—this tormented man who felt himself totally unworthy, the slave of his Mistress, who had no lust for lust, but for whom lust lusted, a sinner and man of conscience. One might think that at seventy-five a man is no longer held in such awful enthrallment to servile lust—but one would be mistaken. For that endures until a man's last sigh. True, the spear may be a little duller, but release from the hand of the Mistress—that will never be. In deepest shame Judah bent low for his blessing—but then what a strange thing happened! As the oil of promise flowed from the horn upon his head, his own heart, in equal measure to the high solemnity of the occasion, grew more secure, found manifest consolation, said to itself with growing pride, "Well, well, in spite of everything, it seems. It wasn't so bad after all, and evidently not an obstacle to the blessing. Maybe it's not such a serious matter. This purity I thirsted for, was, it turns out, not essential for salvation, and all of it, even hell itself, played its part. Who would have thought it, blessing drips upon my head. God have mercy on me—I am the one!"

It didn't drip, it gushed, it surged. In blessing Judah, Jacob almost ruthlessly spent himself, so that later several brothers heard only brief, vague words spoken in a frail voice.

"You are the one, Jehuda! For your hand is on the neck of your enemies—your brothers shall praise you. Yes, your father's sons shall bow down before you and the children of each mother praise

the anointed one in you." Then came the lion. For a good while
there was nothing but the lion and fierce leonine metaphors. Judah
was a lion's whelp, from the litter of a lioness, a true king of beasts.
The ravenous lion rose up from his prey, snarling and thundering.
He retreated to his desert mountain, made his den there, stretching
out like the maned king that he was and like the son of a grim lioness. Who would dare rouse him? No one dared that. How peculiar—considering how he heaped blame on those he chose not to
bless for their attachment to instruments of violence—that the father
praised the sons he wished to bless as ravenous brigands. Just as in
his utter weakness he had seen himself in the role of the warrior,
with sword and bow, so now he praised his sons—especially the tormented Judah, but even little Benjamin toward the end as well—as
bloodthirsty beasts of prey and savage brutes. It is remarkable: the
weakness of gentle, spiritual souls is a weakness for heroics.

And yet in blessing Judah, Jacob intended no such brutal heroics. The hero at whom he was aiming, whom he had long ago formed
in his mind, was not of that splendidly roaring sort that weakness
has a fondness for—no, Shiloh was his name. It was a long way from
lions to him—which is why the blessing now first made a transition:
the old man added the vision of a great king. The king sat on his
throne, and his scepter was braced between his feet, from where it
would never depart, nor be taken from him until "the hero" came,
until Shiloh appeared. For Judah, the king with the ruler's staff between his feet, this name of promise was something totally new—it
came as a surprise to the entire assembly, and they all listened in
amazement. Only one person among them all already knew of it and
had been waiting eagerly to hear it. We cannot help casting a glance
outside to the outline of her shadow—there she stood very erect, in
darkling pride, as Jacob proclaimed this woman's seed. Grace would
never depart from Judah, he would never die, nor would his eye fail
until his greatness became exceeding great, for from him would
come the one to whom all peoples would be obedient, the bringer of
peace, the man of the star.

These high and solemn proceedings above Judah's head, still
bowed in shame, exceeded all expectations. His person, or rather his
tribe, was blended—whether intentionally or due to a confusion of
mind, or to both, which is to say, due to a confusion intentionally
exploited for high and solemn poetic purpose—was blended and

merged with the figure of Shiloh, so that when it came to the vision of the fullness of blessing and grace to which Jacob now devoted himself, no one could say whether his words concerned Judah or this man of promise. It all swam in wine—sparkling wine turned everything red before the listeners' eyes. It was a land, this king's kingdom, a land where someone bound his animal to the vine and his ass's colt to the choice vine. Were these the vineyards of Hebron, the wine-clad hills of Engedi? Into his city "he" rode on an ass and upon the foal of a she-ass, a beast of burden. There was nothing but the drunken delight of red wine at the sight of him, and he himself was like a drunken god of wine stomping in the winepress, holding skirts high in exultation—the blood of the wine drenched his apron and the red juice of the grape his garments. How beautiful he was wading there, dancing the dance of the winepress—more beautiful than any other man, white as snow, red as blood, black as ebony . . .

Jacob's voice died away. His head drooped, his eyes gazed up from below. He had spent himself in this blessing, had husbanded his energies rather poorly. He appeared to be praying for their renewal. Judah, realizing that his blessing was at an end, stepped back, ashamed and amazed that a lack of purity was in fact no obstacle. For those assembled around the deathbed, the proclamation of Shiloh, that completely new revelation and announcement that had come with Judah's blessing, was so extraordinary, so sensational that they could barely contain themselves. A spirited whispering passed through the tent and the crowd outside. Out there it even grew to a murmur, voices could be heard excitedly repeating the name Shiloh. But all commotion came to a halt the moment Jacob raised his head and hand again. Zebulun's name came from his lips.

Zebulun placed his head under the hand, and since his name was "dwelling place" and "habitation," no one was surprised when Jacob told him about his future dwelling and habitation: he would dwell at the shore of the sea, near treasure-laden ships, and his border would be at Sidon. That sufficed, he had always wanted it that way, even if the pronouncement had come in rather perfunctory and faint tones. Issakhar . . .

Issakhar would be like a raw-boned ass crouching between two sheepfolds. The Little Asses in Cancer were his sponsors, but despite this connection, Jacob did not seem to expect much from him. He briefly spoke of him in the past tense, but meant the future.

Issakhar saw a resting place that was good and a land that was pleasant. He was strong and phlegmatic. It did not matter to him that he would offer his bones for bearing burdens like a caravan ass. To serve, to bend the shoulder that it might be laden with its burden, seemed easiest to him. So much for Issakhar. He touched the Jordan, or so Jacob claimed to see. Enough of him. Now for Dan.

Dan held the balance scale and judged with discernment. He was so subtle of mind and tongue that he stung and was like a viper. This son offered Jacob the opportunity to raise his finger and insert a brief zoological lesson for his audience: In the beginning, as God busied himself with Creation, He had crossed a hedgehog with a lizard, from which had come the adder. Dan was an adder. He was a serpent in the way and a viper by the path, not easy to spot in the sand and very cunning. In him heroics took the form of cunning. He bit his enemy's horse in the heel, so that the rider fell backward. That was Dan, Bilhah's son.

"I wait for your help, eternal Lord." It was here that Jacob heaved this sigh and prayer, both out of a sense of exhaustion and a concern that he might not finish. He had sired so many sons that the sum of them almost exceeded his strength in his last hour. He would manage, however, with God's help.

He now demanded burly Gad in his coat sewn with brass plates.

"Gaddiel, you are burdened by troops bursting forth, but in the end you shall burst upon them. Burden them well, my burly son. And now Asher.

"Asher, of the sweet tooth and lips, had rich land on the mountain slope toward Tyre. The lowlands waved with grain and dripped with oil, so that he dined on rich food and to anoint himself made fine salves such as kings exchange to please one another. From him came pleasure and the delight of a well-groomed body, which has its value too. Asher, you will also amount to something. And since song has come from you and sweet annunciation, may you be praised before your brother Naphtali, whom I now summon beneath my hand.

"Naphtali was a doe bounding over ditches, and a leaping hind. His was the swiftness and the gallop, he was a running ram when it lowers its horns and plunges ahead. His tongue was swift as well, delivering nimble tidings, and the fruits of the plain of Genessaret ripened quickly. May your trees be filled with quickly ripening fruit, Naphtali, and may rapid, if not all too significant, success be your judgment and portion."

And, his blessing done, this son now stepped back as well. The old man rested in deep silence, his eyes closed, his chin on his breast. And after a while he smiled. Everyone saw the smile and was touched, for they knew the summons it signaled. It was a happy, yes, a sly smile and yet a little sad as well, but the slyness came from the way the fervor of love and tenderness conquered sadness and renunciation. "Joseph!" the old man said. And a fifty-six-year-old man, who had once been thirty and seventeen and nine and had lain in his cradle as the lamb of a mother sheep, a child of his times, beautiful of countenance, dressed in Egyptian white, Pharaoh's heavenly ring on his finger, a man full of favor, bent down beneath the pale hand of blessing.

"Joseph, my sprout, son of the virgin, son of loveliness, son of the fruit tree beside a spring, fruitful bough whose branches run over the wall, I greet you. You who mark the beginning of spring, firstling bullock in his adornment, my greetings to you."

Jacob had spoken this solemn salutation in loud, clear tones for everyone to hear. But then he dropped his voice almost to a whisper, his obvious intent being, if not to exclude the public entirely, at least to limit its size. Only those standing nearest to him heard his farewell words to the son set apart; those farther away caught only fragments, and for now those outside were left with nothing whatever. But later it all was repeated, spread from one to another, and discussed.

"Most dearly beloved son," came the words from painfully smiling lips, "son favored by a bold heart for the sake of the only beloved wife, who lived in you, and with whose eyes you gazed, just as she once gazed at me beside the well, when she first appeared among Laban's sheep and I rolled the cover away for her—I was permitted to kiss her and the shepherds rejoiced, singing 'loo, loo, loo.' In you, my darling, I clung to her when the Almighty tore her from me, she dwelt in your charms, and what is sweeter than what is double and mutable? I know well that what is double is not one with the spirit for which we stand, but is the folly of nations. And yet I fell under its ancient and mighty spell. Can a man belong to that spirit always and totally, avoiding all folly? Behold, I myself am double, am Jacob and Rachel. I am she, who found it so hard to leave you for the demanding land that demands that I depart from you today as well—it demands it of us all. You, too, my joy and my care, have now advanced halfway toward that land and yet you were once small and then young and were everything my heart understood charm to be—my heart was serious, but soft, and thus weak before your charms. Called to lofty heights and to diamond-bright cliffs, it still secretly loved the charm of the hills."

His words dried up for a few minutes, and he smiled with closed eyes, as if his mind were wandering in those same charming hills that he had suddenly pictured in blessing Joseph.

When he began to speak again he appeared to have forgotten that Joseph's head was under his hand, because for a while he spoke of him, too, as if of some third person.

"Seventeen years he lived for me and by God's grace lived for me yet another seventeen years; but in between lay my numbness and the fate of a man set apart. Foes lay in wait to snare his charms— what folly, for these were bound up as one with a cleverness that brought their covetousness to naught. More alluring than any man's eye has ever seen are the women who climb up to look upon him from walls and towers and from windows, but look in vain. And so they made life bitter for him and assailed him with the arrows of slander. But his bow held in strength, his muscles held in strength, and the hands of the Eternal held him fast. Not without rapture will his name be remembered, for he succeeded where few ever succeed: to find favor before God and man. That is a rare blessing, for one usually has the choice of pleasing either God or the world; but to him was given the spirit of charming mediation, so that he pleased both. Be not proud, my child—need I warn you? No, I know that your cleverness shields you from arrogance. For it is a lovely blessing, but not the highest or most stern. Behold, your precious life lies in all its truth before the eyes of a dying man. It was play, it was allusion, a confiding, cordial state of favor, hinting at salvation and yet not fully summoned and admitted to true seriousness. It is such a mixture of high delight and sadness that it stirs my heart with love— and none can love you so, my child, who knows only the luster of your life, but does not see, as does a father's heart, its sadness. And so I bless you, my blessed son, from the strength of my heart and in the name of the Eternal, who gave you and took you and gave you and now takes me from you. My blessing shall ascend higher than the blessings of my fathers upon my own head. Be blessed as you are, with blessings from above and blessings from the deep below, a surge of blessing from the breast of heaven and the womb of earth. Blessing, blessing upon Joseph's head, and those who come from you shall bask in the sun of your name. Broad be the river of song that celebrates the playful story of your life, singing it ever new, for it was a holy game, and you suffered and could forgive. Just as I also forgive you that you have made me suffer. And God forgive us all."

He finished and hesitantly withdrew his hand from that head. So one life takes leave of another and must depart; yet a little while and the other will depart as well.

Joseph stepped back to join his brothers. He had not exaggerated when he said that he, too, would receive his due share and be judged by a dying man's sense of truth. He took Benjamin by the hand and brought him forward, for the old man had failed to call him. His strength was obviously at an end, and Joseph had to place the hand of blessing on his little brother's head, for it would no longer have found its way on its own. The old man surely still knew that it was his youngest who awaited his judgment, but what his faltering lips muttered had nothing to do with the little man. Perhaps they would make sense to his descendants. Benjamin, they strained to hear, was a ravenous wolf who devours the prey of the morning and will divide the spoils of evening. He was baffled to hear it.

Jacob's final thoughts were once again about the cave, that double cave in the field of Ephron, son of Zohar, and his wish to be buried there beside his fathers. "I charge you to do it," he rasped. "It has been paid for, purchased by Abram from the children of Heth for four hundred shekels of silver according to weights current at . . ." Here death interrupted him, he stretched out his feet, sank back deep into his bed, and his life stood still.

And when it happened, their breath, their lives, stood still a little too. Then Mai-Sakhme, who was Joseph's steward, but a physician as well, calmly approached the bed. He laid an ear to the silent heart, placed a feather to the mute lips, and drawing his own lips in a little circle of concentration, he observed the down, which did not stir. He struck fire before the pupils, but they paid no attention now. Then he turned to Joseph, his master, and reported to him: "He is gathered to his people."

With a motion of his head, Joseph indicated, however, that Judah and not he should receive this report. And while the good man stood before his brother and repeated, "He is gathered to his people," Joseph stepped up to the deathbed and closed the dead man's eyes— for that is why he had directed Mai to Judah, so that he might do this. Then he laid his brow to his father's brow and wept for Jacob.

Judah, the heir, ordered all things proper to the occasion: the hiring of male and female mourners, as well as singers of both sexes and flute players, and the washing, anointing, and wrapping of the corpse. Damasek–Eliezer burnt an offering of incense there in the tent: stacte, periwinkles from the Red Sea, galbanum, and frankincense mixed with salt; and as the spicy clouds enveloped the dead man, the guests at his bedside streamed from the tent, joining those who had been standing outside, and departed with them, eagerly discussing the judgments and decrees that Jacob had meted out to the twelve.

Now They Wrap Jacob

And so this story, one grain of sand at a time, has silently, steadily run through the neck of its glass; the sand lies in a mound below, and only a few grains are still left in the chalice at the top. Nothing remains of all its happenings except to tell of what happened to the dead man. But that is no small thing—so take our advice and watch reverently as the last grains run through and gently come to rest on those heaped below. For what happened to Jacob's mortal shell was something quite extraordinary and the ceremonies honoring it were almost without parallel. No king has been borne to his grave as was this man of solemnity—all according to measures designed and ordered by his son Joseph.

After his father's demise, he indeed left the first preliminary arrangements to his brother Jehuda, the inheritor of the blessing; later, however, he took the matter in hand himself, for only he could plan things and issue decrees for which he first had to be empowered by a quickly assembled council of brothers. These plans were dictated by circumstances, dictated by Jacob's charge and testament, and with all his heart Joseph was glad such was the case. For in having been set apart for so long, he thought like an Egyptian, and his ardent wish to commemorate his father and treat his remains in only the finest and most expensive fashion was in perfect accord with the Egyptian way of thinking.

Jacob had not wished to be buried in the land of dead gods, but had made them swear that he would be interred with his fathers in that cave at home. This entailed a major transport, for which Joseph had exceedingly grand plans that would demand time: time for equipping the solemn transport and time for the journey itself, a matter of at least seventeen days. The corpse, moreover, had to be preserved, preserved according to the arts of Egypt, pickled and embalmed; and if the man now gathered to his people would have found that idea objectionable, then he should have refrained from enjoining them to carry him home. His instruction that he not be buried in Egypt meant that he had to be buried in the Egyptian manner, be splendidly stuffed and laced as an Osiris mummy—which may offend some people. But we have not lived in Egypt for forty years as his son Joseph had, have not been nourished by the juices and attitudes of this peculiar land. In his sorrow, he found it both a joy and a consolation that his father's testament allowed him to treat these precious remains according to that land's most exquisite rites of honor and to bestow permanency upon them, cost what it might.

Accordingly, no sooner had he returned home to Menfe, where he went into mourning, than he sent men to Goshen, for whom the brothers used the term "physicians," though they were nothing of the sort, but specialists in mummification, eternity artists, the most skilled and sought-after in their trade, nor was it by chance that they lived in the city of the wrapped god. With them came carpenters and stonemasons, goldsmiths and engravers, who at once set up a workshop beside the dead man's house of felt, while inside the "physicians" performed on the corpse what the brothers termed "anointing." But that was not the right word. With a hooked iron tool they extracted the brain through the nostrils and filled the hollow skull with spices. An extremely sharp knife of Ethiopian obsidian, wielded with great elegance and fingers spread wide, was used to open the left side of the abdomen so that they could remove the viscera, which were destined to be preserved in special alabaster jars whose lids would bear the image of the deceased. They rinsed the empty abdominal cavity with date wine and replaced the innards with their finest wares: myrrh and the spicy bark from the runner roots of the laurel. They did it with the devotion of craftsmen, for death was their artistic medium, and they took joy in making the man's body look so much tidier and more appealing than when it had contained a living soul.

They then carefully sewed up the incision and laid the corpse in a caustic saltpeter bath for a total of seventy days. During this time they were on holiday, with nothing to do but eat and drink, and were paid for every hour. When this period came to an end and the dead man was well pickled, the wrapping could begin—a task of great importance. Bandages of byssus, four hundred ells long and painted with a sticky gum, were wrapped around Jacob, with the finest of these endless strips of linen placed closest to the body—wrapped round and round, now in parallel, now overlapping, and in between they laid a golden collar around his tightly bound neck and on his breast another piece of jewelry cut from hammered gold: the image of a vulture, its wings outspread.

For all this time the artisans who had come with the physicians had likewise been hard at work and could contribute their articles of beauty: ribbons, wrought from gold foil and inscribed with the name of the deceased and eulogies to his name, were bound around the wrapping linens, around shoulders, waist, and knees, and then tied to others that ran the length of the body at the front and back. Nor was that the end of it, for what had once been Jacob, was now an eternal, ornate doll of death, purified from all corruption, which they encased from head to foot in thin, supple plates of pure gold and then lifted into an *arôn*, a perfectly measured casket in the shape of a human being, richly adorned with gemstones and colorful glass beads, all supplied by cabinetmakers, jewelers, and sculptors, who had been working all this time. One figure rested within another; the head of the external figure was of chiseled wood overlaid with a mask of gold foil and bore the beard of Usir on its chin.

This, then, was what happened to Jacob—with all due splendor and honor, though not in accord with his wishes, but solely with those of his transplanted son. But it is probably best that these things are done in accord with the emotions of the man with living guts in his body, for it can make no difference to the other one.

To commemorate his father in death by elevating the man's final wish to an occasion of highest pomp and circumstance—that was Joseph's sole desire and purpose, and while the corpse was being readied for transport, the exalted son had taken steps to turn this journey into a grand triumph, a marvelous event worthy of chronicling. For this he needed Pharaoh's approval, but because he was observing several weeks of mourning with the attendant neglect of his own person, he could not speak with the god himself, but sent an envoy up to the city of the horizon, in the nome of the Rabbit, who in his stead begged the beautiful child of Atôn for Joseph to be allowed to accompany his father's body to its resting place beyond the borders of the land. It was Mai-Sakhme, his steward, to whom he entrusted this mission—first because it offered the good man an opportunity to be part of this story until the very end, but also because he knew he could place highest trust in the man's calmness and loyalty when carrying out the delicate diplomacy the task required. For the point was to obtain from Pharaoh orders that one could only suggest to him, but not directly ask of him; the point was to win his consent to a full ceremonial state funeral for the man who had sired his First Servant, or, in other words, to induce him to decree a Grand Procession.

Once again we see that Rachel's lamb had become quite accustomed to thinking in the Egyptian mode. A Grand Procession was a peculiarly Egyptian notion, a festive and ceremonial spectacle beloved by the people of Keme, and Joseph had at once interpreted Jacob's last testament to include not only an embalmment in the highest price range, but also a Grand Procession that would be talked about beyond the Euphrates and as far as the Islands of the Sea. It was to vie with the most famous ambassadorial corteges that Egypt had ever sent abroad—to Babel, Mitanniland, or the great King Hattusil in the land of Hetti—and to deserve being recorded for posterity in the annals of the kingdom. Pharaoh would have to grant him official leave for seventy days so that he could join his eleven brothers, as well as his own sons and theirs, in accompanying their father along the special route of honor that he had selected and that led to his grave beyond the border—this was the first and easiest part. But it was not enough, it was not a Grand Procession, not a king's cortege, and this worldly son wanted his father carried to his grave as no less than a king. Pharaoh had to be convinced to permit this, to order it; he had to command the state—that is, both court and army—to provide an escort, including a considerable military force to guard them on the long journey across the desert. And once the steward had spoken to him, the idea occurred to Pharaoh and he ordered it done, decreeing it in part because he himself was touched and wanted to show love and favor to his most deserving servant, who had done so much for him, but in part also because he was worried that if Joseph were to travel to the land of his origin without an Egyptian escort, he might not return in the end. That Meni was seriously worried about this, and that Joseph was also counting on his worry, can be seen clearly shimmering through the words our basic report puts in his mouth during negotiations at court: "Now therefore let me go up and bury my father; then I will *return*." It may be that he obligingly made this promise to return on his own; but it is equally likely that Pharaoh demanded it of him. In any case, there stood between master and servant the suspicion that Joseph might use his departure in order never to return, and Pharaoh was glad that he could unite favor and caution, that with the assistance of a heavy escort of honor he could prevent the loss of this irreplaceable man.

The Lord of the Two Crowns was no longer the youngest himself by now; the years of his life were more than forty, and that life had been fragile and sad. He himself had encountered death: one of his daughters, the second of six, Meketatôn, the most anemic of them all, had died at age nine; and Ikhnatôn, the father of daughters, had given himself over to far more tears than Nefernefruatôn, his queen. He wept a great deal; quite apart from death, tears came easily to him just in general on any occasion, for he was lonely and unhappy, and the opulence of his existence, the soft civilized splendor in which he lived, did not help make him any less sensitive to loneliness and not being understood. True, he liked to say that whoever has things hard, should also have it good. But the two were combined for him only amid tears; he had things too good for it to be hard for him as well, and he wept a great deal over his lot. His little morning cloud edged in gold, the queen, and his diaphanous daughters were constantly having to use fine batiste to dry the tears from his now aging boyish face.

There in the splendid court of the magnificent temple that he had built for his father in heaven at Akhet-Atôn, the sole capital, his one great joy was to offer sacrifices of flowers while choirs sang hymns to his god, whom he pictured as a gentle friend of nature who wept copious tears as well. But such joy was soured by his mistrust of the sincerity of his courtiers, who lived off him and had accepted the "doctrine," but who—as every test of their knowledge showed—did not understand it, for it was beyond them. No one could fathom the doctrine of a father who lived at an infinite distance in heaven and nevertheless blessed every little mouse and worm with his tender concern, of whom the solar disk was merely a mediating symbol, and who whispered the truth of his nature to Ikhnatôn, his beloved child—no one, as he admitted to himself, believed any of it with all his heart. He was alienated from his people and shunned all contact with them. As for the religious powers of his kingdom, the temples and priests, and not just Amun, but all the other ancient and time-honored national divinities, he lived in hopeless strife with them all—with the exception, at best, of the sun's house at On—and out of pained zeal for his own revelation had gone so far as to issue orders and decrees to suppress and destroy Egypt's gods (and again, not just Amun-Rê, but also Usir, the Lord of the West, and Eset, the mother, Anup, Khnum, Thoth, Setekh, and even Ptah, the lord of art), which only widened the chasm between him and his land, with its deeply rooted religious concern to preserve and remain faithful to its oldest traditions in all things, until, shut off in a world of royal luxury, he was a stranger in his own land.

Was it any wonder, then, that this dreamer's gray, half-veiled eyes were almost always red with weeping? And when Mai-Sakhme spoke before him as Joseph's envoy and presented his master's petition that he be given a leave of absence in connection with the news of Jacob's demise, he immediately began weeping—he was always on the verge of it, and his tears made good use of this occasion as well.

"How terribly sad," he said. "He has died? That very old man? That comes as a shock to My Majesty. He visited me, I recall, while he was still alive, and made no small impression on me. In his youth he was a rascal, My Majesty knows of some of his pranks, with hides and rods—I could still laugh until I cry even today. Now his life has attained its limit, and my little uncle, the Overseer of All That Heaven Gives, is orphaned? How infinitely sad! He is sitting there and weeping, is he, your master and my Unique Friend? I know that he is no stranger to tears, that they come easily to him, and for that reason my heart goes out to him, for it is always a good and dear sign in a man. When he revealed himself to his brothers with the words 'It is I,' he wept then too, I know. And he is requesting a leave of absence? A leave of seventy days? That is a good many for burying a father, no matter how great a rascal he may have been. Must it really be seventy? It is so hard to do without him. Somewhat easier perhaps than in the years of the fat and lean cows, but even in these steadier times I shall find it very difficult to spare the man who attends to the Kingdom of Blackness for me, since My Majesty understands little of all that—my interest has always been the light above. Ah, what small thanks one receives—people are much more grateful to the man who provides them blackness than to him who proclaims the light to them. Do not think that I bear any envy toward your dear master. He is to be as Pharaoh in the Two Lands until the end of his life, for far beyond any thanks I might render, he has helped My poor Majesty—as best it could be helped."

He wept a little more and then said, "But of course he should bury his worthy father, that old rascal, with full honors and take him to a foreign land in the company of his sons and brothers and his brothers' sons, in short, with all the male seed of his house—that will make a great cortege. It will look like an exodus, and it will appear to people as if he were departing from Egypt with his family to the land from whence he came. One must avoid such a misleading impression. It could lead to unrest in the land and to scenes of upheaval if the people were to believe their Provider was leaving them—I surmise they would feel it far more bitterly than if My Majesty were to depart and leave this land out of grief at their ingratitude. Hearken, my friend: What sort of procession would that be that consisted only of children and children's children? In my opinion there is but one choice, and this transport provides fully sufficient cause for arranging for a Grand Procession. It should be one of the grandest ever sent forth into foreign lands, so that it may return from there with equal pomp. What sort of Pharaoh would I be were I to grant the Provider, my Unique Friend, a request without going beyond the mere granting of it? Tell him: 'Pharaoh, who covers you with kisses, gives you seventy-five days that you may bury your father in Asia, but not only your family and their households shall travel with you and the corpse. Pharaoh will also decree a true Grand Procession, and the crème of Egypt shall bring your father to his grave. I shall, so says Ikhnatôn to you, assign my entire court, the noblest of those who serve me and the noblest in all the land, the administrators of the state and their households, together with chariots and an armed escort, a very great force. They shall all follow the bier with you, apple of my eye, both before and after you and to both sides, and shall accompany you in the same fashion on your return to me, once you have delivered your precious cargo to that place where you wish to leave it.' "

The Grand Procession

This was the answer that Mai-Sakhme brought back from Akhet-Atôn for Joseph, and everything was set in motion and arranged accordingly. Invitations, tantamount to orders, issued by a high official of the palace, who called himself Privy Councilor of the Morning Levee and of Secret Decisions, were sent by express messenger in all directions, and a date was set for all those called from throughout the kingdom to participate in the procession to assemble in the desert outside Menfe. It was an inconvenient honor that had been bestowed upon Pharaoh's servants, upon the great men of his house and the great men of the Two Lands of Egypt. And yet there was no one who would not have been wary of declining it—in fact, dignitaries not included were objects of malicious remarks by those invited and fell ill with worry. Organizing the Grand Procession as its various components and contingents flowed into the desert valley was no small task—it fell to a troop commander who usually bore the title Driver of the King's Chariot of the First Rank, but on this occasion and for the duration of the enterprise was given the title Orderer of the Grand Funeral Procession of Osiris Yaaqov ben Yitzchak, Father of the King's Spender of Shade. It was this field officer who, working from a list of participants, had drawn up the order of march and now at the point of assembly brought the beauty of clear hierarchical order to the muddle of chariots and sedan chairs, of riding animals and beasts of burden. The armed escort that was to protect them was also under his command.

The procession was ordered as follows: With a division of soldiers, trumpeters, and drummers in the lead, it was opened by Nubian archers, Libyans armed with scimitars, and Egyptian lance-bearers. This was followed by the flower of Pharaoh's court—as many as could possibly be included without entirely depriving the person of the god of a noble entourage: Friends and Sole Friends of the King, Fan-Bearers at the King's Right Hand, palace officials ranking as high as the Supreme Keeper of Secrets and Privy Coun-cilor of the King's Commands, and other highly placed persons such as His Majesty's Chief Baker and Chief Butler, the Lord High Stew-ard, the Overseer of the King's Wardrobe, the Chief Launderer and Bleacher of the Great House, the Sandal-Bearer to Pharaoh, his Chief Wigmaker, who was also a Privy Councilor to the Two Crowns, and so forth.

This gaggle of flunkeys formed the vanguard to the catafalque, which was incorporated into the procession once it arrived in Goshen and from there on glistened high above it. With its sparkling gemstones and face and beard of gold, the sarcophagus bearing Jacob's image had been placed on a bier, which was then set on a gilded sledge, and this upon a wagon whose wheels were draped and that was drawn by twelve white oxen; and now the towering cargo swayed along, just ahead of the professional mourners who broke into occasional wailing to the accompaniment of flutes and preceded the house of the dead man, his entire clan, for they were next in line. This included Joseph, with his sons and household staff, of whom Mai-Sakhme was the oldest; it included Joseph's eleven brothers with their sons and sons' sons—all who bore a male name in Israel followed after the casket, along with the dead man's closest atten-dants, especially Eliezer, his oldest servant, plus a good many other menials, so that the contingent from his house was very numerous and very long. But what a retinue was in their wake!

For now came the administrative officialdom of the Two Lands: the Viziers of Upper and Lower Egypt, Joseph's immediate subordi-nates; the chief bookkeepers of the House of Provisions; people like the Overseer of Cattle and All Domestic Beasts, who also bore the title Overseer of Horns, Claws, and Feathers; the Head of the Royal Fleet; the True Head of the Cabinet and the Warden of the Treasury Scales; the General Overseer of All Horses and a great number of True Judges and Chief Scribes. Who can list all the titles and offices borne by all those who decided it was an honor to be obliged to accompany the mummy of the father of Joseph the Provider to foreign shores. Military, with standards and cornets, now followed the civil servants. And finally at the rear was the baggage train, with tents, wagonloads of fodder, mules, and drivers—imagine the supplies of food and drink that such a procession would need for a journey across the desert.

A very great company, as tradition rightly says, for one need only picture this long-drawn-out hurly-burly of vehicles and resplendent teams, of colorful plumage and flashing weapons, of snorting beasts, rolling wheels, and marching feet, of whinnies, brays, and lows, of blaring coronets, drumbeats, and well-trained lamentation, and rising from its midst, dominating everything, the tiered structure for the sarcophagus, with its well-wrapped traveler inside. Joseph had reason to be satisfied. His father's heart had once lost him to Egypt, and now all of Egypt had to pay homage to that heart's heartfelt grief by bearing the dead Jacob to his grave on its shoulders.

And so the marvelous procession that awakened universal marvel wended its way toward the eastern frontier and now entered those bleak stretches that had to be overcome once one left behind Hapi's meadows in Pharaoh's eastern provinces to arrive in the lands of Haru and Emor. It moved along the upper edge of the mountainous desert of Sinai, but then turned in a direction that would have surprised anyone with a knowledge of its goal: for it did not take the usual, shortest route to Gaza by the sea and then through the land of the Philistines by way of Beersheba to Hebron, but instead passed below the port of Khazati and followed a road that fell away with the land to the East, through Amalek and toward Edom at the southern end of the Salt Sea. It skirted those caustic waters along their eastern shore as far as the mouth of the Jardên and then continued a short distance up that river's valley. It was from there, that is, from Gilead and the east, that it crossed the river and entered the land of Kenana.

A huge detour for Jacob's huge funeral cortege; it made a seventeen-day trip twice that long, which was the reason why Joseph had demanded a leave of seventy days—and even then he had not demanded enough and in fact slightly exceeded the seventy-five Pharaoh had granted him out of love. He had decided early on, however, to make this long detour and immediately revealed his intentions to the man in charge, the colonel who kept order in the procession and thought it a very good idea. He had been worried that the incursion of an Egyptian force of such size, with so many men under arms, entering Canaan on the highway from Gaza, would result in turmoil, misunderstanding, and difficulties and much preferred an evasive route that led through quieter country. In Joseph's mind, however, this very extensive detour was meant to enhance the honors of the journey. For him this solemn transport could not demand time and effort enough; no distances could be too great through which proud Egypt had to bear his father on its shoulders. That is why he had wanted to extend their route and saw his plan carried out.

When they had completed circling Sodom's sea and advanced a little way against the current of the Jardên, they came to a spot along its bank that was called Goren Atad; in ancient times it had been no more than a threshing floor surrounded by thorns and briars, but it was now a populous market. Nearby, along the river, was a broad meadow where they spread out and made camp under the curious eye of the locals. They stayed there for seven days and wept loudly, held a seven-day lamentation, begun anew each day in bitter and shrill tones, so that, just as had been the intention, the children of the land were very impressed, especially since even the animals were in mourning. "A very large camp," these people said, raising their eyebrows, "and a grievous mourning on the part of Egypt." And from then on they had no other name for this meadow but Abel-Mizraim, or "Egypt's meadow of mourning."

After delaying to pay these honors, the procession re-formed and crossed the Jordan at a ford that, to further their own commerce, the children of the land had made much more passable by sinking tree trunks and stones there. The sledge bearing Jacob's coffin was taken from its wagon and his twelve sons carried it on poles across the river.

They were in their own country and now ascended from the steamy river valley to fresher heights. They followed the well-maintained road that held to the mountain ridge, and on the third day they came to Hebron. Encircled on its slope lay Kiriath-Arba, from where many of its residents hastened down to behold the wandering splendor that had entered the region with its holy burden and now filled the plain of the valley, in one rocky wall of which was the bricked-shut entrance to the double cave, that ancient funereal heirloom. Supplied by nature, but enlarged and improved upon by human hand, it did not appear double on the outside, for it had only one door. When the wall was broken open, however, as was now done, it opened onto a circular shaft leading downward and then branching to the right and left into two corridors blocked with slabs of stone, behind which lay the two barrel-vaulted crypts—this was why the cave was called "double." At the mere thought of who all had found an eternal home in these rocky chambers, one turns pale—as the brothers now turned pale when the cave was opened before them. It left the Egyptians unmoved; indeed, there were even some wrinkled noses at such a homemade grave. But all that was Israel turned pale.

The shaft and corridors were very narrow and low, and two people from the house of Jacob, his oldest and second-oldest servants, one in front, the other behind, were just barely able to maneuver the mummy down into its chamber—whether into the one on the right or on the left, that has been forgotten. If dust and bones could marvel, there certainly would have been much marveling in the cave at this newcomer in his foolish foreign finery. But instead there reigned only total indifference, out of whose musty smell the crouching bearers hastened back up the shaft into the sweet airs of life. There slave artisans stood at the ready with trowel and mortar, and in an instant the final refuge, which would receive no one else after this, was closed again.

The house closed, the father disposed of—ten pairs of eyes stared at the last brick in the last hole. What is wrong with them? How sallow they look, these ten men, chewing at their lips. They cast furtive glances at the eleventh, and lower their eyes. It is quite obvious: they are afraid. They feel abandoned, anxious in their abandonment. Their father is gone, the hundred-year-old father of these seventy-year-olds. He has always been there until now, even as a wrapped mummy—but now he is behind that wall, and suddenly their hearts sink. Suddenly it seems as if he, he alone, has been their shield and protection, standing—where no one and nothing now stand—between them and retribution.

They stood off to one side, muttering among themselves as dusk fell. The moon rose, the eternal images emerged, the cool and damp of the mountains rose from the earth among the tents of Jacob's escort of honor. Then they called over the twelfth of their number, Benjamin, Rachel's child.

"Benjamin," they said with faltering lips, "pay attention, here's the thing. We have a message from him who has been gathered to his people to be given to Jehosiph, your brother, and you are best suited to bring it to him. For shortly before his death, in his final days, when Joseph was not there, our father commanded us, saying: 'When I am dead, you are to tell your brother Joseph for me: Forgive your brothers their transgression and their sin, that they did evil to you. For as in life so also in death, I shall be between you and them, and I lay it upon you as my bequest and last testament that you shall not do them evil and take revenge for old matters, even when I am seemingly no longer there. Let them shear their sheep, but leave them unshorn.'"

"Is that true?" Benjamin asked. "I wasn't present when he said it."

"You were never present for anything," they replied, "and so you have nothing to say. Such a little fellow need not be present everywhere. But surely you will not refuse to bring His Grace, your brother Joseph, our father's last wish and purpose. Go now to him at once. We, however, shall follow after you and await what news you have for us."

And so Benjamin went in to his exalted brother in his tent and said in some embarrassment, "Joseph-el, forgive me for disturbing you, but your brothers have asked me to inform you that on his deathbed Father implored by all that is holy that after his death you would inflict no pain for what happened years ago, for even after death he wanted to be a shield between you and to prevent your taking revenge."

"Is that true?" Joseph asked, his eyes welling with tears.

"It's probably not exactly true," Benjamin replied.

"No, for he knew it was not necessary," Joseph added, and two tears dropped from his eyelashes. "They are right behind you, I suppose, outside the tent?" he asked.

"They are," his little brother answered.

"Then let us go out to them," Joseph said.

And he stepped outside beneath starry luster and the weft of moonlight. There they were, and they fell down before him and said, "Here we are, servants of the God of your father, and we are your slaves. As your brother has told you, we ask that you forgive us our evil deed and not repay us according to your power. As you forgave us while Jacob was alive, so forgive us now after his death."

"But brothers, dear old brothers," he replied, bowing to them with arms spread wide, "what are you saying! You speak exactly as if you feared me and wanted me to forgive you. Am I as God? In the land below, it is said, I am as Pharaoh, and though he is called god, he is but a dear, poor thing. But in asking for my forgiveness, you have not, it appears, really understood the whole story we are in. I do not scold you for that. One can very easily be in a story without understanding it. Perhaps it was meant to be that way, and I have only myself to blame for always understanding too well the game that was being played. Did you not hear it from our father's lips as he gave me my blessing, that in my case it has always been merely a playful game and an echo? And in his departing words to you did he even mention the nasty thing that happened between you and me? No, he said nothing of it, for he was also part of the game, of God's playful game. Under his protection I had to rouse you, by my brazen immaturity, to do evil, but God indeed turned it to good, so that I fed many people and matured a little myself besides. But if it is a question of pardon among us human beings, then I am the one who should beg it of you, for you had to play the evildoers so that everything might turn out this way. And now I am supposed to make use of Pharaoh's power, merely because it is mine, to revenge myself on you for three days of chastisement in a well, and again turn to evil what God has turned to good? Don't make me laugh! For a man who, contrary to all justice and reason, uses power simply because he has it—one can only laugh at him. If not today, then sometime in the future—and it is the future we shall hold to. Sleep in peace. Tomorrow, by God's counsel, we shall begin our journey back to the comical land of Egypt."

This is what he said to them, and they laughed and wept together, and they all reached their hands out to him as he stood there
in their midst and they touched him, and he caressed them as well.
And so ends this invention of God, this beautiful story of

Joseph and his brothers.

ABOUT THE TRANSLATOR

John E. Woods is the distinguished translator of many books—most notably Arno Schmidt's *Evening Edged in Gold*, for which he won both the American Book Award for translation and the PEN Translation Prize in 1981; Patrick Süskind's *Perfume*, for which he again won the PEN Translation Prize, in 1987; Christoph Ransmayr's *The Terrors of Ice and Darkness*, *The Last World* (for which he was awarded the Schlegel-Tieck Prize in 1991), and *The Dog King*; Thomas Mann's *Buddenbrooks*, *The Magic Mountain* (for which he was awarded the Helen and Kurt Wolff Prize in 1996), and *Doctor Faustus*; Ingo Schulze's *33 Moments of Happiness*, and *Simple Stories*; Jan Philip Reemtsma's *More Than a Champion*; *The Good Man of Nanking: The Diaries of John Rabe*; and Bernhard Schlink's *Flights of Love*. He lives in San Diego, California.